JEAN-CHRISTOPHE

JEAN-CHRISTOPHE

ROMAIN ROLLAND

**INTRODUCTION BY
LOUIS AUCHINCLOSS**

CARROLL & GRAF PUBLISHERS, INC.
NEW YORK

COPYRIGHT © 1996 BY CARROLL & GRAF PUBLISHERS, INC.

INTRODUCTION COPYRIGHT © 1996 BY LOUIS AUCHINCLOSS

ALL RIGHTS RESERVED.

ORIGINALLY PUBLISHED IN THE UNITED STATES IN 1910
BY HENRY HOLT AND COMPANY.

FIRST CARROLL & GRAF EDITION 1996.

CARROLL & GRAF PUBLISHERS, INC.
260 FIFTH AVENUE
NEW YORK, NY 10001

LIBRARY OF CONGRESS CATALOGING-IN-PUBLICATION DATA
IS AVAILABLE.

ISBN 0-7867-0307-5

MANUFACTURED IN THE UNITED STATES OF AMERICA.

INTRODUCTION

It is a rare occurence, if not a unique one, for a novelist of the first rank to be an accomplished musician and a specialist in the history of music, but such was the case with Romain Rolland. Born in Burgundy in 1866 he spent a solitary childhood with a widowed mother; music and reading provided his principal occupations. His most important educational years were those spent in Rome at the French School of Archaeology and History. It was there that he met Malwida von Meysenburg, a friend of Wagner and Nietzsche, under whose tutelage he developed his lifelong emancipation from the limitations of nationalism, race, and religion.

Upon his return to France he subsequently published a life of Beethoven, studies of Michelangelo and Tolstoy, and taught history of music at the Sorbonne. He had already retired at the outbreak of the First World War and was living in Switzerland in self-imposed exile, where he published a plea for peace called *Au-dessus de la Mêlée,* which aroused great anger and cries of pro-Germanism in France. When he won the Nobel Prize in Literature in 1915, the French Academy protested that they had not nominated him, but it turned out that Anatole France secretly had. Rolland died in Vézelay in 1944, under house arrest by the Vichy government for his anti-Nazi views. However much he might have been in favor of a world understanding between the hostile nations of the globe, he would never have sought it at the price of liberty.

Rolland wrote a considerable amount of fiction and drama in addition to his published correspondence with Richard Strauss and Malwilda von Meysenburg, but he is remembered chiefly today for his mammoth *roman fleuve, Jean-Christophe.* It is the life story of Jean-Christophe Krafft, a German Rhinelander composer who escapes to France after his involvement in a village fracas with the soldiers of a neighboring garrison and spends some dozen years in Paris before he has again to flee, this time to Switzerland, having killed a policeman in a socialist riot. He is obviously a violent man, but his honesty and integrity are complete, almost alarmingly so. He is absolutely incapable of the smallest hypocrisy or prevarication, no matter how grave the cost be to his career, his welfare, or his very life. He refuses to admit the least concession to good manners or even good fellowship; he expresses himself loudly and forcibly about his tastes in music and art; he judges the virtues and failings of his fellow men. He dislikes most of the great music and art of his own era as well as that of the past. He cannot abide Brahms; both Massenet and Leoncavallo positively sicken him. He will not consent to any compromise in the performance of his own works that does not meet with his highest standards, even when played by those professionals who like his music. With an exceedingly sharp eye for the smallest failing in loyalty or sincerity by his friends, he is clearly a hard man to live with.

How then can the reader, let alone the hero's multitudinous acquaintances, abide him? Because he is so clearly a genius; his creator has totally succeeded in making him that. If at one moment he seems absurdly impractical and idealistic, at the next he appears to be actually realistic. For if a man, a genius, has the gift of so brilliant a vision of beauty—and who is to say that such a thing is impossible?—wouldn't it be a sacrilege to dilute it with ordinary stuff for the momentary gain of an applauding audience or a sympathetic critic?

To me the greatness of the novel lies in the effect of the hero on the cast of characters he meets, hates, likes, and sometimes loves. These people are drawn in vivid and fascinating psychological detail, and their life stories are given sometimes at greater length than seems strictly appropriate to their importance in relation to Jean-Christophe, but in a *roman fleuve,* or at least in this one, the parts can be as good, if not greater than the whole. The unifying factor is that most of the characters, at one point or another, ultimately turn against the hero. It is not only because they are mean, although many of them are; it is because there is something about genius and personal integrity on such a scale, that creates in them a passion to belittle it, or even to extinguish it. So glaring a light shows them up, warts and all.

As Rolland says: "Most men are essentially dead by thirty; after that they are only a reflection of what they used to be; for the rest of their lives they ape their old selves, repeating mechanically and grimacingly the things they said, did, thought, or loved in the days when they *were*."

It is perhaps small wonder that the saints of old were flayed, burned, crucified, or thrown to the beasts.

So real are the people to Rolland with whom he surrounds his hero that he sometimes muses as to what might have happened had a particular pair of them grown more intimate than his plot allows. He speculates as to what might have happened had Jean-Christophe and a girl called Rosa decided to unite their destinies: "And so they lost sight of each other. It was perhaps just as well. For all her goodness she wasn't vital enough to fathom him. And despite his fondness of and esteem for her, he would have stifled in an airless, joyless life—they would both have suffered."

Jean-Christophe is full, perhaps too full, of the passion for life. He has no need of the urgent advice which Henry James's Strether offers Little Bilham in *The Ambassadors*: "Live all you can; it's a mistake not to. It doesn't so much matter what you do in particular, so long as you *have* your life. If you haven't had that, what *have* you had?" Jean-Christophe as a friendless and penniless German in a hostile Paris reflects: "He was alone! What a joy to be alone, to be oneself! What a joy to have cast off one's chains, one's memories, the whole hallucination of loved and hated faces!"

There are moments, however, in a novel of such length when at least this reader began a bit to lose patience with the hero, and to find his constant denunciations of the current social and artistic scene too sweeping, even perhaps a bit too Teutonic. Here are his thoughts on Paris of the *Belle Époque*:

"He who would see God living, face to face, must seek him not in the celestial desert of his mind but in the love of his fellow man. The artists of the day were far from that love. They wrote for the vain, anarchistic, rootless elite of the social world who gloried in not sharing the passions of ordinary men or who made a joke of them. The glory of cutting themselves off from the crowd, of being different! Death take them! Let us go to the living, let us drink to the breasts of the earth, to the sacred love of family!"

While Rolland does not mention the ultrafashionable portrait painter of the era, Giovanni Boldini, I wonder if the latter's svelte stylish ladies, with their mocking and suggestive smiles, their ivory shoulders and breasts half revealed by coyly draped dresses and their full hips shaped by shimmering skirts—yet all executed with undeniable virtuosity—were not what our author was snorting at. Was he too blind to see that behind Boldini was Marcel Proust? If the France of that era produced a Robert de Montesquieu, it also produced a Cézanne. A good argument could be made that they were not opposites but very much wines from the same vineyard, if of a different quality.

Jean-Christophe has several romances during the course of his tale but none so odd as the penultimate one, which occurs in Switzerland after his flight from the French police. He takes refuge with Dr. Braun, a Swiss, whose wife, Anna, is a strange, tense, silent woman of a deeply superstitious nature. She appears at first to dislike Jean-Christophe but is in fact passionately drawn to him. The urge is both mutual and so strong that the pair have no option but to enter into a violent physical affair, even though there is no love between them. He is heartbroken at deceiving the friend who has taken him in, and she believes that hellfire will be her inevitable punishment. She insists finally that she must kill herself; and he sees no alternative but to follow suit when she has done so. He watches her as she twice aims a revolver at her heart and twice pulls the trigger, but when it fails to fire they give up the attempt, and she collapses in a nervous breakdown. Jean-Christophe returns to Paris where he carries on a curious relationship with a charming Frenchwoman, the widow of a Hungarian diplomat, who loves him but for some reason prefers a platonic affair to a passionate one. I found both these incidents inconsistent with the hero whom I thought I had come to know so well in the first thousand pages of the novel.

The only way, it seemed, for Rolland to end his epic was to kill off the hero, which he does in 1912—a bit prematurely, perhaps, since Jean-Christophe would have been only in his fifties. Despite his relatively young age, he dies, in peace, with the sense that he has accomplished in music everything that he could have expected to accomplish.

The end of the tale is shrouded in the darkness of the approaching world conflict. Rolland foresaw with a shrewd prescience just how devastating that war would be, and he describes effectively the folly and lightness with which all of Europe seemed to accept its inevitability. He saw the animosity of France and Germany as the seed of the ensuing catastrophe: the desire of the former for *revanche* for the defeat of 1870 and the lust of the latter to dominate the Continent. He saw the virtues and failings of both nations, and that hardly made him popular with either. He was an idealist, but even he was willing to overlook—or at least palliate—the violence in men whose fancied high morality he valued. He never criticizes his hero for killing a policeman in a riot where he did not belong. In his dramas about the French Revolution he boldly asserts that the Thermidorian conspirators who brought about the deaths of Robespierre and Saint-Just hereby destroyed the revolution and ushered in an era of capitalistic greed. For Jean-Christophe, Robespierre is an unsung hero of France, and that is something I cannot entirely forget in assessing the remarkable character of Jean-Christophe Krafft.

Louis Auchincloss
January, 1996

CONTENTS

BOOK I

THE DAWN	3
MORNING	107
YOUTH	215
REVOLT	357

BOOK II

THE MARKET-PLACE	3
ANTOINETTE	197
THE HOUSE	301

BOOK III

LOVE AND FRIENDSHIP	3
THE BURNING BUSH	165
THE NEW DAWN	349

BOOK I

THE DAWN

Dianzi, nell'alba che precede al giorno,
Quando l'anima tua dentro dormìa. . . .
                                        Purgatorio, ix.

JEAN-CHRISTOPHE

I

> Come, quando i vapori umidi e spessi
> A diradar cominciansi, la spera
> Del sol debilemente entra per essi. . . .
> *Purgatorio,* xvii.

FROM behind the house rises the murmuring of the river. All day long the rain has been beating against the window-panes; a stream of water trickles down the window at the corner where it is broken. The yellowish light of the day dies down. The room is dim and dull.

The new-born child stirs in his cradle. Although the old man left his sabots at the door when he entered, his footsteps make the floor creak. The child begins to whine. The mother leans out of her bed to comfort it; and the grandfather gropes to light the lamp, so that the child shall not be frightened by the night when he awakes. The flame of the lamp lights up old Jean Michel's red face, with its rough white beard and morose expression and quick eyes. He goes near the cradle. His cloak smells wet, and as he walks he drags his large blue list slippers. Louisa signs to him not to go too near. She is fair, almost white; her features are drawn; her gentle, stupid face is marked with red in patches; her lips are pale and swollen, and they are parted in a timid smile; her eyes devour the child—and her eyes are blue and vague; the pupils are small, but there is an infinite tenderness in them.

The child wakes and cries, and his eyes are troubled. Oh! how terrible! The darkness, the sudden flash of the lamp, the hallucinations of a mind as yet hardly detached from chaos, the stifling, roaring night in which it is enveloped, the illimitable gloom from which, like blinding shafts of light, there emerge acute sensations, sorrows, phantoms—those enormous faces leaning over him, those eyes that pierce through him, penetrating, are beyond his comprehension! . . . He has not the strength to cry out; terror holds him motionless, with eyes and mouth wide open and he rattles in his throat. His large head, that seems to have swollen up, is wrinkled with the grotesque and lamentable grimaces that he makes; the skin of his face and hands is brown and purple, and spotted with yellow. . . .

"Dear God!" said the old man with conviction: "How ugly he is!"

He put the lamp down on the table.

Louisa pouted like a scolded child. Jean Michel looked at her out of the corner of his eye and laughed.

"You don't want me to say that he is beautiful? You would not believe it. Come, it is not your fault. They are all like that."

The child came out of the stupor and immobility into which he had been thrown by the light of the lamp and the eyes of the old man. He began to cry. Perhaps he instinctively felt in his mother's eyes a caress which made it possible for him to complain. She held out her arms for him and said:

"Give him to me."

The old man began, as usual, to air his theories:

"You ought not to give way to children when they cry. You must just let them cry."

But he came and took the child and grumbled:

"I never saw one quite so ugly."

Louisa took the child feverishly and pressed it to her bosom. She looked at it with a bashful and delighted smile.

"Oh, my poor child!" she said shamefacedly. "How ugly you are—how ugly! and how I love you!"

Jean Michel went back to the fireside. He began to poke the fire in protest, but a smile gave the lie to the moroseness and solemnity of his expression.

"Good girl!" he said. "Don't worry about it. He has plenty of time to alter. And even so, what does it matter? Only one thing is asked of him: that he should grow into an honest man."

The child was comforted by contact with his mother's warm

body. He could be heard sucking her milk and gurgling and snorting. Jean Michel turned in his chair, and said once more, with some emphasis:

"There's nothing finer than an honest man."

He was silent for a moment, pondering whether it would not be proper to elaborate this thought; but he found nothing more to say, and after a silence he said irritably:

"Why isn't your husband here?"

"I think he is at the theater," said Louisa timidly. "There is a rehearsal."

"The theater is closed. I passed it just now. One of his lies."

"No. Don't be always blaming him. I must have misunderstood. He must have been kept for one of his lessons."

"He ought to have come back," said the old man, not satisfied. He stopped for a moment, and then asked, in a rather lower voice and with some shame:

"Has he been . . . again?"

"No, father—no, father," said Louisa hurriedly.

The old man looked at her; she avoided his eyes.

"It's not true. You're lying."

She wept in silence.

"Dear God!" said the old man, kicking at the fire with his foot. The poker fell with a clatter. The mother and the child trembled.

"Father, please—please!" said Louisa. "You will make him cry."

The child hesitated for a second or two whether to cry or to go on with his meal; but not being able to do both at once, he went on with the meal.

Jean Michel continued in a lower tone, though with outbursts of anger:

"What have I done to the good God to have this drunkard for my son? What is the use of my having lived as I have lived, and of having denied myself everything all my life! But you—you—can't you do anything to stop it? Heavens! That's what you ought to do. . . . You should keep him at home! . . ."

Louisa wept still more.

"Don't scold me! . . . I am unhappy enough as it is! I have done everything I could. If you knew how terrified I am when I am alone! Always I seem to hear his step on the stairs. Then I wait for the door to open, or I ask myself: 'O God! what will he look like?' . . . It makes me ill to think of it!"

She was shaken by her sobs. The old man grew anxious. He went to her and laid the disheveled bedclothes about her trembling shoulders and caressed her head with his hands.

"Come, come, don't be afraid. I am here."

She calmed herself for the child's sake, and tried to smile.

"I was wrong to tell you that."

The old man shook his head as he looked at her.

"My poor child, it was not much of a present that I gave you."

"It's my own fault," she said. "He ought not to have married me. He is sorry for what he did."

"What, do you mean that he regrets? . . ."

"You know. You were angry yourself because I became his wife."

"We won't talk about that. It is true I was vexed. A young man like that—I can say so without hurting you—a young man whom I had carefully brought up, a distinguished musician, a real artist—might have looked higher than you, who had nothing and were of a lower class, and not even of the same trade. For more than a hundred years no Krafft has ever married a woman who was not a musician! But, you know, I bear you no grudge, and am fond of you, and have been ever since I learned to know you. Besides, there's no going back on a choice once it's made; there's nothing left but to do one's duty honestly."

He went and sat down again, thought for a little, and then said, with the solemnity in which he invested all his aphorisms:

"The first thing in life is to do one's duty."

He waited for contradiction, and spat on the fire. Then, as neither mother nor child raised any objection, he was for going on, but relapsed into silence.

.   .   .   .

They said no more. Both Jean Michel, sitting by the fireside, and Louisa, in her bed, dreamed sadly. The old man, in spite of what he had said, had bitter thoughts about his son's marriage, and Louisa was thinking of it also, and blaming herself, although she had nothing wherewith to reproach herself.

She had been a servant when, to everybody's surprise, and her own especially, she married Melchior Krafft, Jean Michel's son. The Kraffts were without fortune, but were considerable people in the little Rhine town in which the old man had settled down more than fifty years before. Both father and son were musicians, and known to all the musicians of the country from Cologne to Mannheim. Melchior played the violin at the Hof-Theater, and Jean Michel had formerly been director of the grand-ducal concerts. The old man had been profoundly humiliated by his son's marriage, for he had built great hopes upon Melchior; he had wished to make him the distinguished man which he had failed to become himself. This mad freak destroyed all his ambitions. He had stormed at first, and showered curses upon Melchior and Louisa. But, being a good-hearted creature, he forgave his daughter-in-law when he learned to know her better; and he even came by a paternal affection for her, which showed itself for the most part in snubs.

No one ever understood what it was that drove Melchior to such a marriage—least of all Melchior. It was certainly not Louisa's beauty. She had no seductive quality: she was small, rather pale, and delicate, and she was a striking contrast to Melchior and Jean Michel, who were both big and broad, red-faced giants, heavy-handed, hearty eaters and drinkers, laughter-loving and noisy. She seemed to be crushed by them; no one noticed her, and she seemed to wish to escape even what little notice she attracted. If Melchior had been a kind-hearted man, it would have been credible that he should prefer Louisa's simple goodness to every other advantage; but a vainer man never was. It seemed incredible that a young man of his kidney, fairly good-looking, and quite conscious of it, very foolish, but not without talent, and in a position to look for some well-dowered match, and capable even—who knows?—of turning the head of one of his pupils among the people of the town, should suddenly have chosen a girl of the people—poor, uneducated, without beauty, a girl who could in no way advance his career.

But Melchior was one of those men who always do the opposite of what is expected of them and of what they expect of themselves. It is not that they are not warned—a man who is warned is worth two men, says the proverb. They profess never to be the dupe of anything, and that they steer their ship with unerring hand towards a definite point. But they reckon without themselves, for they do not know themselves. In one of those moments of forgetfulness which are habitual with them they let go the tiller, and, as is natural when things are left to themselves, they take a naughty pleasure in rounding on their masters. The ship which is released from its course at once strikes a rock, and Melchior, bent upon intrigue, married a cook. And yet he was neither drunk nor in a stupor on the day when he bound himself to her for life, and he was not under any passionate impulse; far from it. But perhaps there are in us forces other than mind and heart, other even than the senses—mysterious forces which take hold of us in the moments when the others are asleep; and perhaps it was such forces that Melchior had found in the depths of those pale eyes which had looked at him so timidly one evening when he had accosted the girl on the bank of the river, and had sat down beside her in the reeds—without knowing why—and had given her his hand.

Hardly was he married than he was appalled by what he had done, and he did not hide what he felt from poor Louisa, who humbly asked his pardon. He was not a bad fellow, and he willingly granted her that; but immediately remorse would seize him again when he was with his friends or in the houses of his rich pupils, who were disdainful in their treatment of him, and no longer trembled at the touch of his hand when he corrected the position of their fingers on the keyboard. Then he would return gloomy of countenance, and Louisa, with a catch at her heart, would read in it with the first glance the customary reproach; or he would stay out late at one inn or another, there to seek self-respect or kindliness from others. On such evenings he would return shouting with laughter, and this was more doleful for Louisa than the hidden reproach and gloomy rancor that prevailed on other days. She felt that she was to a certain extent responsible for the fits of madness in which the small remnant of her husband's sense would disappear, together with the household money. Melchior sank lower and lower. At an age when he should have been engaged in unceasing toil to develop his mediocre talent, he just let things slide, and others took his place.

But what did that matter to the unknown force which had thrown him in with the little flaxen-haired servant? He had played his part, and little Jean-Christophe had just set foot on this earth whither his destiny had thrust him.

. . . .

Night was fully come. Louisa's voice roused old Jean Michel from the torpor into which he had sunk by the fireside as he thought of the sorrows of the past and present.

"It must be late, father," said the young woman affectionately. "You ought to go home; you have far to go."

"I am waiting for Melchior," replied the old man.

"Please, no. I would rather you did not stay."

"Why?"

The old man raised his head and looked fiercely at her. She did not reply.

He resumed.

"You are afraid. You do not want me to meet him?"

"Yes, yes; it would only make things worse. You would make each other angry, and I don't want that. Please, please go!"

The old man sighed, rose, and said:

"Well . . . I'll go."

He went to her and brushed her forehead with his stiff beard. He asked if she wanted anything, put out the lamp, and went stumbling against the chairs in the darkness of the room. But he had no sooner reached the staircase than he thought of his son returning drunk, and he stopped at each step, imagining a thousand dangers that might arise if Melchior were allowed to return alone. . . .

In the bed by his mother's side the child was stirring again. An unknown sorrow had arisen from the depths of his being. He stiffened himself against her. He twisted his body, clenched his fists, and knitted his brows. His suffering increased steadily, quietly, certain of its strength. He knew not what it was, nor whence it came. It appeared immense,—infinite, and he began to cry lamentably. His mother caressed him with her gentle hands. Already his suffering was less acute. But he went on weeping, for he felt it still near, still inside himself. A man who suffers can lessen his anguish by knowing whence it comes. By thought he can locate it in a certain portion of his body which can be cured, or, if necessary, torn away. He fixes the bounds of it, and separates it from himself. A child has no such illusive resource. His first encounter with suffering is more tragic and more true. Like his own being, it seems infinite. He feels that it is seated in his bosom, housed in his heart, and is mistress of his flesh. And it is so. It will not leave his body until it has eaten it away.

His mother hugs him to her, murmuring: " It is done—it is done! Don't cry, my little Jesus, my little goldfish. . . ." But his intermittent outcry continues. It is as though this wretched, unformed, and unconscious mass had a presentiment of a whole life of sorrow awaiting him, and nothing can appease him. . . .

The bells of St. Martin rang out in the night. Their voices are solemn and slow. In the damp air they come like footsteps on moss. The child became silent in the middle of a sob. The marvelous music, like a flood of milk, surged sweetly through him. The night was lit up; the air was moist and tender. His sorrow disappeared, his heart began to laugh, and he slid into his dreams with a sigh of abandonment.

The three bells went on softly ringing in the morrow's festival. Louisa also dreamed, as she listened to them, of her own past misery and of what would become in the future of the dear little child sleeping by her side. She had been for hours lying in her bed, weary and suffering. Her hands and her body were burning; the heavy eiderdown crushed her; she felt crushed and oppressed by the darkness; but she dared not move. She looked at the child, and the night did not prevent her reading his features, that looked so old. Sleep overcame her; fevered images passed through her brain. She thought she heard Melchior open the door, and her heart leaped. Occasionally the murmuring of the stream rose more loudly through the silence, like the roaring of some beast. The window once or twice gave a sound under the beating of the rain. The bells rang out more slowly, and then died down, and Louisa slept by the side of her child.

All this time Jean Michel was waiting outside the house, dripping with rain, his beard wet with the mist. He was waiting for the return of his wretched son: for his mind, never ceasing, had insisted on telling him all sorts of tragedies brought about by drunkenness; and although he did not believe them, he could not have slept a wink if he had gone away without having seen his son return. The sound of the bells made him melancholy, for he remembered all his shattered hopes. He thought of what he was doing at such an hour in the street, and for very shame he wept.

.   .   .   .

The vast tide of the days moves slowly. Day and night come up and go down with unfailing regularity, like the ebb and flow of an infinite ocean. Weeks and months go by, and then begin again, and the succession of days is like one day.

The day is immense, inscrutable, marking the even beat of light and darkness, and the beat of the life of the torpid creature dreaming in the depths of his cradle—his imperious needs, sorrowful or glad—so regular that the night and the day which bring them seem by them to be brought about.

The pendulum of life moves heavily, and in its slow beat the whole creature seems to be absorbed. The rest is no more than dreams, snatches of dreams, formless and swarming, and dust of atoms dancing aimlessly, a dizzy whirl passing, and bringing laughter or horror. Outcry, moving shadows, grinning shapes, sorrows, terrors, laughter, dreams, dreams. . . . All is a dream, both day and night. . . . And in such chaos the light of friendly eyes that smile upon him, the flood of joy that surges through his body from his mother's body, from her breasts filled with milk—the force that is in him, the immense, unconscious force gathering in him, the turbulent ocean roaring in the narrow prison of the child's body. For eyes that could see into it there would be revealed whole worlds half buried in the darkness, nebulæ taking shape, a universe in the making. His being is limitless. He is all that there is. . . .

Months pass. . . . Islands of memory begin to rise above the river of his life. At first they are little uncharted islands, rocks just peeping above the surface of the waters. Round about them and behind in the twilight of the dawn stretches the great untroubled sheet of water; then new islands, touched to gold by the sun.

So from the abyss of the soul there emerge shapes definite, and scenes of a strange clarity. In the boundless day which dawns once more, ever the same, with its great monotonous beat, there begins to show forth the round of days, hand in hand, and some of their forms are smiling, others sad. But ever the links of the chain are broken, and memories are linked together above weeks and months. . . .

The River . . . the Bells . . . as long as he can remember— far back in the abysses of time, at every hour of his life— always their voices, familiar and resonant, have rung out. . . .

Night—half asleep—a pale light made white the window. . . . The river murmurs. Through the silence its voice rises omnipotent; it reigns over all creatures. Sometimes it caresses their sleep, and seems almost itself to die away in the roaring of its torrent. Sometimes it grows angry, and howls like a furious beast about to bite. The clamor ceases. Now there is a murmuring of infinite tenderness, silvery sounds like clear little bells, like the laughter of children, or soft singing voices, or dancing music—a great mother voice that never, never goes to sleep! It rocks the child, as it has rocked through the ages, from birth to death, the generations that were before him; it fills all his thoughts, and lives in all his dreams, wraps him round with the cloak of its fluid harmonies, which still will be about him when he lies in the little cemetery that sleeps by the water's edge, washed by the Rhine. . . .

The bells. . . . It is dawn! They answer each other's call, sad, melancholy, friendly, gentle. At the sound of their slow voices there rise in him hosts of dreams—dreams of the past, desires, hopes, regrets for creatures who are gone, unknown to the child, although he had his being in them, and they live again in him. Ages of memory ring out in that music. So much mourning, so many festivals! And from the depths of the room it is as though, when they are heard, there passed lovely waves of sound through the soft air, free winging birds, and the moist soughing of the wind. Through the window smiles a patch of blue sky; a sunbeam slips through the curtains to the bed. The little world known to the eyes of the child, all that he can see from his bed every morning as he awakes, all that with so much effort he is beginning to recognize and classify, so that he may be master of it—his kingdom is lit up. There is the table where people eat, the cupboard where he hides to play, the tiled floor along which he crawls, and the wall-paper which in its antic shapes holds for him so many humorous or terrifying stories, and the clock which chatters and stammers so many words which he alone can understand. How many things there are in this room! He does not know them all. Every day he sets out on a voyage of exploration in this universe which is his. Everything is his. Nothing is immaterial; everything has its worth, man or fly. Everything lives—the cat, the fire, the table, the grains of dust which dance in a sunbeam. The room is a country, a day is a lifetime. How is a creature to know himself in the midst of these vast spaces? The world is so large! A creature is lost in it. And the faces, the actions, the movement, the noise, which make round about him an unending turmoil! . . . He is weary; his eyes close; he goes to sleep. That sweet deep sleep that overcomes him suddenly at any time, and wherever he may be—on his mother's lap, or under the table, where he loves to hide! . . . It is good. All is good. . . .

These first days come buzzing up in his mind like a field of corn or a wood stirred by the wind, and cast in shadow by the great fleeting clouds. . .

The shadows pass; the sun penetrates the forest. Jean-Christophe begins to find his way through the labyrinth of the day.

It is morning. His parents are asleep. He is in his little bed, lying on his back. He looks at the rays of light dancing on the ceiling. There is infinite amusement in it. Now he laughs out loud with one of those jolly children's laughs which

stir the hearts of those that hear them. His mother leans
out of her bed towards him, and says: " What is it, then, little
mad thing? " Then he laughs again, and perhaps he makes
an effort to laugh because he has an audience. His mamma
looks severe, and lays a finger on her lips to warn him lest
he should wake his father: but her weary eyes smile in spite of
herself. They whisper together. Then there is a furious growl
from his father. Both tremble. His mother hastily turns her
back on him, like a naughty little girl: she pretends to be asleep.
Jean-Christophe buries himself in his bed, and holds his
breath. . . . Dead silence.

After some time the little face hidden under the clothes comes
to the surface again. On the roof the weathercock creaks.
The rain-pipe gurgles; the Angelus sounds. When the wind
comes from the east, the distant bells of the villages on the
other bank of the river give answer. The sparrows foregathered
in the ivy-clad wall make a deafening noise, from which three
or four voices, always the same, ring out more shrilly than the
others, just as in the games of a band of children. A pigeon
coos at the top of a chimney. The child abandons himself to
the lullaby of these sounds. He hums to himself softly, then
a little more loudly, then quite loudly, then very loudly, until
once more his father cries out in exasperation: " That little
donkey never will be quiet! Wait a little, and I'll pull your
ears! " Then Jean-Christophe buries himself in the bedclothes
again, and does not know whether to laugh or cry. He is terrified and humiliated; and at the same time the idea of the
donkey with which his father has compared him makes him
burst out laughing. From the depths of his bed he imitates
its braying. This time he is whipped. He sheds every tear that
is in him. What has he done? He wanted so much to laugh
and to get up! And he is forbidden to budge. How do people
sleep forever? When will they get up? . . .

One day he could not contain himself. He heard a cat and
a dog and something queer in the street. He slipped out of
bed, and, creeping awkwardly with his bare feet on the tiles,
he tried to go down the stairs to see what it was; but the door
was shut. To open it, he climbed on to a chair; the whole thing
collapsed, and he hurt himself and howled. And once more

at the top of the stairs he was whipped. He is always being whipped! . . .

He is in church with his grandfather. He is bored. He is not very comfortable. He is forbidden to stir, and all the people are saying all together words that he does not understand. They all look solemn and gloomy. It is not their usual way of looking. He looks at them, half frightened. Old Lena, their neighbor, who is sitting next to him, looks very cross; there are moments when he does not recognize even his grandfather. He is afraid a little. Then he grows used to it, and tries to find relief from boredom by every means at his disposal. He balances on one leg, twists his neck to look at the ceiling, makes faces, pulls his grandfather's coat, investigates the straws in his chair, tries to make a hole in them with his finger, listens to the singing of birds, and yawns so that he is like to dislocate his jaw.

Suddenly there is a deluge of sound: the organ is played. A thrill goes down his spine. He turns and stands with his chin resting on the back of his chair, and he looks very wise. He does not understand this noise; he does not know the meaning of it; it is dazzling, bewildering, and he can hear nothing clearly. But it is good. It is as though he were no longer sitting there on an uncomfortable chair in a tiresome old house. He is suspended in mid-air, like a bird; and when the flood of sound rushes from one end of the church to the other, filling the arches, reverberating from wall to wall, he is carried with it, flying and skimming hither and thither, with nothing to do but to abandon himself to it. He is free; he is happy. The sun shines. . . . He falls asleep.

His grandfather is displeased with him. He behaves ill at Mass.

He is at home, sitting on the ground, with his feet in his hands. He has just decided that the door-mat is a boat, and the tiled floor a river. He all but drowned in stepping off the carpet. He is surprised and a little put out that the others pay no attention to the matter as he does when he goes into the room. He seizes his mother by the skirts. " You see, it is water! You must go across by the bridge." (The bridge is a series of holes between the red tiles.) His mother crosses without even listening to him. He is vexed, as a dramatic author is vexed when he sees his audience talking during his great work.

Next moment he thinks no more of it. The tiled floor is no longer the sea. He is lying down on it, stretched full-length, with his chin on the tiles, humming music of his own composition, and gravely sucking his thumb and dribbling. He is lost in contemplation of a crack between the tiles. The lines of the tiles grimace like faces. The imperceptible hole grows larger, and becomes a valley; there are mountains about it. A centipede moves: it is as large as an elephant. Thunder might crash, the child would not hear it.

No one bothers about him, and he has no need of any one. He can even do without door-mat boats, and caverns in the tiled floor, with their fantastic fauna. His body is enough. What a source of entertainment! He spends hours in looking at his nails and shouting with laughter. They have all different faces, and are like people that he knows. And the rest of his body! . . . He goes on with the inspection of all that he has. How many surprising things! There are so many marvels. He is absorbed in looking at them.

But he was very roughly picked up when they caught him at it.

Sometimes he takes advantage of his mother's back being turned, to escape from the house. At first they used to run after him and bring him back. Then they got used to letting him go alone, only so he did not go too far away. The house is at the end of the town; the country begins almost at once. As long as he is within sight of the windows he goes without stopping, very deliberately, and now and then hopping on one foot. But as soon as he has passed the corner of the road, and the brushwood hides him from view, he changes abruptly. He stops there, with his finger in his mouth, to find out what story he shall tell himself that day; for he is full of stories. True, they are all very much like each other, and every one of them could be told in a few lines. He chooses. Generally he takes up the same story, sometimes from the point where it left off, sometimes from the beginning, with variations. But any trifle—a word heard by chance—is enough to set his mind off on another direction.

Chance was fruitful of resources. It is impossible to imagine what can be made of a simple piece of wood, a broken bough found alongside a hedge. (You break them off when you do not find them.) It was a magic wand. If it were long and thin, it became a lance, or perhaps a sword; to brandish it aloft was enough to cause armies to spring from the earth. Jean-Christophe was their general, marching in front of them, setting them an example, and leading them to the assault of a hillock. If the branch were flexible, it changed into a whip. Jean-Christophe mounted on horseback and leaped precipices. Sometimes his mount would slip, and the horseman would find himself at the bottom of the ditch, sorrily looking at his dirty hands and barked knees. If the wand were lithe, then Jean-Christophe would make himself the conductor of an orchestra: he would be both conductor and orchestra; he conducted and he sang; and then he would salute the bushes, with their little green heads stirring in the wind.

He was also a magician. He walked with great strides through the fields, looking at the sky and waving his arms. He commanded the clouds. He wished them to go to the right, but they went to the left. Then he would abuse them, and repeat his command. He would watch them out of the corner of his eye, and his heart would beat as he looked to see if there were not at least a little one which would obey him. But they went on calmly moving to the left. Then he would stamp his foot, and threaten them with his stick, and angrily order them to go to the left; and this time, in truth, they obeyed him. He was happy and proud of his power. He would touch the flowers and bid them change into golden carriages, as he had been told they did in the stories; and, although it never happened, he was quite convinced that it would happen if only he had patience. He would look for a grasshopper to turn into a hare; he would gently lay his stick on its back, and speak a rune. The insect would escape: he would bar its way. A few moments later he would be lying on his belly near to it, looking at it. Then he would have forgotten that he was a magician, and just amuse himself with turning the poor beast on its back, while he laughed aloud at its contortions.

It occurred to him also to tie a piece of string to his magic wand, and gravely cast it into the river, and wait for a fish to come and bite. He knew perfectly well that fish do not usually bite at a piece of string without bait or hook; but he thought that for once in a way, and for him, they might make an exception to their rule; and in his inexhaustible confidence, he carried it so far as to fish in the street with a whip through the grating of a sewer. He would draw up the whip from time to time excitedly, pretending that the cord of it was more heavy, and that he had caught a treasure, as in a story that his grandfather had told him. . . .

And always in the middle of all these games there used to occur to him moments of strange dreaming and complete forgetfulness. Everything about him would then be blotted out; he would not know what he was doing, and was not even conscious of himself. These attacks would take him unawares. Sometimes as he walked or went upstairs a void would suddenly open before him. He would seem then to have lost all thought. But when he came back to himself, he was shocked and bewildered to find himself in the same place on the dark staircase. It was as though he had lived through a whole lifetime—in the space of a few steps.

His grandfather used often to take him with him on his evening walk. The little boy used to trot by his side and give him his hand. They used to go by the roads, across plowed fields, which smelled strong and good. The grasshoppers chirped. Enormous crows poised along the road used to watch them approach from afar, and then fly away heavily as they came up with them.

His grandfather would cough. Jean-Christophe knew quite well what that meant. The old man was burning with the desire to tell a story; but he wanted it to appear that the child had asked him for one. Jean-Christophe did not fail him; they understood each other. The old man had a tremendous affection for his grandson, and it was a great joy to find in him a willing audience. He loved to tell of episodes in his own life, or stories of great men, ancient and modern. His voice would then become emphatic and filled with emotion, and would tremble with a childish joy, which he used to try to stifle. He seemed delighted to hear his own voice. Unhappily, words used to fail him when he opened his mouth to speak. He was used to such disappointment, for it always came upon him with his outbursts of eloquence. And as he used to forget it with each new attempt, he never succeeded in resigning himself to it.

He used to talk of Regulus, and Arminius, of the soldiers of Lützow, of Kœrner, and of Frédéric Stabs, who tried to kill the Emperor Napoleon. His face would glow as he told of incredible deeds of heroism. He used to pronounce historic words in such a solemn voice that it was impossible to hear them, and he used to try artfully to keep his hearer on tenter-hooks at the thrilling moments. He would stop, pretend to choke, and noisily blow his nose; and his heart would leap when the child asked, in a voice choking with impatience: " And then, grandfather? "

There came a day, when Jean-Christophe was a little older, when he perceived his grandfather's method; and then he wick-edly set himself to assume an air of indifference to the rest of the story, and that hurt the poor old man. But for the moment Jean-Christophe is altogether held by the power of the story-teller. His blood leaped at the dramatic passages. He did not know what it was all about, neither where nor when these deeds were done, or whether his grandfather knew Ar-minius, or whether Regulus were not—God knows why!—some one whom he had seen at church last Sunday. But his heart and the old man's heart swelled with joy and pride in the tale of heroic deeds, as though they themselves had done them; for the old man and the child were both children.

Jean-Christophe was less happy when his grandfather inter-polated in the pathetic passages one of those abstruse discourses so dear to him. There were moral thoughts generally traceable to some idea, honest enough, but a little trite, such as " Gentle-ness is better than violence," or " Honor is the dearest thing in life," or " It is better to be good than to be wicked "—only they were much more involved. Jean-Christophe's grandfather had no fear of the criticism of his youthful audience, and abandoned himself to his habitual emphatic manner; he was not afraid of repeating the same phrases, or of not finishing them, or even, if he lost himself in his discourse, of saying anything that came into his head, to stop up the gaps in his thoughts; and he used to punctuate his words, in order to give them greater force, with inappropriate gestures. The boy used to listen with profound respect, and he thought his grandfather very eloquent, but a little tiresome.

Both of them loved to return again and again to the fabulous legend of the Corsican conqueror who had taken Europe. Jean-Christophe's grandfather had known him. He had almost fought against him. But he was a man to admit the greatness of his adversaries: he had said so twenty times. He would have given one of his arms for such a man to have been born on this side of the Rhine. Fate had decreed otherwise; he admired him, and had fought against him—that is, he had been on the point of fighting against him. But when Napoleon had been no farther than ten leagues away, and they had marched out to meet him, a sudden panic had dispersed the little band in a forest, and every man had fled, crying, " We are betrayed! " In vain, as the old man used to tell, in vain did he endeavor to rally the fugitives; he threw himself in front of them, threatening them and weeping: he had been swept away in the flood of them, and on the morrow had found himself at an extraordinary distance from the field of battle— For so he called the place of the rout. But Jean-Christophe used impatiently to bring him back to the exploits of the hero, and he was delighted by his marvelous progress through the world. He saw him followed by innumerable men, giving vent to great cries of love, and at a wave of his hand hurling themselves in swarms upon flying enemies—they were always in flight. It was a fairy-tale. The old man added a little to it to fill out the story; he conquered Spain, and almost conquered England, which he could not abide.

Old Krafft used to intersperse his enthusiastic narratives with indignant apostrophes addressed to his hero. The patriot awoke in him, more perhaps when he told of the Emperor's defeats than of the Battle of Jena. He would stop to shake his fist

at the river, and spit contemptuously, and mouth noble insults
—he did not stoop to less than that. He would call him
" rascal," " wild beast," " immoral." And if such words were
intended to restore to the boy's mind a sense of justice, it must
be confessed that they failed in their object; for childish logic
leaped to this conclusion: " If a great man like that had no
morality, morality is not a great thing, and what matters most
is to be a great man." But the old man was far from suspecting
the thoughts which were running along by his side.

They would both be silent, pondering, each after his own
fashion, these admirable stories—except when the old man used
to meet one of his noble patrons taking a walk. Then he would
stop, and bow very low, and breathe lavishly the formulæ
of obsequious politeness. The child used to blush for it without knowing why. But his grandfather at heart had a vast
respect for established power and persons who had " arrived ";
and possibly his great love for the heroes of whom he told
was only because he saw in them persons who had arrived at
a point higher than the others.

When it was very hot, old Krafft used to sit under a tree,
and was not long in dozing off. Then Jean-Christophe used
to sit near him on a heap of loose stones or a milestone, or
some high seat, uncomfortable and peculiar; and he used to
wag his little legs, and hum to himself, and dream. Or sometimes he used to lie on his back and watch the clouds go by;
they looked like oxen, and giants, and hats, and old ladies,
and immense landscapes. He used to talk to them in a low
voice, or be absorbed in a little cloud which a great one was
on the point of devouring. He was afraid of those which
were very black, almost blue, and of those which went very
fast. It seemed to him that they played an enormous part in
life, and he was surprised that neither his grandfather nor
his mother paid any attention to them. They were terrible
beings if they wished to do harm. Fortunately, they used to
go by, kindly enough, a little grotesque, and they did not stop.
The boy used in the end to turn giddy with watching them
too long, and he used to fidget with his legs and arms, as
though he were on the point of falling from the sky. His
eyelids then would wink, and sleep would overcome him. Si-

lence. . . . The leaves murmur gently and tremble in the sun;
a faint mist passes through the air; the uncertain flies hover,
booming like an organ; the grasshoppers, drunk with the summer, chirp eagerly and hurriedly; all is silent. . . . Under the
vault of the trees the cry of the green woodpecker has magic
sounds. Far away on the plain a peasant's voice harangues
his oxen; the shoes of a horse ring out on the white road. Jean-
Christophe's eyes close. Near him an ant passes along a dead
branch across a furrow. He loses consciousness. . . . Ages have
passed. He wakes. The ant has not yet crossed the twig.

Sometimes the old man would sleep too long, and his face
would grow rigid, and his long nose would grow longer, and
his mouth stand open. Jean-Christophe used then to look at
him uneasily, and in fear of seeing his head change gradually
into some fantastic shape. He used to sing loudly, so as to
wake him up, or tumble down noisily from his heap of stones.
One day it occurred to him to throw a handful of pine-needles
in his grandfather's face, and tell him that they had fallen
from the tree. The old man believed him, and that made
Jean-Christophe laugh. But, unfortunately, he tried the trick
again, and just when he had raised his hand he saw his grandfather's eyes watching him. It was a terrible affair. The old
man was solemn, and allowed no liberty to be taken with the
respect due to himself. They were estranged for more than
a week.

The worse the road was, the more beautiful it was to Jean-
Christophe. Every stone had a meaning for him; he knew them
all. The shape of a rut seemed to him to be a geographical
accident almost of the same kind as the great mass of the
Taunus. In his head he had the map of all the ditches and
hillocks of the region extending two kilometers round about
the house, and when he made any change in the fixed ordering
of the furrows, he thought himself no less important than an
engineer with a gang of navvies; and when with his heel he
crushed the dried top of a clod of earth, and filled up the
valley at the foot of it, it seemed to him that his day had
not been wasted.

Sometimes they would meet a peasant in his cart on the
highroad, and if the peasant knew Jean-Christophe's grand-

father they would climb up by his side. That was a Paradise on earth. The horse went fast, and Jean-Christophe laughed with delight, except when they passed other people walking; then he would look serious and indifferent, like a person accustomed to drive in a carriage, but his heart was filled with pride. His grandfather and the man would talk without bothering about him. Hidden and crushed by their legs, hardly sitting, sometimes not sitting at all, he was perfectly happy. He talked aloud, without troubling about any answer to what he said. He watched the horse's ears moving. What strange creatures those ears were! They moved in every direction—to right and left; they hitched forward, and fell to one side, and turned backwards in such a ridiculous way that he burst out laughing. He would pinch his grandfather to make him look at them; but his grandfather was not interested in them. He would repulse Jean-Christophe, and tell him to be quiet. Jean-Christophe would ponder. He thought that when people grow up they are not surprised by anything, and that when they are strong they know everything; and he would try to be grown up himself, and to hide his curiosity, and appear to be indifferent.

He was silent then. The rolling of the carriage made him drowsy. The horse's little bells danced—ding, ding; dong, ding. Music awoke in the air, and hovered about the silvery bells, like a swarm of bees. It beat gaily with the rhythm of the cart—an endless source of song, and one song came on another's heels. To Jean-Christophe they were superb. There was one especially which he thought so beautiful that he tried to draw his grandfather's attention to it. He sang it aloud. They took no heed of him. He began it again in a higher key, then again shrilly, and then old Jean Michel said irritably: "Be quiet; you are deafening me with your trumpet-call!" That took away his breath. He blushed and was silent and mortified. He crushed with his contempt the two stockish imbeciles who did not understand the sublimity of his song, which opened wide the heavens! He thought them very ugly, with their week-old beards, and they smelled very ill.

He found consolation in watching the horse's shadow. That was an astonishing sight. The beast ran along with them lying on its side. In the evening, when they returned, it covered a part of the field. They came upon a rick, and the shadow's head would rise up and then return to its place when they had passed. Its snout was flattened out like a burst balloon; its ears were large, and pointed like candles. Was it really a shadow or a creature? Jean-Christophe would not have liked to encounter it alone. He would not have run after it as he did after his grandfather's shadow, so as to walk on its head and trample it under foot. The shadows of the trees when the sun was low were also objects of meditation. They made barriers along the road, and looked like phantoms, melancholy and grotesque, saying, " Go no farther! " and the creaking axles and the horse's shoes repeated, " No farther! "

Jean-Christophe's grandfather and the driver never ceased their endless chatter. Sometimes they would raise their voices, especially when they talked of local affairs or things going wrong. The child would cease to dream, and look at them uneasily. It seemed to him that they were angry with each other, and he was afraid that they would come to blows. However, on the contrary, they best understood each other in their common dislikes. For the most part, they were without hatred or the least passion; they talked of small matters loudly, just for the pleasure of talking, as is the joy of the people. But Jean-Christophe, not understanding their conversation, only heard the loud tones of their voices and saw their agitated faces, and thought fearfully: " How wicked he. looks! Surely they hate each other! How he rolls his eyes, and how wide he opens his mouth! He spat on my nose in his fury. O Lord, he will kill my grandfather! . . ."

The carriage stopped. The peasant said: " Here you are." The two deadly enemies shook hands. Jean-Christophe's grandfather got down first; the peasant handed him the little boy. The whip flicked the horse, the carriage rolled away, and there they were by the little sunken road near the Rhine. The sun dipped down below the fields. The path wound almost to the water's edge. The plentiful soft grass yielded under their feet, crackling. Alder-trees leaned over the river, almost half in the water. A cloud of gnats danced. A boat passed poiselessly, drawn on by the peaceful current, striding along. The water sucked the branches of the willows with a little noise like lips. The light was soft and misty, the air fresh, the river silvery gray. They reached their home, and the crickets chirped, and on the threshold smiled his mother's dear face. . . .

Oh, delightful memories, kindly visions, which will hum their melody in their tuneful flight through life! . . . Journeys in later life, great towns and moving seas, dream countries and loved faces, are not so exactly graven in the soul as these childish walks, or the corner of the garden seen every day through the window, through the steam and mist made by the child's mouth glued to it for want of other occupation. . . .

Evening now, and the house is shut up. Home . . . the refuge from all terrifying things—darkness, night, fear, things unknown. No enemy can pass the threshold. . . . The fire flares. A golden duck turns slowly on the spit; a delicious smell of fat and of crisping flesh scents the room. The joy of eating, incomparable delight, a religious enthusiasm, thrills of joy! The body is too languid with the soft warmth, and the fatigues of the day, and the familiar voices. The act of digestion plunges it in ecstasy, and faces, shadows, the lamp-shade, the tongues of flame dancing with a shower of stars in the fireplace—all take on a magical appearance of delight. Jean-Christophe lays his cheek on his plate, the better to enjoy all this happiness. . . .

He is in his soft bed. How did he come there? He is overcome with weariness. The buzzing of the voices in the room and the visions of the day are intermingled in his mind. His father takes his violin; the shrill sweet sounds cry out complaining in the night. But the crowning joy is when his mother comes and takes Jean-Christophe's hands. He is drowsy, and, leaning over him, in a low voice she sings, as he asks, an old song with words that have no meaning. His father thinks such music stupid, but Jean-Christophe never wearies of it. He holds his breath, and is between laughing and crying. His heart is intoxicated. He does not know where he is, and he is overflowing with tenderness. He throws his little arms round his mother's neck, and hugs her with all his strength. She says, laughing:

"You want to strangle me?"

He hugs her close. How he loves her! How he loves everything! Everybody, everything! All is good, all is beautiful. . . . He sleeps. The cricket on the hearth cheeps. His grandfather's tales, the great heroes, float by in the happy night. . . . To be a hero like them! . . . Yes, he will be that . . . he is that. . . . Ah, how good it is to live!

What an abundance of strength, joy, pride, is in that little creature! What superfluous energy! His body and mind never cease to move; they are carried round and round breathlessly. Like a little salamander, he dances day and night in the flames. His is an unwearying enthusiasm finding its food in all things. A delicious dream, a bubbling well, a treasure of inexhaustible hope, a laugh, a song, unending drunkenness. Life does not hold him yet; always he escapes it. He swims in the infinite. How happy he is! He is made to be happy! There is nothing in him that does not believe in happiness, and does not cling to it with all his little strength and passion! . . .

Life will soon see to it that he is brought to reason.

II

L' alba vinceva l'ora mattutina
Che fuggia nnanzi, sì che di lontano
Conobbi il tremolar della marina. . . .
Purgatorio, i.

The Kraffts came originally from Antwerp. Old Jean Michel had left the country as a result of a boyish freak, a violent quarrel, such as he had often had, for he was devilish pugnacious, and it had had an unfortunate ending. He settled down, almost fifty years ago, in the little town of the principality, with its red-pointed roofs and shady gardens, lying on the slope of a gentle hill, mirrored in the pale green eyes of *Vater Rhein*. An excellent musician, he had readily gained appreciation in a country of musicians. He had taken root there by marrying, forty years ago, Clara Sartorius, daughter of the Prince's *Kapellmeister,* whose duties he took over. Clara was a placid German with two passions—cooking and music.

She had for her husband ·a veneration only equaled by that which she had for her father. Jean Michel no less admired his wife. They had lived together in perfect amity for fifteen years, and they had four children. Then Clara died, and Jean Michel bemoaned her loss, and then, five months later, married Ottilia Schütz, a girl of twenty, with red cheeks, robust and smiling. After eight years of marriage she also died, but in that time she gave him seven children—eleven children in all, of whom only one had survived. Although he loved them much, all these bereavements had not shaken his good-humor. The greatest blow had been the death of Ottilia, three years ago, which had come to him at an age when it is difficult to start life again and to make a new home. But after a moment's confusion old Jean Michel regained his equilibrium, which no misfortune seemed able to disturb.

He was an affectionate man, but health was the strongest thing in him. He had a physical repugnance from sadness, and a need of gaiety, great gaiety, Flemish fashion—an enormous and childish laugh. Whatever might be his grief, he did not drink one drop the less, nor miss one bite at table, and his band never had one day off. Under his direction the Court orchestra won a small celebrity in the Rhine country, where Jean Michel had become legendary by reason of his athletic stature and his outbursts of anger. He could not master them, in spite of all his efforts, for the violent man was at bottom timid and afraid of compromising himself. He loved decorum and feared opinion. But his blood ran away with him. He used to see red, and he used to be the victim of sudden fits of crazy impatience, not only at rehearsals, but at the concerts, where once in the Prince's presence he had hurled his bâton and had stamped about like a man possessed, as he apostrophized one of the musicians in a furious and stuttering voice. The Prince was amused, but the artists in question were rancorous against him. In vain did Jean Michel, ashamed of his outburst, try to pass it by immediately in exaggerated obsequiousness. On the next occasion he would break out again, and as this extreme irritability increased with age, in the end it made his position very difficult. He felt it himself, and one day, when his outbursts had all but caused the whole orchestra to

strike, he sent in his resignation. He hoped that in consideration of his services they would make difficulties about accepting
it, and would ask him to stay. There was nothing of the kind,
and as he was too proud to go back on his offer, he left, broken-
hearted, and crying out upon the ingratitude of mankind.

Since that time he had not known how to fill his days. He
was more than seventy, but he was still vigorous, and he went
on working and going up and down the town from morning
to night, giving lessons, and entering into discussions, pronouncing perorations, and entering into everything. He was
ingenious, and found all sorts of ways of keeping himself occupied. He began to repair musical instruments; he invented,
experimented, and sometimes discovered improvements. He
composed also, and set store by his compositions. He had
once written a *Missa Solennis*, of which he used often to talk,
and it was the glory of his family. It had cost him so much
trouble that he had all but brought about a congestion of the
mind in the writing of it. He tried to persuade himself that
it was a work of genius, but he knew perfectly well with what
emptiness of thought it had been written, and he dared not
look again at the manuscript, because every time he did so
he recognized in the phrases that he had thought to be his
own, rags taken from other authors, painfully pieced together
haphazard. It was a great sorrow to him. He had ideas sometimes which he thought admirable. He would run tremblingly
to his table. Could he keep his inspiration this time? But
hardly had he taken pen in hand than he found himself alone
in silence, and all his efforts to call to life again the vanished
voices ended only in bringing to his ears familiar melodies of
Mendelssohn or Brahms.

"There are," says George Sand, "unhappy geniuses who
lack the power of expression, and carry down to their graves
the unknown region of their thoughts, as has said a member
of that great family of illustrious mutes or stammerers—
Geoffrey Saint-Hilaire." Old Jean Michel belonged to that
family. He was no more successful in expressing himself in
music than in words, and he always deceived himself. He
would so much have loved to talk, to write, to be a great
musician, an eloquent orator! It was his secret sore. He told

no one of it, did not admit it to himself, tried not to think of it; but he did think of it, in spite of himself, and so there was the seed of death in his soul.

Poor old man! In nothing did he succeed in being absolutely himself. There were in him so many seeds of beauty and power, but they never put forth fruit; a profound and touching faith in the dignity of Art and the moral value of life, but it was nearly always translated in an emphatic and ridiculous fashion; so much noble pride, and in life an almost servile admiration of his superiors; so lofty a desire for independence, and, in fact, absolute docility; pretensions to strength of mind, and every conceivable superstition; a passion for heroism, real courage, and so much timidity!—a nature to stop by the wayside.

Jean Michel had transferred all his ambitions to his son, and at first Melchior had promised to realize them. From childhood he had shown great musical gifts. He learned with extraordinary facility, and quickly acquired as a violinist a virtuosity which for a long time made him the favorite, almost the idol, of the Court concerts. He played the piano and other instruments pleasantly. He was a fine talker, well, though a little heavily, built, and was of the type which passes in Germany for classic beauty; he had a large brow that expressed nothing, large regular features, and a curled beard—a Jupiter of the banks of the Rhine. Old Jean Michel enjoyed his son's success; he was ecstatic over the virtuoso's *tours de force,* he who had never been able properly to play any instrument. In truth, Melchior would have had no difficulty in expressing what he thought. The trouble was that he did not think; and he did not even bother about it. He had the soul of a mediocre comedian who takes pains with the inflexions of his voice without caring about what they express, and, with anxious vanity, watches their effect on his audience.

The odd thing was that, in spite of his constant anxiety about his stage pose, there was in him, as in Jean Michel, in spite of his timid respect for social conventions, a curious, irregular, unexpected and chaotic quality, which made people say that the Kraffts were a bit crazy. It did not harm him

at first; it seemed as though these very eccentricities were the
proof of the genius attributed to him; for it is understood
among people of common sense that an artist has none. But
it was not long before his extravagances were traced to their
source—usually the bottle. Nietzsche says that Bacchus is the
God of Music, and Melchior's instinct was of the same opinion;
but in his case his god was very ungrateful to him; far from
giving him the ideas he lacked, he took away from him the few
that he had. After his absurd marriage—absurd in the eyes
of the world, and therefore also in his own—he gave himself
up to it more and more. He neglected his playing—so secure
in his own superiority that very soon he lost it. Other *virtuosi*
came to succeed him in public favor. That was bitter to
him, but instead of rousing his energy, these rebuffs only discouraged him. He avenged himself by crying down his rivals
with his pot-fellows. In his absurd conceit he counted on
succeeding his father as musical director: another man was
appointed. He thought himself persecuted, and took on the
airs of a misunderstood genius. Thanks to the esteem in which
old Krafft was held, he kept his place as a violin in the orchestra,
but gradually he lost all his lessons in the town. And if this
blow struck most at his vanity, it touched his purse even more.
For several years the resources of his household had grown less
and less, following on various reverses of fortune. After having
known plenty, want came, and every day increased. Melchior
refused to take notice of it; he did not spend one penny the
less on his toilet or his pleasures.

He was not a bad man, but a half-good man, which is perhaps
worse—weak, without spring, without moral strength, but for
the rest, in his own opinion, a good father, a good son, a good
husband, a good man—and perhaps he was good, if to be so
it is enough to possess an easy kindness, which is quickly
touched, and that animal affection by which a man loves his
kin as a part of himself. It cannot even be said that he was
very egoistic; he had not personality enough for that. He was
nothing. They are a terrible thing in life, these people who
are nothing. Like a dead weight thrown into the air, they
fall, and must fall; and in their fall they drag with them
everything that they have.

It was when the situation of his family had reached its most
difficult point, that little Jean-Christophe began to understand
what was going on about him.

He was no longer the only child. Melchior gave his wife
a child every year, without troubling to think what was to
become of it later. Two had died young; two others were three
and four years old. Melchior never bothered about them.
Louisa, when she had to go out, left them with Jean-Christophe,
now six years old.

The charge cost Jean-Christophe something, for he had to
sacrifice to his duty his splendid afternoons in the fields. But
he was proud of being treated as a man, and gravely fulfilled
his task. He amused the children as best he could by showing
them his games, and he set himself to talk to them as he had
heard his mother talking to the baby. Or he would carry them
in his arms, one after another, as he had seen her do; he bent
under their weight, and clenched his teeth, and with all his
strength clutched his little brother to his breast, so as to prevent
his falling. The children always wanted to be carried—they
were never tired of it; and when Jean-Christophe could do no
more, they wept without ceasing. They made him very unhappy, and he was often troubled about them. They were very
dirty, and needed maternal attentions. Jean-Christophe did
not know what to do. They took advantage of him. Sometimes he wanted to slap them, but he thought, "They are little;
they do not know," and, magnanimously, he let them pinch him,
and beat him, and tease him. Ernest used to howl for nothing;
he used to stamp his feet and roll about in a passion; he was
a nervous child, and Louisa had bidden Jean-Christophe not
to oppose his whims. As for Rodolphe, he was as malicious
as a monkey; he always took advantage of Jean-Christophe
having Ernest in his arms, to play all sorts of silly pranks
behind his back; he used to break toys, spill water, dirty his
frock, and knock the plates over as he rummaged in the cupboard.

And when Louisa returned, instead of praising Jean-Christophe, she used to say to him, without scolding him, but with
an injured air, as she saw the havoc: "My poor child, you are
not very clever!"

Jean-Christophe would be mortified, and his heart would grow big within him.

Louisa, who let no opportunity escape of earning a little money, used to go out as cook for exceptional occasions, such as marriages or baptismal feasts. Melchior pretended to know nothing about it—it touched his vanity—but he was not annoyed with her for doing it, so long as he did not know. Jean-Christophe had as yet no idea of the difficulties of life; he knew no other limit to his will than the will of his parents, and that did not stand much in his way, for they let him do pretty much as he pleased. His one idea was to grow up, so as to be able to do as he liked. He had no conception of obstacles standing in the way at every turn, and he had never the least idea but that his parents were completely their own masters. It was a shock to his whole being when, for the first time, he perceived that among men there are those who command, and those who are commanded, and that his own people were not of the first class; it was the first crisis of his life.

It happened one afternoon. His mother had dressed him in his cleanest clothes, old clothes given to her which Louisa's ingenuity and patience had turned to account. He went to find her, as they had agreed, at the house in which she was working. He was abashed at the idea of entering alone. A footman was swaggering in the porch; he stopped the boy, and asked him patronizingly what he wanted. Jean-Christophe blushed, and murmured that he had come to see " Frau Krafft " —as he had been told to say.

" Frau Krafft? What do you want with Frau Krafft?" asked the footman, ironically emphasizing the word *Frau*. " Your mother? Go down there. You will find Louisa in the kitchen at the end of the passage."

He went, growing redder and redder. He was ashamed to hear his mother called familiarly *Louisa*. He was humiliated; he would have liked to run away down to his dear river, and the shelter of the brushwood where he used to tell himself stories.

In the kitchen he came upon a number of other servants,

who greeted him with noisy exclamations. At the back, near
the stove, his mother smiled at him with tender embarrassment.
He ran to her, and clung to her skirts. She was wearing a
white apron, and holding a wooden spoon. She made him more
unhappy by trying to raise his chin so as to look in his face,
and to make him hold out his hand to everybody there and say
good-day to them. He would not; he turned to the wall and
hid his face in his arms. Then gradually he gained courage,
and peeped out of his hiding-place with merry bright eyes,
which hid again every time any one looked at him. He stole
looks at the people there. His mother looked busy and important, and he did not know her like that; she went from one
saucepan to another, tasting, giving advice, in a sure voice
explaining recipes, and the cook of the house listened respectfully. The boy's heart swelled with pride as he saw how much
his mother was appreciated, and the great part that she played
in this splendid room, adorned with magnificent objects of
gold and silver.

Suddenly conversation ceased. The door opened. A lady
entered with a rustling of the stuffs she was wearing. She
cast a suspicious look about her. She was no longer young,
and yet she was wearing a light dress with wide sleeves. She
caught up her dress in her hand, so as not to brush against
anything. It did not prevent her going to the stove and looking at the dishes, and even tasting them. When she raised her
hand a little, her sleeve fell back, and her arm was bare to the
elbow. Jean-Christophe thought this ugly and improper. How
dryly and abruptly she spoke to Louisa! And how humbly
Louisa replied! Jean-Christophe hated it. He hid away in
his corner, so as not to be observed, but it was no use. The
lady asked who the little boy might be. Louisa fetched him
and presented him; she held his hands to prevent his hiding
his face. And, though he wanted to break away and flee,
Jean-Christophe felt instinctively that this time he must not
resist. The lady looked at the boy's scared face, and at first
she gave him a kindly, motherly smile. But then she resumed
her patronizing air, and asked him about his behavior, and his
piety, and put questions to him, to which he did not reply.
She looked to see how his clothes fitted him, and Louisa eagerly

declared that they were magnificent. She pulled down his waistcoat to remove the creases. Jean-Christophe wanted to cry, it fitted so tightly. He did not understand why his mother was giving thanks.

The lady took him by the hand and said that she would take him to her own children. Jean-Christophe cast a look of despair at his mother; but she smiled at the mistress so eagerly that he saw that there was nothing to hope for from her, and he followed his guide like a sheep that is led to the slaughter.

They came to a garden, where two cross-looking children, a boy and a girl, about the same age as Jean-Christophe, were apparently sulky with each other. Jean-Christophe's advent created a diversion. They came up to examine the new arrival. Jean-Christophe, left with the children by the lady, stood stock-still in a pathway, not daring to raise his eyes. The two others stood motionless a short distance away, and looked him up and down, nudged each other, and tittered. Finally, they made up their minds. They asked him who he was, whence he came, and what his father did. Jean-Christophe, turned to stone, made no reply; he was terrified almost to the point of tears, especially of the little girl, who had fair hair in plaits, a short skirt, and bare legs.

They began to play. Just as Jean-Christophe was beginning to be a little happier, the little boy stopped dead in front of him, and touching his coat, said:

"Hullo! That's mine!"

Jean-Christophe did not understand. Furious at this assertion that his coat belonged to some one else, he shook his head violently in denial.

"I know it all right," said the boy. "It's my old blue waistcoat. There's a spot on it."

And he put his finger on the spot. Then, going on with his inspection, he examined Jean-Christophe's feet, and asked what his mended-up shoes were made of. Jean-Christophe grew crimson. The little girl pouted and whispered to her brother—Jean-Christophe heard it—that it was a little poor boy. Jean-Christophe resented the word. He thought he would succeed in combating the insulting opinions, as he stammered in a

choking voice that he was the son of Melchior Krafft, and that
his mother was Louisa the cook. It seemed to him that this
title was as good as any other, and he was right. But the
two children, interested in the news, did not seem to esteem
him any the more for it. On the contrary, they took on a
patronizing tone. They asked him what he was going to be—
a cook or a coachman. Jean-Christophe revolted. He felt an
iciness steal into his heart.

Encouraged by his silence, the two rich children, who had
conceived foɪ the little poor boy one of those cruel and unreasoning antipathies which children have, tried various amusing ways of tormenting him. The little girl especially was
implacable. She observed that Jean-Christophe could hardly
run, because his clothes were so tight, and she conceived the
subtle idea of making him jump. They made an obstacle of
little seats, and insisted on Jean-Christophe clearing it. The
wretched child dared not say what it was that prevented his
jumping. He gathered himself together, hurled himself through
the air; and measured his length on the ground. They roared
with laughter at him. He had to try again. Tears in his
eyes, he made a desperate attempt, and this time succeeded in
jumping. That did not satisfy his tormentors, who decided
that the obstacle was not high enough, and they built it up
until it became a regular break-neck affair. Jean-Christophe
tried to rebel, and declared that he would not jump. Then the
little girl called him a coward, and said that he was afraid.
Jean-Christophe could not stand that, and, knowing that he
must fall, he jumped, and fell. His feet caught in the obstacle;
the whole thing toppled over with him. He grazed his hands
and almost broke his head, and, as a crowning misfortune, his
trousers tore at the knees and elsewhere. He was sick with
shame; he heard the two children dancing with delight round
him; he suffered horribly. He felt that they despised and
hated him. Why? Why? He would gladly have died! There
is no more cruel suffering than that of a child who discovers
for the first time the wickedness of others; he believes then that
he is persecuted by the whole world, and there is nothing to
support him; there is nothing then—nothing! . . . Jean-Christophe tried to get up; the little boy pushed him down again;

the little girl kicked him.   He tried again, and they both jumped on him, and sat on his back and pressed his face down into the ground.   Then rage seized him—it was too much.   His hands were bruised, his fine coat was torn—a catastrophe for him!—shame, pain, revolt against the injustice of it, so many misfortunes all at once, plunged him in blind fury.   He rose to his hands and knees, shook himself like a dog, and rolled his tormentors over; and when they returned to the assault he butted at them, head down, bowled over the little girl, and, with one blow of his fist, knocked the boy into the middle of a flower-bed.

They howled.   The children ran into the house with piercing cries.   Doors slammed, and cries of anger were heard.   The lady ran out as quickly as her long dress would let her.   Jean-Christophe saw her coming, and made no attempt to escape. He was terrified at what he had done; it was a thing unheard of, a crime; but he regretted nothing.   He waited.   He was lost.   So much the better!   He was reduced to despair.

The lady pounced on him.   He felt her beat him.   He heard her talking in a furious voice, a flood of words; but he could distinguish nothing.   His little enemies had come back to see his shame, and screamed shrilly.   There were servants—a babel of voices.   To complete his downfall, Louisa, who had been summoned, appeared, and, instead of defending him, she began to scold him—she, too, without knowing anything—and bade him beg pardon.   He refused angrily.   She shook him, and dragged him by the hand to the lady and the children, and bade him go on his knees.   But he stamped and roared, and bit his mother's hand.   Finally, he escaped among the servants, who laughed.

He went away, his heart beating furiously, his face burning with anger and the slaps which he had received.   He tried not to think, and he hurried along because he did not want to cry in the street.   He wanted to be at home, so as to be able to find the comfort of tears.   He choked; the blood beat in his head; he was at bursting-point.

Finally, he arrived; he ran up the old black staircase to his usual nook in the bay of a window above the river; he hurled himself into it breathlessly, and then there came a flood of tears. He did not know exactly why he was crying, but he had to cry; and when the first flood of them was done, he wept again because he wanted, with a sort of rage, to make himself suffer, as if he could in this way punish the others as well as himself. Then he thought that his father must be coming home, and that his mother would tell him everything, and that his own miseries were by no means at an end. He resolved on flight, no matter whither, never to return.

Just as he was going downstairs, he bumped into his father, who was coming up.

"What are you doing, boy? Where are you going?" asked Melchior.

He did not reply.

"You are up to some folly. What have you done?"

Jean-Christophe held his peace.

"What have you done?" repeated Melchior. "Will you answer?"

The boy began to cry and Melchior to shout, vying with each other until they heard Louisa hurriedly coming up the stairs. She arrived, still upset. She began with violent reproach and further chastisement, in which Melchior joined as soon as he understood—and probably before—with blows that would have felled an ox. Both shouted; the boy roared. They ended by angry argument. All the time that he was beating his son, Melchior maintained that he was right, and that this was the sort of thing that one came by, by going out to service with people who thought they could do everything because they had money; and as she beat the child, Louisa shouted that her husband was a brute, that she would never let him touch the boy, and that he had really hurt him. Jean-Christophe was, in fact, bleeding a little from the nose, but he hardly gave a thought to it, and he was not in the least thankful to his mother for stopping it with a wet cloth, since she went on scolding him. In the end they pushed him away in a dark closet, and shut him up without any supper.

He heard them shouting at each other, and he did not know which of them he detested most. He thought it must be his mother, for he had never expected any such wickedness from her. All the misfortunes of the day overwhelmed him: all that he had suffered—the injustice of the children, the injustice of the lady, the injustice of his parents, and—this he felt like an open wound, without quite knowing why—the degradation of his parents, of whom he was so proud, before these evil and contemptible people. Such cowardice, of which for the first time he had become vaguely conscious, seemed ignoble to him. Everything was upset for him—his admiration for his own people, the religious respect with which they inspired him, his confidence in life, the simple need that he had of loving others and of being loved, his moral faith, blind but absolute. It was a complete cataclysm. He was crushed by brute force, without any means of defending himself or of ever again escaping. He choked. He thought himself on the point of death. All his body stiffened in desperate revolt. He beat with fists, feet, head, against the wall, howled, was seized with convulsions, and fell to the floor, hurting himself against the furniture.

His parents, running up, took him in their arms. They vied with each other now as to who should be the more tender with him. His mother undressed him, carried him to his bed, and sat by him and remained with him until he was calmer. But he did not yield one inch. He forgave her nothing, and pretended to be asleep to get rid of her. His mother seemed to him bad and cowardly. He had no suspicion of all the suffering that she had to go through in order to live and give a living to her family, and of what she had borne in taking sides against him.

After he had exhausted to the last drop the incredible store of tears that is in the eyes of a child, he felt somewhat comforted. He was tired and worn out, but his nerves were too much on stretch for him to sleep. The visions that had been with him floated before him again in his semi-torpor. Especially he saw again the little girl with her bright eyes and her turned-up, disdainful little nose, her hair hanging down to her shoulders, her bare legs and her childish, affected way of talking. He trembled, as it seemed to him that he could hear her voice. He remembered how stupid he had been with her, and he conceived a savage hatred for her. He did not pardon her for having brought him low, and was consumed with the desire to humiliate her and to make her weep. He sought means of

doing this, but found none. There was no sign of her ever
caring about him. But by way of consoling himself he supposed that everything was as he wished it to be. He supposed
that he had become very powerful and famous, and decided
that she was in love with him. Then he began to tell himself
one of those absurd stories which in the end he would regard
as more real than reality.

She was dying of love, but he spurned her. When he passed
before her house she watched him pass, hiding behind the
curtains, and he knew that she watched him, but he pretended
to take no notice, and talked gaily. Even he left the country,
and journeyed far to add to her anguish. He did great things.
Here he introduced into his narrative fragments chosen from
his grandfather's heroic tales, and all this time she was falling
ill of grief. Her mother, that proud dame, came to beg of
him: " My poor child is dying. I beg you to come! " He went.
She was in her bed. Her face was pale and sunken. She
held out her arms to him. She could not speak, but she took
his hands and kissed them as she wept. Then he looked at
her with marvelous kindness and tenderness. He bade her
recover, and consented to let her love him. At this point of
the story, when he amused himself by drawing out the coming
together by repeating their gestures and words several times,
sleep overcame him, and he slept and was consoled.

But when he opened his eyes it was day, and it no longer
shone so lightly or so carelessly as its predecessor. There was
a great change in the world. Jean-Christophe now knew the
meaning of injustice.

There were now times of extremely straitened circumstances
at home. They became more and more frequent. They lived
meagerly then. No one was more sensible of it than Jean-
Christophe. His father saw nothing. He was served first,
and there was always enough for him. He talked noisily, and
roared with laughter at his own jokes, and he never noticed
his wife's glances as she gave a forced laugh, while she watched
him helping himself. When he passed the dish it was more
than half empty. Louisa helped the children—two potatoes
each. When it came to Jean-Christophe's turn there were

sometimes only three left, and his mother was not helped. He knew that beforehand; he had counted them before they came to him. Then he summoned up courage, and said carelessly:

"Only one, mother."

She was a little put out.

"Two, like the others."

"No, please; only one."

"Aren't you hungry?"

"No, I'm not very hungry."

But she, too, only took one, and they peeled them care-fully, cut them up in little pieces, and tried to eat them as slowly as possible. His mother watched him. When he had finished:

"Come, take it!"

"No, mother."

"But you are ill?"

"I am not ill, but I have eaten enough."

Then his father would reproach him with being obstinate, and take the last potato for himself. But Jean-Christophe learned that trick, and he used to keep it on his plate for Ernest, his little brother, who was always hungry, and watched him out of the corner of his eyes from the beginning of dinner, and ended by asking:

"Aren't you going to eat it? Give it me, then, Jean-Christophe."

Oh, how Jean-Christophe detested his father, how he hated him for not thinking of them, or for not even dreaming that he was eating their share! He was so hungry that he hated him, and would gladly have told him so; but he thought in his pride that he had no right, since he could not earn his own living. His father had earned the bread that he took. He himself was good for nothing; he was a burden on everybody; he had no right to talk. Later on he would talk— if there were any later on. Oh, he would die of hunger first! . . .

He suffered more than another child would have done from these cruel fasts. His robust stomach was in agony. Some-times he trembled because of it; his head ached. There was a hole in his chest—a hole which turned and widened, as if a

gimlet were being twisted in it. But he did not complain. He
felt his mother's eyes upon him, and assumed an expression of
indifference. Louisa, with a clutching at her heart, understood
vaguely that her little boy was denying himself so that the
others might have more. She rejected the idea, but always
returned to it. She dared not investigate it or ask Jean-Christophe if it were true, for, if it were true, what could she
do? She had been used to privation since her childhood.
What is the use of complaining when there is nothing to be
done? She never suspected, indeed—she, with her frail health
and small needs—that the boy might suffer more than herself.
She did not say anything, but once or twice, when the others
were gone, the children to the street, Melchior about his business, she asked her eldest son to stay to do her some small
service. Jean-Christophe would hold her skein while she un-
wound it. Suddenly she would throw everything away, and
draw him passionately to her. She would take him on her
knees, although he was quite heavy, and would hug and hug
him. He would fling his arms round her neck, and the two
of them would weep desperately, embracing each other.
" My poor little boy! . . ."
" Mother, mother! . . ."
They said no more, but they understood each other.

It was some time before Jean-Christophe realized that his
father drank. Melchior's intemperance did not—at least, in
the beginning—exceed tolerable limits. It was not brutish. It
showed itself rather by wild outbursts of happiness. He used
to make foolish remarks, and sing loudly for hours together as
he drummed on the table, and sometimes he insisted on dancing
with Louisa and the children. Jean-Christophe saw that his
mother looked sad. She would shrink back and bend her face
over her work; she avoided the drunkard's eyes, and used to try
gently to quiet him when he said coarse things that made her
blush. But Jean-Christophe did not understand, and he was
in such need of gaiety that these noisy home-comings of his
father were almost a festival to him. The house was melancholy, and these follies were a relaxation for him. He used
to laugh heartily at Melchior's crazy antics and stupid jokes;

he sang and danced with him; and he was put out when his mother in an angry voice ordered him to cease. How could it be wrong, since his father did it? Although his ever keen observation, which never forgot anything it had seen, told him that there were in his father's behavior several things which did not accord with his childish and imperious sense of justice, yet he continued to admire him. A child has so much need of an object of admiration! Doubtless it is one of the eternal forms of self-love. When a man is, or knows himself to be, too weak to accomplish his desires and satisfy his pride, as a child he transfers them to his parents, or, as a man who has failed, he transfers them to his children. They are, or shall be, all that he dreamed of being—his champions, his avengers— and in this proud abdication in their favor, love and egoism are mingled so forcefully and yet so gently as to bring him keen delight. Jean-Christophe forgot all his grudges against his father, and cast about to find reasons for admiring him. He admired his figure, his strong arms, his voice, his laugh, his gaiety, and he shone with pride when he heard praise of his father's talents as a virtuoso, or when Melchior himself recited with some amplification the eulogies he had received. He believed in his father's boasts, and looked upon him as a genius, as one of his grandfather's heroes.

One evening about seven o'clock he was alone in the house His little brothers had gone out with Jean Michel. Louisa was washing the linen in the river. The door opened, and Melchior plunged in. He was hatless and disheveled. He cut a sort of caper to cross the threshold, and then plumped down in a chair by the table. Jean-Christophe began to laugh, thinking it was a part of one of the usual buffooneries, and he approached him. But as soon as he looked more closely at him the desire to laugh left him. Melchior sat there with his arms hanging, and looking straight in front of him, seeing nothing, with his eyes blinking. His face was crimson, his mouth was open, and from it there gurgled every now and then a silly laugh. Jean-Christophe stood stock-still. He thought at first that his father was joking, but when he saw that he did not budge he was panic-stricken.

" Papa, papa ! " he cried.

Melchior went on gobbling like a fowl. Jean-Christophe took him by the arm in despair, and shook him with all his strength.

"Papa, dear papa, answer me, please, please!"

Melchior's body shook like a boneless thing, and all but fell. His head flopped towards Jean-Christophe; he looked at him and babbled incoherently and irritably. When Jean-Christophe's eyes met those clouded eyes he was seized with panic terror. He ran away to the other end of the room, and threw himself on his knees by the bed, and buried his face in the clothes. He remained so for some time. Melchior swung heavily on the chair, sniggering. Jean-Christophe stopped his ears, so as not to hear him, and trembled. What was happening within him was inexpressible. It was a terrible upheaval— terror, sorrow, as though for some one dead, some one dear and honored.

No one came; they were left alone. Night fell, and Jean-Christophe's fear grew as the minutes passed. He could not help listening, and his blood froze as he heard the voice that he did not recognize. The silence made it all the more terrifying; the limping clock beat time for the senseless babbling. He could bear it no longer; he wished to fly. But he had to pass his father to get out, and Jean-Christophe shuddered at the idea of seeing those eyes again; it seemed to him that he must die if he did. He tried to creep on hands and knees to the door of the room. He could not breathe; he would not look; he stopped at the least movement from Melchior, whose feet he could see under the table. One of the drunken man's legs trembled. Jean-Christophe reached the door. With one trembling hand he pushed the handle, but in his terror he let go. It shut to again. Melchior turned to look. The chair on which he was balanced toppled over; he fell down with a crash. Jean-Christophe in his terror had no strength left for flight. He remained glued to the wall, looking at his father stretched there at his feet, and he cried for help.

His fall sobered Melchior a little. He cursed and swore, and thumped on the chair that had played him such a trick. He tried vainly to get up, and then did manage to sit up with his back resting against the table, and he recognized his surroundings. He saw Jean-Christophe crying; he called him. Jean-Christophe wanted to run away; he could not stir. Melchior called him again, and as the child did not come, he swore angrily. Jean-Christophe went near him, trembling in every limb. Melchior drew the boy near him, and made him sit on his knees. He began by pulling his ears, and in a thick, stuttering voice delivered a homily on the respect due from a son to his father. Then he went off suddenly on a new train of thought, and made him jump in his arms while he rattled off silly jokes. He wriggled with laughter. From that he passed immediately to melancholy ideas. He commiserated the boy and himself; he hugged him so that he was like to choke, covered him with kisses and tears, and finally rocked him in his arms, intoning the *De Profundis*. Jean-Christophe made no effort to break loose; he was frozen with horror. Stifled against his father's bosom, feeling his breath hiccoughing and smelling of wine upon his face, wet with his kisses and repulsive tears, he was in an agony of fear and disgust. He would have screamed, but no sound would come from his lips. He remained in this horrible condition for an age, as it seemed to him, until the door opened, and Louisa came in with a basket of linen on her arm. She gave a cry, let the basket fall, rushed at Jean-Christophe, and with a violence which seemed incredible in her she wrenched Melchior's arm, crying:

" Drunken, drunken wretch ! "

Her eyes flashed with anger.

Jean-Christophe thought his father was going to kill her. But Melchior was so startled by the threatening appearance of his wife that he made no reply, and began to weep. He rolled on the floor; he beat his head against the furniture, and said that she was right, that he was a drunkard, that he brought misery upon his family, and was ruining his poor children, and wished he were dead. Louisa had contemptuously turned her back on him. She carried Jean-Christophe into the next room, and caressed him and tried to comfort him. The boy went on trembling, and did not answer his mother's questions; then he burst out sobbing. Louisa bathed his face with water. She kissed him, and used tender words, and wept with

him. In the end they were both comforted. She knelt, and
made him kneel by her side. They prayed to God to cure father
of his disgusting habit, and make him the kind, good man that
he used to be. Louisa put the child to bed. He wanted her to
stay by his bedside and hold his hand. Louisa spent part
of the night sitting on Jean-Christophe's bed. He was feverish.
The drunken man snored on the floor.

Some time after that, one day at school, when Jean-Christophe was spending his time watching the flies on the ceiling,
and thumping his neighbors, to make them fall off the form,
the schoolmaster, who had taken a dislike to him, because he
was always fidgeting and laughing, and would never learn anything, made an unhappy allusion. Jean-Christophe had fallen
down himself, and the schoolmaster said he seemed to be like
to follow brilliantly in the footsteps of a certain well-known
person. All the boys burst out laughing, and some of them
took upon themselves to point the allusion with comment both
lucid and vigorous. Jean-Christophe got up, livid with shame,
seized his ink-pot, and hurled it with all his strength at the
nearest boy whom he saw laughing. The schoolmaster fell on
him and beat him. He was thrashed, made to kneel, and set
to do an enormous imposition.

He went home, pale and storming, though he said never a
word. He declared frigidly that he would not go to school
again. They paid no attention to what he said. Next morning,
when his mother reminded him that it was time to go, he
replied quietly that he had said that he was not going any more.
In vain Louisa begged and screamed and threatened; it was
no use. He stayed sitting in his corner, obstinate. Melchior
thrashed him. He howled, but every time they bade him go
after the thrashing was over he replied angrily, " No! " They
asked him at least to say why. He clenched his teeth, and
would not. Melchior took hold of him, carried him to school,
and gave him into the master's charge. They set him on his
form, and he began methodically to break everything within
reach—his inkstand, his pen. He tore up his copy-book and
lesson-book, all quite openly, with his eye on the schoolmaster,
provocative. They shut him up in a dark room. A few moments later the schoolmaster found him with his handkerchief

tied round his neck, tugging with all his strength at the two ends of it. He was trying to strangle himself.

They had to send him back.

Jean-Christophe was impervious to sickness. He had in-herited from his father and grandfather their robust constitu-tions. They were not mollycoddles in that family; well or ill, they never worried, and nothing could bring about any change in the habits of the two Kraffts, father and son. They went out winter and summer, in all weathers, and stayed for hours together out in rain or sun, sometimes bareheaded and with their coats open, from carelessness or bravado, and walked for miles without being tired, and they looked with pity and disdain upon poor Louisa, who never said anything, but had to stop. She would go pale, and her legs would swell, and her heart would thump. Jean-Christophe was not far from sharing the scorn of his mother; he did not understand people being ill. When he fell, or knocked himself, or cut himself, or burned himself, he did not cry; but he was angry with the thing that had injured him. His father's brutalities and the roughness of his little playmates, the urchins of the street, with whom he used to fight, hardened him. He was not afraid of blows, and more than once he returned home with bleeding nose and bruised forehead. One day he had to be wrenched away, almost suffocated, from one of these fierce tussles in which he had bowled over his adversary, who was savagely banging his head on the ground. That seemed natural enough to him, for he was prepared to do unto others as they did unto himself.

And yet he was afraid of all sorts of things, and although no one knew it—for he was very proud—nothing brought him so much suffering during a part of his childhood as these same terrors. For two or three years especially they gnawed at him like a disease.

He was afraid of the mysterious something that lurks in darkness—evil powers that seemed to lie in wait for his life, the roaring of monsters which fearfully haunt the mind of every child and appear in everything that he sees, the relic perhaps of a form long dead, hallucinations of the first days

after emerging from chaos, from the fearful slumber in his
mother's womb, from the awakening of the larva from the
depths of matter.

He was afraid of the garret door. It opened on to the stairs,
and was almost always ajar. When he had to pass it he felt
his heart beating; he would spring forward and jump by it
without looking. It seemed to him that there was some one
or something behind it. When it was closed he heard distinctly
something moving behind it. That was not surprising, for
there were large rats; but he imagined a monster, with rattling
bones, and flesh hanging in rags, a horse's head, horrible and
terrifying eyes, shapeless. He did not want to think of it,
but did so in spite of himself. With trembling hand he would
make sure that the door was locked; but that did not keep him
from turning round ten times as he went downstairs.

He was afraid of the night outside. Sometimes he used to
stay late with his grandfather, or was sent out in the evening on some errand. Old Krafft lived a little outside the town
in the last house on the Cologne road. Between the house and
the first lighted windows of the town there was a distance of
two or three hundred yards, which seemed three times as long
to Jean-Christophe. There were places where the road twisted
and it was impossible to see anything. The country was
deserted in the evening, the earth grew black, and the sky
was awfully pale. When he came out from the hedges that
lined the road, and climbed up the slope, he could still see
a yellowish gleam on the horizon, but it gave no light, and
was more oppressive than the night; it made the darkness
only darker; it was a deathly light. The clouds came down
almost to earth. The hedges grew enormous and moved. The
gaunt trees were like grotesque old men. The sides of the
wood were stark white. The darkness moved. There were
dwarfs sitting in the ditches, lights in the grass, fearful flying
things in the air, shrill cries of insects coming from nowhere.
Jean-Christophe was always in anguish, expecting some fear-
some or strange putting forth of Nature. He would run, with
his heart leaping in his bosom.

When he saw the light in his grandfather's room he would
gain confidence. But worst of all was when old Krafft was

not at home. That was most terrifying. The old house, lost
in the country, frightened the boy even in daylight. He forgot
his fears when his grandfather was there, but sometimes the
old man would leave him alone, and go out without warning
him. Jean-Christophe did not mind that. The room was
quiet. Everything in it was familiar and kindly. There was
a great white wooden bedstead, by the bedside was a great
Bible on a shelf, artificial flowers were on the mantelpiece,
with photographs of the old man's two wives and eleven children—and at the bottom of each photograph he had written
the date of birth and death—on the walls were framed texts
and vile chromolithographs of Mozart and Beethoven. A little
piano stood in one corner, a great violoncello in another; rows
of books higgledy-piggledy, pipes, and in the window pots of
geraniums. It was like being surrounded with friends. The
old man could be heard moving about in the next room, and
planing or hammering, and talking to himself, calling himself
an idiot, or singing in a loud voice, improvising a *potpourri*
of scraps of chants and sentimental *Lieder,* warlike marches,
and drinking songs. Here was shelter and refuge. Jean-
Christophe would sit in the great armchair by the window, with
a book on his knees, bending over the pictures and losing himself in them. The day would die down, his eyes would grow
weary, and then he would look no more, and fall into vague
dreaming. The wheels of a cart would rumble by along the
road, a cow would moo in the fields; the bells of the town,
weary and sleepy, would ring the evening Angelus. Vague
desires, happy presentiments, would awake in the heart of the
dreaming child.

Suddenly Jean-Christophe would awake, filled with dull uneasiness. He would raise his eyes—night! He would listen—
silence! His grandfather had just gone out. He shuddered.
He leaned out of the window to try to see him. The road was
deserted; things began to take on a threatening aspect. Oh
God! If *that* should be coming! What? He could not tell.
The fearful thing. The doors were not properly shut. The
wooden stairs creaked as under a footstep. The boy leaped
up, dragged the armchair, the two chairs and the table, to
the most remote corner of the room: he made a barrier of

them; the armchair against the wall, a chair to the right, a chair to the left, and the table in front of him. In the middle he planted a pair of steps, and, perched on top with his book and other books, like provisions against a siege, he breathed again, having decided in his childish imagination that the enemy could not pass the barrier—that was not to be allowed.

But the enemy would creep forth, even from his book. Among the old books which the old man had picked up were some with pictures which made a profound impression on the child: they attracted and yet terrified him. There were fantastic visions—temptations of St. Anthony—in which skeletons of birds hung in bottles, and thousands of eggs writhe like worms in disemboweled frogs, and heads walk on feet, and asses play trumpets, and household utensils and corpses of animals walk gravely, wrapped in great cloths, bowing like old ladies. Jean-Christophe was horrified by them, but always returned to them, drawn on by disgust. He would look at them for a long time, and every now and then look furtively about him to see what was stirring in the folds of the curtains. A picture of a flayed man in an anatomy book was still more horrible to him. He trembled as he turned the page when he came to the place where it was in the book. This shapeless medley was grimly etched for him. The creative power inherent in every child's mind filled out the meagerness of the setting of them. He saw no difference between the daubs and the reality. At night they had an even more powerful influence over his dreams than the living things that he saw during the day.

He was afraid to sleep. For several years nightmares poisoned his rest. He wandered in cellars, and through the manhole saw the grinning flayed man entering. He was alone in a room, and he heard a stealthy footstep in the corridor; he hurled himself against the door to close it, and was just in time to hold the handle; but it was turned from the outside; he could not turn the key, his strength left him, and he cried for help. He was with his family, and suddenly their faces changed; they did crazy things. He was reading quietly, and he felt that an invisible being was all *round* him. He tried to fly, but felt himself bound. He tried to cry out, but he was gagged. A loathsome grip was about his neck. He awoke, suffocating, and with his teeth chattering; and he went on trembling long after he was awake; he could not be rid of his agony.

The room in which he slept was a hole without door or windows; an old curtain hung up by a curtain-rod over the entrance was all that separated it from the room of his father and mother. The thick air stifled him. His brother, who slept in the same bed, used to kick him. His head burned, and he was a prey to a sort of hallucination in which all the little troubles of the day reappeared infinitely magnified. In this state of nervous tension, bordering on delirium, the least shock was an agony to him. The creaking of a plank terrified him. His father's breathing took on fantastic proportions. It seemed to be no longer a human breathing, and the monstrous sound was horrible to him; it seemed to him that there must be a beast sleeping there. The night crushed him; it would never end; it must always be so; he was lying there for months and months. He gasped for breath; he half raised himself on his bed, sat up, dried his sweating face with his shirt-sleeve. Sometimes he nudged his brother Rodolphe to wake him up; but Rodolphe moaned, drew away from him the rest of the bedclothes, and went on sleeping.

So he stayed in feverish agony until a pale beam of light appeared on the floor below the curtain. This timorous paleness of the distant dawn suddenly brought him peace. He felt the light gliding into the room, when it was still impossible to distinguish it from darkness. Then his fever would die down, his blood would grow calm, like a flooded river returning to its bed; an even warmth would flow through all his body, and his eyes, burning from sleeplessness, would close in spite of himself.

In the evening it was terrible to him to see the approach of the hour of sleep. He vowed that he would not give way to it, to watch the whole night through, fearing his nightmares. But in the end weariness always overcame him, and it was always when he was least on his guard that the monsters returned.

Fearful night! So sweet to most children, so terrible to some! . . . He was afraid to sleep. He was afraid of not sleeping. Waking or sleeping, he was surrounded by monstrous shapes, the phantoms of his own brain, the larvæ floating in the half-day and twilight of childhood, as in the dark chiaroscuro of sickness.

But these fancied terrors were soon to be blotted out in the great Fear—that which is in the hearts of all men; that Fear which Wisdom does in vain preen itself on forgetting or denying—Death.

One day when he was rummaging in a cupboard, he came upon several things that he did not know—a child's frock and a striped bonnet. He took them in triumph to his mother, who, instead of smiling at him, looked vexed, and bade him take them back to the place where he had found them. When he hesitated to obey, and asked her why, she snatched them from him without reply, and put them on a shelf where he could not reach them. Roused to curiosity, he plied her with questions. At last she told him that there had been a little brother who had died before Jean-Christophe came into the world. He was taken aback—he had never heard tell of him. He was silent for a moment, and then tried to find out more. His mother seemed to be lost in thought; but she told him that the little brother was called Jean-Christophe like himself, but was more sensible. He put more questions to her, but she would not reply readily. She told him only that his brother was in Heaven, and was praying for them all. Jean-Christophe could get no more out of her; she bade him be quiet, and to let her go on with her work. She seemed to be absorbed in her sewing; she looked anxious, and did not raise her eyes. But after some time she looked at him where he was in the corner, whither he had retired to sulk, began to smile, and told him to go and play outside.

These scraps of conversation profoundly agitated Jean-Christophe. There had been a child, a little boy, belonging to his mother, like himself, bearing the same name, almost exactly the same, and he was dead! Dead! He did not exactly know what that was, but it was something terrible. And they never talked of this other Jean-Christophe; he was quite forgotten. It would be the same with him if he were to die? This thought

was with him still in the evening at table with his family,
when he saw them all laughing and talking of trifles. So, then,
it was possible that they would be gay after he was dead!
Oh! he never would have believed that his mother could be
selfish enough to laugh after the death of her little boy! He
hated them all. He wanted to weep for himself, for his own
death, in advance. At the same time he wanted to ask a
whole heap of questions, but he dared not; he remembered the
voice in which his mother had bid him be quiet. At last he
could contain himself no longer, and one night when he had
gone to bed, and Louisa came to kiss him, he asked:

"Mother, did he sleep in my bed?"

The poor woman trembled, and, trying to take on an indifferent tone of voice, she asked:.

"Who?"

"The little boy who is dead," said Jean-Christophe in a
whisper.

His mother clutched him with her hands.

"Be quiet—quiet," she said.

Her voice trembled. Jean-Christophe, whose head was leaning against her bosom, heard her heart beating. There was a
moment of silence, then she said:

"You must never talk of that, my dear. . . . Go to sleep.
. . . No, it was not his bed."

She kissed him. He thought he felt her cheek wet against
his. He wished he could have been sure of it. He was a little
comforted. There was grief in her then! Then he doubted it
again the next moment, when he heard her in the next room
talking in a quiet, ordinary voice. Which was true—that or
what had just been? He turned about for long in his bed without finding any answer. He wanted his mother to suffer; not
that he also did not suffer in the knowledge that she was sad,
but it would have done him so much good, in spite of everything! He would have felt himself less alone. He slept, and
next day thought no more of it.

Some weeks afterwards one of the urchins with whom he
played in the street did not come at the usual time. One of
them said that he was ill, and they got used to not seeing him
in their games. It was explained, it was quite simple. One

evening Jean-Christophe had gone to bed; it was early, and from the recess in which his bed was, he saw the light in the room. There was a knock at the door. A neighbor had come to have a chat. He listened absently, telling himself stories as usual. The words of their talk did not reach him. Suddenly he heard the neighbor say: " He is dead." His blood stopped, for he had understood who was dead. He listened and held his breath. His parents cried out. Melchior's booming voice said:

" Jean-Christophe, do you hear? Poor Fritz is dead."
Jean-Christophe made an effort, and replied quietly:
" Yes, papa."
His bosom was drawn tight as in a vise.
Melchior went on:
" ' Yes, papa.' Is that all you say? You are not grieved by it."
Louisa, who understood the child, said:
" 'Ssh! Let him sleep! "
And they talked in whispers. But Jean-Christophe, pricking his ears, gathered all the details of illness—typhoid fever, cold baths, delirium, the parents' grief. He could not breathe, a lump in his throat choked him. He shuddered. All these horrible things took shape in his mind. Above all, he gleaned that the disease was contagious—that is, that he also might die in the same way—and terror froze him, for he remembered that he had shaken hands with Fritz the last time he had seen him, and that very day had gone past the house. But he made no sound, so as to avoid having to talk, and when his father, after the neighbor had gone, asked him: " Jean-Christophe, are you asleep?" he did not reply. He heard Melchior saying to Louisa:
" The boy has no heart."
Louisa did not reply, but a moment later she came and gently raised the curtain and looked at the little bed. Jean-Christophe only just had time to close his eyes and imitate the regular breathing which his brothers made when they were asleep. Louisa went away on tip-toe. And yet how he wanted to keep her! How he wanted to tell her that he was afraid, and to ask her to save him, or at least to comfort him! But

he was afraid of their laughing at him, and treating him as a coward; and besides, he knew only too well that nothing that they might say would be any good. And for hours he lay there in agony, thinking that he felt the disease creeping over him, and pains in his head, a stricture of the heart, and thinking in terror: " It is the end. I am ill. I am going to die. I am going to die!" . . . Once he sat up in his bed and called to his mother in a low voice; but they were asleep, and he dared not wake them.

From that time on his childhood was poisoned by the idea of death. His nerves delivered him up to all sorts of little baseless sicknesses, to depression, to sudden transports, and fits of choking. His imagination ran riot with these troubles, and thought it saw in all of them the murderous beast which was to rob him of his life. How many times he suffered agonies, with his mother sitting only a few yards away from him, and she guessing nothing! For in his cowardice he was brave enough to conceal all his terror in a strange jumble of feeling —pride in not turning to others, shame of being afraid, and the scrupulousness of a tenderness which forbade him to trouble his mother. But he never ceased to think: " This time I am ill. I am seriously ill. It is diphtheria. . . ." He had chanced on the word " diphtheria." . . . " Dear God! not this time! . . ."

He had religious ideas: he loved to believe what his mother had told him, that after death the soul ascended to the Lord, and if it were pious entered into the garden of paradise. But the idea of this journey rather frightened than attracted him. He was not at all envious of the children whom God, as a recompense, according to his mother, took in their sleep and called to Him without having made them suffer. He trembled, as he went to sleep, for fear that God should indulge this whimsy at his expense. It must be terrible to be taken suddenly from the warmth of one's bed and dragged through the void into the presence of God. He imagined God as an enormous sun, with a voice of thunder. How it must hurt! It must burn the eyes, ears—all one's soul! Then, God could punish— you never know. . . . And besides, that did not prevent all the other horrors which he did not know very well, though he could guess them from what he had heard—your body in a box, all alone at the bottom of a hole, lost in the crowd of those revolting cemeteries to which he was taken to pray. . . God! God! How sad! how sad! . . .

And yet it was not exactly joyous to live, and be hungry, and see your father drunk, and to be beaten, to suffer in so many ways from the wickedness of other children, from the insulting pity of grown-up persons, and to be understood by no one, not even by your mother. Everybody humiliates you, no one loves you. You are alone—alone, and matter so little! Yes; but it was just this that made him want to live. He felt in himself a surging power of wrath. A strange thing, that power! It could do nothing yet; it was as though it were afar off and gagged, swaddled, paralyzed; he had no idea what it wanted, what, later on, it would be. But it was in him; he was sure of it; he felt it stirring and crying out. To-morrow —to-morrow, what a voyage he would take! He had a savage desire to live, to punish the wicked, to do great things. "Oh! but how I will live when I am . . ." he pondered a little— "when I am eighteen!" Sometimes he put it at twenty-one; that was the extreme limit. He thought that was enough for the domination of the world. He thought of the heroes dearest to him—of Napoleon, and of that other more remote hero, whom he preferred, Alexander the Great. Surely he would be like them if only he lived for another twelve—ten years. He never thought of pitying those who died at thirty. They were old; they had lived their lives; it was their fault if they had failed. But to die now . . . despair! Too terrible to pass while yet a little child, and forever to be in the minds of men a little boy whom everybody thinks he has the right to scold! He wept with rage at the thought, as though he were already dead.

This agony of death tortured his childish years—corrected only by disgust with all life and the sadness of his own.

It was in the midst of these gloomy shadows, in the stifling night that every moment seemed to intensify about him, that there began to shine, like a star lost in the dark abysm of space the light which was to illuminate his life: divine music. . .

His grandfather gave the children an old piano, which one
of his clients, anxious to be rid of it, had asked him to take.
His patient ingenu.ty had almost put it in order. The present
had not been very well received. Louisa thought her room
already too small, without filling it up any more; and Melchior
said that Jean Michel had not ruined himself over it: just
firewood. Only Jean-Christophe was glad of it without exactly
knowing why. It seemed to him a magic box, full of marvelous
stories. just like the ones in the fairy-book—a volume of the
"Thousand and One Nights"—which his grandfather read
to him sometimes to their mutual delight. He had heard his
father try the piano on the day of its arrival, and draw from it a
little rain of arpeggios like the drops that a puff of wind shakes
from the wet branches of a tree after a shower. He clapped
his hands, and cried "Encore!" but Melchior scornfully closed
the piano, saying that it was worthless. Jean-Christophe did
not insist, but after that he was always hovering about the
instrument. As soon as no one was near he would raise the
lid, and softly press down a key, just as if he were moving
with his finger the living shell of some great insect; he wanted
to push out the creature that was locked up in it. Sometimes
in his haste he would strike too hard, and then his mother would
cry out, "Will you not be quiet? Don't go touching everything!" or else he would pinch himself cruelly in closing the
piano, and make piteous faces as he sucked his bruised fingers. . . .

Now his greatest joy is when his mother is gone out for a
day's service, or to pay some visit in the town. He listens as
she goes down the stairs, and into the street, and away. He
is alone. He opens the piano, and brings up a chair, and perches
on it. His shoulders just about reach the keyboard; it is
enough for what he wants. Why does he wait until he is alone?
No one would prevent his playing so long as he did not make
too much noise. But he is ashamed before the others, and
dare not. And then they talk and move about: that spoils his
pleasure. It is so much more beautiful when he is alone!
Jean-Christophe holds his breath so that the silence may be
even greater, and also because he is a little excited, as though
he were going to let off a gun. His heart beats as he lays

his finger on the key; sometimes he lifts his finger after he
has the key half pressed down, and lays it on another. Does he
know what will come out of it, more than what will come out
of the other? Suddenly a sound issues from it; there are deep
sounds and high sounds, some tinkling, some roaring. The
child listens to them one by one as they die away and finally
cease to be; they hover in the air like bells heard far off, coming
near in the wind, and then going away again; then when you
listen you hear in the distance other voices, different, joining
in and droning like flying insects; they seem to call to you,
to draw you away farther—farther and farther into the mysterious regions, where they dive down and are lost. . . . They
are gone! . . . No; still they murmur. . . . A little beating
of wings. . . . How strange it, all is! They are like spirits.
How is it that they are so obedient? how is it that they are
held captive in this old box? But best of all is when you lay
two fingers on two keys at once. Then you never know exactly
what will happen. Sometimes the two spirits are hostile; they
are angry with each other, and fight; and hate each other, and
buzz testily. Then voices are raised; they cry out, angrily,
now sorrowfully. Jean-Christophe adores that; it is as though
there were monsters chained up, biting at their fetters, beating
against the bars of their prison; they are like to break them,
and burst out like the monsters in the fairy-book—the genii
imprisoned in the Arab bottles under the seal of Solomon.
Others flatter you; they try to cajole you, but you feel that
they only want to bite, that they are hot and fevered. Jean-
Christophe does not know what they want, but they lure him
and disturb him; they make him almost blush. And sometimes there are notes that love each other; sounds embrace,
as people do with their arms when they kiss: they are gracious
and sweet. These are the good spirits; their faces are smiling,
and there are no lines in them; they love little Jean-Christophe, and little Jean-Christophe loves them. Tears come to
his eyes as he hears them, and he is never weary of calling
them up. They are his friends, his dear, tender friends. . . .

So the child journeys through the forest of sounds, and
round him he is conscious of thousands of forces lying in wait
for him, and calling to him to caress or devour him. . . .

One day Melchior came upon him thus. He made him jump with fear at the sound of his great voice. Jean-Christophe, thinking he was doing wrong, quickly put his hands up to his ears to ward off the blows he feared. But Melchior did not scold him, strange to say; he was in a good temper, and laughed.

"You like that, boy?" he asked, patting his head kindly. "Would you like me to teach you to play it?"

Would he like! . . . Delighted, he murmured: "Yes." The two of them sat down at the piano, Jean-Christophe perched this time on a pile of big books, and very attentively he took his first lesson. He learned first of all that the buzzing spirits have strange names, like Chinese names, of one syllable, or even of one letter. He was astonished; he imagined them to be different from that: beautiful, caressing names, like the princesses in the fairy stories. He did not like the familiarity with which his father talked of them. Again, when Melchior evoked them they were not the same; they seemed to become indifferent as they rolled out from under his fingers. But Jean-Christophe was glad to learn about the relationships between them, their hierarchy, the scales, which were like a King commanding an army, or like a band of negroes marching in single file. He was surprised to see that each soldier, or each negro, could become a monarch in his turn, or the head of a similar band, and that it was possible to summon whole battalions from one end to the other of the keyboard. It amused him to hold the thread which made them march. But it was a small thing compared with what he had seen at first; his enchanted forest was lost. However, he set himself to learn, for it was not tiresome, and he was surprised at his father's patience. Melchior did not weary of it either; he made him begin the same thing over again ten times. Jean-Christophe did not understand why he should take so much trouble; his father loved him, then? That was good! The boy worked away; his heart was filled with gratitude.

He would have been less docile had he known what thoughts were springing into being in his father's head.

From that day on Melchior took him to the house of a neighbor, where three times a week there was chamber music. Melchior played first violin, Jean Michel the violoncello. The other two were a bank-clerk and the old watchmaker of the *Schillerstrasse*. Every now and then the chemist joined them with his flute. They began at five, and went on till nine. Between each piece they drank beer. Neighbors used to come in and out, and listen without a word, leaning against the wall, and nodding their heads, and beating time with their feet, and filling the room with clouds of tobacco-smoke. Page followed page, piece followed piece, but the patience of the musicians was never exhausted. They did not speak; they were all attention; their brows were knit, and from time to time they grunted with pleasure, but for the rest they were perfectly incapable not only of expressing, but even of feeling, the beauty of what they played. They played neither very accurately nor in good time, but they never went off the rails, and followed faithfully the marked changes of tone. They had that musical facility which is easily satisfied, that mediocre perfection which is so plentiful in the race which is said to be the most musical in the world. They had also that great appetite which does not stickle for the quality of its food, so only there be quantity —that healthy appetite to which all music is good, and the more substantial the better—it sees no difference between Brahms and Beethoven, or between the works of the same master, between an empty concerto and a moving sonata, because they are fashioned of the same stuff.

Jean-Christophe sat apart in a corner, which was his own, behind the piano. No one could disturb him there, for to reach it he had to go on all fours. It was half dark there, and the boy had just room to lie on the floor if he huddled up. The smoke of the tobacco filled his eyes and throat: dust, too; there were large flakes of it like sheepskin, but he did not mind that, and listened gravely, squatting there Turkish fashion, and widening the holes in the cloth of the piano with his dirty little fingers. He did not like everything that they played; but nothing that they played bored him, and he never tried to formulate his opinions, for he thought himself too small to know anything. Only some music sent him to sleep, some woke him up; it was never disagreeable to him. Without his knowing it, it was nearly always good music that excited him. Sure of not

being seen, he made faces, he wrinkled his nose, ground his
teeth, or stuck out his tongue; his eyes flashed with anger or
drooped languidly; he moved his arms and legs with a defiant
and valiant air; he wanted to march, to lunge out, to pulverize
the world. He fidgeted so much that in the end a head would
peer over the piano, and say: "Hullo, boy, are you mad?
Leave the piano. . . . Take your hand away, or I'll pull your
ears!" And that made him crestfallen and angry. Why did
they want to spoil his pleasure? He was not doing any harm.
Must he always be tormented! His father chimed in. They
chid him for making a noise, and said that he did not like
music. And in the end he believed it. These honest citizens
grinding out concertos would have been astonished if they had
been told that the only person in the company who really felt
the music was the little boy.

If they wanted him to keep quiet, why did they play airs
which make you march? In those pages were rearing horses,
swords, war-cries, the pride of triumph; and they wanted him,
like them, to do no more than wag his head and beat time with
his feet! They had only to play placid dreams or some of those
chattering pages which talk so much and say nothing. There
are plenty of them, for example, like that piece of Goldmark's,
of which the old watchmaker had just said with a delighted
smile: "It is pretty. There is no harshness in it. All the
corners are rounded off. . . ." The boy was very quiet then.
He became drowsy. He did not know what they were playing,
hardly heard it; but he was happy; his limbs were numbed,
and he was dreaming.

His dreams were not a consecutive story; they had neither
head nor tail. It was rarely that he saw a definite picture:
his mother making a cake, and with a knife removing the paste
that clung to her fingers; a water-rat that he had seen the
night before swimming in the river; a whip that he wanted
to make with a willow wand. . . . Heaven knows why these
things should have cropped up in his memory at such a time!
But most often he saw nothing at all, and yet he felt things
innumerable and infinite. It was as though there were a
number of very important things not to be spoken of, or
not worth speaking of, because they were so well known, and

because they had always been so. Some of them were sad, terribly sad; but there was nothing painful in them, as there is in the things that belong to real life; they were not ugly and debasing, like the blows that Jean-Christophe had from his father, or like the things that were in his head when, sick at heart with shame, he thought of some humiliation; they filled the mind with a melancholy calm. And some were bright and shining, shedding torrents of joy. And Jean-Christophe thought: "Yes, it is *thus*—thus that I will do by-and-by." He did not know exactly what *thus* was, nor why he said it, but he felt that he had to say it, and that it was clear as day. He heard the sound of a sea, and he was quite near to it, kept from it only by a wall of dunes. Jean-Christophe had no idea what sea it was, or what it wanted with him, but he was conscious that it would rise above the barrier of dunes. And then! . . . Then all would be well, and he would be quite happy. Nothing to do but to hear it, then, quite near, to sink to sleep to the sound of its great voice, soothing away all his little griefs and humiliations. They were sad still, but no longer shameful nor injurious; everything seemed natural and almost sweet.

Very often it was mediocre music that produced this intoxication in him. The writers of it were poor devils, with no thought in their heads but the gaining of money, or the hiding away of the emptiness of their lives by tagging notes together according to accepted formulæ—or to be original, in defiance of formulæ. But in the notes of music, even when handled by an idiot, there is such a power of life that they can let loose storms in a simple soul. Perhaps even the dreams suggested by the idiots are more mysterious and more free than those breathed by an imperious thought which drags you along by force, for aimless movement and empty chatter do not disturb the mind in its own pondering. . . .

So, forgotten and forgetting, the child stayed in his corner behind the piano, until suddenly he felt ants climbing up his legs. And he remembered then that he was a little boy with dirty nails, and that he was rubbing his nose against a whitewashed wall, and holding his feet in his hands.

On the day when Melchior, stealing on tiptoe, had surprised

the boy at the keyboard that was too high for him, he had stayed to watch him for a moment, and suddenly there had flashed upon him: " A little prodigy! . . . Why had he not thought of it? . . . What luck for the family! . . ." No doubt he had thought that the boy would be a little peasant like his mother. " It would cost nothing to try. What a great thing it would be! He would take him all over Germany, perhaps abroad. It would be a jolly life, and noble to boot." Melchior never failed to look for the nobility hidden in all he did, for it was not often that he failed to find it, after some reflection.

Strong in this assurance, immediately after supper, as soon as he had taken his last mouthful, he dumped the child once more in front of the piano, and made him go through the day's lesson until his eyes closed in weariness. Then three times the next day. Then the day after that. Then every day. Jean-Christophe soon tired of it; then he was sick to death of it; finally he could stand it no more, and tried to revolt against it. There was no point in what he was made to do: nothing but learning to run as fast as possible over the keys, by loosening the thumb, or exercising the fourth finger, which would cling awkwardly to the two next to it. It got on his nerves; there was nothing beautiful in it. There was an end of the magic sounds, and fascinating monsters, and the universe of dreams felt in one moment. . . . Nothing but scales and exercises—dry, monotonous, dull—duller than the conversation at meal-time, which was always the same—always about the dishes, and always the same dishes. At first the child listened absently to what his father said. When he was severely reprimanded he went on with a bad grace. He paid no attention to abuse; he met it with bad temper. The last straw was when one evening he heard Melchior unfold his plans in the next room. So it was in order to put him on show like a trick animal that he was so badgered and forced every day to move bits of ivory! He was not even given time to go and see his beloved river. What was it made them so set against him? He was angry, hurt in his pride, robbed of his liberty. He decided that he would play no more, or as badly as possible, and would discourage his father. It would be hard, but at all costs he must keep his independence.

The very next lesson he began to put his plan into execution. He set himself conscientiously to hit the notes awry, or to bungle every touch. Melchior cried out, then roared, and blows began to rain. He had a heavy ruler. At every false note he struck the boy's fingers, and at the same time shouted in his ears, so that he was like to deafen him. Jean-Christophe's face twitched under the pain of it; he bit his lips to keep himself from crying, and stoically went on hitting the notes all wrong, bobbing his head down whenever he felt a blow coming. But his system was not good, and it was not long before he began to see that it was so. Melchior was as obstinate as his son, and he swore that even if they were to stay there two days and two nights he would not let him off a single note until it had been properly played. Then Jean-Christophe tried too deliberately to play wrongly, and Melchior began to suspect the trick, as he saw that the boy's hand fell heavily to one side at every note with obvious intent. The blows became more frequent; Jean-Christophe was no longer conscious of his fingers. He wept pitifully and silently, sniffing, and swallowing down his sobs and tears. He understood that he had nothing to gain by going on like that, and that he would have to resort to desperate measures. He stopped, and, trembling at the thought of the storm which was about to let loose, he said valiantly:

"Papa, I won't play any more."

Melchior choked.

"What! What! . . ." he cried.

He took and almost broke the boy's arm with shaking it. Jean-Christophe, trembling more and more, and raising his elbow to ward off the blows, said again:

"I won't play any more. First, because I don't like being beaten. And then . . ."

He could not finish. A terrific blow knocked the wind out of him, and Melchior roared:

"Ah! you don't like being beaten? You don't like it? . . ."

Blows rained. Jean-Christophe bawled through his sobs:

"And then . . . I don't like music! . . . I don't like music! . . ."

He slipped down from his chair. Melchior roughly put him back, and knocked his knuckles against the keyboard. He cried:

" You shall play! "

And Jean-Christophe shouted:

" No! No! I won't play! "

Melchior had to surrender. He thrashed the boy, thrust him from the room, and said that he should have nothing to eat all day, or the whole month, until he had played all his exercises without a mistake. He kicked him out and slammed the door after him.

Jean-Christophe found himself on the stairs, the dark and dirty stairs, worm-eaten. A draught came through a broken pane in the skylight, and the walls were dripping. Jean-Christophe sat on one of the greasy steps; his heart was beating wildly with anger and emotion. In a low voice he cursed his father:

" Beast! That's what you are! A beast . . . a gross creature . . . a brute! Yes, a brute! . . . and I hate you, I hate you! . . . Oh, I wish you were dead! I wish you were dead! "

His bosom swelled. He looked desperately at the sticky staircase and the spider's web swinging in the wind above the broken pane. He felt alone, lost in his misery. He looked at the gap in the banisters. . . . What if he were to throw himself down? . . . or out of the window? . . . Yes, what if he were to kill himself to punish them? How remorseful they would be! He heard the noise of his fall from the stairs. The door upstairs opened suddenly. Agonized voices cried: " He has fallen!—He has fallen! " Footsteps clattered downstairs. His father and mother threw themselves weeping upon his body. His mother sobbed: " It is your fault! You have killed him! " His father waved his arms, threw himself on his knees, beat his head against the banisters, and cried: " What a wretch am I! What a wretch am I! " The sight of all this softened his misery. He was on the point of taking pity on their grief; but then he thought that it was well for them, and he enjoyed his revenge. . . .

When his story was ended, he found himself once more at

the top of the stairs in the dark; he looked down once more,
and his desire to throw himself down was gone. He even
shuddered a little, and moved away from the edge, thinking
that he might fall. Then he felt that he was a prisoner, like
a poor bird in a cage—a prisoner forever, with nothing to do
but to break his head and hurt himself. He wept, wept, and
he rubbed his eyes with his dirty little hands, so that in a
moment he was filthy. As he wept he never left off looking at
the things about him, and he found some distraction in that.
He stopped moaning for a moment to look at the spider which
had just begun to move. Then he began with less conviction.
He listened to the sound of his own weeping, and went on
mechanically with his sobbing, without much knowing why he
did so. Soon he got up; he was attracted by the window. He
sat on the window-sill, retiring into the background, and
watched the spider furtively. It interested while it revolted
him.

Below the Rhine flowed, washing the walls of the house. In
the staircase window it was like being suspended over the river
in a moving sky. Jean-Christophe never limped down the
stairs without taking a long look at it, but he had never yet
seen it as it was to-day. Grief sharpens the senses; it is as
though everything were more sharply graven on the vision
after tears have washed away the dim traces of memory. The
river was like a living thing to the child—a creature inexplicable, but how much more powerful than all the creatures that
he knew! Jean-Christophe leaned forward to see it better; he
pressed his mouth and flattened his nose against the pane.
Where was *it* going? What did *it* want? *It* looked free, and
sure of its road. . . . Nothing could stop *it*. At all hours of
the day or night, rain or sun, whether there were joy or sorrow
in the house, *it* went on going by, and it was as though nothing
mattered to *it*, as though *it* never knew sorrow, and rejoiced
in *its* strength. What joy to be like *it*, to run through the fields,
and by willow-branches, and over little shining pebbles and
crisping sand, and to care for nothing, to be cramped by nothing, to be free! . . .

The boy looked and listened greedily; it was as though he
were borne along by the river, moving by with it. . . . When

he closed his eyes he saw color—blue, green, yellow, red, and great chasing shadows and sunbeams. . . . What he sees takes shape. Now it is a large plain, reeds, corn waving under a breeze scented with new grass and mint. Flowers on every side —cornflowers, poppies, violets. How lovely it is! How sweet the air! How good it is to lie down in the thick, soft grass! . . . Jean-Christophe feels glad and a little bewildered, as he does when on feast-days his father pours into his glass a little Rhine wine. . . . The river goes by. . . . The country is changed. . . . Now there are trees leaning over the water; their delicate leaves, like little hands, dip, move, and turn about in the water. A village among the trees is mirrored in the river. There are cypress-trees, and the crosses of the cemetery showing above the white wall washed by the stream. Then there are rocks, a mountain gorge, vines on the slopes, a little pine-wood, and ruined castles. . . . And once more the plain, corn, birds, and the sun. . . .

The great green mass of the river goes by smoothly, like a single thought; there are no waves, almost no ripples—smooth, oily patches. Jean-Christophe does not see it; he has closed his eyes to hear it better. The ceaseless roaring fills him, makes him giddy; he is exalted by this eternal, masterful dream which goes no man knows whither. Over the turmoil of its depths rush waters, in swift rhythm, eagerly, ardently. And from the rhythm ascends music, like a vine climbing a trellis— arpeggios from silver keys, sorrowful violins, velvety and smooth-sounding flutes. . . . The country has disappeared. The river has disappeared. There floats by only a strange, soft, and twilight atmosphere. Jean-Christophe's heart flutters with emotion. What does he see now? Oh! Charming faces! . . . A little girl with brown tresses calls to him, slowly, softly, and mockingly. . . . A pale boy's face looks at him with melancholy blue eyes. . . . Others smile; other eyes look at him—curious and provoking eyes, and their glances make him blush—eyes affectionate and mournful, like the eyes of a dog—eyes imperious, eyes suffering. . . . And the pale face of a woman, with black hair, and lips close pressed, and eyes so large that they obscure her other features, and they gaze upon Jean-Christophe with an ardor that hurts him. . . . And, dearest of

all, that face which smiles upon him with clear gray eyes and
lips a little open, showing gleaming white teeth. . . . Ah!
how kind and tender is that smile! All his heart is tenderness
from it! How good it is to love! Again! Smile upon me
again! Do not go! . . . Alas! it is gone! . . . But it leaves
in his heart sweetness ineffable. Evil, sorrow, are no more;
nothing is left. . . . Nothing, only an airy dream, like serene
music, floating down a sunbeam, like the gossamers on fine
summer days. . . . What has happened? What are these
visions that fill the child with sadness and sweet sorrow? Never
had he seen them before, and yet he knew them and recognized
them. Whence come they? From what obscure abysm of
creation? Are they what has been . . . *or what will
be?* . . .

Now all is done, every haunting form is gone. Once more
through a misty veil, as though he were soaring high above
it, the river in flood appears, covering the fields, and rolling
by, majestic, slow, almost still. And far, far away, like a steely
light upon the horizon, a watery plain, a line of trembling waves
—the sea. The river runs down to it. The sea seems to run
up to the river. She fires him. He desires her. He must lose
himself in her. . . . The music hovers; lovely dance rhythms
swing out madly; all the world is rocked in their triumphant
whirligig. . . . The soul, set free, cleaves space, like swallows'
flight, like swallows drunk with the air, skimming across the
sky with shrill cries. . . . Joy! Joy! There is nothing, nothing! . . . Oh, infinite happiness! . . .

Hours passed; it was evening; the staircase was in darkness.
Drops of rain made rings upon the river's gown, and the current
bore them dancing away. Sometimes the branch of a tree or
pieces of black bark passed noiselessly and disappeared. The
murderous spider had withdrawn to her darkest corner. And
little Jean-Christophe was still leaning forward on the window-
sill. His face was pale and dirty; happiness shone in him.
He was asleep.

III

E la faccia del sol nascere ombrata.
Purgatorio, xxx.

HE had to surrender. In spite of an obstinate and heroic resistance, blows triumphed over his ill-will. Every morning for three hours, and for three hours every evening, Jean-Christophe was set before the instrument of torture. All on edge with attention and weariness, with large tears rolling down his cheeks and nose, he moved his little red hands over the black and white keys—his hands were often stiff with cold—under the threatening ruler, which descended at every false note, and the harangues of his master, which were more odious to him than the blows. He thought that he hated music. And yet he applied himself to it with a zest which fear of Melchior did not altogether explain. Certain words of his grandfather had made an impression on him. The old man, seeing his grandson weeping, had told him, with that gravity which he always maintained for the boy, that it was worth while suffering a little for the most beautiful and noble art given to men for their consolation and glory. And Jean-Christophe, who was grateful to his grandfather for talking to him like a man, had been secretly touched by these simple words, which sorted well with his childish stoicism and growing pride. But, more than by argument, he was bound and enslaved by the memory of certain musical emotions, bound and enslaved to the detested art, against which he tried in vain to rebel.

There was in the town, as usual in Germany, a theater, where opera, opéra-comique, operetta, drama, comedy, and vaudeville are presented—every sort of play of every style and fashion. There were performances three times a week from six to nine in the evening. Old Jean Michel never missed one, and was equally interested in everything. Once he took his grandson with him. Several days beforehand he told him at length what the piece was about. Jean-Christophe did not understand it, but he did gather that there would be terrible things in it, and while he was consumed with the desire to see them he was much afraid, though he dared not confess it. He knew that there was to be a storm, and he was fearful of being struck by lightning. He knew that there was to be a battle, and he was not at all sure that he would not be killed. On the night before, in bed, he went through real agony, and on the day of the performance he almost wished that his grandfather might be prevented from coming for him. But when the hour was near, and his grandfather did not come, he began to worry, and every other minute looked out of the window. At last the old man appeared, and they set out together. His heart leaped in his bosom; his tongue was dry, and he could not speak.

They arrived at the mysterious building which was so often talked about at home. At the door Jean Michel met some acquaintances, and the boy, who was holding his hand tight because he was afraid of being lost, could not understand how they could talk and laugh quietly at such a moment.

Jean Michel took his usual place in the first row behind the orchestra. He leaned on the balustrade, and began a long conversation with the contra-bass. He was at home there; there he was listened to because of his authority as a musician, and he made the most of it; it might almost be said that he abused it. Jean-Christophe could hear nothing. He was overwhelmed by his expectation of the play, by the appearance of the theater, which seemed magnificent to him, by the splendor of the audience, who frightened him terribly. He dared not turn his head, for he thought that all eyes were fixed on him. He hugged his little cap between his knees, and he stared at the magic curtain with round eyes.

At last three blows were struck. His grandfather blew his nose, and drew the *libretto* from his pocket. He always followed it scrupulously, so much so that sometimes he neglected what was happening on the stage. The orchestra began to play. With the opening chords Jean-Christophe felt more at ease. He was at home in this world of sound, and from that moment, however extravagant the play might be, it seemed natural to him.

The curtain was raised, to reveal pasteboard trees and creatures who were not much more real. The boy looked at it all, gaping with admiration, but he was not surprised. The piece

was set in a fantastic East, of which he could have had no
idea. The poem was a web of ineptitudes, in which no human
quality was perceptible. Jean-Christophe hardly grasped it at
all; he made extraordinary mistakes, took one character for
another, and pulled at his grandfather's sleeve to ask him absurd
questions, which showed that he had understood nothing. He
was not bored: passionately interested, on the contrary. Round
the idiotic *libretto* he built a romance of his own invention,
which had no sort of relation to the one that was represented
on the stage. Every moment some incident upset his romance,
and he had to repair it, but that did not worry him. He had
made his choice of the people who moved upon the stage, making all sorts of different sounds, and breathlessly he followed
the fate of those upon whom he had fastened his sympathy.
He was especially concerned with a fair lady, of uncertain age,
who had long, brilliantly fair hair, eyes of an unnatural size,
and bare feet. The monstrous improbabilities of the setting
did not shock him. His keen, childish eyes did not perceive
the grotesque ugliness of the actors, large and fleshy, and the
deformed chorus of all sizes in two lines, nor the pointlessness
of their gestures, nor their faces bloated by their shrieks, nor
the full wigs, nor the high heels of the tenor, nor the make-up
of his lady-love, whose face was streaked with variegated pen-
ciling. He was in the condition of a lover, whose passion blinds
him to the actual aspect of the beloved object. The marvelous
power of illusion, natural to children, stopped all unpleasant
sensations on the way, and transformed them.

The music especially worked wonders. It bathed the whole
scene in a misty atmosphere, in which everything became beautiful, noble, and desirable. It bred in the soul a desperate
need of love, and at the same time showed phantoms of love
on all sides, to fill the void that itself had created. Little
Jean-Christophe was overwhelmed by his emotion. There were
words, gestures, musical phrases which disturbed him; he dared
not then raise his eyes; he knew not whether it were well
or ill; he blushed and grew pale by turns; sometimes there
came drops of sweat upon his brow, and he was fearful lest
all the people there should see his distress. When the catastrophe came about which inevitably breaks upon lovers in the

fourth act of an opera so as to provide the tenor and the *prima donna* with an opportunity for showing off their shrillest screams, the child thought he must choke; his throat hurt him as though he had caught cold; he clutched at his neck with his hands, and could not swallow his saliva; tears welled up in him; his hands and feet were frozen. Fortunately, his grandfather was not much less moved. He enjoyed the theater with a childish simplicity. During the dramatic passages he coughed carelessly to hide his distress, but Jean-Christophe saw it, and it delighted him. It was horribly hot; Jean-Christophe was dropping with sleep, and he was very uncomfortable. But he thought only: " Is there much longer? It cannot be finished ! " Then suddenly it was finished, without his knowing why. The curtain fell; the audience rose; the enchantment was broken.

They went home through the night, the two children—the old man and the little boy. What a fine night! What a serene moonlight! They said nothing; they were turning over their memories. At last the old man said:

" Did you like it, boy? "

Jean-Christophe could not reply; he was still fearful from emotion, and he would not speak, so as not to break the spell; he had to make an effort to whisper, with a sigh:

" Oh yes."

The old man smiled. After a time he went on:

" It's a fine thing—a musician's trade! To create things like that, such marvelous spectacles—is there anything more glorious? It is to be God on earth! "

The boy's mind leaped to that. What! a man had made all that! That had not occurred to him. It had seemed that it must have made itself, must be the work of Nature. A man, a musician, such as he would be some day! Oh, to be that for one day, only one day! And then afterwards . . . afterwards, whatever you like! Die, if necessary! He asked:

" What man made that, grandfather? "

The old man told him of François Marie Hassler, a young German artist who lived at Berlin. He had known him once. Jean-Christophe listened, all ears. Suddenly he said:

"And you, grandfather?"

The old man trembled.

"What?" he asked.

"Did you do things like that—you too?"

"Certainly," said the old man a little crossly.

He was silent, and after they had walked a little he sighed heavily. It was one of the sorrows of his life. He had always longed to write for the theater, and inspiration had always betrayed him. He had in his desk one or two acts written, but he had so little illusion as to their worth that he had never dared to submit them to an outside judgment.

They said no more until they reached home. Neither slept. The old man was troubled. He took his Bible for consolation. In bed Jean-Christophe turned over and over the events of the evening; he recollected the smallest details, and the girl with the bare feet reappeared before him. As he dozed off a musical phrase rang in his ears as distinctly as if the orchestra were there. All his body leaped; he sat up on his pillow, his head buzzing with music, and he thought: "Some day I also shall write. Oh, can I ever do it?"

From that moment he had only one desire, to go to the theater again, and he set himself to work more keenly, because they made a visit to the theater his reward. He thought of nothing but that; half the week he thought of the last performance, and the other half he thought of the next. He was fearful of being ill on a theater day, and this fear made him often find in himself the symptoms of three or four illnesses. When the day came he did not eat; he fidgeted like a soul in agony; he looked at the clock fifty times, and thought that the evening would never come; finally, unable to contain himself, he would go out an hour before the office opened, for fear of not being able to procure a seat, and, as he was the first in the empty theater, he used to grow uneasy. His grandfather had told him that once or twice the audience had not been large enough, and so the players had preferred not to perform, and to give back the money. He watched the arrivals and counted them, thinking: "Twenty-three, twenty-four, twenty-five. . . . Oh, it is not enough . . . there will never be

enough!" And when he saw some important person enter
the circle or the stalls, his heart was lighter, and he 'said to
himself: "They will never dare to send him away. Surely
they will play for him." But he was not convinced; he would
not be reassured until the musicians took their places. And
even then he would be afraid that the curtain would rise, and
they would announce, as they had done one evening, a change
of programme. With lynx eyes he watched the stand of the
contra-bass to see if the title written on his music was that of
the piece announced. And when he had seen it there, two
minutes later he would look again to make quite sure that he
had not been wrong. The conductor was not there. He must
be ill. There was a stirring behind the curtain, and a sound
of voices and hurried footsteps. Was there an accident, some
untoward misfortune? Silence again. The conductor was at
his post. Everything seemed ready at last. . . . They did not
begin! What was happening? He boiled over with impatience.
Then the bell rang. His heart thumped away. The orchestra
began the overture, and for a few hours Jean-Christophe would
swim in happiness, troubled only by the idea that it must soon
come to an end.

Some time after that a musical event brought even more
excitement into Jean-Christophe's thoughts. François Marie
Hassler, the author of the first opera which had so bowled him
over, was to visit the town. He was to conduct a concert con-
sisting of his compositions. The town was excited. The young
musician was the subject of violent discussion in Germany,
and for a fortnight he was the only topic of conversation. It
was a different matter when he arrived. The friends of Melchior and old Jean Michel continually came for news, and
they went away with the most extravagant notions of the musician's habits and eccentricities. The child followed these narratives with eager attention. The idea that the great man was
there in the town, breathing the same air as himself, treading
the same stones, threw him into a state of dumb exaltation.
He lived only in the hope of seeing him.

Hassler was staying at the Palace as the guest of the Grand
Duke. He hardly went out, except to the theater for rehearsals,

to which Jean-Christophe was not admitted, and as he was very lazy, he went to and fro in the Prince's carriage. Therefore, Jean-Christophe did not have many opportunities of seeing him, and he only succeeded once in catching sight of him as he drove in the carriage. He saw his fur coat, and wasted hours in waiting in the street, thrusting and jostling his way to right and left, and before and behind, to win and keep his place in front of the loungers. He consoled himself with spending half his days watching the windows of the Palace which had been pointed out as those of the master. Most often he only saw the shutters, for Hassler got up late, and the windows were closed almost all morning. This habit had made well-informed persons say that Hassler could not bear the light of day, and lived in eternal night.

At length Jean-Christophe was able to approach his hero. It was the day of the concert. All the town was there. The Grand Duke and his Court occupied the great royal box, surmounted with a crown supported by two chubby cherubims. The theater was in gala array. The stage was decorated with branches of oak and flowering laurel. All the musicians of any account made it a point of honor to take their places in the orchestra. Melchior was at his post, and Jean Michel was conducting the chorus.

When Hassler appeared there was loud applause from every part of the house, and the ladies rose to see him better. Jean-Christophe devoured him with his eyes. Hassler had a young, sensitive face, though it was already rather puffy and tired-looking; his temples were bald, and his hair was thin on the crown of his head; for the rest, fair, curly hair. His blue eyes looked vague. He had a little fair mustache and an expressive mouth, which was rarely still, but twitched with a thousand imperceptible movements. He was tall, and held himself badly— not from awkwardness, but from weariness or boredom. He conducted capriciously and lithely, with his whole awkward body swaying, like his music, with gestures, now caressing, now sharp and jerky. It was easy to see that he was very nervous, and his music was the exact reflection of himself. The quivering and jerky life of it broke through the usual apathy of the orchestra. Jean-Christophe breathed heavily; in spite of his

fear of drawing attention to himself, he could not stand still
in his place; he fidgeted, got up, and the music gave him such
violent and unexpected shocks that he had to move his head,
arms, and legs, to the great discomfort of his neighbors, who
warded off his kicks as best they could. The whole audience
was enthusiastic, fascinated by the success, rather than by the
compositions. At the end there was a storm of applause and
cries, in which the trumpets in the orchestra joined, German
fashion, with their triumphant blare in salute of the conqueror.
Jean-Christophe trembled with pride, as though these honors
were for himself. He enjoyed seeing Hassler's face light up
with childish pleasure. The ladies threw flowers, the men
waved their hats, and the audience rushed for the platform.
Every one wanted to shake the master's hand. Jean-Christophe
saw one enthusiast raise the master's hand to his lips, another
steal a handkerchief that Hassler had left on the corner of his
desk. He wanted to reach the platform also, although he did
not know why, for if at that moment he had found himself
near Hassler, he would have fled at once in terror and emotion.
But he butted with all his force, like a ram, among the skirts
and legs that divided him from Hassler. He was too small;
he could not break through.

Fortunately, when the concert was over, his grandfather came
and took him to join in a party to serenade Hassler. It was
night, and torches were lighted. All the musicians of the
orchestra were there. They talked only of the marvelous compositions they had heard. They arrived outside the Palace,
and took up their places without a sound under the master's
windows. They took on an air of secrecy, although everybody,
including Hassler, knew what was to come. In the silence of
the night they began to play certain famous fragments of
Hassler's compositions. He appeared at the window with the
Prince, and they roared in their honor. Both bowed. A servant came from the Prince to invite the musicians to enter the
Palace. They passed through great rooms, with frescoes representing naked men with helmets; they were of a reddish color,
and were making gestures of defiance. The sky was covered with
great clouds like sponges. There were also men and women of
marble clad in waist-cloths made of iron. The guests walked on

carpets so thick that their tread was inaudible, and they came
at length to a room which was as light as day, and there were
tables laden with drinks and good things.

The Grand Duke was there, but Jean-Christophe did not see
him; he had eyes only for Hassler. Hassler came towards
them; he thanked them. He picked his words carefully, stopped
awkwardly in the middle of a sentence, and extricated himself
with a quip which made everybody laugh. They began to eat.
Hassler took four or five musicians aside. He singled out
Jean-Christophe's grandfather, and addressed very flattering
words to him: he recollected that Jean Michel had been one
of the first to perform his works, and he said that he had often
heard tell of his excellence from a friend of his who had been
a pupil of the old man's. Jean-Christophe's grandfather expressed his gratitude profusely; he replied with such extraordinary eulogy that, in spite of his adoration of Hassler, the
boy was ashamed. But to Hassler they seemed to be pleasant
and in the rational order. Finally, the old man, who had
lost himself in his rigmarole, took Jean-Christophe by the hand,
and presented him to Hassler. Hassler smiled at Jean-Christophe, and carelessly patted his head, and when he learned that
the boy liked his music, and had not slept for several nights
in anticipation of seeing him, he took him in his arms and
plied him with questions. Jean-Christophe, struck dumb and
blushing with pleasure, dared not look at him. Hassler took
him by the chin and lifted his face up. Jean-Christophe ventured to look. Hassler's eyes were kind and smiling; he began
to smile too. Then he felt so happy, so wonderfully happy in
the great man's arms, that he burst into tears. Hassler was
touched by this simple affection, and was more kind than ever.
He kissed the boy and talked to him tenderly. At the same
time he said funny things and tickled him to make him laugh;
and Jean-Christophe could not help laughing through his tears.
Soon he became at ease, and answered Hassler readily, and of
his own accord he began to whisper in his ear all his small
ambitions, as though he and Hassler were old friends; he told
him how he wanted to be a musician like Hassler, and, like
Hassler, to make beautiful things, and to be a great man. He,
who was always ashamed, talked confidently; he did not know

what he was saying; he was in a sort of ecstasy. Hassler smiled
at his prattling and said:

"When you are a man, and have become a good musician,
you shall come and see me in Berlin. I shall make something
of you."

Jean-Christophe was too delighted to reply.

Hassler teased him.

"You don't want to?"

Jean-Christophe nodded his head violently five or six times,
meaning "Yes."

"It is a bargain, then?"

Jean-Christophe nodded again.

"Kiss me, then."

Jean-Christophe threw his arms round Hassler's neck and
hugged him with all his strength.

"Oh, you are wetting me! Let go! Your nose wants
wiping!"

Hassler laughed, and wiped the boy's nose himself, a little
self-consciously, though he was quite jolly. He put him down,
then took him by the hand and led him to a table, where he
filled his pockets with cake, and left him, saying:

"Good-bye! Remember your promise."

Jean-Christophe swam in happiness. The rest of the world
had ceased to exist for him. He could remember nothing of
what had happened earlier in the evening; he followed lovingly
Hassler's every expression and gesture. One thing that he said
struck him. Hassler was holding a glass in his hand; he was
talking, and his face suddenly hardened, and he said:

"The joy of such a day must not make us forget our enemies.
We must never forget our enemies. It is not their fault that
we are not crushed out of existence. It will not be our fault
if that does not happen to them. That is why the toast I
propose is that there are people whose health . . . we will not
drink!"

Everybody applauded and laughed at this original toast.
Hassler had laughed with the others and his good-humored
expression had returned. But Jean-Christophe was put out
by it. Although he did not permit himself to criticise any
action of his hero, it hurt him that he had thought ugly things,

when on such a night there ought to be nothing but brilliant
thoughts and fancies. But he did not examine what he felt,
and the impression that it made was soon driven out by his
great joy and the drop of champagne which he drank out of
his grandfather's glass.

On the way back the old man never stopped talking; he was
delighted with the praise that Hassler had given him; he cried
out that Hassler was a genius such as had not been known
for a century. Jean-Christophe said nothing, locking up in
his heart his intoxication of love. *He* had kissed him. *He*
had held him in his arms! How good *he* was! How great!
"Ah," he thought in bed, as he kissed his pillow passionately,
"I would die for him—die for him!"

The brilliant meteor which had flashed across the sky of the
little town that night had a decisive influence on Jean-Christophe's mind. All his childhood Hassler was the model on
which his eyes were fixed, and to follow his example the little
man of six decided that he also would write music. To tell
the truth, he had been doing so for long enough without knowing it, and he had not waited to be conscious of composing
before he composed.

Everything is music for the born musician. Everything that
throbs, or moves, or stirs, or palpitates—sunlit summer days,
nights when the wind howls, flickering light, the twinkling of
the stars, storms, the song of birds, the buzzing of insects, the
murmuring of trees, voices, loved or loathed, familiar fireside
sounds, a creaking door, blood moving in the veins in the silence
of the night—everything that is is music; all that is needed
is that it should be heard. All the music of creation found
its echo in Jean-Christophe. Everything that he saw, everything that he felt, was translated into music without his being
conscious of it. He was like a buzzing hive of bees. But no
one noticed it, himself least of all.

Like all children, he hummed perpetually at every hour of
the day. Whatever he was doing—whether he were walking in
the street, hopping on one foot, or lying on the floor at his
grandfather's, with his ·head in his hands, absorbed in the
pictures of a book, or sitting in his little chair in the darkest
corner of the kitchen. dreaming aimlessly in the twilight—al-

ways the monotonous murmuring of his little trumpet was to be heard, played with lips closed and cheeks blown out. His mother seldom paid any heed to it, but, once in a while, she would protest.

When he was tired of this state of half-sleep he would have to move and make a noise. Then he made music, singing it at the top of his voice. He had made tunes for every occasion. He had a tune for splashing in his wash-basin in the morning, like a little duck. He had a tune for sitting on the piano-stool in front of the detested instrument, and another for getting off it, and this was a more brilliant affair than the other. He had one for his mother putting the soup on the table; he used to go before her then blowing a blare of trumpets. He played triumphal marches by which to go solemnly from the dining-room to the bedroom. Sometimes he would organize little processions with his two small brothers; all then would file out gravely, one after another, and each had a tune to march to. But, as was right and proper, Jean-Christophe kept the best for himself. Every one of his tunes was strictly appropriated to its special occasion, and Jean-Christophe never by any chance confused them. Anybody else would have made mistakes, but he knew the shades of difference between them exactly.

One day at his grandfather's house he was going round the room clicking his heels, head up and chest out; he went round and round and round, so that it was a wonder he did not turn sick, and played one of his compositions. The old man, who was shaving, stopped in the middle of it, and, with his face covered with lather, came to look at him, and said:

" What are you singing, boy? "

Jean-Christophe said he did not know.

" Sing it again! " said Jean Michel.

Jean-Christophe tried; he could not remember the tune. Proud of having attracted his grandfather's attention, he tried to make him admire his voice, and sang after his own fashion an air from some opera, but that was not what the old man wanted. Jean Michel said nothing, and seemed not to notice him any more. But he left the door of his room ajar while the boy was playing alone in the next room.

A few days later Jean-Christophe, with the chairs arranged

about him, was playing a comedy in music, which he had made
up of scraps that he remembered from the theater, and he was
making steps and bows, as he had seen them done in a minuet,
and addressing himself to the portrait of Beethoven which
hung above the table. As he turned with a pirouette he saw
his grandfather watching him through the half-open door. He
thought the old man was laughing at him; he was abashed, and
stopped dead; he ran to the window, and pressed his face
against the panes, pretending that he had been watching something of the greatest interest. But the old man said nothing;
he came to him and kissed him, and Jean-Christophe saw that
he was pleased. His vanity made the most of these signs;
he was clever enough to see that he had been appreciated;
but he did not know exactly which his grandfather had admired
most—his talent as a dramatic author, or as a musician, or
as a singer, or as a dancer. He inclined to the latter, for he
prided himself on this.

A week later, when he had forgotten the whole affair, his
grandfather said mysteriously that he had something to show
him. He opened his desk, took out a music-book, and put it
on the rack of the piano, and told the boy to play. Jean-Christophe was very much interested, and deciphered it fairly well.
The notes were written by hand in the old man's large handwriting, and he had taken especial pains with it. The headings
were adorned with scrolls and flourishes. After some moments
the old man, who was sitting beside Jean-Christophe turning
the pages for him, asked him what the music was. Jean-
Christophe had been too much absorbed in his playing to notice
what he had played, and said that he did not know it.
" Listen! . . . You don't know it? "
Yes; he thought he knew it, but he did not know where
he had heard it. The old man laughed.
" Think."
Jean-Christophe shook his head.
" I don't know."
A light was fast dawning in his mind; it seemed to him that
the air . . . But, no! He dared not. . . . He would not recog-
nize it.
" I don't know, grandfather."

He blushed.

"What, you little fool, don't you see that it is your own?"

He was sure of it, but to hear it said made his heart thump.

"Oh! grandfather! . . ."

Beaming, the old man showed him the book.

"See: *Aria*. It is what you were singing on Tuesday when you were lying on the floor. *March*. That is what I asked you to sing again last week, and you could not remember it. *Minuet*. That is what you were dancing by the armchair. Look!"

On the cover was written in wonderful Gothic letters:

"*The Pleasures of Childhood: Aria, Minuetto, Valse, and Marcia, Op. 1, by Jean-Christophe Krafft.*"

Jean-Christophe was dazzled by it. To see his name, and that fine title, and that large book—his work! . . . He went on murmuring:

"Oh! grandfather! grandfather! . . ."

The old man drew him to him. Jean-Christophe threw himself on his knees, and hid his head in Jean Michel's bosom. He was covered with blushes from his happiness. The old man was even happier, and went on, in a voice which he tried to make indifferent, for he felt that he was on the point of breaking down:

"Of course, I added the accompaniment and the harmony to fit the song. And then "—he coughed—" and then, I added a *trio* to the minuet, because . . . because it is usual . . . and then . . . I think it is not at all bad."

He played it. Jean-Christophe was very proud of collaborating with his grandfather.

"But, grandfather, you must put your name to it too."

"It is not worth while. It is not worth while others besides yourself knowing it. Only "—here his voice trembled—" only, later on, when I am no more, it will remind you of your old grandfather . . . eh? You won't forget him?"

The poor old man did not say that he had been unable to resist the quite innocent pleasure of introducing one of his own unfortunate airs into his grandson's work, which he felt was destined to survive him; but his desire to share in this imagi-

nary glory was very humble and very touching, since it was
enough for him anonymously to transmit to posterity a scrap
of his own thought, so as not altogether to perish. Jean-
Christophe was touched by it, and covered his face with kisses,
and the old man, growing more and more tender, kissed his
hair.

"You will remember me? Later on, when you are a good
musician, a great artist, who will bring honor to his family,
to his art, and to his country, when you are famous, you will
remember that it was your old grandfather who first perceived it,
and foretold what you would be?"

There were tears in his eyes as he listened to his own words.
He was reluctant to let such signs of weakness be seen. He
had an attack of coughing, became moody, and sent the boy
away hugging the precious manuscript.

Jean-Christophe went home bewildered by his happiness. The
stones danced about him. The reception he had from his family
sobered him a little. When he blurted out the splendor of his
musical exploit they cried out upon him. His mother laughed
at him. Melchior declared that the old man was mad, and
that he would do better to take care of himself than to set
about turning the boy's head. As for Jean-Christophe, he
would oblige by putting such follies from his mind, and sitting
down *illico* at the piano and playing exercises for four hours.
He must first learn to play properly; and as for composing,
there was plenty of time for that later on when he had nothing
better to do.

Melchior was not, as these words of wisdom might indicate,
trying to keep the boy from the dangerous exaltation of a too
early pride. On the contrary, he proved immediately that this
was not so. But never having himself had any idea to express
in music, and never having had the least need to express an
idea, he had come, as a *virtuoso,* to consider composing a secondary matter, which was only given value by the art of the
executant. He was not insensible of the tremendous enthusiasm
roused by great composers like Hassler. For such ovations
he had the respect which he always paid to success—mingled,
perhaps, with a little secret jealousy—for it seemed to him that
such applause was stolen from him. But he knew by experience

that the successes of the great *virtuosi* are no less remarkable, and are more personal in character, and therefore more fruitful of agreeable and flattering consequences. He affected to pay profound homage to the genius of the master musicians; but he took a great delight in telling absurd anecdotes of them, presenting their intelligence and morals in a lamentable light. He placed the *virtuoso* at the top of the artistic ladder, for, he said, it is well known that the tongue is the noblest member of the body, and what would thought be without words? What would music be without the executant? But whatever may have been the reason for the scolding that he gave Jean-Christophe, it was not without its uses in restoring some common sense to the boy, who was almost beside himself with his grandfather's praises. It was not quite enough. Jean-Christophe, of course, decided that his grandfather was much cleverer than his father, and though he sat down at the piano without sulking, he did so not so much for the sake of obed:ence as to be able to dream in peace, as he always did while his fingers ran mechanically over the keyboard. While he played his interminable exercises he heard a proud voice inside himself saying over and over again: "I am a composer—a great composer."

From that day on, since he was a composer, he set himself to composing. Before he had even learned to write, he continued to cipher crotchets and quavers on scraps of paper, which he tore from the household account-books. But in the effort to find out what he was thinking, and to set it down in black and white, he arrived at thinking nothing, except when he wanted to think something. But he did not for that give up making musical phrases, and as he was a born musician he made them somehow, even if they meant nothing at all. Then he would take them in triumph to his grandfather, who wept with joy over them—he wept easily now that he was growing old—and vowed that they were wonderful.

All this was like to spoil him altogether. Fortunately, his own good sense saved him, helped by the influence of a man who made no pretension of having any influence over anybody, and set nothing before the eyes of the world but a common-sense point of view. This man was Louisa's brother.

Like her, he was small, thin, puny, and rather round-shouldered. No one knew exactly how old he was; he could not be more than forty, but he looked more than fifty. He had a little wrinkled face, with a pink complexion, and kind pale blue eyes, like faded forget-me-nots. When he took off his cap, which he used fussily to wear everywhere from his fear of draughts, he exposed a little pink bald head, conical in shape, which was the great delight of Jean-Christophe and his brothers. They never left off teasing him about it, asking him what he had done with his hair, and, encouraged by Melchior's pleasantries, threatening to smack it. He was the first to laugh at them, and put up with their treatment of him patiently. He was a peddler; he used to go from village to village with a pack on his back, containing everything—groceries, stationery, confectionery, handkerchiefs, scarves, shoes, pickles, almanacs, songs, and drugs. Several attempts had been made to make him settle down, and to buy him a little business—a store or a drapery shop. But he could not do it. One night he would get up, push the key under the door, and set off again with his pack. Weeks and months went by before he was seen again. Then he would reappear. Some evening they would hear him fumbling at the door; it would half open, and the little bald head, politely uncovered, would appear with its kind eyes and timid smile. He would say, " Good-evening, everybody," carefully wipe his shoes before entering, salute everybody, beginning with the eldest, and go and sit in the most remote corner of the room. There he would light his pipe, and sit huddled up, waiting quietly until the usual storm of questions was over. The two Kraffts, Jean-Christophe's father and grandfather, had a jeering contempt for him. The little freak seemed ridiculous to them, and their pride was touched by the low degree of the peddler. They made him feel it, but he seemed to take no notice of it, and showed them a profound respect which disarmed them, especially the old man, who was very sensitive to what people thought of him. They used to crush him with heavy pleasantries, which often brought the blush to Louisa's cheeks. Accustomed to bow without dispute to the intellectual superiority of the Kraffts, she had no doubt that her husband and father-in-law were right; but she loved her brother, and her brother had for her a dumb adoration. They were the only members of their family, and they were both humble, crushed, and thrust aside by life; they were united in sadness and tenderness by a bond of mutual pity and common suffering, borne in secret. With the Kraffts—robust, noisy, brutal, solidly built for living, and living joyously—these two weak, kindly creatures, out of their setting, so to speak, outside life, understood and pitied each other without ever saying anything about it.

Jean-Christophe, with the cruel carelessness of childhood, shared the contempt of his father and grandfather for the little peddler. He made fun of him, and treated him as a comic figure; he worried him with stupid teasing, which his uncle bore with his unshakable phlegm. But Jean-Christophe loved him, without quite knowing why. He loved him first of all as a plaything with which he did what he liked. He loved him also because he always gave him something nice—a dainty, a picture, an amusing toy. The little man's return was a joy for the children, for he always had some surprise for them. Poor as he was, he always contrived to bring them each a present, and he never forgot the birthday of any one of the family. He always turned up on these august days, and brought out of his pocket some jolly present, lovingly chosen. They were so used to it that they hardly thought of thanking him; it seemed natural, and he appeared to be sufficiently repaid by the pleasure he had given. But Jean-Christophe, who did not sleep very well, and during the night used to turn over in his mind the events of the day, used sometimes to think that his uncle was very kind, and he used to be filled with floods of gratitude to the poor man. He never showed it when the day came, because he thought that the others would laugh at him. Besides, he was too little to see in kindness all the rare value that it has. In the language of children, kind and stupid are almost synonymous, and Uncle Gottfried seemed to be the living proof of it.

One evening when Melchior was dining out, Gottfried was left alone in the living-room, while Louisa put the children to bed. He went out, and sat by the river a few yards away from the house. Jean-Christophe, having nothing better to do, followed him, and, as usual, tormented him with his puppy tricks until he was out of breath, and dropped down on the grass at his feet. Lying on his belly, he buried his nose in the turf. When he had recovered his breath, he cast about for some new crazy thing to say. When he found it he shouted it out, and rolled about with laughing, with his face still buried in the earth. He received no answer. Surprised by the silence, he raised his head, and began to repeat his joke. He saw Gottfried's face lit up by the last beams of the setting sun cast through golden mists. He swallowed down his words. Gottfried smiled with his eyes half closed and his mouth half open, and in his sorrowful face was an expression of sadness and unutterable melancholy. Jean-Christophe, with his face in his hands, watched him. The night came; little by little Gottfried's face disappeared. Silence reigned. Jean-Christophe in his turn was filled with the mysterious impressions which had been reflected on Gottfried's face. He fell into a vague stupor. The earth was in darkness, the sky was bright; the stars peeped out. The little waves of the river chattered against the bank. The boy grew sleepy. Without seeing them, he bit off little blades of grass. A grasshopper chirped near him. It seemed to him that he was going to sleep.

Suddenly, in the dark, Gottfried began to sing. He sang in a weak, husky voice, as though to himself; he could not have been heard twenty yards away. But there was sincerity and emotion in his voice; it was as though he were thinking aloud, and that through the song, as through clear water, the very inmost heart of him was to be seen. Never had Jean-Christophe heard such singing, and never had he heard such a song. Slow, simple, childish, it moved gravely, sadly, a little monotonously, never hurrying—with long pauses—then setting out again on its way, careless where it arrived, and losing itself in the night. It seemed to come from far away, and it went no man knows whither. Its serenity was full of sorrow, and beneath its seeming peace there dwelt an agony of the ages. Jean-Christophe held his breath; he dared not move; he was cold with emotion. When it was done he crawled towards Gottfried, and in a choking voice said:

" Uncle ! "

Gottfried did not reply.

"Uncle!" repeated the boy, placing his hands and chin on Gottfried's knees.

Gottfried said kindly:

"Well, boy . . ."

"What is it, uncle? Tell me! What were you sing. ing?"

"I don't know."

"Tell me what it is!"

"I don't know. Just a song."

"A song that you made."

"No, not I! What an idea! . . . It is an old song."

"Who made it?"

"No one knows. . . ."

"When?"

"No one knows. . . ."

"When you were little?"

"Before I was born, before my father was born, and before his father, and before his father's father. . . . It has always been."

"How strange! No one has ever told me about it."

He thought for a moment.

"Uncle, do you know any other?"

"Yes."

"Sing another, please."

"Why should I sing another? One is enough. One sings when one wants to sing, when one has to sing. One must not sing for the fun of it."

"But what about when one makes music?"

"That is not music."

The boy was lost in thought. He did not quite understand. But he asked for no explanation. It was true, it was not music, not like all the rest. He went on:

"Uncle, have you ever made them?"

"Made what?"

"Songs!"

"Songs? Oh! How should I make them? They can't be made."

With his usual logic the boy insisted:

"But, uncle, it must have been made once. . . ."

Gottfried shook his head obstinately.

" It has always been."

The boy returned to the attack:

" But, uncle, isn't it possible to make other songs, new songs? "

" Why make them? There are enough for everything. There are songs for when you are sad, and for when you are gay; for when you are weary, and for when you are thinking of home; for when you despise yourself, because you have been a vile sinner, a worm upon the earth; for when you want to weep, because people have not been kind to you; and for when your heart is glad because the world is beautiful, and you see God's heaven, which, like Him, is always kind, and seems to laugh at you. . . . There are songs for everything, everything. Why should I make them? "

" To be a great man! " said the boy, full of his grandfather's teaching and his simple dreams.

Gottfried laughed softly. Jean-Christophe, a little hurt, asked him:

" Why are you laughing? "

Gottfried said:

" Oh! I? . . . I am nobody."

He kissed the boy's head, and said:

" You want to be a great man? "

" Yes," said Jean-Christophe proudly. He thought Gottfried would admire him. But Gottfried replied:

" What for? "

Jean-Christophe was taken aback. He thought for a moment, and said:

" To make beautiful songs! "

Gottfried laughed again, and said:

" You want to make beautiful songs, so as to be a great man; and you want to be a great man, so as to make beautiful songs. You are like a dog chasing its own tail."

Jean-Christophe was dashed. At any other time he would not have borne his uncle laughing at him, he at whom he was used to laughing. And, at the same time, he would never have thought Gottfried clever enough to stump him with an argument. He cast about for some answer or some imper-

tinence to throw at him, but could find none. Gottfried went
on:

"When you are as great as from here to Coblentz, you will
never make a single song."

Jean-Christophe revolted on that.

"And if I will! . . ."

"The more you want to, the less you can. To make songs,
you have to be like those creatures. Listen. . . ."

The moon had risen, round and gleaming, behind the fields.
A silvery mist hovered above the ground and the shimmering
waters. The frogs croaked, and in the meadows the melodious
fluting of the toads arose. The shrill tremolo of the grasshoppers seemed to answer the twinkling of the stars. The wind
rustled softly in the branches of the alders. From the hills
above the river there came down the sweet light song of a
nightingale.

"What need is there to sing?" sighed Gottfried, after a long
silence. (It was not clear whether he were talking to himself
or to Jean-Christophe.) "Don't they sing sweeter than anything that you could make?"

Jean-Christophe had often heard these sounds of the night,
and he loved them. But never had he heard them as he heard
them now. It was true: what need was there to sing? . . . His
heart was full of tenderness and sorrow. He was fain to embrace the meadows, the river, the sky, the clear stars. He was
filled with love for his uncle Gottfried, who seemed to him
now the best, the cleverest, the most beautiful of men. He
thought how he had misjudged him, and he thought that his
uncle was sad because he, Jean-Christophe, had misjudged him.
He was remorseful. He wanted to cry out: "Uncle, do not
be sad! I will not be naughty again. Forgive me, I love you!"
But he dared not. And suddenly he threw himself into Gottfried's arms, but the words would not come, only he repeated,
"I love you!" and kissed him passionately. Gottfried was surprised and touched, and went on saying, "What? What?"
and kissed him. Then he got up, took him by the hand, and
said: "We must go in." Jean-Christophe was sad because
his uncle had not understood him. But as they came to the
house, Gottfried said: "If you like we'll go again to hear God's

music, and I will sing you some more songs." And when Jean-Christophe kissed him gratefully as they said good-night, he saw that his uncle had understood.

Thereafter they often went for walks together in the evening, and they walked without a word along by the river, or through the fields. Gottfried slowly smoked his pipe, and Jean-Christophe, a little frightened by the darkness, would give him his hand. They would sit down on the grass, and after a few moments of silence Gottfried would talk to him about the stars and the clouds; he taught him to distinguish the breathing of the earth, air, and water, the songs, cries, and sounds of the little worlds of flying, creeping, hopping, and swimming things swarming in the darkness, and the signs of rain and fine weather, and the countless instruments of the symphony of the night. Sometimes Gottfried would sing tunes, sad or gay, but always of the same kind, and always in the end Jean-Christophe would be brought to the same sorrow. But he would never sing more than one song in an evening, and Jean-Christophe noticed that he did not sing gladly when he was asked to do so; it had to come of itself, just when he wanted to. Sometimes they had to wait for a long time without speaking, and just when Jean-Christophe was beginning to think, " He is not going to sing this evening," Gottfried would make up his mind.

One evening, when nothing would induce Gottfried to sing, Jean-Christophe thought of submitting to him one of his own small compositions, in the making of which he found so much trouble and pride. He wanted to show what an artist he was. Gottfried listened very quietly, and then said:

" That is very ugly, my poor dear Jean-Christophe! "

Jean-Christophe was so hurt that he could find nothing to say. Gottfried went on pityingly:

" Why did you do it? It is so ugly! No one forced you to do it."

Hot with anger, Jean-Christophe protested:

" My grandfather thinks my music fine."

" Ah! " said Gottfried, not turning a hair. " No doubt he is right. He is a learned man. He knows all about music. I know nothing about it. . . ."

And after a moment:

"But I think that is very ugly."

He looked quietly at Jean-Christophe, and saw his angry face, and smiled, and said:

"Have you composed any others? Perhaps I shall like the others better than that."

Jean-Christophe thought that his other compositions might wipe out the impression of the first, and he sang them all. Gottfried said nothing; he waited until they were finished. Then he shook his head, and with profound conviction said:

"They are even more ugly."

Jean-Christophe shut his lips, and his chin trembled; he wanted to cry. Gottfried went on as though he himself were upset.

"How ugly they are!"

Jean-Christophe, with tears in his voice, cried out:

"But why do you say they are ugly?"

Gottfried looked at him with his frank eyes.

"Why? . . . I don't know. . . . Wait. . . . They are ugly . . . first, because they are stupid. . . . Yes, that's it. . . . They are stupid, they don't mean anything. . . . You see? When you wrote, you had nothing to say. Why did you write them?"

"I don't know," said Jean-Christophe, in a piteous voice. "I wanted to write something pretty."

"There you are! You wrote for the sake of writing. You wrote because you wanted to be a great musician, and to be admired. You have been proud; you have been a liar; you have been punished. . . . You see! A man is always punished when he is proud and a liar in music. Music must be modest and sincere—or else, what is it? Impious, a blasphemy of the Lord, who has given us song to tell the honest truth."

He saw the boy's distress, and tried to kiss him. But Jean-Christophe turned angrily away, and for several days he sulked. He hated Gottfried. But it was in vain that he said over and over to himself: "He is an ass! He knows nothing—nothing! My grandfather, who is much cleverer, likes my music." In his heart he knew that his uncle was right, and Gottfried's words were graven on his inmost soul; he was ashamed to have been a liar.

And, in spite of his resentment, he always thought of it
when he was writing music, and often he tore up what he had
written, being ashamed already of what Gottfried would have
thought of it. When he got over it, and wrote a melody which
he knew to be not quite sincere, he hid it carefully from his
uncle; he was fearful of his judgment, and was quite happy
when Gottfried just said of one of his pieces: "That is not so
very ugly. . . . I like it. . . ."

Sometimes, by way of revenge, he used to trick him by giving
him as his own melodies from the great musicians, and he was
delighted when it happened that Gottfried disliked them heartily. But that did not trouble Gottfried. He would laugh loudly
when he saw Jean-Christophe clap his hands and dance about
him delightedly, and he always returned to his usual argument:
"It is well enough written, but it says nothing." He always
refused to be present at one of the little concerts given in
Melchior's house. However beautiful the music might be, he
would begin to yawn and look sleepy with boredom. Very soon
he would be unable to bear it any longer, and would steal away
quietly. He used to say:

"You see, my boy, everything that you write in the house
is not music. Music in a house is like sunshine in a room.
Music is to be found outside where you breathe God's dear fresh
air."

He was always talking of God, for he was very pious, unlike
the two Kraffts, father and son, who were free-thinkers, and
took care to eat meat on Fridays.

Suddenly, for no apparent reason, Melchior changed his
opinion. Not only did he approve of his father having put
together Jean-Christophe's inspirations, but, to the boy's great
surprise, he spent several evenings in making two or three copies
of his manuscript. To every question put to him on the subject,
he replied impressively, "We shall see; . . ." or he would rub
his hands and laugh, smack the boy's head by way of a joke,
or turn him up and blithely spank him. Jean-Christophe loathed
these familiarities, but he saw that his father was pleased, and
did not know why.

Then there were mysterious confabulations between Melchior

and his father. And one evening Jean-Christophe, to his astonishment, learned that he, Jean-Christophe, had dedicated to
H.S.H. the Grand Duke Leopold the *Pleasures of Childhood.*
Melchior had sounded the disposition of the Prince, who had
shown himself graciously inclined to accept the homage. Thereupon Melchior declared that without losing a moment they must,
primo, draw up the official request to the Prince; *secondo,*
publish the work; *tertio,* organize a concert to give it a hearing.

There were further long conferences between Melchior and
Jean Michel. They argued heatedly for two or three evenings.
It was forbidden to interrupt them. Melchior wrote, erased;
erased, wrote. The old man talked loudly, as though he were
reciting verses. Sometimes they squabbled or thumped on the
table because they could not find a word.

Then Jean-Christophe was called, made to sit at the table
with a pen in his hand, his father on his right, his grandfather
on his left, and the old man began to dictate words which
he did not understand, because he found it difficult to write
every word in his enormous letters, because Melchior was shouting in his ear, and because the old man declaimed with such
emphasis that Jean-Christophe, put out by the sound of the
words, could not bother to listen to their meaning. The old
man was no less in a state of emotion. He could not sit still,
and he walked up and down the room, involuntarily illustrating
the text of what he read with gestures, but he came every minute
to look over what the boy had written, and Jean-Christophe,
frightened by the two large faces looking over his shoulder,
put out his tongue, and held his pen clumsily. A mist floated
before his eyes; he made too many strokes, or smudged what
he had written; and Melchior roared, and Jean Michel stormed;
and he had to begin again, and then again, and when he thought
that they had at last come to an end, a great blot fell on the
immaculate page. Then they pulled his ears, and he burst
into tears; but they forbade him to weep, because he was spoiling
the paper, and they began to dictate, beginning all over again,
and he thought it would go on like that to the end of his
life.

At last it was finished, and Jean Michel leaned against the
mantelpiece, and read over their handiwork in a voice trembling

with pleasure, while Melchior sat straddled across a chair, and looked at the ceiling and wagged his chair and, as a connoisseur, rolled round his tongue the style of the following epistle:

> "*Most Noble and Sublime Highness! Most Gracious Lord!*

"From my fourth year Music has been the first occupation of my childish days. So soon as I allied myself to the noble Muse, who roused my soul to pure harmony, I loved her, and, as it seemed to me, she returned my love. Now I am in my sixth year, and for some time my Muse in hours of inspiration has whispered in my ears: 'Be bold! Be bold! Write down the harmonies of thy soul!' 'Six years old,' thought I, 'and how should I be bold? What would the learned in the art say of me?' I hesitated. I trembled. But my Muse insisted. I obeyed. I wrote.

"And now shall I,

> *O Most Sublime Highness!*

—shall I have the temerity and audacity to place upon the steps of Thy Throne the first-fruits of my youthful labors? . . . Shall I make so bold as to hope that Thou wilt let fall upon them the august approbation of Thy paternal regard? . . .

"Oh, yes! For Science and the Arts have ever found in Thee their sage Mæcenas, their generous champion, and talent puts forth its flowers under the ægis of Thy holy protection.

"In this profound and certain faith I dare, then, approach Thee with these youthful efforts. Receive them as a pure offering of my childish veneration, and of Thy goodness deign,

> *O Most Sublime Highness!*

to glance at them, and at their young author, who bows at Thy feet deeply and in humility!

> "*From the most submissive, faithful, and obedient servant of His Most Noble and Most Sublime Highness,*

> "JEAN-CHRISTOPHE KRAFFT."

Jean-Christophe heard nothing. He was very happy to have finished, and, fearing that he would be made to begin again, he ran away to the fields. He had no idea of what he had written, and he cared not at all. But when the old man had finished his reading he began again to taste the full flavor of it, and when the second reading came to an end Melchior and he declared that it was a little masterpiece. That was also the opinion of the Grand Duke, to whom the letter was presented, with a copy of the musical work. He was kind enough to send word that he found both quite charming. He granted permission for the concert, and ordered that the hall of his Academy of Music should be put at Melchior's disposal, and deigned to promise that he would have the young artist presented to himself on the day of the performance.

Melchior set about organizing the concert as quickly as possible. He engaged the support of the *Hof Musik Verein,* and as the success of his first ventures had blown out his sense of proportion, he undertook at the same time to publish a magnificent edition of the *Pleasures of Childhood.* He wanted to have printed ·on the cover of it a portrait of Jean-Christophe at the piano, with himself, Melchior, standing by his side, violin in hand. He had to abandon that, not on account of the cost—Melchior did not stop at any expense—but because there was not time enough. He fell back on an allegorical design representing a cradle, a trumpet, a drum, a wooden horse, grouped round a lyre which put forth rays like the sun. The title-page bore, together with a long dedication, in which the name of the Prince stood out in enormous letters, a notice to the effect that " Herr Jean-Christophe Krafft was six years old." He was, in fact, seven and a half. The printing of the design was very expensive. To meet the bill for it, Jean Michel had to sell an old eighteenth-century chest, carved with faces, which he had never consented to sell, in spite of the repeated offers of Wormser, the furniture-dealer. But Melchior had no doubt but the subscriptions would cover the cost, and beyond that the expenses of printing the composition.

One other question occupied his mind : how to dress Jean-Christophe on the day of the concert. There was a family council to decide the matter. Melchior would have liked the boy to appear in a short frock and bare legs, like a child or four. But Jean-Christophe was very large for his age, and everybody knew him. They could not hope to deceive any one. Melchior had a great idea. He decided that the boy should wear a dress-coat and white tie. In vain did Louisa protest that they would make her poor boy ridiculous. Melchior anticipated exactly the success and merriment that would be produced by such an unexpected appearance. It was decided on, and the tailor came and measured Jean-Christophe for his little coat. He had also to have fine linen and patent-leather pumps, and all that swallowed up their last penny. Jean-Christophe was very uncomfortable in his new clothes. To make him used to them they made him try on his various garments. For a whole month he hardly left the piano-stool. They taught him to bow. He had never a moment of liberty. He raged against it, but dared not rebel, for he thought that he was going to accomplish something startling. He was both proud and afraid of it. They pampered him; they were afraid he would catch cold; they swathed his neck in scarves; they warmed his boots in case they were wet; and at table he had the best of everything.

At last the great day arrived. The barber came to preside over his toilet and curl Jean-Christophe's rebellious hair. He did not leave it until he had made it look like a sheep-skin. All the family walked round Jean-Christophe and declared that he was superb. Melchior, after looking him up and down, and turning him about and about, was seized with an idea, and went off to fetch a large flower, which he put in his buttonhole. But when Louisa saw him she raised her hands, and cried out distressfully that he looked like a monkey. That hurt him cruelly. He did not know whether to be ashamed or proud of his garb. Instinctively he felt humiliated, and he was more so at the concert. Humiliation was to be for him the outstanding emotion of that memorable day.

The concert was about to begin. The hall was half empty; the Grand Duke had not arrived. One of those kindly and well-informed friends who always appear on these occasions came and told them that there was a Council being held at

the Palace, and that the Grand Duke would not come. He had
it on good authority. Melchior was in despair. He fidgeted,
paced up and down, and looked repeatedly out of the window.
Old Jean Michel was also in torment, but he was concerned
for his grandson. He bombarded him with instructions. Jean-
Christophe was infected by the nervousness of his family. He
was not in the least anxious about his compositions, but he was
troubled by the thought of the bows that he had to make to the
audience, and thinking of them brought him to agony.

However, he had to begin; the audience was growing impatient. The orchestra of the *Hof Musik Verein* began the
Coriolan Overture. The boy knew neither Coriolan nor Beethoven, for though he had often heard Beethoven's music, he
had not known it. He never bothered about the names of the
works he heard. He gave them names of his own invention,
while he created little stories or pictures for them. He classi-
fied them usually in three categories: fire, water, and earth,
with a thousand degrees between each. Mozart belonged almost
always to water. He was a meadow by the side of a river, a
transparent mist floating over the water, a spring shower, or
a rainbow. Beethoven was fire—now a furnace with gigantic
flames and vast columns of smoke; now a burning forest, a
heavy and terrible cloud, flashing lightning; now a wide sky
full of quivering stars, one of which breaks free, swoops, and
dies on a fine September night setting the heart beating. Now
the imperious ardor of that heroic soul burned him like fire.
Everything else disappeared. What was it all to him?—Melchior in despair, Jean Michel agitated, all the busy world, the
audience, the Grand Duke, little Jean-Christophe. What had
he to do with all these? What lay between them and him?
Was that he—he, himself? . . . He was given up to the furious
will that carried him headlong. He followed it breathlessly,
with tears in his eyes, and his legs numb, thrilling from the
palms of his hands to the soles of his feet. His blood drummed
" Charge! " and he trembled in every limb. And as he listened
so intensely, hiding behind a curtain, his heart suddenly leaped
violently. The orchestra had stopped short in the middle of a
bar, and after a moment's silence, it broke into a crashing of
brass and cymbals with a military march, officially strident.

The transition from one sort of music to another was so brutal, so unexpected, that Jean-Christophe ground his teeth and stamped his foot with rage, and shook his fist at the wall. But Melchior rejoiced. The Grand Duke had come in, and the orchestra was saluting him with the National Anthem. And in a trembling voice Jean Michel gave his last instructions to his grandson.

The overture began again, and this time was finished. It was now Jean-Christophe's turn. Melchior had arranged the programme to show off at the same time the skill of both father and son. They were to play together a sonata of Mozart for violin and piano. For the sake of effect he had decided that Jean-Christophe should enter alone. He was led to the entrance of the stage and showed the piano at the front, and for the last time it was explained what he had to do, and then he was pushed on from the wings.

He was not much afraid, for he was used to the theater; but when he found himself alone on the platform, with hundreds of eyes staring at him, he became suddenly so frightened that instinctively he moved backwards and turned towards the wings to go back again. He saw his father there gesticulating and with his eyes blazing. He had to go on. Besides, the audience had seen him. As he advanced there arose a twittering of curiosity, followed soon by laughter, which grew louder and louder. Melchior had not been wrong, and the boy's garb had all the effect anticipated. The audience rocked with laughter at the sight of the child with his long hair and gipsy complexion timidly trotting across the platform in the evening dress of a man of the world. They got up to see him better. Soon the hilarity was general. There was nothing unkindly in it, but it would have made the most hardened musician lose his head. Jean-Christophe, terrified by the noise, and the eyes watching, and the glasses turned upon him, had only one idea: to reach the piano as quickly as possible, for it seemed to him a refuge, an island in the midst of the sea. With head down, looking neither to right nor left, he ran quickly across the platform, and when he reached the middle of it, instead of bowing to the audience, as had been arranged, he turned his back on it, and plunged straight for the piano. The chair was too high

for him to sit down without his father's help, and in his distress, instead of waiting, he climbed up on to it on his knees.
That increased the merriment of the audience, but now Jean-
Christophe was safe. Sitting at his instrument, he was afraid
of no one.

Melchior came at last. He gained by the good-humor of
the audience, who welcomed him with warm applause. The
sonata began. The boy played it with imperturbable certainty,
with his lips pressed tight in concentration, his eyes fixed on
the keys, his little legs hanging down from the chair. He
became more at ease as the notes rolled out; he was among
friends that he knew. A murmur of approbation reached him,
and waves of pride and satisfaction surged through him as he
thought that all these people were silent to listen to him and
to admire him. But hardly had he finished when fear overcame
him again, and the applause which greeted him gave him more
shame than pleasure. His shame increased when Melchior took
him by the hand, and advanced with him to the edge of the
platform, and made him bow to the public. He obeyed, and
bowed very low, with a funny awkwardness; but he was humiliated, and blushed for what he had done, as though it were
a thing ridiculous and ugly.

He had to sit at the piano again, and he played the *Pleasures
of Childhood*. Then the audience was enraptured. After each
piece they shouted enthusiastically. They wanted him to begin
again, and he was proud of his success and at the same time
almost hurt by such applause, which was also a command. At
the end the whole audience rose to acclaim him; the Grand
Duke led the applause. But as Jean-Christophe was now alone
on the platform he dared not budge from his seat. The applause redoubled. He bent his head lower and lower, blushing
and hang-dog in expression, and he looked steadily away from
the audience. Melchior came. He took him in his arms, and
told him to blow kisses. He pointed out to him the Grand
Duke's box. Jean-Christophe turned a deaf ear. Melchior took
his arm, and threatened him in a low voice. Then he did as
he was told passively, but he did not look at anybody, he did
not raise his eyes, but went on turning his head away, and he
was unhappy. He was suffering; how, he did not know. His

vanity was suffering. He did not like the people who were
there at all. It was no use their applauding; he could not
forgive them for having laughed and for being amused by his
humiliation; he could not forgive them for having seen him
in such a ridiculous position—held in mid-air to blow kisses.
He disliked them even for applauding, and when Melchior did
at last put him down, he ran away to the wings. A lady threw
a bunch of violets up at him as he went. It brushed his face.
He was panic-stricken and ran as fast as he could, turning
over a chair that was in his way. The faster he ran the more
they laughed, and the more they laughed the faster he ran.

At last he reached the exit, which was filled with people
looking at him. He forced his way through, butting, and ran
and hid himself at the back of the anteroom. His grandfather
was in high feather, and covered him with blessings. The
musicians of the orchestra shouted with laughter, and congratulated the boy, who refused to look at them or to shake
hands with them. Melchior listened intently, gaging the applause, which had not yet ceased, and wanted to take Jean-
Christophe on to the stage again. But the boy refused angrily,
clung to his grandfather's coat-tails, and kicked at everybody
who came near him. At last he burst into tears, and they
had to let him be.

Just at this moment an officer came to say that the Grand
Duke wished the artists to go to his box. How could the child
be presented in such a state? Melchior swore angrily, and his
wrath only had the effect of making Jean-Christophe's tears
flow faster. To stop them, his grandfather promised him a
pound of chocolates if he would not cry any more, and Jean-
Christophe, who was greedy, stopped dead, swallowed down
his tears, and let them carry him off; but they had to swear
at first most solemnly that they would not take him on to
the platform again.

In the anteroom of the Grand Ducal box he was presented
to a gentleman in a dress-coat, with a face like a pug-dog,
bristling mustaches, and a short, pointed beard—a little red-
faced man, inclined to stoutness, who addressed him with bantering familiarity, and called him "Mozart *redivivus!*" This
was the Grand Duke. Then he was presented in turn to the

Grand Duchess and her daughter, and their suite. But as he did not dare raise his eyes, the only thing he could remember of this brilliant company was a series of gowns and uniforms from the waist down to the feet. He sat on the lap of the young Princess, and dared not move or breathe. She asked him questions, which Melchior answered in an obsequious voice with formal replies, respectful and servile; but she did not listen to Melchior, and went on teasing the child. He grew redder and redder, and, thinking that everybody must have noticed it, he thought he must explain it away and said with a long sigh:

"My face is red. I am hot."

That made the girl shout with laughter. But Jean-Christophe did not mind it in her, as he had in his audience just before, for her laughter was pleasant, and she kissed him, and he did not dislike that.

Then he saw his grandfather in the passage at the door of the box, beaming and bashful. The old man was fain to show himself, and also to say a few words, but he dared not, because no one had spoken to him. He was enjoying his grandson's glory at a distance. Jean-Christophe became tender, and felt an irresistible impulse to procure justice also for the old man, so that they should know his worth. His tongue was loosed, and he reached up to the ear of his new friend and whispered to her:

"I will tell you a secret."

She laughed, and said:

"What?"

"You know," he went on—"you know the pretty *trio* in my *minuetto*, the *minuetto* I played? . . . You know it? . . ." (He hummed it gently.) ". . . Well, grandfather wrote it, not I. All the other airs are mine. But that is the best. Grand-father wrote it. Grandfather did not want me to say anything. You won't tell anybody? . . ." (He pointed out the old man.) "That is my grandfather. I love him; he is very kind to me."

At that the young Princess laughed again, said that he was a darling, covered him with kisses, and, to the consternation of Jean-Christophe and his grandfather, told everybody. Everybody laughed then, and the Grand Duke congratulated the old man, who was covered with confusion, tried in vain to explain himself, and stammered like a guilty criminal. But Jean-Christophe said not another word to the girl, and in spite of her wheedling he remained dumb and stiff. He despised her for having broken her promise. His idea of princes suffered considerably from this disloyalty. He was so angry about it that he did not hear anything that was said, or that the Prince had appointed him laughingly his pianist in ordinary, his *Hof Musicus.*

He went out with his relatives, and found himself surrounded in the corridors of the theater, and even in the street, with people congratulating him or kissing him. That displeased him greatly, for he did not like being kissed, and did not like people meddling with him without asking his permission.

At last they reached home, and then hardly was the door closed than Melchior began to call him a " little idiot " because he had said that the *trio* was not his own. As the boy was under the impression that he had done a fine thing, which deserved praise, and not blame, he rebelled, and was impertinent. Melchior lost his temper, and said that he would box his ears, although he had played his music well enough, because with his idiocy he had spoiled the whole effect of the concert. Jean-Christophe had a profound sense of justice. He went and sulked in a corner; he visited his contempt upon his father, the Princess, and the whole world. He was hurt also because the neighbors came and congratulated his parents and laughed with them, as if it were they who had played, and as if it were their affair.

At this moment a servant of the Court came with a beautiful gold watch from the Grand Duke and a box of lovely sweets from the young Princess. Both presents gave great pleasure to Jean-Christophe, and he did not know which gave him the more; but he was in such a bad temper that he would not admit it to himself. and he went on sulking, scowling at the sweets, and wondering whether he could properly accept a gift from a person who had betrayed his confidence. As he was on the point of giving in his father wanted to set him down at once at the table, and make him write at his dictation a letter of thanks. This was too much. Either from the nervous strain of the day, or from instinctive shame at beginning the letter, as Melchior wanted him to, with the words, " The little servant and musician—*Knecht und Musicus*—of Your Highness . . ." he burst into tears, and was inconsolable. The servant waited and scoffed. Melchior had to write the letter. That did not make him exactly kindly disposed towards Jean-Christophe. As a crowning misfortune, the boy let his watch fall and broke it. A storm of reproaches broke upon him. Melchior shouted that he would have to go without dessert. Jean-Christophe said angrily that that was what he wanted. To punish him, Louisa said that she would begin by confiscating his sweets. Jean-Christophe was up in arms at that, and said that the box was his, and no one else's, and that no one should take it away from him! He was smacked, and in a fit of anger snatched the box from his mother's hands, hurled it on the floor, and stamped on it. He was whipped, taken to his room, undressed, and put to bed.

In the evening he heard his parents dining with friends— a magnificent repast, prepared a week before in honor of the concert. He was like to die with wrath at such injustice. They laughed loudly, and touched glasses. They had told the guests that the boy was tired, and no one bothered about him. Only after dinner, when the party was breaking up, he heard a slow, shuffling step come into his room, and old Jean Michel bent over his bed and kissed him, and said: " Dear little Jean-Christophe! . . ." Then, as if he were ashamed, he went away without another word. He had slipped into his hand some sweetmeats which he had hidden in his pocket.

That softened Jean-Christophe; but he was so tired with all the day's emotions that he had not the strength to think about what his grandfather had done. He had not even the strength to reach out to the good things the old man had given him. He was worn out, and went to sleep almost at once.

His sleep was light. He had acute nervous attacks, like electric shocks, which shook his whole body. In his dreams he was haunted by wild music. He awoke in the night. The Beethoven overture that he had heard at the concert was roaring in his ears. It filled the room with its mighty beat. He sat up in his bed, rubbed his eyes and ears, and asked himself if he were asleep. No; he was not asleep. He recognized the sound, he recognized those roars of anger, those savage cries; he heard the throbbing of that passionate heart leaping in his bosom, that tumult of the blood; he felt on his face the frantic beating of the wind, lashing and destroying, then stopping suddenly, cut off by an Herculean will. That Titanic soul entered his body, blew out his limbs and his soul, and seemed to give them colossal proportions. He strode over all the world. He was like a mountain, and storms raged within him —storms of wrath, storms of sorrow! . . . Ah, what sorrow! . . . But they were nothing! He felt so strong! . . . To suffer —still to suffer! . . . Ah, how good it is to be strong! How good it is to suffer when a man is strong! . . .

He laughed. His laughter rang out in the silence of the night. His father woke up and cried:

"Who is there?"

His mother whispered:

"Ssh! the boy is dreaming!"

All then were silent; round them all was silence. The music died away, and nothing sounded but the regular breathing of the human creatures asleep in the room, comrades in misery, thrown together by Fate in the same frail barque, bound onwards by a wild whirling force through the night.

(Jean–Christophe's letter to the Grand Duke Leopold is inspired by Beethoven's letter to the Prince Elector of Bonn, written when he was eleven.)

MORNING

I

THE DEATH OF JEAN MICHEL

YEARS have passed. Jean-Christophe is nearly eleven. His musical education is proceeding. He is learning harmony with Florian Holzer, the organist of St. Martin's, a friend of his grandfather's, a very learned man, who teaches him that the chords and series of chords that he most loves, and the harmonies which softly greet his heart and ear, those that he cannot hear without a little thrill running down his spine, are bad and forbidden. When he asks why, no reply is forthcoming but that it is so; the rules forbid them. As he is naturally in revolt against discipline, he loves them only the more. His delight is to find examples of them in the great and admired musicians, and to take them to his grandfather or his master. His grandfather replies that in the great musicians they are admirable, and that Beethoven and Bach can take any liberty. His master, less conciliatory, is angry, and says acidly that the masters did better things.

Jean-Christophe has a free pass for the concerts and the theater. He has learned to play every instrument a little. He is already quite skilful with the violin, and his father procured him a seat in the orchestra. He acquitted himself so well there that after a few months' probation he was officially appointed second violin in the *Hof Musik Verein*. He has begun to earn his living. Not too soon either, for affairs at home have gone from bad to worse. Melchior's intemperance has swamped him, and his grandfather is growing old.

Jean-Christophe has taken in the melancholy situation. He is already as grave and anxious as a man. He fulfils his task valiantly, though it does not interest him, and he is apt to fall asleep in the orchestra in the evenings, because it is late and he is tired. The theater no longer rouses in him the emotion it used to do when he was little. When he was little—four

years ago—his greatest ambition had been to occupy the place
that he now holds. But now he dislikes most of the music he
is made to play. He dare not yet pronounce judgment upon
it, but he does find it foolish; and if by chance they do play
lovely things, he is displeased by the carelessness with which
they are rendered, and his best-beloved works are made to
appear like his neighbors and colleagues in the orchestra, who,
as soon as the curtain has fallen, when they have done with
blowing and scraping, mop their brows and smile and chatter
quietly, as though they had just finished an hour's gymnastics.
And he has been close to his former flame, the fair barefooted
singer. He meets her quite often during the *entr'acte* in the
saloon. She knows that he was once in love with her, and she
kisses him often. That gives him no pleasure. He is disgusted by her paint and scent and her fat arms and her greediness. He hates her now.

The Grand Duke did **not** forget his pianist in ordinary.
Not that the small pension which was granted to him with this
title was regularly paid—it had to be asked for—but from time
to time Jean-Christophe used to receive orders to go to the
Palace when there were distinguished guests, or simply when
Their Highnesses took it into their heads that they wanted to
hear him. It was almost always in the evening, at the time
when Jean-Christophe wanted to be alone. He had to leave
everything and hurry off. Sometimes he was made to wait
in the anteroom, because dinner was not finished. The servants, accustomed to see him, used to address him familiarly.
Then he would be led into a great room full of mirrors and
lights, in which well-fed men and women used to stare at him
with horrid curiosity. He had to cross the waxed floor to kiss
Their Highnesses' hands, and the more he grew the more awkward he became, for he felt that he was in a ridiculous position,
and his pride used to suffer.

When it was all done he used to sit at the piano and have
to play for these idiots. He thought them idiots. There were
moments when their indifference so oppressed him as he played
that he was often on the point of stopping in the middle of a
piece. There was no air about him; he was near suffocation,
seemed losing his senses. When he finished he was overwhelmed

with congratulations and laden with compliments; he was introduced all round. He thought they looked at him like some
strange animal in the Prince's menagerie, and that the words
of praise were addressed rather to his master than to himself.
He thought himself brought low, and he developed a morbid
sensibility from which he suffered the more as he dared not
show it. He saw offense in the most simple actions. If any
one laughed in a corner of the room, he imagined himself to
be the cause of it, and he knew not whether it were his manners,
or his clothes, or his person, or his hands, or his feet, that
caused the laughter. He was humiliated by everything. He
was humiliated if people did not talk to him, humiliated if they
did, humiliated if they gave him sweets like a child, humiliated
especially when the Grand Duke, as sometimes happened, in
princely fashion dismissed him by pressing a piece of money
into his hand. He was wretched at being poor and at being
treated as a poor boy. One evening, as he was going home,
the money that he had received weighed so heavily upon him
that he threw it through a cellar window, and then immediately
he would have done anything to get it back, for at home there
was a month's old account with the butcher to pay.

His relatives never suspected these injuries to his pride.
They were delighted at his favor with the Prince. Poor Louisa
could conceive of nothing finer for her son than these evenings
at the Palace in splendid society. As for Melchior, he used
to brag of it continually to his boon-fellows. But Jean-Christophe's grandfather was happier than any. He pretended to
be independent and democratic, and to despise greatness, but
he had a simple admiration for money, power, honors, social
distinction, and he took unbounded pride in seeing his grandson
moving among those who had these things. He delighted in
them as though such glory was a reflection upon himself, and
in spite of all his efforts to appear calm and indifferent, his
face used to glow. On the evenings when Jean-Christophe went
to the Palace, old Jean Michel used always to contrive to stay
about the house on some pretext or another. He used to await
his grandson's return with childish impatience, and when Jean-
Christophe came in he would begin at once with a careless air
to ply him with seeming idle questions, such as:

"Well, did things go well to-night?"

Or he would make little hints like:

"Here's our Jean-Christophe; he can tell us some news."

Or he would produce some ingenious compliment by way of flattery:

"Here's our young nobleman!"

But Jean-Christophe, out of sorts and out of temper, would reply with a curt "Good-evening!" and go and sulk in a corner. But the old man would persist, and ply him with more direct questions, to which the boy replied only "Yes," or "No." Then the others would join in and ask for details. Jean-Christophe would look more and more thunderous. They had to drag the words from his lips until Jean Michel would lose his temper and hurl insults at him. Then Jean-Christophe would reply with scant respect, and the end would be a rumpus. The old man would go out and slam the door. So Jean-Christophe spoiled the joy of these poor people, who had no inkling of the cause of his bad temper. It was not their fault if they had the souls of servants, and never dreamed that it is possible to be otherwise.

Jean-Christophe was turned into himself, and though he never judged his family, yet he felt a gulf between himself and them. No doubt he exaggerated what lay between them, and in spite of their different ways of thought it is quite probable that they could have understood each other if he had been able to talk intimately to them. But it is known that nothing is more difficult than absolute intimacy between children and parents, even when there is much love between them, for on the one side respect discourages confidence, and on the other the idea, often erroneous, of the superiority of age and experience prevents them taking seriously enough the child's feelings, which are often just as interesting as those of grown-up persons, and almost always more sincere.

But the people that Jean-Christophe saw at home and the conversation that he heard there widened the distance between himself and his family.

Melchior's friends used to frequent the house—mostly musicians of the orchestra, single men and hard drinkers. They were not bad fellows, but vulgar. They made the house shake with their footsteps and their laughter. They loved music, but they spoke of it with a stupidity that was revolting. The coarse indiscretion of their enthusiasm wounded the boy's modesty of feeling. When they praised a work that he loved it was as though they were insulting him personally. He would stiffen himself and grow pale, frozen, and pretend not to take any interest in music. He would have hated it had that been possible. Melchior used to say:

" The fellow has no heart. He feels nothing. I don't know where he gets it from."

Sometimes they used to sing German four-part songs—four-footed as well—and these were all exactly like themselves—slow-moving, solemn and broad, fashioned of dull melodies. Then Jean-Christophe used to fly to the most distant room and hurl insults at the wall.

His grandfather also had friends : the organist, the furniture-dealer, the watch-maker, the contra-bass—garrulous old men, who used always to pass round the same jokes and plunge into interminable discussions on art, politics, or the family trees of the country-side, much less interested in the subjects of which they talked than happy to talk and to find an audience.

As for Louisa, she used only to see some of her neighbors who brought her the gossip of the place, and at rare intervals a " kind lady," who, under pretext of taking an interest in her, used to come and engage her services for a dinner-party, and pretend to watch over the religious education of the children.

But of all who came to the house, none was more repugnant to Jean-Christophe than his Uncle Theodore, a stepson of his grandfather's, a son by a former marriage of his grandmother Clara, Jean Michel's first wife. He was a partner in a great commercial house which did business in Africa and the Far East. He was the exact type of one of those Germans of the new style, whose affectation it is scoffingly to repudiate the old idealism of the race, and, intoxicated by conquest, to maintain a cult of strength and success which shows that they are not accustomed to seeing them on their side. But as it is difficult at once to change the age-old nature of a people, the despised idealism sprang up again in him at every turn in language, manners, and moral habits and the quotations from Goethe to fit the smallest incidents of domestic life, for he was a singular compound of conscience and self-interest. There was in him a curious effort to reconcile the honest principles of the old German *bourgeoisie* with the cynicism of these new commercial *condottieri*—a compound which forever gave out a repulsive flavor of hypocrisy, forever striving to make of German strength, avarice, and self-interest the symbols of all right, justice, and truth.

Jean-Christophe's loyalty was deeply injured by all this. He could not tell whether his uncle were right or no, but he hated him, and marked him down for an enemy. His grandfather had no great love for him either, and was in revolt against his theories; but he was easily crushed in argument by Theodore's fluency, which was never hard put to it to turn into ridicule the old man's simple generosity. In the end Jean Michel came to be ashamed of his own good-heartedness, and by way of showing that he was not so much behind the times as they thought, he used to try to talk like Theodore; but the words came hollow from his lips, and he was ill at ease with them. Whatever he may have thought of him, Theodore did impress him. He felt respect for such practical skill, which he admired the more for knowing himself to be absolutely incapable of it. He used to dream of putting one of his grandsons to similar work. That was Melchior's idea also. He intended to make Rodolphe follow in his uncle's footsteps. And so the whole family set itself to flatter this rich relation of whom they expected help. He, seeing that he was necessary to them, took advantage of it to cut a fine masterful figure. He meddled in everything, gave advice upon everything, and made no attempt to conceal his contempt for art and artists. Rather, he blazoned it abroad for the mere pleasure of humiliating his musicianly relations, and he used to indulge in stupid jokes at their expense, and the cowards used to laugh.

Jean-Christophe, especially, was singled out as a butt for his uncle's jests. He was not patient under them. He would say nothing, but he used to grind his teeth angrily, and his uncle used to laugh at his speechless rage. But one day, when Theodore went too far in his teasing, Jean-Christophe, losing control of himself, spat in his face. It was a fearful affair. The insult was so monstrous that his uncle was at first paralyzed by it; then words came back to him, and he broke out into a flood of abuse. Jean-Christophe sat petrified by the enormity of the thing that he had done, and did not even feel the blows that rained down upon him; but when they tried to force him down on his knees before his uncle, he broke away, jostled his mother aside, and ran out of the house. He did not stop until he could breathe no more, and then he was right out in the country. He heard voices calling him, and he debated within himself whether he had not better throw himself into the river, since he could not do so with his enemy. He spent the night in the fields. At dawn he went and knocked at his grandfather's door. The old man had been so upset by Jean-Christophe's disappearance—he had not slept for it—that he had not the heart to scold him. He took him home, and then nothing was said to him, because it was apparent that he was still in an excited condition, and they had to smooth him down, for he had to play at the Palace that evening. But for several weeks Melchior continued to overwhelm him with his complaints, addressed to nobody in particular, about the trouble that a man takes to give an example of an irreproachable life and good manners to unworthy creatures who dishonor him. And when his Uncle Theodore met him in the street, he turned his head and held his nose by way of showing his extreme disgust.

Finding so little sympathy at home, Jean-Christophe spent as little time there as possible. He chafed against the continual restraint which they strove to set upon him. There were too many things, too many people, that he had to respect, and he was never allowed to ask why, and Jean-Christophe did not possess the bump of respect. The more they tried to discipline him and to turn him into an honest little German *bourgeois,* the more he felt the need of breaking free from it all. It would have been his pleasure after the dull, tedious, formal performances which he had to attend in the orchestra or at the Palace to roll in the grass like a fowl, and to slide down the grassy slope on the seat of his new trousers, or to have a stone-fight with the urchins of the neighborhood. It was not because he was afraid of scoldings and thwackings that he did not do these things more often, but because he had no playmates. He

could not get on with other children. Even the little gutter-
snipes did not like playing with him, because he took every
game too seriously, and struck too lustily. He had grown used
to being driven in on himself, and to living apart from children
of his own age. He was ashamed of not being clever at games,
and dared not take part in their sport. And he used to pretend
to take no interest in it, although he was consumed by the
desire to be asked to play with them. But they never said
anything to him, and then he would go away hurt, but assuming indifference.

He found consolation in wandering with Uncle Gottfried
when he was in the neighborhood. He became more and more
friendly with him, and sympathized with his independent temper. He understood so well now Gottfried's delight in tramping
the roads without a tie in the world! Often they used to
go out together in the evening into the country, straight on,
aimlessly, and as Gottfried always forgot the time, they used to
come back very late, and then were scolded. Gottfried knew
that it was wrong, but Jean-Christophe used to implore, and
he could not himself resist the pleasure of it. About midnight
he would stand in front of the house and whistle, an agreed
signal. Jean-Christophe would be in his bed fully dressed.
He would slip out with his shoes in his hand, and, holding his
breath, creep with all the artful skill of a savage to the kitchen
window, which opened on to the road. He would climb on to
the table; Gottfried would take him on his shoulders, and then
off they would go, happy as truants.

Sometimes they would go and seek out Jeremy the fisherman,
a friend of Gottfried's, and then they would slip out in his
boat under the moon. The water dropping from the oars gave
out little arpeggios, then chromatic scales. A milky vapor hung
tremulous over the surface of the waters. The stars quivered.
The cocks called to each other from either bank, and sometimes in the depths of the sky they heard the trilling of larks
ascending from earth, deceived by the light of the moon. They
were silent. Gottfried hummed a tune. Jeremy told strange
tales of the lives of the beasts—tales that gained in mystery
from the curt and enigmatic manner of their telling. The moon
hid herself behind the woods. They skirted the black mass

of the hills. The darkness of the water and the sky mingled. There was never a ripple on the water. Sounds died down. The boat glided through the night. Was she gliding? Was she moving? Was she still? . . . The reeds parted with a sound like the rustling of silk. The boat grounded noiselessly. They climbed out on to the bank, and returned on foot. They would not return until dawn. They followed the river-bank. Clouds of silver ablets, green as ears of corn, or blue as jewels, teemed in the first light of day. They swarmed like the serpents of Medusa's head, and flung themselves greedily at the bread thrown to them; they plunged for it as it sank, and turned in spirals, and then darted away in a flash, like a ray of light. The river took on rosy and purple hues of reflection. The birds woke one after another. The truants hurried back. Just as carefully as when they had set out, they returned to the room, with its thick atmosphere, and Jean-Christophe, worn out, fell into bed, and slept at once, with his body sweet-smelling with the smell of the fields.

All was well, and nothing would have been known, but that one day Ernest, his younger brother, betrayed Jean-Christophe's midnight sallies. From that moment they were forbidden, and he was watched. But he contrived to escape, and he preferred the society of the little peddler and his friends to any other. His family was scandalized. Melchior said that he had the tastes of a laborer. Old Jean Michel was jealous of Jean-Christophe's affection for Gottfried, and used to lecture him about lowering himself so far as to like such vulgar company when he had the honor of mixing with the best people and of being the servant of princes. It was considered that Jean-Christophe was lacking in dignity and self-respect.

In spite of the penury which increased with Melchior's intemperance and folly, life was tolerable as long as Jean Michel was there. He was the only creature who had any influence over Melchior, and who could hold him back to a certain extent from his vice. The esteem in which he was generally held did serve to pass over the drunkard's freaks, and he used constantly to come to the aid of the household with money. Besides the modest pension which he enjoyed as retired *Kapellmeister*, he was still able to earn small sums by giving lessons and tuning pianos. He gave most of it to his daughter-in-law, for he perceived her difficulties, though she strove to hide them from him. Louisa hated the idea that he was denying himself for them, and it was all the more to the old man's credit in that he had always been accustomed to a large way of living and had great needs to satisfy. Sometimes even his ordinary sacrifices were not sufficient, and to meet some urgent debt Jean Michel would have secretly to sell a piece of furniture or books, or some relic that he set store by. Melchior knew that his father made presents to Louisa that were concealed from himself, and very often he would lay hands on them, in spite of protest. But when this came to the old man's ears—not from Louisa, who said nothing of her troubles to him, but from one of his grandchildren—he would fly into a terrible passion, and there were frightful scenes between the two men. They were both extraordinarily violent, and they would come to round oaths and threats—almost it seemed as though they would come to blows. But even in his most angry passion respect would hold Melchior in check, and, however drunk he might be, in the end he would bow his head to the torrent of insults and humiliating reproach which his father poured out upon him. But for that he did not cease to watch for the first opportunity of breaking out again, and with his thoughts on the future, Jean Michel would be filled with melancholy and anxious fears.

"My poor children," he used to say to Louisa, "what will become of you when I am no longer here? . . . Fortunately," he would add, fondling Jean-Christophe, "I can go on until this fellow pulls you out of the mire." But he was out in his reckoning; he was at the end of his road. No one would have suspected it. He was surprisingly strong. He was past eighty; he had a full head of hair, a white mane, still gray in patches, and in his thick beard were still black hairs. He had only about ten teeth left, but with these he could chew lustily. It was a pleasure to see him at table. He had a hearty appetite, and though he reproached Melchior for drinking, he always emptied his bottle himself. He had a preference for white Moselle. For the rest—wine, beer, cider—he could do justice to all the good things that the Lord hath made. He was not so foolish as to lose his reason in his cups, and he kept to his allowance. It is true that it was a plentiful allowance, and that a feebler intelligence must have been made drunk by it. He was strong of foot and eye, and indefatigably active. He got up at six, and performed his ablutions scrupulously, for he cared for his appearance and respected his person. He lived alone in his house, of which he was sole occupant, and never let his daughter-in-law meddle with his affairs. He cleaned out his room, made his own coffee, sewed on his buttons, nailed, and glued, and altered; and going to and fro and up and down stairs in his shirt-sleeves, he never stopped singing in a sounding bass which he loved to let ring out as he accompanied himself with operatic gestures. And then he used to go out in all weathers. He went about his business, omitting none, but he was not often punctual. He was to be seen at every street corner arguing with some acquaintance or joking with some woman whose face he had remembered, for he loved pretty women and old friends. And so he was always late, and never knew the time. But he never let the dinner-hour slip by. He dined wherever he might be, inviting himself, and he would not go home until late—after nightfall, after a visit to his grandchildren. Then he would go to bed, and before he went to sleep read a page of his old Bible, and during the night—for he never slept for more than an hour or two together—he would get up to take down one of his old books, bought second-hand—history, theology, belles-lettres, or science. He used to read at random a few pages, which interested and bored him, and he did not rightly understand them, though he did not skip a word, until sleep came to him again. On Sunday he would go to church, walk with the children, and play bowls. He had never been ill, except for a little gout in his toes, which used to make him swear at night while he was reading his Bible. It seemed as though he might live to be a hundred, and he himself could see no reason why he should not live longer. When people said that he would die a centenarian, he used to think, like another illustrious old man, that no limit can be appointed to the goodness of Providence. The only sign that he was growing old was that he was more easily brought to tears, and was becoming every day more irritable. The smallest impatience with him could throw him into a violent fury. His red face and short neck would grow redder than ever. He would stutter angrily, and have to stop, choking. The family doctor, an old friend, had warned him to take care and to moderate both his anger and his appetite. But with an old man's obstinacy he plunged into acts of still greater recklessness out of bravado, and he laughed at medicine and doctors. He pretended to despise death, and did not mince his language when he declared that he was not afraid of it.

One summer day, when it was very hot, and he had drunk copiously, and argued in the market-place, he went home and began to work quietly in his garden. He loved digging. Bareheaded under the sun, still irritated by his argument, he dug angrily. Jean-Christophe was sitting in the arbor with a book in his hand, but he was not reading. He was dreaming and listening to the cheeping of the crickets, and mechanically following his grandfather's movements. The old man's back was towards him; he was bending and plucking out weeds. Suddenly Jean-Christophe saw him rise, beat against the air with his arms, and fall heavily with his face to the ground. For a moment he wanted to laugh; then he saw that the old man did not stir. He called to him, ran to him, and shook him with all his strength. Fear seized him. He knelt, and with his two hands tried to raise the great head from the ground. It was so heavy and he trembled so that he could hardly move it. But when he saw the eyes turned up, white and bloody, he was frozen with horror and, with a shrill cry, let the head fall. He got up in terror, ran away and out of the place. He cried and wept. A man passing by stopped the boy. Jean-Christophe could not speak, but he pointed to the house. The man went in, and Jean-Christophe followed him. Others had heard his cries, and they came from the neighboring houses. Soon the garden was full of people. They trampled the flowers, and bent down over the old man. They cried aloud. Two or three men lifted him up. Jean-Christophe stayed by the gate, turned to the wall, and hid his face in his hands. He was afraid to look, but he could not help himself, and when they passed him he saw through his fingers the old man's huge body, limp and flabby. One arm dragged along the ground, the head, leaning against the knee of one of the men carrying the body, bobbed at every step, and the face was scarred, covered with mud, bleeding. The mouth was open and the eyes were fearful. He howled again, and took to flight. He ran as though something were after him, and never stopped until he reached home. He burst into the kitchen with frightful cries. Louisa was cleaning vegetables. He hurled himself at her, and hugged her desperately, imploring her help. His face was distorted with his sobs; he could hardly speak. But at the first word she understood. She went white, let the things fall from her hands, and without a word rushed from the house.

Jean-Christophe was left alone, crouching against a cupboard. He went on weeping. His brothers were playing. He could not make out quite what had happened. He did not think of his grandfather; he was thinking only of the dreadful sights he had just seen, and he was in terror lest he should be made to return to see them again.

And as it turned out in the evening, when the other children, tired of doing every sort of mischief in the house, were beginning to feel wearied and hungry, Louisa rushed in again, took them by the hand, and led them to their grandfather's house. She walked very fast, and Ernest and Rodolphe tried to complain, as usual; but Louisa bade them be silent in such a tone of voice that they held their peace. An instinctive fear seized them, and when they entered the house they began to weep. It was not yet night. The last hours of the sunset cast strange lights over the inside of the house—on the door-handle, on the mirror, on the violin hung on the wall in the chief room, which was half in darkness. But in the old man's room a candle was alight, and the flickering flame, vying with the livid, dying day, made the heavy darkness of the room more oppressive. Melchior was sitting near the window, loudly weeping. The doctor, leaning over the bed, hid from sight what was lying there. Jean-Christophe's heart beat so that it was like to break. Louisa made the children kneel at the foot of the bed. Jean-Christophe stole a glance. He expected something so terrifying after what he had seen in the afternoon that at the first glimpse he was almost comforted. His grandfather lay motionless, and seemed to be asleep. For a moment the child believed that the old man was better, and that all was at an end. But when he heard his heavy breathing; when, as he looked closer, he saw the swollen face, on which the wound that he had come by in the fall had made a broad scar; when he understood that here was a man at point of death, he began to tremble; and while he repeated Louisa's prayer for the restoration of his grandfather, in his heart he prayed that if the old man could not get well he might be already dead. He was terrified at the prospect of what was going to happen.

The old man had not been conscious since the moment of his fall. He only returned to consciousness for a moment, enough to learn his condition, and that was lamentable. The priest was there, and recited the last prayers over him. They raised the old man on his pillow. He opened his eyes slowly, and they seemed no longer to obey his will. He breathed noisily, and with unseeing eyes looked at the faces and the lights, and suddenly he opened his mouth. A nameless terror showed on his features.

" But then . . ." he gasped—" but I am going to die! "

The awful sound of his voice pierced Jean-Christophe's heart. Never, never was it to fade from his memory. The old man said no more. He moaned like a little child. The stupor took him once more, but his breathing became more and more difficult. He groaned, he fidgeted with his hands, he seemed to struggle against the mortal sleep. In his semi-consciousness he cried once:

" Mother! "

Oh, the biting impression that it made, this mumbling of the old man, calling in anguish on his mother, as Jean-Christophe would himself have done—his mother, of whom he was never known to talk in life, to whom he now turned instinctively, the last futile refuge in the last terror! . . . Then he seemed to be comforted for a moment. He had once more a flicker of consciousness. His heavy eyes, the pupils of which seemed to move aimlessly, met those of the boy frozen in his fear. They lit up. The old man tried to smile and speak. Louisa took Jean-Christophe and led him to the bedside. Jean Michel moved his lips, and tried to caress his head with his hand, but then he fell back into his torpor. It was the end.

They sent the children into the next room, but they had too

much to do to worry about them, and Jean-Christophe, under
the attraction of the horror of it, peeped through the half-open
door at the tragic face on the pillow; the man strangled by
the firm clutch that had him by the neck; the face which grew
ever more hollow as he watched; the sinking of the creature
into the void, which seemed to suck it down like a pump; and
the horrible death-rattle, the mechanical breathing, like a bubble
of air bursting on the surface of waters; the last efforts of the
body, which strives to live when the soul is no longer. Then
the head fell on one side on the pillow. All, all was silence.

A few moments later, in the midst of the sobs and prayers
and the confusion caused by the death, Louisa saw the child,
pale, wide-eyed, with gaping mouth, clutching convulsively at
the handle of the door. She ran to him. He had a seizure
in her arms. She carried him away. He lost consciousness.
He woke up to find himself in his bed. He howled in terror,
because he had been left alone for a moment, had another
seizure, and fainted again. For the rest of the night and the
next day he was in a fever. Finally, he grew calm, and on the
next night fell into a deep sleep, which lasted until the middle
of the following day. He felt that some one was walking in
his room, that his mother was leaning over his bed and kissing
him. He thought he heard the sweet distant sound of bells.
But he would not stir; he was in a dream.   .

When he opened his eyes again his Uncle Gottfried was sitting at the foot of his bed. Jean-Christophe was worn out,
and could remember nothing. Then his memory returned, and
he began to weep. Gottfried got up and kissed him.

" Well, my boy—well? " he said gently.

" Oh, uncle, uncle! " sobbed the boy, clinging to him.

" Cry, then . . ." said Gottfried. " Cry! "

He also was weeping.

When he was a little comforted Jean-Christophe dried his
eyes and looked at Gottfried. Gottfried understood that he
wanted to ask something.

" No," he said, putting a finger to his lips, " you must not
talk. It is good to cry, bad to talk."

The boy insisted.

" It is no good."

" Only one thing—only one ! . . ."

" What ? "

Jean-Christophe hesitated.

" Oh, uncle ! " he asked, " where is he now ? "

Gottfried answered:

" He is with the Lord, my boy."

But that was not what Jean-Christophe had asked.

" No; you do not understand. Where is he—he *himself ?* "
(He meant the body.)

He went on in a trembling voice:

" Is *he* still in the house ? "

" They buried the good man this morning," said Gottfried.
" Did you not hear the bells ? "

Jean-Christophe was comforted. Then, when he thought that
he would never see his beloved grandfather again, he wept once
more bitterly.

" Poor little beast ! " said Gottfried, looking pityingly at the
child.

Jean-Christophe expected Gottfried to console him, but Gottfried made no attempt to do so, knowing that it was useless.

" Uncle Gottfried," asked the boy, " are not you afraid of it,
too ? "

(Much did he wish that Gottfried should not have been afraid,
and would tell him the secret of it !)

" 'Ssh ! " he said, in a troubled voice. . . .

" And how is one not to be afraid ? " he said, after a moment.
" But what can one do ? It is so. One must put up with
it."

Jean-Christophe shook his head in protest.

" One has to put up with it, my boy," said Gottfried. " *He*
ordered it up yonder. One has to love what *He* has ordered."

" I hate Him ! " said Jean-Christophe, angrily shaking his
fist at the sky.

Gottfried fearfully bade him be silent. Jean-Christophe himself was afraid of what he had just said, and he began to pray
with Gottfried. But blood boiled, and as he repeated the words
of servile humility and resignation there was in his inmost
heart a feeling of passionate revolt and horror of the abominable
thing and the monstrous Being who had been able to create it.

Days passed and nights of rain over the freshly-turned earth under which lay the remains of poor old Jean Michel. At the moment Melchior wept and cried and sobbed much, but the week was not out before Jean-Christophe heard him laughing heartily. When the name of the dead man was pronounced in his presence, his face grew longer and a lugubrious expression came into it, but in a moment he would begin to talk and gesticulate excitedly. He was sincerely afflicted, but it was impossible for him to remain sad for long.

Louisa, passive and resigned, accepted the misfortune as she accepted everything. She added a prayer to her daily prayers; she went regularly to the cemetery, and cared for the grass as if it were part of her household.

Gottfried paid touching attention to the little patch of ground where the old man slept. When he came to the neighborhood, he brought a little souvenir—a cross that he had made, or flowers that Jean Michel had loved. He never missed, even if he were only in the town for a few hours, and he did it by stealth.

Sometimes Louisa took Jean-Christophe with her on her visits to the cemetery. Jean-Christophe revolted in disgust against the fat patch of earth clad in its sinister adornment of flowers and trees, and against the heavy scent which mounts to the sun, mingling with the breath of the sonorous cypress. But he dared not confess his disgust, because he condemned it in himself as cowardly and impious. He was very unhappy. His grandfather's death haunted him incessantly, and yet he had long known what death was, and had thought about it and been afraid of it. But he had never before seen it, and he who sees it for the first time learns that he knew nothing, neither of death nor of life. One moment brings everything tottering. Reason is of no avail. You thought you were alive, you thought you had some experience of life; you see then that you knew nothing, that you have been living in a veil of illusions spun by your own mind to hide from your eyes the awful countenance of reality. There is no connection between the idea of suffering and the creature who bleeds and suffers. There is no connection between the idea of death and the convulsions of body and soul in combat and in death. Human language, human wisdom, are only a puppet-show of stiff mechanical dolls by the side of the grim charm of reality and the creatures of mind and blood, whose desperate and vain efforts are strained to the fixing of a life which crumbles away with every day.

Jean-Christophe thought of death day and night. Memories of the last agony pursued him. He heard that horrible breathing; every night, whatever he might be doing, he saw his grandfather again. All Nature was changed; it seemed as though there were an icy vapor drawn over her. Round him, everywhere, whichever way he turned, he felt upon his face the fatal breathing of the blind, all-powerful Beast; he felt himself in the grip of that fearful destructive Form, and he felt that there was nothing to be done. But, far from crushing him, the thought of it set him aflame with hate and indignation. He was never resigned to it. He butted head down against the impossible; it mattered nothing that he broke his head, and was forced to realize that he was not the stronger. He never ceased to revolt against suffering. From that time on his life was an unceasing struggle against the savagery of a Fate which he could not admit.

The very misery of his life afforded him relief from the obsession of his thoughts. The ruin of his family, which only Jean Michel had withheld, proceeded apace when he was removed. With him the Kraffts had lost their chief means of support, and misery entered the house.

Melchior increased it. Far from working more, he abandoned himself utterly to his vice when he was free of the only force that had held him in check. Almost every night he returned home drunk, and he never brought back his earnings. Besides, he had lost almost all his lessons. One day he had appeared at the house of one of his pupils in a state of complete intoxication, and, as a consequence of this scandal, all doors were closed to him. He was only tolerated in the orchestra out of regard for the memory of his father, but Louisa trembled lest he should be dismissed any day after a scene. He had already been threatened with it on several evenings when he had turned up in his place about the end of the performance.

Twice or thrice he had forgotten altogether to put in an appearance. And of what was he not capable in those moments of stupid excitement when he was taken with the itch to do and say idiotic things! Had he not taken it into his head one evening to try and play his great violin concerto in the middle of an act of the *Valkyrie?* They were hard put to it to stop him. Sometimes, too, he would shout with laughter in the middle of a performance at the amusing pictures that were presented on the stage or whirling in his own brain. He was a joy to his colleagues, and they passed over many things because he was so funny. But such indulgence was worse than severity, and Jean-Christophe could have died for shame.

The boy was now first violin in the orchestra. He sat so that he could watch over his father, and, when necessary, beseech him, and make him be silent. It was not easy, and the best thing was not to pay any attention to him, for if he did, as soon as the sot felt that eyes were upon him, he would take to making faces or launch out into a speech. Then Jean-Christophe would turn away, trembling with fear lest he should commit some outrageous prank. He would try to be absorbed in his work, but he could not help hearing Melchior's utterances and the laughter of his colleagues. Tears would come into his eyes. The musicians, good fellows that they were, had seen that, and were sorry for him. They would hush their laughter, and only talk about his father when Jean-Christophe was not by. But Jean-Christophe was conscious of their pity. He knew that as soon as he had gone their jokes would break out again, and that Melchior was the laughing-stock of the town. He could not stop him, and he was in torment. He used to bring his father home after the play. He would take his arm, put up with his pleasantries, and try to conceal the stumbling in his walk. But he deceived no one, and in spite of all his efforts it was very rarely that he could succeed in leading Melchior all the way home. At the corner of the street Melchior would declare that he had an urgent appointment with some friends, and no argument could dissuade him from keeping this engagement. Jean-Christophe took care not to insist too much, so as not to expose himself to a scene and paternal imprecations which might attract the neighbors to their windows.

All the household money slipped away in this fashion. Melchior was not satisfied with drinking away his earnings; he drank away all that his wife and son so hardly earned. Louisa used to weep, but she dared not resist, since her husband had harshly reminded her that nothing in the house belonged to her, and that he had married her without a sou. Jean-Christophe tried to resist. Melchior boxed his ears, treated him like a naughty child, and took the money out of his hands. The boy was twelve or thirteen. He was strong, and was beginning to kick against being beaten; but he was still afraid to rebel, and rather than expose himself to fresh humiliations of the kind he let himself be plundered. The only resource that Louisa and Jean-Christophe had was to hide their money; but Melchior was singularly ingenious in discovering their hiding-places when they were not there.

Soon that was not enough for him. He sold the things that he had inherited from his father. Jean-Christophe sadly saw the precious relics go—the books, the bed, the furniture, the portraits of musicians. He could say nothing. But one day, when Melchior had crashed into Jean Michel's old piano, he swore as he rubbed his knee, and said that there was no longer room to move about in his own house, and that he would rid the house of all such gimcrackery. Jean-Christophe cried aloud. It was true that the rooms were too full, since all Jean Michel's belongings were crowded into them, so as to be able to sell the house, that dear house in which Jean-Christophe had spent the happiest hours of his childhood. It was true also that the old piano was not worth much, that it was husky in tone, and that for a long time Jean-Christophe had not used it, since he played on the fine new piano due to the generosity of the Prince; but however old and useless it might be, it was Jean-Christophe's best friend. It had awakened the child to the boundless world of music; on its worn yellow keys he had discovered with his fingers the kingdom of sounds and its laws; it had been his grandfather's work (months had gone to repairing it for his grandson), and he was proud of it; it was in some sort a holy relic, and Jean-Christophe protested that his father had no right to sell it. Melchior bade him be silent. Jean-Christophe cried louder than ever that the piano was his, and that he forbade any one to touch it; but Melchior looked at him with an evil smile, and said nothing

Next day Jean-Christophe had forgotten the affair. He came home tired, but in a fairly good temper. He was struck by the sly looks of his brothers. They pretended to be absorbed in their books, but they followed him with their eyes, and watched all his movements, and bent over their books again when he looked at them. He had no doubt that they had played some trick upon him, but he was used to that, and did not worry about it, but determined, when he had found it out, to give them a good thrashing, as he always did on such occasions. He scorned to look into the matter, and he began to talk to his father, who was sitting by the fire, and questioned him as to the doings of the day with an affectation of interest which suited him but ill; and while he talked he saw that Melchior was exchanging stealthy nods and winks with the two children. Something caught at his heart. He ran into his room. The place where the piano had stood was empty! He gave a cry of anguish. In the next room he heard the stifled laughter of his brothers. The blood rushed to his face. He rushed in to them, and cried:

"My piano!"

Melchior raised his head with an air of calm bewilderment which made the children roar with laughter. He could not contain himself when he saw Jean-Christophe's piteous look, and he turned aside to guffaw. Jean-Christophe no longer knew what he was doing. He hurled himself like a mad thing on his father. Melchior, lolling in his chair, had no time to protect himself. The boy seized him by the throat and cried:

"Thief! Thief!"

It was only for a moment. Melchior shook himself, and sent Jean-Christophe rolling down on to the tile floor, though in his fury he was clinging to him like grim death. The boy's head crashed against the tiles. Jean-Christophe got upon his knees. He was livid, and he went on saying in a choking voice:

"Thief, thief! . . . You are robbing us—mother and me. . . . Thief! . . . You are selling my grandfather!"

Melchior rose to his feet, and held his fist above Jean-Christophe's head. The boy stared at him with hate in his eyes. He was trembling with rage. Melchior began to tremble, too.

He sat down, and hid his face in his hands. The two children had run away screaming. Silence followed the uproar. Melchior groaned and mumbled. Jean-Christophe, against the wall, never ceased glaring at him with clenched teeth, and he trembled in every limb. Melchior began to blame himself.

"I am a thief! I rob my family! My children despise me! It were better if I were dead!"

When he had finished whining, Jean-Christophe did not budge, but asked him harshly:

"Where is the piano?"

"At Wormser's," said Melchior, not daring to look at him.

Jean-Christophe took a step forward, and said:

"The money!"

Melchior, crushed, took the money from his pocket and gave it to his son. Jean-Christophe turned towards the door. Melchior called him:

"Jean-Christophe!"

Jean-Christophe stopped. Melchior went on in a quavering voice:

"Dear Jean-Christophe . . . do not despise me!"

Jean-Christophe flung his arms round his neck and sobbed:

"No, father—dear father! I do not despise you! I am so unhappy!"

They wept loudly. Melchior lamented:

"It is not my fault. I am not bad. That's true, Jean-Christophe? I am not bad?"

He promised that he would drink no more. Jean-Christophe wagged his head doubtfully, and Melchior admitted that he could not resist it when he had money in his hands. Jean-Christophe thought for a moment and said:

"You see, father, we must . . ."

He stopped.

"What then?"

"I am ashamed . . ."

"Of whom?" asked Melchior naïvely

"Of you."

Melchior made a face and said:

"That's nothing."

Jean-Christophe explained that they would have to put all

the family money, even Melchior's contribution, into the hands
of some one else, who would dole it out to Melchior day by
day, or week by week, as he needed it. Melchior, who was
in humble mood—he was not altogether starving—agreed to
the proposition, and declared that he would then and there
write a letter to the Grand Duke to ask that the pension which
came to him should be regularly paid over in his name to Jean-
Christophe. Jean-Christophe refused, blushing for his father's
humiliation. But Melchior, thirsting for self-sacrifice, insisted
on writing. He was much moved by his own magnanimity.
Jean-Christophe refused to take the letter, and when Louisa
came in and was acquainted with the turn of events, she declared
that she would rather beg in the streets than expose her husband to such an insult. She added that she had every confidence
in him, and that she was sure he would make amends out of
love for the children and herself. In the end there was a
scene of tender reconciliation and Melchior's letter was left on
the table, and then fell under the cupboard, where it remained
concealed.

But a few days later, when she was cleaning up, Louisa
found it there, and as she was very unhappy about Melchior's
fresh outbreaks—he had forgotten all about it—instead of tearing it up, she kept it. She kept it for several months, always
rejecting the idea of making use of it, in spite of the suffering
she had to endure. But one day, when she saw Melchior once
more beating Jean-Christophe and robbing him of his money,
she could bear it no longer, and when she was left alone with
the boy, who was weeping, she went and fetched the letter, and
gave it him, and said:

" Go! "

Jean-Christophe hesitated, but he understood that there was
no other way if they wished to save from the wreck the little
that was left to them. He went to the Palace. He took nearly
an hour to walk a distance that ordinarily took twenty minutes.
He was overwhelmed by the shame of what he was doing. His
pride, which had grown great in the years of sorrow and isolation, bled at the thought of publicly confessing his father's
vice. He knew perfectly well that it was known to everybody,
but by a strange and natural inconsequence he would not admit

it, and pretended to notice nothing, and he would rather have been hewn in pieces than agree. And now, of his own accord, he was going! . . . Twenty times he was on the point of turning back. He walked two or three times round the town, turning away just as he came near the Palace. He was not alone in his plight. His mother and brothers had also to be considered. Since his father had deserted them and betrayed them, it was his business as eldest son to take his place and come to their assistance. There was no room for hesitation or pride; he had to swallow down his shame. He entered the Palace. On the staircase he almost turned and fled. He knelt down on a step; he stayed for several minutes on the landing, with his hand on the door, until some one coming made him go in.

Every one in the offices knew him. He asked to see His Excellency the Director of the Theaters, Baron de Hammer Langbach. A young clerk, sleek, bald, pink-faced, with a white waistcoat and a pink tie, shook his hand familiarly, and began to talk about the opera of the night before. Jean-Christophe repeated his question. The clerk replied that His Excellency was busy for the moment, but that if Jean-Christophe had a request to make they could present it with other documents which were to be sent in for His Excellency's signature. Jean-Christophe held out his letter. The clerk read it, and gave a cry of surprise.

"Oh, indeed!" he said brightly. "That is a good idea. He ought to have thought of that long ago! He never did anything better in his life! Ah, the old sot! How the devil did he bring himself to do it?"

He stopped short. Jean-Christophe had snatched the paper out of his hands, and, white with rage, shouted:

"I forbid you! . . . I forbid you to insult me!"

The clerk was staggered.

"But, my dear Jean-Christophe," he began to say, "whoever thought of insulting you? I only said what everybody thinks, and what you think yourself."

"No!" cried Jean-Christophe angrily.

"What! you don't think so? You don't think that he drinks?"

"It is not true!" said Jean-Christophe.

He stamped his foot.

The clerk shrugged his shoulders.

"In that case, why did he write this letter?"

"Because," said Jean-Christophe (he did not know what to say)—"because, when I come for my wages every month, I prefer to take my father's at the same time. It is no good our both putting ourselves out. . . . My father is very busy."

He reddened at the absurdity of his explanation. The clerk looked at him with pity and irony in his eyes. Jean-Christophe crumpled the paper in his hands, and turned to go. The clerk got up and took him by the arm.

"Wait a moment," he said. "I'll go and fix it up for you."

He went into the Director's office. Jean-Christophe waited, with the eyes of the other clerks upon him. His blood boiled. He did not know what he was doing, what to do, or what he ought to do. He thought of going away before the answer was brought to him, and he had just made up his mind to that when the door opened.

"His Excellency will see you," said the too obliging clerk.

Jean-Christophe had to go in.

His Excellency Baron de Hammer Langbach, a little neat old man with whiskers, mustaches, and a shaven chin, looked at Jean-Christophe over his golden spectacles without stopping writing, nor did he give any response to the boy's awkward bow.

"So," he said, after a moment, "you are asking, Herr Krafft . . . ?"

"Your Excellency," said Jean-Christophe hurriedly, "I ask your pardon. I have thought better of it. I have nothing to ask."

The old man sought no explanation for this sudden reconsideration. He looked more closely at Jean-Christophe, coughed, and said:

"Herr Krafft, will you give me the letter that is in your hand?"

Jean-Christophe saw that the Director's gaze was fixed on the paper which he was still unconsciously holding crumpled up in his hand.

"It is no use, Your Excellency," he murmured. "It is not worth while now."

" Please give it me," said the old man quietly, as though he had not heard.

Mechanically Jean-Christophe gave him the crumpled letter, but he plunged into a torrent of stuttered words while he held out his hand for the letter. His Excellency carefully smoothed out the paper, read it, looked at Jean-Christophe, let him flounder about with his explanations, then checked him, and said with a malicious light in his eyes:

" Very well, Herr Krafft; the request is granted."

He dismissed him with a wave of his hand and went on with his writing.

Jean-Christophe went out, crushed.

" No offense, Jean-Christophe! " said the clerk kindly, when the boy came into the office again. Jean-Christophe let him shake his hand without daring to raise his eyes. He found himself outside the Palace. He was cold with shame. Everything that had been said to him recurred in his memory, and he imagined that there was an insulting irony in the pity of the people who honored and were sorry for him. He went home, and answered only with a few irritable words Louisa's questions, as though he bore a grudge against her for what he had just done. He was racked by remorse when he thought of his father. He wanted to confess everything to him, and to beg his pardon. Melchior was not there. Jean-Christophe kept awake far into the night, waiting for him. The more he thought of him the more his remorse quickened. He idealized him; he thought of him as weak, kind, unhappy, betrayed by his own family. As soon as he heard his step on the stairs he leaped from his bed to go and meet him, and throw himself in his arms; but Melchior was in such a disgusting state of intoxication that Jean-Christophe had not even the courage to go near him, and he went to bed again, laughing bitterly at his own illusions.

When Melchior learned a few days later of what had happened, he was in a towering passion, and, in spite of all Jean-Christophe's entreaties, he went and made a scene at the Palace. But he returned with his tail between his legs, and breathed not a word of what had happened. He had been very badly received. He had been told that he would have to take a very different tone about the matter, that the pension had only been

continued out of consideration for the worth of his son, and
that if in the future there came any scandal concerning him
to their ears, it would be suppressed. And so Jean-Christophe
was much surprised and comforted to see his father accept his
living from day to day, and even boast about having taken the
initiative in the *sacrifice*.

But that did not keep Melchior from complaining outside
that he had been robbed by his wife and children, that he had
put himself out for them all his life, and that now they let
him want for everything. He tried also to extract money from
Jean-Christophe by all sorts of ingenious tricks and devices,
which often used to make Jean-Christophe laugh, although he
was hardly ever taken in by them. But as Jean-Christophe
held firm, Melchior did not insist. He was curiously intimidated by the severity in the eyes of this boy of fourteen who
judged him. He used to avenge himself by some stealthy,
dirty trick. He used to go to the cabaret and eat and drink
as much as he pleased, and then pay nothing, pretending that
his son would pay his debts. Jean-Christophe did not protest,
for fear of increasing the scandal, and he and Louisa exhausted
their resources in discharging Melchior's debts. In the end
Melchior more and more lost interest in his work as violinist,
since he no longer received his wages, and his absence from
the theater became so frequent that, in spite of Jean-Christophe's entreaties, they had to dismiss him. The boy was left
to support his father, his brothers, and the whole household.

So at fourteen Jean-Christophe became the head of the
family.

He stoutly faced his formidable task. His pride would not
allow him to resort to the charity of others. He vowed that
he would pull through alone. From his earliest days he had
suffered too much from seeing his mother accept and even ask
for humiliating charitable offerings. He used to argue the
matter with her when she returned home triumphant with some
present that she had obtained from one of her patronesses.
She saw no harm in it, and was glad to be able, thanks to the
money, to spare Jean-Christophe a little, and to bring another
meager dish forth for supper. But Jean-Christophe would be-

come gloomy, and would not talk all evening, and would even refuse, without giving any reason, to touch food gained in this way. Louisa was vexed, and clumsily urged her son to eat. He was not to be budged, and in the end she would lose her temper, and say unkind things to him, and he would retort. Then he would fling his napkin on the table and go out. His father would shrug his shoulders and call him a *poseur;* his brothers would laugh at him and eat his portion.

But he had somehow to find a livelihood. His earnings from the orchestra were not enough. He gave lessons. His talents as an instrumentalist, his good reputation, and, above all, the Prince's patronage, brought him a numerous *clientèle* among the middle classes. Every morning from nine o'clock on he taught the piano to little girls, many of them older than himself, who frightened him horribly with their coquetry and maddened him with the clumsiness of their playing. They were absolutely stupid as far as music went, but, on the other hand, they had all, more or less, a keen sense of ridicule, and their mocking looks spared none of Jean-Christophe's awkwardnesses. It was torture for him. Sitting by their side on the edge of his chair, stiff, and red in the face; bursting with anger, and not daring to stir; controlling himself so as not to say stupid things, and afraid of the sound of his own voice, so that he could hardly speak a word; trying to look severe, and feeling that his pupil was looking at him out of the corner of her eye, he would lose countenance, grow confused in the middle of a remark; fearing to make himself ridiculous, he would become so, and break out into violent reproach. But it was very easy for his pupils to avenge themselves, and they did not fail to do so, and upset him by a certain way of looking at him, and by asking him the simplest questions, which made him blush up to the roots of his hair; or they would ask him to do them some small service, such as fetching something they had forgotten from a piece of furniture, and that was for him a most painful ordeal, for he had to cross the room under fire of malicious looks, which pitilessly remarked the least awkwardness in his movements and his clumsy legs. his stiff arms, his body cramped by his shyness.

From these lessons he had to hasten to rehearsal at the theater.

Often he had no time for lunch, and he used to carry a piece
of bread and some cold meat in his pocket to eat during the
interval. Sometimes he had to take the place of Tobias Pfeiffer,
the *Musik Direktor,* who was interested in him, and sometimes
had him to conduct the orchestra rehearsals instead of himself.
And he had also to go on with his own musical education.
Other piano lessons filled his day until the hour of the performance, and very often in the evening after the play he was
sent for to play at the Palace. There he had to play for an
hour or two. The Princess laid claim to a knowledge of music.
She was very fond of it, but had never been able to perceive
the difference between good and bad. She used to make Jean-
Christophe play through strange programmes, in which dull
rhapsodies stood side by side with masterpieces. But her
greatest pleasure was to make him improvise, and she used to
provide him with heartbreakingly sentimental themes.

Jean-Christophe used to leave about midnight, worn out, with
his hands burning, his head aching, his stomach empty. He
was in a sweat, and outside snow would be falling, or there
would be an icy fog. He had to walk across half the town to
reach home. He went on foot, his teeth chattering, longing
to sleep and to cry, and he had to take care not to splash his
only evening dress-suit in the puddles.

He would go up to his room, which he still shared with his
brothers, and never was he so overwhelmed by disgust and
despair with his life as at the moment when in his attic,
with its stifling smell, he was at last permitted to take off
the halter of his misery. He had hardly the heart to undress
himself. Happily, no sooner did his head touch the pillow
than he would sink into a heavy sleep which deprived him of
all consciousness of his troubles.

But he had to get up by dawn in summer, and before dawn
in winter. He wished to do his own work. It was all the
free time that he had between five o'clock and eight. Even
then he had to waste some of it by work to command, for his
title of *Hof Musicus* and his favor with the Grand Duke exacted
from him official compositions for the Court festivals.

So the very source of his life was poisoned. Even his dreams
were not free, but as usual, this restraint made them only the

stronger. When nothing hampers action, the soul has fewer reasons for action, and the closer the walls of Jean-Christophe's prison of care and banal tasks were drawn about him, the more his heart in its revolt felt its independence. In a life without obstacles he would doubtless have abandoned himself to chance and to the voluptuous sauntering of adolescence. As he could be free only for an hour or two a day, his strength flowed into that space of time like a river between walls of rock. It is a good discipline for art for a man to confine his efforts between unshakable bounds. In that sense it may be said that misery is a master, not only of thought, but of style; it teaches sobriety to the mind as to the body. When time is doled out and thoughts measured, a man says no word too much, and grows accustomed to thinking only what is essential; so he lives at double pressure, having less time for living.

This had happened in Jean-Christophe's case. Under his yoke he took full stock of the value of liberty and he never frittered away the precious minutes with useless words or actions. His natural tendency to write diffusely, given up to all the caprice of a mind sincere but indiscriminating, found correction in being forced to think and do as much as possible in the least possible time. Nothing had so much influence on his artistic and moral development—not the lessons of his masters, nor the example of the masterpieces. During the years when the character is formed he came to consider music as an exact language, in which every sound has a meaning, and at the same time he came to loathe those musicians who talk without saying anything.

And yet the compositions which he wrote at this time were still far from expressing himself completely, because he was still very far from having completely discovered himself. He was seeking himself through the mass of acquired feelings which education imposes on a child as second nature. He had only intuitions of his true being, until he should feel the passions of adolescence, which strip the personality of its borrowed garments as a thunder-clap purges the sky of the mists that hang over it. Vague and great forebodings were mingled in him with strange memories, of which he could not rid himself. He raged against these lies; he was wretched to see how inferior

what he wrote was to what he thought; he had bitter doubts
of himself. But he could not resign himself to such a stupid
defeat. He longed passionately to do better, to write great
things, and always he missed fire. After a moment of illusion
as he wrote, he saw that what he had done was worthless. He
tore it up; he burned everything that he did; and, to crown
his humiliation, he had to see his official works, the most
mediocre of all, preserved, and he could not destroy them—
the concerto, *The Royal Eagle*, for the Prince's birthday and
the cantata, *The Marriage of Pallas*, written on the occasion
of the marriage of Princess Adelaide—published at great expense in *éditions de luxe*, which perpetuated his imbecilities
for posterity; for he believed in posterity. He wept in his
humiliation.

Fevered years! No respite, no release—nothing to create
a diversion from such maddening toil; no games, no friends.
How should he have them? In the afternoon, when other
children played, young Jean-Christophe, with his brows knit
in attention, was at his place in the orchestra in the dusty
and ill-lighted theater; and in the evening, when other children
were abed, he was still there, sitting in his chair, bowed with
weariness.

No intimacy with his brothers. The younger, Ernest, was
twelve. He was a little ragamuffin, vicious and impudent,
who spent his days with other rapscallions like himself, and
from their company had caught not only deplorable manners,
but shameful habits which good Jean-Christophe, who had never
so much as suspected their existence, was horrified to see one
day. The other, Rodolphe, the favorite of Uncle Theodore,
was to go into business. He was steady, quiet, but sly. He
thought himself much superior to Jean-Christophe, and did not
admit his authority in the house, although it seemed natural
to him to eat the food that he provided. He had espoused the
cause of Theodore and Melchior's ill-feeling against Jean-Christophe and used to repeat their absurd gossip. Neither of
the brothers cared for music, and Rodolphe, in imitation of his
uncle, affected to despise it. Chafing against Jean-Christophe's
authority and lectures—for he took himself very seriously as
the head of the family—the two boys had tried to rebel; but

Jean-Christophe, who had lusty fists and the consciousness of right, sent them packing. Still they did not for that cease to do with him as they liked. They abused his credulity, and laid traps for him, into which he invariably fell. They used to extort money from him with barefaced lies, and laughed at him behind his back. Jean-Christophe was always taken in. He had so much need of being loved that an affectionate word was enough to disarm his rancor. He would have forgiven them everything for a little love. But his confidence was cruelly shaken when he heard them laughing at his stupidity after a scene of hypocritical embracing which had moved him to tears, and they had taken advantage of it to rob him of a gold watch, a present from the Prince, which they coveted. He despised them, and yet went on letting himself be taken in from his unconquerable tendency to trust and to love. He knew it. He raged against himself, and he used to thrash his brothers soundly when he discovered once more that they had tricked him. That did not keep him from swallowing almost immediately the fresh hook which it pleased them to bait for him.

A more bitter cause of suffering was in store for him. He learned from officious neighbors that his father was speaking ill of him. After having been proud of his son's successes, and having boasted of them everywhere, Melchior was weak and shameful enough to be jealous of them. He tried to decry them. It was stupid to weep; Jean-Christophe could only shrug his shoulders in contempt. It was no use being angry about it, for his father did not know what he was doing, and was embittered by his own downfall. The boy said nothing. He was afraid, if he said anything, of being too hard; but he was cut to the heart.

They were melancholy gatherings at the family evening meal round the lamp, with a spotted cloth, with all the stupid chatter and the sound of the jaws of these people whom he despised and pitied, and yet loved in spite of everything. Only between himself and his brave mother did Jean-Christophe feel a bond of affection. But Louisa, like himself, exhausted herself during the day, and in the evening she was worn out and hardly spoke, and after dinner used to sleep in her chair over her darning. And she was so good that she seemed to make no difference

in her love between her husband and her three sons. She loved
them all equally. Jean-Christophe did not find in her the
trusted friend that he so much needed.

So he was driven in upon himself. For days together he
would not speak, fulfilling his tiresome and wearing task with
a sort of silent rage. Such a mode of living was dangerous,
especially for a child at a critical age, when he is most sensitive,
and is exposed to every agent of destruction and the risk of
being deformed for the rest of his life. Jean-Christophe's
health suffered seriously. He had been endowed by his parents
with a healthy constitution and a sound and healthy body; but
his very healthiness only served to feed his suffering when the
weight of weariness and too early cares had opened up a gap
by which it might enter. Quite early in life there were signs
of grave nervous disorders. When he was a small boy he was
subject to fainting-fits and convulsions and vomiting whenever
he encountered opposition. When he was seven or eight, about
the time of the concert, his sleep had been troubled. He used
to talk, cry, laugh and weep in his sleep, and this habit returned to him whenever he had too much to think of. Then
he had cruel headaches, sometimes shooting pains at the base
of his skull or the top of his head, sometimes a leaden heaviness. His eyes troubled him. Sometimes it was as though
red-hot needles were piercing his eyeballs. He was subject to
fits of dizziness, when he could not see to read, and had to
stop for a minute or two. Insufficient and unsound food and
irregular meals ruined the health of his stomach. He was
racked by internal pains or exhausted by diarrhea. But nothing brought him more suffering than his heart. It beat with
a crazy irregularity. Sometimes it would leap in his bosom,
and seem like to break; sometimes it would hardly beat at
all, and seem like to stop. At night his temperature would
vary alarmingly; it would change suddenly from fever-point
to next to nothing. He would burn, then shiver with cold,
pass through agony. His throat would go dry; a lump in it
would prevent his breathing. Naturally his imagination
took fire. He dared not say anything to his family of what
he was going through, but he was continually dissecting it with
a minuteness which either enlarged his sufferings or created

new ones. He decided that he had every known illness one
after the other. He believed that he was going blind, and as
he sometimes used to turn giddy as he walked, he thought
that he was going to fall down dead. Always that dreadful
fear of being stopped on his road, of dying before his time,
obsessed him, overwhelmed him, and pursued him. Ah, if he
had to die, at least let it not be now, not before he had tasted
victory! . . .

Victory . . . the fixed idea which never ceases to burn within
him without his being fully aware of it—the idea which bears
him up through all his disgust and fatigues and the stagnant
morass of such a life! A dim and great foreknowledge of
what he will be some day, of what he is already! . . . What
is he? A sick, nervous child, who plays the violin in the
orchestra and writes mediocre concertos? No; far more than
such a child. That is no more than the wrapping, the seeming
of a day; that is not his Being. There is no connection between
his Being and the existing shape of his face and thought. He
knows that well. When he looks at himself in the mirror he
does not know himself. That broad red face, those prominent
eyebrows, those little sunken eyes, that short thick nose, that
sullen mouth—the whole mask, ugly and vulgar, is foreign to
himself. Neither does he know himself in his writings.
He judges, he knows that what he does and what he is are
nothing; and yet he is sure of what he will be and do. Sometimes he falls foul of such certainty as a vain lie. He takes
pleasure in humiliating himself and bitterly mortifying himself by way of punishment. But his certainty endures; nothing
can alter it. Whatever he does, whatever he thinks, none of
his thoughts, actions, or writings contain him or express him.
He knows, he has this strange presentiment, that the more that
he is, is not contained in the present but is what he *will be,*
what he *will be to-morrow.* *He will be!* . . . He is fired by
that faith, he is intoxicated by that light! Ah, if only *To-day*
does not block the way! If only he does not fall into one
of the cunning traps which *To-day* is forever laying for him!

So he steers his bark across the sea of days, turning his eyes
neither to right nor left, motionless at the helm, with his gaze
fixed on the bourne, the refuge, the end that he has in sight.

In the orchestra, among the talkative musicians, at table with his own family, at the Palace, while he is playing without a thought of what he is playing, for the entertainment of Royal folk—it is in that future, that future which a speck may bring toppling to earth—no matter, it is in that that he lives.

He is at his old piano, in his garret, alone. Night falls. The dying light of day is cast upon his music. He strains his eyes to read the notes until the last ray of light is dead. The tenderness of hearts that are dead breathed forth from the dumb page fills him with love. His eyes are filled with tears. It seems to him that a beloved creature is standing behind him, that soft breathing caresses his cheek, that two arms are about his neck. He turns, trembling. He feels, he knows, that he is not alone. A soul that loves and is loved is there, near him. He groans aloud because he cannot perceive it, and yet that shadow of bitterness falling upon his ecstasy has sweetness, too. Even sadness has its light. He thinks of his beloved masters, of the genius that is gone, though its soul lives on in the music which it had lived in its life. His heart is overflowing with love; he dreams of the superhuman happiness which must have been the lot of these glorious men, since the reflection only of their happiness is still so much aflame. He dreams of being like them, of giving out such love as this, with lost rays to lighten his misery with a godlike smile. In his turn to be a god, to give out the warmth of joy, to be a sun of life! . . .

Alas! if one day he does become the equal of those whom he loves, if he does achieve that brilliant happiness for which he longs, he will see the illusion that was upon him. . . .

II

OTTO

ONE Sunday when Jean-Christophe had been invited by his *Musik Direktor* to dine at the little country house which Tobias Pfeiffer owned an hour's journey from the town, he took the Rhine steamboat. On deck he sat next to a boy about his own

age, who eagerly made room for him. Jean-Christophe paid
no attention, but after a moment, feeling that his neighbor
had never taken his eyes off him, he turned and looked at him.
He was a fair boy, with round pink cheeks, with his hair parted
on one side, and a shade of down on his lip. He looked frankly
what he was—a hobbledehoy—though he made great efforts to
seem grown up. He was dressed with ostentatious care—flannel
suit, light gloves, white shoes, and a pale blue tie—and he carried a little stick in his hand. He looked at Jean-Christophe
out of the corner of his eye without turning his head, with
his neck stiff, like a hen; and when Jean-Christophe looked
at him he blushed up to his ears, took a newspaper from his
pocket, and pretended to be absorbed in it, and to look important over it. But a few minutes later he dashed to pick up
Jean-Christophe's hat, which had fallen. Jean-Christophe, surprised at such politeness, looked once more at the boy, and
once more he blushed. Jean-Christophe thanked him curtly, for
he did not like such obsequious eagerness, and he hated to be
fussed with. All the same, he was flattered by it.

Soon it passed from his thoughts; his attention was occupied
by the view. It was long since he had been able to escape
from the town, and so he had keen pleasure in the wind that
beat against his face, in the sound of the water against the
boat, in the great stretch of water and the changing spectacle
presented by the banks—bluffs gray and dull, willow-trees half
under water, pale vines, legendary rocks, towns crowned with
Gothic towers and factory chimneys belching black smoke.
And as he was in ecstasy over it all, his neighbor in a choking
voice timidly imparted a few historic facts concerning the ruins
that they saw, cleverly restored and covered with ivy. He
seemed to be lecturing to himself. Jean-Christophe, roused to
interest, plied him with questions. The other replied eagerly,
glad to display his knowledge, and with every sentence he addressed himself directly to Jean-Christophe, calling him "*Herr
Hof Violinist.*"

"You know me, then?" said Jean-Christophe.

"Oh yes," said the boy, with a simple admiration that tickled
Jean-Christophe's vanity.

They talked. The boy had often seen Jean-Christophe at

concerts, and his imagination had been touched by everything that he had heard about him. He did not say so to Jean-Christophe, but Jean-Christophe felt it, and was pleasantly surprised by it. He was not used to being spoken to in this tone of eager respect. He went on questioning his neighbor about the history of the country through which they were passing. The other set out all the knowledge that he had, and Jean-Christophe admired his learning. But that was only the peg on which their conversation hung. What interested them was the making of each other's acquaintance. They dared not frankly approach the subject; they returned to it again and again with awkward questions. Finally they plunged, and Jean-Christophe learned that his new friend was called Otto Diener, and was the son of a rich merchant in the town. It appeared, naturally, that they had friends in common, and little by little their tongues were loosed. They were talking eagerly when the boat arrived at the town at which Jean-Christophe was to get out. Otto got out, too. That surprised them, and Jean-Christophe proposed that they should take a walk together until dinner-time. They struck out across the fields. Jean-Christophe had taken Otto's arm familiarly, and was telling him his plans as if he had known him from his birth. He had been so much deprived of the society of children of his own age that he found an inexpressible joy in being with this boy, so learned and well brought up, who was in sympathy with him.

Time passed, and Jean-Christophe took no count of it. Diener, proud of the confidence which the young musician showed him, dared not point out that the dinner-hour had rung. At last he thought that he must remind him of it, but Jean-Christophe, who had begun the ascent of a hill in the woods, declared that they must go to the top, and when they reached it he lay down on the grass as though he meant to spend the day there. After a quarter of an hour Diener, seeing that he seemed to have no intention of moving, hazarded again:

" And your dinner? "

Jean-Christophe, lying at full length, with his hands behind his head, said quietly:

" Tssh! "

Then he looked at Otto, saw his scared look, and began to laugh.

"It is too good here," he explained. "I shan't go. Let them wait for me!"

He half rose.

"Are you in a hurry? No? Do you know what we'll do? We'll dine together. I know of an inn."

Diener would have had many objections to make—not that any one was waiting for him, but because it was hard for him to come to any sudden decision, whatever it might be. He was methodical, and needed to be prepared beforehand. But Jean-Christophe's question was put in such a tone as allowed of no refusal. He let himself be dragged off, and they began to talk again.

At the inn their eagerness died down. Both were occupied with the question as to who should give the dinner, and each within himself made it a point of honor to give it—Diener because he was the richer, Jean-Christophe because he was the poorer. They made no direct reference to the matter, but Diener made great efforts to assert his right by the tone of authority which he tried to take as he asked for the menu. Jean-Christophe understood what he was at and turned the tables on him by ordering other dishes of a rare kind. He wanted to show that he was as much at his ease as anybody, and when Diener tried again by endeavoring to take upon himself the choice of wine, Jean-Christophe crushed him with a look, and ordered a bottle of one of the most expensive vintages they had in the inn.

When they found themselves seated before a considerable repast, they were abashed by it. They could find nothing to say, ate mincingly, and were awkward and constrained in their movements. They became conscious suddenly that they were strangers, and they watched each other. They made vain efforts to revive the conversation; it dropped immediately. Their first half-hour was a time of fearful boredom. Fortunately, the meat and drink soon had an effect on them, and they looked at each other more confidently. Jean-Christophe especially, who was not used to such good things, became extraordinarily loquacious. He told of the difficulties of his life, and Otto, breaking through his reserve, confessed that he also was not happy. He was weak and timid, and his schoolfellows put upon him. They laughed at him, and could not forgive him for despising their vulgar manners. They played all sorts of tricks on him. Jean-Christophe clenched his fists, and said they had better not try it in his presence. Otto also was misunderstood by his family. Jean-Christophe knew the unhappiness of that, and they commiserated each other on their common misfortunes. Diener's parents wanted him to become a merchant, and to step into his father's place, but he wanted to be a poet. He would be a poet, even though he had to fly the town, like Schiller, and brave poverty! (His father's fortune would all come to him, and it was considerable.) He confessed blushingly that he had already written verses on the sadness of life, but he could not bring himself to recite them, in spite of Jean-Christophe's entreaties. But in the end he did give two or three of them, dithering with emotion. Jean-Christophe thought them admirable. They exchanged plans. Later on they would work together; they would write dramas and song-cycles. They admired each other. Besides his reputation as a musician, Jean-Christophe's strength and bold ways made an impression on Otto, and Jean-Christophe was sensible of Otto's elegance and distinguished manners—everything in this world is relative—and of his ease of manner—that ease of manner which he looked and longed for.

Made drowsy by their meal, with their elbows on the table, they talked and listened to each other with softness in their eyes. The afternoon drew on; they had to go. Otto made a last attempt to procure the bill, but Jean-Christophe nailed him to his seat with an angry look which made it impossible for him to insist. Jean-Christophe was only uneasy on one point— that he might be asked for more than he had. He would have given his watch and everything that he had about him rather than admit it to Otto. But he was not called on to go so far. He had to spend on the dinner almost the whole of his month's money.

They went down the hill again. The shades of evening were beginning to fall over the pine-woods. Their tops were still bathed in rosy light; they swung slowly with a surging sound.

The carpet of purple pine-needles deadened the sound of their footsteps. They said no word. Jean-Christophe felt a strange sweet sadness welling through his heart. He was happy; he wished to talk, but was weighed down with his sweet sorrow. He stopped for a moment, and so did Otto. All was silence. Flies buzzed high above them in a ray of sunlight; a rotten branch fell. Jean-Christophe took Otto's hand, and in a trembling voice said:

" Will you be my friend? "

Otto murmured:

" Yes."

They shook hands; their hearts beat; they dared hardly look at each other.

After a moment they walked on. They were a few paces away from each other, and they dared say no more until they were out of the woods. They were fearful of each other, and of their strange emotion. They walked very fast, and never stopped until they had issued from the shadow of the trees; then they took courage again, and joined hands. They marveled at the limpid evening falling, and they talked disconnectedly.

On the boat, sitting at the bows in the brilliant twilight, they tried to talk of trivial matters, but they gave no heed to what they were saying. They were lost in their own happiness and weariness. They felt no need to talk, or to hold hands, or even to look at each other; they were near each other.

When they were near their journey's end they agreed to meet again on the following Sunday. Jean-Christophe took Otto to his door. Under the light of the gas they timidly smiled and murmured *au revoir*. They were glad to part, so wearied were they by the tension at which they had been living for those hours and by the pain it cost them to break the silence with a single word.

Jean-Christophe returned alone in the night. His heart was singing: " I have a friend! I have a friend! " He saw nothing, he heard nothing, he thought of nothing else.

He was very sleepy, and fell asleep as soon as he reached

47

his room; but he was awakened twice or thrice during the night, as by some fixed idea. He repeated, " I have a friend," and went to sleep again at once.

Next morning it seemed to be all a dream. To test the reality of it, he tried to recall the smallest details of the day. He was absorbed by this occupation while he was giving his lessons, and even during the afternoon he was so absent during the orchestra rehearsal that when he left he could hardly remember what he had been playing.

When he returned home he found a letter waiting for him. He had no need to ask himself whence it came. He ran and shut himself up in his room to read it. It was written on pale blue paper in a labored, long, uncertain hand, with very correct flourishes:

" Dear Herr Jean-Christophe—dare I say Honored
    Friend?—

" I am thinking much of our doings yesterday, and I do thank you tremendously for your kindness to me. I am so grateful for all that you have done, and for your kind words, and the delightful walk and the excellent dinner! I am only worried that you should have spent so much money on it. What a lovely day! Do you not think there was something providential in that strange meeting? It seems to me that it was Fate decreed that we should meet. How glad I shall be to see you again on Sunday! I hope you will not have had too much unpleasantness for having missed the *Hof Musik Direktor's* dinner. I should be so sorry if you had any trouble because of me.

" Dear Herr Jean-Christophe, I am always
    " Your very devoted servant and friend,
                                " Otto Diener.

" P. S.—On Sunday please do not call for me at home. It would be better, if you will, for us to meet at the *Schloss Garten.*"

Jean-Christophe read the letter with tears in his eyes. He kissed it; he laughed aloud; he jumped about on his bed. Then

he ran to the table and took pen in hand to reply at once. He
could not wait a moment. But he was not used to writing.
He could not express what was swelling in his heart; he dug
into the paper with his pen, and blackened his fingers with
ink; he stamped impatiently. At last, by dint of putting out
his tongue and making five or six drafts, he succeeded in writing in malformed letters, which flew out in all directions, and
with terrific mistakes in spelling:

" My Soul,—

   " How dare you speak of gratitude, because I love you? Have
I not told you how sad I was and lonely before I knew you?
Your friendship is the greatest of blessings. Yesterday I was
happy, happy!—for the first time in my life. I weep for joy
as I read your letter. Yes, my beloved, there is no doubt
that it was Fate brought us together. Fate wishes that we
should be friends to do great things. Friends! The lovely
word! Can it be that at last I have a friend? Oh! you will
never leave me? You will be faithful to me? Always! always!
. . . How beautiful it will be to grow up together, to work
together, to bring together—I my musical whimsies, and all
the crazy things that go chasing through my mind; you your
intelligence and amazing learning! How much you know! I
have never met a man so clever as you. There are moments
when I am uneasy. I seem to be unworthy of your friendship.
You are so noble and so accomplished, and I am so grateful
to you for loving so coarse a creature as myself! . . . But no!
I have just said, let there be no talk of gratitude. In friendship there is no obligation nor benefaction. I would not accept
any benefaction! We are equal, since we love. How impatient
I am to see you! I will not call for you at home, since you
do not wish it—although, to tell the truth, I do not understand
all these precautions—but you are the wiser; you are surely
right. . . .

   " One word only! No more talk of money. I hate money—
the word and the thing itself. If I am not rich, I am yet rich
enough to give to my friend, and it is my joy to give all I
can for him. Would not you do the same? And if I needed
it, would you not be the first to give me all your fortune? But

that shall never be! I have sound fists and a sound head, and
I shall always be able to earn the bread that I eat. Till Sunday! Dear God, a whole week without seeing you! And for
two days I have not seen you! How have I been able to live
so long without you?

"The conductor tried to grumble, but do not bother about it
any more than I do. What are others to me? I care nothing
what they think or what they may ever think of me. Only
you matter. Love me well, my soul; love me as I love you!-
I cannot tell you how much I love you. I am yours, yours,
yours, from the tips of my fingers to the apple of my
eye.

"Yours always,

"JEAN-CHRISTOPHE."

Jean-Christophe was devoured with impatience for the rest
of the week. He would go out of his way, and make long turns
to pass by Otto's house. Not that he counted on seeing him,
but the sight of the house was enough to make him grow pale
and red with emotion. On the Thursday he could bear it no
longer, and sent a second letter even more high-flown than the
first. Otto answered it sentimentally.

Sunday came at length, and Otto was punctually at the meeting-place. But Jean-Christophe had been there for an hour,
waiting impatiently for the walk. He began to imagine dreadfully that Otto would not come. He trembled lest Otto should
be ill, for he did not suppose for a moment that Otto might
break his word. He whispered over and over again, "Dear
God, let him come—let him come!" and he struck at the pebbles
in the avenue with his stick, saying to himself that if he
missed three times Otto would not come, but if he hit them
Otto would appear at once. In spite of his care and the
easiness of the test, he had just missed three times when he
saw Otto coming at his easy, deliberate pace; for Otto was
above all things correct, even when he was most moved. Jean-
Christophe ran to him, and with his throat dry wished him
"Good-day!" Otto replied, "Good-day!" and they found
that they had nothing more to say to each other, except that
the weather was fine and that it was five or six minutes past

ten, or it might be ten past, because the castle clock was always slow.

They went to the station, and went by rail to a neighboring place which was a favorite excursion from the town. On the way they exchanged not more than ten words. They tried to make up for it by eloquent looks, but they were no more successful. In vain did they try to tell each other what friends they were; their eyes would say nothing at all. They were just play-acting. Jean-Christophe saw that, and was humiliated. He did not understand how he could not express or even feel all that had filled his heart an hour before. Otto did not, perhaps, so exactly take stock of their failure, because he was less sincere, and examined himself with more circumspection, but he was just as disappointed. The truth is that the boys had, during their week of separation, blown out their feelings to such a diapason that it was impossible for them to keep them actually at that pitch, and when they met again their first impression must of necessity be false. They had to break away from it, but they could not bring themselves to agree to it.

All day they wandered in the country without ever breaking through the awkwardness and constraint that were upon them. It was a holiday. The inns and woods were filled with a rabble of excursionists—little *bourgeois* families who made a great noise and ate everywhere. That added to their ill-humor. They attributed to the poor people the impossibility of again finding the carelessness of their first walk. But they talked, they took great pains to find subjects of conversation; they were afraid of finding that they had nothing to say to each other. Otto displayed his school-learning; Jean-Christophe entered into technical explanations of musical compositions and violin-playing. They oppressed each other; they crushed each other by talking; and they never stopped talking, trembling lest they should, for then there opened before them abysses of silence which horrified them. Otto came near to weeping, and Jean-Christophe was near leaving him and running away as hard as he could, he was so bored and ashamed.

Only an hour before they had to take the train again did they thaw. In the depths of the woods a dog was barking; he was hunting on his own account. Jean-Christophe proposed

that they should hide by his path to try and see his quarry.
They ran into the midst of the thicket. The dog came near
them, and then went away again. They went to right and left,
went forward and doubled. The barking grew louder: the
dog was choking with impatience in his lust for slaughter. He
came near once more. Jean-Christophe and Otto, lying on the
dead leaves in the rut of a path, waited and held their breath.
The barking stopped; the dog had lost the scent. They heard his
yap once again in the distance; then silence came upon the
woods. Not a sound, only the mysterious hum of millions of
creatures, insects, and creeping things, moving unceasingly, destroying the forest—the measured breathing of death, which
never stops. The boys listened, they did not stir. Just
when they got up, disappointed, and said, "It is all over;
he will not come!" a little hare plunged out of the thicket.
He came straight upon them. They saw him at the same
moment, and gave a cry of joy. The hare turned in his tracks
and jumped aside. They saw him dash into the brushwood
head over heels. The stirring of the rumpled leaves vanished
away like a ripple on the face of waters. Although they were
sorry for having cried out, the adventure filled them with joy.
They rocked with laughter as they thought of the hare's terrified leap, and Jean-Christophe imitated it grotesquely. Otto
did the same. Then they chased each other. Otto was the
hare, Jean-Christophe the dog. They plunged through woods
and meadows, dashing through hedges and leaping ditches. A
peasant shouted at them, because they had rushed over a field
of rye. They did not stop to hear him. Jean-Christophe
imitated the hoarse barking of the dog to such perfection that
Otto laughed until he cried. At last they rolled down a slope,
shouting like mad things. When they could not utter another
sound they sat up and looked at each other, with tears of
laughter in their eyes. They were quite happy and pleased
with themselves. They were no longer trying to play the heroic
friend; they were frankly what they were—two boys.

They came back arm-in-arm, singing senseless songs, and yet,
when they were on the point of returning to the town, they
thought they had better resume their pose, and under the last
tree of the woods they carved their initials intertwined. But

then good temper had the better of their sentimentality, and in the train they shouted with laughter whenever they looked at each other. They parted assuring each other that they had had a "hugely delightful" (*kolossal entzückend*) day, and that conviction gained with them when they were alone once more.

They resumed their work of construction more patient and ingenious even than that of the bees, for of a few mediocre scraps of memory they fashioned a marvelous image of themselves and their friendship. After having idealized each other during the week, they met again on the Sunday, and in spite of the discrepancy between the truth and their illusion, they got used to not noticing it and to twisting things to fit in with their desires.

They were proud of being friends. The very contrast of their natures brought them together. Jean-Christophe knew nothing so beautiful as Otto. His fine hands, his lovely hair, his fresh complexion, his shy speech, the politeness of his manners, and his scrupulous care of his appearance delighted him. Otto was subjugated by Jean-Christophe's brimming strength and independence. Accustomed by age-old inheritance to religious respect for all authority, he took a fearful joy in the company of a comrade in whose nature was so little reverence for the established order of things. He had a little voluptuous thrill of terror whenever he heard him decry every reputation in the town, and even mimic the Grand Duke himself. Jean-Christophe knew the fascination that he exercised over his friend, and used to exaggerate his aggressive temper. Like some old revolutionary, he hewed away at social conventions and the laws of the State. Otto would listen, scandalized and delighted. He used timidly to try and join in, but he was always careful to look round to see if any one could hear.

Jean-Christophe never failed, when they walked together, to leap the fences of a field whenever he saw a board forbidding it, or he would pick fruit over the walls of private grounds. Otto was in terror lest they should be discovered. But such feelings had for him an exquisite savor, and in the evening, when he had returned, he would think himself a hero. He

admired Jean-Christophe fearfully. His instinct of obedience
found a satisfying quality in a friendship in which he had
only to acquiesce in the will of his friend. Jean-Christophe
never put him to the trouble of coming to a decision. He
decided everything, decreed the doings of the day, decreed even
the ordering of life, making plans, which admitted of no discussion, for Otto's future, just as he did for his own family.
Otto fell in with them, though he was a little put aback by hearing Jean-Christophe dispose of his fortune for the building later
on of a theater of his own contriving. But, intimidated by his
friend's imperious tones, he did not protest, being convinced
also by his friend's conviction that the money amassed by
Commerzienrath Oscar Diener could be put to no nobler use.
Jean-Christophe never for a moment had any idea that he
might be violating Otto's will. He was instinctively a despot,
and never imagined that his friend's wishes might be different
from his own. Had Otto expressed a desire different from his own,
he would not have hesitated to sacrifice his own personal preference. He would have sacrificed even more for him. He was
consumed by the desire to run some risk for him. He wished
passionately that there might appear some opportunity of putting his friendship to the test. When they were out walking
he used to hope that they might meet some danger, so that he
might fling himself forward to face it. He would have loved
to die for Otto. Meanwhile, he watched over him with a restless solicitude, gave him his hand in awkward places, as though
he were a girl. He was afraid that he might be tired, afraid
that he might be hot, afraid that he might be cold. When
they sat down under a tree he took off his coat to put it about
his friend's shoulders; when they walked he carried his cloak.
He would have carried Otto himself. He used to devour him
with his eyes like a lover, and, to tell the truth, he was in
love.

He did not know it, not knowing yet what love was. But
sometimes, when they were together, he was overtaken by a
strange unease—the same that had choked him on that first
day of their friendship in the pine-woods—and the blood would
rush to his face and set his cheeks aflame. He was afraid. By
an instinctive unanimity the two boys used furtively to separate

and run away from each other, and one would lag behind on the road. They would pretend to be busy looking for blackberries in the hedges, and they did not know what it was that so perturbed them.

But it was in their letters especially that their feelings flew high. They were not then in any danger of being contradicted by facts, and nothing could check their illusions or intimidate them. They wrote to each other two or three times a week in a passionately lyric style. They hardly ever spoke of real happenings or common things; they raised great problems in an apocalyptic manner, which passed imperceptibly from enthusiasm to despair. They called each other, " My blessing, my hope, my beloved, my Self." They made a fearful hash of the word " Soul." They painted in tragic colors the sadness of their lot, and were desolate at having brought into the existence of their friend the sorrows of their existence.

" I am sorry, my love," wrote Jean-Christophe, " for the pain which I bring you. I cannot bear that you should suffer. It must not be. *I will not have it.*" (He underlined the words with a stroke of the pen that dug into the paper.) " If you suffer, where shall I find strength to live? I have no happiness but in you. Oh, be happy! I will gladly take all the burden of sorrow upon myself! Think of me! Love me! I have such great need of being loved. From your love there comes to me a warmth which gives me life. If you knew how I shiver! There is winter and a biting wind in my heart. I embrace your soul."

" My thought kisses yours," replied Otto.

" I take your face in my hands," was Jean-Christophe's answer, " and what I have not done and will not do with my lips I do with all my being. I kiss you as I love you, Prudence! "

Otto pretended to doubt him.

" Do you love me as much as I love you? "

" O God," wrote Jean-Christophe, " not as much, but ten, a hundred, a thousand times more! What! Do you not feel it? What would you have me do to stir your heart? "

" What a lovely friendship is ours! " sighed Otto. " Was there ever its like in history? It is sweet and fresh as a dream. If only it does not pass away! If you were to cease to love me!"

"How stupid you are, my beloved!" replied Jean-Christophe. "Forgive me, but your weakling fear enrages me. How can you ask whether I shall cease to love you! For me to live is to love you. Death is powerless against my love. You yourself could do nothing if you wished to destroy it. Even if you betrayed me, even if you rent my heart, I should die with a blessing upon you for the love with which you fill me. Once for all, then, do not be uneasy, and vex me no more with these cowardly doubts!"

But a week later it was he who wrote:

"It is three days now since I heard a word fall from your lips. I tremble. Would you forget me? My blood freezes at the thought. . . . Yes, doubtless. . . . The other day only I saw your coldness towards me. You love me no longer! You are thinking of leaving me! . . . Listen! If you forget me, if you ever betray me, I will kill you like a dog!"

"You do me wrong, my dear heart," groaned Otto. "You draw tears from me. I do not deserve this. But you can do as you will. You have such rights over me that, if you were to break my soul, there would always be a spark left to live and love you always!"

"Heavenly powers!" cried Jean-Christophe. "I have made my friend weep! . . . Heap insults on me, beat me, trample me underfoot! I am a wretch! I do not deserve your love!"

They had special ways of writing the address on their letters, of placing the stamp—upside down, askew, at bottom in a corner of the envelope—to distinguish their letters from those which they wrote to persons who did not matter. These childish secrets had the charm of the sweet mysteries of love.

One day, as he was returning from a lesson, Jean-Christophe saw Otto in the street with a boy of his own age. They were laughing and talking familiarly. Jean-Christophe went pale, and followed them with his eyes until they had disappeared round the corner of the street. They had not seen him. He went home. It was as though a cloud had passed over the sun; all was dark.

When they met on the following Sunday, Jean-Christophe said nothing at first; but after they had been walking for half an hour he said in a choking voice:

"I saw you on Wednesday in the *Königgasse*."

"Ah!" said Otto.

And he blushed.

Jean-Christophe went on:

"You were not alone."

"No," said Otto; "I was with some one."

Jean-Christophe swallowed down his spittle and asked in a voice which he strove to make careless:

"Who was it?"

"My cousin Franz."

"Ah!" said Jean-Christophe; and after a moment: "You have never said anything about him to me."

"He lives at Rheinbach."

"Do you see him often?"

"He comes here sometimes."

"And you, do you go and stay with him?"

"Sometimes."

"Ah!" said Jean-Christophe again.

Otto, who was not sorry to turn the conversation, pointed out a bird who was pecking at a tree. They talked of other things. Ten minutes later Jean-Christophe broke out again:

"Are you friends with him?"

"With whom?" asked Otto.

(He knew perfectly who was meant.)

"With your cousin."

"Yes. Why?"

"Oh, nothing!"

Otto did not like his cousin much, for he used to bother him with bad jokes; but a strange malign instinct made him add a few moments later:

"He is very nice."

"Who?" asked Jean-Christophe.

(He knew quite well who was meant.)

"Franz."

Otto waited for Jean-Christophe to say something, but he

seemed not to have heard. He was cutting a switch from a hazel-tree. Otto went on:

"He is amusing. He has all sorts of stories."

Jean-Christophe whistled carelessly.

Otto renewed the attack:

"And he is so clever . . . and distinguished! . . ."

Jean-Christophe shrugged his shoulders as though to say: "What interest can this person have for me?"

And as Otto, piqued, began to go on, he brutally cut him short, and pointed out a spot to which to run.

They did not touch on the subject again the whole afternoon, but they were frigid, affecting an exaggerated politeness which was unusual for them, especially for Jean-Christophe. The words stuck in his throat. At last he could contain himself no longer, and in the middle of the road he turned to Otto, who was lagging five yards behind. He took him fiercely by the hands, and let loose upon him:

"Listen, Otto! I will not—I will not let you be so friendly with Franz, because . . . because you are my friend, and I will not let you love any one more than me! I will not! You see, you are everything to me! You cannot . . . you must not! . . . If I lost you, there would be nothing left but death. I do not know what I should do. I should kill myself; I should kill you! No, forgive me! . . ."

Tears fell from his eyes.

Otto, moved and frightened by the sincerity of such grief, growling out threats, made haste to swear that he did not and never would love anybody so much as Jean-Christophe, that Franz was nothing to him, and that he would not see him again if Jean-Christophe wished it. Jean-Christophe drank in his words, and his heart took new life. He laughed and breathed heavily; he thanked Otto effusively. He was ashamed of having made such a scene, but he was relieved of a great weight. They stood face to face and looked at each other, not moving, and holding hands. They were very happy and very much embarrassed. They became silent; then they began to talk again, and found their old gaiety. They felt more at one than ever.

But it was not the last scene of the kind. Now that Otto

felt his power over Jean-Christophe, he was tempted to abuse
it. He knew his sore spot, and was irresistibly tempted to
place his finger on it. Not that he had any pleasure in Jean-
Christophe's anger; on the contrary, it made him unhappy—
but he felt his power by making Jean-Christophe suffer. He
was not bad; he had the soul of a girl.

In spite of his promises, he continued to appear arm in
arm with Franz or some other comrade. They made a great
noise between them, and he used to laugh in an affected way.
When Jean-Christophe reproached him with it, he used to titter
and pretend not to take him seriously, until, seeing Jean-Christophe's eyes change and his lips tremble with anger, he would
change his tone, and fearfully promise not to do it again, and
the next day he would do it. Jean-Christophe would write
him furious letters, in which he called him:

"Scoundrel! Let me never hear of you again! I do not
know you! May the devil take you and all dogs of your
kidney!"

But a tearful word from Otto, or, as he ever did, the sending
of a flower as a token of his eternal constancy, was enough for
Jean-Christophe to be plunged in remorse, and to write:

"My angel, I am mad! Forget my idiocy. You are the
best of men. Your little finger alone is worth more than all
stupid Jean-Christophe. You have the treasures of an ingenuous and delicate tenderness. I kiss your flower with tears
in my eyes. It is there on my heart. I thrust it into my
skin with blows of my fist. I would that it could make me
bleed, so that I might the more feel your exquisite goodness
and my own infamous folly! . . ."

But they began to weary of each other. It is false to pretend that little quarrels feed friendship. Jean-Christophe was
sore against Otto for the injustice that Otto made him be
guilty of. He tried to argue with himself; he laid the blame
upon his own despotic temper. His loyal and eager nature,
brought for the first time to the test of love, gave itself utterly,
and demanded a gift as utter without the reservation of one
particle of the heart. He admitted no sharing in friendship.
Being ready to sacrifice all for his friend, he thought it right
and even necessary that his friend should wholly sacrifice him-

self and everything for him. But he was beginning to feel
that the world was not built on the model of his own inflexible
character, and that he was asking things which others could
not give. Then he tried to submit. He blamed himself, he
regarded himself as an egoist, who had no right to encroach
upon the liberty of his friend, and to monopolize his affection.
He did sincerely endeavor to leave him free, whatever it might
cost himself. In a spirit of humiliation he did set himself to
pledge Otto not to neglect Franz; he tried to persuade himself
that he was glad to see him finding pleasure in society other
than his own. But when Otto, who was not deceived, maliciously
obeyed him, he could not help lowering at him, and then he
broke out again.

If necessary, he would have forgiven Otto for preferring
other friends to himself; but what he could not stomach was
the lie. Otto was neither liar nor hypocrite, but it was as difficult
for him to tell the truth as for a stutterer to pronounce words.
What he said was never altogether true nor altogether false.
Either from timidity or from uncertainty of his own feelings
he rarely spoke definitely. His answers were equivocal, and,
above all, upon every occasion he made mystery and was secret
in a way that set Jean-Christophe beside himself. When he
was caught tripping, or was caught in what, according to the
conventions of their friendship, was a fault, instead of admitting it he would go on denying it and telling absurd stories
One day Jean-Christophe, exasperated, struck him. He thought
it must be the end of their friendship and that Otto would
never forgive him; but after sulking for a few hours Otto
came back as though nothing had happened. He had no resentment for Jean-Christophe's violence—perhaps even it was not
unpleasing to him, and had a certain charm for him—and yet
he resented Jean-Christophe letting himself be tricked, gulping
down all his mendacities. He despised him a little, and thought
himself superior. Jean-Christophe, for his part, resented Otto's
receiving blows without revolting.

They no longer saw each other with the eyes of those first
days. Their failings showed up in full light. Otto found Jean-
Christophe's independence less charming. Jean-Christophe was
a tiresome companion when they went walking. He had no sort

of concern for correctness. He used to dress as he liked, take off his coat, open his waistcoat, walk with open collar, roll up his shirt-sleeves, put his hat on the end of his stick, and fling out his chest in the air. He used to swing his arms as he walked, whistle, and sing at the top of his voice. He used to be red in the face, sweaty, and dusty. He looked like a peasant returning from a fair. The aristocratic Otto used to be mortified at being seen in his company. When he saw a carriage coming he used to contrive to lag some ten paces behind, and to look as though he were walking alone.

Jean-Christophe was no less embarrassing company when he began to talk at an inn or in a railway-carriage when they were returning home. He used to talk loudly, and say anything that came into his head, and treat Otto with a disgusting familiarity. He used to express opinions quite recklessly concerning people known to everybody, or even about the appearance of people sitting only a few yards away from him, or he would enter into intimate details concerning his health and domestic affairs. It was useless for Otto to roll his eyes and to make signals of alarm. Jean-Christophe seemed not to notice them, and no more controlled himself than if he had been alone. Otto would see smiles on the faces of his neighbors, and would gladly have sunk into the ground. He thought Jean-Christophe coarse, and could not understand how he could ever have found delight in him.

What was most serious was that Jean-Christophe was just as reckless and indifferent concerning all the hedges, fences, inclosures, walls, prohibitions of entry, threats of fines, *Verbot* of all sorts, and everything that sought to confine his liberty and protect the sacred rights of property against it. Otto lived in fear from moment to moment, and all his protests were useless. Jean-Christophe grew worse out of bravado.

One day, when Jean-Christophe, with Otto at his heels, was walking perfectly at home across a private wood, in spite of, or because of, the walls fortified with broken bottles which they had had to clear, they found themselves suddenly face to face with a gamekeeper, who let fire a volley of oaths at them, and after keeping them for some time under a threat of legal proceedings, packed them off in the most ignominious fashion.

Otto did not shine under this ordeal. He thought that he was already in jail, and wept, stupidly protesting that he had gone in by accident, and that he had followed Jean-Christophe without knowing whither he was going. When he saw that he was safe, instead of being glad, he bitterly reproached Jean-Christophe. He complained that Jean-Christophe had brought him into trouble. Jean-Christophe quelled him with a look, and called him "Lily-liver!" There was a quick passage of words. Otto would have left Jean-Christophe if he had known how to find the way home. He was forced to follow him, but they affected to pretend that they were not together.

A storm was brewing. In their anger they had not seen it coming. The baking countryside resounded with the cries of insects. Suddenly all was still. They only grew aware of the silence after a few minutes. Their ears buzzed. They raised their eyes; the sky was black; huge, heavy, livid clouds overcast it. They came up from every side like a cavalry-charge. They seemed all to be hastening towards an invisible point, drawn by a gap in the sky. Otto, in terror, dare not tell his fears, and Jean-Christophe took a malignant pleasure in pretending not to notice anything. But without saying a word they drew nearer together. They were alone in the wide country. Silence. Not a wind stirred,—hardly a fevered tremor that made the little leaves of the trees shiver now and then. Suddenly a whirling wind raised the dust, twisted the trees and lashed them furiously. And the silence came again, more terrible than before. Otto, in a trembling voice, spoke at last.

"It is a storm. We must go home."

Jean-Christophe said:

"Let us go home."

But it was too late. A blinding, savage light flashed, the heavens roared, the vault of clouds rumbled. In a moment they were wrapped about by the hurricane, maddened by the lightning, deafened by the thunder, drenched from head to foot. They were in deserted country, half an hour from the nearest house. In the lashing rain, in the dim light, came the great red flashes of the storm. They tried to run but, their wet clothes clinging, they could hardly walk. Their shoes slipped on their feet, the water trickled down their bodies. It was difficult to breathe. Otto's teeth were chattering, and he was mad with rage. He said biting things to Jean-Christophe. He wanted to stop; he declared that it was dangerous to walk; he threatened to sit down on the road, to sleep on the soil in the middle of the plowed fields. Jean-Christophe made no reply. He went on walking, blinded by the wind, the rain, and the lightning; deafened by the noise; a little uneasy, but unwilling to admit it.

And suddenly it was all over. The storm had passed, as it had come. But they were both in a pitiful condition. In truth, Jean-Christophe was, as usual, so disheveled that a little more disorder made hardly any difference to him. But Otto, so neat, so careful of his appearance, cut a sorry figure. It was as though he had just taken a bath in his clothes, and Jean-Christophe, turning and seeing him, could not help roaring with laughter. Otto was so exhausted that he could not even be angry. Jean-Christophe took pity and talked gaily to him. Otto replied with a look of fury. Jean-Christophe made him stop at a farm. They dried themselves before a great fire, and drank hot wine. Jean-Christophe thought the adventure funny, and tried to laugh at it; but that was not at all to Otto's taste, and he was morose and silent for the rest of their walk. They came back sulking and did not shake hands when they parted.

As a result of this prank they did not see each other for more than a week. They were severe in their judgment of each other. But after inflicting punishment on themselves by depriving themselves of one of their Sunday walks, they got so bored that their rancor died away. Jean-Christophe made the first advances as usual. Otto condescended to meet them, and they made peace.

In spite of their disagreement it was impossible for them to do without each other. They had many faults; they were both egoists. But their egoism was naïve; it knew not the self-seeking of maturity which makes it so repulsive; it knew not itself even; it was almost lovable, and did not prevent them from sincerely loving each other! Young Otto used to weep on his pillow as he told himself stories of romantic devotion of which he was the hero; he used to invent pathetic adventures, in which he was strong, valiant, intrepid, and protected Jean-Christophe, whom he used to imagine that he adored. Jean-Christophe never saw or heard anything beautiful or strange without thinking: " If only Otto were here! " He carried the image of his friend into his whole life, and that image used to be transfigured, and become so gentle that, in spite of all that he knew about Otto, it used to intoxicate him. Certain words of Otto's which he used to remember long after they were spoken, and to embellish by the way, used to make him tremble with emotion. They imitated each other. Otto aped Jean-Christophe's manners, gestures, and writing. Jean-Christophe was sometimes irritated by the shadow which repeated every word that he said and dished up his thoughts as though they were its own. But he did not see that he himself was imitating Otto, and copying his way of dressing, walking, and pronouncing certain words. They were under a fascination. They were infused one in the other; their hearts were over-flowing with tenderness. They trickled over with it on every side like a fountain. Each imagined that his friend was the cause of it. They did not know that it was the waking of their adolescence.

Jean-Christophe, who never distrusted any one, used to leave his papers lying about. But an instinctive modesty made him keep together the drafts of the letters which he scrawled to Otto, and the replies. But he did not lock them up; he just placed them between the leaves of one of his music-books, where he felt certain that no one would look for them. He reckoned without his brothers' malice.

He had seen them for some time laughing and whispering and looking at him; they were declaiming to each other frag-ments of speech which threw them into wild laughter. Jean-Christophe could not catch the words, and, following his usual tactics with them, he feigned utter indifference to everything they might do or say. A few words roused his attention; he thought he recognized them. Soon he was left without doubt that they had read his letters. But when he challenged Ernest and Rodolphe, who were calling each other " My dear soul," with pretended earnestness, he could get nothing from them. The little wretches pretended not to understand, and said that they had the right to call each other whatever they liked. Jean-Christophe, who had found all the letters in their places, did not insist farther.

Shortly afterwards he caught Ernest in the act of thieving; the little beast was rummaging in the drawer of the chest in which Louisa kept her money. Jean-Christophe shook him, and took advantage of the opportunity to tell him everything that he had stored up against him. He enumerated, in terms of scant courtesy, the misdeeds of Ernest, and it was not a short catalogue. Ernest took the lecture in bad part; he replied impudently that Jean-Christophe had nothing to reproach him with, and he hinted at unmentionable things in his brother's friendship with Otto. Jean-Christophe did not understand; but when he grasped that Otto was being dragged into the quarrel he demanded an explanation of Ernest. The boy tittered; then, when he saw Jean-Christophe white with anger, he refused to say any more. Jean-Christophe saw that he would obtain nothing in that way; he sat down, shrugged his shoulders, and affected a profound contempt for Ernest. Ernest, piqued by this, was impudent again; he set himself to hurt his brother, and set forth a litany of things each more cruel and more vile than the last. Jean-Christophe kept a tight hand on himself. When at last he did understand, he saw red; he leaped from his chair. Ernest had no time to cry out. Jean-Christophe had hurled himself on him, and rolled with him into the middle of the room, and beat his head against the tiles. On the frightful cries of the victim, Louisa, Melchior, everybody, came running. They rescued Ernest in a parlous state. Jean-Christophe would not loose his prey; they had to beat and beat him. They called him a savage beast, and he looked it. His eyes were bursting from his head, he was grinding his teeth, and his only thought was to hurl himself again on Ernest. When they asked him what had happened, his fury increased, and he cried out that he would kill him. Ernest also refused to tell.

Jean-Christophe could not eat nor sleep. He was shaking with fever, and wept in his bed. It was not only for Otto that he was suffering. A revolution was taking place in him. Ernest had no idea of the hurt that he had been able to do his brother. Jean-Christophe was at heart of a puritanical intolerance, which could not admit the dark ways of life, and was discovering them one by one with horror. At fifteen, with his free life and strong instincts, he remained strangely simple. His natural purity and ceaseless toil had protected him. His brother's words had opened up abyss on abyss before him. Never would he have conceived such infamies, and now that the idea of it had come to him, all his joy in loving and being loved was spoiled. Not only his friendship with Otto, but friendship itself was poisoned.

It was much worse when certain sarcastic allusions made him think, perhaps wrongly, that he was the object of the unwholesome curiosity of the town, and especially, when, some time afterwards, Melchior made a remark about his walks with Otto. Probably there was no malice in Melchior, but Jean-Christophe, on the watch, read hidden meanings into every word, and almost he thought himself guilty. At the same time Otto was passing through a similar crisis.

They tried still to see each other in secret. But it was impossible for them to regain the carelessness of their old relation. Their frankness was spoiled. The two boys who loved each other with a tenderness so fearful that they had never dared exchange a fraternal kiss, and had imagined that there could be no greater happiness than in seeing each other, and in being friends, and sharing each other's dreams, now felt that they were stained and spotted by the suspicion of evil minds. They came to see evil even in the most innocent acts: a look, a hand-clasp—they blushed, they had evil thoughts. Their relation became intolerable.

Without saying anything they saw each other less often. They tried writing to each other, but they set a watch upon their expressions. Their letters became cold and insipid. They grew disheartened. Jean-Christophe excused himself on the ground of his work, Otto on the ground of being too busy, and their correspondence ceased. Soon afterwards Otto left for the University, and the friendship which had lightened a few months of their lives died down and out.

And also, a new love, of which this had been only the fore-runner, took possession of Jean-Christophe's heart, and made every other light seem pale by its side.

III

MINNA

Four or five months before these events Frau Josepha von Kerich, widow of Councilor Stephan von Kerich, had left Berlin, where her husband's duties had hitherto detained them, and settled down with her daughter in the little Rhine town, in her native country. She had an old house with a large garden, almost a park, which sloped down to the river, not far from Jean-Christophe's home. From his attic Jean-Christophe could see the heavy branches of the trees hanging over the walls, and the high peak of the red roof with its mossy tiles. A little sloping alley, with hardly room to pass, ran alongside the park to the right; from there, by climbing a post, you could look over the wall. Jean-Christophe did not fail to make use of it. He could then see the grassy avenues, the lawns like open meadows, the trees interlacing and growing wild, and the white front of the house with its shutters obsti-nately closed. Once or twice a year a gardener made the rounds, and aired the house. But soon Nature resumed her sway over the garden, and silence reigned over all.

That silence impressed Jean-Christophe. He used often stealthily to climb up to his watch-tower, and as he grew taller, his eyes, then his nose, then his mouth reached up to the top of the wall; now he could put his arms over it if he stood on tiptoe, and, in spite of the discomfort of that position, he used to stay so, with his chin on the wall, looking, listening, while the evening unfolded over the lawns its soft waves of gold, which lit up with bluish rays the shade of the pines. There he could forget himself until he heard footsteps approaching in the street. The night scattered its scents over the garden: lilac in spring, acacia in summer, dead leaves in the autumn. When Jean-Christophe was on his way home in the evening from the

Palace, however weary he might be, he used to stand by the door to drink in the delicious scent, and it was hard for him to go back to the smells of his room. And often he had played —when he used to play—in the little square with its tufts of grass between the stones, before the gateway of the house of the Kerichs. On each side of the gate grew a chestnut-tree a hundred years old; his grandfather used to come and sit beneath them, and smoke his pipe, and the children used to use the nuts for missiles and toys.

One morning, as he went up the alley, he climbed up the post as usual. He was thinking of other things, and looked absently. He was just going to climb down when he felt that there was something unusual about it. He looked towards the house. The windows were open; the sun was shining into them and, although no one was to be seen, the old place seemed to have been roused from its fifteen years' sleep, and to be smiling in its awakening. Jean-Christophe went home uneasy in his mind.

At dinner his father talked of what was the topic of the neighborhood: the arrival of Frau Kerich and her daughter with an incredible quantity of luggage. The chestnut square was filled with rascals who had turned up to help unload the carts. Jean-Christophe was excited by the news, which, in his limited life, was an important event, and he returned to his work, trying to imagine the inhabitants of the enchanted house from his father's story, as usual hyperbolical. Then he became absorbed in his work, and had forgotten the whole affair when, just as he was about to go home in the evening, he remembered it all, and he was impelled by curiosity to climb his watch-tower to spy out what might be toward within the walls. He saw nothing but the quiet avenue, in which the motionless trees seemed to be sleeping in the last rays of the sun. In a few moments he had forgotten why he was looking, and abandoned himself as he always did to the sweetness of the silence. That strange place—standing erect, perilously balanced on the top of a post—was meet for dreams. Coming from the ugly alley, stuffy and dark, the sunny gardens were of a magical radiance. His spirit wandered freely through these regions of harmony, and music sang in him; they lulled him, and he forgot time

and material things, and was only concerned to miss none of
the whisperings of his heart.

So he dreamed open-eyed and open-mouthed, and he could
not have told how long he had been dreaming, for he saw nothing. Suddenly his heart leaped. In front of him, at a bend
in an avenue, were two women's faces looking at him. One,
a young lady in black, with fine irregular features and fair hair,
tall, elegant, with carelessness and indifference in the poise of
her head, was looking at him with kind, laughing eyes. The
other, a girl of fifteen, also in deep mourning, looked as though
she were going to burst out into a fit of wild laughter; she was
standing a l.ttle behind her mother, who, without looking at
her, signed to her to be quiet. She covered her lips with her
hands, as if she were hard put to it not to burst out laughing.
She was a little creature with a fresh face, white, pink, and
round-cheeked; she had a plump little nose, a plump little
mouth, a plump little chin, firm eyebrows, bright eyes, and a
mass of fair hair plaited and wound round her head in a crown
to show her rounded neck and her smooth white forehead—a
Cranach face.

Jean-Christophe was turned to stone by this apparition. He
could not go away, but stayed, glued to his post, with his mouth
wide open. It was only when he saw the young lady coming
towards him with her kindly mocking smile that he wrenched
himself away, and jumped—tumbled—down into the alley, dragging with him pieces of plaster from the wall. He heard a kind
voice calling him, "Little boy!" and a shout of childish laughter, clear and liquid as the song of a bird. He found himself
in the alley on hands and knees, and, after a moment's bewilderment, he ran away as hard as he could go, as though he was
afraid of being pursued. He was ashamed, and his shame kept
bursting upon him again when he was alone in his room at
home. After that he dared not go down the alley, fearing
oddly that they might be lying in wait for him. When he had
to go by the house, he kept close to the walls, lowered his head,
and almost ran without ever looking back. At the same time
he never ceased to think of the two faces that he had seen;
he used to go up to the attic, taking off his shoes so as not
to be heard, and to look his hardest out through the skylight

in the direction of the Kerichs' house and park, although he
knew perfectly well that it was impossible to see anything but
the tops of the trees and the topmost chimneys.

About a month later, at one of the weekly concerts of the
Hof Musik Verein, he was playing a concerto for piano and
orchestra of his own composition. He had reached the last
movement when he chanced to see in the box facing him Frau
and Fräulein Kerich looking at him. He so little expected
to see them that he was astounded, and almost missed out his
reply to the orchestra. He went on playing mechanically to
the end of the piece. When it was finished he saw, although
he was not looking in their direction, that Frau and Fräulein
Kerich were applauding a little exaggeratedly, as though they
wished him to see that they were applauding. He hurried away
from the stage. As he was leaving the theater he saw Frau
Kerich in the lobby, separated from him by several rows of
people, and she seemed to be waiting for him to pass. It was
impossible for him not to see her, but he pretended not to do
so, and, brushing his way through, he left hurriedly by the
stage-door of the theater. Then he was angry with himself,
for he knew quite well that Frau Kerich meant no harm. But
he knew that in the same situation he would do the same again.
He was in terror of meeting her in the street. Whenever he
saw at a distance a figure that resembled her, he used to turn
aside and take another road.

It was she who came to him. She sought him out at home.

One morning when he came back to dinner Louisa proudly
told him that a lackey in breeches and livery had left a letter
for him, and she gave him a large black-edged envelope, on the
back of which was engraved the Kerich arms. Jean-Christophe
opened it, and trembled as he read these words:

"Frau Josepha von Kerich requests the pleasure of *Hof
Musicus* Jean-Christophe Krafft's company at tea to-day at half-
past five."

"I shall not go," declared Jean-Christophe.
"What!" cried Louisa. "I said that you would go."

Jean-Christophe made a scene, and reproached his mother with meddling in affairs that were no concern of hers.

"The servant waited for a reply. I said that you were free to-day. You have nothing to do then."

In vain did Jean-Christophe lose his temper, and swear that he would not go; he could not get out of it now. When the appointed time came, he got ready fuming; in his heart of hearts he was not sorry that chance had so done violence to his whims.

Frau von Kerich had had no difficulty in recognizing in the pianist at the concert the little savage whose shaggy head had appeared over her garden wall on the day of her arrival. She had made inquiries about him of her neighbors, and what she learned about Jean-Christophe's family and the boy's brave and difficult life had roused interest in him, and a desire to talk to him.

Jean-Christophe, trussed up in an absurd coat, which made him look like a country parson, arrived at the house quite ill with shyness. He tried to persuade himself that Frau and Fräulein Kerich had had no time to remark his features on the day when they had first seen him. A servant led him down a long corridor, thickly carpeted, so that his footsteps made no sound, to a room with a glass-paneled door which opened on to the garden. It was raining a little, and cold; a good fire was burning in the fireplace. Near the window, through which he had a peep of the wet trees in the mist, the two ladies were sitting. Frau Kerich was working and her daughter was reading a book when Jean-Christophe entered. When they saw him they exchanged a sly look.

"They know me again," thought Jean-Christophe, abashed.

He bobbed awkwardly, and went on bobbing.

Frau von Kerich smiled cheerfully, and held out her hand.

"Good-day, my dear neighbor," she said. "I am glad to see you. Since I heard you at the concert I have been wanting to tell you how much pleasure you gave me. And as the only way of telling you was to invite you here, I hope you will forgive me for having done so."

In the kindly, conventional words of welcome there was so

much cordiality, in spite of a hidden sting of irony, that Jean-Christophe grew more at his ease.

"They do not know me again," he thought, comforted.

Frau von Kerich presented her daughter, who had closed her book and was looking interestedly at Jean-Christophe.

"My daughter Minna," she said. "She wanted so much to see you."

"But, mamma," said Minna, "it is not the first time that we have seen each other."

And she laughed aloud.

"They do know me again," thought Jean-Christophe, crest-fallen.

"True," said Frau von Kerich, laughing too, "you paid us a visit the day we came."

At these words the girl laughed again, and Jean-Christophe looked so pitiful that when Minna looked at him she laughed more than ever. She could not control herself, and she laughed until she cried. Frau von Kerich tried to stop her, but she, too, could not help laughing, and Jean-Christophe, in spite of his constraint, fell victim to the contagiousness of it. Their merriment was irresistible; it was impossible to take offense at it. But Jean-Christophe lost countenance altogether when Minna caught her breath again, and asked him whatever he could be doing on the wall. She was tickled by his uneasiness. He murmured, altogether at a loss. Frau von Kerich came to his aid, and turned the conversation by pouring out tea.

She questioned him amiably about his life. But he did not gain confidence. He could not sit down; he could not hold his cup, which threatened to upset; and whenever they offered him water, milk, sugar or cakes, he thought that he had to get up hurriedly and bow his thanks, stiff, trussed up in his frock-coat, collar, and tie, like a tortoise in its shell, not daring and not being able to turn his head to right or left, and over-whelmed by Frau von Kerich's innumerable questions, and the warmth of her manner, frozen by Minna's looks, which he felt were taking in his features, his hands, his movements, his clothes. They made him even more uncomfortable by trying to put him at his ease—Frau von Kerich by her flow of words,

Minna by the coquettish eyes which instinctively she made at him to amuse herself.

Finally they gave up trying to get anything more from him than bows and monosyllables, and Frau von Kerich, who had the whole burden of the conversation, asked him, when she was worn out, to play the piano. Much more shy of them than of a concert audience, he played an adagio of Mozart. But his very shyness, the uneasiness which was beginning to fill his heart from the company of the two women, the ingenuous emotion with which his bosom swelled, which made him happy and unhappy, were in tune with the tenderness and youthful modesty of the music, and gave it the charm of spring. Frau von Kerich was moved by it; she said so with the exaggerated words of praise customary among men and women of the world; she was none the less sincere for that, and the very excess of the flattery was sweet coming from such charming lips. Naughty Minna said nothing, and looked astonished at the boy who was so stupid when he talked, but was so eloquent with his fingers. Jean-Christophe felt their sympathy, and grew bold under it. He went on playing; then, half turning towards Minna, with an awkward smile and without raising his eyes, he said timidly:

"This is what I was doing on the wall."

He played a little piece in which he had, in fact, developed the musical ideas which had come to him in his favorite spot as he looked into the garden, not, be it said, on the evening when he had seen Minna and Frau von Kerich—for some obscure reason, known only to his heart, he was trying to persuade himself that it was so—but long before, and in the calm rhythm of the *andante con moto,* there were to be found the serene impression of the singing of birds, mutterings of beasts, and the majestic slumber of the great trees in the peace of the sunset.

The two hearers listened delightedly. When he had finished Frau von Kerich rose, took his hands with her usual vivacity, and thanked him effusively. Minna clapped her hands, and cried that it was "admirable," and that to make him compose other works as "sublime" as that, she would have a ladder placed against the wall, so that he might work there at his

ease. Frau von Kerich told Jean-Christophe not to listen to
silly Minna; she begged him to come as often as he liked to
her garden, since he loved it, and she added that he need never
bother to call on them if he found it tiresome.

" You need never bother to come and see us," added Minna.
" Only if you do not come, beware! "

She wagged her finger in menace.

Minna was possessed by no imperious desire that Jean-Christophe should come to see her, or should even follow the rules
of politeness with regard to herself, but it pleased her to produce a little effect which instinctively she felt to be charming.

Jean-Christophe blushed delightedly. Frau von Kerich won
him completely by the tact with which she spoke of his mother
and grandfather, whom she had known. The warmth and kindness of the two ladies touched his heart; he exaggerated their
easy urbanity, their worldly graciousness, in his desire to think
it heartfelt and deep. He began to tell them, with his naïve
trustfulness, of his plans and his wretchedness. He did not
notice that more than an hour had passed, and he jumped with
surprise when a servant came and announced dinner. But
his confusion turned to happiness when Frau von Kerich told
him to stay and dine with them, like the good friends that they
were going to be, and were already. A place was laid for
him between the mother and daughter, and at table his talents
did not show to such advantage as at the piano. That part
of his education had been much neglected; it was his impression
that eating and drinking were the essential things at table,
and not the manner of them. And so tidy Minna looked at
him, pouting and a little horrified.

They thought that he would go immediately after supper.
But he followed them into the little room, and sat with them,
and had no idea of going. Minna stifled her yawns, and made
signs to her mother. He did not notice them, because he was
dumb with his happiness, and thought they were like himself—
because Minna, when she looked at him, made eyes at him from
habit—and finally, once he was seated, he did not quite know
how to get up and take his leave. He would have stayed all
night had not Frau von Kerich sent him away herself, without
ceremony, but kindly.

He went, carrying in his heart the soft light of the brown eyes of Frau von Kerich and the blue eyes of Minna; on his hands he felt the sweet contact of soft fingers, soft as flowers, and a subtle perfume, which he had never before breathed, enveloped him, bewildered him, brought him almost to swooning.

He went again two days later, as was arranged, to give Minna a music-lesson. Thereafter, under this arrangement, he went regularly twice a week in the morning, and very often he went again in the evening to play and talk.

Frau von Kerich was glad to see him. She was a clever and a kind woman. She was thirty-five when she lost her husband, and although young in body and at heart, she was not sorry to withdraw from the world in which she had gone far since her marriage. Perhaps she left it the more easily because she had found it very amusing, and thought wisely that she could not both eat her cake and have it. She was devoted to the memory of Herr von Kerich, not that she had felt anything like love for him when they married; but good-fellowship was enough for her; she was of an easy temper and an affectionate disposition.

She had given herself up to her daughter's education; but the same moderation which she had had in her love, held in check the impulsive and morbid quality which is sometimes in motherhood, when the child is the only creature upon whom the woman can expend her jealous need of loving and being loved. She loved Minna much, but was clear in her judgment of her, and did not conceal any of her imperfections any more than she tried to deceive herself about herself. Witty and clever, she had a keen eye for discovering at a glance the weakness, and ridiculous side, of any person; she took great pleasure in it, without ever being the least malicious, for she was as indulgent as she was scoffing, and while she laughed at people she loved to be of use to them.

Young Jean-Christophe gave food both to her kindness and to her critical mind. During the first days of her sojourn in the little town, when her mourning kept her out of society, Jean-Christophe was a distraction for her—primarily by his talent. She loved music, although she was no musician; she found in it a physical and moral well-being in which her thoughts could idly sink into a pleasant melancholy. Sitting by the fire—while Jean-Christophe played—a book in her hands, and smiling vaguely, she took a silent delight in the mechanical movements of his fingers, and the purposeless wanderings of her reverie, hovering among the sad, sweet images of the past.

But more even than the music, the musician interested her. She was clever enough to be conscious of Jean-Christophe's rare gifts, although she was not capable of perceiving his really original quality. It gave her a curious pleasure to watch the waking of those mysterious fires which she saw kindling in him. She had quickly appreciated his moral qualities, his uprightness, his courage, the sort of Stoicism in him, so touching in a child. But for all that she did not view him the less with the usual perspicacity of her sharp, mocking eyes. His awkwardness, his ugliness, his little ridiculous qualities amused her; she did not take him altogether seriously; she did not take many things seriously. Jean-Christophe's antic outbursts, his violence, his fantastic humor, made her think sometimes that he was a little unbalanced; she saw in him one of the Kraffts, honest men and good musicians, but always a little wrong in the head. Her light irony escaped Jean-Christophe; he was conscious only of Frau von Kerich's kindness. He was so unused to any one being kind to him! Although his duties at the Palace brought him into daily contact with the world, poor Jean-Christophe had remained a little savage, untutored and uneducated. The selfishness of the Court was only concerned in turning him to its profit and not in helping him in any way. He went to the Palace, sat at the piano, played, and went away again, and nobody ever took the trouble to talk to him, except absently to pay him some banal compliment. Since his grandfather's death, no one, either at home or outside, had ever thought of helping him to learn the conduct of life, or to be a man. He suffered cruelly from his ignorance and the roughness of his manners. He went through an agony and bloody sweat to shape himself alone, but he did not succeed. Books, conversation, example—all were lacking. He would fain have confessed his distress to a friend, but could not bring himself to do so. Even with Otto he had not dared, because at the first words he had uttered, Otto had assumed a tone of disdainful superiority which had burned into him like hot iron.

And now with Frau von Kerich it all became easy. Of her own accord, without his having to ask anything—it cost Jean-Christophe's pride so much!—she showed him gently what he should not do, told him what he ought to do, advised him how to dress, eat, walk, talk, and never passed over any fault of manners, taste, or language; and he could not be hurt by it, so light and careful was her touch in the handling of the boy's easily injured van ty. She took in hand also his literary education without seeming to be concerned with it; she never showed surprise at his strange ignorance, but never let slip an opportunity of correcting his mistakes simply, easily, as if it were natural for him to have been in error; and, instead of alarming him with pedantic lessons, she conceived the idea of employing their evening meetings by making Minna or Jean-Christophe read passages of history, or of the poets, German and foreign. She treated him as a son of the house, with a few fine shades of patronizing familiarity which he never saw. She was even concerned with his clothes, gave him new ones, knitted him a woolen comforter, presented him with little toilet things, and all so gently that he never was put about by her care or her presents. In short, she gave him all the little attentions and the quasi-maternal care which come to every good woman instinctively for a child who is intrusted to her, or trusts himself to her, without her having any deep feeling for it. But Jean-Christophe thought that all the tenderness was given to him personally, and he was filled with gratitude; he would break out into little awkward, passionate speeches, which seemed a little ridiculous to Frau von Kerich, though they did not fail to give her pleasure.

With Minna his relation was very different. When Jean-Christophe met her again at her first lesson, he was still intoxicated by his memories of the preceding evening and of the girl's soft looks, and he was greatly surprised to find her an altogether different person from the girl he had seen only

a few hours before. She hardly looked at him, and did not
listen to what he said, and when she raised her eyes to him, he
saw in them so icy a coldness that he was chilled by it. He
tortured himself for a long time to discover wherein lay his
offense. He had given none, and Minna's feelings were neither
more nor less favorable than on the preceding day; just as she
had been then, Minna was completely indifferent to him. If
on the first occasion she had smiled upon him in welcome, it
was from a girl's instinctive coquetry, who delights to try the
power of her eyes on the first comer, be it only a trimmed poodle
who turns up to fill her idle hours. But since the preceding
day the too-easy conquest had already lost interest for her. She
had subjected Jean-Christophe to a severe scrutiny and she
thought him an ugly boy, poor, ill-bred, who played the piano
well, though he had ugly hands, held his fork at table abomi-
nably, and ate his fish with a knife. Then he seemed to her
very uninteresting. She wanted to have music-lessons from
him; she wanted, even, to amuse herself with him, because for
the moment she had no other companion, and because in spite
of her pretensions of being no longer a child, she had still
in gusts a crazy longing to play, a need of expending her
superfluous gaiety, which was, in her as in her mother, still
further roused by the constraint imposed by their mourning.
But she took no more account of Jean-Christophe than of a
domestic animal, and if it still happened occasionally during
the days of her greatest coldness that she made eyes at him,
it was purely out of forgetfulness, and because she was thinking
of something else, or simply so as not to get out of practice.
And when she looked at him like that, Jean-Christophe's heart
used to leap. It is doubtful if she saw it; she was telling herself
stories. For she was at the age when we delight the senses
with sweet fluttering dreams. She was forever absorbed in
thoughts of love, filled with a curiosity which was only innocent
from ignorance. And she only thought of love, as a well-taught
young lady should, in terms of marriage. Her ideal was far
from having taken definite shape. Sometimes she dreamed
of marrying a lieutenant, sometimes of marrying a poet, prop
erly sublime, à la Schiller. One project devoured another
and the last was always welcomed with the same gravity and

just the same amount of conviction. For the rest, all of them were quite ready to give way before a profitable reality, for it is wonderful to see how easily romantic girls forget their dreams, when something less ideal, but more certain, appears before them.

As it was, sentimental Minna was, in spite of all, calm and cold. In spite of her aristocratic name, and the pride with which the ennobling particle filled her, she had the soul of a little German housewife in the exquisite days of adolescence.

Naturally Jean-Christophe did not in the least understand the complicated mechanism—more complicated in appearance than in reality—of the feminine heart. He was often baffled by the ways of his friends, but he was so happy in loving them that he credited them with all that disturbed and made him sad with them, so as to persuade himself that he was as much loved by them as he loved them himself. A word or an affectionate look plunged him in delight. Sometimes he was so bowled over by it that he would burst into tears.

Sitting by the table in the quiet little room, with Frau von Kerich a few yards away sewing by the light of the lamp—Minna reading on the other side of the table, and no one talking, he looking through the half-open garden-door at the gravel of the avenue glistening under the moon, a soft murmur coming from the tops of the trees—his heart would be so full of happiness that suddenly, for no reason, he would leap from his chair, throw himself at Frau von Kerich's feet, seize her hand, needle or no needle, cover it with kisses, press it to his lips, his cheeks, his eyes, and sob. Minna would raise her eyes, lightly shrug her shoulders, and make a face. Frau von Kerich would smile down at the big boy groveling at her feet, and pat his head with her free hand, and say to him in her pretty voice, affectionately and ironically:

"Well, well, old fellow! What is it?"

Oh, the sweetness of that voice, that peace, that silence, that soft air in which were no shouts, no roughness, no violence, that oasis in the harsh desert of life, and—heroic light gilding with its rays people and things—the light of the enchanted world conjured up by the reading of the divine poets! Goethe,

Schiller, Shakespeare, springs of strength, of sorrow, and of love! . . .

Minna, with her head down over the book, and her face faintly colored by her animated delivery, would read in her fresh voice, with its slight lisp, and try to sound important when she spoke in the characters of warriors and kings. Sometimes Frau von Kerich herself would take the book; then she would lend to tragic histories the spiritual and tender graciousness of her own nature, but most often she would listen, lying back in her chair, her never-ending needlework in her lap; she would smile at her own thoughts, for always she would come back to them through every book.

Jean-Christophe also had tried to read, but he had had to give it up; he stammered, stumbled over the words, skipped the punctuation, seemed to understand nothing, and would be so moved that he would have to stop in the middle of the pathetic passages, feeling tears coming. Then in a tantrum he would throw the book down on the table, and his two friends would burst out laughing. . . . How he loved them! He carried the image of them everywhere with him, and they were mingled with the persons in Shakespeare and Goethe. He could hardly distinguish between them. Some fragrant word of the poets which called up from the depths of his being passionate emotions could not in him be severed from the beloved lips that had made him hear it for the first time. Even twenty years later he could never read Egmont or Romeo, or see them played, without there leaping up in him at certain lines the memory of those quiet evenings, those dreams of happiness, and the beloved faces of Frau von Kerich and Minna.

He would spend hours looking at them in the evening when they were reading; in the night when he was dreaming in his bed, awake, with his eyes closed; during the day, when he was dreaming at his place in the orchestra, playing mechanically with his eyes half closed. He had the most innocent tenderness for them, and, knowing nothing of love, he thought he was in love. But he did not quite know whether it was with the mother or the daughter. He went into the matter gravely, and did not know which to choose. And yet, as it seemed to him that he must at all costs make his choice, he inclined towards Frau von Kerich. And he did in fact discover, as soon as he had made up his mind to it, that it was she that he loved. He loved her quick eyes, the absent smile upon her half-open lips, her pretty forehead, so young in seeming, and the parting to one side in her fine, soft hair, her rather husky voice, with its little cough, her motherly hands, the elegance of her movements, and her mysterious soul. He would thrill with happiness when, sitting by his side, she would kindly explain to him the meaning of some passage in a book which he did not understand; she would lay her hand on Jean-Christophe's shoulder; he would feel the warmth of her fingers, her breath on his cheek, the sweet perfume of her body; he would listen in ecstasy, lose all thought of the book, and understand nothing at all. She would see that and ask him to repeat what she had said; then he would say nothing, and she would laughingly be angry, and tap his nose with her book, telling him that he would always be a little donkey. To that he would reply that he did not care so long as he was *her* little donkey, and she did not drive him out of her house. She would pretend to make objections; then she would say that although he was an ugly little donkey, and very stupid, she would agree to keep him—and perhaps even to love him—although he was good for nothing, if at the least he would be just *good*. Then they would both laugh, and he would go swimming in his joy.

When he discovered that he loved Frau von Kerich, Jean-Christophe broke away from Minna. He was beginning to be irritated by her coldness and disdain, and as, by dint of seeing her often, he had been emboldened little by little to resume his freedom of manner with her, he did not conceal his exasperation from her. She loved to sting him, and he would reply sharply. They were always saying unkind things to each other, and Frau von Kerich only laughed at them. Jean-Christophe, who never got the better in such passages of words, used sometimes to issue from them so infuriated that he thought he detested Minna; and he persuaded himself that he only went to her house again because of Frau von Kerich.

He went on giving her music lessons. Twice a week, from nine to ten in the morning, he superintended the girl's scales and exercises. The room in which they did this was Minna's studio—an odd workroom, which, with an amusing fidelity, reflected the singular disorder of her little feminine mind.

On the table were little figures of musical cats—a whole orchestra—one playing a violin, another the violoncello—a little pocket-mirror, toilet things and writing things, tidily arranged. On the shelves were tiny busts of musicians—Beethoven frowning, Wagner with his velvet cap, and the Apollo Belvedere. On the mantelpiece, by a frog smoking a red pipe, a paper fan on which was painted the Bayreuth Theater. On the two bookshelves were a few books—Lübke, Mommsen, Schiller, " Sans Famille," Jules Verne, Montaigne. On the walls large photographs of the Sistine Madonna, and pictures by Herkomer, edged with blue and green ribbons. There was also a view of a Swiss hotel in a frame of silver thistles; and above all, everywhere in profusion, in every corner of the room, photographs of officers, tenors, conductors, girl-friends, all with inscriptions, almost all with verse—or at least what is accepted as verse in Germany. In the center of the room, on a marble pillar, was enthroned a bust of Brahms, with a beard; and, above the piano, little plush monkeys and cotillion trophies hung by threads.

Minna would arrive late, her eyes still puffy with sleep, sulky; she would hardly reach out her hand to Jean-Christophe, coldly bid him good-day, and, without a word, gravely and with dignity sit down at the piano. When she was alone, it pleased her to play interminable scales, for that allowed her agreeably to prolong her half-somnolent condition and the dreams which she was spinning for herself. But Jean-Christophe would compel her to fix her attention on difficult exercises, and so sometimes she would avenge herself by playing them as badly as she could. She was a fair musician, but she did not like music —like many German women. But, like them, she thought she ought to like it, and she took her lessons conscientiously enough, except for certain moments of diabolical malice indulged in to enrage her master. She could enrage him much more by the icy indifference with which she set herself to her task. But the worst was when she took it into her head that it was her duty to throw her soul into an expressive passage: then she would become sentimental and feel nothing.

Young Jean-Christophe, sitting by her side, was not very polite. He never paid her compliments—far from it. She resented that, and never let any remark pass without answering it. She would argue about everything that he said, and when she made a mistake she would insist that she was playing what was written. He would get cross, and they would go on exchanging ungracious words and impertinences. With her eyes on the keys, she never ceased to watch Jean-Christophe and enjoy his fury. As a relief from boredom she would invent stupid little tricks, with no other object than to interrupt the lesson and to annoy Jean-Christophe. She would pretend to choke, so as to make herself interesting; she would have a fit of coughing, or she would have something very important to say to the maid. Jean-Christophe knew that she was play-acting; and Minna knew that Jean-Christophe knew that she was play-acting; and it amused her, for Jean-Christophe could not tell her what he was thinking.

One day, when she was indulging in this amusement and was coughing languidly, hiding her mouth in her handkerchief, as if she were on the point of choking, but in reality watching Jean-Christophe's exasperation out of the corner of her eye, she conceived the ingenious idea of letting the handkerchief fall, so as to make Jean-Christophe pick it up, which he did with the worst grace in the world. She rewarded him with a " Thank you! " in her grand manner, which nearly made him explode.

She thought the game too good not to be repeated. Next day she did it again. Jean-Christophe did not budge; he was boiling with rage. She waited a moment, and then said in an injured tone:

" Will you please pick up my handkerchief? "

Jean-Christophe could not contain himself.

" 1 am not your servant! " he cried roughly. " Pick it up yourself! "

Minna choked with rage. She got up suddenly from her stool, which fell over.

" Oh, this is too much! " she said, and angrily thumped the piano; and she left the room in a fury.

Jean-Christophe waited. She did not come back. He was

ashamed of what he had done; he felt that he had behaved like
a little cad. And he was at the end of his tether: she made
fun of him too impudently! He was afraid lest Minna should
complain to her mother, and he should be forever banished from
Frau von Kerich's thoughts. He knew not what to do; for if
he was sorry for his brutality, no power on earth would have
made him ask pardon.

He came again on the chance the next day, although he
thought that Minna would refuse to take her lesson. But
Minna, who was too proud to complain to anybody—Minna,
whose conscience was not shielded against reproach—appeared
again, after making him wait five minutes more than usual;
and she sat down at the piano, stiff, upright, without turning
her head or saying a word, as though Jean-Christophe no longer
existed for her. But she did not fail to take her lesson, and
all the subsequent lessons, because she knew very well that Jean-
Christophe was a fine musician, and that she ought to learn
to play the piano properly if she wished to be—what she wished
to be—a well-bred young lady of finished education.

But how bored she was! How they bored each other!

One misty morning in March, when little flakes of snow
were flying, like feathers, in the gray air, they were in the
studio. It was hardly daylight. Minna was arguing, as usual,
about a false note that she had struck, and pretending that it
"was written so." Although he knew perfectly well that she
was lying, Jean-Christophe bent over the book to look at the
passage in question closely. Her hand was on the rack, and
she did not move it. His lips were near her hand. He tried
to read and could not; he was looking at something else—a
thing soft, transparent, like the petals of a flower. Suddenly—
he did not know what he was thinking of—he pressed his lips
as hard as he could on the little hand.

They were both dumfounded by it. He flung backwards;
she withdrew her hand—both blushing. They said no word;
they did not look at each other. After a moment of confused
silence she began to play again; she was very uneasy: her
bosom rose and fell as though she were under some weight:
she struck wrong note after wrong note. He did not notice it:

he was more uneasy than she. His temples throbbed; he heard
nothing; he knew not what she was playing; and, to break the
silence, he made a few random remarks in a choking voice.
He thought that he was forever lost in Minna's opinion. He
was confounded by what he had done, thought it stupid and
rude. The lesson-hour over, he left Minna without looking at
her, and even forgot to say good-bye. She did not mind. She
had no thought now of deeming Jean-Christophe ill-mannered;
and if she made so many mistakes in playing, it was because
all the time she was watching him out of the corner of her
eye with astonishment and curiosity, and—for the first time—
sympathy.

When she was left alone, instead of going to look for her
mother as usual, she shut herself up in her room and examined
this extraordinary event. She sat with her face in her hands
in front of the mirror. Her eyes seemed to her soft and gleaming. She bit gently at her lip in the effort of thinking. And
as she looked complacently at her pretty face, she visualized
the scene, and blushed and smiled. At dinner she was animated
and merry. She refused to go out at once, and stayed in the
drawing-room for part of the afternoon; she had some work
in her hand, and did not make ten stitches without a mistake,
but what did that matter! In a corner of the room, with her
back turned to her mother, she smiled; or, under a sudden
impulse to let herself go, she pranced about the room and
sang at the top of her voice. Frau von Kerich started and
called her mad. Minna flung her arms round her neck, shaking with laughter, and hugged and kissed her.

In the evening, when she went to her room, it was a long
time before she went to bed. She went on looking at herself
in the mirror, trying to remember, and having thought all
through the day of the same thing—thinking of nothing. She
undressed slowly; she stopped every moment, sitting on the
bed, trying to remember what Jean-Christophe was like. It
was a Jean-Christophe of fantasy who appeared, and now he
did not seem nearly so uncouth to her. She went to bed and
put out the light. Ten minutes later the scene of the morning
rushed back into her mind, and she burst out laughing. Her
mother got up softly and opened the door, thinking that, against

orders, she was reading in bed. She found Minna lying quietly
in her bed, with her eyes wide open in the dim candlelight.
"What is it?" she asked. "What is amusing you?"
"Nothing," said Minna gravely. "I was thinking."
"You are very lucky to find your own company so amusing.
But go to sleep."
"Yes, mamma," replied Minna meekly. Inside herself she
was grumbling: "Go away! Do go away!" until the door
was closed, and she could go on enjoying her dreams. She
fell into a sweet drowsiness. When she was nearly asleep, she
leaped for joy:
"He loves me. . . . What happiness! How good of him to
love me! . . . How I love him!"
She kissed her pillow and went fast asleep.

When next they were together Jean-Christophe was surprised
at Minna's amiability. She gave him "Good-day," and asked
him how he was in a very soft voice; she sat at the piano,
looking wise and modest; she was an angel of docility. There
were none of her naughty schoolgirl's tricks, but she listened
religiously to Jean-Christophe's remarks, acknowledged that
they were right, gave little timid cries herself when she made a
mistake and set herself to be more accurate. Jean-Christophe
could not understand it. In a very short time she made
astounding progress. Not only did she play better, but with
musical feeling. Little as he was given to flattery, he had to
pay her a compliment. She blushed with pleasure, and thanked
him for it with a look tearful with gratitude. She took pains
with her toilet for him; she wore ribbons of an exquisite shade;
she gave Jean-Christophe little smiles and soft glances, which
he disliked, for they irritated him, and moved him to the
depths of his soul. And now it was she who made conversation,
but there was nothing childish in what she said; she talked
gravely, and quoted the poets in a pedantic and pretentious
way. He hardly ever replied; he was ill at ease. This new
Minna that he did not know astonished and disquieted him.
    Always she watched him. She was waiting. . . . For what?
. . . Did she know herself? . . . She was waiting for him to
do it again. He took good care not to, for he was convinced

that he had behaved like a clod; he seemed never to give a
thought to it. She grew restless, and one day when he was
sitting quietly at a respectful distance from her dangerous little
paws, she was seized with impatience: with a movement so quick
that she had no time to think of it, she herself thrust her little
hand against his lips. He was staggered by it, then furious
and ashamed. But none the less he kissed it very passionately.
Her naïve effrontery enraged him; he was on the point of
leaving her there and then.

But he could not. He was entrapped. Whirling thoughts
rushed in his mind; he could make nothing of them. Like mists
ascending from a valley they rose from the depths of his heart.
He wandered hither and thither at random through this mist
of love, and whatever he did, he did but turn round and round
an obscure fixed idea, a Desire unknown, terrible and fascinating as a flame to an insect. It was the sudden eruption of the
blind forces of Nature.

They passed through a period of waiting. They watched
each other, desired each other, were fearful of each other.
They were uneasy. But they did not for that desist from their
little hostilities and sulkinesses; only there were no more familiarities between them; they were silent. Each was busy constructing their love in silence.

Love has curious retroactive effects. As soon as Jean-
Christophe discovered that he loved Minna, he discovered at the
same time that he had always loved her. For three months
they had been seeing each other almost every day without ever
suspecting the existence of their love. But from the day when
he did actually love her, he was absolutely convinced that he
had loved her from all eternity.

It was a good thing for him to have discovered at last *whom*
he loved. He had loved for so long without knowing whom!
It was a sort of relief to him, like a sick man, who, suffering
from a general illness, vague and enervating, sees it become
definite in sharp pain in some portion of his body. Nothing
is more wearing than love without a definite object; it eats
away and saps the strength like a fever. A known passion
leads the mind to excess; that is exhausting, but at least one

knows why. It is an excess; it is not a wasting away. Anything rather than emptiness.

Although Minna had given Jean-Christophe good reason to believe that she was not indifferent to him, he did not fail to torture himself with the idea that she despised him. They had never had any very clear idea of each other, but this idea had never been more confused and false than it was now; it consisted of a series of strange fantasies which could never be made to agree, for they passed from one extreme to the other, endowing each other in turn with faults and charms which they did not possess—charms when they were parted, faults when they were together. In either case they were wide of the mark.

They did not know themselves what they desired. For Jean-Christophe his love took shape as that thirst for tenderness, imperious, absolute, demanding reciprocation, which had burned in him since childhood, which he demanded from others, and wished to impose on them by will or force. Sometimes this despotic desire of full sacrifice of himself and others—especially others, perhaps—was mingled with gusts of a brutal and obscure desire, which set him whirling, and he did not understand it. Minna, curious above all things, and delighted to have a romance, tried to extract as much pleasure as possible from it for her vanity and sentimentality; she tricked herself whole-heartedly as to what she was feeling. A great part of their love was purely literary. They fed on the books they had read, and were forever ascribing to themselves feelings which they did not possess.

But the moment was to come when all these little lies and small egoisms were to vanish away before the divine light of love. A day, an hour, a few seconds of eternity. . . . And it was so unexpected! . . .

One evening they were alone and talking. The room was growing dark. Their conversation took a serious turn. They talked of the infinite, of Life, and Death. It made a larger frame for their little passion. Minna complained of her loneliness, which led naturally to Jean-Christophe's answer that she was not so lonely as she thought.

"No," she said, shaking her head. "That is only words.

Every one lives for himself; no one is interested in you; nobody loves you."

Silence.

" And I ? " said Jean-Christophe suddenly, pale with emotion. Impulsive Minna jumped to her feet, and took his hands. The door opened. They flung apart. Frau von Kerich entered. Jean-Christophe buried himself in a book, which he held upside down. Minna bent over her work, and pricked her finger with her needle.

They were not alone together for the rest of the evening, and they were afraid of being left. When Frau von Kerich got up to look for something in the next room, Minna, not usually obliging, ran to fetch it for her, and Jean-Christophe took advantage of her absence to take his leave without saying goodnight to her.

Next day they met again, impatient to resume their interrupted conversation. They did not succeed. Yet circumstances were favorable to them. They went a walk with Frau von Kerich, and had plenty of opportunity for talking as much as they liked. But Jean-Christophe could not speak, and he was so unhappy that he stayed as far away as possible from Minna. And she pretended not to notice his discourtesy; but she was piqued by it, and showed it. When Jean-Christophe did at last contrive to utter a few words, she listened icily; he had hardly the courage to finish his sentence. They were coming to the end of the walk. Time was flying. And he was wretched at not having been able to make use of it.

A week passed. They thought they had mistaken their feeling for each other. They were not sure but that they had dreamed the scene of that evening. Minna was resentful against Jean-Christophe. Jean-Christophe was afraid of meeting her alone. They were colder to each other than ever.

A day came when it had rained all morning and part of the afternoon. They had stayed in the house without speaking, reading, yawning, looking out of the window; they were bored and cross. About four o'clock the sky cleared. They ran into the garden. They leaned their elbows on the terrace wall, and looked down at the lawns sloping to the river. The earth was steaming; a soft mist was ascending to the sun; little rain-

drops glittered on the grass; the smell of the damp earth and
the perfume of the flowers intermingled; around them buzzed
a golden swarm of bees. They were side by side, not looking
at each other; they could not bring themselves to break the
silence. A bee came up and clung awkwardly to a clump of
wistaria heavy with rain, and sent a shower of water down on
them. They both laughed, and at once they felt that they
were no longer cross with each other, and were friends again.
But still they did not look at each other. Suddenly, without
turning her head, she took his hand, and said:

"Come!"

She led him quickly to the little labyrinth with its box-
bordered paths, which was in the middle of the grove. They
climbed up the slope, slipping on the soaking ground, and
the wet trees shook out their branches over them. Near the
top she stopped to breathe.

"Wait . . . wait . . ." she said in a low voice, trying to
take breath.

He looked at her. She was looking away; she was smiling,
breathing hard, with her lips parted; her hand was trembling
in Jean-Christophe's. They felt the blood throbbing in their
linked hands and their trembling fingers. Around them all
was silent. The pale shoots of the trees were quivering in the
sun; a gentle rain dropped from the leaves with silvery sounds,
and in the sky were the shrill cries of swallows.

She turned her head towards him; it was a lightning flash.
She flung her arms about his neck; he flung himself into her
arms.

"Minna! Minna! My darling! . . ."

"I love you, Jean Christophe! I love you!"

They sat on a wet wooden seat. They were filled with love,
sweet, profound, absurd. Everything else had vanished. No
more egoism, no more vanity, no more reservation. Love, love
—that is what their laughing, tearful eyes were saying. The
cold coquette of a girl, the proud boy, were devoured with the
need of self-sacrifice, of giving, of suffering, of dying for each
other. They did not know each other; they were not the same;
everything was changed; their hearts, their faces, their eyes,
gave out a radiance of the most touching kindness and tender-

ness. Moments of purity, of self-denial, of absolute giving of themselves, which through life will never return!

After a desperate murmuring of words and passionate promises to belong to each other forever, after kisses and incoherent words of delight, they saw that it was late, and they ran back hand in hand, almost falling in the narrow paths, bumping into trees, feeling nothing, blind and drunk with the joy of it.

When he left her he did not go home; he could not have gone to sleep. He left the town, and walked over the fields; he walked blindly through the night. The air was fresh, the country dark and deserted. A screech-owl hooted shrilly. Jean-Christophe went on like a sleep-walker. The little lights of the town quivered on the plain, and the stars in the dark sky. He sat on a wall by the road and suddenly burst into tears. He did not know why. He was too happy, and the excess of his joy was compounded of sadness and delight; there was in it thankfulness for his happiness, pity for those who were not happy, a melancholy and sweet feeling of the frailty of things, the mad joy of living. He wept for delight, and slept in the midst of his tears. When he awoke dawn was peeping. White mists floated over the river, and veiled the town, where Minna, worn out, was sleeping, while in her heart was the light of her smile of happiness.

They contrived to meet again in the garden next morning and told their love once more, but now the divine unconsciousness of it all was gone. She was a little playing the part of the girl in love, and he, though more sincere, was also playing a part. They talked of what their life should be. He regretted his poverty and humble estate. She affected to be generous, and enjoyed her generosity. She said that she cared nothing for money. That was true, for she knew nothing about it, having never known the lack of it. He promised that he would become a great artist; that she thought fine and amusing, like a novel. She thought it her duty to behave really like a woman in love. She read poetry; she was sentimental. He was touched by the infection. He took pains with his dress; he was absurd; he set a guard upon his speech; he was pretentious. Frau von Kerich watched him and laughed, and asked herself what could have made him so stupid.

But they had moments of marvelous poetry, and these would suddenly burst upon them out of dull days, like sunshine through a mist. A look, a gesture, a meaningless word, and they were bathed in happiness; they had their good-byes in the evening on the dimly-lighted stairs, and their eyes would seek each other, divine each other through the half darkness, and the thrill of their hands as they touched, the trembling in their voices, all those little nothings that fed their memory at night, as they slept so lightly that the chiming of each hour would awake them, and their hearts would sing " I am loved," like the murmuring of a stream.

They discovered the charm of things. Spring smiled with a marvelous sweetness. The heavens were brilliant, the air was soft, as they had never been before. All the town—the red roofs, the old walls, the cobbled streets—showed with a kindly charm that moved Jean-Christophe. At night, when everybody was asleep, Minna would get up from her bed, and stand by the window, drowsy and feverish. And in the afternoon, when he was not there, she would sit in a swing, and dream, with a book on her knees, her eyes half closed, sleepy and lazily happy, mind and body hovering in the spring air. She would spend hours at the piano, with a patience exasperating to others, going over and over again scales and passages which made her turn pale and cold with emotion. She would weep when she heard Schumann's music. She felt full of pity and kindness for all creatures, and so did he. They would give money stealthily to poor people whom they met in the street, and would then exchange glances of compassion; they were happy in their kindness.

To tell the truth, they were kind only by fits and starts. Minna suddenly discovered how sad was the humble life of devotion of old Frida, who had been a servant in the house since her mother's childhood, and at once she ran and hugged her, to the great astonishment of the good old creature, who was busy mending the linen in the kitchen. But that did not keep her from speaking harshly to her a few hours later, when Frida did not come at once on the sound of the bell. And

Jean-Christophe, who was consumed with love for all humanity, and would turn aside so as not to crush an insect, was entirely indifferent to his own family. By a strange reaction he was colder and more curt with them the more affectionate he was to all other creatures; he hardly gave thought to them; he spoke abruptly to them, and found no interest in seeing them. Both in Jean-Christophe and Minna their kindness was only a surfeit of tenderness which overflowed at intervals to the benefit of the first comer. Except for these overflowings they were more egoistic than ever, for their minds were filled only with the one thought, and everything was brought back to that.

How much of Jean-Christophe's life was filled with the girl's face! What emotion was in him when he saw her white frock in the distance, when he was looking for her in the garden; when at the theater, sitting a few yards away from their empty places, he heard the door of their box open, and the mocking voice that he knew so well; when in some outside conversation the dear name of Kerich cropped up! He would go pale and blush; for a moment or two he would see and hear nothing. And then there would be a rush of blood over all his body, the assault of unknown forces.

The little German girl, naïve and sensual, had odd little tricks. She would place her ring on a little pile of flour, and he would have to get it again and again with his teeth without whitening his nose. Or she would pass a thread through a biscuit, and put one end of it in her mouth and one in his, and then they had to nibble the thread to see who could get to the biscuit first. Their faces would come together; they would feel each other's breathing; their lips would touch, and they would laugh forcedly, while their hands would turn to ice. Jean-Christophe would feel a desire to bite, to hurt; he would fling back, and she would go on laughing forcedly. They would turn away, pretend indifference, and steal glances at each other.

These disturbing games had a disquieting attraction for them; they wanted to play them, and yet avoided them. Jean-Christophe was fearful of them, and preferred even the constraint of the meetings when Frau von Kerich or some one else was present. No outside presence could break in upon the converse of their loving hearts; constraint only made their love sweeter and more intense. Everything gained infinitely in value; a word, a movement of the lips, a glance were enough to make the rich new treasure of their inner life shine through the dull veil of ordinary existence. They alone could see it, or so they thought, and smiled, happy in their little mysteries. Their words were no more than those of a drawing-room conversation about trivial matters; to them they were an unending song of love. They read the most fleeting changes in their faces and voices as in an open book; they could have read as well with their eyes closed, for they had only to listen to their hearts to hear in them the echo of the heart of the beloved. They were full of confidence in life, in happiness, in themselves. Their hopes were boundless. They loved, they were loved, happy, without a shadow, without a doubt, without a fear of the future. Wonderful serenity of those days of spring! Not a cloud in the sky. A faith so fresh that it seems that nothing can ever tarnish it. A joy so abounding that nothing can ever exhaust it. Are they living? Are they dreaming? Doubtless they are dreaming. There is nothing in common between life and their dream—nothing, except in that moment of magic: they are but a dream themselves; their being has melted away at the touch of love.

It was not long before Frau von Kerich perceived their little intrigue, which they thought very subtly managed, though it was very clumsy. Minna had suspected it from the moment when her mother had entered suddenly one day when she was talking to Jean-Christophe, and standing as near to him as she could, and on the click of the door they had darted apart as quickly as possible, covered with confusion. Frau von Kerich had pretended to see nothing. Minna was almost sorry. She would have liked a tussle with her mother; it would have been more romantic.

Her mother took care to give her no opportunity for it; she was too clever to be anxious, or to make any remark about it. But to Minna she talked ironically about Jean-Christophe, and made merciless fun of his foibles; she demolished him in a few words. She did not do it deliberately; she acted upon instinct, with the treachery natural to a woman who is defending her own. It was useless for Minna to resist, and sulk, and be impertinent, and go on denying the truth of her remarks; there was only too much justification for them, and Frau von Kerich had a cruel skill in flicking the raw spot. The largeness of Jean-Christophe's boots, the ugliness of his clothes, his ill-brushed hat, his provincial accent, his ridiculous way of bowing, the vulgarity of his loud-voicedness, nothing was forgotten which might sting Minna's vanity. Such remarks were always simple and made by the way; they never took the form of a set speech, and when Minna, irritated, got upon her high horse to reply, Frau von Kerich would innocently be off on another subject. But the blow struck home, and Minna was sore under it.

She began to look at Jean-Christophe with a less indulgent eye. He was vaguely conscious of it, and uneasily asked her:

" Why do you look at me like that? "

And she answered:

" Oh, nothing! "

But a moment after, when he was merry, she would harshly reproach him for laughing so loudly. He was abashed; he never would have thought that he would have to take care not to laugh too loudly with her: all his gaiety was spoiled. Or when he was talking absolutely at his ease, she would absently interrupt him to make some unpleasant remark about his clothes, or she would take exception to his common expressions with pedantic aggressiveness. Then he would lose all desire to talk, and sometimes would be cross. Then he would persuade himself that these ways which so irritated him were a proof of Minna's interest in him, and she would persuade herself also that it was so. He would try humbly to do better. But she was never much pleased with him, for he hardly ever succeeded.

But he had no time—nor had Minna—to perceive the change that was taking place in her. Easter came, and Minna had to go with her mother to stay with some relations near Weimar.

During the last week before the separation they returned to the intimacy of the first days. Except for little outbursts of impatience Minna was more affectionate than ever. On the eve of her departure they went for a long walk in the park;

she led Jean-Christophe mysteriously to the arbor, and put about his neck a little scented bag, in which she had placed a lock of her hair; they renewed their eternal vows, and swore to write to each other every day; and they chose a star out of the sky, and arranged to look at it every evening at the same time.

The fatal day arrived. Ten times during the night he had asked himself, " Where will she be to-morrow? " and now he thought, " It is to-day. This morning she is still here; to-night she will be here no longer." He went to her house before eight o'clock. She was not up; he set out to walk in the park; he could not; he returned. The passages were full of boxes and parcels; he sat down in a corner of the room listening for the creaking of doors and floors, and recognizing the footsteps on the floor above him. Frau von Kerich passed, smiled as she saw him and, without stopping, threw him a mocking good-day. Minna came at last; she was pale, her eyelids were swollen; she had not slept any more than he during the night. She gave orders busily to the servants; she held out her hand to Jean-Christophe, and went on talking to old Frida. She was ready to go. Frau von Kerich came back. They argued about a hat-box. Minna seemed to pay no attention to Jean-Christophe, who was standing, forgotten and unhappy, by the piano. She went out with her mother, then came back; from the door she called out to Frau von Kerich. She closed the door. They were alone. She ran to him, took his hand, and dragged him into the little room next door; its shutters were closed. Then she put her face up to Jean-Christophe's and kissed him wildly. With tears in her eyes she said:

" You promise—you promise that you will love me always? "

They sobbed quietly, and made convulsive efforts to choke their sobs down so as not to be heard. They broke apart as they heard footsteps approaching. Minna dried her eyes, and resumed her busy air with the servants, but her voice trembled.

He succeeded in snatching her handkerchief, which she had let fall—her little dirty handkerchief, crumpled and wet with her tears.

He went to the station with his friends in their carriage. Sitting opposite each other Jean-Christophe and Minna hardly

dared look at each other for fear of bursting into tears. Their
hands sought each other, and clasped until they hurt. Frau
von Kerich watched them with quizzical good-humor, and
seemed not to see anything. The time arrived. Jean-Christophe was standing by the door of the train when it began to
move, and he ran alongside the carriage, not looking where
he was going, jostling against porters, his eyes fixed on Minna's
eyes, until the train was gone. He went on running until it
was lost from sight. Then he stopped, out of breath, and
found himself on the station platform among people of no
importance. He went home, and, fortunately, his family were
all out, and all through the morning he wept.

For the first time he knew the frightful sorrow of parting,
an intolerable torture for all loving hearts. The world is
empty; life is empty; all is empty. The heart is choked; it
is impossible to breathe; there is mortal agony; it is difficult,
impossible, to live—especially when all around you there are
the traces of the departed loved one, when everything about
you is forever calling up her image, when you remain in the
surroundings in which you lived together, she and you, when
it is a torment to try to live again in the same places the
happiness that is gone. Then it is as though an abyss were
opened at your feet; you lean over it; you turn giddy; you
almost fall. You fall. You think you are face to face with
Death. And so you are; parting is one of his faces. You
watch the beloved of your heart pass away; life is effaced; only
a black hole is left—nothingness.

Jean-Christophe went and visited all the beloved spots, so
as to suffer more. Frau von Kerich had left him the key of
the garden, so that he could go there while they were away.
He went there that very day, and was like to choke with sorrow.
It seemed to him as he entered that he might find there a little
of her who was gone; he found only too much of her; her
image hovered over all the lawns; he expected to see her appear
at all the corners of the paths; he knew well that she would
not appear, but he tormented himself with pretending that she
might, and he went over the tracks of his memories of love—
the path to the labyrinth, the terrace carpeted with wistaria,

the seat in the arbor, and he inflicted torture on himself by
saying: " A week ago . . . three days ago . . . yesterday, it
was so. Yesterday she was here . . . this very morning. . . ."
He racked his heart with these thoughts until he had to stop,
choking, and like to die. In his sorrow was mingled anger with
himself for having wasted all that time, and not having made
use of it. So many minutes, so many hours, when he had
enjoyed the infinite happiness of seeing her, breathing her, and
feeding upon her. And he had not appreciated it! He had
let the time go by without having tasted to the full every tiny
moment! And now! . . . Now it was too late. . . . Irreparable! Irreparable!

He went. home. His family seemed odious to him. He could
not bear their faces, their gestures, their fatuous conversation,
the same as that of the preceding day, the same as that of all
the preceding days—always the same. They went on living
their usual life, as though no such misfortune had come to
pass in their midst. And the town had no more idea of it
than they. The people were all going about their affairs, laughing, noisy, busy; the crickets were chirping; the sky was bright.
He hated them all; he felt himself crushed by this universal
egoism. But he himself was more egoistic than the whole
universe. Nothing was worth while to him. He had no kindness. He loved nobody.

He passed several lamentable days. His work absorbed him
again automatically: but he had no heart for living.

One evening when he was at supper with his family, silent
and depressed, the postman knocked at the door and left a
letter for him. His heart knew the sender of it before he had
seen the handwriting. Four pairs of eyes, fixed on him with
undisguised curiosity, waited for him to read it, clutching at
the hope that this interruption might take them out of their
usual boredom. He placed the letter by his plate, and would
not open it, pretending carelessly that he knew what it was
about. But his brothers, annoyed, would not believe it, and
went on prying at it; and so he was in tortures until the meal
was ended. Then he was free to lock himself up in his room.
His heart was beating so that he almost tore the letter as he
opened it. He trembled to think what might be in it; but

as soon as he had glanced over the first words he was filled with joy.

A few very affectionate words. Minna was writing to him by stealth. She called him "Dear *Christlein,*" and told him that she had wept much, had looked at the star every evening, that she had been to Frankfort, which was a splendid town, where there were wonderful shops, but that she had never bothered about anything because she was thinking of him. She reminded him that he had sworn to be faithful to her, and not to see anybody while she was away, so that he might think only of her. She wanted him to work all the time while she was gone, so as to make himself famous, and her too. She ended by asking him if he remembered the little room where they had said good-bye on the morning when she had left him: she assured him that she would be there still in thought, and that she would still say good-bye to him in the same way. She signed herself, " Eternally yours! Eternally! . . ." and she had added a postscript bidding him buy a straw hat instead of his ugly felt—all the distinguished people there were wearing them—a coarse straw hat, with a broad blue ribbon.

Jean-Christophe read the letter four times before he could quite take it all in. He was so overwhelmed that he could not even be happy; and suddenly he felt so tired that he lay down and read and re-read the letter and kissed it again and again. He put it under his pillow, and his hand was forever making sure that it was there. An ineffable sense of well-being permeated his whole soul. He slept all through the night.

His life became more tolerable. He had ever sweet, soaring thoughts of Minna. He set about answering her; but he could not write freely to her; he had to hide his feelings: that was painful and difficult for him. He continued clumsily to conceal his love beneath formulæ of ceremonious politeness, which he always used in an absurd fashion.

When he had sent it he awaited Minna's reply, and only lived in expectation of it. To win patience he tried to go for walks and to read. But his thoughts were only of Minna: he went on crazily repeating her name over and over again; he was so abject in his love and worship of her name that he carried everywhere with him a volume of Lessing, because the

name of Minna occurred in it, and every day when he left
the theater he went a long distance out of his way so as to
pass a mercery shop, on whose signboard the five adored letters
were written.

He reproached himself for wasting time when she had bid
him so urgently to work, so as to make her famous. The naïve
vanity of her request touched him, as a mark of her confidence
in him. He resolved, by way of fulfilling it, to write a work
which should be not only dedicated, but consecrated, to her.
He could not have written any other at that time. Hardly
had the scheme occurred to him than musical ideas rushed in
upon him. It was like a flood of water accumulated in a
reservoir for several months, until it should suddenly rush down,
breaking all its dams. He did not leave his room for a week.
Louisa left his dinner at the door; for he did not allow even
her to enter.

He wrote a quintette for clarionet and strings. The first
movement was a poem of youthful hope and desire; the last
a lover's joke, in which Jean-Christophe's wild humor peeped
out. But the whole work was written for the sake of the second
movement, the *larghetto,* in which Jean-Christophe had depicted
an ardent and ingenuous little soul, which was, or was meant
to be, a portrait of Minna. No one would have recognized it,
least of all herself; but the great thing was that it was perfectly
recognizable to himself; and he had a thrill of pleasure in the
illusion of feeling that he had caught the essence of his beloved.
No work had ever been so easily or happily written; it was an
outlet for the excess of love which the parting had stored up
in him; and at the same time his care for the work of art, the
effort necessary to dominate and concentrate his passion into
a beautiful and clear form, gave him a healthiness of mind, a
balance in his faculties, which gave him a sort of physical
delight—a sovereign enjoyment known to every creative artist.
While he is creating he escapes altogether from the slavery of
desire and sorrow; he becomes then master in his turn; and
all that gave him joy or suffering seems then to him to be
only the fine play of his will. Such moments are too short;
for when they are done he finds about him, more heavy than
ever, the chains of reality.

While Jean-Christophe was busy with his work he hardly had time to think of his parting from Minna; he was living with her. Minna was no longer in Minna; she was in himself. But when he had finished he found that he was alone, more alone than before, more weary, exhausted by the effort; he remembered that it was a fortnight since he had written to Minna and that she had not replied.

He wrote to her again, and this time he could not bring himself altogether to exercise the constraint which he had imposed on himself for the first letter. He reproached Minna jocularly—for he did not believe it himself—with having forgotten him. He scolded her for her laziness and teased her affectionately. He spoke of his work with much mystery, so as to rouse her curiosity, and because he wished to keep it as a surprise for her when she returned. He described minutely the hat that he had bought; and he told how, to carry out the little despot's orders—for he had taken all her commands literally—he did not go out at all, and said that he was ill as an excuse for refusing invitations. He did not add that he was even on bad terms with the Grand Duke, because, in excess of zeal, he had refused to go to a party at the Palace to which he had been invited. The whole letter was full of a careless joy, and conveyed those little secrets so dear to lovers. He imagined that Minna alone had the key to them, and thought himself very clever, because he had carefully replaced every word of love with words of friendship.

After he had written he felt comforted for a moment; first, because the letter had given him the illusion of conversation with his absent fair, but chiefly because he had no doubt but that Minna would reply to it at once. He was very patient for the three days which he had allowed for the post to take his letter to Minna and bring back her answer; but when the fourth day had passed he began once more to find life difficult. He had no energy or interest in things, except during the hour before the post's arrival. Then he was trembling with impatience. He became superstitious, and looked for the smallest sign—the crackling of the fire, a chance word—to give him an assurance that the letter would come. Once that hour was passed he would collapse again. No more work, no more walks;

the only object of his existence was to wait for the next post, and all his energy was expended in finding strength to wait for so long. But when evening came, and all hope was gone for the day, then he was crushed; it seemed to him that he could never live until the morrow, and he would stay for hours, sitting at his table, without speaking or thinking, without even the power to go to bed, until some remnant of his will would take him off to it; and he would sleep heavily, haunted by stupid dreams, which made him think that the night would never end.

This continual expectation became at length a physical torture, an actual illness. Jean-Christophe went so far as to suspect his father, his brother, even the postman, of having taken the letter and hidden it from him. He was racked with uneasiness. He never doubted Minna's fidelity for an instant. If she did not write, it must be because she was ill, dying, perhaps dead. Then he rushed to his pen and wrote a third letter, a few heartrending lines, in which he had no more thought of guarding his feelings than of taking care with his spelling. The time for the post to go was drawing near; he had crossed out and smudged the sheet as he turned it over, dirtied the envelope as he closed it. No matter! He could not wait until the next post. He ran and hurled his letter into the box and waited in mortal agony. On the next night but one he had a clear vision of Minna, ill, calling to him; he got up, and was on the point of setting out on foot to go to her. But where? Where should he find her?

On the fourth morning Minna's letter came at last—hardly a half-sheet—cold and stiff. Minna said that she did not understand what could have filled him with such stupid fears, that she was quite well, that she had no time to write, and begged him not to get so excited in future, and not to write any more.

Jean-Christophe was stunned. He never doubted Minna's sincerity. He blamed himself; he thought that Minna was justly annoyed by the impudent and absurd letters that he had written. He thought himself an idiot, and beat at his head with his fist. But it was all in vain; he was forced to feel that Minna did not love him as much as he loved her.

The days that followed were so mournful that it is impossible to describe them. Nothingness cannot be described. Deprived of the only boon that made living worth while for him—his letters to Minna—Jean-Christophe now only lived mechanically, and the only thing which interested him at all was when in the evening, as he was going to bed, he ticked off on the calendar, like a schoolboy, one of the interminable days which lay between himself and Minna's return. The day of the return was past. They ought to have been at home a week. Feverish excitement had succeeded Jean-Christophe's prostration. Minna had promised when she left to advise him of the day and hour of their arrival. He waited from moment to moment to go and meet them; and he tied himself up in a web of guesses as to the reasons for their delay.

One evening one of their neighbors, a friend of his grandfather, Fischer, the furniture dealer, came in to smoke and chat with Melchior after dinner as he often did. Jean-Christophe, in torment, was going up to his room after waiting for the postman to pass when a word made him tremble. Fischer said that next day he had to go early in the morning to the Kerichs' to hang up the curtains. Jean-Christophe stopped dead, and asked:

" Have they returned? "

" You wag! You know that as well as I do," said old Fischer roguishly. " Fine weather! They came back the day before yesterday."

Jean-Christophe heard no more; he left the room, and got ready to go out. His mother, who for some time had secretly been watching him without his knowing it, followed him into the lobby, and asked him timidly where he was going. He made no answer, and went out. He was hurt.

He ran to the Kerichs' house. It was nine o'clock in the evening. They were both in the drawing-room and did not appear to be surprised to see him. They said " Good-evening " quietly. Minna was busy writing, and held out her hand over the table and went on with her letter, vaguely asking him for his news. She asked him to forgive her discourtesy, and pretended to be listening to what he said, but she interrupted him to ask something of her mother. He had prepared touching words concerning all that he had suffered during her absence; he could hardly summon a few words; no one was interested in them, and he had not the heart to go on—it all rang so false.

When Minna had finished her letter she took up some work, and, sitting a little away from him, began to tell him about her travels. She talked about the pleasant weeks she had spent —riding on horseback, country-house life, interesting society; she got excited gradually, and made allusions to events and people whom Jean-Christophe did not know, and the memory of them made her mother and herself laugh. Jean-Christophe felt that he was a stranger during the story; he did not know how to take it, and laughed awkwardly. He never took his eyes from Minna's face, beseeching her to look at him, imploring her to throw him a glance for alms. But when she did look at him—which was not often, for she addressed herself more to her mother than to him—her eyes, like her voice, were cold and indifferent. Was she so constrained because of her mother, or was it that he did not understand? He wished to speak to her alone, but Frau von Kerich never left them for a moment. He tried to bring the conversation round to some subject interesting to himself; he spoke of his work and his plans; he was dimly conscious that Minna was evading him, and instinctively he tried to interest her in himself. Indeed, she seemed to listen attentively enough; she broke in upon his narrative with various interjections, which were never very apt, but always seemed to be full of interest. But just as he was beginning to hope once more, carried off his feet by one of her charming smiles, he saw Minna put her little hand to her lips and yawn. He broke off short. She saw that, and asked his pardon amiably, saying that she was tired. He got up, thinking that they would persuade him to stay, but they said nothing. He spun out his " Good-bye," and waited for a word to ask him to come again next day; there was no suggestion of it. He had to go. Minna did not take him to the door. She held out her hand to him—an indifferent hand that drooped limply in his—and he took his leave of them in the middle of the room.

He went home with terror in his heart. Of the Minna of two months before, of his beloved Minna, nothing was left. What had happened? What had become of her? For a poor boy who has never yet experienced the continual change, the complete disappearance, and the absolute renovation of living souls, of which the majority are not so much souls as collections of souls in succession changing and dying away continually, the simple truth was too cruel for him to be able to believe it. He rejected the idea of it in terror, and tried to persuade himself that he had not been able to see properly, and that Minna was just the same. He decided to go again to the house next morning, and to talk to her at all costs.

He did not sleep. Through the night he counted one after another the chimes of the clock. From one o'clock on he was rambling round the Kerichs' house; he entered it as soon as he could. He did not see Minna, but Frau von Kerich. Always busy and an early riser, she was watering the pots of flowers on the veranda. She gave a mocking cry when she saw Jean-Christophe.

"Ah!" she said. "It is you! . . . I am glad you have come. I have something to talk to you about. Wait a moment. . . ."

She went in for a moment to put down her watering can and to dry her hands, and came back with a little smile as she saw Jean-Christophe's discomfiture; he was conscious of the approach of disaster.

"Come into the garden," she said; "we shall be quieter."

In the garden that was full still of his love he followed Frau von Kerich. She did not hasten to speak, and enjoyed the boy's uneasiness.

"Let us sit here," she said at last. They were sitting on the seat in the place where Minna had held up her lips to him on the eve of her departure.

"I think you know what is the matter," said Frau von Kerich, looking serious so as to complete his confusion. "I should never have thought it of you, Jean-Christophe. I thought you a serious boy. I had every confidence in you. I should never have thought that you would abuse it to try and turn my daughter's head. She was in your keeping. You ought to have shown respect for her, respect for me, respect for your-self."

There was a light irony in her accents. Frau von Kerich attached not the least importance to this childish love affair; but Jean-Christophe was not conscious of it, and her reproaches, which he took, as he took everything, tragically, went to his heart.

"But, Madam . . . but, Madam . . ." he stammered, with tears in his eyes, "I have never abused your confidence. . . . Please do not think that. . . . I am not a bad man, that I swear! . . . I love Fräulein Minna. I love her with all my soul, and I wish to marry her."

Frau von Kerich smiled.

"No, my poor boy," she said, with that kindly smile in which was so much disdain, as at last he was to understand, "no, it is impossible; it is just a childish folly."

"Why? Why?" he asked.

He took her hands, not believing that she could be speaking seriously, and almost reassured by the new softness in her voice. She smiled still, and said:

"Because . . ."

He insisted. With ironical deliberation—she did not take him altogether seriously—she told him that he had no fortune, that Minna had different tastes. He protested that that made no difference; that he would be rich, famous; that he would win honors, money, all that Minna could desire. Frau von Kerich looked skeptical; she was amused by his self-confidence, and only shook her head by way of saying no. But he stuck to it.

"No, Jean-Christophe," she said firmly, "no. It is not worth arguing. It is impossible. It is not only a question of money. So many things! The position . . ."

She had no need to finish. That was a needle that pierced to his very marrow. His eyes were opened. He saw the irony of the friendly smile, he saw the coldness of the kindly look, he understood suddenly what it was that separated him from this woman whom he loved as a son, this woman who seemed to treat him like a mother; he was conscious of all that was patronizing and disdainful in her affection. He got up. He was pale. Frau von Kerich went on talking to him in her caressing voice, but it was the end; he heard no more the music of the words; he perceived under every word the falseness of that elegant soul. He could not answer a word. He went. Everything about him was going round and round.

When he regained his room he flung himself on his bed, and gave way to a fit of anger and injured pride, just as he used to do when he was a little boy. He bit his pillow; he crammed his handkerchief into his mouth, so that no one should hear him crying. He hated Frau von Kerich. He hated Minna. He despised them mightily. It seemed to him that he had been insulted, and he trembled with shame and rage. He had to reply, to take immediate action. If he could not avenge himself he would die.

He got up, and wrote an idiotically violent letter:

"MADAM,—

"I do not know if, as you say, you have been deceived in me. But I do know that I have been cruelly deceived in you. I thought that you were my friends. You said so. You pretended to be so, and I loved you more than my life. I see now that it was all a lie, that your affection for me was only a sham; you made use of me. I amused you, provided you with entertainment, made music for you. I was your servant. Your servant: that I am not! I am no man's servant!

"You have made me feel cruelly that I had no right to love your daughter. Nothing in the world can prevent my heart from loving where it loves, and if I am not your equal in rank, I am as noble as you. It is the heart that ennobles a man. If I am not a Count, I have perhaps more honor than many Counts. Lackey or Count, when a man insults me, I despise him. I despise as much any one who pretends to be noble, and is not noble of soul.

"Farewell! You have mistaken me. You have deceived me. I detest you!

"He who, in spite of you, loves, and will love till death, Fräulein Minna, *because she is his,* and nothing can take her from him."

Hardly had he thrown his letter into the box than he was
filled with terror at what he had done.   He tried not to think
of it, but certain phrases cropped up in his memory; he was
in a cold sweat as he thought of Frau von Kerich reading those
enormities.   At first he was upheld by his very despair, but
next day he saw that his letter could only bring about a final
separation from Minna, and that seemed to him the direst of
misfortunes.   He still hoped that Frau von Kerich, who knew
his violent fits, would not take it seriously, that she would only
reprimand him severely, and—who knows?—that she would
be touched perhaps by the sincerity of his passion.   One word,
and he would have thrown himself at her feet.   He waited for
five days.   Then came a letter.   She said:

" DEAR SIR,—
    " Since, as you say, there has been a misunderstanding be-
tween us, it would be wise not any further to prolong it.   I
should be very sorry to force upon you a relationship which
has become painful to you.   You will think it natural, therefore, that we should break it off.   I hope that you will in time
to come have no lack of other friends who will be able to
appreciate you as you wish to be appreciated.   I have no doubt
as to your future, and from a distance shall, with sympathy,
follow your progress in your musical career.   Kind regards.
                              " JOSEPHA VON KERICH."

The most bitter reproaches would have been less cruel.   Jean-
Christophe saw that he was lost.   It is possible to reply to an
unjust accusation.   But what is to be done against the negative-
ness of such polite indifference?   He raged against it.   He
thought that he would never see Minna again, and he could
not bear it.   He felt how little all the pride in the world weighs
against a little love.   He forgot his dignity; he became cowardly; he wrote more letters, in which he implored forgiveness.
They were no less stupid than the letter in which he had railed
against her.   They evoked no response.   And everything was said.

He nearly died of it.   He thought of killing himself.   He
thought of murder.   At least, he imagined that he thought of

it. He was possessed by incendiary and murderous desires.
People have little idea of the paroxysm of love or hate which
sometimes devours the hearts of children. It was the most
terrible crisis of his childhood. It ended his childhood. It
stiffened his will. But it came near to breaking it forever.

He found life impossible. He would sit for hours with his
elbows on the window-sill looking down into the courtyard,
and dreaming, as he used to when he was a little boy, of some
means of escaping from the torture of life when it became too
great. The remedy was there, under his eyes. Immediate . . .
immediate? How could one know? . . . Perhaps after hours
—centuries—horrible sufferings! . . . But so utter was his
childish despair that he let himself be carried away by the
giddy round of such thoughts.

Louisa saw that he was suffering. She could not gauge
exactly what was happening to him, but her instinct gave her
a dim warning of danger. She tried to approach her son, to
discover his sorrow, so as to console him. But the poor woman
had lost the habit of talking intimately to Jean-Christophe. For
many years he had kept his thoughts to himself, and she had
been too much taken up by the material cares of life to find time
to discover them or divine them. Now that she would so gladly
have come to his aid she knew not what to do. She hovered
about him like a soul in torment; she would gladly have found
words to bring him comfort, and she dared not speak for fear
of irritating him. And in spite of all her care she did irritate
him by her every gesture and by her very presence, for she
was not very adroit, and he was not very indulgent. And yet
he loved her; they loved each other. But so little is needed
to part two creatures who are dear to each other, and love each
other with all their hearts! A too violent expression, an awkward gesture, a harmless twitching of an eye or a nose, a
trick of eating, walking, or laughing, a physical constraint
which is beyond analysis. . . . You say that these things are
nothing, and yet they are all the world. Often they are enough
to keep a mother and a son, a brother and a brother, a friend
and a friend, who live in proximity to each other, forever
strangers to each other.

Jean-Christophe did not find in his mother's grief a sufficient

prop ... the crisis through which he was passing. Besides,
what is the affection of others to the egoism of passion preoccupied with itself?

One night when his family were sleeping, and he was sitting
by his desk, not thinking or moving, he was engulfed in his
perilous ideas, when a sound of footsteps resounded down the
little silent street, and a knock on the door brought him from
his stupor. There was a murmuring of thick voices. He
remembered that his father had not come in, and he thought
angrily that they were bringing him back drunk, as they had
done a week or two before, when they had found him lying in
the street. For Melchior had abandoned all restraint, and was
more and more the victim of his vice, though his athletic health
seemed not in the least to suffer from an excess and a recklessness which would have killed any other man. He ate enough
for four, drank until he dropped, passed whole nights out of
doors in icy rain, was knocked down and stunned in brawls,
and would get up again next day, with his rowdy gaiety, wanting
everybody about him to be gay too.

Louisa, hurrying up, rushed to open the door. Jean-Christophe, who had not budged, stopped his ears so as not to hear
Melchior's vicious voice and the tittering comments of the
neighbors. . . .

. . . Suddenly a strange terror seized him; for no reason
he began to tremble, with his face hidden in his hands. And
on the instant a piercing cry made him raise his head. He
rushed to the door. . . .

In the midst of a group of men talking in low voices, in
the dark passage, lit only by the flickering light of a lantern,
lying, just as his grandfather had done, on a stretcher, was
a body dripping with water, motionless. Louisa was clinging
to it and sobbing. They had just found Melchior drowned in
the mill-race.

Jean-Christophe gave a cry. Everything else vanished; all
his other sorrows were swept aside. He threw himself on his
father's body by Louisa's side, and they wept together.

'Seated by the bedside, watching Melchior's last sleep, on
whose face was now a severe and solemn expression, he felt
the dark peace of death enter into his soul. His childish passion

was gone from him like a fit of fever; the icy breath of the
grave had taken it all away. Minna, his pride, his love, and
himself. . . . Alas! What misery! How small everything
showed by the side of this reality, the only reality—death!
Was it worth while to suffer so much, to desire so much, to
be so much put about to come in the end to that! . . .

He watched his father's sleep, and he was filled with an
infinite pity. He remembered the smallest of his acts of kindness and tenderness. For with all his faults Melchior was not
bad; there was much good in him. He loved his family. He
was honest. He had a little of the uncompromising probity of
the Kraffts, which, in all questions of morality and honor,
suffered no discussion, and never would admit the least of those
small moral impurities which so many people in society regard
not altogether as faults. He was brave, and whenever there
was any danger faced it with a sort of enjoyment. If he was
extravagant himself, he was so for others too; he could not bear
anybody to be sad, and very gladly gave away all that belonged
to him—and did not belong to him—to the poor devils he met
by the wayside. All his qualities appeared to Jean-Christophe
now, and he invented some of them, or exaggerated them. It
seemed to him that he had misunderstood his father. He reproached himself with not having loved him enough. He saw
him as broken by Life; he thought he heard that unhappy soul,
drifting, too weak to struggle, crying out for the life so uselessly lost. He heard that lamentable entreaty that had so cut
him to the heart one day:

"Jean-Christophe! Do not despise me!"

And he was overwhelmed by remorse. He threw himself on
the bed, and kissed the dead face and wept. And as he had
done that day, he said again:

"Dear father, I do not despise you. I love you. Forgive
me!"

But that piteous entreaty was not appeased, and went on:

"Do not despise me! Do not despise me!" And suddenly
Jean-Christophe saw himself lying in the place of the dead
man; he heard the terrible words coming from his own lips;
he felt weighing on his heart the despair of a useless life,
irreparably lost. And he thought in terror: "Ah! everything,

all the suffering, all the misery in the world, rather than come to that! . . ." How near he had been to it! Had he not all but yielded to the temptation to snap off his life himself, cowardly to escape his sorrow? ·As if all the sorrows, all betrayals, were not childish griefs beside the torture and the crime of self-betrayal, denial of faith, of self-contempt in death!

He saw that life was a battle without armistice, without mercy, in which he who wishes to be a man worthy of the name of a man must forever fight against whole armies of invisible enemies; against the murderous forces of Nature, uneasy desires, dark thoughts, treacherously leading him to degradation and destruction. He saw that he had been on the point of falling into the trap. He saw that happiness and love were only the friends of a moment to lead the heart to disarm and abdicate. And the little puritan of fifteen heard the voice of his God:

" Go, go, and never rest."

" But whither, Lord, shall I go? Whatsoever I do, whithersoever I go, is not the end always the same? Is not the end of all things in that? "

" Go on to Death, you who must die! Go and suffer, you who must suffer! You do not live to be happy. You live to fulfil my Law. Suffer; die. But be what you must be—a Man."

YOUTH

Christofori faciem die quacunque tueris,
Illa nempe die non morte mala morieris.

THE house was plunged in silence. Since Melchior's death everything seemed dead. Now that his loud voice was stilled, from morning to night nothing was heard but the wearisome murmuring of the river.

Christophe hurled himself into his work. He took a fiercely angry pleasure in self-castigation for having wished to be happy. To expressions of sympathy and kind words he made no reply, but was proud and stiff. Without a word he went about his daily task, and gave his lessons with icy politeness. His pupils who knew of his misfortune were shocked by his insensibility. But those who were older and had some experience of sorrow knew that this apparent coldness might, in a child, be used only to conceal suffering: and they pitied him. He was not grateful for their sympathy. Even music could bring him no comfort. He played without pleasure, and as a duty. It was as though he found a cruel joy in no longer taking pleasure in anything, or in persuading himself that he did not: in depriving himself of every reason for living, and yet going on.

His two brothers, terrified by the silence of the house of death, ran away from it as quickly as possible. Rodolphe went into the office of his uncle Theodore, and lived with him, and Ernest, after trying two or three trades, found work on one of the Rhine steamers plying between Mainz and Cologne, and he used to come back only when he wanted money. Christophe was left alone with his mother in the house, which was too large for them; and the meagerness of their resources, and the payment of certain debts which had been discovered after his father's death, forced them, whatever pain it might cost, to seek another more lowly and less expensive dwelling.

They found a little flat,—two or three rooms on the second

floor of a house in the Market Street. It was a noisy district in the middle of the town, far from the river, far from the trees, far from the country and all the familiar places. But they had to consult reason, not sentiment, and Christophe found in it a fine opportunity for gratifying his bitter creed of self-mortification. Besides, the owner of the house, old registrar Euler, was a friend of his grandfather, and knew the family: that was enough for Louisa, who was lost in her empty house, and was irresistibly drawn towards those who had known the creatures whom she had loved.

They got ready to leave. They took long draughts of the bitter melancholy of the last days passed by the sad, beloved fireside that was to be left forever. They dared hardly tell their sorrow: they were ashamed of it, or afraid. Each thought that they ought not to show their weakness to the other. At table, sitting alone in a dark room with half-closed shutters, they dared not raise their voices: they ate hurriedly and did not look at each other for fear of not being able to conceal their trouble. They parted as soon as they had finished. Christophe went back to his work; but as soon as he was free for a moment, he would come back, go stealthily home, and creep on tiptoe to his room or to the attic. Then he would shut the door, sit down in a corner on an old trunk or on the window-ledge, or stay there without thinking, letting the indefinable buzzing and humming of the old house, which trembled with the lightest tread, thrill through him. His heart would tremble with it. He would listen anxiously for the faintest breath in or out of doors, for the creaking of floors, for all the imperceptible familiar noises: he knew them all. He would lose consciousness, his thoughts would be filled with the images of the past, and he would issue from his stupor only at the sound of St. Martin's clock, reminding him that it was time to go.

In the room below him he could hear Louisa's footsteps passing softly to and fro, then for hours she could not be heard; she made no noise. Christophe would listen intently. He would go down, a little uneasy, as one is for a long time after a great misfortune. He would push the door ajar; Louisa would turn her back on him; she would be sitting in front of a cupboard in the midst of a heap of things—rags, old belongings, odd garments, treasures, which she had brought out intending to sort them. But she had no strength for it; everything reminded her of something; she would turn and turn it in her hands and begin to dream; it would drop from her hands; she would stay for hours together with her arms hanging down, lying back exhausted in a chair, given up to a stupor of sorrow.

Poor Louisa was now spending most of her life in the past— that sad past, which had been very niggardly of joy for her; but she was so used to suffering that she was still grateful for the least tenderness shown to her, and the pale lights which had shone here and there in the drab days of her life, were still enough to make them bright. All the evil that Melchior had done her was forgotten; she remembered only the good. Her marriage had been the great romance of her life. If Melchior had been drawn into it by a caprice, of which he had quickly repented, she had given herself with her whole heart; she thought that she was loved as much as she had loved; and to Melchior she was ever most tenderly grateful. She did not try to understand what he had become in the sequel. Incapable of seeing reality as it is, she only knew how to bear it as it is, humbly and honestly, as a woman who has no need of understanding life in order to be able to live. What she could not explain, she left to God for explanation. In her singular piety, she put upon God the responsibility for all the injustice that she had suffered at the hands of Melchior and the others, and only visited them with the good that they had given her. And so her life of misery had left her with no bitter memory. She only felt worn out—weak as she was—by those years of privation and fatigue. And now that Melchior was no longer there, now that two of her sons were gone from their home, and the third seemed to be able to do without her, she had lost all heart for action; she was tired, sleepy; her will was stupefied. She was going through one of those crises of neurasthenia which often come upon active and industrious people in the decline of life, when some unforeseen event deprives them of every reason for living. She had not the heart even to finish the stocking she was knitting, to tidy the drawer in which she was looking, to get up to shut the window; she would sit there, without a thought, without strength—save for recollection.

She was conscious of her collapse, and was ashamed of it or blushed for it; she tried to hide it from her son; and Christophe, wrapped up in the egoism of his own grief, never noticed it. No doubt he was often secretly impatient with his mother's slowness in speaking, and acting, and doing the smallest thing; but different though her ways were from her usual activity, he never gave a thought to the matter until then.

Suddenly on that day it came home to him for the first time when he surprised her in the midst of her rags, turned out on the floor, heaped up at her feet, in her arms, and in her lap. Her neck was drawn out, her head was bowed, her face was stiff and rigid. When she heard him come in she started; her white cheeks were suffused with red; with an instinctive movement she tried to hide the things she was holding, and muttered with an awkward smile:

"You see, I was sorting . . ."

The sight of the poor soul stranded among the relics of the past cut to his heart, and he was filled with pity. But he spoke with a bitter asperity and seemed to scold, to drag her from her apathy:

"Come, come, mother; you must not stay there, in the middle of all that dust, with the room all shut up! It is not good for you. You must pull yourself together, and have done with all this."

"Yes," said she meekly.

She tried to get up to put the things back in the drawer. But she sat down again at once and listlessly let them fall from her hands.

"Oh! I can't . . . I can't," she moaned. "I shall never finish!"

He was frightened. He leaned over her. He caressed her forehead with his hands.

"Come, mother, what is it?" he said. "Shall I help you? Are you ill?"

She did not answer. She gave a sort of stifled sob. He took her hands, and knelt down by her side, the better to see her in the dusky room.

"Mother!" he said anxiously.

Louisa laid her head on his shoulder and burst into tears.

"My boy, my boy," she cried, holding close to him. "My boy! . . . You will not leave me? Promise me that you will not leave me?"

His heart was torn with pity.

"No, mother, no. I will not leave you. What made you think of such a thing?"

"I am so unhappy! They have all left me, all. . . ."

She pointed to the things all about her, and he did not know whether she was speaking of them or of her sons and the dead.

"You will stay with me? You will not leave me? . . . What should I do, if you went too?"

"I will not go, I tell you; we will stay together. Don't cry. I promise."

She went on weeping. She could not stop herself. He dried her eyes with his handkerchief.

"What is it, mother dear? Are you in pain?"

"I don't know; I don't know what it is." She tried to calm herself and to smile.

"I do try to be sensible. I do. But just nothing at all makes me cry. . . . You see, I'm doing it again. . . . Forgive me. I am so stupid. I am old. I have no strength left. I have no taste for anything any more. I am no good for anything. I wish I were buried with all the rest. . . ."

He held her to him, close, like a child.

"Don't worry, mother; be calm; don't think about it. . . ."

Gradually she grew quiet.

"It is foolish. I am ashamed. . . . But what is it? What is it?"

She who had always worked so hard could not understand why her strength had suddenly snapped, and she was humiliated to the very depths of her being. He pretended not to see it.

"A little weariness, mother," he said, trying to speak carelessly. "It is nothing; you will see; it is nothing."

But he too was anxious. From his childhood he had been accustomed to see her brave, resigned, in silence withstanding every test. And he was astonished to see her suddenly broken: he was afraid.

He helped her to sort the things scattered on the floor. Every now and then she would linger over something, but he would gently take it from her hands, and she suffered him.

From that time on he took pains to be more with her. As soon as he had finished his work, instead of shutting himself up in his room, as he loved to do, he would return to her. He felt her loneliness and that she was not strong enough to be left alone: there was danger in leaving her alone.

He would sit by her side in the evening near the open window looking on to the road. The view would slowly disappear. The people were returning home. Little lights appeared in the houses far off. They had seen it all a thousand times. But soon they would see it no more. They would talk disjointedly. They would point out to each other the smallest of the familiar incidents and expectations of the evening, always with fresh interest. They would have long intimate silences, or Louisa, for no apparent reason, would tell some reminiscence, some disconnected story that passed through her mind. Her tongue was loosed a little now that she felt that she was with one who loved her. She tried hard to talk. It was difficult for her, for she had grown used to living apart from her family; she looked upon her sons and her husband as too clever to talk to her, and she had never dared to join in their conversation. Christophe's tender care was a new thing to her and infinitely sweet, though it made her afraid. She deliberated over her words; she found it difficult to express herself; her sentences were left unfinishd and obscure. Sometimes she was ashamed of what she was saying; she would look at her son, and stop in the middle of her narrative. But he would press her hand, and she would be reassured. He was filled with love and pity for the childish, motherly creature, to whom he had turned when he was a child, and now she turned to him for support. And he took a melancholy pleasure in her prattle, that had no interest for anybody but himself, in her trivial memories of a life that had always been joyless and mediocre, though it seemed to Louisa to be of infinite worth. Sometimes he would try to interrupt her; he was afraid that her memories would make her sadder than ever, and he would urge her to sleep. She would understand what he was at, and would say with gratitude in her eyes:

" No. I assure you, it does one good; let us stay a little longer."

They would stay until the night was far gone and the neigh-bors were abed. Then they would say good-night, she a little comforted by being rid of some of her trouble, he with a heavy heart under this new burden added to that which already he had to bear.

The day came for their departure. On the night before they stayed longer than usual in the unlighted room. They did not speak. Every now and then Louisa moaned: " Fear God! Fear God! " Christophe tried to keep her attention fixed on the thousand details of the morrow's removal. She would not go to bed until he gently compelled her. But he went up to his room and did not go to bed for a long time. When leaning out of the window he tried to gaze through the darkness to see for the last time the moving shadows of the river beneath the house. He heard the wind in the tall trees in Minna's garden. The sky was black. There was no one in the street. A cold rain was just falling. The weathercocks creaked. In a house near by a child was crying. The night weighed with an overwhelming heaviness upon the earth and upon his soul. The dull chiming of the hours, the cracked note of the halves and quarters, dropped one after another into the grim silence, broken only by the sound of the rain on the roofs and the cobbles.

When Christophe at last made up his mind to go to bed, chilled in body and soul, he heard the window below him shut. And, as he lay, he thought sadly that it is cruel for the poor to dwell on the past, for they have no right to have a past, like the rich: they have no home, no corner of the earth wherein to house their memories: their joys, their sor-rows, all their days, are scattered in the wind.

Next day in beating rain they moved their scanty furniture to their new dwelling. Fischer, the old furniture dealer, lent them a cart and a pony; he came and helped them himself. But they could not take everything, for the rooms to which they were going were much smaller than the old. Chris-tophe had to make his mother leave the oldest and most useless of their belongings. It was not altogether easy; the least thing had its worth for her: a shaky table, a broken chair, she wished to leave nothing behind. Fischer, fortified by the authority of his old friendship with Jean Michel, had to join Christophe in complaining, and, good-fellow that he was and understanding her grief, had even to promise to keep some of her precious rubbish for her against the day when she should want it again. Then she agreed to tear herself away.

The two brothers had been told of the removal, but Ernest came on the night before to say that he could not be there, and Rodolphe appeared for a moment about noon; he watched them load the furniture, gave some advice, and went away again looking mightily busy.

The procession set out through the muddy streets. Christophe led the horse, which slipped on the greasy cobbles. Louisa walked by her son's side, and tried to shelter him from the rain. And so they had a melancholy homecoming in the damp rooms, that were made darker than ever by the dull light coming from the lowering sky. They could not have fought against the depression that was upon them had it not been for the attentions of their landlord and his family. But, when the cart had driven away, as night fell, leaving the furniture heaped up in the room; and Christophe and Louisa were sitting, worn out, one on a box, the other on a sack; they heard a little dry cough on the staircase; there was a knock at the door. Old Euler came in. He begged pardon elaborately for disturbing his guests, and said that by way of celebrating their first evening he hoped that they would be kind enough to sup with himself and his family. Louisa, stunned by her sorrow, wished to refuse. Christophe was not much more tempted than she by this friendly gathering, but the old man insisted and Christophe, thinking that it would be better for his mother not to spend their first evening in their new home alone with her thoughts, made her accept.

They went down to the floor below, where they found the whole family collected: the old man, his daughter, his son-in-law, Vogel, and his grandchildren, a boy and a girl, both a little younger than Christophe. They clustered around their guests, bade them welcome, asked if they were tired, if they were pleased with their rooms, if they needed anything; putting so many questions that Christophe in bewilderment could make nothing of them, for everybody spoke at once. The soup was placed on the table; they sat down. But the noise went on. Amalia, Euler's daughter, had set herself at once to acquaint Louisa with local details: with the topography of the district, the habits and advantages of the house, the time when the milkman called, the time when she got up, the various trades-people and the prices that she paid. She did not stop until she had explained everything. Louisa, half-asleep, tried hard to take an interest in the information, but the remarks which she ventured showed that she had understood not a word, and provoked Amalia to indignant exclamations and repetition of every detail. Old Euler, a clerk, tried to explain to Christophe the difficulties of a musical career. Christophe's other neighbor, Rosa, Amalia's daughter, never stopped talking from the moment when they sat down,—so volubly that she had no time to breathe; she lost her breath in the middle of a sentence, but at once she was off again. Vogel was gloomy and complained of the food, and there were embittered arguments on the subject. Amalia, Euler, the girl, left off talking to take part in the discussion; and there were endless controversies as to whether there was too much salt in the stew or not enough; they called each other to witness, and, naturally, no two opinions were the same. Each despised his neighbor's taste, and thought only his own healthy and reasonable. They might have gone on arguing until the Last Judgment.

But, in the end, they all joined in crying out upon the bad weather. They all commiserated Louisa and Christophe upon their troubles, and in terms which moved him greatly they praised him for his courageous conduct. They took great pleasure in recalling not only the misfortunes of their guests, but also their own, and those of their friends and all their acquaintance, and they all agreed that the good are always unhappy, and that there is joy only for the selfish and dishonest. They decided that life is sad, that it is quite useless, and that they were all better dead, were it not the indubitable will of God that they should go on living so as to suffer. As these ideas came very near to Christophe's actual pessimism, he thought the better of his landlord, and closed his eyes to their little oddities.

When he went upstairs again with his mother to the disordered rooms, they were weary and sad, but they felt a little less lonely; and while Christophe lay awake through the night, for he could not sleep because of his weariness and the noise of the neighborhood, and listened to the heavy carts shaking the walls, and the breathing of the family sleeping below, he tried to persuade himself that he would be, if not happy, at least less unhappy here, with these good people—a little tiresome, if the truth be told—who suffered from like misfortunes, who seemed to understand him, and whom, he thought, he understood.

But when at last he did fall asleep, he was roused unpleasantly at dawn by the voices of his neighbors arguing, and the creaking of a pump worked furiously by some one who was in a hurry to swill the yard and the stairs.

Justus Euler was a little bent old man, with uneasy, gloomy eyes, a red face, all lines and pimples, gap-toothed, with an unkempt beard, with which he was forever fidgeting with his hands. Very honest, quite able, profoundly moral, he had been on quite good terms with Christophe's grandfather. He was said to be like him. And, in truth, he was of the same generation and brought up with the same principles; but he lacked Jean Michel's strong physique, that is, while he was of the same opinion on many points, fundamentally he was hardly at all like him, for it is temperament far more than ideas that makes a man, and whatever the divisions, fictitious or real, marked between men by intellect, the great divisions between men and men are into those who are healthy and those who are not. Old Euler was not a healthy man. He talked morality, like Jean Michel, but his morals were not the same as Jean Michel's; he had not his sound stomach, his lungs, or his jovial strength. Everything in Euler and his family was built on a more parsimonious and niggardly plan. He had been an official for forty years, was now retired, and suffered from that melancholy that comes from inactivity and weighs so heavily upon old men, who have not made provision in their inner life for their last years. All his habits, natural and acquired, all the habits of his trade had given him a meticulous and peevish quality, which was reproduced to a certain extent in each of his children.

His son-in-law, Vogel, a clerk at the Chancery Court, was fifty years old. Tall, strong, almost bald, with gold spectacles, fairly good-looking, he considered himself ill, and no doubt was so, although obviously he did not have the diseases which he thought he had, but only a mind soured by the stupidity of his calling and a body ruined to a certain extent by his sedentary life. Very industrious, not without merit, even cultured up to a point, he was a victim of our ridiculous modern life, or like so many clerks, locked up in their offices, he had succumbed to the demon of hypochondria. One of those unfortunates whom Goethe called " *ein trauriger, ungriechischer Hypochondrist* "—" a gloomy and un-Greek hypochondriac,"— and pitied, though he took good care to avoid them.

Amalia was neither the one nor the other. Strong, loud, and active, she wasted no sympathy on her husband's jeremiads; she used to shake him roughly. But no human strength can bear up against living together, and when in a household one or other is neurasthenic, the chances are that in time they will both be so. In vain did Amalia cry out upon Vogel, in vain did she go on protesting either from habit or because it was necessary; next moment she herself was lamenting her condition more loudly even than he, and, passing imperceptibly from scolding to lamentation, she did him no good; she increased his ills tenfold by loudly singing chorus to his follies. In the end not only did she crush the unhappy Vogel, terrified by the proportions assumed by his own outcries sent sounding back by this echo, but she crushed everybody, even herself. In her turn she caught the trick of unwarrantably bemoaning her health, and her father's, and her daughter's, and her son's. It became a mania; by constant repetition she came to believe what she said. She took the least chill tragically; she was uneasy and worried about everybody. More than that, when they were well, she still worried, because of the sickness that was bound to come. So life was passed in perpetual fear. Outside that they were all in fairly good health, and it seemed as though their state of continual moaning and groaning did serve to keep them well. They all ate and slept and worked as usual, and the life of this household was not relaxed for it all. Amalia's activity was not satisfied with working from morning to night up and down the house; they all had to toil with her, and there was forever a moving of furniture, a washing of floors, a polishing of wood, a sound of voices, footsteps, quivering, movement.

The two children, crushed by such loud authority, leaving nobody alone, seemed to find it natural enough to submit to it. The boy, Leonard, was good looking, though insignificant of feature, and stiff in manner. The girl, Rosa, fair-haired, with pretty blue eyes, gentle and affectionate, would have been pleasing especially with the freshness of her delicate complexion, and her kind manner, had her nose not been quite so large or so awkwardly placed; it made her face heavy and gave her a foolish expression. She was like a girl of Holbein, in the gallery at Basle—the daughter of burgomaster Meier—sitting, with eyes cast down, her hands on her knees, her fair hair falling down to her shoulders, looking embarrassed and ashamed of her uncomely nose. But so far Rosa had not been troubled by it, and it never had broken in upon her inexhaustible chatter. Always her shrill voice was heard in the house telling stories, always breathless, as though she had no time to say everything, always excited and animated, in spite of the protests which she drew from her mother, her father, and even her grandfather, exasperated, not so much because she was forever talking as because she prevented them talking themselves. For these good people, kind, loyal, devoted—the very cream of good people—had almost all the virtues, but they lacked one virtue which is capital, and is the charm of life: the virtue of silence.

Christophe was in tolerant mood. His sorrow had softened his intolerant and emphatic temper. His experience of the cruel indifference of the elegant made him more conscious of the worth of these honest folk, graceless and devilish tiresome, who had yet an austere conception of life, and because they lived joylessly, seemed to him to live without weakness. Having decided that they were excellent, and that he ought to like them, like the German that he was, he tried to persuade himself that he did in fact like them. But he did not succeed; he lacked that easy Germanic idealism, which does not wish to see, and does not see, what would be displeasing to its sight, for fear of disturbing the very proper tranquillity of its judgment and the pleasantness of its existence. On the contrary, he never was so conscious of the defects of these people as when he loved them, when he wanted to love them absolutely without reservation; it was a sort of unconscious loyalty, and an inexorable demand for truth, which, in spite of himself, made him more clear-sighted, and more exacting, with what was dearest to him. And it was not long before he began to be irritated by the oddities of the family. They made no attempt to conceal them. Contrary to the usual habit they displayed every intolerable quality they possessed, and all the good in them was hidden. So Christophe told himself, for he judged himself to have been unjust, and tried to surmount his first impressions, and to discover in them the excellent qualities which they so carefully concealed.

He tried to converse with old Justus Euler, who asked nothing better. He had a secret sympathy with him, remembering that his grandfather had liked to praise him. But good old Jean Michel had more of the pleasant faculty of deceiving himself about his friends than Christophe, and Christophe soon saw that. In vain did he try to accept Euler's memories of his grandfather. He could only get from him a discolored caricature of Jean Michel, and scraps of talk that were utterly uninteresting. Euler's stories used invariably to begin with:

"As, I used to say to your poor grandfather . . ." He could remember nothing else. He had heard only what he had said himself.

Perhaps Jean Michel used only to listen in the same way. Most friendships are little more than arrangements for mutual satisfaction, so that each party may talk about himself to the other. But at least Jean Michel, however naïvely he used to give himself up to the delight of talking, had sympathy which he was always ready to lavish on all sides. He was interested in everything; he always regretted that he was no longer fifteen, so as to be able to see the marvelous inventions of the new generations, and to share their thoughts. He had the quality, perhaps the most precious in life, a curiosity always fresh, never changing with the years, born anew every morning. He had not the talent to turn this gift to account; but how many men of talent might envy him! Most men die at twenty or thirty; thereafter they are only reflections of themselves: for the rest of their lives they are aping themselves, repeating from day to day more and more mechanically and affectedly what they said and did and thought and loved when they were alive.

It was so long since old Euler had been alive, and he had been such a small thing then, that what was left of him now was very poor and rather ridiculous. Outside his former trade and his family life he knew nothing, and wished to know nothing. On every subject he had ideas ready-made, dating from his youth. He pretended to some knowledge of the arts, but he clung to certain hallowed names of men, about whom he was forever reiterating his emphatic formulæ: everything else was naught and had never been. When modern interests were mentioned he would not listen, and talked of something else. He declared that he loved music passionately, and he would ask Christophe to play. But as soon as Christophe, who had been caught once or twice, began to play, the old fellow would begin to talk loudly to his daughter, as though the music only increased his interest in everything but music. Christophe would get up exasperated in the middle of his piece, so one would notice it. There were only a few old airs—three or four—some very beautiful, others very ugly, but all equally sacred, which were privileged to gain comparative silence and absolute approval. With the very first notes the old man would go into ecstasies, tears would come to his eyes, not so much for the pleasure he was enjoying as for the pleasure which once he had enjoyed. In the end Christophe had a horror of these airs, though some of them, like the *Adelaïde* of Beethoven, were very dear to him; the old man was always humming the first bars of them, and never failed to declare, " There, that is music," contemptuously comparing it with " all the blessed modern music, in which there is no melody." Truth to tell, he knew nothing whatever about it.

His son-in-law was better educated and kept in touch with artistic movements: but that was even worse, for in his judgment there was always a disparaging tinge. He was lacking neither in taste nor intelligence; but he could not bring himself to admire anything modern. He would have disparaged Mozart and Beethoven, if they had been contemporary, just as he would have acknowledged the merits of Wagner and Richard Strauss had they been dead for a century. His discontented temper refused to allow that there might be great men living during his own lifetime; the idea was distasteful to him. He was so embittered by his wasted life that he insisted on pretending that every life was wasted, that it could not be otherwise, and that those who thought the opposite, or pretended to think so, were one of two things: fools or humbugs.

And so he never spoke of any new celebrity except in a tone of bitter irony, and as he was not stupid he never failed to discover at the first glance the weak or ridiculous sides of them. Any new name roused him to distrust; before he knew anything about the man he was inclined to criticise him—because he knew nothing about him. If he was sympathetic towards Christophe it was because he thought that the misanthropic boy found life as evil as he did himself, and that he was not a genius. Nothing so unites the small of soul in their suffering and discontent as the statement of their common impotence. Nothing so much restores the desire for health or life to those who are healthy and made for the joy of life as contact with the stupid pessimism of the mediocre and the sick, who, because they are not happy, deny the happiness of others. Christophe felt this. And yet these gloomy thoughts were familiar to him; but he was surprised to find them on Vogel's lips, where they were unrecognizable; more than that, they were repugnant to him; they offended him.

He was even more in revolt against Amalia's ways. The good creature did no more than practise Christophe's theories of duty. The word was upon her lips at every turn. She worked unceasingly, and wanted everybody to work as she did. Her work was never directed towards making herself and others happier; on the contrary. It almost seemed as though it was mainly intended to incommode everybody and to make life as disagreeable as possible so as to sanctify it. Nothing would induce her for a moment to relinquish her holy duties in the household, that sacro-sanct institution which in so many women takes the place of all other duties, social and moral. She would have thought herself lost had she not on the same day, at the same time, polished the wooden floors, washed the tiles, cleaned the door-handles, beaten the carpets, moved the chairs, the cupboards, the tables. She was ostentatious about it. It was as though it was a point of honor with her. And after all, is it not in much the same spirit that many women conceive and defend their honor? It is a sort of piece of furniture which they have to keep polished, a well waxed floor, cold, hard—and slippery.

The accomplishment of her task did not make Frau Vogel more amicable. She sacrificed herself to the trivialities of the household, as to a duty imposed by God. And she despised those who did not do as she did, those who rested, and were able to enjoy life a little in the intervals of work. She would go and rouse Louisa in her room when from time to time she sat down in the middle of her work to dream. Louisa would sigh, but she submitted to it with a half-shamed smile. Fortunately, Christophe knew nothing about it; Amalia used to wait until he had gone out before she made these irruptions into their rooms, and so far she had not directly attacked him; he would not have put up with it. When he was with her he was conscious of a latent hostility within himself. What he could least forgive her was the noise she made. He was maddened by it. When he was locked in his room—a little low room looking out on the yard—with the window hermetically sealed, in spite of the want of air, so as not to hear the clatter in the house, he could not escape from it. Involuntarily he was forced to listen attentively for the least sound coming up from below, and when the terrible voice which penetrated all the walls broke out again after a moment of silence he was filled with rage; he would shout, stamp with his foot, and roar insults at her through the wall. In the general uproar, no one ever noticed it; they thought he was composing. He would consign Frau Vogel to the depths of hell. He had no respect for her, nor esteem to check him. At such times it seemed to him that he would have preferred the loosest and most stupid of women, if only she did not talk, to cleverness, honesty, all the virtues, when they make too much noise.

His hatred of noise brought him in touch with Leonard. In the midst of the general excitement the boy was the only one to keep calm, and never to raise his voice more at one moment than another. He always expressed himself correctly and deliberately, choosing his words, and never hurrying. Amalia, simmering, never had patience to wait until he had finished; the whole family cried out upon his slowness. He did not worry about it. Nothing could upset his calm, respectful deference. Christophe was the more attracted to him when he learned that Leonard intended to devote his life to the Church, and his curiosity was roused.

With regard to religion, Christophe was in a queer position; he did not know himself how he stood towards it. He had never had time to think seriously about it. He was not well enough educated, and he was too much absorbed by the difficulties of existence to be able to analyze himself and to set his ideas in order. His violence led him from one extreme to the other, from absolute facts to complete negation, without troubling to find out whether in either case he agreed with himself. When he was happy he hardly thought of God at all, but he was quite ready to believe in Him. When he was unhappy he thought of Him, but did not believe; it seemed to him impossible that a God could authorize unhappiness and injustice. But these difficulties did not greatly exercise him. He was too fundamentally religious to think much about God. He lived in God; he had no need to believe in Him. That is well enough for the weak and worn, for those whose lives are anæmic. They aspire to God, as a plant does to the sun. The dying cling to life. But he who bears in his soul the sun and life, what need has he to seek them outside himself?

Christophe would probably never have bothered about these questions had he lived alone. But the obligations of social life forced him to bring his thoughts to bear on these puerile and useless problems, which occupy a place out of all proportion in the world; it is impossible not to take them into account since at every step they are in the way. As if a healthy, generous creature, overflowing with strength and love, had not a

thousand more worthy things to do than to worry as to whether
God exists or no! . . . If it were only a question of believing
in God! But it is needful to believe in *a* God, of whatever
shape or size and color and race. So far Christophe never
gave a thought to the matter. Jesus hardly occupied his
thoughts at all. It was not that he did not love him: he loved
him when he thought of him: but he never thought of him.
Sometimes he reproached himself for it, was angry with himself,
could not understand why he did not take more interest in him.
And yet he professed, all his family professed; his grandfather
was forever reading the Bible; he went regularly to Mass;
he served it in a sort of way, for he was an organist; and he
set about his task conscientiously and in an exemplary manner.
But when he left the church he would have been hard put to
it to say what he had been thinking about. He set himself
to read the Holy Books in order to fix his ideas, and he found
amusement and even pleasure in them, just as in any beautiful
strange books, not essentially different from other books, which
no one ever thinks of calling sacred. In truth, if Jesus ap·
pealed to him, Beethoven did no less. And at his organ in
Saint Florian's Church, where he accompanied on Sundays, he
was more taken up with his organ than with Mass, and he
was more religious when he played Bach than when he played
Mendelssohn. Some of the ritual brought him to a fervor of
exaltation. But did he then love God, or was it only the music,
as an impudent priest said to him one day in jest, without
thinking of the unhappiness which his quip might cause in
him? Anybody else would not have paid any attention to it,
and would not have changed his mode of living—(so many
people put up with not knowing what they think!) But
Christophe was cursed with an awkward need for sincerity,
which filled him with scruples at every turn. And when scruples
came to him they possessed him forever. He tortured himself;
he thought that he had acted with duplicity. Did he believe
or did he not? . . . He had no means, material or intellectual—
(knowledge and leisure are necessary)—of solving the problem by himself. And yet it had to be solved, or he was either
indifferent or a hypocrite. Now, he was incapable of being
either one or the other.

He tried timidly to sound those about him. They all seemed to be sure of themselves. Christophe burned to know their reasons. He could not discover them. Hardly did he receive a definite answer; they always talked obliquely. Some thought him arrogant, and said that there is no arguing these things, that thousands of men cleverer and better than himself had believed without argument, and that he needed only to do as they had done. There were some who were a little hurt, as though it were a personal affront to ask them such a question, and yet they were of all perhaps the least certain of their facts. Others shrugged their shoulders and said with a smile: "Bah! it can't do any harm." And their smile said: "And it is so useful! . . ." Christophe despised them with all his heart.

He had tried to lay his uncertainties before a priest, but he was discouraged by the experiment. He could not discuss the matter seriously with him. Though his interlocution was quite pleasant, he made Christophe feel, quite politely, that there was no real equality between them; he seemed to assume in advance that his superiority was beyond dispute, and that the discussion could not exceed the limits which he laid down for it, without a kind of impropriety; it was just a fencing bout, and was quite inoffensive. When Christophe wished to exceed the limits and to ask questions, which the worthy man was pleased not to answer, he stepped back with a patronizing smile, and a few Latin quotations, and a fatherly objurgation to pray, pray that God would enlighten him. Christophe issued from the interview humiliated and wounded by his love of polite superiority. Wrong or right, he would never again for anything in the world have recourse to a priest. He admitted that these men were his superiors in intelligence or by reason of their sacred calling; but in argument there is neither superiority, nor inferiority, nor title, nor age, nor name; nothing is of worth but truth, before which all men are equal.

So he was glad to find a boy of his own age who believed. He asked no more than belief, and he hoped that Leonard would give him good reason for believing. He made advances to him. Leonard replied with his usual gentleness, but without eagerness; he was never eager about anything. As they could not carry on a long conversation in the house without being interrupted every moment by Amalia or the old man, Christophe proposed that they should go for a walk one evening after dinner. Leonard was too polite to refuse, although he would gladly have got out of it, for his indolent nature disliked walking, talking, and anything that cost him an effort.

Christophe had some difficulty in opening up the conversation. After two or three awkward sentences about trivialities he plunged with a brusqueness that was almost brutal. He asked Leonard if he were really going to be a priest, and if he liked the idea. Leonard was nonplussed, and looked at him uneasily, but when he saw that Christophe was not hostilely disposed he was reassured.

"Yes," he replied. "How could it be otherwise?"

"Ah!" said Christophe. "You are very happy." Leonard was conscious of a shade of envy in Christophe's voice and was agreeably flattered by it. He altered his manner, became expansive, his face brightened.

"Yes," he said, "I am happy." He beamed.

"What do you do to be so?" asked Christophe.

Before replying Leonard proposed that they should sit down on a quiet seat in the cloisters of St. Martin's. From there they could see a corner of the little square, planted with acacias, and beyond it the town, the country, bathed in the evening mists. The Rhine flowed at the foot of the hill. An old deserted cemetery, with graves lost under the rich grass, lay in slumber beside them behind the closed gates.

Leonard began to talk. He said, with his eyes shining with contentment, how happy he was to escape from life, to have found a refuge, where a man is, and forever will be, in shelter. Christophe, still sore from his wounds, felt passionately the desire for rest and forgetfulness; but it was mingled with regret. He asked with a sigh:

"And yet, does it cost you nothing to renounce life altogether?"

"Oh!" said Leonard quietly. "What is there to regret? Isn't life sad and ugly?"

"There are lovely things too," said Christophe, looking at the beautiful evening.

"There are some beautiful things, but very few."

" The tew that there are are yet many to me."

" Oh, well! it is simply a matter of common sense. On the one hand a little good and much evil; on the other neither good nor evil on earth, and after, infinite happiness—how can one hesitate?"

Christophe was not very pleased with this sort of arithmetic. So economic a life seemed to him very poor. But he tried to persuade himself that it was wisdom.

" So," he asked a little ironically, " there is no risk of your being seduced by an hour's pleasure?"

" How foolish! When you know that it is only an hour, and that after it there is all eternity!"

" You are quite certain of eternity?"

" Of course."

Christophe questioned him. He was thrilled with hope and desire. Perhaps Leonard would at last give him impregnable reasons for believing. With what a passion he would himself renounce all the world to follow him to God.

At first Leonard, proud of his rôle of apostle, and convinced that Christophe's doubts were only a matter of form, and that they would of course give way before his first arguments, relied upon the Holy Books, the authority of the Gospel, the miracles, and traditions. But he began to grow gloomy when, after Christophe had listened for a few minutes, he stopped him and said that he was answering questions with questions, and that he had not asked him to tell exactly what it was that he was doubting, but to give some means of resolving his doubts. Leonard then had to realize that Christophe was much more ill than he seemed, and that he would only allow himself to be convinced by the light of reason. But he still thought that Christophe was playing the free thinker—(it never occurred to him that he might be so sincerely).—He was not discouraged, and, strong in his recently acquired knowledge, he turned back to his school learning: he unfolded higgledy. piggledy, with more authority than order, his metaphysical proofs of the existence of God and the immortality of the soul. Christophe, with his mind at stretch, and his brow knit in the effort, labored in silence, and made him say it all over again; tried hard to gather the mean ing, and to take it to himself, and to follow the reasoning. Then suddenly he burst out, vowed that Leonard was laughing at him, that it was all tricks, jests of the fine talkers who forged words and then amused themselves with pretending that these words were things. Leonard was nettled, and guaranteed the good faith of his authors. Christophe shrugged his shoulders, and said with an oath that they were only humbugs, infernal writers; and he demanded fresh proof.

Leonard perceived to his horror that Christophe was incurably attainted, and took no more interest in him. He remembered that he had been told not to waste his time in arguing with skeptics,—at least when they stubbornly refuse to believe. There was the risk of being shaken himself, without profiting the other. It was better to leave the unfortunate fellow to the will of God, who, if He so designs, would see to it that the skeptic was enlightened: or if not, who would dare to go against the will of God? Leonard did not insist then on carrying on the discussion. He only said gently that for the time being there was nothing to be done, that no reasoning could show the way to a man who was determined not to see it, and that Jean-Christophe must pray and appeal to Grace: nothing is possible without that: he must desire grace and the will to believe.

"The will," thought Christophe bitterly. "So then, God will exist because I will Him to exist? So then, death will not exist, because it pleases me to deny it! . . . Alas! How easy life is to those who have no need to see the truth, to those who can see what they wish to see, and are forever forging pleasant dreams in which softly to sleep!" In such a bed, Christophe knew well that he would never sleep. . . .

Leonard went on talking. He had fallen back on his favorite subject, the sweets of the contemplative life, and once on this neutral ground, he was inexhaustible. In his monotonous voice, that shook with the pleasure in him, he told of the joys of the life in God, outside, above the world, far from noise, of which he spoke in a sudden tone of hatred (he detested it almost as much as Christophe), far from violence, far from frivolity, far from the little miseries that one has to suffer every day, in the warm, secure nest of faith, from which you can contemplate in peace the wretchedness of a strange and distant world. And as Christophe listened, he perceived the egoism of that faith. Leonard saw that. He hurriedly explained: the contemplative life was not a lazy life. On the contrary, a man is more active in prayer than in action. What would the world be without prayer? You expiate the sins of others, you bear the burden of their misdeeds, you offer up your talents, you intercede between the world and God.

Christophe listened in silence with increasing hostility. He was conscious of the hypocrisy of such renunciation in Leonard. He was not unjust enough to assume hypocrisy in all those who believe. He knew well that with a few, such abdication of life comes from the impossibility of living, from a bitter despair, an appeal to death,—that with still fewer, it is an ecstasy of passion. . . . (How long does it last?) . . . But with the majority of men is it not too often the cold reasoning of souls more busied with their own ease and peace than with the happiness of others, or with truth? And if sincere men are conscious of it, how much they must suffer by such profanation of their ideal! . . .

Leonard was quite happy, and now set forth the beauty and harmony of the world, seen from the loftiness of the divine roost: below all was dark, unjust, sorrowful; seen from on high, it all became clear, luminous, ordered: the world was like the works of a clock, perfectly ordered. . . .

Now Christophe only listened absently. He was asking himself: " Does he believe, or does he believe that he believes? " And yet his own faith, his own passionate desire for faith was not shaken. Not the mediocrity of soul, and the poverty of argument of a fool like Leonard could touch that. . . .

Night came down over the town. The seat on which they were sitting was in darkness: the stars shone out, a white mist came up from the river, the crickets chirped under the trees in the cemetery. The bells began to ring: first the highest of them, alone, like a plaintive bird, challenging the sky: then the second, a third lower, joined in its plaint: at last came the deepest, on the fifth, and seemed to answer them. The three voices were merged in each other. At the bottom of the

towers there was a buzzing, as of a gigantic hive of bees. The
air and the boy's heart quivered. Christophe held his breath,
and thought how poor was the music of musicians compared with such an ocean of music, with all the sounds of
thousands of creatures: the former, the free world of sounds,
compared with the world tamed, catalogued, coldly labeled by
human intelligence. He sank and sank into that sonorous and
immense world without continents or bounds. . . .

And when the great murmuring had died away, when the
air had ceased at last to quiver, Christophe woke up.
He looked about him startled. . . . He knew nothing. Around
him and in him everything was changed. There was no
God. . . .

As with faith, so the loss of faith is often equally a flood
of grace, a sudden light. Reason counts for nothing: the
smallest thing is enough—a word, silence, the sound of bells.
A man walks, dreams, expects nothing. Suddenly the world
crumbles away. All about him is in ruins. He is alone. He
no longer believes.

Christophe was terrified, and could not understand how
it had come about. It was like the flooding of a river in the
spring. . . .

Leonard's voice was still sounding, more monotonous than
the voice of a cricket. Christophe did not hear it: he heard
nothing. Night was fully come. Leonard stopped. Surprised
to find Christophe motionless, uneasy because of the lateness
of the hour, he suggested that they should go home. Christophe
did not reply. Leonard took his arm. Christophe trembled,
and looked at Leonard with wild eyes.

"Christophe, we must go home," said Leonard.

"Go to hell!" cried Christophe furiously.

"Oh! Christophe! What have I done?" asked Leonard
tremulously. He was dumfounded.

Christophe came to himself.

"Yes. You are right," he said more gently. "I do not
know what I'm saying. Go to God! Go to God!"

He was alone. He was in bitter distress.

"Ah! my God! my God!" he cried, wringing his hands,
passionately raising his face to the dark sky. "Why do I no

longer believe? Why can I believe no more? What has happened to me? . . ."

The disproportion between the wreck of his faith and the conversation that he had just had with Leonard was too great: it was obvious that the conversation had no more brought it about than that the boisterousness of Amalia's gabble and the pettiness of the people with whom he lived were not the cause of the upheaval which for some days had been taking place in his moral resolutions. These were only pretexts. The uneasiness had not come from without. It was within himself. He felt stirring in his heart monstrous and unknown things, and he dared not rely on his thoughts to face the evil. The evil? Was it evil? A languor, an intoxication, a voluptuous agony filled all his being. He was no longer master of himself. In vain he sought to fortify himself with his former stoicism. His whole being crashed down. He had a sudden consciousness of the vast world, burning, wild, a world immeasurable. . . . How it swallows up God!

Only for a moment. But the whole balance of his old life was in that moment destroyed.

There was only one person in the family to whom Christophe paid no attention: this was little Rosa. She was not beautiful: and Christophe, who was far from beautiful himself, was very exacting of beauty in others. He had that calm cruelty of youth, for which a woman does not exist if she be ugly,—unless she has passed the age for inspiring tenderness, and there is then no need to feel for her anything but grave, peaceful, and quasi-religious sentiments. Rosa also was not distinguished by any especial gift, although she was not without intelligence: and she was cursed with a chattering tongue which drove Christophe from her. And he had never taken the trouble to know her, thinking that there was in her nothing to know; and the most he ever did was to glance at her.

But she was of better stuff than most girls: she was certainly better than Minna, whom he had so loved. She was a good girl, no coquette, not at all vain, and until Christophe came it had never occurred to her that she was plain, or if it had it had not worried her: for none of her family bothered about it. Whenever her grandfather or her mother told her so out of a desire to grumble, she only laughed: she did not believe it, or she attached no importance to it: nor did they. So many others, just as plain, and more, had found some one to love them! The Germans are very mildly indulgent to physical imperfections: they cannot see them: they are even able to embellish them, by virtue of an easy imagination which finds unexpected qualities in the face of their desire to make them like the most illustrious examples of human beauty. Old Euler would not have needed much urging to make him declare that his granddaughter had the nose of the Juno Ludovisi. Happily he was too grumpy to pay compliments: and Rosa, unconcerned about the shape of her nose, had no vanity except in the accomplishment, with all the ritual, of the famous household duties. She had accepted as Gospel all that she had been taught. She hardly ever went out, and she had very little standard of comparison; she admired her family naïvely, and believed what they said. She was of an expansive and confiding nature, easily satisfied, and tried to fall in with the mournfulness of her home, and docilely used to repeat the pessimistic ideas which she heard. She was a creature of devotion—always thinking of others, trying to please, sharing anxieties, guessing at what others wanted; she had a great need of loving without demanding anything in return. Naturally her family took advantage of her, although they were kind and loved her: but there is always a temptation to take advantage of the love of those who are absolutely delivered into your hands. Her family were so sure of her attentions that they were not at all grateful for them: whatever she did, they expected more. And then, she was clumsy; she was awkward and hasty; her movements were jerky and boyish; she had outbursts of tenderness which used to end in disaster: a broken glass, a jug upset, a door slammed to: things which let loose upon her the wrath of everybody in the house. She was always being snubbed and would go and weep in a corner. Her tears did not last long. She would soon smile again, and begin to chatter without a suspicion of rancor against anybody.

Christophe's advent was an important event in her life. She had often heard of him. Christophe had some place in the gossip of the town: he was a sort of little local celebrity: his name used often to recur in the family conversation, especially when old Jean Michel was alive, who, proud of his grandson, used to sing his praises to all of his acquaintance. Rosa had seen the young musician once or twice at concerts. When she heard that he was coming to live with them, she clapped her hands. She was sternly rebuked for her breach of manners and became confused. She saw no harm in it. In a life so monotonous as hers, a new lodger was a great distraction. She spent the last few days before his arrival in a fever of expectancy. She was fearful lest he should not like the house, and she tried hard to make every room as attractive as possible. On the morning of his arrival, she even put a little bunch of flowers on the mantelpiece to bid him welcome. As to herself, she took no care at all to look her best; and one glance was enough to make Christophe decide that she was plain, and slovenly dressed. She did not think the same of him, though she had good reason to do so: for Christophe, busy, exhausted, ill-kempt, was even more ugly than usual. But Rosa, who was incapable of thinking the least ill of anybody, Rosa, who thought her grandfather, her father, and her mother, all perfectly beautiful, saw Christophe exactly as she had expected to see him, and admired him with all her heart. She was frightened at sitting next to him at table; and unfortunately her shyness took the shape of a flood of words, which at once alienated Christophe's sympathies. She did not see this, and that first evening remained a shining memory in her life. When she was alone in her room, after they had all gone upstairs, she heard the tread of the new lodgers as they walked over her head; and the sound of it ran joyously through her; the house seemed to her to have taken new life.

The next morning for the first time in her life she looked at herself in the mirror carefully and uneasily, and without exactly knowing the extent of her misfortune she began to be conscious of it. She tried to decide about her features, one by one; but she could not. She was filled with sadness and apprehension. She sighed· deeply, and thought of introducing certain changes in her toilet, but she only made herself look still more plain. She conceived the unlucky idea of overwhelming Christophe with her kindness. In her naïve desire to be always seeing her new friends, and doing them service, she was forever going up and down the stairs, bringing them some utterly useless thing, insisting on helping them, and always laughing and talking and shouting. Her zeal and her stream of talk could only be interrupted by her mother's impatient voice calling her. Christophe looked grim; but for his good resolutions he must have lost his temper quite twenty times. He restrained himself for two days; on the third, he locked his door. Rosa knocked, called, understood, went downstairs in dismay, and did not try again. When he saw her he explained that he was very busy and could not be disturbed. She humbly begged his pardon. She could not deceive herself as to the failure of her innocent advances: they had accomplished the opposite of her intention: they had alienated Christophe. He no longer took the trouble to conceal his ill-humor; he did not listen when she talked, and did not disguise his impatience. She felt that her chatter irritated him, and by force of will she succeeded in keeping silent for a part of the evening: but the thing was stronger than herself: suddenly she would break out again and her words would tumble over each other more tumultuously than ever. Christophe would leave her in the middle of a sentence. She was not angry with him. She was angry with herself. She thought herself stupid, tiresome, ridiculous: all her faults assumed enormous proportions and she tried to wrestle with them: but she was discouraged by the check upon her first attempts, and said to herself that she could not do it, that she was not strong enough. But she would try again.

But there were other faults against which she was powerless: what could she do against her plainness? There was no doubt about it. The certainty of her misfortune had suddenly been revealed to her one day when she was looking at herself in the mirror; it came like a thunderclap. Of course she exaggerated the evil, and saw her nose as ten times larger than it was; it seemed to her to fill all her face; she dared not show herself; she wished to die. But there is in youth such a power of hope that these fits of discouragement never lasted long: she would end by pretending that she had been mistaken; she would try to believe it, and for a moment or two would actually succeed in thinking her nose quite ordinary and almost shapely. Her instinct made her attempt, though very clumsily, certain childish tricks, a way of doing her hair so as not so much to show her forehead and so accentuate the disproportion of her face. And yet, there was no coquetry in her; no thought of love had crossed her mind, or she was unconscious of it. She asked little: nothing but a little friendship: but Christophe did not show any inclination to give her that little. It seemed to Rosa that she would have been perfectly happy had he only condescended to say good-day when they met. A friendly good-evening with a little kindness. But Christophe usually looked so hard and so cold! It chilled her. He never said anything disagreeable to her, but she would rather have had cruel reproaches than such cruel silence.

One evening Christophe was playing his piano. He had taken up his quarters in a little attic at the top of the house so as not to be so much disturbed by the noise. Downstairs Rosa was listening to him, deeply moved. She loved music though her taste was bad and unformed. While her mother was there, she stayed in a corner of the room and bent over her sewing, apparently absorbed in her work; but her heart was with the sounds coming from upstairs, and she wished to miss nothing. As soon as Amalia went out for a walk in the neighborhood, Rosa leaped to her feet, threw down her sewing, and went upstairs with her heart beating until she came to the attic door. She held her breath and laid her ear against the door. She stayed like that until Amalia returned. She went on tiptoe, taking care to make no noise, but as she was not very sure-footed, and was always in a hurry, she was always tripping upon the stairs; and once while she was listening, leaning forward with her cheek glued to the keyhole, she lost her balance, and banged her forehead against the door. She was so alarmed that she lost her breath. The piano stopped dead: she could not escape. She was getting up when the door opened. Christophe saw her, glared at her furiously, and

then without a word, brushed her aside, walked angrily downstairs, and went out. He did not return until dinner time,
paid no heed to the despairing looks with which she asked his
pardon, ignored her existence, and for several weeks he never
played at all. Rosa secretly shed many tears; no one noticed
it, no one paid any attention to her. Ardently she prayed to
God . . . for what? She did not know. She had to confide
her grief in some one. She was sure that Christophe detested
her.

And, in spite of all, she hoped. It was enough for her if
Christophe seemed to show any sign of interest in her, if he
appeared to listen to what she said, if he pressed her hand
with a little more friendliness than usual. . . .

A few imprudent words from her relations set her imagination off upon a false road.

The whole family was filled with sympathy for Christophe.
The big boy of sixteen, serious and solitary, who had such lofty
ideas of his duty, inspired a sort of respect in them all. His
fits of ill-temper, his obstinate silences, his gloomy air, his
brusque manner, were not surprising in such a house as that.
Frau Vogel, herself, who regarded every artist as a loafer, dared
not reproach him aggressively, as she would have liked to do,
with the hours that he spent in star-gazing in the evening,
leaning, motionless, out of the attic window overlooking the
yard, until night fell; for she knew that during the rest of the
day he was hard at work with his lessons; and she humored
him—like the rest—for an ulterior motive which no one expressed though everybody knew it.

Rosa had seen her parents exchanging looks and mysterious
whisperings when she was talking to Christophe. At first she
took no notice of it. Then she was puzzled and roused by
it; she longed to know what they were saying, but dared not
ask.

One evening when she had climbed on to a garden seat to
untie the clothes-line hung between two trees, she leaned on
Christophe's shoulder to jump down. Just at that moment
her eyes met her grandfather's and her father's; they were
sitting smoking their pipes, and leaning against the wall of

the house. The two men winked at each other, and Justus
Euler said to Vogel:

"They will make a fine couple."

Vogel nudged him, seeing that the girl was listening, and
he covered his remark very cleverly—(or so he thought)—with
a loud "Hm! hm!" that could have been heard twenty yards
away. Christophe, whose back was turned, saw nothing, but
Rosa was so bowled over by it that she forgot that she was
jumping down, and sprained her foot. She would have fallen
had not Christophe caught her, muttering curses on her clumsiness. She had hurt herself badly, but she did not show it;
she hardly thought of it; she thought only of what she had
just heard. She walked to her room; every step was agony to
her; she stiffened herself against it so as not to let it be seen.
A delicious, vague uneasiness surged through her. She fell
into a chair at the foot of her bed and hid her face in the
coverlet. Her cheeks were burning; there were tears in her
eyes, and she laughed She was ashamed, she wished to sink
into the depths of the earth, she could not fix her ideas; her
blood beat in her temples, there were sharp pains in her ankle;
she was in a feverish stupor. Vaguely she heard sounds outside, children crying and playing in the street, and her grandfather's words were ringing in her ears; she was thrilled, she
laughed softly, she blushed, with her face buried in the eiderdown: she prayed, gave thanks, desired, feared—she loved.

Her mother called her. She tried to get up. At the first
step she felt a pain so unbearable that she almost fainted; her
head swam. She thought she was going to die, she wished to
die, and at the same time she wished to live with all the forces
of her being, to live for the promised happiness. Her mother
came at last, and the whole household was soon excited. She
was scolded as usual, her ankle was dressed, she was put to
bed, and sank into the sweet bewilderment of her physical pain
and her inward joy. The night was sweet. . . . The smallest
memory of that dear evening was hallowed for her. She did
not think of Christophe, she knew not what she thought. She
was happy.

The next day, Christophe, who thought himself in some
measure responsible for the accident, came to make inquiries,

and for the first time he made some show of affection for her. She was filled with gratitude, and blessed her sprained ankle. She would gladly have suffered all her life, if, all her life, she might have such joy.—She had to lie down for several days and never move; she spent them in turning over and over her grandfather's words, and considering them. Had he said:
"They will . . ."
Or:
"They would . . .?"
But it was possible that he had never said anything of this kind?—Yes. He had said it; she was certain of it. . . . What! Did they not see that she was ugly, and that Christophe could not bear her? . . . But it was so good to hope! She came to believe that perhaps she had been wrong, that she was not as ugly as she thought; she would sit up on her sofa to try and see herself in the mirror on the wall opposite, above the mantelpiece; she did not know what to think. After all, her father and her grandfather were better judges than herself; people cannot tell about themselves. . . . Oh! Heaven, if it were possible! . . . If it could be . . . if, she never dared think it, if . . . if she were pretty! . . . Perhaps, also, she had exaggerated Christophe's antipathy. No doubt he was indifferent, and after the interest he had shown in her the day after the accident did not bother about her any more; he forgot to inquire; but Rosa made excuses for him, he was so busy! How should he think of her? An artist cannot be judged like other men. . . .

And yet, resigned though she was, she could not help expecting with beating heart a word of sympathy from him when he came near her. A word only, a look . . . her imagination did the rest. In the beginning love needs so little food! It is enough to see, to touch as you pass; such a power of dreams flows from the soul in such moments, that almost of itself it can create its love: a trifle can plunge it into ecstasy that later, when it is more satisfied, and in proportion more exacting, it will hardly find again when at last it does possess the object of its desire.—Rosa lived absolutely, though no one knew it, in a romance of her own fashioning, pieced together by herself: Christophe loved her secretly, and was too shy to confess his love, or there was some stupid reason, fantastic or romantic, delightful to the imagination of the sentimental little ninny. She fashioned endless stories, and all perfectly absurd; she knew it herself, but tried not to know it; she lied to herself voluptuously for days and days as she bent over her sewing. It made her forget to talk: her flood of words was turned inward, like a river which suddenly disappears underground. But then the river took its revenge. What a debauch of speeches, of unuttered conversations which no one heard but herself! Sometimes her lips would move as they do with people who have to spell out the syllables to themselves as they read so as to understand them.

When her dreams left her she was happy and sad. She knew that things were not as she had just told herself: but she was left with a reflected happiness, and had greater confidence for her life. She did not despair of winning Christophe.

She did not admit it to herself, but she set about doing it. With the sureness of instinct that great affection brings, the awkward, ignorant girl contrived immediately to find the road by which she might reach her beloved's heart. She did not turn directly to him. But as soon as she was better and could once more walk about the house she approached Louisa. The smallest excuse served. She found a thousand little services to render her. When she went out she never failed to undertake various errands: she spared her going to the market, arguments with tradespeople, she would fetch water for her from the pump in the yard; she cleaned the windows and polished the floors in spite of Louisa's protestations, who was confused when she did not do her work alone; but she was so weary that she had not the strength to oppose anybody who came to help her. Christophe was out all day. Louisa felt that she was deserted, and the companionship of the affectionate, chattering girl was pleasant to her. Rosa took up her quarters in her room. She brought her sewing, and talked all the time. By clumsy devices she tried to bring conversation round to Christophe. Just to hear of him, even to hear his name, made her happy; her hands would tremble; she would sit with downcast eyes. Louisa was delighted to talk of her beloved Christophe, and would tell little tales of his childhood, trivial and just a little ridiculous; but there was no fear of Rosa thinking them so: she took a great joy, and there was a dear emotion for her in imagining Christophe as a child, and doing all the tricks and having all the darling ways of children: in her the motherly tenderness which lies in the hearts of all women was mingled deliciously with that other tenderness: she would laugh heartily and tears would come to her eyes. Louisa was touched by the interest that Rosa took in her. She guessed dimly what was in the girl's heart, but she never let it appear that she did so; but she was glad of it; for of all in the house she only knew the worth of the girl's heart. Sometimes she would stop talking to look at her. Rosa, surprised by her silence, would raise her eyes from her work. Louisa would smile at her. Rosa would throw herself into her arms, suddenly, passionately, and would hide her face in Louisa's bosom. Then they would go on working and talking, as if nothing had happened.

In the evening when Christophe came home, Louisa, grateful for Rosa's attentions, and in pursuance of the little plan she had made, always praised the girl to the skies. Christophe was touched by Rosa's kindness. He saw how much good she was doing his mother, in whose face there was more serenity: and he would thank her effusively. Rosa would murmur, and escape to conceal her embarrassment: so she appeared a thousand times more intelligent and sympathetic to Christophe than if she had spoken. He looked at her less with a prejudiced eye, and did not conceal his surprise at finding unsuspected qualities in her. Rosa saw that; she marked the progress that she made in his sympathy and thought that his sympathy would lead to love. She gave herself up more than ever to her dreams. She came near to believing with the beautiful presumption of youth that what you desire with all your being is always accomplished in the end. Besides, how was her desire unreasonable? Should not Christophe have been more sensible than any other of her goodness and her affectionate need of self-devotion?

But Christophe gave no thought to her. He esteemed her; but she filled no room in his thoughts. He was busied with far other things at the moment. Christophe was no longer Christophe. He did not know himself. He was in a mighty travail that was like to sweep everything away, a complete upheaval.

Christophe was conscious of extreme weariness and great uneasiness. He was for no reason worn out; his head was heavy, his eyes, his ears, all his senses were dumb and throbbing. He could not give his attention to anything. His mind leaped from one subject to another, and was in a fever that sucked him dry. The perpetual fluttering of images in his mind made him giddy. At first he attributed it to fatigue and the enervation of the first days of spring. But spring passed and his sickness only grew worse.

It was what the poets who only touch lightly on things call the unease of adolescence, the trouble of the cherubim, the waking of the desire of love in the young body and soul. As if the fearful crisis of all a man's being, breaking up, dying, and coming to full rebirth, as if the cataclysm in which everything, faith, thought, action, all life, seems like to be blotted out, and then to be new-forged in the convulsions of sorrow and joy, can be reduced to terms of a child's folly!

All his body and soul were in a ferment. He watched them, having no strength to struggle, with a mixture of curiosity and disgust. He did not understand what was happening in himself. His whole being was disintegrated. He spent days together in absolute torpor. Work was torture to him. At night he slept heavily and in snatches, dreaming monstrously, with gusts of desire; the soul of a beast was racing madly in him. Burning, bathed in sweat, he watched himself in horror; he tried to break free of the crazy and unclean thoughts that possessed him, and he wondered if he were going mad.

The day gave him no shelter from his brutish thoughts. In the depths of his soul he felt that he was slipping down and down; there was no stay to clutch at; no barrier to keep back chaos. All his defenses, all his citadels, with the quadruple rampart that hemmed him in so proudly—his God, his art, his pride, his moral faith, all was crumbling away, falling piece by piece from him. He saw himself naked, bound, lying unable to move, like a corpse on which vermin swarm. He had spasms of revolt: where was his will, of which he was so proud? He called to it in vain: it was like the efforts that one makes in sleep, knowing that one is dreaming, and trying to awake. Then one succeeds only in falling from one dream to another like a lump of lead, and in being more and more choked by the suffocation of the soul in bondage. At last he found that it was less painful not to struggle. He decided not to do so, with fatalistic apathy and despair.

The even tenor of his life seemed to be broken up. Now he slipped down a subterranean crevasse and was like to disappear; now he bounded up again with a violent jerk. The chain of his days was snapped. In the midst of the even plain of the hours great gaping holes would open to engulf his soul. Christophe looked on at the spectacle as though it did not concern him. Everything, everybody,—and himself—were strange to him. He went about his business, did his work, automatically: it seemed to him that the machinery of his life might stop at any moment: the wheels were out of gear. At dinner with his mother and the others, in the orchestra with the musicians and the audience, suddenly there would be a void and emptiness in his brain: he would look stupidly at the grinning faces about him: and he could not understand. He would ask himself:

" What is there between these creatures and . . .? "

He dared not even say:

". . . and me."

For he knew not whether he existed. He would speak and his voice would seem to issue from another body. He would move, and he saw his movements from afar, from above—from the top of a tower. He would pass his hand over his face, and his eyes would wander. He was often near doing crazy things.

It was especially when he was most in public that he had to keep guard on himself. For example, on the evenings when he went to the Palace or was playing in public. Then he would suddenly be seized by a terrific desire to make a face, or say something outrageous, to pull the Grand Duke's nose, or to take a running kick at one of the ladies. One whole evening while he was conducting the orchestra, he struggled against an insensate desire to undress himself in public: and he was haunted by the idea from the moment when he tried to check it: he had to exert all his strength not to give way to it. When he issued from the brute struggle he was dripping with sweat and his mind was blank. He was really mad. It was enough for him to think that he must not do a thing for it to fasten on him with the maddening tenacity of a fixed idea.

So his life was spent in a series of unbridled outbreaks and of endless falls into emptiness. A furious wind in the desert. Whence came this wind? From what abyss came these desires that wrenched his body and mind? He was like a bow stretched to breaking point by a strong hand,—to what end unknown?— which then springs back like a piece of dead wood. Of what force was he the prey? He dared not probe for it. He felt that he was beaten, humiliated, and he would not face his defeat. He was weary and broken in spirit. He understood now the people whom formerly he had despised: those who will not seek awkward truth. In the empty hours, when he remembered that time was passing, his work neglected, the future lost, he was frozen with terror. But there was no reaction: and his cowardice found excuses in desperate affirmation of the void in which he lived: he took a bitter delight in abandoning himself to it like a wreck on the waters. What was the good of fighting? There was nothing beautiful, nor good; neither God, nor life, nor being of any sort. In the street as he walked, suddenly the earth would sink away from him: there was neither ground, nor air, nor light, nor himself: there was nothing. He would fall, his head would drag him down, face forwards: he could hardly hold himself up; he was on the point of collapse. He thought he was going to die, suddenly, struck down. He thought he was dead. . . .

Christophe was growing a new skin. Christophe was growing a new soul. And seeing the worn out and rotten soul of his childhood falling away he never dreamed that he was taking on a new one, young and stronger. As through life we change our bodies, so also do we change our souls: and the metamorphosis does not always take place slowly over many days; there are times of crisis when the whole is suddenly renewed. The adult changes his soul. The old soul that is cast off dies. In those hours of anguish we think that all is at an end. And the whole thing begins again. A life dies. Another life has already come into being.

One night he was alone in his room, with his elbow on his desk under the light of a candle. His back was turned to the window. He was not working. He had not been able to work for weeks. Everything was twisting and turning in his head. He had brought everything under scrutiny at once: religion, morals, art, the whole of life. And in the general dissolution of his thoughts was no method, no order: he had plunged into the reading of books taken haphazard from his grandfather's heterogeneous library or from Vogel's collection of books: books of theology, science, philosophy, an odd lot, of which he understood nothing, having everything to learn: he could not finish any of them, and in the middle of them went off on divagations, endless whimsies, which left him weary, empty, and in mortal sorrow.

So, that evening, he was sunk in an exhausted torpor. The whole house was asleep. His window was open. Not a breath came up from the yard. Thick clouds filled the sky. Christophe mechanically watched the candle burn away at the bottom of the candlestick. He could not go to bed. He had no thought of anything. He felt the void growing, growing from moment to moment. He tried not to see the abyss that drew him to its brink: and in spite of himself he leaned over and his eyes gazed into the depths of the night. In the void, chaos was stirring, and faint sounds came from the darkness. Agony filled him: a shiver ran down his spine: his skin tingled: he clutched the table so as not to fall. Convulsively he awaited nameless things, a miracle, a God. . . .

Suddenly, like an opened sluice, in the yard behind him, a deluge of water, a heavy rain, large drops, down pouring, fell. The still air quivered. The dry, hard soil rang out like a bell. And the vast scent of the earth, burning, warm as that of an animal, the smell of the flowers, fruit, and amorous flesh rose in a spasm of fury and pleasure. Christophe, under illusion, at fullest stretch, shook. He trembled. . . . The veil was rent. He was blinded. By a flash of lightning, he saw, in the depths of the night, he saw—he was God. God was in himself; He burst the ceiling of the room, the walls of the house; He cracked the very bounds of existence. He filled the sky, the universe, space. The world coursed through Him, like a cataract. In the horror and ecstasy of that cataclysm, Christophe fell too, swept along by the whirlwind which brushed away and crushed like straws the laws of nature. He was breathless: he was drunk with the swift hurtling down into God . . . God-abyss! God-gulf! Fire of Being! Hurricane of life! Madness of living, —aimless, uncontrolled, beyond reason,—for the fury of living!

When the crisis was over, he fell into a deep sleep and slept as he had not done for long enough. Next day when he awoke his head swam: he was as broken as though he had been drunk. But in his inmost heart he had still a beam of that somber and great light that had struck him down the night before. He tried to relight it. In vain. The more he pursued it, the more it eluded him. From that time on, all his energy was directed towards recalling the vision of a moment. The endeavor was futile. Ecstasy does not answer the bidding of the will.

But that mystic exaltation was not the only experience that he had of it: it recurred several times, but never with the intensity of the first. It came always at moments when Christophe was least expecting it, for a second only, a time so short, so sudden,—no longer than a wink of an eye or a raising of a hand—that the vision was gone before he could discover that it was: and then he would wonder whether he had not dreamed it. After that fiery bolt that had set the night aflame, it was a gleaming dust, shedding fleeting sparks, which the eye could hardly see as they sped by. But they reappeared more and more often: and in the end they surrounded Christophe with a halo of perpetual misty dreams, in which his spirit melted. Everything that distracted him in his state of semi-hallucination was an irritation to him. It was impossible to work; he gave up thinking about it. Society was odious to him; and more than any, that of his intimates, even that of his mother, because they arrogated to themselves more rights over his soul.

He left the house: he took to spending his days abroad, and never returned until nightfall. He sought the solitude of the fields, and delivered himself up to it, drank his fill of it, like a maniac who wishes not to be disturbed by anything in the obsession of his fixed ideas.—But in the great sweet air, in

contact with the earth, his obsession relaxed, his ideas ceased
to appear like specters.　His exaltation was no less: rather it
was heightened, but it was no longer a dangerous delirium of
the mind but a healthy intoxication of his whole being: body
and soul crazy in their strength.

He rediscovered the world, as though he had never seen it.
It was a new childhood.　It was as though a magic word had
been uttered.　An " Open Sesame! "—Nature flamed with gladness.　The sun boiled.　The liquid sky ran like a clear river.
The earth steamed and cried aloud in delight.　The plants,
the trees, the insects, all the innumerable creatures were like
dazzling tongues of flame in the fire of life writhing upwards.
Everything sang aloud in joy.

And that joy was his own.　That strength was his own.　He
was no longer cut off from the rest of the world.　Till then,
even in the happy days of childhood, when he saw nature with
ardent and delightful curiosity, all creatures had seemed to
him to be little worlds shut up, terrifying and grotesque, un-
related to himself, and incomprehensible.　He was not even
sure that they had feeling and life.　They were strange machines.
And sometimes Christophe had even, with the unconscious
cruelty of a child, dismembered wretched insects without dreaming that they might suffer—for the pleasure of watching their
queer contortions.　His uncle Gottfried, usually so calm, had
one day indignantly to snatch from his hands an unhappy
fly that he was torturing.　The boy had tried to laugh at first:
then he had burst into tears, moved by his uncle's emotion:
he began to understand that his victim did really exist, as well
as himself, and that he had committed a crime.　But if thereafter nothing would have induced him to do harm to the beasts,
he never felt any sympathy for them: he used to pass them
by without ever trying to feel what it was that worked their
machinery: rather he was afraid to think of it: it was something like a bad dream.—And now everything was made plain.
These humble, obscure creatures became in their turn centers
of light.

Lying on his belly in the grass where creatures swarmed,
in the shade of the trees that buzzed with insects, Christophe
would watch the fevered movements of the ants, the long-legged

spiders, that seemed to dance as they walked, the bounding grasshoppers, that leap aside, the heavy, bustling beetles, and the naked worms, pink and glabrous, mottled with white, or with his hands under his head and his eyes closed he would listen to the invisible orchestra, the roundelay of the frenzied insects circling in a sunbeam about the scented pines, the trumpeting of the mosquitoes, the organ notes of the wasps, the brass of the wild bees humming like bells in the tops of the trees, and the godlike whispering of the swaying trees, the sweet moaning of the wind in the branches, the soft whispering of the waving grass, like a breath of wind rippling the limpid surface of a lake, like the rustling of a light dress and lovers' footsteps coming near, and passing, then lost upon the air.

He heard all these sounds and cries within himself. Through all these creatures from the smallest to the greatest flowed the same river of life: and in it he too swam. So, he was one of them, he was of their blood, and, brotherly, he heard the echo of their sorrows and their joys: their strength was merged in his like a river fed with thousands of streams. He sank into them. His lungs were like to burst with the wind, too freely blowing, too strong, that burst the windows and forced its way into the closed house of his suffocating heart. The change was too abrupt: after finding everywhere a void, when he had been buried only in his own existence, and had felt it slipping from him and dissolving like rain, now everywhere he found infinite and unmeasured Being, now that he longed to forget himself, to find rebirth in the universe. He seemed to have issued from the grave. He swam voluptuously in life flowing free and full: and borne on by its current he thought that he was free. He did not know that he was less free than ever, that no creature is ever free, that even the law that governs the universe is not free, that only death—perhaps—can bring deliverance.

But the chrysalis issuing from its stifling sheath, joyously stretched its limbs in its new shape, and had no time as yet to mark the bounds of its new prison.

There began a new cycle of days. Days of gold and fever, mysterious, enchanted, like those of his childhood, when one

by one he discovered things for the first time. From dawn
to set of sun he lived in one long mirage. He deserted all his
business. The conscientious boy, who for years had never
missed a lesson, or an orchestra rehearsal, even when he was
ill, was forever finding paltry excuses for neglecting his work.
He was not afraid to lie. He had no remorse about it. The
stoic principles of life, to which he had hitherto delighted to
bend his will, morality, duty, now seemed to him to have no
truth, nor reason. Their jealous despotism was smashed against
Nature. Human nature, healthy, strong, free, that alone was
virtue: to hell with all the rest! It provoked pitying laughter
to see the little peddling rules of prudence and policy which
the world adorns with the name of morality, while it pretends
to inclose all life within them. A preposterous mole-hill, an
ant-like people! Life sees to it that they are brought to reason.
Life does but pass, and all is swept away.

Bursting with energy Christophe had moments when he was
consumed with a desire to destroy, to burn, to smash, to glut
with actions blind and uncontrolled the force which choked
him. These outbursts usually ended in a sharp reaction: he
would weep, and fling himself down on the ground, and kiss
the earth, and try to dig into it with his teeth and hands, to
feed himself with it, to merge into it: he trembled then with
fever and desire.

One evening he was walking in the outskirts of a wood.
His eyes were swimming with the light, his head was whirling:
he was in that state of exaltation when all creatures and things
were transfigured. To that was added the magic of the
soft warm light of evening. Rays of purple and gold hovered
in the trees. From the meadows seemed to come a phosphorescent glimmer. In a field near by a girl was making hay.
In her blouse and short skirt, with her arms and neck bare,
she was raking the hay and heaping it up. She had a short
nose, wide cheeks, a round face, a handkerchief thrown over
her hair. The setting sun touched with red her sunburned
skin, which, like a piece of pottery, seemed to absorb the last
beams of the day.

She fascinated Christophe   Leaning against a beech-tree
he watched her come towards the verge of the woods, eagerly,

passionately. Everything else had disappeared. She took no notice of him. For a moment she looked at him cautiously: he saw her eyes blue and hard in her brown face. She passed so near to him that, when she leaned down to gather up the hay, through her open blouse he saw a soft down on her shoulders and back. Suddenly the vague desire which was in him leaped forth. He hurled himself at her from behind, seized her neck and waist, threw back her head and fastened his lips upon hers. He kissed her dry, cracked lips until he came against her teeth that bit him angrily. His hands ran over her rough arms, over her blouse wet with her sweat. She struggled. He held her tighter, he wished to strangle her. She broke loose, cried out, spat, wiped her lips with her hand, and hurled insults at him. He let her go and fled across the fields. She threw stones at him and went on discharging after him a litany of filthy epithets. He blushed, less for anything that she might say or think, but for what he was thinking himself. The sudden unconscious act filled him with terror. What had he done? What should he do? What he was able to understand of it all only filled him with disgust. And he was tempted by his disgust. He fought against himself and knew not on which side was the real Christophe. A blind force beset him: in vain did he fly from it: it was only to fly from himself. What would she do about him? What should he do to-morrow . . . in an hour . . . the time it took to cross the plowed field to reach the road? . . . Would he ever reach it? Should he not stop, and go back, and run back to the girl? And then? . . . He remembered that delirious moment when he had held her by the throat. Everything was possible. All things were worth while. A crime even. . . . Yes, even a crime. . . . The turmoil in his heart made him breathless. When he reached the road he stopped to breathe. Over there the girl was talking to another girl who had been attracted by her cries: and with arms akimbo, they were looking at each other and shouting with laughter.

II

SABINE

HE went home. He shut himself up in his room and never stirred for several days. He only went out even into the town when he was compelled. He was fearful of ever going out beyond the gates and venturing forth into the fields: he was afraid of once more falling in with the soft, maddening breath that had blown upon him like a rushing wind during a calm in a storm. He thought that the walls of the town might preserve him from it. He never dreamed that for the enemy to slip within there needed be only the smallest crack in the closed shutters, no more than is needed for a peep out.

In a wing of the house, on the other side of the yard, there lodged on the ground floor a young woman of twenty, some months a widow, with a little girl. Frau Sabine Froehlich was also a tenant of old Euler's. She occupied the shop which opened on to the street, and she had as well two rooms looking on to the yard, together with a little patch of garden, marked off from the Eulers' by a wire fence up which ivy climbed. They did not often see her: the child used to play down in the garden from morning to night making mud pies: and the garden was left to itself, to the great distress of old Justus, who loved tidy paths and neatness in the beds. He had tried to bring the matter to the attention of his tenant: but that was probably why she did not appear: and the garden was not improved by it.

Frau Froehlich kept a little draper's shop which might have had customers enough, thanks to its position in a street of shops in the center of the town: but she did not bother about it any more than about her garden. Instead of doing her housework herself, as, according to Frau Vogel, every self-respecting woman ought to do—especially when she is in circumstances which do not permit much less excuse idleness— she had hired a little servant, a girl of fifteen, who came in for a few hours in the morning to clean the rooms and look

after the shop, while the young woman lay in bed or dawdled
over her toilet.

Christophe used to see her sometimes, through his windows,
walking about her room, with bare feet, in her long nightgown,
or sitting for hours together before her mirror: for she was
so careless that she used to forget to draw her curtains: and
when she saw him, she was so lazy that she could not take
the trouble to go and lower them. Christophe, more modest
than she, would leave the window so as not to incommode her:
but the temptation was great. He would blush a little and
steal a glance at her bare arms, which were rather thin, as
she drew them languidly around her flowing hair, and with her
hands clasped behind her head, lost herself in a dream, until
they were numbed, and then she would let them fall. Christophe
would pretend that he only saw these pleasant sights inadver-
tently as he happened to pass the window, and that they did not
disturb him in his musical thoughts: but he liked it, and in the
end he wasted as much time in watching Frau Sabine, as she
did over her toilet. Not that she was a coquette: she was
rather careless, generally, and did not take anything like the
meticulous care with her appearance that Amalia or Rosa did.
If she dawdled in front of her dressing table it was from pure
laziness: every time she put in a pin she had to rest from the
effort of it, while she made little piteous faces at herself in
the mirrors. She was never quite properly dressed at the end
of the day.

Often her servant used to go before Sabine was ready: and
a customer would ring the shop-bell. She would let him ring
and call once or twice before she could make up her mind
to get up from her chair. She would go down, smiling, and
never hurrying,—never hurrying would look for the article
required,—and if she could not find it after looking for some
time, or even (as happened sometimes) if she had to take
too much trouble to reach it, as for instance, taking the ladder
from one end of the shop to the other,—she would say calmly
that she did not have it in stock: and as she never bothered
to put her stock in order, or to order more of the articles of
which she had run out, her customers used to lose patience
and go elsewhere. But she never minded. How could you be

angry with such a pleasant creature who spoke so sweetly, and was never excited about anything! She did not mind what anybody said to her: and she made this so plain that those who began to complain never had the courage to go on: they used to go, answering her charming smile with a smile: but they never came back. She never bothered about it. She went on smiling.

She was like a little Florentine figure. Her well marked eyebrows were arched: her gray eyes were half open behind the curtain of her lashes. The lower eyelid was a little swollen, with a little crease below it. Her little, finely drawn nose turned up slightly at the end. Another little curve lay between it and her upper lip, which curled up above her half-open mouth, pouting in a weary smile. Her lower lip was a little thick: the lower part of her face was rounded, and had the serious expression of the little virgins of Filippo Lippi. Her complexion was a little muddy, her hair was light brown, always untidy, and done up in a slovenly chignon. She was slight of figure, small-boned. And her movements were lazy. Dressed carelessly—a gaping bodice, buttons missing, ugly, worn shoes, always looking a little slovenly—she charmed by her grace and youth, her gentleness, her instinctively coaxing ways. When she appeared to take the air at the door of her shop, the young men who passed used to look at her with pleasure: and although she did not bother about them, she noticed it none the less. Always then she wore that grateful and glad expression which is in the eyes of all women when they know that they have been seen with sympathetic eyes. It seemed to say:

"Thank you! . . . Again! Look at me again!" But though it gave her pleasure to please, her indifference would never let her make the smallest effort to please.

She was an object of scandal to the Euler-Vogels. Everything about her offended them: her indolence, the untidiness of her house, the carelessness of her dress, her polite indifference to their remarks, her perpetual smile, the impertinent serenity with which she had accepted her husband's death, her child's illnesses, her straitened circumstances, the great and small annoyances of her daily life, while nothing could change one jot of her favorite habits, or her eternal longing,—everything about her offended them: and the worst of all was that, as she was, she did give pleasure. Frau Vogel could not forgive her that. It was almost as though Sabine did it on purpose, on purpose, ironically, to set at naught by her conduct the great traditions, the true principles, the savorless duty, the pleasureless labor, the restlessness, the noise, the quarrels, the mooning ways, the healthy pessimism which was the motive power of the Euler family, as it is that of all respectable persons, and made their life a foretaste of purgatory. That a woman who did nothing but dawdle about all the blessed day should take upon herself to defy them with her calm insolence, while they bore their suffering in silence like galley-slaves,—and that people should approve of her into the bargain—that was beyond the limit, that was enough to turn you against respectability! . . . Fortunately, thank God, there were still a few sensible people left in the world. Frau Vogel consoled herself with them. They exchanged remarks about the little widow, and spied on her through her shutters. Such gossip was the joy of the family when they met at supper. Christophe would listen absently. He was so used to hearing the Vogels set themselves up as censors of their neighbors that he never took any notice of it. Besides he knew nothing of Frau Sabine except her bare neck and arms, and though they were pleasing enough, they did not justify his coming to a definite opinion about her. However, he was conscious of a kindly feeling towards her: and in a contradictory spirit he was especially grateful to her for displeasing Frau Vogel.

After dinner in the evening when it was very hot it was impossible to stay in the stifling yard, where the sun shone the whole afternoon. The only place in the house where it was possible to breathe was the rooms looking into the street. Euler and his son-in-law used sometimes to go and sit on the doorstep with Louisa. Frau Vogel and Rosa would only appear for a moment: they were kept by their housework: Frau Vogel took a pride in showing that she had no time for dawdling: and she used to say, loudly enough to be overheard, that all the people sitting there and yawning on their doorsteps, with out doing a stitch of work, got on her nerves. As she could not—(to her sorrow)—compel them to work, she would pretend not to see them, and would go in and work furiously. Rosa thought she must do likewise. Euler and Vogel would discover draughts everywhere, and fearful of catching cold, would go up to their rooms: they used to go to bed early, and would have thought themselves ruined had they changed the least of their habits. After nine o'clock only Louisa and Christophe would be left. Louisa spent the day in her room: and, in the evening, Christophe used to take pains to be with her, whenever he could, to make her take the air. If she were left alone she would never go out: the noise of the street frightened her. Children were always chasing each other with shrill cries. All the dogs of the neighborhood took it up and barked. The sound of a piano came up, a little farther off a clarinet, and in the next street a cornet à piston. Voices chattered. People came and went and stood in groups in front of their houses. Louisa would have lost her head if she had been left alone in all the uproar. But when her son was with her it gave her pleasure. The noise would gradually die down. The children and the dogs would go to bed first. The groups of people would break up. The air would become more pure. Silence would descend upon the street. Louisa would tell in her thin voice the little scraps of news that she had heard from Amalia or Rosa. She was not greatly interested in them. But she never knew what to talk about to her son, and she felt the need of keeping in touch with him, of saying something to him. And Christophe, who felt her need, would pretend to be interested in everything she said: but he did not listen. He was off in vague dreams, turning over in his mind the doings of the day.

One evening when they were sitting there—while his mother was talking he saw the door of the draper's shop open. A woman came out silently and sat in the street. Her chair was only a few yards from Louisa. She was sitting in the darkest shadow. Christophe could not see her face: but he recognized her. His dreams vanished. The air seemed sweeter to him. Louisa had not noticed Sabine's presence, and went on with her chatter in a low voice. Christophe paid more attention to her, and he felt impelled to throw out a remark here and there, to talk, perhaps to be heard. The slight figure sat there without stirring, a little limp, with her legs lightly crossed and her hands lying crossed in her lap. She was looking straight in front of her, and seemed to hear nothing. Louisa was overcome with drowsiness. She went in. Christophe said he would stay a little longer.

It was nearly ten. The street was empty. The people were going indoors. The sound of the shops being shut was heard. The lighted windows winked and then were dark again. One or two were still lit: then they were blotted out. Silence. . . . They were alone, they did not look at each other, they held their breath, they seemed not to be aware of each other. From the distant fields came the smell of the new-mown hay, and from a balcony in a house near by the scent of a pot of cloves. No wind stirred. Above their heads was the Milky Way. To their right red Jupiter. Above a chimney Charles' Wain bent its axles: in the pale green sky its stars flowered like daisies. From the bells of the parish church eleven o'clock rang out and was caught up by all the other churches, with their voices clear or muffled, and, from the houses, by the dim chiming of the clock or husky cuckoos.

They awoke suddenly from their dreams, and got up at the same moment. And just as they were going indoors they both bowed without speaking. Christophe went up to his room. He lighted his candle, and sat down by his desk with his head in his hands, and stayed so for a long time without a thought. Then he sighed and went to bed.

Next day when he got up, mechanically he went to his window to look down into Sabine's room. But the curtains were drawn. They were drawn the whole morning. They were drawn ever after.

Next evening Christophe proposed to his mother that they should go again to sit by the door. He did so regularly. Louisa was glad of it: she did not like his shutting himself up in his room immediately after dinner with the window and shutters closed.—The little silent shadow never failed to come and sit in its usual place. They gave each other a quick nod, which Louisa never noticed. Christophe would talk to his mother.

Sabine would smile at her little girl, playing in the street: about nine she would go and put her to bed and would then return noiselessly. If she stayed a little Christophe would begin to be afraid that she would not come back. He would listen for sounds in the house, the laughter of the little girl who would not go to sleep: he would hear the rustling of Sabine's dress before she appeared on the threshold of the shop. Then he would look away and talk to his mother more eagerly. Sometimes he would feel that Sabine was looking at him. In turn he would furtively look at her. But their eyes would never meet.

The child was a bond between them. She would run about in the street with other children. They would find amusement in teasing a good-tempered dog sleeping there with his nose in his paws: he would cock a red eye and at last would emit a growl of boredom: then they would fly this way and that screaming in terror and happiness. The little girl would give piercing shrieks, and look behind her as though she were being pursued: she would throw herself into Louisa's lap, and Louisa would smile fondly. She would keep the child and question her: and so she would enter into conversation with Sabine. Christophe never joined in. He never spoke to Sabine. Sabine never spoke to him. By tacit agreement they pretended to ignore each other. But he never lost a word of what they said as they talked over him. His silence seemed unfriendly to Louisa. Sabine never thought it so: but it would make her shy, and she would grow confused in her remarks. Then she would find some excuse for going in.

For a whole week Louisa kept indoors for a cold. Christophe and Sabine were left alone. The first time they were frightened by it. Sabine, to seem at her ease, took her little girl on her knees and loaded her with caresses. Christophe was embarrassed and did not know whether he ought to go on ignoring what was happening at his side. It became difficult: although they had not spoken a single word to each other, they did know each other, thanks to Louisa. He tried to begin several times: but the words stuck in his throat. Once more the little girl extricated them from their difficulty. She played hide-and-seek, and went round Christophe's chair. He caught

her as she passed and kissed her. He was not very fond of
children: but it was curiously pleasant to him to kiss the little
girl. She struggled to be free, for she was busy with her game.
He teased her, she bit his hands: he let her fall. Sabine laughed.
They looked at the child and exchanged a few trivial words.
Then Christophe tried—(he thought he must)—to enter into
conversation: but he had nothing very much to go upon: and
Sabine did not make his task any the easier: she only repeated
what he said:

" It is a fine evening."

" Yes. It is a very fine evening."

" Impossible to breathe in the yard."

" Yes. The yard was stifling."

Conversation became very difficult. Sabine discovered that
it was time to take the little girl in, and went in herself: and
she did not appear again.

Christophe was afraid she would do the same on the evenings
that followed and that she would avoid being left alone with
him, as long as Louisa was not there. But on the contrary,
the next evening Sabine tried to resume their conversation.
She did so deliberately rather than for pleasure: she was
obviously taking a great deal of trouble to find subjects of
conversation, and bored with the questions she put: questions
and answers came between heartbreaking silences. Christophe
remembered his first interviews with Otto: but with Sabine
their subjects were even more limited than then, and she had
not Otto's patience. When she saw the small success of her
endeavors she did not try any more: she had to give herself
too much trouble, and she lost interest in it. She said no more,
and he followed her lead.

And then there was sweet peace again. The night was calm
once more, and they returned to their inward thoughts. Sabine
rocked slowly in her chair, dreaming. Christophe also was
dreaming. They said nothing. After half an hour Christophe
began to talk to himself, and in a low voice cried out with
pleasure in the delicious scent brought by the soft wind that
came from a cart of strawberries. Sabine said a word or two
in reply. Again they were silent. They were enjoying the
charm of these indefinite silences, and trivial words. Their

dreams were the same, they had but one thought: they did **not**
know what it was: they did not admit it to themselves. **At**
eleven they smiled and parted.

Next day they did not even try to talk: they resumed **their**
sweet silence. At long intervals a word or two let them **know**
that they were thinking of the same things.

Sabine began to laugh.

"How much better it is," she said, "not to try to talk! **One**
thinks one must, and it is so tiresome!"

"Ah!" said Christophe with conviction, "if only everybody
thought the same."

They both laughed. They were thinking of Frau Vogel.

"Poor woman!" said Sabine; "how exhausting she is!"

"She is never exhausted," replied Christophe gloomily.

She was tickled by his manner and his jest.

"You think it amusing?" he asked. "That is easy for **you**.
You are sheltered."

"So I am," said Sabine. "I lock myself in." She had **a**
little soft laugh that hardly sounded. Christophe heard it **with**
delight in the calm of the evening. He snuffed the fresh **air**
luxuriously.

"Ah! It is good to be silent!" he said, stretching his limbs.

"And talking is no use!" said she.

"Yes," returned Christophe, "we understand each other **so**
well!"

They relapsed into silence. In the darkness they could **not**
see each other. They were both smiling.

And yet, though they felt the same, when they were together—
or imagined that they did—in reality they knew nothing **of**
each other. Sabine did not bother about it. Christophe **was**
more curious. One evening he asked her:

"Do you like music?"

"No," she said simply. "It bores me. I don't understand
it."

Her frankness charmed him. He was sick of the lies of people
who said that they were mad about music, and were bored **to**
death when they heard it: and it seemed to him almost **a virtue**
not to like it and to say so. He asked if Sabine read.

"No. She had no books."

He offered to lend her his.

" Serious books? " she asked uneasily.

" Not serious books if she did not want them. Poetry."

" But those are serious books."

" Novels, then."

She pouted.

" They don't interest you? "

" Yes. She was interested in them: but they were always too long: she never had the patience to finish them. She forgot the beginning: skipped chapters and then lost the thread. And then she threw the book away."

" Fine interest you take! "

" Bah! Enough for a story that is not true. She kept her interest for better things than books."

" For the theater, then? "

" No. . . . No."

" Didn't she go to the theater? "

" No. It was too hot. There were too many people. So much better at home. The lights tired her eyes. And the actors were so ugly! "

He agreed with her in that. But there were other things in the theater: the play, for instance.

" Yes," she said absently. " But I have no time."

" What do you do all day? "

She smiled.

" There is so much to do."

" True," said he. " There is your shop."

" Oh! " she said calmly. " That does not take much time."

" Your little girl takes up your time then? "

" Oh! no, poor child! She is very good and plays by herself."

" Then? "

He begged pardon for his indiscretion. But she was amused by it.

" There are so many things."

" What things? "

" She could not say. All sorts of things. Getting up, dressing, thinking of dinner, cooking dinner, eating dinner, thinking of supper, cleaning her room. . . . And then the day was over.

. . . And besides you must have a little time for doing nothing!"

"And you are not bored?"

"Never."

"Even when you are doing nothing?"

"Especially when I am doing nothing.   It is much worse doing something: that bores me."

They looked at each other and laughed.

"You are very happy!" said Christophe.   "I can't do nothing."

"It seems to me that you know how."

"I have been learning lately."

"Ah! well, you'll learn."

When he left off talking to her he was at his ease and comfortable.   It was enough for him to see her.   He was rid of his anxieties, and irritations, and the nervous trouble that made him sick at heart.   When he was talking to her he was beyond care: and so when he thought of her.   He dared not admit it to himself: but as soon as he was in her presence, he was filled with a delicious soft emotion that brought him almost to unconsciousness.   At night he slept as he had never done.

When he came back from his work he would look into this shop.   It was not often that he did not see Sabine.   They bowed and smiled.   Sometimes she was at the door and then they would exchange a few words: and he would open the door and call the little girl and hand her a packet of sweets.

One day he decided to go in.   He pretended that he wanted some waistcoat buttons.   She began to look for them: but she could not find them.   All the buttons were mixed up: it was impossible to pick them out.   She was a little put out that he should see her untidiness.   He laughed at it and bent over the better to see it.

"No," she said, trying to hide the drawers with her hands. "Don't look!   It is a dreadful muddle. . . ."

She went on looking.   But Christophe embarrassed her.   She was cross, and as she pushed the drawer back she said:

"I can't find any. Go to Lisi, in the next street. She is sure to have them. She has everything that people want."

He laughed at her way of doing business.

"Do you send all your customers away like that?"

"Well. You are not the first," said Sabine warmly.

And yet she was a little ashamed.

"It is too much trouble to tidy up," she said. "I put off doing it from day to day. . . . But I shall certainly do it to-morrow."

"Shall I help you?" asked Christophe.

She refused. She would gladly have accepted: but she dared not, for fear of gossip. And besides it humiliated her.

They went on talking.

"And your buttons?" she said to Christophe a moment later. "Aren't you going to Lisi?"

"Never," said Christophe. "I shall wait until you have tidied up."

"Oh!" said Sabine, who had already forgotten what she had just said, "don't wait all that time!"

Her frankness delighted them both.

Christophe went to the drawer that she had shut.

"Let me look."

She ran to prevent his doing so.

"No, now please. I am sure I haven't any."

"I bet you have."

At once he found the button he wanted, and was triumphant. He wanted others. He wanted to go on rummaging: but she snatched the box from his hands, and, hurt in her vanity, she began to look herself.

The light was fading. She went to the window. Christophe sat a little away from her: the little girl clambered on to his knees. He pretended to listen to her chatter and answered her absently. He was looking at Sabine and she knew that he was looking at her. She bent over the box. He could see her neck and a little of her cheek.—And as he looked he saw that she was blushing. And he blushed too.

The child went on talking. No one answered her. Sabine did not move. Christophe could not see what she was doing he was sure she was doing nothing: she was not even looking at the box in her hands. The silence went on and on. The little girl grew uneasy and slipped down from Christophe's knees.

"Why don't you say anything?"

Sabine turned sharply and took her in her arms. The box was spilled on the floor: the little girl shouted with glee and ran on hands and knees after the buttons rolling under the furniture. Sabine went to the window again and laid her cheek against the pane. She seemed to be absorbed in what she saw outside.

"Good-night!" said Christophe, ill at ease. She did not turn her head, and said in a low voice:

"Good-night."

On Sundays the house was empty during the afternoon. The whole family went to church for Vespers. Sabine did not go. Christophe jokingly reproached her with it once when he saw her sitting at her door in the little garden, while the lovely bells were bawling themselves hoarse summoning her. She replied in the same tone that only Mass was compulsory: not Vespers: it was then no use, and perhaps a little indiscreet to be too zealous: and she liked to think that God would be rather pleased than angry with her.

"You have made God in your own image," said Christophe.

"I should be so bored if I were in His place," replied she with conviction.

"You would not bother much about the world if you were in His place."

"All that I should ask of it would be that it should not bother itself about me."

"Perhaps it would be none the worse for that," said Christophe.

"Tssh!" cried Sabine, "we are being irreligious."

"I don't see anything irreligious in saying that God is like you. I am sure He is flattered."

"Will you be silent!" said Sabine, half laughing, half angry. She was beginning to be afraid that God would be scandalized. She quickly turned the conversation.

"Besides," she said, "it is the only time in the week when one can enjoy the garden in peace."

"Yes," said Christophe. "They are gone." They looked at each other.

"How silent it is," muttered Sabine. "We are not used to it. One hardly knows where one is. . . ."

"Oh!" cried Christophe suddenly and angrily.

"There are days when I would like to strangle her!" There was no need to ask of whom he was speaking.

"And the others?" asked Sabine gaily.

"True," said Christophe, a little abashed. "There is Rosa."

"Poor child!" said Sabine.

They were silent.

"If only it were always as it is now!" sighed Christophe.

She raised her laughing eyes to his, and then dropped them. He saw that she was working.

"What are you doing?" he asked.

(The fence of ivy that separated the two gardens was between them.)

"Look!" she said, lifting a basin that she was holding in her lap. "I am shelling peas."

She sighed.

"But that is not unpleasant," he said, laughing.

"Oh!" she replied, "it is disgusting, always having to think of dinner."

"I bet that if it were possible," he said, "you would go without your dinner rather than have the trouble of cooking it."

"That's true," cried she.

"Wait! I'll come and help you."

He climbed over the fence and came to her.

She was sitting in a chair in the door. He sat on a step at her feet. He dipped into her lap for handfuls of green pods: and he poured the little round peas into the basin that Sabine held between her knees. He looked down. He saw Sabine's black stockings clinging to her ankles and feet—one of her feet was half out of its shoe. He dared not raise his eyes to look at her.

The air was heavy. The sky was dull and clouds hung low: there was no wind. No leaf stirred. The garden was inclosed within high walls: there was no world beyond them.

The child had gone out with one of the neighbors. They were alone. They said nothing. They could say nothing. Without looking he went on taking handfuls of peas from Sabine's lap: his fingers trembled as he touched her: among the fresh smooth pods they met Sabine's fingers, and they trembled too. They could not go on. They sat still, not looking at each other: she leaned back in her chair with her lips half-open and her arms hanging: he sat at her feet leaning against her: along his shoulder and arm he could feel the warmth of Sabine's leg. They were breathless. Christophe laid his hands against the stones to cool them: one of his hands touched Sabine's foot, that she had thrust out of her shoe, and he left it there, could not move it. They shivered. Almost they lost control. Christophe's hand closed on the slender toes of Sabine's little foot. Sabine turned cold, the sweat broke out on her brow, she leaned towards Christophe. . . .

Familiar voices broke the spell. They trembled. Christophe leaped to his feet and crossed the fence again. Sabine picked up the shells in her lap and went in. In the yard he turned. She was at her door. They looked at each other. Drops of rain were beginning to patter on the leaves of the trees. . . . She closed her door. Frau Vogel and Rosa came in. . . . He went up to his room. . . .

In the yellow light of the waning day drowned in the torrents of rain, he got up from his desk in response to an irresistible impulse: he ran to his window and held out his arms to the opposite window. At the same moment through the opposite window in the half-darkness of the room he saw—he thought he saw—Sabine holding out her arms to him.

He rushed from his room. He went downstairs. He ran to the garden fence. At the risk of being seen he was about to clear it. But when he looked at the window at which she had appeared, he saw that the shutters were closed. The house seemed to be asleep. He stopped. Old Euler, going to his cellar, saw him and called him. He retraced his footsteps. He thought he must have been dreaming.

It was not long before Rosa began to see what was happening. She had no diffidence and she did not yet know what jealousy was. She was ready to give wholly and to ask nothing in return. But if she was sorrowfully resigned to not being loved by Christophe, she had never considered the possibility of Christophe loving another.

One evening, after dinner, she had just finished a piece of embroidery at which she had been working for months. She was happy, and wanted for once in a way to leave her work and go and talk to Christophe. She waited until her mother's back was turned and then slipped from the room. She crept from the house like a truant. She wanted to go and confound Christophe, who had vowed scornfully that she would never finish her work. She thought it would be a good joke to go and take them by surprise in the street. It was no use the poor child knowing how Christophe felt towards her: she was always inclined to measure the pleasure which others should have at seeing her by that which she had herself in meeting them.

She went out. Christophe and Sabine were sitting as usual in front of the house. There was a catch at Rosa's heart. And yet she did not stop for the irrational idea that was in her: and she chaffed Christophe warmly. The sound of her shrill voice in the silence of the night struck on Christophe like a false note. He started in his chair, and frowned angrily. Rosa waved her embroidery in his face triumphantly. Christophe snubbed her impatiently.

" It is finished—finished! " insisted Rosa.

" Oh! well—go and begin another," said Christophe curtly.

Rosa was crestfallen. All her delight vanished. Christophe went on crossly:

" And when you have done thirty, when you are very old, you will at least be able to say to yourself that your life has not been wasted! "

Rosa was near weeping.

" How cross you are, Christophe! " she said.

Christophe was ashamed and spoke kindly to her. She was satisfied with so little that she regained confidence: and she began once more to chatter noisily: she could not speak low, she shouted deafeningly, like everybody in the house. In spite of himself Christophe could not conceal his ill-humor. At first he answered her with a few irritated monosyllables: then he said nothing at all, turned his back on her, fidgeted in his chair, and ground his teeth as she rattled on. Rosa saw that he was losing his temper and knew that she ought to stop: but she went on louder than ever. Sabine, a few yards away, in the dark, said nothing, watched the scene with ironic impassivity. Then she was weary and, feeling that the evening was wasted, she got up and went in. Christophe only noticed her departure after she had gone. He got up at once and without ceremony went away with a curt " Good-evening."

Rosa was left alone in the street, and looked in bewilderment at the door by which he had just gone in. Tears came to her eyes. She rushed in, went up to her room without a sound, so as not to have to talk to her mother, undressed hurriedly, and when she was in her bed, buried under the clothes, sobbed and sobbed. She made no attempt to think over what had passed: she did not ask herself whether Christophe loved Sabine, or whether Christophe and Sabine could not bear her: she knew only that all was lost, that life was useless, that there was nothing left to her but death.

Next morning thought came to her once more with eternal illusive hope. She recalled the events of the evening and told herself that she was wrong to attach so much importance to them. No doubt Christophe did not love her: she was resigned to that, though in her heart she thought, though she did not admit the thought, that in the end she would win his love by her love for him. But what reason had she for thinking that there was anything between Sabine and him? How could he, so clever as he was, love a little creature whose insignificance and mediocrity were patent? She was reassured,—but for that she did not watch Christophe any the less closely. She saw nothing all day, because there was nothing to see: but Christophe seeing her prowling about him all day long without any sort of explanation was peculiarly irritated by it. She set the crown on her efforts in the evening when she appeared again and sat with them in the street. The scene of the previous evening was repeated. Rosa talked alone. But Sabine did not wait so long before she went indoors: and Christophe followed her example. Rosa could no longer pretend that her presence was not unwelcome: but the unhappy girl tried to deceive herself. She did not perceive that she could have done nothing worse than to try so to impose on herself: and with her usual clumsiness she went on through the succeeding days.

Next day with Rosa sitting by his side Christophe waited in vain for Sabine to appear.

The day after Rosa was alone. They had given up the struggle. But she gained nothing by it save resentment from Christophe, who was furious at being robbed of his beloved evenings, his only happiness. He was the less inclined to forgive her, for being absorbed with his own feelings, he had no suspicion of Rosa's.

Sabine had known them for some time: she knew that Rosa was jealous even before she knew that she herself was in love: but she said nothing about it: and, with the natural cruelty of a pretty woman, who is certain of her victory, in quizzical silence she watched the futile efforts of her awkward rival.

Left mistress of the field of battle Rosa gazed piteously upon the results of her tactics. The best thing she could have done would have been not to persist, and to leave Christophe alone, at least for the time being: but that was not what she did: and as the worst thing she could have done was to talk to him about Sabine, that was precisely what she did.

With a fluttering at her heart, by way of sounding him, she said timidly that Sabine was pretty. Christophe replied curtly that she was very pretty. And although Rosa might have foreseen the reply she would provoke, her heart thumped when she heard him. She knew that Sabine was pretty: but she had never particularly remarked it: now she saw her for the first time with the eyes of Christophe: she saw her delicate features, her short nose, her fine mouth, her slender figure, her graceful movements. . . . Ah! how sad! . . . What would not she have given to possess Sabine's body, and live in it! She did not go closely into why it should be preferred to her own! . . . Her own! . . . What had she done to possess such a body? What a burden it was upon her. How ugly it seemed to her! It was odious to her. And to think that nothing but death could ever free her from it! . . . She was at once too proud and too humble to complain that she was not loved: she had no right to do so: and she tried even more to humble herself. But her instinct revolted. . . . No. It was not just! . . . Why should she have such a body, she, and not Sabine? . . . And why should Sabine be loved? What had she done to be loved? . . . Rosa saw her with no kindly eye, lazy, careless, egoistic, indifferent towards everybody, not looking after her house, or her child, or anybody, loving only herself, living only for sleeping, dawdling, and doing nothing. . . . And it was such a woman who pleased . . . who pleased Christophe. . . . Christophe who was so severe, Christophe who was so discerning, Christophe whom she esteemed and admired more than anybody! . . . How could Christophe be blind to it?—She could not help from time to time dropping an unkind remark about Sabine in his hearing. She did not wish to do so: but the impulse was stronger than herself. She was always sorry for it, for she was a kind creature and disliked speaking ill of anybody. But she was the more sorry because she drew down on herself such cruel replies as showed how much Christophe was in love. He did not mince matters. Hurt in his love, he tried to hurt in return: and succeeded. Rosa would make no reply and go out with her head bowed, and her lips tight pressed to keep from crying. She thought that it was her own fault, that she deserved it for having hurt Christophe by attacking the object of his love.

Her mother was less patient. Frau Vogel, who saw everything, and old Euler, also, had not been slow to notice Christophe's interviews with their young neighbor: it was not difficult to guess their romance. Their secret projects of one day marrying Rosa to Christophe were set at naught by it: and that seemed to them a personal affront of Christophe, although he was not supposed to know that they had disposed of him without consulting his wishes. But Amalia's despotism did not admit of ideas contrary to her own: and it seemed scandalous to her that Christophe should have disregarded the contemptuous opinion she had often expressed of Sabine.

She did not hesitate to repeat it for his benefit. Whenever

he was present she found some excuse for talking about her neighbor: she cast about for the most injurious things to say of her, things which might sting Christophe most cruelly: and with the crudity of her point of view and language she had no difficulty in finding them. The ferocious instinct of a woman, so superior to that of a man in the art of doing evil, as well as of doing good, made her insist less on Sabine's laziness and moral failings than on her uncleanliness. Her indiscreet and prying eye had watched through the window for proofs of it in the secret processes of Sabine's toilet: and she exposed them with coarse complacency. When from decency she could not say everything she left the more to be understood.

Christophe would go pale with shame and anger: he would go white as a sheet and his lips would quiver. Rosa, foreseeing what must happen, would implore her mother to have done: she would even try to defend Sabine. But she only succeeded in making Amalia more aggressive.

And suddenly Christophe would leap from his chair. He would thump on the table and begin to shout that it was monstrous to speak of a woman, to spy upon her, to expose her misfortunes: only an evil mind could so persecute a creature who was good, charming, quiet, keeping herself to herself, and doing no harm to anybody, and speaking no ill of anybody. But they were making a great mistake if they thought they could do her harm: they only made him more sympathetic and made her kindness shine forth only the more clearly.

Amalia would feel then that she had gone too far: but she was hurt by feeling it: and, shifting her ground, she would say that it was only too easy to talk of kindness: that the word was called in as an excuse for everything. Heavens! It was easy enough to be thought kind when you never bothered about anything or anybody, and never did your duty!

To which Christophe would reply that the first duty of all was to make life pleasant for others, but that there were people for whom duty meant only ugliness, unpleasantness, tiresomeness, and everything that interferes with the liberty of others and annoys and injures their neighbors, their servants, their families, and themselves. God save us from such people, and such a notion of duty, as from the plague! . . .

They would grow venomous. Amalia would be very bitter. Christophe would not budge an inch.—And the result of it all was that henceforth Christophe made a point of being seen continually with Sabine. He would go and knock at her door. He would talk gaily and laugh with her. He would choose moments when Amalia and Rosa could see him. Amalia would avenge herself with angry words. But the innocent Rosa's heart was rent and torn by this refinement of cruelty: she felt that he detested them and wished to avenge himself: and she wept bitterly.

So, Christophe, who had suffered so much from injustice, learned unjustly to inflict suffering.

Some time after that Sabine's brother, a miller at Landegg, a little town a few miles away, was to celebrate the christening of a child. Sabine was to be godmother. She invited Christophe. He had no liking for these functions: but for the pleasure of annoying the Vogels and of being with Sabine he accepted eagerly.

Sabine gave herself the malicious satisfaction of inviting Amalia and Rosa also, being quite sure that they would refuse. They did. Rosa was longing to accept. She did not dislike Sabine: sometimes even her heart was filled with tenderness for her because Christophe loved her: sometimes she longed to tell her so and to throw her arms about her neck. But there was her mother and her mother's example. She stiffened herself in her pride and refused. Then, when they had gone, and she thought of them together, happy together, driving in the country on the lovely July day, while she was left shut up in her room, with a pile of linen to mend, with her mother grumbling by her side, she thought she must choke: and she cursed her pride. Oh! if there were still time! . . . Alas! if it were all to do again, she would have done the same. . . .

The miller had sent his wagonette to fetch Christophe and Sabine. They took up several guests from the town and the farms on the road. It was fresh dry weather. The bright sun made the red berries of the brown trees by the road and the wild cherry trees in the fields shine. Sabine was smiling. Her pale face was rosy under the keen wind. Christophe had her little girl on his knees. They did not try to talk to each other: they talked to their neighbors without caring to whom or of what: they were glad to hear each other's voices: they were glad to be driving in the same carriage. They looked at each other in childish glee as they pointed out to each other a house, a tree, a passerby. Sabine loved the country: but she hardly ever went into it: her incurable laziness made excursions impossible: it was almost a year since she had been outside the town: and so she delighted in the smallest things she saw. They were not new to Christophe: but he loved Sabine, and like all lovers he saw everything through her eyes, and felt all her thrills of pleasure, and all and more than the emotion that was in her: for, merging himself with his beloved, he endowed her with all that he was himself.

When they came to the mill they found in the yard all the people of the farm and the other guests, who received them with a deafening noise. The fowls, the ducks, and the dogs joined in. The miller, Bertold, a great fair-haired fellow, square of head and shoulders, as big and tall as Sabine was slight, took his little sister in his arms and put her down gently as though he were afraid of breaking her. It was not long before Christophe saw that the little sister, as usual, did just as she liked with the giant, and that while he made heavy fun of her whims, and her laziness, and her thousand and one failings, he was at her feet, her slave. She was used to it, and thought it natural. She did nothing to win love: it seemed to her right that she should be loved: and if she were not, did not care: that is why everybody loved her.

Christophe made another discovery not so pleasing. For a christening a godfather is necessary as well as a godmother, and the godfather has certain rights over the godmother, rights which he does not often renounce, especially when she is young and pretty. He learned this suddenly when he saw a farmer, with fair curly hair, and rings in his ears, go up to Sabine laughing and kiss her on both cheeks. Instead of telling himself that he was an ass to have forgotten this privilege, and more than an ass to be huffy about it, he was cross with Sabine, as though she had deliberately drawn him into the snare. His crossness grew worse when he found himself separated from her during the ceremony. Sabine turned round every now and then as the procession wound across the fields and threw him a friendly glance. He pretended not to see it. She felt that he was annoyed, and guessed why: but it did not trouble her: it amused her. If she had had a real squabble with some one she loved, in spite of all the pain it might have caused her, she would never have made the least effort to break down any misunderstanding: it would have been too much trouble. Everything would come right if it were only left alone.

At dinner, sitting between the miller's wife and a fat girl with red cheeks whom he had escorted to the service without ever paying any attention to her, it occurred to Christophe to turn and look at his neighbor: and, finding her comely, out of revenge, he flirted desperately with her with the idea of catching Sabine's attention. He succeeded: but Sabine was not the sort of woman to be jealous of anybody or anything: so long as she was loved, she did not care whether her lover did or did not pay court to others: and instead of being angry, she was delighted to see Christophe amusing himself. From the other end of the table she gave him her most charming smile. Christophe was disgruntled: there was no doubt then that Sabine was indifferent to him: and he relapsed into his sulky mood from which nothing could draw him, neither the soft eyes of his neighbor, nor the wine that he drank. Finally, when he was half asleep, he asked himself angrily what on earth he was doing at such an interminable orgy, and did not hear the miller propose a trip on the water to take certain of the guests home. Nor did he see Sabine beckoning him to come with her so that they should be in the same boat. When it occurred to him, there was no room for him: and he had to go in another boat. This fresh mishap was not likely to make him more amiable until he discovered that he was to be rid of almost all his companions on the way. Then he relaxed and was pleasant. Besides the pleasant afternoon on the water, the pleasure of rowing, the merriment of these good people, rid him of his ill-humor. As Sabine was no longer there he lost his self-consciousness, and had no scruple about being frankly amused like the others.

They were in their boats. They followed each other closely,

and tried to pass each other. They threw laughing insults at each other. When the boats bumped Christophe saw Sabine's smiling face: and he could not help smiling too: they felt that peace was made. He knew that very soon they would return together.

They began to sing part songs. Each voice took up a line in time and the refrain was taken up in chorus. The people in the different boats, some way from each other, now echoed each other. The notes skimmed over the water like birds. From time to time a boat would go in to the bank: a few peasants would climb out: they would stand there and wave to the boats as they went further and further away. Little by little they were disbanded. One by one voices left the chorus. At last they were alone, Christophe, Sabine, and the miller.

They came back in the same boat, floating down the river. Christophe and Bertold held the oars, but they did not row. Sabine sat in the stern facing Christophe, and talked to her brother and looked at Christophe. Talking so, they were able to look at each other undisturbedly. They could never have done so had the words ceased to flow. The deceitful words seemed to say: " It is not you that I see." But their eyes said to each other: " Who are you? Who are you? You that I love! . . . You that I love, whoever you be! . . ."

The sky was clouded, mists rose from the fields, the river steamed, the sun went down behind the clouds. Sabine shivered and wrapped her little black shawl round her head and shoulders. She seemed to be tired. As the boat, hugging the bank, passed under the spreading branches of the willows, she closed her eyes: her thin face was pale: her lips were sorrowful: she did not stir, she seemed to suffer,—to have suffered,—to be dead. Christophe's heart ached. He leaned over to her. She opened her eyes again and saw Christophe's uneasy eyes upon her and she smiled into them. It was like a ray of sunlight to him. He asked in a whisper:

" Are you ill? "

She shook her head and said:

" I am cold."

The two men put their overcoats about her, wrapped up her feet, her legs, her knees, like a child being tucked up in bed. She suffered it and thanked them with her eyes. A fine, cold rain was beginning to fall. They took the oars and went quietly home. Heavy clouds hung in the sky. The river was inky black. Lights showed in the windows of the houses here and there in the fields. When they reached the mill the rain was pouring down and Sabine was numbed.

They lit a large fire in the kitchen and waited until the deluge should be over. But it only grew worse, and the wind rose. They had to drive three miles to get back to the town. The miller declared that he would not let Sabine go in such weather: and he proposed that they should both spend the night in the farmhouse. Christophe was reluctant to accept: he looked at Sabine for counsel: but her eyes were fixed on the fire on the hearth: it was as though they were afraid of influencing Christophe's decision. But when Christophe had said " Yes," she turned to him and she was blushing—(or was it the reflection of the fire?)—and he saw that she was pleased.

A jolly evening. . . . The rain stormed outside. In the black chimney the fire darted jets of golden sparks. They spun round and round. Their fantastic shapes were marked against the wall. The miller showed Sabine's little girl how to make shadows with her hands. The child laughed and was not altogether at her ease. Sabine leaned over the fire and poked it mechanically with a heavy pair of tongs: she was a little weary, and smiled dreamily, while, without listening, she nodded to her sister-in-law's chatter of her domestic affairs. Christophe sat in the shadow by the miller's side and watched Sabine smiling. He knew that she was smiling at him. They never had an opportunity of being alone all evening, or of looking at each other: they sought none.

They parted early. Their rooms were adjoining, and communicated by a door. Christophe examined the door and found that the lock was on Sabine's side. He went to bed and tried to sleep. The rain was pattering against the windows. The wind howled in the chimney. On the floor above him a door was banging. Outside the window a poplar bent and groaned under the tempest. Christophe could not close his eyes. He was thinking that he was under the same roof, near her. A wall only divided them. He heard no sound in Sabine's room. But he thought he could see her. He sat up in his bed and called to her in a low voice through the wall: tender, passionate words he said: he held out his arms to her. And it seemed to him that she was holding out her arms to him. In his heart he heard the beloved voice answering him, repeating his words, calling low to him: and he did not know whether it was he who asked and answered all the questions, or whether it was really she who spoke. The voice came louder, the call to him: he could not resist: he leaped from his bed: he groped his way to the door: he did not wish to open it: he was reassured by the closed door. And when he laid his hand once more on the handle he found that the door was opening. . . .

He stopped dead. He closed it softly: he opened it once more: he closed it again. Was it not closed just now? Yes. He was sure it was. Who had opened it? . . . His heart beat so that he choked. He leaned over his bed, and sat down to breathe again. He was overwhelmed by his passion. It robbed him of the power to see or hear or move: his whole body shook. He was in terror of this unknown joy for which for months he had been craving, which was with him now, near him, so that nothing could keep it from him. Suddenly the violent boy filled with love was afraid of these desires newly realized and revolted from them. He was ashamed of them, ashamed of what he wished to do. He was too much in love to dare to enjoy what he loved: he was afraid: he would have done anything to escape his happiness. Is it only possible to love, to love, at the cost of the profanation of the beloved? . . .

He went to the door again: and trembling with love and fear, with his hand on the latch he could not bring himself to open it.

And on the other side of the door, standing barefooted on the tiled floor, shivering with cold, was Sabine.

So they stayed . . . for how long? Minutes? Hours? . . . They did not know that they were there: and yet they did know. They held out their arms to each other,—he was overwhelmed by a love so great that he had not the courage to enter,—she called to him, waited for him, trembled lest he should enter.

. . And when at last he made up his mind to enter, she had just made up her mind to turn the lock again.

Then he cursed himself for a fool. He leaned against the door with all his strength. With his lips to the lock he implored her:

" Open."

He called to Sabine in a whisper: she could hear his heated breathing. She stayed motionless near the door: she was frozen: her teeth were chattering: she had no strength either to open the door or to go to bed again. . . .

The storm made the trees crack and the doors in the house bang. . . . They turned away and went to their beds, worn out, sad and sick at heart. The cocks crowed huskily. The first light of dawn crept through the wet windows, a wretched, pale dawn, drowned in the persistent rain. . . .

Christophe got up as soon as he could: he went down to the kitchen and talked to the people there. He was in a hurry to be gone and was afraid of being left alone with Sabine again. He was almost relieved when the miller's wife said that Sabine was unwell, and had caught cold during the drive and would not be going that morning.

His journey home was melancholy. He refused to drive, and walked through the soaking fields, in the yellow mist that covered the earth, the trees, the houses, with a shroud. Like the light, life seemed to be blotted out. Everything loomed like a specter. He was like a specter himself.

At home he found angry faces. They were all scandalized at his having passed the night God knows where with Sabine. He shut himself up in his room and applied himself to his work. Sabine returned the next day and shut herself up also. They avoided meeting each other. The weather was still wet and cold: neither of them went out. They saw each other through their closed windows. Sabine was wrapped up by her fire, dreaming. Christophe was buried in his papers. They bowed to each other a little coldly and reservedly and then pretended to be absorbed again. They did not take stock of what they were feeling: they were angry with each other, with themselves, with things generally. The night at the farmhouse had been thrust aside in their memories: they were ashamed of it, and did not know whether they were more ashamed of their

folly or of not having yielded to it. It was painful to them
to see each other: for that made them remember things from
which they wished to escape: and by joint agreement they
retired into the depths of their rooms so as utterly to forget
each other. But that was impossible, and they suffered keenly
under the secret hostility which they felt was between them.
Christophe was haunted by the expression of dumb rancor which
he had once seen in Sabine's cold eyes. From such thoughts
her suffering was not less: in vain did she struggle against
them, and even deny them: she could not rid herself of them.
They were augmented by her shame that Christophe should have
guessed what was happening within her: and the shame of
having offered herself . . . the shame of having offered herself
without having given.

Christophe gladly accepted an opportunity which cropped up
to go to Cologne and Düsseldorf for some concerts. He was
glad to spend two or three weeks away from home. Preparation for the concerts and the composition of a new work that
he wished to play at them took up all his time and he succeeded
in forgetting his obstinate memories. They disappeared from
Sabine's mind too, and she fell back into the torpor of her
usual life. They came to think of each other with indifference.
Had they really loved each other? They doubted it. Christophe was on the point of leaving for Cologne without saying
good-bye to Sabine.

On the evening before his departure they were brought together again by some imperceptible influence. It was one of
the Sunday afternoons when everybody was at church. Christophe had gone out too to make his final preparations for the
journey. Sabine was sitting in her tiny garden warming herself in the last rays of the sun. Christophe came home: he
was in a hurry and his first inclination when he saw her was
to bow and pass on. But something held him back as he was
passing: was it Sabine's paleness, or some indefinable feeling:
remorse, fear, tenderness? . . . He stopped, turned to Sabine,
and, leaning over the fence, he bade her good-evening. Without
replying she held out her hand. Her smile was all kindness,—
such kindness as he had never seen in her. Her gesture seemed
to say: "Peace between us. . . ." He took her hand over the

fence, bent over it, and kissed it. She made no attempt to withdraw it. He longed to go down on his knees and say, "I love you." . . . They looked at each other in silence. But they offered no explanation. After a moment she removed her hand and turned her head. He turned too to hide his emotion. Then they looked at each other again with untroubled eyes. The sun was setting. Subtle shades of color, violet, orange, and mauve, chased across the cold clear sky. She shivered and drew her shawl closer about her shoulders with a movement that he knew well. He asked:

"How are you?"

She made a little grimace, as if the question were not worth answering. They went on looking at each other and were happy. It was as though they had lost, and had just found each other again. . . .

At last he broke the silence and said:

"I am going away to-morrow."

There was alarm in Sabine's eyes.

"Going away?" she said.

He added quickly:

"Oh! only for two or three weeks." .

"Two or three weeks," she said in dismay.

He explained that he was engaged for the concerts, but that when he came back he would not stir all winter.

"Winter," she said. "That is a long time off. . . ."

"Oh! no. It will soon be here."

She saddened and did not look at him.

"When shall we meet again?" she asked a moment later.

Tle did not understand the question: he had already answered it.

"As soon as I come back: in a fortnight, or three weeks at most."

She still looked dismayed. He tried to tease her:

"It won't be long for you," he said. "You will sleep."

"Yes," said Sabine.

She looked down, she tried to smile: but her eyes trembled. "Christophe! . . ." she said suddenly, turning towards him. There was a note of distress in her voice. She seemed to say: "Stay! Don't go! . . ."

He took her hand, looked at her, did not understand the importance she attached to his fortnight's absence: but he was only waiting for a word from her to say:

" I will stay. . . ."

And just as she was going to speak, the front door was opened and Rosa appeared. Sabine withdrew her hand from Christophe's and went hurriedly into her house. At the door she turned and looked at him once more—and disappeared.

Christophe thought he should see her again in the evening. But he was watched by the Vogels, and followed everywhere by his mother: as usual, he was behindhand with his preparations for his journey and could not find time to leave the house for a moment.

Next day he left very early. As he passed Sabine's door he longed to go in, to tap at the window: it hurt him to leave her without saying good-bye: for he had been interrupted by Rosa before he had had time to do so. But he thought she must be asleep and would be cross with him if he woke her up. And then, what could he say to her? It was too late now to abandon his journey: and what if she were to ask him to do so? . . . He did not admit to himself that he was not averse to exercising his power over her,—if need be, causing her a little pain. . . . He did not take seriously the grief that his departure brought Sabine: and he thought that his short absence would increase the tenderness which, perhaps, she had for him.

He ran to the station. In spite of everything he was a little remorseful. But as soon as the train had started it was all forgotten. There was youth in his heart. Gaily he saluted the old town with its roofs and towers rosy under the sun: and with the carelessness of those who are departing he said good-bye to those whom he was leaving, and thought no more of them.

The whole time that he was at Düsseldorf and Cologne Sabine never once recurred to his mind. Taken up from morning till night with rehearsals and concerts, dinners and talk, busied with a thousand and one new things and the pride and satisfaction of his success he had no time for recollection. Once only, on the fifth night after he left home, he woke suddenly after a dream and knew that he had been thinking of *her* in his sleep and that the thought of *her* had wakened him up: but he could not remember how he had been thinking of her. He was unhappy and feverish. It was not surprising: he had been playing at a concert that evening, and when he left the hall he had been dragged off to a supper at which he had drunk several glasses of champagne. He could not sleep and got up. He was obsessed by a musical idea. He pretended that it was that which had broken in upon his sleep and he wrote it down. As he read through it he was astonished to see how sad it was. There was no sadness in him when he wrote: at least, so he thought. But he remembered that on other occasions when he had been sad he had only been able to write joyous music, so gay that it offended his mood. He gave no more thought to it. He was used to the surprises of his mind world without ever being able to understand them. He went to sleep at once, and knew no more until the next morning.

He extended his stay by three or four days. It pleased him to prolong it, knowing he could return whenever he liked: he was in no hurry to go home. It was only when he was on the way, in the train, that the thought of Sabine came back to him. He had not written to her. He was even careless enough never to have taken the trouble to ask at the post-office for any letters that might have been written to him. He took a secret delight in his silence: he knew that at home he was expected, that he was loved. . . . Loved? She had never told him so: he had never told her so. No doubt they knew it and had no need to tell it. And yet there was nothing so precious as the certainty of such an avowal. Why had they waited so long to make it? When they had been on the point of speaking always something —some mischance, shyness, embarrassment,—had hindered them. Why? Why? How much time they had lost! . . . He longed to hear the dear words from the lips of the beloved. He longed to say them to her: he said them aloud in the empty carriage. As he neared the town he was torn with impatience, a sort of agony. . . . Faster! Faster! Oh! To think that in an hour he would see her again! . . .

It was half-past six in the morning when he reached home. Nobody was up yet. Sabine's windows were closed. He went

into the yard on tiptoe so that she should not hear him. He
chuckled at the thought of taking her by surprise. He went
up to his room. His mother was asleep. He washed and brushed
his hair without making any noise. He was hungry: but he was
afraid of waking Louisa by rummaging in the pantry. He
heard footsteps in the yard: he opened his window softly and
saw Rosa, first up as usual, beginning to sweep. He called her
gently. She started in glad surprise when she saw him: then
she looked solemn. He thought she was still offended with him:
but for the moment he was in a very good temper. He went
down to her.

"Rosa, Rosa," he said gaily, "give me something to eat or
I shall eat you! I am dying of hunger!"

Rosa smiled and took him to the kitchen on the ground floor.
She poured him out a bowl of milk and then could not refrain
from plying him with a string of questions about his travels
and his concerts. But although he was quite ready to answer
them,—(in the happiness of his return he was almost glad to
hear Rosa's chatter once more)—Rosa stopped suddenly in the
middle of her cross-examination, her face fell, her eyes turned
away, and she became sorrowful. Then her chatter broke out
again: but soon it seemed that she thought it out of place
and once more she stopped short. And he noticed it then and
said:

"What is the matter, Rosa? Are you cross with me?"

She shook her head violently in denial, and turning towards him with her usual suddenness took his arm with both
hands:

"Oh! Christophe! . . ." she said.

He was alarmed. He let his piece of bread fall from his
hands.

"What! What is the matter?" he stammered.

She said again:

"Oh! Christophe! . . . Such an awful thing has happened!"

He thrust away from the table. He stuttered:

"H—here?"

She pointed to the house on the other side of the yard.

He cried:

"Sabine!"

She wept:

"She is dead."

Christophe saw nothing. He got up: he almost fell: he clung to the table, upset the things on it: he wished to cry out. He suffered fearful agony. He turned sick.

Rosa hastened to his side: she was frightened: she held his head and wept.

As soon as he could speak he said:

"It is not true!"

He knew that it was true. But he wanted to deny it, he wanted to pretend that it could not be. When he saw Rosa's face wet with tears he could doubt no more and he sobbed aloud.

Rosa raised her head:

"Christophe!" she said.

He hid his face in his hands. She leaned towards him.

"Christophe! . . . Mamma is coming! . . ."

Christophe got up.

"No, no," he said. "She must not see me."

She took his hand and led him, stumbling and blinded by his tears, to a little woodshed which opened on to the yard. She closed the door. They were in darkness. He sat on a block of wood used for chopping sticks. She sat on the fagots. Sounds from without were deadened and distant. There he could weep without fear of being heard. He let himself go and sobbed furiously. Rosa had never seen him weep: she had even thought that he could not weep: she knew only her own girlish tears and such despair in a man filled her with terror and pity. She was filled with a passionate love for Christophe. It was an absolutely unselfish love: an immense need of sacrifice, a maternal self-denial, a hunger to suffer for him, to take his sorrow upon herself. She put her arm round his shoulders.

"Dear Christophe," she said, "do not cry!"

Christophe turned from her.

"I wish to die!"

Rosa clasped her hands.

"Don't say that, Christophe!"

"I wish to die. I cannot . . . cannot live now. . . . What is the good of living?"

" Christophe, dear Christophe! You are not alone. You are loved. . . ."

" What is that to me? I love nothing now. It is nothing to me whether everything else live or die. I love nothing: I loved only her. I loved only her!"

He sobbed louder than ever with his face buried in his hands. Rosa could find nothing to say. The egoism of Christophe's passion stabbed her to the heart. Now when she thought herself most near to him, she felt more isolated and more miserable than ever. Grief instead of bringing them together thrust them only the more widely apart. She wept bitterly.

After some time, Christophe stopped weeping and asked:
" How? . . . How? . . ."

Rosa understood.

" She fell ill of influenza on the evening you left. And she was taken suddenly. . . ."

He groaned.

" Dear God! . . . Why did you not write to me?"

She said:

" I did write. I did not know your address: you did not give us any. I went and asked at the theater. Nobody knew it."

He knew how timid she was, and how much it must have cost her. He asked:

" Did she . . . did she tell you to do that?"

She shook her head:

" No. But I thought . . ."

He thanked her with a look. Rosa's heart melted.

" My poor . . . poor Christophe!" she said.

She flung her arms round his neck and wept. Christophe felt the worth of such pure tenderness. He had so much need of consolation! He kissed her:

" How kind you are," he said. " You loved her too?"

She broke away from him, she threw him a passionate look, did not reply, and began to weep again.

That look was a revelation to him. It meant:

" It was not she whom I loved. . . ."

Christophe saw at last what he had not known—what for months he had not wished to see. He saw that she loved him.

" 'Ssh," she said. " They are calling me." They heard
Amalia's voice.

Rosa asked:

" Do you want to go back to your room? "

He said:

" No. I could not yet: I could not bear to talk to my
mother. . . . Later on. . . ."

She said:

" Stay here. I will come back soon."

He stayed in the dark woodshed to which only a thread of
light penetrated through a small airhole filled with cobwebs.
From the street there came up the cry of a hawker, against the
wall a horse in a stable next door was snorting and kicking.
The revelation that had just come to Christophe gave him no
pleasure: but it held his attention for a moment. It made plain
many things that he had not understood. A multitude of little
things that he had disregarded occurred to him and were explained. He was surprised to find himself thinking of it: he
was ashamed to be turned aside even for a moment from his
misery. But that misery was so frightful, so irrepressible that
the mistrust of self-preservation, stronger than his will, than
his courage, than his love, forced him to turn away from it,
seized on this new idea, as the suicide drowning seizes in spite
of himself on the first object which can help him, not to save
himself, but to keep himself for a moment longer above the
water. And it was because he was suffering that he was able
to feel what another was suffering—suffering through him. He
understood the tears that he had brought to her eyes. He was
filled with pity for Rosa. He thought how cruel he had been
to her—how cruel he must still be. For he did not love her.
What good was it for her to love him? Poor girl! . . . In vain
did he tell himself that she was good (she had just proved
it). What was her goodness to him? What was her life to
him? . . .

He thought:

" Why is it not she who is dead, and the other who is alive? "

He thought:

" She is alive: she loves me: she can tell me that to-day, to-
morrow, all my life: and the other, the woman I love, she is

dead and never told me that she loved me: I never have told
her that I loved her: I shall never hear her say it: she will never
know it. . . ."

And suddenly he remembered that last evening: he remembered that they were just going to talk when Rosa came and
prevented it. And he hated Rosa. . . .

The door of the woodshed was opened. Rosa called Christophe softly, and groped towards him. She took his hand. He
felt an aversion in her near presence: in vain did he reproach
himself for it: it was stronger than himself.

Rosa was silent: her great pity had taught her silence. Christophe was grateful to her for not breaking in upon his grief
with useless words. And yet he wished to know . . . she was
the only creature who could talk to him of *her*. He asked in
a whisper:

" When did she . . ."

(He dared not say: die.)

She replied:

" Last Saturday week."

Dimly he remembered. He said: ·

" At night? "

Rosa looked at him in astonishment and said:

" Yes. At night. Between two and three."

The sorrowful melody came back to him. He asked, trembling:

" Did she suffer much? "

" No, no. God be thanked, dear Christophe: she hardly suffered at all. She was so weak. She did not struggle against
it. Suddenly they saw that she was lost. . . ."

" And she . . . did she know it? "

" I don't know. I think . . ."

" Did she say anything? "

" No. Nothing. She was sorry for herself like a child."

" You were there? "

" Yes. For the first two days I was there alone, before her
brother came."

He pressed her hand in gratitude.

" Thank you."

She felt the blood rush to her heart.

After a silence he said, he murmured the question which was choking him:

" Did she say anything . . . for me? "

Rosa shook her head sadly. She would have given much to be able to let him have the answer he expected: she was almost sorry that she could not lie about it. She tried to console him:

" She was not conscious."

" But she did speak? "

" One could not make out what she said. It was in a very low voice."

" Where is the child? "

" Her brother took her away with him to the country."

" And *she?* "

" She is there too. She was taken away last Monday week."

They began to weep again.

Frau Vogel's voice called Rosa once more. Christophe, left alone again, lived through those days of death. A week, already a week ago. . . . O God! What had become of her? How it had rained that week! . . . And all that time he was laughing, he was happy!

In his pocket he felt a little parcel wrapped up in soft paper: they were silver buckles that he had brought her for her shoes. He remembered the evening when he had placed his hand on the little stockinged foot. Her little feet: where were they now? How cold they must be! . . . He thought the memory of that warm contact was the only one that he had of the beloved creature. He had never dared to touch her, to take her in his arms, to hold her to his breast. She was gone forever, and he had never known her. He knew nothing of her, neither soul nor body. He had no memory of her body, of her life, of her love. . . . Her love? . . . What proof had he of that? . . . He had not even a letter, a token,—nothing. Where could he seek to hold her, in himself, or outside himself? . . . Oh! Nothing! There was nothing left him but the love he had for her, nothing left him but himself.—And in spite of all, his desperate desire to snatch her from destruction, his need of denying death, made him cling to the last piece of wreckage, in an act of blind faith:

"... *he son gia morto: e ben c'albergo cangi resto in te vivo. C'or mi vedi e piangi, se l'un nell' altro amante si trasforma.*"

"... I am not dead: I have changed my dwelling. I live still in thee who art faithful to me. The soul of the beloved is merged in the soul of the lover."

He had never read these sublime words: but they were in him. Each one of us in turn climbs the Calvary of the age. Each one of us finds anew the agony, each one of us finds anew the desperate hope and folly of the ages. Each one of us follows in the footsteps of those who were, of those before us who struggled with death, denied death—and are dead.

He shut himself up in his room. His shutters were closed all day so as not to see the windows of the house opposite. He avoided the Vogels: they were odious to his sight. He had nothing to reproach them with: they were too honest, and too pious not to have thrust back their feelings in the face of death. They knew Christophe's grief and respected it, whatever they might think of it: they never uttered Sabine's name in his presence. But they had been her enemies when she was alive: that was enough to make him their enemy now that she was dead.

Besides they had not altered their noisy habits: and in spite of the sincere though passing pity that they had felt, it was obvious that at bottom they were untouched by the misfortune—(it was too natural)—perhaps even they were secretly relieved by it. Christophe imagined so at least. Now that the Vogels' intentions with regard to himself were made plain he exaggerated them in his own mind. In reality they attached little importance to him: he set too great store by himself. But he had no doubt that the death of Sabine, by removing the greatest obstacle in the way of his landlords' plans, did seem to them to leave the field clear for Rosa. So he detested her. That they—(the Vogels, Louisa, and even Rosa)—should have tacitly disposed of him, without consulting him, was enough in any case to make him lose all affection for the person whom he was destined to love. He shied whenever he thought an attempt was made upon his umbrageous sense of liberty. But now it was not only a question of himself. The rights which these others had assumed over him did not only infringe upon his own rights but upon those of the dead woman to whom his heart was given. So he defended them doggedly, although no one was for attacking them. He suspected Rosa's goodness. She suffered in seeing him suffer and would often come and knock at his door to console him and talk to him about the other. He did not drive her away: he needed to talk of Sabine with some one who had known her: he wanted to know the smallest of what had happened during her illness. But he was not grateful to Rosa: he attributed ulterior motives to her. Was it not plain that her family, even Amalia, permitted these visits and long colloquies which she would never have allowed if they had not fallen in with her wishes? Was not Rosa in league with her family? He could not believe that her pity was absolutely sincere and free of personal thoughts.

And, no doubt, it was not. Rosa pitied Christophe with all her heart. She tried hard to see Sabine through Christophe's eyes, and through him to love her: she was angry with herself for all the unkind feelings that she had ever had towards her, and asked her pardon in her prayers at night. But could she forget that she was alive, that she was seeing Christophe every moment of the day, that she loved him, that she was no longer afraid of the other, that the other was gone, that her memory would also fade away in its turn, that she was left alone, that one day perhaps . . .? In the midst of her sorrow, and the sorrow of her friend more hers than her own, could she repress a glad impulse, an unreasoning hope? For that too she was angry with herself. It was only a flash. It was enough. He saw it. He threw her a glance which froze her heart: she read in it hateful thoughts: he hated her for being alive while the other was dead.

The miller brought his cart for Sabine's little furniture. Coming back from a lesson Christophe saw heaped up before the door in the street the bed, the cupboard, the mattress, the linen, all that she had possessed, all that was left of her. It was a dreadful sight to him. He rushed past it. In the doorway he bumped into Bertold, who stopped him.

"Ah! my dear sir," he said, shaking his hand effusively.

"Ah! who would have thought it when we were together? How happy we were! And yet it was because of that day, because of that cursed row on the water, that she fell ill. Oh! well. It is no use complaining! She is dead. It will be our turn next. That is life. . . . And how are you? I'm very well, thank God!"

He was red in the face, sweating, and smelled of wine. The idea that he was her brother, that he had rights in her memory, hurt Christophe. It offended him to hear this man talking of his beloved. The miller on the contrary was glad to find a friend with whom he could talk of Sabine: he did not understand Christophe's coldness. He had no idea of all the sorrow that his presence, the sudden calling to mind of the day at his farm, the happy memories that he recalled so blunderingly, the poor relics of Sabine, heaped upon the ground, which he kicked as he talked, set stirring in Christophe's soul. He made some excuse for stopping Bertold's tongue. He went up the steps: but the other clung to him, stopped him, and went on with his harangue. At last when the miller took to telling him of Sabine's illness, with that strange pleasure which certain people, and especially the common people, take in talking of illness, with a plethora of painful details, Christophe could bear it no longer—(he took a tight hold of himself so as not to cry out in his sorrow). He cut him short:

"Pardon," he said curtly and icily. "I must leave you."

He left him without another word.

His insensibility revolted the miller. He had guessed the secret affection of his sister and Christophe. And that Christophe should now show such indifference seemed monstrous to him: he thought he had no heart.

Christophe had fled to his room: he was choking. Until the removal was over he never left his room. He vowed that he would never look out of the window, but he could not help doing so: and hiding in a corner behind the curtain he followed the departure of the goods and chattels of the beloved eagerly and with profound sorrow. When he saw them disappearing forever he all but ran down to the street to cry: "No! no! Leave them to me! Do not take them from me!" He longed to beg at least for some little thing, only one little thing, so that she should not be altogether taken from him. But how could he ask such a thing of the miller? It was nothing to him. She herself had not known his love: how dared he then reveal it to another? And besides, if he had tried to say a word he would have burst out crying. . . . No. No. He had to say nothing, to watch all go, without being able—without daring to save one fragment from the wreck. . . .

And when it was all over, when the house was empty, when the yard gate was closed after the miller, when the wheels of his cart moved on, shaking the windows, when they were out of hearing, he threw himself on the floor—not a tear left in him, not a thought of suffering, of struggling, frozen, and like one dead.

There was a knock at the door. He did not move. Another knock. He had forgotten to lock the door. Rosa came in. She cried out on seeing him stretched on the floor and stopped in terror. He raised his head angrily:

"What? What do you want? Leave me!"

She did not go: she stayed, hesitating, leaning against the door, and said again:

"Christophe. . . ."

He got up in silence: he was ashamed of having been seen so. He dusted himself with his hand and asked harshly:

"Well. What do you want?"

Rosa said shyly:

"Forgive me . . . Christophe . . . I came in . . . I was bringing you . . ."

He saw that she had something in her hand.

"See," she said, holding it out to him. "I asked Bertold to give me a little token of her. I thought you would like it. . . ."

It was a little silver mirror, the pocket mirror in which she used to look at herself for hours, not so much from coquetry as from want of occupation. Christophe took it, took also the hand which held it.

"Oh! Rosa! . . ." he said.

He was filled with her kindness and the knowledge of his own injustice. On a passionate impulse he knelt to her and kissed her hand.

" Forgive . . . Forgive . . ." he said.

Rosa did not understand at first: then she understood only too well: she blushed, she trembled, she began to weep. She understood that he meant:

" Forgive me if I am unjust. . . . Forgive me if I do not love you. . . . Forgive me if I cannot . . . if I cannot love you, if I can never love you! . . ."

She did not withdraw her hand from him: she knew that it was not herself that he was kissing. And with his cheek against Rosa's hand, he wept hot tears, knowing that she was reading through him: there was sorrow and bitterness in being unable to love her and making her suffer.

They stayed so, both weeping, in the dim light of the room. At last she withdrew her hand. He went on murmuring: " Forgive! . . ."

She laid her hand gently on his hand. He rose to his feet. They kissed in silence: they felt on their lips the bitter savor of their tears.

" We shall always be friends," he said softly. She bowed her head and left him, too sad to speak.

They thought that the world is ill made. The lover is unloved. The beloved does not love. The lover who is loved is sooner or later torn from his love. . . . There is suffering. There is the bringing of suffering. And the most wretched is not always the one who suffers.

Once more Christophe took to avoiding the house. He could not bear it. He could not bear to see the curtainless windows, the empty rooms.

A worse sorrow awaited him. Old Euler lost no time in reletting the ground floor. One day Christophe saw strange faces in Sabine's room. New lives blotted out the traces of the life that was gone.

It became impossible for him to stay in his rooms. He passed whole days outside, not coming back until nightfall, when it was too dark to see anything. Once more he took to making expeditions in the country. Irresistibly he was drawn to Bertold's farm. But he never went in, dared not go near it, wandered about it at a distance. He discovered a place on a hill

from which he could see the house, the plain, the river: it was
thither that his steps usually turned. From thence he could
follow with his eyes the meanderings of the water down to the
willow clump under which he had seen the shadow of death pass
across Sabine's face. From thence he could pick out the two
windows of the rooms in which they had waited, side by side,
so near, so far, separated by a door—the door to eternity. From
thence he could survey the cemetery. He had never been able
to bring himself to enter it: from childhood he had had a horror
of those fields of decay and corruption, and refused to think of
those whom he loved in connection with them. But from a
distance and seen from above, the little graveyard never looked
grim, it was calm, it slept with the sun. . . . Sleep! . . . She
loved to sleep! Nothing would disturb her there. The crowing
cocks answered each other across the plains. From the home-
stead rose the roaring of the mill, the clucking of the poultry
yard, the cries of children playing. He could make out Sabine's
little girl, he could see her running, he could mark her laughter.
Once he lay in wait for her near the gate of the farmyard, in a
turn of the sunk road made by the walls: he seized her as
she passed and kissed her. The child was afraid and began
to cry. She had almost forgotten him already. He asked
her:

"Are you happy here?"

"Yes. It is fun. . . ."

"You don't want to come back?"

"No!"

He let her go. The child's indifference plunged him in sorrow.
Poor Sabine! . . . And yet it was she, something of her. . . .
So little! The child was hardly at all like her mother: had
lived in her, but was not she: in that mysterious passage through
her being the child had hardly retained more than the faintest
perfume of the creature who was gone: inflections of her voice,
a pursing of the lips, a trick of bending the head. The rest
of her was another being altogether: and that being mingled
with the being of Sabine was repulsive to Christophe though
he never admitted it to himself.

It was only in himself that Christophe could find the image
of Sabine. It followed him everywhere, hovering above him:

but he only felt himself really to be with her when he was
alone. Nowhere was she nearer to him than in this refuge,
on the hill, far from strange eyes, in the midst of the country
that was so full of the memory of her. He would go miles to it,
climbing at a run, his heart beating as though he were going to
a meeting with her: and so it was indeed. When he reached
it he would lie on the ground—the same earth in which *her*
body was laid: he would close his eyes: and *she* would come to
him. He could not see her face: he could not hear her voice:
he had no need: she entered into him, held him, he possessed
her utterly. In this state of passionate hallucination he would
lose the power of thought, he would be unconscious of what
was happening: he was unconscious of everything save that he
was with her.

That state of things did not last long.—To tell the truth
he was only once altogether sincere. From the day following,
his will had its share in the proceedings. And from that time
on Christophe tried in vain to bring it back to life. It was
only then that he thought of evoking in himself the face and
form of Sabine: until then he had never thought of it. He
succeeded spasmodically and he was fired by it. But it was only
at the cost of hours of waiting and of darkness.

"Poor Sabine!" he would think. "They have all forgotten
you. There is only I who love you, who keep your memory
alive forever. Oh, my treasure, my precious! I have you, I
hold you, I will never let you go! . . ."

He spoke these words because already she was escaping him:
she was slipping from his thoughts like water through his
fingers. He would return again and again, faithful to the tryst.
He wished to think of her and he would close his eyes. But
after half an hour, or an hour, or sometimes two hours, he
would begin to see that he had been thinking of nothing. The
sounds of the valley, the roar of the wind, the little bells of the
two goats browsing on the hill, the noise of the wind in the
little slender trees under which he lay, were sucked up by his
thoughts soft and porous like a sponge. He was angry with
his thoughts: they tried to obey him, and to fix the vanished
image to which he was striving to attach his life: but his
thoughts fell back weary and chastened and once more with a

sigh of comfort abandoned themselves to the listless stream of
sensations.

He shook off his torpor.   He strode through the country
hither and thither seeking Sabine.   He sought her in the mirror
that once had held her smile.   He sought her by the river bank
where her hands had dipped in the water.   But the mirror and
the water gave him only the reflection of himself.   The excitement of walking, the fresh air, the beating of his own healthy
blood awoke music in him once more.   He wished to find
change.

"Oh! Sabine! . . ." he sighed.

He dedicated his songs to her: he strove to call her to life in
his music, his love, and his sorrow. . . . In vain: love and sorrow came to life surely: but poor Sabine had no share in them.
Love and sorrow looked towards the future, not towards the past.
Christophe was powerless against his youth.   The sap of life
swelled up again in him with new vigor.   His grief, his regrets,
his chaste and ardent love, his baffled desires, heightened the
fever that was in him.   In spite of his sorrow, his heart beat
in lively, sturdy rhythm: wild songs leaped forth in mad, intoxicated strains: everything in him hymned life and even sadness took on a festival shape.   Christophe was too frank to
persist in self-deception: and he despised himself.   But life
swept him headlong: and in his sadness, with death in his heart,
and life in all his limbs, he abandoned himself to the forces
newborn in him, to the absurd, delicious joy of living, which
grief, pity, despair, the aching wound of an irreparable loss,
all the torment of death, can only sharpen and kindle into being
in the strong, as they rowel their sides with furious spur.

And Christophe knew that, in himself, in the secret hidden
depths of his soul, he had an inaccessible and inviolable sanctuary where lay the shadow of Sabine.   That the flood of life
could not bear away. . . . Each of us bears in his soul as it
were a little graveyard of those whom he has loved.   They sleep
there, through the years, untroubled.   But a day cometh,—this
we know,—when the graves shall reopen.   The dead issue from
the tomb and smile with their pale lips—loving, always—on
the beloved, and the lover, in whose breast their memory dwells,
like the child sleeping in the mother's womb.

III

ADA

AFTER the wet summer the autumn was radiant. In the orchards the trees were weighed down with fruit. The red apples shone like billiard balls. Already some of the trees were taking on their brilliant garb of the falling year: flame color, fruit color, color of ripe melon, of oranges and lemons, of good cooking, and fried dishes. Misty lights glowed through the woods: and from the meadows there rose the little pink flames of the saffron.

He was going down a hill. It was a Sunday afternoon. He was striding, almost running, gaining speed down the slope. He was singing a phrase, the rhythm of which had been obsessing him all through his walk. He was red, disheveled: he was walking, swinging his arms, and rolling his eyes like a madman, when as he turned a bend in the road he came suddenly on a fair girl perched on a wall tugging with all her might at a branch of a tree from which she was greedily plucking and eating purple plums. Their astonishment was mutual. She looked at him, stared, with her mouth full. Then she burst out laughing. So did he. She was good to see, with her round face framed in fair curly hair, which was like a sunlit cloud about her, her full pink cheeks, her wide blue eyes, her rather large nose, impertinently turned up, her little red mouth showing white teeth—the canine little, strong, and projecting—her plump chin, and her full figure, large and plump, well built, solidly put together. He called out:

"Good eating!" And was for going on his road. But she called to him:

"Sir! Sir! Will you be very nice? Help me to get down. I can't . . ."

He returned and asked her how she had climbed up.

"With my hands and feet. . . . It is easy enough to get up. . . ."

"Especially when there are tempting plums hanging above your head. . . ."

" Yes. . . . But when you have eaten your courage goes
You can't find the way to get down."

He looked at her on her perch. He said:

" You are all right there. Stay there quietly. I'll come and
see you to-morrow. Good-night! "

But he did not budge, and stood beneath her. She pretended
to be afraid, and begged him with little glances not to leave
her. They stayed looking at each other and laughing. She
showed him the branch to which she was clinging and asked:

" Would you like some? "

Respect for property had not developed in Christophe since
the days of his expeditions with Otto: he accepted without
hesitation. She amused herself with pelting him with plums.
When he had eaten she said:

" Now! . . ."

He took a wicked pleasure in keeping her waiting. She grew
impatient on her wall. At last he said:

" Come, then! " and held his hand up to her.

But just as she was about to jump down she thought a
moment.

" Wait! We must make provision first! "

She gathered the finest plums within reach and filled the
front of her blouse with them.

" Carefully! Don't crush them! "

He felt almost inclined to do so.

She lowered herself from the wall and jumped into his arms.
Although he was sturdy he bent under her weight and all but
dragged her down. They were of the same height. Their
faces came together. He kissed her lips, moist and sweet with
the juice of the plums: and she returned his kiss without more
ceremony.

" Where are you going? " he asked.

" I don't know."

" Are you out alone? "

" No. I am with friends. But I have lost them. . . . Hi!
Hi! " she called suddenly as loudly as she could.

No answer.

She did not bother about it any more. They began to walk,
at random, following their noses.

"And you . . . where are you going?" said she.

"I don't know, either."

"Good. We'll go together."

She took some plums from her gaping blouse and began to munch them.

"You'll make yourself sick," he said.

"Not I! I've been eating them all day."

Through the gap in her blouse he saw the white of her chemise.

"They are all warm now," she said.

"Let me see!"

She held him one and laughed. He ate it. She watched him out of the corner of her eye as she sucked at the fruit like a child. He did not know how the adventure would end. It is probable that she at least had some suspicion. She waited.

"Hi! Hi!" Voices in the woods.

"Hi! Hi!" she answered. "Ah! There they are!" she said to Christophe. "Not a bad thing, either!"

But on the contrary she was thinking that it was rather a pity. But speech was not given to woman for her to say what she is thinking. . . . Thank God! for there would be an end of morality on earth. . . .

The voices came near. Her friends were near the road. She leaped the ditch, climbed the hedge, and hid behind the trees. He watched her in amazement. She signed to him imperiously to come to her. He followed her. She plunged into the depths of the wood.

"Hi! Hi!" she called once more when they had gone some distance. "You see, they must look for me!" she explained to Christophe.

Her friends had stopped on the road and were listening for her voice to mark where it came from. They answered her and in their turn entered the woods. But she did not wait for them. She turned about on right and on left. They bawled loudly after her. She let them, and then went and called in the opposite direction. At last they wearied of it, and, making sure that the best way of making her come was to give up seeking her, they called:

"Good-bye!" and went off singing.

She was furious that they should not have bothered about her any more than that. She had tried to be rid of them: but she had not counted on their going off so easily. Christophe looked rather foolish: this game of hide-and-seek with a girl whom he did not know did not exactly enthrall him: and he had no thought of taking advantage of their solitude. Nor did she think of it: in her annoyance she forgot Christophe.

" Oh! It's too much," she said, thumping her hands together. " They have left me."

" But," said Christophe, " you wanted them to."

" Not at all."

" You ran away."

" If I ran away from them that is my affair, not theirs. They ought to look for me. What if I were lost? . . ."

Already she was beginning to be sorry for herself because of what might have happened if . . . if the opposite of what actually had occurred had come about.

" Oh! " she said. " I'll shake them! " She turned back and strode off.

As she went she remembered Christophe and looked at him once more.—But it was too late. She began to·laugh. The little demon which had been in her the moment before was gone. While she was waiting for another to come she saw Christophe with the eyes of indifference. And then, she was hungry. Her stomach was reminding her that it was supper-time: she was in a hurry to rejoin her friends at the inn. She took Christophe's arm, leaned on it with all her weight, groaned, and said that she was exhausted. That did not keep her from dragging Christophe down a slope, running, and shouting, and laughing like a mad thing.

They talked. She learned who he was: she did not know his name, and seemed not to be greatly impressed by his title of musician. He learned that she was a shop-girl from a dress-maker's in the *Kaiserstrasse* (the most fashionable street in the town): her name was Adelheid—to friends, Ada. Her companions on the excursion were one of her friends, who worked at the same place as herself, and two nice young men, a clerk at Weiller's bank, and a clerk from a big linen-draper's. They

were turning their Sunday to account: they had decided to
dine at the Brochet inn, from which there is a fine view over
the Rhine, and then to return by boat.

The others had already established themselves at the inn
when they arrived. Ada made a scene with her friends: she
complained of their cowardly desertion and presented Christophe as her savior. They did not listen to her complaints:
but they knew Christophe, the bank-clerk by reputation, the
clerk from having heard some of his compositions—(he thought
it a good idea to hum an air from one of them immediately
afterwards)—and the respect which they showed him made an
impression on Ada, the more so as Myrrha, the other young
woman—(her real name was Hansi or Johanna)—a brunette
with blinking eyes, bumpy forehead, hair screwed back, Chinese
face, a little too animated, but clever and not without charm,
in spite of her goat-like head and her oily golden-yellow
complexion,—at once began to make advances to their *Hof
Musicus.* They begged him to be so good as to honor their
repast with his presence.

Never had he been in such high feather: for he was overwhelmed with attentions, and the two women, like good friends
as they were, tried each to rob the other of him. Both courted
him: Myrrha with ceremonious manners, sly looks, as she rubbed
her leg against his under the table—Ada, openly making play
with her fine eyes, her pretty mouth, and all the seductive
resources at her command. Such coquetry in its almost coarseness incommoded and distressed Christophe. These two bold
young women were a change from the unkindly faces he was
accustomed to at home. Myrrha interested him, he guessed her
to be more intelligent than Ada: but her obsequious manners
and her ambiguous smile were curiously attractive and repulsive
to him at the same time. She could do nothing against Ada's
radiance of life and pleasure: and she was aware of it. When
she saw that she had lost the bout, she abandoned the effort,
turned in upon herself, went on smiling, and patiently waited
for her day to come. Ada, seeing herself mistress of the field,
did not seek to push forward the advantage she had gained:
what she had done had been mainly to despite her friend: she
had succeeded, she was satisfied. But she had been caught in

her own game. She felt as she looked into Christophe's eyes the passion that she had kindled in him: and that same passion began to awake in her. She was silent: she left her vulgar teasing: they looked at each other in silence: on their lips they had the savor of their kiss. From time to time by fits and starts they joined vociferously in the jokes of the others: then they relapsed into silence, stealing glances at each other. At last they did not even look at each other, as though they were afraid of betraying themselves. Absorbed in themselves they brooded over their desire.

When the meal was over they got ready to go. They had to go a mile and a half through the woods to reach the pier. Ada got up first: Christophe followed her. They waited on the steps until the others were ready: without speaking, side by side, in the thick mist that was hardly at all lit up by the single lamp hanging by the inn door.—Myrrha was dawdling by the mirror.

Ada took Christophe's hand and led him along the house towards the garden into the darkness. Under a balcony from which hung a curtain of vines they hid. All about them was dense darkness. They could not even see each other. The wind stirred the tops of the pines. He felt Ada's warm fingers entwined in his and the sweet scent of a heliotrope flower that she had at her breast.

Suddenly she dragged him to her: Christophe's lips found Ada's hair, wet with the mist, and kissed her eyes, her eyebrows, her nose, her cheeks, the corners of her mouth, seeking her lips, and finding them, staying pressed to them.

The others had gone. They called:

"Ada! . . ."

They did not stir, they hardly breathed, pressed close to each other, lips and bodies.

They heard Myrrha:

"They have gone on."

The footsteps of their companions died away in the night. They held each other closer, in silence, stifling on their lips a passionate murmuring.

In the distance a village clock rang out. They broke apart. They had to run to the pier. Without a word they set out, arms and hands entwined, keeping step—a little quick, firm step, like hers. The road was deserted: no creature was abroad: they could not see ten yards ahead of them: they went, serene and sure, into the beloved night. They never stumbled over the pebbles on the road. As they were late they took a short cut. The path led for some way down through vines and then began to ascend and wind up the side of the hill. Through the mist they could hear the roar of the river and the heavy paddles of the steamer approaching. They left the road and ran across the fields. At last they found themselves on the bank of the Rhine but still far from the pier. Their serenity was not disturbed. Ada had forgotten her fatigue of the evening. It seemed to them that they could have walked all night like that, on the silent grass, in the hovering mists, that grew wetter and more dense along the river that was wrapped in a whiteness as of the moon. The steamer's siren hooted: the invisible monster plunged heavily away and away. They said, laughing:

" We will take the next."

By the edge of the river soft lapping waves broke at their feet. At the landing stage they were told:

" The last boat has just gone."

Christophe's heart thumped. Ada's hand grasped his arm more tightly.

" But," she said, " there will be another one to-morrow."

A few yards away in a halo of mist was the flickering light of a lamp hung on a post on a terrace by the river. A little farther on were a few lighted windows—a little inn. They went into the tiny garden. The sand ground under their feet. They groped their way to the steps. When they entered, the lights were being put out. Ada, on Christophe's arm, asked for a room. The room to which they were led opened on to the little garden. Christophe leaned out of the window and saw the phosphorescent flow of the river, and the shade of the lamp on the glass of which were crushed mosquitoes with large wings. The door was closed. Ada was standing by the bed and smiling. He dared not look at her. She did not look at him: but through her lashes she followed Christophe's every movement. The floor creaked with every step. They could hear the least noise in the house. They sat on the bed and embraced in silence.

The flickering light of the garden is dead. All is dead. . . . Night. . . . The abyss. . . . Neither light nor consciousness. . . . Being. The obscure, devouring forces of Being. Joy all-powerful. Joy rending. Joy which sucks down the human creature as the void a stone. The sprout of desire sucking up thought. The absurd delicious law of the blind intoxicated worlds which roll at night. . . .

. . . A night which is many nights, hours that are centuries, records which are death. . . . Dreams shared, words spoken with eyes closed, tears and laughter, the happiness of loving in the voice, of sharing the nothingness of sleep, the swiftly passing images flouting in the brain, the hallucinations of the roaring night. . . . The Rhine laps in a little creek by the house: in the distance his waters over the dams and breakwaters make a sound as of a gentle rain falling on sand. The hull of the boat cracks and groans under the weight of water. The chain by which it is tied sags and grows taut with a rusty clattering. The voice of the river rises: it fills the room. The bed is like a boat. They are swept along side by side by a giddy current— hung in mid-air like a soaring bird. The night grows ever more dark, the void more empty. Ada weeps, Christophe loses consciousness: both are swept down under the flowing waters of the night. . . .

Night. . . . Death. . . . Why wake to life again? . . .

The light of the dawning day peeps through the dripping panes. The spark of life glows once more in their languorous bodies. He awakes. Ada's eyes are looking at him. A whole life passes in a few moments: days of sin, greatness, and peace. . . .

"Where am I? And am I two? Do I still exist? I am no longer conscious of being. All about me is the infinite: I have the soul of a statue, with large tranquil eyes, filled with Olympian peace. . . ."

They fall back into the world of sleep. And the familiar sounds of the dawn, the distant bells, a passing boat, oars dripping water, footsteps on the road, all caress without disturbing their happy sleep, reminding them that they are alive, and making them delight in the savor of their happiness. . . .

The puffing of the steamer outside the window brought Christophe from his torpor. They had agreed to leave at seven so as to return to the town in time for their usual occupations. He whispered:

" Do you hear? "

She did not open her eyes; she smiled, she put out her lips, she tried to kiss him and then let her head fall back on his shoulder. . . . Through the window panes he saw the funnel of the steamer slip by against the sky, he saw the empty deck, and clouds of smoke. Once more he slipped into dreaminess. . . .

An hour passed without his knowing it. He heard it strike and started in astonishment.

" Ada! . . ." he whispered to the girl. " Ada! " he said again. " It's eight o'clock."

Her eyes were still closed: she frowned and pouted pettishly. " Oh! let me sleep! " she said.

She sighed wearily and turned her back on him and went to sleep once more.

He began to dream. His blood ran bravely, calmly through him. His limpid senses received the smallest impressions simply and freshly. He rejoiced in his strength and youth. Unwittingly he was proud of being a man. He smiled in his happiness, and felt himself alone: alone as he had always been, more lonely even but without sadness, in a divine solitude. No more fever. No more shadows. Nature could freely cast her reflection upon his soul in its serenity. Lying on his back, facing the window, his eyes gazing deep into the dazzling air with its luminous mists, he smiled:

" How good it is to live! . . ."

To live! . . . A boat passed. . . . The thought suddenly of those who were no longer alive, of a boat gone by on which they were together: he—she. . . . She? . . . Not that one, sleeping by his side.—She, the only she, the beloved, the poor little woman who was dead.—But is it that one? How came she there? How did they come to this room? He looks at her, he does not know her: she is a stranger to him: yesterday morning she did not exist for him. What does he know of her? —He knows that she is not clever. He knows that she is not good. He knows that she is not even beautiful with her face spiritless and bloated with sleep, her low forehead, her mouth open in breathing, her swollen dried lips pouting like a fish. He knows that he does not love her. And he is filled with a bitter sorrow when he thinks that he kissed those strange lips, in the first moment with her, that he has taken this beautiful body for which he cares nothing on the first night of their meeting,—and that she whom he loved, he watched her live and die by his side and never dared touch her hair with his lips, that he will never know the perfume of her being. Nothing more. All is crumbled away. The earth has taken all from him. And he never defended what was his. . . .

And while he leaned over the innocent sleeper and scanned her face, and looked at her with eyes of unkindness, she felt his eyes upon her. Uneasy under his scrutiny she made a great effort to raise her heavy lids and to smile: and she said, stammering a little like a waking child:

"Don't look at me. I'm ugly. . . ."

She fell back at once, weighed down with sleep, smiled once more, murmured.

"Oh! I'm so . . . so sleepy! . . ." and went off again into her dreams.

He could not help laughing: he kissed her childish lips more tenderly. He watched the girl sleeping for a moment longer, and got up quietly. She gave a comfortable sigh when he was gone. He tried not to wake her as he dressed, though there was no danger of that: and when he had done he sat in the chair near the window and watched the steaming smoking river which looked as though it were covered with ice: and he fell into a brown study in which there hovered music, pastoral, melancholy.

From time to time she half opened her eyes and looked at him vaguely, took a second or two, smiled at him, and passed from one sleep to another. She asked him the time.

"A quarter to nine."

Half asleep she pondered:

" What! Can it be a quarter to nine?"

At half-past nine she stretched, sighed, and said that she was going to get up.

It was ten o'clock before she stirred. She was petulant.

" Striking again! . . . The clock is fast! . . ." He laughed and went and sat on the bed by her side. She put her arms round his neck and told him her dreams. He did not listen very attentively and interrupted her with little love words. But she made him be silent and went on very seriously, as though she were telling something of the highest importance:

" She was at dinner: the Grand Duke was there: Myrrha was a Newfoundland dog . . . No, a frizzy sheep who waited at table. . . . Ada had discovered a method of rising from the earth, of walking, dancing, and lying down in the air. You see it was quite simple: you had only to do . . thus . . . thus . . . and it was done. . . ."

Christophe laughed at her. She laughed too, though a little ruffled at his laughing. She shrugged her shoulders.

" Ah! you don't understand! . . ."

They breakfasted on the bed from the same cup, with the same spoon.

At last she got up: she threw off the bedclothes and slipped down from the bed. Then she sat down to recover her breath and looked at her feet. Finally she clapped her hands and told him to go out: and as he was in no hurry about it she took him by the shoulders and thrust him out of the door and then locked it.

After she had dawdled, looked over and stretched each of her handsome limbs, she sang, as she washed, a sentimental *Lied* in fourteen couplets, threw water at Christophe's face—he was outside drumming on the window—and as they left she plucked the last rose in the garden and then they took the steamer. The mist was not yet gone: but the sun shone through it: they floated through a creamy light. Ada sat at the stern with Christophe: she was sleepy and a little sulky: she grumbled about the light in her eyes, and said that she would have a headache all day. And as Christophe did not take her complaints seriously enough she returned into morose silence. Her eyes were hardly opened and in them was the funny gravity of children who have just woke up. But at the next landing-stage an elegant lady came and sat not far from her, and she grew lively at once: she talked eagerly to Christophe about things sentimental and distinguished. She had resumed with him the ceremonious *Sie*.

Christophe was thinking about what she could say to her employer by way of excuse for her lateness. She was hardly at all concerned about it.

"Bah! It's not the first time."

"The first time that . . . what?"

"That I have been late," she said, put out by the question.

He dared not ask her what had caused her lateness.

"What will you tell her?"

"That my mother is ill, dead . . . how do I know?"

He was hurt by her talking so lightly.

"I don't want you to lie."

She took offense:

"First of all, I never lie. . . . And then, I cannot very well tell her . . ."

He asked her half in jest, half in earnest:

"Why not?"

She laughed, shrugged, and said that he was coarse and ill-bred, and that she had already asked him not to use the *Du* to her.

"Haven't I the right?"

"Certainly not."

"After what has happened?"

"Nothing has happened."

She looked at him a little defiantly and laughed: and although she was joking, he felt most strongly that it would not have cost her much to say it seriously and almost to believe it. But some pleasant memory tickled her: for she burst out laughing and looked at Christophe and kissed him loudly without any concern for the people about, who did not seem to be in the least surprised by it.

Now on all his excursions he was accompanied by shop-girls and clerks: he did not like their vulgarity, and used to try to

lose them: but Ada out of contrariness was no longer disposed
for wandering in the woods. When it rained or for some other
reason they did not leave the town he would take her to the
theater, or the museum, or the *Thiergarten:* for she insisted
on being seen with him. She even wanted him to go to church
with her; but he was so absurdly sincere that he would not set
root inside a church since he had lost his belief—(on some other
excuse he had resigned his position as organist)—and at the
same time, unknown to himself, remained much too religious
not to think Ada's proposal sacrilegious.

He used to go to her rooms in the evening. Myrrha would
be there, for she lived in the same house. Myrrha was not at
all resentful against him: she would hold out her soft hand
caressingly, and talk of trivial and improper things and then
slip away discreetly. The two women had never seemed to be
such friends as since they had had small reason for being so:
they were always together. Ada had no secrets from Myrrha:
she told her everything: Myrrha listened to everything: they
seemed to be equally pleased with it all.

Christophe was ill at ease in the company of the two women.
Their friendship, their strange conversations, their freedom of
manner, the crude way in which Myrrha especially viewed and
spoke of things—(not so much in his presence, however, as
when he was not there, but Ada used to repeat her sayings to
him)—their indiscreet and impertinent curiosity, which was
forever turned upon subjects that were silly or basely sensual,
the whole equivocal and rather animal atmosphere oppressed
him terribly, though it interested him: for he knew nothing like
it. He was at sea in the conversations of the two little beasts,
who talked of dress, and made silly jokes, and laughed in an
inept way with their eyes shining with delight when they were
off on the track of some spicy story. He was more at ease when
Myrrha left them. When the two women were together it was
like being in a foreign country without knowing the language.
It was impossible to make himself understood: they did not
even listen: they poked fun at the foreigner.

When he was alone with Ada they went on speaking different
languages: but at least they did make some attempt to understand each other. To tell the truth, the more he understood

her, the less he understood her. She was the first woman he had known. For if poor Sabine was a woman he had known, he had known nothing of her: she had always remained for him a phantom of his heart. Ada took upon herself to make him make up for lost time. In his turn he tried to solve the riddle of woman: an enigma which perhaps is no enigma except for those who seek some meaning in it.

Ada was without intelligence: that was the least of her faults. Christophe would have commended her for it, if she had approved it herself. But although she was occupied only with stupidities, she claimed to have some knowledge of the things of the spirit: and she judged everything with complete assurance. She would talk about music, and explain to Christophe things which he knew perfectly, and would pronounce absolute judgment and sentence. It was useless to try to convince her: she had pretensions and susceptibilities in everything; she gave herself airs, she was obstinate, vain: she would not—she could not understand anything. Why would she not accept that she could understand nothing? He loved her so much better when she was content with being just what she was, simply, with her own qualities and failings, instead of trying to impose on others and herself!

In fact, she was little concerned with thought. She was concerned with eating, drinking, singing, dancing, crying, laughing, sleeping: she wanted to be happy: and that would have been all right if she had succeeded. But although she had every gift for it: she was greedy, lazy, sensual, and frankly egoistic in a way that revolted and amused Christophe: although she had almost all the vices which make life pleasant for their fortunate possessor, if not for their friends—(and even then does not a happy face, at least if it be pretty, shed happiness on all those who come near it?)—in spite of so many reasons for being satisfied with life and herself Ada was not even clever enough for that. The pretty, robust girl, fresh, hearty, healthy-looking, endowed with abundant spirits and fierce appetites, was anxious about her health. She bemoaned her weakness, while she ate enough for four. She was always sorry for herself: she could not drag herself along, she could not breathe, she had a headache, feet-ache, her eyes ached, her stomach ached, her soul ached. She was afraid of everything, and madly superstitious, and saw omens everywhere: at meals the crossing of knives and forks, the number of the guests, the upsetting of a salt-cellar: then there must be a whole ritual to turn aside misfortune. Out walking she would count the crows, and never failed to watch which side they flew to: she would anxiously watch the road at her feet, and when a spider crossed her path in the morning she would cry out aloud: then she would wish to go home and there would be no other means of not interrupting the walk than to persuade her that it was after twelve, and so the omen was one of hope rather than of evil. She was afraid of her dreams: she would recount them at length to Christophe; for hours she would try to recollect some detail that she had forgotten; she never spared him one; absurdities piled one on the other, strange marriages, deaths, dressmakers' prices, burlesque, and sometimes, obscene things. He had to listen to her and give her his advice. Often she would be for a whole day under the obsession of her inept fancies. She would find life ill-ordered, she would see things and people rawly and overwhelm Christophe with her jeremiads: and it seemed hardly worth while to have broken away from the gloomy middle-class people with whom he lived to find once more the eternal enemy: the "*trauriger ungriechischer Hypochondrist.*"

But suddenly in the midst of her sulks and grumblings, she would become gay, noisy, exaggerated: there was no more dealing with her gaiety than with her moroseness: she would burst out laughing for no reason and seem as though she were never going to stop: she would rush across the fields, play mad tricks and childish pranks, take a delight in doing silly things, in mixing with the earth, and dirty things, and the beasts, and the spiders, and worms, in teasing them, and hurting them, and making them eat each other: the cats eat the birds, the fowls the worms, the ants the spiders, not from any wickedness, or perhaps from an altogether unconscious instinct for evil, from curiosity, or from having nothing better to do. She seemed to be driven always to say stupid things, to repeat senseless words again and again, to irritate Christophe, to exasperate him, set his nerves on edge, and make him almost beside himself. And her coquetry as soon as anybody—no matter who—appeared on the road! . . . Then she would talk excitedly, laugh noisily, make faces, draw attention to herself: she would assume an affected mincing gait. Christophe would have a horrible presentiment that she was going to plunge into serious discussion.—And, indeed, she would do so. She would become sentimental, uncontrolledly, just as she did everything: she would unbosom herself in a loud voice. Christophe would suffer and long to beat her. Least of all could he forgive her her lack of sincerity. He did not yet know that sincerity is a gift as rare as intelligence or beauty and that it cannot justly be expected of everybody. He could not bear a lie: and Ada gave him lies in full measure. She was always lying, quite calmly, in spite of evidence to the contrary. She had that astounding faculty for forgetting what is displeasing to them—or even what has been pleasing to them—which those women possess who live from moment to moment.

And, in spite of everything, they loved each other with all their hearts. Ada was as sincere as Christophe in her love. Their love was none the less true for not being based on intellectual sympathy: it had nothing in common with base passion. It was the beautiful love of youth: it was sensual, but not vulgar, because it was altogether youthful: it was naïve, almost chaste, purged by the ingenuous ardor of pleasure. Although Ada was not, by a long way, so ignorant as Christophe, yet she had still the divine privilege of youth of soul and body, that freshness of the senses, limpid and vivid as a running stream, which almost gives the illusion of purity and through life is never replaced. Egoistic, commonplace, insincere in her ordinary life,—love made her simple, true, almost good: she understood in love the joy that is to be found in self-forgetfulness. Christophe saw this with delight: and he would gladly have died for her. Who can tell all the absurd and touching illusions that a loving heart brings to its love! And the natural illusion of the lover was magnified an hundredfold in Christophe by the power of illusion which is born in the artist. Ada's smile held profound meanings for him: an affectionate word was the proof of the goodness of her heart. He loved in her all that is good and beautiful in the universe. He called her his own, his soul, his life. They wept together over their love.

Pleasure was not the only bond between them: there was an indefinable poetry of memories and dreams,—their own? or those of the men and women who had loved before them, who had been before them,—in them? . . . Without a word, perhaps without knowing it, they preserved the fascination of the first moments of their meeting in the woods, the first days, the first nights together: those hours of sleep in each other's arms, still, unthinking, sinking down into a flood of love and silent joy. Swift fancies, visions, dumb thoughts, titillating, and making them go pale, and their hearts sink under their desire, bringing all about them a buzzing as of bees. A fine light, and tender. . . . Their hearts sink and beat no more, borne down in excess of sweetness. Silence, languor, and fever, the mysterious weary smile of the earth quivering under the first sunlight of spring. . . . So fresh a love in two young creatures is like an April morning. Like April it must pass. Youth of the heart is like an early feast of sunshine.

Nothing could have brought Christophe closer to Ada in his love than the way in which he was judged by others.

The day after their first meeting it was known all over the town. Ada made no attempt to cover up the adventure, and rather plumed herself on her conquest. Christophe would have liked more discretion: but he felt that the curiosity of the people was upon him: and as he did not wish to seem to fly from it, he threw in his lot with Ada. The little town buzzed with tattle. Christophe's colleagues in the orchestra paid him sly compliments to which he did not reply, because he would not allow any meddling with his affairs. The respectable people of the town judged his conduct very severely. He lost his music lessons with certain families. With others, the mothers thought that they must now be present at the daughters' lessons, watching with suspicious eyes, as though Christophe were intending to carry off the precious darlings. The young ladies were supposed to know nothing. Naturally they knew everything: and while they were cold towards Christophe for his lack of taste, they were longing to have further details. It was only among the small tradespeople, and the shop people, that Christophe was popular: but not for long: he was just as annoyed by their approval as by the condemnation of the rest: and being unable to do anything against that condemnation, he took steps not to keep their approval: there was no difficulty about that. He was furious with the general indiscretion.

The most indignant of all with him were Justus Euler and the Vogels. They took Christophe's misconduct as a personal outrage. They had not made any serious plans concerning him: they distrusted—especially Frau Vogel—these artistic temperaments. But as they were naturally discontented and always inclined to think themselves persecuted by fate, they persuaded themselves that they had counted on the marriage of Christophe and Rosa; as soon as they were quite certain that such a marriage would never come to pass, they saw in it the mark of the usual ill luck. Logically, if fate were responsible for their miscalculation, Christophe could not be: but the Vogels' logic was that which gave them the greatest opportunity for finding reasons for being sorry for themselves. So they decided that if Christophe had misconducted himself it was not so much for his own pleasure as to give offense to them. They were scandalized. Very religious, moral, and oozing domestic virtue, they were of those to whom the sins of the flesh are the most shameful, the most serious, almost the only sins, because they are the only dreadful sins—(it is obvious that respectable people are never likely to be tempted to steal or murder).—And so Christophe seemed to them absolutely wicked, and they changed their demeanor towards him. They were icy towards him and turned away as they passed him. Christophe, who was in no particular need of their conversation, shrugged his shoulders at all the fuss. He pretended not to notice Amalia's insolence: who, while she affected contemptuously to avoid him, did all that she could to make him fall in with her so that she might tell him all that was rankling in her.

Christophe was only touched by Rosa's attitude. The girl condemned him more harshly even than his family. Not that this new love of Christophe's seemed to her to destroy her last chances of being loved by him: she knew that she had no chance

left—(although perhaps she went on hoping: she always
hoped).—But she had made an idol of Christophe: and that
idol had crumbled away. It was the worst sorrow for her . . .
yes, a sorrow more cruel to the innocence and honesty of her
heart, than being disdained and forgotten by him. Brought up
puritanically, with a narrow code of morality, in which she
believed passionately, what she had heard about Christophe
had not only brought her to despair but had broken her heart.
She had suffered already when he was in love with Sabine:
she had begun then to lose some of her illusions about her hero.
That Christophe could love so commonplace a creature seemed
to her inexplicable and inglorious. But at least that love was
pure, and Sabine was not unworthy of it. And in the end
death had passed over it and sanctified it. . . . But that at once
Christophe should love another woman,—and such a woman!—
was base, and odious! She took upon herself the defense of
the dead woman against him. She could not forgive him for
having forgotten her. . . . Alas! He was thinking of her
more than she: but she never thought that in a passionate heart
there might be room for two sentiments at once: she thought
it impossible to be faithful to the past without sacrifice of the
present. Pure and cold, she had no idea of life or of Christophe:
everything in her eyes was pure, narrow, submissive to duty,
like herself. Modest of soul, modest of herself, she had only
one source of pride: purity: she demanded it of herself and of
others. She could not forgive Christophe for having so lowered
himself, and she would never forgive him.

Christophe tried to talk to her, though not to explain himself
—(what could he say to her? what could he say to a little
puritanical and naïve girl?).—He would have liked to assure
her that he was her friend, that he wished for her esteem, and
had still the right to it. He wished to prevent her absurdly
estranging herself from him.—But Rosa avoided him in stern
silence: he felt that she despised him.

He was both sorry and angry. He felt that he did not deserve
such contempt: and yet in the end he was bowled over by it:
and thought himself guilty. Of all the reproaches cast against
him the most bitter came from himself when he thought of
Sabine. He tormented himself.

"Oh! God, how is it possible? What sort of creature am I? . . ."

But he could not resist the stream that bore him on. He thought that life is criminal: and he closed his eyes so as to live without seeing it. He had so great a need to live, and be happy, and love, and believe! . . . No: there was nothing despicable in his love! He knew that it was impossible to be very wise, or intelligent, or even very happy in his love for Ada: but what was there in it that could be called vile? Suppose— (he forced the idea on himself)—that Ada were not a woman of any great moral worth, how was the love that he had for her the less pure for that? Love is in the lover, not in the beloved. Everything is worthy of the lover, everything is worthy of love. To the pure all is pure. All is pure in the strong and the healthy of mind. Love, which adorns certain birds with their loveliest colors, calls forth from the souls that are true all that is most noble in them. The desire to show to the beloved only what is worthy makes the lover take pleasure only in those thoughts and actions which are in harmony with the beautiful image fashioned by love. And the waters of youth in which the soul is bathed, the blessed radiance of strength and joy, are beautiful and health-giving, making the heart great.

That his friends misunderstood him filled him with bitterness. But the worst trial of all was that his mother was beginning to be unhappy about it.

The good creature was far from sharing the narrow views of the Vogels. She had seen real sorrows too near ever to try to invent others. Humble, broken by life, having received little joy from it, and having asked even less, resigned to everything that happened, without even trying to understand it, she was careful not to judge or censure others: she thought she had no right. She thought herself too stupid to pretend that they were wrong when they did not think as she did: it would have seemed ridiculous to try to impose on others the inflexible rules of her morality and belief. Besides that, her morality and her belief were purely instinctive: pious and pure in herself she closed her eyes to the conduct of others, with the indulgence of her class for certain faults and certain weaknesses.

That had been one of the complaints that her father-in-law, Jean Michel, had lodged against her: she did not sufficiently distinguish between those who were honorable and those who were not: she was not afraid of stopping in the street or the market-place to shake hands and talk with young women, notorious in the neighborhood, whom a respectable woman ought to pretend to ignore. She left it to God to distinguish between good and evil, to punish or to forgive. From others she asked only a little of that affectionate sympathy which is so necessary to soften the ways of life. If people were only kind she asked no more.

But since she had lived with the Vogels a change had come about in her. The disparaging temper of the family had found her an easier prey because she was crushed and had no strength to resist. Amalia had taken her in hand: and from morning to night when they were working together alone, and Amalia did all the talking, Louisa, broken and passive, unconsciously assumed the habit of judging and criticising everything. Frau Vogel did not fail to tell her what she thought of Christophe's conduct. Louisa's calmness irritated her. She thought it indecent of Louisa to be so little concerned about what put him beyond the pale: she was not satisfied until she had upset her altogether. Christophe saw it. Louisa dared not reproach him: but every day she made little timid remarks, uneasy, insistent: and when he lost patience and replied sharply, she said no more: but still he could see the trouble in her eyes: and when he came home sometimes he could see that she had been weeping. He knew his mother too well not to be absolutely certain that her uneasiness did not come from herself.—And he knew well whence it came.

He determined to make an end of it. One evening when Louisa was unable to hold back her tears and had got up from the table in the middle of supper without Christophe being able to discover what was the matter, he rushed downstairs four steps at a time and knocked at the Vogels' door. He was boiling with rage. He was not only angry about Frau Vogel's treatment of his mother: he had to avenge himself for her having turned Rosa against him, for her bickering against Sabine, for all that he had had to put up with at her hands for months. For months he had borne his pent-up feelings against her and now made haste to let them loose.

He burst in on Frau Vogel and in a voice that he tried to keep calm, though it was trembling with fury, he asked her what she had told his mother to bring her to such a state.

Amalia took it very badly: she replied that she would say what she pleased, and was responsible to no one for her actions—to him least of all. And seizing the opportunity to deliver the speech which she had prepared, she added that if Louisa was unhappy he had to go no further for the cause of it than his own conduct, which was a shame to himself and a scandal to everybody else.

Christophe was only waiting for her onslaught to strike out. He shouted angrily that his conduct was his own affair, that he did not care a rap whether it pleased Frau Vogel or not, that if she wished to complain of it she must do so to him, and that she could say to him whatever she liked: that rested with her, but he *forbade* her—(did she hear?)—*forbade* her to say anything to his mother: it was cowardly and mean so to attack a poor sick old woman.

Frau Vogel cried loudly. Never had any one dared to speak to her in such a manner. She said that she was not to be lectured by a rapscallion,—and in her own house, too!—And she treated him with abuse.

The others came running up on the noise of the quarrel,—except Vogel, who fled from anything that might upset his health. Old Euler was called to witness by the indignant Amalia and sternly bade Christophe in future to refrain from speaking to or visiting them. He said that they did not need him to tell them what they ought to do, that they did their duty and would always do it.

Christophe declared that he would go and would never again set foot in their house. However, he did not go until he had relieved his feelings by telling them what he had still to say about their famous Duty, which had become to him a personal enemy. He said that their Duty was the sort of thing to make him love vice. It was people like them who discouraged good, by insisting on making it unpleasant. It was their fault that so many find delight by contrast among those who are dishonest, but amiable and laughter-loving. It was a profanation of the name of duty to apply it to everything, to the most stupid tasks, to trivial things, with a stiff and arrogant severity which ends by darkening and poisoning life. Duty, he said, was exceptional: it should be kept for moments of real sacrifice, and not used to lend the lover of its name to ill-humor and the desire to be disagreeable to others. There was no reason, because they were stupid enough or ungracious enough to be sad, to want everybody else to be so too and to impose on everybody their decrepit way of living. . . . The first of all virtues is joy. Virtue must be happy, free, and unconstrained. He who does good must give pleasure to himself. But this perpetual upstart Duty, this pedagogic tyranny, this peevishness, this futile discussion, this acrid, puerile quibbling, this ungraciousness, this charmless life, without politeness, without silence, this mean-spirited pessimism, which lets slip nothing that can make existence poorer than it is, this vainglorious unintelligence, which finds it easier to despise others than to understand them, all this middle-class morality, without greatness, without largeness, without happiness, without beauty, all these things are odious and hurtful: they make vice appear more human than virtue.

So thought Christophe: and in his desire to hurt those who had wounded him, he did not see that he was being as unjust as those of whom he spoke.

No doubt these unfortunate people were almost as he saw them. But it was not their fault: it was the fault of their ungracious life, which had made their faces, their doings, and their thoughts ungracious. They had suffered the deformation of misery—not that great misery which swoops down and slays or forges anew—but the misery of ever recurring ill-fortune, that small misery which trickles down drop by drop from the first day to the last. . . . Sad, indeed! For beneath these rough exteriors what treasures in reserve are there, of uprightness, of kindness, of silent heroism! . . . The whole strength of a people, all the sap of the future.

Christophe was not wrong in thinking duty exceptional. But love is so no less. Everything is exceptional. Everything that is of worth has no worse enemy—not the evil (the vices are of

worth)—but the habitual. The mortal enemy of the soul is
the daily wear and tear.

Ada was beginning to weary of it. She was not clever enough
to find new food for her love in an abundant nature like that
of Christophe. Her senses and her vanity had extracted from
it all the pleasure they could find in it. There was left her
only the pleasure of destroying it. She had that secret instinct
common to so many women, even good women, to so many
men, even clever men, who are not creative either of art, or of
children, or of pure action,—no matter what: of life—and yet
have too much life in apathy and resignation to bear with their
uselessness. They desire others to be as useless as themselves
and do their best to make them so. Sometimes they do so
in spite of themselves: and when they become aware of their
criminal desire they hotly thrust it back. But often they hug
it to themselves: and they set themselves according to their
strength—some modestly in their own intimate circle—others
largely with vast audiences—to destroy everything that has life,
everything that loves life, everything that deserves life. The
critic who takes upon himself to diminish the stature of
great men and great thoughts—and the girl who amuses
herself with dragging down her lovers, are both mischievous
beasts of the same kind.—But the second is the pleasanter of
the two.

Ada then would have liked to corrupt Christophe a little, to
humiliate him. In truth, she was not strong enough. More
intelligence was needed, even in corruption. She felt that:
and it was not the least of her rankling feelings against Christophe that her love could do him no harm. She did not admit
the desire that was in her to do him harm: perhaps she would
have done him none if she had been able. But it annoyed her
that she could not do it. It is to fail in love for a woman
not to leave her the illusion of her power for good or evil over
her lover: to do that must inevitably be to impel her irresistibly
to the test of it. Christophe paid no attention to it. When
Ada asked him jokingly:

" Would you leave your music for me? "

(Although she had no wish for him to do so.)

He replied frankly:

" No, my dear : neither you nor anybody else can do anything against that. I shall always make music."

" And you say you love ? " cried she, put out.

She hated his music—the more so because she did not understand it, and it was impossible for her to find a means of coming to grips with this invisible enemy and so to wound Christophe in his passion. If she tried to talk of it contemptuously, or scornfully to judge Christophe's compositions, he would shout with laughter; and in spite of her exasperation Ada would relapse into silence : for she saw that she was being ridiculous.

But if there was nothing to be done in that direction, she had discovered another weak spot in Christophe, one more easy of access : his moral faith. In spite of his squabble with the Vogels, and in spite of the intoxication of his adolescence, Christophe had preserved an instinctive modesty, a need of purity, of which he was entirely unconscious. At first it struck Ada, attracted and charmed her, then made her impatient and irritable, and finally, being the woman she was, she detested it. She did not make a frontal attack. She would ask insidiously :

" Do you love me ? "

" Of course ! "

" How much do you love me ? "

" As much as it is possible to love."

" That is not much . . . after all ! . . . What would you do for me ? "

" Whatever you like."

" Would you do something dishonest."

" That would be a queer way of loving."

" That is not what I asked. Would you ? "

" It is not necessary."

" But if I wished it ? "

" You would be wrong."

" Perhaps. . . . Would you do it ? "

He tried to kiss her. But she thrust him away.

" Would you do it ? Yes or no ? "

" No, my dear."

She turned her back on him and was furious.

" You do not love me. You do not know what love is."

" That is quite possible," he said good-humoredly. He knew that, like anybody else, he was capable in a moment of passion of committing some folly, perhaps something dishonest, and—who knows?—even more: but he would have thought shame of himself if he had boasted of it in cold blood, and certainly it would be dangerous to confess it to Ada. Some instinct warned him that the beloved foe was lying in ambush, and taking stock of his smallest remark: he would not give her any weapon against him.

She would return to the charge again, and ask him:

" Do you love me because you love me, or because I love you? "

" Because I love you."

" Then if I did not love you, you would still love me? "

" Yes."

" And if I loved some one else you would still love me? "

" Ah! I don't know about that. . . . I don't think so. . . . In any case you would be the last person to whom I should say so."

" How would it be changed? "

" Many things would be changed. Myself, perhaps. You, certainly."

" And if I changed, what would it matter? "

" All the difference in the world. I love you as you are. If you become another creature I can't promise to love you."

" You do not love, you do not love! What is the use of all this quibbling? You love or you do not love. If you love me you ought to love me just as I am, whatever I do, always."

" That would be to love you like an animal."

" I want to be loved like that."

" Then you have made a mistake," said he jokingly. " I am not the sort of man you want. I would like to be, but I cannot. And I will not."

" You are very proud of your intelligence! You love your intelligence more than you do me."

" But I love you, you wretch, more than you love yourself. The more beautiful and the more good you are, the more I love you."

"You are a schoolmaster," she said with asperity.

"What would you? I love what is beautiful. Anything ugly disgusts me."

"Even in me?"

"Especially in you."

She drummed angrily with her foot.

"I will not be judged."

"Then complain of what I judge you to be, and of what I love in you," said he tenderly to appease her.

She let him take her in his arms, and deigned to smile, and let him kiss her. But in a moment when he thought she had forgotten she asked uneasily:

"What do you think ugly in me?"

He would not tell her: he replied cowardly:

"I don't think anything ugly in you."

She thought for a moment, smiled, and said:

"Just a moment, Christli: you say that you do not like lying?"

"I despise it."

"You are right," she said. "I despise it too. I am of a good conscience. I never lie."

He stared at her: she was sincere. Her unconsciousness disarmed him.

"Then," she went on, putting her arms about his neck, "why would you be cross with me if I loved some one else and told you so?"

"Don't tease me."

"I'm not teasing: I am not saying that I do love some one else: I am saying that I do not. . . . But if I did love some one later on . . ."

"Well, don't let us think of it."

"But I want to think of it. . . . You would not be angry with me? You could not be angry with me?"

"I should not be angry with you. I should leave you. That is all."

"Leave me? Why? If I still loved you. . . .?"

"While you loved some one else?"

"Of course. It happens sometimes."

"Well, it will not happen with us."

" Why ? "

" Because as soon as you love some one else, I shall love you no longer, my dear, never, never again."

" But just now you said perhaps. . . . Ah! you see you do not love me ! "

" Well then : all the better for you."

" Because . . . ? "

" Because if I loved you when you loved some one else it might turn out badly for you, me, and him."

" Then ! . . . Now you are mad. Then I am condemned to stay with you all my life ? "

" Be calm. You are free. You shall leave me when you like. Only it will not be *au revoir* : it will be good-bye."

" But if I still love you ? "

" When people love, they sacrifice themselves to each other."

" Well, then . . . sacrifice yourself ! "

He could not help laughing at her egoism : and she laughed too.

" The sacrifice of one only," he said, " means the love of one only."

" Not at all. It means the love of both. I shall not love you much longer if you do not sacrifice yourself for me. And think, Christli, how much you will love me, when you have sacrificed yourself, and how happy you will be."

They laughed and were glad to have a change from the seriousness of the disagreement.

He laughed and looked at her. At heart, as she said, she had no desire to leave Christophe at present : if he irritated her and often bored her she knew the worth of such devotion as his : and she loved no one else. She talked so for fun, partly because she knew he disliked it, partly because she took pleasure in playing with equivocal and unclean thoughts like a child which delights to mess about with dirty water. He knew this. He did not mind. But he was tired of these unwholesome discussions, of the silent struggle against this uncertain and uneasy creature whom he loved, who perhaps loved him : he was tired from the effort that he had to make to deceive himself about her, sometimes tired almost to tears. He would think : " Why, why is she like this ? Why are people like this ? How second-

rate life is!" . . . At the same time he would smile as he
saw her pretty face above him, her blue eyes, her flower-like
complexion, her laughing, chattering lips, foolish a little, half
open to reveal the brilliance of her tongue and her white teeth.
Their lips would almost touch: and he would look at her as
from a distance, a great distance, as from another world: he
would see her going farther and farther from him, vanishing
in a mist. . . . And then he would lose sight of her. He could
hear her no more. He would fall into a sort of smiling oblivion
in which he thought of his music, his dreams, a thousand things
foreign to Ada. . . . Ah! beautiful music! . . . so sad, so mortally sad! and yet kind, loving. . . . Ah! how good it is! . . .
It is that, it is that. . . . Nothing else is true. . . .

She would shake his arm. A voice would cry:

"Eh, what's the matter with you? You are mad, quite mad.
Why do you look at me like that? Why don't you answer?"

Once more he would see the eyes looking at him. Who was
it? . . . Ah! yes. . . . He would sigh.

She would watch him. She would try to discover what he
was thinking of. She did not understand: but she felt that it
was useless: that she could not keep hold of him, that there
was always a door by which he could escape. She would conceal
her irritation.

"Why are you crying?" she asked him once as he returned
from one of his strange journeys into another life.

He drew his hands across his eyes. He felt that they were
wet.

"I do not know," he said.

"Why don't you answer? Three times you have said the
same thing."

"What do you want?" he asked gently.

She went back to her absurd discussions. He waved his hand
wearily.

"Yes," she said. "I've done. Only a word more!" And
off she started again.

Christophe shook himself angrily.

"Will you keep your dirtiness to yourself!"

"I was only joking."

"Find cleaner subjects, then!"

" Tell me why, then. Tell me why you don't like it."

" Why? You can't argue as to why a dump-heap smells. It does smell, and that is all! I hold my nose and go away."

He went away, furious: and he strode along taking in great breaths of the cold air.

But she would begin again, once, twice, ten times. She would bring forward every possible subject that could shock him and offend his conscience.

He thought it was only a morbid jest of a neurasthenic girl, amusing herself by annoying him. He would shrug his shoulders or pretend not to hear her: he would not take her seriously. But sometimes he would long to throw her out of the window: for neurasthenia and the neurasthenics were very little to his taste. . . .

But ten minutes away from her were enough to make him forget everything that had annoyed him. He would return to Ada with a fresh store of hopes and new illusions. He loved her. Love is a perpetual act of faith. Whether God exist or no is a small matter: we believe, because we believe. We love because we love: there is no need of reasons! . . .

After Christophe's quarrel with the Vogels it became impossible for them to stay in the house, and Louisa had to seek another lodging for herself and her son.

One day Christophe's younger brother Ernest, of whom they had not heard for a long time, suddenly turned up. He was out of work, having been dismissed in turn from all the situations he had procured: his purse was empty and his health ruined: and so he had thought it would be as well to re-establish himself in his mother's house.

Ernest was not on bad terms with either of his brothers: they thought very little of him and he knew it: but he did not bear any grudge against them, for he did not care. They had no ill-feeling against him. It was not worth the trouble. Everything they said to him slipped off his back without leaving a mark. He just smiled with his sly eyes, tried to look contrite, thought of something else, agreed, thanked them, and in the end always managed to extort money from one or other of them. In spite of himself Christophe was fond of the pleasant mortal who, like himself, and more than himself, resembled their father Melchior in feature. Tall and strong like Christophe, he had regular features, a frank expression, a straight nose, a laughing mouth, fine teeth, and endearing manners. When even Christophe saw him he was disarmed and could not deliver half the reproaches that he had prepared : in his heart he had a sort of motherly indulgence for the handsome boy who was of his blood, and physically at all events did him credit. He did not believe him to be bad : and Ernest was not a fool. Without culture, he was not without brains : he was even not incapable of taking an interest in the things of the mind. He enjoyed listening to music : and without understanding his brother's compositions he would listen to them with interest. Christophe, who did not receive too much sympathy from his family, had been glad to see him at some of his concerts.

But Ernest's chief talent was the knowledge that he possessed of the character of his two brothers, and his skill in making use of his knowledge. It was no use Christophe knowing Ernest's egoism and indifference : it was no use his seeing that Ernest never thought of his mother or himself except when he had need of them : he was always taken in by his affectionate ways and very rarely did he refuse him anything. He much preferred him to his other brother Rodolphe, who was orderly and correct, assiduous in his business, strictly moral, never asked for money, and never gave any either, visited his mother regularly every Sunday, stayed an hour, and only talked about himself, boasting about himself, his firm, and everything that concerned him, never asking about the others, and taking no interest in them, and going away when the hour was up, quite satisfied with having done his duty. Christophe could not bear him. He always arranged to be out when Rodolphe came. Rodolphe was jealous of him : he despised artists, and Christophe's success really hurt him, though he did not fail to turn his small fame to account in the commercial circles in which he moved : but he never said a word about it either to his mother or to Christophe : he pretended to ignore it. On the other hand, he never ignored the least of the unpleasant things that happened to Christophe. Christophe despised such pettiness, and pretended not to notice it : but it would really have hurt him to know, though he never thought about it, that much of the unpleasant information that Rodolphe had about him came from Ernest. The young rascal fed the differences between Christophe and Rodolphe: no doubt he recognized Christophe's superiority and perhaps even sympathized a little ironically with his candor. But he took good care to turn it to account: and while he despised Rodolphe's ill-feeling he exploited it shamefully. He flattered his vanity and jealousy, accepted his rebukes deferentially and kept him primed with the scandalous gossip of the town, especially with everything concerning Christophe,—of which he was always marvelously informed. So he attained his ends, and Rodolphe, in spite of his avarice, allowed Ernest to despoil him just as Christophe did.

So Ernest made use and a mock of them both, impartially. And so both of them loved him.

In spite of his tricks Ernest was in a pitiful condition when he turned up at his mother's house. He had come from Munich, where he had found and, as usual, almost immediately lost a situation. He had had to travel the best part of the way on foot, through storms of rain, sleeping God knows where. He was covered with mud, ragged, looking like a beggar, and coughing miserably. Louisa was upset and Christophe ran to him in alarm when they saw him come in. Ernest, whose tears flowed easily, did not fail to make use of the effect he had produced: and there was a general reconciliation: all three wept in each other's arms.

Christophe gave up his room: they warmed the bed, and laid the invalid in it, who seemed to be on the point of death. Louisa and Christophe sat by his bedside and took it in turns to watch by him. They called in a doctor, procured medicines, made a good fire in the room, and gave him special food.

Then they had to clothe him from head to foot: linen, shoes, clothes, everything new. Ernest left himself in their hands. Louisa and Christophe sweated to squeeze the money from their expenditure. They were very straitened at the moment: the removal, the new lodgings, which were dearer though just as uncomfortable, fewer lessons for Christophe and more expenses. They could just make both ends meet. They managed

somehow. No doubt Christophe could have applied to
Rodolphe, who was more in a position to help Ernest,
but he would not: he made it a point of honor to help his
brother alone. He thought himself obliged to do so as the
eldest,—and because he was Christophe. Hot with shame he
had to accept, to declare his willingness to accept an offer which
he had indignantly rejected a fortnight before,—a proposal from
an agent of an unknown wealthy amateur who wanted to
buy a musical composition for publication under his own name.
Louisa took work out, mending linen. They hid their sacrifice
from each other: they lied about the money they brought
home.

When Ernest was convalescent and sitting huddled up by
the fire, he confessed one day between his fits of coughing that
he had a few debts.—They were paid. No one reproached him.
That would not have been kind to an invalid and a prodigal
son who had repented and returned home. For Ernest seemed
to have been changed by adversity and sickness. With tears
in his eyes he spoke of his past misdeeds: and Louisa kissed
him and told him to think no more of them. He was fond:
he had always been able to get round his mother by his demonstrations of affection: Christophe had once been a little jealous
of him. Now he thought it natural that the youngest and the
weakest son should be the most loved. In spite of the small
difference in their ages he regarded him almost as a son rather
than as a brother. Ernest showed great respect for him: sometimes he would allude to the burdens that Christophe was taking
upon himself, and to his sacrifice of money: but Christophe
would not let him go on, and Ernest would content himself
with showing his gratitude in his eyes humbly and affectionately.
He would argue with the advice that Christophe gave him: and
he would seem disposed to change his way of living and to
work seriously as soon as he was well again.

He recovered: but had a long convalescence. The doctor
declared that his health, which he had abused, needed to be
fostered. So he stayed on in his mother's house, sharing
Christophe's bed, eating heartily the bread that his brother
earned, and the little dainty dishes that Louisa prepared for
him. He never spoke of going. Louisa and Christophe never

mentioned it either. They were too happy to have found again the son and the brother they loved.

Little by little in the long evenings that he spent with Ernest Christophe began to talk intimately to him. He needed to confide in somebody. Ernest was clever: he had a quick mind and understood—or seemed to understand—on a hint only. There was pleasure in talking to him. And yet Christophe dared not tell him about what lay nearest to his heart: his love. He was kept back by a sort of modesty. Ernest, who knew all about it, never let it appear that he knew.

One day when Ernest was quite well again he went in the sunny afternoon and lounged along the Rhine. As he passed a noisy inn a little way out of the town, where there were drinking and dancing on Sundays, he saw Christophe sitting with Ada and Myrrha, who were making a great noise. Christophe saw him too, and blushed. Ernest was discreet and passed on without acknowledging him.

Christophe was much embarrassed by the encounter: it made him more keenly conscious of the company in which he was: it hurt him that his brother should have seen him then: not only because it made him lose the right of judging Ernest's conduct, but because he had a very lofty, very naïve, and rather archaic notion of his duties as an elder brother which would have seemed absurd to many people: he thought that in failing in that duty, as he was doing, he was lowered in his own eyes.

In the evening when they were together in their room, he waited for Ernest to allude to what had happened. But Ernest prudently said nothing and waited also. Then while they were undressing Christophe decided to speak about his love. He was so ill at ease that he dared not look at Ernest: and in his shyness he assumed a gruff way of speaking. Ernest did not help him out: he was silent and did not look at him, though he watched him all the same: and he missed none of the humor of Christophe's awkwardness and clumsy words. Christophe hardly dared pronounce Ada's name: and the portrait that he drew of her would have done just as well for any woman who was loved. But he spoke of his love: little by little he was carried away by the flood of tenderness that filled his heart: he said how good it was to love, how wretched he had been before

he had found that light in the darkness, and that life was
nothing without a dear, deep-seated love. His brother listened
gravely: he replied tactfully, and asked no questions: but a
warm handshake showed that he was of Christophe's way of
thinking. They exchanged ideas concerning love and life.
Christophe was happy at being so well understood. They exchanged a brotherly embrace before they went to sleep.

Christophe grew accustomed to confiding his love to Ernest,
though always shyly and reservedly. Ernest's discretion reassured him. He let him know his uneasiness about Ada: but
he never blamed her: he blamed himself: and with tears in
his eyes he would declare that he could not live if he were to
lose her.

He did not forget to tell Ada about Ernest: he praised his
wit and his good looks.

Ernest never approached Christophe with a request to be
introduced to Ada: but he would shut himself up in his room
and sadly refuse to go out, saying that he did not know anybody. Christophe would think ill of himself on Sundays for
going on his excursions with Ada, while his brother stayed
at home. And yet he hated not to be alone with his beloved:
he accused himself of selfishness and proposed that Ernest
should come with them.

The introduction took place at Ada's door, on the landing.
Ernest and Ada bowed politely. Ada came out, followed by
her inseparable Myrrha, who when she saw Ernest gave a little
cry of surprise. Ernest smiled, went up to Myrrha, and
kissed her: she seemed to take it as a matter of course.

"What! You know each other?" asked Christophe in astonishment.

"Why, yes!" said Myrrha, laughing.

"Since when?"

"Oh, a long time!"

"And you knew?" asked Christophe, turning to Ada. "Why
did you not tell me?"

"Do you think I know all Myrrha's lovers?" said Ada, shrugging her shoulders.

Myrrha took up the word and pretended in fun to be angry.
Christophe could not find out any more about it. He was

depressed. It seemed to him that Ernest and Myrrha and Ada had been lacking in honesty, although indeed he could not have brought any lie up against them : but it was difficult to believe that Myrrha, who had no secrets from Ada, had made a mystery of this, and that Ernest and Ada were not already acquainted with each other. He watched them. But they only exchanged a few trivial words and Ernest only paid attention to Myrrha all the rest of the day. Ada only spoke to Christophe : and she was much more amiable to him than usual.

From that time on Ernest always joined them. Christophe could have done without him : but he dared not say so. He had no other motive for wanting to leave his brother out than his shame in having him for boon companion. He had no suspicion of him. Ernest gave him no cause for it : he seemed to be in love with Myrrha and was always reserved and polite with Ada, and even affected to avoid her in a way that was a little out of place : it was as though he wished to show his brother's mistress a little of the respect he showed to himself. Ada was not surprised by it and was none the less careful.

They went on long excursions together. The two brothers would walk on in front. Ada and Myrrha, laughing and whispering, would follow a few yards behind. They would stop in the middle of the road and talk. Christophe and Ernest would stop and wait for them. Christophe would lose patience and go on : but soon he would turn back annoyed and irritated, by hearing Ernest talking and laughing with the two young women. He would want to know what they were saying : but when they came up with him their conversation would stop.

"What are you three always plotting together?" he would ask.

They would reply with some joke. They had a secret understanding like thieves at a fair.

Christophe had a sharp quarrel with Ada. They had been cross with each other all day. Strange to say, Ada had not assumed her air of offended dignity, to which she usually resorted in such cases, so as to avenge herself, by making herself as intolerably tiresome as usual. Now she simply pretended to ignore Christophe's existence and she was in excellent

spirits with the other two. It was as though in her heart she
was not put out at all by the quarrel.

Christophe, on the other hand, longed to make peace: he
was more in love than ever. His tenderness was now mingled
with a feeling of gratitude for all the good things love had
brought him, and regret for the hours he had wasted in stupid
argument and angry thoughts—and the unreasoning fear, the
mysterious idea that their love was nearing its end. Sadly he
looked at Ada's pretty face and she pretended not to see him
while she was laughing with the others: and the sight of her
woke in him so many dear memories, of great love, of sincere
intimacy.—Her face had sometimes—it had now—so much goodness in it, a smile so pure, that Christophe asked himself why
things were not better between them, why they spoiled their
happiness with their whimsies, why she would insist on forgetting their bright hours, and denying and combating all that
was good and honest in her—what strange satisfaction she
could find in spoiling, and smudging, if only in thought, the
purity of their love. He was conscious of an immense need
of believing in the object of his love, and he tried once more
to bring back his illusions. He accused himself of injustice:
he was remorseful for the thoughts that he attributed to her,
and of his lack of charity.

He went to her and tried to talk to her: she answered him
with a few curt words: she had no desire for a reconciliation
with him. He insisted: he begged her to listen to him for a
moment away from the others. She followed him ungraciously.
When they were a few yards away so that neither Myrrha nor
Ernest could see them, he took her hands and begged her
pardon, and knelt at her feet in the dead leaves of the wood.
He told her that he could not go on living so at loggerheads
with her: that he found no pleasure in the walk, or the fine
day: that he could enjoy nothing, and could not even breathe,
knowing that she detested him: he needed her love. Yes: he
was often unjust, violent, disagreeable: he begged her to forgive
him: it was the fault of his love, he could not bear anything
second-rate in her, nothing that was altogether unworthy of
her and their memories of their dear past. He reminded her
of it all, of their first meeting, their first days together: he

said that he loved her just as much, that he would always love
her, that she should not go away from him! She was everything to him. . . .

Ada listened to him, smiling, uneasy, almost softened. She
looked at him with kind eyes, eyes that said that they loved
each other, and that she was no longer angry. They kissed,
and holding each other close they went into the leafless woods.
She thought Christophe good and gentle, and was grateful to
him for his tender words: but she did not relinquish the naughty
whims that were in her mind. But she hesitated, she did not
cling to them so tightly: and yet she did not abandon what she
had planned to do. Why? Who can say? . . . Because she
had vowed what she would do?—Who knows? Perhaps she
thought it more entertaining to deceive her lover that day, to
prove to him, to prove to herself her freedom. She had no
thought of losing him: she did not wish for that. She thought
herself more sure of him than ever.

They reached a clearing in the forest. There were two
paths. Christophe took one. Ernest declared that the other
led more quickly to the top of the hill whither they were going.
Ada agreed with him. Christophe, who knew the way, having
often been there, maintained that they were wrong. They did
not yield. Then they agreed to try it: and each wagered that
he would arrive first. Ada went with Ernest. Myrrha accompanied Christophe: she pretended that she was sure that he
was right: and she added, "As usual." Christophe had taken
the game seriously: and as he never liked to lose, he walked
quickly, too quickly for Myrrha's liking, for she was in much
less of a hurry than he.

"Don't be in a hurry, my friend," she said, in her quiet,
ironic voice, "we shall get there first."

He was a little sorry.

"True," he said, "I am going a little too fast: there is no
need."

He slackened his pace.

"But I know them," he went on. "I am sure they will
run so as to be there before us."

Myrrha burst out laughing.

"Oh! no," she said. "Oh! no: don't you worry about that."

She hung on his arm and pressed close to him. She was
a little shorter than Christophe, and as they walked she raised
her soft eyes to his. She was really pretty and alluring. He
hardly recognized her: the change was extraordinary. Usually
her face was rather pale and puffy: but the smallest excitement,
a merry thought, or the desire to please, was enough to make
her worn expression vanish, and her cheeks go pink, and the
little wrinkles in her eyelids round and below her eyes disappear, and her eyes flash, and her whole face take on a youth,
a life, a spiritual quality that never was in Ada's. Christophe
was surprised by this metamorphosis, and turned his eyes away
from hers: he was a little uneasy at being alone with her. She
embarrassed him and prevented him from dreaming as he
pleased: he did not listen to what she said, he did not answer
her, or if he did it was only at random: he was thinking—
he wished to think only of Ada. He thought of the kindness
in her eyes, her smile, her kiss: and his heart was filled with
love. Myrrha wanted to make him admire the beauty of the
trees with their little branches against the clear sky. . . . Yes:
it was all beautiful: the clouds were gone, Ada had returned
to him, he had succeeded in breaking the ice that lay between
them: they loved once more: near or far, they were one. He
sighed with relief: how light the air was! Ada had come back
to him. . . . Everything brought her to mind: . . . It was a
little damp: would she not be cold? . . . The lovely trees were
powdered with hoar-frost: what a pity she should not see them!
. . . But he remembered the wager, and hurried on: he was
concerned only with not losing the way. He shouted joyfully
as they reached the goal:

" We are first! "

He waved his hat gleefully. Myrrha watched him and smiled.

The place where they stood was a high, steep rock in the
middle of the woods. From this flat summit with its fringe
of nut-trees and little stunted oaks they could see, over the
wooded slopes, the tops of the pines bathed in a purple mist,
and the long ribbon of the Rhine in the blue valley. Not a bird
called. Not a voice. Not a breath of air. A still, calm winter's
day, its chilliness faintly warmed by the pale beams of a misty
sun. Now and then in the distance there came the sharp

whistle of a train in the valley. Christophe stood at the edge of the rock and looked down at the countryside. Myrrha watched Christophe.

He turned to her amiably:

"Well! The lazy things. I told them so! . . . Well: we must wait for them. . . ."

He lay stretched out in the sun on the cracked earth.

"Yes. Let us wait . . ." said Myrrha, taking off her hat.

In her voice there was something so quizzical that he raised his head and looked at her.

"What is it?" she asked quietly.

"What did you say?"

"I said: Let us wait. It was no use making me run so fast."

"True."

They waited lying on the rough ground. Myrrha hummed a tune. Christophe took it up for a few phrases. But he stopped every now and then to listen.

"I think I can hear them."

Myrrha went on singing.

"Do stop for a moment."

Myrrha stopped.

"No. It is nothing."

She went on with her song.

Christophe could not stay still.

"Perhaps they have lost their way."

"Lost? They could not. Ernest knows all the paths."

A fantastic idea passed through Christophe's mind.

"Perhaps they arrived first, and went away before we came!"

Myrrha was lying on her back and looking at the sun. She was seized with a wild burst of laughter in the middle of her song and all but choked. Christophe insisted. He wanted to go down to the station, saying that their friends would be there already. Myrrha at last made up her mind to move.

"You would be certain to lose them! . . . There was never any talk about the station. We were to meet here."

He sat down by her side. She was amused by his eagerness. He was conscious of the irony in her gaze as she looked at him. He began to be seriously troubled—to be anxious about them: he did not suspect them. He got up once more. He spoke of going down into the woods again and looking for them, calling to them. Myrrha gave a little chuckle: she took from her pocket a needle, scissors, and thread: and she calmly undid and sewed in again the feathers in her hat: she seemed to have established herself for the day.

"No, no, silly," she said. "If they wanted to come do you think they would not come of their own accord?"

There was a catch at his heart. He turned towards her: she did not look at him: she was busy with her work. He went up to her.

"Myrrha!" he said.

"Eh?" she replied without stopping. He knelt now to look more nearly at her.

"Myrrha!" he repeated.

"Well?" she asked, raising her eyes from her work and looking at him with a smile. "What is it?"

She had a mocking expression as she saw his downcast face.

"Myrrha!" he asked, choking, "tell me what you think . . ."

She shrugged her shoulders, smiled, and went on working.

He caught her hands and took away the hat at which she was sewing.

"Leave off, leave off, and tell me. . . ."

She looked squarely at him and waited. She saw that Christophe's lips were trembling.

"You think," he said in a low voice, "that Ernest and Ada . . .?"

She smiled.

"Oh! well!"

He started back angrily.

"No! No! It is impossible! You don't think that! . . . No! No!"

She put her hands on his shoulders and rocked with laughter.

"How dense you are, how dense, my dear!"

He shook her violently.

"Don't laugh! Why do you laugh? You would not laugh if it were true. You love Ernest. . . ."

She went on laughing and drew him to her and kissed him. In spite of himself he returned her kiss. But when he felt her

lips on his, her lips, still warm with his brother's kisses, he
flung her away from him and held her face away from his
own: he asked:

"You knew it? It was arranged between you?"

She said "Yes," and laughed.

Christophe did not cry out, he made no movement of anger.
He opened his mouth as though he could not breathe: he closed
his eyes and clutched at his breast with his hands: his heart
was bursting. Then he lay down on the ground with his face
buried in his hands and he was shaken by a crisis of disgust
and despair like a child.

Myrrha, who was not very soft-hearted, was sorry for him:
involuntarily she was filled with motherly compassion, and
leaned over him, and spoke affectionately to him, and tried to
make him sniff at her smelling-bottle. But he thrust her away
in horror and got up so sharply that she was afraid. He had
neither strength nor desire for revenge. He looked at her with
his face twisted with grief.

"You drab,* he said in despair. "You do not know the
harm you have done. . . ."

She tried to hold him back. He fled through the woods,
spitting out his disgust with such ignominy, with such muddy
hearts, with such incestuous sharing as that to which they had
tried to bring him. He wept, he trembled: he sobbed with disgust. He was filled with horror, of them all, of himself, of
his body and soul. A storm of contempt broke loose in him:
it had long been brewing: sooner or later there had to come
the reaction against the base thoughts, the degrading compromises, the stale and pestilential atmosphere in which he had
been living for months: but the need of loving, of deceiving
himself about the woman he loved, had postponed the crisis
as long as possible. Suddenly it burst upon him: and it was
better so. There was a great gust of wind of a biting purity,
an icy breeze which swept away the miasma. Disgust in one
swoop had killed his love for Ada.

If Ada thought more firmly to establish her domination over
Christophe by such an act, that proved once more her gross
inappreciation of her lover. Jealousy which binds souls that
are besmirched could only revolt a nature like Christophe's,

young, proud, and pure. But what he could not forgive, what
he never would forgive, was that the betrayal was not the outcome of passion in Ada, hardly even of one of those absurd
and degrading though often irresistible caprices to which the
reason of a woman is sometimes hard put to it not to surrender.
No—he understood now,—it was in her a secret desire to degrade him, to humiliate him, to punish him for his moral
resistance, for his inimical faith, to lower him to the common
level, to bring him to her feet, to prove to herself her own
power for evil. And he asked himself with horror: what is
this impulse towards dirtiness, which is in the majority of
human beings—this desire to besmirch the purity of themselves
and others,—these swinish souls, who take a delight in rolling
in filth, and are happy when not one inch of their skins is left
clean! . . .

Ada waited two days for Christophe to return to her. Then
she began to be anxious, and sent him a tender note in which
she made no allusion to what had happened. Christophe did
not even reply. He hated Ada so profoundly that no words
could express his hatred. He had cut her out of his life. She
no longer existed for him.

Christophe was free of Ada, but he was not free of himself.
In vain did he try to return into illusion and to take up again
the calm and chaste strength of the past. We cannot return
to the past. We have to go onward: it is useless to turn back,
save only to see the places by which we have passed, the distant
smoke from the roofs under which we have slept, dying away
on the horizon in the mists of memory. But nothing so distances us from the soul that we had as a few months of
passion. The road takes a sudden turn: the country is changed:
it is as though we were saying good-bye for the last time to
all that we are leaving behind.

Christophe could not yield to it. He held out his arms to
the past: he strove desperately to bring to life again the soul
that had been his, lonely and resigned. But it was gone.
Passion itself is not so dangerous as the ruins that it heaps up
and leaves behind. In vain did Christophe not love, in vain—
for a moment—did he despise love: he bore the marks of its

talons: his whole being was steeped in it: there was in his heart a void which must be filled. With that terrible need of tenderness and pleasure which devours men and women when they have once tasted it, some other passion was needed, were it only the contrary passion, the passion of contempt, of proud purity, of faith in virtue.—They were not enough, they were not enough to stay his hunger: they were only the food of a moment. His life consisted of a succession of violent reactions— leaps from one extreme to the other. Sometimes he would bend his passion to rules inhumanly ascetic: not eating, drinking water, wearing himself out with walking, heavy tasks, and so not sleeping, denying himself every sort of pleasure. Sometimes he would persuade himself that strength is the true morality for people like himself: and he would plunge into the quest of joy. In either case he was unhappy. He could no longer be alone. He could no longer not be alone.

The only thing that could have saved him would have been to find a true friendship,—Rosa's perhaps: he could have taken refuge in that. But the rupture was complete between the two families. They no longer met. Only once had Christophe seen Rosa. She was just coming out from Mass. He had hesitated to bow to her: and when she saw him she had made a movement towards him: but when he had tried to go to her through the stream of the devout walking down the steps, she had turned her eyes away: and when he approached her she bowed coldly and passed on. In the girl's heart he felt intense, icy contempt. And he did not feel that she still loved him and would have liked to tell him so: but she had come to think of her love as a fault and foolishness: she thought Christophe bad and corrupt, and further from her than ever. So they were lost to each other forever. And perhaps it was as well for both of them. In spite of her goodness, she was not near enough to life to be able to understand him. In spite of his need of affection and respect he would have stifled in a commonplace and confined existence, without joy, without sorrow, without air. They would both have suffered. The unfortunate occurrence which cut them apart was, when all was told, perhaps, fortunate as often happens—as always happens—to those who are strong and endure.

But at the moment it was a great sorrow and a great misfortune for them. Especially for Christophe. Such virtuous intolerance, such narrowness of soul, which sometimes seems to deprive those who have the most of them of all intelligence, and those who are most good of kindness, irritated him, hurt him, and flung him back in protest into a freer life.

During his loafing with Ada in the beer gardens of the neighborhood he had made acquaintance with several good fellows—Bohemians, whose carelessness and freedom of manners had not been altogether distasteful to him. One of them, Friedemann, a musician like himself, an organist, a man of thirty, was not without intelligence, and was good at his work, but he was incurably lazy and rather than make the slightest effort to be more than mediocre, he would have died of hunger, though not, perhaps, of thirst. He comforted himself in his indolence by speaking ill of those who lived energetically, God knows why: and his sallies, rather heavy for the most part, generally made people laugh. Having more liberty than his companions, he was not afraid,—though timidly, and with winks and nods and suggestive remarks,—to sneer at those who held positions: he was even capable of not having ready-made opinions about music, and of having a sly fling at the forged reputations of the great men of the day. He had no mercy upon women either: when he was making his jokes he loved to repeat the old saying of some misogynist monk about them, and Christophe enjoyed its bitterness just then more than anybody:

"*Femina mors animae.*"

In his state of upheaval Christophe found some distraction in talking to Friedemann. He judged him, he could not long take pleasure in this vulgar bantering wit: his mockery and perpetual denial became irritating before long and he felt the impotence of it all: but it did soothe his exasperation with the self-sufficient stupidity of the Philistines. While he heartily despised his companion, Christophe could not do without him. They were continually seen together sitting with the unclassed and doubtful people of Friedemann's acquaintance, who were even more worthless than himself. They used to play, and harangue, and drink the whole evening. Christophe would suddenly wake up in the midst of the dreadful smell of food

and tobacco: he would look at the people about him with strange
eyes: he would not recognize them: he would think in
agony:

"Where am I? Who are these people? What have I to do
with them?"

Their remarks and their laughter would make him sick. But
he could not bring himself to leave them: he was afraid of
going home and of being left alone face to face with his soul,
his desires, and remorse. He was going to the dogs: he knew
it: he was doing it deliberately,—with cruel clarity he saw in
Friedemann the degraded image of what he was—of what he
would be one day: and he was passing through a phase of
such disheartenedness and disgust that instead of being brought
to himself by such a menace, it actually brought him low.

He would have gone to the dogs, if he could. Fortunately,
like all creatures of his kind, he had a spring, a succor against
destruction which others do not possess: his strength, his instinct for life, his instinct against letting himself perish, an
instinct more intelligent than his intelligence, and stronger than
his will. And also, unknown to himself, he had the strange
curiosity of the artist, that passionate, impersonal quality, which
is in every creature really endowed with creative power. In
vain did he love, suffer, give himself utterly to all his passions:
he saw them. They were in him but they were not himself.
A myriad of little souls moved obscurely in him towards a fixed
point unknown, yet certain, just like the planetary worlds
which are drawn through space into a mysterious abyss. That
perpetual state of unconscious action and reaction was shown
especially in those giddy moments when sleep came over his
daily life, and from the depths of sleep and the night rose the
multiform face of Being with its sphinx-like gaze. For a year
Christophe had been obsessed with dreams in which in a second
of time he felt clearly with perfect illusion that he *was* at one
and the same time several different creatures, often far removed
from each other by countries, worlds, centuries. In his waking
state Christophe was still under his hallucination and uneasiness, though he could not remember what had caused it. It
was like the weariness left by some fixed idea that is gone,
though traces of it are left and there is no understanding it.

But while his soul was so troublously struggling through the network of the days, another soul, eager and serene, was watching all his desperate efforts. He did not see it: but it cast over him the reflection of its hidden light. That soul was joyously greedy to feel everything, to suffer everything, to observe and understand men, women, the earth, life, desires, passions, thoughts, even those that were torturing, even those that were mediocre, even those that were vile: and it was enough to lend them a little of its light, to save Christophe from destruction. It made him feel—he did not know how—that he was not altogether alone. That love of being and of knowing everything, that second soul, raised a rampart against his destroying passions.

But if it was enough to keep his head above water, it did not allow him to climb out of it unaided. He could not succeed in seeing clearly into himself, and mastering himself, and regaining possession of himself. Work was impossible for him. He was passing through an intellectual crisis: the most fruitful of his life: all his future life was germinating in it: but that inner wealth for the time being only showed itself in extravagance: and the immediate effect of such superabundance was not different from that of the flattest sterility. Christophe was submerged by his life. All his powers had shot up and grown too fast, all at once, suddenly. Only his will had not grown with them: and it was dismayed by such a throng of monsters. His personality was cracking in every part. Of this earthquake, this inner cataclysm others saw nothing. Christophe himself could see only his impotence to will, to create, to be. Desires, instincts, thoughts issued one after another like clouds of sulphur from the fissures of a volcano: and he was forever asking himself: "And now, what will come out? What will become of me? Will it always be so? or is this the end of all? Shall I be nothing, always?"

And now there sprang up in him his hereditary fires, the vices of those who had gone before him.—He got drunk. He would return home smelling of wine, laughing, in a state of collapse.

Poor Louisa would look at him, sigh, say nothing, and pray.

But one evening when he was coming out of an inn by the

gates of the town he saw, a few yards in front of him on the
road, the droll shadow of his uncle Gottfried, with his pack
on his back. The little man had not been home for months,
and his periods of absence were growing longer and longer.
Christophe hailed him gleefully. Gottfried, bending under
his load, turned round: he looked at Christophe, who was making extravagant gestures, and sat down on a milestone to wait
for him. Christophe came up to him with a beaming face,
skipping along, and shook his uncle's hand with great demonstrations of affection. Gottfried took a long look at him and
then he said:

"Good-day, Melchior."

Christophe thought his uncle had made a mistake, and burst
out laughing.

"The poor man is breaking up," he thought; "he is losing
his memory."

Indeed, Gottfried did look old, shriveled, shrunken, and dried:
his breathing came short and painfully. Christophe went on
talking. Gottfried took his pack on his shoulders again and
went on in silence. They went home together, Christophe
gesticulating and talking at the top of his voice, Gottfried
coughing and saying nothing. And when Christophe questioned
him, Gottfried still called him Melchior. And then Christophe
asked him:

"What do you mean by calling me Melchior? My name is
Christophe, you know. Have you forgotten my name?"

Gottfried did not stop. He raised his eyes toward Christophe
and looked at him, shook his head, and said coldly:

"No. You are Melchior: I know you."

Christophe stopped dumfounded. Gottfried trotted along:
Christophe followed him without a word. He was sobered.
As they passed the door of a café he went up to the dark panes
of glass, in which the gas-jets of the entrance and the empty
streets were reflected, and he looked at himself: he recognized
Melchior. He went home crushed.

He spent the night—a night of anguish—in examining himself, in soul-searching. He understood now. Yes: he recognized the instincts and vices that had come to light in him:
they horrified him. He thought of that dark watching by the

body of Melchior, of all that he had sworn to do, and, surveying his life since then, he knew that he had failed to keep his vows. What had he done in the year? What had he done for his God, for his art, for his soul? What had he done for eternity? There was not a day that had not been wasted, botched, besmirched. Not a single piece of work, not a thought, not an effort of enduring quality. A chaos of desires destructive of each other. Wind, dust, nothing. . . . What did his intentions avail him? He had fulfilled none of them. He had done exactly the opposite of what he had intended. He had become what he had no wish to be: that was the balance-sheet of his life.

He did not go to bed. About six in the morning it was still dark,—he heard Gottfried getting ready to depart.—For Gottfried had had no intentions of staying on. As he was passing the town he had come as usual to embrace his sister and nephew: but he had announced that he would go on next morning.

Christophe went downstairs. Gottfried saw his pale face and his eyes hollow with a night of torment. He smiled fondly at him and asked him to go a little of the way with him. They set out together before dawn. They had no need to talk: they understood each other. As they passed the cemetery Gottfried said:

" Shall we go in? "

When he came to the place he never failed to pay a visit to Jean Michel and Melchior. Christophe had not been there for a year. Gottfried knelt by Melchior's grave and said:

" Let us pray that they may sleep well and not come to torment us."

His thought was a mixture of strange superstitions and sound sense: sometimes it surprised Christophe: but now it was only too clear to him. They said no more until they left the cemetery.

When they had closed the creaking gate, and were walking along the wall through the cold fields, waking from slumber, by the little path which led them under the cypress trees from which the snow was dropping, Christophe began to weep.

" Oh! uncle," he said, " how wretched I am! "

He dared not speak of his experience in love, from an odd fear of embarrassing or hurting Gottfried · but he spoke of his shame, his mediocrity, his cowardice, his broken vows.

"What am I to do, uncle? I have tried, I have struggled: and after a year I am no further on than before. Worse: I have gone back. I am good for nothing. I am good for nothing! I have ruined my life. I am perjured! . . ."

They were walking up the hill above the town. Gottfried said kindly:

"Not for the last time, my boy. We do not do what we will to do. We will and we live: two things. You must be comforted. The great thing is, you see, never to give up willing and living. The rest does not depend on us."

Christophe repeated desperately:

"I have perjured myself."

"Do you hear?" said Gottfried.

(The cocks were crowing in all the countryside.)

"They, too, are crowing for another who is perjured. They crow for every one of us, every morning."

"A day will come," said Christophe bitterly, "when they will no longer crow for me. . . . A day to which there is no to-morrow. And what shall I have made of my life?"

"There is always a to-morrow," said Gottfried.

"But what can one do, if willing is no use?"

"Watch and pray."

"I do not believe."

Gottfried smiled.

"You would not be alive if you did not believe. Every one believes. Pray."

"Pray to what?"

Gottfried pointed to the sun appearing on the horizon, red and frozen.

"Be reverent before the dawning day. Do not think of what will be in a year, or in ten years. Think of to-day. Leave your theories. All theories, you see, even those of virtue, are bad, foolish, mischievous. Do not abuse life. Live in to-day. Be reverent towards each day. Love it, respect it, do not sully it, do not hinder it from coming to flower. Love it even when

it is gray and sad like to-day. Do not be anxious. See. It
is winter now. Everything is asleep. The good earth will
awake again. You have only to be good and patient like the
earth. Be reverent. Wait. If you are good, all will go well.
If you are not, if you are weak, if you do not succeed, well,
you must be happy in that. No doubt it is the best you can
do. So, then, why *will?* Why be angry because of what you
cannot do? We all have to do what we can. . . . *Als ich kann.*"

"It is not enough," said Christophe, making a face.

Gottfried laughed pleasantly.

"It is more than anybody does. You are a vain fellow. You
want to be a hero. That is why you do such silly things. . . .
A hero! . . . I don't quite know what that is: but, you see,
I imagine that a hero is a man who does what he can. The
others do not do it."

"Oh!" sighed Christophe. "Then what is the good of
living? It is not worth while. And yet there are people who
say: 'He who wills can!'" . . .

Gottfried laughed again softly.

"Yes? . . . Oh! well, they are liars, my friend. Or they
do not will anything much. . . ."

They had reached the top of the hill. They embraced affectionately. The little peddler went on, treading wearily. Christophe stayed there, lost in thought, and watched him go. He
repeated his uncle's saying:

"*Als ich kann* (The best I can)."

And he smiled, thinking:

"Yes. . . . All the same. . . . It is enough."

He returned to the town. The frozen snow crackled under
his feet. The bitter winter wind made the bare branches
of the stunted trees on the hill shiver. It reddened his cheeks,
and made his skin tingle, and set his blood racing. The red
roofs of the town below were smiling under the brilliant, cold
sun. The air was strong and harsh. The frozen earth seemed
to rejoice in bitter gladness. And Christophe's heart was like
that. He thought:

"I, too, shall wake again."

There were still tears in his eyes. He dried them with
the back of his hand, and laughed to see the sun dipping down

behind a veil of mist. The clouds, heavy with snow, were floating over the town, lashed by the squall. He laughed at them. The wind blew icily. . . .

"Blow, blow! . . . Do what you will with me. Bear me with you! . . . I know now where I am going."

REVOLT

SHIFTING SANDS

FREE! He felt that he was free! . . . Free of others and of himself! The network of passion in which he had been enmeshed for more than a year had suddenly been burst asunder. How? He did not know. The filaments had given before the growth of his being. It was one of those crises of growth in which robust natures tear away the dead casing of the year that is past, the old soul in which they are cramped and stifled.

Christophe breathed deeply, without understanding what had happened. An icy whirlwind was rushing through the great gate of the town as he returned from taking Gottfried on his way. The people were walking with heads lowered against the storm. Girls going to their work were struggling against the wind that blew against their skirts: they stopped every now and then to breathe, with their nose and cheeks red, and they looked exasperated, and as though they wanted to cry. He thought of that other torment through which he had passed. He looked at the wintry sky, the town covered with snow, the people struggling along past him: he looked about him, into himself: he was no longer bound. He was alone! . . . Alone! How happy to be alone, to be his own! What joy to have escaped from his bonds, from his torturing memories, from the hallucinations of faces that he loved or detested! What joy at last to live, without being the prey of life, to have become his own master! . . .

He went home white with snow. He shook himself gaily like a dog. As he passed his mother, who was sweeping the passage, he lifted her up, giving little inarticulate cries of affection such as one makes to a tiny child. Poor old Louisa struggled in her son's arms: she was wet with the melting snow: and she called him, with a jolly laugh, a great gaby.

He went up to his room three steps at a time.—He could hardly see himself in his little mirror it was so dark. But his heart was glad. His room was low and narrow and it was difficult to move in it, but it was like a kingdom to him. He locked the door and laughed with pleasure. At last he was finding himself! How long he had been gone astray! He was eager to plunge into thought like a bather into water. It was like a great lake afar off melting into the mists of blue and gold. After a night of fever and oppressive heat he stood by the edge of it, with his legs bathed in the freshness of the water, his body kissed by the wind of a summer morning. He plunged in and swam: he knew not whither he was going, and did not care: it was joy to swim whithersoever he listed. He was silent, then he laughed, and listened for the thousand thousand sounds of his soul: it swarmed with life. He could make out nothing: his head was swimming: he felt only a bewildering happiness. He was glad to feel in himself such unknown forces: and indolently postponing putting his powers to the test he sank back into the intoxication of pride in the inward flowering, which, held back for months, now burst forth like a sudden spring.

His mother called him to breakfast. He went down: he was giddy and light-headed as though he had spent a day in the open air: but there was such a radiance of joy in him that Louisa asked what was the matter. He made no reply: he seized her by the waist and forced her to dance with him round the table on which the tureen was steaming. Out of breath Louisa cried that he was mad: then she clasped her hands.

"Dear God!" she said anxiously. "Sure, he is in love again!"

Christophe roared with laughter. He hurled his napkin into the air.

"In love? . . ." he cried. "Oh! Lord! . . . but no! I've had enough! You can be easy on that score. That is done, done, forever! . . . Ouf!"

He drank a glassful of water.

Louisa looked at him, reassured, wagged her head, and smiled.

"That's a drunkard's pledge," she said. "It won't last until to-night."

"Then the day is clear gain," he replied good-humoredly.

"Oh, yes!" she said. "But what has made you so happy?"

"I am happy. That is all."

Sitting opposite her with his elbows on the table he tried to tell her all that he was going to do. She listened with kindly skepticism and gently pointed out that his soup was going cold. He knew that she did not hear what he was saying: but he did not care: he was talking for his own satisfaction.

They looked at each other smiling: he talking: she hardly listening. Although she was proud of her son she attached no great importance to his artistic projects: she was thinking: "He is happy: that matters most."—While he was growing more and more excited with his discourse he watched his mother's dear face, with her black shawl tightly tied round her head, her white hair, her young eyes that devoured him lovingly, her sweet and tranquil kindliness. He knew exactly what she was thinking. He said to her jokingly:

"It is all one to you, eh? You don't care about what I'm telling you?"

She protested weakly:

"Oh, no! Oh, no!"

He kissed her.

"Oh, yes! Oh, yes! You need not defend yourself. You are right. Only love me. There is no need to understand me—either for you or for anybody else. I do not need anybody or anything now: I have everything in myself. . . ."

"Oh!" said Louisa. "Another maggot in his brain! . . . But if he must have one I prefer this to the other."

What sweet happiness to float on the surface of the lake of his thoughts! . . . Lying in the bottom of a boat with his body bathed in sun, his face kissed by the light fresh wind that skims over the face of the waters, he goes to sleep: he is swung by threads from the sky. Under his body lying at full length, under the rocking boat he feels the deep, swelling water: his hand dips into it. He rises: and with his chin on the edge of the boat he watches the water flowing by as he did when he was a child. He sees the reflection of strange creatures darting by like lightning. . . . More, and yet more. . . . They are never the same. He laughs at the fantastic spectacle that is unfolded within him: he laughs at his own thoughts: he has no need to catch and hold them. Select? Why select among so many thousands of dreams? There is plenty of time! . . . Later on! . . . He has only to throw out a line at will to draw in the monsters whom he sees gleaming in the water. He lets them pass. . . . Later on! . . .

The boat floats on at the whim of the warm wind and the insentient stream. All is soft, sun, and silence.

At last languidly he throws out his line. Leaning out over the lapping water he follows it with his eyes until it disappears. After a few moments of torpor he draws it in slowly: as he draws it in it becomes heavier: just as he is about to fish it out of the water he stops to take breath. He knows that he has his prey: he does not know what it is: he prolongs the pleasure of expectancy.

At last he makes up his mind: fish with gleaming, many-colored scales appear from the water: they writhe like a nest of snakes. He looks at them curiously, he stirs them with his finger: but hardly has he drawn them from the water than their colors fade and they slip between his fingers. He throws them back into the water and begins to fish for others. He is more eager to see one after another all the dreams stirring in him than to catch at any one of them: they all seem more beautiful to him when they are freely swimming in the transparent lake. . . .

He caught all kinds of them, each more extravagant than the last. Ideas had been heaped up in him for months and he had not drawn upon them, so that he was bursting with riches. But it was all higgledy-piggledy: his mind was a Babel, an old Jew's curiosity shop in which there were piled up in the one room rare treasures, precious stuffs, scrap-iron, and rags. He could not distinguish their values: everything amused him. There were thrilling chords, colors which rang like bells, harmonies which buzzed like bees, melodies smiling like lovers' lips. There were visions of the country, faces, passions, souls, characters, literary ideas, metaphysical ideas. There were great

projects, vast and impossible, tetralogies, decalogies, pretending
to depict everything in music, covering whole worlds. And,
most often there were obscure, flashing sensations, called forth
by a trifle, the sound of a voice, a man or a woman passing in
the street, the pattering of rain. An inward rhythm.—Many
of these projects advanced no further than their title: most
of them were never more than a note or two: it was enough.
Like all very young people, he thought he had created what he
dreamed of creating.

But he was too keenly alive to be satisfied for long with such
fantasies. He wearied of an illusory possession: he wished to
seize his dreams.—How to begin? They seemed to him all
equally important. He turned and turned them: he rejected
them, he took them up again. . . . No, he never took them up
again: they were no longer the same, they were never to be
caught twice: they were always changing: they changed in his
hands, under his eyes, while he was watching them. He must
make haste: he could not: he was appalled by the slowness
with which he worked. He would have liked to do everything
in one day, and he found it horribly difficult to complete the
smallest thing. His dreams were passing and he was passing
himself: while he was doing one thing it worried him not to
be doing another. It was as though it was enough to have
chosen one of his fine subjects for it to lose all interest for
him. And so all his riches availed him nothing. His thoughts
had life only on condition that he did not tamper with
them: everything that he succeeded in doing was still-born.
It was the torment of Tantalus: within reach were fruits that
became stones as soon as he plucked them: near his lips was
a clear stream which sank away whenever he bent down to
drink.

To slake his thirst he tried to sip at the springs that he had
conquered, his old compositions. . . . Loathsome in taste! At
the first gulp he spat it out again, cursing. What! That tepid
water, that insipid music, was that his music?—He read through
all his compositions: he was horrified: he understood not a
note of them, he could not even understand how he had come
to write them. He blushed. Once after reading through a

page more foolish than the rest he turned round to make sure
that there was nobody in the room, and then he went and hid
his face in his pillow like a child ashamed. Sometimes they
seemed to him so preposterously silly that they were quite funny,
and he forgot that they were his own. . . .

" What an idiot! " he would cry, rocking with laughter.

But nothing touched him more than those compositions in
which he had set out to express his own passionate feelings: the
sorrows and joys of love. Then he would bound in his chair
as though a fly had stung him: he would thump on the table,
beat his head, and roar angrily: he would coarsely apostrophize
himself: he would vow himself to be a swine, trebly a scoundrel,
a clod, and a clown—a whole litany of denunciation. In the
end he would go and stand before his mirror, red with shouting,
and then he would take hold of his chin and say:

" Look, look, you scurvy knave, look at the ass-face that is
yours! I'll teach you to lie, you blackguard! Water, sir,
water."

He would plunge his face into his basin, and hold it under
water until he was like to choke. When he drew himself up,
scarlet, with his eyes starting from his head, snorting like a
seal, he would rush to his table, without bothering to sponge
away the water trickling down him: he would seize the unhappy compositions, angrily tear them in pieces, growling:

" There, you beast! . . . There, there, there! . . ."

Then he would recover.

What exasperated him most in his compositions was their untruth. Not a spark of feeling in them. A phraseology got
by heart, a schoolboy's rhetoric: he spoke of love like a blind
man of color: he spoke of it from hearsay, only repeating the
current platitudes. And it was not only love: it was the same
with all the passions, which had been used for themes and
declamations.—And yet he had always tried to be sincere.—
But it is not enough to wish to be sincere: it is necessary to
have the power to be so: and how can a man be so when as
yet he knows nothing of life? What had revealed the falseness
of his work, what had suddenly digged a pit between himself
and his past was the experience which he had had during the
last six months of life. He had left fantasy: there was now

in him a real standard to which he could bring all the thoughts
for judgment as to their truth or untruth.

The disgust which his old work, written without passion,
roused in him, made him decide with his usual exaggeration
that he would write no more until he was forced to write by
some passionate need: and leaving the pursuit of his ideas at
that, he swore that he would renounce music forever, unless
creation were imposed upon him in a thunderclap.

He made this resolve because he knew quite well that the
storm was coming.

Thunder falls when it will, and where it will. But there
are peaks which attract it. Certain places—certain souls—
breed storms: they create them, or draw them from all points
of the horizon: and certain ages of life, like certain months
of the year, are so saturated with electricity, that thunderstorms
are produced in them,—if not at will—at any rate when they
are expected.

The whole being of a man is taut for it. Often the storm
lies brooding for days and days. The pale sky is hung with
burning, fleecy clouds. No wind stirs. The still air ferments,
and seems to boil. The earth lies in a stupor: no sound comes
from it. The brain hums feverishly: all nature awaits the
explosion of the gathering forces, the thud of the hammer which
is slowly rising to fall back suddenly on the anvil of the clouds.
Dark, warm shadows pass: a fiery wind rises through the body,
the nerves quiver like leaves. . . . Then silence falls again.
The sky goes on gathering thunder.

In such expectancy there is voluptuous anguish. In spite
of the discomfort that weighs so heavily upon you, you feel
in your veins the fire which is consuming the universe. The
soul surfeited boils in the furnace, like wine in a vat. Thousands of germs of life and death are in labor in it. What will
issue from it? The soul knows not. Like a woman with child,
it is silent: it gazes in upon itself: it listens anxiously for the
stirring in its womb, and thinks: " What will be born of
me? " . . .

Sometimes such waiting is in vain. The storm passes without
breaking: but you wake heavy, cheated, enervated, disheartened

But it is only postponed: the storm will break: if not to-day, then to-morrow: the longer it is delayed, the more violent will it be. . . .

Now it comes! . . . The clouds have come up from all corners of the soul. Thick masses, blue and black, torn by the frantic darting of the lightning: they advance heavily, drunkenly, darkening the soul's horizon, blotting out light. An hour of madness! . . . The exasperated Elements, let loose from the cage in which they are held bound by the Laws which hold the balance between the mind and the existence of things, reign, formless and colossal, in the night of consciousness. The soul is in agony. There is no longer the will to live. There is only longing for the end, for the deliverance of death. . . .

And suddenly there is lightning!

Christophe shouted for joy.

Joy, furious joy, the sun that lights up all that is and will be, the godlike joy of creation! There is no joy but in creation. There are no living beings but those who create. All the rest are shadows, hovering over the earth, strangers to life. All the joys of life are the joys of creation: love, genius, action, —quickened by flames issuing from one and the same fire. Even those who cannot find a place by the great fireside: the ambitious, the egoists, the sterile sensualists,—try to gain warmth in the pale reflections of its light.

To create in the region of the body, or in the region of the mind, is to issue from the prison of the body: it is to ride upon the storm of life: it is to be He who Is. To create is to triumph over death.

Wretched is the sterile creature, that man or that woman who remains alone and lost upon the earth, scanning their withered bodies, and the sight of themselves from which no flame of life will ever leap! Wretched is the soul that does not feel its own fruitfulness, and know itself to be big with life and love, as a tree with blossom in the spring! The world may heap honors and benefits upon such a soul: it does but crown a corpse.

When Christophe was struck by the flash of lightning, an electric fluid coursed through his body: he trembled under the shock. It was as though on the high seas, in the dark night, he had suddenly sighted land. Or it was as though in a crowd he had gazed into two eyes saluting him. Often it would happen to him after hours of prostration when his mind was leaping desperately through the void. But more often still it came in moments when he was thinking of something else, talking to his mother, or walking through the streets. If he were in the street a certain human respect kept him from too loudly demonstrating his joy. But if he were at home nothing could keep him back. He would stamp. He would sound a blare of triumph: his mother knew that well, and she had come to know what it meant. She used to tell Christophe that he was like a hen that has laid an egg.

He was permeated with his musical imagination. Sometimes it took shape in an isolated phrase complete in itself: more often it would appear as a nebula enveloping a whole work: the structure of the work, its general lines, could be perceived through a veil, torn asunder here and there by dazzling phrases which stood out from the darkness with the clarity of sculpture. It was only a flash: sometimes others would come in quick succession: each lit up other corners of the night. But usually, the capricious force having once shown itself unexpectedly, would disappear again for several days into its mysterious retreats, leaving behind it a luminous ray.

This delight in inspiration was so vivid that Christophe was disgusted by everything else. The experienced artist knows that inspiration is rare and that intelligence is left to complete the work of intuition: he puts his idea under the press and squeezes out of them the last drop of the divine juices that are in them—(and if need be sometimes he does not shrink from diluting them with clear water).—Christophe was too young and too sure of himself not to despise such contemptible practices. He dreamed impossibly of producing nothing that was not absolutely spontaneous. If he had not been deliberately blind he would certainly have seen the absurdity of his aims. No doubt he was at that time in a period of inward abundance in which there was no gap, no chink, through which boredom or emptiness could creep. Everything served as an excuse to his inexhaustible fecundity: everything that his eyes saw or his ears heard, everything with which he came in contact in his daily life: every look, every word, brought forth a crop of dreams. In the boundless heaven of his thoughts he saw circling millions of milky stars, rivers of living light.—And yet, even then, there were moments when everything was suddenly blotted out. And although the night could not endure, although he had hardly time to suffer from these long silences of his soul, he did not escape a secret terror of that unknown power which came upon him, left him, came again, and disappeared. . . . How long, this time? Would it ever come again?—His pride rejected that thought and said: " This force is myself. When it ceases to be, I shall cease to be: I shall kill myself."—He never ceased to tremble: but it was only another delight.

But, if, for the moment, there was no danger of the spring running dry, Christophe was able already to perceive that it was never enough to fertilize a complete work. Ideas almost always appeared rawly: he had painfully to dig them out of the ore. And always they appeared without any sort of sequence, and by fits and starts: to unite them he had to bring to bear on them an element of reflection and deliberation and cold will, which fashioned them into new form. Christophe was too much of an artist not to do so: but he would not accept it: he forced himself to believe that he did no more than transcribe what was within himself, while he was always compelled more or less to transform it so as to make it intelligible.— More than that: sometimes he would absolutely forge a meaning for it. However violently the musical idea might come upon him it would often have been impossible for him to say what it meant. It would come surging up from the depths of life, from far beyond the limits of consciousness: and in that absolutely pure Force, which eluded common rhythms, consciousness could never recognize in it any of the motives which stirred in it, none of the human feelings which it defines and classifies: joys, sorrows, they were all merged in one single passion which was unintelligible, because it was above the intelligence. And yet, whether it understood or no, the intelligence needed to give a name to this form, to bind it down to one or other of the structures of logic, which man is forever building indefatigably in the hive of his brain.

So Christophe convinced himself—he wished to do so—that the obscure power that moved him had an exact meaning, and that its meaning was in accordance with his will. His free instinct, risen from the unconscious depths, was willy-nilly forced to plod on under the yoke of reason with perfectly clear ideas which had nothing at all in common with it. And work so produced was no more than a lying juxtaposition of one of those great subjects that Christophe's mind had marked out for itself, and those wild forces which had an altogether different meaning unknown to himself.

He groped his way, head down, borne on by the contradictory forces warring in him, and hurling into his incoherent works a fiery and strong quality of life which he could not express, though he was joyously and proudly conscious of it.

The consciousness of his new vigor made him able for the first time to envisage squarely everything about him, everything that he had been taught to honor, everything that he had respected without question: and he judged it all with insolent freedom. The veil was rent: he saw the German lie.

Every race, every art has its hypocrisy. The world is fed with a little truth and many lies. The human mind is feeble: pure truth agrees with it but ill: its religion, its morality, its states, its poets, its artists, must all be presented to it swathed in lies. These lies are adapted to the mind of each race: they vary from one to the other: it is they that make it so difficult for nations to understand each other, and so easy for them to despise each other. Truth is the same for all of us: but every nation has its own lie, which it calls its idealism: every creature therein breathes it from birth to death: it has become a condition of life: there are only a few men of genius who can break free from it through heroic moments of crisis, when they are alone in the free world of their thoughts.

It was a trivial thing which suddenly revealed to Christophe the lie of German art. It was not because it had not always been visible that he had not seen it: he was not near it, he had not recoiled from it. Now the mountain appeared to his gaze because he had moved away from it.

He was at a concert of the *Städtische Townhalle.* The concert was given in a large hall occupied by ten or twelve rows of little tables—about two or three hundred of them. At the end of the room was a stage where the orchestra was sitting. All round Christophe were officers dressed up in their long, dark coats,—with broad, shaven faces, red, serious, and commonplace: women talking and laughing noisily, ostentatiously at their ease: jolly little girls smiling and showing all their teeth: and large men hidden behind their beards and spectacles, looking like kindly spiders with round eyes. They got up with every fresh glass to drink a toast: they did this almost religiously: their faces, their voices changed: it was as though they were saying Mass: they offered each other the libations, they drank of the chalice with a mixture of solemnity and buffoonery. The music was drowned under the conversation and the clinking of glasses. And yet everybody was trying to talk and eat quietly. The *Herr Konzertmeister,* a tall, bent old man, with a white beard hanging like a tail from his chin, and a long aquiline nose, with spectacles, looked like a philologist.—All these types were familiar to Christophe. But on that day he had an inclination—he did not know why—to see them as caricatures. There are days like that when, for no apparent reason, the grotesque in people and things which in ordinary life passes unnoticed, suddenly leaps into view.

The programme of the music included the *Egmont* overture, a valse of Waldteufel, *Tannhäuser's Pilgrimage to Rome,* the overture to the *Merry Wives* of Nicolai, the religious march of *Athalie,* and a fantasy on the *North Star.* The orchestra played the Beethoven overture correctly, and the valse deliciously. During the *Pilgrimage of Tannhäuser,* the uncorking of bottles was heard. A big man sitting at the table next to Christophe beat time to the *Merry Wives* by imitating Falstaff. A stout old lady, in a pale blue dress, with a white belt, golden pince-nez on her flat nose, red arms, and an enormous waist, sang in a loud voice *Lieder* of Schumann and Brahms. She raised her eyebrows, made eyes at the wings, smiled with a smile that seemed to curdle on her moon-face, made exaggerated gestures which must certainly have called to mind the *café-concert* but

for the majestic honesty which shone in her: this mother of a
family played the part of the giddy girl, youth, passion: and
Schumann's poetry had a faint smack of the nursery. The
audience was in ecstasies.—But they grew solemn and attentive
when there appeared the Choral Society of the Germans of
the South (*Süddeutschen Männer Liedertafel*), who alternately
cooed and roared part songs full of feeling. There were forty,
and they sang four parts: it seemed as though they had set
themselves to free their execution of every trace of style that
could properly be called choral: a hotch-potch of little melodious
effects, little timid puling shades of sound, dying *pianissimos,*
with sudden swelling, roaring *crescendos,* like some one beating
on an empty box: no breadth or balance, a mawkish style: it was
like Bottom:

"Let me play the lion. I will roar you as gently as any
sucking dove. I will roar you as it were a nightingale."

Christophe listened from the beginning with growing amazement. There was nothing new in it all to him. He knew
these concerts, the orchestra, the audience. But suddenly it
all seemed to him false. All of it: even to what he most loved,
the *Egmont* overture, in which the pompous disorder and correct agitation hurt him in that hour like a want of frankness.
No doubt it was not Beethoven or Schumann that he heard,
but their absurd interpreters, their cud-chewing audience whose
crass stupidity was spread about their works like a heavy mist.—
No matter, there was in the works, even the most beautiful of
them, a disturbing quality which Christophe had never before
felt.—What was it? He dared not analyze it, deeming it a
sacrilege to question his beloved masters. But in vain did he
shut his eyes to it: he had seen it. And, in spite of himself,
he went on seeing it: like the *Vergognosa* at Pisa he looked
between his fingers.

He saw German art stripped. All of them—the great and
the idiots—laid bare their souls with a complacent tenderness.
Emotion overflowed, moral nobility trickled down, their hearts
melted in distracted effusions: the sluice gates were opened to
the fearful German tender-heartedness: it weakened the energy
of the stronger, it drowned the weaker under its grayish waters:
it was a flood: in the depths of it slept German thought. And

what thoughts were those of a Mendelssohn, a Brahms, a Schumann, and, following them, the whole legion of little writers of affected and tearful *Lieder!* Built on sand. Never rock. Wet and shapeless clay.—It was all so foolish, so childish often, that Christophe could not believe that it never occurred to the audience. He looked about him: but he saw only gaping faces, convinced in advance of the beauties they were hearing and the pleasure that they ought to find in it. How could they admit their own right to judge for themselves? They were filled with respect for these hallowed names. What did they not respect? They were respectful before their programmes, before their glasses, before themselves. It was clear that mentally they dubbed everything excellent that remotely or nearly concerned them.

Christophe passed in review the audience and the music alternately: the music reflected the audience, the audience reflected the music. Christophe felt laughter overcoming him and he made faces. However, he controlled himself. But when the Germans of the South came and solemnly sang the *Confession* that reminded him of the blushes of a girl in love, Christophe could not contain himself. He shouted with laughter. Indignant cries of "Ssh!" were raised. His neighbors looked at him, scared: their honest, scandalized faces filled him with joy: he laughed louder than ever, he laughed, he laughed until he cried. Suddenly the audience grew angry. They cried: "Put him out!" He got up, and went, shrugging his shoulders, shaking with suppressed laughter. His departure caused a scandal. It was the beginning of hostilities between Christophe and his birthplace.

After that experience Christophe shut himself up and set himself to read once more the works of the "hallowed" musicians. He was appalled to find that certain of the masters whom he loved most had *lied*. He tried hard to doubt it at first, to believe that he was mistaken.—But no, there was no way out of it. He was staggered by the conglomeration of mediocrity and untruth which constitutes the artistic treasure of a great people. How many pages could bear examination! From that time on he could begin to read other works, other

masters, who were dear to him, only with a fluttering heart.
. . . Alas! There was some spell cast upon him: always there
was the same discomfiture. With some of them his heart was
rent: it was as though he had lost a dear friend, as if he had
suddenly seen that a friend in whom he had reposed entire
confidence had been deceiving him for years. He wept for it.
He did not sleep at night: he could not escape his torment.
He blamed himself: perhaps he had lost his judgment? Perhaps he had become altogether an idiot?—No, no. More than
ever he saw the radiant beauty of the day and with more freshness and love than ever he felt the generous abundance of life:
his heart was not deceiving him. . . .

But for a long time he dared not approach those who were
the best for him, the purest, the Holy of Holies. He trembled
at the thought of bringing his faith in them to the test. But
how resist the pitiless instinct of a brave and truthful soul,
which will go on to the end, and see things as they are, whatever
suffering may be got in doing so?—So he opened the sacred
works, he called upon the last reserve, the imperial guard. . . .
At the first glance he saw that they were no more immaculate
than the others. He had not the courage to go on. Every now
and then he stopped and closed the book: like the son of Noah,
he threw his cloak about his father's nakedness. . . .

Then he was prostrate in the midst of all these ruins. He
would rather have lost an arm, than have tampered with his
blessed illusions. In his heart he mourned. But there was so
much sap in him, so much reserve of life, that his confidence
in art was not shaken. With a young man's naïve presumption he began life again as though no one had ever lived it
before him. Intoxicated by his new strength, he felt—not without reason, perhaps—that with a very few exceptions there is
almost no relation between living passion and the expression
which art has striven to give to it. But he was mistaken in
thinking himself more happy or more true when he expressed
it. As he was filled with passion it was easy for him to discover it at the back of what he had written: but no one else
would have recognized it through the imperfect vocabulary
with which he designated its variations. Many artists whom
he condemned were in the same case. They had had, and had

translated profound emotions: but the secret of their language had died with them.

Christophe was no psychologist: he was not bothered with all these arguments: what was dead for him had always been so. He revised his judgment of the past with all the confident and fierce injustice of youth. He stripped the noblest souls, and had no pity for their foibles. There were the rich melancholy, the distinguished fantasy, the kindly thinking emptiness of Mendelssohn. There were the bead-stringing and the affectation of Weber, his dryness of heart, his cerebral emotion. There was Liszt, the noble priest, the circus rider, neo-classical and vagabond, a mixture in equal doses of real and false nobility, of serene idealism and disgusting virtuosity. Schubert, swallowed up by his sentimentality, drowned at the bottom of leagues of stale, transparent water. The men of the heroic ages, the demi-gods, the Prophets, the Fathers of the Church, were not spared. Even the great Sebastian, the man of ages, who bore in himself the past and the future,—Bach,—was not free of untruth, of fashionable folly, of school-chattering. The man who had seen God, the man who lived in God, seemed sometimes to Christophe to have had an insipid and sugared religion, a Jesuitical style, rococo. In his cantatas there were languorous and devout airs—(dialogues of the Soul coquetting with Jesus)—which sickened Christophe: then he seemed to see chubby cherubims with round limbs and flying draperies. And also he had a feeling that the genial *Cantor* always wrote in a closed room: his work smacked of stuffiness: there was not in his music that brave outdoor air that was breathed in others, not such great musicians, perhaps, but greater men— more human—than he. Like Beethoven or Händel. What hurt him in all of them, especially in the classics, was their lack of freedom: almost all their works were " constructed." Sometimes an emotion was filled out with all the commonplaces of musical rhetoric, sometimes with a simple rhythm, an ornamental design, repeated, turned upside down, combined in every conceivable way in a mechanical fashion. These symmetrical and twaddling constructions—classical and neo-classical sonatas and symphonies—exasperated Christophe, who, at that time, was not very sensible of the beauty of order, and vast and well-conceived plans. That seemed to him to be rather masons' work than musicians'.

But he was no less severe with the romantics. It was a strange thing, and he was more surprised by it than anybody,— but no musicians irritated him more than those who had pretended to be—and had actually been—the most free, the most spontaneous, the least constructive,—those, who, like Schumann, had poured drop by drop, minute by minute, into their innumerable little works, their whole life. He was the more indignantly in revolt against them as he recognized in them his adolescent soul and all the follies that he had vowed to pluck out of it. In truth, the candid Schumann could not be taxed with falsity: he hardly ever said anything that he had not felt. But that was just it: his example made Christophe understand that the worst falsity in German art came into it not when the artists tried to express something which they had not felt, but rather when they tried to express the feelings which they did in fact feel—*feelings which were false*. Music is an implacable mirror of the soul. The more a German musician is naïve and in good faith, the more he displays the weaknesses of the German soul, its uncertain depths, its soft tenderness, its want of frankness, its rather sly idealism, its incapacity for seeing itself, for daring to come face to face with itself. That false idealism is the secret sore even of the greatest—of Wagner. As he read his works Christophe ground his teeth. *Lohengrin* seemed to him a blatant lie. He loathed the huxtering chivalry, the hypocritical mummery, the hero without fear and without a heart, the incarnation of cold and selfish virtue admiring itself and most patently self-satisfied. He knew it too well, he had seen it in reality, the type of German Pharisee, foppish, impeccable, and hard, bowing down before its own image, the divinity to which it has no scruple about sacrificing others. *The Flying Dutchman* overwhelmed him with its massive sentimentality and its gloomy boredom. The loves of the barbarous decadents of the *Tetralogy* were of a sickening staleness. Siegmund carrying off his sister sang a tenor drawing-room song. Siegfried and Brünnhilde, like respectable German married people, in the *Götterdämmerung* laid bare before each other, especially for the benefit of the audience, their pompous and voluble conjugal passion. Every sort of lie had arranged to meet in that work: false idealism, false Christianity, false Gothicism, false legend, false gods, false humans. Never did more monstrous convention appear than in that theater which was to upset all the convent.ons. Neither eyes, nor mind, nor heart could be deceived by it for a moment: if they were, then they must wish to be so.—They did wish to be so. Germany was delighted with that doting, child.sh art, an art of brutes let loose, and mystic, namby-pamby little girls.

And Christophe could do nothing: as soon as he heard the music he was caught up like the others, more than the others, by the flood, and the diabolical will of the man who had let it loose. He laughed, and he trembled, and his cheeks burned, and he felt galloping armies rushing through him! And he thought that those who bore such storms within themselves might have all allowances made for them. What cries of joy he uttered when in the hallowed works which he could not read without trembling he felt once more his old emotion, ardent st.ll, with nothing to tarnish the purity of what he loved! These were glorious relics that he saved from the wreck. What happiness they gave him! It seemed to him that he had saved a part of himself. And was it not himself? These great Germans, against whom he revolted, were they not his blood, his flesh, his most precious life? He was only severe with them because he was severe with himself. Who loved them better than he? Who felt more than he the goodness of Schubert, the innocence of Haydn, the tenderness of Mozart, the great heroic heart of Beethoven? Who more often than he took refuge in the murmuring of the forests of Weber, and the cool shade of the cathedrals of John Sebastian, raising against the gray sky of the North, above the plains of Germany, their pile of stone, and their gigantic towers with their sun-tipped spires?—But he suffered from their lies, and he could not forget them. He attributed them to the race, their greatness to themselves. He was wrong. Greatness and weaknesses belong equally to the race whose great, shifting thought flows like the greatest river of music and poetry at which Europe comes to drink.— And in what other people would he have found the simple purity which now made it possible for him to condemn it so harshly?

He had no notion of that. With the ingratitude of a spoiled child he turned against his mother the weapons which he had received from her. Later, later, he was to feel all that he owed to her, and how dear she was to him. . . .

But he was in a phase of blind reaction against all the idols of his childhood. He was angry with himself and with them because he had believed in them absolutely and passionately—and it was well that it was so. There is an age in life when we must dare to be unjust, when we must make a clean sweep of all admiration and respect got at second-hand, and deny everything—truth and untruth—everything which we háve not of ourselves known for truth. Through education, and through everything that he sees and hears about him, a child absorbs so many lies and blind follies mixed with the essential verities of life, that the first duty of the adolescent who wishes to grow into a healthy man is to sacrifice everything.

Christophe was passing through that crisis of healthy disgust. His instinct was impelling him to eliminate from his life all the undigested elements which encumbered it.

First of all to go was that sickening sweet tenderness which sucked away the soul of Germany like a damp and moldy river-bed. Light! Light! A rough, dry wind which should sweep away the miasmas of the swamp, the misty staleness of the *Lieder, Liedchen, Liedlein,* as numerous as drops of rain in which inexhaustibly the Germanic *Gemüt* is poured forth: the countless things like *Sehnsucht* (Desire), *Hcimweh* (Home-sickness), *Aufschwung* (Soaring), *Trage* (A question), *Warum?* (Why?), *an den Mond* (To the Moon), *an die Sterne* (To the Stars), *an die Nachtigall* (To the Nightingale), *an den Frühling* (To Spring), *an den Sonnenschein* (To Sunshine): like *Frühlingslied* (Spring Song), *Frühlingslust* (Delights of Spring), *Frühlingsgruss* (Hail to the Spring), *Frühlingsfahrt* (A Spring Journey), *Frühlingsnacht* (A Spring Night), *Frühlingsbotschaft* (The Message of Spring): like *Stimme der Liebe* (The Voice of Love), *Sprache der Liebe* (The Language of Love), *Trauer der Liebe* (Love's Sorrow),

Geist der Liebe (The Spirit of Love), *Fülle der Liebe* (The Fullness of Love) : like *Blumenlied* (The Song of the Flowers), *Blumenbrief* (The Letter of the Flowers), *Blumengruss* (Flowers' Greeting) : like *Herzeleid* (Heart Pangs), *Mein Herz ist schwer* (My Heart is Heavy), *Mein Herz ist betrübt* (My Heart is Troubled), *Mein Aug' ist trüb* (My Eye is Heavy) : like the candid and silly dialogues with the *Röselein* (The Little Rose), with the brook, with the turtle dove, with the lark : like those idiotic questions : " *If the briar could have no thorns?* "— " *Is an old husband like a lark who has built a nest?* "—" *Is she newly plighted?* " : the whole deluge of stale tenderness, stale emotion, stale melancholy, stale poetry. . . . How many lovely things profaned, rare things, used in season or out! For the worst of it was that it was all useless : a habit of undressing their hearts in public, a fond and foolish propensity of the honest people of Germany for plunging loudly into confidences. With nothing to say they were always talking! Would their chatter never cease?—As well bid frogs in a pond be silent.

It was in the expression of love that Christophe was most rawly conscious of untruth : for he was in a position to compare it with the reality. The conventional love songs, lacrymose and proper, contained nothing like the desires of man or the heart of woman. And yet the people who had written them must have loved at least once in their lives! Was it possible that they could have loved like that? No, no, they had lied, as they always did, they had lied to themselves : they had tried to idealize themselves. . . . Idealism! That meant that they were afraid of looking at life squarely, were incapable of seeing things like a man, as they are.—Everywhere the same timidity, the same lack of manly frankness. Everywhere the same chilly enthusiasm, the same pompous lying solemnity, in their patriotism, in their drinking, in their religion. The *Trinklieder* (Drinking Songs) were prosopopeia to wine and the bowl : " *Du, herrlich Glas . . .* " ("Thou, noble glass . . ."). Faith—the one thing in the world which should be spontaneous, springing from the soul like an unexpected sudden stream—was a manufactured article, a commodity of trade. Their patriotic songs were made for docile flocks of sheep basking in unison. . . .

Shout, then!—What! Must you go on lying—"*idealizing*" —till you are surfeited, till it brings you to slaughter and madness! . . .

Christophe ended by hating all idealism. He preferred frank brutality to such lying. But at heart he was more of an idealist than the rest, and he had not—he could not have—any more real enemies than the brutal realists whom he thought he preferred.

He was blinded by passion. He was frozen by the mist, the anæmic lying, "the sunless phantom Ideas." With his whole being he reached upwards to the sun. In his youthful contempt for the hypocrisy with which he was surrounded, or for what he took to be hypocrisy, he did not see the high, practical wisdom of the race which little by little had built up for itself its grandiose idealism in order to suppress its savage instincts, or to turn them to account. Not arbitrary reasons, not moral and religious codes, not legislators and statesmen, priests and philosophers, transform the souls of peoples and often impose upon them a new nature: but centuries of misfortune and experience, which forge the life of peoples who have the will to live.

And yet Christophe went on composing: and his compositions were not examples of the faults which he found in others. In him creation was an irresistible necessity which would not submit to the rules which his intelligence laid down for it. No man creates from reason, but from necessity.—It is not enough to have recognized the untruth and affectation inherent in the majority of the feelings to avoid falling into them: long and painful endeavor is necessary: nothing is more difficult than to be absolutely true in modern society with its crushing heritage of indolent habits handed down through generations. It is especially difficult for those people, those nations who are possessed by an indiscreet mania for letting their hearts speak— for making them speak—unceasingly, when most generally it had much better have been silent.

Christophe's heart was very German in that: it had not yet learned the virtue of silence: and that virtue did not belong to his age. He had inherited from his father a need for talk-

ing, and talking loudly. He knew it and struggled against it:
but the conflict paralyzed part of his forces.—And he had another gift of heredity, no less burdensome, which had come to
him from his grandfather: an extraordinary difficulty—in expressing himself exactly.—He was the son of a *virtuoso*. He
was conscious of the dangerous attraction of virtuosity: a physical pleasure, the pleasure of skill, of agility, of satisfied muscular activity, the pleasure of conquering, of dazzling, of en-
thralling in his own person the many-headed audience: an
excusable pleasure, in a young man almost an innocent pleasure,
though none the less destructive of art and soul: Christophe
knew it: it was in his blood: he despised it, but all the same
he yielded to it.

And so, torn between the instincts of his race and those of
his genius, weighed down by the burden of a parasitical past,
which covered him with a crust that he could not break through,
he floundered along, and was much nearer than he thought to
all that he shunned and banned. All his compositions were a
mixture of truth and turgidness, of lucid strength and faltering
stupidity. It was only in rare moments that his personality
could pierce the casing of the dead personality which hampered
his movements.

He was alone. He had no guide to help him out of the mire.
When he thought he was out of it he slipped back again. He
went blindly on, wasting his time and strength in futile efforts.
He was spared no trial: and in the disorder of his creative
striving he never knew what was of greatest worth in what he
created. He tied himself up in absurd projects, symphonic
poems, which pretended to philosophy and were of monstrous
dimensions. He was too sincere to be able to hold to them for
long together: and he would discard them in disgust before
he had stretched out a single movement. Or he would set out
to translate into overtures the most inaccessible works of poetry.
Then he would flounder about in a domain which was not his
own. When he drew up scenarios for himself—(for he stuck
at nothing)—they were idiotic: and when he attacked the great
works of Goethe, Hebbel, Kleist, or Shakespeare, he understood them all wrong. It was not want of intelligence but want
of the critical spirit: he could not yet understand others, he

was too much taken up with himself: he found himself everywhere with his naïve and turgid soul.

But besides these monsters who were not really begotten, he wrote a quantity of small pieces, which were the immediate expression of passing emotions—the most eternal of all: musical thoughts, *Lieder.* In this as in other things he was in passionate reaction against current practices. He would take up the most famous poems, already set to music, and was impertinent enough to try to treat them differently and with greater truth than Schumann and Schubert. Sometimes he would try to give to the poetic figures of Goethe—to Mignon, the Harpist in *Wilhelm Meister,* their individual character, exact and changing. Sometimes he would tackle certain love songs which the weakness of the artists and the dullness of the audience in tacit agreement had clothed about with sickly sentimentality: and he would unclothe them: he would restore to them their rough, crude sensuality. In a word, he set out to make passions and people live for themselves and not to serve as toys for German families seeking an easy emotionalism on Sundays when they sat about in some *Biergarten.*

But generally he would find the poets, even the greatest of them, too literary: and he would select the simplest texts for preference: texts of old *Lieder,* jolly old songs, which he had read perhaps in some improving work: he would take care not to preserve their choral character: he would treat them with a fine, lively, and altogether lay audacity. Or he would take words from the Gospel, or proverbs, sometimes even words heard by chance, scraps of dialogues of the people, children's thoughts: words often awkward and prosaic in which there was only pure feeling. With them he was at his ease, and he would reach a depth with them which was not in his other compositions, a depth which he himself never suspected.

Good or bad, more often bad than good, his works as a whole had abounding vitality. They were not altogether new: far from it. Christophe was often banal, through his very sincerity: he repeated sometimes forms already used because they exactly rendered his thought, because he also felt in that way and not otherwise. Nothing would have induced him to try to be original: it seemed to him that a man must be very commonplace to burden himself with such an idea. He tried to be himself, to say what he felt, without worrying as to whether what he said had been said before him or not. He took a pride in believing that it was the best way of being original and that Christophe had only been and only would be alive once. With the magnificent impudence of youth, nothing seemed to him to have been done before: and everything seemed to him to be left for doing—or for doing again. And the feeling of this inward fullness of life, of a life stretching endless before him, brought him to a state of exuberant and rather indiscreet happiness. He was perpetually in a state of jubilation, which had no need of joy: it could adapt itself to sorrow: its source overflowed with life, was, in its strength, mother of all happiness and virtue. To live, to live too much! . . . A man who does not feel within himself this intoxication of strength, this jubilation in living—even in the depths of misery,—is not an artist. That is the touchstone. True greatness is shown in this power of rejoicing through joy and sorrow. A Mendelssohn or a Brahms, gods of the mists of October, and of fine rain, have never known the divine power.

Christophe was conscious of it: and he showed his joy simply, impudently. He saw no harm in it, he only asked to share it with others. He did not see how such joy hurts the majority of men, who never can possess it and are always envious of it. For the rest he never bothered about pleasing or displeasing: he was sure of himself, and nothing seemed to him simpler than to communicate his conviction to others,—to conquer. Instinctively he compared his riches with the general poverty of the makers of music: and he thought that it would be very easy to make his superiority recognized. Too easy, even. He had only to show himself.

He showed himself.

They were waiting for him.

Christophe had made no secret of his feelings. Since he had become aware of German Pharisaism, which refuses to see things as they are, he had made it a law for himself that he should be absolutely, continually, uncompromisingly sincere in everything without regard for anything or anybody or himself.

And as he could do nothing without going to extremes, he
was extravagant in his sincerity: he would say outrageous things
and scandalize people a thousand times less naïve than himself. He never dreamed that it might annoy them. When he
realized the idiocy of some hallowed composition he would make
haste to impart his discovery to everybody he encountered:
musicians of the orchestra, or amateurs of his acquaintance.
He would pronounce the most absurd judgments with a beaming face. At first no one took him seriously: they laughed
at his freaks. But it was not long before they found that he
was always reverting to them, insisting on them in a way that
was really bad taste. It became evident that Christophe believed in his paradoxes: and they became less amusing. He
was a nuisance: at concerts he would make ironic remarks in
a loud voice, or would express his scorn for the glorious masters
in no veiled fashion wherever he might be.

Everything passed from mouth to mouth in the little town:
not a word was lost. People were already affronted by his conduct during the past year. They had not forgotten the scandalous fashion in which he had shown himself abroad with
Ada and the troublous times of the sequel. He had forgotten
it himself: one day wiped out another, and he was very different
from what he had been two months before. But others had
not forgotten: those who, in all small towns, take upon themselves scrupulously to note down all the faults, all the imperfections, all the sad, ugly, and unpleasant happenings concerning their neighbors, so that nothing is ever forgotten. Christophe's new extravagances were naturally set, side by side with
his former indiscretions, in the scroll. The former explained
the latter. The outraged feelings of offended morality were now
bolstered up by those of scandalized good taste. The kindliest
of them said:

"He is trying to be particular."

But most alleged:

"*Total verrückt!*" (Absolutely mad.)

An opinion no less severe and even more dangerous was
beginning to find currency—an opinion assured of success by
reason of its illustrious origin: it was said that, at the Palace,
whither Christophe still went upon his official duties, he had

had the bad taste in conversation with the Grand Duke himself, with revolting lack of decency, to give vent to his ideas concerning the illustrious masters: it was said that he had called Mendelssohn's *Elijah* "a clerical humbug's paternoster," and he had called certain *Lieder* of Schumann "*Backfisch Musik*": and that in the face of the declared preference of the august Princess for those works! The Grand Duke had cut short his impertinences by saying dryly:

"To hear you, sir, one would doubt your being a German."

This vengeful utterance, coming from so lofty an eminence, reached the lowest depths: and everybody who thought he had reason to be annoyed with Christophe, either for his success, or for some more personal if not more cogent reason, did not fail to call to mind that he was not in fact pure German. His father's family, it was remembered, came originally from Belgium. It was not surprising, therefore, that this immigrant should decry the national glories. That explained everything and German vanity found reasons there.n for greater self-esteem, and at the same time for despising its adversary.

Christophe himself most substantially fed this Platonic vengeance. It is very imprudent to criticise others when you are yourself on the point of challenging criticism. A cleverer or less frank artist would have shown more modesty and more respect for his predecessors. But Christophe could see no reason for hiding his contempt for mediocrity or his joy in his own strength, and his joy was shown in no temperate fashion. Although from childhood Christophe had been turned in upon himself for want of any creature to confide in, of late he had come by a need of expansiveness. He had too much joy for himself: his breast was too small to contain it: he would have burst if he had not shared his delight. Failing a friend, he had confided in his colleague in the orchestra, the second *Kapellmeister*. Siegmund Ochs, a young Wurtemberger, a good fellow, though crafty, who showed him an effusive deference. Christophe did not distrust him: and, even if he had, how could it have occurred to him that it might be harmful to confide his joy to one who did not care, or even to an enemy? Ought they not rather to be grateful to him? Was it not for them also that he was working? He brought happiness for all, friends and enemies alike.—He had no idea that there is nothing more difficult than to make men accept a new happiness: they almost prefer their old misery: they need food that has been masticated for ages. But what is most intolerable to them is the thought that they owe such happiness to another. They cannot forgive that offense until there is no way of evading it: and in any case, they do contrive to make the giver pay dearly for it.

There were, then, a thousand reasons why Christophe's confidences should not be kindly received by anybody. But there were a thousand and one reasons why they should not be acceptable to Siegmund Ochs. The first *Kapellmeister,* Tobias Pfeiffer, was on the point of retiring: and, in spite of his youth, Christophe had every chance of succeeding him. Ochs was too good a German not to recognize that Christophe was worthy of the position, since the Court was on his side. But he had too good an opinion of himself not to believe that he would have been more worthy had the Court known him better. And so he received Christophe's effusions with a strange smile when he arrived at the theater in the morning with a face that he tried hard to make serious, though it beamed in spite of himself.

" Well? " he would say slyly as he came up to him, " another masterpiece? "

Christophe would take his arm.

" Ah! my friend. It is the best of all. . . . If you could hear it! . . . Devil take me, it is too beautiful! There has never been anything like it. God help the poor audience! They will only long for one thing when they have heard it: to die."

His words did not fall upon deaf ears. Instead of smiling, or of chaffing Christophe about his childish enthusiasm—he would have been the first to laugh at it and beg pardon if he had been made to feel the absurdity of it—Ochs went into ironic ecstasies: he drew Christophe on to further enormities: and when he left him made haste to repeat them all, making them even more grotesque. The little circle of musicians chuckled over them: and every one was impatient for the opportunity of judging the unhappy compositions.—They were all judged beforehand.

At last they appeared—Christophe had chosen from the better of his works an overture to the *Judith* of Hebbel, the savage energy of which had attracted him, in his reaction against German atony, although he was beginning to lose his taste for it, knowing intuitively the unnaturalness of such assumption of genius, always and at all costs. He had added a symphony which bore the bombastic title of the Basle Boecklin, "*The Dream of Life*," and the motto: "*Vita somnium breve*." A song-cycle completed the programme, with a few classical works, and a *Festmarsch* by Ochs, which Christophe had kindly offered to include in his concert, though he knew it to be mediocre.

Nothing much happened during the rehearsals. Although the orchestra understood absolutely nothing of the composition it was playing and everybody was privately disconcerted by the oddities of the new music, they had no time to form an opinion: they were not capable of doing so until the public had pronounced on it. Besides, Christophe's confidence imposed on the artists, who, like every good German orchestra, were docile and disciplined. His only difficulties were with the singer. She was the blue lady of the *Townhalle* concert. She was famous through Germany: the domestic creature sang Brünnhilde and Kundry at Dresden and Bayreuth with undoubted lung-power. But if in the Wagnerian school she had learned the art of which that school is justly proud, the art of good articulation, of projecting the consonants through space, and of battering the gaping audience with the vowels as with a club, she had not learned—designedly—the art of being natural. She provided for every word: everything was accentuated: the syllables moved with leaden feet, and there was a tragedy in every sentence. Christophe implored her to moderate her dramatic power a little. She tried at first graciously enough: but her natural heaviness and her need for letting her voice go carried her away. Christophe became nervous. He told the respectable lady that he had tried to make human beings speak with his speaking-trumpet and not the dragon Fafner. She took his insolence in bad part—naturally. She said that, thank Heaven! she knew what singing was, and that she had had the honor of interpreting the *Lieder* of Maestro Brahms, in the presence of that great man, and that he had never tired of hearing her.

" So much the worse! So much the worse: " cried Christophe.

She asked him with a haughty smile to be kind enough to
explain the meaning of his energetic remark. He replied that
never in his life had Brahms known what it was to be natural,
that his eulogies were the worst possible censure, and that
although he—Christophe—was not very polite, as she had justly
observed, never would he have gone so far as to say anything so
unpleasant.

The argument went on in this fashion: and the lady insisted
on singing in her own way, with heavy pathos and melodramatic
effects—until one day when Christophe declared coldly that he
saw the truth: it was her nature and nothing could change it:
but since the *Lieder* could not be sung properly, they should
not be sung at all: he withdrew them from the programme.—It
was on the eve of the concert and they were counting on the
Lieder: she had talked about them: she was musician enough
to appreciate certain of their qualities: Christophe insulted her:
and as she was not sure that the morrow's concert would not
set the seal on the young man's fame, she did not wish to quarrel
with a rising star. She gave way suddenly: and during the
last rehearsal she submitted docilely to all Christophe's wishes.
But she had made up her mind—at the concert—to have her
own way.

The day came. Christophe had no anxiety. He was too full
of his music to be able to judge it. He realized that some of
his works in certain places bordered on the ridiculous. But
what did that matter? Nothing great can be written without
touching the ridiculous. To reach the heart of things it is
necessary to dare human respect, politeness, modesty, the timidity of social lies under which the heart is stifled. If nobody
is to be affronted and success attained, a man must be resigned
all his life to remain bound by convention and to give to second-
rate people the second-rate truth, mitigated, diluted, which they
are capable of receiving: he must dwell in prison all his life.
A man is great only when he has set his foot on such anxieties
Christophe trampled them underfoot. Let them hiss him: he
was sure of not leaving them indifferent. He conjured up the
faces that certain people of his acquaintance would make as

they heard certain rather bold passages. He expected bitter criticism: he smiled at it already. In any case they would have to be blind—or deaf—to deny that there was force in it—pleasant or otherwise, what did it matter?—Pleasant! Pleasant! . . . Force! That is enough. Let it go its way, and bear all before it, like the Rhine! . . .

He had one setback. The Grand Duke did not come. The royal box was only occupied by Court people, a few ladies-in-waiting. Christophe was irritated by it. He thought: "The fool is cross with me. He does not know what to think of my work: he is afraid of compromising himself." He shrugged his shoulders, pretending not to be put out by such idiocy. Others paid more attention to it: it was the first lesson for him, a menace of his future.

The public had not shown much more interest than the Grand Duke: quite a third of the hall was empty. Christophe could not help thinking bitterly of the crowded halls at his concerts when he was a child. He would not have been surprised by the change if he had had more experience: it would have seemed natural to him that there were fewer people come to hear him when he made good music than when he made bad: for it is not music but the musician in which the greater part of the public is interested: and it is obvious that a musician who is a man and like everybody else is much less interesting than a musician in a child's little trowsers or short frock, who tickles sentimentality or amuses idleness.

After waiting in vain for the hall to fill, Christophe decided to begin. He tried to pretend that it was better so, saying, " A few friends but good."—His optimism did not last long.

His pieces were played in silence.—There is a silence in an audience which seems big and overflowing with love. But there was nothing in this. Nothing. Utter sleep. Blankness. Every phrase seemed to drop into depths of indifference. With his back turned to the audience, busy with his orchestra, Christophe was fully aware of everything that was happening in the hall, with those inner antennæ, with which every true musician is endowed, so that he knows whether what he is playing is waking an echo in the hearts about him. He went on conducting and growing excited while he was frozen by the cold

mist of boredom rising from the stalls and the boxes behind
him.

At last the overture was ended: and the audience applauded.
It applauded coldly, politely, and was then silent. Christophe
would rather have had them hoot. . . . A hiss! One hiss!
Anything to give a sign of life, or at least of reaction against
his work! . . . Nothing.—He looked at the audience. The
people were looking at each other, each trying to find out what
the other thought. They did not succeed and relapsed into
indifference.

The music went on. The symphony was played.—Christophe
found it hard to go on to the end. Several times he was on
the point of throwing down his bâton and running away. Their
apathy overtook him: at last he could not understand what he
was conducting: he could not breathe: he felt that he was falling
into fathomless boredom. There was not even the whispered
ironic comment which he had anticipated at certain passages:
the audience were reading their programmes. Christophe heard
the pages turned all together with a dry rustling: and then
once more there was silence until the last chord, when the same
polite applause showed that they had not understood that the
symphony was finished.—And yet there were four pairs of hands
went on clapping when the others had finished: but they awoke
no echo, and stopped ashamed: that made the emptiness seem
more empty, and the little incident served to show the audience
how bored it had been.

Christophe took a seat in the middle of the orchestra: he
dared not look to right or left. He wanted to cry: and at the
same time he was quivering with rage. He was fain to get
up and shout at them: " You bore me! Ah! How you bore
me! I cannot bear it! . . . Go away! Go away, all of
you! . . ."

The audience woke up a little: they were expecting the singer,
—they were accustomed to applauding her. In that ocean of new
music in which they were drifting without a compass, she at
least was sure, a known land, and a solid, in which there was
no danger of being lost. Christophe divined their thoughts
exactly: and he laughed bitterly. The singer was no less conscious of the expectancy of the audience: Christophe saw that

in her regal airs when he came and told her that it was her turn
to appear. They looked at each other inimically. Instead of
offering her his arm, Christophe thrust his hands into his
pockets and let her go on alone. Furious and out of countenance she passed him. He followed her with a bored expression.
As soon as she appeared the audience gave her an ovation: that
made everybody happier: every face brightened, the audience
grew interested, and glasses were brought into play. Certain
of her power she tackled the *Lieder,* in her own way, of course,
and absolutely disregarded Christophe's remarks of the evening
before. Christophe, who was accompanying her, went pale. He
had foreseen her rebellion. At the first change that she made
he tapped on the piano and said angrily:
" No! "
She went on. He whispered behind her back in a low voice
of fury:
" No! No! Not like that! . . . Not that! "
Unnerved by his fierce growls, which the audience could not
hear, though the orchestra caught every syllable, she stuck to
it, dragging her notes, making pauses like organ stops. He
paid no heed to them and went ahead: in the end they got
out of time. The audience did not notice it: for some time
they had been saying that Christophe's music was not made
to seem pleasant or right to the ear: but Christophe, who was
not of that opinion, was making lunatic grimaces: and at last
he exploded. He stopped short in the middle of a bar:
" Stop," he shouted.
She was carried on by her own impetus for half a bar and
then stopped:
" That's enough," he said dryly.
There was a moment of amazement in the audience. After
a few seconds he said icily:
" Begin again! "
She looked at him in stupefaction: her hands trembled: she
thought for a moment of throwing his book at his head: afterwards she did not understand how it was that she did not do
so. But she was overwhelmed by Christophe's authority and his
unanswerable tone of voice: she began again. She sang the
whole song-cycle, without changing one shade of meaning, or

a single movement: for she felt that he would spare her nothing: and she shuddered at the thought of a fresh insult.

When she had finished the audience recalled her frantically. They were not applauding the *Lieder*—(they would have applauded just the same if she had sung any others)—but the famous singer who had grown old in harness: they knew that they could safely admire her. Besides, they wanted to make up to her for the insult she had just received. They were not quite sure, but they did vaguely understand that the singer had made a mistake: and they thought it indecent of Christophe to call their attention to it. They encored the songs. But Christophe shut the piano firmly.

The singer did not notice his insolence: she was too much upset to think of singing again. She left the stage hurriedly and shut herself up in her box: and then for a quarter of an hour she relieved her heart of the flood of wrath and rage that was pent up in it: a nervous attack, a deluge of tears, indignant outcries and imprecations against Christophe,—she omitted nothing. Her cries of anger could be heard through the closed door. Those of her friends who had made their way there told everybody when they left that Christophe had behaved like a cad. Opinion travels quickly in a concert hall. And so when Christophe went to his desk for the last piece of music the audience was stormy. But it was not his composition: it was the *Festmarsch* by Ochs, which Christophe had kindly included in his programme. The audience—who were quite at their ease with the dull music—found a very simple method of displaying their disapproval of Christophe without going so far as to hiss him: they acclaimed Ochs ostentatiously, recalled the composer two or three times, and he appeared readily. And that was the end of the concert.

The Grand Duke and everybody at the Court—the bored, gossiping little provincial town—lost no detail of what had happened. The papers which were friendly towards the singer made no allusion to the incident: but they all agreed in exalting her art while they only mentioned the titles of the *Lieder* which she had sung. They published only a few lines about Christophe's other compositions, and they all said almost the same things: ". . . Knowledge of counterpoint. Complicated writing. Lack of inspiration. No melody. Written with the head, not with the heart. Want of sincerity. Trying to be original. . . ." Followed a paragraph on true originality, that of the masters who are dead and buried, Mozart, Beethoven, Loewe, Schubert, Brahms, "those who are original without thinking of it."—Then by a natural transition they passed to the revival at the Grand Ducal Theater of the *Nachtlager von Granada* of Konradin Kreutzer: a long account was given of "the delicious music, as fresh and jolly as when it was first written."

Christophe's compositions met with absolute and astonished lack of comprehension from the most kindly disposed critics: veiled hostility from those who did not like him, and were arming themselves for later ventures: and from the general public, guided by neither friendly nor hostile critics, silence. Left to its own thoughts the general public does not think at all: that goes without saying.

Christophe was bowled over.

And yet there was nothing surprising in his defeat. There were reasons, three to one, why his compositions should not please. They were immature. They were, secondly, too advanced to be understood at once. And, lastly, people were only too glad to give a lesson to the impertinent youngster.—But Christophe was not cool-headed enough to admit that his reverse was legitimate. He had none of that serenity which the true artist gains from the mournful experience of long misunderstanding at the hands of men and their incurable stupidity. His naïve confidence in the public and in success which he thought he could easily gain because he deserved it, crumbled away. He would have thought it natural to have enemies. But what staggered him was to find that he had not a single friend. Those on whom he had counted, those who hitherto had seemed to be interested in everything that he wrote, had not given him a single word of encouragement since the concert. He tried to probe them: they took refuge behind vague words. He insisted, he wanted to know what they really thought: the most sincere of them referred back to his former works, his foolish early efforts.—More than once in his life he was to hear his

new works condemned by comparison with the older ones,—
and that by the same people who, a few years before, had condemned his older works when they were new: that is the usual
ordering of these things. Christophe did not like it: he exclaimed loudly. If people did not like him, well and good:
he accepted that: it even pleased him since he could not be
friends with everybody. But that people should pretend to
be fond of him and not allow him to grow up, that they should
try to force him all his life to remain a child, was beyond the
pale! What is good at twelve is not good at twenty: and he
hoped not to stay at that, but to change and to go on changing
always. . . . These idiots who tried to stop life! . . . What
was interesting in his childish compositions was not their childishness and silliness, but the force in them hungering for the
future. And they were trying to kill his future! . . . No, they
had never understood what he was, they had never loved him,
never then or now: they only loved the weakness and vulgarity
in him, everything that he had in common with others, and not
himself, not what he really was: their friendship was a misunderstanding. . . .

He was exaggerating, perhaps. It often happens with quite
nice people who are incapable of liking new work which they
sincerely love when it is twenty years old. New life smacks
too strong for their weak senses: the scent of it must evaporate
in the winds of Time. A work of art only becomes intelligible
to them when it is crusted over with the dust of years.

But Christophe could not admit of not being understood
when he was *present,* and of being understood when he was *past.*
He preferred to think that he was not understood at all, in
any case, even. And he raged against it. He was foolish
enough to want to make himself understood, to explain himself,
to argue. Although no good purpose was served thereby: he
would have had to reform the taste of his time. But he was
afraid of nothing. He was determined by hook or by crook to
clean up German taste. But it was utterly impossible: he
could not convince anybody by means of conversation, in which
he found it difficult to find words, and expressed himself with
an excess of violence about the great musicians and even about
the men to whom he was talking: he only succeeded in making

a few more enemies. He would have had to prepare his ideas beforehand, and then to force the public to hear him. . . .

And just then, at the appointed hour, his star—his evil star— gave him the means of doing so.

He was sitting in the restaurant of the theater in a group of musicians belonging to the orchestra whom he was scandalizing by his artistic judgments. They were not all of the same opinion: but they were all ruffled by the freedom of his language. Old Krause, the alto, a good fellow and a good musician, who sincerely loved Christophe, tried to turn the conversation: he coughed, then looked out for an opportunity of making a pun. But Christophe did not hear him: he went on: and Krause mourned and thought:

"What makes him say such things? God bless him! You can think these things: but you must not say them."

The odd thing was that he also thought "these things": at least, he had a glimmering of them, and Christophe's words roused many doubts in him: but he had not the courage to confess it, or openly to agree—half from fear of compromising himself, half from modesty and distrust of himself.

Weigl, the cornet-player, did not want to know anything: he was ready to admire anything, or anybody, good or bad, star or gas-jet: everything was the same to him: there were no degrees in his admiration: he admired, admired, admired. It was a vital necessity to him: it hurt him when anybody tried to curb him.

Old Kuh, the violoncellist, suffered even more. He loved bad music with all his heart. Everything that Christophe hounded down with his sarcasm and invective was infinitely dear to him: instinctively his choice pitched on the most conventional works: his soul was a reservoir of tearful and high-flown emotion. Indeed, he was not dishonest in his tender regard for all the sham great men. It was when he tried to pretend that he liked the real great men that he was lying to himself—in perfect innocence. There are "Brahmins" who think to find in their God the breath of old men of genius: they love Beethoven in Brahms. Kuh went one better: he loved Brahms in Beethoven.

But the most enraged of all with Christophe's paradoxes was Spitz, the bassoon. It was not so much his musical instinct that was wounded as his natural servility. One of the Roman Emperors wished to die standing. Spitz wished to die, as he had lived, crawling: that was his natural position: it was delightful to him to grovel at the feet of everything that was official, hallowed, " arrived ": and he was beside himself when anybody tried to keep him from playing the lackey, comfortably.

So, Kuh groaned, Weigl threw up his hands in despair, Krause made jokes, and Spitz shouted in a shrill voice. But Christophe went on imperturbably shouting louder than the rest: and saying monstrous things about Germany and the Germans.

At the next table a young man was listening to him and rocking with laughter. He had black curly hair, fine, intelligent eyes, a large nose, which at its end could not make up its mind to go either to right or left, and rather than go straight on, went to both sides at once, thick lips, and a clever, mobile face: he was following everything that Christophe said, hanging on his lips, reflecting every word with a sympathetic and yet mocking attention, wrinkling up his forehead, his temples, the corners of his eyes, round his nostrils and cheeks, grimacing with laughter, and every now and then shaking all over convulsively. He did not join in the conversation, but he did not miss a word of it. He showed his joy especially when he saw Christophe, involved in some argument and heckled by Spitz, flounder about, stammer, and stutter with anger, until he had found the word he was seeking,—a rock with which to crush his adversary. And his delight knew no bounds when Christophe, swept along by his passions far beyond the capacity of his thought, enunciated monstrous paradoxes which made his hearers snort.

At last they broke up, each of them tired out with feeling and alleging his own superiority. As Christophe, the last to go, was leaving the room he was accosted by the young man who had listened to his words with such pleasure. He had not yet noticed him. The other politely removed his hat, smiled, and asked permission to introduce himself:

" Franz Mannheim."

He begged pardon for his indiscretion in listening to the argument, and congratulated Christophe on the *maestria* with which he had pulverized his opponents. He was still laughing at the thought of it. Christophe was glad to hear it, and looked at him a little distrustfully:

" Seriously? " he asked. " You are not laughing at me? "

The other swore by the gods. Christophe's face lit up.

" Then you think I am right? You are of my opinion? "

" Well," said Mannheim, " I am not a musician. I know nothing of music. The only music I like—(if it is not too flattering to say so)—is yours. . . . That may show you that my taste is not so bad. . . ."

" Oh! " said Christophe skeptically, though he was flattered all the same, " that proves nothing."

" You are difficult to please. . . . Good! . . . I think as you do: that proves nothing. And I don't venture to judge what you say of German musicians. But, anyhow, it is so true of the Germans in general, the old Germans, all the romantic idiots with their rancid thought, their sloppy emotion, their senile reiteration which we are asked to admire, ' *the eternal Yesterday, which has always been, and always will be, and will be law to-morrow because it is law to-day.*' . . .! "

He recited a few lines of the famous passage in Schiller:

"*. . . Das ewig Gestrige,*
Das immer war und immer wiederkehrt. . . ."

" Himself, first of all! " He stopped in the middle of his recitation.

" Who? " asked Christophe.

" The pump-maker who wrote that! "

Christophe did not understand. But Mannheim went on:

" I should like to have a general cleaning up of art and thought every fifty years—nothing to be left standing."

" A little drastic," said Christophe, smiling.

" No, I assure you. Fifty years is too much: I should say

thirty. . . . And even less! . . . It is a hygienic measure. One does not keep one's ancestors in one's house. One gets rid of them, when they are dead, and sends them elsewhere, there politely to rot, and one places stones on them to be quite sure that they will not come back. Nice people put flowers on them, too. I don't mind if they like it. All I ask is to be left in peace. I leave them alone! Each for his own side, say I : the dead and the living."

" There are some dead who are more alive than the living."

" No, no! It would be more true to say that there are some living who are more dead than the dead."

" Maybe. In any case, there are old things which are still young."

" Then if they are still young we can find them for ourselves. . . . But I don't believe it. What has been good once never is good again. Nothing is good but change. Before all we have to rid ourselves of the old men and things. There are too many of them in Germany. Death to them, say I ! "

Christophe listened to these squibs attentively and labored to discuss them : he was in part in sympathy with them, he recognized certain of his own thoughts in them : and at the same time he felt a little embarrassed at having them so blown out to the point of caricature. But as he assumed that everybody else was as serious as himself, he thought that perhaps Mannheim, who seemed to be more learned than himself and spoke more easily, was right, and was drawing the logical conclusions from his principles. Vain Christophe, whom so many people could not forgive for his faith in himself, was really most naïvely modest, often tricked by his modesty when he was with those who were better educated than himself,—especially when they consented not to plume themselves on it to avoid an awkward discussion. Mannheim, who was amusing himself with his own paradoxes, and from one sally to another had reached extravagant quips and cranks, at which he was laughing immensely, was not accustomed to being taken seriously : he was delighted with the trouble that Christophe was taking to discuss his nonsense, and even to understand it : and while he laughed, he was grateful for the importance which Christophe gave him : he thought him absurd and charming.

They parted very good friends: and Christophe was not a little surprised three hours later at rehearsal to see Mannheim's head poked through the little door leading to the orchestra, smiling and grimacing, and making mysterious signs at him. When the rehearsal was over Christophe went to him. Mannheim took his arm familiarly.

"You can spare a moment? . . . Listen. I have an idea. Perhaps you will think it absurd. . . . Would not you like for once in a way to write what you think of music and the musicos? Instead of wasting your breath in haranguing four dirty knaves of your band who are good for nothing but scraping and blowing into bits of wood, would it not be better to address the general public?"

"Not better? Would I like? . . . My word! And when do you want me to write? It *is* good of you! . . ."

"I've a proposal for you. . . . Some friends and I: Adalbert von Waldhaus, Raphael Goldenring, Adolf Mai, and Lucien Ehrenfeld,—have started a Review, the only intelligent Review in the town: the *Dionysos.*—(You must know it. . . .)—We all admire each other and should be glad if you would join us. Will you take over our musical criticism?"

Christophe was abashed by such an honor: he was longing to accept: he was only afraid of not being worthy: he could not write.

"Oh! come," said Mannheim, "I am sure you can. And besides, as soon as you are a critic you can do anything you like. You've no need to be afraid of the public. The public is incredibly stupid. It is nothing to be an artist: an artist is only a sort of comedian: an artist can be hissed. But a critic has the right to say: 'Hiss me that man!' The whole audience lets him do its thinking. Think whatever you like. Only look as if you were thinking something. Provided you give the fools their food, it does not much matter what, they will gulp down anything."

In the end Christophe consented, with effusive thanks. He only made it a condition that he should be allowed to say what he liked.

"Of course, of course," said Mannheim. "Absolute freedom! We are all free."

He looked him up at the theater once more after the performance to introduce him to Adalbert von Waldhaus and his friends.
They welcomed him warmly.

With the exception of Waldhaus, who belonged to one of
the noble families of the neighborhood, they were all Jews and
all very rich: Mannheim was the son of a banker: Mai the son
of the manager of a metallurgical establishment: and Ehrenfeld's father was a great jeweler. Their fathers belonged to
the older generation of Jews, industrious and acquisitive, attached to the spirit of their race, building their fortunes with
keen energy, and enjoying their energy much more than their
fortunes. Their sons seemed to be made to destroy what their
fathers had builded: they laughed at family prejudice and their
ant-like mania for economy and delving: they posed as artists,
affected to despise money and to fling it out of window. But
in reality they hardly ever let it slip through their fingers: and
in vain did they do all sorts of foolish things: they never could
altogether lead astray their lucidity of mind and practical sense.
For the rest, their parents kept an eye on them, and reined
them in. The most prodigal of them, Mannheim, would sincerely have given away all that he had: but he never had anything: and although he was always loudly inveighing against
his father's niggardliness, in his heart he laughed at it and
thought that he was right. In fine, there was only Waldhaus
really who was in control of his fortune, and went into it whole-
heartedly and reckless of cost, and bore that of the Review.
He was a poet. He wrote "Polymètres," in the manner of
Arno Holz and Walt Whitman, with lines alternately very long
and very short, in which stops, double and triple stops, dashes,
silences, commas, italics and italics, played a great part. And so
did alliteration and repetition—of a word—of a line—of a
whole phrase. He interpolated words of every language. He
wanted—(no one has ever known why)—to render the Cézanne
into verse. In truth, he was poetic enough and had a distinguished taste for stale things. He was sentimental and dry,
naïve and foppish: his labored verses affected a cavalier carelessness. He would have been a good poet for men of the world.
But there are too many of the kind in the Reviews and artistic
circles: and he wished to be alone. He had taken it into his

head to play the great gentleman who is above the prejudices of his caste. He had more prejudices than anybody. He did not admit their existence. He took a delight in surrounding himself with Jews in the Review which he edited, to rouse the indignation of his family, who were very anti-Semite, and to prove his own freedom of mind to himself. With his colleagues he assumed a tone of courteous equality. But in his heart he had a calm and boundless contempt for them. He was not unaware that they were very glad to make use of his name and money: and he let them do so because it pleased him to despise them.

And they despised him for letting them do so: for they knew very well that it served his turn. A fair exchange. Waldhaus lent them his name and fortune: and they brought him their talents, their eye for business and subscribers. They were much more intelligent than he. Not that they had more personality. They had perhaps even less. But in the little town they were, as the Jews are everywhere and always,—by the mere fact of their difference of race which for centuries has isolated them and sharpened their faculty for making observation—they were the most advanced in mind, the most sensible of the absurdity of its moldy institutions and decrepit thought. Only, as their character was less free than their intelligence, it did not help them, while they mocked, from trying rather to turn those institutions and ideas to account than to reform them. In spite of their independent professions of faith, they were like the noble Adalbert, little provincial snobs, rich, idle young men of family, who dabbled and flirted with letters for the fun of it. They were very glad to swagger about as giant-killers: but they were kindly enough and never slew anybody but a few inoffensive people or those whom they thought could never harm them. They cared nothing for setting by the ears a society to which they knew very well they would one day return and embrace all the prejudices which they had combated. And when they did venture to make a stir on a little scandal, or loudly to declare war on some idol of the day,—who was beginning to totter,—they took care never to burn their boats: in case of danger they re-embarked. Whatever then might be the issue of the campaign,—when it was finished it was a long

time before war would break out again: the Philistines could
sleep in peace.   All that these new *Davidsbündler* wanted to
do was to make it appear that they could have been terrible if
they had so desired: but they did not desire.   They preferred
to be on friendly terms with artists and to give suppers to
actresses.

Christophe was not happy in such a set.   They were always
talking of women and horses: and their talk was not refined.
They were stiff and formal.   Adalbert spoke in a mincing, slow
voice, with exaggerated, bored, and boring politeness.   Adolf
Mai, the secretary of the Review, a heavy, thick-set, bull-necked,
brutal-looking young man, always pretended to be in the right:
he laid down the law, never listened to what anybody said,
seemed to despise the opinion of the person he was talking to,
and also that person.   Goldenring, the art critic, who had a
twitch, and eyes perpetually winking behind his large spectacles,
—no doubt in imitation of the painters whose society he cultivated, wore long hair, smoked in silence, mumbled scraps of
sentences which he never finished, and made vague gestures in
the air with his thumb.   Ehrenfeld was little, bald, and smiling, had a fair beard and a sensitive, weary-looking face, a
hooked nose, and he wrote the fashions and the society notes
in the Review.   In a silky voice he used to talk obscurely: he had
a wit, though of a malignant and often ignoble kind.—All these
young millionaires were anarchists, of course: when a man pos-
sesses everything it is the supreme luxury for him to deny society: for in that way he can evade his responsibilities.   So might
a robber, who has just fleeced a traveler, say to him: " What
are you staying for?   Get along!   I have no more use for you."

Of the whole bunch Christophe was only in sympathy with
Mannheim: he was certainly the most lively of the five: he
was amused by everything that he said and everything that
was said to him: stuttering, stammering, blundering, sniggering, talking nonsense, he was incapable of following an argument, or of knowing exactly what he thought himself: but he
was quite kindly, bearing no malice, having not a spark of
ambition.   In truth, he was not very frank: he was always
playing a part: but quite innocently, and he never did anybody
any harm.

He espoused all sorts of strange Utopias—most often generous. He was too subtle and too skeptical to keep his head even in his enthusiasms, and he never compromised himself by applying his theories. But he had to have some hobby: it was a game to him, and he was always changing from one to another. For the time being his craze was for kindness. It was not enough for him to be kind naturally: he wished to be thought kind: he professed kindness, and acted it. Out of reaction against the hard, dry activity of his kinsfolk, and against German austerity, militarism, and Philistinism, he was a Tolstoyan, a Nirvanian, an evangelist, a Buddhist,—he was not quite sure what,—an apostle of a new morality that was soft, boneless, indulgent, placid, easy-living, effusively forgiving every sin, especially the sins of the flesh, a morality which did not conceal its predilection for those sins and much less readily forgave the virtues—a morality which was only a compact of pleasure, a libertine association of mutual accommodations, which amused itself by donning the halo of sanctity. There was in it a spice of hypocrisy which was a little offensive to delicate palates, and would have even been frankly nauseating if it had taken itself seriously. But it made no pretensions towards that: it merely amused itself. His blackguardly Christianity was only meant to serve until some other hobby came along to take its place—no matter what: brute force, imperialism, "laughing lions."—Mannheim was always playing a part, playing with his whole heart: he was trying on all the feelings that he did not possess before becoming a good Jew like the rest and with all the spirit of his race. He was very sympathetic, and extremely irritating. For some time Christophe was one of his hobbies. Mannheim swore by him. He blew his trumpet everywhere. He dinned his praises into the ears of his family. According to him Christophe was a genius, an extraordinary man, who made strange music and talked about it in an astonishing fashion, a witty man—and a handsome: fine lips, magnificent teeth. He added that Christophe admired him.—One evening he took him home to dinner. Christophe found himself talking to his new friend's father, Lothair Mannheim, the banker, and Franz's sister, Judith.

It was the first time that he had been in a Jew's house. Although there were many Jews in the little town, and although they played an important part in its life by reason of their wealth, cohesion, and intelligence, they lived a little apart. There were always rooted prejudices in the minds of the people and a secret hostility that was credulous and injurious against them. Christophe's family shared these prejudices. His grandfather did not love Jews: but the irony of fate had decreed that his two best pupils should be of the race—(one had become a composer, the other a famous *virtuoso*): for there had been moments when he was fain to embrace these two good musicians: and then he would remember sadly that they had crucified the Lord: and he did not know how to reconcile his two incompatible currents of feeling. But in the end he did embrace them. He was inclined to think that the Lord would forgive them because of their love for music.—Christophe's father, Melchior, who pretended to be broad-minded, had had fewer scruples about taking money from the Jews: and he even thought it good to do so: but he ridiculed them, and despised them.—As for his mother, she was not sure that she was not committing a sin when she went to cook for them. Those whom she had had to do with were disdainful enough with her: but she had no grudge against them, she bore nobody any ill-will: she was filled with pity for these unhappy people whom God had damned: sometimes she would be filled with compassion when she saw the daughter of one of them go by or heard the merry laughter of their children.

" So pretty she is! . . . Such pretty children! . . . How dreadful! . . ." she would think.

She dared not say anything to Christophe, when he told her that he was going to dine with the Mannheims: but her heart sank. She thought that it was unnecessary to believe everything bad that was said about the Jews—(people speak ill of everybody)—and that there are honest people everywhere, but that it was better and more proper to keep themselves to themselves, the Jews on their side, the Christians on theirs.

Christophe shared none of these prejudices. In his perpetual reaction against his surroundings he was rather attracted towards the different race. But he hardly knew them. He had only come in contact with the more vulgar of the Jews: little shopkeepers, the populace swarming in certain streets between the Rhine and the cathedral, forming, with the gregarious instinct of all human beings, a sort of little ghetto. He had often strolled through the neighborhood, catching sight of and feeling a sort of sympathy with certain types of women with hollow cheeks, and full lips, and wide cheek-bones, a da Vinci smile, rather depraved, while the coarse language and shrill laughter destroyed this harmony that was in their faces when in repose. Even in the dregs of the people, in those large-headed, beady-eyed creatures with their bestial faces, their thick-set, squat bodies, those degenerate descendants of the most noble of all peoples, even in that thick, fetid muddiness there were strange phosphorescent gleams, like will-o'-the-wisps dancing over a swamp: marvelous glances, minds subtle and brilliant, a subtle electricity emanating from the ooze which fascinated and disturbed Christophe. He thought that hidden deep were fine souls struggling, great hearts striving to break free from the dung: and he would have liked to meet them, and to aid them: without knowing them, he loved them, while he was a little fearful of them. And he had never had any opportunity of meeting the best of the Jews.

His dinner at the Mannheims' had for him the attraction of novelty and something of that of forbidden fruit. The Eve who gave him the fruit sweetened its flavor. From the first moment Christophe had eyes only for Judith Mannheim. She was utterly different from all the women he had known. Tall and slender, rather thin, though solidly built, with her face framed in her black hair, not long, but thick and curled low on her head, covering her temples and her broad, golden brow; rather short-sighted, with large pupils, and slightly prominent eyes: with a largish nose and wide nostrils, thin cheeks, a heavy chin, strong coloring, she had a fine profile showing much energy and alertness: full face, her expression was more changing, uncertain, complex: her eyes and her cheeks were irregular. She seemed to give revelation of a strong race, and in the mold of that race, roughly thrown together, were manifold incongruous elements, of doubtful and unequal quality, beautiful and vulgar at the same time. Her beauty lay especially in her silent

lips, and in her eyes, in which there seemed to be greater depth
by reason of their short-sightedness, and darker by reason of
the bluish markings round them.

It needed to be more used than Christophe was to those eyes,
which are more those of a race than of an individual, to be
able to read through the limpidity that unveiled them with
such vivid quality, the real soul of the woman whom he thus
encountered. It was the soul of the people of Israel that he
saw in her sad and burning eyes, the soul that, unknown to
them, shone forth from them. He lost himself as he gazed into
them. It was only after some time that he was able, after losing his way again and again, to strike the track again on that
oriental sea.

She looked at him: and nothing could disturb the clearness
of her gaze: nothing in his Christian soul seemed to escape
her. He felt that. Under the seduction of the woman's eyes
upon him he was conscious of a virile desire, clear and cold,
which stirred in him brutally, indiscreetly. There was no evil
in the brutality of it. She took possession of him: not like a
coquette, whose desire is to seduce without caring whom she se-
duces. Had she been a coquette she would have gone to greatest
lengths: but she knew her power, and she left it to her natural
instinct to make use of it in its own way,—especially when she
had so easy a prey as Christophe.—What interested her more
was to know her adversary—(any man, any stranger, was an
adversary for her,—an adversary with whom later on, if occasion served, she could sign a compact of alliance).—She wished
to know his quality. Life being a game, in which the cleverest
wins, it was a matter of reading her opponent's cards and of
not showing her own. When she succeeded she tasted the sweets
of victory. It mattered little whether she could turn it to any
account. It was purely for her pleasure. She had a passion
for intelligence: not abstract intelligence, although she had
brains enough, if she had liked, to have succeeded in any
branch of knowledge and would have made a much better successor to Lothair Mannheim, the banker, than her brother. But
she preferred intelligence in the quick, the sort of intelligence
which studies men. She loved to pierce through to the soul
and to weigh its value—(she gave as scrupulous an attention

to it as the Jewess of Matsys to the weighing of her gold)—
with marvelous divination she could find the weak spot in the
armor, the imperfections and foibles which are the key to the
soul,—she could lay her hands on its secrets: it was her way
of feeling her sway over it. But she never dallied with her
victory: she never did anything with her prize. Once her
curiosity and her vanity were satisfied she lost her interest
and passed on to another specimen. All her power was sterile.
There was something of death in her living soul. She had
the genius of curiosity and boredom.

And so she looked at Christophe and he looked at her. She
hardly spoke. An imperceptible smile was enough, a little
movement of the corners of her mouth: Christophe was hypnotized by her. Every now and then her smile would fade away,
her face would become cold, her eyes indifferent: she would
attend to the meal or speak coldly to the servants: it was as
though she were no longer listening. Then her eyes would light
up again: and a few words coming pat would show that she
had heard and understood everything.

She coldly examined her brother's judgment of Christophe:
she knew Franz's crazes: her irony had had fine sport when
she saw Christophe appear, whose looks and distinction had been
vaunted by her brother—(it seemed to her that Franz had
a special gift for seeing facts as they are not: or perhaps he
only thought it a paradoxical joke).—But when she looked at
Christophe more closely she recognized that what Franz had
said was not altogether false: and as she went on with her
scrutiny she discovered in Christophe a vague, unbalanced,
though robust and bold power: that gave her pleasure, for she
knew, better than any, the rarity of power. She was able to
make Christophe talk about whatever she liked, and reveal his
thoughts, and display the limitations and defects of his mind:
she made him play the piano: she did not love music but she
understood it: and she saw Christophe's musical originality,
although his music had roused no sort of emotion in her. Without the least change in the coldness of her manner, with a few
short, apt, and certainly not flattering, remarks she showed her
growing interest in Christophe.

Christophe saw it: and he was proud of it: for he felt the worth of such judgment and the rarity of her approbation. He made no secret of his desire to win it: and he set about it so naïvely as to make the three of them smile: he talked only to Judith and for Judith: he was as unconcerned with the others as though they did not exist.

Franz watched him as he talked: he followed his every word, with his lips and eyes, with a mixture of admiration and amusement: and he laughed aloud as he glanced at his father and his sister, who listened impassively and pretended not to notice him.

Lothair Mannheim,—a tall old man, heavily built, stooping a little, red-faced, with gray hair standing straight up on end, very black mustache and eyebrows, a heavy though energetic and jovial face, which gave the impression of great vitality— had also studied Christophe during the first part of the dinner, slyly but good-naturedly: and he too had recognized at once that there was "something" in the boy. But he was not interested in music or musicians: it was not in his line: he knew nothing about it and made no secret of his ignorance: he even boasted of it—(when a man of that sort confesses his ignorance of anything he does so to feed his vanity).—As Christophe had clearly shown at once, with a rudeness in which there was no shade of malice, that he could without regret dispense with the society of the banker, and that the society of Fräulein Judith Mannheim would serve perfectly to fill his evening, old Lothair in some amusement had taken his seat by the fire: he read his paper, listening vaguely and ironically to Christophe's crotchets and his queer music, which sometimes made him laugh inwardly at the idea that there could be people who understood it and found pleasure in it. He did not trouble to follow the conversation: he relied on his daughter's cleverness to tell him exactly what the newcomer was worth. She discharged her duty conscientiously.

When Christophe had gone Lothair asked Judith:

" Well, you probed him enough: what do you think of the artist? "

She laughed, thought for a moment, reckoned up, and said:

" He is a little cracked: but he is not stupid."

" Good," said Lothair. " I thought so too. He will succeed, then ? "

" Yes, I think so. He has power."

" Very good," said Lothair with the magnificent logic of the strong who are only interested in the strong, " we must help him."

Christophe went away filled with admiration for Judith Mannheim. He was not in love with her as Judith thought. They were both—she with her subtlety, he with his instinct which took the place of mind in him,—mistaken about each other. Christophe was fascinated by the enigma and the intense activity of her mind: but he did not love her. His eyes and his intelligence were ensnared: his heart escaped.—Why?—It were difficult to tell. Because he had caught a glimpse of some doubtful, disturbing quality in her?—In other circumstances that would have been a reason the more for loving: love is never stronger than when it goes out to one who will make it suffer.—If Christophe did not love Judith it was not the fault of either of them. The real reason, humiliating enough for both, was that he was still too near his last love. Experience had not made him wiser. But he had loved Ada so much, he had consumed so much faith, force, and illusion in that passion that there was not enough left for a new passion. Before another flame could be kindled he would have to build a new pyre in his heart: short of that there could only be a few flickerings, remnants of the conflagration that had escaped by chance, which asked only to be allowed to burn, cast a brief and brilliant light and then died down for want of food. Six months later, perhaps, he might have loved Judith blindly. Now he saw in her only a friend,—a rather disturbing friend in truth—but he tried to drive his uneasiness back: it reminded him of Ada: there was no attraction in that memory: he preferred not to think of it. What attracted him in Judith was everything in her which was different from other women, not that which she had in common with them. She was the first intelligent woman he had met. She was intelligent from head to foot. Even her beauty—her gestures, her movements, her features, the fold of her lips, her eyes, her hands, her slender elegance—was the reflection of her intelligence: her body was molded by her intelligence: without her intelligence she would have passed unnoticed: and no doubt she would even have been thought plain by most people. Her intelligence delighted Christophe. He thought it larger and more free than it was: he could not yet know how deceptive it was. He longed ardently to confide in her and to impart his ideas to her. He had never found anybody to take an interest in his dreams: he was turned in upon himself: what joy then to find a woman to be his friend! That he had not a sister had been one of the sorrows of his childhood: it seemed to him that a sister would have understood him more than a brother could have done. And when he met Judith he felt that childish and illusory hope of having a brotherly love spring up in him. Not being in love, love seemed to him a poor thing compared with friendship.

Judith felt this little shade of feeling and was hurt by it. She was not in love with Christophe, and as she had excited other passions in other young men of the town, rich young men of better position, she could not feel any great satisfaction in knowing Christophe to be in love with her. But it piqued her to know that he was not in love. No doubt she was pleased with him for confiding his plans: she was not surprised by it: but it was a little mortifying for her to know that she could only exercise an intellectual influence over him—(an unreasoning influence is much more precious to a woman).—She did not even exercise her influence: Christophe only courted her mind. Judith's intellect was imperious. She was used to molding to her will the soft thoughts of the young men of her acquaintance. As she knew their mediocrity she found no pleasure in holding sway over them. With Christophe the pursuit was more interesting because more difficult. She was not interested in his projects: but she would have liked to direct his originality of thought, his ill-grown power, and to make them good,—in her own way, of course, and not in Christophe's, which she did not take the trouble to understand. She saw at once that she could not succeed without a struggle: she had marked down in Christophe all sorts of notions and ideas which she thought childish and extravagant: they were weeds to her: she tried hard to eradicate them. She did not get rid of a single one. She did not gain the least satisfaction for her vanity. Christophe was intractable. Not being in love he had no reason for surrendering his ideas to her.

She grew keen on the game and instinctively tried for some time to overcome him. Christophe was very nearly taken in again in spite of h:s lucidity of mind at that time. Men are easily taken in by any flattery of their vanity or their desires: and an artist is twice as easy to trick as any other man because he has more imagination. Judith had only to draw Christophe into a dangerous flirtation to bowl him over once more more thoroughly than ever. But as usual she soon wearied of the game: she found that such a conquest was hardly worth while: Christophe was already boring her: she did not understand him.

She did not understand him beyond a certain point. Up to that she understood everything. Her admirable intelligence could not take her beyond it: she needed a heart, or in default of that the thing which could give the illusion of one for a time: love. She understood Christophe's criticism of people and things: it amused her and seemed to her true enough: she had thought much the same herself. But what she did not understand was that such ideas might have an influence on practical life when it might be dangerous or awkward to apply them. The attitude of revolt against everybody and everything which Christophe had taken up led to nothing: he could not imagine that he was going to reform the world. . . . And then? . . . It was waste of time to knock one's head against a wall. A clever man judges men, laughs at them in secret, despises them a little: but he does as they do—only a little better: it is the only way of mastering them. Thought is one world: action is another. What boots it for a man to be the victim of his thoughts? Since men are so stupid as not to be able to bear the truth, why force it on them? To accept their weakness, to seem to bow to it, and to feel free to despise them in his heart, is there not a secret joy in that? The joy of a clever slave? Certainly. But all the world is a slave: there is no getting away from that: it is useless to protest against it: better to be a slave deliberately of one's own free will and to avoid ridiculous and futile conflict. Besides, the

worst slavery of all is to be the slave of one's own thoughts
and to sacrifice everything to them. There is no need to deceive
one's self.—She saw clearly that if Christophe went on, as
he seemed determined to do, with his aggressive refusal to compromise with the prejudices of German art and German mind,
he would turn everybody against him, even his patrons: he
was courting inevitable ruin. She did not understand why he
so obstinately held out against himself, and so took pleasure in
digging his own ruin.

To have understood him she would have had to be able to
understand that his aim was not success but his own faith.
He believed in art: he believed in *his* art: he believed in himself, as realities not only superior to interest, but also to his
own life. When he was a little out of patience with her remarks and told her so in his naïve arrogance, she just shrugged
her shoulders: she did not take him seriously. She thought he
was using big words such as she was accustomed to hearing
from her brother when he announced periodically his absurd
and ridiculous resolutions, which he never by any chance put
into practice. And then when she saw that Christophe really
believed in what he said, she thought him mad and lost interest
in him.

After that she took no trouble to appear to advantage, and
she showed herself as she was: much more German, and average
German, than she seemed to be at first, more perhaps than she
thought.—The Jews are quite erroneously reproached with not
belonging to any nation and with forming from one end of
Europe to the other a homogeneous people impervious to the
influence of the different races with which they have pitched
their tents. In reality there is no race which more easily takes
on the impress of the country through which it passes: and
if there are many characteristics in common between a French
Jew and a German Jew, there are many more different characteristics derived from their new country, of which with incredible rapidity they assimilate the habits of mind: more the
habits than the mind, indeed. But habit, which is a second
nature to all men, is in most of them all the nature that they
have, and the result is that the majority of the autochthonous
citizens of any country have very little right to reproach the

Jews with the lack of a profound and reasonable national feeling of which they themselves possess nothing at all.

The women, always more sensible to external influences, more easily adaptable to the conditions of life and to change with them—Jewish women throughout Europe assume the physical and moral customs, often exaggerating them, of the country in which they live,—without losing the shadow and the strange fluid, solid, and haunting quality of their race.—This idea came to Christophe. At the Mannheims' he met Judith's aunts, cousins, and friends. Though there was little of the German in their eyes, ardent and too close together, their noses going down to their lips, their strong features, their red blood coursing under their coarse brown skins: though almost all of them seemed hardly at all fashioned to be German—they were all extraordinarily German: they had the same way of talking, of dressing,—of overdressing.—Judith was much the best of them all: and comparison with them made all that was exceptional in her intelligence, all that she had made of herself, shine forth. But she had most of their faults just as much as they. She was much more free than they morally—almost absolutely free —but socially she was no more free: or at least her practical sense usurped the place of her freedom of mind. She believed in society, in class, in prejudice, because when all was told she found them to her advantage. It was idle for her to laugh at the German spirit: she followed it like any German. Her intelligence made her see the mediocrity of some artist of reputation: but she respected him none the less because of his reputation: and if she met him personally she would admire him: for her vanity was flattered. She had no love for the works of Brahms and she suspected him of being an artist of the second rank: but his fame impressed her: and as she had received five or six letters from him the result was that she thought him the greatest musician of the day. She had no doubt as to Christophe's real worth, or as to the stupidity of Lieutenant Detlev von Fleischer: but she was more flattered by the homage the lieutenant deigned to pay to her millions than by Christophe's friendship: for a dull officer is a man of another caste: it is more difficult for a German Jewess to enter that caste than for any other woman. Although she was not deceived by these feudal follies, and although she knew quite well that if she did marry Lieutenant Detlev von Fleischer she would be doing him a great honor, she set herself to the conquest: she stooped so low as to make eyes at the fool and to flatter his vanity. The proud Jewess, who had a thousand reasons for her pride—the clever, disdainful daughter of Mannheim the banker lowered herself, and acted like any of the little middle-class German women whom she despised.

That experience was short. Christophe lost his illusions about Judith as quickly as he had found them. It is only just to say that Judith did nothing to preserve them. As soon as a woman of that stamp has judged a man she is done with him: he ceases to exist for her: she will not see him again. And she no more hesitates to reveal her soul to him, with calm impudence, that to appear naked before her dog, her cat, or any other domestic animal. Christophe saw Judith's egoism and coldness, and the mediocrity of her character. He had not had time to be absolutely caught. But he had been enough caught to make him suffer and to bring him to a sort of fever. He did not so much love Judith as what she might have been—what she ought to have been. Her fine eyes exercised a melancholy fascination over him: he could not forget them: although he knew now the drab soul that slumbered in their depths he went on seeing them as he wished to see them, as he had first seen them. It was one of those loveless hallucinations of love which take up so much of the hearts of artists when they are not entirely absorbed by their work. A passing face is enough to create it: they see in it all the beauty that is in it, unknown to its indifferent possessor. And they love it the more for its indifference. They love it as a beautiful thing that must die without any man having known its worth or that it even had life. Perhaps he was deceiving himself, and Judith Mannheim could not have been anything more than she was. But for a moment Christophe had believed in her: and her charm endured: he could not judge her impartially. All her beauty seemed to him to be hers, to be herself. All that was vulgar in her he cast back upon her twofold race, Jew and German, and perhaps he was more indignant with the German than with the Jew, for it had made him suffer more. As he did not yet know any other nation, the German spirit was for him a sort of scapegoat: he put upon it all the sins of the world. That Judith had deceived him was a reason the more for combating it: he could not forgive it for having crushed the life out of such a soul.

Such was his first encounter with Israel. He had hoped much from it. He had hoped to find in that strong race living apart from the rest an ally for his fight. He lost that hope. With the flexibility of his passionate intuition, which made him leap from one extreme to another, he persuaded himself that the Jewish race was much weaker than it was said to be, and much more open—much too open—to outside influence. It had all its own weaknesses augmented by those of the rest of the world picked up on its way. It was not in them that he could find assistance in working the lever of his art. Rather he was in danger of being swallowed with them in the sands of the desert.

Having seen the danger, and not feeling sure enough of himself to brave it, he suddenly gave up going to the Mannheims'. He was invited several times and begged to be excused without giving any reason. As up till then he had shown an excessive eagerness to accept, such a sudden change was remarked: it was attributed to his "originality": but the Mannheims had no doubt that the fair Judith had something to do with it: Lothair and Franz joked about it at dinner. Judith shrugged her shoulders and said it was a fine conquest, and she asked her brother frigidly not to make such a fuss about it. But she left no stone unturned in her effort to bring Christophe back. She wrote to him for some musical information which no one else could supply: and at the end of her letter she made a friendly allusion to the rarity of his visits and the pleasure it would give them to see him. Christophe replied, giving the desired information, said that he was very busy, and did not go. They met sometimes at the theater. Christophe obstinately looked away from the Mannheims' box: and he would pretend not to see Judith, who held herself in readiness to give him her most charming smile. She did not persist. As she did not

count on him for anything she was annoyed that the little
artist should let her do all the labor of their friendship, and
pure waste at that. If he wanted to come, he would. If not—
oh, well, they could do without him. . . .

They did without him: and his absence left no very great
gap in the Mannheims' evenings. But in spite of herself Judith
was really annoyed with Christophe. It seemed natural enough
not to bother about him when he was there: and she could
allow him to show his displeasure at being neglected: but that
his displeasure should go so far as to break off their relationship altogether seemed to her to show a stupid pride and a
heart more egoistic than in love.—Judith could not tolerate
her own faults in others.

She followed the more attentively everything that Christophe
did and wrote. Without seeming to do so, she would lead her
brother to the subject of Christophe: she would make him tell
her of his intercourse with him: and she would punctuate the
narrative with clever ironic comment, which never let any
ridiculous feature escape, and gradually destroyed Franz's enthusiasm without his knowing it.

At first all went well with the Review. Christophe had not
yet perceived the mediocrity of his colleagues: and, since he
was one of them, they hailed him as a genius. Mannheim,
who had discovered him, went everywhere repeating that Christophe was an admirable critic, though he had never read anything he had written, that he had mistaken his vocation, and
that he, Mannheim, had revealed it to him. They advertised
his articles in mysterious terms which roused curiosity: and his
first effort was in fact like a stone falling into a duck-pond in
the atony of the little town. It was called: *Too much music.*

" Too much music, too much drinking, too much eating,"
wrote Christophe. "Eating, drinking, hearing, without hunger, thirst, or need, from sheer habitual gormandizing. Living like Strasburg geese. These people are sick from a diseased
appetite. It matters little what you give them: *Tristram* or the
Trompeter von Säkkingen, Beethoven or Mascagni, a fugue or
a two-step, Adam, Bach, Puccini, Mozart, or Marschner: they do
not know what they are eating: the great thing is to eat. They
find no pleasure in it. Look at them at a concert. Talk of

German gaiety! These people do not know what gaiety means: they are always gay! Their gaiety, like their sorrow, drops like rain: their joy is dust: there is neither life nor force in it. They would stay for hours smilingly and vaguely drinking in sounds, sounds, sounds. They think of nothing: they feel nothing: they are sponges. True joy, or true sorrow—strength— is not drawn out over hours like beer from a cask. They take you by the throat and have you down: after they are gone there is no desire left in a man to drink in anything: he is full! . . .

"Too much music! You are slaying each other and it. If you choose to murder each other that is your affair: I can't help it. But where music is concerned,—hands off! I will not suffer you to debase the loveliness of the world by heaping up in the same basket things holy and things shameful, by giving, as you do at present, the prelude to *Parsifal* between a fantasia on the *Daughter of the Regiment* and a saxophone quartette, or an adagio of Beethoven between a cakewalk and the rubbish of Leoncavallo. You boast of being a musical people. You pretend to love music. What sort of music do you love? Good or bad? You applaud both equally. Well, then, choose! What exactly do you want? You do not know yourselves. You do not want to know: you are too fearful of taking sides and compromising yourselves. . . . To the devil with your prudence!—You are above party, do you say?— Above? You mean below. . . ."

And he quoted the lines of old Gottfried Keller, the rude citizen of Zurich—one of the German writers who was most dear to him by reason of his vigorous loyalty and his keen savor of the soil:

"*Wer über den Partein sich wähnt mit stolzen Mienen*
Der steht zumeist vielmehr beträchtlich unter ihnen."

("He who proudly preens himself on being above parties is rather immeasurably beneath them.")

"Have courage and be true," he went on. "Have courage and be ugly. If you like bad music, then say so frankly Show yourselves, see yourselves as you are. Rid your souls of the loathsome burden of all your compromise and equivocation. Wash it in pure water. How long is it since you have seen yourselves in a mirror? I will show you yourselves. Composers, *virtuosi,* conductors, singers, and you, dear public. You shall for once know yourselves. . . . Be what you like: but, for any sake, be true! Be true even though art and artists—and I myself—have to' suffer for it! If art and truth cannot live together, then let art disappear. Truth is life. Lies are death."

Naturally, this youthful, wild outburst, which was all of a piece, and in very bad taste, produced an outcry. And yet, as everybody was attacked and nobody in particular, its pertinency was not recognized. Every one is, or believes himself to be, or says that he is the best friend of truth: there was therefore no danger of the conclusions of the article being attacked. Only people were shocked by its general tone: everybody agreed that it was hardly proper, especially from an artist in a semi-official position. A few musicians began to be uneasy and protested bitterly: they saw that Christophe would not stop at that. Others thought themselves more clever and congratulated Christophe on his courage: they were no less uneasy about his next articles.

Both tactics produced the same result. Christophe had plunged: nothing could stop him: and as he had promised, everybody was passed in survey, composers and interpreters alike.

The first victims were the *Kapellmeisters.* Christophe did not confine himself to general remarks on the art of conducting an orchestra. He mentioned his colleagues of his own town and the neighboring towns by name: or if he did not name them his allusions were so transparent that nobody could be mistaken. Everybody recognized the apathetic conductor of the Court, Alois von Werner, a cautious old man, laden with honors, who was afraid of everything, dodged everything, was too timid to make a remark to his musicians and meekly followed whatever they chose to do,—who never risked anything on his programme that had not been consecrated by twenty years of success, or, at least, guaranteed by the official stamp of some academic dignity. Christophe ironically applauded his boldness: he congratulated him on having discovered Gade, Dvorak, or Tschaikowsky: he waxed enthusiastic over his unfailing correctness, his metronomic equality, the always *fein-nunciert* (finely shaded) playing of his orchestra: he proposed to orchestrate the *École de la Vélocité* of Czerny for his next concert, and implored him not to try himself so much, not to give rein to his passions, to look after his precious health.—Or he cried out indignantly upon the way in which he had conducted the *Eroica* of Beethoven:

"A cannon! A cannon! Mow me down these people! . . . But have you then no idea of the conflict, the fight between human stupidity and human ferocity,—and the strength which tramples them underfoot with a glad shout of laughter?—How could you know it? It is you against whom it fights! You expend all the heroism that is in you in listening or in playing the *Eroica* of Beethoven without a yawn—(for it bores you. . . . Confess that it bores you to death!)—or in risking a draught as you stand with bare head and bowed back to let some Serene Highness pass."

He could not be sarcastic enough about the pontiffs of the Conservatories who interpreted the great men of the past as "classics."

"Classical! That word expresses everything. Free passion, arranged and expurgated for the use of schools! Life, that vast plain swept by the winds,—inclosed within the four walls of a school playground! The fierce, proud beat of a heart in anguish, reduced to the tic-tacs of a four-tune pendulum, which goes its jolly way, hobbling and imperturbably leaning on the crutch of time! . . . To enjoy the Ocean you need to put it in a bowl with goldfish. You only understand life when you have killed it."

If he was not kind to the "bird-stuffers," as he called them, he was even less kind to the ringmen of the orchestra, the illustrious *Kapellmeisters* who toured the country to show off their flourishes and their dainty hands, those who exercised their virtuosity at the expense of the masters, tried hard to make the most familiar works unrecognizable, and turned somersaults through the hoop of the *Symphony in C minor*. He made them appear as old coquettes, *prima donnas* of the orchestra, gipsies, and rope-dancers.

The *virtuosi* naturally provided him with splendid material.

He declared himself incompetent when he had to criticise their conjuring performances. He said that such mechanical exercises belonged to the School of Arts and Crafts, and that not musical criticism but charts registering the duration, and number of the notes, and the energy expended, could decide the merit of such labors. Sometimes he would set at naught some famous piano *virtuoso* who during a two hours' concert had surmounted the formidable difficulties, with a smile on his lips and his hair hanging down into his eyes—of executing a childish *andante* of Mozart.—He did not ignore the pleasure of overcoming difficulties. He had tasted it himself: it was one of the joys of life to him. But only to see the most material aspect of it, and to reduce all the heroism of art to that, seemed to him grotesque and degrading. He could not forgive the " lions " or " panthers " of the piano.—But he was not very indulgent either towards the town pedants, famous in Germany, who, while they are rightly anxious not to alter the text of the masters, carefully suppress every flight of thought, and, like E. d'Albert and H. von Bülow, seem to be giving a lesson in diction when they are rendering a passionate sonata.

The singers had their turn. Christophe was full to the brim of things to say about their barbarous heaviness and their provincial affectations. It was not only because of his recent misadventures with the enraged lady, but because of all the torture he had suffered during so many performances. It was difficult to know which had suffered most, ears or eyes. And Christophe had not enough standards of comparison to be able to have any idea of the ugliness of the setting, the hideous costumes, the screaming colors. He was only shocked by the vulgarity of the people, their gestures and attitudes, their unnatural playing, the inability of the actors to take on other souls than their own, and by the stupefying indifference with which they passed from one rôle to another, provided they were written more or less in the same register. Matrons of opulent flesh, hearty and buxom, appeared alternately as Ysolde and Carmen. Amfortas played Figaro.—But what most offended Christophe was the ugliness of the singing, especially in the classical works in which the beauty of melody is essential. No one in Germany could sing the perfect music of the eighteenth century: no one would take the trouble. The clear, pure style of Gluck and Mozart which, like that of Goethe, seems to be bathed in the light of Italy—the style which begins to change and to become vibrant and dazzling with Weber—the style ridiculed by the ponderous caricatures of the author of *Crociato*—had been killed by the triumph of Wagner. The wild flight of the Valkyries with their strident cries had passed over the Grecian sky. The heavy clouds of Odin dimmed the light. No one now thought of singing music: they sang poems. Ugliness and carelessness of detail, even false notes were let pass under pretext that only the whole, only the thought behind it mattered. . . .

"Thought! Let us talk of that. As if you understood it! . . . But whether or no you do understand it, I pray you respect the form that thought has chosen for itself. Above all, let music be and remain music!"

And the great concern of German artists with expression and profundity of thought was, according to Christophe, a good joke. Expression? Thought? Yes, they introduced them into everything—everything impartially. They would have found thought in a skein of wool just as much—neither more nor less—as in a statue of Michael Angelo. They played anything, anybody's music with exactly the same energy. For most of them the great thing in music—so he declared—was the volume of sound, just a musical noise. The pleasure of singing so potent in Germany was in some sort a pleasure of vocal gymnastics. It was just a matter of being inflated with air and then letting it go vigorously, powerfully, for a long time together and rhythmically.—And by way of compliment he accorded a certain great singer a certificate of good health. He was not content with flaying the artists. He strode over the footlights and trounced the public for coming, gaping, to such performances. The public was staggered and did not know whether it ought to laugh or be angry. They had every right to cry out upon his injustice: they had taken care not to be mixed up in any artistic conflict: they stood aside prudently from any burning question: and to avoid making any mistake they applauded everything! And now Christophe declared that it was a crime to applaud! . . . To applaud bad works?—That would have been enough! But Christophe went further: he stormed at them for applauding great works:

"Humbugs!" he said. "You would have us believe that you have as much enthusiasm as that? . . . Oh! Come! Spare yourselves the trouble! You only prove exactly the opposite of what you are trying to prove. Applaud if you like those works and passages which in some measure deserve applause. Applaud those loud final movements which are written, as Mozart said, "for long ears." Applaud as much as you like, then: your braying is anticipated: it is part of the concert.— But after the *Missa Solemnis* of Beethoven! . . . Poor wretches! . . . It is the Last Judgment. You have just seen the maddening *Gloria* pass like a storm over the ocean. You have seen the waterspout of an athletic and tremendous well, which stops, breaks, reaches up to the clouds clinging by its two hands above the abyss, then plunging once more into space in full swing. The squall shrieks and whirls along. And when the hurricane is at its height there is a sudden modulation, a radiance of sound which cleaves the darkness of the sky and falls upon the livid sea like a patch of light. It is the end: the furious flight of the destroying angel stops short, its wings transfixed by these flashes of lightning. Around you all is buzzing and quivering. The eye gazes fixedly forward in stupor. The heart beats, breathing stops, the limbs are paralyzed. . . . And hardly has the last note sounded than already you are gay and merry. You shout, you laugh, you criticise, you applaud. . . . But you have seen nothing, heard nothing, felt nothing, understood nothing, nothing, nothing, absolutely nothing! The sufferings of an artist are a show to you. You think the tears of agony of a Beethoven are finely painted. You would cry 'Encore' to the Crucifixion. A great soul struggles all its life long in sorrow to divert your idleness for an hour! . . ."

So, without knowing it, he confirmed Goethe's great words: but he had not yet attained his lofty serenity:

"The people make a sport of the sublime. If they could see it as it is, they would be unable to bear its aspect."

If he had only stopped at that!—But, whirled along by his enthusiasm, he swept past the public and plunged like a cannon ball into the sanctuary, the tabernacle, the inviolable refuge of mediocrity: Criticism. He bombarded his colleagues. One of them had taken upon himself to attack the most gifted of living composers, the most advanced representative of the new school, Hassler, the writer of programme symphonies, extravagant in truth, but full of genius. Christophe who—as perhaps will be remembered—had been presented to him when he was a child, had always had a secret tenderness for him in his gratitude for the enthusiasm and emotion that he had had then. To see a stupid critic, whose ignorance he knew, instructing a man of that caliber, calling him to order, and reminding him of set principles, infuriated him:

" Order! Order! " he cried. " You do not know any order but that of the police. Genius is not to be dragged along the beaten track. It creates order, and makes its will a law."

After this arrogant declaration he took the unlucky critic, considered all the idiocies he had written for some time past, and administered correction.

All the critics felt the affront. Up to that time they had stood aside from the conflict. They did not care to risk a rebuff: they knew Christophe, they knew his efficiency, and they knew also that he was not long-suffering. Certain of them had discreetly expressed their regret that so gifted a composer should dabble in a profession not his own. Whatever might be their opinion (when they had one), and however hurt they might be by Christophe, they respected in him their own privilege of being able to criticise everything without being criticised themselves. But when they saw Christophe rudely break the tacit convention which bound them, they saw in him an enemy of public order. With one consent it seemed revolting to them that a very young man should take upon himself to show scant respect for the national glories: and they began a furious campaign against him. They did not write long articles or consecutive arguments—(they were unwilling to venture upon such ground with an adversary better armed than themselves: although a journalist has the special faculty of being able to discuss without taking his adversary's arguments into consideration, and even without having read them)—but long experience had taught them that, as the reader of a paper always

agrees with it, even to appear to argue was to weaken its credit
with him: it was necessary to affirm, or better still, to deny—
(negation is twice as powerful as affirmation: it is a direct
consequence of the law of gravity: it is much easier to drop
a stone than to throw it up).—They adopted, therefore, a system of little notes, perfidious, ironic, injurious, which were repeated day by day, in an easily accessible position, with unwearying assiduity. They held the insolent Christophe up to
ridicule, though they never mentioned him by name, but always
transparently alluded to him. They twisted his words to make
them look absurd: they told anecdotes about him, true for
the most part, though the rest were a tissue of lies, nicely
calculated to set him at loggerheads with the whole town, and,
worse still, with the Court: even his physical appearance, his
features, his manner of dressing, were attacked and caricatured
in a way that by dint of repetition came to be like him.

It would have mattered little to Christophe's friends if their
Review had not also come in for blows in the battle. In truth,
it served rather as an advertisement: there was no desire to
commit the Review to the quarrel: rather the attempt was made
to cut Christophe off from it: there was astonishment that
it should so compromise its good name, and they were given
to understand that if they did not take care steps would be
taken, however unpleasant it might be, to make the whole
editorial staff responsible. There were signs of attack, gentle
enough, upon Adolf Mai and Mannheim, which stirred up the
wasps' nest. Mannheim only laughed at it: he thought that
it would infuriate his father, his uncles, cousins, and his innumerable family, who took upon themselves to watch everything he did and to be scandalized by it. But Adolf Mai took
it very seriously and blamed Christophe for compromising the
Review. Christophe sent him packing. The others who had
not been attacked found it rather amusing that Mai, who was
apt to pontificate over them, should be their scapegoat. Waldhaus was secretly delighted: he said that there was never a
fight without a few heads being broken. Naturally he took
good care that it should not be his own: he thought he was
sheltered from onslaught by the position of his family and his

relatives: and he saw no harm in the Jews, his allies, being mauled a little. Ehrenfeld and Goldenring, who were so far untouched, would not have been worried by attack: they could reply. But what did touch them on the raw was that Christophe should go on persistently putting them in the wrong with their friends, and especially their women friends. They had laughed loudly at the first articles and thought them good fun: they admired Christophe's vigorous window-smashing: they thought they had only to give the word to check his combativeness, or at least to turn his attack from men and women whom they might mention.—But no. Christophe would listen to nothing: he paid no heed to any remark and went on like a madman. If they let him go on there would be no living in the place. Already their young women friends, furious and in tears, had come and made scenes at the offices of the Review. They brought all their diplomacy to bear on Christophe to persuade him at least to moderate certain of his criticisms: Christophe changed nothing. They lost their tempers: Christophe lost his, but he changed nothing. Waldhaus was amused by the unhappiness of his friends, which in no wise touched him, and took Christophe's part to annoy them. Perhaps also he was more capable than they of appreciating Christophe's extravagance, who with head down hurled himself upon everything without keeping any line of retreat, or preparing any refuge for the future. As for Mannheim he was royally amused by the farce: it seemed to him a good joke to have introduced this madman among these correct people, and he rocked with laughter both at the blows which Christophe dealt and at those which he received. Although under his sister's influence he was beginning to think that Christophe was decidedly a little cracked, he only liked him the more for it—(it was necessary for him to find those who were in sympathy with him a little absurd).—And so he joined Waldhaus in supporting Christophe against the others.

As he was not wanting in practical sense, in spite of all his efforts to pretend to the contrary, he thought very justly that it would be to his friend's advantage to ally himself with the cause of the most advanced musical party in the country.

As in most German towns, there was in the town a *Wagner-*

Verein, which represented new ideas against the conservative element.—In truth, there was no great risk in defending Wagner when his fame was acknowledged everywhere and his works included in the repertory of every Opera House in Germany. And yet his victory was rather won by force than by universal accord, and at heart the majority were obstinately conservative, especially in the small towns such as this which have been rather left outside the great modern movements and are rather proud of their ancient fame. More than anywhere else there reigned the distrust, so innate in the German people, of anything new, the sort of laziness in feeling anything true or powerful which has not been pondered and digested by several generations. It was apparent in the reluctance with which— if not the works of Wagner which are beyond discussion— every new work inspired by the Wagnerian spirit was accepted. And so the *Wagner-Vereine* would have had a useful task to fulfil if they had set themselves to defend all the young and original forces in art. Sometimes they did so, and Bruckner or Hugo Wolf found in some of them their best allies. But too often the egoism of the master weighed upon his disciples: and just as Bayreuth serves only monstrously to glorify one man, the *offshoots* of Bayreuth were little churches in which Mass was eternally sung in honor of the one God. At the most the faithful disciples were admitted to the side chapels, the disciples who applied the hallowed doctrines to the letter, and, prostrate in the dust, adored the only Divinity with His many faces: music, poetry, drama, and metaphysics.

The *Wagner-Verein* of the town was in exactly this case.— However, they went through the form of activity: they were always trying to enroll young men of talent who looked as though they might be useful to it: and they had long had their eyes on Christophe. They had discreetly made advances to him, of which Christophe had not taken any notice, because he felt no need of being associated with anybody: he could not understand the necessity which drove his compatriots always to be banding themselves together in groups, being unable to do anything alone: neither to sing, nor to walk, nor to drink. He was averse to all *Vereinswesen.* But on the whole he was more kindly disposed to the *Wagner-Verein* than to any other

Verein: at least they did provide an excuse for fine concerts: and although he did not share all the Wagnerian ideas on art, he was much nearer them than to those of any other group in music. He could he thought find common ground with a party which was as unjust as himself towards Brahms and the "Brahmins." So he let himself be put up for it. Mannheim introduced him: he knew everybody. Without being a musician he was a member of the *Wagner-Verein.*—The managing committee had followed the campaign which Christophe was conducting in the Review. His slaughter in the opposing camp had seemed to them to give signs of a strong grip which it would be as well to have in their service. Christophe had also let fly certain disrespectful remarks about the sacred fetish: but they had preferred to close their eyes to that: and perhaps his attacks, not yet very offensive, had not been without their influence, unconsciously, in making them so eager to enroll Christophe before he had time to deliver himself manfully. They came and very amiably asked his permission to play some of his compositions at one of the approaching concerts of the Association. Christophe was flattered, and accepted: he went to the *Wagner-Verein,* and, urged by Mannheim, he was made a member.

At that time there were at the head of the *Wagner-Verein* two men, of whom one enjoyed a certain notoriety as a writer, and the other as a conductor. Both had a Mohammedan belief in Wagner. The first, Josias Kling, had compiled a Wagner Dictionary—*Wagner Lexikon*—which made it possible in a moment to know the master's thoughts *de omni re scibili:* it had been his life's work. He was capable of reciting whole chapters of it at table, as the French provincials used to troll the songs of the Maid. He used also to publish in the *Bayreuther Blätter* articles on Wagner and the Aryan Spirit. Of course, Wagner was to him the type of the pure Aryan, of whom the German race had remained the last inviolable refuge against the corrupting influences of Latin Semitism, especially the French. He declared that the impure French spirit was finally destroyed, though he did not desist from attacking it bitterly day by day as though the eternal enemy were still a menace. He would only acknowledge one great man in France: the

Count of Gobineau. Kling was a little man, very little, and he used to blush like a girl.—The other pillar of the *Wagner-Verein,* Erich Lauber, had been manager of a chemical works until four years before: then he had given up everything to become a conductor. He had succeeded by force of will, and because he was very rich. He was a Bayreuth fanatic: it was said that he had gone there on foot, from Munich, wearing pilgrim's sandals. It was a strange thing that a man who had read much, traveled much, practised divers professions, and in everything displayed an energetic personality, should have become in music a sheep of Panurge: all his originality was expended in his being a little more stupid than the others. He was not sure enough of himself in music to trust to his own personal feelings, and so he slavishly followed the interpretations of Wagner given by the *Kapellmeisters,* and the licensees of Bayreuth. He desired to reproduce even to the smallest detail the setting and the variegated costumes which delighted the puerile and barbarous taste of the little Court of Wahnfried. He was like the fanatical admirer of Michael Angelo who used to reproduce in his copies even the cracks in the wall of the moldy patches which had themselves been hallowed by their appearance in the hallowed pictures.

Christophe was not likely to approve greatly of the two men. But they were men of the world, pleasant, and both well-read: and Lauber's conversation was always interesting on any other subject than music. He was a bit of a crank: and Christophe did not dislike cranks: they were a change from the horrible banality of reasonable people. He did not yet know that there is nothing more devastating than an irrational man, and that originality is even more rare among those who are called " originals " than among the rest. For these " originals " are simply maniacs whose thoughts are reduced to clockwork.

Josias Kling and Lauber, being desirous of winning Christophe's support, were at first very keenly interested in him. Kling wrote a eulogistic article about him and Lauber followed all his directions when he conducted his compositions at one of the concerts of the Society. Christophe was touched by it all. Unfortunately all their attentions were spoiled by the

stupidity of those who paid them. He had not the faculty of
pretending about people because they admired him. He was
exacting. He demanded that no one should admire him for
the opposite of what he was: and he was always prone to regard
as enemies those who were his friends, by mistake. And so
he was not at all pleased with Kling for seeing in him a disciple
of Wagner, and trying to see connections between passages of
his *Lieder* and passages of the *Tetralogy,* which had nothing in
common but certain notes of the scale. And he had no pleasure
in hearing one of his works sandwiched—together with a worthless imitation by a Wagnerian student—between two enormous
blocks of Wagnerian drama.

It was not long before he was stifled in the little chapel.
It was just another Conservatoire, as narrow as the old Con-
servatoires, and more intolerant because it was the latest comer
in art. Christophe began to lose his illusions about the absolute
value of a form of art or of thought. Hitherto he had always
believed that great ideas bear their own light within themselves. Now he saw that ideas may change, but that men
remain the same: and, in fine, nothing counted but men: ideas
were what they were. If they were born mediocre and servile,
even genius became mediocre in its passage through their souls,
and the shout of freedom of the hero breaking his bonds became
the act of slavery of succeeding generations.—Christophe could
not refrain from expressing his feelings. He let no opportunity
slip of jeering at fetishism in art. He declared that there was
no need of idols, or classics of any sort, and that he only had
the right to call himself the heir of the spirit of Wagner who
was capable of trampling Wagner underfoot and so walking
on and keeping himself in close communion with life. . Kling's
stupidity made Christophe aggressive. He set out all the faults
and absurdities he could see in Wagner. The Wagnerians at
once credited him with a grotesque jealousy of their God.
Christophe for his part had no doubt that these same people
who exalted Wagner since he was dead would have been the
first to strangle him in his life: and he did them an injustice.
The Klings and the Laubers also had had their hour of illumina-
tion: they had been advanced twenty years ago: and then like
most people they had stopped short at that. Man has so little

force that he is out of breath after the first ascent: very few are long-winded enough to go on.

Christophe's attitude quickly alienated him from his new friends. Their sympathy was a bargain: he had to side with them if they were to side with him: and it was quite evident that Christophe would not yield an inch: he would not join them. They lost their enthusiasm for him. The eulogies which he refused to accord to the gods and demi-gods who were approved by the cult, were withheld from him. They showed less eagerness to welcome his compositions: and some of the members began to protest against his name being too often on the programmes. They laughed at him behind his back, and criticism went on: Kling and Lauber by not protesting seemed to take part in it. They would have avoided a breach with Christophe if possible: first because the minds of the Germans of the Rhine like mixed solutions, solutions which are not solutions, and have the privilege of prolonging indefinitely an ambiguous situation: and secondly, because they hoped in spite of everything to be able to make use of him, by wearing him down, if not by persuasion.

Christophe gave them no time for it. Whenever he thought he felt that at heart any man disliked him, but would not admit it and tried to cover it up so as to remain on good terms with him, he would never rest until he had succeeded in proving to him that he was his enemy. One evening at the *Wagner-Verein* when he had come up against a wall of hypocritical hostility, he could bear it no longer and sent in his resignation to Lauber without wasting words. Lauber could not understand it: and Mannheim hastened to Christophe to try and pacify him. At his first words Christophe burst out:

"No, no, no,—no! Don't talk to me about these people. I will not see them again. . . . I cannot. I cannot. . . . I am disgusted, horribly, with men: I can hardly bear to look at one."

Mannheim laughed heartily. He was thinking much less of smoothing Christophe down than of having the fun of it.

"I know that they are not beautiful," he said; "but that is nothing new: what new thing has happened?"

"Nothing. I have had enough, that is all. . . . Yes, laugh,

laugh at me: everybody knows I am mad. Prudent people
act in accordance with the laws of logic and reason and sanity.
I am not like that: I am a man who acts only on his own
impulse. When a certain quantity of electricity is accumulated
in me it has to expend itself, at all costs: and so much the
worse for the others if it touches them! And so much the
worse for them! I am not made for living in society. Henceforth I shall belong only to myself."

"You think you can do without everybody else?" said Mannheim. "You cannot play your music all by yourself. You
need singers, an orchestra, a conductor, an audience, a
claque. . . ."

Christophe shouted.

"No! no! no!"

But the last word made him jump.

"A claque! Are you not ashamed?"

"I am not talking of a paid claque—(although, indeed, it is
the only means yet discovered of revealing the merit of a composition to the audience).—But you must have a claque: the
author's coterie is a claque, properly drilled by him: every
author has his claque: that is what friends are for."

"I don't want any friends!"

"Then you will be hissed."

"I want to be hissed!"

Mannheim was in the seventh heaven.

"You won't have even that pleasure for long. They won't
play you."

"So be it, then! Do you think I care about being a famous
man? . . . Yes. I was making for that with all my might. . . .
Nonsense! Folly! Idiocy! . . . As if the satisfaction of the
vulgarest sort of pride could compensate for all the sacrifices—
weariness, suffering, infamy, insults, degradation, ignoble con-
cessions—which are the price of fame! Devil take me if I ever
bother my head about such things again! Never again! Publicity is a vulgar infamy. I will be a private citizen and live
for myself and those whom I love. . . ."

"Good," said Mannheim ironically. "You must choose a
profession. Why shouldn't you make shoes?"

"Ah! if I were a cobbler like the incomparable Sachs!"

cried Christophe. " How happy my life would be! A cobbler
all through the week,—and a musician on Sunday, privately,
intimately, for my own pleasure and that of my friends! What
a life that would be! . . . Am I mad, to waste my time and
trouble for the magnificent pleasure of being a prey to the
judgment of idiots? Is it not much better and finer to be
loved and understood by a few honest men than to be heard,
criticised, and toadied by thousands of fools? . . . The devil
of pride and thirst for fame shall never again take me: trust
me for that!"

" Certainly," said Mannheim. He thought:

" In an hour he will say just the opposite." He remarked
quietly :

" Then I am to go and smooth things down with the *Wagner-
Verein?*"

Christophe waved his arms.

" What is the good of my shouting myself hoarse with telling
you ' No,' for the last hour? . . . I tell you that I will never
set foot inside it again! I loathe all these *Wagner-Vereine*,
all these *Vereine*, all these flocks of sheep who have to huddle
together to be able to baa in unison. Go and tell those sheep
from me that I am a wolf, that I have teeth, and am not made
for the pasture!"

" Good, good. I will tell them," said Mannheim, as he
went. He was delighted with his morning's entertainment.
He thought :

" He is mad, mad, mad as a hatter. . . ."

His sister, to whom he reported the interview, at once
shrugged her shoulders and said :

" Mad? He would like us to think so! . . . He is stupid,
and absurdly vain. . . ."

.. Christophe went on with his fierce campaign in Waldhaus's
Review. It was not that it gave him pleasure : criticism disgusted him, and he was always wishing it at the bottom of the
sea. But he stuck to it because people were trying to stop him :
he did not wish to appear to have given in.

Waldhaus was beginning to be uneasy. As long as he was
out of reach he had looked on at the affray with the calmness

of an Olympian god. But for some weeks past the other papers
had seemed to be beginning to disregard his inviolability: they
had begun to attack his vanity as a writer with a rare malevolence in which, had Waldhaus been more subtle, he might have
recognized the hand of a friend. As a matter of fact, the
attacks were cunningly instigated by Ehrenfeld and Goldenring: they could see no other way of inducing him to stop
Christophe's polemics. Their perception was justified. Waldhaus at once declared that Christophe was beginning to weary
him: and he withdrew his support. All the staff of the Review
then tried hard to silence Christophe! But it were as easy to
muzzle a dog who is about to devour his prey! Everything they
said to him only excited him more. He called them poltroons
and declared that he would say everything—everything that he
ought to say. If they wished to get rid of him, they were free
to do so! The whole town would know that they were as
cowardly as the rest: but he would not go of his own accord.

They looked at each other in consternation, bitterly blaming
Mannheim for the trick he had played them in bringing such
a madman among them. Mannheim laughed and tried hard
to curb Christophe himself: and he vowed that with the next
article Christophe would water his wine. They were incredulous: but the event proved that Mannheim had not boasted
vainly. Christophe's next article, though not a model of courtesy, did not contain a single offensive remark about anybody.
Mannheim's method was very simple: they were all amazed
at not having thought of it before: Christophe never read what
he wrote in the Review, and he hardly read the proofs of his
articles, only very quickly and carelessly. Adolf Mai had more
than once passed caustic remarks on the subject: he said that
a printer's error was a disgrace to a Review: and Christophe,
who did not regard criticism altogether as an art, replied that
those who were upbraided in it would understand well enough.
Mannheim turned this to account: he said that Christophe was
right and that correcting proofs was printers' work: and he
offered to take it over. Christophe was overwhelmed with
gratitude: but they told him that such an arrangement would
be of service to them and a saving of time for the Review. So
Christophe left his proofs to Mannheim and asked him to

correct them carefully. Mannheim did: it was sport for him. At first he only ventured to tone down certain phrases and to delete here and there certain ungracious epithets. Emboldened by success, he went further with his experiments: he began to alter sentences and their meaning: and he was really skilful in it. The whole art of it consisted in preserving the general appearance of the sentence and its characteristic form while making it say exactly the opposite of what Christophe had meant. Mannheim took far more trouble to disfigure Christophe's articles than he would have done to write them himself: never had he worked so hard. But he enjoyed the result: certain musicians whom Christophe had hitherto pursued with his sarcasms were astounded to see him grow gradually gentle and at last sing their praises. The staff of the Review were delighted. Mannheim used to read aloud his lucubrations to them. They roared with laughter. Ehrenfeld and Goldenring would say to Mannheim occasionally:

"Be careful! You are going too far."

"There's no danger," Mannheim would say. And he would go on with it.

Christophe never noticed anything. He used to go to the office of the Review, leave his copy, and not bother about it any more. Sometimes he would take Mannheim aside and say:

"This time I really have done for the swine. Just read. . . ." Mannheim would read.

"Well, what do you think of it?"

"Terrible, my dear fellow, there's nothing left of them!"

"What do you think they will say?"

"Oh! there will be a fine row."

But there never was a row. On the contrary, everybody beamed at Christophe: people whom he detested would bow to him in the street. One day he came to the office uneasy and scowling: and, throwing a visiting card on the table, he asked:

"What does this mean?"

It was the card of a musician whom he slaughtered.

"A thousand thanks."

Mannheim replied with a laugh:

"It is ironical."

Christophe was set at rest.

"Oh!" he said. "I was afraid my article had pleased him."

"He is furious," said Ehrenfeld: "but he does not wish to seem so: he is posing as the strong man, and is just laughing."

"Laughing? . . . Swine!" said Christophe, furious once more. "I shall write another article about him. He laughs best who laughs last."

"No, no," said Waldhaus anxiously. "I don't think he is laughing at you. It is humility: he is a good Christian. He is holding out the other cheek to the smiter."

"So much the better!" said Christophe. "Ah! Coward! He has asked for it: he shall have his flogging."

Waldhaus tried to intervene. But the others laughed.

"Let him be . . ." said Mannheim.

"After all . . ." replied Waldhaus, suddenly reassured, "a little more or less makes no matter! . . ."

Christophe went away. His colleagues rocked and roared with laughter. When they had had their fill of it Waldhaus said to Mannheim:

"All the same, it was a narrow squeak. . . . Please be careful. We shall be caught yet."

"Bah!" said Mannheim. "We have plenty of time. . . . And besides, I am making friends for him."

II

ENGULFED

CHRISTOPHE had got so far with his clumsy efforts towards the reform of German art when there happened to pass through the town a troupe of French actors. It would be more exact to say, a band; for, as usual, they were a collection of poor devils, picked up goodness knows where, and young unknown players too happy to learn their art, provided they were allowed to act. They were all harnessed to the chariot of a famous and elderly actress who was making tour of Germany, and passing through the little princely town, gave their performances there.

Waldhaus' review made a great fuss over them. Mannheim and his friends knew or pretended to know about the literary and

social life of Paris: they used to repeat gossip picked up in
the boulevard newspapers and more or less understood; they
represented the French spirit in Germany. That robbed Christophe of any desire to know more about it. Mannheim used
to overwhelm him with praises of Paris. He had been there
several times; certain members of his family were there. He
had relations in every country in Europe, and they had everywhere assumed the nationality and aspect of the country: this
tribe of the seed of Abraham included an English baronet,
a Belgian senator, a French minister, a deputy in the *Reichstag*,
and a Papal Count; and all of them, although they were united
and filled with respect for the stock from which they sprang,
were sincerely English, Belgian, French, German, or Papal, for
their pride never allowed of doubt that the country of their
adoption was the greatest of all. Mannheim was paradoxically
the only one of them who was pleased to prefer all the countries
to which he did not belong. He used often to talk of Paris enthusiastically, but as he was always extravagant in his talk, and,
by way of praising the Parisians, used to represent them as a
species of scatterbrains, lewd and rowdy, who spent their time
in love-making and revolutions without ever taking themselves seriously, Christophe was not greatly attracted by the
" Byzantine and decadent republic beyond the Vosges." He used
rather to imagine Paris as it was presented in a naïve engraving
which he had seen as a frontispiece to a book that had recently
appeared in a German art publication; the Devil of Notre Dame
appeared huddled up above the roofs of the town with the
legend:

*"Eternal luxury like an insatiable Vampire devours its prey
above the great city."*

Like a good German he despised the debauched Volcae and
their literature, of which he only knew lively buffooneries like
L'Aiglon, Madame Sans Gêne, and a few café songs. The snobbishness of the little town, where those people who were most
notoriously incapable of being interested in art flocked noisily
to take places at the box office, brought him to an affectation
of scornful indifference towards the great actress. He vowed
that he would not go one yard to hear her. It was the easier

for him to keep his promise as seats had reached an exorbitant price which he could not afford.

The repertory which the French actors had brought included a few classical pieces; but for the most part it was composed of those idiotic pieces which are expressly manufactured in Paris for exportation, for nothing is more international than mediocrity. Christophe knew *La Tosca,* which was to be the first production of the touring actors; he had seen it in translation adorned with all those easy graces which the company of a little Rhenish theater can give to a French play: and he laughed scornfully and declared that he was very glad, when he saw his friends go off to the theater, not to have to see it again. But next day he listened none the less eagerly, without seeming to listen, to the enthusiastic tales of the delightful evening they had had: he was angry at having lost the right to contradict them by having refused to see what everybody was talking about.

The second production announced was a French translation of *Hamlet.* Christophe had never missed an opportunity of seeing a play of Shakespeare's. Shakespeare was to him of the same order as Beethoven, an inexhaustible spring of life. *Hamlet* had been specially dear to him during the period of stress and tumultuous doubts through which he had just passed. In spite of his fear of seeing himself reflected in that magic mirror he was fascinated by it: and he prowled about the theater notices, though he did not admit that he was longing to book a seat. But he was so obstinate that after what he had said to his friends he would not eat his words: and he would have stayed at home that evening if chance had not brought him in contact with Mannheim just as he was sadly going home.

Mannheim took his arm and told him angrily, though he never ceased his banter, that an old beast of a relation, his father's sister, had just come down upon them with all her retinue and that they had all to stay at home to welcome her. He had time to get out of it: but his father would brook no trifling with questions of family etiquette and the respect due to elderly relatives: and as he had to handle his father carefully because he wanted presently to get money out of him, he had had to give in and not go to the play.

" You had tickets? " asked Christophe.

" An excellent box: and I have to go and give it—(I am just going now)—to that old pig, Grünebaum, papa's partner, so that he can swagger there with the she Grünebaum and their turkey hen of a daughter. Jolly! . . . I want to find something very disagreeable to say to them. They won't mind so long as I give them the tickets—although they would much rather they were banknotes."

He stopped short with his mouth open and looked at Christophe:

" Oh! but—but just the man I want!" He chuckled:

" Christophe, are you going to the theater? "

" No."

" Good. You shall go. I ask it as a favor. You cannot refuse."

Christophe did not understand.

" But I have no seat."

" Here you are!" said Mannheim triumphantly, thrusting the ticket into his hand.

" You are mad," said Christophe. " What about your father's orders? "

Mannheim laughed:

" He will be furious!" he said.

He dried his eyes and went on:

" I shall tap him to-morrow morning as soon as he is up before he knows anything."

" I cannot accept," said Christophe, " knowing that he would not like it."

" It does not concern you: you know nothing about it."

Christophe had unfolded the ticket:

" And what would I do with a box for four? "

" Whatever you like. You can sleep in it, dance if you like. Take some women. You must know some? If need be w* can lend you some."

Christophe held out the ticket to Mannheim:

" Certainly not. Take it back."

" Not I," said Mannheim, stepping back a pace. " I can't force you to go if it bores you, but I shan't take it back. You

can throw it in the fire or even take it virtuously to the Grünebaums. I don't care. Good-night!"

He left Christophe in the middle of the street, ticket in
hand, and went away.

Christophe was unhappy about it. He said to himself that
he ought to take it to the Grünebaums: but he was not keen
about the idea. He went home still pondering, and when later
he looked at the clock he saw that he had only just time
enough to dress for the theater. It would be too silly to waste
the ticket. He asked his mother to go with him. But Louisa
declared that she would rather go to bed. He went. At heart
he was filled with childish glee at the thought of his evening.
Only cne thing worried him: the thought of having to be
alone in such a pleasure. He had no remorse about Mannheim's father or the Grünebaums, whose box he was taking:
but he was remorseful about those whom he might have taken
with him. He thought of the joy it could give to other young
people like himself: and it hurt him not to be able to give it
them. He cast about but could find nobody to whom he could
offer his ticket. Besides, it was late and he must hurry.

As he entered the theater he passed by the closed window
on which a poster announced that there was not a single seat
left in the office. Among the people who were turning away
from it disappointedly he noticed a girl who could not make
up her mind to leave and was enviously watching the people
going in. She was dressed very simply in black; she was not very
tall; her face was thin and she looked delicate; and at the
moment he did not notice whether she were pretty or plain.
He passed her: then he stopped, turned, and without stopping
to think:

"You can't get a seat, Fräulein?" he asked point-blank.

She blushed and said with a foreign accent:

"No, sir."

"I have a box which I don't know what to do with. Will
you make use of it with me?"

She blushed again and thanked him and said she could not
accept. Christophe was embarrassed by her refusal, begged her
pardon and tried to insist, but he could not persuade her,

although it was obvious that she was dying to accept. He was very perplexed. He made up his mind suddenly.

"There is a way out of the difficulty," he said. "You take the ticket. I don't want it. I have seen the play." (He was boasting). "It will give you more pleasure than me. Take it, please."

The girl was so touched by his proposal and the cordial manner in which it was made that tears all but came to her eyes. She murmured gratefully that she could not think of depriving him of it.

"Then, come," he said, smiling.

He looked so kind and honest that she was ashamed of having refused, and she said in some confusion:

"Thank you. I will come."

They went in. The Mannheims' box was wide, big, and faced the stage: it was impossible not to be seen in it if they had wished. It is useless to say that their entry passed unnoticed. Christophe made the girl sit at the front, while he stayed a little behind so as not to embarrass her. She sat stiffly upright, not daring to turn her head: she was horribly shy: she would have given much not to have accepted. To give her time to recover her composure and not knowing what to talk to her about, Christophe pretended to look the other way. Whichever way he looked it was easily seen that his presence with an unknown companion among the brilliant people of the boxes was exciting much curiosity and comment. He darted furious glances at those who were looking at him: he was angry that people should go on being interested in him when he took no interest in them. It did not occur to him that their indiscreet curiosity was more busied with his companion than with himself and that there was more offense in it. By way of showing his utter indifference to anything they might say or think he leaned towards the girl and began to talk to her. She looked so scared by his talking and so unhappy at having to reply, and it seemed to be so difficult for her to wrench out a "Yes" or a "No" without ever daring to look at him, that he took pity on her shyness, and drew back to a corner. Fortunately the play began.

Christophe had not seen the play bill and he hardly cared to know what part the great actress was playing: he was one of those simple people who go to the theater to see the play and not the actors. He had never wondered whether the famous player would be Ophelia or the Queen; if he had wondered about it he would have inclined towards the Queen, bearing in mind the ages of the two ladies. But it could never have occurred to him that she would play Hamlet. When he saw Hamlet, and heard his mechanical dolly squeak, it was some time before he could believe it; he wondered if he were not dreaming.

"But who? Who is it?" he asked half aloud. "It can't be . . ."

And when he had to accept that it *was* Hamlet, he rapped out an oath, which fortunately his companion did not hear, because she was a foreigner, though it was heard perfectly in the next box: for he was at once indignantly bidden to be silent. He withdrew to the back of the box to swear his fill. He could not recover his temper. If he had been just he would have given homage to the elegance of the travesty and the *tour de force* of nature and art, which made it possible for a woman of sixty to appear in a youth's costume and even to seem beautiful in it—at least to kindly eyes. But he hated all *tours de force,* everything which violates and falsifies Nature. He liked a woman to be a woman, and a man a man. (It does not often happen nowadays.) The childish and absurd travesty of the Leonora of Beethoven did not please him much. But this travesty of Hamlet was beyond all dreams of the preposterous. To make of the robust Dane, fat and pale, choleric, cunning, intellectual, subject to hallucinations, a woman—not even a woman: for a woman playing the man can only be a monster,—to make of Hamlet a eunuch or an androgynous betwixt and between,—the times must be flabby indeed, criticism must be idiotic, to let such disgusting folly be tolerated for a single day and not hissed off the boards! The actress's voice infuriated Christophe. She had that singing, labored diction, that monotonous melopœia which seems to have been dear to the least poetic people in the world since the days of the *Champmeslé* and the *Hôtel de Bourgogne.*

Christophe was so exasperated by it that he wanted to go away. He turned his back on the scene, and he made hideous faces against the wall of the box like a child put in the corner. Fortunately his companion dared not look at him: for if she had seen him she would have thought him. mad.

Suddenly Christophe stopped making faces. He stopped still and made no sound. A lovely musical voice, a young woman's voice, grave and sweet, was heard. Christophe pricked his ears. As she went on with her words he turned again, keenly interested to see what bird could warble so. He saw Ophelia. In truth she was nothing like the Ophelia of Shakespeare. She was a beautiful girl, tall, big and fine like a young fresh statue —Electra or Cassandra. She was brimming with life. In spite of her efforts to keep within her part, the force of youth and joy that was in her shone forth from her body, her movements, her gestures, her brown eyes that laughed in spite of herself. Such is the power of physical beauty that Christophe who a moment before had been merciless in judging the interpretation of Hamlet never for a moment thought of regretting that Ophelia was hardly at all like his image of her: and he sacrificed his image to the present vision of her remorselessly. With the unconscious faithlessness of people of passion he even found a profound truth in the youthful ardor brimming in the depths of the chaste and unhappy virgin heart. But the magic of the voice, pure, warm, and velvety, worked the spell: every word sounded like a lovely chord: about every syllable there hovered like the scent of thyme or wild mint the laughing accent of the Midi with its full rhythm. Strange was this vision of an Ophelia from Arles! In it was something of that golden sun and its wild northwest wind, its *mistral*.

Christophe forgot his companion and came and sat by her side at the front of the box: he never took his eyes off the beautiful actress whose name he did not know. But the audience who had not come to see an unknown player paid no attention to her, and only applauded when the female Hamlet spoke. That made Christophe growl and call them: " Idiots ! " in a low voice which could be heard ten yards away.

It was not until the curtain was lowered upon the first act that he remembered the existence of his companion, and seeing that she was still shy he thought with a smile of how he must have scared her with his extravagances. He was not far wrong: the girl whom chance had thrown in his company for a few hours was almost morbidly shy; she must have been in an abnormal state of excitement to have accepted Christophe's invitation. She had hardly accepted it than she had wished at any cost to get out of it, to make some excuse and to escape. It had been much worse for her when she had seen that she was an object of general curiosity, and her unhappiness had been increased almost past endurance when she heard behind her back—(she dared not turn round)—her companion's low growls and imprecations. She expected anything now, and when he came and sat by her she was frozen with terror: what eccentricity would he commit next? She would gladly have sunk into the ground fathoms down. She drew back instinctively: she was afraid of touching him.

But all her fears vanished when the interval came and she heard him say quite kindly:

"I am an unpleasant companion, eh? I beg your pardon."

Then she looked at him and saw his kind smile which had induced her to come with him.

He went on:

"I cannot hide what I think. . . . But you know it is too much! . . . That woman, that old woman! . . ."

He made a face of disgust.

She smiled and said in a low voice:

"It is fine in spite of everything."

He noticed her accent and asked:

"You are a foreigner?"

"Yes," said she.

He looked at her modest gown.

"A governess?" he said.

"Yes."

"What nationality?"

She said:

"I am French."

He made a gesture of surprise:

"French? I should not have thought it."

"Why?" she asked timidly.

"You are so . . . serious!" said he.

(She thought it was not altogether a compliment from him.)

"There are serious people also in France," said she confusedly.

He looked at her honest little face, with its broad forehead, little straight nose, delicate chin, and thin cheeks framed in her chestnut hair. It was not she that he saw: he was thinking of the beautiful actress. He repeated:

"It is strange that you should be French! . . . Are you really of the same nationality as Ophelia? One would never think it."

After a moment's silence he went on:

"How beautiful she is!" without noticing that he seemed to be making a comparison between the actress and his companion that was not at all flattering to her. But she felt it: but she did not mind: for she was of the same opinion. He tried to find out about the actress from her: but she knew nothing: it was plain that she did not know much about the theater.

"You must be glad to hear French?" he asked. He meant it in jest, but he touched her.

"Ah!" she said with an accent of sincerity which struck him, "it does me so much good! I am stifled here."

He looked at her more closely: she clasped her hands, and seemed to be oppressed. But at once she thought of how her words might hurt him:

"Forgive me," she said. "I don't know what I am saying."

He laughed:

"Don't beg pardon! You are quite right. You don't need to be French to be stifled here. Ouf!"

He threw back his shoulders and took a long breath.

But she was ashamed of having been so free and relapsed into silence. Besides she had just seen that the people in the boxes next to them were listening to what they were saying: he noticed it too and was wrathful. They broke off: and until the end of the interval he went out into the corridor. The girl's words were ringing in his ears, but he was lost in dreams: the image of Ophelia filled his thoughts. During the succeeding acts she took hold of him completely, and when the beautiful actress came to the mad scene and the melancholy songs of

love and death, her voice gave forth notes so moving that he
was bowled over: he felt that he was going to burst into tears.
Angry with himself for what he took to be a sign of weakness—
(for he would not admit that a true artist can weep)—and
not wishing to make an object of himself, he left the box
abruptly. The corridors and the foyer were empty. In his
agitation he went down the stairs of the theater and went out
without knowing it. He had to breathe the cold night air,
and to go striding through the dark, half-empty streets. He
came to himself by the edge of a canal, and leaned on the parapet of the bank and watched the silent water whereon the reflections of the street lamps danced in the darkness. His soul
was like that: it was dark and heaving: he could see nothing
in it but great joy dancing on the surface. The clocks rang
the hour. It was impossible for him to go back to the theater
and hear the end of the play. To see the triumph of Fortin-
bras? No, that did not tempt him. A fine triumph that!
Who thinks of envying the conqueror? Who would be he after
being gorged with all the wild and absurd savagery of life?
The whole play is a formidable indictment of life. But there
is such a power of life in it that sadness becomes joy, and
bitterness intoxicates. . . .

Christophe went home without a thought for the unknown
girl, whose name even he had not ascertained.

Next morning he went to see the actress at the little third-
rate hotel in which the impresario had quartered her with her
comrades while the great actress had put up at the best hotel
in the town. He was conducted to a very untidy room where
the remains of breakfast were left on an open piano, together
with hairpins and torn and dirty sheets of music. In the next
room Ophelia was singing at the top of her voice, like a child,
for the pleasure of making a noise. She stopped for a moment
when her visitor was announced to ask merrily in a loud voice
without ever caring whether she were heard through the wall:
"What does he want? What is his name? Christophe?
Christophe what? Christophe Krafft? What a name!"
(She repeated it two or three times, rolling her *r*'s terribly.)
"It is like a swear——"

(She swore.)

"Is he young or old? Pleasant? Very well. I'll come."
She began to sing again:

"Nothing is sweeter than my love . . ." while she rushed about her room cursing a tortoise-shell pin which had got lost in all the rubbish. She lost patience, began to grumble, and roared. Although he could not see her Christophe followed all her movements on the other side of the wall in imagination and laughed to himself. At last he heard steps approaching, the door was flung open, and Ophelia appeared.

She was half dressed, in a loose gown which she was holding about her waist: her bare arms showed in her wide sleeves; her hair was carelessly done, and locks of it fell down into her eyes and over her cheeks. Her fine brown eyes smiled, her lips smiled, her cheeks smiled, and a charming dimple in her chin smiled. In her beautiful grave melodious voice she asked him to excuse her appearance. She knew that there was nothing to excuse and that he could only be very grateful to her for it. She thought he was a journalist come to interview her. Instead of being annoyed when he told her that he had come to her entirely of his own accord and because he admired her, she was delighted. She was a good girl, affectionate, delighted to please, and making no effort to conceal her delight. Christophe's visit and his enthusiasm made her very happy—(she was not yet spoiled by flattery). She was so natural in all her movements and ways, even in her little vanities and her naïve delight in giving pleasure, that he was not embarrassed for a single moment. They became old friends at once. He could jabber a few words of French: and she could jabber a few words of German: after an hour they told each other all their secrets. She never thought of sending him away. The splendid gay southern creature, intelligent and warm-hearted, who would have been bored to tears with her stupid companions and in a country whose language she did not know, a country without the natural joy that was in herself, was glad to find some one to talk to. As for Christophe it was an untold blessing for him to meet the free-hearted girl of the Midi filled with the life of the people, in the midst of his narrow and insincere fellow citizens. He did not yet know the workings of such natures which, unlike the Germans, have no more in their minds and hearts than they show, and often not even as much. But at the least she was young, she was alive, she said frankly, rawly, what she thought: she judged everything freely from a new and a fresh point of view: in her it was possible to breathe a little of the northwest wind that sweeps away mists. She was gifted. Uneducated and unthinking, she could at once feel with her whole heart and be sincerely moved by things which were beautiful and good; and then, a moment later, she would burst out laughing. She was a coquette and made eyes; she did not mind showing her bare arms and neck under her half open gown; she would have liked to turn Christophe's head, but it was all purely instinctive. There was no thought of gaining her own ends in her, and she much preferred to laugh, and talk blithely, to be a good fellow, a good chum, without ceremony or awkwardness. She told him about the under-world of the theater, her little sorrows, the silly susceptibilities of her comrades, the bickerings of Jezebel—(so she called the great actress)—who took good care not to let her shine. He confided his sufferings at the hands of the Germans: she clapped her hands and played chords to him. She was kind and would not speak ill of anybody; but that did not keep her from doing so, and while she blamed herself for her malice, when she laughed at anybody, she had a fund of mocking humor and that realistic and witty gift of observation which belongs to the people of the South; she could not resist it and drew cuttingly satirical portraits. With her pale lips she laughed merrily to show her teeth, like those of a puppy, and dark eyes shone in her pale face, which was a little discolored by grease paint.

They noticed suddenly that they had been talking for more than an hour. Christophe proposed to come for Corinne—(that was her stage name)—in the afternoon and show her over the town. She was delighted with the idea, and they arranged to meet immediately after dinner.

At the appointed hour, he turned up. Corinne was sitting in the little drawing-room of the hotel, with a book in her hand, which she was reading aloud. She greeted him with smiling eyes but did not stop reading until she had finished her sentence. Then she signed to him to sit down on the sofa by her side:

"Sit there," she said, "and don't talk. I am going over my part. I shall have finished in a quarter of an hour."

She followed the script with her finger nail and read very quickly and carelessly like a little girl in a hurry. He offered to hear her her words. She passed him the book and got up to repeat what she had learned. She floundered and would repeat the end of one sentence four times before going on to the next. She shook her head as she recited her part; her hairpins fell down and all over the room. When she could not recollect sometimes some word she was as impatient as a naughty child; sometimes she swore comically or she would use big words—one word with which she apostrophized herself was very big and very short. Christophe was astonished by the mixture of talent and childishness in her. She would produce moving tones of voice quite aptly, but in the middle of a speech into which she seemed to be throwing her whole heart she would say a whole string of words that had absolutely no meaning. She recited her lesson like a parrot, without troubling about its meaning, and then she produced burlesque nonsense. She did not worry about it. When she saw it she would shout with laughter. At last she said: "Zut!", snatched the book from him, flung it into a corner of the room, and said:

"Holidays! The hour has struck! . . . Now let us go out."

He was a little anxious about her part and asked:

"You think you will know it?"

She replied confidently:

"Certainly. What is the prompter for?" She went into her room to put on her hat. Christophe sat at the piano while he was waiting for her and struck a few chords. From the next room she called:

"Oh! What is that? Play some more! How pretty it is!"

She ran in, pinning on her hat. He went on. When he had finished she wanted him to play more. She went into ecstasies with all the little arch exclamations habitual to Frenchwomen which they make about *Tristan* and a cup of chocolate equally. It made Christophe laugh; it was a change from the tremendous

affected, clumsy exclamations of the Germans; they were both
exaggerated in different directions; one made a mountain out
of a mole-hill, the other made a mole-hill out of a mountain;
the French was not less ridiculous than the German, but for
the moment it seemed more pleasant because he loved the lips
from which it came. Corinne wanted to know what he was
playing, and when she learned that he had composed it she
gave a shout. He had told her during their conversation in
the morning that he was a composer, but she had hardly
listened to him. She sat by him and insisted on his playing
everything that he had composed. Their walk was forgotten.
It was not mere politeness on her part; she adored music and
had an admirable instinct for it which supplied the deficiencies
of her education. At first he did not take her seriously and
played his easiest melodies. But when he had played a passage
by which he set more store and saw that she preferred it too,
although he had not said anything about it, he was joyfully
surprised. With the naïve astonishment of the Germans when
they meet a Frenchman who is a good musician he said:
"Odd. How good your taste is! I should never have thought
it . . ."
Corinne laughed in his face.
He amused himself then by selecting compositions more and
more difficult to understand, to see how far she would go
with him. But she did not seem to be put out by his boldness,
and after a particularly new melody which Christophe himself
had almost come to doubt because he had never succeeded in
having it accepted in Germany, he was greatly astonished when
Corinne begged him to play it again, and she got up and began
to sing the notes from memory almost without a mistake! He
turned towards her and took her hands warmly:
"But you are a musician!" he cried.
She began to laugh and explained that she had made her
début as a singer in provincial opera houses, but that an impresario of touring companies had recognized her disposition
towards the poetic theater and had enrolled her in its services.
He exclaimed:
"What a pity!"

"Why?" said she. "Poetry also is a sort of music."

She made him explain to her the meaning of his *Lieder;* he told her the German words, and she repeated them with easy mimicry, copying even the movements of his lips and eyes as he pronounced the words. When she had these to sing from memory, then she made grotesque mistakes, and when she forgot, she invented words, guttural and barbarously sonorous, which made them both laugh. She did not tire of making him play, nor he of playing for her and hearing her pretty voice; she did not know the tricks of the trade and sang a little from the throat like little girls, and there was a curious fragile quality in her voice that was very touching. She told him frankly what she thought. Although she could not explain why she liked or disliked anything there was always some grain of sense hidden in her judgment. The odd thing was that she found least pleasure in the most classical passages which were most appreciated in Germany; she paid him a few compliments out of politeness; but they obviously meant nothing. As she had no musical culture she had not the pleasure which amateurs and even artists find in what is *already heard,* a pleasure which often makes them unconsciously reproduce, or, in a new composition, like forms or formulæ which they have already used in old compositions. Nor did she have the German taste for melodious sentimentality (or, at least, her sentimentality was different; Christophe did not yet know its failings)—she did not go into ecstasies over the soft insipid music preferred in Germany; she did not single out the most melodious of his *Lieder,*—a melody which he would have liked to destroy because his friends, only too glad to be able to compliment him on something, were always talking about it. Corinne's dramatic instinct made her prefer the melodies which frankly reproduced a certain passion; he also set most store by them. And yet she did not hesitate to show her lack of sympathy with certain rude harmonies which seemed quite natural to Christophe; they gave her a sort of shock when she came upon them; she would stop then and ask " if it was really so." When he said "Yes," then she would rush at the difficulty; but she would make a little grimace which did not escape Christophe. Sometimes even she would prefer to skip the bar. Then he would play it again on the piano.

"You don't like that?" he would ask.

She would screw up her nose.

"It is wrong," she would say.

"Not at all," he would reply with a laugh. "It is quite right. Think of its meaning. It is rhymthic, isn't it?"

(He pointed to her heart.)

But she would shake her head:

"May be; but it is wrong here." (She pulled her ear.)

And she would be a little shocked by the sudden outbursts of German declamation.

"Why should he talk so loud?" she would ask. "He is all alone. Aren't you afraid of his neighbors overhearing him? It is as though—(Forgive me! You won't be angry?)—he were hailing a boat."

He was not angry; he laughed heartily, he recognized that there was some truth in what she said. Her remarks amused him; nobody had ever said such things before. They agreed that declamation in singing generally deforms the natural word like a magnifying glass. Corinne asked Christophe to write music for a piece in which she would speak to the accompaniment of the orchestra, singing a few sentences every now and then. He was fired by the idea in spite of the difficulties of the stage setting which, he thought, Corinne's musical voice would easily overcome, and they made plans for the future. It was not far short of five o'clock when they thought of going out. Night fell early. They could not think of going for a walk. Corinne had a rehearsal at the theater in the evening; nobody was allowed to be present. She made him promise to come and fetch her during the next afternoon to take the walk they had planned.

Next day they did almost the same again. He found Corinne in front of her mirror, perched on a high stool, swinging her legs; she was trying on a wig. Her dresser was there and a hair dresser of the town to whom she was giving instructions about a curl which she wished to have higher up. As she looked in the glass she saw Christophe smiling behind her back; she put out her tongue at him. The hair dresser went away with the wig and she turned gaily to Christophe:

"Good-day, my friend!" she said.

She held up her cheek to be kissed. He had not expected such intimacy, but he took advantage of it all the same. She did not attach so much importance to the favor; it was to her a greeting like any other.

"Oh! I am happy!" said she. "It will do very well to-night." (She was talking of her wig.) "I was so wretched! If you had come this morning you would have found me absolutely miserable."

He asked why.

It was because the Parisian hair dresser had made a mistake in packing and had sent a wig which was not suitable to the part.

"Quite flat," she said, "and falling straight down. When I saw it I wept like a Magdalen. Didn't I, Désirée?"

"When I came in," said Désirée, "I was afraid for Madame. Madame was quite white. Madame looked like death."

Christophe laughed. Corinne saw him in her mirror:

"Heartless wretch; it makes you laugh," she said indignantly.

She began to laugh too.

He asked her how the rehearsal had gone. Everything had gone off well. She would have liked the other parts to be cut more and her own less. They talked so much that they wasted part of the afternoon. She dressed slowly; she amused herself by asking Christophe's opinion about her dresses. Christophe praised her elegance and told her naïvely in his Franco-German jargon, that he had never seen anybody so "luxurious." She looked at him for a moment and then burst out laughing.

"What have I said?" he asked. "Have I said anything wrong?"

"Yes, yes," she cried, rocking with laughter. "You have indeed."

At last they went out. Her striking costume and her exuberant chatter attracted attention. She looked at everything with her mocking eyes and made no effort to conceal her impressions. She chuckled at the dressmakers' shops, and at the picture post-card shops in which sentimental scenes, comic and obscene drawings, the town prostitutes, the imperial family, the Emperor as a sea-dog holding the wheel of the *Germania* and defying the heavens, were all thrown together higgledy-piggledy. She giggled at a dinner-service decoration with Wagner's cross-grained face, or at a hair dresser's shop-window in which there was the wax head of a man. She made no attempt to modify her hilarity over the patriotic monument representing the old Emperor in a traveling coat and a peaked cap, together with Prussia, the German States, and a nude Genius of War. She made remarks about anything in the faces of the people or their way of speaking that struck her as funny. Her victims were left in no doubt about it as she maliciously picked out their absurdities. Her instinctive mimicry made her sometimes imitate with her mouth and nose their broad grimaces and frowns, without thinking; and she would blow out her cheeks as she repeated fragments of sentences and words that struck her as grotesque in sound as she caught them. He laughed heartily and was not at all embarrassed by her impertinence, for he was no longer easily embarrassed. Fortunately he had no great reputation to lose, or his walk would have ruined it for ever.

They visited the cathedral. Corinne wanted to go to the top of the spire, in spite of her high heels, and long dress which swept the stairs or was caught in a corner of the staircase; she did not worry about it, but pulled the stuff which split, and went on climbing, holding it up. She wanted very much to ring the bells. From the top of the tower she declaimed Victor Hugo (he did not understand it), and sang a popular French song. After that she played the muezzin. Dusk was falling. They went down into the cathedral where the dark shadows were creeping along the gigantic walls in which the magic eyes of the windows were shining. Kneeling in one of the side chapels, Christophe saw the girl who had shared his box at *Hamlet*. She was so absorbed in her prayers that she did not see him: he saw that she was looking sad and strained. He would have liked to speak to her, just to say, " How do you do? " but Corinne dragged him off like a whirlwind.

They parted soon afterwards. She had to get ready for the performance, which began early, as usual in Germany. He had hardly reached home when there was a ring at the door and a letter from Corinne was handed in:

"Luck! Jezebel ill! No performance! No school! Come! Let us dine together!   Your friend,
                                                  "CORINETTE.
"P. S. Bring plenty of music!"

It was some time before he understood. When he did understand he was as happy as Corinne, and went to the hotel at once. He was afraid of finding the whole company assembled at dinner; but he saw nobody. Corinne herself was not there. At last he heard her laughing voice at the back of the house: he went to look for her and found her in the kitchen. She had taken it into her head to cook a dish in her own way, one of those southern dishes which fills the whole neighborhood with its aroma and would awaken a stone. She was on excellent terms with the large proprietress of the hotel, and they were jabbering in a horrible jargon that was a mixture of German, French, and negro, though there is no word to describe it in any language. They were laughing loudly and making each other taste their cooking. Christophe's appearance made them noisier than ever. They tried to push him out; but he struggled and succeeded in tasting the famous dish. He made a face. She said he was a barbarous Teuton and that it was no use putting herself out for him.

They went up to the little sitting-room when the table was laid; there were only two places, for himself and Corinne. He could not help asking her where her companions were. Corinne waved her hands carelessly:

"I don't know."

"Don't you sup together?"

"Never! We see enough of each other at the theater! . . . And it would be awful if we had to meet at meals! . . ."

It was so different from German custom that he was surprised and charmed by it.

"I thought," he said, "you were a sociable people!"

"Well," said she, "am I not sociable?"

"Sociable means living in society. We have to see each

other! Men, women, children, we all belong to societies from
birth to death. We are always making societies: we eat, sing,
think in societies. When the societies sneeze, we sneeze too:
we don't have a drink except with our societies."

"That must be amusing," said she. "Why not out of the
same glass?"

"Brotherly, isn't it?"

"That for fraternity! I like being 'brotherly' with people
I like: not with the others . . . Pooh! That's not society:
that is an ant heap."

"Well, you can imagine how happy I am here, for I think
as you do."

"Come to us, then!"

He asked nothing better. He questioned her about Paris
and the French. She told him much that was not perfectly
accurate. Her southern propensity for boasting was mixed
with an instinctive desire to shine before him. According to
her, everybody in Paris was free: and as everybody in Paris
was intelligent, everybody made good use of their liberty, and
no one abused it. Everybody did what they liked: thought,
believed, loved or did not love, as they liked; nobody had anything to say about it. There nobody meddled with other people's
beliefs, or spied on their consciences or tried to regulate their
thoughts. There politicians never dabbled in literature or the
arts, and never gave orders, jobs, and money to their friends
or clients. There little cliques never disposed of reputation or
success, journalists were never bought; there men of letters
never entered into controversies with the church, that could lead
to nothing. There criticism never stifled unknown talent, or
exhausted its praises upon recognized talent. There success, success at all costs, did not justify the means,
and command the adoration of the public. There were only
gentle manners, kindly and sweet. There was never any bitterness, never any scandal. Everybody helped everybody else.
Every worthy newcomer was certain to find hands held out to
him and the way made smooth for him. Pure love of beauty
filled the chivalrous and disinterested souls of the French, and
they were only absurd in their idealism, which, in spite of their
acknowledged wit, made them the dupes of other nations.

Christophe listened open-mouthed. It was certainly marvelous. Corinne marveled herself as she heard her words. She had forgotten what she had told Christophe the day before about the difficulties of her past life. He gave no more thought to it than she.

And yet Corinne was not only concerned with making the Germans love her country: she wanted to make herself loved, too. A whole evening without flirtation would have seemed austere and rather absurd to her. She made eyes at Christophe; but it was trouble wasted: he did not notice it. Christophe did not know what it was to flirt. He loved or did not love. When he did not love he was miles from any thought of love. He liked Corinne enormously. He felt the attraction of her southern nature; it was so new to him. And her sweetness and good humor, her quick and lively intelligence: many more reasons than he needed for loving. But the spirit blows where it listeth. It did not blow in that direction, and as for playing at love, in love's absence, the idea had never occurred to him.

Corinne was amused by his coldness. She sat by his side at the piano while he played the music he had brought with him, and put her arm round his neck, and to follow the music she leaned towards the keyboard, almost pressing her cheek against his. He felt her hair touch his face, and quite close to him saw the corner of her mocking eye, her pretty little mouth, and the light down on her tip-tilted nose. She waited, smiling—she waited. Christophe did not understand the invitation. Corinne was in his way: that was all he thought of. Mechanically he broke free from her and moved his chair. And when, a moment later, he turned to speak to Corinne, he saw that she was choking with laughter: her cheeks were dimpled, her lips were pressed together, and she seemed to be holding herself in.

"What is the matter?" he said, in his astonishment.

She looked at him and laughed aloud.

He did not understand.

"Why are you laughing?" he asked. "Did I say anything funny?"

The more he insisted, the more she laughed. When she

had almost finished she had only to look at his crestfallen appearance to break out again. She got up, ran to the sofa at
the other end of the room, and buried her face in the cushions
to laugh her fill; her whole body shook with it. He began to
laugh too, came towards her, and slapped her on the back.
When she had done laughing she raised her head, dried the
tears in her eyes, and held out her hands to him.

"What a good boy you are!" she said.

"No worse than another."

She went on, shaking occasionally with laughter, still holding his hands.

"Frenchwomen are not serious?" she asked. (She pronounced it: "*Françouése.*")

"You are making fun of me," he said good-humoredly.

She looked at him kindly, shook his hands vigorously, and
said:

"Friends?"

"Friends!" said he, shaking her hand.

"You will think of Corinette when she is gone? You won't
be angry with the Frenchwoman for not being serious?"

"And Corinette won't be angry with the barbarous Teuton
for being so stupid?"

"That is why she loves him. . . . You will come and see
her in Paris?"

"It is a promise. . . . And she—she will write to him?"

"I swear it. . . . You say: 'I swear.'"

"I swear."

"No, not like that. You must hold up your hand." She
recited the oath of the Horatii. She made him promise to
write a play for her, a melodrama, which could be translated
into French and played in Paris by her. She was going away
next day with her company. He promised to go and see her
again the day after at Frankfort, where they were giving a
performance.

They stayed talking for some time. She presented Christophe with a photograph in which she was much décolletée,
draped only in a garment fastening below her shoulders. They
parted gaily, and kissed like brother and sister. And, indeed,
once Corinne had seen that Christophe was fond of her, but

not at all in love, she began to be fond of him, too, without love, as a good friend.

Their sleep was not troubled by it. He could not see her off next day, because he was occupied by a rehearsal. But on the day following he managed to go to Frankfort as he had promised. It was a few hours' journey by rail. Corinne hardly believed Christophe's promise. But he had taken it seriously, and when the performance began he was there. When he knocked at her dressing-room door during the interval, she gave a cry of glad surprise and threw her arms round his neck with her usual exuberance. She was sincerely grateful to him for having come. Unfortunately for Christophe, she was much more sought after in the city of rich, intelligent Jews, who could appreciate her actual beauty and her future success. Almost every minute there was a knock at the door, and it opened to reveal men with heavy faces and quick eyes, who said the conventional things with a thick accent. Corinne naturally made eyes, and then she would go on talking to Christophe in the same affected, provoking voice, and that irritated him. And he found no pleasure in the calm lack of modesty with which she went on dressing in his presence, and the paint and grease with which she larded her arms, throat, and face filled him with profound disgust. He was on the point of going away without seeing her again after the performance; but when he said good-bye and begged to be excused from going to the supper that was to be given to her after the play, she was so hurt by it and so affectionate, too, that he could not hold out against her. She had a time-table brought, so as to prove that he could and must stay an hour with her. He only needed to be convinced, and he was at the supper. He was even able to control his annoyance with the follies that were indulged in and his irritation at Corinne's coquetries with all and sundry. It was impossible to be angry with her. She was an honest girl, without any moral principles, lazy, sensual, pleasure-loving, childishly coquettish; but at the same time so loyal, so kind, and all her faults were so spontaneous and so healthy that it was only possible to smile at them and even to love them. Christophe, who was sitting opposite her, watched her animation, her radiant eyes, her sticky lips, with their Italian smile—that smile in which there is kindness, subtlety, and a sort of heavy greediness. He saw her more clearly than he had yet done. Some of her features reminded him of Ada: certain gestures, certain looks, certain sensual and rather coarse tricks—the eternal feminine. But what he loved in her was her southern nature, that generous nature which is not niggardly with its gifts, which never troubles to fashion drawing-room beauties and literary cleverness, but harmonious creatures who are made body and mind to grow in the air and the sun. When he left she got up from the table to say good-bye to him away from the others. They kissed and renewed their promises to write and meet again.

He took the last train home. At a station the train coming from the opposite direction was waiting. In the carriage opposite his—a third-class compartment—Christophe saw the young Frenchwoman who had been with him to the performance of *Hamlet*. She saw Christophe and recognized him. They were both astonished. They bowed and did not move, and dared not look again. And yet he had seen at once that she was wearing a little traveling toque and had an old valise by her side. It did not occur to him that she was leaving the country. He thought she must be going away for a few days. He did not know whether he ought to speak to her. He stopped, turned over in his mind what to say, and was just about to lower the window of the carriage to address a few words to her, when the signal was given. He gave up the idea. A few seconds passed before the train moved. They looked straight at each other. Each was alone, and their faces were pressed against the windows and they looked into each other's eyes through the night. They were separated by two windows. If they had reached out their hands they could have touched each other. So near. So far. The carriages shook heavily. She was still looking at him, shy no longer, now that they were parting. They were so absorbed in looking at each other that they never even thought of bowing for the last time. She was slowly borne away. He saw her disappear, and the train which bore her plunged into the night. Like two circling worlds, they had passed close to each other in infinite space, and now they sped apart perhaps for eternity.

When she had disappeared he felt the emptiness that her strange eyes had left in him, and he did not understand why; but the emptiness was there. Sleepy, with eyes half-closed, lying in a corner of the carriage, he felt her eyes looking into his, and all other thoughts ceased, to let him feel them more keenly. The image of Corinne fluttered outside his heart like an insect breaking its wings against a window; but he did not let it in.

He found it again when he got out of the train on his arrival, when the keen night air and his walk through the streets of the sleeping town had shaken off his drowsiness. He scowled at the thought of the pretty actress, with a mixture of pleasure and irritation, according as he recalled her affectionate ways or her vulgar coquetries.

"Oh! these French people," he growled, laughing softly, while he was undressing quietly, so as not to waken his mother, who was asleep in the next room.

A remark that he had heard the other evening in the box occurred to him:

"There are others also."

At his first encounter with France she laid before him the enigma of her double nature. But, like all Germans, he did not trouble to solve it, and as he thought of the girl in the train he said quietly:

"She does not look like a Frenchwoman."

As if a German could say what is French and what is not.

French or not, she filled his thoughts; for he woke in the middle of the night with a pang: he had just remembered the valise on the seat by the girl's side; and suddenly the idea that she had gone forever crossed his mind. The idea must have come to him at the time, but he had not thought of it. It filled him with a strange sadness. He shrugged his shoulders.

"What does it matter to me?" he said. "It is not my affair."

He went to sleep.

But next day the first person he met when he went out was Mannheim, who called him "Blücher," and asked him if he had made up his mind to conquer all France. From the garrulous newsmonger he learned that the story of the box had had a success exceeding all Mannheim's expectations.

"Thanks to you! Thanks to you!" cried Mannheim. "You are a great man. I am nothing compared with you."

"What have I done?" said Christophe.

"You are wonderful!" Mannheim replied. "I am jealous of you. To shut the box in the Grünebaums' faces, and then to ask the French governess instead of them—no, that takes the cake! I should never have thought of that!"

"She was the Grünebaums' governess?" said Christophe in amazement.

"Yes. Pretend you don't know, pretend to be innocent. You'd better! . . . My father is beside himself. The Grünebaums are in a rage! . . . It was not for long: they have sacked the girl."

"What!" cried Christophe. "They have dismissed her? Dismissed her because of me?"

"Didn't you know?" said Mannheim. "Didn't she tell you?"

Christophe was in despair.

"You mustn't be angry, old man," said Mannheim. "It does not matter. Besides, one had only to expect that the Grünebaums would find out . . ."

"What?" cried Christophe. "Find out what?"

"That she was your mistress, of course!"

"But I do not even know her. I don't know who she is."

Mannheim smiled, as if to say:

"You take me for a fool."

Christophe lost his temper and bade Mannheim do him the honor of believing what he said. Mannheim said:

"Then it is even more humorous."

Christophe worried about it, and talked of going to the Grünebaums and telling them the facts and justifying the girl. Mannheim dissuaded him.

"My dear fellow," he said, "anything you may say will only convince them of the contrary. Besides, it is too late. The girl has gone away."

Christophe was utterly sick at heart and tried to trace the

young Frenchwoman. He wanted to write to her to beg her
pardon. But nothing was known of her. He applied to the
Grünebaums, but they snubbed him. They did not know
themselves where she had gone, and they did not care. The
idea of the harm he had done in trying to do good tortured
Christophe: he was remorseful. But added to his remorse
was a mysterious attraction, which shone upon him from the
eyes of the woman who was gone. Attraction and remorse
both seemed to be blotted out, engulfed in the flood of the
day's new thoughts. But they endured in the depths of his
heart. Christophe did not forget the woman whom he called
his victim. He had sworn to meet her again. He knew how
small were the chances of his ever seeing her again: and he
was sure that he would see her again.

As for Corinne, she never answered his letters. But three
months later, when he had given up expecting to hear from
her, he received a telegram of forty words of utter nonsense,
in which she addressed him in little familiar terms, and
asked " if they were still fond of each other." Then, after
nearly a year's silence, there came a scrappy letter scrawled in
her enormous childish zigzag writing, in which she tried to
play the lady.—a few affectionate, droll words. And there
she left it. She did not forget him, but she had no time
to think of him.

Still under the spell of Corinne and full of the ideas they
had exchanged about art, Christophe dreamed of writing the
music for a play in which Corinne should act and sing a few
airs—a sort of poetic melodrama. That form of art once so
much in favor in Germany, passionately admired by Mozart,
and practised by Beethoven, Weber, Mendelssohn and Schumann, and all the great classics, had fallen into discredit
since the triumph of Wagnerism, which claimed to have realized
the definite formula of the theater and music. The Wagnerian
pedants, not content with proscribing every new melodrama,
busied themselves with dressing up the old melodramas and
operas. They carefully effaced every trace of spoken dialogue and
wrote for Mozart, Beethoven, or Weber, recitations in their own
manner; they were convinced that they were doing a service to

the fame of the masters and filling out their thoughts by the pious deposit of their dung upon masterpieces.

Christophe, who had been made more sensible of the heaviness, and often the ugliness, of Wagnerian declamation by Corinne, had for some time been debating whether it was not nonsense and an offense against nature to harness and yoke together the spoken word and the word sung in the theater: it was like harnessing a horse and a bird to a cart. Speech and singing each had its rhythm. It was comprehensible that an artist should sacrifice one of the two arts to the triumph of that which he preferred. But to try to find a compromise between them was to sacrifice both: it was to want speech no longer to be speech, and singing no longer to be singing; to want singing to let its vast flood be confined between the banks of monotonous canals, to want speech to cloak its lovely naked limbs with rich, heavy stuffs which must paralyze its gestures and movements. Why not leave both with their spontaneity and freedom of movement? Like a beautiful girl walking tranquilly, lithely along a stream, dreaming as she goes: the gay murmur of the water lulls her dreams, and unconsciously she brings her steps and her thoughts in tune with the song of the stream. So being both free, music and poesy would go side by side, dreaming, their dreams mingling. Assuredly all music was not good for such a union, nor all poetry. The opponents of melodrama had good ground for attack in the coarseness of the attempts which had been made in that form, and of the interpreters. Christophe had for long shared their dislike: the stupidity of the actors who delivered these recitations spoken to an instrumental accompaniment, without bothering about the accompaniment, without trying to merge their voices in it, rather, on the contrary, trying to prevent anything being heard but themselves, was calculated to revolt any musical ear. But since he had tasted the beauty of Corinne's harmonious voice—that liquid and pure voice which played upon music like a ray of light on water, which wedded every turn of a melody, which was like the most fluid and most free singing,—he had caught a glimpse of the beauty of a new art.

Perhaps he was right, but he was still too inexperienced to venture without peril upon a form which—if it is meant to

be beautiful and really artistic—is the most difficult of all.
That art especially demands one essential condition, the perfect harmony of the combined efforts of the poet, the musicians,
and the actors. Christophe had no tremors about it: he
hurled himself blindly at an unknown art of which the laws
were only known to himself.

His first idea had been to clothe in music a fairy fantasy of
Shakespeare or an act of the second part of *Faust*. But the
theaters showed little disposition to make the experiment. It
would be too costly and appeared absurd. They were quite
willing to admit Christophe's efficiency in music, but that he
should take upon himself to have ideas about poetry and the
theater made them smile. They did not take him seriously.
The world of music and the world of poesy were like two foreign and secretly hostile states. Christophe had to accept the
collaboration of a poet to be able to set foot upon poetic territory, and he was not allowed to choose his own poet. He
would not have dared to choose himself. He did not trust his
taste in poetry. He had been told that he knew nothing about
it; and, indeed, he could not understand the poetry which was
admired by those about him. With his usual honesty and
stubbornness, he had tried hard sometimes to feel the beauty of
some of these works, but he had always been bewildered and a
little ashamed of himself. No, decidedly he was not a poet.
In truth, he loved passionately certain old poets, and that
consoled him a little. But no doubt he did not love them as
they should be loved. Had he not once expressed the ridiculous idea that those poets only are great who remain great even
when they are translated into prose, and even into the prose
of a foreign language, and that words have no value apart
from the soul which they express? His friends had laughed
at him. Mannheim had called him a goose. He did not try
to defend himself. As every day he saw, through the example
of writers who talk of music, the absurdity of artists who
attempt to image any art other than their own, he resigned
himself—though a little incredulous at heart—to his incom-
petence in poetry, and he shut his eyes and accepted the judgments of those whom he thought were better informed than
himself. So he let his friends of the Review impose one of

their number on him, a great man of a decadent coterie, Stephen von Hellmuth, who brought him an *Iphigenia*. It was at the time when German poets (like their colleagues in France) were recasting all the Greek tragedies. Stephen von Hellmuth's work was one of those astounding Græco-German plays in which Ibsen, Homer, and Oscar Wilde are compounded —and, of course, a few manuals of archæology. Agamemnon was neurasthenic and Achilles impotent: they lamented their condition at length, and naturally their outcries produced no change. The energy of the drama was concentrated in the rôle of Iphigenia—a nervous, hysterical, and pedantic Iphigenia, who lectured the hero, declaimed furiously, laid bare for the audience her Nietzschian pessimism and, glutted with death, cut her throat, shrieking with laughter.

Nothing could be more contrary to Christophe's mind than such pretentious, degenerate, Ostrogothic stuff, in Greek dress. It was hailed as a masterpiece by everybody about him. He was cowardly and was overpersuaded. In truth, he was bursting with music and thinking much more of his music than of the text. The text was a new bed into which to let loose the flood of his passions. He was as far as possible from the state of abnegation and intelligent impersonality proper to musical translation of a poetic work. He was thinking only of himself and not at all of the work. He never thought of adapting himself to it. He was under an illusion: he saw in the poem something absolutely different from what was actually in it—just as when he was a child he used to compose in his mind a play entirely different from that which was upon the stage.

It was not until it came to rehearsal that he saw the real play. One day he was listening to a scene, and he thought it so stupid that he fancied the actors must be spoiling it, and went so far as to explain it to them in the poet's presence; but also to explain it to the poet himself, who was defending his interpretation. The author refused bluntly to hear him, and said with some asperity that he thought he knew what he had meant to write. Christophe would not give in, and maintained that Hellmuth knew nothing about it. The general merriment told him that he was making himself ridiculous. He said no

more, agreeing that after all it was not he who had written
the poem. Then he saw the appalling emptiness of the play
and was overwhelmed by it: he wondered how he could ever
have been persuaded to try it. He called himself an idiot and
tore his hair. He tried in vain to reassure himself by saying:
" You know nothing about it; it is not your business. Keep
to your music." He was so much ashamed of certain idiotic
things in it, of the pretentious pathos, the crying falsity of
the words, the gestures and attitudes, that sometimes, when
he was conducting the orchestra, he hardly had the strength to
raise his bâton. He wanted to go and hide in the prompter's
box. He was too frank and too little politic to conceal what
he thought. Every one noticed it: his friends, the actors, and
the author. Hellmuth said to him with a frigid smile:
" Is it not fortunate enough to please you? "
Christophe replied honestly:
" Truth to tell, no. I don't understand it."
" Then you did not read it when you set it to music? "
" Yes," said Christophe naïvely, " but I made a mistake. I
understood it differently."
" It is a pity you did not write what you understood yourself."
" Oh! If only I could have done so!" said Christophe.
The poet was vexed, and in his turn criticised the music.
He complained that it was in the way and prevented his words
being heard.
If the poet did not understand the musician or the musician
the poet, the actors understood neither the one nor the other,
and did not care. They were only asking for sentences in their
parts on which to bring in their usual effects. They had no
idea of adapting their declamation to the formality of the piece
and the musical rhythm. They went one way, the music another. It was as though they were constantly singing out of
tune. Christophe ground his teeth and shouted the note at
them until he was hoarse. They let him shout and went on
imperturbably, not even understanding what he wanted them
to do.
Christophe would have flung the whole thing up if the rehearsals had not been so far advanced, and he had not been

bound to go on by fear of legal proceedings. Mannheim, to whom he confided his discouragement, laughed at him:

"What is it?" he asked. "It is all going well. You don't understand each other? What does that matter? Who has ever understood his work but the author? It is a toss-up whether he understands it himself!"

Christophe was worried about the stupidity of the poem, which, he said, would ruin the music. Mannheim made no difficulty about admitting that there was no common sense in the poem and that Hellmuth was "a muff," but he would not worry about him: Hellmuth gave good dinners and had a pretty wife. What more did criticism want?

Christophe shrugged his shoulders and said that he had no time to listen to nonsense.

"It is not nonsense!" said Mannheim, laughing. "How serious people are! They have no idea of what matters in life."

And he advised Christophe not to bother so much about Hellmuth's business, but to attend to his own. He wanted him to advertise a little. Christophe refused indignantly. To a reporter who came and asked for a history of his life, he replied furiously:

"It is not your affair!"

And when they asked for his photograph for a review, he stamped with rage and shouted that he was not, thank God! an emperor, to have his face passed from hand to hand. It was impossible to bring him into touch with influential people. He never replied to invitations, and when he had been forced by any chance to accept, he would forget to go or would go with such a bad grace that he seemed to have set himself to be disagreeable to everybody.

But the climax came when he quarreled with his review, two days before the performance.

The thing was bound to happen. Mannheim had gone on revising Christophe's articles, and he no longer scrupled about deleting whole lines of criticism and replacing them with compliments.

One day, out visiting, Christophe met a certain virtuoso—a

foppish pianist whom he had slaughtered. The man came and
thanked him with a smile that showed all his white teeth.   He
replied brutally that there was no reason for it.   The other
insisted and poured forth expressions of gratitude.   Christophe
cut him short by saying that if he was satisfied with the article
that was his affair, but that the article had certainly not been
written with a view to pleasing him.   And he turned his back
on him.   The virtuoso thought him a kindly boor and went
away laughing.   But Christophe remembered having received a
card of thanks from another of his victims, and a suspicion
flashed upon him.   He went out, bought the last number of the
Review at a news-stand, turned to his article, and read . . .
At first he wondered if he were going mad.   Then he understood, and, mad with rage, he ran to the office of the *Dionysos*.

Waldhaus and Mannheim were there, talking to an actress
whom they knew.   They had no need to ask Christophe what
brought him.   Throwing a number of the Review on the table,
Christophe let fly at them without stopping to take breath, with
extraordinary violence, shouting, calling them rogues, rascals,
forgers, thumping on the floor with a chair.   Mannheim began
to laugh.   Christophe tried to kick him.   Mannheim took
refuge behind the table and rolled with laughter.   But Waldhaus took it very loftily.   With dignity, formally, he tried to
make himself heard through the row, and said that he would
not allow any one to talk to him in such a tone, that Christophe
should hear from him, and he held out his card.   Christophe
flung it in his face.

" Mischief-maker !—I don't need your card to know what
you are. . . .   You are a rascal and a forger ! . . .   And you
think I would fight with you . . . a thrashing is all you deserve ! . . ."

His voice could be heard in the street.   People stopped to
listen.   Mannheim closed the windows.   The actress tried to
escape, but Christophe was blocking the way.   Waldhaus was
pale and choking.   Mannheim was stuttering and stammering
and trying to reply.   Christophe did not let them speak.   He let
loose upon them every expression he could think of, and never
stopped until he was out of breath and had come to an end of
his insults.   Waldhaus and Mannheim only found their tongues

after he had gone. Mannheim quickly recovered himself: insults slipped from him like water from a duck's back. But Waldhaus was still sore: his dignity had been outraged, and what made the affront more mortifying was that there had been witnesses. He would never forgive it. His colleagues joined chorus with him. Mannheim only of the staff of the Review was not angry with Christophe. He had had his fill of entertainment out of him: it did not seem to him a heavy price to pay for his pound of flesh, to suffer a few violent words. It had been a good joke. If he had been the butt of it he would have been the first to laugh. And so he was quite ready to shake hands with Christophe as though nothing had happened. But Christophe was more rancorous and rejected all advances. Mannheim did not care. Christophe was a toy from which he had extracted all the amusement possible. He was beginning to want a new puppet. From that very day all was over between them. But that did not prevent Mannheim still saying, whenever Christophe was mentioned in his presence, that they were intimate friends. And perhaps he thought they were.

Two days after the quarrel the first performance of *Iphigenia* took place. It was an utter failure. Waldhaus' review praised the poem and made no mention of the music. The other papers and reviews made merry over it. They laughed and hissed. The piece was withdrawn after the third performance, but the jokes at its expense did not disappear so quickly. People were only too glad of the opportunity of having a fling at Christophe, and for several weeks the *Iphigenia* remained an unfailing subject for joking. They knew that Christophe had no weapon of defense, and they took advantage of it. The only thing which held them back a little was his position at the Court. Although his relation with the Grand Duke had become quite cold, for the Prince had several times made remarks to which he had paid no attention whatever, he still went to the Palace at intervals, and still enjoyed, in the eye of the public, a sort of official protection, though it was more visionary than real. He took upon himself to destroy even that last support.

He suffered from the criticisms. They were concerned not only with his music, but also with his idea of a new form of art, which the writers did not take the trouble to understand. It was very easy to travesty it and make fun of it. Christophe was not yet wise enough to know that the best reply to dishonest critics is to make none and to go on working. For some months past he had fallen into the bad habit of not letting any unjust attack go unanswered. He wrote an article in which he did not spare certain of his adversaries. The two papers to which he took it returned it with ironically polite excuses for being unable to publish it. Christophe stuck to his guns. He remembered that the socialist paper in the town had made advances to him. He knew one of the editors. They used to meet and talk occasionally. Christophe was glad to find some one who would talk freely about power, the army and oppression and archaic prejudices. But they could not go far with each other, for the socialist always came back to Karl Marx, about whom Christophe cared not a rap. Moreover, Christophe used to find in his speeches about the free man—besides a materialism which was not much to his taste—a pedantic severity and a despotism of thought, a secret cult of force, an inverse militarism, all of which did not sound very different from what he heard every day in German.

However, he thought of this man and his paper when he saw all other doors in journalism closed to him. He knew that his doing so would cause a scandal. The paper was violent, malignant, and always being condemned. But as Christophe never read it, he only thought of the boldness of its ideas, of which he was not afraid, and not of the baseness of its tone, which would have repelled him. Besides, he was so angry at seeing the other papers in alliance to suppress him that perhaps he would have gone on even if he had been warned. He wanted to show people that he was not so easily got rid of. So he took his article to the socialist paper, which received it with open arms. The next day the article appeared, and the paper announced in large letters that it had engaged the support of the young and talented maestro, Jean-Christophe Krafft, whose keen sympathy with the demands of the working classes was well known.

Christophe read neither the note nor the article, for he had gone out before dawn for a walk in the country, it being Sunday. He was in fine fettle. As he saw the sun rise he shouted, laughed, yodeled, leaped, and danced. No more review, no more criticisms to do! It was spring and there was once more the music of the heavens and the earth, the most beautiful of all. No more dark concert rooms, stuffy and smelly, unpleasant people, dull performers. Now the marvelous song of the murmuring forests was to be heard, and over the fields like waves there passed the intoxicating scents of life, breaking through the crust of the earth and issuing from the grave.

He went home with his head buzzing with light and music, and his mother gave him a letter which had been brought from the Palace while he was away. The letter was in an impersonal form, and told Herr Krafft that he was to go to the Palace that morning. The morning was past, it was nearly one o'clock. Christophe was not put about.

"It is too late now," he said. "It will do to-morrow."

But his mother said anxiously:

"No, no. You cannot put off an appointment with His Highness like that: you must go at once. Perhaps it is a matter of importance."

Christophe shrugged his shoulders.

"Important! As if those people could have anything important to say! . . . He wants to tell me his ideas about music. That will be funny! . . . If only he has not taken it into his head to rival Siegfried Meyer[1] and wants to show me a *Hymn to Aegis!* I vow that I will not spare him. I shall say: 'Stick to politics. You are master there. You will always be right. But beware of art! In art you are seen without your plumes, your helmet, your uniform, your money, your titles, your ancestors, your policemen—and just think for a moment what will be left of you then!'"

Poor Louisa took him quite seriously and raised her hands in horror.

"You won't say that! . . . You are mad! Mad!"

It amused him to make her uneasy by playing upon her

[1] A nickname given by German pamphleteers to H. M. (His Majesty) the Emperor.

credulity until he became so extravagant that Louisa began to see that he was making fun of her.

" You are stupid, my boy! "

He laughed and kissed her. He was in a wonderfully good humor. On his walk he had found a beautiful musical theme, and he felt it frolicking in him like a fish in water. He refused to go to the Palace until he had had something to eat. He was as hungry as an ape. Louisa then supervised his dressing, for he was beginning to tease her again, pretending that he was quite all right as he was with his old clothes and dusty boots. But he changed them all the same, and cleaned his boots, whistling like a blackbird and imitating all the instruments in an orchestra. When he had finished his mother inspected him and gravely tied his tie for him again. For once in a way he was very patient, because he was pleased with himself—which was not very usual. He went off saying that he was going to elope with Princess Adelaide—the Grand Duke's daughter, quite a pretty woman, who was married to a German princeling and had come to stay with her parents for a few weeks. She had shown sympathy for Christophe when he was a child, and he had a soft side for her. Louisa used to declare that he was in love with her, and he would pretend to be so in fun.

He did not hurry; he dawdled and looked into the shops, and stopped to pat some dog that he knew as it lay on its side and yawned in the sun. He jumped over the harmless railings which inclosed the Palace square—a great empty square, surrounded with houses, with two little fountains, two symmetrical bare flower-beds, divided, as by a parting, by a gravel path, carefully raked and bordered by orange trees in tubs. In the middle was the bronze statue of some unknown Grand Duke in the costume of Louis Philippe, on a pediment adorned at the four corners by allegorical figures representing the Virtues. On a seat one solitary man was dozing over his paper. Behind the silly moat of the earthworks of the Palace two sleepy cannon yawned upon the sleepy town. Christophe laughed at the whole thing.

He entered the Palace without troubling to take on a more official manner. At most he stopped humming, but his thoughts went dancing on inside him. He threw his hat on the table in the hall and familiarly greeted the old usher, whom he had known since he was a child. (The old man had been there on the day when Christophe had first entered the Palace, on the evening when he had seen Hassler.) But to-day the old man, who always used to reply good-humoredly to Christophe's disrespectful sallies, now seemed a little haughty. Christophe paid no heed to it. A little farther on, in the ante-chamber, he met a clerk of the chancery, who was usually full of conversation and very friendly. He was surprised to see him hurry past him to avoid having to talk. However, he did not attach any significance to it, and went on and asked to be shown in.

He went in. They had just finished dinner. His Highness was in one of the drawing-rooms. He was leaning against the mantelpiece, smoking, and talking to his guests, among whom Christophe saw *his* princess, who was also smoking. She was lying back in an armchair and talking in a loud voice to some officers who made a circle about her. The gathering was lively. They were all very merry, and when Christophe entered he heard the Grand Duke's thick laugh. But he stopped dead when he saw Christophe. He growled and pounced on him.

"Ah! There you are!" he said. "You have condescended to come at last? Do you think you can go on making fun of me any longer? You're a blackguard, sir!"

Christophe was so staggered by this brutal attack that it was some time before he could utter a word. He was thinking that he was only late, and that that could not have provoked such violence. He murmured:

"What have I done, Your Highness?"

His Highness did not listen and went on angrily:

"Be silent! I will not be insulted by a blackguard!" Christophe turned pale, and gulped so as to try to speak, for he was choking. He made an effort, and said:

"Your Highness, you have no right—you have no right to insult me without telling me what I have done."

The Grand Duke turned to his secretary, who produced a paper from his pocket and held it out to him. He was in such a state of exasperation as could not be explained only by his anger: the fumes of good wine had their share in it, too. He

came and stood in front of Christophe, and like a toreador with
his cape, furiously waved the crumpled newspaper in his face
and shouted:

"Your muck, sir! . . . You deserve to have your nose
rubbed in it!"

Christophe recognized the socialist paper.

"I don't see what harm there is in it," he said.

"What! What!" screamed the Grand Duke. "You are impudent! . . . This rascally paper, which insults me from day
to day, and spews out filthy insults upon me! . . ."

"Sire," said Christophe, "I have not read it."

"You lie!" shouted the Grand Duke.

"You shall not call me a liar," said Christophe. "I have
not read it. I am only concerned with reviews, and besides, I
have the right to write in whatever paper I like."

"You have no right but to hold your tongue. I have been
too kind to you. I have heaped kindness upon you, you and
yours, in spite of your misconduct and your father's, which
would have justified me in cutting you off. I forbid you to
go on writing in a paper which is hostile to me. And further:
I forbid you altogether to write anything in future without my
authority. I have had enough of your musical polemics. I
will not allow any one who enjoys my patronage to spend his
time in attacking everything which is dear to people of taste
and feeling, to all true Germans. You would do better to
write better music, or if that is impossible, to practise your
scales and exercises. I don't want to have anything to do with a
musical Bebel who amuses himself by decrying all our national
glories and upsetting the minds of the people. We know what
is good, thank God. We do not need to wait for you to tell
us. Go to your piano, sir, or leave us in peace!"

Standing face to face with Christophe the fat man glared
at him insultingly. Christophe was livid, and tried to speak.
His lips moved; he stammered:

"I am not your slave. I shall say what I like and write
what I like . . ."

He choked. He was almost weeping with shame and rage.
His legs were trembling. He jerked his elbow and upset an
ornament on a table by his side. He felt that he was in a

ridiculous position. He heard people laughing. He looked down the room, and as through a mist saw the princess watching the scene and exchanging ironically commiserating remarks with her neighbors. He lost count of what exactly happened. The Grand Duke shouted. Christophe shouted louder than he without knowing what he said. The Prince's secretary and another official came towards him and tried to stop him. He pushed them away, and while he talked he waved an ash-tray which he had mechanically picked up from the table against which he was leaning. He heard the secretary say:

"Put it down! Put it down!"

And he heard himself shouting inarticulately and knocking on the edge of the table with the ash-tray.

"Go!" roared the Grand Duke, beside himself with rage. "Go! Go! I'll have you thrown out!"

The officers had come up to the Prince and were trying to calm him. The Grand Duke looked apoplectic. His eyes were starting from his head, he shouted to them to throw the rascal out. Christophe saw red. He longed to thrust his fist in the Grand Duke's face; but he was crushed under a weight of conflicting feelings: shame, fury, a remnant of shyness, of German loyalty, traditional respect, habits of humility in the Prince's presence. He tried to speak; he could not. He tried to move; he could not. He could not see or hear. He suffered them to push him along and left the room.

He passed through the impassive servants who had come up to the door, and had missed nothing of the quarrel. He had to go thirty yards to cross the ante-chamber, and it seemed a lifetime. The corridor grew longer and longer as he walked up it. He would never get out! . . . The light of day which he saw shining downstairs through the glass door was his haven. He went stumbling down the stairs. He forgot that he was bareheaded. The old usher reminded him to take his hat. He had to gather all his forces to leave the castle, cross the court, reach his home. His teeth were chattering when he opened the door. His mother was terrified by his face and his trembling. He avoided her and refused to answer her questions. He went up to his room, shut himself in, and lay down. He was shaking so that he could not undress. His breathing

came in jerks and his whole body seemed shattered. . . . Oh!
If only he could see no more, feel no more, no longer have
to bear with his wretched body, no longer have to struggle
against ignoble life, and fall, fall, breathless, without thought,
and no longer be anywhere! . . . With frightful difficulty
he tore off his clothes and left them on the ground, and
then flung himself into his bed and drew the coverings over
him. There was no sound in the room save that of the little
iron be⁻ rattling on the tiled floor.

Louisa listened at the door. She knocked in vain. She called
softly. There was no reply. She waited, anxiously listening
through the silence. Then she went away. Once or twice
during the day she came and listened, and again at night, before
she went to bed. Day passed, and the night. The house was
still. Christophe was shaking with fever. Every now and
then he wept, and in the night he got up several times and
shook his fist at the wall. About two o'clock, in an access of
madness, he got up from his bed, sweating and half naked. He
wanted to go and kill the Grand Duke. He was devoured by
hate and shame. His body and his heart writhed in the fire of
it. Nothing of all the storm in him could be heard outside;
not a word, not a sound. With clenched teeth he fought it
down and forced it back into himself.

Next morning he came down as usual. He was a wreck. He
said nothing and his mother dared not question him. She
knew, from the gossip of the neighborhood. All day he stayed
sitting by the fire, silent, feverish, and with bent head, like a
little old man. And when he was alone he wept in silence.

In the evening the editor of the socialist paper came to see
him. Naturally he had heard and wished to have details.
Christophe was touched by his coming, and interpreted it
naïvely as a mark of sympathy and a desire for forgiveness
on the part of those who had compromised him. He made a
point of seeming to regret nothing and he let himself go and
said everything that was rankling in him. It was some solace
for him to talk freely to a man who shared his hatred of oppression. The other urged him on. He saw a good chance for his
journal in the event, and an opportunity for a scandalous ar-

ticle, for which he expected Christophe to provide him with
material if he did not write it himself; for he thought that
after such an explosion the Court musician would put his very
considerable political talents and his no less considerable little
tit-bits of secret information about the Court at the service
of "the cause." As he did not plume himself on his subtlety
he presented the thing rawly in the crudest light. Christophe
started. He declared that he would write nothing and said that
any attack on the Grand Duke that he might make would be
interpreted as an act of personal vengeance, and that he would
be more reserved now that he was free than when, not being
free, he ran some risk in saying what he thought. The journalist could not understand his scruples. He thought Christophe
narrow and clerical at heart, but he also decided that Christophe
was afraid. He said:

"Oh, well! Leave it to us. I will write it myself. You
need not bother about it."

Christophe begged him to say nothing, but he had no means
of restraining him. Besides, the journalist declared that the
affair was not his concern only: the insult touched the paper,
which had the right to avenge itself. There was nothing to be
said to that. All that Christophe could do was to ask him on
his word of honor not to abuse certain of his confidences which
had been made to his friend and not to the journalist. The
other made no difficulty about that. Christophe was not reassured by it. He knew too well how imprudent he had been.
When he was left alone he turned over everything that he had
said, and shuddered. Without hesitating for a moment, he
wrote to the journalist imploring him once more not to repeat
what he had confided to him. (The poor wretch repeated it
in part himself in the letter.)

Next day, as he opened the paper with feverish haste, the
first thing he read was his story at great length on the front
page. Everything that he had said on the evening before was
immeasurably enlarged, having suffered that peculiar deformation which everything has to suffer in its passage through the
mind of a journalist. The article attacked the Grand Duke
and the Court with low invective. Certain details which it
gave were too personal to Christophe, too obviously known only

to him, for the article not to be attributed to him in its entirety.

Christophe was crushed by this fresh blow. As he read a cold sweat came out on his face. When he had finished he was dumfounded. He wanted to rush to the office of the paper, but his mother withheld him, not unreasonably being fearful of his violence. He was afraid of it himself. He felt that if he went there he would do something foolish; and he stayed—and did a very foolish thing. He wrote an indignant letter to the journalist in which he reproached him for his conduct in insulting terms, disclaimed the article, and broke with the party. The disclaimer did not appear.

Christophe wrote again to the paper, demanding that his letter should be published. They sent him a copy of his first letter, written on the night of the interview and confirming it. They asked if they were to publish that, too. He felt that he was in their hands. Thereupon he unfortunately met the indiscreet interviewer in the street. He could not help telling him of his contempt for him. Next day the paper, without a spark of shame, published an insulting paragraph about the servants of the Court, who even when they are dismissed remain servants and are incapable of being free. A few allusions to recent events left no room for doubt that Christophe was meant.

When it became evident to everybody that Christophe had no single support, there suddenly cropped up a host of enemies whose existence he had never suspected. All those whom he had offended, directly or indirectly, either by personal criticism or by attacking their ideas and taste, now took the offensive and avenged themselves with interest. The general public whom Christophe had tried to shake out of their apathy were quite pleased to see the insolent young man, who had presumed to reform opinion and disturb the rest of people of property, taken down a peg. Christophe was in the water. Everybody did their best to duck him.

They did not come down upon him all at once. One tried first, to spy out the land. Christophe made no response, and he struck more lustily. Others followed, and then the whole gang of them. Some joined in the sport simply for fun, like puppies who think it funny to leave their mark in inappropriate places. They were the flying squadron of incompetent journalists, who, knowing nothing, try to hide their ignorance by belauding the victors and belaboring the vanquished. Others brought the weight of their principles and they shouted like deaf people. Nothing was left of anything when they had passed. They were the critics—with the criticism which kills.

Fortunately for Christophe, he did not read the papers. A few devoted friends took care to send him the most insulting. But he left them in a heap on his desk and never thought of opening them. It was only towards the end of it that his eyes were attracted by a great red mark round an article. He read that his *Lieder* were like the roaring of a wild beast; that his symphonies seemed to have come from a madhouse; that his art was hysterical, his harmony spasmodic, as a change from the dryness of his heart and the emptiness of his thought. The critic, who was well known, ended with these words:

" Herr Krafft as a journalist has lately given astounding proof of his style and taste, which roused irresistible merriment in musical circles. He was then given the friendly advice rather to devote himself to composition. But the latest products of his muse have shown that this advice, though well-meant, was bad. Herr Krafft should certainly devote himself to journalism."

After reading the article, which prevented Christophe working the whole morning, naturally he began to look for the other hostile papers, and became utterly demoralized. But Louisa, who had a mania for moving everything lying about, by way of " tidying up," had already burned them. He was irritated at first and then comforted, and he held out the last of the papers to her, and said that she had better do the same with that.

Other rebuffs hurt him more. A quartette which he had sent in manuscript to a well-known society at Frankfort was rejected unanimously and returned without explanation. An overture which an orchestra at Cologne seemed disposed to perform was returned after a month as unplayable. But the worst of all was inflicted on him by an orchestral society in the town. The *Kapellmeister*, H. Euphrat, its conductor, was quite a

good musician, but like many conductors, he had no curiosity
of mind. He suffered (or rather he carried to extremes) the
laziness peculiar to his class, which consists in going on and
on investigating familiar works, while it shuns any really new
work like the plague. He was never tired of organizing Beethoven, Mozart, or Schumann festivals: in conducting these works
he had only to let himself be carried along by the purring of
the familiar rhythms. On the other hand, contemporary music
was intolerable to him. He dared not admit it and pretended
to be friendly towards young talent; in fact, whenever he was
brought a work built on the old lines—a sort of hotch-potch of
works that had been new fifty years before—he would receive
it very well, and would even produce it ostentatiously and force it
upon the public. It did not disturb either his effects or the way
in which the public was accustomed to be moved. On the other
hand, he was filled with a mixture of contempt and hatred for
anything which threatened to disturb that arrangement and
put him to extra trouble. Contempt would predominate if
the innovator had no chance of emerging from obscurity. But
if there were any danger of his succeeding, then hatred would
predominate—of course until the moment when he had gained
an established success.

Christophe was not yet in that position: far from it. And
so he was much surprised when he was informed, by indirect
overtures, that Herr H. Euphrat would be very glad to produce one of his compositions. It was all the more unexpected as he knew that the *Kapellmeister* was an intimate friend
of Brahms and others whom he had maltreated in his criticisms.
Being honest himself, he credited his adversaries with the
same generous feelings which he would have had himself. He
supposed that now that he was down they wished to show him
that they were above petty spite. He was touched by it. He
wrote effusively to Herr Euphrat and sent him a symphonic
poem. The conductor replied through his secretary coldly but
politely, acknowledging the receipt of his work, and adding
that, in accordance with the rules of the society, the symphony
would be given out to the orchestra immediately and put to
the test of a general rehearsal before it could be accepted for
public hearing. A rule is a rule. Christophe had to bow to it,

though it was a pure formality which served to weed out the lucubrations of amateurs which were sometimes a nuisance.

A few weeks later Christophe was told that his composition was to be rehearsed. On principle everything was done privately and even the author was not permitted to be present at the rehearsal. But by a generally agreed indulgence the author was always admitted; only he did not show himself. Everybody knew it and everybody pretended not to know it. On the appointed day one of his friends brought Christophe to the hall, where he sat at the back of a box. He was surprised to see that at this private rehearsal the hall—at least the ground floor seats—were almost all filled; a crowd of dilettante idlers and critics moved about and chattered to each other. The orchestra had to ignore their presence.

They began with the Brahms *Rhapsody* for alto, chorus of male voices, and orchestra on a fragment of the *Harzreise im Winter* of Goethe. Christophe, who detested the majestic sentimentality of the work, thought that perhaps the "Brahmins" had introduced it politely to avenge themselves by forcing him to hear a composition of which he had written irreverently. The idea made him laugh, and his good humour increased when after the *Rhapsody* there came two other productions by known musicians whom he had taken to task; there seemed to be no doubt about their intentions. And while he could not help making a face at it he thought that after all it was quite fair tactics; and, failing the music, he appreciated the joke. It even amused him to applaud ironically with the audience, which made manifest its enthusiasm for Brahms and his like.

At last it came to Christophe's symphony. He saw from the way the orchestra and the people in the hall were looking at his box that they were aware of his presence. He hid himself. He waited with the catch at his heart which every musician feels at the moment when the conductor's wand is raised and the waters of the music gather in silence before bursting their dam. He had never yet heard his work played. How would the creatures of his dreams live? How would their voices sound? He felt their roaring within him; and he leaned over the abyss of sounds waiting fearfully for what should come forth.

What did come forth was a nameless thing, a shapeless hotch-potch. Instead of the bold columns which were to support the front of the building the chords came crumbling down like a building in ruins; there was nothing to be seen but the dust of mortar. For a moment Christophe was not quite sure whether they were really playing his work. He cast back for the train, the rhythm of his thoughts; he could not recognize it; it went on babbling and hiccoughing like a drunken man clinging close to the wall, and he was overcome with shame, as though he had himself been seen in that condition. It was of no avail to think that he had not written such stuff; when an idiotic interpreter destroys a man's thoughts he has always a moment of doubt when he asks himself in consternation if he is himself responsible for it. The audience never asks such a question; the audience believes in the interpreter, in the singers, in the orchestra whom they are accustomed to hear as they believe in their newspaper; they cannot make a mistake; if they say absurd things, it is the absurdity of the author. This audience was the less inclined to doubt because it liked to believe. Christophe tried to persuade himself that the *Kapell-meister* was aware of the hash and would stop the orchestra and begin again. The instruments were not playing together. The horn had missed his beat and had come in a bar too late; he went on for a few minutes, and then stopped quietly to clean his instrument. Certain passages for the oboe had absolutely disappeared. It was impossible for the most skilled ear to pick up the thread of the musical idea, or even to imagine that there was one. Fantastic instrumentations, hu-moristic sallies became grotesque through the coarseness of the execution. It was lamentably stupid, the work of an idiot, of a joker who knew nothing of music. Christophe tore his hair. He tried to interrupt, but the friend who was with him held him back, assuring him that the *Herr Kapellmeister* must surely see the faults of the execution and would put everything right —that Christophe must not show himself and that if he made any remark it would have a very bad effect. He made Chris-tophe sit at the very back of the box. Christophe obeyed, but he beat his head with his fists; and every fresh monstrosity drew from him a groan of indignation and misery.

"The wretches! The wretches! . . ."

He groaned, and squeezed his hands tight to keep himself from crying out.

Now mingled with the wrong notes there came up to him the muttering of the audience, who were beginning to be restless. At first it was only a tremor; but soon Christophe was left without a doubt; they were laughing. The musicians of the orchestra had given the signal; some of them did not conceal their hilarity. The audience, certain then that the music was laughable, rocked with laughter. This merriment became general; it increased at the return of a very rhythmical motif which the double-basses accentuated in a burlesque fashion. Only the *Kapellmeister* went on through the uproar inperturbably beating time.

At last they reached the end (the best things come to an end). It was the turn of the audience. They exploded with delight, an explosion which lasted for several minutes. Some hissed; others applauded ironically; the wittiest of all shouted "Encore!" A bass voice coming from a stage box began to imitate the grotesque motif. Other jokers followed suit and imitated it also. Some one shouted "Author!" It was long since these witty folk had been so highly entertained.

When the tumult was calmed down a little the *Kapellmeister*, standing quite impassive with his face turned towards the audience though he was pretending not to see it—(the audience was still supposed to be non-existent)—made a sign to the audience that he was about to speak. There was a cry of "Ssh," and silence. He waited a moment longer; then—(his voice was curt, cold, and cutting) :

"Gentlemen," he said, "I should certainly not have let *that* be played through to the end if I had not wished to make an example of the gentleman who has dared to write offensively of the great Brahms."

That was all; and jumping down from his stand he went out amid cheers from the delighted audience. They tried to recall him; the applause went on for a few minutes longer. But he did not return. The orchestra went away. The audience decided to go too. The concert was over.

It had been a good day.

REVOLT   481

Christophe had gone already. Hardly had he seen the wretched conductor leave his desk when he had rushed from the box; he plunged down the stairs from the first floor to meet him and slap his face. His friend who had brought him followed and tried to hold him back, but Christophe brushed him aside and almost threw him downstairs;—(he had reason to believe that the fellow was concerned in the trick which had been played him). Fortunately for H. Euphrat and himself the door leading to the stage was shut; and his furious knocking could not make them open it. However the audience was beginning to leave the hall. Christophe could not stay there. He fled.

He was in an indescribable condition. He walked blindly, waving his arms, rolling his eyes, talking aloud like a madman; he suppressed his cries of indignation and rage. The street was almost empty. The concert hall had been built the year before in a new neighborhood a little way out of the town; and Christophe instinctively fled towards the country across the empty fields in which were a few lonely shanties and scaffoldings surrounded by fences. His thoughts were murderous; he could have killed the man who had put such an affront upon him. Alas! and when he had killed him would there be any change in the animosity of those people whose insulting laughter was still ringing in his ears? They were too many; he could do nothing against them; they were all agreed—they who were divided about so many things—to insult and crush him. It was past understanding; there was hatred in them. What had he done to them all? There were beautiful things in him, things to do good and make the heart big; he had tried to say them, to make others enjoy them; he thought they would be happy like himself. Even if they did not like them they should be grateful to him for his intentions; they could, if need be, show him kindly where he had been wrong; but that they should take such a malignant joy in insulting and odiously travestying his ideas, in trampling them underfoot, and killing him by ridicule, how was it possible? In his excitement he exaggerated their hatred; he thought it much more serious than such mediocre people could ever be. He sobbed: " What have I done to them? " He choked, he thought that all was lost, just as he did when he was a child coming into contact for the first time with human wickedness.

And when he looked about him he suddenly saw that he had reached the edge of the mill-race, at the very spot where a few years before his father had been drowned. And at once he thought of drowning himself too. He was just at the point of making the plunge.

But as he leaned over the steep bank, fascinated by the calm clean aspect of the water, a tiny bird in a tree by his side began to sing—to sing madly. He held his breath to listen. The water murmured. The ripening corn moaned as it waved under the soft caressing wind; the poplars shivered. Behind the hedge on the road, out of sight, bees in hives in a garden filled the air with their scented music. From the other side of the stream a cow was chewing the cud and gazing with soft eyes. A little fair-haired girl was sitting on a wall, with a light basket on her shoulders, like a little angel with wings, and she was dreaming, and swinging her bare legs and humming aimlessly. Far away in a meadow a white dog was leaping and running in wide circles. Christophe leaned against a tree and listened and watched the earth in Spring; he was caught up by the peace and joy of these creatures; he could forget, he could forget. Suddenly he clasped the tree with his arms and leaned his cheek against it. He threw himself on the ground; he buried his face in the grass; he laughed nervously, happily. All the beauty, the grace, the charm of life wrapped him round, imbued his soul, and he sucked them up like a sponge. He thought:

"Why are you so beautiful, and they—men—so ugly?"

No matter! He loved it, he loved it, he felt that he would always love it, and that nothing could ever take it from him. He held the earth to his breast. He held life to his breast:

"I love you! You are mine. They cannot take you from me. Let them do what they will! Let them make me suffer! . . . Suffering also is life!"

Christophe began bravely to work again. He refused to have anything more to do with "men of letters"—well named—makers of phrases, the sterile babblers, journalists, critics, the exploiters and traffickers of art. As for musicians he would waste no more time in battling with their prejudices and jealousy. They did not want him? Very well! He did not want them. He had his work to do; he would do it. The Court had given him back his liberty; he was grateful for it. He was grateful to the people for their hostility; he could work in peace.

Louisa approved with all her heart. She had no ambition; she was not a Krafft; she was like neither his father nor his grandfather. She did not want honors or reputation for her son. She would have liked him to be rich and famous; but if those advantages could only be bought at the price of so much unpleasantness she much preferred not to bother about them. She had been more upset by Christophe's grief over his rupture with the Palace than by the event itself; and she was heartily glad that he had quarreled with the review and newspaper people. She had a peasant's distrust of blackened paper; it was only a waste of time and made enemies. She had sometimes heard his young friends of the Review talking to Christophe; she had been horrified by their malevolence; they tore everything to pieces and said horrible things about everybody; and the worse things they said the better pleased they were. She did not like them. No doubt they were very clever and very learned, but they were not kind, and she was very glad that Christophe saw no more of them. She was full of common sense: what good were they to him?

" They may say, write, and think what they like of me," said Christophe. " They cannot prevent my being myself. What do their ideas or their art matter to me? I deny them! "

It is all very fine to deny the world. But the world is not so easily denied by a young man's boasting. Christophe was sincere, but he was under illusion; he did not know himself. He was not a monk; he had not the temperament for renouncing the world, and besides he was not old enough to do so. At first he did not suffer much, he was plunged in composition; and while his work lasted he did not feel the want of anything. But when he came to the period of depression which follows the completion of a work and lasts until a new work takes possession of the mind, he looked about him and was horrified by his loneliness. He asked himself why he wrote. While a man is writing he never asks himself that question; he must write, there is no arguing about it. And then he finds himself with the work that he has begotten: the great instinct which caused it to spring forth is silent; he does not understand why it was born: he hardly recognizes it, it is almost a stranger to him; he longs to forget it. And that is impossible as long as it is not published or played, or living its own life in the world. Till then it is like a new-born child attached to its mother, a living thing bound fast to his living flesh; it must be amputated at all costs or it will not live. The more Christophe composed the more he suffered under the weight of these creatures who had sprung forth from himself and could neither live nor die. He was haunted by them. Who could deliver him from them? Some obscure impulse would stir in these children of his thoughts; they longed desperately to break away from him to expand into other souls like the quick and fruitful seed which the wind scatters over the universe. Must he remain imprisoned in his sterility? He raged against it.

Since every outlet—theaters, concerts—was closed to him, and nothing would induce him to approach those managers who had once failed him, there was nothing left but for him to publish his writings, but he could not flatter himself that it would be easier to find a publisher to produce his work than an orchestra to play it. The two or three clumsy attempts that he had made were enough; rather than expose himself to another rebuff, or to bargain with one of these music merchants and put up with his patronizing airs, he preferred to publish it at his own expense. It was an act of madness; he had some small savings out of his Court salary and the proceeds of a few concerts, but the source from which the money had come was dried up and it would be a long time before he could find another; and he should have been prudent enough to be careful with his scanty funds which had to help him over the difficult period upon which he was entering. Not only did he not do so; but, as his savings were not enough to cover the expenses of publication, he did not shrink from getting into debt. Louisa dared not say anything; she found him absolutely unreasonable, and did not understand how anybody could spend money for the sake of seeing his name on a book; but since it was a way of making him be patient and of keeping him with her, she was only too happy for him to have that satisfaction.

Instead of offering the public compositions of a familiar and undisturbing kind, in which it could feel at home, Christophe chose from among his manuscripts a suite very individual in character, which he valued highly. They were piano pieces mixed with *Lieder,* some very short and popular in style, others very elaborate and almost dramatic. The whole formed a series of impressions, joyous or mild, linked together naturally and written alternately for the piano and the voice, alone or accompanied. " For," said Christophe, " when I dream, I do not always formulate what I feel. I suffer, I am happy, and have no words to say; but then comes a moment when I must say what I am feeling, and I sing without thinking of what I am doing; sometimes I sing only vague words, a few disconnected phrases, sometimes whole poems; then I begin to dream again. And so the day goes by; and I have tried to give the impression of a day. Why these gathered impressions composed only of songs or preludes? There is nothing more false or less harmonious. One must try to give the free play of the soul." He had called his suite: *A Day.* The different parts of the composition bore sub-titles, shortly indicating the succession of his inward dreams. Christophe had written mysterious dedications, initials, dates, which only he could understand, as they reminded him of poetic moments or beloved faces: the gay Corinne, the languishing Sabine, and the little unknown Frenchwoman.

Besides this work he selected thirty of his *Lieder*—those which pleased him most, and consequently pleased the public least. He avoided choosing the most " melodious " of his melodies, but he did choose the most characteristic. (The public always has a horror of anything " characteristic." Characterless things are more likely to please them.)

These *Lieder* were written to poems of old Silesian poets of the seventeenth century that Christophe had read by chance in a popular collection, and whose loyalty he had loved. Two especially were dear to him, dear as brothers, two creatures full of genius and both had died at thirty: the charming Paul Fleming, the traveler to the Caucasus and to Ispahan, who preserved his soul pure, loving and serene in the midst of the savagery of war, the sorrows of life, and the corruption of his time, and Johann Christian Günther, the unbalanced genius who wore himself out in debauchery and despair, casting his life to the four winds. He had translated Günther's cries of provocation and vengeful irony against the hostile God who overwhelms His creatures, his furious curses like those of a Titan overthrown hurling the thunder back against the heavens. He had selected Fleming's love songs to Anemone and Basilene, soft and sweet as flowers, and the rondo of the stars, the *Tanzlied* (dancing song) of hearts glad and limpid—and the calm heroic sonnet To Himself (*An Sich*), which Christophe used to recite as a prayer every morning.

The smiling optimism of the pious Paul Gerhardt also had its charm for Christophe. It was a rest for him on recovering from his own sorrows. He loved that innocent vision of nature as God, the fresh meadows, where the storks walk gravely among the tulips and white narcissus, by little brooks singing on the sands, the transparent air wherein there pass the wide-winged swallows and flying doves, the gaiety of a sunbeam piercing the rain, and the luminous sky smiling through the clouds, and the serene majesty of the evening, the sweet peace of the forests, the cattle, the bowers and the fields. He had had the impertinence to set to music several of those mystic canticles which are still sung in Protestant communities. And he had avoided preserving the choral character. Far from it: he had a horror of it; he had given them a free and vivacious character. Old Gerhardt would have shuddered at the devilish pride which was breathed forth now in certain lines of his *Song of the Christian Traveler,* or the pagan delight which made this peaceful stream of his *Song of Summer* bubble over like a torrent.

The collection was published without any regard for common sense, of course. The publisher whom Christophe paid for printing and storing his *Lieder* had no other claim to his choice than that of being his neighbor. He was not equipped for such important work; the printing went on for months; there were mistakes and expensive corrections. Christophe knew nothing about it and the whole thing cost more by a third than it need have done; the expenses far exceeded anything he had anticipated. Then when it was done, Christophe found an enormous edition on his hands and did not know what to do with it. The publisher had no customers; he took no steps to circulate the work. And his apathy was quite in accord with Christophe's attitude. When he asked him, to satisfy his conscience, to write him a short advertisement of it, Christophe replied that "he did not want any advertisement; if his music was good it would speak for itself." The publisher religiously respected his wishes; he put the edition away in his warehouse. It was well kept; for in six months not a copy was sold.

While he was waiting for the public to make up its mind Christophe had to find some way of repairing the hole he had made in his means; and he could not be nice about it, for he had to live and pay his debts. Not only were his debts larger than he had imagined but he saw that the moneys on which he had counted were less than he had thought. Had he lost money without knowing it or—what was infinitely more probable—had he reckoned up wrongly? (He had never been able to add correctly.) It did not matter much why the money was missing; it was missing without a doubt. Louisa had to give her all to help her son. He was bitterly remorseful and tried to pay her back as soon as possible and at all costs. He tried to get lessons, though it was painful to him to ask and to put up with refusals. He was out of favor altogether; he found it very difficult to obtain pupils again. And so when it was suggested that he should teach at a school he was only too glad.

It was a semi-religious institution. The director, an astute gentleman, had seen, though he was no musician, how useful Christophe might be, and how cheaply in his present position. He was pleasant and paid very little. When Christophe ventured to make a timid remark the director told him with a kindly smile that as he no longer held an official position he could not very well expect more.

It was a sad task! It was not so much a matter of teaching the pupils music as of making their parents and themselves believe that they had learned it. The chief thing was to make them able to sing at the ceremonies to which the public were admitted. It did not matter how it was done. Christophe was in despair; he had not even the consolation of telling himself as he fulfilled his task that he was doing useful work; his conscience reproached him with it as hypocrisy. He tried to give the children more solid instruction and to make them acquainted with and love serious music; but they did not care for it a bit. Christophe could not succeed in making them listen to it; he had no authority over them; in truth he was not made for teaching children. He took no interest in their floundering; he tried to explain to them all at once the theory of music. When he had to give a piano lesson he would set his pupil a symphony of Beethoven which he would play as a duet with her. Naturally that could not succeed; he would explode angrily, drive the pupil from the piano and go on playing alone for a long time. He was just the same with his private pupils outside the school. He had not an ounce of patience; for instance he would tell a young lady who prided herself on her aristocratic appearance and position, that she played like a kitchen maid; or he would even write to her mother and say that he gave it up, that it would kill him if he went on long bothering about a girl so devoid of talent. All of which did not improve his position. His few pupils left him; he could not keep any of them more than a few months. His mother argued with him; he would argue with himself. Louisa made him promise that at least he would not break with the school he had joined; for if he lost that position he did not know what he should do for a living. And so he restrained himself in spite of his disgust; he was most exemplarily punctual. But how could he conceal his thoughts when a donkey of a pupil blundered for the tenth time in some passages, or when he had to coach his class for the next concert in some foolish chorus!—(For he was not even allowed to choose

his programme: his taste was not trusted)—He was not exactly
zealous about it all. And yet he went stubbornly on, silent,
frowning, only betraying his secret wrath by occasionally
thumping on his desk and making his pupils jump in their
seats. But sometimes the pill was too bitter; he could not
bear it any longer. In the middle of the chorus he would interrupt the singers:

"Oh! Stop! Stop! I'll play you some Wagner instead."

They asked nothing better. They played cards behind his
back. There was always someone who reported the matter to
the director; and Christophe would be reminded that he was
not there to make his pupils like music but to make them
sing. He received his scoldings with a shudder; but he accepted them; he did not want to lose his work. Who would
have thought a few years before, when his career looked so
assured and brilliant (when he had done nothing), that he
would be reduced to such humiliation just as he was beginning
to be worth something?

Among the hurts to his vanity that he came by in his work
at the school, one of the most painful was having to call on
his colleagues. He paid two calls at random; and they bored
him so that he had not the heart to go on. The two privileged
persons were not at all pleased about it, but the others were
personally affronted. They all regarded Christophe as their
inferior in position and intelligence; and they assumed a
patronizing manner towards him. Sometimes he was overwhelmed by it, for they seemed to be so sure of themselves and
the opinion they had of him that he began to share it; he felt
stupid with them; what could he have found to say to them?
They were full of their profession and saw nothing beyond it.
They were not men. If only they had been books! But they
were only notes to books, philological commentaries.

Christophe avoided meeting them. But sometimes he was
forced to do so. The director was at home once a month in
the afternoon; and he insisted on all his people being there.
Christophe, who had cut the first afternoon, without excuse,
in the vain hope that his absence would not be noticed, was
ever afterwards the object of sour attention. Next time he was

lectured by his mother and decided to go; he was as solemn about it as though he were going to a funeral.

He found himself at a gathering of the teachers of the school and other institutions of the town, and their wives and daughters. They were all huddled together in a room too small for them, and grouped hierarchically. They paid no attention to him. The group nearest him was talking of pedagogy and cooking. All the wives of the teachers had culinary recipes which they set out with pedantic exuberance and insistence. The men were no less interested in these matters and hardly less competent. They were as proud of the domestic talents of their wives as they of their husbands' learning. Christophe stood by a window leaning against the wall, not knowing how to look, now trying to smile stupidly, now gloomy with a fixed stare and unmoved features, and he was bored to death. A little away from him, sitting in the recess of the window, was a young woman to whom nobody was talking and she was as bored as he. They both looked at the room and not at each other. It was only after some time that they noticed each other just as they both turned away to yawn, both being at the limit of endurance. Just at that moment their eyes met. They exchanged a look of friendly understanding. He moved towards her. She said in a low voice:

" Are you amused? "

He turned his back on the room, and, looking out of the window, put out his tongue. She burst out laughing, and suddenly waking up she signed to him to sit down by her side. They introduced themselves; she was the wife of Professor Reinhart, who lectured on natural history at the school, and was newly come to the town, where they knew nobody. She was not beautiful; she had a large nose, ugly teeth, and she lacked freshness; but she had keen, clever eyes and a kindly smile. She chattered like a magpie; he answered her solemnly; she had an amusing frankness and a droll wit; they laughingly exchanged impressions out loud without bothering about the people round them. Their neighbors, who had not deigned to notice their existence when it would have been charitable to help them out of their loneliness, now threw angry looks at them; it was in bad taste to be so much amused. But they did not care what the others might think of them; they were taking their revenge in their chatter.

In the end Frau Reinhart introduced her husband to Christophe. He was extremely ugly; he had a pale, greasy, pock-marked, rather sinister face, but he looked very kind. He spoke low down in his throat and pronounced his words sententiously, stammeringly, pausing between each syllable.

They had been married a few months only and these two plain people were in love with each other; they had an affectionate way of looking at each other, talking to each other, taking each other's hands in the presence of everybody—which was comic and touching. If one wanted anything the other would want it too. And so they invited Christophe to go and sup with them after the reception. Christophe began jokingly to beg to be excused; he said that the best thing to do that evening would be to go to bed; he was quite worn out with boredom, as tired as though he had walked ten miles. But Frau Reinhart said that he could not be left in that condition; it would be dangerous to spend the night with such gloomy thoughts. Christophe let them drag him off. In his loneliness he was glad to have met these good people, who were not very distinguished in their manners but were simple and *gemütlich.*

The Reinharts' little house was *gemütlich* like themselves. It was a rather chattering *Gemüt,* a *Gemüt* with inscriptions. The furniture, the utensils, the china all talked, and went on repeating their joy in seeing their " charming guest," asked after his health, and gave him pleasant and virtuous advice. On the sofa—which was very hard—was a little cushion which murmured amiably:

" Only a quarter of an hour! " (*Nur ein Viertelstündchen.*)

The cup of coffee which was handed to Christophe insisted on his taking more:

" Just a drop! " (*Noch ein Schlückchen.*)

The plates seasoned the cooking with morality and otherwise the cooking was quite excellent. One plate said:

" Think of everything: otherwise no good will come to you! "

Another:

"Affection and gratitude please everybody. Ingratitude pleases nobody."

Although Christophe did not smoke, the ash-tray on the mantelpiece insisted on introducing itself to him:

"A little resting place for burning cigars." (*Ruheplätzchen für brennende Cigarren.*)

He wanted to wash his hands. The soap on the washstand said:

"For our charming guest." (*Für unseren lieben Gast.*)

And the sententious towel, like a person who has nothing to say, but thinks he must say something all the same, gave him this reflection, full of good sense but not very apposite, that "to enjoy the morning you must rise early."

"*Morgenstund hat Gold im Mund.*"

At length Christophe dared not even turn in his chair for fear of hearing himself addressed by other voices coming from every part of the room. He wanted to say:

"Be silent, you little monsters! We don't understand each other."

And he burst out laughing crazily and then tried to explain to his host and hostess that he was thinking of the gathering at the school. He would not have hurt them for the world. And he was not very sensible of the ridiculous. Very soon he grew accustomed to the loquacious cordiality of these people and their belongings. He could have tolerated anything in them! They were so kind! They were not tiresome either; if they had no taste they were not lacking in intelligence.

They were a little lost in the place to which they had come. The intolerable susceptibilities of the little provincial town did not allow people to enter it as though it were a mill, without having properly asked for the honor of becoming part of it. The Reinharts had not sufficiently attended to the provincial code which regulated the duties of new arrivals in the town towards those who had settled in it before them. Reinhart would have submitted to it mechanically. But his wife, to whom such drudgery was oppressive—she disliked being put out —postponed her duties from day to day. She had selected those calls which bored her least, to be paid first, or she had put the others off indefinitely. The distinguished persons who were comprised in the last category choked with indignation at such a want of respect. Angelica Reinhart—(her husband called her Lili)—was a little free in her manners; she could not take on the official tone. She would address her superiors in the hierarchy familiarly and make them go red in the face with indignation; and if need be she was not afraid of contradicting them. She had a quick tongue and always had to say whatever was in her head; sometimes she made extraordinarily foolish remarks at which people laughed behind her back; and also she could be malicious whole-heartedly, and that made her mortal enemies. She would bite her tongue as she was saying rash things and wish she had not said them, but it was too late. Her husband, the gentlest and most respectful of men, would chide her timidly about it. She would kiss him and say that she was a fool and that he was right. But the next moment she would break out again; and she would always say things at the least suitable moment; she would have burst if she had not said them. She was exactly the sort of woman to get on with Christophe.

Among the many ridiculous things which she ought not to have said, and consequently was always saying, was her trick of perpetually comparing the way things were done in Germany and the way they were done in France. She was a German— (nobody more so)—but she had been brought up in Alsace among French Alsatians, and she had felt the attraction of Latin civilization which so many Germans in the annexed countries, even those who seem the least likely to feel it, cannot resist. Perhaps, to tell the truth, the attraction had become stronger out of a spirit of contradiction since Angelica had married a North German and lived with him in purely German society.

She opened up her usual subject of discussion on her first evening with Christophe. She loved the pleasant freedom of conversation in France. Christophe echoed her. France to him was Corinne; bright blue eyes, smiling lips, frank free manners, a musical voice; he loved to know more about it.

Lili Reinhart clapped her hands on finding herself so thoroughly agreeing with Christophe.

"It is a pity," she said, "that my little French friend has gone, but she could not stand it; she has gone."

The image of Corinne was at once blotted out. As a match going out suddenly makes the gentle glimmer of the stars shine out from the dark sky, another image and other eyes appeared.

"Who?" asked Christophe with a start, "the little governess?"

"What?" said Frau Reinhart, "you knew her too?"

He described her; the two portraits were identical.

"You knew her?" repeated Christophe. "Oh! Tell me everything you know about her! . . ."

Frau Reinhart began by declaring that they were bosom friends and had no secrets from each other. But when she had to go into detail her knowledge was reduced to very little. They had met out calling. Frau Reinhart had made advances to the girl; and with her usual cordiality had invited her to come and see her. The girl had come two or three times and they had talked. But the curious Lili had not so easily succeeded in finding out anything about the life of the little Frenchwoman; the girl was very reserved; she had had to worm her story out of her, bit by bit. Frau Reinhart knew that she was called Antoinette Jeannin; she had no fortune, and no friends, except a younger brother who lived in Paris and to whom she was devoted. She used always to talk of him; he was the only subject about which she could talk freely; and Lili Reinhart had gained her confidence by showing sympathy and pity for the boy living alone in Paris without relations, without friends, at a boarding school. It was partly to pay for his education that Antoinette had accepted a post abroad. But the two children could not live without each other; they wanted to be with each other every day, and the least delay in the delivery of their letters used to make them quite ill with anxiety. Antoinette was always worrying about her brother, the poor child could not always manage to hide his sadness and loneliness from her; every one of his complaints used to sound through Antoinette's heart and seemed like to break it; the thought that he was suffering used to torture her and she used often to imagine that he was ill and would not say so. Frau Reinhart in her kindness had often had to rebuke her for her groundless fears, and she used to succeed in restoring her confidence for a moment. She had not been able to find out anything about Antoinette's family or position or her inner self. The girl was wildly shy and used to draw into herself at the first question. The little she said showed that she was cultured and intelligent; she seemed to have a precocious knowledge of life; she seemed to be at once naïve and undeceived, pious and disillusioned. She had not been happy in the town in a tactless and unkind family. She used not to complain, but it was easy to see that she used to suffer—Frau Reinhart did not exactly know why she had gone. It had been said that she had behaved badly. Angelica did not believe it; she was ready to swear that it was all a disgusting calumny, worthy of the foolish rotten town. But there had been stories; it did not matter what, did it?

" No," said Christophe, bowing his head.

" And so she has gone."

" And what did she say—anything to you when she went? "

" Ah! " said Lili Reinhart, " I had no chance. I had gone to Cologne for a few days just then! When I came back—*Zu spät*" (too late).—She stopped to scold her maid, who had brought her lemon too late for her tea.

And she added sententiously with the solemnity which the true German brings naturally to the performance of the familiar duties of daily life:

" Too late, as one so often is in life! "

(It was not clear whether she meant the lemon or her interrupted story.)

She went on:

" When I returned I found a line from her thanking me for all I had done and telling me that she was going; she was returning to Paris; she gave no address."

" And she did not write again? "

" Not again."

Once more Christophe saw her sad face disappear into the night; once more he saw her eyes for a moment just as he had seen them for the last time looking at him through the carriage window.

The enigma of France was once more set before him more

insistently than ever. Christophe never tired of asking Frau Reinhart about the country which she pretended to know so well. And Frau Reinhart who had never been there was not reluctant to tell him about it. Reinhart, a good patriot, full of prejudices against France, which he knew better than his wife, sometimes used to qualify her remarks when her enthusiasm went too far; but she would repeat her assertions only the more vigorously, and Christophe, knowing nothing at all about it, backed her up confidently.

What was more precious even than Lili Reinhart's memories were her books. She had a small library of French books: school books, a few novels, a few volumes bought at random. Christophe, greedy of knowledge and ignorant of France, thought them a treasure when Reinhart went and got them for him and put them at his disposal.

He began with volumes of select passages, old school books, which had been used by Lili Reinhart or her husband in their school days. Reinhart had assured him that he must begin with them if he wished to find his way about French literature, which was absolutely unknown to him. Christophe was full of respect for those who knew more than himself, and obeyed religiously; and that very evening he began to read. He tried first of all to take stock of the riches in his possession.

He made the acquaintance of certain French writers, namely: Thédore-Henri Barrau, François Pétis de la Croix, Frédéric Baudry, Émile Delérot, Charles-Auguste-Désiré Filon, Samuel Descombaz, and Prosper Baur. He read the poetry of Abbé Joseph Reyre, Pierre Lachambaudie, the Duc de Nivernois, André van Hasselt, Andrieux, Madame Colet, Constance-Marie Princesse de Salm-Dyck, Henriette Hollard, Gabriel-Jean-Baptiste-Ernest-Wilfrid Legouvé, Hippolyte Violeau, Jean Reboul, Jean Racine, Jean de Béranger, Frédéric Béchard, Gustave Nadaud, Édouard Plouvier, Eugène Manuel, Hugo, Millevoye, Chênedollé, James Lacour Delâtre, Félix Chavannes, Francis-Édouard-Joachim, known as François Coppée, and Louis Belmontet. Christophe was lost, drowned, submerged under such a deluge of poetry and turned to prose. He found Gustave de Molinari, Fléchier, Ferdinand-Édouard Buisson, Mérimée, Malte-Brun, Voltaire, Lamé-Fleury, Dumas père, J.-J. Rousseau, Mézières, Mirabeau, de Mazade, Claretie, Cortambert, Frédéric II, and M. de Voguë. The most often quoted of French historians was Maximilien Samson-Frédéric Schœll. In the French anthology Christophe found the Proclamation of the New German Empire; and he read a description of the Germans by Frédéric-Constant de Rougemont, in which he learned that *" the German was born to live in the region of the soul. He has not the light noisy gaiety of the Frenchman. His is a great soul; his affections are tender and profound. He is indefatigable in toil and persevering in enterprise. There is no more moral or long-lived people. Germany has an extraordinary number of writers. She has the genius of art. While the inhabitants of other countries pride themselves on being French, English, Spanish, the German on the other hand embraces all humanity in his love. And though its position is the very center of Europe the German nation seems to be at once the heart and the higher reason of humanity."*

Christophe closed the book. He was astonished and tired. He thought:

" The French are good fellows; but they are not strong."

He took another volume. It was on a higher plane: it was meant for high schools. Musset occupied three pages, and Victor Duruy thirty, Lamartine seven pages and Thiers almost forty. The whole of the *Cid* was included—or almost the whole:—(ten monologues of Don Diègue and Rodrigue had been suppressed because they were too long.)—Lanfrey exalted Prussia against Napoleon I and so he had not been cut down; he alone occupied more space than all the great classics of the eighteenth century. Copious narrations of the French defeats of 1870 had been extracted from *La Débâcle* of Zola. Neither Montaigne, nor La Rochefoucauld, nor La Bruyère, nor Diderot, nor Stendhal, nor Balzac, nor Flaubert appeared. On the other hand, Pascal, who did not appear in the other book, found a place in this as a curiosity; and Christophe learned by the way that the convulsionary *"was one of the fathers of Port-Royal, a girls' school, near Paris . . ."*[1]

_____

[1] The anthologies of French literature which Jean-Christophe borrowed from his friends the Reinharts were:

Christophe was on the point of throwing the book away; his head was swimming; he could not see. He said to himself: " I shall never get through with it." He could not formulate any opinion. He turned over the leaves idly for hours without knowing what he was reading. He did not read French easily, and when he had labored to make out a passage, it was almost always something meaningless and highfalutin.

And yet from the chaos there darted flashes of light, like rapier thrusts, words that looked and stabbed, heroic laughter. Gradually an impression emerged from his first reading, perhaps through the biased scheme of the selections. Voluntarily or involuntarily the German editors had selected those pieces of French which could seem to establish by the testimony of the French themselves the failings of the French and the superiority of the Germans. But they had no notion that what they most exposed to the eyes of an independent mind like Christophe's was the surprising liberty of these Frenchmen who criticised everything in their own country and praised their adversaries. Michelet praised Frederick II, Lanfrey the English of Trafalgar, Charras the Prussia of 1813. No enemy of Napoleon had ever dared to speak of him so harshly. Nothing was too greatly respected to escape their disparagement. Even under the great King the previous poets had had their freedom of speech. Molière spared nothing, La Fontaine laughed at everything. Even Boileau gibed at the nobles. Voltaire derided war, flogged religion, scoffed at his country. Moralists, satirists, pamphleteers, comic writers. they all vied one with another in gay or somber audacity. Want of respect was universal. The honest German editors were sometimes scared by it, they had to throw a rope to their consciences by trying to excuse Pascal, who lumped together cooks, porters, soldiers, and camp followers; they protested in a note that Pascal would not have written thus if he had been acquainted

---

I. *Selected French passages for the use of secondary schools,* by Hubert H. Wingerath. Ph. D.. director of the real-school of Saint John at Strasburg. Part II: Middle forms.—7th Edition, 1902, Dumont-Schauberg.

II. L. Herrig and G. F. Burguy: *Literary France,* arranged by F. Tendering, director of the real-gymnasium of the Johanneum, Hamburg.—1904, Brunswick.

with the noble armies of modern times. They did not fail to
remind the reader how happily Lessing had corrected the
Fables of La Fontaine by following, for instance, the advice
of the Genevese Rousseau and changing the piece of cheese of
Master Crow to a piece of poisoned meat of which the vile fox
dies.

*"May you never gain anything but poison. You cursed
flatterers!"*

They blinked at naked truth; but Christophe was pleased with
it; he loved this light. Here and there he was even a little
shocked; he was not used to such unbridled independence
which looks like anarchy to the eyes even of the freest of
Germans, who in spite of everything is accustomed to order
and discipline. And he was led astray by the way of the
French; he took certain things too seriously; and other things
which were implacable denials seemed to him to be amusing
paradoxes. No matter! Surprised or shocked he was drawn
on little by little. He gave up trying to classify his impressions; he passed from one feeling to another; he lived. The
gaiety of the French stories—Chamfort, Ségur, Dumas père,
Mérimée all lumped together—delighted him; and every now
and then in gusts there would creep forth from the printed
page the wild intoxicating scent of the Revolutions.

It was nearly dawn when Louisa, who slept in the next room,
woke up and saw the light through the chinks of Christophe's
door. She knocked on the wall and asked if he were ill. A
chair creaked on the floor: the door opened and Christophe
appeared, pale, in his nightgown, with a candle and a book
in his hand, making strange, solemn, and grotesque gestures.
Louisa was in terror and got up in her bed, thinking that he
was mad. He began to laugh, and, waving his candle, he declaimed a scene from Molière. In the middle of a sentence he
gurgled with laughter; he sat at the foot of his mother's bed
to take breath; the candle shook in his hand. Louisa was reassured, and scolded him forcibly:

"What is the matter with you? What is it? Go to bed.
. . . My poor boy, are you going out of your senses?"

But he began again:

"You must listen to this!"

And he sat by her bedside and read the play, going back to the beginning again. He seemed to see Corinne; he heard her mocking tones, cutting and sonorous. Louisa protested:

" Go away! Go away! You will catch cold. How tiresome you are. Let me go to sleep! "

He went on relentlessly. He raised his voice, waved his arms, choked with laughter; and he asked his mother if she did not think it wonderful. Louisa turned her back on him, buried herself in the bedclothes, stopped her ears, and said:

" Do leave me alone! . . . "

But she laughed. inwardly at hearing his laugh. At last she gave up protesting. And when Christophe had finished the act, and asked her, without eliciting any reply, if she did not think what he had read interesting, he bent over her and saw that she was asleep. Then he smiled, gently kissed her hair, and stole back to his own room.

He borrowed more and more books from the Reinharts' library. There were all sorts of books in it. Christophe devoured them all. He wanted so much to love the country of Corinne and the unknown young woman. He had so much enthusiasm to get rid of that he found a use for it in his reading. Even in second-rate works there were sentences and pages which had the effect on him of a gust of fresh air. He exaggerated the effect, especially when he was talking to Frau Reinhart, who always went a little better than he. Although she was as ignorant as a fish, she delighted to contrast French and German culture and to decry the German to the advantage of the French, just to annoy her husband and to avenge herself for the boredom she had to suffer in the little town.

Reinhart was really amused. Notwithstanding his learning, he had stopped short at the ideas he had learned at school. To him the French were a clever people, skilled in practical things, amiable, talkative, but frivolous, susceptible, and boastful, incapable of being serious, or sincere, or of feeling strongly—a people without music, without philosophy, without poetry (except for *l'Art Poétique,* Béranger and François Coppée)—a people of pathos, much gesticulation, exaggerated speech, and pornography. There were not words strong enough for the denunciation of Latin immorality; and for want of a better he always came back to *frivolity*, which for him, as for the majority of his compatriots, had a particularly unpleasant meaning. And he would end with the usual couplet in praise of the noble German people,—the moral people (" *By that,*" Herder has said, " *it is distinguished from all other nations.*")—the faithful people (*treues Volk . . . Treu* meaning everything: sincere, faithful, loyal and upright)—*the People par excellence,* as Fichte says—German Force, the symbol of justice and truth —German thought—the German *Gemüt*—the German language, the only original language, the only language that, like the race itself, has preserved its purity—German women, German wine, German song . . . " *Germany, Germany above everything in the world!* "

Christophe would protest. Frau Reinhart would cry out. They would all shout. They did not get on the less for it. They knew quite well that they were all three good Germans.

Christophe used often to go and talk, dine and walk with his new friends. Lili Reinhart made much of him, and used to cook dainty suppers for him. She was delighted to have the excuse for satisfying her own greediness. She paid him all sorts of sentimental and culinary attentions. For Christophe's birthday she made a cake, on which were twenty candles and in the middle a little wax figure in Greek costume which was supposed to represent Iphigenia holding a bouquet. Christophe, who was profoundly German in spite of himself, was touched by these rather blunt and not very refined marks of true affection.

The excellent Reinharts found other more subtle ways of showing their real friendship. On his wife's instigation Reinhart, who could hardly read a note of music, had bought twenty copies of Christophe's *Lieder*—(the first to leave the publisher's shop)—he had sent them to different parts of Germany to university acquaintances. He had also sent a certain number to the libraries of Leipzig and Berlin, with which he had dealings through his classbooks. For the moment at least their touching enterprise, of which Christophe knew nothing, bore no fruit. The *Lieder* which had been scattered broadcast seemed to miss fire:

nobody talked of them : and the Reinharts, who were hurt by this indifference, were glad they had not told Christophe about what they had done, for it would have given him more pain than consolation. But in truth nothing is lost, as so often appears in life; no effort is in vain. For years nothing happens. Then one day it appears that your idea has made its way. It was impossible to be sure that Christophe's *Lieder* had not reached the hearts of a few good people buried in the country, who were too timid or too tired to tell him so.

One person wrote to him. Two or three months after the Reinharts had sent them, a letter came for Christophe. It was warm, ceremonious, enthusiastic, old-fashioned in form, and came from a little town in Thuringia, and was signed " *Universitäts Musikdirektor Professor Dr. Peter Schulz.*"

It was a great joy for Christophe, and even greater for the Reinharts, when at their house he opened the letter, which he had left lying in his pocket for two days. They read it together. Reinhart made signs to his wife which Christophe did not notice. He looked radiant, until suddenly Reinhart saw his face grow gloomy, and he stopped dead in the middle of his reading.

" Well, why do you stop? " he asked.

(They used the familiar *du.*)

Christophe flung the letter on the table angrily.

" No. It is too much! " he said.

" What is? "

" Read! "

He turned away and went and sulked in a corner.

Reinhart and his wife read the letter, and could find in it only fervent admiration.

" I don't see," he said in astonishment.

" You don't see? You don't see? . . ." cried Christophe, taking the letter and thrusting it in his face. " Can't you read? Don't you see that he is a *'Brahmin'* "?

And then Reinhart noticed that in one sentence the *Universitäts Musikdirektor* compared Christophe's *Lieder* with those of Brahms. Christophe moaned :

" A friend! I have found a friend at last! . . . And I have hardly found him when I have lost him! . . ."

The comparison revolted him. If they had let him, he
would have replied with a stupid letter, or perhaps, upon reflection, he would have thought himself very prudent and
generous in not replying at all. Fortunately, the Reinharts
were amused by his ill-humor, and kept him from committing
any further absurdity. They succeeded in making him write
a letter of thanks. But the letter, written reluctantly, was cold
and constrained. The enthusiasm of Peter Schulz was not
shaken by it. He sent two or three more letters, brimming
over with affection. Christophe was not a good correspondent,
and although he was a little reconciled to his unknown friend
by the sincerity and real sympathy which he could feel behind
his words, he let the correspondence drop. Schulz wrote no
more. Christophe never thought about him.

He now saw the Reinharts every day and frequently several
times a day. They spent almost all the evenings together.
After spending the day alone in concentration he had a physical need of talking, of saying everything that was in his mind,
even if he were not understood, and of laughing with or without reason, of expanding and stretching himself.

He played for them. Having no other means of showing his
gratitude, he would sit at the piano and play for hours together. Frau Reinhart was no musician, and she had difficulty in keeping herself from yawning; but she sympathized
with Christophe, and pretended to be interested in everything
he played. Reinhart was not much more of a musician than his
wife, but was sometimes touched quite materially by certain
pieces of music, certain passages, certain bars, and then he
would be violently moved sometimes even to tears, and that
seemed silly to him. The rest of the time he felt nothing; it
was just music to him. That was the general rule. He was
never moved except by the least good passages of a composition
—absolutely insignificant passages. Both of them persuaded
themselves that they understood Christophe, and Christophe
tried to pretend that it was so. Every now and then he would
be seized by a wicked desire to make fun of them. He would
lay traps for them and play things without any meaning, inapt
potpourris; and he would let them think that he had com-

posed them. Then, when they had admired it, he would tell
them what it was. Then they would grow wary, and when
Christophe played them a piece with an air of mystery, they
would imagine that he was trying to catch them again, and
they would criticise it. Christophe would let them go on and
back them up, and argue that such music was worthless, and
then he would break out:

"Rascals! You are right! . . . It is my own!" He
would be as happy as a boy at having taken them in. Frau
Reinhart would be cross and come and give him a little slap;
but he would laugh so good-humoredly that they would laugh
with him. They did not pretend to be infallible. And as
they had no leg to stand on, Lili Reinhart would criticise everything and her husband would praise everything, and so they
were certain that one or other of them would always be in
agreement with Christophe.

For the rest, it was not so much the musician that attracted
them in Christophe as the crack-brained boy, with his affectionate ways and true reality of life. The ill that they had
heard spoken of him had rather disposed them in his favor.
Like him, they were rather oppressed by the atmosphere of the
little town; like him, they were frank, they judged for themselves, and they regarded him as a great baby, not very clever
in the ways of life, and the victim of his own frankness.

Christophe was not under many illusions concerning his new
friends, and it made him sad to think that they did not understand the depths of his character, and that they would never
understand it. But he was so much deprived of friendship and
he stood in such sore need of it, that he was infinitely grateful
to them for wanting to like him a little. He had learned
wisdom in his experiences of the last year; he no longer
thought he had the right to be overwise. Two years earlier
he would not have been so patient. He remembered with amusement and remorse his severe judgment of the honest and tiresome Eulers! Alas! How wisdom had grown in him! He
sighed a little. A secret voice whispered: "Yes, but for how
long?"

That made him smile and consoled him a little. What
would he not have given to have a friend, one friend who

would understand him and share his soul! But although he
was still young he had enough experience of the world to know
that his desire was one of those which are most difficult to
realize in life, and that he could not hope to be happier than
the majority of the true artists who had gone before him. He
had learned the histories of some of them. Certain books, borrowed from the Reinharts, had told him about the terrible
trials through which the German musicians of the seventeenth
century had passed, and the calmness and resolution with which
one of these great souls—the greatest of all, the heroic Schütz—
had striven, as unshakably he went on his way in the midst
of wars and burning towns, and provinces ravaged by the
plague, with his country invaded, trampled underfoot by the
hordes of all Europe, and—worst of all—broken, worn out,
degraded by misfortune, making no fight, indifferent to everything, longing only for rest. He thought: "With such an
example, what right has any man to complain? They had
no audience, they had no future; they wrote for themselves and
God. What they wrote one day would perhaps be destroyed
by the next. And yet they went on writing and they were not
sad. Nothing made them lose their intrepidity, their joviality.
They were satisfied with their song; they asked nothing of
life but to live, to earn their daily bread, to express their
ideas, and to find a few honest men, simple, true, not artists,
who no doubt did not understand them, but had confidence in
them and won their confidence in return. How dared he
have demanded more than they? There is a minimum of happiness which it is permitted to demand. But no man has the
right to more; it rests with a man's self to gain the surplus of
happiness, not with others."

Such thoughts brought him new serenity, and he loved his
good friends the Reinharts the more for them. He had no
idea that even this affection was to be denied him.

He reckoned without the malevolence of small towns. They
are tenacious in their spite—all the more tenacious because their
spite is aimless. A healthy hatred which knows what it wants
is appeased when it has achieved its end. But men who are
mischievous from boredom never lay down their arms, for

they are always bored. Christophe was a natural prey for
their want of occupation. He was beaten without a doubt;
but he was bold enough not to seem crushed. He did not
bother anybody, but then he did not bother about anybody.
He asked nothing. They were impotent against him. He
was happy with his new friends and indifferent to anything
that was said or thought of him. That was intolerable.—Frau
Reinhart roused even more irritation. Her open friendship
with Christophe in the face of the whole town seemed, like his
attitude, to be a defiance of public opinion. But the good Lili
Reinhart defied nothing and nobody. She had no thought to
provoke others; she did what she thought fit without asking
anybody else's advice. That was the worst provocation.

All their doings were watched. They had no idea of it.
He was extravagant, she scatter-brained, and both even wanting in prudence when they went out together, or even at home
in the evening, when they leaned over the balcony talking and
laughing. They drifted innocently into a familiarity of speech
and manner which could easily supply food for calumny.

One morning Christophe received an anonymous letter. He
was accused in basely insulting terms of being Frau Reinhart's lover. His arms fell by his sides. He had never had
the least thought of love or even of flirtation with her. He
was too honest. He had a Puritanical horror of adultery.
The very idea of such a dirty sharing gave him a physical and
moral feeling of nausea. To take the wife of a friend would
have been a crime in his eyes, and Lili Reinhart would have
been the last person in the world with whom he could have
been tempted to commit such an offense. The poor woman
was not beautiful, and he would not have had even the excuse
of passion.

He went to his friends ashamed and embarrassed. They
also were embarrassed. Each of them had received a similar
letter, but they had not dared to tell each other, and all three
of them were on their guard and watched each other and dared
not move or speak, and they just talked nonsense. If Lili
Reinhart's natural carelessness took the ascendant for a moment, or if she began to laugh and talk wildly, suddenly a
look from her husband or Christophe would stop her dead;

the letter would cross her mind; she would stop in the middle
of a familiar gesture and grow uneasy. Christophe and Reinhart were in the same plight. And each of them was thinking:
" Do the others know? "

However, they said nothing to each other and tried to go
on as though nothing had happened.

But the anonymous letters went on, growing more and more
insulting and dirty. They were plunged into a condition of
depression and intolerable shame. They hid themselves when
they received the letters, and had not the strength to burn
them unopened. They opened them with trembling hands,
and as they unfolded the letters their hearts would sink; and
when they read what they feared to read, with some new vari-
ation on the same theme—the injurious and ignoble inventions of a mind bent on causing a hurt—they wept in silence.
They racked their brains to discover who the wretch might be
who so persistently persecuted them.

One day Frau Reinhart, at the end of her letter, confessed
the persecution of which she was the victim to her husband,
and with tears in his eyes he confessed that he was suffering
in the same way. Should they mention it to Christophe?
They dared not. But they had to warn him to make him be
cautious.—At the first words that Frau Reinhart said to him,
with a blush, she saw to her horror that Christophe had also
received letters. Such utter malignance appalled them. Frau
Reinhart had no doubt that the whole town was in the secret.
Instead of helping each other, they only undermined each
other's fortitude. They did not know what to do. Christophe talked of breaking somebody's head.—But whose? And
besides, that would be to justify the calumny! . . . Inform
the police of the letters?—That would make their insinuations
public. . . . Pretend to ignore them? It was no longer possible. Their friendly relations were now disturbed. It was
useless for Reinhart to have absolute faith in the honesty of
his wife and Christophe. He suspected them in spite of himself. He felt that his suspicions were shameful and absurd,
and tried hard not to pay any heed to them, and to leave Christophe and his wife alone together. But he suffered, and his
wife saw that he was suffering.

It was even worse for her. She had never thought of flirting with Christophe, any more than he had thought of it with her. The calumnious letters brought her imperceptibly to the ridiculous idea that after all Christophe was perhaps in love with her; and although he was never anywhere near showing any such feeling for her, she thought she must defend herself, not by referring directly to it, but by clumsy precautions, which Christophe did not understand at first, though, when he did understand, he was beside himself. It was so stupid that it made him laugh and cry at the same time! He in love with the honest little woman, kind enough as she was, but plain and common! . . . And to think that she should believe it! . . . And that he could not deny it, and tell her and her husband:

" Come! There is no danger! Be calm! . . ." But no; he could not offend these good people. And besides, he was beginning to think that if she held out against being loved by him it was because she was secretly on the point of loving him. The anonymous letters had had the fine result of having given him so foolish and fantastic an idea.

The situation had become at once so painful and so silly that it was impossible for this to go on. Besides, Lili Reinhart, who, in spite of her brave words, had no strength of character, lost her head in the face of the dumb hostility of the little town. They made shamefaced excuses for not meeting:

" Frau Reinhart was unwell. . . . Reinhart was busy. . . . They were going away for a few days. . . ."

Clumsy lies which were always unmasked by chance, which seemed to take a malicious pleasure in doing so.

Christophe was more frank, and said:

" Let us part, my friends. We are not strong enough."

The Reinharts wept.—But they were happier when the breach was made.

The town had its triumph. This time Christophe was quite alone. It had robbed him of his last breath of air:—the affection, however humble, without which no heart can live.

III

DELIVERANCE

He had no one. All his friends had disappeared. His dear Gottfried, who had come to his aid in times of difficulty, and whom now he so sorely needed, had gone some months before. This time forever. One evening in the summer of the last year a letter in large handwriting, bearing the address of a distant village, had informed Louisa that her brother had died upon one of his vagabond journeys which the little peddler had insisted on making, in spite of his ill health. He was buried there in the cemetery of the place. The last manly and serene friendship which could have supported Christophe had been swallowed up. He was left alone with his old mother, who cared nothing for his ideas—could only love him and not understand him. About him was the immense plain of Germany, the green ocean. At every attempt to climb out of it he only slipped back deeper than ever. The hostile town watched him drown. . . .

And as he was struggling a light flashed upon him in the middle of the night, the image of Hassler, the great musician whom he had loved so much when he was a child. His fame shone over all Germany now. He remembered the promises that Hassler had made him then. And he clung to this piece of wreckage in desperation. Hassler could save him! Hassler must save him! What was he asking? Not help, nor money, nor material assistance of any kind. Nothing but understanding. Hassler had been persecuted like him. Hassler was a free man. He would understand a free man, whom German mediocrity was pursuing with its spite and trying to crush. They were fighting the same battle.

He carried the idea into execution as soon as it occurred to him. He told his mother that he would be away for a week, and that very evening he took the train for the great

town in the north of Germany where Hassler was *Kapellmeister.*
He could not wait. It was a last effort to breathe.

Hassler was famous. His enemies had not disarmed, but his
friends cried that he was the greatest musician, present, past
and future. He was surrounded by partisans and detractors who
were equally absurd. As he was not of a very firm character,
he had been embittered by the last, and mollified by the first.
He devoted his energy to writing things to annoy his critics
and make them cry out. He was like an urchin playing pranks.
These pranks were often in the most detestable taste. Not
only did he devote his prodigious talent to musical eccentricities which made the hair of the pontiffs stand on end, but he
showed a perverse predilection for queer themes, bizarre subjects, and often for equivocal and scabrous situations; in a
word, for everything which could offend ordinary good sense
and decency. He was quite happy when the people howled,
and the people did not fail him. Even the Emperor, who
dabbled in art, as every one knows, with the insolent presumption of upstarts and princes, regarded Hassler's fame as a
public scandal, and let no opportunity slip of showing his
contemptuous indifference to his impudent works. Hassler
was enraged and delighted by such august opposition, which
had almost become a consecration for the advanced paths in
German art, and went on smashing windows. At every new
folly his friends went into ecstasies and cried that he was a
genius.

Hassler's coterie was chiefly composed of writers, painters,
and decadent critics who certainly had the merit of representing the party of revolt against the reaction—always a menace in
North Germany—of the pietistic spirit and State morality;
but in the struggle the independence had been carried to a
pitch of absurdity of which they were unconscious. For, if
many of them were not lacking in a rude sort of talent, they
had little intelligence and less taste. They could not rise above
the fastidious atmosphere which they had created, and like
all cliques, they had ended by losing all sense of real life.
They legislated for themselves and hundreds of fools who read
their reviews and gulped down everything they were pleased to

promulgate. Their adulation had been fatal to Hassler, for it
had made him too pleased with himself. He accepted without
examination every musical idea that came into his head, and
he had a private conviction, however he might fall below his
own level, he was still superior to that of all other musicians.
And though that idea was only too true in the majority of
cases, it did not follow that it was a very fit state of mind
for the creation of great works. At heart Hassler had a
supreme contempt for everybody, friends and enemies alike;
and this bitter jeering contempt was extended to himself and life
in general. He was all the more driven back into his
ironic skepticism because he had once believed in a number
of generous and simple things. As he had not been strong
enough to ward off the slow destruction of the passing of the
days, nor hypocritical enough to pretend to believe in the
faith he had lost, he was forever gibing at the memory of it.
He was of a Southern German nature, soft and indolent, not
made to resist excess of fortune or misfortune, of heat or cold,
needing a moderate temperature to preserve its balance. He
had drifted insensibly into a lazy enjoyment of life. He loved
good food, heavy drinking, idle lounging, and sensuous thoughts.
His whole art smacked of these things, although he was too
gifted for the flashes of his genius not still to shine forth from
his lax music which drifted with the fashion. No one was
more conscious than himself of his decay. In truth, he was
the only one to be conscious of it—at rare moments which,
naturally, he avoided. Besides, he was misanthropic, absorbed
by his fearful moods, his egoistic preoccupations, his concern
about his health—he was indifferent to everything which had
formerly excited his enthusiasm or hatred.

Such was the man to whom Christophe came for assistance.
With what joy and hope he arrived, one cold, wet morning,
in the town wherein then lived the man who symbolized for
him the spirit of independence in his art! He expected words
of friendship and encouragement from him—words that he
needed to help him to go on with the ungrateful, inevitable
battle which every true artist has to wage against the world
until he breathes his last, without even for one day laying

down his arms; for, as Schiller has said, "*the only relation with the public of which a man never repents—is war.*"

Christophe was so impatient that he just left his bag at the first hotel he came to near the station, and then ran to the theater to find out Hassler's address. Hassler lived some way from the center of the town, in one of the suburbs. Christophe took an electric train, and hungrily ate a roll. His heart thumped as he approached his goal.

The district in which Hassler had chosen his house was almost entirely built in that strange new architecture into which young Germany has thrown an erudite and deliberate barbarism struggling laboriously to have genius. In the middle of the commonplace town, with its straight, characterless streets, there suddenly appeared Egyptian hypogea, Norwegian chalets, cloisters, bastions, exhibition, pavilions, pot-bellied houses, fakirs, buried in the ground, with expressionless faces, with only one enormous eye; dungeon gates, ponderous gates, iron hoops, golden cryptograms on the panes of grated windows, belching monsters over the front door, blue porcelain tiles plastered on in most unexpected places; variegated mosaics representing Adam and Eve; roofs covered with tiles of jarring colors; houses like citadels with castellated walls, deformed animals on the roofs, no windows on one side, and then suddenly, close to each other, gaping holes, square, red, angular, triangular, like wounds; great stretches of empty wall from which suddenly there would spring a massive balcony with one window—a balcony supported by Nibelungesque Caryatides, balconies from which there peered through the stone balustrade two pointed heads of old men, bearded and long-haired, mermen of Bœcklin. On the front of one of these prisons—a Pharaohesque mansion, low and one-storied, with two naked giants at the gate—the architect had written:

> Let the artist show his universe,
> Which never was and yet will ever be.
>
> *Seine Welt zeige der Künstler,*
> *Die niemals war noch jemals sein wird.*

Christophe was absorbed by the idea of seeing Hassler, and looked with the eyes of amazement and under no attempt to

understand. He reached the house he sought, one of the
simplest—in a Carolingian style. Inside was rich luxury, commonplace enough. On the staircase was the heavy atmosphere
of hot air. There was a small lift which Christophe did not use,
as he wanted to gain time to prepare himself for his call by going up the four flights of stairs slowly, with his legs giving and
his heart thumping with his excitement. During that short
ascent his former interview with Hassler, his childish enthusiasm, the image of his grandfather were as clearly in his mind
as though it had all been yesterday.

It was nearly eleven when he rang the bell. He was received
by a sharp maid, with a *serva padrona* manner, who looked at
him impertinently and began to say that " Herr Hassler could
not see him, as Herr Hassler was tired." Then the naïve disappointment expressed in Christophe's face amused her; for
after making an unabashed scrutiny of him from head to foot,
she softened suddenly and introduced him to Hassler's study,
and said she would go and see if Herr Hassler would receive
him. Thereupon she gave him a little wink and closed the
door.

On the walls were a few impressionist paintings and some
gallant French engravings of the eighteenth century: for
Hassler pretended to some knowledge of all the arts, and
Manet and Watteau were joined together in his taste in accordance with the prescription of his coterie. The same mixture of
styles appeared in the furniture, and a very fine Louis XV
bureau was surrounded by new art armchairs and an oriental
divan with a mountain of multi-colored cushions. The doors
were ornamented with mirrors, and Japanese bric-a-brac covered
the shelves and the mantelpiece, on which stood a bust of
Hassler. In a bowl on a round table was a profusion of photographs of singers, female admirers and friends, with witty
remarks and enthusiastic interjections. The bureau was incredibly untidy. The piano was open. The shelves were
dusty, and half-smoked cigars were lying about everywhere.

In the next room Christophe heard a cross voice grumbling.
It was answered by the shrill tones of the little maid. It
was clear that Hassler was not very pleased at having to appear. It was clear, also, that the young woman had decided

that Hassler should appear; and she answered him with extreme familiarity and her shrill voice penetrated the walls. Christophe was rather upset at hearing some of the remarks she made to her master. But Hassler did not seem to mind. On the contrary, it rather seemed as though her impertinence amused him; and while he went on growling, he chaffed the girl and took a delight in exciting her. At last Christophe heard a door open, and, still growling and chaffing, Hassler came shuffling.

He entered. Christophe's heart sank. He recognized him. Would to God he had not! It was Hassler, and yet it was not he. He still had his great smooth brow, his face as unwrinkled as that of a babe; but he was bald, stout, yellowish, sleepy-looking; his lower lip drooped a little, his mouth looked bored and sulky. He hunched his shoulders, buried his hands in the pockets of his open waistcoat; old shoes flopped on his feet; his shirt was bagged above his trousers, which he had not finished buttoning. He looked at Christophe with his sleepy eyes, in which there was no light as the young man murmured his name. He bowed automatically, said nothing, nodded towards a chair, and with a sigh, sank down on the divan and piled the cushions about himself. Christophe repeated:

"I have already had the honor . . . You were kind enough . . . My name is Christophe Krafft. . . ."

Hassler lay back on the divan, with his legs crossed, his hands clasped together on his right knee, which he held up to his chin as he replied:

"I don't remember."

Christophe's throat went dry, and he tried to remind him of their former meeting. Under any circumstances it would have been difficult for him to talk of memories so intimate; now it was torture for him. He bungled his sentences, could not find words, said absurd things which made him blush. Hassler let him flounder on and never ceased to look at him with his vague, indifferent eyes. When Christophe had reached the end of his story, Hassler went on rocking his knee in silence for a moment, as though he were waiting for Christophe to go on. Then he said:

"Yes . . . That does not make us young again . . ." and stretched his legs.

After a yawn he added:

". . . I beg pardon . . . Did not sleep . . . Supper at the theater last night . . ." and yawned again.

Christophe hoped that Hassler would make some reference to what he had just told him, but Hassler, whom the story had not interested at all, said nothing about it, and he did not ask Christophe anything about his life. When he had done yawning he asked:

"Have you been in Berlin long?"

"I arrived this morning," said Christophe.

"Ah!" said Hassler, without any surprise. "What hotel?"

He did not seem to listen to the reply, but got up lazily and pressed an electric bell.

"Allow me," he said.

The little maid appeared with her impertinent manner.

"Kitty," said he, "are you trying to make me go without breakfast this morning?"

"You don't think I am going to bring it here while you have some one with you?"

"Why not?" he said, with a wink and a nod in Christophe's direction. "He feeds my mind: I must feed my body."

"Aren't you ashamed to have some one watching you eat— like an animal in a menagerie?"

Instead of being angry, Hassler began to laugh and corrected her:

"Like a domestic animal," he went on. "But do bring it. I'll eat my shame with it."

Christophe saw that Hassler was making no attempt to find out what he was doing, and tried to lead the conversation back. He spoke of the difficulties of provincial life, of the mediocrity of the people, the narrow-mindedness, and of his own isolation. He tried to interest him in his moral distress. But Hassler was sunk deep in the divan, with his head lying back on a cushion and his eyes half closed, and let him go on talking without even seeming to listen; or he would raise his eyelids for a moment and pronounce a few coldly ironical words, some ponderous jest at the expense of provincial people, which cut short Christophe's attempts to talk more intimately. Kitty returned with the breakfast tray: coffee, butter, ham, etc. She put it down crossly on the desk in the middle of the untidy papers. Christophe waited until she had gone before he went on with his sad story which he had such difficulty in continuing. Hassler drew the tray towards himself. He poured himself out some coffee and sipped at it. Then in a familiar and cordial though rather contemptuous way he stopped Christophe in the middle of a sentence to ask if he would take a cup.

Christophe refused. He tried to pick up the thread of his sentence, but he was more and more nonplussed, and did not know what he was saying. He was distracted by the sight of Hassler with his plate under his chin, like a child, gorging pieces of bread and butter and slices of ham which he held in his fingers. However, he did succeed in saying that he composed, that he had had an overture in the *Judith* of Hebbel performed. Hassler listened absently.

" *Was?* " (What?) he asked.

Christophe repeated the title.

" *Ach! So, so!* " (Ah! Good, good!) said Hassler, dipping his bread and his fingers into his cup. That was all.

Christophe was discouraged and was on the point of getting up and going, but he thought of his long journey in vain, and summoning up all his courage he murmured a proposal that he should play some of his works to Hassler. At the first mention of it Hassler stopped him.

" No, no. I don't know anything about it," he said, with his chaffing and rather insulting irony. " Besides, I haven't the time."

Tears came to Christophe's eyes. But he had vowed not to leave until he had Hassler's opinion about his work. He said, with a mixture of confusion and anger:

" I beg your pardon, but you promised once to hear me. I came to see you for that from the other end of Germany. You shall hear me."

Hassler, who was not used to such ways, looked at the awkward young man, who was furious, blushing, and near tears.

That amused him, and wearily shrugging his shoulders, he pointed to the piano, and said with an air of comic resignation:
"Well, then! . . . There you are!"

On that he lay back on his divan, like a man who is going to sleep, smoothed out his cushions, put them under his outstretched arms, half closed his eyes, opened them for a moment to take stock of the size of the roll of music which Christophe had brought from one of his pockets, gave a little sigh, and lay back to listen listlessly.

Christophe was intimidated and mortified, but he began to play. It was not long before Hassler opened his eyes and ears with the professional interest of the artist who is struck in spite of himself by a beautiful thing. At first he said nothing and lay still, but his eyes became less dim and his sulky lips moved. Then he suddenly woke up, growling his surprise and approbation. He only gave inarticulate interjections, but the form of them left no doubt as to his feelings, and they gave Christophe an inexpressible pleasure. Hassler forgot to count the number of pages that had been played and were left to be played. When Christophe had finished a piece, he said:
"Go on! . . . Go on! . . ."

He was beginning to use human language.

"That's good! Good!" he exclaimed to himself. "Famous! . . . Awfully famous! (*Schrecklich famos!*) But, damme!" He growled in astonishment. "What is it?"

He had risen on his seat, was stretching for wind, making a trumpet with his hand, talking to himself, laughing with pleasure, or at certain odd harmonies, just putting out his tongue as though to moisten his lips. An unexpected modulation had such an effect on him that he got up suddenly with an exclamation, and came and sat at the piano by Christophe's side. He did not seem to notice that Christophe was there. He was only concerned with the music, and when the piece was finished he took the book and began to read the page again, then the following pages, and went on ejaculating his admiration and surprise as though he had been alone in the room.

"The devil!" he said. "Where did the little beast find that? . . ."

He pushed Christophe away with his shoulders and himself

played certain passages. He had a charming touch on the piano, very soft, caressing and light. Christophe noticed his fine long, well-tended hands, which were a little morbidly aristocratic and out of keeping with the rest. Hassler stopped at certain chords and repeated them, winking, and clicking with his tongue. He hummed with his lips, imitating the sounds of the instruments, and went on interspersing the music with his apostrophes in which pleasure and annoyance were mingled. He could not help having a secret initiative, an unavowed jealousy, and at the same time he greedily enjoyed it all.

Although he went on talking to himself as though Christophe did not exist, Christophe, blushing with pleasure, could not help taking Hassler's exclamations to himself, and he explained what he had tried to do. At first Hassler seemed not to pay any attention to what the young man was saying, and went on thinking out loud; then something that Christophe said struck him and he was silent, with his eyes still fixed on the music, which he turned over as he listened without seeming to hear. Christophe grew more and more excited, and at last he plumped into confidence, and talked with naïve enthusiasm about his projects and his life.

Hassler was silent, and as he listened he slipped back into his irony. He had let Christophe take the book from his hands; with his elbow on the rack of the piano and his hand on his forehead, he looked at Christophe, who was explaining his work with youthful ardor and eagerness. And he smiled bitterly as he thought of his own beginning, his own hopes, and of Christophe's hopes, and all the disappointments that lay in wait for him.

Christophe spoke with his eyes cast down, fearful of losing the thread of what he had to say. Hassler's silence encouraged him. He felt that Hassler was watching him and not missing a word that he said, and he thought he had broken the ice between them, and he was glad at heart. When he had finished he shyly raised his head—confidently, too—and looked at Hassler. All the joy welling in him was frozen on the instant, like too early birds, when he saw the gloomy, mocking eyes that looked into his without kindness. He was silent.

After an icy moment, Hassler spoke dully. He had changed

once more; he affected a sort of harshness towards the young man. He teased him cruelly about his plans, his hopes of success, as though he were trying to chaff himself, now that he had recovered himself. He set himself coldly to destroy his faith in life, his faith in art, his faith in himself. Bitterly he gave himself as an example, speaking of his actual works in an insulting fashion.

"Hog-waste!" he said. "That is what these swine want. Do you think there are ten people in the world who love music? Is there a single one?"

"There is myself!" said Christophe emphatically. Hassler looked at him, shrugged his shoulders, and said wearily:

"You will be like the rest. You will do as the rest have done. You will think of success, of amusing yourself, like the rest. . . . And you will be right. . . ."

Christophe tried to protest, but Hassler cut him short; he took the music and began bitterly to criticise the works which he had first been praising. Not only did he harshly pick out the real carelessness, the mistakes in writing, the faults of taste or of expression which had escaped the young man, but he made absurd criticisms, criticisms which might have been made by the most narrow and antiquated of musicians, from which he himself, Hassler, had had to suffer all his life. He asked what was the sense of it all. He did not even criticise: he denied; it was as though he were trying desperately to efface the impression that the music had made on him in spite of himself.

Christophe was horrified and made no attempt to reply. How could he reply to absurdities which he blushed to hear on the lips of a man whom he esteemed and loved? Besides, Hassler did not listen to him. He stopped at that, stopped dead, with the book in his hands, shut; no expression in his eyes and his lips drawn down in bitterness. At last he said, as though he had once more forgotten Christophe's presence:

"Ah! the worst misery of all is that there is not a single man who can understand you!"

Christophe was racked with emotion. He turned suddenly, laid his hand on Hassler's, and with love in his heart he repeated:

" There is myself ! "

But Hassler did not move his hand, and if something stirred in his heart for a moment at that boyish cry, no light shone in his dull eyes, as they looked at Christophe. Irony and evasion were in the ascendant. He made a ceremonious and comic little bow in acknowledgment.

" Honored ! " he said.

He was thinking:

" Do you, though? Do you think I have lost my life for you ? "

He got up, threw the book on the piano, and went with his long spindle legs and sat on the divan again. Christophe had divined his thoughts and had felt the savage insult in them, and he tried proudly to reply that a man does not need to be understood by everybody; certain souls are worth a whole people; they think for it, and what they have thought the people have to think.—But Hassler did not listen to him. He had fallen back into his apathy, caused by the weakening of the life slumbering in him. Christophe, too sane to understand the sudden change, felt that he had lost. But he could not resign himself to losing after seeming to be so near victory. He made desperate efforts to excite Hassler's attention once more. He took up his music book and tried to explain the reason for the irregularities which Hassler had remarked. Hassler lay back on the sofa and preserved a gloomy silence. He neither agreed nor contradicted; he was only waiting for him to finish.

Christophe saw that there was nothing more to be done. He stopped short in the middle of a sentence. He rolled up his music and got up. Hassler got up, too. Christophe was shy and ashamed, and murmured excuses. Hassler bowed slightly, with a certain haughty and bored distinction, coldly held out his hand politely, and accompanied him to the door without a word of suggestion that he should stay or come again.

Christophe found himself in the street once more, absolutely crushed. He walked at random; he did not know where he was going. He walked down several streets mechanically, and then found himself at a station of the train by which he had come. He went back by it without thinking of what he was doing. He sank down on the seat with his arms and legs limp. It was impossible to think or to collect his ideas; he thought of nothing, he did not try to think. He was afraid to envisage himself. He was utterly empty. It seemed to him that there was emptiness everywhere about him in that town. He could not breathe in it. The mists, the massive houses stifled him. He had only one idea, to fly, to fly as quickly as possible,—as if by escaping from the town he would leave in it the bitter disillusion which he had found in it.

He returned to his hotel. It was half-past twelve. It was two hours since he had entered it,—with what a light shining in his heart! Now it was dead.

He took no lunch. He did not go up to his room. To the astonishment of the people of the hotel, he asked for his bill, paid as though he had spent the night there, and said that he was going. In vain did they explain to him that there was no hurry, that the train he wanted to go by did not leave for hours, and that he had much better wait in the hotel. He insisted on going to the station at once. He was like a child. He wanted to go by the first train, no matter which, and not to stay another hour in the place. After the long journey and all the expense he had incurred,—although he had taken his holiday not only to see Hassler, but the museums, and to hear concerts and to make certain acquaintances—he had only one idea in his head: To go . . .

He went back to the station. As he had been told, his train did not leave for three hours. And also the train was not express—(for Christophe had to go by the cheapest class)— stopped on the way. Christophe would have done better to go by the next train, which went two hours later and caught up the first. But that meant spending two more hours in the place, and Christophe could not bear it. He would not even leave the station while he was waiting.—A gloomy period of waiting in those vast and empty halls, dark and noisy, where strange shadows were going in and out, always busy, always hurrying; strange shadows who meant nothing to him, all unknown to him, not one friendly face. The misty day died down. The electric lamps, enveloped in fog, flushed the night and made it darker than ever. Christophe grew more and more depressed as time went on, waiting in agony for the time to go. Ten times an hour he went to look at the train indicators to make sure that he had not made a mistake. As he was reading them once more from end to end to pass the time, the name of a place caught his eye. He thought he knew it. It was only after a moment that he remembered that it was where old Schulz lived, who had written him such kind and enthusiastic letters. In his wretchedness the idea came to him of going to see his unknown friend. The town was not on the direct line on his way home, but a few hours away, by a little local line. It meant a whole night's journey, with two or three changes and interminable waits. Christophe never thought about it. He decided suddenly to go. He had an instinctive need of clinging to sympathy of some sort. He gave himself no time to think, and telegraphed to Schulz to say that he would arrive next morning. Hardly had he sent the telegram than he regretted it. He laughed bitterly at his eternal illusions. Why go to meet a new sorrow?—But it was done now. It was too late to change his mind.

These thoughts filled his last hour of waiting—his train at last was ready. He was the first to get into it, and he was so childish that he only began to breathe again when the train shook, and through the carriage window he could see the outlines of the town fading into the gray sky under the heavy downpour of the night. He thought he must have died if he had spent the night in it.

At the very hour—about six in the evening—a letter from Hassler came for Christophe at his hotel. Christophe's visit stirred many things in him. The whole afternoon he had been thinking of it bitterly, and not without sympathy for the poor boy who had come to him with such eager affection to be received so coldly. He was sorry for that reception and a little angry with himself. In truth, it had been only one of those fits of sulky whimsies to which he was subject. He thought to make it good by sending Christophe a ticket for the opera and a few words appointing a meeting after the performance.— Christophe never knew anything about it. When he did not see him, Hassler thought:

"He is angry. So much the worse for him!"

He shrugged his shoulders and did not wait long for him.

Next day Christophe was far away—so far that all eternity would not have been enough to bring them together. And they were both separated forever.

Peter Schulz was seventy-five. He had always had delicate health and age had not spared him. He was fairly tall, but stooping, and his head hung down to his chest. He had a weak throat and difficulty in breathing. Asthma, catarrh, bronchitis were always upon him, and the marks of the struggles he had to make—many a night sitting up in his bed, bending forward, dripping with sweat in the effort to force a breath of air into his stifling lungs—were in the sorrowful lines on his long, thin, clean-shaven face. His nose was long and a little swollen at the top. Deep lines came from under his eyes and crossed his cheeks, that were hollow from his toothlessness. Age and infirmity had not been the only sculptors of that poor wreck of a man: the sorrows of life also had had their share in its making.—And in spite of all he was not sad. There was kindness and serenity in his large mouth. But in his eyes especially there was that which gave a touching softness to the old face. They were light gray, limpid, and transparent. They looked straight, calmly and frankly. They hid nothing of the soul. Its depths could be read in them.

His life had been uneventful. He had been alone for years. His wife was dead. She was not very good, or very intelligent, and she was not at all beautiful. But he preserved a tender memory of her. It was twenty-five years since he had lost her, and he had never once failed a night to have a little imaginary conversation, sad and tender, with her before he went to sleep. He shared all his doings with her.—He had had no children. That was the great sorrow of his life. He had transferred his need of affection to his pupils, to whom he was attached as a father to his sons. He had found very little return. An old heart can feel very near to a young heart and almost of the same age; knowing how brief are the years that lie between them. But the young man never has any idea of that. To him an old man is a man of another age, and besides, he is absorbed by his immediate anxieties and instinctively turns away from the melancholy end of all his efforts. Old Schulz had sometimes found gratitude in his pupils who were touched by the keen and lively interest he took in everything good or ill that happened to them. They used to come and see him from time to time. They used to write and thank him when they left the university. Some of them used to go on writing occasionally during the years following. And then old Schulz would hear nothing more of them except in the papers which kept him informed of their advancement, and he would be as glad of their success as though it was his own. He was never hurt by their silence. He found a thousand excuses for it. He never doubted their affection and used to ascribe even to the most selfish the feelings that he had for them.

But his books were his greatest refuge. They neither forgot nor deceived him. The souls which he cherished in them had risen above the flood of time. They were inscrutable, fixed for eternity in the love they inspired and seemed to feel, and gave forth once more to those who loved them. He was Professor of Æsthetics and the History of Music, and he was like an old wood quivering with the songs of birds. Some of these songs sounded very far away. They came from the depths of the ages. But they were not the least sweet and mysterious of all.—Others were familiar and intimate to him, dear companions; their every phrase reminded him of the joys and sorrows of his past life, conscious or unconscious:—(for under every day lit by the light of the sun there are unfolded other days lit by a light unknown)—And there were some songs that he had never yet heard, songs which said the things that he had been long awaiting and needing; and his heart opened to receive them like the earth to receive rain. And so old Schulz listened, in the silence of his solitary life, to the forest filled with birds, and, like the monk of the legend, who slept in the ecstasy of the song of the magic bird, the years passed over him and the evening of life was come, but still he had the heart of a boy of twenty.

He was not only rich in music. He loved the poets—old and new. He had a predilection for those of his own country, especially for Goethe; but he also loved those of other countries. He was a learned man and could read several languages.

In mind he was a contemporary of Herder and the great.
Weltbürger—the "citizens of the world," of the end of the
eighteenth century. He had lived through the years of bitter
struggle which preceded and followed seventy, and was im-
mersed in their vast idea. And although he adored Germany,
he was not "vainglorious" about it. He thought, with Herder,
that "*among all vainglorious men, he who is vainglorious of
his nationality is the completest fool,*" and, with Schiller, that
"*it is a poor ideal only to write for one nation.*" And he was
timid of mind. but his heart was large, and ready to welcome
lovingly everything beautiful in the world. Perhaps he was
too indulgent with mediocrity; but his instinct never doubted
as to what was the best; and if he was not strong enough to
condemn the sham artists admired by public opinion, he was
always strong enough to defend the artists of originality and
power whom public opinion disregarded. His kindness often
led him astray. He was fearful of committing any injustice,
and when he did not like what others liked, he never doubted
but that it must be he who was mistaken, and he would manage to love it. It was so sweet to him to love! Love and
admiration were even more necessary to his moral being than
air to his miserable lungs. And so how grateful he was to
those who gave him a new opportunity of showing them!—
Christophe could have no idea of what his *Lieder* had been to
him. He himself had not felt them nearly so keenly when he
had written them. His songs were to him only a few sparks
thrown out from his inner fire. He had cast them forth
and would cast forth others. But to old Schulz they were a
whole world suddenly revealed to him—a whole world to be
loved. His life had been lit up by them.

A year before he had had to resign his position at the university. His health, growing more and more precarious,
prevented his lecturing. He was ill and in bed when Wolf's
Library had sent him as usual a parcel of the latest music they
had received, and in it were Christophe's *Lieder*. He was alone.
He was without relatives. The few that he had had were long
since dead. He was delivered into the hands of an old servant,
who profited by his weakness to make him do whatever she liked

A few friends hardly younger than himself used to come and see him from time to time, but they were not in very good health either, and when the weather was bad they too stayed indoors and missed their visits. It was winter then and the streets were covered with melting snow. Schulz had not seen anybody all day. It was dark in the room. A yellow fog was drawn over the windows like a screen, making it impossible to see out. The heat of the stove was thick and oppressive. From the church hard by an old peal of bells of the seventeenth century chimed every quarter of an hour, haltingly and horribly out of tune, scraps of monotonous chants, which seemed grim in their heartiness to Schulz when he was far from gay himself. He was coughing, propped up by a heap of pillows. He was trying to read Montaigne, whom he loved; but now he did not find as much pleasure in reading him as usual. He let the book fall, and was breathing with difficulty and dreaming. The parcel of music was on the bed. He had not the courage to open it. He was sad at heart. At last he sighed, and when he had very carefully untied the string, he put on his spectacles and began to read the pieces of music. His thoughts were elsewhere, always returning to memories which he was trying to thrust aside.

The book he was holding was Christophe's. His eyes fell on an old canticle the words of which Christophe had taken from a simple, pious poet of the seventeenth century, and had modernized them. The *Christliches Wanderlied* (The Christian Wanderer's Song) of Paul Gerhardt.

> *Hoff! O du arme Seele.*
> *Hoff! und sei unverzagt.*
>
> *Erwarte nur der Zeit.*
> *So wirst du schon erblicken*
> *Die Sonne der schönsten Freud.*
>
> Hope, oh! thou wretched soul,
> Hope, hope and be valiant!
>
> *   *   *   *   *
>
> Only wait then, wait,
> And surely thou shalt see
> The sun of lovely Joy.

Old Schulz knew the ingenuous words, but never had they so spoken to him, never so nearly. . . . It was not the tranquil piety, soothing and lulling the soul by its monotony. It was a soul like his own. It was his own soul, but younger and stronger, suffering, striving to hope, striving to see, and seeing, Joy. His hands trembled, great tears trickled down his cheeks. He read on:

> *Auf! Auf! gieb deinem Schmerze*
> *Und Sorgen gute Nacht!*
> *Lass fahren was das Herze*
> *Betrübt und traurig macht!*

> Up! Up! and give thy sorrow
> And all thy cares good-night:
> And all that grieves and saddens
> Thy heart be put to flight.

Christophe brought to these thoughts a boyish and valiant ardor, and the heroic laughter in it showed forth in the last naïve and confident verses:

> *Bist du doch nicht Regente,*
> *Der alles führen soll,*
> *Gott sitzt im Regimente,*
> *Und führct alles wohl.*

> Not thou thyself art ruler
> Whom all things must obey,
> But God is Lord decreeing—
> All follows in His way.

And when there came the superbly defiant stanzas which in his youthful barbarian insolence he had calmly plucked from their original position in the poem to form the conclusion of his *Lied:*

> *Und obgleich alle Teufel*
> *Hier wollten wiederstehn,*
> *So wird doch ohne Zweifel,*
> *Gott nicht zurücke gehn.*

> *Was er ihm vorgenommen,*
> *Und was er haben will,*
> *Das muss doch endlich kommen*
> *Zu seinem Zweck und Ziel.*

> And even though all Devils
> Came and opposed his will,
> There were no cause for doubting,
> God will be steadfast still:
>
> What He has undertaken,
> All His divine decree—
> Exactly as He ordered
> At last shall all things be.

. . . then there were transports of delight, the intoxication of war, the triumph of a Roman *Imperator*.

The old man trembled all over. Breathlessly he followed the impetuous music like a child dragged along by a companion. His heart beat. Tears trickled down. He stammered:

"Oh! My God! . . . Oh! My God! . . ."

He began to sob and he laughed; he was happy. He choked. He was attacked by a terrible fit of coughing. Salome, the old servant, ran to him, and she thought the old man was going to die. He went on crying, and coughing, and saying over and over again:

"Oh! My God! . . . My God! . . ."

And in the short moments of respite between the fits of coughing he laughed a little hysterically.

Salome thought he was going mad. When at last she understood the cause of his agitation, she scolded him sharply:

"How can anybody get into such a state over a piece of foolery! . . . Give it me! I shall take it away. You shan't see it again."

But the old man held firm, in the midst of his coughing, and he cried to Salome to leave him alone. As she insisted, he grew angry, swore, and choked himself with his oaths. Never had she known him to be angry and to stand out against her. She was aghast and surrendered her prize. But she did not mince her words with him. She told him he was an old fool and said that hitherto she had thought she had to do with a gentleman, but that now she saw her mistake; that he said things which would make a plowman blush, that his eyes were starting from his head, and if they had been pistols would have killed her . . . She would have gone on for a long time in that strain if he had not got up furiously on his pillow and shouted at her:

" Go! " in so peremptory a voice that she went, slamming the door and declaring that he might call her as much as he liked, only she would not put herself out and would leave him alone to kick the bucket.

Then silence descended upon the darkening room. Once more the bells pealed placidly and grotesquely through the calm evening. A little ashamed of his anger, old Schulz was lying on his back, motionless, waiting, breathless, for the tumult in his heart to die down. He was clasping the precious *Lieder* to his breast and laughing like a child.

He spent the following days of solitude in a sort of ecstasy. He thought no more of his illness, of the winter, of the gray light, or of his loneliness. Everything was bright and filled with love about him. So near to death, he felt himself living again in the young soul of an unknown friend.

He tried to imagine Christophe. He did not see him as anything like what he was. He saw him rather as an idealized version of himself, as he would have liked to be: fair, slim, with blue eyes, and a gentle, quiet voice, soft, timid and tender. He idealized everything about him: his pupils, his neighbors, his friends, his old servant. His gentle, affectionate disposition and his want of the critical faculty—in part voluntary, so as to avoid any disturbing thought—surrounded him with serene, pure images like himself. It was the kindly lying which he needed if he were to live. He was not altogether deceived by it, and often in his bed at night he would sigh as he thought of a thousand little things which had happened during the day to contradict his idealism. He knew quite well that old Salome used to laugh at him behind his back with her gossips, and that she used to rob him regularly every week. He knew that his pupils were obsequious with him while they had need of him, and that after they had received all the services they could expect from him they deserted him. He knew that his former colleagues at the university had forgotten him altogether since he had retired, and that his successor attacked him in his articles, not by name, but by some treacherous allusion, and by quoting some worthless thing that he had said or by pointing out his mistakes—(a procedure

very common in the world of criticism). He knew that his
old friend Kunz had lied to him that very afternoon, and that
he would never see again the books which his other friend,
Pottpetschmidt, had borrowed for a few days,—which was hard
for a man who, like himself, was as attached to his books as
to living people. Many other sad things, old or new, would
come to him. He tried not to think of them, but they were
there all the same. He was conscious of them. Sometimes
the memory of them would pierce him like some rending sorrow.

"Oh! My God! My God! . . ."

He would groan in the silence of the night.—And then
he would discard such hurtful thoughts; he would deny them;
he would try to be confident, and optimistic, and to believe in
human truth; and he would believe. How often had his
illusions been brutally destroyed!—But always others springing into life, always, always. . . . He could not do without
them.

The unknown Christophe became a fire of warmth to his
life. The first cold, ungracious letter which he received from
him would have hurt him—(perhaps it did so)—but he would
not admit it, and it gave him a childish joy. He was so
modest and asked so little of men that the little he received
from them was enough to feed his need of loving and being
grateful to them. To see Christophe was a happiness which
he had never dared to hope for, for he was too old now to
journey to the banks of the Rhine, and as for asking Christophe
to come to him, the idea had never even occurred to him.

Christophe's telegram reached him in the evening, just as
he was sitting down to dinner. He did not understand at first.
He thought he did not know the signature. He thought there
was some mistake, that the telegram was not for him. He
read it three times. In his excitement his spectacles would
not stay on his nose. The lamp gave a very bad light, and
the letters danced before his eyes. When he did understand
he was so overwhelmed that he forgot to eat. In vain did
Salome shout at him. He could not swallow a morsel. He
threw his napkin on the table, unfolded,—a thing he never did.
He got up, hobbled to get his hat and stick, and went out. Old

Schulz's first thought on receiving such good news was to go and share it with others, and to tell his friends of Christophe's coming.

He had two friends who were music mad like himself, and he had succeeded in making them share his enthusiasm for Christophe. Judge Samuel Kunz and the dentist, Oscar Pottpetschmidt, who was an excellent singer. The three old friends had often talked about Christophe, and they had played all his music that they could find. Pottpetschmidt sang, Schulz accompanied, and Kunz listened. They would go into ecstasies for hours together. How often had they said while they were playing:

" Ah! If only Krafft were here! "

Schulz laughed to himself in the street .for the joy he had and was going to give. Night was falling, and Kunz lived in a little village half an hour away from the town. But the sky was clear; it was a soft April evening. The nightingales were singing. Old Schulz's heart was overflowing with happiness. He breathed without difficulty, he walked like a boy. He strode along gleefully, without heeding the stones against which he kicked in the darkness. He turned blithely into the side of the road when carts came along, and exchanged a merry greeting with the drivers, who looked at him in astonishment when the lamps showed the old man climbing up the bank of the road.

Night was fully come when he reached Kunz's house, a little way out of the village in a little garden. He drummed on the door and shouted at the top of his voice. A window was opened and Kunz appeared in alarm. He peered through the door and asked:

" Who is there? What is it? "

Schulz was out of breath, but he called gladly:

" Krafft—Krafft is coming to-morrow . . ." Kunz did not understand; but he recognized the voice:

" Schulz! . . . What! At this hour? What is it? " Schulz repeated:

" To-morrow, he is coming to-morrow morning! . . . "

" What? " asked Kunz, still mystified.

"Krafft!" cried Schulz.

Kunz pondered the word for a moment; then a loud exclamation showed that he had understood.

"I am coming down!" he shouted.

The window was closed. He appeared on the steps with a lamp in his hand and came down into the garden. He was a little stout old man, with a large gray head, a red beard, red hair on his face and hands. He took little steps and he was smoking a porcelain pipe. This good natured, rather sleepy little man had never worried much about anything. For all that, the news brought by Schulz excited him; he waved his short arms and his lamp and asked:

"What? Is it him? Is he really coming?"

"To-morrow morning!" said Schulz, triumphantly waving the telegram.

The two old friends went and sat on a seat in the arbor. Schulz took the lamp. Kunz carefully unfolded the telegram and read it slowly in a whisper. Schulz read it again aloud over his shoulder. Kunz went on looking at the paper, the marks on the telegram, the time when it had been sent, the time when it had arrived, the number of words. Then he gave the precious paper back to Schulz, who was laughing happily, looked at him and wagged his head and said:

"Ah! well . . . Ah! well! . . ."

After a moment's thought and after drawing in and expelling a cloud of tobacco smoke he put his hand on Schulz's knee and said:

"We must tell Pottpetschmidt."

"I was going to him," said Schulz.

"I will go with you," said Kunz.

He went in and put down his lamp and came back immediately. The two old men went on arm in arm. Pottpetschmidt lived at the other end of the village. Schulz and Kunz exchanged a few absent words, but they were both pondering the news. Suddenly Kunz stopped and whacked on the ground with his stick:

"Oh! Lord!" he said. . . . "He is away!"

He had remembered that Pottpetschmidt had had to go away that afternoon for an operation at a neighboring town where he had to spend the night and stay a day or two. Schulz was distressed. Kunz was equally put out. They were proud of Pottpetschmidt; they would have liked to show him off. They stood in the middle of the road and could not make up their minds what to do.

"What shall we do? What shall we do?" asked Kunz.

"Krafft absolutely must hear Pottpetschmidt," said Schulz. He thought for a moment and said:

"We must sent him a telegram."

They went to the post office and together they composed a long and excited telegram of which it was very difficult to understand a word. Then they went back. Schulz reckoned:

"He could be here to-morrow morning if he took the first train."

But Kunz pointed out that it was too late and that the telegram would not be sent until the morning. Schulz nodded, and they said:

"How unfortunate!"

They parted at Kunz's door; for in spite of his friendship for Schulz it did not go so far as to make him commit the imprudence of accompanying Schulz outside the village, and even to the end of the road by which he would have had to come back alone in the dark. It was arranged that Kunz should dine on the morrow with Schulz. Schulz looked anxiously at the sky:

"If only it is fine to-morrow!"

And his heart was a little lighter when Kunz, who was supposed to have a wonderful knowledge of meteorology, looked gravely at the sky—(for he was no less anxious than Schulz that Christophe should see their little countryside in all its beauty)—and said:

"It will be fine to-morrow."

Schulz went along the road to the town and came to it not without having stumbled more than once in the ruts and the heaps of stones by the wayside. Before he went home he called in at the confectioner's to order a certain tart which was the envy of the town. Then he went home, but just as he was going in he turned back to go to the station to find out the exact time at which the train arrived. At last he did go home and called Salome and discussed at length the dinner for the morrow. Then only he went to bed worn out; but he was as excited as a child on Christmas Eve, and all night he turned about and about and never slept a wink. About one o'clock in the morning he thought of getting up to go and tell Salome to cook a stewed carp for dinner; for she was marvelously successful with that dish. He did not tell her; and it was as well, no doubt. But he did get up to arrange all sorts of things in the room he meant to give Christophe; he took a thousand precautions so that Salome should not hear him, for he was afraid of being scolded. All night long he was afraid of missing the train although Christophe could not arrive before eight o'clock. He was up very early. He first looked at the sky; Kunz had not made a mistake; it was glorious weather. On tiptoe Schulz went down to the cellar; he had not been there for a long time, fearing the cold and the steep stairs; he selected his best wines, knocked his head hard against the ceiling as he came up again, and thought he was going to choke when he reached the top of the stairs with his full basket. Then he went to the garden with his shears; ruthlessly he cut his finest roses and the first branches of lilac in flower. Then he went up to his room again, shaved feverishly, and cut himself more than once. He dressed carefully and set out for the station. It was seven o'clock. Salome had not succeeded in making him take so much as a drop of milk, for he declared that Christophe would not have had breakfast when he arrived and that they would have breakfast together when they came from the station.

He was at the station three-quarters of an hour too soon. He waited and waited for Christophe and finally missed him. Instead of waiting patiently at the gate he went on to the platform and lost his head in the crowd of people coming and going. In spite of the exact information of the telegram he had imagined, God knows why, that Christophe would arrive by a different train from that which brought him; and besides it had never occurred to him that Christophe would get out of a fourth-class carriage. He stayed on for more than half an hour waiting at the station, when Christophe, who had long since arrived, had gone straight to his house. As a crowning misfortune Salome had just gone out to do her shopping; Christophe found the door shut. The woman next door whom Salome had told to say, in case any one should ring, that she would soon be back, gave the message without any addition to it. Christophe, who had not come to see Salome and did not even know who she was, thought it a very bad joke; he asked if *Herr Universitäts Musikdirektor* Schulz was not at home. He was told "Yes," but the woman could not tell him where he was. Christophe was furious and went away.

When old Schulz came back with a face an ell long and learned from Salome, who had just come in too, what had happened he was in despair; he almost wept. He stormed at his servant for her stupidity in going out while he was away and not having even given instructions that Christophe was to be kept waiting. Salome replied in the same way that she could not imagine that he would be so foolish as to miss a man whom he had gone to meet. But the old man did not stay to argue with her; without losing a moment he hobbled out of doors again and went off to look for Christophe armed with the very vague clues given him by his neighbors.

Christophe had been offended at finding nobody and not even a word of excuse. Not knowing what to do until the next train he went and walked about the town and the fields, which he thought very pretty. It was a quiet reposeful little town sheltered between gently sloping hills; there were gardens round the houses, cherry-trees and flowers, green lawns, beautiful shady trees, pseudo-antique ruins, white busts of bygone princesses on marble columns in the midst of the trees, with gentle and pleasing faces. All about the town were meadows and hills. In the flowering trees blackbirds whistled joyously, for many little orchestras of flutes gay and solemn. It was not long before Christophe's ill-humor vanished; he forgot Peter Schulz.

The old man rushed vainly through the streets questioning people; he went up to the old castle on the hill above the town and was coming back in despair when, with his keen, far-sighted eyes, he saw some distance away a man lying in a meadow in the shade of a thorn. He did not know Christophe; he had no means of being sure that it was he. Besides, the man's back was turned towards him and his face was half hidden in the grass. Schulz prowled along the road and about the meadow with his heart beating:

"It is he . . . No, it is not he . . ."

He dared not call to him. An idea struck him; he began to sing the last bars of Christophe's *Lied:*

"*Auf! Auf!* . . ." (Up! Up! . . .)

Christophe rose to it like a fish out of the water and shouted the following bars at the top of his voice. He turned gladly. His face was red and there was grass in his hair. They called to each other by name and ran together. Schulz strode across the ditch by the road; Christophe leaped the fence. They shook hands warmly and went back to the house laughing and talking loudly. The old man told how he had missed him. Christophe, who a moment before had decided to go away without making any further attempt to see Schulz, was at once conscious of his kindness and simplicity and began to love him. Before they arrived they had already confided many things to each other.

When they reached the house they found Kunz, who, having learned that Schulz had gone to look for Christophe, was waiting quietly. They were given *café au lait.* But Christophe said that he had breakfasted at an inn. The old man was upset; it was a real grief to him that Christophe's first meal in the place should not have been in his house; such small things were of vast importance to his fond heart. Christophe. who understood him, was amused by it secretly, and loved him the more for it. And to console him he assured him that he had appetite enough for two breakfasts; and he proved his assertion.

All his troubles had gone from his mind; he felt that he was among true friends and he began to recover. He told them about his journey and his rebuffs in a humorous way; he looked like a schoolboy on holiday. Schulz beamed and devoured him with his eyes and laughed heartily.

It was not long before conversation turned upon the secret bond that united the three of them: Christophe's music. Schulz was longing to hear Christophe play some of his compositions;

but he dared not ask him to do so. Christophe was striding about the room and talking. Schulz watched him whenever he went near the open piano; and he prayed inwardly that he might stop at it. The same thought was in Kunz. Their hearts beat when they saw him sit down mechanically on the piano stool, without stopping talking, and then without looking at the instrument run his fingers over the keys at random. As Schulz expected hardly had Christophe struck a few arpeggios than the sound took possession of him; he went on striking chords and still talking; then there came whole phrases; and then he stopped talking and began to play. The old men exchanged a meaning glance, sly and happy.

"Do you know that?" asked Christophe, playing one of his *Lieder*.

"Do I know it?" said Schulz delightedly. Christophe said without stopping, half turning his head:

"Euh! It is not very good. Your piano!" The old man was very contrite. He begged pardon:

"It is old," he said humbly. "It is like myself." Christophe turned round and looked at the old man, who seemed to be asking pardon for his age, took both his hands, and laughed. He looked into his honest eyes:

"Oh!" he said, "you are younger than I." Schulz laughed aloud and spoke of his old body and his infirmities.

"Ta, ta, ta!" said Christophe, "I don't mean that; I know what I am saying. It is true, isn't it, Kunz?"

(They had already suppressed the "*Herr.*")

Kunz agreed emphatically.

Schulz tried to find the same indulgence for his piano.

"It has still some beautiful notes," he said timidly.

And he touched them—four or five notes that were fairly true, half an octave in the middle register of the instrument. Christophe understood that it was an old friend and he said kindly,—thinking of Schulz's eyes:

"Yes. It still has beautiful eyes."

Schulz's face lit up. He launched out on an involved eulogy of his old piano, but he dropped immediately, for Christophe had begun to play again. *Lieder* followed *Lieder;* Christophe sang them softly. With tears in his eyes Schulz followed his every movement. With his hands folded on his stomach Kunz closed his eyes the better to enjoy it. From time to time Christophe turned beaming towards the two old men who were absolutely delighted, and he said with a naïve enthusiasm at which they never thought of laughing:

"Hein! It is beautiful! . . . And this! What do you say about this? . . . And this again! . . . This is the most beautiful of all. . . . Now I will play you something which will make your hair curl. . . ."

As he was finishing a dreamy fragment the cuckoo clock began to call. Christophe started and shouted angrily. Kunz was suddenly awakened and rolled his eyes fearfully. Even Schulz did not understand at first. Then when he saw Christophe shaking his fist at the calling bird and shouting to someone in the name of Heaven to take the idiot and throw it away, the ventriloquist specter, he too discovered for the first time in his life that the noise was intolerable; and he took a chair and tried to mount it to take down the spoil-sport. But he nearly fell and Kunz would not let him try again; he called Salome. She came without hurrying herself, as usual, and was staggered to find the clock thrust into her hands, which Christophe in his impatience had taken down himself.

"What am I to do with it?" she asked.

"Whatever you like. Take it away! Don't let us see it again!" said Schulz, no less impatient than Christophe.

(He wondered how he could have borne such a horror for so long.)

Salome thought that they were surely all cracked.

The music went on. Hours passed. Salome came and announced that dinner was served. Schulz bade her be silent. She came again ten minutes later, then once again, ten minutes after that; this time she was beside herself and boiling with rage while she tried to look unperturbed; she stood firmly in the middle of the room and in spite of Schulz's desperate gestures she asked in a brazen voice:

"Do the gentlemen prefer to eat their dinner cold or burned? It does not matter to me. I only await your orders."

Schulz was confused by her scolding and tried to retort; but Christophe burst out laughing. Kunz followed his exam-

ple and at length Schulz laughed too. Salome, satisfied with
the effect she had produced, turned on her heels with the air of
a queen who is graciously pleased to pardon her repentant
subjects.

"That's a good creature!" said Christophe, getting up from
the piano. "She is right. There is nothing so intolerable as
an audience arriving in the middle of a concert."

They sat at table. There was an enormous and delicious
repast. Schulz had touched Salome's vanity and she only
asked an excuse to display her art. There was no lack of
opportunity for her to exercise it. The old friends were tremendous feeders. Kunz was a different man at table; he expanded like a sun; he would have done well as a sign for a
restaurant. Schulz was no less susceptible to good cheer; but
his ill health imposed more restraint upon him. It is true that
generally he did not pay much heed to that; and he had to pay
for it. In that event he did not complain, if he were ill at
least he knew why. Like Kunz he had recipes of his own
handed down from father to son for generations. Salome was
accustomed therefore to work for connoisseurs. But on this occasion she had contrived to include all her masterpieces in one
menu; it was like an exhibition of the unforgettable cooking
of Germany, honest and unsophisticated, with all the scents
of all the herbs, and thick sauces, substantial soups, perfect
stews, wonderful carp, sauerkraut, geese, plain cakes, aniseed
and caraway seed bread. Christophe was in raptures with his
mouth full, and he ate like an ogre; he had the formidable
capacity of his father and grandfather, who would have devoured a whole goose. But he could live just as well for a whole
week on bread and cheese, and cram when occasion served.
Schulz was cordial and ceremonious and watched him with kind
eyes, and plied him with all the wines of the Rhine. Kunz
was shining and recognized him as a brother. Salome's large
face was beaming happily. At first she had been deceived when
Christophe came. Schulz had spoken about him so much
beforehand that she had fancied him as an Excellency, laden
with letters and honors. When she saw him she cried out:

"What! Is that all?"

But at table Christophe won her good graces; she had never

seen anybody so splendidly do justice to her talent. Instead of going back to her kitchen she stayed by the door to watch Christophe, who was saying all sorts of absurd things without missing a bite, and with her hands on her hips she roared with laughter. They were all glad and happy. There was only one shadow over their joy: the absence of Pottpetschmidt. They often returned to it.

"Ah! If he were here! How he would eat! How he would drink! How he would sing!"

Their praises of him were inexhaustible.

"If only Christophe could see him! . . . But perhaps he would be able to. Perhaps Pottpetschmidt would return in the evening, on that night at latest. . . ."

"Oh! I shall be gone to-night," said Christophe.

A shadow passed over Schulz's beaming face.

"What! Gone!" he said in a trembling voice. "But you are not going."

"Oh, yes," said Christophe gaily. "I must catch the train to-night."

Schulz was in despair. He had counted on Christophe spending the night, perhaps several nights, in his house. He murmured:

"No, no. You can't go! . . ."

Kunz repeated:

"And Pottpetschmidt! . . ."

Christophe looked at the two of them; he was touched by the dismay on their kind friendly faces and said:

"How good you are! . . . If you like I will go to-morrow morning."

Schulz took him by the hand.

"Ah!" he said. "How glad I am! Thank you! Thank you!"

He was like a child to whom to-morrow seems so far, so far, that it will not bear thinking on. Christophe was not going to-day; to-day was theirs; they would spend the whole evening together; he would sleep under his roof; that was all that Schulz saw; he would not look further.

They became merry again. Schulz rose suddenly, looked very solemn, and excitedly and slowly proposed the toast of

their guest, who had given him the immense joy and honor
of visiting the little town and his humble house; he drank to his
happy return, to his success, to his glory, to every happiness in
the world, which with all his heart he wished him. And then
he proposed another toast "to noble music,"—another to his
old friend Kunz,—another to spring,—and he did not forget
Pottpetschmidt. Kunz in his turn drank to Schulz and the
others, and Christophe, to bring the toasts to an end, proposed
the health of dame Salome, who blushed crimson. Upon that,
without giving the orators time to reply, he began a familiar
song which the two old men took up; after that another, and
then another for three parts which was all about friendship and
music and wine; the whole was accompanied by loud laughter
and the clink of glasses continually touching.

It was half-past three when they got up from the table.
They were rather drowsy. Kunz sank into a chair; he was
longing to have a sleep. Schulz's legs were worn out by his
exertions of the morning and by standing for his toasts. They
both hoped that Christophe would sit at the piano again and
go on playing for hours. But the terrible boy, who was in fine
form, first struck two or three chords on the piano, shut it
abruptly, looked out of the window, and asked if they could
not go for a walk until supper. The country attracted him.
Kunz showed little enthusiasm, but Schulz at once thought it an
excellent idea and declared that he must show their guest the
walk round the *Schönbuchwälder*. Kunz made a face; but he did
not protest and got up with the others; he was as desirous as
Schulz of showing Christophe the beauties of the country.

They went out. Christophe took Schulz's arm and made him
walk a little faster than the old man liked. Kunz followed
mopping his brow. They talked gaily. The people standing
at their doors watched them pass and thought that *Herr Professor* Schulz looked like a young man. When they left the
town they took to the fields. Kunz complained of the heat
Christophe was merciless and declared that the air was exquisite. Fortunately for the two old men, they stopped frequently to argue and they forgot the length of the walk in their
conversation. They went into the woods. Schulz recited verses
of Goethe and Mörike. Christophe loved poetry, but he could

not remember any, and while he listened he stepped into a
vague dream in which music replaced the words and made him
forget them. He admired Schulz's memory. What a difference
there was between the vivacity of mind of this poor rich old
man, almost impotent, shut up in his room for a great part of
the year, shut up in his little provincial town almost all his
life,—and Hassler, young, famous, in the very thick of the
artistic movement, and touring over all Europe for his concerts
and yet interested in nothing and unwilling to know anything!
Not only was Schulz in touch with every manifestation of the
art of the day that Christophe knew, but he knew an immense
amount about musicians of the past and of other countries of
whom Christophe had never heard. His memory was a great
reservoir in which all the beautiful waters of the heavens were
collected. Christophe never wearied of dipping into it, and
Schulz was glad of Christophe's interest. He had sometimes
found willing listeners or docile pupils, but he had never yet
found a young and ardent heart with which he could share
his enthusiasms, which sometimes so swelled in him that he
was like to choke.

They had become the best friends in the world when unhappily the old man chanced to express his admiration for
Brahms. Christophe was at once coldly angry; he dropped
Schulz's arm and said harshly that anyone who loved Brahms
could not be his friend. That threw cold water on their happiness. Schulz was too timid to argue, too honest to lie, and
murmured and tried to explain. But Christophe stopped him:

" Enough ! "

It was so cutting that it was impossible to reply. There was
an icy silence. They walked on. The two old men dared not
look at each other. Kunz coughed and tried to take up the
conversation again and to talk of the woods and the weather;
but Christophe sulked and would not talk and only answered
with monosyllables. Kunz, finding no response from him, tried
to break the silence by talking to Schulz; but Schulz's throat
was dry, he could not speak. Christophe watched him out of
the corner of his eyes and he wanted to laugh; he had forgiven
him already. He had never been seriously angry with him;
he even thought it brutal to make the poor old man sad; but

he abused his power and would not appear to go back on what he had said. They remained so until they left the woods; nothing was to be heard but the weary steps of the two down-cast old men; Christophe whistled through his teeth and pretended not to see them. Suddenly he could bear it no longer. He burst out laughing, turned towards Schulz and gripped his arm:

"My dear good old Schulz!" he said, looking at him affec-tionately. "Isn't it beautiful? Isn't it beautiful?"

He was speaking of the country and the fine day, but his laughing eyes seemed to say:

"You are good. I am a brute. Forgive me! I love you much."

The old man's heart melted. It was as though the sun had shone again after an eclipse. But a short time passed before he could utter a word. Christophe took his arm and went on talking to him more amiably than ever; in his eagerness he went faster and faster without noticing the strain upon his two companions. Schulz did not complain; he did not even notice his fatigue; he was so happy. He knew that he would have to pay for that day's rashness; but he thought:

"So much the worse for to-morrow! When he is gone I shall have plenty of time to rest."

But Kunz, who was not so excited, followed fifteen yards behind and looked a pitiful object. Christophe noticed it at last. He begged his pardon confusedly and proposed that they should lie down in a meadow in the shade of the poplars. Of course Schulz acquiesced without a thought for the effect it might have on his bronchitis. Fortunately Kunz thought of it for him; or at least he made it an excuse for not running any risk from the moisture of the grass when he was in such a perspiration. He suggested that they should take the train back to the town from a station close by. They did so. In spite of their fatigue they had to hurry, so as not to be late, and they reached the station just as the train came in.

At the sight of them a big man threw himself out of the door of a carriage and roared the names of Schulz and Kunz, to-gether with all their titles and qualities, and he waved his arms like a madman. Schulz and Kunz shouted in reply and also waved their arms; they rushed to the big man's compartment and he ran to meet them, jostling the people on the platform. Christophe was amazed and ran after them asking:

"What is it?"

And the others shouted exultantly:

"It is Pottpetschmidt!"

The name did not convey much to him. He had forgotten the toasts at dinner. Pottpetschmidt in the carriage and Schulz and Kunz on the step were making a deafening noise, they were marveling at their encounter. They climbed into the train as it was going. Schulz introduced Christophe. Pottpetschmidt bowed as stiff as a poker and his features lost all expression; then when the formalities were over he caught hold of Christophe's hand and shook it five or six times, as though he were trying to pull his arm out, and then began to shout again. Christophe was able to make out that he thanked God and his stars for the extraordinary meeting. That did not keep him from slapping his thigh a moment later and crying out upon the misfortune of having had to go away—he who never went away—just when the *Herr Kapellmeister* was coming. Schulz's telegram had only reached him that morning an hour after the train went; he was asleep when it arrived and they had not thought it worth while to wake him. He had stormed at the hotel people all morning. He was still storming. He had sent his patients away, cut his business appointments and taken the first train in his haste to return, but the infernal train had missed the connection on the main line; Pottpetschmidt had had to wait three hours at a station; he had exhausted all the expletives in his vocabulary and fully twenty times had narrated his misadventures to other travelers who were also waiting, and a porter at the station. At last he had started again. He was fearful of arriving too late . . . But, thank God! Thank God! . . .

He took Christophe's hands again and crushed them in his vast paws with their hairy fingers. He was fabulously stout and tall in proportion; he had a square head, close cut red hair, a clean-shaven pock-marked face, big eyes, large nose, thin lips, a double chin, a short neck, a monstrously wide back, a stomach like a barrel, arms thrust out by his body, enormous feet and hands; a gigantic mass of flesh, deformed by excess in eating and drinking; one of those human tobacco-jars that one sees sometimes rolling along the streets in the towns of Bavaria, which keep the secret of that race of men that is produced by a system of gorging similar to that of the Strasburg geese. He listened with joy and warmth like a pot of butter, and with his two hands on his outstretched knees, or on those of his neighbors, he never stopped talking, hurling consonants into the air like a catapult and making them roll along. Occasionally he would have a fit of laughing which made him shake all over; he would throw back his head, open his mouth, snorting, gurgling, choking. His laughter would infect Schulz and Kunz and when it was over they would look at Christophe as they dried their eyes. They seemed to be asking him:

"Hein! . . . And what do you say?"

Christophe said nothing; he thought fearfully:

"And this monster sings my music?"

They went home with Schulz. Christophe hoped to avoid Pottpetschmidt's singing and made no advances in spite of Pottpetschmidt's hints. He was itching to be heard. But Schulz and Kunz were too intent on showing their friend off; Christophe had to submit. He sat at the piano rather ungraciously; he thought:

"My good man, my good man, you don't know what is in store for you; have a care! I will spare you nothing."

He thought that he would hurt Schulz and he was angry at that; but he was none the less determined to hurt him rather than have this Falstaff murdering his music. He was spared the pain of hurting his old friend: the fat man had an admirable voice. At the first bars Christophe gave a start of surprise. Schulz, who never took his eyes off him, trembled; he thought that Christophe was dissatisfied; and he was only reassured when he saw his face grow brighter and brighter as he went on playing. He was lit up by the reflection of Christophe's delight; and when the song was finished and Christophe turned round and declared that he had never heard any of his songs sung so well, Schulz found a joy in all sweeter and greater than Christophe's in his satisfaction, sweeter and greater than Pottpetschmidt's in his triumph; for they had only their own pleasure, and Schulz had that of his two friends. They went on with the music. Christophe cried aloud; he could not understand how so ponderous and common a creature could succeed in reading the idea of his *Lieder*. No doubt there were not exactly all the shades of meaning, but there was the impulse and the passion which he had never quite succeeded in imparting to professional singers. He looked at Pottpetschmidt and wondered:

" Does he really feel that? "

But he could not see in his eyes any other light than that of satisfied vanity. Some unconscious force stirred in that solid flesh. The blind passion was like an army fighting without knowing against whom or why. The spirit of the *Lieder* took possession of it and it obeyed gladly, for it had need of action; and, left to itself, it never would have known how.

Christophe fancied that on the day of the Creation the Great Sculptor did not take very much trouble to put in order the scattered members of his rough-hewn creatures, and that He had adjusted them anyhow without bothering to find out whether they were suited to each other, and so every one was made up of all sorts of pieces; and one man was scattered among five or six different men; his brain was with one, his heart with another, and the body belonging to his soul with yet another; the instrument was on one side, the performer on the other. Certain creatures remained like wonderful violins, forever shut up in their cases, for want of anyone with the art to play them. And those who were fit to play them were found all their lives to put up with wretched scraping fiddles. He had all the more reason for thinking so as he was furious with himself for never having been able properly to sing a page of music. He had an untuned voice and could never hear himself without disgust.

However, intoxicated by his success, Pottpetschmidt began to " put expression " into Christophe's *Lieder,* that is to say he substituted his own for Christophe's. Naturally he did not think that the music gained by the change, and he grew gloomy. Schulz saw it. His lack of the critical faculty and his admiration for his friends would not have allowed him of his own

accord to set it down to Pottpetschmidt's bad taste. But his
affection for Christophe made him perceptive of the young
man's finest shades of thought; he was no longer in himself,
he was in Christophe; and he too suffered from Pottpetschmidt's
affectations. He tried hard to stop his going down that perilous slope. It was not easy to silence Pottpetschmidt. Schulz
found it enormously difficult, when the singer had exhausted
Christophe's repertory, to keep him from breaking out into
the lucubrations of mediocre compositions at the mention of
whose names Christophe curled up and bristled like a porcu-
pine.

Fortunately the announcement of supper muzzled Pottpetschmidt. Another field for his valor was opened for him;
he had no rival there; and Christophe, who was a little weary
with his exploits in the afternoon, made no attempt to vie with
him.

It was getting late. They sat round the table and the three
friends watched Christophe; they drank in his words. It
seemed very strange to Christophe to find himself in the remote
little town among these old men whom he had never seen until
that day and to be more intimate with them than if they had
been his relations. He thought how fine it would be for an
artist if he could know of the unknown friends whom his
ideas find in the world,—how gladdened his heart would be and
how fortified he would be in his strength. But he is rarely
that; every one lives and dies alone, fearing to say what he
feels the more he feels and the more he needs to express it.
Vulgar flatterers have no difficulty in speaking. Those who
love most have to force their lips open to say that they love.
And so he must be grateful indeed to those who dare to speak;
they are unconsciously collaborators with the artist.—Christophe was filled with gratitude for old Schulz. He did not confound him with his two friends; he felt that he was the soul
of the little group; the others were only reflections of that living
fire of goodness and love. The friendship that Kunz and
Pottpetschmidt had for him was very different. Kunz was
selfish; music gave him a comfortable satisfaction like a fat
cat when it is stroked. Pottpetschmidt found in it the pleasure

of tickled vanity and physical exercise. Neither of them troubled to understand him. But Schulz absolutely forgot himself;
he loved.

It was late. The two friends went away in the night. Christophe was left alone with Schulz. He said:

"Now I will play for you alone."

He sat at the piano and played,—as he knew how to play
when he had some one dear to him by his side. He played his
latest compositions. The old man was in ecstasies. He sat
near Christophe and never took his eyes from him and held
his breath. In the goodness of his heart he was incapable of
keeping the smallest happiness to himself, and in spite of
himself he said:

"Ah! What a pity Kunz is not here!"

That irritated Christophe a little.

An hour passed; Christophe was still playing; they had not
exchanged a word. When Christophe had finished neither
spoke a word. There was silence, the house, the street, was
asleep. Christophe turned and saw that the old man was weeping; he got up and went and embraced him. They talked in
whispers in the stillness of the night. The clock ticked dully
in the next room. Schulz talked in a whisper, with his hands
clasped, and leaning forward; he was telling Christophe, in
answer to his questions, about his life and his sorrow; at every
turn he was ashamed of complaining and had to say:

"I am wrong . . . I have no right to complain . . .
Everybody has been very good to me . . ."

And indeed he was not complaining; it was only an involuntary melancholy emanating from the dull story of his
lonely life. At the most sorrowful moments he wove into it
professions of faith vaguely idealistic and very sentimental
which amazed Christophe, though it would have been too cruel
to contradict him. At bottom there was in Schulz not so much
a firm belief as a passionate desire to believe—an uncertain hope
to which he clung as to a buoy. He sought the confirmation of
it in Christophe's eyes. Christophe understood the appeal in
the eyes of his friend, who clung to him with touching confidence, imploring him,—and dictating his answer. Then he
spoke of the calm faith or strength, sure of itself, words which

the old man was expecting, and they comforted him. The old man and the young had forgotten the years that lay between them; they were near each other, like brothers of the same age, loving and helping each other; the weaker sought the support of the stronger; the old man took refuge in the young man's soul.

They parted after midnight; Christophe had to get up early to catch the train by which he had come. And so he did not loiter as he undressed. The old man had prepared his guest's room as though for a visit of several months. He had put a bowl of roses on the table and a branch of laurel. He had put fresh blotting paper on the bureau. During the morning he had had an upright piano carried up. On the shelf by the bed he had placed books chosen from among his most precious and beloved. There was no detail that he had not lovingly thought out. But it was a waste of trouble: Christophe saw nothing. He flung himself on his bed and went sound asleep at once.

Schulz could not sleep. He was pondering the joy that he had had and the sorrow he must have at the departure of his friend. He was turning over in his mind the words that had been spoken. He was thinking that his dear Christophe was sleeping near him on the other side of the wall against which his bed lay. He was worn out, stiff all over, depressed; he felt that he had caught cold during the walk and that he was going to have a relapse; but he had only one thought:

"If only I can hold out until he has gone!" And he was fearful of having a fit of coughing and waking Christophe. He was full of gratitude to God, and began to compose verses to the song of old Simeon: *"Nunc dimittis . . ."* He got up in a sweat to write the verses down and sat at his desk until he had carefully copied them out with an affectionate dedication, and his signature, and the date and hour. Then he lay down again with a shiver and could not get warm all night.

Dawn came. Schulz thought regretfully of the dawn of the day before. But he was angry with himself for spoiling with such thoughts the few minutes of happiness left to him; he knew that on the morrow he would regret the time fleeting then, and he tried not to waste any of it. He listened, eager for the least sound in the next room. But Christophe did not stir. He lay still just as he had gone to bed; he had not moved. Half-past six rang and he still slept. Nothing would have been easier than to make him miss the train, and doubtless he would have taken it with a laugh. But the old man was too scrupulous to use a friend so without his consent. In vain did he say to himself:

"It will not be my fault. I could not help it. It will be enough to say nothing. And if he does not wake in time I shall have another whole day with him."

He answered himself:

"No, I have no right."

And he thought it his duty to go and wake him. He knocked at his door. Christophe did not hear at first; he had to knock again. That made the old man's heart thump as he thought: "Ah! How well he sleeps! He would stay like that till midday! . . ."

At last Christophe replied gaily through the partition. When he learned the time he cried out; he was heard bustling about his room, noisily dressing himself, singing scraps of melody, while he chattered with Schulz through the wall and cracked jokes while the old man laughed in spite of his sorrow. The door opened; Christophe appeared, fresh, rested, and happy; he had no thought of the pain he was causing. In reality there was no hurry for him to go; it would have cost him nothing to stay a few days longer; and it would have given Schulz so much pleasure! But Christophe could not know that. Besides, although he was very fond of the old man, he was glad to go; he was worn out by the day of perpetual conversation, by these people who clung to him in desperate fondness. And then he was young, he thought there would be plenty of time to meet again; he was not going to the other ends of the earth!—The old man knew that he would soon be much farther than the other ends of the earth, and he looked at Christophe for all eternity.

In spite of his extreme weariness he took him to the station. A fine cold rain was falling noiselessly. At the station when he opened his purse Christophe found that he had not enough money to buy his ticket home. He knew that Schulz would gladly lend him the money, but he would nót ask him for it. . . . Why? Why deny those who love you the opportunity—the happiness of doing you a service? . . . He would not out of discretion—perhaps out of vanity. He took a ticket for a station on the way, saying that he would do the rest of the journey on foot.

The time for leaving came. They embraced on the footboard of the carriage. Schulz slipped the poem he had written during the night into Christophe's hand. He stayed on the platform below the compartment. They had nothing more to say to each other, as usual when good-byes are too long drawn out, but Schulz's eyes went on speaking, they never left Christophe's face until the train went.

The carriage disappeared round a curve. Schulz was left alone. He went back by the muddy path; he dragged along; suddenly he felt all his weariness, the cold, the melancholy of the rainy day. He was hardly able to reach home and to go upstairs again. Hardly had he reached his room than he was seized with an attack of asthma and coughing. Salome came to his aid. Through his involuntary groans, he said:

" What luck ! . . . What luck that I was prepared for it. . . ." He felt very ill. He went to bed. Salome fetched the doctor. In bed he became as limp as a rag. He could not move; only his breast was heaving and panting like a million billows. His head was heavy and feverish. He spent the whole day in living through the day before, minute by minute; he tormented himself, and then was angry with himself for complaining after so much happiness. With his hands clasped and his heart big with love he thanked God.

Christophe was soothed by his day and restored to confidence in himself by the affection that he had left behind him,—so he returned home. When he had gone as far as his ticket would take him he got out blithely and took to the road on foot. He had sixty kilometers to do. He was in no hurry and dawdled like a school-boy. It was April. The country was not very far on. The leaves were unfolding like little wrinkled hands at the ends of the black branches; the apple trees were in flower, and along the hedges the frail eglantine smiled.

Above the leafless forest, where a soft greenish down was beginning to appear, on the summit of a little hill, like a trophy on the end of a lance, there rose an old Romanic castle. Three black clouds sailed across the soft blue sky. Shadows chased over the country in spring, showers passed, then the bright sun shone forth again and the birds sang.

Christophe found that for some time he had been thinking of Uncle Gottfried. He had not thought of the poor man for a long time, and he wondered why the memory of him should so obstinately obsess him now; he was haunted by it as he walked along a path along a canal that reflected the poplars; and the image of his uncle was so actual that as he turned a great wall he thought he saw him coming towards him.

The sky grew dark. A heavy downpour of rain and hail fell, and thunder rumbled in the distance. Christophe was near a village; he could see its pink walls and red roofs among the clumps of trees. He hurried and took shelter under the projecting roof of the nearest house. The hail-stones came lashing down; they rang out on the tiles and fell down into the street like pieces of lead. The ruts were overflowing. Above the blossoming orchards a rainbow flung its brilliant garish scarf over the dark blue clouds.

On the threshold a girl was standing knitting. She asked Christophe to enter. He accepted the invitation. The room into which he stepped was used as a kitchen, a dining-room, and a bed-room. At the back a stew-pot hung over a great fire. A peasant woman who was cleaning vegetables wished Christophe good-day, and bade him go near the fire to dry himself. The girl fetched a bottle of wine and gave him to drink. She sat on the other side of the table and went on knitting, while at the same time she looked after two children who were playing at testing each other's eyes with those grasses which are known in the country as "thiefs" or "sweeps." She began to talk to Christophe. It was only after a moment that he saw that she was blind. She was not pretty. She was a big girl, with red cheeks, white teeth, and strong arms, but her features were irregular; she had the smiling, rather expressionless air of many blind people, and also their mania for talking of things and people as though they could see them.

At first Christophe was startled and wondered if she were making fun of him when she said that he looked well and that the country was looking very pretty. But after looking from the blind girl to the woman who was cleaning the vegetables he saw that nobody was surprised and that it was no joke— (there was nothing to joke about indeed).—The two women asked Christophe friendly questions as to whither he was going and whence he had come. The blind girl joined in the conversation with a rather exaggerated eagerness; she agreed with, or commented on, Christophe's remarks about the road and the fields. Naturally her observations were often wide of the mark. She seemed to be trying to pretend that she could see as well as he.

Other members of the family came in: a healthy peasant of thirty and his young wife. Christophe talked to them all, and watched the clearing sky, waiting for the moment to set out again. The blind girl hummed an air while she plied her knitting needles. The air brought back all sorts of old memories to Christophe.

"What!" he said. "You know that." (Gottfried had taught her it.)

He hummed the following notes. The girl began to laugh. She sang the first half of the phrases and he finished them. He had just got up to go and look at the weather and he was walking round the room, mechanically taking stock of every corner of it, when near the dresser he saw an object which made him start. It was a long twisted stick, the handle of which was roughly carved to represent a little bent man bowing. Christophe knew it well, he had played with it as a child. He pounced on the stick and asked in a choking voice:

"Where did you get this? . . . Where did you get it?"

The man looked up and said:

"A friend left it here—an old friend who is dead."

Christophe cried:

"Gottfried?"

They all turned and asked:

"How do you know . . . ?"

And when Christophe told them that Gottfried was his uncle, they were all greatly excited. The blind girl got up; her ball

of wool rolled across the room; she stopped her work and took
Christophe's hands and said in a great state of emotion:

" You are his nephew? "

They all talked at once. Christophe asked:

" But how . . . how do you come to know him? " The
man replied:

" It was here that he died."

They sat down again, and when the excitement had gone
down a little, the mother told, as she went on with her work,
that Gottfried used to go to the house for many years; he always used to stay there on his way to and fro from his journeys. The last time he came—(it was in last July)—he
seemed very tired, and when he took off his pack it was some
time before he could speak a word, but they did not take any
notice of it because they were used to seeing him like that when
he arrived and knew that he was short of breath. He did not
complain either. He never used to complain; he always used
to find some happiness in the most unpleasant things. When
he was doing some exhausting work he used to be glad thinking
how good it would be in bed at night, and when he was ill he
used to say how good it would be when he was not ill any
longer. . . .

" And, sir, it is wrong to be always content," added the
woman, " for if you are not sorry for yourself, nobody will
pity you. I always complain . . ."

Well, nobody had paid any attention to him. They had even
chaffed him about looking so well and Modesta—(that was the
blind girl's name)—who had just relieved him of his pack had
asked him if he was never going to be tired of running like a
young man. He smiled in reply, for he could not speak. He
sat on the seat by the door. Everybody went about their work,
the men to the fields, the woman to her cooking. Modesta went
near the seat, she stood leaning against the door with her
knitting in her hands and talked to Gottfried. He did not
reply; she did not ask him for any reply and told him everything that had happened since his last visit. He breathed
with difficulty and she heard him trying hard to speak. Instead of being anxious about him she said:

" Don't speak. Just rest. You shall talk presently. . . How can people tire themselves out like that! . . ."

And then he did not talk or even try to talk. She went on with her story thinking that he was listening. He sighed and said nothing. When the mother came a little later she found Modesta still talking and Gottfried motionless on the seat with his head flung back facing the sky; for some minutes Modesta had been talking to a dead man. She understood then that the poor man had been trying to say a few words before he died but had not been able to; then with his sad smile he had accepted that and had closed his eyes in the peace of the summer evening. . . .

The rain had ceased. The daughter-in-law went to the stables, the son took his mattock and cleared the little gutter in front of the door which the mud had obstructed. Modesta had disappeared at the beginning of the story. Christophe was left alone in the room with the mother, and was silent and much moved. The old woman, who was rather talkative, could not bear a prolonged silence; and she began to tell him the whole history of her acquaintance with Gottfried. It went far back. When she was quite young Gottfried loved her. He dared not tell her, but it became a joke; she made fun of him, everybody made fun of him,—(it was the custom wherever he went)—Gottfried used to come faithfully every year. It seemed natural to him that people should make fun of him, natural that she should have married and been happy with another man. She had been too happy, she had boasted too much of her happiness; then unhappiness came. Her husband died suddenly. Then his daughter,—a fine strong girl whom everybody admired, who was to be married to the son of the richest farmer of the district,—lost her sight as the result of an accident. One day when she had climbed to the great pear tree behind the house to pick the fruit the ladder slipped; as she fell a broken branch struck a blow near the eye. At first it was thought that she would escape with a scar, but later she had had unceasing pains in her forehead; one eye lost its sight, then the other; and all their remedies had been useless. Of course the marriage was broken off; her betrothed had vanished without any explanation, and of all the young men who a month before had actually fought for a dance with her, not one had the courage—(it is quite comprehensible)—to take a blind girl to his arms. And so Modesta, who till then had been careless and gay, had fallen into such despair that she wanted to die. She refused to eat; she did nothing but weep from morning to evening, and during the night they used to hear her still moaning in her bed. They did not know what to do, they could only join her in her despair; and she only wept the more. At last they lost patience with her moaning; then they scolded her and she talked of throwing herself into the canal. The minister would come sometimes; he would talk of the good God, and eternal things, and the merit she was gaining for the next world by bearing her sorrows, but that did not console her at all. One day Gottfried came. Modesta had never been very kind to him. Not that she was naturally unkind, but she was disdainful, and besides she never thought; she loved to laugh, and there was no malice in what she said or did to him. When he heard of her misfortune he was as overwhelmed by it as though he were a member of the family. However he did not let her see it the first time he saw her. He went and sat by her side, made no allusion to her accident and began to talk quietly as he had always done before. He had no word of pity for her; he even seemed not to notice that she was blind. Only he never talked to her of things she could not see; he talked to her about what she could hear or notice in her blindness; and he did it quite simply as though it were a natural thing; it was as though he too were blind. At first she did not listen and went on weeping. But next day she listened better and even talked to him a little. . . .

"And," the woman went on, "I do not know what he can have said to her. For we were hay-making and I was too busy to notice her. But in the evening when we came in from the fields we found her talking quietly. And after that she went on getting better. She seemed to forget her affliction. But every now and then she would think of it again; she would weep alone or try to talk to Gottfried of sad things; but he seemed not to hear, or he would not reply in the same tone; he would go on talking gravely or merrily of things which soothed

and interested her. At last he persuaded her to go out of the
house, which she had never left since her accident. He made
her go a few yards round the garden at first, and then for a
longer distance in the fields. And at last she learned to find
her way everywhere and to make out everything as though she
could see. She even notices things to which we never pay any
attention, and she is interested in everything, whereas before
she was never interested in much outside herself. That time
Gottfried stayed with us longer than usual. We dared not ask
him to postpone his departure, but he stayed of his own accord
until he saw that she was calmer. And one day—she was out
there in the yard,—I heard her laughing. I cannot tell you
what an effect that had on me. Gottfried looked happy too.
He was sitting near me. We looked at each other, and I am
not ashamed to tell you, sir, that I kissed him with all my
heart. Then he said to me:

"'Now I think I can go. I am not needed any more.'

"I tried to keep him. But he said:

"'No. I must go now. I cannot stay any longer.'

"Everybody knew that he was like the Wandering Jew: he
could not stay anywhere; we did not insist. Then he went, but
he arranged to come here more often, and every time it was a
great joy for Modesta; she was always better after his visits.
She began to work in the house again; her brother married:
she looks after the children; and now she never complains and
always looks happy. I sometimes wonder if she would be so
happy if she had her two eyes. Yes, indeed, sir, there are days
when I think that it would be better to be like her and not to
see certain ugly people and certain evil things. The world is
growing very ugly, it grows worse every day. . . . And
yet I should be very much afraid of God taking me at my
word, and for my part I would rather go on seeing the world,
ugly as it is. . . ."

Modesta came back and the conversation changed. Christophe wished to go now that the weather was fair again, but they
would not let him. He had to agree to stay to supper and to
spend the night with them. Modesta sat near Christophe and
did not leave him all the evening. He would have liked to talk
intimately to the girl whose lot filled him with pity. But she

gave him no opportunity. She would only try to ask him about Gottfried. When Christophe told her certain things she did not know, she was happy and a little jealous. She was a little unwilling to talk of Gottfried herself; it was apparent that she did not tell everything, and when she did tell everything she was sorry for it at once; her memories were her property, she did not like sharing them with another; in her affection she was as eager as a peasant woman in her attachment to her land; it hurt her to think that anybody could love Gottfried as much as she. It is true that she refused to believe it; and Christophe, understanding, left her that satisfaction. As he listened to her he saw that, although she had seen Gottfried and had even seen him with indulgent eyes, since her blindness she had made of him an image absolutely different from the reality, and she had transferred to the phantom of her mind all the hunger for love that was in her. Nothing had disturbed her illusion. With the bold certainty of the blind, who calmly invent what they do not know, she said to Christophe:

"You are like him."

He understood that for years she had grown used to living in a house with closed shutters through which the truth could not enter. And now that she had learned to see in the darkness that surrounded her, and even to forget the darkness, perhaps she would have been afraid of a ray of light filtering through the gloom. With Christophe she recalled a number of rather silly trivialities in a smiling and disjointed conversation in which Christophe could not be at his ease. He was irritated by her chatter; he could not understand how a creature who had suffered so much had not become more serious in her suffering, and he could not find tolerance for such futility; every now and then he tried to talk of graver things, but they found no echo; Modesta could not—or would not—follow him.

They went to bed. It was long before Christophe could sleep. He was thinking of Gottfried and trying to disengage him from the image of Modesta's childish memories. He found it difficult and was irritated. His heart ached at the thought that Gottfried had died there and that his body had no doubt lain in that very bed. He tried to live through the agony of his last moments, when he could neither speak nor make the blind girl understand, and had closed his eyes in death. He longed to have been able to raise his eyelids and to read the thoughts hidden under them, the mystery of that soul, which had gone without making itself known, perhaps even without knowing itself! It never tried to know itself, and all its wisdom lay in not desiring wisdom, or in not trying to impose its will on circumstance, but in abandoning itself to the force of circumstance, in accepting it and loving it. So he assimilated the mysterious essence of the world without even thinking of it. And if he had done so much good to the blind girl, to Christophe, and doubtless to many others who would be forever unknown, it was because, instead of bringing the customary words of the revolt of man against nature, he brought something of the indifferent peace of Nature, and reconciled the submissive soul with her. He did good like the fields, the woods, all Nature with which he was impregnated. Christophe remembered the evenings he had spent with Gottfried in the country, his walks as a child, the stories and songs in the night. He remembered also the last walk he had taken with his uncle, on the hill above the town, on a cold winter's morning, and the tears came to his eyes once more. He did not try to sleep, so as to remain with his memories. He did not wish to lose one moment of that night in the little place, filled with the soul of Gottfried, to which he had been led as though impelled by some unknown force. But while he lay listening to the irregular trickling of the fountain and the shrill cries of the bats, the healthy fatigue of youth mastered his will, and he fell asleep.

When he awoke the sun was shining: everybody on the farm was already at work. In the hall he found only the old woman and the children. The young couple were in the fields, and Modesta had gone to milk. They looked for her in vain. She was nowhere to be found. Christophe said he would not wait for her return. He did not much want to see her, and he said that he was in a hurry. He set out after telling the old woman to bid the others good-bye for him.

As he was leaving the village at a turn of the road he saw

the blind girl sitting on a bank under a hawthorn hedge. She got up as she heard him coming, approached him smiling, took his hand, and said:

"Come."

They climbed up through meadows to a little shady flowering field filled with tombstones, which looked down on the village. She led him to a grave and said:

"He is there."

They both knelt down. Christophe remembered another grave by which he had knelt with Gottfried, and he thought:

"Soon it will be my turn."

But there was no sadness in his thought. A great peace was ascending from the earth. Christophe leaned over the grave and said in a whisper to Gottfried:

"Enter into me! . . ."

Modesta was praying, with her hands clasped and her lips moving in silence. Then she went round the grave on her knees, feeling the ground and the grass and the flowers with her hands. She seemed to caress them, her quick fingers seemed to see. They gently plucked the dead stalks of the ivy and the faded violets. She laid her hand on the curb to get up. Christophe saw her fingers pass furtively over Gottfried's name, lightly touching each letter. She said:

"The earth is sweet this morning."

She held out her hand to him. He gave her his. She made him touch the moist warm earth. He did not loose her hand. Their locked fingers plunged into the earth. He kissed Modesta. She kissed him, too.

They both rose to their feet. She held out to him a few fresh violets she had gathered, and put the faded ones into her bosom. They dusted their knees and left the cemetery without a word. In the fields the larks were singing. White butterflies danced about their heads. They sat down in a meadow a few yards away from each other. The smoke of the village was ascending direct to the sky that was washed by the rain. The still canal glimmered between the poplars. A gleaming blue mist wrapped the meadows and woods in its folds.

Modesta broke the silence. She spoke in a whisper of the beauty of the day as though she could see it. She drank in the air through her half-open lips; she listened for the sounds of creatures and things. Christophe also knew the worth of such music. He said what she was thinking and could not have said. He named certain of the cries and imperceptible tremors that they could hear in the grass, in the depths of the air. She said:

" Ah! You see that, too? "

He replied that Gottfried had taught him to distinguish them.

" You, too? " she said a little crossly.

He wanted to say to her:

" Do not be jealous."

But he saw the divine light smiling all about them: he looked at her blind eyes and was filled with pity.

" So," he asked, " it was Gottfried taught you? "

She said " Yes," and that they gave her more delight than ever before. . . . She did not say before " what." She never mentioned the words " eyes " or " blind."

They were silent for a moment. Christophe looked at her in pity. She felt that he was looking at her. He would have liked to tell her how much he pitied her. He would have liked her to complain, to confide in him. He asked kindly:

" You have been very unhappy? "

She sat dumb and unyielding. She plucked the blades of grass and munched them in silence. After a few moments,— (the song of a lark was going farther and farther from them in the sky),—Christophe told her how he too had been unhappy, and how Gottfried had helped him. He told her all his sorrows, his trials, as though he were thinking aloud or talking to a sister. The blind girl's face lit up as he told his story, which she followed eagerly. Christophe watched her and saw that she was on the point of speaking. She made a movement to come near him and hold his hand. He moved, too—but already she had relapsed into her impassiveness, and when he had finished, she only replied with a few banal words. Behind her broad forehead, on which there was not a line, there was the obstinacy of a peasant, hard as a stone. She said that she must go home to look after her brother's children. She talked of them with a calm smile.

He asked her:

" You are happy? "

She seemed to be more happy to hear him say the word. She said she was happy and insisted on the reasons she had for being so: she was trying to persuade herself and him that it was so. She spoke of the children, and the house, and all that she had to do. . . .

" Oh! yes," she said, " I am very happy! " Christophe did not reply. She rose to go. He rose too. They said good-bye gaily and carelessly. Modesta's hand trembled a little in Christophe's. She said:

" You will have fine weather for your walk to-day." And she told him of a crossroads where he must not go wrong. It was as though, of the two, Christophe were the blind one.

They parted. He went down the hill. When he reached the bottom he turned. She was standing at the summit in the same place. She waved her handkerchief and made signs to him as though she saw him.

There was something heroic and absurd in her obstinacy in denying her misfortune, something which touched Christophe and hurt him. He felt how worthy Modesta was of pity and even of admiration,—and he could not have lived two days with her. As he went his way between flowering hedges he thought of dear old Schulz, and his old eyes, bright and tender, before which so many sorrows had passed which they refused to see, for they would not see hurtful realities.

" How does he see me, I wonder? " thought Christophe. " I am so different from his idea of me! To him I am what he wants me to be. Everything is in his own image, pure and noble like himself. He could not bear life if he saw it as it is."

And he thought of the girl living in darkness who denied the darkness, and tried to pretend that what was was not, and that what was not was.

Then he saw the greatness of German idealism, which he had so often loathed because in vulgar souls it is a source of hypocrisy and stupidity. He saw the beauty of the faith which

begets a world within the world, different from the world, like
a little island in the ocean.—But he could not bear such a
faith for himself, and refused to take refuge upon such an
Island of the Dead. Life! Truth! He would not be a lying
hero. Perhaps that optimistic lie which a German Emperor
tried to make law for all his people was indeed necessary for
weak creatures if they were to live. And Christophe would
have thought it a crime to snatch from such poor wretches the
illusion which upheld them. But for himself he never could
have recourse to such subterfuges. He would rather die than
live by illusion. Was not Art also an illusion? No. It must
not be. Truth! Truth! Eyes wide open, let him draw in
through every pore the all-puissant breath of life, see things
as they are, squarely face his misfortunes,—and laugh.

Several months passed. Christophe had lost all hope of escaping from the town. Hassler, the only man who could have
saved him, had refused to help him. And old Schulz's friendship had been taken from him almost as soon as it had been
given.

He had written once on his return, and he had received
two affectionate letters, but from sheer laziness, and especially
because of the difficulty he had expressing himself in a letter,
he delayed thanking him for his kind words. He put off writing from day to day. And when at last he made up his mind
to write he had a word from Kunz announcing the death of
his old friend. Schulz had had a relapse of his bronchitis
which had developed into pneumonia. He had forbidden them
to bother Christophe, of whom he was always talking. In spite
of his extreme weakness and many years of illness, he was
not spared a long and painful end. He had charged Kunz
to convey the tidings to Christophe and to tell him that he
had thought of him up to the last hour; that he thanked him
for all the happiness he owed him, and that his blessing would
be on Christophe as long as he lived. Kunz did not tell him
that the day with Christophe had probably been the reason of
his relapse and the cause of his death.

Christophe wept in silence, and he felt then all the worth
of the friend he had lost, and how much he loved him, and he

was grieved not to have told him more of how he loved him. It was too late now. And what was left to him? The good Schulz had only appeared enough to make the void seem more empty, the night more black after he ceased to be. As for Kunz and Pottpetschmidt, they had no value outside the friendship they had for Schulz and Schulz for them. Christophe valued them at their proper worth. He wrote to them once and their relation ended there. He tried also to write to Modesta, but she answered with a commonplace letter in which she spoke only of trivialities. He gave up the correspondence. He wrote to nobody and nobody wrote to him.

Silence. Silence. From day to day the heavy cloak of silence descended upon Christophe. It was like a rain of ashes falling on him. It seemed already to be evening, and Christophe was losing his hold on life. He would not resign himself to that. The hour of sleep was not yet come. He must live.

And he could not live in Germany. The sufferings of his genius cramped by the narrowness of the little town lashed him into injustice. His nerves were raw: everything drew blood. He was like one of those wretched wild animals who perished of boredom in the holes and cages in which they were imprisoned in the *Stadtgarten* (town gardens). Christophe used often to go and look at them in sympathy. He used to look at their wonderful eyes, in which there burned—or every day grew fainter—a fierce and desperate fire. Ah! How they would have loved the brutal bullet which sets free, or the knife that strikes into their bleeding hearts! Anything rather than the savage indifference of those men who prevented them from either living or dying!

Not the hostility of the people was the hardest for Christophe to bear, but their inconsistency, their formless, shallow natures. There was no knowing how to take them. The pig-headed opposition of one of those stiff-necked, hard races who refuse to understand any new thought were much better. Against force it is possible to oppose force—the pick and the mine which hew away and blow up the hard rock. But what can be done against an amorphous mass which gives like a jelly, collapses under the least pressure, and retains no imprint of it? All thought and energy and everything disappeared in the slough. When a stone fell there were hardly more than a few ripples quivering on the surface of the gulf: the monster opened and shut its maw, and there was left no trace of what had been.

They were not enemies. Dear God! if they only had been enemies! They were people who had not the strength to love or hate, or believe or disbelieve,—in religion, in art, in politics, in daily life; and all their energies were expended in trying to reconcile the irreconcilable. Especially since the German victories they had been striving to make a compromise, a revolting intrigue between their new power and their old principles. The old idealism had not been renounced. There should have been a new effort of freedom of which they were incapable. They were content with a forgery, with making it subservient to German interests. Like the serene and subtle Schwabian, Hegel, who had waited until after Leipzig and Waterloo to assimilate the cause of his philosophy with the Prussian State—their interests having changed, their principles had changed too. When they were defeated they said that Germany's ideal was humanity. Now that they had defeated others, they said that Germany was the ideal of humanity. When other countries were more powerful, they said, with Lessing, that *" patriotism is a heroic weakness which it is well to be without,"* and they called themselves *" citizens of the world."* Now that they were in the ascendant, they could not enough despise the Utopias *" à la Française."* Universal peace, fraternity, pacific progress, the rights of man, natural equality: they said that the strongest people had absolute rights against the others, and that the others, being weaker, had no rights against themselves. It was the living God and the Incarnate Idea, the progress of which is accomplished by war, violence, and oppression. Force had become holy now that it was on their side. Force had become the only idealism and the only intelligence.

In truth, Germany had suffered so much for centuries from having idealism and no fame that she had every excuse after so many trials for making the sorrowful confession that at all costs Force must be hers. But what bitterness was hidden in such a confession from the people of Herder and Goethe! And

what an abdication was the German victory, what a degradation
of the German ideal! Alas! There were only too many facili-
ties for such an abdication in the deplorable tendency even of
the best Germans to submit.

"*The chief characteristic of Germany,*" said Moser, more than
a century ago, "*is obedience.*" And Madame de Staël:

"*They have submitted doughtily. They find philosophic
reasons for explaining the least philosophic theory in the world:
respect for power and the chastening emotion of fear which
changes that respect into admiration.*"

Christophe found that feeling everywhere in Germany, from
the highest to the lowest—from the William Tell of Schiller,
that limited little bourgeois with muscles like a porter, who, as
the free Jew Börne says, "*to reconcile honor and fear passes
before the pillar of dear Herr Gessler, with his eyes down so
as to be able to say that he did not see the hat; did not dis-
obey,*"—to the aged and respectable Professor Weisse, a man
of seventy, and one of the most honored men of learning in the
town, who, when he saw a *Herr Lieutenant* coming, would make
haste to give him the path and would step down into the road.
Christophe's blood boiled whenever he saw one of these small
acts of daily servility. They hurt him as much as though he
had demeaned himself. The arrogant manners of the officers
whom he met in the street, their haughty insolence, made him
speechless with anger. He never would make way for them.
Whenever he passed them he returned their arrogant stare.
More than once he was very near causing a scene. He seemed
to be looking for trouble. However, he was the first to understand the futility of such bravado; but he had moments of
aberration, the perpetual constraint which he imposed on himself and the accumulation of force in him that had no outlet
made him furious. Then he was ready to go any length, and
he had a feeling that if he stayed a year longer in the place
he would be lost. He loathed the brutal militarism which he
felt weighing down upon him, the sabers clanking on the pavement, the piles of arms, and the guns placed outside the barracks, their muzzles gaping down on the town, ready to fire.
Scandalous novels, which were then making a great stir, denounced the corruption of the garrisons, great and small: the

officers were represented as mischievous creatures, who, outside
their automatic duties, were only idle and spent their time in
drinking, gambling, getting into debt, living on their families,
slandering one another, and from top to bottom of the hierarchy they abused their authority at the expense of their inferiors. The idea that he would one day have to obey them
stuck in Christophe's throat. He could not, no, he could never
bear it, and lose his own self-respect by submitting to their
humiliations and injustice. . . . He had no idea of the moral
strength in some of them, or of all that they might be suffering themselves: lost illusions, so much strength and youth
and honor and faith, and passionate desire for sacrifice, turned
to ill account and spoiled,—the pointlessness of a career, which,
if it is only a career, if it has not sacrifice as its end, is only a
grim activity, an inept display, a ritual which is recited without belief in the words that are said. . . .

His country was not enough for Christophe. He felt in
himself that unknown force which wakes suddenly, irresistibly,
in certain species of birds, at definite times, like the ebb and
flow of the tides:—the instinct of the great migrations. As
he read the volumes of Herder and Fichte which old Schulz
had left him, he found souls like his own, not "*sons of the
soil,*" slavishly bound to the globe, but "*spirits, sons of the
sun,*" turning invincibly to the light wheresoever it comes.

Whither should he go? He did not know. But instinctively
his eyes turned to the Latin South. And first to France—
France, the eternal refuge of Germany in distress. How often
had German thought turned to France, without ceasing to
slander her! Even since seventy, what an attraction emanated
from the town which had been shattered and smoking under
the German guns! The most revolutionary and the most re-
actionary forms of thought and art had found alternately and
sometimes at once example and inspiration there. Like so many
other great German musicians in distress, Christophe turned
towards Paris. . . . What did he know of the French? Two
women's faces and some chance reading. That was enough for
him to imagine a country of light, of gaiety, of courage, and
even of a little Gallic boasting, which does not sort ill with the
bold youth of the heart. He believed it all, because he needed

to believe it all, because, with all his soul, he would have liked it to be so.

He made up his mind to go. But he could not go because of his mother.

Louisa was growing old. She adored her son, who was her only joy, and she was all that he most loved on earth. And yet they were always hurting each other. She hardly understood Christophe, and did not try to understand him. She was only concerned to love him. She had a narrow, timid, dull mind, and a fine heart; an immense need of loving and being loved in which there was something touching and sad. She respected her son because he seemed to her to be very learned; but she did all she could to stifle his genius. She thought he would stay all his life with her in their little town. They had lived together for years, and she could not imagine that he would not always be the same. She was happy: why should he not be happy, too? All her dreams for him soared no higher than seeing him married to some prosperous citizen of the town, hearing him play the organ at church on Sundays, and never having him leave her. She regarded her son as though he were still twelve years old. She would have liked him never to be more than that. Innocently she inflicted torture on the unhappy man who was suffocated in that narrow world.

And yet there was much truth—moral greatness—in that unconscious philosophy of the mother, who could not understand ambition and saw all the happiness of life in the family affections and the accomplishment of humble duties. She was a creature who wished to love and only to love. Sooner renounce life, reason, logic, the material world, everything, rather than love! And that love was infinite, suppliant, exacting: it gave everything—it wished to be given everything; it renounced life for love, and it desired that renunciation from others, from the beloved. What a power is the love of a simple soul! It makes it find at once what the groping reasoning of an uncertain genius like Tolstoy, or the too refined art of a dying civilization, discovers after a lifetime—ages—of bitter struggle and exhausting effort! But the imperious world which was seething in

Christophe had very different laws and demanded another wisdom.

For a long time he had been wanting to announce his determination to his mother. But he was fearful of the grief it would bring to her, and just as he was about to speak he would lose his courage and put it off. Two or three times he did timidly allude to his departure, but Louisa did not take him seriously:—perhaps she preferred not to take him seriously, so as to persuade him that he was talking in jest. Then he dared not go on; but he would remain gloomy and thoughtful, or it was apparent that he had some secret burden upon his soul. And the poor woman, who had an intuition as to the nature of that secret, tried fearfully to delay the confession of it. Sometimes in the evening, when they were sitting, silent, in the light of the lamp, she would suddenly feel that he was going to speak, and then in terror she would begin to talk, very quickly, at random, about nothing in particular. She hardly knew what she was saying, but at all costs she must keep him from speaking. Generally her instinct made her find the best means of imposing silence on him: she would complain about her health, about the swelling of her hands and feet, and the cramps in her legs. She would exaggerate her sickness: call herself an old, useless, bed-ridden woman. He was not deceived by her simple tricks. He would look at her sadly in dumb reproach, and after a moment he would get up, saying that he was tired, and go to bed.

But all her devices could not save Louisa for long. One evening, when she resorted to them once more, Christophe gathered his courage and put his hand on his mother's and said:

"No, mother. I have something to say to you." Louisa was horrified, but she tried to smile and say chokingly:

"What is it, my dear?"

Christophe stammered out his intention of going. She tried to take it as a joke and to turn the conversation as usual, but he was not to be put off, and went on so deliberately and so seriously that there was no possibility of doubt. Then she said nothing. Her pulse stopped, and she sat there dumb, frozen, looking at him with terror in her eyes. Such sorrow showed in her eyes as he spoke that he too stopped, and they sat, both speechless. When at last she was able to recover her breath, she said—(her lips trembled)—:

"It is impossible . . . It is impossible . . ."

Two large tears trickled down her cheeks. He turned his head away in despair and hid his face in his hands. They wept. After some time he went to his room and shut himself up until the morrow. They made no reference to what had happened, and as he did not speak of it again she tried to pretend that he had abandoned the project. But she lived on tenterhooks.

There came a time when he could hold himself in no longer. He had to speak even if it broke his heart: he was suffering too much. The egoism of his sorrow mastered the idea of the suffering he would bring to her. He spoke. He went through with it, never looking at his mother, for fear of being too greatly moved. He fixed the day for his departure so as to avoid a second discussion—(he did not know if he could again win the sad courage that was in him that day). Louisa cried:

"No, no! Stop, stop! . . ."

He set his teeth and went on implacably. When he had finished (she was sobbing) he took her hands and tried to make her understand how it was absolutely necessary for his art and his life for him to go away for some time. She refused to listen. She wept and said:

"No, no! . . . I will not . . ."

After trying to reason with her, in vain, he left her, thinking that the night would bring about a change in her ideas. But when they met next day at breakfast he began once more to talk of his plans. She dropped the piece of bread she was raising to her lips and said sorrowfully and reproachfully:

"Why do you want to torture me?"

He was touched, but he said:

"Dear mother, I must."

"No, no!" she replied. "You must not . . . You want to hurt me . . . It is a madness . . ."

They tried to convince each other, but they did not listen to each other. He saw that argument was wasted; it would

only make her suffer more, and he began ostentatiously to prepare for his departure.

When she saw that no entreaty would stop him, Louisa relapsed into a gloomy stupor. She spent her days locked up in
her room and without a light, when evening came. She did not
speak or eat. At night he could hear her weeping. He was
racked by it. He could have cried out in his grief, as he lay
all night twisting and turning in his bed, sleeplessly, a prey to
his remorse. He loved her so. Why must he make her suffer? . . . Alas! She would not be the only one: he saw that
clearly. . . . Why had destiny given him the desire and strength
of a mission which must make those whom he loved suffer?

" Ah ! " he thought. " If I were free, if I were not drawn on
by the cruel need of being what I must be, or else of dying in
shame and disgust with myself, how happy would I make you—
you whom I love! Let me live first; do, fight, suffer, and then
I will come back to you and love you more than ever. How I
would like only to love, love, love! . . ."

He never could have been strong enough to resist the perpetual reproach of the grief-stricken soul had that reproach
been strong enough to remain silent. But Louisa, who was
weak and rather talkative, could not keep the sorrow that was
stifling her to herself. She told her neighbors. She told her
two other sons. They could not miss such a fine opportunity of
putting Christophe in the wrong. Rodolphe especially, who
had never ceased to be jealous of his elder brother, although
there was little enough reason for it at the time—Rodolphe,
who was cut to the quick by the least praise of Christophe, and
was secretly afraid of his future success, though he never dared
admit so base a thought—(for he was clever enough to feel his
brother's force, and to be afraid that others would feel it, too),
Rodolphe was only too happy to crush Christophe beneath the
weight of his superiority. He had never worried much about
his mother, though he knew her straitened circumstances: although he was well able to afford to help her, he left it all to
Christophe. But when he heard of Christophe's intention he
discovered at once hidden treasures of affection. He was
furious at his proposing to leave his mother and called it monstrous egoism. He was impudent enough to tell Christophe

so. He lectured him loftily like a child who deserves smacking: he told him stiffly of his duty towards his mother and of all that she had sacrificed for him. Christophe almost burst with rage. He kicked Rodolphe out and called him a rascal and a hypocrite. Rodolphe avenged himself by feeding his mother's indignation. Excited by him, Louisa began to persuade herself that Christophe was behaving l'ke a bad son. She tried to declare that he had no right to go, and she was only too willing to believe it. Instead of using only her tears, which were her strongest weapon, she reproached Christophe bitterly and unjustly, and disgusted him. They said cruel things to each other: the result was that Christophe, who, till then, had been hesitating, only thought of hastening his preparations for his departure He knew that the charitable neighbors were commiserating his mother and that in the opinion of the neighborhood she was regarded as a victim and himself as a monster. He set his teeth and would not go back on his resolve.

The days passed. Christophe and Louisa hardly spoke to each other. Instead of enjoying to the last drop their last days together, these two who loved each other wasted the time that was left—as too often happens—in one of those sterile fits of sullenness in which so many affections are swallowed up. They only met at meals, when they sat opposite each other, not looking at each other, never speaking, forcing themselves to eat a few mouthfuls, not so much for the sake of eating as for the sake of appearances. Christophe would contrive to mumble a few words, but Louisa would not reply; and when she tried to talk he would be silent. This state of things was intolerable to both of them, and the longer it went on the more difficult it became to break it. Were they going to part like that? Louisa admitted that she had been unjust and awkward, but she was suffering too much to know how to win back her son's love, which she thought she had lost, and at all costs to prevent his departure, the idea of which she refused to face. Christophe stole glances at his mother's pale, swollen face and he was torn by remorse; but he had made up his mind to go, and knowing that he was going forever out of her life, he wished cowardly to be gone to escape his remorse.

His departure was fixed for the next day but one. One of

their sad meals had just come to an end. When they finished their supper, during which they had not spoken a word, Christophe withdrew to his room; and sitting at his desk, with his head in his hands—he was incapable of working—he became lost in thought. The night was drawing late: it was nearly one o'clock in the morning. Suddenly he heard a noise, a chair upset in the next room. The door opened and his mother appeared in her nightgown, barefooted, and threw her arms round his neck and sobbed. She was feverish. She kissed her son and moaned through her despairing sobs:

"Don't go! Don't go! I implore you! I implore you! My dear, don't go! . . . I shall die . . . I can't, I can't bear it! . . ."

He was alarmed and upset. He kissed her and said: "Dear mother, calm yourself, please, please!"

But she went on:

"I can't bear it . . . I have only you. If you go, what will become of me? I shall die if you go. I don't want to die away from you. I don't want to die alone. Wait until I am dead! . . ."

Her words rent his heart. He did not know what to say to console her. What arguments could hold good against such an outpouring of love and sorrow! He took her on his knees and tried to calm her with kisses and little affectionate words. The old woman gradually became silent and wept softly. When she was a little comforted, he said:

"Go to bed. You will catch cold."

She repeated: "Don't go!"

He said in a low voice: "I will not go."

She trembled and took his hand. "Truly?" she said. "Truly?"

He turned his head away sadly. "To-morrow," he answered, "I will tell you to-morrow. . . . Leave me now, please! . . ."

She got up meekly and went back to her room. Next morning she was ashamed of her despairing outburst which had come upon her like a madness in the middle of the night, and she was fearful of what her son would say to her. She waited for him, sitting in a corner of the room. She had taken up some knitting for occupation, but her hands refused to hold it.

She let it fall. Christophe entered. They greeted each other in a whisper, without looking at each other. He was gloomy, and went and stood by the window, with his back to his mother, and he stayed without speaking. There was a great struggle in him. He knew the result of it already, and was trying to delay the issue. Louisa dared not speak a word to him and provoke the answer which she expected and feared. She forced herself to take up her knitting again, but she could not see what she was doing, and she dropped her stitches. Outside it was raining. After a long silence Christophe came to her. She did not stir, but her heart was beating. Christophe stood still and looked at her, then, suddenly, he went down on his knees and hid his face in his mother's dress, and without saying a word, he wept. Then she understood that he was going to stay, and her heart was filled with a mortal agony of joy—but at once she was seized by remorse, for she felt all that her son was sacrificing for her, and she began to suffer all that Christophe had suffered when it was she whom he sacrificed. She bent over him and covered his brow and his hair with kisses. In silence their tears and their sorrow mingled. At last he raised his head, and Louisa took his face in her hands and looked into his eyes. She would have liked to say to him:
"Go!"
But she could not.
He would have liked to say to her:
"I am glad to stay."
But he could not.
The situation was hopeless; neither of them could alter it. She sighed in her sorrow and love:
"Ah! if we could all be born and all die together!" Her simple way filled him with tenderness; he dried his tears and tried to smile and said:
"We shall die together."
She insisted:
"Truly you will not go?"
He got up:
"I have said so. Don't let us talk about it. There is nothing more to be said."
Christophe kept his word; he never talked of going again,

but he could not help thinking of it. He stayed, but he made
his mother pay dearly for his sacrifice by his sadness and bad
temper. And Louisa tactlessly—much more tactlessly than she
knew, never failing to do what she ought not to have done—
Louisa, who knew only too well the reason of his grief, insisted
on his telling her what it was. She worried him with her affection, uneasy, vexing, argumentative, reminding him every
moment that they were very different from each other—and
that he was trying to forget. How often he had tried to open
his heart to her! But just as he was about to speak the Great
Wall of China would rise between them, and he would keep his
secrets buried in himself. She would guess, but she never dared
invite his confidence, or else she could not. When she tried she
would succeed only in flinging back in him those secrets which
weighed so sorely on him and which he was so longing to tell.

A thousand little things, harmless tricks, cut her off from
him and irritated Christophe. The good old creature was
doting. She had to talk about the local gossip, and she had
that nurse's tenderness which will recall all the silly little things
of the earliest years, and everything that is associated with the
cradle. We have such difficulty in issuing from it and growing
into men and women! And Juliet's nurse must forever be laying before us our duty-swaddling clothes, commonplace thoughts,
the whole unhappy period in which the growing soul struggles
against the oppression of vile matter or stifling surroundings!

And with it all she had little outbursts of touching tenderness
—as though to a little child—which used to move him greatly
and he would surrender to them—like a little child.

The worst of all to bear was living from morning to night
as they did, together, always together, isolated from the rest
of the world. When two people suffer and cannot help each
other's suffering, exasperation is fatal; each in the end holds the
other responsible for the suffering; and each in the end believes
it. It were better to be alone; alone in suffering.

It was a daily torment for both of them. They would never
have broken free if chance had not come to break the cruel
indecision, against which they were struggling, in a way that
seemed unfortunate—but it was really fortunate.

It was a Sunday in October. Four o'clock in the afternoon. The weather was brilliant. Christophe had stayed in his room all day, chewing the cud of melancholy.

He could bear it no longer; he wanted desperately to go out, to walk, to expend his energy, to tire himself out, so as to stop thinking.

Relations with his mother had been strained since the day before. He was just going out without saying good-bye to her; but on the stairs he thought how it would hurt her the whole evening when she was left alone. He went back, making an excuse of having left something in his room. The door of his mother's room was ajar. He put his head in through the aperture. He watched his mother for a few moments. . . . (What a place those two seconds were to fill in his life ever after!) . . .

Louisa had just come in from vespers. She was sitting in her favorite place, the recess of the window. The wall of the house opposite, dirty white and cracked, obstructed the view, but from the corner where she sat she could see to the right through the yards of the next houses a little patch of lawn the size of a pocket-handkerchief. On the window sill a pot of convolvulus climbed along its threads and over this frail ladder stretched its tendrils which were caressed by a ray of sunlight. Louisa was sitting in a low chair bending over her great Bible which was open on her lap, but she was not reading. Her hands were laid flat on the book—her hands with their swollen veins, worker's nails, square and a little bent—and she was devouring with loving eyes the little plant and the patch of sky she could see through it. A sunbeam, basking on the green gold leaves, lit up her tired face, with its rather blotchy complexion, her white, soft, and rather thick hair, and her lips, parted in a smile. She was enjoying her hour of rest. It was the best moment of the week to her. She made use of it to sink into that state so sweet to those who suffer, when thoughts dwell on nothing, and in torpor nothing speaks save the heart and that is half asleep.

"Mother," he said, "I want to go out. I am going by Buir. I shall be rather late."

Louisa, who was dozing off, trembled a little. Then she

turned her head towards him and looked at him with her calm, kind eyes.

"Yes, my dear, go," she said. "You are right; make use of the fine weather."

She smiled at him. He smiled at her. They looked at each other for a moment, then they said good-night affectionately, nodding and smiling with the eyes.

He closed the door softly. She slipped back into her reverie, which her son's smile had lit up with a bright ray of light like the sunbeam on the pale leaves of the convolvulus.

So he left her—forever.

An October evening. A pale watery sun. The drowsy country is sinking to sleep. Little village bells are slowly ringing in the silence of the fields. Columns of smoke rise slowly in the midst of the plowed fields. A fine mist hovers in the distance. The white fogs are awaiting the coming of the night to rise. . . . A dog with his nose to the ground was running in circles in a field of beat. Great flocks of crows whirled against the gray sky.

Christophe went on dreaming, having no fixed object, but yet instinctively he was walking in a definite direction. For several weeks his walks round the town had gravitated whether he liked it or not towards another village where he was sure to meet a pretty girl who attracted him. It was only an attraction, but it was very vivid and rather disturbing. Christophe could hardly do without loving some one; and his heart was rarely left empty; it always had some lovely image for its idol. Generally it did not matter whether the idol knew of his love; his need was to love, the fire must never be allowed to go out; there must never be darkness in his heart.

The object of this new flame was the daughter of a peasant whom he had met, as Eliézer met Rebecca, by a well; but she did not give him to drink; she threw water in his face. She was kneeling by the edge of a stream in a hollow in the bank between two willows, the roots of which made a sort of nest about her; she was washing linen vigorously; and her tongue was not less active than her arms; she was talking and laughing loudly with other girls of the village who were washing opposite her on the other side of the stream. Christophe was lying in the grass a few yards away, and, with his chin resting in his hands, he watched them. They were not put out by it; they went on chattering in a style which sometimes did not lack bluntness. He hardly listened; he heard only the sound of their merry voices, mingling with the noise of their washing pots, and with the distant lowing of the cows in the meadows, and he was dreaming, never taking his eyes off the beautiful washerwoman. A bright young face would make him glad for a whole day. It was not long before the girls made out which of them he was looking at; and they made caustic remarks to each other; the girl he preferred was not the least cutting in the observations she threw at him. As he did not budge, she got up, took a bundle of linen washed and wrung, and began to lay it out on the bushes near him so as to have an excuse for looking at him. As she passed him she continued to splash him with her wet clothes and she looked at him boldly and laughed. She was thin and strong: she had a fine chin, a little underhung, a short nose, arching eyebrows, deep-set blue eyes, bold, bright and hard, a pretty mouth with thick lips, pouting a little like those of a Greek maid, a mass of fair hair turned up in a knot on her head, and a full color. She carried her head very erect, tittered at every word she said and even when she said nothing, and walked like a man, swinging her sunburned arms. She went on laying out her linen while she looked at Christophe with a provoking smile—waiting for him to speak. Christophe stared at her too; but he had no desire to talk to her. At last she burst out laughing to his face and turned back towards her companions. He stayed lying where he was until evening fell and he saw her go with her bundle on her back and her bare arms crossed, her back bent under her load, still talking and laughing.

He saw her again a few days later at the town market among heaps of carrots and tomatoes and cucumbers and cabbages. He lounged about watching the crowd of women, selling, who were standing in a line by their baskets like slaves for sale. The police official went up to each of them with his satchel and roll of tickets, receiving a piece of money and giving a paper. The coffee seller went from row to row with a basket full of little coffee pots. And an old nun, plump and jovial, went round the market with two large baskets on her arms and without any sort of humility begged vegetables, or talked of the good God. The women shouted: the old scales with their green painted pans jingled and clanked with the noise of their chains; the big dogs harnessed to the little carts barked loudly, proud of their importance. In the midst of the rabble Christophe saw Rebecca.—Her real name was Lorchen (Eleanor).—On her fair hair she had placed a large cabbage leaf, green and white, which made a dainty lace cap for her. She was sitting on a basket by a heap of golden onions, little pink turnips, haricot beans, and ruddy apples, and she was munching her own apples one after another without trying to sell them. She never stopped eating. From time to time she would dry her chin and wipe it with her apron, brush back her hair with her arm, rub her cheek against her shoulder, or her nose with the back of her hand. Or, with her hands on her knees, she would go on and on throwing a handful of shelled peas from one to the other. And she would look to right and left idly and indifferently. But she missed nothing of what was going on about her. And without seeming to do so she marked every glance cast in her direction. She saw Christophe. As she talked to her customers she had a way of raising her eyebrows and looking at her admirer over their heads. She was as dignified and serious as a Pope; but inwardly she was laughing at Christophe. And he deserved it; he stood there a few yards away devouring her with his eyes, then he went away without speaking to her. He had not the least desire to do so.

He came back more than once to prowl round the market and the village where she lived. She would be about the yard of the farm; he would stop on the road to look at her. He did not admit that he came to see her, and indeed he did so almost unconsciously. When, as often happened, he was absorbed by the composition of some work he would be rather like a somnambulist: while his conscious soul was following its musical ideas the rest of him would be delivered up to the other unconscious soul which is forever watching for the smallest distraction of the mind to take the freedom of the fields. He was often bewildered by the buzzing of his musical ideas when he was face to face with her; and he would go on dreaming as he watched her. He could not have said that he loved her; he did not even think of that; it gave him pleasure to see her, nothing more. He did not take stock of the desire which was always bringing him back to her.

His insistence was remarked. The people at the farm joked about it, for they had discovered who Christophe was. But they left him in peace; for he was quite harmless. He looked silly enough in truth; but he never bothered about it.

There was a holiday in the village. Little boys were crushing crackers between stones and shouting "God save the Emperor!" ("*Kaiser lebe! Hoch!*"). A cow shut up in the barn and the men drinking at the inn were to be heard. Kites with long tails like comets dipped and swung in the air above the fields. The fowls were scratching frantically in the straw and the golden dung-heap; the wind blew out their feathers like the skirts of an old lady. A pink pig was sleeping voluptuously on his side in the sun.

Christophe made his way towards the red roof of the inn of the *Three Kings* above which floated a little flag. Strings of onions hung by the door, and the windows were decorated with red and yellow flowers. He went into the saloon, filled with tobacco smoke, where yellowing chromos hung on the walls and in the place of honor a colored portrait of the Emperor-King surrounded with a wreath of oak leaves. People were dancing. Christophe was sure his charmer would be there. He sat in a corner of the room from which he could watch the movement of the dancers undisturbed. But in spite of all his care to pass unnoticed Lorchen spied him out in his corner. While she waltzed indefatigably she threw quick glances at him over her partner's shoulder to make sure that he was still looking at her; and it amused her to excite him; she coquetted with the young men of the village, laughing the while with her wide mouth. She talked a great deal and said silly things and was not very different from the girls of the polite world who think they must laugh and move about and play to the gallery when anybody looks at them, instead of keeping their foolishness to

themselves. But they are not so very foolish either; for they
know quite well that the gallery only looks at them and does not
listen to what they say.—With his elbows on the table and his
chin in his hands Christophe watched the girl's tricks with
burning, furious eyes; his mind was free enough not to be taken
in by her wiles, but he was not enough himself not to be led
on by them; and he growled with rage and he laughed in silence
and shrugged his shoulders in falling into the snare.

Not only the girl was watching him; Lorchen's father also
had his eyes on him. Thick-set and short, bald-headed—a big
head with a short nose—sunburned skull with a fringe of hair
that had been fair and hung in thick curls like Dürer's St. John,
clean-shaven, expressionless face, with a long pipe in the corner
of his mouth, he was talking very deliberately to some other
peasants while all the time he was watching Christophe's pantomime out of the corner of his eye; and he laughed softly. After
a moment he coughed and a malicious light shone in his little gray
eyes and he came and sat at Christophe's table. Christophe was annoyed and turned and scowled at him; he met the cunning look
of the old man, who addressed Christophe familiarly without taking his pipe from his lips. Christophe knew him; he knew him
for a common old man; but his weakness for his daughter made
him indulgent towards the father and even gave him a queer
pleasure in being with him; the old rascal saw that. After talking about rain and fine weather and some chaffing reference to
the pretty girls in the room, and a remark on Christophe's not
dancing he concluded that Christophe was right not to put
himself out and that it was much better to sit at table with a
mug in his hand; without ceremony he invited himself
to have a drink. While he drank the old man went on talking
deliberately as always. He spoke about his affairs, the difficulty
of gaining a livelihood, the bad weather and high prices. Christophe hardly listened and only replied with an occasional grunt;
he was not interested; he was looking at Lorchen. Christophe
wondered what had procured him the honor of the old man's
company and confidences. At last he understood. When the
old man had exhausted his complaints he passed on to another
chapter; he praised the quality of his produce, his vegetables,

his fowls, his eggs, his milk, and suddenly he asked if Christophe could not procure him the custom of the Palace. Christophe started:

" How the devil did he know? . . . He knew him then? "

" Oh, yes," said the old man. " Everything is known . . ."

He did not add:

". . . when you take the trouble to make enquiries."

But Christophe added it for him. He took a wicked pleasure in telling him that although everything was known, " he was no doubt unaware that he had just quarreled with the Court and that if he had ever been able to flatter himself on having some credit with the servants' quarters and butchers of the Palace—(which he doubted strongly)—that credit at present was dead and buried. The old man's lips twitched imperceptibly. However, he was not put out and after a moment he asked if Christophe could not at least recommend him to such and such a family. And he mentioned all those with whom Christophe had had dealings; for he had informed himself of them at the market, and there was no danger of his forgetting any detail that might be useful to him. Christophe would have been furious at such spying upon him had he not rather wanted to laugh at the thought that the old man would be robbed in spite of all his cunning (for he had no doubt of the value of the recommendation he was asking—a recommendation more likely to make him lose his customers than to procure him fresh ones). So he let him empty all his bag of clumsy tricks and answered neither " Yes " nor " No." But the peasant persisted and finally he came down to Christophe and Louisa whom he had kept for the end, and expressed his keen desire to provide them with milk, butter and cream. He added that as Christophe was a musician nothing was so good for the voice as a fresh egg swallowed raw morning and evening; and he tried hard to make him let him provide him with these, warm from the hen. The idea of the old peasant taking him for a singer made Christophe roar with laughter. The peasant took advantage of that to order another bottle. And then having got all he could out of Christophe for the time being he went away without further ceremony.

Night had fallen. The dancing had become more and more

excited. Lorchen had ceased to pay any attention to Christophe; she was too busy turning the head of a young lout of the village, the son of a rich farmer, for whom all the girls were competing. Christophe was interested by the struggle; the young women smiled at each other and would have been only too pleased to scratch each other. Christophe forgot himself and prayed for the triumph of Lorchen. But when her triumph was won he felt a little downcast. He was enraged by it. He did not love Lorchen; he did not want to be loved by her; it was natural that she should love anybody she liked.—No doubt. But it was not pleasant to receive so little sympathy himself when he had so much need of giving and receiving. Here, as in the town, he was alone. All these people were only interested in him while they could make use of him and then laugh at him. He sighed, smiled as he looked at Lorchen, whom her joy in the discomfiture of her rivals had made ten times prettier than ever, and got ready to go. It was nearly nine. He had fully two miles to go to the town.

He got up from the table when the door opened and a handful of soldiers burst in. Their entry dashed the gaiety of the place. The people began to whisper. A few couples stopped dancing to look uneasily at the new arrivals. The peasants standing near the door deliberately turned their backs on them and began to talk among themselves; but without seeming to do so they presently contrived to leave room for them to pass. For some time past the whole neighborhood had been at loggerheads with the garrisons of the fortresses round it. The soldiers were bored to death and wreaked their vengeance on the peasants. They made coarse fun of them, maltreated them, and used the women as though they were in a conquered country. The week before some of them, full of wine, had disturbed a feast at a neighboring village and had half killed a farmer. Christophe, who knew these things, shared the state of mind of the peasant, and he sat down again and waited to see what would happen.

The soldiers were not worried by the ill-will with which their entry was received, and went noisily and sat down at the full tables, jostling the people away from them to make room; it was the affair of a moment. Most of the people went away grumbling. An old man sitting at the end of a bench did not move quickly enough; they lifted the bench and the old man toppled over amid roars of laughter. Christophe felt the blood rushing to his head; he got up indignantly; but, as he was on the point of interfering, he saw the old man painfully pick himself up and instead of complaining humbly crave pardon. Two of the soldiers came to Christophe's table; he watched them come and clenched his fists. But he did not have to defend himself. They were two tall, strong, good-humored louts, who had followed sheepishly one or two daredevils and were trying to imitate them. They were intimidated by Christophe's defiant manner, and when he said curtly: "This place is taken," they hastily begged his pardon and withdrew to their end of the bench so as not to disturb him. There had been a masterful inflection in his voice; their natural servility came to the fore. They saw that Christophe was not a peasant.

Christophe was a little mollified by their submission, and was able to watch things more coolly. It was not difficult to see that the gang were led by a non-commissioned officer—a little bull-dog of a man with hard eyes—with a rascally, hypocritical and wicked face; he was one of the heroes of the affray of the Sunday before. He was sitting at the table next to Christophe. He was drunk already and stared at the people and threw insulting sarcasms at them which they pretended not to hear. He attacked especially the couples dancing, describing their physical advantages or defects with a coarseness of expression which made his companions laugh. The girls blushed and tears came to their eyes; the young men ground their teeth and raged in silence. Their tormentor's eyes wandered slowly round the room, sparing nobody; Christophe saw them moving towards himself. He seized his mug, and clenched his fist on the table and waited, determined to throw the liquor at his head on the first insult. He said to himself:

"I am mad. It would be better to go away. They will slit me up; and then if I escape they will put me in prison; the game is not worth the candle. I'd better go before he provokes me."

But his pride would not let him, he would not seem to be running away from such brutes as these. The officer's cunning brutal stare was fixed on him. Christophe stiffened and glared at him angrily. The officer looked at him for a moment; Christophe's face irritated him; he nudged his neighbor and pointed out the young man with a snigger; and he opened his lips to insult him. Christophe gathered himself together and was just about to fling his mug at him. . . . Once more chance saved him. Just as the drunken man was about to speak an awkward couple of dancers bumped into him and made him drop his glass. He turned furiously and let loose a flood of insults. His attention was distracted; he forgot Christophe. Christophe waited for a few minutes longer; then seeing that his enemy had no thought of going on with his remarks he got up, slowly took his hat and walked leisurely towards the door. He did not take his eyes off the bench where the other was sitting, just to let him feel that he was not giving in to him. But the officer had forgotten him altogether; no one took any notice of him.

He was just turning the handle of the door; in a few seconds he would have been outside. But it was ordered that he should not leave so soon. An angry murmur rose at the end of the room. When the soldiers had drunk they had decided to dance. And as all the girls had their cavaliers they drove away their partners, who submitted to it. But Lorchen was not going to put up with that. It was not for nothing that she had her bold eyes and her firm chin which so charmed Christophe. She was waltzing like a mad thing when the officer who had fixed his choice upon her came and pulled her partner away from her. She stamped with her foot, screamed, and pushed the soldier away, declaring that she would never dance with such a boor. He pursued her. He dispersed with his fists the people behind whom she was trying to hide. At last she took refuge behind a table; and then protected from him for a moment she took breath to scream abuse at him; she saw that all her resistance would be useless and she stamped with rage and groped for the most violent words to fling at him and compared his face to that of various animals of the farm-yard. He leaned towards her over the table, smiled wickedly, and his eyes glittered with rage. Suddenly he pounced and jumped over the table. He caught hold of her. She struggled with feet and fists

like the cow-woman she was. He was not too steady on his
legs and almost lost his balance. In his fury he flung her
against the wall and slapped her face. He had no time to do it
again; some one had jumped on his back, and was cuffing him
and kicking him back into the crowd. It was Christophe who
had flung himself on him, overturning tables and people without
stopping to think of what he was doing. Mad with rage, the
officer turned and drew his saber. Before he could make use
of it Christophe felled him with a stool. The whole thing had
been so sudden that none of the spectators had time to think of
interfering. The other soldiers ran to Christophe drawing their
sabers. The peasants flung themselves at them. The uproar
became general. Mugs flew across the room; the tables were
overturned. The peasants woke up; they had old scores to pay
off. The men rolled about on the ground and bit each other
savagely. Lorchen's partner, a stolid farm-hand, had caught
hold of the head of the soldier who had just insulted him and
was banging it furiously against the wall. Lorchen, armed with
a cudgel, was striking out blindly. The other girls ran away
screaming, except for a few wantons who joined in heartily.
One of them—a fat little fair girl—seeing a gigantic soldier—
the same who had sat at Christophe's table—crushing in the
chest of his prostrate adversary with his boot, ran to the fire,
came back, dragged the brute's head backwards and flung a
handful of burning ashes into his eyes. The man bellowed.
The girl gloated, abused the disarmed enemy, whom the peasants now thwacked at their ease. At last the soldiers finding
themselves on the losing side rushed away leaving two of their
number on the floor. The fight went on in the village street.
They burst into the houses crying murder, and trying to smash
everything. The peasants followed them with forks, and set
their savage dogs on them. A third soldier fell with his
belly cleft by a fork. The others had to fly and were hunted
out of the village, and from a distance they shouted as they
ran across the fields that they would fetch their comrades and
come back immediately.

The peasants, left masters of the field, returned to the inn;
they were exultant; it was a revenge for all the outrages they
had suffered for so long. They had as yet no thought of the

consequences of the affray. They all talked at once and boasted of their prowess. They fraternized with Christophe, who was delighted to feel in touch with them. Lorchen came and took his hand and held it for a moment in her rough paw while she giggled at him. She did not think him ridiculous for the moment.

They looked to the wounded. Among the villagers there were only a few teeth knocked out, a few ribs broken and a few slight bruises and scars. But it was very different with the soldiers. They were seriously injured: the giant whose eyes had been burned had had his shoulder half cut off with a hatchet; the man whose belly had been pierced was dying; and there was the officer who had been knocked down by Christophe. They were laid out by the hearth. The officer, who was the least injured of the three, had just opened his eyes. He took a long look at the ring of peasants leaning over him, a look filled with hatred. Hardly had he regained consciousness of what had happened than he began to abuse them. He swore that he would be avenged and would settle their hash, the whole lot of them; he choked with rage; it was palpable that if he could he would exterminate them. They tried to laugh, but their laughter was forced. A young peasant shouted to the wounded man:

"Hold your gab or I'll kill you."

The officer tried to get up, and he glared at the man who had just spoken to him with blood-shot eyes:

"Swine!" he said. "Kill me! They'll cut your heads off."

He went on shouting. The man who had been ripped up screamed like a bleeding pig. The third was stiff and still like a dead man. A crushing terror came over the peasants. Lorchen and some women carried the wounded men to another room. The shouts of the officer and the screams of the dying man died away. The peasants were silent; they stood fixed in the circle as though the three bodies were still lying at their feet; they dared not budge and looked at each other in panic. At last Lorchen's father said:

"You have done a fine piece of work!"

There was an agonized murmuring; their throats were dry. Then they began all to talk at once. At first they whispered as

though they were afraid of eavesdroppers, but soon they raised
their voices and became more vehement; they accused each other;
they blamed each other for the blows they had struck. The
dispute became acrid; they seemed to be on the point of going
for each other. Lorchen's father brought them to unanimity.
With his arms folded he turned towards Christophe and jerked
his chin at him:

"And," he said, "what business had this fellow here?"

The wrath of the rabble was turned on Christophe:

"True! True!" they cried. "He began it! But for him
nothing would have happened."

Christophe was amazed. He tried to reply:

"You know perfectly that what I did was for you, not for
myself."

But they replied furiously:

"Aren't we capable of defending ourselves? Do you think
we need a gentleman from the town to tell us what we should
do? Who asked your advice? And besides who asked you to
come? Couldn't you stay at home?"

Christophe shrugged his shoulders and turned towards the
door. But Lorchen's father barred the way, screaming:

"That's it! That's it!" he shouted. "He would like to
cut away now after getting us all into a scrape. He shan't go!"

The peasants roared:

"He shan't go! He's the cause of it all. He shall pay for it
all!"

They surrounded him and shook their fists at him. Christophe saw the circle of threatening faces closing in upon him;
fear had infuriated them. He said nothing, made a face of
disgust, threw his hat on the table, went and sat at the end of
the room, and turned his back on them.

But Lorchen was angry and flung herself at the peasants.
Her pretty face was red and scowling with rage. She pushed
back the people who were crowding round Christophe:

"Cowards! Brute beasts!" she cried. "Aren't you
ashamed? You want to pretend that he brought it all on you!
As if they did not see you all! As if there was a single one
of you who had not hit out his hand as he could! . . . If
there had been a man who had stayed with his arms folded

while the others were fighting I would spit in his face and call
him: Coward! Coward! . . ."

The peasants, surprised by this unexpected outburst, stayed
for a moment in silence; they began to shout again:

" He began it! Nothing would have happened but for him.'

In vain did Lorchen's father make signs to his daughter.
She went on:

" Yes. He did begin it! That is nothing for you to boast
about. But for him you would have let them insult you. You
would have let them insult you. You cowards! You funks!"

She abused her partner:

" And you, you said nothing. Your heart was in your mouth;
you held out your bottom to be kicked. You would have
thanked them for it! Aren't you ashamed? . . . Aren't
you all ashamed? You are not men! You're as brave as sheep
with your noses to the ground all the time! He had to give
you an example!—And now you want to make him bear everything? . . . Well, I tell you, that shan't happen! He
fought for us. Either you save him or you'll suffer along with
him. I give you my word for it!"

Lorchen's father caught her arm. He was beside himself and
shouted:

" Shut up! Shut up! . . . Will you shut up, you
bitch!"

But she thrust him away and went on again. The peasants
yelled. She shouted louder than they in a shrill, piercing
scream:

" What have you to say to it all? Do you think I did not
see you just now kicking the man who is lying half dead in
the next room? And you, show me your hands! . . .
There's blood on them. Do you think I did not see you with
your knife? I shall tell everything I saw if you do the least
thing against him. I will have you all condemned."

The infuriated peasants thrust their faces into Lorchen's
and bawled at her. One of them made as though to box her
ears, but Lorchen's lover seized him by the scruff of the neck
and they jostled each other and were on the point of coming
to blows. An old man said to Lorchen:

" If we are condemned, you will be too."

"I shall be too," she said, "I am not so cowardly as you."
And she burst out again.

They did not know what to do. They turned to her father:
"Can't you make her be silent?"

The old man had understood that it was not wise to push
Lorchen too far. He signed to them to be calm. Silence came.
Lorchen went on talking alone; then as she found no response,
like a fire without fuel, she stopped. After a moment her
father coughed and said:

"Well, then, what do you want? You don't want to ruin
us."

She said:

"I want him to be saved."

They began to think. Christophe had not moved from where
he sat; he was stiff and proud and seemed not to understand
that they were discussing him; but he was touched by Lorchen's
intervention. Lorchen seemed not to be aware of his presence;
she was leaning against the table by which he was sitting, and
glaring defiantly at the peasants, who were smoking and looking
down at the ground. At last her father chewed his pipe for a
little and said:

"Whether we say anything or not,—if he stays he is done
for. The sergeant major recognized him; he won't spare him.
There is only one thing for him to do—to get away at once to
the other side of the frontier."

He had come to the conclusion it would be better for them all
if Christophe escaped; in that way he would admit his guilt,
and when he was no longer there to defend himself it would
not be difficult to put upon him the burden of the affair. The
others agreed. They understood each other perfectly.—Now
that they had come to a decision they were all in a hurry for
Christophe to go. Without being in the least embarrassed by
what they had been saying a moment before they came up to
him and pretended to be deeply interested in his welfare.

"There is not a moment to lose, sir," said Lorchen's father.
"They will come back. Half an hour to go to the fortress.
Half an hour to come back. . . . There is only just time to
slip away."

Christophe had risen. He too had been thinking. He knew

that if he stayed he was lost. But to go, to go without seeing
his mother? . . . No. It was impossible. He said that
he would first go back to the town and would still have time
to go during the night and cross the frontier. But they protested loudly. They had barred the door just before to prevent
his going; now they wanted to prevent his not going. If he
went back to the town he was certain to be caught; they would
know at the fortress before he got there; they would await him
at home.—He insisted. Lorchen had understood him:

"You want to see your mother? . . . I will go instead
of you."

"When?"

"To-night."

"Really! You will do that?"

"I will go."

She took her shawl and put it round her head.

"Write a letter. I will take it to her. Come with me. I
will give you some ink."

She took him into the inner room. At the door she turned,
and addressing her lover:

"And do you get ready," she said. "You must take him.
You must not leave him until you have seen him over the
frontier."

He was as eager as anybody to see Christophe over into
France and farther if possible.

Lorchen went into the next room with Christophe. He was
still hesitating. He was torn by grief at the thought that
he would not be able to embrace his mother. When would he
see her again? She was so old, so worn out, so lonely! This
fresh blow would be too much for her. What would become of
her without him? . . . But what would become of him if
he stayed and were condemned and put in prison for years?
Would not that even more certainly mean destitution and misery for her? If he were free, though far away, he could always
help her, or she could come to him.—He had not time to see
clearly in his mind. Lorchen took his hands—she stood near
him and looked at him; their faces were almost touching; she
threw her arms round his neck and kissed his mouth:

"Quick! Quick!" she whispered, pointing to the table.

JEAN-CHRISTOPHE

He gave up trying to think. He sat down. She tore a sheet of squared paper with red lines from an account book.

He wrote:

"MY DEAR MOTHER: Forgive me. I am going to hurt you much. I cannot do otherwise. I have done nothing wrong. But now I must fly and leave the country. The girl who brings you this letter will tell you everything. I wanted to say good-bye to you. They will not let me. They say that I should be arrested. I am so unhappy that I have no will left. I am going over the frontier but I shall stay near it until you have written to me; the girl who brings you my letter will bring me your reply. Tell me what to do. I will do whatever you say. Do you want me to come back? Tell me to come back! I cannot bear the idea of leaving you alone. What will you do to live? Forgive me! Forgive me! I love you and I kiss you . . ."

"Be quick, sir, or we shall be too late," said Lorchen's swain, pushing the door open.

Christophe wrote his name hurriedly and gave the letter to Lorchen.

"You will give it to her yourself?"

"I am going," she said.

She was already ready to go.

"To-morrow," she went on, "I will bring you her reply; you must wait for me at Leiden,—(the first station beyond the German frontier)—on the platform."

(She had read Christophe's letter over his shoulder as he wrote.)

"You will tell me everything and how she bore the blow and everything she says to you? You will not keep anything from me?" said Christophe beseechingly.

"I will tell you everything."

They were not so free to talk now, for the young man was at the door watching them:

"And then, Herr Christophe," said Lorchen, "I will go and see her sometimes and I will send you news of her; do not be anxious."

She shook hands with him vigorously like a man.

"Let us go!" said the peasant.

"Let us go!" said Christophe.

All three went out. On the road they parted. Lorchen went one way and Christophe, with his guide, the other. They did not speak. The crescent moon veiled in mists was disappearing behind the woods. A pale light hovered over the fields. In the hollows the mists had risen thick and milky white. The shivering trees were bathed in the moisture of the air.—They were not more than a few minutes gone from the village when the peasant flung back sharply and signed to Christophe to stop. They listened. On the road in front of them they heard the regular tramp of a troop of soldiers coming towards them. The peasant climbed the hedge into the fields. Christophe followed him. They walked away across the plowed fields. They heard the soldiers go by on the road. In the darkness the peasant shook his fist at them. Christophe's heart stopped like a hunted animal that hears the baying of the hounds. They returned to the road again, avoiding the villages and isolated farms where the barking of the dogs betrayed them to the countryside. On the slope of a wooded hill they saw in the distance the red lights of the railway. They took the direction of the signals and decided to go to the first station. It was not easy. As they came down into the valley they plunged into the fog. They had to jump a few streams. Soon they found themselves in immense fields of beetroot and plowed land; they thought they would never be through. The plain was uneven; there were little rises and hollows into which they were always in danger of falling. At last after walking blindly through the fog they saw suddenly a few yards away the signal light of the railway at the top of an embankment. They climbed the bank. At the risk of being run over they followed the rails until they were within a hundred yards of the station; then they took to the road again. They reached the station twenty minutes before the train went. In spite of Lorchen's orders the peasant left Christophe; he was in a hurry to go back to see what had happened to the others and to his own property.

Christophe took a ticket for Leiden and waited alone in the empty third-class waiting room. An official who was asleep

on a seat came and looked at Christophe's ticket and opened
the door for him when the train came in. There was nobody
in the carriage. Everybody in the train was asleep. In the
fields all was asleep. Only Christophe did not sleep in
spite of his weariness. As the heavy iron wheels approached
the frontier he felt a fearful longing to be out of reach. In
an hour he would be free. But till then a word would be
enough to have him arrested. . . . Arrested! His whole
being revolted at the word. To be stifled by odious force!
. . . He could not breathe. His mother, his country, that
he was leaving, were no longer in his thoughts. In the egoism
of his threatened liberty he thought only of that liberty of his
life which he wished to save. Whatever it might cost! Even
at the cost of crime. He was bitterly sorry that he had taken
the train instead of continuing the journey to the frontier on
foot. He had wanted to gain a few hours. A fine gain! He
was throwing himself into the jaws of the wolf. Surely they
were waiting for him at the frontier station; orders must have
been given; he would be arrested. . . . He thought for a
moment of leaving the train while it was moving, before it
reached the station; he even opened the door of the carriage,
but it was too late; the train was at the station. It stopped.
Five minutes. An eternity. Christophe withdrew to the end of
the compartment and hid behind the curtain and anxiously
watched the platform on which a gendarme was standing motionless. The station master came out of his office with a telegram in his hand and went hurriedly up to the gendarme. Christophe had no doubt that it was about himself. He looked for a
weapon. He had only a strong knife with two blades. He
opened it in his pocket. An official with a lamp on his chest
had passed the station master and was running along the train.
Christophe saw him coming. His fist closed on the handle of
the knife in his pocket and he thought:

"I am lost."

He was in such a state of excitement that he would have
been capable of plunging the knife into the man's breast if he
had been unfortunate enough to come straight to him and open
his compartment. But the official stopped at the next carriage

to look at the ticket of a passenger who had just taken his
seat. The train moved on again. Christophe repressed the
throbbing of his heart. He did not stir. He dared hardly say to
himself that he was saved. He would not say it until he had
crossed the frontier. . . . Day was beginning to dawn. The
silhouettes of the trees were starting out of the night. A carriage was passing on the road like a fantastic shadow with a
jingle of bells and a winking eye. . . . With his face close
pressed to the window Christophe tried to see the post with the
imperial arms which marked the bounds of his servitude. He
was still looking for it in the growing light when the train
whistled to announce its arrival at the first Belgian station.

He got up, opened the door wide, and drank in the icy air.
Free! His whole life before him! The joy of life! . . .
And at once there came upon him suddenly all the sadness
of what he was leaving, all the sadness of what he was going
to meet; and he was overwhelmed by the fatigue of that night
of emotion. He sank down on the seat. He had hardly been
in the station a minute. When a minute later an official opened
the door of the carriage he found Christophe asleep. Christophe awoke, dazed, thinking he had been asleep an hour; he got
out heavily and dragged himself to the customs, and when he
was definitely accepted on foreign territory, having no more to
defend himself, he lay down along a seat in the waiting room
and dropped off and slept like a log.

He awoke about noon. Lorchen could hardly come before
two or three o'clock. While he was waiting for the trains he
walked up and down the platform of the little station. Then
he went straight on into the middle of the fields. It was a
gray and joyless day giving warning of the approach of winter.
The light was dim. The plaintive whistle of a train stopping
was all that broke the melancholy silence. Christophe stopped
a few yards away from the frontier in the deserted country.
Before him was a little pond, a clear pool of water, in which
the gloomy sky was reflected. It was inclosed by a fence and
two trees grew by its side. On the right, a poplar with leafless
trembling top. Behind, a great walnut tree with black naked

branches like a monstrous polypus. The black fruit of it swung heavily on it. The last withered leaves were decaying and falling one by one upon the still pond. . . .

It seemed to him that he had already seen them, the two trees, the pond . . . —and suddenly he had one of those moments of giddiness which open great distances in the plain of life. A chasm in Time. He knew not where he was, who he was, in what age he lived, through how many ages he had been so. Christophe had a feeling that it had already been, that what was, now, was not, now, but in some other time. He was no longer himself. He was able to see himself from outside, from a great distance, as though it were some one else standing there in that place. He heard the buzzing of memory and of an unknown creature within himself; the blood boiled in his veins and roared:

"Thus . . . Thus . . . Thus . . ."

The centuries whirled through him. . . . Many other Kraffts had passed through the experiences which were his on that day, and had tasted the wretchedness of the last hour on their native soil. A wandering race, banished everywhere for their independence and disturbing qualities. A race always the prey of an inner demon that never let it settle anywhere. A race attached to the soil from which it was torn, and never, never ceasing to love it.

Christophe in his turn was passing through these same sorrowful experiences; and he was finding on the way the footsteps of those who had gone before him. With tears in his eyes he watched his native land disappear in the mist, his country to which he had to say farewell.—Had he not ardently desired to leave it?—Yes; but now that he was actually leaving it he felt himself racked by anguish. Only a brutish heart can part without emotion from the motherland. Happy or unhappy he had lived with her; she was his mother and his comrade; he had slept in her, he had slept on her bosom, he was impregnated with her; in her bosom she held the treasure of his dreams, all his past life, the sacred dust of those whom he had loved. Christophe saw now in review the days of his life, and the dear men and women whom he was leaving on that soil or beneath it. His sufferings were not less dear to him than his joys. Minna,

Sabine, Ada, his grandfather, Uncle Gottfried, old Schulz—all
passed before him in the space of a few minutes. He could not
tear himself away from the dead—(for he counted Ada also
among the dead)—the idea of his mother whom he was leaving,
the only living creature of all those whom he loved, among these
phantoms was intolerable to him.

He was almost on the point of crossing the frontier again,
so cowardly did his flight seem to him. He made up his mind
that if the answer Lorchen was to bring him from his mother
betrayed too great grief he would return at all costs. But if
he received nothing? If Lorchen had not been able to reach
Louisa, or to bring back the answer? Well, he would go back.

He returned to the station. After a grim time of waiting the
train at last appeared. Christophe expected to see Lorchen's
bold face in the train; for he was sure she would keep her
promise; but she did not appear. He ran anxiously from one
compartment to another; he said to himself that if she had been
in the train she would have been one of the first to get out.
As he was plunging through the stream of passengers coming
from the opposite direction he saw a face which he seemed to
know. It was the face of a little girl of thirteen or fourteen,
chubby, dimpled, and ruddy as an apple, with a little turned-up
nose and a large mouth, and a thick plait coiled around her
head. As he looked more closely at her he saw that she had
in her hand an old valise very much like his own. She was
watching him too like a sparrow; and when she saw that he
was looking at her she came towards him; but she stood firmly
in front of Christophe and stared at him with her little mouse-
like eyes, without speaking a word. Christophe knew her; she
was a little milkmaid at Lorchen's farm. Pointing to the valise
he said:

" That is mine, isn't it? "

The girl did not move and replied cunningly:

" I'm not sure. Where do you come from, first of all? "

" Buir."

" And who sent it you? "

" Lorchen. Come. Give it me."

The little girl held out the valise.

" There it is."

And she added:

"Oh! But I knew you at once!"

"What were you waiting for then?"

"I was waiting for you to tell me that it was you."

"And Lorchen?" asked Christophe. "Why didn't she come?"

The girl did not reply. Christophe understood that she did not want to say anything among all the people. They had first to pass through the customs. When that was done Christophe took the girl to the end of the platform:

"The police came," said the girl, now very talkative. "They came almost as soon as you had gone. They went into all the houses. They questioned everybody, and they arrested big Sami and Christian and old Kaspar. And also Mélanie and Gertrude, though they declared they had done nothing, and they wept; and Gertrude scratched the gendarmes. It was not any good then saying that you had done it all."

"I?" exclaimed Christophe.

"Oh! yes," said the girl quietly. "It was no good as you had gone. Then they looked for you everywhere and hunted for you in every direction."

"And Lorchen?"

"Lorchen was not there. She came back afterwards after she had been to the town."

"Did she see my mother?"

"Yes. Here is the letter. And she wanted to come herself, but she was arrested too."

"How did you manage to come?"

"Well, she came back to the village without being seen by the police, and she was going to set out again. But Irmina, Gertrude's sister, denounced her. They came to arrest her. Then when she saw the gendarmes coming she went up to her room and shouted that she would come down in a minute, that she was dressing. I was in the vineyard behind the house; she called to me from the window: 'Lydia! Lydia!' I went to her; she threw down your valise and the letter which your mother had given her, and she explained where I should find you. I ran, and here I am."

"Didn't she say anything more?"

" Yes. She told me to give you this shawl to show you that I came from her."

Christophe recognized the white shawl with red spots and embroidered flowers which Lorchen had tied round her head when she left him on the night before. The naïve improbability of the excuse she had made for sending him such a love-token did not make him smile.

" Now," said the girl, " here is the return train. I must go home. Good-night."

" Wait," said Christophe. " And the fare, what did you do about that?"

" Lorchen gave it me."

" Take this," said Christophe, pressing a few pieces of money into her hand.

He held her back as she was trying to go.

" And then . . ." he said.

He stooped and kissed her cheeks. The girl affected to protest.

" Don't mind," said Christophe jokingly. " It was not for you."

" Oh! I know that," said the girl mockingly. " It was for Lorchen."

It was not only Lorchen that Christophe kissed as he kissed the little milkmaid's chubby cheeks; it was all Germany.

The girl slipped away and ran towards the train which was just going. She hung out of the window and waved her handkerchief to him until she was out of sight. He followed with his eyes the rustic messenger who had brought him for the last time the breath of his country and of those he loved.

When she had gone he found himself utterly alone, this time, a stranger in a strange land. He had in his hand his mother's letter and the shawl love-token. He pressed the shawl to his breast and tried to open the letter. But his hands trembled. What would he find in it? What suffering would be written in it?—No; he could not bear the sorrowful words of reproach which already he seemed to hear; he would retrace his steps.

At last he unfolded the letter and read: " My poor child, do not be anxious about me. I will be wise. God has punished me. I must not be selfish and keep you here. Go to Paris. Perhaps it will be better for you. Do not worry about me. I can manage somehow. The chief thing is that you should be happy. I kiss you.   MOTHER.

"Write to me when you can."

Christophe sat down on his valise and wept.

The porter was shouting the train for Paris.

The heavy train was slowing down with a terrific noise. Christophe dried his tears, got up and said:

"I must go."

He looked at the sky in the direction in which Paris must be. The sky, dark everywhere, was even darker there. It was like a dark chasm. Christophe's heart ached, but he said again:

"I must go."

He climbed into the train and leaning out of the window went on looking at the menacing horizon:

"O, Paris!" he thought, "Paris! Come to my aid! Save me! Save my thoughts!"

The thick fog grew denser still. Behind Christophe, above the country he was leaving, a little patch of sky, pale blue, large, like two eyes—like the eyes of Sabine—smiled sorrowfully through the heavy veil of clouds and then was gone. The train departed. Rain fell. Night fell.

BOOK II

THE MARKET-PLACE

THE MARKETPLACE

JEAN-CHRISTOPHE IN PARIS

I

DISORDER in order. Untidy officials offhanded in manner. Travelers protesting against the rules and regulations, to which they submitted all the same. Christophe was in France.

After having satisfied the curiosity of the customs, he took his seat again in the train for Paris. Night was over the fields that were soaked with the rain. The hard lights of the stations accentuated the sadness of the interminable plain buried in darkness. The trains, more and more numerous, that passed, rent the air with their shrieking whistles, which broke upon the torpor of the sleeping passengers. The train was nearing Paris.

Christophe was ready to get out an hour before they ran in; he had jammed his hat down on his head; he had buttoned his coat up to his neck for fear of the robbers, with whom he had been told Paris was infested; twenty times he had got up and sat down; twenty times he had moved his bag from the rack to the seat, from the seat to the rack, to the exasperation of his fellow-passengers, against whom he knocked every time with his usual clumsiness.

Just as they were about to run into the station the train suddenly stopped in the darkness. Christophe flattened his nose against the window and tried vainly to look out. He turned towards his fellow-travelers, hoping to find a friendly glance which would encourage him to ask where they were. But they were all asleep or pretending to be so: they were bored and scowling: not one of them made any attempt to

discover why they had stopped. Christophe was surprised by
their indifference: these stiff, somnolent creatures were so utterly unlike the French of his imagination! At last he sat
down, discouraged, on his bag, rocking with every jolt of the
train, and in his turn he was just dozing off when he was
roused by the noise of the doors being opened. . . . Paris!
. . . His fellow-travelers were already getting out.

Jostling and jostled, he walked towards the exit of the station, refusing the porter who offered to carry his bag. With
a peasant's suspiciousness he thought every one was going to
rob him. He lifted his precious bag on to his shoulder and
walked straight ahead, indifferent to the curses of the people
as he forced his way through them. At last he found himself
in the greasy streets of Paris.

He was too much taken up with the business in hand, the
finding of lodgings, and too weary of the whirl of carriages
into which he was swept, to think of looking at anything. The
first thing was to look for a room. There was no lack of
hotels: the station was surrounded with them on all sides:
their names were flaring in gas letters. Christophe wanted to
find a less dazzling place than any of these: none of them
seemed to him to be humble enough for his purse. At last
in a side street he saw a dirty inn with a cheap eating-house
on the ground floor. It was called *Hôtel de la Civilisation*.
A fat man in his shirt-sleeves was sitting smoking at a table:
he hurried forward as he saw Christophe enter. He could not
understand a word of his jargon: but at the first glance he
marked and judged the awkward childish German, who refused to let his bag out of his hands, and struggled hard to
make himself understood in an incredible language. He took
him up an evil-smelling staircase to an airless room which
opened on to a closed court. He vaunted the quietness of
the room, to which no noise from outside could penetrate: and
he asked a good price for it. Christophe only half understood
him; knowing nothing of the conditions of life in Paris, and
with his shoulder aching with the weight of his bag, he ac-

cepted everything: he was eager to be alone. But hardly was
he left alone when he was struck by the dirtiness of it all: and
to avoid succumbing to the melancholy which was creeping
over him, he went out again very soon after having dipped
his face in the dusty water, which was greasy to the touch.
He tried hard not to see and not to feel, so as to escape
disgust.

He went down into the street. The October mist was thick
and keenly cold: it had that stale Parisian smell, in which
are mingled the exhalations of the factories of the outskirts
and the heavy breath of the town. He could not see ten yards
in front of him. The light of the gas-jets flickered like a
candle on the point of going out. In the semi-darkness there
were crowds of people moving in all directions. Carriages
moved in front of each other, collided, obstructed the road,
stemming the flood of people like a dam. The oaths of the
drivers, the horns and bells of the trams, made a deafening
noise. The roar, the clamor, the smell of it all, struck fearfully
on the mind and heart of Christophe. He stopped for a moment, but was at once swept on by the people behind him and
borne on by the current. He went down the *Boulevard de
Strasbourg,* seeing nothing, bumping awkwardly into the
passers-by. He had eaten nothing since morning. The cafés,
which he found at every turn, abashed and revolted him, for
they were all so crowded. He applied to a policeman; but
he was so slow in finding words that the man did not even
take the trouble to hear him out, and turned his back on him
in the middle of a sentence and shrugged his shoulders. He
went on walking mechanically. There was a small crowd in
front of a shop-window. He stopped mechanically. It was a
photograph and picture-postcard shop: there were pictures of
girls in chemises, or without them: illustrated papers displayed
obscene jests. Children and young girls were looking at them
calmly. There was a slim girl with red hair who saw Christophe lost in contemplation and accosted him. He looked at her
and did not understand. She took his arm with a silly smile

He shook her off, and rushed away, blushing angrily. There were rows of café concerts: outside the doors were displayed grotesque pictures of the comedians. The crowd grew thicker and thicker. Christophe was struck by the number of vicious faces, prowling rascals, vile beggars, painted women sickeningly scented. He was frozen by it all. Weariness, weakness, and the horrible feeling of nausea, which more and more came over him, turned him sick and giddy. He set his teeth and walked on more quickly. The fog grew denser as he approached the Seine. The whirl of carriages became bewildering. A horse slipped and fell on its side: the driver flogged it to make it get up: the wretched beast, held down by its harness, struggled and fell down again, and lay still as though it were dead. The sight of it—common enough—was the last drop that made the wretchedness that filled the soul of Christophe flow over. The miserable struggles of the poor beast, surrounded by indifferent and careless faces, made him feel bitterly his own insignificance among these thousands of men and women—the feeling of revulsion, which for the last hour had been choking him, his disgust with all these human beasts, with the unclean atmosphere, with the morally repugnant people, burst forth in him with such violence that he could not breathe. He burst into tears. The passers-by looked in amazement at the tall young man whose face was twisted with grief. He strode along with the tears running down his cheeks, and made no attempt to dry them. People stopped to look at him for a moment: and if he had been able to read the soul of the mob, which seemed to him to be so hostile, perhaps in some of them he might have seen—mingled, no doubt, with a little of the ironic feeling of the Parisians for any sorrow so simple and ridiculous as to show itself—pity and brotherhood. But he saw nothing: his tears blinded him.

He found himself in a square, near a large fountain. He bathed his hands and dipped his face in it. A little news-vendor watched him curiously and passed comment on him, waggishly though not maliciously: and he picked up his hat for him—Christophe had let it fall. The icy coldness of the water revived Christophe. He plucked up courage again. He retraced his steps, but did not look about him: he did not even think of eating: it would have been impossible for him to speak to anybody: it needed the merest trifle to set him off weeping again. He was worn out. He lost his way, and wandered about aimlessly until he found himself in front of his hotel, just when he had made up his mind that he was lost. He had forgotten even the name of the street in which he lodged.

He went up to his horrible room. He was empty, and his eyes were burning: he was aching body and soul as he sank down into a chair in the corner of the room: he stayed like that for a couple of hours and could not stir. At last he wrenched himself out of his apathy and went to bed. He fell into a fevered slumber, from which he awoke every few minutes, feeling that he had been asleep for hours. The room was stifling: he was burning from head to foot: he was horribly thirsty: he suffered from ridiculous nightmares, which clung to him even after he had opened his eyes: sharp pains thudded in him like the blows of a hammer. In the middle of the night he awoke, overwhelmed by despair, so profound that he all but cried out: he stuffed the bedclothes into his mouth so as not to be heard: he felt that he was going mad. He sat up in bed, and struck a light. He was bathed in sweat. He got up, opened his bag to look for a handkerchief. He laid his hand on an old Bible, which his mother had hidden in his linen. Christophe had never read much of the Book: but it was a comfort beyond words for him to find it at that moment. The Bible had belonged to his grandfather and to his grandfather's father. The heads of the family had inscribed on a blank page at the end their names and the important dates of their lives—births, marriages, deaths. His grandfather had written in pencil, in his large hand, the dates when he had read and re-read each chapter: the Book was full of tags of yellowed paper, on which the old man had jotted down his simple thoughts. The Book used to rest on a shelf above his bed, and he used often to take it down during the long, sleepless nights and hold converse with it rather than read it. It had been with him to the hour of his death, as it had been with his father. A century of the joys and sorrows of the family was breathed forth from the pages of the Book. Holding it in his hands, Christophe felt less lonely.

He opened it at the most somber words of all:

Is there not an appointed time to man upon earth? Are not his days also like the days of an hireling?

When I lie down, I say, When shall I arise and the night be gone? and I am full of tossings to and fro unto the dawn of the day.

When I say, My bed shall comfort me, my couch shall ease my complaint, then Thou searest me with dreams and terrifiest me through visions. . . . How long wilt Thou not depart from me, nor let me alone till I swallow down my spittle? I have sinned; what shall I do unto Thee, O Thou preserver of men?

Though He slay me yet will I trust in Him.

All greatness is good, and the height of sorrow tops deliverance. What casts down and overwhelms and blasts the soul beyond all hope is mediocrity in sorrow and joy, selfish and niggardly suffering that has not the strength to be rid of the lost pleasure, and in secret lends itself to every sort of degradation to steal pleasure anew. Christophe was braced up by the bitter savor that he found in the old Book: the wind of Sinai coming from vast and lonely spaces and the mighty sea to sweep away the steamy vapors. The fever in Christophe subsided. He was calm again, and lay down and slept peacefully until the morrow. When he opened his eyes again it was day. More acutely than ever he was conscious of the horror of his room: he felt his loneliness and wretchedness: but he faced them. He was no longer disheartened: he was left only with a sturdy melancholy. He read over now the words of Job:

Even though God slay me yet would I trust in Him.

He got up. He was ready calmly to face the fight.

He made up his mind there and then to set to work. He knew only two people in Paris: two young fellow-countrymen: his old friend Otto Diener, who was in the office of his uncle, a cloth merchant in the *Mail* quarter: and a young Jew from Mainz, Sylvain Kohn, who had a post in a great publishing house, the address of which Christophe did not know.

He had been very intimate with Diener when he was fourteen or fifteen. He had had for him one of those childish friendships which precede love, and are themselves a sort of love.[1] Diener had loved him too. The shy, reserved boy had been attracted by Christophe's gusty independence: he had tried hard to imitate him, quite ridiculously: that had both irritated and flattered Christophe. Then they had made plans for the overturning of the world. In the end Diener had gone abroad for his education in business, and they did not see each other again: but Christophe had news of him from time to time from the people in the town with whom Diener remained on friendly terms.

As for Sylvain Kohn, his relation with Christophe had been of another kind altogether. They had been at school together, where the young monkey had played many pranks on Christophe, who thrashed him for it when he saw the trap into which he had fallen. Kohn did not put up a fight: he let Christophe knock him down and rub his face in the dust, while he howled; but he would begin again at once with a malice that never tired—until the day when he became really afraid, Christophe having seriously threatened to kill him.

Christophe went out early. He stopped to breakfast at a café. In spite of his self-consciousness, he forced himself to lose no opportunity of speaking French. Since he had to live in Paris, perhaps for years, he had better adapt himself as quickly as possible to the conditions of life there, and overcome his repugnance. So he forced himself, although he suffered horribly, to take no notice of the sly looks of the waiter as he listened to his horrible lingo. He was not discouraged, and

[1] See *Jean-Christophe*—I: " The Morning."

went on obstinately constructing ponderous, formless sentences and repeating them until he was understood.

He set out to look for Diener. As usual, when he had an idea in his head, he saw nothing of what was going on about him. During that first walk his only impression of Paris was that of an old and ill-kept town. Christophe was accustomed to the towns of the new German Empire, that were both very old and very young, towns in which there is expressed a new birth of pride: and he was unpleasantly surprised by the shabby streets, the muddy roads, the hustling people, the confused traffic—vehicles of every sort and shape: venerable horse omnibuses, steam trams, electric trams, all sorts of trams—booths on the pavements, merry-go-rounds of wooden horses (or monsters and gargoyles) in the squares that were choked up with statues of gentlemen in frock-coats: all sorts of relics of a town of the Middle Ages endowed with the privilege of universal suffrage, but quite incapable of breaking free from its old vagabond existence. The fog of the preceding day had turned to a light, soaking rain. In many of the shops the gas was lit, although it was past ten o'clock.

Christophe lost his way in the labyrinth of streets round the *Place des Victoires,* but eventually found the shop he was looking for in the *Rue de la Banque.* As he entered he thought he saw Diener at the back of the long, dark shop, arranging packages of goods, together with some of the assistants. But he was a little short-sighted, and could not trust his eyes, although it was very rarely that they deceived him. There was a general movement among the people at the back of the shop when Christophe gave his name to the clerk who approached him: and after a confabulation a young man stepped forward from the group, and said in German:

" Herr Diener is out."

" Out? For long?"

" I think so. He has just gone."

Christophe thought for a moment; then he said:

" Very well. I will wait."

The clerk was taken aback, and hastened to add:

"But he won't be back before two or three."

"Oh! That's nothing," replied Christophe calmly. "I haven't anything to do in Paris. I can wait all day if need be."

The young man looked at him in amazement, and thought he was joking. But Christophe had forgotten him already. He sat down quietly in a corner, with his back turned towards the street: and it looked as though he intended to stay there.

The clerk went back to the end of the shop and whispered to his colleagues: they were most comically distressed, and cast about for some means of getting rid of the insistent Christophe.

After a few uneasy moments, the door of the office was opened and Herr Diener appeared. He had a large red face, marked with a purple scar down his cheek and chin, a fair mustache, smooth hair, parted on one side, a gold-rimmed eyeglass, gold studs in his shirt-front, and rings on his fat fingers. He had his hat and an umbrella in his hands. He came up to Christophe in a nonchalant manner. Christophe, who was dreaming as he sat, started with surprise. He seized Diener's hands, and shouted with a noisy heartiness that made the assistants titter and Diener blush. That majestic personage had his reasons for not wishing to resume his former relationship with Christophe: and he had made up his mind from the first to keep him at a distance by a haughty manner. But he had no sooner come face to face with Christophe than he felt like a little boy again in his presence: he was furious and ashamed. He muttered hurriedly:

"In my office. . . . We shall be able to talk bettei there."

Christophe recognized Diener's habitual prudence.

But when they were in the office and the door was shut, Diener showed no eagerness to offer him a chair. He remained standing, making clumsy explanations:

"Very glad. . . . I was just going out. . . . They thought I had gone. . . . But I must go . . . I have only a minute . . . a pressing appointment. . . ."

Christophe understood that the clerk had lied to him, **and** that the lie had been arranged by Diener to get rid of him. His blood boiled: but he controlled himself, and said dryly:

" There is no hurry."

Diener drew himself up. He was shocked by such off-handedness.

" What! " he said. " No hurry! In business . . ." Christophe looked him in the face.

" No."

Diener looked away. He hated Christophe for having so put him to shame. He murmured irritably. Christophe cut him short:

" Come," he said. " You know . . ."

(He used the " *Du,*" which maddened Diener, who from the first had been vainly trying to set up between Christophe and himself the barrier of the " *Sie.*")

" You know why I am here? "

" Yes," said Diener. " I know."

(He had heard of Christophe's escapade, and the warrant out against him, from his friends.)

" Then," Christophe went on, " you know that I am not here for fun. I have had to fly. I have nothing. I must live."

Diener was waiting for that, for the request. He took it with a mixture of satisfaction—(for it made it possible for him to feel his superiority over Christophe)—and embarrassment— (for he dared not make Christophe feel his superiority as much as he would have liked).

" Ah! " he said pompously. " It is very tiresome, very tiresome. Life here is hard. Everything is so dear. We have enormous expenses. And all these assistants . . ."

Christophe cut him short contemptuously:

" I am not asking you for money."

Diener was abashed. Christophe went on:

" Is your business doing well? Have you many customers? "

" Yes. Yes. Not bad, thank God! . . ." said Diener cautiously. (He was on his guard.)

Christophe darted a look of fury at him, and went on:

" You know many people in the German colony? "

" Yes."

" Very well: speak for me. They must be musical. They have children. I will give them lessons."

Diener was embarrassed at that.

" What is it? " asked Christophe. " Do you think I'm not competent to do the work? "

He was asking a service as though it were he who was rendering it. Diener, who would not have done a thing for Christophe except for the sake of putting him under an obligation, was resolved not to stir a finger for him.

" It isn't that. You're a thousand times too good for it. Only . . ."

" What, then? "

" Well, you see, it's very difficult—very difficult—on account of your position."

" My position? "

" Yes. . . . You see, that affair, the warrant. . . . If that were to be known. . . . It is difficult for me. It might do me harm."

He stopped as he saw Christophe's face go hot with anger: and he added quickly:

" Not on my own account. . . . I'm not afraid. . . . Ah! If I were alone! . . . But my uncle . . . you know, the business is his. I can do nothing without him. . . . "

He grew more and more alarmed at Christophe's expression, and at the thought of the gathering explosion he said hurriedly—(he was not a bad fellow at bottom: avarice and vanity were struggling in him: he would have liked to help Christophe, at a price):

" Can I lend you fifty francs? "

Christophe went crimson. He went up to Diener, who stepped back hurriedly to the door and opened it, and held himself in readiness to call for help, if necessary. But Christophe only thrust his face near his and bawled:

" You swine ! "

And he flung him aside and walked out through the little
throng of assistants.   At the door he spat in disgust.

He strode along down the street.   He was blind with fury.
The rain sobered him.   Where was he going?   He did not
know.   He did not know a soul.   He stopped to think outside a book-shop, and he stared stupidly at the rows of books.
He was struck by the name of a publisher on the cover of one of
them.   He wondered why.   Then he remembered that it was
the name of the house in which Sylvain Kohn was employed.
He made a note of the address. . . .   But what was the good?
He would not go. . . .   Why should he not go? . . .   If
that scoundrel Diener, who had been his friend, had given him
such a welcome, what had he to expect from a rascal whom he
had handled roughly, who had good cause to hate him?   Vain
humiliations!   His blood boiled at the thought.   But his native pessimism, derived perhaps from his Christian education,
urged him on to probe to the depths of human baseness.

" I have no right to stand on ceremony.   I must try everything before I give in."

And an inward voice added:

" And I shall not give in."

He made sure of the address, and went to hunt up Kohn.
He made up his mind to hit him in the eye at the first show
of impertinence.

The publishing house was in the neighborhood of the
Madeleine.   Christophe went up to a room on the second
floor, and asked for Sylvain Kohn.   A man in livery told him
that " Kohn was not known."   Christophe was taken aback,
and thought his pronunciation must be at fault, and he repeated his question: but the man listened attentively, and
repeated that no one of that name was known in the place.
Quite out of countenance, Christophe begged pardon, and was
turning to go when a door at the end of the corridor opened,
and he saw Kohn himself showing a lady out.   Still suffering

from the affront put upon him by Diener, he was inclined to think that everybody was having a joke at his expense. His first thought was that Kohn had seen him, and had given orders to the man to say that he was not there. His gorge rose at the impudence of it. He was on the point of going in a huff, when he heard his name: Kohn, with his sharp eyes, had recognized him: and he ran up to him, with a smile on his lips, and his hands held out with every mark of extraordinary delight.

Sylvain Kohn was short, thick-set, clean-shaven, like an American; his complexion was too red, his hair too black; he had a heavy, massive face, coarse-featured; little darting, wrinkled eyes, a rather crooked mouth, a heavy, cunning smile. He was modishly dressed, trying to cover up the defects of his figure, high shoulders, and wide hips. That was the only thing that touched his vanity: he would gladly have put up with any insult if only he could have been a few inches taller and of a better figure. For the rest, he was very well pleased with himself: he thought himself irresistible, as indeed he was. The little German Jew, clod as he was, had made himself the chronicler and arbiter of Parisian fashion and smartness. He wrote insipid society paragraphs and articles in a delicately involved manner. He was the champion of French style, French smartness, French gallantry, French wit—Regency, red heels, Lauzun. People laughed at him: but that did not prevent his success. Those who say that in Paris ridicule kills do not know Paris: so far from dying of it, there are people who live on it: in Paris ridicule leads to everything, even to fame and fortune. Sylvain Kohn was far beyond any need to reckon the good-will that every day accumulated to him through his Frankfortian affectations.

He spoke with a thick accent through his nose.

"Ah! What a surprise!" he cried gaily, taking Christophe's hands in his own clumsy paws, with their stubby fingers that looked as though they were crammed into too tight a skin. He could not let go of Christophe's hands. It was as though he were encountering his best friend. Christophe **was** so staggered that he wondered again if Kohn was not making fun of him. But Kohn was doing nothing of the kind—or, rather, if he was joking, it was no more than usual. There was no rancor about Kohn: he was too clever for that. He had long ago forgotten the rough treatment he had suffered at Christophe's hands: and if ever he did remember it, it did not worry him. He was delighted to have the opportunity of showing his old schoolfellow his importance and his new duties, and the elegance of his Parisian manners. He was not lying in expressing his surprise: a visit from Christophe was the last thing in the world that he expected: and if he was too worldly-wise not to know that the visit was of set material purpose, he took it as a reason the more for welcoming him, as it was, in fact, a tribute to his power.

"And you have come from Germany? How is your mother?" he asked, with a familiarity which at any other time would have annoyed Christophe, but now gave him comfort in the strange city.

"But how was it," asked Christophe, who was still inclined to be suspicious, "that they told me just now that Herr Kohn did not belong here?"

"Herr Kohn doesn't belong here," said Sylvain Kohn, laughing. "My name isn't Kohn now. My name is Hamilton."

He broke off.

"Excuse me," he said.

He went and shook hands with a lady who was passing and smiled grimacingly. Then he came back. He explained that the lady was a writer famous for her voluptuous and passionate novels. The modern Sappho had a purple ribbon on her bosom, a full figure, bright golden hair round a painted face; she made a few pretentious remarks in a mannish fashion with the accent of Franche-Comté.

Kohn plied Christophe with questions. He asked about all the people at home, and what had become of so-and-so, pluming himself on the fact that he remembered everybody. Christophe had forgotten his antipathy; he replied cordially and gratefully, giving a mass of detail about which Kohn cared nothing at all, and presently he broke off again.

"Excuse me," he said.

And he went to greet another lady who had come in.

"Dear me!" said Christophe. "Are there only women writers in France?"

Kohn began to laugh, and said fatuously:

"France is a woman, my dear fellow. If you want to succeed, make up to the women."

Christophe did not listen to the explanation, and went on with his own story. To put a stop to it, Kohn asked:

"But how the devil do you come here?"

"Ah!" thought Christophe, "he doesn't know. That is why he was so amiable. He'll be different when he knows."

He made it a point of honor to tell everything against himself: the brawl with the soldiers, the warrant out against him, his flight from the country.

Kohn rocked with laughter.

"Bravo!" he cried. "Bravo! That's a good story!"

He shook Christophe's hand warmly. He was delighted by any smack in the eye of authority: and the story tickled him the more as he knew the heroes of it: he saw the funny side of it.

"I say," he said, "it is past twelve. Will you give me the pleasure . . .? Lunch with me?"

Christophe accepted gratefully. He thought:

"This is a good fellow—decidedly a good fellow. I was mistaken."

They went out together. On the way Christophe put forward his request:

"You see how I am placed. I came here to look for work—music lessons—until I can make my name. Could you speak for me?"

"Certainly," said Kohn. "To any one you like. I know everybody here. I'm at your service."

He was glad to be able to show how important he was.

Christophe covered him with expressions of gratitude. He felt that he was relieved of a great weight of anxiety.

At lunch he gorged with the appetite of a man who has not broken fast for two days. He tucked his napkin round his neck, and ate with his knife. Kohn-Hamilton was horribly shocked by his voracity and his peasant manners. And he was hurt, too, by the small amount of attention that his guest gave to his bragging. He tried to dazzle him by telling of his fine connections and his prosperity: but it was no good: Christophe did not listen, and bluntly interrupted him. His tongue was loosed, and he became familiar. His heart was full, and he overwhelmed Kohn with his simple confidences of his plans for the future. Above all, he exasperated him by insisting on taking his hand across the table and pressing it effusively. And he brought him to the pitch of irritation at last by wanting to clink glasses in the German fashion, and, with sentimental speeches, to drink to those at home and to *Vater Rhein*. Kohn saw, to his horror, that he was on the point of singing. The people at the next table were casting ironic glances in their direction. Kohn made some excuse on the score of pressing business, and got up. Christophe clung to him: he wanted to know when he could have a letter of introduction, and go and see some one, and begin giving lessons.

"I'll see about it. To-day—this evening," said Kohn. "I'll talk about you at once. You can be easy on that score."

Christophe insisted.

"When shall I know?"

"To-morrow . . . to-morrow . . . or the day after."

"Very well. I'll come back to-morrow."

"No, no!" said Kohn quickly. "I'll let you know. Don't you worry."

"Oh! it's no trouble. Quite the contrary. Eh? I've nothing else to do in Paris in the meanwhile."

"Good God!" thought Kohn. . . . "No," he said aloud.

"But I would rather write to you. You wouldn't find me the next few days. Give me your address."

Christophe dictated it.

"Good. I'll write you to-morrow."

"To-morrow?"

"To-morrow. You can count on it."

He cut short Christophe's hand-shaking, and escaped. "Ugh!" he thought. "What a bore!"

As he went into his office he told the boy that he would not be in when "the German" came to see him. Ten minutes later he had forgotten him.

Christophe went back to his lair. He was full of gentle thoughts.

"What a good fellow! What a good fellow!" he thought. "How unjust I was about him. And he bears me no ill-will!"

He was remorseful, and he was on the point of writing to tell Kohn how sorry he was to have misjudged him, and to beg his forgiveness for all the harm he had done him. The tears came to his eyes as he thought of it. But it was harder for him to write a letter than a score of music: and after he had cursed and cursed the pen and ink of the hotel—which were, in fact, horrible—after he had blotted, criss-crossed, and torn up five or six sheets of paper, he lost patience and dropped it.

The rest of the day dragged wearily: but Christophe was so worn out by his sleepless night and his excursions in the morning that at length he dozed off in his chair. He only woke up in the evening, and then he went to bed: and he slept for twelve hours on end.

Next day from eight o'clock on he sat waiting for the promised letter. He had no doubt of Kohn's sincerity. He did not go out, telling himself that perhaps Kohn would come round by the hotel on his way to his office. So as not to be out, about midday he had his lunch sent up from the eating-house downstairs. Then he sat waiting again. He was sure Kohn would come on his way back from lunch. He paced up and

down his room, sat down, paced up and down again, opened his
door whenever he heard footsteps on the stairs. He had no
desire to go walking about Paris to stay his anxiety. He lay
down on his bed. His thoughts went back and back to his old
mother, who was thinking of him too—she alone thought of
him. He had an infinite tenderness for her, and he was remorseful at having left her. But he did not write to her. He
was waiting until he could tell her that he had found work.
In spite of the love they had for each other, it would never have
occurred to either of them to write just to tell their love: letters were for things more definite than that. He lay on the
bed with his hands locked behind his head, and dreamed. Although his room was away from the street, the roar of Paris
invaded the silence: the house shook. Night came again, and
brought no letter.

Came another day like unto the last.

On the third day, exasperated by his voluntary seclusion,
Christophe decided to go out. But from the impression of his
first evening he was instinctively in revolt against Paris. He
had no desire to see anything: no curiosity: he was too much
taken up with the problem of his own life to take any pleasure
in watching the lives of others: and the memories of lives past,
the monuments of a city, had always left him cold. And so,
hardly had he set foot out of doors, than, although he had
made up his mind not to go near Kohn for a week, he went
straight to his office.

The boy obeyed his orders, and said that M. Hamilton had
left Paris on business. It was a blow to Christophe. He gasped
and asked when M. Hamilton would return. The boy replied
at random:

" In ten days."

Christophe went back utterly downcast, and buried himself
in his room during the following days. He found it impossible to work. His heart sank as he saw that his small supply
of money—the little sum that his mother had sent him, carefully wrapped up in a handkerchief at the bottom of his bag—

was rapidly decreasing. He imposed a severe régime on himself. He only went down in the evening to dinner in the little pot-house, where he quickly became known to the frequenters of it as the " Prussian," or " Sauerkraut." With frightful effort, he wrote two or three letters to French musicians whose names he knew hazily. One of them had been dead for ten years. He asked them to be so kind as to give him a hearing. His spelling was wild, and his style was complicated by those long inversions and ceremonious formulæ which are the custom in Germany. He addressed his letters: " To the Palace of the Academy of France." The only man to read his gave it to his friends as a joke.

After a week Christophe went once more to the publisher's office. This time he was in luck. He met Sylvain Kohn going out, on the doorstep. Kohn made a face as he saw that he was caught: but Christophe was so happy that he did not see that. He took his hands in his usual uncouth way, and asked gaily:

" You've been away? Did you have a good time? "

Kohn said that he had had a very good time, but he did not unbend. Christophe went on:

" I came, you know. . . . They told you, I suppose? . . . Well, any news? You mentioned my name? What did they say? "

Kohn looked blank. Christophe was amazed at his frigid manner: he was not the same man.

" I mentioned you," said Kohn: " but I haven't heard yet. I haven't had time. I have been very busy since I saw you— up to my ears in business. I don't know how I can get through. It is appalling. I shall be ill with it all."

" Aren't you well? " asked Christophe anxiously and solicitously.

Kohn looked at him slyly, and replied:

" Not at all well. I don't know what's the matter, the last few days. I'm very unwell."

" I'm so sorry," said Christophe, taking his arm. " Do be

careful. You must rest. I'm so sorry to have been a bother to you. You should have told me. What is the matter with you, really?"

He took Kohn's sham excuses so seriously that the little Jew was hard put to it to hide his amusement, and disarmed by his funny simplicity. Irony is so dear a pleasure to the Jews —(and a number of Christians in Paris are Jewish in this respect)—that they are indulgent with bores, and even with their enemies, if they give them the opportunity of tasting it at their expense. Besides, Kohn was touched by Christophe's interest in himself. He felt inclined to help him.

"I've got an idea," he said. "While you are waiting for lessons, would you care to do some work for a music publisher?"

Christophe accepted eagerly.

"I've got the very thing," said Kohn. "I know one of the partners in a big firm of music publishers—Daniel Hecht. I'll introduce you. You'll see what there is to do. I don't know anything about it, you know. But Hecht is a real musician. You'll get on with him all right."

They parted until the following day. Kohn was not sorry to be rid of Christophe by doing him this service.

Next day Christophe fetched Kohn at his office. On his advice, he had brought several of his compositions to show to Hecht. They found him in his music-shop near the Opéra. Hecht did not put himself out when they went in: he coldly held out two fingers to take Kohn's hand, did not reply to Christophe's ceremonious bow, and at Kohn's request he took them into the next room. He did not ask them to sit down. He stood with his back to the empty chimney-place, and stared at the wall.

Daniel Hecht was a man of forty, tall, cold, correctly dressed, a marked Phenician type; he looked clever and disagreeable: there was a scowl on his face: he had black hair and a beard like that of an Assyrian King, long and square-cut. He hardly ever looked straight forward, and he had an icy brutal way of talking which sounded insulting even when he only said "Good-day." His insolence was more apparent than real. No doubt it emanated from a contemptuous strain in his character: but really it was more a part of the automatic and formal element in him. Jews of that sort are quite common: opinion is not kind towards them: that hard stiffness of theirs is looked upon as arrogance, while it is often in reality the outcome of an incurable boorishness in body and soul.

Sylvain Kohn introduced his protégé, in a bantering, pretentious voice, with exaggerated praises. Christophe was abashed by his reception, and stood shifting from one foot to the other, holding his manuscripts and his hat in his hand. When Kohn had finished, Hecht, who up to then had seemed to be unaware of Christophe's existence, turned towards him disdainfully, and, without looking at him, said:

"Krafft . . . Christophe Krafft. . . . Never heard the name."

To Christophe it was as though he had been struck, full in the chest. The blood rushed to his cheeks. He replied angrily:

"You'll hear it later on."

Hecht took no notice, and went on imperturbably, as though Christophe did not exist:

"Krafft . . . no, never heard it."

He was one of those people for whom not to be known to them is a mark against a man.

He went on in German:

"And you come from the *Rhine-land?* . . . It's wonderful how many people there are there who dabble in music! But I don't think there is a man among them who has any claim to be a musician."

He meant it as a joke, not as an insult: but Christophe did not take it so. He would have replied in kind if Kohn had not anticipated him.

"Oh, come, come!" he said to Hecht. "You must do me the justice to admit that I know nothing at all about it."

"That's to your credit," replied Hecht

"If I am to be no musician in order to please you," said Christophe dryly, "I am sorry, but I'm not that."

Hecht, still looking aside, went on, as indifferently as ever.

"You have written music? What have you written? *Lieder,* I suppose?"

"*Lieder,* two symphonies, symphonic poems, quartets, piano suites, theater music," said Christophe, boiling.

"People write a great deal in Germany," said Hecht, with scornful politeness.

It made him all the more suspicious of the newcomer to think that he had written so many works, and that he, Daniel Hecht, had not heard of them.

"Well," he said, "I might perhaps find work for you as you are recommended by my friend Hamilton. At present we are making a collection, a 'Library for Young People,' in which we are publishing some easy pianoforte pieces. Could you 'simplify' the *Carnival* of Schumann, and arrange it for six and eight hands?"

Christophe was staggered.

"And you offer that to me, to me—me . . . ?"

His naïve "Me" delighted Kohn: but Hecht was offended.

"I don't see that there is anything surprising in that," he said. "It is not such easy work as all that! If you think it too easy, so much the better. We'll see about that later on. You tell me you are a good musician. I must believe you. But I've never heard of you."

He thought to himself:

"If one were to believe all these young sparks, they would knock the stuffing out of Johannes Brahms himself."

Christophe made no reply—(for he had vowed to hold himself in check)—clapped his hat on his head, and turned towards the door. Kohn stopped him, laughing:

"Wait, wait!" he said. And he turned to Hecht: "He has brought some of his work to give you an idea."

"Ah!" said Hecht warily. "Very well, then: let us see them."

Without a word Christophe held out his manuscripts. Hecht cast his eyes over them carelessly.

"What's this? *A suite for piano* . . . (reading) : *A Day.* . . . Ah! Always program music! . . ."

In spite of his apparent indifference he was reading carefully. He was an excellent musician, and knew his job : he knew nothing outside it : with the first bar or two he gauged his man. He was silent as he turned over the pages with a scornful air : he was struck by the talent revealed in them : but his natural reserve and his vanity, piqued by Christophe's manner, kept him from showing anything. He went on to the end in silence, not missing a note.

"Yes," he said, in a patronizing tone of voice, "they're well enough."

Violent criticism would have hurt Christophe less.

"I don't need to be told that," he said irritably.

"I fancy," said Hecht, "that you showed me them for me to say what I thought."

"Not at all."

"Then," said Hecht coldly, "I fail to see what you have come for."

"I came to ask for work, and nothing else."

"I have nothing to offer you for the time being, except what I told you. And I'm not sure of that. I said it was possible, that's all."

"And you have no other work to offer a musician like myself?"

"A musician like you?" said Hecht ironically and cuttingly. "Other musicians at least as good as yourself have not thought the work beneath their dignity. There are men whose names I could give you, men who are now very well known in Paris, have been very grateful to me for it."

"Then they must have been—swine!" bellowed Christophe. —(He had already learned certain of the most useful words in the French language)—"You are wrong if you think you have to do with a man of that kidney. Do you think you can take

me in with looking anywhere but at me, and clipping your
words? You didn't even deign to acknowledge my bow when
I came in. . . . But what the hell are you to treat me like
that? Are you even a musician? Have you ever written anything? . . . And you pretend to teach me how to write—
me. to whom writing is life! . . . And you can find nothing
better to offer me, when you have read my music, than a
hashing up of great musicians, a filthy scrabbling over their
works to turn them into parlor tricks for little girls! . . .
You go to your Parisians who are rotten enough to be taught
their work by you! I'd rather die first!"

It was impossible to stem the torrent of his words.

Hecht said icily:

"Take it or leave it."

Christophe went out and slammed the doors. Hecht
shrugged, and said to Sylvain Kohn, who was laughing:

"He will come to it like the rest."

At heart he valued Christophe. He was clever enough to
feel not only the worth of a piece of work, but also the worth
of a man. Behind Christophe's outburst he had marked a
force. And he knew its rarity—in the world of art more than
anywhere else. But his vanity was ruffled by it: nothing would
ever induce him to admit himself in the wrong. He desired
loyally to be just to Christophe, but he could not do it unless
Christophe came and groveled to him. He expected Christophe to return: his melancholy skepticism and his experience
of men had told him how inevitably the will is weakened and
worn down by poverty.

Christophe went home. Anger had given place to despair.
He felt that he was lost. The frail prop on which he had
counted had failed him. He had no doubt but that he had
made a deadly enemy, not only of Hecht, but of Kohn, who had
introduced him. He was in absolute solitude in a hostile city.
Outside Diener and Kohn he knew no one. His friend Corinne,
the beautiful actress whom he had met in Germany, was not

in Paris: she was still touring abroad, in America, this time
on her own account: the papers published clamatory descriptions of her travels. As for the little French governess whom
he had unwittingly robbed of her situation,—the thought of her
had long filled him with remorse—how often had he vowed
that he would find her when he reached Paris.[1] But now that
he was in Paris he found that he had forgotten one important
thing: her name. He could not remember it. He could only
recollect her Christian name: Antoinette. And then, even if he
remembered, how was he to find a poor little governess in that
ant-heap of human beings?

He had to set to work as soon as possible to find a livelihood. He had five francs left. In spite of his dislike of him,
he forced himself to ask the innkeeper if he did not know of
anybody in the neighborhood to whom he could give music-
lessons. The innkeeper, who had no great opinion of a lodger
who only ate once a day and spoke German, lost what respect
he had for him when he heard that he was only a musician.
He was a Frenchman of the old school, and music was to him
an idler's job. He scoffed:

"The piano! . . . I don't know. You strum the piano!
Congratulations! . . . But 'tis a queer thing to take to that
trade as a matter of taste! When I hear music, it's just for
all the world like listening to the rain. . . . But perhaps
you might teach me. What do you say, you fellows?" he
cried, turning to some fellows who were drinking.

They laughed loudly.

"It's a fine trade," said one of them. "Not dirty work.
And the ladies like it."

Christophe did not rightly understand the French or the
jest: he floundered for his words: he did not know whether to
be angry or not. The innkeeper's wife took pity on him:

"Come, come, Philippe, you're not serious," she said to her
husband. "All the same," she went on, turning to Christophe,
"there is some one who might do for you."

[1] See *Jean-Christophe*—I: "Revolt."

" Who? " asked her husband.

" The Grasset girl.   You know, they've bought a piano."

" Ah!   Those stuck-up folk!   So they have."

They told Christophe that the girl in question was the
daughter of a butcher: her parents were trying to make a lady
of her; they would perhaps like her to have lessons, if only
for the sake of making people talk.   The innkeeper's wife
promised to see to it.

Next day she told Christophe that the butcher's wife would
like to see him.   He went to her house, and found her in the
shop, surrounded with great pieces of meat.   She was a pretty,
rather florid woman, and she smiled sweetly, but stood on her
dignity when she heard why he had come.   Quite abruptly she
came to the question of payment, and said quickly that she
did not wish to give much, because the piano is quite an agreeable thing, but not necessary: she offered him fifty centimes an
hour.   In any case, she would not pay more than four francs
a week.   After that she asked Christophe a little doubtfully if
he knew much about music.   She was reassured, and became
more amiable when he told her that not only did he know
about music, but wrote it into the bargain: that flattered her
vanity: it would be a good thing to spread about the neighborhood that her daughter was taking lessons with a composer.

Next day, when Christophe found himself sitting by the
piano—a horrible instrument, bought second-hand, which
sounded like a guitar—with the butcher's little daughter, whose
short, stubby fingers fumbled with the keys; who was unable
to tell one note from another; who was bored to tears; who
began at once to yawn in his face; and he had to submit to
the mother's superintendence, and to her conversation, and to
her ideas on music and the teaching of music—then he felt so
miserable, so wretchedly humiliated, that he had not even the
strength to be angry about it.   He relapsed into a state of
despair: there were evenings when he could not eat.   If in a
few weeks he had fallen so low, where would he end?   What

good was it to have rebelled against Hecht's offer? The thing to which he had submitted was even more degrading.

One evening, as he sat in his room, he could not restrain his tears: he flung himself on his knees by his bed and prayed. . . . To whom did he pray? To whom could he pray? He did not believe in God; he believed that there was no God. . . . But he had to pray—he had to pray within his soul. Only the mean of spirit never need to pray. They never know the need that comes to the strong in spirit of taking refuge within the inner sanctuary of themselves. As he left behind him the humiliations of the day, in the vivid silence of his heart Christophe felt the presence of his eternal Being, of his God. The waters of his wretched life stirred and shifted above Him and never touched Him: what was there in common between that and Him? All the sorrows of the world rushing on to destruction dashed against that rock. Christophe heard the blood beating in his veins, beating like an inward voice, crying:

"Eternal . . . I am . . . I am. . . ."

Well did he know that voice: as long as he could remember he had heard it. Sometimes he forgot it: often for months together he would lose consciousness of its mighty monotonous rhythm: but he knew that it was there, that it never ceased, like the ocean roaring in the night. In the music of it he found once more the same energy that he gained from it whenever he bathed in its waters. He rose to his feet. He was fortified. No: the hard life that he led contained nothing of which he need be ashamed: he could eat the bread he earned, and never blush for it: it was for those who made him earn it at such a price to blush and be ashamed. Patience! Patience! The time would come. . . .

But next day he began to lose patience again: and, in spite of all his efforts, he did at last explode angrily, one day during a lesson, at the silly little ninny, who had been maddeningly impertinent and laughed at his accent, and had taken a malicious delight in doing exactly the opposite of what he told her. The girl screamed in response to Christophe's angry shouts.

She was frightened and enraged at a man whom she paid daring to show her no respect. She declared that he had struck her—(Christophe had shaken her arm rather roughly). Her mother bounced in on them like a Fury, and covered her daughter with kisses and Christophe with abuse. The butcher also appeared, and declared that he would not suffer any infernal Prussian to take upon himself to touch his daughter. Furious, pale with rage, itching to choke the life out of the butcher and his wife and daughter, Christophe rushed away. His host and hostess, seeing him come in in an abject condition, had no difficulty in worming the story out of him: and it fed the malevolence with which they regarded their neighbors. But by the evening the whole neighborhood was saying that the German was a brute and a child-beater.

Christophe made fresh advances to the music-vendors: but in vain. He found the French lacking in cordiality: and the whirl and confusion of their perpetual agitation crushed him. They seemed to him to live in a state of anarchy, directed by a cunning and despotic bureaucracy.

One evening, he was wandering along the boulevards, discouraged by the futility of his efforts, when he saw Sylvain Kohn coming from the opposite direction. He was convinced that they had quarreled irrevocably and looked away and tried to pass unnoticed. But Kohn called to him:

"What became of you after that great day?" he asked with a laugh. "I've been wanting to look you up, but I lost your address. . . . Good Lord, my dear fellow, I didn't know you! You were epic: that's what you were, epic!"

Christophe stared at him. He was surprised and a little ashamed.

"You're not angry with me?"

"Angry? What an idea!"

So far from being angry, he had been delighted with the way in which Christophe had trounced Hecht: it had been a treat to him. It really mattered nothing to him whether Chris-

tophe or Hecht was right: he only regarded people as source of
entertainment: and he saw in Christophe a spring of high
comedy, which he intended to exploit to the full.

"You should have come to see me," he went on. "I was
expecting you. What are you doing this evening? Come to
dinner. I won't let you off. Quite informal: just a few artists:
we meet once a fortnight. You should know these people.
Come. I'll introduce you."

In vain did Christophe beg to be excused on the score of his
clothes. Sylvain Kohn carried him off.

They entered a restaurant on one of the boulevards, and
went up to the second floor. Christophe found himself among
about thirty young men, whose ages ranged from twenty to
thirty-five, and they were all engaged in animated discussion.
Kohn introduced him as a man who had just escaped from a
German prison. They paid no attention to him and did not
stop their passionate discussion, and Kohn plunged into it at
once.

Christophe was shy in this select company, and said nothing:
but he was all ears. He could not grasp—he had great difficulty in following the volubility of the French—what great
artistic interests were in dispute. He listened attentively, but
he could only make out words like "trust," "monopoly," "fall
in prices," "receipts," mixed up with phrases like "the dignity
of art," and the "rights of the author." And at last he saw that
they were talking business. A certain number of authors, it
appeared, belonged to a syndicate and were angry about certain
attempts which had been made to float a rival concern, which,
according to them, would dispute their monopoly of exploita-
tion. The defection of certain of their members who had
found it to their advantage to go over bag and baggage to the
rival house had roused them to the wildest fury. They talked
of decapitation. ". . . Burked. . . . Treachery. . . .
Shame. . . . Sold. . . ."

Others did not worry about the living: they were incensed
against the dead, whose sales without royalties choked up the

market. It appeared that the works of De Musset had just become public property, and were selling far too well. And so they demanded that the State should give them rigorous protection, and heavily tax the masterpieces of the past so as to check their circulation at reduced prices, which, they declared, was unfair competition with the work of living artists.

They stopped each other to hear the takings of such and such a theater on the preceding evening. They all went into ecstasies over the fortune of a veteran dramatist, famous in two continents—a man whom they despised, though they envied him even more. From the incomes of authors they passed to those of the critics. They talked of the sum—(pure calumny, no doubt)—received by one of their colleagues for every first performance at one of the theaters on the boulevards, the consideration being that he should speak well of it. He was an honest man: having made his bargain he stuck to it: but his great secret lay—(so they said)—in so eulogizing the piece that it would be taken off as quickly as possible so that there might be many new plays. The tale—(or the account)—caused laughter, but nobody was surprised.

And mingled with all that talk they threw out fine phrases: they talked of " poetry " and " art for art's sake." But through it all there rang " art for money's sake "; and this jobbing spirit, newly come into French literature, scandalized Christophe. As he understood nothing at all about their talk of money he had given it up. But then they began to talk of letters, or rather of men of letters.—Christophe pricked up his ears as he heard the name of Victor Hugo.

They were debating whether he had been cuckolded: they argued at length about the love of Sainte-Beuve and Madame Hugo. And then they turned to the lovers of George Sand and their respective merits. That was the chief occupation of criticism just then: when they had ransacked the houses of great men, rummaged through the closets, turned out the drawers, ransacked the cupboards, they burrowed down to their inmost lives. The attitude of Monsieur de Lauzun lying flat under the bed of the King and Madame de Montespan was the attitude of criticism in its cult of history and truth— (everybody just then, of course, made a cult of truth). These young men were subscribers to the cult: no detail was too small for them in their search for truth. They applied it to the art of the present as well as to that of the past: and they analyzed the private life of certain of the more notorious of their contemporaries with the same passion for exactness. It was a queer thing that they were possessed of the smallest details of scenes which are usually enacted without witnesses. It was really as though the persons concerned had been the first to give exact information to the public out of their great devotion to the truth.

Christophe was more and more embarrassed and tried to talk to his neighbors of something else; but nobody listened to him. At first they asked him a few vague questions about Germany— questions which, to his amazement, displayed the almost complete ignorance of these distinguished and apparently cultured young men concerning the most elementary things of their work —literature and art—outside Paris; at most they had heard of a few great names: Hauptmann, Sudermann, Liebermann, Strauss (David, Johann, Richard), and they picked their way gingerly among them for fear of getting mixed. If they had questioned Christophe it was from politeness rather than from curiosity: they had no curiosity: they hardly seemed to notice his replies: and they hurried back at once to the Parisian topics which were regaling the rest of the company.

Christophe timidly tried to talk of music. Not one of these men of letters was a musician. At heart they considered music an inferior art. But the growing success of music during the last few years had made them secretly uneasy: and since it was the fashion they pretended to be interested in it. They frothed especially about a new opera and declared that music dated from its performance, or at least the new era in music. This idea made things easy for their ignorance and snobbishness, for it relieved them of the necessity of knowing anything else.

The author of the opera, a Parisian, whose name Christophe heard for the first time, had, said some, made a clean sweep of all that had gone before him, cleaned up, renovated, and recreated music. Christophe started at that. He asked nothing better than to believe in genius. But such a genius as that, a genius who had at one swoop wiped out the past. . . . Good heavens! He must be a lusty lad: how the devil had he done it? He asked for particulars. The others, who would have been hard put to it to give any explanation and were disconcerted by Christophe, referred him to the musician of the company, Théophile Goujart, the great musical critic, who began at once to talk of sevenths and ninths. Goujart knew music much as Sganarelle knew Latin. . . .

". . . *You don't know Latin?*"

"*No.*"

(*With enthusiasm*) "*Cabricias, arci thuram, catalamus, singulariter . . . bonus, bona, bonum.*"

Finding himself with a man who "understood Latin" he prudently took refuge in the chatter of esthetics. From that impregnable fortress he began to bombard Beethoven, Wagner, and classical art, which was not before the house (but in France it is impossible to praise an artist without making as an offering a holocaust of all those who are unlike him). He announced the advent of a new art which trampled under foot the conventions of the past. He spoke of a new musical language which had been discovered by the Christopher Columbus of Parisian music, and he said it made an end of the language of the classics: that was a dead language.

Christophe reserved his opinion of this reforming genius to wait until he had seen his work before he said anything: but in spite of himself he felt an instinctive distrust of this musical Baal to whom all music was sacrificed. He was scandalized to hear the Masters so spoken of: and he forgot that he had said much the same sort of thing in Germany. He who at home had thought himself a revolutionary in art, he who had scandalized others by the boldness of his judgments and the frankness of his expressions, felt, as soon as he heard these words spoken in France, that he was at heart a conservative. He tried to argue, and was tactless enough to speak, not like a man of culture, who advances arguments without exposition, but as a professional, bringing out disconcerting facts. He did not hesitate to plunge into technical explanations: and his voice, as he talked, struck a note which was well calculated to offend the ears of a company of superior persons to whom his arguments and the vigor with which he supported them were alike ridiculous. The critic tried to demolish him with an attempt at wit, and to end the discussion which had shown Christophe to his stupefaction that he had to deal with a man who did not in the least know what he was talking about. And so they came to the opinion that the German was pedantic and superannuated: and without knowing anything about it they decided that his music was detestable. But Christophe's bizarre personality had made an impression on the company of young men, and with their quickness in seizing on the ridiculous they had marked the awkward, violent gestures of his thin arms with their enormous hands, and the furious glances that darted from his eyes as his voice rose to a falsetto. Sylvain Kohn saw to it that his friends were kept amused.

Conversation had deserted literature in favor of women. As a matter of fact they were only two aspects of the same subject: for their literature was concerned with nothing but women, and their women were concerned with nothing but literature, they were so much taken up with the affairs and men of letters.

They spoke of one good lady, well known in Parisian society, who had, it was said, just married her lover to her daughter, the better to keep him. Christóphe squirmed in his chair, and tactlessly made a face of disgust. Kohn saw it, and nudged his neighbor and pointed out that the subject seemed to excite the German—that no doubt he was longing to know the lady. Christophe blushed, muttered angrily, and finally said hotly that such women ought to be whipped. His proposition was received with a shout of Homeric laughter: and Sylvain Kohn

cooingly protested that no man should touch a woman, even
with a flower, etc., etc.   (In Paris he was the very Knight of
Love.)   Christophe replied that a woman of that sort was
neither more nor less than a bitch, and that there was only one
remedy for vicious dogs: the whip.   They roared at him.
Christophe said that their gallantry was hypocritical, and that
those who talked most of their respect for women were those
who possessed the least of it: and he protested against these
scandalous tales.   They replied that there was no scandal in
it, and that it was only natural: and they were all agreed
that the heroine of the story was not only a charming woman,
but *the* Woman, *par excellence*.   The German waxed indignant.
Sylvain Kohn asked him slyly what he thought Woman was
like.   Christophe felt that they were pulling his leg and laying
a trap for him: but he fell straight into it in the violent expression of his convictions.   He began to explain his ideas on
love to these bantering Parisians.   He could not find his words,
floundered about after them, and finally fished up from the
phrases he remembered such impossible words, such enormities,
that he had all his hearers rocking with laughter, while all the
time he was perfectly and admirably serious, never bothered
about them, and was touchingly impervious to their ridicule: for
he could not help seeing that they were making fun of him.
At last he tied himself up in a sentence, could not extricate
himself, brought his fist down on the table, and was silent.

They tried to bring him back into the discussion: he scowled
and did not flinch, but sat with his elbows on the table,
ashamed and irritated.   He did not open his lips again, except to eat and drink, until the dinner was over.   He drank
enormously, unlike the Frenchmen, who only sipped their wine.
His neighbor wickedly encouraged him, and went on filling his
glass, which he emptied absently.   But, although he was not
used to these excesses, especially after the weeks of privation
through which he had passed, he took his liquor well, and did
not cut so ridiculous a figure as the others hoped.   He sat there
lost in thought: they paid no attention to him: they thought he

was made drowsy by the wine. He was exhausted by the effort of following the conversation in French, and tired of hearing about nothing but literature—actors, authors, publishers, the chatter of the *coulisses* and literary life: everything seemed to be reduced to that. Amid all these new faces and the buzz of words he could not fix a single face, nor a single thought. His short-sighted eyes, dim and dreamy, wandered slowly round the table, and they rested on one man after another without seeming to see them. And yet he saw them better than any one, though he himself was not conscious of it. He did not, like these Jews and Frenchmen, peck at the things he saw and dissect them, tear them to rags, and leave them in tiny, tiny pieces. Slowly, like a sponge, he sucked up the essence of men and women, and bore away their image in his soul. He seemed to have seen nothing and to remember nothing. It was only long afterwards—hours, often days—when he was alone, gazing in upon himself, that he saw that he had borne away a whole impression.

But for the moment he seemed to be just a German boor, stuffing himself with food, concerned only with not missing a mouthful. And he heard nothing clearly, except when he heard the others calling each other by name, and then, with a silly drunken insistency, he wondered why so many Frenchmen have foreign names: Flemish, German, Jewish, Levantine, Anglo- or Spanish-American.

He did not notice when they got up from the table. He went on sitting alone: and he dreamed of the Rhenish hills, the great woods, the tilled fields, the meadows by the waterside, his old mother. Most of the others had gone. At last he thought of going, and got up, too, without looking at anybody, and went and took down his hat and cloak, which were hanging by the door. When he had put them on he was turning away without saying good-night, when through a half-open door he saw an object which fascinated him: a piano. He had not touched a musical instrument for weeks. He went in and lovingly touched the keys, sat down just as he was, with his hat on his head and his cloak on his shoulders, and began to play. He had altogether forgotten where he was. He did not notice that two men crept into the room to listen to him. One was Sylvain Kohn, a passionate lover of music—God knows why! for he knew nothing at all about it, and he liked bad music just as well as good. The other was the musical critic, Théophile Goujart. He—it simplifies matters so much—neither understood nor loved music: but that did not keep him from talking about it. On the contrary: nobody is so free in mind as the man who knows nothing of what he is talking about: for to such a man it does not matter whether he says one thing more than another.

Théophile Goujart was tall, strong, and muscular: he had a black beard, thick curls on his forehead, which was lined with deep inexpressive wrinkles, short arms, short legs, a big chest: a type of woodman or porter of the Auvergne. He had common manners and an arrogant way of speaking. He had gone into music through politics, at that time the only road to success in France. He had attached himself to the fortunes of a Minister to whom he had discovered that he was distantly related—a son "of the bastard of his apothecary." Ministers are not eternal, and when it seemed that the day of his Minister was over Théophile Goujart deserted the ship, taking with him all that he could lay his hands on, notably several orders: for he loved glory. Tired of politics, in which for some time past he had received various snubs, both on his own account and on that of his patron, he looked out for a shelter from the storm, a restful position in which he could annoy others without being himself annoyed. Everything pointed to criticism. Just at that moment there fell vacant the post of musical critic to one of the great Parisian papers. The previous holder of the post, a young and talented composer, had been dismissed because he insisted on saying what he thought of the authors and their work. Goujart had never taken any interest in music, and knew nothing at all about it: he was chosen without a moment's hesitation. They had had enough of competent critics: with

Goujart there was at least nothing to fear: he did not attach an absurd importance to his opinions: he was always at the editor's orders, and ready to comply with a slashing article or enthusiastic approbation. That he was no musician was a secondary consideration. Everybody in France knows a little about music. Goujart quickly acquired the requisite knowledge. His method was quite simple: it consisted in sitting at every concert next to some good musician, a composer if possible, and getting him to say what he thought of the works performed. At the end of a few months of this apprenticeship, he knew his job: the fledgling could fly. He did not, it is true, soar like an eagle: and God knows what howlers Goujart committed with the greatest show of authority in his paper! He listened and read haphazard, stirred the mixture up well in his sluggish brains, and arrogantly laid down the law for others; he wrote in a pretentious style, interlarded with puns, and plastered over with an aggressive pedantry: he had the mind of a schoolmaster. Sometimes, every now and then, he drew down on himself cruel replies: then he shammed dead, and took good care not to answer them. He was a mixture of cunning and thick-headedness, insolent or groveling as circumstances demanded. He cringed to the masters who had an official position or an established fame (he had no other means of judging merit in music). He scorned everybody else, and exploited writers who were starving. He was no fool.

In spite of his reputation and the authority he had acquired, he knew in his heart of hearts that he knew nothing about music: and he recognized that Christophe knew a great deal about it. Nothing would have induced him to say so: but it was borne in upon him. And now he heard Christophe play: and he made great efforts to understand him, looking absorbed, profound, without a thought in his head: he could not see a yard ahead of him through the fog of sound, and he wagged his head solemnly as one who knew and adjusted the outward and visible signs of his approval to the fluttering of the eyelids of Sylvain Kohn, who found it hard to stand still.

At last Christophe, emerging to consciousness from the fumes of wine and music, became dimly aware of the pantomime going on behind his back: he turned and saw the two amateurs of music. They rushed at him and violently shook hands with him—Sylvain Kohn gurgling that he had played like a god, Goujart declaring solemnly that he had the left hand of Rubinstein and the right hand of Paderewski (or it might be the other way round). Both agreed that such talent ought not to be hid under a bushel, and they pledged themselves to reveal it. And, incidentally, they were both resolved to extract from it as much honor and profit as possible.

From that day on Sylvain Kohn took to inviting Christophe to his rooms, and put at his disposal his excellent piano, which he never used himself. Christophe, who was bursting with suppressed music, did not need to be urged, and accepted: and for a time he made good use of the invitation.

At first all went well. Christophe was only too happy to play: and Sylvain Kohn was tactful enough to leave him to play in peace. He enjoyed it thoroughly himself. By one of those queer phenomena which must be in everybody's observation, the man, who was no musician, no artist, cold-hearted and devoid of all poetic feeling and real kindness, was enslaved sensually by Christophe's music, which he did not understand, though he found in it a strongly voluptuous pleasure. Unfortunately, he could not hold his tongue. He had to talk, loudly, while Christophe was playing. He had to underline the music with affected exclamations, like a concert snob, or else he passed ridiculous comment on it. Then Christophe would thump the piano, and declare that he could not go on like that. Kohn would try hard to be silent: but he could not do it: at once he would begin again to sniffle, sigh, whistle, beat time, hum, imitate the various instruments. And when the piece was ended he would have burst if he had not given Christophe the benefit of his inept comment.

He was a queer mixture of German sentimentality, Parisian humbug, and intolerable fatuousness. Sometimes he expressed second-hand precious opinions; sometimes he made extravagant comparisons; and then he would make dirty, obscene remarks, or propound some insane nonsense. By way of praising Beethoven, he would point out some trickery, or read a lascivious sensuality into his music. The *Quartet in C Minor* seemed to him jolly spicy. The sublime *Adagio of the Ninth Symphony* made him think of Cherubino. After the three crashing chords at the opening of the *Symphony in C Minor,* he called out: "Don't come in! I've some one here." He admired the Battle of *Heldenleben* because he pretended that it was like the noise of a motor-car. And always he had some image to explain each piece, a puerile incongruous image. Really, it seemed impossible that he could have any love for music. However, there was no doubt about it: he really did love it: at certain passages to which he attached the most ridiculous meanings the tears would come into his eyes. But after having been moved by a scene from Wagner, he would strum out a gallop of Offenbach, or sing some music-hall ditty after the *Ode to Joy.* Then Christophe would bob about and roar with rage. But the worst of all to bear was not when Sylvain Kohn was absurd so much as when he was trying to be profound and subtle, when he was trying to impress Christophe, when it was Hamilton speaking, and not Sylvain Kohn. Then Christophe would scowl blackly at him, and squash him with cold contempt, which hurt Hamilton's vanity: very often these musical evenings would end in a quarrel. But Kohn would forget it next day, and Christophe, sorry for his rudeness, would make a point of going back.

That would not have mattered much if Kohn had been able to refrain from inviting his friends to hear Christophe. But he could not help wanting to show off his musician. The first time Christophe found in Kohn's rooms three or four little Jews and Kohn's mistress—a large florid woman, all paint and powder, who repeated idiotic jokes and talked about her food, and thought herself a musician because she showed her legs every evening in the Revue of the Variétés—Christophe looked black. Next time he told Sylvain Kohn curtly that he would never again play in his rooms. Sylvain Kohn swore by all his gods that he would not invite anybody again. But he did so by stealth, and hid his guests in the next room. Naturally, Christophe found that out, and went away in a fury, and this time did not return.

And yet he had to accommodate Kohn, who had introduced him to various cosmopolitan families, and found him pupils.

A few days after Théophile Goujart hunted Christophe up in his lair. He did not seem to mind his being in such a horrible place. On the contrary, he was charming. He said:

"I thought perhaps you would like to hear a little music from time to time: and as I have tickets for everything, I came to ask if you would care to come with me."

Christophe was delighted. He was glad of the kindly attention, and thanked him effusively. Goujart was a different man from what he had been at their first meeting. He had dropped his conceit, and, man to man, he was timid, docile, anxious to learn. It was only when they were with others that he resumed his superior manner and his blatant tone of voice. His eagerness to learn had a practical side to it. He had no curiosity about anything that was not actual. He wanted to know what Christophe thought of a score he had received which he would have been hard put to it to write about, for he could hardly read a note.

They went to a symphony concert. They had to go in by the entrance to a music-hall. They went down a winding passage to an ill-ventilated hall: the air was stifling: the seats were very narrow, and placed too close together: part of the audience was standing and blocking up every way out:—the uncomfortable French. A man who looked as though he were hopelessly bored was racing through a Beethoven symphony as though he were in a hurry to get to the end of it. The voluptuous strains of a stomach-dance coming from the music-hall next door were mingled with the funeral march of the *Eroica*. People kept coming in and taking their seats, and turning their glasses on the audience. As soon as the last person had arrived, they began to go out again. Christophe strained every nerve to try and follow the thread of the symphony through the babel: and he did manage to wrest some pleasure from it— (for the orchestra was skilful, and Christophe had been deprived of symphony music for a long time)—and then Goujart took his arm and, in the middle of the concert, said:

" Now let us go. We'll go to another concert."

Christophe frowned: but he made no reply and followed his guide. They went half across Paris, and then reached another hall, that smelled of stables, in which at other times fairy plays and popular pieces were given—(in Paris music is like those poor workingmen who share a lodging: when one of them leaves the bed, the other creeps into the warm sheets). No air, of course: since the reign of Louis XIV the French have considered air unhealthy: and the ventilation of the theaters, like that of old at Versailles, makes it impossible for people to breathe. A noble old man, waving his arms like a lion-tamer, was letting loose an act of Wagner: the wretched beast —the act—was like the lions of a menagerie, dazzled and cowed by the footlights, so that they have to be whipped to be reminded that they are lions. The audience consisted of female Pharisees and foolish women, smiling inanely. After the lion had gone through its performance, and the tamer had bowed, and they had both been rewarded by the applause of the audience, Goujart suggested that they should go to yet another concert. But this time Christophe gripped the arms of his stall, and declared that he would not budge: he had had enough of running from concert to concert, picking up the crumbs of a symphony and scraps of a concert on the way. In vain did Goujart try to explain to him that musical criticism in Paris was a trade in which it was more important to see than to hear. Christophe protested that music was not written to be heard in a cab, and needed more concentration. Such a hotch-potch of concerts was sickening to him: one at a time was enough for him.

He was much surprised at the extraordinary number of concerts in Paris. Like most Germans, he thought that music held a subordinate place in France: and he expected that it would be served up in small delicate portions. By way of a beginning, he was given fifteen concerts in seven days. There was one for every evening in the week, and often two or three an evening at the same time in different quarters of the city. On Sundays there were four, all at the same time. Christophe marveled at this appetite for music. And he was no less amazed at the length of the programs. Till then he had thought that his fellow-countrymen had a monopoly of these orgies of sound which had more than once disgusted him in Germany. He saw now that the Parisians could have given them points in the matter of gluttony. They were given full measure: two symphonies, a concerto, one or two overtures, an act from an opera. And they came from all sources: German, Russian, Scandinavian, French—beer, champagne, orgeat, wine —they gulped down everything without winking. Christophe was amazed that these indolent Parisians should have had such capacious stomachs. They did not suffer for it at all. It was the cask of the Danaïdes. It held nothing.

It was not long before Christophe perceived that this mass of music amounted to very little really. He saw the same faces and heard the same pieces at every concert. Their copious programs moved in a circle. Practically nothing earlier than Beethoven. Practically nothing later than Wagner. And what gaps between them! It seemed as though music were reduced to five or six great German names, three or four French names, and, since the Franco-Russian alliance, half a dozen Muscovites. None of the old French Masters. None of the great Italians. None of the German giants of the seventeenth and eighteenth centuries. No contemporary German music, with the single exception of Richard Strauss, who was more acute than the rest, and came once a year to plant his new works on the Parisian public. No Belgian music. No Tschek music. But, most surprising of all, practically no contem-porary French music. And yet everybody was talking about it mysteriously as a thing that would revolutionize the world. Christophe was yearning for an opportunity of hearing it: he was very curious about it, and absolutely without prejudice: he was longing to hear new music, and to admire the works of genius. But he never succeeded in hearing any of it: for he did not count a few short pieces, quite cleverly written, but cold and brain-spun, to which he had not listened very attentively.

While he was waiting to form an opinion, Christophe tried to find out something about it from musical criticism.

That was not easy. It was like the Court of King Pétaud. Not only did the various papers lightly contradict each other: but they contradicted themselves in different articles—almost on different pages. To read them all was enough to drive a man crazy. Fortunately, the critics only read their own articles, and the public did not read any of them. But Christophe, who wanted to gain a clear idea about French musicians, labored hard to omit nothing: and he marveled at the agility of the critics, who darted about in a sea of contradictions like fish in water.

But amid all these divergent opinions one thing struck him: the pedantic manner of most of the critics. Who was it said that the French were amiable fantastics who believed in nothing? Those whom Christophe saw were more hag-ridden by the science of music—even when they knew nothing—than all the critics on the other side of the Rhine.

At that time the French musical critics had set about learn-ing what music was. There were even a few who knew some-thing about it: they were men of original thought, who had taken the trouble to think about their art, and to think for themselves. Naturally, they were not very well known: they were shelved in their little reviews: with only one or two ex-ceptions. the newspapers were not for them. They were honest

men—intelligent, interesting, sometimes driven by their isolation to paradox and the habit of thinking aloud, intolerance, and
garrulity. The rest had hastily learned the rudiments of harmony: and they stood gaping in wonder at their newly acquired
knowledge. Like Monsieur Jourdain when he learned the
rules of grammar, they marvelled at their knowledge:

"*D, a, Da; F, a, Fa; R, a, Ra. . . . Ah! How fine it
is! . . . Ah! How splendid it is to know something! . . .*"

They only babbled of theme and counter-theme, of harmonies
and resultant sounds, of consecutive ninths and tierce major.
When they had labeled the succeeding harmonies which made
up a page of music, they proudly mopped their brows: they
thought they had explained the music, and almost believed that
they had written it. As a matter of fact, they had only repeated
it in school language, like a boy making a grammatical analysis
of a page of Cicero. But it was so difficult for the best of them
to conceive music as a natural language of the soul that, when
they did not make it an adjunct to painting, they dragged it
into the outskirts of science, and reduced it to the level of a
problem in harmonic construction. Some who were learned
enough took upon themselves to show a thing or two to past
musicians. They found fault with Beethoven, and rapped Wagner over the knuckles. They laughed openly at Berlioz and
Gluck. Nothing existed for them just then but Johann Sebastian Bach, and Claude Debussy. And Bach, who had lately
been roundly abused, was beginning to seem pedantic, a periwig,
and in fine. a hack. Quite distinguished men extolled Rameau
in mysterious terms—Rameau and Couperin. called the Great.

There were tremendous conflicts waged between these learned
men. They were all musicians: but as they all affected different styles, each of them claimed that his was the only true
style, and cried "Raca!" to that of their colleagues. They accused each other of sham writing and sham culture, and
hurled at each other's heads the words "idealism" and "materialism," "symbolism" and "verism," "subjectivism" and
"objectivism." Christophe thought it was hardly worth while

leaving Germany to find the squabbles of the Germans in Paris. Instead of being grateful for having good music presented in so many different fashions, they would only tolerate their own particular fashion: and a new *Lutrin,* a fierce war, divided musicians into two hostile camps, the camp of counterpoint and the camp of harmony. Like the *Gros-boutiens* and the *Petits-boutiens,* one side maintained with acrimony that music should be read horizontally, and the other that it should be read vertically. One party would only hear of full-sounding chords, melting concatenations, succulent harmonies: they spoke of music as though it were a confectioner's shop. The other party would not hear of the ear, that trumpery organ, being considered: music was for them a lecture, a Parliamentary assembly, in which all the orators spoke at once without bothering about their neighbors, and went on talking until they had done: if people could not hear, so much the worse for them! They could read their speeches next day in the *Official Journal:* music was made to be read, and not to be heard. When Christophe first heard of this quarrel between the *Horizontalists* and the *Verticalists,* he thought they were all mad. When he was summoned to join in the fight between the army of *Succession* and the army of *Superposition,* he replied, with his usual formula, which was very different from that of Sosia:

" Gentlemen, I am everybody's enemy."

And when they insisted, saying:

" Which matters most in music, harmony or counterpoint? "

He replied:

" Music. Show me what you have done."

They were all agreed about their own music. These intrepid warriors who, when they were not pummeling each other, were whacking away at some dead Master whose fame had endured too long, were reconciled by the one passion which was common to them all: an ardent musical patriotism. France was to them *the* great musical nation. They were perpetually proclaiming the decay of Germany. That did not hurt Christophe. He had declared so himself, and therefore was not in a position to contradict them. But he was a little surprised to hear of the supremacy of French music: there was, in fact, very little trace of it in the past. And yet French musicians maintained that their art had been admirable from the earliest period. By way of glorifying French music, they set to work to throw ridicule on the famous men of the last century, with the exception of one Master, who was very good and very pure— and a Belgian. Having done that amount of slaughter, they were free to admire the archaic Masters, who had been forgotten, while a certain number of them were absolutely unknown. Unlike the lay schools of France which date the world from the French Revolution, the musicians regarded it as a chain of mighty mountains, to be scaled before it could be possible to look back on the Golden Age of music, the Eldorado of art. After a long eclipse the Golden Age was to emerge again: the hard wall was to crumble away: a magician of sound was to call forth in full flower a marvelous spring: the old tree of music was to put forth young green leaves: in the bed of harmony thousands of flowers were to open their smiling eyes upon the new dawn: and silvery trickling springs were to bubble forth with the vernal sweet song of streams—a very idyl.

Christophe was delighted. But when he looked at the bills of the Parisian theaters, he saw the names of Meyerbeer, Gounod, Massenet, and Mascagni and Leoncavallo—names with which he was only too familiar: and he asked his friends if all this brazen music, with its girlish rapture, its artificial flowers, like nothing so much as a perfumery shop, was the garden of Armide that they had promised him. They were hurt and protested: if they were to be believed, these things were the last vestiges of a moribund age: no one attached any value to them. But the fact remained that *Cavalleria Rusticana* flourished at the Opéra Comique, and *Pagliacci* at the Opéra: Massenet and Gounod were more frequently performed than anybody else, and the musical trinity—*Mignon, Les Huguenots,* and *Faust*—had safely crossed the bar of the thousandth performance. But these were only trivial accidents: there was

no need to go and see them. When some untoward fact up-
sets a theory, nothing is more simple than to ignore it. The
French critics shut their eyes to these blatant works and to
the public which applauded them: and only a very little more
was needed to make them ignore the whole music-theater in
France. The music-theater was to them a literary form, and
therefore impure. (Being all literary men, they set a ban on
literature.) Any music that was expressive, descriptive, suggestive—in short, any music with any meaning—was condemned as impure. In every Frenchman there is a Robespierre.
He must be for ever chopping the head off something or somebody to purify it. The great French critics only recognized
pure music: the rest they left to the rabble.

Christophe was rather mortified when he thought how vulgar his taste must be. But he found some comfort in the discovery that all these musicians who despised the theater spent
their time in writing for it: there was not one of them who
did not compose operas. But no doubt that was also a trivial
accident. They were to be judged, as they desired, by
their pure music. Christophe looked about for their pure
music.

Théophile Goujart took him to the concerts of a Society
dedicated to the national art. There the new glories of French
music were elaborated and carefully hatched. It was a club,
a little church, with several side-chapels. Each chapel had its
saint, each saint his devotees, who blackguarded the saint in
the next chapel. It was some time before Christophe could
differentiate between the various saints. Naturally enough, being accustomed to a very different sort of art, he was at first
baffled by the new music, and the more he thought he understood it, the farther was he from a real understanding.

It all seemed to him to be bathed in a perpetual twilight.
It was a dull gray ground on which were drawn lines, shad-
ing off and blurring into each other, sometimes starting from
the mist, and then sinking back into it again. Among all these

lines there were stiff, crabbed, and cramped designs, as though
they were drawn with a set-square—patterns with sharp corners, like the elbow of a skinny woman. There were patterns
in curves floating and curling like the smoke of a cigar. But
they were all enveloped in the gray light. Did the sun never
shine in France? Christophe had only had rain and fog since
his arrival, and was inclined to believe so; but it is the artist's
business to create sunshine when the sun fails. These men lit
up their little lanterns, it is true: but they were like the glow-
worm's lamp, giving no warmth and very little light. The
titles of their works were changed: they dealt with Spring, the
South, Love, the Joy of Living, Country Walks; but the music
never changed: it was uniformly soft, pale, enervated, anemic,
wasting away. It was then the mode in France, among the
fastidious, to whisper in music. And they were quite right:
for as soon as they tried to talk aloud they shouted: there
was no mean. There was no alternative but distinguished
somnolence and melodramatic declamation.

Christophe shook off the drowsiness that was creeping over
him, and looked at his program; and he was surprised to read
that the little puffs of cloud floating across the gray sky claimed
to represent certain definite things. For, in spite of theory, all
their pure music was almost always program music, or at least
music descriptive of a certain subject. It was in vain that they
denounced literature: they needed the support of a literary
crutch. Strange crutches they were, too, as a rule! Christophe observed the odd puerility of the subjects which they
labored to depict—orchards, kitchen-gardens, farmyards, musical menageries, a whole Zoo. Some musicians transposed for
orchestra or piano the pictures in the Louvre, or the frescoes
of the Opéra: they turned into music Cuyp, Baudry, and Paul
Potter: explanatory notes helped the hearer to recognize the
apple of Paris, a Dutch inn, or the crupper of a white horse.
To Christophe it was like the production of children obsessed
by images, who, not knowing how to draw, scribble down in
their exercise-books anything that comes into their heads, and

naïvely write down under it in large letters an inscription to the effect that it is a house or a tree.

But besides these blind image-fanciers who saw with their ears, there were the philosophers: they discussed metaphysical problems in music: their symphonies were composed of the struggle between abstract principles and stated symbols or religions. And in their operas they affected to study the judicial and social questions of the day: the Declaration of the Rights of Woman and the Citizen, elaborated by the metaphysicians of the Butte and the Palais-Bourbon. They did not shrink from bringing the question of divorce on to the platform together with the inquiry into the birth-rate and the separation of the Church and State. Among them were to be found lay symbolists and clerical symbolists. They introduced philosophic rag-pickers, sociological grisettes, prophetic bakers, and apostolic fishermen to the stage. Goethe spoke of the artists of his day, "who reproduced the ideas of Kant in allegorical pictures." The artists of Christophe's day wrote sociology in semi-quavers. Zola, Nietzsche, Maeterlinck, Barrès, Jaurès, Mendès, the Gospel, and the Moulin Rouge, all fed the cistern whence the writers of operas and symphonies drew their ideas. Many of them, intoxicated by the example of Wagner, cried: "And I, too, am a poet!" And with perfect assurance they tacked on to their music verses in rhyme, or unrhymed, written in the style of an elementary school or a decadent feuilleton.

All these thinkers and poets were partisans of pure music. But they preferred talking about it to writing it. And yet they did sometimes manage to write it. Then they wrote music that was not intended to say anything. Unfortunately, they often succeeded: their music was meaningless—at least, to Christophe. It is only fair to say that he had not the key to it.

In order to understand the music of a foreign nation a man must take the trouble to learn the language, and not make up his mind beforehand that he knows it. Christophe, like every good German, thought he knew it. That was excusable. Many Frenchmen did not understand it any more than he. Like the Germans of the time of Louis XIV, who tried so hard to speak French that in the end they forgot their own language, the French musicians of the nineteenth century had taken so much pains to unlearn their language that their music had become a foreign lingo. It was only of recent years that a movement had sprung up to speak French in France. They did not all succeed: the force of habit was very strong: and with a few exceptions their French was Belgian, or still smacked faintly of Germany. It was quite natural, therefore, that a German should be mistaken, and declare, with his usual assurance, that it was very bad German, and meant nothing, since he could make nothing of it.

Christophe was in exactly that case. The symphonies of the French seemed to him to be abstract, dialectic, and musical themes were opposed and superposed arithmetically in them: their combinations and permutations might just as well have been expressed in figures or the letters of the alphabet. One man would construct a symphony on the progressive development of a sonorous formula which did not seem to be complete until the last page of the last movement, so that for nine-tenths of the work it never advanced beyond the grub stage of its existence. **Another** would erect variations on a theme which was not stated until the end, so that the symphony gradually descended from the complex to the simple. They were very clever toys. But a man would need to be both very old and very young to be able to enjoy them. They had cost their inventors untold effort. They took years to write a fantasy. They worried their hair white in the search for new combinations of chords—to express . . .? No matter! New expressions. As the organ creates the need, they say, so the expression must in the end create the idea: the chief thing is that the expression should be novel. Novelty at all costs! They had a morbid horror of anything that "had been said." The best of them were paralyzed by it all. They seemed always to be keeping a fearful guard on themselves, and crossing out what they had written, wondering: " Good Lord! Where did I read that? " . . . There are some musicians—especially in Germany—who spend their time in piecing together other people's music. The musicians of France were always looking out at every bar to see that they had not included in their catalogues melodies that had already been used by others, and erasing, erasing, changing the shape of the note until it was like no known note, and even ceased to be like a note at all.

But they did not take Christophe in: in vain did they muffle themselves up in a complicated language, and make superhuman and prodigious efforts, go into orchestral fits, or cultivate inorganic harmonies, an obsessing monotony, declamations à la Sarah Bernhardt, beginning in a minor key, and going on for hours plodding along like mules, half asleep, along the edge of the slippery slope—always under the mask Christophe found the souls of these men, cold, weary, horribly scented, like Gounod and Massenet, but even less natural. And he repeated the unjust comment on the French of Gluck:

" Let them be: they always go back to their giddy-go-round."

Only they did try so hard to be learned. They took popular songs as themes for learned symphonies, like dissertations for the Sorbonne. That was the great game at the time. All sorts and kinds of popular songs, songs of all nations, were pressed into the service. And they worked them up into things like the *Ninth Symphony* and the *Quartet* of César Franck, only much more difficult. A musician would conceive quite a simple air. At once he would mix it up with another, which meant nothing at all, though it jarred hideously with the first. And all these people were obviously so calm, so perfectly balanced! . . .

And there was a young conductor, properly haggard and dressed for the part, who produced these works: he flung himself about, darted lightnings, made Michael Angelesque gestures as though he were summoning up the armies of Beethoven or Wagner. The audience, which was composed of society people,

was bored to tears, though nothing would have induced them
to renounce the honor of paying a high price for such glorious
boredom: and there were young tyros who were only too glad to
bring their school knowledge into play as they picked up the
threads of the music, and they applauded with an enthusiasm
as frantic as the gestures of the conductor, and the fearful
noise of the music. . . .

"What rot!" said Christopher. (For he was well up in
Parisian slang by now.)

But it is easier to penetrate the mystery of Parisian slang
than the mystery of Parisian music. Christophe judged it
with the passion which he brought to bear on everything, and
the native incapacity of the Germans to understand French
art. At least, he was sincere, and only asked to be put right if
he was mistaken. And he did not regard himself as bound by
his judgment, but left it open to any new impression that
might alter it.

As matters stood, he readily admitted that there was much
talent in the music he heard, interesting stuff, certain odd
happy rhythms and harmonies, an assortment of fine materials,
mellow and brilliant, glittering colors, a perpetual outpouring
of invention and cleverness. Christophe was entertained by it,
and learned a thing or two. All these small masters had infinitely more freedom of thought than the musicians of Germany: they bravely left the highroad and plunged through
the woods. They did their best to lose themselves. But they
were so clever that they could not manage it. Some of them
found themselves on the road again in twenty yards. Others
tired at once, and stopped wherever they might be. There
were a few who almost discovered new paths, but instead of
following them up they sat down at the edge of the wood and
fell to musing under a tree. What they most lacked was will-
power, force: they had all the gifts save one—vigor and life.
And all their multifarious efforts were confusedly directed, and
were lost on the road. It was only rarely that these artists

became conscious of the nature of their efforts, and could join forces to a common and a given end. It was the usual result of French anarchy, which wastes the enormous wealth of talent and good intentions through the paralyzing influence of its uncertainty and contradictions. With hardly an exception, all the great French musicians, like Berlioz and Saint-Saens—to mention only the most recent—have been hopelessly muddled, self-destructive, and forsworn, for want of energy, want of faith, and, above all, for want of an inward guide.

Christophe, with the insolence and disdain of the latter-day German, thought:

"The French do no more than fritter away their energy in inventing things which they are incapable of using. They need a master of another race, a Gluck or a Napoleon, to turn their Revolutions to any account."

And he smiled at the notion of an Eighteenth of Brumaire.

And yet, in the midst of all this anarchy, there was a group striving to restore order and discipline to the minds of artists and public. By way of a beginning, they had taken a Latin name reminiscent of a clerical institution which had flourished thirteen or fourteen centuries ago at the time of the great Invasion of the Goths and Vandals. Christophe was rather surprised at their going back so far. It was a good thing, certainly, to dominate one's generation. But it looked as though a watch-tower fourteen centuries high might be a little inconvenient, and more suitable perhaps for observing the movements of the stars than those of the men of the present day. But Christophe was soon reassured when he saw that the sons of St. Gregory spent very little time on their tower: they only went up it to ring the bells, and spent the rest of their time in the church below. It was some time before Christophe, who attended some of their services, saw that it was a Catholic cult: he had been sure at the outset that their rites were those of some little Protestant sect. The audience groveled: the disciples were pious, intolerant, aggressive on the smallest provocation: at their head was a man of a cold sort of purity, rather childish and wilful, maintaining the integrity of his doctrine, religious, moral, and artistic, explaining in abstract terms the Gospel of music to the small number of the Elect, and calmly damning Pride and Heresy. To these two states of mind he attributed every defect in art and every vice of humanity: the Renaissance, the Reformation, and present-day Judaism, which he lumped together in one category. The Jews of music were burned in effigy after being ignominiously dressed. The colossal Handel was soundly trounced. Only Johann Sebastian Bach attained salvation by the grace of the Lord, who recognized that he had been a Protestant by mistake.

The temple of the *Rue Saint-Jacques* fulfilled an apostolic function: souls and music found salvation there. The rules of genius were taught there most methodically. Laborious pupils applied the formulæ with infinite pains and absolute certainty. It looked as though by their pious labors they were trying to regain the criminal levity of their ancestors: the Aubers, the Adams, and the trebly damned, the diabolical Berlioz, the devil himself, *diabolus in musica*. With laudable ardor and a sincere piety they spread the cult of the acknowledged masters. In ten years the work they had to show was considerable: French music was transformed. Not only the French critics, but the musicians themselves had learned something about music. There were now composers, and even virtuosi, who were acquainted with the works of Bach. And that was not so common even in Germany! But, above all, a great effort had been made to combat the stay-at-home spirit of the French, who will shut themselves up in their homes, and cannot be induced to go out. So their music lacks air: it is sealed-chamber music, sofa music, music with no sort of vigor. Think of Beethoven composing as he strode across country, rushing down the hillsides, swinging along through sun and rain, terrifying the cattle with his wild shouts and gestures! There was no danger of the musicians of Paris upsetting their neighbors with the noise of their inspiration, like the bear of

Bonn. When they composed they muted the strings of their thought: and the heavy hangings of their rooms prevented any sound from outside breaking in upon them.

The *Schola* had tried to let in fresh air, and had opened the windows upon the past. But only on the past. The windows were opened upon a courtyard, not into the street. And it was not much use. Hardly had they opened the windows than they closed the shutters, like old women afraid of catching cold. And there came up a gust or two of the Middle Ages, Bach, Palestrina, popular songs. But what was the good of that? The room still smelt of stale air. But really that suited them very well: they were afraid of the great modern draughts of air. And if they knew more than other people, they also denied more in art. Their music took on a doctrinal character: there was no relaxation: their concerts were history lectures, or a string of edifying examples. Advanced ideas became academic. The great Bach, he whose music is like a torrent, was received into the bosom of the Church and then tamed. His music was submitted to a transformation in the minds of the *Schola* very like the transformation to which the savagely sensual Bible has been submitted in the minds of the English. As for modern music, the doctrine promulgated was aristocratic and eclectic, an attempt to compound the distinctive characteristics of the three or four great periods of music from the sixth to the twentieth century. If it had been possible to carry it out, the resulting music would have been like those hybrid structures raised by a Viceroy of India on his return from his travels, with rare materials collected in every corner of the earth. But the good sense of the French saved them from any such barbarically erudite excesses: they carefully avoided any application of their theories: they treated them as Molière treated his doctors: they took their prescriptions, but did not carry them out. The best of them went their own way. The rest of them contented themselves in practice with very intricate and difficult exercises in counterpoint: they called them sonatas, quartets, and symphonies. . . . " Sonata, what do you desire of me?" The poor thing desired nothing at all except to be a sonata. The idea behind it was abstract and anonymous, heavy and joyless. So might a lawyer conceive an art. Christophe, who had at first been by way of being pleased with the French for not liking Brahms, now thought that there were many, many little Brahms in France. These laborious, conscientious, honest journeymen had many qualities and virtues. Christophe left them edified, but bored to distraction. It was all very good, very good. . . .

How fine it was outside!

And yet there were a few independent musicians in Paris, men belonging to no school. They alone were interesting to Christophe. It was only through them that he could gauge the vitality of the art. Schools and coteries only express some superficial fashion or manufactured theory. But the independent men who stand apart have more chance of really discovering the ideas of their race and time. It is true that that makes them all the more difficult for a foreigner to understand.

That was, in fact, what happened when Christophe first heard the famous work which the French had so extravagantly praised, while some of them were announcing the coming of the greatest musical revolution of the last ten centuries. (It was easy for them to talk about centuries: they knew hardly anything of any except their own.)

Théophile Goujart and Sylvain Kohn took Christophe to the Opéra Comique to hear *Pelleas and Melisande*. They were proud to display the opera to him—as proud as though they had written it themselves. They gave Christophe to understand that it would be the road to Damascus for him. And they went on eulogizing it even after the piece had begun. Christophe shut them up and listened intently. After the first act he turned to Sylvain Kohn, who asked him, with glittering eyes:

" Well, old man, what do you think of it?"

And he said:

" Is it like that all through? "

" Yes."

" But it's nothing."

Kohn protested loudly, and called him a Philistine.

" Nothing at all," said Christophe. " No music. No de-velopment. No sequence. No cohesion. Very nice harmony. Quite good orchestral effects, quite good. But it's nothing— nothing at all. . . ."

He listened through the second act. Little by little the lantern gathered light and glowed: and he began to perceive something through the twilight. Yes: he could understand the sober-minded rebellion against the Wagnerian ideal which swamped the drama with floods of music; but he wondered a little ironically if the ideal of sacrifice did not mean the sacrifice of something which one does not happen to possess. He felt the easy fluency of the opera, the production of an effect with the minimum of trouble, the indolent renunciation of the sturdy effort shown in the vigorous Wagnerian structures. And he was quite struck by the unity of it, the simple, modest, rather dragging declamation, although it seemed monotonous to him, and, to his German ears, it sounded false:—(and it even seemed to him that the more it aimed at truth the more it showed how little the French language was suited to music: it is too logical, too precise, too definite,—a world perfect in itself, but hermetically sealed).—However, the attempt was in-teresting, and Christophe gladly sympathized with the spirit of revolt and reaction against the over-emphasis and violence of Wagnerian art. The French composer seemed to have de-voted his attention discreetly and ironically to all the things that sentiment and passion only whisper. He showed love and death inarticulate. It was only by the imperceptible throbbing of a melody, a little thrill from the orchestra that was no more than a quivering of the corners of the lips, that the drama passing through the souls of the characters was brought home to the audience. It was as though the artist were

fearful of letting himself go. He had the genius of taste—
except at certain moments when the Massenet slumbering in the
heart of every Frenchman awoke and waxed lyrical. Then
there showed hair that was too golden, lips that were too red—
the Lot's wife of the Third Republic playing the lover. But
such moments were the exception: they were a relaxation of
the writer's self-imposed restraint: throughout the rest of the
opera there reigned a delicate simplicity, a simplicity which
was not so very simple, a deliberate simplicity, the subtle
flower of an ancient society. That young Barbarian, Christophe, only half liked it. The whole scheme of the play, the
poem, worried him. He saw a middle-aged Parisienne posing
childishly and having fairy-tales told to her. It was not the
Wagnerian sickliness, sentimental and clumsy, like a girl from
the Rhine provinces. But the Franco-Belgian sickliness was
not much better, with its simpering parlor-tricks:—" the hair,"
" the little father," " the doves,"—and the whole trick of mystery for the delectation of society women. The soul of the
Parisienne was mirrored in the little piece, which, like a flattering picture, showed the languid fatalism, the boudoir Nirvana, the soft, sweet melancholy. Nowhere a trace of will-
power. No one knew what he wanted. No one knew what he
was doing.

" It is not my fault! It is not my fault! " these grown-up
children groaned. All through the five acts, which took place
in a perpetual half-light—forests, caves, cellars, death-cham-
bers—little sea-birds struggled: hardly even that. Poor little
birds! Pretty birds, soft, pretty birds. . . . They were so
afraid of too much light, of the brutality of deeds, words, passions—life! Life is not soft and pretty. Life is no kid-glove
matter. . . .

Christophe could hear in the distance the rumbling of cannon, coming to batter down that worn-out civilization, that
perishing little Greece.

Was it that proud feeling of melancholy and pity that made
him in spite of all sympathize with the opera? It interested

him more than he would admit. Although he went on telling
Sylvain Kohn, as they left the theater, that it was "very fine,
very fine, but lacking in *Schwung* (impulse), and did not contain enough music for him," he was careful not to confound
Pelleas with the other music of the French. He was attracted
by the lamp shining through the fog. And then he saw other
lights, vivid and fantastic, flickering round it. His attention
was caught by these will-o'-the-wisps: he would have liked to
go near them to find out how it was that they shone: but they
were not easy to catch. These independent musicians, whom
Christophe did not understand, were not very approachable.
They seemed to lack that great need of sympathy which possessed Christophe. With a few exceptions they seemed to read
very little, know very little, desire very little. They almost
all lived in retirement, some outside Paris, others in Paris, but
isolated, by circumstances or purposely, shut up in a narrow
circle—from pride, shyness, disgust, or apathy. There were
very few of them, but they were split up into rival groups,
and could not tolerate each other. They were extremely
susceptible, and could not bear with their enemies, or their
rivals, or even their friends, when they dared to admire any
other musician than themselves, or when they admired too
coldly, or too fervently, or in too commonplace or too ec-
centric a manner. It was extremely difficult to please them.
Every one of them had actually sanctioned a critic, armed
with letters patent, who kept a jealous watch at the foot of
the statue. Visitors were requested not to touch. They did
not gain any greater understanding from being understood
only by their own little groups. They were deformed by the
adulation and the opinion that their partisans and they themselves held of their work, and they lost grip of their art and
their genius. Men with a pleasing fantasy thought themselves
reformers, and Alexandrine artists posed as rivals of Wagner.
They were almost all the victims of competition. Every day
they had to leap a little higher than the day before, and,
especially, higher than their rivals. These exercises in high

jumping were not always successful, and were certainly not attractive except to professionals. They took no account of
the public, and the public never bothered about them. Their
art was out of touch with the people, music which was only fed
from music. Now, Christophe was under the impression,
rightly or wrongly, that there was no music that had a greater
need of outside support than French music. That supple
climbing plant needed a prop: it could not do without literature, but did not find in it enough of the breath of life. French
music was breathless, bloodless, will-less. It was like a woman
languishing for her lover. But, like a Byzantine Empress, slender and feeble in body, laden with precious stones, it was
surrounded with eunuchs: snobs, esthetes, and critics. The
nation was not musical: and the craze, so much talked of during the last twenty years, for Wagner, Beethoven, Bach, or
Debussy, never reached farther than a certain class. The
enormous increase in the number of concerts, the flowing tide
of music at all costs, found no real response in the development of public taste. It was just a fashionable craze confined
to the few, and leading them astray. There was only a handful
of people who really loved music, and these were not the
people who were most occupied with it, composers and critics.
There are so few musicians in France who really love music!

So thought Christophe: but it did not occur to him that
it is the same everywhere, that even in Germany there are not
many more real musicians, and that the people who matter in
art are not the thousands who understand nothing about it,
but the few who love it and serve it in proud humility. Had
he ever set eyes on them in France? Creators and critics—
the best of them were working in silence, far from the racket,
as César Franck had done, and the most gifted composers of
the day were doing, and a number of artists who would live
out their lives in obscurity, so that some day in the future
some journalist might have the glory of discovering them and
posing as their friend—and the little army of industrious and
obscure men of learning who, without ambition and careless

of their fame, were building stone by stone the greatness of the past history of France, or, being vowed to the musical education of the country, were .preparing the greatness of the France of the future. There were minds there whose wealth and liberty and world-wide curiosity would have attracted Christophe if he had been able to discover them! But at most he only caught a cursory glimpse of two or three of them: he only made their acquaintance in the villainous caricatures of their ideas. He saw only their defects copied and exaggerated by the apish mimics of art and the bagmen of the Press.

But what most disgusted him with these vulgarians of music was their formalism. They never seemed to consider anything but form. Feeling, character, life—never a word of these! It never seemed to occur to them that every real musician lives in a world of sound, as other men live in a visible world, and that his days are liyed in and borne onward by a flood of music. Music is the air he breathes, the sky above him. Nature wakes answering music in his soul. His soul itself is music: music is in all that it loves, hates, suffers, fears, hopes. And when the soul of a musician loves a beautiful body, it sees music in that, too. The beloved eyes are not blue, or brown, or gray: they are music: their tenderness is like caressing notes, like a delicious chord. That inward music is a thousand times more rich than the music that finds expression, and the instrument is inferior to the player. Genius is measured by the power of life, by the power of evoking life through the imperfect instrument of art. But to how many men in France does that ever occur? To these chemists music seems to be no more than the art of resolving sounds. They mistake the alphabet for a book. Christophe shrugged his shoulders when he heard them say complacently that to understand art it must be abstracted from the man. They were extraordinarily pleased with this paradox: for by it they fancied they were proving their own musical quality. And even Goujart subscribed to it— Goujart, the idiot who had never been able to understand how people managed to learn by heart a piece of music—(he had tried to get Christophe to explain the mystery to him)—and had tried to prove to him that Beethoven's greatness of soul and Wagner's sensuality had no more to do with their music than a painter's model has to do with his portraits.

Christophe lost patience with him, and said:

" That only proves that a beautiful body is of no more artistic value to you than a great passion. Poor fellow! . . . You have no notion of the beauty given to a portrait by the beauty of a perfect face, or of the glow of beauty given to music by the beauty of the great soul which is mirrored in it? . . . Poor fellow! . . . You are interested only in the handiwork? So long as it is well done you are not concerned with the meaning of a piece of work. . . . Poor fellow! . . . You are like those people who do not listen to what an orator says, but only to the sound of his voice, and watch his gestures without understanding them, and then say he speaks devilish well. . . . Poor fellow! Poor wretch! . . . Oh, you rotten swine!"

But it was not only a particular theory that irritated Christophe; it was all their theories. He was appalled by their unending arguments, their Byzantine discussions, the everlasting talk, talk, talk, of musicians about music, and nothing else. It was enough to make the best of musicians heartily sick of music. Like Moussorgski, Christophe thought that it would be as well for musicians every now and then to leave their counterpoint and harmony in favor of books or experience of life. Music is not enough for a present-day musician; not thus will he dominate his age and raise his head above the stream of time. . . . Life! All life! To see everything, to know everything, to feel everything. To love, to seek, to grasp Truth—the lovely Penthesilea, Queen of the Amazons, whose teeth bite in answer to a kiss!

Away with your musical discussion-societies, away with your chord-factories! Not all the twaddle of the harmonic kitchens would ever help him to find a new harmony that was alive, alive, and not a monstrous birth.

He turned his back on these Doctor Wagners, brooding on
their alembics to hatch out some homunculus in bottle: and,
running away from French music, he sought to enter literary
circles and Parisian society.   Like many millions of people
in France, Christophe made his first acquaintance with modern French literature through the newspapers.   He wanted
to get the measure of Parisian thought as quickly as possible,
and at the same time to perfect his knowledge of the language.
And so he set himself conscientiously to read the papers which
he was told were most Parisian.   On the first day after a hor-
rific chronicle of events, which filled several pages with paragraphs and snapshots, he read a story about a father and a
daughter, a girl of fifteen: it was narrated as though it were
a matter of course, and even rather moving.   Next day, in the
same paper, he read a story about a father and a son, a boy of
twelve, and the girl was mixed up in it again.   On the following day he read a story about a brother and a sister.   Next
day, the story was about two sisters.   On the fifth day . . .
On the fifth day he hurled the paper away with a shudder, and
said to Sylvain Kohn:
"But what's the matter with you all?   Are you ill?"
Sylvain Kohn began to laugh, and said:
"That is art."
Christophe shrugged his shoulders:
"You're pulling my leg."
Kohn laughed once more:
"Not at all.   Read a little more."
And he pointed to the report of a recent inquiry into Art
and Morality, which set out that "Love sanctified everything,"
that "Sensuality was the leaven of Art," that "Art could not
be Immoral," that "Morality was a convention of Jesuit edu-
cation," and that nothing mattered except "the greatness of
Desire."   A number of letters from literary men witnessed the
artistic purity of a novel depicting the life of bawds.   Some of
the signatories were among the greatest names in contemporary literature, or the most austere of critics.   A domestic

poet, *bourgeois* and a Catholic, gave his blessing as an artist to a detailed description of the decadence of the Greeks. There were enthusiastic praises of novels in which the course of Lewdness was followed through the ages: Rome, Alexandria, Byzantium, the Italian and French Renaissance, the Age of Greatness . . . Nothing was omitted. Another cycle of studies was devoted to the various countries of the world: conscientious writers had devoted their energies, with a monkish patience, to the study of the low quarters of the five continents. And it was no matter for surprise to discover among these geographers and historians of Pleasure distinguished poets and very excellent writers. They were only marked out from the rest by their erudition. In their most impeccable style they told archaic stories, highly spiced.

But what was most alarming was to see honest men and real artists, men who rightly enjoyed a high place in French literature, struggling in such a traffic, for which they were not at all suited. Some of them with great travail wrote, like the rest, the sort of trash that the newspapers serialize. They had to produce it by a fixed time, once or twice a week: and it had been going on for years. They went on producing and producing, long after they had ceased to have anything to say, racking their brains to find something new, something more sensational, more bizarre: for the public was surfeited and sick of everything, and soon wearied of even the most wanton imaginary pleasures: they had always to go one better—better than the rest, better than their own best—and they squeezed out their very life-blood, they squeezed out their guts: it was a pitiable sight, a grotesque spectacle.

Christophe, who did not know the ins and outs of that melancholy traffic, and if he had known them would not have been more indulgent; for in his eyes nothing in the world could excuse an artist for selling his art for thirty pieces of silver. . . .

(Not even to assure the well-being of those whom he loves? Not even then.

That is not human.

It is not a question of being human; it is a question of being a man. . . . Human! . . . May God have mercy on your white-livered humanitarianism, it is so bloodless! . . . No man loves twenty things at once, no man can serve many gods! . . .)

. . . Christophe, who, in his hard-working life, had hardly yet seen beyond the limits of his little German town, could have no idea that this artistic degradation, which showed so rawly in Paris, was common to nearly all the great towns: and the hereditary prejudices of chaste Germany against Latin immorality awoke in him once more. And yet Sylvain Kohn might easily have pointed to what was going on by the banks of the Spree, and the impurity of Imperial Germany, where brutality made shame and degradation even more repulsive. But Sylvain Kohn never thought of it: he was no more shocked by that than by the life of Paris. He thought ironically: "Every nation has its little ways," and the ways of the world in which he lived seemed so natural to him that Christophe could be excused for thinking it was in the nature of the people. And so, like so many of his compatriots, he saw in the secret sore which is eating away the intellectual aristocracies of Europe the vice proper to French art, and the bankruptcy of the Latin races.

Christophe was hurt by his first encounter with French literature, and it took him some time to get over it. And yet there were plenty of books which were not solely occupied with what one of these writers has nobly called "the taste for fundamental entertainments." But he never laid hands on the best and finest of them. Such books were not written for the like of Sylvain Kohn and his friends: they did not bother about them, and certainly Kohn and the rest never bothered about the better class of books: they ignored each other. Sylvain Kohn would never have thought of mentioning them to Christophe. He was quite sincerely convinced that his friends and himself were the incarnation of French

Art, and thought there was no talent, no art, no France outside the men who had been consecrated as great by their opinion and the press of the boulevards. Christophe knew nothing about the poets who were the glory of French literature, the very crown of France. Very few of the novelists reached him, or emerged from the ocean of mediocre writers: a few books of Barrès and Anatole France. But he was not sufficiently familiar with the language to be able to enjoy the universal dilettantism, and erudition, and irony of the one, or the unequal but superior art of the other. He spent some time in watching the little orange-trees in tubs growing in the hothouse of Anatole France, and the delicate, perfect flowers clambering over the gravelike soul of Barrès. He stayed for a moment or two before the genius, part sublime, part silly, of Maeterlinck: from that there issued a polite mysticism, monotonous, numbing like some vague sorrow. He shook himself, and plunged into the heavy, sluggish stream, the muddy romanticism of Zola, with whom he was already acquainted, and when he emerged from that it was to sink back and drown in a deluge of literature.

The submerged lands exhaled an *odor di femina*. The literature of the day teemed with effeminate men and women. It is well that women should write if they are sincere enough to describe what no man has yet seen: the depths of the soul of a woman. But only very few dared do that: most of them only wrote to attract the men: they were as untruthful in their books as in their drawing-rooms: they jockeyed their facts and flirted with the reader. Since they were no longer religious, and had no confessor to whom to tell their little lapses, they told them to the public. There was a perfect shower of novels, almost all scabrous, all affected, written in a sort of lisping style, a style scented with flowers and fine perfumes—sometimes too fine—sometimes not fine at all—and the eternal stale, warm, sweetish smell. Their books reeked of it. Christophe thought, like Goethe: " Let women do what they like with poetry and writing: but men must not write like women! That I cannot stand." He could not help being disgusted by their tricks, their sly coquetry, their sentimentality, which seemed to expend itself by preference upon creatures hardly worthy of interest, their style crammed with metaphor, their love-making and sensuality, their hotch-potch of subtlety and brutality.

But Christophe was ready to admit that he was not in a position to judge. He was deafened by the row of this babel of words. It was impossible to hear the little fluting sounds that were drowned in it all. For even among such books as these there were some, from the pages of which, behind all the nonsense, there shone the limpid sky and the harmonious outline of the hills of Attica—so much talent, so much grace, a sweet breath of life, and charm of style, a thought like the voluptuous women or the languid boys of Perugino and the young Raphael, smiling, with half-closed eyes, at their dream of love. But Christophe was blind to that. Nothing could reveal to him the dominant tendencies, the currents of public opinion. Even a Frenchman would have been hard put to it to see them. And the only definite impression that he had at this time was that of a flood of writing which looked like a national disaster. It seemed as though everybody wrote: men, women, children, officers, actors, society people, blackguards. It was an epidemic.

For the time being Christophe gave it up. He felt that such a guide as Sylvain Kohn must lead him hopelessly astray. His experience of a literary coterie in Germany gave him very properly a profound distrust of the people whom he met: it was impossible to know whether or no they only represented the opinion of a few hundred idle people, or even, in certain cases, whether or no the author was his own public. The theater gave a more exact idea of the society of Paris. It played an enormous part in the daily life of the city. It was an enormous kitchen, a Pantagruelesque restaurant, which could not cope with the appetite of the two million inhabitants. There were thirty leading theaters, without counting the local houses, café concerts, all sorts of shows—a hundred halls, all giving performances every evening, and, every evening, almost all full. A whole nation of actors and officials. Vast sums were swallowed up in the gulf. The four State-aided theaters gave work to three thousand people, and cost the country ten million francs. The whole of Paris re-echoed with the glory of the play-actors. It was impossible to go anywhere without seeing innumerable photographs, drawings, caricatures, reproducing their features and mannerisms, gramophones reproducing their voices, and the newspapers their opinions on art and politics. They had special newspapers devoted to them. They published their heroic and domestic Memoirs. These big self-conscious children, who spent their time in aping each other, these wonderful apes reigned and held sway over the Parisians: and the dramatic authors were their chief ministers. Christophe asked Sylvain Kohn to conduct him into the kingdom of shadows and reflections.

But Sylvain Kohn was no safer as a guide in that world than in the world of books, and, thanks to him, Christophe's first impression was almost as repulsive as that of his first essay in literature. It seemed that there was everywhere the same spirit of mental prostitution.

The pleasure-mongers were divided into two schools. On the one hand there was the good old way, the national way, of providing a coarse and unclean pleasure, quite frankly; a delight in ugliness, strong meat, physical deformities, a show of drawers, barrack-room jests, risky stories, red pepper, high game, private rooms—" a manly frankness," as those people say who try to reconcile looseness and morality by pointing out that, after four acts of dubious fun, order is restored and the Code triumphs by the fact that the wife is really with the husband whom she thinks she is deceiving—(so long as the law is observed, then virtue is all right):—that vicious sort of virtue which defends marriage by endowing it with all the charm of lewdness:—the Gallic way.

The other school was in the modern style. It was much

more subtle and much more disgusting. The Parisianized Jews and the Judaicized Christians who frequented the theater had introduced into it the usual hash of sentiment which is the distinctive feature of a degenerate cosmopolitanism. Those sons who blushed for their fathers set themselves to abnegate their racial conscience: and they succeeded only too well. Having plucked out the soul that was their birthright, all that was left them was a mixture of the moral and intellectual values of other races: they made a *macédoine* of them, an *olla podrida:* it was their way of taking possession of them. The men who who were at that time in control of the theaters in Paris were extraordinarily skilful at beating up filth and sentiment, and giving virtue a flavoring of vice, vice a flavoring of virtue, and turning upside down every human relation of age, sex, the family, and the affections. Their art, therefore, had an odor *sui generis,* which smelt both good and bad at once—that is to say, it smelled very bad indeed: they called it " amoralism."

One of their favorite heroes at that time was the amorous old man. Their theaters presented a rich gallery of portraits of the type: and in painting it they introduced a thousand pretty touches. Sometimes the sexagenarian hero would take his daughter into his confidence, and talk to her about his mistress: and she would talk about her lovers: and they would give each other friendly advice: the kindly father would aid his daughter in her indiscretions: and the precious daughter would intervene with the unfaithful mistress, beg her to return, and bring her back to the fold. Sometimes the good old man would listen to the confidences of his mistress: he would talk to her about her lovers, or, if nothing better was forthcoming, he would listen to the tale of her gallantries, and even take a delight in them. And there were portraits of lovers, distinguished gentlemen, who presided in the houses of their former mistresses, and helped them in their nefarious business. Society women were thieves. The men were bawds, the girls were Lesbian. And all these things happened in the highest society: the society of rich people—the only society that mattered. For

that made it possible to offer the patrons of the theater dam-
aged goods under cover of the delights of luxury. So tricked
out, it was displayed in the market, to the joy of old gentlemen and young women. And it all reeked of death and the
seraglio.

Their style was not less mixed than their sentiments. They
had invented a composite jargon of expressions from all classes
of society and every country under the sun—pedantic, slangy,
classical, lyrical, precious, prurient, and low—a mixture of
bawdy jests, affectations, coarseness, and wit, all of which
seemed to have a foreign accent. Ironical, and gifted with a
certain clownish humor, they had not much natural wit: but
they were clever enough, and they manufactured their goods in
imitation of Paris. If the stone was not always of the first
water, and if the setting was always strange and overdone,
at least it shone in artificial light, and that was all it was
meant to do. They were intelligent, keen, though short-
sighted observers—their eyes had been dulled by centuries of
the life of the counting-house—turning the magnifying-glass on
human sentiments, enlarging small things, not seeing big things.
With a marked predilection for finery, they were incapable of
depicting anything but what seemed to their upstart snobbishness the ideal of polite society: a little group of worn-out rakes
and adventurers, who quarreled among themselves for the possession of certain stolen moneys and a few virtueless females.

And yet upon occasion the real nature of these Jewish writers
would suddenly awake, come to the surface from the depths
of their being, in response to some mysterious echo called forth
by some vivid word or sensation. Then there appeared a strange
hotch-potch of ages and races, a breath of wind from the Desert,
bringing over the seas to their Parisian rooms the musty smell
of a Turkish bazaar, the dazzling shimmer of the sands, the
mirage, blind sensuality, savage invective, nervous disorder,
only a hair's-breadth away from epilepsy, a destructive frenzy
—Samson, suddenly rising like a lion—after ages of squatting
in the shade—and savagely tearing down the columns of the

Temple, which comes crashing down on himself and on his enemies.

Christophe blew his nose and said to Sylvain Kohn:

"There's power in it: but it stinks. That's enough! Let's go and see something else."

"What?" asked Sylvain Kohn.

"France."

"That's it!" said Kohn.

"Can't be," replied Christophe. "France isn't like that."

"It's France, and Germany, too."

"I don't believe it. A nation that was anything like that wouldn't last for twenty years: why, it's decomposing already. There must be something else."

"There's nothing better."

"There must be something else," insisted Christophe.

"Oh, yes," said Sylvain Kohn. "We have fine people, of course, and theaters for them, too. Is that what you want? We can give you that."

He took Christophe to the Théâtre Français.

That evening they happened to be playing a modern comedy, in prose, dealing with some legal problem.

From the very beginning Christophe was baffled to make out in what sort of world the action was taking place. The voices of the actors were out of all reason, full, solemn, slow, formal: they rounded every syllable as though they were giving a lesson in elocution, and they seemed always to be scanning Alexandrines with tragic pauses. Their gestures were solemn and almost hieratic. The heroine, who wore her gown as though it were a Greek peplus, with arm uplifted, and head lowered, was nothing else but Antigone, and she smiled with a smile of eternal sacrifice, carefully modulating the lower notes of her beautiful contralto voice. The heavy father walked about like a fencing-master, with automatic gestures, a funereal dignity,—romanticism in a frock-coat. The juvenile lead gulped and gasped and squeezed out a sob or two. The piece was written in the style of a tragic serial story: abstract phrases, bureaucratic epithets, academic periphrases. No movement, not a sound unrehearsed. From beginning to end it was clockwork, a set problem, a scenario, the skeleton of a play, with not a scrap of flesh, only literary phrases. Timid ideas lay behind discussions that were meant to be bold: the whole spirit of the thing was hopelessly middle-class and respectable.

The heroine had divorced an unworthy husband, by whom she had had a child, and she had married a good man whom she loved. The point was, that even in such a case as this divorce was condemned by Nature, as it is by prejudice. Nothing could be easier than to prove it: the author contrived that the woman should be surprised, for one occasion only, into yielding to the first husband. After that, instead of a perfectly natural remorse, perhaps a profound sense of shame, together with a greater desire to love and honor the second and good husband, the author trotted out an heroic case of conscience, altogether beyond Nature. French writers never seem to be on good terms with virtue: they always force the note when they talk of it: they make it quite incredible. They always seem to be dealing with the heroes of Corneille, and tragedy Kings. And are they not Kings and Queens, these millionaire heroes, and these heroines who would not be interesting unless they had at least a mansion in Paris and two or three country-houses? For such writers and such a public wealth itself is a beauty, and almost a virtue.

The audience was even more amazing than the play. They were never bored by all the tiresomely repeated improbabilities. They laughed at the good points, when the actors said things that were *meant* to be laughed at: it was made obvious that they were coming, so that the audience could be ready to laugh. They mopped their eyes and coughed, and were deeply moved when the puppets gasped, and gulped, and roared, and fainted away in accordance with the hallowed tragic ritual.

"And people say the French are gay!" exclaimed Christophe as they left the theater.

"There's a time for everything," said Sylvain Kohn chaffingly. "You wanted virtue. You see, there's still virtue in France."

"But that's not virtue!" cried Christophe. "That's rhetoric!"

"In France," said Sylvain Kohn. "Virtue in the theater is always rhetorical."

"A pretorium virtue," said Christophe, "and the prize goes to the best talker. I hate lawyers. Have you no poets in France?"

Sylvain Kohn took him to the poetic drama.

There were poets in France. There were even great poets. But the theater was not for them. It was for the versifiers. The theater is to poetry what the opera is to music. As Berlioz said: *Sicut amori lupanar.*

Christophe saw Princesses who were virtuously promiscuous, who prostituted themselves for their honor, who were compared with Christ ascending Calvary:—friends who deceived their friends out of devotion to them:—glorified triangular relations:—heroic cuckoldry: (the cuckold, like the blessed prostitute, had become a European commodity: the example of King Mark had turned the heads of the poets: like the stag of Saint Hubert, the cuckold never appeared without a halo.) And Christophe saw also lovely damsels torn between passion and duty: their passion bade them follow a new lover: duty bade them stay with the old one, an old man who gave them money and was deceived by them. And in the end they plumped heroically for Duty. Christophe could not see how Duty differed from sordid interest: but the public was satisfied. The word Duty was enough for them: they did not insist on having the thing itself; they took the author's word for it.

The summit of art was reached and the greatest pleasure was given when, most paradoxically, sexual immorality and Corneillian heroics could be combined. In that way every need of the Parisian public was satisfied: mind, senses, rhetoric. But it is only just to say that the public was fonder even of words than of lewdness. Eloquence could send it into ecstasies. It would have suffered anything for a fine tirade. Virtue or vice, heroics hobnobbing with the basest prurience, there was no pill that it would not swallow if it were gilded with sonorous rhymes and redundant words. Anything that came to hand was ground into couplets, antitheses, arguments: love, suffering, death. And when that was done, they thought they had felt love, suffering, and death. Nothing but phrases. It was all a game. When Hugo brought thunder on to the stage, at once (as one of his disciples said) he muted it so as not to frighten even a child. (The disciple fancied he was paying him a compliment.) It was never possible to feel any of the forces of Nature in their art. They made everything polite. Just as in music—and even more than in music, which was a younger art in France, and therefore relatively more simple— they were terrified of anything that had been "already said." The most gifted of them coldly devoted themselves to working contrariwise. The process was childishly simple: they pitched on some beautiful legend or fairy-story, and turned it upside down. Thus, Bluebeard was beaten by his wives, or Polyphemus was kind enough to pluck out his eye by way of sacrificing himself to the happiness of Acis and Galatea. And they thought of nothing but form. And once more it seemed to Christophe (though he was not a good judge) that these masters of form were rather coxcombs and imitators than great writers creating their own style and giving breadth and depth to their work.

They played at being artists. They played at being poets. Nowhere was the poetic lie more insolently reared than in the heroic drama. They put up a burlesque conception of a hero:

> "*The great thing is to have a soul magnificent,*
> *An eagel's eye ; broad brow like portico ; present*
> *An air of strength, grave mien, most touchingly to show*
> *A heart that throbs, eyes full of dreams of worlds they know.*"

Verses like that were taken seriously. Behind the hocus-pocus of such fine-sounding words, the bombast, the theatrical clash and clang of the swords and pasteboard helmets, there was always the incurable futility of a Sardou, the intrepid vaudevillist, playing Punch and Judy with history. When in the world was the like of the heroism of Cyrano ever to be found? These writers moved heaven and earth; they summoned from their tombs the Emperor and his legions, the bandits of the Ligue, the *condottieri* of the Renaissance, called up the human cyclones that once devastated the universe:—just to display a puppet, standing unmoved through frightful massacres, surrounded by armies, soldiers, and whole hosts of captive women, dying of a silly calfish love for a woman whom he had seen ten or fifteen years before—or King Henri IV submitting to assassination because his mistress no longer loved him.

So, and no otherwise, did these good people present their parlor Kings, and *condottieri,* and heroic passion. They were worthy scions of the illustrious nincompoops of the days of *Grand Cyrus,* those Gascons of the ideal—Scudéry, La Calprenède—an everlasting brood, the songsters of sham heroism, impossible heroism, which is the enemy of truth. Christophe observed to his amazement that the French, who are said to be so clever, had no sense of the ridiculous.

He was lucky when religion was not dragged in to fit the fashion! Then, during Lent, certain actors read the sermons of Bossuet at the Gaîté to the accompaniment of an organ. Jewish authors wrote tragedies about Saint Theresa for Jewish actresses. The *Way of the Cross* was acted at the Bodinière, the *Child Jesus* at the Ambigu, the *Passion* at the Porte-Saint-Martin, *Jesus* at the Odéon, orchestral suites on the subject of *Christ* at the Botanical Gardens. And a certain brilliant talker —a poet who wrote passionate love-songs—gave a lecture on the *Redemption* at the Châtelet. And, of course, the passages of the Gospel that were most carefully preserved by these people were those relating to Pilate and Mary Magdalene:—" *What is truth?*" and the story of the blessed foolish virgin.—And their boulevard Christs were horribly loquacious and well up in all the latest tricks of worldly casuistry.

Christophe said:

" That is the worst yet. It is untruth incarnate. I'm stifling. Let's get out."

And yet there was a great classic art that held its ground among all these modern industries, like the ruins of the splendid ancient temples among all the pretentious buildings of modern Rome. But, outside Molière, Christophe was not yet able to appreciate it. He was not yet familiar enough with the language, and, therefore, could not grasp the genius of the race. Nothing baffled him so much as the tragedy of the seventeenth century—one of the least accessible provinces of French art to foreigners, precisely because it lies at the very heart of France. It bored him horribly; he found it cold, dry, and revolting in its tricks and pedantry. The action was thin or forced, the characters were rhetorical abstractions or as insipid as the conversation of society women. They were caricatures of the ancient legends and heroes: a display of reason, arguments, quibbling, and antiquated psychology and archeology. Speeches, speeches, speeches; the eternal loquacity of the French. Christophe ironically refused to say whether it was beautiful or not: there was nothing to interest him in it: whatever the arguments put forward in turn by the orators of *Cinna,* he did not care a rap which of the talking-machines won in the end.

However, he had to admit that the French audience was not of his way of thinking, and that they did applaud these plays that bored him. But that did not help to dissipate his confusion: he saw the plays through the audience: and he recognized in the modern French certain of the features, distorted, of the classics. So might a critical eye see in the faded charms of an old coquette the clear, pure features of her daughter:—(such a discovery is not calculated to foster the illusion of love). Like the members of a family who are used to seeing each other, the French could not see the resemblance.

But Christophe was struck by it, and exaggerated it: he could see nothing else. Every work of art he saw seemed to him to be full of old-fashioned caricatures of the great ancestors of the French: and he saw these same great ancestors also in caricature. He could not see any difference between Corneille and the long line of his followers, those rhetorical poets whose mania it was to present nothing but sublime and ridiculous cases of conscience. And Racine he confounded with his offspring of pretentiously introspective Parisian psychologists.

None of these people had really broken free from the classics. The critics were for ever discussing *Tartuffe* and *Phèdre*. They never wearied of hearing the same plays over and over again. They delighted in the same old words, and when they were old men they laughed at the same jokes which had been their joy when they were children. And so it would be while the French nation endured. No country in the world has so firmly rooted a cult of its great-great-grandfathers. The rest of the universe did not interest them. There were many, many men and women, even intelligent men and women, who had never read anything, and never wanted to read anything outside the works that had been written in France under the Great King! Their theaters presented neither Goethe, nor Schiller, nor Kleist, nor Grillparzer, nor Hebbel, nor any of the great dramatists of other nations, with the exception of the ancient Greeks, whose heirs they declared themselves to be—(like every other nation in Europe). Every now and then they felt they ought to include Shakespeare. That was the touchstone. There were two schools of Shakespearean interpreters: the one played *King Lear,* with a commonplace realism, like a comedy of Emile Augier: the other turned *Hamlet* into an opera, with bravura airs and vocal exercises à la Victor Hugo. It never occurred to them that reality could be poetic or that poetry was the spontaneous language of hearts bursting with life. Shakespeare seemed false. They very quickly went back to Rostand.

And yet, during the last twenty years, there had been sturdy

efforts made to vitalize the theater: the narrow circle of subjects drawn from Parisian literature had been widened: the
theater laid hands on everything with a show of audacity. Two
or three times even the outer world, public life, had torn down
the curtain of convention. But the theatrists made haste to
piece it together again. They lived in blinkers, and were
afraid of seeing things as they are. A sort of clannishness, a
classical tradition, a routine of form and spirit, and a lack of
real seriousness, held them back from pushing their audacity
to its logical extremity. They turned the acutest problems into
ingenious games: and they always came back to the problem of
women—women of a certain class. And what a sorry figure did
the phantoms of great men cut on their boards: the heroic
Anarchy of Ibsen, the Gospel of Tolstoy, the Superman of
Nietzsche! . . .

The literary men of Paris took a great deal of trouble to seem
to be advanced thinkers. But at heart they were all conservative. There was no literature in Europe in which the past,
the old, the "eternal yesterday," held a completer and more
unconscious sway: in the great reviews, in the great newspapers,
in the State-aided theaters, in the Academy, Paris was in
literature what London was in Politics: the check on the mind
of Europe. The French Academy was a House of Lords. A
certain number of the institutions of the *Ancien Régime* forced
the spirit of the old days on the new society. Every revolutionary element was rejected or promptly assimilated. They
asked nothing better. In vain did the Government pretend
to a socialistic polity. In art it truckled under to the Academies
and the Academic Schools. Against the Academies there was
no opposition save from a few coteries, and they put up a very
poor fight. For as soon as a member of a coterie could, he fell
into line with an Academy, and became more academic than
the rest. And even if a writer were in the advance guard or
in the van of the army, he was almost always trammeled by
his group and the ideas of his group. Some of them were
hidebound by their academic *Credo,* others by their revolution-

ary *Credo:* and, when all was done, they both amounted to the same thing.

By way of rousing Christophe, on whom academic art had acted as a soporific, Sylvain Kohn proposed to take him to certain eclectic theaters,—the very latest thing. There they saw murder, rape, madness, torture, eyes plucked out, bellies gutted —anything to thrill the nerves, and satisfy the barbarism lurking beneath a too civilized section of the people. It had a great attraction for pretty women and men of the world—the people who would go and spend whole afternoons in the stuffy courts of the Palais de Justice, listening to scandalous cases, laughing, talking, and eating chocolates. But Christophe indignantly refused. The more closely he examined that sort of art, the more acutely he became aware of the odor that from the very first he had detected, faintly in the beginning, then more strongly, and finally it was suffocating: the odor of death.

Death: it was everywhere beneath all the luxury and uproar. Christophe discovered the explanation of the feeling of repugnance with which certain French plays had filled him. It was not their immorality that shocked him. Morality, immorality, amorality,—all these words mean nothing. Christophe had never invented any moral theory: he loved the great poets and great musicians of the past, and they were no saints: when he came across a great artist he did not inquire into his morality: he asked him rather:

" Are you healthy? "

To be healthy was the great thing. " If the poet is ill, let him first of all cure himself," as Goethe says. " When he is cured, he will write."

The writers of Paris were unhealthy: or if one of them happened to be healthy, the chances were that he was ashamed of it: he disguised it, and did his best to catch some disease. Their sickness was not shown in any particular feature of their art:—the love of pleasure, the extreme license of mind,

or the universal trick of criticism which examined and dis-
sected every idea that was expressed. All these things could
be—and were, as the case might be—healthy or unhealthy. If
death was there, it did not come from the material, but from
the use that these people made of it; it was in the people themselves. And Christophe himself loved pleasure. He, too, loved
liberty. He had drawn down upon himself the displeasure
of his little German town by his frankness in defending many
things, which he found here, promulgated by these Parisians,
in such a way as to disgust him. And yet they were the same
things. But nothing sounded the same to the Parisians and to
himself. When Christophe impatiently shook off the yoke of
the great Masters of the past, when he waged war against the
esthetics and the morality of the Pharisees, it was not a game
to him as it was to these men of intellect: and his revolt was
directed only towards life, the life of fruitfulness, big with
the centuries to come. With these people all tended to sterile
enjoyment. Sterile, Sterile, Sterile. That was the key to the
enigma. Mind and senses were fruitlessly debauched. A
brilliant art, full of wit and cleverness—a lovely form, in truth,
a tradition of beauty, impregnably seated, in spite of foreign
alluvial deposits—a theater which was a theater, a style which
was a style, authors who knew their business, writers who could
write, the fine skeleton of an art, and a thought that had been
great. But a skeleton. Sonorous words, ringing phrases, the
metallic clang of ideas hurtling down the void, witticisms,
minds haunted by sensuality, and senses numbed with thought.
It was all useless, save for the sport of egoism. It led to death.
It was a phenomenon analogous to the frightful decline in the
birth-rate of France, which Europe was observing—and reckoning—in silence. So much wit, so much cleverness, so many
acute senses, all wasted and wasting in a sort of shameful
onanism! They had no notion of it, and wished to have none.
They laughed. That was the only thing that comforted Christophe a little: these people could still laugh: all was not lost.
He liked them even less when they tried to take themselves

seriously: and nothing hurt him more than to see writers, who regarded art as no more than an instrument of pleasure, giving themselves airs as priests of a disinterested religion:

"We are artists," said Sylvain Kohn once more complacently. "We follow art for art's sake. Art is always pure: everything in art is chaste. We explore life as tourists, who find everything amusing. We are amateurs of rare sensations, lovers of beauty."

"You are hypocrites," replied Christophe bluntly. "Excuse my saying so. I used to think my own country had a monopoly. In Germany our hypocrisy consists in always talking about idealism while we think of nothing but our interests, and we even believe that we are idealists while we think of nothing but ourselves. But you are much worse: you cover your national lewdness with the names of Art and Beauty (with capitals)—when you do not shield your Moral Pilatism behind the names of Truth, Science, Intellectual Duty, and you wash your hands of the possible consequences of your haughty inquiry. Art for art's sake! . . . That's a fine faith! But it is the faith of the strong. Art! To grasp life, as the eagle claws its prey, to bear it up into the air, to rise with it into the serenity of space! . . . For that you need talons, great wings, and a strong heart. But you are nothing but sparrows who, when they find a piece of carrion, rend it here and there, squabbling for it, and twittering. . . . Art for art's sake! . . . Oh! wretched men! Art is no common ground for the feet of all who pass it by. Why, it is a pleasure, it is the most intoxicating of all. But it is a pleasure which is only won at the cost of a strenuous fight: it is the laurel-wreath that crowns the victory of the strong. Art is life tamed. Art is the Emperor of life. To be Cæsar a man must have the soul of Cæsar. But you are only limelight Kings: you are playing a part, and do not even deceive yourselves. And, like those actors, who turn to profit their deformities, you manufacture literature out of your own deformities and those of your public. Lovingly do you cultivate the diseases of your people, their fear of effort, their love of pleasure, their sensual minds, their chimerical humanitarianism, everything in them that drugs the will, everything in them that saps their power for action. You deaden their minds with the fumes of opium. Behind it all is death: you know it: but you will not admit it. Well, I tell you: Where death is, there art is not. Art is the spring of life. But even the most honest of your writers are so cowardly that even when the bandage is removed from their eyes they pretend not to see: they have the effrontery to say:

" ' It is dangerous, I admit: it is poisonous: but it is full of talent.'

" It is as if a judge, sentencing a hooligan, were to say:

" ' He's a blackguard, certainly: but he has so much talent! . . .' "

Christophe wondered what was the use of French criticism. There was no lack of critics: they swarmed all over and about French art. It was impossible to see the work of the artists: they were swamped by the critics.

Christophe was not indulgent towards criticism in general. He found it difficult to admit the utility of these thousands of artists who formed a Fourth or Fifth Estate in the modern community: he read in it the signs of a worn-out generation which relegates to others the business of regarding life—feeling vicariously. And, to go farther, it seemed to him not a little shameful that they could not even see with their own eyes the reflection of life, but must have yet more intermediaries, reflections of the reflection—the critics. At least, they ought to have seen to it that the reflections were true. But the critics reflected nothing but the uncertainty of the mob that moved round them. They were like those trick mirrors which reflect again and again the faces of the sightseers who gaze into them against a painted background.

There had been a time when the critics had enjoyed a tremendous authority in France. The public bowed down to their

decrees: and they were not far from regarding them as superior
to the artists, as artists with intelligence:—(apparently the two
words do not go together naturally). Then they had multiplied
too rapidly: there were too many oracles: that spoiled the trade.
When there are so many people, each of whom declares that he
is the sole repository of truth, it is impossible to believe them:
and in the end they cease to believe it themselves. They were
discouraged: in the passage from night to day, according to
the French custom, they passed from one extreme to the other.
Where they had before professed to know everything, they now
professed to know nothing. It was a point of honor with them,
quite fatuously. Renan had taught those milksop generations
that it is not correct to affirm anything without denying it at
once, or at least casting a doubt on it. He was one of those
men of whom St. Paul speaks: "For whom there is always
Yes, Yes, and then No, No." All the superior persons in France
had wildly embraced this amphibious *Credo*. It exactly suited
their indolence of mind and weakness of character. They no
longer said of a work of art that it was good or bad, true or
false, intelligent or idiotic. They said:

"It may be so. . . . Nothing is impossible. . . . I
don't know. . . . I wash my hands of it."

If some objectionable piece were put up, they did not
say:

"That is nasty rubbish!"

They said:

"Sir Sganarelle, please do not talk like that. Our philosophy bids us talk of everything open-mindedly: and therefore
you ought not to say: 'That is nasty rubbish!' but: 'It
seems to me that that is nasty rubbish. . . . But it is not
certain that it is so. It may be a masterpiece. Who can say
that it is not?'"

There was no danger of their being accused of tyranny over
the arts. Schiller once taught them a lesson when he reminded
the petty tyrants of the Press of his time of what he called
bluntly:

" The Duty of Servants.

" First, the house must be clean that the Queen is to enter. Bustle about, then!   Sweep the rooms.   That is what you are there for, gentlemen!

" But as soon as She appears, out you go!   Let not the serving-wench sit in her lady's chair!"

But, to be just to the critics of that time, it must be said that they never did sit in their lady's chair.   It was ordered that they should be servants: and servants they were.   But bad servants: they never took a broom in their hands: the room was thick with dust.   Instead of cleaning and tidying, they folded their arms, and left the work to be done by the master, the divinity of the day:—Universal Suffrage.

In fact, there had been for some time a wave of reaction passing through the popular conscience.   A few people had set out—feebly enough—on a campaign of public health: but Christophe could see no sign of it among the people with whom he lived.   They gained no hearing, and were laughed at.   When every now and then some honest man did raise a protest against unclean art, the authors replied haughtily that they were in the right, since the public was satisfied.   That was enough to silence every objection.   The public had spoken: that was the supreme law of art!   It never occurred to anybody to impeach the evidence of a debauched public in favor of those who had debauched them, or that it was the artist's business to lead the public, not the public the artist.   A numerical religion— the number of the audience, and the sum total of the receipts— dominated the artistic thought of that commercialized democracy.   Following the authors, the critics docilely declared that the essential function of a work of art was to please.   Success is law: and when success endures, there is nothing to be done but to bow to it.   And so they devoted their energies to anticipating the fluctuations of the Exchange of pleasure, in trying to find out what the public thought of the various plays. The joke of it was that the public was always trying frantically to find out what the critics thought.   And so there they were.

looking at each other: and in each other's eyes they saw nothing but their own indecision.

And yet never had there been such crying need of a fearless critic. In an anarchical Republic, fashion, which is all-powerful in art, very rarely looks backward, as it does in a conservative State: it goes onwards always: and there is a perpetual competition of libertinism which hardly anybody dare resist. The mob is incapable of forming an opinion: at heart it is shocked: but nobody dares to say what everybody secretly feels. If the critics were strong, if they dared to be strong, what a power they would have! A vigorous critic would in a few years become the Napoleon of public taste, and sweep away all the diseases of art. But there is no Napoleon in France. All the critics live in that vitiated atmosphere, and do not notice it. And they dare not speak. They all know each other. They are a more or less close company, and they have to consider each other: not one of them is independent. To be so, they would have to renounce their social life, and even their friendships. Who is there that would have the courage, in such a knock-kneed time, when even the best critics doubt whether a just notice is worth the annoyance it may cause to the writer and the object of it? Who is there so devoted to duty that he would condemn himself to such a hell on earth: dare to stand out against opinion, fight the imbecility of the public, expose the mediocrity of the successes of the day, defend the unknown artist who is alone and at the mercy of the beasts of prey, and subject the minds of those who were born to obey to the dominion of the master-mind? Christophe actually heard the critics at a first night in the vestibule of the theater say: "H'm! Pretty bad, isn't it? Utter rot!" And next day in their notices they talked of masterpieces, Shakespeare, the wings of genius beating above their heads.

"It is not so much talent that your art lacks as character," said Christophe to Sylvain Kohn. "You need a great critic, a Lessing, a . . ."

"A Boileau?" said Sylvain quizzically.

"A Boileau, perhaps, more than these artists of genius."

"If we had a Boileau," said Sylvain Kohn, "no one would listen to him."

"If they did not listen to him," replied Christophe, "he would not be a Boileau. I bet you that if I set out and told you the truth about yourselves, quite bluntly, however clumsy I might be, you would have to gulp it down."

"My dear good fellow!" laughed Sylvain Kohn.

That was all the reply he made.

He was so cocksure and so satisfied with the general flabbiness of the French that suddenly it occurred to Christophe that Kohn was a thousand times more of a foreigner in France than himself: and there was a catch at his heart.

"It is impossible," he said once more, as he had said that evening when he had left the theater on the boulevards in disgust. "There must be something else."

"What more do you want?" asked Sylvain Kohn.

"France."

"We are France," said Sylvain Kohn, gurgling with laughter.

Christophe stared hard at him for a moment, then shook his head, and said once more:

"There must be something else."

"Well, old man, you'd better look for it," said Sylvain Kohn, laughing louder than ever.

Christophe had to look for it. It was well hidden.

II

THE more clearly Christophe saw into the vat of ideas in which Parisian art was fermenting, the more strongly he was impressed by the supremacy of women in that cosmopolitan community. They had an absurdly disproportionate importance. It was not enough for woman to be the helpmeet of man. It was not even enough for her to be his equal. Her pleasure must be law both for herself and for man. And man

truckled to it. When a nation is growing old, it renounces
its will, its faith, the whole essence of its being, in favor of the
giver of pleasure. Men make works of art: but women make
men,—(except when they tamper with the work of the men, as
happened in France at that time):—and it would be more
just to say that they unmake what they make. No doubt the
Eternal Feminine has been an uplifting influence on the best
of men: but for the ordinary men, in ages of weariness and
fatigue, there is, as some one has said, another Feminine, just
as eternal, who drags them down. This other Feminine was
the mistress of Parisian thought, the Queen of the Republic.

Christophe closely observed the Parisian women at the houses
at which Sylvain Kohn's introduction or his own skill at the
piano had made him welcome. Like most foreigners, he gen-
eralized freely and unsparingly about French women from the
two or three types he had met: young women, not very tall,
and not at all fresh, with neat figures, dyed hair, large hats
on their pretty heads that were a little too large for their bodies:
they had trim features, but their faces were just a little too
fleshy: good noses, vulgar sometimes, characterless always: quick
eyes without any great depth, which they tried to make as
brilliant and large as possible: well-cut lips that were perfectly
under control: plump little chins; and the lower part of their
faces revealed their utter materialism; they were elegant little
creatures who, amid all their preoccupations with love and intrigue, never lost sight of public opinion and their domestic
affairs. They were pretty, but they belonged to no race.
In all these polite ladies there was the savor of the respectable woman perverted, or wanting to be so, together
with all the traditions of her class; prudence, economy, coldness, practical common sense, egoism. A poor sort of life.
A desire for pleasure emanating rather from a cerebral
curiosity than from a need of the senses. Their will was
mediocre in quality, but firm. They were very well dressed,
and had little automatic gestures. They were always patting

their hair or their gowns with the backs or the palms of their hands, with little delicate movements. And they always managed to sit so that they could admire themselves—and watch other women—in a mirror, near or far, not to mention, at tea or dinner, the spoons, knives, silver coffee-pots, polished and shining, in which they always peeped at the reflections of their faces, which were more interesting to them than anything or anybody else. At meals they dieted sternly: drinking water and depriving themselves altogether of any food that might stand in the way of their ideal of a complexion of a floury whiteness.

There was a fairly large proportion of Jewesses among Christophe's acquaintance: and he was always attracted by them, although, since his encounter with Judith Mannheim, he had hardly any illusions about them. Sylvain Kohn had introduced him to several Jewish houses where he was received with the usual intelligence of the race, which loves intelligence. Christophe met financiers there, engineers, newspaper proprietors, international brokers, slave-dealers of a sort from Algiers—the men of affairs of the Republic. They were clear-headed and energetic, indifferent to other people, smiling, affable, and secretive. Christophe felt sometimes that behind their hard faces was the knowledge of crime in the past, and the future, of these men gathered round the sumptuous table laden with food, flowers, and wine. They were almost all ugly. But the women, taken as a whole, were quite brilliant, though it did not do to look at them too closely: in most of them there was a want of subtlety in their coloring. But brilliance there was, and a fair show of material life, beautiful shoulders generously exposed to view, and a genius for making their beauty and even their ugliness a lure for the men. An artist would have recognized in some of them the old Roman type, the women of the time of Nero, down to the time of Hadrian. And there were Palmaesque faces, with a sensual expression, heavy chins solidly modeled with the neck, and not without a certain bestial beauty. Some of them had thick curly hair, and bold, fiery eyes: they seemed to be subtle, incisive, ready for everything, more virile than other women. And also more feminine. Here and there a more spiritual profile would stand out. Those pure features came from beyond Rome, from the East, the country of Laban: there was expressed in them the poetry of silence, of the Desert. But when Christophe went nearer, and listened to the conversations between Rebecca and Faustina the Roman, or Saint Barbe the Venetian, he found her to be just a Parisian Jewess, just like the others, even more Parisian than the Parisian women, more artificial and sophisticated, talking quietly, and maliciously stripping the assembled company, body and soul, with her Madonna's eyes.

Christophe wandered from group to group, but could identify himself with none of them. The men talked savagely of hunting, brutally of love, and only of money with any sort of real appreciation. And that was cold and cunning. They talked business in the smoking-room. Christophe heard some one say of a certain fop who was sauntering from one lady to another, with a buttonhole in his coat, oozing heavy compliments:

"So! He is free again?"

In a corner of the room two ladies were talking of the love-affairs of a young actress and a society woman. There was occasional music. Christophe was asked to play. Large women, breathless and heavily perspiring, declaimed in an apocalyptic tone verses of Sully-Prudhomme or Auguste Dorchain. A famous actor solemnly recited a *Mystic Ballad* to the accompaniment of an American organ. Words and music were so stupid that they turned Christophe sick. But the Roman women were delighted, and laughed heartily to show their magnificent teeth. Scenes from Ibsen were performed. It was a fine epilogue to the struggle of a great man against the Pillars of Society that it should be used for their diversion!

And then they all began, of course, to prattle about art. That was horrible. The women especially began to talk of Ibsen, Wagner, Tolstoy, flirtatiously, politely, boredly, or idiotically. Once the conversation had started, there was no stopping it.

The disease was contagious. Christophe had to listen to the ideas of bankers, brokers, and slave-dealers on art. In vain did he refuse to speak or try to turn the conversation: they insisted on talking about music and poetry. As Berlioz said: "Such people use the words quite coolly: just as though they were talking of wine, women, or some such trash." An alienist physician recognized one of his patients in an Ibsen heroine, though to his way of thinking she was infinitely more silly. An engineer quite sincerely declared that the husband was the sympathetic character in the *Doll's House*. The famous actor —a well-known Comedian—brayed his profound ideas on Nietzsche and Carlyle: he assured Christophe that he could not see a picture of Velasquez—(the idol of the hour)—"without the tears coursing down his cheeks." And he confided—still to Christophe's private ear—that, though he esteemed art very highly, yet he esteemed still more highly the art of living, acting, and that if he were asked to choose what part he would play, it would be that of Bismarck. . . . Sometimes there would be of the company a professed wit, but the level of the conversation was not appreciably higher for that. Generally they said nothing; they confined themselves to a jerky remark or an enigmatic smile: they lived on their reputations, and were saved further trouble. But there were a few professional talkers, generally from the South. They talked about anything and everything. They had no sense of proportion: everything came alike to them. One was a Shakespeare. Another a Molière. Another a Pascal, if not a Jesus Christ. They compared Ibsen with Dumas *fils*, Tolstoy with George Sand: and the gist of it all was that everything came from France. Generally they were ignorant of foreign languages. But that did not disturb them. It mattered so little to their audience whether they told the truth or not! What did matter was that they should say amusing things, things as flattering as possible to national vanity. Foreigners had to put up with a good deal—with the exception of the idol of the hour: for there was always a fashionable idol: Grieg, or Wagner, or

Nietzsche, or Gorki, or D'Annunzio. It never lasted long, and the idol was certain one fine morning to be thrown on to the rubbish-heap.

For the moment the idol was Beethoven. Beethoven—save the mark!—was in the fashion: at least, among literary and polite persons: for musicians had dropped him at once, in accordance with the see-saw system which is one of the laws of artistic taste in France. A Frenchman needs to know what his neighbor thinks before he knows what he thinks himself, so that he can think the same thing or the opposite. Thus, when they saw Beethoven in popular favor, the most distinguished musicians began to discover that he was not distinguished enough for them: they claimed to lead opinion, not to follow it: and rather than be in agreement with it they turned their backs on it. They began to regard Beethoven as a man afflicted with deafness, crying in a voice of bitterness: and some of them declared that he might be an excellent moralist, but that he was certainly overpraised as a musician. That sort of joke was not at all to Christophe's taste. Still less did he like the enthusiasm of polite society. If Beethoven had come to Paris just then, he would have been the lion of the hour: it was such a pity that he had been dead for more than a century. His vogue grew not so much out of his music as out of the more or less romantic circumstances of his life which had been popularized by sentimental and virtuous biographies. His rugged face and lion's mane had become a romantic figure. Ladies wept for him: they hinted that if they had known him he should not have been so unhappy: and in their greatness of heart they were the more ready to sacrifice all for him, in that there was no danger of Beethoven taking them at their word: the old fellow was beyond all need of anything. That was why the virtuosi, the conductors, and the *impresarii* bowed down in pious worship before him: and, as the representatives of Beethoven, they gathered the homage destined for him. There were sumptuous festivals at exorbitant prices, which afforded society people an opportunity of showing their generosity—and incidentally also of discovering Beethoven's symphonies. There were committees of actors, men of the world, Bohemians, and politicians, appointed by the Republic to preside over the destinies of art, and they informed the world of their intention to erect a monument to Beethoven: and on these committees, together with a few honest men whose names guaranteed the rest, were all the riffraff who would have stoned Beethoven if he had been alive, if Beethoven had not crushed the life out of them. Christophe watched and listened. He ground his teeth to keep himself from saying anything outrageous. He was on tenterhooks the whole evening. He could not talk, nor could he keep silent. It seemed to him humiliating and shameful to talk neither for pleasure nor from necessity, but out of politeness, because he had to talk. He was not allowed to say what he thought, and it was impossible for him to make conversation. And he did not even know how to be polite without talking. If he looked at anybody, he glared too fixedly and intently: in spite of himself he studied that person, and that person was offended. If he spoke at all, he believed too much in what he was saying; and that was disturbing for everybody, and even for himself. He quite admitted that he was out of his element: and, as he was clever enough to sound the general note of the company, in which his presence was a discord, he was as upset by his manners as his hosts. He was angry with himself and with them.

When at last he stood in the street once more, very late at night, he was so worn out with the boredom of it all that he could hardly drag himself home: he wanted to lie down just where he was, in the street, as he had done many times when he was returning as a boy from his performances at the Palace of the Grand Duke. Although he had only five or six francs to take him to the end of the week, he spent two of them on a cab. He flung himself into it the more quickly to escape: and as he drove along he groaned aloud from sheer exhaustion. When he reached home and got to bed, he groaned in his sleep. . . . And then, suddenly, he roared with laughter as he remembered some ridiculous saying. He woke up repeating it, and imitating the features of the speaker. Next day, and for several days after, as he walked about, he would suddenly bellow like a bull. . . . Why did he visit these people? Why did he go on visiting them? Why force himself to gesticulate and make faces, like the rest, and pretend to be interested in things that did not appeal to him in the very least? Was it true that he was not in the least interested? A year ago he would not have been able to put up with them for a moment. Now, at heart, he was amused by it all, while at the same time it exasperated him. Was a little of the indifference of the Parisians creeping over him? He would sometimes wonder fearfully whether he had lost strength. But, in truth, he had gained in strength. He was more free in mind in strange surroundings. In spite of himself, his eyes were opened to the great Comedy of the world.

Besides, whether he liked it or not, he had to go on with it if he wanted his art to be recognized by Parisian society, which is only interested in art in so far as it knows the artist. And he had to make himself known if he were to find among these Philistines the pupils necessary to keep him alive.

And, then, Christophe had a heart: his heart must have affection: wherever he might be, there he would find food for his affections: without it he could not live.

Among the few girls of that class of society—few enough —whom Christophe taught, was the daughter of a rich motor-car manufacturer, Colette Stevens. Her father was a Belgian, a naturalized Frenchman, the son of an Anglo-American settled at Antwerp, and a Dutchwoman. Her mother was an Italian. A regular Parisian family. To Christophe—and to many others —Colette Stevens was the type of French girl.

She was eighteen, and had velvety, soft black eyes, which she used skilfully upon young men—regular Spanish eyes, with enormous pupils; a rather long and fantastic nose, which wrinkled up and moved at the tip as she talked, with little fractious pouts and shrugs; rebellious hair; a pretty little face; rather sallow complexion, dabbed with powder; heavy, rather thick features: altogether she was like a plump kitten.

She was slight, very well dressed, attractive, provoking: she had sly, affected, rather silly manners: her pose was that of a little girl, and she would sit rocking her chair for hours at a time, and giving little exclamations like: " No? Impossible. . . ."

At meals she would clap her hands when there was a dish she loved: in the drawing-room she would smoke cigarette after cigarette, and, when there were men present, display an exuberant affection for her girl-friends, flinging her arms round their necks, kissing their hands, whispering in their ears, making ingenuous and naughty remarks, doing it most brilliantly, in a soft, twittering voice; and in the lightest possible way she would say improper things, without seeming to do more than hint at them, and was even more skilful in provoking them from others; she had the ingenuous air of a little girl, who knows perfectly well what she is about, with her large brilliant eyes, slyly and voluptuously looking sidelong, maliciously taking in all the gossip, and catching at all the dubious remarks of the conversation, and all the time angling for hearts.

All these tricks and shows, and her sophisticated ingenuity, were not at all to Christophe's liking. He had better things to do than to lend himself to the practices of an artful little girl, and did not even care to look on at them for his amusement. He had to earn his living, to keep his life and ideas from death. He had no interest in these drawing-room parakeets beyond the gaining of a livelihood. In return for their money, he gave them lessons, conscientiously concentrating all his energies on the task, to keep the boredom of it from mastering him, and his attention from being distracted by the tricks of his pupils when they were coquettes, like Colette Stevens. He paid no more attention to her than to Colette's little cousin, a. child of twelve, shy and silent, whom the Stevens had adopted, to whom also Christophe gave lessons on the piano.

But Colette was too clever not to feel that all her charms were lost on Christophe, and too adroit not to adapt herself at once to his character. She did not even need to do so deliberately. It was a natural instinct with her. She was a woman. She was like water, formless. The soul of every man she met was a vessel, whose form she took immediately out of curiosity. It was a law of her existence that she should always be some one else. Her whole personality was for ever shifting. She was for ever changing her vessel.

Christophe attracted her for many reasons, the chief of which was that he was not attracted by her. He attracted her also because he was different from all the young men of her acquaintance: she had never tried to pour herself into a vessel of such a rugged form. And, finally, he attracted her, because, being naturally and by inheritance expert in the valuation at the first glance of men and vessels, she knew perfectly well that what he lacked in polish Christophe made up in a solidity of character which none of her smart young Parisians could offer her.

She played as well and as badly as most idle young women. She played a great deal and very little—that is to say, that she was always working at it, but knew nothing at all about it. She strummed on her piano all day long, for want of anything else to do, or from affectation, or because it gave her pleasure. Sometimes she rattled along mechanically. Sometimes she would play well, very well, with taste and soul—(it was almost as though she had a soul: but, as a matter of fact, she only borrowed one). Before she knew Christophe, she was capable of liking Massenet, Grieg, Thomé. But after she met Christophe she ceased to like them. Then she played Bach and Beethoven very correctly—(which is not very high praise): but the great thing was that she loved them. At bottom it was not Beethoven, nor Thomé, nor Bach, nor Grieg that she loved, but the notes, the sounds, the fingers running over the keys, the thrills she got from the chords which tickled her nerves and made her wriggle with pleasure.

In the drawing-room of the great house, decorated with faded tapestry, and on an easel in the middle room, a portrait of the stout Madame Stevens by a fashionable painter who had represented her in a languishing attitude, like a flower dying for want of water, with a die-away expression in her eyes, and her body draped in impossible curves, by way of expressing the rare quality of her millionaire soul—in the great drawing-room, with its bow-windows looking on to a clump of old trees powdered with snow, Christophe would find Colette sitting at her piano, repeating the same passage over and over again, delighting her ear with mellifluous dissonance.

"Ah!" Christophe would say as he entered, "the cat is still purring!"

"How wicked of you!" she would laugh. . . . (And she would hold out her soft little hand.)

". . . Listen. Isn't it pretty?"

"Very pretty," he would say indifferently.

"You aren't listening! . . . Will you please listen?"

"I am listening. . . . It's the same thing over and over again."

"Ah! you are no musician," she would say pettishly.

"As if that were music or anything like it!"

"What! Not music! . . . What is it, then, if you please?"

"You know quite well: I won't tell you, because it would not be polite."

"All the more reason why you should say it."

"You want me to? . . . So much the worse for you! . . . Well, do you know what you are doing with your piano? . . . You are flirting with it."

"Indeed!"

"Certainly. You say to it: 'Dear piano, dear piano, say pretty things to me; kiss me; give me just one little kiss!'"

"You need not say any more," said Colette, half vexed, half laughing. "You haven't the least idea of respect."

" Not the least."

" You are impertinent. . . . And then, even if it were so, isn't that the right way to love music? "

" Oh, come, don't mix music up with that."

" But that is music! A beautiful chord is a kiss."

" I never told you that."

" But isn't it true? . . . Why do you shrug your shoulders and make faces? "

" Because it annoys me."

" So much the better."

" It annoys me to hear music spoken of as though it were a sort of indulgence. . . . Oh, it isn't your fault. It's the fault of the world you live in. The stale society in which you live regards music as a sort of legitimate vice. . . . Come, sit down! Play me your sonata."

" No. Let us talk a little longer."

" I'm not here to talk. I'm here to teach you the piano. . . . Come, play away! "

" You're so rude! " said Colette, rather vexed—but at heart delighted to be handled so roughly.

She played her piece carefully: and, as she was clever, she succeeded fairly well, and sometimes even very well. Christophe, who was not deceived, laughed inwardly at the skill " of the little beast, who played as though she felt what she was playing, while really she felt nothing at all." And yet he had a sort of amused sympathy for her. Colette, on her part, seized every excuse for going on with the conversation, which interested her much more than her lesson. It was no good Christophe drawing back on the excuse that he could not say what he thought without hurting her feelings: she always wheedled it out of him: and the more insulting it was, the less she was hurt by it: it was an amusement for her. But, as she was quick enough to see that Christophe liked nothing so much as sincerity, she would contradict him flatly, and argue tenaciously, They would part very good friends.

However, Christophe would never have had the least illusion about their friendship, and there would never have been the smallest intimacy between them, had not Colette one day taken it into her head, out of sheer instinctive coquetry, to confide in him.

The evening before her parents had given an At Home. She had laughed, chattered, flirted outrageously: but next morning, when Christophe came for her lesson, she was worn out, drawn-looking, gray-faced, and haggard. She hardly spoke: she seemed utterly depressed. She sat at the piano, played softly, made mistakes. tried to correct them, made them again, stopped short, and said:

" I can't. . . . Please forgive me. . . . Please wait a little. . . ."

He asked if she were unwell. She said: " No. . . . She was out of sorts. . . . She had bouts of it. . . . It was absurd, but he must not mind."

He proposed to go away and come again another day: but she insisted on his staying:

" Just a moment. . . . I shall be all right presently. . . . It's silly of me, isn't it? "

He felt that she was not her usual self: but he did not question her: and, to turn the conversation, he said:

" That's what comes of having been so brilliant last night. You took too much out of yourself."

She smiled a little ironically.

" One can't say the same of you," she replied.

He laughed.

" I don't believe you said a word," she went on.

" Not a word."

" But there were interesting people there."

" Oh yes. All sorts of lights and famous people, all talking at once. But I'm lost among all your boneless Frenchmen who understand everything, and explain everything, and excuse everything—and feel nothing at all. People who talk for hours together about art and love! Isn't it revolting? "

"But you ought to be interested in art if not in love."

"One doesn't talk about these things: one does them."

"But when one cannot do them?" said Colette, pouting.
Christophe replied with a laugh:

"Well, leave it to others. Everybody is not fit for art."

"Nor for love?"

"Nor for love."

"How awful! What is left for us?"

"Housekeeping."

"Thanks," said Colette, rather annoyed. She turned to the
piano and began again, made mistakes, thumped the keyboard,
and moaned:

"I can't! . . . I'm no good at all. I believe you are right.
Women aren't any good."

"It's something to be able to say so," said Christophe
genially.

She looked at him rather sheepishly, like a little girl who
has been scolded, and said:

"Don't be so hard."

"I'm not saying anything hard about good women," replied
Christophe gaily. "A good woman is Paradise on earth. Only,
Paradise on earth . . ."

"I know. No one has ever seen it."

"I'm not so pessimistic. I say only that I have never seen
it: but that's no reason why it should not exist. I'm determined to find it, if it does exist. But it is not easy. A good
woman and a man of genius are equally rare."

"And all the other men and women don't count?"

"On the contrary, it is only they who count—for the
world."

"But for you?"

"For me, they don't exist."

"You *are* hard," repeated Colette.

"A little. Somebody has to be hard, if only in the interest
of the others! . . . If there weren't a few pebbles here and
there in the world, the whole thing would go to pulp."

"Yes. You are right. It is a good thing for you that you are strong," said Colette sadly. "But you must not be too hard on men,—and especially on women who aren't strong. . . . You don't know how terrible our weakness is to us. Because you see us flirting, and laughing, and doing silly things, you think we never dream of anything else, and you despise us. Ah! if you could see all that goes on in the minds of the girls of from fifteen to eighteen as they go out into society, and have the sort of success that comes to their youth and freshness—when they have danced, and talked smart nonsense, and said bitter things at which people laugh because they laugh, when they have given themselves to imbeciles, and sought in vain in their eyes the light that is nowhere to be found, —if you could see them in their rooms at night, in silence, alone, kneeling in agony to pray! . . ."

"Is it possible?" said Christophe, altogether amazed. "What! you, too, have suffered?"

Colette did not reply: but tears came to her eyes. She tried to smile and held out her hand to Christophe: he grasped it warmly.

"What would you have us do? There is nothing to do. You men can free yourselves and do what you like. But we are bound for ever and ever within the narrow circle of the duties and pleasures of society: we cannot break free."

"There is nothing to prevent your freeing yourselves, finding some work you like, and winning your independence just as we do."

"As you do? Poor Monsieur Krafft! Your work is not so very certain! . . . But at least you like your work. But what sort of work can we do? There isn't any that we could find interesting—for, I know, we dabble in all sorts of things, and pretend to be interested in a heap of things that do not concern us: we do so want to be interested in something! I do what the others do. I do charitable work and sit on social work committees. I go to lectures at the Sorbonne by Bergson and Jules Lemaître, historical concerts, classical matinées, and I

take notes and notes. . . . I never know what I am writing!
. . . and I try to persuade myself that I am absorbed by it,
or at least that it is useful. Ah! but I know that it is not true.
I know that I don't care a bit, and that I am bored by it all!
. . . Don't despise me because I tell you frankly what everybody thinks in secret. I'm no sillier than the rest. But what
use are philosophy, history, and science to me? As for art,—
you see,—I strum and daub and make messy little water-color
sketches;—but is that enough to fill a woman's life? There is
only one end to our life: marriage. But do you think there is
much fun in marrying this or that young man whom I know
as well as you do? I see them as they are. I am not fortunate enough to be like your German Gretchens, who can always create an illusion for themselves. . . . That is terrible,
isn't it? To look around and see girls who have married and
their husbands, and to think that one will have to do as they
have done, be cramped in body and mind, and become dull like
them! . . . One needs to be stoical, I tell you, to accept such
a life with such obligations. All women are not capable of it.
. . . And time passes, the years go by, youth fades: and yet
there were lovely things and good things in us—all useless, for
day by day they die, and one has to surrender them to the fools
and people whom one despises, people who will despise oneself!
. . . And nobody understands! One would think that we
were sphinxes. One can forgive the men who find us dull and
strange! But the women ought to understand us! They have
been like us: they have only to look back and remember. . . .
But no. There is no help from them. Even our mothers ignore us, and actually try not to know what we are. They only
try to get us married. For the rest, they say, live, die, do as
you like! Society absolutely abandons us."

"Don't lose heart," said Christophe. "Every one has to
face the experience of life all over again. If you are brave,
it will be all right. Look outside your own circle. There
must be a few honest men in France."

"There are. I know. But they are so tedious! . . . And

then, I tell you, I detest the circle in which I live: but I don't think I could live outside it, now. It has become a habit. I need a certain degree of comfort, certain refinements of luxury and comfort, which, no doubt, money alone cannot provide, though it is an indispensable factor. That sounds pretty poor, I know. But I know myself: I am weak. . . . Please, please, don't draw away from me because I tell you of my cowardice. Be kind and listen to me. It helps me so to talk to you! I feel that you are strong and sound: I have such confidence in you. Will you be my friend?"

"Gladly," said Christophe. "But what can I do?"

"Listen to me, advise me, give me courage. I am often so depressed! And then I don't know what to do. I say to myself: 'What is the good of fighting? What's the good of tormenting myself? One way or the other, what does it matter? Nothing and nobody matters!' That is a dreadful condition to be in. I don't want to get like that. Help me. Help me."

She looked utterly downcast; she looked older by ten years: she looked at Christophe with abject, imploring eyes. He promised what she asked. Then she revived, smiled, and was gay once more.

And in the evening she was laughing and flirting as usual.

Thereafter they had many intimate conversations. They were alone together: she confided in him: he tried hard to understand and advise her: she listened to his advice, or, if necessary, to his remonstrances, gravely, attentively, like a good little girl: it was a distraction, an interest, even a support for her: she thanked him coquettishly with a depth of feeling in her eyes.—But her life was changed in nothing: it was only a distraction the more.

Her day was passed in a succession of metamorphoses. She got up very late, about midday, after a sleepless night: for she rarely went to sleep before dawn. All day long she did nothing. She would vaguely call to mind a poem, an idea, a scrap of an

idea, or a face that had pleased her. She was never quite
awake until about four or five in the afternoon. Till then her
eyelids were heavy, her face was puffy, and she was sulky and
sleepy. She would revive on the arrival of a few girl-friends as
talkative as herself, and all sharing the same interest in the
gossip of Paris. They chattered endlessly about love. The
psychology of love: that was the unfailing topic, mixed up with
dress, the indiscretions of others, and scandal. She had also
a circle of idle young men to whom it was necessary to spend
three hours a day among skirts: they ought to have worn them
really, for they had the souls and the conversation of girls.
Christophe had his hour as her confessor. At once Colette
would become serious and intense. She was like the young
Frenchwoman, of whom Bodley speaks, who, at the confessional,
" developed a calmly prepared essay, a model of clarity and
order, in which everything that was to be said was properly arranged in distinct categories."—And after that she flung herself
once more into the business of amusement. As the day went on
she grew younger. In the evening she went to the theater: and
there was the eternal pleasure of recognizing the same eternal
faces in the audience:—her pleasure lay not in the play that
was performed, but in the actors whom she knew, whose familiar
mannerisms she remarked once more. And she exchanged
spiteful remarks with the people who came to see her in her
box about the people in the other boxes and about the actresses.
The *ingénue* was said to have a thin voice " like sour mayonnaise," or the great comédienne was dressed " like a lamp-
shade."—Or else she went out to a party: and there the pleasure, for a pretty girl like Colette, lay in being seen:—(but
there were bad days: nothing is more capricious than good looks
in Paris):—and she renewed her store of criticisms of people,
and their dresses, and their physical defects. There was no
conversation.—She would go home late, and take her time
about going to bed (that was the time when she was most
awake). She would dawdle about her dressing-table: skim
through a book: laugh to herself at the memory of something

said or done.   She was bored and very unhappy.   She could not go to sleep, and in the night there would come frightful moments of despair.

Christophe, who only saw Colette for a few hours at intervals, and could only be present at a few of these transformations, found it difficult to understand her at all.   He wondered when she was sincere,—or if she were always sincere—or if she were never sincere.   Colette herself could not have told him.   Like most girls who are idle and circumscribed in their desires, she was in darkness.   She did not know what she was, because she did not know what she wanted, because she could not know what she wanted without having tried it.   She would try it, after her fashion, with the maximum of liberty and the minimum of risk, trying to copy the people about her and to take their moral measure.   She was in no hurry to choose.   She would have liked to try everything, and turn everything to account.

But that did not work with a friend like Christophe.   He was perfectly willing to allow her to prefer people whom he did not admire, even people whom he despised: but he would not suffer her to put him on the same level with them.   Everybody to his own taste: but at least let everybody have his own taste.

He was the less inclined to be patient with Colette, as she seemed to take a delight in gathering round herself all the young men who were most likely to exasperate Christophe: disgusting little snobs, most of them wealthy, all of them idle, or jobbed into a sinecure in some government office—which amounts to the same thing.   They all wrote—or pretended to write.   That was an itch of the Third Republic.   It was a sort of indolent vanity,—intellectual work being the hardest of all to control, and most easily lending itself to the game of bluff.   They never gave more than a discreet, though respectful hint, of their great labors.   They seemed to be convinced of the importance of their work, staggering under the weight of it.   At first Christophe was a little embarrassed by the fact that he had never heard of them or their works.   He tried bashfully to ask about them: he was especially anxious to know what one of them had written, a young man who was declared by the others to be a master of the theater. He was surprised to hear that this great dramatist had written a one-act play taken from a novel, which had been pieced together from a number of short stories, or, rather, sketches, which he had published in one of the Reviews during the past ten years. The baggage of the others was not more considerable: a few one-act plays, a few short stories, a few verses. Some of them had won fame with an article, others with a book "which they were going to write." They professed scorn for long-winded books. They seemed to attach extreme importance to the handling of words. And yet the word "thought" frequently occurred in their conversation: but it did not seem to have the same meaning as is usually given to it: they applied it to the details of style. However, there were among them great thinkers, and great ironists, who, when they wrote, printed their subtle and profound remarks in *italics,* so that there might be no mistake.

They all had the cult of the letter *I:* it was the only cult they had. They tried to proselytize. But, unfortunately, other people were subscribers to the cult. They were always conscious of their audience in their way of speaking, walking, smoking, reading a paper, carrying their heads, looking, bowing to each other.—Such players' tricks are natural to young people, and the more insignificant—that is to say, unoccupied —they are, the stronger hold do they have on them. They are more especially paraded before women: for they covet women, and long—even more—to be coveted by them. But even on a chance meeting they will trot out their bag of tricks: even for a passer-by from whom they can expect only a glance of amazement. Christophe often came across these young strutting peacocks: budding painters, and musicians, art-students who modeled their appearance on some famous portrait: Van Dyck, Rembrandt, Velasquez, Beethoven; or fitted it to the parts they wish to play: painter, musician, workman, the profound thinker, the jolly fellow, the Danubian peasant, the

natural man. . . . They were always on the lookout to see
if they were attracting attention. When Christophe met them
in the street he took a malicious pleasure in looking the other
way and ignoring them. But their discomfiture never lasted
long: a yard or so farther on they would start strutting for the
next comer.—But the young men of Colette's little circle were
rather more subtle: their coxcombry was mental: they had two
or three models, who were not themselves original. Or else
they would mimic an idea: Force, Joy, Pity, Solidarity, Socialism, Anarchism, Faith, Liberty: all these were parts for their
playing. They were horribly clever in making the dearest and
rarest thoughts mere literary stuff, and in degrading the most
heroic impulses of the human soul to the level of drawing-room
commodities, fashionable neckties.

But in love they were altogether in their element: that was
their special province. The casuistry of pleasure had no secrets
for them: they were so clever that they could invent new problems so as to have the honor of solving them. That has always been the occupation of people who have nothing else to
do: in default of love, they "make love": above all, they explain it. Their notes took up far more room than their text,
which, as a matter of fact, was very short. Sociology gave a
relish to the most scabrous thoughts: everything was sheltered
beneath the flag of sociology: though they might have had
pleasure in indulging their vices, there would have been something lacking if they had not persuaded themselves that they
were laboring in the cause of the new world. That was an
eminently Parisian sort of socialism: erotic socialism.

Among the problems that were then exercising the little
Court of Love was the equality of men and women in marriage, and their respective rights in love. There had been
young men, honest, protestant, and rather ridiculous,—Scan-
dinavians and Swiss—who had based equality on virtue: saying that men should come to marriage as chaste as women.
The Parisian casuists looked for another sort of equality, an
equality based on loss of virtue, saying that women should

come to marriage as besmirched as men,—the right to take lovers. The Parisians had carried adultery, in imagination and practice, to such a pitch that they were beginning to find it rather insipid: and in the world of letters attempts were being made to support it by a new invention: the prostitution of young girls,—I mean regularized, universal, virtuous, decent, domestic, and, above all, social prostitution.—There had just appeared a book on the question, full of talent, which apparently said all there was to be said: through four hundred pages of playful pedantry, "strictly in accordance with the rules of the Baconian method," it dealt with the "best method of controlling the relations of the sexes." It was a lecture on free love, full of talk about manners, propriety, good taste, nobility, beauty, truth, modesty, morality,—a regular Berquin for young girls who wanted to go wrong.—It was, for the moment, the Gospel in which Colette's little court rejoiced, while they paraphrased it. It goes without saying, that, like all disciples, they discarded all the justice, observation, and even humanity that lay behind the paradox, and only retained the evil in it. They plucked all the most poisonous flowers from the little bed of sweetened blossoms,—aphorisms of this sort: "The taste for pleasure can only sharpen the taste for work":—"It is monstrous that a girl should become a mother before she has tasted the sweets of life."—"To have had the love of a worthy and pure-souled man as a girl is the natural preparation of a woman for a wise and considered motherhood":—"Mothers," said this author, "should organize the lives of their daughters with the same delicacy and decency with which they control the liberty of their sons."—"The time would come when girls would return as naturally from their lovers as now they return from a walk or from taking tea with a friend."

Colette laughingly declared that such teaching was very reasonable.

Christophe had a horror of it. He exaggerated its importance and the evil that it might do. The French are too clever to bring their literature into practice. These Diderots

in miniature are, in ordinary life, like the genial Panurge of
the encyclopedia, honest citizens, not really a whit less timorous
than the rest. It is precisely because they are so timid in action that they amuse themselves with carrying action (in
thought) to the limit of possibility. It is a game without any
risk.

But Christophe was not a French dilettante.

Among the young men of Colette's circle, there was one
whom she seemed to prefer, and, of course, he was the most objectionable of all to Christophe.

He was one of those young parvenus of the second generation
who form an aristocracy of letters, and are the patricians of
the Third Republic. His name was Lucien Lévy-Cœur. He
had quick eyes, set wide apart, an aquiline nose, a fair Van Dyck
beard clipped to a point: he was prematurely bald, which did
not become him: and he had a silky voice, elegant manners, and
fine soft hands, which he was always rubbing together. He
always affected an excessive politeness, an exaggerated courtesy,
even with people he did not like, and even when he was bent
on snubbing them.

Christophe had met him before at the literary dinner, to
which he was taken by Sylvain Kohn: and though they had
not spoken to each other, the sound of Lévy-Cœur's voice
had been enough to rouse a dislike which he could not explain,
and he was not to discover the reason for it until much later.
There are sudden outbursts of love: and so there are of hate,—
or—(to avoid hurting those tender souls who are afraid of the
word as of every passion)—let us call it the instinct of health
scenting the enemy, and mounting guard against him.

Lévy-Cœur was exactly the opposite of Christophe, and
represented the spirit of irony and decay which fastened gently,
politely, inexorably, on all the great things that were left of
the dying society: the family, marriage, religion, patriotism:
in art, on everything that was manly, pure, healthy, of the people: faith in ideas, feelings, great men, in Man. Behind that

mode of thought there was only the mechanical pleasure of analysis, analysis pushed to extremes, a sort of animal desire to nibble at thought, the instinct of a worm. And side by side with that ideal of intellectual nibbling was a girlish sensuality, the sensuality of a blue-stocking: for to Lévy-Cœur everything became literature. Everything was literary copy to him: his own adventures, his vices and the vices of his friends. He had written novels and plays in which, with much talent, he described the private life of his relations, and their most intimate adventures, and those of his friends, his own, his *liaisons,* among others one with the wife of his best friend: the portraits were well-drawn: everybody praised them, the public, the wife, and his friend. It was impossible for him to gain the confidence or the favors of a woman without putting them into a book.—One would have thought that his indiscretions would have produced strained relations with his " friends." But there was nothing of the kind; they were hardly more than a little embarrassed: they protested as a matter of form: but at heart they were delighted at being held up to the public gaze, *en déshabille:* so long as their faces were masked, their modesty was undisturbed. But there was never any spirit of vengeance, or even of scandal, in his tale-telling. He was no worse a man or lover than the majority. In the very chapters in which he exposed his father and mother and his mistress, he would write of them with a poetic tenderness and charm. He was really extremely affectionate: but he was one of those men who have no need to respect when they love: quite the contrary: they rather love those whom they can despise a little: that makes the object of their affection seem nearer to them and more human. Such men are of all the least capable of understanding heroism and purity. They are not far from considering them lies or weakness of mind. It goes without saying that such men are convinced that they understand better than anybody else the heroes of art whom they judge with a patronizing familiarity.

He got on excellently well with the young women of the

rich, idle middle-class. He was a companion for them, a sort of depraved servant, only more free and confidential, who gave them instruction and roused their envy. They had hardly any constraint with him: and, with the lamp of Psyche in their hands, they made a careful study of the hermaphrodite, and he suffered them.

Christophe could not understand how a girl like Colette, who seemed to have so refined a nature and a touching eagerness to escape from the degrading round of her life, could find pleasure in such company. Christophe was no psychologist. Lucien Lévy-Cœur could easily beat him on that score. Christophe was Colette's confidant: but Colette was the confidante of Lucien Lévy-Cœur. That gave him a great advantage. It is very pleasant to a woman to feel that she has to deal with a man weaker than herself. She finds food in it at once for her lower and higher instincts: her maternal instinct is touched by it. Lucien Lévy-Cœur knew that perfectly: one of the surest means of touching a woman's heart is to sound that mysterious chord. But in addition, Colette felt that she was weak, and cowardly, and possessed of instincts of which she was not proud, though she was not inclined to deny them. It pleased her to allow herself to be persuaded by the audacious and nicely calculated confessions of her friend that others were just the same, and that human nature must be taken for what it is. And so she gave herself the satisfaction of not resisting inclinations that she found very agreeable, and the luxury of saying that it must be so, and that it was wise not to rebel and to be indulgent with what one could not—" alas! "—prevent. There was a wisdom in that, the practice of which contained no element of pain.

For any one who can envisage life with serenity, there is a peculiar relish in remarking the perpetual contrast which exists in the very bosom of society between the extreme refinement of apparent civilization and its fundamental animalism. In every gathering that does not consist only of fossils and petrified souls, there are, as it were, two conversational strata, one above the other: one—which everybody can hear—between mind and mind: the other—of which very few are conscious, though it is the greater of the two—between instinct and instinct, the beast in man and woman. Often these two strata of conversation are contradictory. While mind and mind are passing the small change of convention, body and body say: Desire, Aversion, or, more often: Curiosity, Boredom, Disgust. The beast in man and woman, though tamed by centuries of civilization, and as cowed as the wretched lions in the tamer's cage, is always thinking of its food.

But Christophe had not yet reached that disinterestedness which comes only with age and the death of the passions. He had taken himself very seriously as adviser to Colette. She had asked for his help: and he saw her in the lightness of her heart exposed to danger. So he made no effort to conceal his dislike of Lucien Lévy-Cœur. At first that gentleman maintained towards Christophe an irreproachable and ironical politeness. He, too, scented the enemy: but he thought he had nothing to fear from him: he made fun of him without seeming to do so. If only he could have had Christophe's admiration he would have been on quite good terms with him, but that he never could obtain: he saw that clearly, for Christophe had not the art of disguising his feelings. And so Lucien Lévy-Cœur passed insensibly from an abstract intellectual antagonism to a little, carefully veiled, war, of which Colette was to be the prize.

She held the balance evenly between her two friends. She appreciated Christophe's talent and moral superiority: but she also appreciated Lucien Lévy-Cœur's amusing immorality and wit: and, at bottom, she found more pleasure in it. Christophe did not mince his protestations: she listened to him with a touching humility which disarmed him. She was quite a good creature, but she lacked frankness, partly from weakness, partly from her very kindness. She was half play-acting: she pretended to think with Christophe. As a matter of fact, she knew the worth of such a friend: but she was not ready to

make any sacrifice for a friendship: she was not ready to
sacrifice anything for anybody: she just wanted everything to
go smoothly and pleasantly.   And so she concealed from Christophe the fact that she went on receiving Lucien Lévy-Cœur:
she lied with the easy charm of the young women of her
class who, from their childhood, are expert in the practice
which is so necessary for those who wish to keep their friends
and please everybody.   She excused herself by pretending that
she wished to avoid hurting Christophe: but in reality it was
because she knew that he was right and wanted to go on doing
as she liked without quarreling with him.   Sometimes Christophe suspected her tricks: then he would scold her, and wax
indignant.   She would go on playing the contrite little girl, and
be affectionate and sorry: and she would look tenderly at him
—*feminæ ultima ratio.*—And really it did distress her to think
of losing Christophe's friendship: she would be charmingly
serious and in that way succeed in disarming Christophe for
a little while longer.   But sooner or later there had to be an explosion.   Christophe's irritation was fed unconsciously by a
little jealousy.   And into Colette's coaxing tricks there crept
a little, a very little, love, all of which made the rupture only
the more violent.

One day when Christophe had caught Colette out in a flagrant
lie he gave her a definite alternative: she must choose between
Lucien Lévy-Cœur and himself.   She tried to dodge the question: and, finally, she vindicated her right to have whatever
friends she liked.   She was perfectly right: and Christophe
admitted that he had been absurd: but he knew also that he
had not been exacting from egoism: he had a sincere affection
for Colette: he wanted to save her even against her will.   He
insisted awkwardly.   She refused to answer.   He said:

" Colette, do you want us not to be friends any more? "

She replied:

" No, no.   I should be sorry if you ceased to be my friend."

" But you will not sacrifice the smallest thing for our
friendship."

"Sacrifice! What a silly word!" she said. "Why should one always be sacrificing one thing for another? It's just a stupid Christian idea. You're nothing but an old parson at heart."

"Maybe," he said. "I want one thing or another. I allow nothing between good and evil, not so much as the breadth of a hair."

"Yes, I know," she said. "That is why I love you. For I do love you: but . . ."

"But you love the other fellow too?"

She laughed, and said, with a soft look in her eyes and a tender note in her voice:

"Stay!"

He was just about to give in once more when Lucien Lévy-Cœur came in: and he was welcomed with the same soft look in her eyes and the same tender note in her voice. Christophe sat for some time in silence watching Colette at her tricks: then he went away, having made up his mind to break with her. He was sick and sorry at heart. It was so stupid to grow so fond, always to be falling into the trap!

When he reached home he toyed with his books, and idly opened his Bible and read:

". . . *The Lord saith, Because the daughters of Zion are haughty and walk with stretched forth necks and wanton eyes, walking and mincing as they go, and making a tinkling with their feet,*

"*Therefore the Lord will smite with a scab the crown of the head of the daughters of Zion, and the Lord will discover their secret parts* . . ."

He burst out laughing as he thought of Colette's little tricks: and he went to bed well pleased with himself. Then he thought that he too must have become tainted with the corruption of Paris for the Bible to have become a humorous work to him. But he did not stop saying over and over again the judgment of the great judiciary humorist: and he tried to imagine its effect on the head of his young friend. He went to sleep laughing like a child.   He had lost all thought of his new sorrow.   One more or less. . . .   He was getting used to it.

He did not give up Colette's music-lessons: but he refused to take the opportunities she gave him of continuing their intimate conversations.   It was no use her being sorry about it or offended, and trying all sorts of tricks: he stuck to his guns: they were rude to each other: of her own accord she took to finding excuses for missing the lessons: and he also made excuses for declining the Stevens' invitations.

He had had enough of Parisian society: he could not bear the emptiness of it, the idleness, the moral impotence, the neurasthenia, its aimless, pointless, self-devouring hypercriticism. He wondered how people could live in such a stagnant atmosphere of art for art's sake and pleasure for pleasure's sake. And yet the French did live in it: they had been a great nation, and they still cut something of a figure in the world: at least, they seemed to do so to the outside spectator.   But where were the springs of their life?   They believed in nothing, nothing but pleasure. . . .

Just as Christophe reached this point in his reflections, he ran into a crowd of young men and women, all shouting at the tops of their voices, dragging a carriage in which was sitting an old priest casting blessings right and left.   A little farther on he found some French soldiers battering down the doors of a church with axes, and there were men attacking them with chairs.   He saw that the French did still believe in something —though he could not understand in what.   He was told that the State and the Church were separated after a century of living together, and that as the Church had refused to go with a good grace, standing on its rights and its power, it was being evicted.   To Christophe the proceeding seemed ungallant: but he was so sick of the anarchical dilettantism of the Parisian artists that he was delighted to find men ready to have their heads broken for a cause, however foolish it might be.

It was not long before he discovered that there were many such people in France. The political journals plunged into the fight like the Homeric heroes: they published daily calls to civil war. It is true that it got no farther than words, and that they very rarely came to blows. But there was no lack of simple souls to put into action what the others declared in words. Strange things happened: departments threatened to break away from France, regiments deserted, prefectures were burned, tax-collectors were on horseback at the head of a company of gendarmes, peasants were armed with scythes, and put their kettles on to boil to defend the churches, which the Free Thinkers were demolishing in the name of liberty: there were popular redeemers who climbed trees to address the provinces of Wine, that had risen against the provinces of Alcohol. Everywhere there were millions of men shaking hands, all red in the face from shouting, and in the end all going for each other. The Republic flattered the people: and then turned arms against them. The people on their side broke the heads of a few of their own young men—officers and soldiers.—And so every one proved to everybody else the excellence of his cause and his fists. Looked at from a distance, through the newspapers, it was as though the country had gone back a few centuries, Christophe discovered that France—skeptical France—was a nation of fanatics. But it was impossible for him to find out the meaning of their fanaticism. For or against religion? For or against Reason? For or against the country?—They were for and against everything. They were fanatics for the pleasure of it.

He spoke about it one evening to a Socialist deputy whom he met sometimes at the Stevens'. Although he had spoken to him before, he had no idea what sort of man he was: till then they had only talked about music. Christophe was very surprised to learn that this man of the world was the leader of a violent party.

Achille Roussin was a handsome man, with a fair beard, a

burring way of talking, a florid complexion, affable manners, a certain polish on his fundamental vulgarity, certain peasant tricks which from time to time he used in spite of himself:— a way of paring his nails in public, a vulgar habit of catching hold of the coat of the man he was talking to, or gripping him by the arm:—he was a great eater, a heavy drinker, a high liver with a gift of laughter, and the appetite of a man of the people pushing his way into power: he was adaptable, quick to alter his manners to sort with his surroundings and the person he was talking to, full of ideas, and reasonable in expounding them, able to listen, and to assimilate at once everything he heard: for the rest he was sympathetic, intelligent, interested in everything, naturally, or as a matter of acquired habit, or merely out of vanity: he was honest so far as was compatible with his interests, or when it was dangerous not to be so.

He had quite a pretty wife, tall, well made, and well set up, with a charming figure which was a little too much shown off by her tight dresses, which accentuated and exaggerated the rounded curves of her anatomy: her face was framed in curly black hair: she had big black eyes, a long, pointed chin: her face was big, but quite charming in its general effect, though it was spoiled by the twitch of her short-sighted eyes, and her silly little pursed-up mouth. She had an affected precise manner, like a bird, and a simpering way of talking: but she was kindly and amiable. She came of a rich shopkeeping family, broad-minded and virtuous, and she was devoted to the countless duties of society, as to a religion, not to mention the duties, social and artistic, which she imposed on herself: she had her *salon,* dabbled in University Extension movements, and was busy with philanthropic undertakings and researches into the psychology of childhood,—all without any enthusiasm or profound interest,—from a mixture of natural kindness, snobbishness, and the harmless pedantry of a young woman of education, who always seems to be repeating a lesson, and taking a pride in showing that she has learned it well. She needed to be busy, but she did not need to be interested in what she was doing. It was like the feverish industry of those women who always have a piece of knitting in their hands, and never stop clicking their needles, as though the salvation of the world depended on their work, which they themselves do not know what to do with. And then there was in her—as in women who knit—the vanity of the good woman who sets an example to other women.

The Deputy had an affectionate contempt for her. He had chosen well both as regards his pleasure and his peace of mind. He enjoyed her beauty and asked no more of her: and she asked no more of him. He loved her and deceived her. She put up with that, provided she had her share of his attention. Perhaps also it gave her a sort of pleasure. She was placid and sensual. She had the attitude of mind of a woman of the harem.

They had two fine children of four and five years old, whom she looked after, like a good mother, with the same amiable, cold attentiveness with which she followed her husband's political career, and the latest fashions in dress and art. And it produced in her the most odd mixture of advanced ideas, ultra-decadent art, polite restlessness, and bourgeois sentiment.

They invited Christophe to go and see them. Madame Roussin was a good musician, and played the piano charmingly: she had a delicate, firm touch: with her little head bowed over the keyboard, and her hands poised above it and darting down, she was like a pecking hen. She was talented and knew more about music than most Frenchwomen, but she was as insensible as a fish to the deeper meaning of music: to her it was only a succession of notes, rhythms, and degrees of sound, to which she listened or reproduced carefully: she never looked for the soul in it, having no use for it herself. This amiable, intelligent, simple woman, who was always ready to do any one a kindness, gave Christophe the graceful welcome which she extended to everybody. Christophe was not particularly grateful to her for it: he was not much in sympathy with her: she hardly existed for him. Perhaps it was that unconsciously he could not forgive her acquiescence in her husband's infidelities, of which she was by no means ignorant. Passive acceptance was of all the vices that which he could least excuse.

He was more intimate with Achille Roussin. Roussin loved music, as he loved the other arts, crudely but sincerely. When he liked a symphony, it became a thing that he could take into his arms. He had a superficial culture and turned it to good account: his wife had been useful to him there. He was interested in Christophe because he saw in him a vigorous vulgarian such as he was himself. And he found it absorbing to study an original of his stamp—(he was unwearying in his observation of humanity)—and to discover his impressions of Paris. The frankness and rudeness of Christophe's remarks amused him. He was skeptic enough to admit their truth. He was not put out by the fact that Christophe was a German. On the contrary: he prided himself on being above national prejudice. And, when all was said and done, he was sincerely "human"—(that was his chief quality);—he sympathized with everything human. But that did not prevent his being quite convinced of the superiority of the French—an old race, and an old civilization—over the Germans, and making fun of the Germans.

At Achille Roussin's Christophe met other politicians, the Ministers of yesterday, and the Ministers of to-morrow. He would have been only too glad to talk to each of them individually, if these illustrious persons had thought him worthy. In spite of the generally accepted opinion he found them much more interesting than the other Frenchmen of his acquaintance. They were more alive mentally, more open to the passions and the great interests of humanity. They were brilliant talkers, mostly men from the South, and they were amazingly dilettante: individually they were almost as much so as the men of letters. Of course, they were very ignorant about art, and especially about foreign art: but they all pretended more or less to some knowledge of it: and often they really loved it. There were

Councils which were very like the coterie of some little Review. One of them would be a playwright: another would scrape on the violin; another would be a besotted Wagnerian. And they all collected Impressionist pictures, read decadent books, and prided themselves on a taste for some ultra-aristocratic art, which was almost always in direct opposition to their ideas. It puzzled Christophe to find these Socialist or Radical-Socialist Ministers, these apostles of the poor and down-trodden, posing as connoisseurs of eclectic art. No doubt they had a perfect right to do so: but it seemed to him rather disloyal.

But the odd thing was when these men who in private conversation were skeptics, sensualists, Nihilists, and anarchists, came to action: at once they became fanatics. Even the most dilettante of them when they came into power became like Oriental despots: they had a mania for ordering everything, and let nothing alone: they were skeptical in mind and tyrannical in temper. The temptation to use the machinery of administrative centralization created by the greatest of despots was too great, and it was difficult not to abuse it. The result was a sort of republican imperialism on to which there had latterly been grafted an atheistic catholicism.

For some time past the politicians had made no claim to do anything but control the body—that is to say, money:—they hardly troubled the soul at all, since the soul could not be converted into money. Their own souls were not concerned with politics: they passed above or below politics, which in France are thought of as a branch—a lucrative, though not very exalted branch—of commerce and industry: the intellectuals despised the politicians, the politicians despised the intellectuals. —But lately there had been a closer understanding, then an alliance, between the politicians and the lowest class of intellectuals. A new power had appeared upon the scene, which had arrogated to itself the absolute government of ideas: the Free Thinkers. They had thrown in their lot with the other power, which had seen in them the perfect machinery of political despotism. They were trying not so much to destroy the

Church as to supplant it: and, in fact, they created a Church of Free Thought which had its catechisms, and ceremonies, its baptisms, its confirmations, its marriages, its regional councils, if not its ecumenicals at Rome. It was most pitifully comic to see these thousands of poor wretches having to band themselves together in order to be able to " think freely." True, their freedom of thought consisted in setting a ban on the thought of others in the name of Reason: for they believed in Reason as the Catholics believed in the Blessed Virgin without ever dreaming for a moment that Reason, like the Virgin, was in itself nothing, or that the real thing lay behind it. And, just as the Catholic Church had its armies of monks and its congregations stealthily creeping through the veins of the nation, propagating its views and destroying every other sort of vitality, so the Anti-Catholic Church had its Free Masons, whose chief Lodge, the Grand-Orient, kept a faithful record of all the secret reports with which their pious informers in all quarters of France supplied them. The Republican State secretly encouraged the sacred espionage of these mendicant friars and Jesuits of Reason, who terrorized the army, the University, and every branch of the State: and it was never noticed that while they pretended to serve the State, they were all the time aiming at supplanting it, and that the country was slowly moving towards an atheistic theocracy; very little, if anything, different from that of the Jesuits of Paraguay.

Christophe met some of these gentry at Roussin's. They were all blind fetish-worshippers. At that time they were rejoicing at having removed Christ from the Courts of Law. They thought they had destroyed religion because they had destroyed a few pieces of wood and ivory. Others were concentrating on Joan of Arc and her banner of the Virgin, which they had just wrested from the Catholics. One of the Fathers of the new Church, a general who was waging war on the French of the old Church, had just given utterance to an anti-clerical speech in honor of Vercingetorix: he proclaimed the ancient Gaul, to whom Free Thought had erected a statue, to be a son of the

people, and the first champion against (the Church of) Rome.
The Ministers of the Marine, by way of purifying the fleet
and showing their horror of war, called their cruisers *Descartes*
and *Ernest Renan*. Other Free Thinkers had set themselves
to purify art. They expurgated the classics of the seventeenth
century, and did not allow the name of God to sully the *Fables*
of La Fontaine. They did not allow it in music either: and
Christophe heard one of them, an old radical,—("*To be a
radical in old age,*" says Goethe, "*is the height of folly*")—
wax indignant at the religious *Lieder* of Beethoven having been
given at a popular concert. He demanded that other words
should be used instead of " God."

" What? " asked Christophe in exasperation. " The Republic? "

Others who were even more radical would accept no compromise and wanted purely and simply to suppress all religious
music and all schools in which it was taught. In vain did a
director of the University of Fine Arts, who was considered
an Athenian in that Bœotia, try to explain that musicians must
be taught music: for, as he said, with great loftiness of thought,
" when you send a soldier to the barracks, you teach him how
to use a gun and then how to shoot. And so it is with a young
composer: his head is buzzing with ideas: but he has not yet
learned to put them in order." And, being a little scared by
his own courage, he protested with every sentence: " I am an
old Free Thinker. . . . I am an old Republican . . ."
and he declared audaciously that " he did not care much whether
the compositions of Pergolese were operas or Masses: all that he
wanted to know was, were they human works of art? "—But
his adversary with implacable logic answered " the old Free
Thinker and Republican " that " there were two sorts of music:
that which was sung in churches and that which was sung in
other places." The first sort was the enemy of Reason and the
State: and the Reason of the State ought to suppress it.

All these silly people would have been more ridiculous than
dangerous if behind them there had not been men of real worth,

supporting them, who were, like them—and perhaps even more —fanatics of Reason. Tolstoy speaks somewhere of those "epidemic influences" which prevail in religion, philosophy, politics, art, and science, "insensate influences, the folly of which only becomes apparent to men when they are clear of them, while as long as they are under their dominion they seem so true to them that they think them beyond all argument." Instances are the craze for tulips, belief in sorcery, and the aberrations of literary fashions.—The religion of Reason was such a craze. It was common to the most ignorant and the most cultured, to the "sub-veterinaries" of the Chamber, and certain of the keenest intellects of the University. It was even more dangerous in the latter than in the former: for with the latter it was mixed up with a credulous and stupid optimism, which sapped its energy: while with the others it was fortified and given a keener edge by a fanatical pessimism which was under no illusion as to the fundamental antagonism of Nature and Reason, and they were only the more desperately resolved to wage the war of abstract Liberty, abstract Justice, abstract Truth, against the malevolence of Nature. There was behind it all the idealism of the Calvinists, the Jansenists, and the Jacobins, the old belief in the fundamental perversity of mankind, which can and must be broken by the implacable pride of the Elect inspired by the breath of Reason,—the Spirit of God. It was a very French type, the type of intelligent Frenchman, who is not at all "human." A pebble as hard as iron: nothing can penetrate it: it breaks everything that it touches.

Christophe was appalled by the conversations that he had at Achille Roussin's with some of these fanatics. It upset all his ideas about France. He had thought, like so many people, that the French were a well-balanced, sociable. tolerant, liberty-loving people. And he found them lunatics with their abstract ideas, their diseased logic. ready to sacrifice themselves and everybody else for one of their syllogisms. They were always talking of liberty, but there never were men less able to understand it or to stand it.   Nowhere in the world were there characters more coldly and atrociously despotic in their passion for intellect or their passion for always being in the right.

And it was not only true of one party.   Every party was the same.   They could not—they would not—see anything above or beyond their political or religious formula, or their country, their province, their group, or their own narrow minds.   There were anti-Semites who expended all the forces of their being in a blind, impotent hatred of all the privileges of wealth: for they hated all Jews, and called those whom they hated "Jews." There were nationalists who hated—(when they were kinder they stopped short at despising)—every other nation, and even among their own people, they called everybody who did not agree with them foreigners, or renegades, or traitors.   There were anti-protestants who persuaded themselves that all Protestants were English or Germans, and would have them all expelled from France.   There were men of the West who denied the existence of anything east of the Rhine: men of the North who denied the existence of everything south of the Loire: men of the South who called all those who lived north of the Loire Barbarians: and there were men who boasted of being of Gallic descent: and, craziest of all, there were "Romans" who prided themselves on the defeat of their ancestors: and Bretons, and Lorrainians, and Félibres, and Albigeois; and men from Carpentras, and Pontoise, and Quimper-Corentin: they all thought only of themselves, the fact of being themselves was sufficient patent of nobility, and they could not put up with the idea of people being anything else.   There is nothing to be done with such people: they will not listen to argument from any other point of view: they must burn everybody else at the stake, or be burned themselves.

Christophe thought that it was lucky that such people should live under a Republic: for all these little despots did at least annihilate each other.   But if any one of them had become Emperor or King, it would have been the end of him.

He did not know that there is one virtue left to work the salvation of people of that temper of mind :—inconsequence.

The French politicians were no exception. Their despotism was tempered with anarchy: they were for ever swinging between two poles. On one hand they relied on the fanatics of thought, on the other they relied on the anarchists of thought. Mixed up with them was a whole rabble of dilettante Socialists, mere opportunists, who held back from taking any part in the fight until it was won, though they followed in the wake of the army of Free Thought, and, after every battle won, they swooped down on the spoils. These champions of Reason did not labor in the cause of Reason. . . . *Sic vos non vobis* . . . but in the cause of the Citizens of the World, who with glad shouts trampled under foot the traditions of the country, and had no intention of destroying one Faith in order to set up another, but in order to set themselves up and break away from all restraint.

There Christophe marked the likeness of Lucien Lévy-Cœur. He was not surprised to learn that Lucien Lévy-Cœur was a Socialist. He only thought that Socialists must be fairly on the road to success to have enrolled Lucien Lévy-Cœur. But he did not know that Lucien Lévy-Cœur had also contrived to figure in the opposite camp, where he had succeeded in allying himself with men of the most anti-Liberal opinions, if not anti-Semite, in politics and art. He asked Achille Roussin:

" How can you put up with such men ? "

Roussin replied :

" He is so clever ! And he is working for us; he is destroying the old world."

" He is doing that all right," said Christophe. " He is destroying it so thoroughly that I don't see what is going to be left for you to build up again. Do you think there'll be timber enough left for your new house? And are you even sure that the worms have not crept into your building-yard ? "

Lucien Lévy-Cœur was not the only nibbler at Socialism. The Socialist papers were staffed by these petty men of letters, with their art for art's sake, these licentious anarchists who had fastened on all the roads that might lead to success. They barred the way to others, and filled the papers, which styled themselves the organs of the people, with their dilettante decadence and their *struggle for life*. They were not content with being jobbed into positions: they wanted fame. Never had there been a time when there were so many premature statues, or so many speeches delivered at the unveiling of them. But queerest of all were the banquets that were periodically offered to one or other of the great men of the fraternity by the sycophants of fame, not in celebration of any of their deeds, but in celebration of some honor given to them: for those were the things that most appealed to them. Esthetes, supermen, Socialist Ministers, they were all agreed when it was a question of feasting to celebrate some promotion in the Legion of Honor founded by the Corsican officer.

Roussin laughed at Christophe's amazement. He did not think the German far out in his estimation of the supporters of his party. When they were alone together he would handle them severely himself. He knew their stupidity and their knavery better than any one: but that did not keep him from supporting them in order to retain their support. And if in private he never hesitated to speak of the people in terms of contempt, on the platform he was a different man. Then he would assume a high-pitched voice, shrill, nasal, labored, solemn tones, a tremolo, a bleat, wide, sweeping, fluttering gestures like the beating of wings: exactly like Mounet-Sully.

Christophe tried hard to discover exactly how far Roussin believed in his Socialism. It was obvious that at heart he did not believe in it at all: he was too skeptical. And yet he did believe in it, to a certain extent: and though he knew perfectly well that it was only a part of his mind that believed in it— (perhaps the most important part)—he had arranged his life and conduct in accordance with it, because it suited him best. It was not only his practical interest that was served by it, but also his vital interests, the foundations of his being and all his actions. His Socialistic Faith was to him a sort of

State religion.—Most people live like that. Their lives are based on religious, moral, social, or purely practical beliefs,—(belief in their profession, in their work, in the utility of the part they play in life)—in which they do not, at heart, believe. But they do not wish to know it: for they must have this apparent faith, this " State religion," of which every man is priest, to live.

Roussin was not one of the worst. There were many, many others who called themselves Socialists and Radicals, from—it can hardly be called ambition, for their ambition was so short-sighted, and did not go beyond immediate plunder and their re-election! They pretended to believe in a new order of society. Perhaps there was a time when they believed in it: and they went on pretending to do so: but, in fact, they had no idea beyond living on the spoils of the dying order of society. This predatory Nihilism was saved by a short-sighted opportunism. The great interests of the future were sacrificed to the egoism of the present. They cut down the army; they would have dislocated the country to please the electors. They were not lacking in cleverness: they knew perfectly well what they ought to have done: but they did not do it, because it would have cost them too much effort, and they were incapable of effort. They wanted to arrange their own lives and the life of the nation with the least possible amount of trouble and sacrifice. All down the scale the point was to get the maximum of pleasure with the minimum of effort. That was their morality, immoral enough, but it was the only guide in the political muddle, in which the leaders set the example of anarchy, and the disordered pack of politicians were chasing ten hares at once, and letting them all escape one after the other, and an aggressive Foreign Office was yoked with a pacific War Office, and Ministers of War were cutting down the army in order to purify it, Naval Ministers were inciting the workmen in the arsenals, military instructors were preaching the horrors of war, and all the officials, judges, revolutionaries, and patriots were dilettante. The political demoralization was universal. Every man was expecting the State to provide him with office, honors, pensions, indemnities: and the Government did, as a matter of fact, feed the appetite of its supporters: honors and pensions were made the quarry of the sons, nephews, grand-nephews, and valets of those in power: the deputies were always voting an increase in their own salaries: revenues, posts, titles, all the possessions of the State, were being blindly squandered.—And, like a sinister echo of the example of the upper classes, the lower classes were always on the verge of a strike: they had men teaching contempt of authority and revolt against the established order; post-office employés burned letters and despatches, workers in factories threw sand or emery-powder into the gears of the machines, men working in the arsenals sacked them, ships were burned, and artisans deliberately made a horrible mess of their work,—the destruction not of riches, but of the wealth of the world.

And to crown it all the intellectuals amused themselves by discovering that this national suicide was based on reason and right, in the sacred right of every human being to be happy. There was a morbid humanitarianism which broke down the distinction between Good and Evil, and developed a sentimental pity for the " sacred and irresponsible human " in the criminal, the doting sentimentality of an old man:—it was a capitulation to crime, the surrender of society to its mercies.

Christophe thought:

" France is drunk with liberty. When she has raved and screamed, she will fall down dead-drunk. And when she wakes up she will find herself in prison."

What hurt Christophe most in this demagogy was to see the most violent political measures coldly carried through by these men whose fundamental instability he knew perfectly well. The disproportion between the shiftiness of these men and the rigorous Acts that they passed or authorized was too scandalous. It was as though there were in them two contradictory things: an inconsistent character, believing in nothing, and discursive Reason, intent on truncating, mowing down, and crushing life, without regard for anything. Christophe wondered why the peaceful middle-class, the Catholics, the officials who were harassed in every conceivable way, did not throw them all out by the window. He dared not tell Roussin what he thought: but, as he was incapable of concealing anything, Roussin had no difficulty in guessing it. He laughed and said:

"No doubt that is what you or I would do. But there is no danger of them doing it. They are just a set of poor devils who haven't the energy: they can't do much more than grumble. They're just the fag end of an aristocracy, idiotic, stultified by their clubs and their sport, prostituted by the Americans and the Jews, and, by way of showing how up to date they are, they play the degraded parts allotted to them in fashionable plays, and support those who have degraded them. They're an apathetic and surly middle-class: they read nothing, understand nothing, don't want to understand anything; they only know how to vilify, vilify, vaguely, bitterly, futilely—and they have only one passion: sleep, to lie huddled in sleep on their money-bags, hating anybody who disturbs them, and even anybody whose tastes differ from theirs, for it does upset them to think of other people working while they are snoozing! If you knew them you would sympathize with us."

But Christophe could find nothing but disgust with both: for he did not hold that the baseness of the oppressed was any excuse for that of the oppressor. Only too frequently had he met at the Stevens' types of the rich dull middle-class that Roussin described,

> "... *L'anime triste di coloro,*
> *Che visser senza infamia esenza lodo,* ...*"*

He saw only too clearly the reason why Roussin and his friends were sure not only of their power over these people, but of their right to abuse it. They had to hand all the instruments of tyranny. Thousands of officials, who had renounced their will and every vestige of personality, and obeyed blindly. A loose, vulgar way of living, a Republic without Republicans: Socialist papers and Socialist leaders groveling before Royalties when they visited Paris: the souls of servants gaping at titles, and gold lace, and orders: they could be kept quiet by just having a bone to gnaw, or the Legion of Honor flung at them. If the Kings had ennobled all the citizens of France, all the citizens of France would have been Royalist.

The politicians were having a fine time. Of the Three Estates of '89 the first was extinct: the second was proscribed, suspect, or had emigrated: the third was gorged by its victory and slept. And, as for the Fourth Estate, which had come into existence at a later date, and had become a public menace in its jealousy, there was no difficulty about squaring that. The decadent Republic treated it as decadent Rome treated the barbarian hordes, that she no longer had the power to drive from her frontiers; she assimilated them, and they quickly became her best watch-dogs. The Ministers of the middle-class called themselves Socialists, lured away and annexed to their own party the most intelligent and vigorous of the working-class: they robbed the proletariat of their leaders, infused their new blood into their own system, and, in return, gorged them with indigestible science and middle-class culture.

One of the most curious features of these attempts at distraint by the middle-class on the people were the Popular Universities. They were little jumble-sales of scraps of knowledge of every period and every country. As one syllabus declared, they set out to teach "every branch of physical, biological, and sociological science: astronomy, cosmology, anthropology, ethnology, physiology, psychology, psychiatry, geography, languages, esthetics, logic, etc." Enough to split the skull of Pico della Mirandola.

In truth there had been originally, and still was in some of them, a certain grand idealism, a keen desire to bring truth, beauty, and morality within the reach of all, which was a very fine thing. It was wonderful and touching to see workmen, after a hard day's toil, crowding into narrow, stuffy lecture-rooms, impelled by a thirst for knowledge that was stronger than fatigue and hunger. But how the poor fellows had been tricked! There were a few real apostles, intelligent human beings, a few upright warm-hearted men, with more good intentions than skill to accomplish them; but, as against them, there were hundreds of fools, idiots, schemers, unsuccessful authors, orators, professors, parsons, speakers, pianists, critics, anarchists, who deluged the people with their productions. Every man jack of them was trying to unload his stock-in-trade. The most thriving of them were naturally the nostrum-mongers, the philosophical lecturers who ladled out general ideas, leavened with a few facts, a scientific smattering, and cosmological conclusions.

The Popular Universities were also an outlet for the ultra-aristocratic works of art: decadent etchings, poetry, and music. The aim was the elevation of the people for the rejuvenation of thought and the regeneration of the race. They began by inoculating them with all the fads and cranks of the middle-class. They gulped them down greedily, not because they liked them, but because they were middle-class. Christophe, who was taken to one of these Popular Universities by Madame Roussin, heard her play Debussy to the people between *la Bonne Chanson* of Gabriel Fauré and one of the later quartets of Beethoven. He who had only begun to grasp the meaning of the later works of Beethoven after many years, and long weary labor, asked some one who sat near him pityingly:

" Do you understand it? "

The man drew himself up like an angry cock, and said:

" Certainly. Why shouldn't I understand it as well as you? "

And by way of showing that he understood it he encored a fugue. glaring defiantly at Christophe.

Christophe went away. He was amazed. He said to himself that the swine had succeeded in poisoning even the living wells of the nation: the People had ceased to be—" People yourselves! " as a working-man said to one of the would-be founders of the Theaters of the People.   " I am as much of the middle-class as you."

One fine evening when above the darkening town the soft sky was like an Oriental carpet, rich in warm faded colors, Christophe walked along by the river from Notre Dame to the Invalides.   In the dim fading light the tower of the cathedral rose like the arms of Moses held up during the battle.   The carved golden spire of the Sainte-Chapelle, the flowering Holy Thorn, flashed out of the labyrinth of houses.   On the other side of the water stretched the royal front of the Louvre, and its windows were like weary eyes lit up with the last living rays of the setting sun.   At the back of the great square of the Invalides behind its trenches and proud walls, majestic, solitary, floated the dull gold dome, like a symphony of bygone victories. And at the top of the hill there stood the Arc de Triomphe, bestriding the hill with the giant stride of the Imperial legions.

And suddenly Christophe thought of it all as of a dead giant lying prone upon the plain.   The terror of it clutched at his heart; he stopped to gaze at the gigantic fossils of a fabulous race, long since extinct, that in its life had made the whole earth ring with the tramp of its armies,—the race whose helmet was the dome of the Invalides, whose girdle was the Louvre, the thousand arms of whose cathedrals had clutched at the heavens, who traversed the whole world with the triumphant stride of the Arch of Napoleon, under whose heel there now swarmed Lilliput.

III

WITHOUT any deliberate effort on his part, Christophe had gained a certain celebrity in the Parisian circles to which he had been introduced by Sylvain Kohn and Goujart.   He was seen everywhere with one or other of his friends at first nights.

and at concerts, and his extraordinary face, his ugliness, the
absurdity of his figure and costume, his brusque, awkward manners, the paradoxical opinions to which he gave vent from time
to time, his undeveloped, but large and healthy intellect, and
the romantic stories spread by Sylvain Kohn about his escapades
in Germany, and his complications with the police and flight
to France, had marked him out for the idle, restless curiosity
of the great cosmopolitan hotel drawing-room that Paris has
become. As long as he held himself in check, observing, listening, and trying to understand before expressing any opinion,
as long as nothing was known of his work or what he really
thought, he was tolerated. The French were pleased with him
for having been unable to stay in Germany. And the French
musicians especially were delighted with Christophe's unjust
pronouncements on German music, and took them all as
homage to themselves:—(as a matter of fact, they heard only
his old youthful opinions, to many of which he would no longer
have subscribed: a few articles published in a German Review
which had been amplified and circulated by Sylvain Kohn).—
Christophe was interesting and did not interfere with anybody: there was no danger of his supplanting anybody. He
needed only to become the great man of a coterie. He needed
only not to write anything, or as little as possible, and not to
have anything performed, and to supply Goujart and his like
with ideas, Goujart and the whole set of men whose motto is the
famous quip—adapted a little:

  "*My glass is small: but I drink . . . the wine of others.*"

  A strong personality sheds its rays especially on young people who are more concerned with feeling than with action.
There were plenty of young people about Christophe. They
were for the most part idle, will-less, aimless, purposeless.
Young men, living in dread of work, fearful of being left
alone with themselves, who sought an armchair immortality,
wandering from café to theater, from theater to café, finding
all sorts of excuses for not going home, to avoid coming face
to face with themselves. They came and stayed for hours,

dawdling, talking, making aimless conversation, and going
away empty, aching, disgusted, satiated, and yet famishing,
forced to go on with it in spite of loathing.   They surrounded
Christophe, like Goethe's water-spaniel, the "lurking specters,"
that lie in wait and seize upon a soul and fasten upon its vitality.

A vain fool would have found pleasure in such a circle of
parasites.   But Christophe had no taste for pedestals.   He
was revolted by the idiotic subtlety of his admirers, who read
into anything he did all sorts of absurd meanings, Renanian,
Nietzschean, hermaphroditic.   He kicked them out.   He was
not made for passivity.   Everything in him cried aloud for
action.   He observed so as to understand: he wished to understand so as to act.   He was free of the constraint of any
school, and of any prejudice, and he inquired into everything,
read everything, and studied all the forms of thought and the
resources of the expression of other countries and other ages in
his art.   He seized on all those which seemed to him effective
and true.   Unlike the French artists whom he studied, who
were ingenious inventors of new forms, and wore themselves
out in the unceasing effort of invention, and gave up the
struggle half-way, he endeavored not so much to invent a new
musical language as to speak the authentic language of music
with more energy: his aim was not to be particular, but to be
strong.   His passion for strength was the very opposite of the
French genius of subtlety and moderation.   He scorned style
for the sake of style and art for art's sake.   The best French
artists seemed to him to be no more than pleasure-mongers.   One
of the most perfect poets in Paris had amused himself with
drawing up a "list of the workers in contemporary French
poetry, with their talents, their productions, and their earnings": and he enumerated "the crystals, the Oriental fabrics, the
gold and bronze medals, the lace for dowagers, the polychromatic
sculpture, the painted porcelain." which had been produced in
the workshops of his various colleagues.   He pictured himself "in the corner of a vast factory of letters, mending old
tapestry, or polishing up rusty halberds."—Such a conception of

the artist as a good workman, thinking only of the perfection of
his craft, was not without an element of greatness. But it did
not satisfy Christophe: and while he admitted in it a certain
professional dignity, he had a contempt for the poor quality of
life which most often it disguised. He could not understand
writing for the sake of writing, or talking for the sake of
talking. He never said words; he said—or wanted to say—
the things themselves.

" Ei dice cose, e voi dite parole . . ."

After a long period of rest, during which he had been entirely occupied with taking in a new world, Christophe suddenly became conscious of an imperious need for creation.
The antagonism which he felt between himself and Paris
called up all his reserve of force by its challenge of his personality. All his passions were brimming in him, and imperiously demanding expression. They were of every kind: and
they were all equally insistent. He tried to create, to fashion
music, into which to turn the love and hatred that were
swelling in his heart, and the will and the renunciation, and
all the daimons struggling within him, all of whom had an
equal right to live. Hardly had he assuaged one passion in
music,—(sometimes he hardly had the patience to finish it)—
than he hurled himself at the opposite passion. But the contradiction was only apparent: if they were always changing,
they were in truth always the same. He beat out roads in
music, roads that led to the same goal: his soul was a mountain:
he tried every pathway up it; on some he wound easily, dally-
ing in the shade: on others he mounted toilsomely with the hot
sun beating up from the dry, sandy track: they all led to God
enthroned on the summit. Love, hatred, evil, renunciation, all
the forces of humanity at their highest pitch, touched eternity,
and were a part of it. For every man the gateway to eternity
is in himself: for the believer as for the atheist, for him who
sees life everywhere as for him who everywhere denies it, and
for him who doubts both life and the denial of it,—and for
Christophe in whose soul there met all these opposing views of

life. All the opposites become one in eternal Force. For Christophe the chief thing was to wake that Force within himself and in others, to fling armfuls of wood upon the fire, to feed the flames of Eternity, and make them roar and flicker. Through the voluptuous night of Paris a great flame darted in his heart. He thought himself free of Faith, and he was a living torch of Faith.

Nothing was more calculated to outrage the French spirit of irony. Faith is one of the feelings which a too civilized society can least forgive: for it has lost it and hates others to possess it. In the blind or mocking hostility of the majority of men towards the dreams of youth there is for many the bitter thought that they themselves were once even as they, and had ambitions and never realized them. All those who have denied their souls, all those who had the seed of work within them, and have not brought it forth rather to accept the security of an easy, honorable life, think:

" Since I could not do the thing I dreamed, why should they do the things they dream? I will not have them do it."

How many Hedda Gablers are ·there among men! What a relentless struggle is there to crush out strength in its new freedom, with what skill is it killed by silence, irony, wear and tear, discouragement,—and, at the crucial moment, betrayed by some treacherous seductive art! . . .

The type is of all nations. Christophe knew it, for he had met it in Germany. Against such people he was armed. His method of defense was simple: he was the first to attack; pounced on the first move, and declared war on them: he forced these dangerous friends to become his enemies. But if such a policy of frankness was an excellent safeguard for his personality, it was not calculated to advance his career as an artist. Once more Christophe began his German tactics. It was too strong for him. Only one thing was altered: his temper: he was in fine fettle.

Lightheartedly, for the benefit of anybody who cared to listen, he expressed his unmeasured criticism of French artists:

and so he made many enemies. He did not take the precaution, as a wise man would have done, of surrounding himself with a little coterie. He would have found no difficulty in gathering about him a number of artists who would gladly have admired him if he had admired them. There were some who admired him in advance, investing admiration as it were. They considered any man they praised as a debtor, of whom, at a given moment, they could demand repayment. But it was a good investment.—But Christophe was a very bad investment. He never paid back. Worse than that, he was barefaced enough to consider poor the works of men who thought his good. Unavowedly they were rancorous, and engaged themselves on the next opportunity to pay him back in kind.

Among his other indiscretions Christophe was foolish enough to declare war on Lucien Lévy-Cœur. He found him in the way, everywhere, and he could not conceal an extraordinary antipathy for the gentle, polite creature who was doing no apparent harm, and even seemed to be kinder than himself, and was, at any rate, far more moderate. He provoked him into argument: and, however insignificant the subject of it might be, Christophe always brought into it a sudden heat and bitterness which surprised their hearers. It was as though Christophe were seizing every opportunity of battering at Lucien Lévy-Cœur, head down: but he could never reach him. His enemy had an extraordinary skill, even when he was most obviously in the wrong, in carrying it off well: he would defend himself with a courtesy which showed up Christophe's bad manners. Christophe still spoke French very badly, interlarding it with slang, and often with very coarse expressions which he had picked up, and, like many foreigners, used wrongly, and he was incapable of outwitting the tactics of Lucien Lévy-Cœur: and he raged furiously against his gentle irony. Everybody thought him in the wrong, for they could not see what Christophe vaguely felt: the hypocrisy of that gentleness, which, when it was brought up against a force which it could not hold in check, tried quietly to stifle it by silence. He was in

no hurry, for, like Christophe, he counted on time, not, as
Christophe did, to build, but to destroy. He had no difficulty
in detaching Sylvain Kohn and Goujart from Christophe, just
as he had gradually forced him out of the Stevens' circle.
He was isolating Christophe.

Christophe himself helped him. He pleased nobody, for he
would not join any party, but was rather against all parties.
He did not like the Jews: but he liked the anti-Semites even
less. He was revolted by the cowardice of the masses stirred
up against a powerful minority, not because it was bad, but because it was powerful, and by the appeal to the basest instincts
of jealousy and hatred. The Jews came to regard him as
an anti-Semite, and the anti-Semites looked on him as a Jew.
As for the artists, they felt his hostility. Instinctively Christophe made himself more German than he was, in art. Revolting against the voluptuous ataraxia of a certain class of
Parisian music, he set up, with violence, a manly, healthy pessimism. When joy appeared in his music, it was with a want of
taste, a vulgar ardor, which were well calculated to disgust even
the aristocratic patrons of popular art. An erudite, crude
form. In his reaction he was not far from affecting an apparent carelessness in style and a disregard of external originality, which were bound to be offensive to the French musicians.
And so those of them, to whom he sent some of his work, without any careful consideration, visited on it the contempt they
had for the belated Wagnerism of the contemporary German
school. Christophe did not care: he laughed inwardly, and repeated the lines of a charming musician of the French Renaissance—adapted to his own case:

*   *   *   *   *

" *Come, come, don't worry about those who will say:*
  ' *Christophe has not the counterpoint of A,*
  And he has not such harmony as Monsieur B.'
  I have something else which they never will see."

But when he tried to have some of his music performed, he
found the doors shut against him. They had quite enough

to do to play—or not to play—the works of young French musicians, and could not bother about those of an unknown German.

Christophe did not go on trying. He shut himself up in his room and went on writing. He did not much care whether the people of Paris heard him or not. He wrote for his own pleasure and not for success. The true artist is not concerned with the future of his work. He is like those painters of the Renaissance who joyously painted mural decorations, knowing full well that in ten years nothing would be left of them. So Christophe worked on in peace, quite good-humoredly resigned to waiting for better times, when help would come to him from some unexpected source.

Christophe was then attracted by the dramatic form. He dared not yet surrender freely to the flood of his own lyrical impulse. He had to run it into definite channels. And, no doubt, it is a good thing for a young man of genius, who is not yet master of himself, and does not even know exactly what he is, to set voluntary bounds upon himself, and to confine therein the soul of which he has so little hold. They are the dikes and sluices which allow the course of thought to be directed.—Unfortunately Christophe had not a poet: he had himself to fashion his subjects out of legend and history.

Among the visions which had been floating before his mind for some months past were certain figures from the Bible.— That Bible, which his mother had given him as a companion in his exile, had been a source of dreams to him. Although he did not read it in any religious spirit, the moral, or, rather, vital energy of that Hebraic Iliad had been to him a spring in which, in the evenings, he washed his naked soul of the smoke and mud of Paris. He was concerned with the sacred meaning of the book: but it was not the less a sacred book to him, for the breath of savage nature and primitive individualities that he found in its pages. He drew in its hymns of the earth, consumed with faith, quivering moun tains, exultant skies, and human lions.

One of the characters in the book for whom he had an especial tenderness was the young David. He did not give him the ironic smile of the Florentine boy, or the tragic intensity of the sublime works of Michael Angelo and Verrochio: he knew them not. His David was a young shepherd-poet, with a virgin soul, in which heroism slumbered, a Siegfried of the South, of a finer race, and more beautiful, and of greater harmony in mind and body.—For his revolt against the Latin spirit was in vain: unconsciously he had been permeated by that spirit. Not only art influences art, not only mind and thought, but everything about the artist:—people, things, gestures, movements, lines, the light of each town. The atmosphere of Paris is very powerful: it molds even the most rebellious souls. And the soul of a German is less capable than any other of resisting it: in vain does he gird himself in his national pride: of all Europeans the German is the most easily denationalized. Unwittingly the soul of Christophe had already begun to assimilate from Latin art a clarity, a sobriety, an understanding of the emotions, and even, up to a point, a plastic beauty, which otherwise it never would have had. His *David* was the proof of it.

He had endeavored to recreate certain episodes of the youth of David: the meeting with Saul, the fight with Goliath: and he had written the first scene. He had conceived it as a symphonic picture with two characters.

On a deserted plateau, on a moor covered with heather in bloom, the young shepherd lay dreaming in the sun. The serene light, the hum and buzz of tiny creatures, the sweet whispering of the waving grass, the silvery tinkling of the grazing sheep, the mighty beat and rhythm of the earth sang through the dreaming boy unconscious of his divine destiny. Drowsing, his voice and the notes of his flute joined the harmonious silence: and his song was so calmly, so limpidly joyous, that, hearing it, there could be no thought of joy or sorrow, only the feeling that it must be so and could not be otherwise.—Suddenly over the moor reached great shadows: the air was still: life seemed to withdraw into the veins of the earth. Only the music of the flute went on calmly. Saul, with his crazy thoughts, passed. The mad King, racked by his fancy, burned like a flame, devouring itself, flung this way and that by the wind. He breathed prayers and violent abuse, hurling defiance at the void about him, the void within himself. And when he could speak no more and fell breathless to the ground, there rang through the silence the smiling peace of the song of the young shepherd, who had never ceased. Then, with a furious beating in his heart, came Saul in silence up to where the boy lay in the heather: in silence he gazed at him: he sat down by his side and placed his fevered hand on the cool brows of the shepherd. Untroubled, David turned, and smiled, and looked at the King. He laid his hand on Saul's knees, and went on singing and playing his flute. Evening came: David went to sleep in the middle of his song, and Saul wept. And through the starry night there rose once more the serene joyous hymn of nature refreshed, the song of thanksgiving of the soul relieved of its burden.

When he wrote the scene, Christophe had thought of nothing but his own joy: he had never given a thought to the manner of its performance: and it had certainly never occurred to him that it might be produced on the stage. He meant it to be sung at a concert at such time as the concert-halls should be open to him.

One evening he spoke of it to Achille Roussin, and when, by request. he had tried to give him an idea of it on the piano, he was amazed to see Roussin burst into enthusiasm, and declare that it must at all costs be produced at one of the theaters, and that he would see to it. He was even more amazed when, a few days later. he saw that Roussin was perfectly serious: and his amazement grew to stupefaction when he heard that Sylvain Kohn, Goujart, and Lucien Lévy-Cœur were taking it up. He had to admit that their personal animosity had yielded to their love of art: and he was much surprised. The only man who was not eager to see his work produced was himself. It was not suited to the theater: it was nonsense, and almost hurtful to stage it. But Roussin was so insistent, Sylvain Kohn so persuasive, and Goujart so positive, that Christophe yielded to the temptation. He was weak. He was so longing to hear his music!

It was quite easy for Roussin. Manager and artist rushed to please him. It happened that a newspaper was organizing a benefit matinée for some charity. It was arranged that the *David* should be produced. A good orchestra was got together. As for the singers, Roussin claimed that he had found the ideal representative of David.

The rehearsals were begun. The orchestra came through the first reading fairly well, although, as usual in France, there was not much discipline about it. Saul had a good, though rather tired, voice: and he knew his business. The David was a handsome, tall, plump, solid lady with a sentimental vulgar voice which she used heavily, with a melodramatic tremolo and all the café-concert tricks. Christophe scowled. As soon as she began to sing it was obvious that she could not be allowed to play the part. After the first pause in the rehearsal he went to the impresario, who had charge of the business side of the undertaking, and was present, with Sylvain Kohn, at the rehearsal. The impresario beamed and said:

" Well, are you satisfied? "

"Yes," said Christophe. " I think it can be made all right. There's only one thing that won't do: the singer. She must be changed. Tell her as gently as you can: you're used to it. . . . It will be quite easy for you to find me another."

The impresario looked disgruntled: he looked at Christophe as though he could not believe that he was serious; and he said:

" But that's impossible! "

" Why is it impossible? " asked Christophe.

The impresario looked cunningly at Sylvain Kohn, and replied:

" But she has so much talent!"

" Not a spark," said Christophe.

" What! . . . She has a fine voice!"

" Not a bit of it."

" And she is beautiful."

" I don't care a damn."

" That won't hurt the part," said Sylvain Kohn, laughing.

" I want a David, a David who can sing: I don't want Helen of Troy," said Christophe.

The impresario rubbed his nose uneasily.

" It's a pity, a great pity . . ." he said. " She is an excellent artist. . . . I give you my word for it! Perhaps she is not at her best to-day. You must give her another trial."

" All right," said Christophe. " But it is a waste of time."

He went on with the rehearsal. It was worse than ever. He found it hard to go on to the end: it got on his nerves: his remarks to the singer, from cold and polite, became dry and cutting, in spite of the obvious pains she was taking to satisfy him, and the way she ogled him by way of winning his favor. The impresario prudently stopped the rehearsal just when it seemed to be hopeless. By way of softening the bad effect of Christophe's remarks, he bustled up to the singer and paid her heavy compliments. Christophe, who was standing by, made no attempt to conceal his impatience, called the impresario, and said:

" There's no room for argument. I won't have the woman. It's unpleasant, I know: but I did not choose her. Do what you can to arrange the matter."

The impresario bowed frigidly, and said coldly:

" I can't do anything. You must see M. Roussin."

" What has it got to do with M. Roussin? I don't want to bother him with this business," said Christophe.

" That won't bother him," said Sylvain Kohn ironically.

And he pointed to Roussin, who had just come in.

Christophe went up to him. Roussin was in high good humor, and cried:

"What! Finished already? I was hoping to hear a bit of it. Well, maestro, what do you say? Are you satisfied?"

"It's going quite well," said Christophe. "I don't know how to thank you . . ."

"Not at all! Not at all!"

"There is only one thing wrong."

"What is it? We'll put it right. I am determined to satisfy you."

"Well . . . the singer. Between ourselves she is detestable."

The beaming smile on Roussin's face froze suddenly. He said, with some asperity:

"You surprise me, my dear fellow."

"She is useless, absolutely useless," Christophe went on. "She has no voice, no taste, no knowledge of her work, no talent. You're lucky not to have heard her! . . ."

Roussin grew more and more acid. He cut Christophe short, and said cuttingly:

"I know Mlle. de Sainte-Ygraine. She is a very talented artiste. I have the greatest admiration for her. Every man of taste in Paris shares my opinion."

And he turned his back on Christophe, who saw him offer his arm to the actress and go out with her. He was dumfounded, and Sylvain Kohn, who had watched the scene delightedly, took his arm and laughed, and said as they went down the stairs of the theater:—

"Didn't you know that she was his mistress?"

Christophe understood. So it was for her sake and not for his own that his piece was to be produced! That explained Roussin's enthusiasm, the money he had laid out, and the eagerness of his sycophants. He listened while Sylvain Kohn told him the story of the Sainte-Ygraine: a music-hall singer, who, after various successes in the little vaudeville theaters, had, like so many of her kind, been fired with the ambition to be heard on a stage more worthy of her talent. She counted on Roussin to procure her an engagement at the Opéra or the Opéra-Comique: and Roussin, who asked nothing better, had seen in the performance of *David* an opportunity of revealing to the Parisian public at no very great risk the lyrical gifts of the new tragedienne, in a part which called for no particular dramatic acting, and gave her an excellent opportunity of displaying the elegance of her figure.

Christophe heard the story through to the end: then he shook off Sylvain Kohn and burst out laughing. He laughed and laughed. When he had done, he said:

"You disgust me. You all disgust me. Art is nothing to you. It's always women, nothing but women. An opera is put on for a dancer, or a singer, for the mistress of M. So-and-So, or Madame Thingummy. You think of nothing but your dirty little intrigues. Bless you, I'm not angry with you: you are like that: very well then, be so and wallow in your mire. But we must part company: we weren't made to live together. Good-night."

He left him, and when he reached home, wrote to Roussin, saying that he withdrew the piece, and did not disguise his reasons for doing so.

It meant a breach with Roussin and all his gang. The consequences were felt at once. The newspapers had made a certain amount of talk about the forthcoming piece, and the story of the quarrel between the composer and the singer appeared in due course. A certain conductor was adventurous enough to play the piece at a Sunday afternoon concert. His good fortune was disastrous for Christophe. The *David* was played—and hissed. All the singer's friends had passed the word to teach the insolent musician a lesson: and the outside public, who had been bored by the symphonic poem, added their voices to the verdict of the critics. To crown his misfortunes, Christophe was ill-advised enough to accept the invitation to display his talents as a pianist at the same concert by giving a *Fantasia* for piano and orchestra. The unkindly disposition

of the audience, which had been to a certain extent restrained
during the performance of the *David,* out of consideration for
the interpreters, broke loose, when they found themselves face
to face with the composer,—whose playing was not all that it
might have been. Christophe was unnerved by the noise in
the hall, and stopped suddenly half-way through a movement:
and he looked jeeringly at the audience, who were startled
into silence, and played *Malbrouck s'en va-t-en guerre!*—and
said insolently:

" That is all you are fit for."

Then he got up and went away.

There was a terrific row. The audience shouted that he had
insulted them, and that he must come and apologize. Next
day the papers unanimously slaughtered the grotesque German
to whom justice had been meted out by the good taste of
Paris.

And then once more he was left in absolute isolation. Once
more Christophe found himself alone, more solitary than ever,
in that great, hostile, stranger city. He did not worry about
it. He began to think that he was fated to be so, and would
be so all his life.

He did not know that a great soul is never alone, that,
however Fortune may cheat him of friendship, in the end a
great soul creates friends by the radiance of the love with
which it is filled, and that even in that hour, when he thought
himself for ever isolated, he was more rich in love than the
happiest men and women in the world.

Living with the Stevens was a little girl of thirteen or
fourteen, to whom Christophe had given lessons at the same
time as Colette. She was a distant cousin of Colette's, and her
name was Grazia Buontempi. She was a little girl with a
golden-brown complexion, with cheeks delicately tinged with
red: healthy-looking: she had a little aquiline nose, a large
well-shaped mouth, always half-open, a round chin, very white,
calm clear eyes, softly smiling, a round forehead framed in

masses of long, silky hair, which fell in long, waving locks loosely down to her shoulders. She was like a little Virgin of Andrea del Sarto, with her wide face and serenely gazing eyes.

She was Italian. Her parents lived almost all the year round in the country on an estate in the North of Italy: plains, fields, little canals. From the loggia on the housetop they looked down on golden vines, from which here and there the black spikes of the cypress-trees emerged. Beyond them were fields, and again fields. Silence. The lowing of the oxen returning from the fields, and the shrill cries of the peasants at the plow were to be heard:

"*Ihi! . . . Fat innanz'! . . .*"

Grasshoppers chirruped in the trees, frogs croaked by the waterside. And at night there was infinite silence under the silver beams of the moon. In the distance, from time to time, the watchers by the crops, sleeping in huts of branches, fired their guns by way of warning thieves that they were awake. To those who heard them drowsily, these noises meant no more than the chiming of a dull clock in the distance, marking the hours of the night. And silence closed again, like a soft cloak, about the soul.

Round little Grazia life seemed asleep. Her people did not give her much attention. In the calmness and beauty that was all about her she grew up peacefully without haste, without fever. She was lazy, and loved to dawdle and to sleep. For hours together she would lie in the garden. She would let herself be borne onward by the silence like a fly on a summer stream. And sometimes, suddenly, for no reason, she would begin to run. She would run like a little animal, head and shoulders a little leaning to the right, moving easily and supply. She was like a kid climbing and slithering among the stones for the sheer joy of leaping about. She would talk to the dogs, the frogs, the grass, the trees, the peasants, and the beasts in the farmyard. She adored all the creatures about her, great and small: but she was less at her ease with the great. She saw very few people. The estate was isolated and far from any town. Very rarely there came along the dusty road some trudging, solemn peasant, or lovely country woman, with bright eyes and sunburnt face, walking with a slow rhythm, head high and chest well out. For days together Grazia lived alone in the silence of the garden: she saw no one: she was never bored: she was afraid of nothing.

One day a tramp came, stealing fowls. He stopped dead when he saw the little girl lying on the grass, eating a piece of bread and butter and humming to herself. She looked up at him calmly, and asked him what he wanted. He said:

" Give me something, or I'll hurt you."

She held out her piece of bread and butter and smiled, and said:

" You must not do harm."

Then he went away.

Her mother died. Her father, a kind, weak man, was an old Italian of a good family, robust, jovial, affectionate, but rather childish, and he was quite incapable of bringing up his child. Old Buontempi's sister, Madame Stevens, came to the funeral, and was struck by the loneliness of the child, and decided to take her back to Paris for a while, to distract her from her grief. Grazia and her father wept: but when Madame Stevens had made up her mind to anything, there was nothing for it but to give in: nobody could stand out against her. She had the brains of the family: and, in her house in Paris, she directed everything, dominated everybody: her husband, her daughter, her lovers:—for she had not denied herself in the matter of love: she went straight at her duties, and her pleasures: she was a practical woman and a passionate—very worldly and very restless.

Transplanted to Paris, Grazia adored her pretty cousin Colette, whom she amused. The pretty little savage was taken out into society and to the theater. They treated her as a child, and she regarded herself as a child, although she was a child no longer. She had feelings which she hid away, for she was fearful of them: accesses of tenderness for some person or thing. She was secretly in love with Colette, and would steal a ribbon or a handkerchief that belonged to her: often in her presence, she could not speak a word: and when she expected her, when she knew that she was going to see her, she would tremble with impatience and happiness. At the theater when she saw her pretty cousin, in evening dress, come into the box and attract general attention, she would smile humbly, affectionately, lovingly: and her heart would leap when Colette spoke to her. Dressed in white, with her beautiful black hair loose and hanging over her shoulders, biting the fingers of her long white cotton gloves, and idly poking her fingers through the holes,—every other minute during the play she would turn towards Colette in the hope of meeting a friendly look, to share the pleasure she was feeling, and to say with her clear brown eyes:

" I love you."

When they were out together in the Bois, outside Paris, she would walk in Colette's shadow, sit at her feet; run in front of her, break off branches that might be in her way, place stones in the mud for her to walk on. And one evening in the garden, when Colette shivered and asked for her shawl, she gave a little cry of delight—she was at once ashamed of it—to think that her beloved would be wrapped in something of hers, and would give it back to her presently filled with the scent of her body.

There were books, certain passages in the poets, which she read in secret—(for she was still given children's books)—which gave her delicious thrills. And there were more even in certain passages in music, although she was told that she could not understand them: and she persuaded herself that she did not understand them:—but she would turn pale and cold with emotion. No one knew what was happening within her at such moments.

Outside that she was just a docile little girl, dreamy, lazy, greedy, blushing on the slightest provocation, now silent for hours together, now talking volubly, easily touched to tears and laughter, breaking suddenly into fits of sobbing or childish laughter. She loved to laugh, and silly little things would amuse her. She never tried to be grown up. She remained a child. She was, above all, kind and could not bear to hurt any-body, and she was hurt by the least angry word addressed to herself. She was very modest and retiring, ready to love and admire anything that seemed good and beautiful to her, and so she attributed to others qualities which they did not possess.

She was being educated, for she was very backward. And that was how she came to be taught music by Christophe.

She saw him for the first time at a crowded party in her aunt's house. Christophe, who was incapable of adapting himself to his audience, played an interminable *adagio* which made everybody yawn: when it seemed to be over he began again: and everybody wondered if it was ever going to end. Madame Stevens was boiling with impatience: Colette was highly amused: she was enjoying the absurdity of it, and rather pleased with Christophe for being so insensible of it: she felt that he was a force, and she liked that: but it was comic too: and she would have been the last person to defend him. Grazia alone was moved to tears by the music. She hid herself away in a corner of the room. When it was over she went away, so that no one should see her emotion, and also because she could not bear to see people making fun of Christophe.

A few days later, at dinner, Madame Stevens in her presence spoke of her having music-lessons from Christophe. Grazia was so upset that she let her spoon drop into her soup-plate, and splashed herself and her neighbor. Colette said she ought first to have lessons in table-manners. Madame Stevens added that Christophe was not the person to go to for that. Grazia was glad to be scolded in Christophe's company.

Christophe began to teach her. She was stiff and frozen, and held her arms close to her sides, and could not stir: and when Christophe placed his hand on hers, to correct the

position of her fingers, and stretched them over the keys, she
nearly fainted. She was fearful of playing badly for him:
but in vain did she practise until she nearly made herself ill,
and evoked impatient protests from her cousin: she always
played vilely when Christophe was present: she was breathless, and her fingers were as stiff as pieces of wood, or as flabby
as cotton: she struck the wrong notes and gave the emphasis
all wrong: Christophe would lose his temper, scold her, and
go away: then she would long to die.

He paid no attention to her, and thought only of Colette.
Grazia was envious of her cousin's intimacy with Christophe:
but, although it hurt her, in her heart she was glad both for
Colette and for Christophe. She thought Colette so superior to
herself that it seemed natural to her that she should monopolize
attention.—It was only when she had to choose between her
cousin and Christophe that she felt her heart turn against
Colette. With her girlish intuition she saw that Christophe
was made to suffer by Colette's coquetry, and the persistent
courtship of her by Lucien Lévy-Cœur. Instinctively she disliked Lévy-Cœur, and she detested him as soon as she knew
that Christophe detested him. She could not understand how
Colette could admit him as a rival to Christophe. She began
secretly to judge him harshly. She discovered certain of his
small hypocrisies, and suddenly changed her manner towards
him. Colette saw it, but did not guess the cause: she pretended
to ascribe it to a little girl's caprice. But it was very certain
that she had lost her power over Grazia: as was shown by a
trifling incident. One evening, when they were walking together in the garden, a gentle rain came on, and Colette,
tenderly, though coquettishly, offered Grazia the shelter of her
cloak: Grazia, for whom, a few weeks before, it would have been
happiness ineffable to be held close to her beloved cousin,
moved away coldly, and walked on in silence at a distance of
some yards. And when Colette said that she thought a piece
of music that Grazia was playing was ugly, Grazia was not
kept from playing and loving it.

She was only concerned with Christophe. She had the insight of her tenderness, and saw that he was suffering, without his saying a word. She exaggerated it in her childish, uneasy regard for him. She thought that Christophe was in love with Colette, when he had really no more than an exacting friendship. She thought he was unhappy, and she was unhappy for him, and she had little reward for her anxiety. She paid for it when Colette had infuriated Christophe: then he was surly and avenged himself on his pupil, waxing wrathful with her mistakes. One morning when Colette had exasperated him more than usual, he sat down by the piano so savagely that Grazia lost the little nerve she had: she floundered: he angrily scolded her for her mistakes: then she lost her head altogether: he fumed, wrung his hands, declared that she would never do anything properly, and that she had better occupy herself with cooking, sewing, anything she liked, only, in Heaven's name, she must not go on with her music! It was not worth the trouble of torturing people with her mistakes. With that he left her in the middle of her lesson. He was furious. And poor Grazia wept, not so much for the humiliation of anything he had said to her, as for despair at not being able to please Christophe, when she longed to do so, and could only succeed in adding to his sufferings. The greatest grief was when Christophe ceased to go to the Stevens' house. Then she longed to go home. The poor child, so healthy, even in her dreams, in whom there was much of the sweet peace of the country, felt ill at ease in the town, among the neurasthenic, restless women of Paris. She never dared say anything, but she had come to a fairly accurate estimation of the people about her. But she was shy, and, like her father, weak, from kindness, modesty, distrust of herself. She submitted to the authority of her domineering aunt and her cousin, who was used to tyrannizing over everybody. She dared not write to her father, to whom she wrote regularly long, affectionate letters:

"Please, please, take me home!"

And her father dared not take her home, in spite of his

own longing: for Madame Stevens had answered his timid
advances by saying that Grazia was very well off where she
was, much better off than she would be with him, and that she
must stay for the sake of her education.

But there came a time when her exile was too hard for the
little southern creature, a time when she had to fly back towards
the light.—That was after Christophe's concert. She went to
it with the Stevens: and she was tortured by the hideous sight
of the rabble amusing themselves with insulting an artist. . . .
An artist? The man who, in Grazia's eyes, was the very type of
art, the personification of all that was divine in life! She
was on the point of tears; she longed to get away. She had
to listen to all the caterwauling, the hisses, the howls, and, when
they reached home, to the laughter of Colette as she exchanged
pitying remarks with Lucien Lévy-Cœur. She escaped to her
room, and through part of the night she sobbed: she spoke to
Christophe, and consoled him: she would gladly have given her
life for him, and she despaired of ever being able to do anything to make him happy. It was impossible for her to stay in
Paris any longer. She begged her father to take her away,
saying:

" I cannot live here any longer; I cannot: I shall die if you
leave me here any longer."

Her father came at once, and though it was very painful to
them both to stand up to her terrible aunt, they screwed up their
courage for it by a desperate effort of will.

Grazia returned to the sleepy old estate. She was glad to
get back to Nature and the creatures that she loved. Every
day she gathered comfort for her sorrow, but in her heart there
remained a little of the melancholy of the North, like a veil
of mist, that very slowly melted away before the sun. Sometimes she thought of Christophe's wretchedness. Lying on the
grass, listening to the familiar frogs and grasshoppers, or sitting
at her piano, which now she played more often than before,
she would dream of the friend her heart had chosen: she would
talk to him, in whispers, for hours together, and it seemed

not impossible to her that one day he would open the door and come in to her. She wrote to him, and, after long hesitation, she sent the letter, unsigned, which, one day, with beating heart, she went secretly and dropped into the box in the village two miles away, beyond the long plowed fields,—a kind, good, touching letter, in which she told him that he was not alone, that he must not be discouraged, that there was one who thought of him, and loved him, and prayed to God for him,—a poor little letter, which was lost in the post, so that he never received it.

Then the serene, monotonous days succeeded each other in the life of his distant friend. And the Italian peace, the genius of tranquillity, calm happiness, silent contemplation, once more took possession of that chaste and silent heart, in whose depths there still burned, like a little constant flame, the memory of Christophe.

But Christophe never knew of the simple love that watched over him from afar, and was later to fill so great a room in his life. Nor did he know that at that same concert, where he had been insulted, there sat the woman who was to be the beloved, the dear companion, destined to walk by his side, shoulder to shoulder, hand in hand.

He was alone. He thought himself alone. But he did not suffer overmuch. He did not feel that bitter anguish that had given him such great agony in Germany. He was stronger. riper: he knew that it must be so. His illusions about Paris were destroyed: men were everywhere the same: he must be a law unto himself, and not waste strength in a childish struggle with the world: he must be himself, calmly, tranquilly. As Beethoven had said, " If we surrender the forces of our lives to life, what, then, will be left for the noblest and highest? " He had firmly grasped a knowledge of his nature and the temper of his race, which formerly he had so harshly judged. The more he was oppressed by the atmosphere of Paris, the more keenly did he feel the need of taking refuge in his own coun·

try, in the arms of the poets and musicians, in whom the best
of Germany is garnered and preserved. As soon as he opened
their books his room was filled with the sound of the sunlit
Rhine and lit by the loving smiles of old friends new found.

How ungrateful he had been to them! How was it he had
failed to feel the treasure of their goodness and honesty? He
remembered with shame all the unjust, outrageous things he
had said of them when he was in Germany. Then he saw
only their defects, their awkward ceremonious manners, their
tearful idealism, their little mental hypocrisies, their
cowardice. Ah! How small were all these things compared
with their great virtues! How could he have been so hard
upon their weaknesses, which now made them even more moving in his eyes: for they were more human for them! In his
reaction he was the more attracted to those of them to whom he
had been most unjust. What things he had said about Schubert
and Bach! And now he felt so near to them. Now it was
as though these noble souls, whose foibles he had so scorned,
leaned over him, now that he was in exile and far from his
own people, and smiled kindly and said:

"Brother, we are here! Courage! We too have had more
than our share of misery. . . . Bah! one wins through
it. . . ."

He heard the soul of Johann Sebastian Bach roaring like
the sea: hurricanes, winds howling, the clouds of life scudding,
—men and women drunk with joy, sorrow, fury, and the
Christ, all meekness, the Prince of Peace, hovering above
them,—towns awakened by the cries of the watchmen, running with glad shouts, to meet the divine Bridegroom, whose
footsteps shake the earth,—the vast store of thoughts, passions,
musical forms, heroic life, Shakespearean hallucinations,
Savonarolaesque prophecies, pastoral, epic, apocalyptic visions,
all contained in the stunted body of the little Thuringian *cantor,*
with his double chin, and little shining eyes under the wrinkled
lids and the raised eyebrows . . .—he could see him so clearly!
somber, jovial, a little absurd, with his head stuffed full of

allegories and symbols, Gothic and rococo, choleric, obstinate, serene, with a passion for life, and a great longing for death . . .—he saw him in his school, a genial pedant, surrounded by his pupils, dirty, coarse, vagabond, ragged, with hoarse voices, the ragamuffins with whom he squabbled, and some-times fought like a navvy, one of whom once gave him a mighty thrashing . . .—he saw him with his family, surrounded by his twenty-one children, of whom thirteen died before him, and one was an idiot, and the rest were good musicians who gave little concerts. . . . Sickness, burial, bitter disputes, want, his genius misunderstood:—and through and above it all, his music, his faith, deliverance and light, joy half seen, felt, desired, grasped,—God, the breath of God kindling his bones, thrilling through his flesh, thundering from his lips. . . . O Force! Force! Thrice joyful thunder of Force! . . .

Christophe took great draughts of that force. He felt the blessing of that power of music which issues from the depths of the German soul. Often mediocre, and even coarse, what does it matter? The great thing is that it is so, and that it flows plenteously. In France music is gathered carefully, drop by drop, and passed through Pasteur filters into bottles, and then corked. And the drinkers of stale water are disgusted by the rivers of German music! They examine minutely the de-fects of the German men of genius!

"Poor little things!"—thought Christophe, forgetting that he himself had once been just as absurd—"they find fault with Wagner and Beethoven! They must have faultless men of genius! . . . As though, when the tempest rages, it would take care not to upset the existing order of things! . . ."

He strode about Paris rejoicing in his strength. If he were misunderstood, so much the better! He would be all the freer. To create, as genius must, a whole world, organically constituted according to his own inward laws, the artist must live in it altogether. An artist can never be too much alone. What is terrible is to see his ideas reflected in a mirror which deforms and stunts them. He must say nothing to others of what he is doing until he has done it: otherwise he would **never** have the courage to go on to the end: for it would no longer be his idea, but the miserable idea of others that would live in him.

Now that there was nothing to disturb his dreams, they bubbled forth like springs from all the corners of his soul, and from every stone of the roads by which he walked. He was living in a visionary state. Everything he saw and heard called forth in him creatures and things different from those he saw and heard. He had only to live to find everywhere about him the life of his heroes. Their sensations came to him of their own accord. The eyes of the passers-by, the sound of a voice borne by the wind, the light on a lawn, the birds singing in the trees of the Luxembourg, a convent-bell ringing so far away, the pale sky, the little patch of sky seen from his room, the sounds and shades of sound of the different hours of the day, all these were not in himself, but in the creatures of his dreams.—Christophe was happy.

But his material position was worse than ever. He had lost his few pupils, his only resource. It was September, and rich people were out of town, and it was difficult to find new pupils. The only one he had was an engineer, a crazy, clever fellow, who had taken it into his head, at forty, to become a great violinist. Christophe did not play the violin very well: but he knew more about it than his pupil: and for some time he gave him three hours a week at two francs an hour. But at the end of six weeks the engineer got tired of it, and suddenly discovered that painting was his vocation.—When he imparted his discovery to Christophe, Christophe laughed heartily: but, when he had done laughing, he reckoned up his finances, and found that he had in hand the twelve francs which his pupil had just paid him for his last lessons. That did **not** worry him: he only said to himself that he must certainly set about finding some other means of living, and start once more going from publisher to publisher. That was not very pleasant. . . . Pff! . . . . It was useless to torment himself in advance. It was a jolly day. He went to Meudon.

He had a sudden longing for a walk. As he walked there
rose in him scraps of music. He was as full of it as a hive
of honey: and he laughed aloud at the golden buzzing of his
bees. For the most part it was changing music. And lively
leaping rhythms, insistent, haunting. . . . Much good it is
to create and fashion music buried within four walls! There
you can only make combinations of subtle, hard, unyielding
harmonies, like the Parisians!

When he was weary he lay down in the woods. The trees
were half in leaf, the sky was periwinkle blue. Christophe
dozed off dreamily, and in his dreams there was the color of
the sweet light falling from October clouds. His blood throbbed.
He listened to the rushing flood of his ideas. They came from
all corners of the earth: worlds, young and old, at war, rags
and tatters of dead souls, guests and parasites that once had
dwelled within him, as in a city. The words that Gottfried
had spoken by the grave of Melchior returned to him: he was
a living tomb, filled with the dead, striving in him,—all his unknown forefathers. He listened to those countless lives, it
delighted him to set the organ roaring, the roaring of that
age-old forest, full of monsters, like the forest of Dante. He
was no longer fearful of them as he had been in his youth.
For the master was there: his will. It was a great joy to him
to crack his whip and make the beasts howl, and feel the
wealth of living creatures in himself. He was not alone. There
was no danger of his ever being alone. He was a host in himself. Ages of Kraffts, healthy and rejoicing in their health.
Against hostile Paris, against a hostile people, he could set a
whole people: the fight was equal.

He had left the modest room—it was too expensive—which
he occupied and taken an attic in the Montrouge district. It
was well aired, though it had no other advantage. There was
a continual draught. But he wanted to breathe. From his
window he had a wide view over the chimneys of Paris to Montmartre in the background. It had not taken him long to move:

a handcart was enough: Christophe pushed it himself. Of all
his possessions the most precious to him, after his old bag,
was one of those casts, which have lately become so popular,
of the death-mask of Beethoven. He packed it with as much
care as though it were a priceless work of art. He never let
it out of his sight. It was an oasis in the midst of the desert
of Paris. And also it served him as a moral thermometer.
The death-mask indicated more clearly than his own conscience
the temperature of his soul, the character of his most secret
thoughts: now a cloudy sky, now the gusty wind of the passions,
now fine calm weather.

He had to be sparing with his food. He only ate once a
day, at one in the afternoon. He bought a large sausage, and
hung it up in his window: a thick slice of it, a hunk of bread,
and a cup of coffee that he made himself were a feast for the
gods. He would have preferred two such feasts. He was angry
with himself for having such a good appetite. He called himself to task, and thought himself a glutton, thinking only of his
stomach. He lost flesh: he was leaner than a famished dog.
But he was solidly built, he had an iron constitution, and his
head was clear.

He did not worry about the morrow, though he had good reason for doing so. As long as he had in hand money enough
for the day he never bothered about it. When he came to the
end of his money he made up his mind to go the round of the
publishers once more. He found no work. He was on his way
home, empty, when, happening to pass the music-shop where he
had been introduced to Daniel Hecht by Sylvain Kohn, he went
in without remembering that he had already been there under
not very pleasant circumstances. The first person he saw was
Hecht. He was on the point of turning tail: but he was too
late: Hecht had seen him. Christophe did not wish to seem to
be avoiding him: he went up to Hecht, not knowing what to
say to him, and fully prepared to stand up to him as arrogantly as need be: for he was convinced that Hecht would be
unsparingly insolent. But he was nothing of the kind. Hecht

coldly held out his hand, muttered some conventional inquiry
after his health, and, without waiting for any request from
Christophe, he pointed to the door of his office, and stepped
aside to let him pass. He was secretly glad of the visit,
which he had foreseen, though he had given up expecting it.
Without seeming to do so, he had carefully followed Christophe's doings: he had missed no opportunity of hearing his
music: he had been at the famous performance of the *David*:
and, despising the public, he had not been greatly surprised
at its hostile reception, since he himself had felt the beauty of
the work. There were probably not two people in Paris more
capable than Hecht of appreciating Christophe's artistic originality. But he took care not to say anything about it, not only
because his vanity was hurt by Christophe's attitude towards
himself, but because it was impossible for him to be amiable:
it was the peculiarly ungracious quality of his nature. He was
sincerely desirous of helping Christophe: but he would not
have stirred a finger to do so: he was waiting for Christophe to
come and ask it of him. And now that Christophe had come,—
instead of generously seizing the opportunity of wiping out the
memory of their previous misunderstanding by sparing his
visitor any humiliation, he gave himself the satisfaction of
hearing him make his request at length: and he even went so
far as to offer Christophe, at least for the time being, the
work which he had formerly refused. He gave him fifty pages
of music to transpose for mandoline and guitar by the next
day. After which, being satisfied that he had made him truckle
down, he found him less distasteful work, but always so ungraciously that it was impossible to be grateful to him for it:
Christophe had to be ground down by necessity before he would
ever go to Hecht again. In any case he preferred to earn his
money by such work, however irritating it might be, than accept it as a gift from Hecht, as it was once more offered to
him:—and, indeed, Hecht meant it kindly: but Christophe had
been conscious of Hecht's original intention to humiliate him:
he was forced to accept his conditions, but nothing would in-

duce him to accept any favor from him: he was willing to work for him:—by giving and giving he squared the account:—but he would not be under any obligation to him. Unlike Wagner, that impudent mendicant where his art was concerned, he did not place his art above himself: the bread that he had not earned himself would have choked him.—One day, when he brought some work that he had sat up all night to finish, he found Hecht at table. Hecht, remarking his pallor and the hungry glances that involuntarily he cast at the dishes, felt sure that he had not eaten that day, and invited him to lunch. He meant kindly, but he made it so apparent that he had noticed Christophe's straits that his invitation looked like charity: Christophe would have died of hunger rather than accept. He could not refuse to sit down at the table—(Hecht said he wanted to talk to him):—but he did not touch a morsel: he pretended that he had just had lunch. His stomach was aching with hunger.

Christophe would gladly have done without Hecht: but the other publishers were even worse.—There were also wealthy amateurs who had conceived some scrap of a musical idea, and could not even write it down. They would send for Christophe, hum over their lucubrations, and say:

" Isn't it fine? "

Then they would give them to him for elaboration,—(to be written):—and then they would appear under their own names through some great publishing house. They were quite convinced that they had composed them themselves. Christophe knew such a one, a distinguished nobleman, a strange, restless creature, who would suddenly call him " Dear friend," grasp him by the arm, and burst into a torrent of enthusiastic demonstrations, talking and giggling, babbling and telling funny stories, interlarded with cries of ecstatic laughter: Beethoven, Verlaine, Fauré, Yvette Guilbert. . . . He made him work, and failed to pay. He worked it out in invitations to lunch and handshakes. Finally he sent Christophe twenty francs, which Christophe gave himself the foolish luxury of returning. That day he had not twenty sous in the world: and he had to buy a twenty-five centimes stamp for a letter to his mother. It was Louisa's birthday, and Christophe would not for the world have failed her: the poor old creature counted on her son's letter, and could not have endured disappointment. For some weeks past she had been writing to him more frequently, in spite of the pain it caused her. She was suffering from her loneliness. But she could not bring herself to join Christophe in Paris: she was too timid, too much attached to her own little town, to her church, her house, and she was afraid of traveling. And besides, if she had wanted to come, Christophe had not enough money: he had not always enough for himself.

He had been given a great deal of pleasure once by receiving a letter from Lorchen, the peasant girl for whose sake he had plunged into the brawl with the Prussian soldiers:[1] she wrote to tell him that she was going to be married: she gave him news of his mother, and sent him a basket of apples and a piece of cake to eat in her honor. They came in the nick of time. That evening with Christophe was a fast, Ember Days, Lent: only the butt end of the sausage hanging by the window was left. Christophe compared himself to the anchorite saints fed by a crow among the rocks. But no doubt the crow was hard put to it to feed all the anchorites, for he never came again.

In spite of all his difficulties Christophe kept his end up. He washed his linen in his basin, and cleaned his boots, whistling like a blackbird. He consoled himself with the saying of Berlioz: "Let us raise our heads above the miseries of life, and let us blithely sing the familiar gay refrain, *Dies iræ.* . . ."—He used to sing it sometimes, to the dismay of his neighbors, who were amazed and shocked to hear him break off in the middle and shout with laughter.

He led a life of stern chastity. As Berlioz remarked: "The lover's life is a life for the idle and the rich." Christophe's poverty, his daily hunt for bread, his excessive sobriety, and

[1] See *Jean-Christophe*—I, "Revolt."

his creative fever left him neither the time nor the taste for any thought of pleasure. He was more than indifferent about it: in his reaction against Paris he had plunged into a sort of moral asceticism. He had a passionate need of purity, a horror of any sort of dirtiness. It was not that he was rid of his passions. At other times he had been swept headlong by them. But his passions remained chaste even when he yielded to them: for he never sought pleasure through them but the absolute giving of himself and fulness of being. And when he saw that he had been deceived he flung them furiously from him. Lust was not to him a sin like any other. It was the great Sin, that which poisons the very springs of life. All those in whom the old Christian belief has not been crusted over with strange conceptions, all those who still feel in themselves the vigor and life of the races, which through the strengthening of an heroic discipline have built up Western civilization, will have no difficulty in understanding him. Christophe despised cosmopolitan society, whose only aim and creed was pleasure.—In truth it is good to seek pleasure, to desire pleasure for all men, to combat the cramping pessimistic beliefs, that have come to weigh upon humanity through twenty centuries of Gothic Christianity. But that can only be upon condition that it is a generous faith, earnestly desirous of the good of others. But instead of that, what happens? The most pitiful egoism. A handful of loose-living men and women trying to give their senses the maximum of pleasure with the minimum of risk, while they take good care that the rest shall drudge for it.—Yes, no doubt, they have their parlor Socialism! . . . But they know perfectly well that their doctrine of pleasure is only practicable for "well-fed" people, for a select pampered few, that it is poison to the poor. . . .

"The life of pleasure is a rich man's life."

Christophe was neither rich nor likely to become so. When he made a little money he spent it at once on music: he went without food to go to concerts. He would take cheap seats in the gallery of the *Théâtre du Châtelet:* and he would steep himself in music: he found both food and love in it. He had such a hunger for happiness and so great a power of enjoying it that the imperfections of the orchestra never worried him: he would stay for two or three hours, drowsy and beatific, and wrong notes or defective taste never provoked in him more than an indulgent smile: he left his critical faculty outside: he was there to love, not to judge. Around him the audience sat motionless, with eyes half closed, letting itself be borne on by the great torrent of dreams. Christophe fancied them as a mass of people curled up in the shade, like an enormous cat, weaving fantastic dreams of lust and carnage. In the deep golden shadows certain faces stood out, and their strange charm and silent ecstasy drew Christophe's eyes and heart: he loved them: he listened through them: he became them, body and soul. One woman in the audience became aware of it, and between her and Christophe during the concert there was woven one of those obscure sympathies, which touch the very depths, though never by one word are they translated into the region of consciousness, while, when the concert is over and the thread that binds soul to soul is snapped, nothing is left of it. It is a state familiar to lovers of music, especially when they are young and do most wholly surrender: the essence of music is so completely love, that the full savor of it is not won unless it be enjoyed through another, and so it is that, at a concert, we instinctively seek among the throng for friendly eyes, for a friend with whom to share a joy too great for ourselves alone.

Among such friends, the friends of one brief hour, whom Christophe marked out for choice of love, the better to taste the sweetness of the music, he was attracted by one face which he saw again and again, at every concert. It was the face of a little grisette who seemed to adore music without understanding it at all. She had an odd little profile, a short, straight nose, almost in line with her slightly pouting lips and delicately molded chin, fine arched eyebrows, and clear eyes: one

of those pretty little faces behind the veil of which one feels
joy and laughter concealed by calm indifference. It is perhaps in such light-hearted girls, little creatures working for
their living, that one finds most the old serenity that is no
more, the serenity of the antique statues and the faces of
Raphael. There is but one moment in their lives, the first
awakening of pleasure: all too soon their lives are sullied.
But at least they have lived for one lovely hour.

It gave Christophe an exquisite pleasure to look at her:
a pretty face would always warm his heart: he could enjoy
without desire: he found joy in it, force, comfort,—almost
virtue. It goes without saying that she quickly became aware
that he was watching her: and, unconsciously, there was set up
between them a magnetic current. And as they met at almost every concert, almost always in the same places, they
quickly learned each other's likes and dislikes. At certain
passages they would exchange meaning glances: when she particularly liked some melody she would just put out her tongue
as though to lick her lips: or, to show that she did not think
much of it, she would disdainfully wrinkle up her pretty nose.
In these little tricks of hers there was a little of that innocent
posing of which hardly any one can be free when he knows
that he is being watched. During serious music she would
sometimes try to look grave and serious: and she would turn
her profile towards him, and look absorbed, and smile to herself, and look out of the corner of her eye to see if he were
watching. They had become very good friends, without exchanging a word, and even without having attempted—at least
Christophe did not—to meet outside.

At last by chance at an evening concert they found themselves sitting next each other. After a moment of smiling
hesitation they began to talk amicably. She had a charming
voice and said many stupid things about music: for she knew
nothing about it and wanted to seem as if she knew: but she
loved it passionately. She loved the worst and the best, Massenet and Wagner: only the mediocre bored her. Music was a

physical pleasure to her: she drank it in through all the pores of her skin as Danaë did the golden rain. The prelude of *Tristan* made her blood run cold: and she loved feeling herself being carried away, like some warrior's prey, by the *Symphonia Eroica.* She told Christophe that Beethoven was deaf and dumb, and that, in spite of it all, if she had known him, she would have loved him, although he was precious ugly. Christophe protested that Beethoven was not so very ugly: then they argued about beauty and ugliness: and she agreed that it was a matter of taste: what was beautiful for one person was not so for another: " We're not golden louis and can't please every one." He preferred her when she did not talk: he understood her better. During the death of Isolde she held out her hand to him: her hand was warm and moist: he held it in his until the end of the piece: they could feel life coursing through the veins of their clasped hands.

They went out together: it was near midnight. They walked back to the Latin Quarter talking eagerly: she had taken his arm and he took her home: but when they reached the door, and she seemed to suggest that he should go up and see her room, he disregarded her smile and the friendliness in her eyes and left her. At first she was amazed, then furious: then she laughed aloud at the thought of his stupidity: and then, when she had reached her room and began to undress, she felt hurt and angry, and finally wept in silence. When next she met him at a concert she tried to be dignified and indifferent and crushing. But he was so kind to her that she could not hold to her resolution. They began to talk once more: only now she was a little reserved with him. He talked to her warmly but very politely and always about serious things, and the music to which they were listening and what it meant to him. She listened attentively and tried to think as he did. The meaning of his words often escaped her: but she believed him all the same. She was grateful to Christophe and had a respect for him which she hardly showed. By tacit agreement they only spoke to each other at concerts. He met her once sur-

rounded with students.   They bowed gravely.   She never talked
about him to any one.   In the depths of her soul there was a
little sanctuary, a quality of beauty, purity, consolation.

And so Christophe, by his presence, by the mere fact of his
existence, exercised an influence that brought strength and
solace.   Wherever he passed he unconsciously left behind the
traces of his inward light.   He was the last to have any notion
of it.   Near him, in the house where he lived, there were people
whom he had never seen, people who, without themselves suspecting it, gradually came under the spell of his beneficent
radiance.

For several weeks Christophe had no money for concerts
even by fasting: and in his attic under the roof, now that
winter was coming in, he was numbed with the cold: he could
not sit still at his table.   Then he would get up and walk
about Paris, trying to warm himself.   He had the faculty of
forgetting the seething town about him, and slipping away
into space and the infinite.   It was enough for him to see
above the noisy street the dead, frozen moon, hung there in the
abysm of the sky, or the sun, like a disc, rolling through the
white mist; then Paris would sink down into the boundless
void and all the life of it would seem to be no more than the
phantom of a life that had been once, long, long ago . . .
ages ago . . .   The smallest tiny sign, imperceptible to the
common lot of men, of the great wild life of Nature, so sparsely
covered with the livery of civilization, was enough to make it
all come rushing mightily up before his gaze.   The grass growing between the stones of the streets, the budding of a tree
strangled by its cast-iron cage, airless, earthless, on some bleak
boulevard: a dog, a passing bird, the last relics of the beasts
and birds that thronged the primeval world, which man has
since destroyed: a whirling cloud of flies: the mysterious epidemic that raged through a whole district:—these were enough
in the thick air of that human hothouse to bring the breath of
the Spirit of the Earth up to slap his cheeks and whip his
energy to action.

During those long walks, when he was often starving, and often had not spoken to a soul for days together, his wealth of dreams seemed inexhaustible. Privation and silence had aggravated his morbid heated condition. At night he slept feverishly, and had exhausting dreams: he saw once more and never ceased to see the old house and the room in which he had lived as a child: he was haunted by musical obsessions. By day he talked and never ceased to talk to the creatures within himself and the beings whom he loved, the absent and the dead.

One cold afternoon in December, when the grass was covered with frost, and the roofs of the houses and the great domes were glistening through the fog, and the trees, with their cold, twisted, naked branches, groping through the mist that hung about them, looked like great weeds at the bottom of the sea,— Christophe, who had been shivering all day and could not get warm again, went into the Louvre, which he hardly knew at all.

Till then painting had never moved him much. He was too much absorbed by the world within himself to grasp the world of color and form. They only acted on him through their music and rhythm, which only brought him an indistinguishable echo of their truth. No doubt his instinct did obscurely divine the selfsame laws that rule the harmony of visible form, as of the form of sounds, and the deep waters of the soul, from which spring the two rivers of color and sound, to flow down the two sides of the mountain of life. But he only knew one side of the mountain, and he was lost in the kingdom of the eye, which was not his. And so he missed the secret of the most exquisite, and perhaps the most natural charm of clear-eyed France, the queen of the world of light.

Even had he been interested in painting, Christophe was too German to adapt himself to so widely different a vision of things. He was not one of those up-to-date Germans who decry the German way of feeling, and persuade themselves that they

admire and love French Impressionism or the artists of the
eighteenth century,—except when they go farther and are convinced that they understand them better than the French.
Christophe was a barbarian, perhaps: but he was frank about it.
The pink flesh of Boucher, the fat chins of Watteau, the bored
shepherds and plump, tight-laced shepherdesses, the whipped-
cream souls, the virtuous oglings of Greuze, the tucked shirts
of Fragonard, all that bare-legged poesy interested him no more
than a fashionable, rather spicy newspaper. He did not see
its rich and brilliant harmony; the voluptuous and sometimes
melancholy dreams of that old civilization, the highest in Europe,
were foreign to him. As for the French school of the seventeenth century, he liked neither its devout ceremony nor its
pompous portraits: the cold reserve of the gravest of the masters,
a certain grayness of soul that clouded the proud works of
Nicolas Poussin and the pale faces of Philippe de Champaigne,
repelled Christophe from old French art. And, once more, he
knew nothing about it. If he had known anything about it he
would have misunderstood it. The only modern painter whose
fascination he had felt at all in Germany, Bœcklin of Basle,
had not prepared him much for Latin art. Christophe remembered the shock of his impact with that brutal genius, which
smacked of earth and the musty smell of the heroic beasts that
it had summoned forth. His eyes, seared by the raw light, used
to the frantic motley of that drunken savage, could hardly
adapt themselves to the half-tints, the dainty and mellifluous
harmonies of French art.

But no man with impunity can live in a foreign land. Unknown to him it sets its seal upon him. In vain does he withdraw into himself: upon a day he must wake up to find that
something has changed.

There was a change in Christophe on that evening when he
wandered through the rooms of the Louvre. He was tired,
cold, hungry; he was alone. Around him darkness was descending upon the empty galleries, and sleeping forms awoke. Christophe was very cold as he walked in silence among Egyptian

sphinxes, Assyrian monsters, bulls of Persepolis, gleaming
snakes from Palissy. He seemed to have passed into a magic
world: and in his heart there was a strange, mysterious emotion. The dream of humanity wrapped him about,—the strange
flowers of the soul. . . .

In the misty gilded light of the picture-galleries, and the
gardens of rich brilliant hues, and painted airless fields, Christophe, in a state of fever, on the very brink of illness, was
visited by a miracle.—He was walking, numbed by hunger, by
the coldness of the galleries, by the bewildering mass of pictures: his head was whirling. When he reached the end of the
gallery that looks on to the river, he stood before the *Good
Samaritan* of Rembrandt, and leaned on the rail in front of
the pictures to keep himself from falling: he closed his eyes
for a moment. When he opened them on the picture in front
of him—he was quite close to it—and he was held spellbound. . . .

Day was spent. Day was already far gone; it was already
dead. The invisible sun was sinking down into the night. It
was the magic hour when dreams and visions come mounting
from the soul, saddened by the labors of the day, still, musing
drowsily. All is silent, only the beating of the heart is heard.
In the body there is hardly the strength to move, hardly to
breathe; sadness; resignation; only an immense longing to fall
into the arms of a friend, a hunger for some miracle, a feeling
that some miracle must come. . . . It comes! A flood of
golden light flames through the twilight, is cast upon the walls
of the hovel, on the shoulder of the stranger bearing the dying
man, touches with its warmth those humble objects, and those
poor creatures, and the whole takes on a new gentleness, a
divine glory. It is the very God, clasping in his terrible, tender
arms the poor wretches, weak, ugly, poor, unclean, the poor
down-at-heel rascal, the miserable creatures, with twisted haggard faces, thronging outside the window, the apathetic, silent
creatures standing in mortal terror,—all the pitiful human beings of Rembrandt, the herd of obscure broken creatures who

know nothing, can do nothing, only wait, tremble, weep, and pray.—-But the Master is there. He will come: it is known that He will come. Not He Himself is seen: only the light that goes before, and the shadow of the light which He casts upon all men. . . .

Christophe left the Louvre, staggering and tottering. His head ached. He could not see. In the street it was raining, but he hardly noticed the puddles between the flags and the water trickling down from his shoes. Over the Seine the yellowish sky was lit up, as the day waned, by an inward flame —like the light of a lamp. Still Christophe was spellbound, hypnotized. It seemed as though nothing existed: not the carriages rattling over the stones with a pitiless noise: the passers-by were not banging into him with their wet umbrellas: he was not walking in the street: perhaps he was sitting at home and dreaming: perhaps he had ceased to exist. . . . And suddenly,—(he was so weak!)—he turned giddy and felt himself falling heavily forward. . . . It was only for the flash of a second: he clenched his fists, hurled himself backward, and recovered his balance.

At that very moment when he emerged into consciousness his eyes met the eyes of a woman standing on the other side of the street, who seemed to be looking for recognition. He stopped dead, trying to remember when he had seen her before. It was only after a moment or two that he could place those sad, soft eyes: it was the little French governess whom, unwittingly, he had had dismissed in Germany, for whom he had been looking for so long to beg her to forgive him. She had stopped, too, in the busy throng, and was looking at him. Suddenly he saw her try to cross through the crowd of people and step down into the road to come to him. He rushed to meet her: but they were separated by a block in the traffic: he saw her again for a moment struggling on the other side of that living wall: he tried to force his way through, was knocked over by a horse, slipped and fell on the slippery asphalt, and was all but run over. When he got up, covered with mud, and succeeded in reaching the other side of the street, she had disappeared.

He tried to follow her, but he had another attack of giddiness, and he had to give it up. Illness was close upon him: he felt that, but he would not submit to it. He set his teeth, and would not go straight home, but went far out of his way. It was just a useless torment to him: he had to admit that he was beaten: his legs ached, he dragged along, and only reached home with frightful difficulty. Half-way up the stairs he choked, and had to sit down. When he got to his icy room he refused to go to bed: he sat in his chair, wet through; his head was heavy and he could hardly breathe, and he drugged himself with music as broken as himself. He heard a few fugitive bars of the *Unfinished Symphony* of Schubert. Poor Schubert! He, too, was alone when he wrote that, feverish, somnolent, in that semitorpid condition which precedes the last great sleep: he sat dreaming by the fireside: all round him were heavy drowsy melodies, like stagnant water: he dwelt on them, like a child half-asleep delighting in some self-told story, and repeating some passage in it twenty times: so sleep comes, then death. . . . And Christophe heard fleetingly that other music, with burning hands, closed eyes, a little weary smile, heart big with sighs, dreaming of the deliverance of death:—the first chorus in the Cantata of J. S. Bach: *"Dear God, when shall I die?"* . . . It was sweet to sink back into the soft melodies slowly floating by, to hear the distant, muffled clangor of the bells. . . . To die, to pass into the peace of earth! . . . *Und dann selber Erde werden.* . . . "And then himself to become earth. . . ."

Christophe shook off these morbid thoughts, the murderous smile of the siren who lies in wait for the hours of weakness of the soul. He got up, and tried to walk about his room: but he could not stand. He was shaking and shivering with fever. He had to go to bed. He felt that it was serious this time: but he did not lay down his arms: he never was of those who, when they are ill, yield utterly to their illness: he struggled, he refused to be ill, and, above all, he was absolutely determined not to die. He had his poor mother waiting for him in Germany. And he had his work to do: he would not yield to death. He clenched his chattering teeth, and firmly grasped his will that was oozing away: he was like a sturdy swimmer battling with the waves dashing over him. At every moment, down he plunged: his mind wandered, endless fancies haunted him, memories of Germany and of Parisian society: he was obsessed by rhythms and scraps of melody which went round, and round, and round, like horses in a circus: the sudden shock of the golden light of the *Good Samaritan*: the tense, stricken faces in the shadow: and then, dark nothingness and night. Then up he would come once more, wrenching away the grimacing mists, clenching his fists, and setting his jaw. He clung to all those whom he loved in the present and the past, to the face of the friend he had just seen in the street. his dear mother, and to the indestructible life within himself, that he felt was like a rock, impervious to death. But once moie the rock was covered by the tide: the waves dashed over it, and tore his soul away from its hold upon it: it was borne headlong and dashed by the foam. And Christophe struggled in delirium, babbling strangely, conducting and playing an imaginary orchestra: trombones, horns, cymbals, timbals, bassoons, double-bass, . . . he scraped, blew, beat the drum, frantically. The poor wretch was bubbling over with suppressed music. For weeks he had been unable to hear or play any music, and he was like a boiler at high pressure. near bursting-point. Certain insistent phrases bored into his brain like gimlets, pierced his skull, and made him scream with agony. After these attacks he would fall back on his pillow, dead tired, wet through, utterly weak, breathless, choking. He had placed his water-jug by his bedside, and he took great draughts of it. The various noises of the adjoining rooms, the banging of the attic doors, made him start. He was filled with a delirious disgust for the creatures swarming round him. But his will fought on, sounded a warlike clarion-note, declaring battle on all devils. . . . *"Und wenn die*

*Welt voll Teufel wär, und wollten uns verschlingen, so fürchten
wir uns nicht so sehr. . . ."* ("And even though the world
were full of devils, all seeking to devour us, we should not be
afraid. . . .").

And over the sea of scalding shadows that dashed over him
there came a sudden calm, glimpses of light, a gentle murmuring of violins and viols, the clear triumphant notes of trumpets
and horns, while, almost motionless, like a great wall, there rose
from the sick man's soul an indomitable song, like a choral of-
J. S. Bach.

While he was fighting against the phantoms of fever and
the choking in his lungs, he was dimly aware that some one
had opened the door, and that a woman entered with a candle
in her hand. He thought it was another hallucination. He
tried to speak, but could not, and fell back on his pillow.
When, every now and then, he was brought for a moment back
to consciousness, he felt that his pillow had been raised, that his
feet had been wrapped up, that there was something burning
his back, or he would see the woman, whose face was not altogether unfamiliar, sitting at the foot of his bed. Then he saw
another face, that of a doctor using a stethoscope. Christophe
could not hear what they were saying, but he gathered that
they were talking of sending him to the hospital. He tried to
protest, to cry out that he would not go, that he would die
where he was, alone: but he could only frame incomprehensible
sounds. But the woman understood him: for she took his part,
and reassured him. He tried hard to find out who she was.
As soon as he could, with frightful effort, frame a sentence, he
asked her. She replied that she lived in the next attic and had
heard him moaning through the wall, and had taken the liberty
of coming in, thinking that he wanted help. She begged him
respectfully not to wear himself out with talking. He obeyed
her. He was worn out with the effort he had made: he lay
still and said nothing: but his brain went on working, painfully gathering together its scattered memories. Where had

he seen her? . . . At last he remembered: yes, he had met her on the attic landing: she was a servant, and her name was Sidonie.

He watched her with half-closed eyes, so that she could not see him. She was little, and had a grave face, a wide forehead, hair drawn back, so that her temples were exposed; her cheeks were pale and high-boned; she had a short nose, pale blue eyes, with a soft, steady look in them, thick lips tightly pressed together, an anemic complexion, a humble, deliberate, and rather stiff manner. She looked after Christophe with busy silent devotion, without a spark of familiarity, and without ever breaking down the reserve of a servant who never forgets class differences.

However, little by little, when he was better and could talk to her, Christophe's affectionate cordiality made Sidonie talk to him a little more freely: but she was always on her guard: there were obviously certain things which she would not tell. She was a mixture of humility and pride. Christophe learned that she came from Brittany, where she had left her father, of whom she spoke very discreetly: but Christophe gathered that he did nothing but drink, have a good time, and live on his daughter: she put up with it, without saying anything, from pride: and she never failed to send him part of her month's wages: but she was not taken in. She had also a younger sister who was preparing for a teacher's examination, and she was very proud of her. She was paying almost all the expenses of her education. She worked frightfully hard, with grim determination.

"Have you a good situation?" asked Christophe.

"Yes. But I am thinking of leaving."

"Why? Aren't they good to you?"

"Oh! no. They're very good to me."

"Don't they pay you enough?"

"Yes. . . ."

He did not quite understand: he tried to understand, and encouraged her to talk. She had nothing to tell him but the

monotony of her life, and the difficulty of earning a living:
she did not lay any stress on it: she was not afraid of work:
it was a necessity to her, almost a pleasure. She never spoke of
the thing that tried her most: boredom. He guessed it. Little
by little, with the intuition of perfect sympathy, he saw that
her suffering was increasing, and it was made more acute
for him by the memory of the trials supported by his own
mother in a similar existence. He saw, as though he had lived
it, the drab, unhealthy, unnatural existence—the ordinary existence imposed on servants by the middle-classes:—employers
who were not so much unkind as indifferent, sometimes leaving her for days together without speaking a word outside her
work. The hours and hours spent in the stuffy kitchen, the one
small window, blocked up by a meat-safe, looking out on to a
white wall. And her only pleasure was when she was told carelessly that her sauce was good or the meat well cooked. A
cramped airless life with no prospect, with no ray of desire or
hope, without interest of any kind.—The worst time of all for
her was when her employers went away to the country. They
economized by not taking her with them: they paid her wages
for the month, but not enough to take her home: they gave
her permission to go at her own expense. She would not, she
could not do that. And so she was left alone in the deserted
house. She had no desire to go out, and did not even talk
to other servants, whose coarseness and immorality she despised.
She never went out in search of amusement: she was naturally
serious, economical, and afraid of misadventure. She sat in
her kitchen, or in her room, from whence across the chimneys
she could see the top of a tree in the garden of a hospital. She
did not read, but tried to work listlessly: she would sit there
dreaming, bored, bored to tears: she had a singular and infinite
capacity for weeping: it was her only pleasure. But when her
boredom weighed too heavily on her she could not even weep:
she was frozen, sick at heart, and dead. Then she would pull
herself together: or life would return of its own accord. She
would think of her sister, listen to a barrel-organ in the distance,

and dream, and slowly count the days until she had gained such and such a sum of money: she would be out in her reckoning, and begin to count all over again: she would fall asleep. So the days passed. . . .

The fits of depression alternated with outbursts of childish chatter and laughter. She would make fun of herself and other people. She watched and judged her employers, and their anxieties fed by their want of occupation, and her mistress's moods and melancholy, and the so-called interests of these so-called people of culture, how they patronized a picture, or a piece of music, or a book of verse. With her rude common sense, as far removed from the snobbishness of the very Parisian servants as from the crass stupidity of the very provincial girls, who only admire what they do not understand, she had a respectful contempt for their dabbling in music, their pointless chatter, and all those perfectly useless and tiresome intellectual smatterings which play so large a part in such hypocritical existences. She could not help silently comparing the real life, with which she grappled, with the imaginary pains and pleasures of that cushioned life, in which everything seems to be the product of boredom. She was not in revolt against it. Things were so: things were so. She accepted everything, knaves and fools alike. She said:

" It takes all sorts to make a world."

Christophe imagined that she was borne up by her religion: but one day she said, speaking of others who were richer and more happy:

" But in the end we shall all be equal."

" When? " asked Christophe. " After the social revolution? "

" The revolution? " said she. " Oh, there'll be much water flowing under bridges before that. I don't believe that stuff. Things will always be the same."

" When shall we all be equal, then? "

" When we're dead, of course! That's the end of everybody."

He was surprised by her calm materialism. He dared not say to her:

" Isn't it a frightful thing, in that case, if there is only one life, that it should be the like of yours, while there are so many others who are happy? "

But she seemed to have guessed his thought: she went on phlegmatically, resignedly, and a little ironically:

" One has to put up with it. Everybody cannot draw a prize. I've drawn a blank: so much the worse! "

She never even thought of looking for a more profitable place outside France. (She had once been offered a situation in America.) The idea of leaving the country never entered her head. She said:

" Stones are hard everywhere."

There was in her a profound, skeptical, and mocking fatalism. She was of the stock that has little or no faith, few considered reasons for living, and yet a tremendous vitality—the stock of the French peasantry, industrious and apathetic, riotous and submissive, who have no great love of life, but cling to it, and have no need of artificial stimulants to keep up their courage.

Christophe, who had not yet come across them, was astonished to find in the girl an absence of all faith: he marveled at her tenacious hold on life, without pleasure or purpose, and most of all he admired her sturdy moral sense that had no need of prop or support. Till then he had only seen the French people through naturalistic novels, and the theories of the mannikins of contemporary literature, who, reacting from the art of the century of pastoral scenes and the Revolution, loved to present natural man as a vicious brute, in order to sanctify their own vices. . . . He was amazed when he discovered Sidonie's uncompromising honesty. It was not a matter of morality but of instinct and pride. She had her aristocratic pride. For it is foolish to imagine that everybody belonging to the people is " popular." The people have their aristocrats just as the upper classes have their vulgarians. The aristocrats are those creatures whose instincts, and perhaps whose blood, are purer than those of the others: those who know and are conscious of what they

are, and must be true to themselves.   They are in the minority:
but, even when they are forced to live apart, the others know
that they are the salt of the earth: and the fact of their existence is a check upon the others, who are forced to model themselves upon them, or to pretend to do so.   Every province, every
village, every congregation of men, is, to a certain degree,
what its aristocrats are: and public opinion varies accordingly,
and is, in one place, severe, in another, lax.   The present anarchy
and upheaval of the majority will not change the unvoiced
power of the minority.   It is more dangerous for them to be
uprooted from their native soil and scattered far and wide in
the great cities.   But even so, lost amid strange surroundings,
living in isolation, yet the individualities of the good stock
persist and never mix with those about them.—Sidonie knew
nothing, wished to know nothing, of all that Christophe had
seen in Paris.   She was no more interested in the sentimental
and unclean literature of the newspapers than in the political
news.   She did not even know that there were Popular Universities: and, if she had known, it is probable that she would
have put herself out as little to go to them as she did to hear
a sermon.   She did her work, and thought for herself: she was
not concerned with what other people thought.   Christophe
congratulated her.

"Why is that surprising?" she asked.   "I am like everybody else.   You haven't met any French people."

"I've been living among them for a year," said Christophe,
"and I haven't met a single one who thought of anything but
amusing himself or of aping those who amuse him."

"That's true," said Sidonie.   "You have only seen rich
people.   The rich are the same everywhere.   You've seen
nothing at all."

"That's true," said Christophe.   "I'm beginning."

For the first time he caught a glimpse of the people of
France, men and women who seem to be built for eternity, who
are one with the earth, who, like the earth, have seen so many

conquering races, so many masters of a day, pass away, while
they themselves endure and do not pass.

When he was getting better and was allowed to get up for
a little, the first thing he thought of was to pay Sidonie back
for the expenses she had incurred during his illness. It was
impossible for him to go about Paris looking for work, and he
had to bring himself to write to Hecht: he asked him for an
advance on account of future work. With his amazing combination of indifference and kindliness Hecht made him wait a
fortnight for a reply—a fortnight during which Christophe tormented himself and practically refused to touch any of the food
Sidonie brought him, and would only accept a little bread and
milk, which she forced him to take, and then he grumbled and
was angry with himself because he had not earned it: then,
without a word, Hecht sent him the sum he asked: and not once
during the months of Christophe's illness did Hecht make any
inquiry after him. He had a genius for making himself disliked even when he was doing a kindness. Even in his kindness Hecht could not be generous.

Sidonie came every day in the afternoon and again in the
evening. She cooked Christophe's dinner for him. She made
no noise, but went quietly about her business: and when she
saw the dilapidated condition of his clothes she took them away
to mend them. Insensibly there had crept an element of affection into their relation. Christophe talked at length about
his mother: and that touched Sidonie: she would put herself
in Louisa's place, alone in Germany: and she had a maternal
feeling for Christophe, and when he talked to her he tried to
trick his need of mothering and love, from which a man suffers most when he is weak and ill. He felt nearer Louisa with
Sidonie than with anybody else. Sometimes he would confide
his artistic troubles to her. She would pity him gently, though
she seemed to regard such sorrows of the intellect ironically.
That, too, reminded him of his mother and comforted him.

He tried to get her to confide in him: but she was much

less open than he.   He asked her jokingly why she did not get married.   And she would reply in her usual tone of mocking resignation that " it was not allowed for servants to marry: it complicates things too much.   Besides, she was sure to make a bad choice, and that is not pleasant.   Men are sordid creatures. They come courting when a woman has money, squeeze it out of her, and then leave her in the lurch.   She had seen too many cases of that and was not inclined to do the same."—She did not tell him of her own unfortunate experience: her future husband had left her when he found that she was giving all her earnings to her family.—Christophe used to see her in the court-yard mothering the children of a family living in the house. When she met them alone on the stairs she would sometimes embrace them passionately.   Christophe would fancy her occupying the place of a lady of his acquaintance: she was not a fool, and she was no plainer than many another woman: he declared that in the lady's place she would have been the better woman of the two.   There are so many splendid lives hidden in the world, unknown and unsuspected!   And, on the other hand, the hosts of the living dead, who encumber the earth, and take up the room and the happiness of others in the light of the sun! . . .

Christophe had no ulterior thought.   He was fond, too fond of her: he let her coddle him like a child.

Some days Sidonie would be queer and depressed: but he attributed that to her work.   Once when they were talking she got up suddenly and left him, making some excuse about her work.   Finally, after a day when Christophe had been more confidential than usual, she broke off her visits for a time: and when she came back she would only talk to him constrainedly. He wondered what he could have done to offend her.   He asked her.   She replied quickly that he had not offended her: but she stayed away again.   A few days later she told him that she was going away: she had given up her situation and was leaving the house.   Coldly and reservedly she thanked him for all his kindness, told him she hoped he would soon recover, and that his mother would remain in good health, and then she said good-by.

He was so astonished at her abrupt departure that he did not know what to say: he tried to discover her reasons: she replied evasively. He asked her where she was going: she did not reply, and, to cut short his questions, she got up to go. As she reached the door he held out his hand: she grasped it warmly: but her face did not betray her, and to the end she maintained her stiff, cold manner. She went away.

He never understood why.

He dragged through the winter—a wet, misty, muddy winter. Weeks on end without sun. Although Christophe was better he was by no means recovered. He still had a little pain in his lungs, a lesion which healed slowly, and fits of coughing which kept him from sleeping at night. The doctor had forbidden him to go out. He might just as well have ordered him to go to the Riviera or the Canary Islands. He had to go out! If he did not go out to look for his dinner, his dinner would certainly not come to look for him.—And he was ordered medicines which he could not afford. And so he gave up consulting doctors: it was a waste of money: and besides he was always ill at ease with them: they could not understand each other: they lived in separate worlds. They had an ironical and rather contemptuous pity for the poor devil of an artist who claimed to be a world to himself, and was swept along like a straw by the river of life. He was humiliated by being examined, and prodded, and handled by these men. He was ashamed of his sick body, and thought:

" How glad I shall be when *it* is dead! "

In spite of loneliness, illness, poverty, and so many other causes of suffering, Christophe bore his lot patiently. He had never been so patient. He was surprised at himself. Illness is often a blessing. By ravaging the body it frees the soul and purifies it: during the nights and days of forced inaction thoughts arise which are fearful of the raw light of day, and are scorched by the sun of health. No man who has never been ill can have a thorough knowledge of himself.

His illness had, in a queer way, soothed Christophe. It had purged him of the coarser elements of his nature. Through his most subtle nerves he felt the world of mysterious forces which dwell in each of us, though the tumult of life prevents our hearing them. Since his visit to the Louvre, in his hours of fever, the smallest memories of which were graven upon his mind, he had lived in an atmosphere like that of the Rembrandt picture, warm, soft, profound. He too felt in his heart the magic beams of an invisible sun. And although he did not believe, he knew that he was not alone: a God was holding him by the hand, and leading him to the predestined goal of his endeavors. He trusted in Him like a little child.

For the first time for years he felt that he must rest. The lassitude of his convalescence was in itself a rest for him after the extraordinary tension of mind that had gone before his illness and had left him still exhausted. Christophe, who for many months had been continually on the alert and strained, upon his guard, felt the fixity of his gaze slowly relax. He was not less strong for it: he was more human. The great though rather monstrous quality of life of the man of genius had passed into the background: he found himself a man like the rest, purged of the fanaticism of his mind, and all the hardness and mercilessness of his actions. He hated nothing: he gave no thought to things that exasperated him, or, if he did, he shrugged them off: he thought less of his own troubles and more of the troubles of others. Since Sidonie had reminded him of the silent suffering of the lowly, fighting on without complaint, all over the world, he forgot himself in them. He who was not usually sentimental now had periods of that mystic tenderness which is the flower of weakness and sickness. In the evening, as he sat with his elbows on the window-sill, gazing down into the courtyard and listening to all the mysterious noises of the night, . . . a voice singing in a house near by, made moving by the distance, or a little girl artlessly strumming Mozart, . . . he thought:

"All you whom I love though I know you not! You whom

life has not sullied; you, who dream of great things, that you know to be impossible, while you fight for them against the envious world,—may you be happy—it is so good to be happy! . . . Oh, my friends, I know that you are there, and I hold my arms out to you. . . . There is a wall between us. Stone by stone I am breaking it down, but I am myself broken in the labor of it. Shall we ever be together? Shall I reach you before another wall is raised up between us: the wall of death? . . . No matter! Though all my life I am alone, so only I may work for you, do you good, and you may love me a little, later on, when I am dead! . . ."

So the convalescent Christophe was nursed by those two good foster-mothers " *Liebe und Noth* " (Love and Poverty).

While his will was thus in abeyance Christophe felt a longing to be with people. And, although he was still very weak, and it was a very foolish thing to do, he used to go out early in the morning when the stream of people poured out of the residential streets on their way to their work, or in the evening, when they were returning. His desire was to plunge into the refreshing bath of human sympathy. Not that he spoke to a soul. He did not even try to do so. It was enough for him to watch the people pass, and guess what they were, and love them. With fond pity he used to watch the workers hurrying along, all, as it were, already worn out by the business of the day, —young men and girls, with pale faces, worn expressions, and strange smiles,—thin, eager faces beneath which there passed desires and anxieties, all with a changing irony,—all so intelligent, too intelligent, a little morbid, the dwellers in a great city. They all hurried along, the men reading the papers, the women nibbling and munching. Christophe would have given a month of his life to let one poor girl, whose eyes were swollen with sleep, who passed near him with a little nervous, mincing walk, sleep on for a few hours more. Oh! how she would have jumped at it, if she had been offered the chance!

He would have loved to pluck all the idle rich people out of their rooms, hermetically sealed at that hour, where they were so ungratefully lying at their ease, and replace them in their beds, in their comfortable existence, with all these eager, weary bodies, these fresh souls, not abounding with life, but alive and greedy of life. In that hour he was full of kindness towards them: and he smiled at their alert, thin little faces, in which there were cunning and ingenuousness, a bold and simple desire for pleasure, and, behind all, honest little souls, true and industrious. And he was not hurt when some of the girls laughed in his face, or nudged each other to point out the strange young man staring at them so hard.

And he would lounge about the riverside, lost in dreams. That was his favorite walk. It did a little satisfy his longing for the great river that had sung the lullaby of his childhood. Ah! it was not *Vater Rhein!* It had none of his all-puissant might: none of the wide horizons, vast plains over which the mind soars and is lost. A river with gray eyes, gowned in pale green, with finely drawn, correct features, a graceful river, with supple movements, wearing with sparkling nonchalance the sumptuous and sober garb of her city, the bracelets of its bridges, the necklets of its monuments, and smiling at her own prettiness, like a lovely woman strolling through the town. . . . The delicious light of Paris! That was the first thing that Christophe had loved in the city: it filled his being sweetly, sweetly: and imperceptibly, slowly, it changed his heart. It was to him the most lovely music, the only music in Paris. He would spend hours in the evening walking by the river, or in the gardens of old France, tasting the harmonies of the light of day touching the tall trees bathed in purple mist, the gray statues and ruins, the worn stones of the royal monuments which had absorbed the light of centuries,—that smooth atmosphere, made of pale sunshine and milky vapor, in which, on a cloud of silvery dust, there floats the laughing spirit of the race.

One evening he was leaning over the parapet near the Saint-

Michel Bridge, and looking at the water and absently turning over the books in one of the little boxes. He chanced upon a battered old volume of Michelet and opened it at random. He had already read a certain amount of that historian, and had been put off by his Gallic boasting, his trick of making himself drunk with words, and his halting style. But that evening he was held from the very first words: he had lighted on the trial of Joan of Arc. He knew the Maid of Orleans through Schiller: but hitherto she had only been a romantic heroine who had been endowed with an imaginary life by a great poet. Suddenly the reality was presented to him and gripped his attention. He read on and on, his heart aching for the tragic horror of the glorious story: and when he came to the moment when Joan learns that she is to die that evening and faints from fear, his hands began to tremble, tears came into his eyes, and he had to stop. He was weak from his illness: he had become absurdly sensitive, and was himself exasperated by it.—When he turned once more to the book it was late and the bookseller was shutting up his boxes. He decided to buy the book and hunted through his pockets: he had exactly six sous. Such scantiness was not rare and did not bother him: he had paid for his dinner, and counted on getting some money out of Hecht next day for some copying he had done. But it was hard to have to wait a day! Why had he spent all he had on his dinner? Ah! if only he could offer the bookseller the bread and sausages that were in his pockets, in payment!

Next morning, very early, he went to Hecht's to get his money: but as he was passing the bridge which bears the name of the archangel of battle—" the brother in Paradise " of Joan of Arc—he could not help stopping. He found the precious book once more in the bookseller's box, and read it right through: he stayed reading it for nearly two hours and missed his appointment with Hecht: and he wasted the whole day waiting to see him. At last he managed to get his new commission and the money for the old. At once he rushed

back to buy the book, although he had read it.   He was afraid
it might have been sold to another purchaser.   No doubt that
would not have mattered much: it was quite easy to get another
copy: but Christophe did not know whether the book was rare
or not: and besides, he wanted that particular book and no other.
Those who love books easily become fetish worshipers.   The
pages from which the well of dreams springs forth are sacred
to them, even when they are dirty and spotted.

In the silence of the night, in his room, Christophe read
once more the Gospel of the Passion of Joan of Arc: and
now there was nothing to make him restrain his emotion.   He
was filled with tenderness, pity, infinite sorrow for the poor
little shepherdess in her coarse peasant clothes, tall, shy, soft-
voiced, dreaming to the sound of bells—(she loved them as he
did)—with her lovely smile, full of understanding and kindness, and her tears, that flowed so readily—tears of love, tears
of pity, tears of weakness: for she was at once so manlike and
so much a woman, the pure and valiant girl, who tamed the
savage lusts of an army of bandits, and calmly, with her intrepid sound good sense, her woman's subtlety, and her gentle
persistency, alone, betrayed on all hands, for months together
foiled the threats and hypocritical tricks of a gang of church-
men and lawyers,—wolves and foxes with bloody eyes and fangs
—who closed a ring about her.

What touched Christophe most nearly was her kindness,
her tenderness of heart,—weeping after her victories, weeping
over her dead enemies, over those who had insulted her, giving
them consolation when they were wounded, aiding them in
death, knowing no bitterness against those who sold her, and
even at the stake, when the flames roared about her, thinking
not of herself, thinking only of the monk who exorcised her,
and compelling him to depart.   She was "gentle in the most
bitter fight, good even amongst the most evil, peaceful even
in war.   Into war, the triumph of Satan, she brought the very
Spirit of God."

And Christophe, thinking of himself, said:

"And into my fight I have not brought enough of the Spirit of God."

He read the fine words of the evangelist of Joan of Arc:

"Be kind, and seek always to be kinder, amid all the injustice of men and the hardships of Fate. . . . Be gentle and of a good countenance even in bitter quarrels, win through experience, and never let it harm that inward treasure. . . ."

And he said within himself:

"I have sinned. I have not been kind. I have not shown good-will towards men. I have been too hard.—Forgive me. Do not think me your enemy, you against whom I wage war! For you too I seek to do good. . . . But you must be kept from doing evil. . . ."

And, as he was no saint, the thought of them was enough to kindle his anger again. What he could least forgive them was that when he saw them, and saw France, through them, he found it impossible to conceive such a flower of purity and poetic heroism ever springing from such a soil. And yet it was so. Who could say that such a flower would not spring from it a second time? The France of to-day could not be worse than that of Charles VII, the debauched and prostituted nation from which the Maid sprang. The temple was empty, fouled, half in ruins. No matter! God had spoken in it.

Christophe was seeking a Frenchman whom he could love for the love of France.

It was about the end of March. For months Christophe had not spoken to a soul nor had a single letter, except every now and then a few lines from his mother, who did not know that he was ill and did not tell him that she herself was ill. His relation with the outside world was confined to his journeys to the music shop to take or bring away his work. He arranged to go there at times when he knew that Hecht would be out—to avoid having to talk to him. The precaution was superfluous, for the only time he met Hecht, he hardly did more than ask him a few indifferent questions about his health.

He was immured in a prison of silence when, one morning, he received an invitation from Madame Roussin to a musical *soirée:* a famous quartet was to play. The letter was very friendly in tone, and Roussin had added a few cordial lines. He was not very proud of his quarrel with Christophe: the less so as he had since quarreled with the singer and now condemned her in no sparing terms. He was a good fellow: he never bore those whom he had wronged any grudge. And he would have thought it preposterous for any of his victims to be more thin-skinned than himself. And so, when he had the pleasure of seeing them again, he never hesitated about holding out his hand.

Christophe's first impulse was to shrug his shoulders and vow that he would not go. But he wavered as the day of the concert came nearer. He was stifling from never hearing a human voice or a note of music. But he vowed again that he would never set foot inside the Roussins' house. But when the day came he went, raging against his own cowardice.

He was ill rewarded. Hardly did he find himself once more in the gathering of politicians and snobs than he was filled with an aversion for them more violent than ever: for during his months of solitude he had lost the trick of such people. It was impossible to hear the music: it was a profanation; Christophe made up his mind to go as soon as the first piece was over.

He glanced round among the faces of those people who were even physically so antipathetic to him. At the other end of the room he saw a face, the face of a young man, looking at him, and then he turned away at once. There was in the face a strange quality of candor which among such bored, indifferent people was most striking. The eyes were timid, but clear and direct. French eyes, which, once they marked a man, went on looking at him with absolute truth, hiding nothing of the soul behind them, missing nothing of the soul of the man at whom they gazed. They were familiar to Christophe. And yet he did not know the face. It was that of a young man between twenty and twenty-five, short, slightly

stooping, delicate-looking, beardless, and melancholy, with chestnut hair, irregular features, though fine, a certain crookedness
which gave it an expression not so much of uneasiness as of
bashfulness, which was not without charm, and seemed to contradict the tranquillity of the eyes. He was standing in an open
door: and nobody was paying any attention to him. Once more
Christophe looked at him: and once more he met his eyes,
which turned away timidly with a delightful awkwardness:
once more he "recognized" them: it seemed to him that he
had seen them in another face.

Christophe, as usual, was incapable of concealing what he
felt, and moved towards the young man: but as he made his
way he wondered what he should say to him: and he hesitated
and stood still looking to right and left, as though he were
moving without any fixed object. But the young man was not
taken in, and saw that Christophe was moving towards himself: he was so nervous at the thought of speaking to him
that he tried to slip into the next room: but he was glued to
his place by his very bashfulness. So they came face to face.
It was some moments before they could find anything to say.
And as they went on standing like that each thought the other
must think him absurd. At last Christophe looked straight
at the young man, and said with a smile, in a gruff voice:

"You're not a Parisian?"

In spite of his embarrassment the young man smiled at this
unexpected question, and replied in the negative. His light
voice, with its hint of a musical quality, was like some delicate
instrument.

"I thought not," said Christophe. And, as he saw that he
was a little confused by the singular remark, he added:

"It is no reproach."

But the young man's embarrassment was only increased.

There was another silence. The young man made an effort
to speak: his lips trembled: it seemed that he had a sentence
on the tip of his tongue, but he could not bring himself to

speak it. Christophe eagerly studied his mobile face, the muscles of which he could see twitching under the clear skin: he did not seem to be of the same clay as the people all about him in the room, with their heavy, coarse faces, which were only a continuation of their necks, part and parcel of their bodies. In the young man's face the soul shone forth: in every part of it there was a spiritual life.

He could not bring himself to speak. Christophe went on genially:

"What are you doing among all these people?"

He spoke out loud with that strange freedom of manner which made him hated. His friend blushed and could not help looking round to see if he had been heard: and Christophe disliked the movement. Then, instead of answering, he asked with a shy, sweet smile:

"And you?"

Christophe began to laugh as usual, rather loudly.

"Yes. And I," he said delightedly.

The young man at last summoned up his courage.

"I love your music so much!" he said, in a choking voice.

Then he stopped and tried once more, vainly, to get the better of his shyness. He was blushing, and knew it: and he blushed the more, up to his temples and round to his ears. Christophe looked at him with a smile, and longed to take him in his arms. The young man looked at him timidly.

"No," he said. "Of course, I can't . . . I can't talk about that . . . not here. . . . ."

Christophe took his hand with a grin. He felt the stranger's thin fingers tremble in his great paw and press it with an involuntary tenderness: and the young man felt Christophe's paw affectionately crush his hand. They ceased to hear the chatter of the people round them. They were alone together and they knew that they were friends.

It was only for a second, for then Madame Roussin touched Christophe on the arm with her fan and said:

"I see that you have introduced yourselves and don't need

me to do so. The boy came on purpose to meet you this evening."

Then, rather awkwardly, they parted.

Christophe asked Madame Roussin:

" Who is he? "

" What? " said she. " You don't know him? He is a young poet and writes very prettily. One of your admirers. He is a good musician and plays the piano quite nicely. It is no good discussing you in his presence: he is mad about you. The other day he all but came to blows about you with Lucien Lévy-Cœur."

" Oh! Bless him for that! " said Christophe.

" Yes, I know you are unjust to poor Lucien. And yet he too loves your work."

" Ah! don't tell me that! I should hate myself."

" It is so, I assure you."

" Never! never! I will not have it. I forbid him to do so."

" Just what your admirer said. You are both mad. Lucien was just explaining one of your compositions to us. The shy boy you met just now got up, trembling with anger, and forbade him to mention your name. Think of it! . . . Fortunately I was there. I laughed it off: Lucien did the same: and the boy was utterly confused and relapsed into silence: and in the end he apologized."

" Poor boy! " said Christophe.

He was touched by it.

" Where did he go? " he asked, without listening to Madame Roussin, who had already begun to talk about something else.

He went to look for him. But his unknown friend had disappeared. Christophe returned to Madame Roussin:

" Tell me, what is his name? "

" Who? " she asked.

" The boy you were talking about just now."

" Your young poet? " she said. " His name is Olivier Jeannin."

The name rang in Christophe's ears like some familiar

melody. The shadowy figure of a girl floated for a moment before his eyes. But the new image, the image of his friend blotted it out at once.

Christophe went home. He strode through the streets of Paris mingling with the throng. He saw nothing, heard nothing; he was insensible to everything about him. He was like a lake cut off from the rest of the world by a ring of mountains. Not a breath stirred, not a sound was heard, all was still. Peace. He said to himself over and over again: " I have a friend."

ANTOINETTE

I

The Jeannins were one of those old French families who have remained stationary for centuries in the same little corner of a province, and have kept themselves pure from any infusion of foreign blood. There are more of them than one would think in France, in spite of all the changes in the social order: it would need a great upheaval to uproot them from the soil to which they are held by so many ties, the profound nature of which is unknown to them. Reason counts for nothing in their devotion to the soil, and interest for very little: and as for sentimental historic memories, they only hold good for a few literary men. What does bind them irresistibly is the obscure though very strong feeling, common to the dull and the intelligent alike, of having been for centuries past a parcel of the land, of living in its life, breathing the same air, hearing the heart of it beating against their own, like the heart of the beloved, feeling its slightest tremor, the changing hours and seasons and days, bright or dull, and hearing the voices and the silence of all things in Nature. It is not always the most beautiful country, nor that which has the greatest charm of life, that most strongly grips the affections, but rather it is the region where the earth seems simplest and most humble, nearest man, speaking to him in a familiar friendly tongue.

Such was the country in the center of France where the Jeannins lived. A flat, damp country, an old sleepy little town, wearily gazing at its reflection in the dull waters of a still canal: round about it were monotonous fields, plowed fields, meadows, little rivers, woods, and again monotonous fields. . . . No scenery, no monuments, no memories. Nothing attractive. It is all dull and oppressive. In its drowsy torpor is a hidden

force.   The soul tasting it for the first time suffers and revolts
against it.   But those who have lived with it for generations
cannot break free: it eats into their very bones: and the stillness of it, the harmonious dullness, the monotony, have a charm
for them and a sweet savor which they cannot analyze, which
they malign, love, and can never forget.

The Jeannins had always lived there.   The family could
be traced back to the sixteenth century, living in the town or
its neighborhood: for of course they had a great-uncle who had
devoted his life to drawing up the genealogical tree of their
obscure line of humble, industrious people: peasants, farmers,
artisans, then clerks, country notaries, working in the sub-
prefecture of the district, where Augustus Jeannin, the father
of the present head of the house, had successfully established
himself as a banker: he was a clever man, with a peasant's cunning and obstinacy, but honest as men go, not over-scrupulous,
a great worker, and a good liver: he had made himself respected
and feared everywhere by his genial malice, his bluntness of
speech, and his wealth.   Short, thick-set, vigorous, with little
sharp eyes set in a big red face, pitted with smallpox, he had
been known as a petticoat-hunter: and he had not altogether
lost his taste for it.   He loved a spicy yarn and good eating.
It was a sight to see him at meals, with his son Antoine sitting
opposite him, with a few old friends of their kidney: the district
judge, the notary, the Archdeacon of the Cathedral:—(old
Jeannin loved stuffing the priest: but also he could stuff with
the priest, if the priest were good at it) :—hearty old fellows
built on the same Rabelaisian lines.   There was a running fire
of terrific stories to the accompaniment of thumps on the table
and roars of laughter, and the row they made could be heard
by the servants in the kitchen and the neighbors in the street.
Then old Augustus caught a chill, which turned to pneumonia, through going down into his cellars one hot summer's
day in his shirt-sleeves to bottle his wine.   In less than twenty-
four hours he had departed this life for the next world, in

which he hardly believed, properly equipped with all the Sacra-
ments of the Church, having, like a good Voltairian provincial,
submitted to it at the last moment in order to pacify his women,
and also because it did not matter one way or the other. . . .
And then, one never knows. . . .

His son Antoine succeeded him in business. He was a fat
little man, rubicund and expansive, clean-shaven, except for
his mutton-chop whiskers, and he spoke quickly and with a
slight stutter, in a loud voice, accompanying his remarks with
little quick, curt gestures. He had not his father's grasp of
finance: but he was quite a good manager. He had only to
look after the established undertakings, which went on de-
veloping day by day, by the mere fact of their existence. He
had the advantage of a business reputation in the district, although he had very little to do with the success of the firm's
ventures. He only contributed method and industry. For the
rest he was absolutely honorable, and was everywhere deservedly
esteemed. His pleasant unctuous manners, though perhaps a
little too familiar for some people, a little too expansive, and
just a little common, had won him a very genuine popularity in
the little town and the surrounding country. He was more
lavish with his sympathy than with his money: tears came readily to his eyes: and the sight of poverty so sincerely moved him
that the victim of it could not fail to be touched by it.

Like most men living in small towns, his thoughts were
much occupied with politics. He was an ardent moderate Republican, an intolerant Liberal, a patriot, and, like his father,
extremely anti-clerical. He was a member of the Municipal
Council: and, like the rest of his colleagues, he delighted in
playing tricks on the *curé* of the parish, or on the Lent preacher,
who roused so much enthusiasm in the ladies of the town. It
must not be forgotten that the anti-clericalism of the little
towns in France is always, more or less, an episode in domestic
warfare, and is a subtle form of that silent, bitter struggle
between husbands and wives, which goes on in almost every
house.

Antoine Jeannin had also some literary pretensions. Like all provincials of his generation, he had been brought up on the Latin Classics, many pages of which he knew by heart, and also a mass of proverbs, and on La Fontaine and Boileau,—the Boileau of *L'Art Poétique,* and, above all, of *Lutrin,*—on the author of *La Pucelle,* and the *poetæ minores* of the eighteenth century, in whose manner he squeezed out a certain number of poems. He was not the only man of his acquaintance possessed by that particular mania, and his reputation gained by it. His rhyming jests, his quatrains, couplets, acrostics, epigrams, and songs, which were sometimes rather risky, though they had a certain coarsely witty quality, were often quoted. He was wont to sing the mysteries of digestion: the Muse of the Loire districts is fain to blow her trumpet like the famous devil of Dante:

"... *Ed egli avea del cul fatto trombetta."*

This sturdy, jovial, active little man had taken to wife a woman of a very different character,—the daughter of a country magistrate, Lucie de Villiers. The De Villiers—or rather Devilliers, for their name had split in its passage through time, like a stone which cracks in two as it goes hurtling down a hillside—were magistrates from father to son; they were of that old parliamentary race of Frenchmen who had a lofty idea of the law, and duty, the social conventions, their personal, and especially their professional, dignity, which was fortified by perfect honesty, tempered with a certain conscious uprightness. During the preceding century they had been infected by nonconformist Jansenism, which had given them a grumbling pessimistic quality, as well as a contempt for the Jesuit attitude of mind. They did not see life as beautiful: and, rather than smooth away life's difficulties, they preferred to exaggerate them so as to have good reason to complain. Lucie de Villiers had certain of these characteristics, which were so directly opposed to the not very refined optimism of her husband. She was tall—taller than he by a head—slender, well made; she dressed well and elegantly, though in a rather sober fashion,

which made her seem—perhaps designedly—older than she was:
she was of a high moral quality: but she was hard on other
people; she would countenance no fault, and hardly even a
caprice: she was thought cold and disdainful. She was very
pious, and that gave rise to perpetual disputes with her husband. For the rest, they were very fond of each other: and,
in spite of their frequent disagreements, they could not have
lived without each other. They were both rather unpractical:
he from want of perception—(he was always in danger of being
taken in by good looks and fine words),—she from her absolute inexperience of business—(she knew nothing about it:
and having always been kept outside it, she took no interest
in it).

They had two children: a girl, Antoinette, the elder by
five years; and a boy, Olivier.

Antoinette was a pretty dark-haired child, with a charming,
honest face of the French type, round, with sharp eyes, a round
forehead, a fine chin, a little straight nose—" one of those very
pretty, fine, noble noses " (as an old French portrait-painter
says so charmingly) " in which there was a certain imperceptible play of expression, which animated the face, and revealed the subtlety of the workings of her mind as she talked
or listened." She had her father's gaiety and carelessness.

Olivier was a delicate fair boy, short, like his father, but
very different in character. His health had been undermined
by one illness after another when he was a child: and although,
as a result, he was petted by his family, his physical weakness
had made him a melancholy, dreamy little boy, who was afraid
of death and very poorly equipped for life. He was shy, and
preferred to be alone: he avoided the society of other children:
he was ill at ease with them: he hated their games and quarrels:
their brutality filled him with horror. He let them strike him,
not from want of courage, but from timidity, because he was
afraid to defend himself, afraid of hurting them: they would
have bullied the life out of him, but for the safeguard of his

father's position. He was tender-hearted and morbidly sensitive: a word, a sign of sympathy, a reproach, were enough to
make him burst into tears. His sister was much sturdier, and
laughed at him, and called him a "little fountain."

The two children were devoted to each other: but they were
too different to live together. They went their own ways and
lived in their own dreams. As Antoinette grew up, she became
prettier: people told her so, and she was well aware of it: it
made her happy, and she wove romances about the future.
Olivier, in his sickly melancholy, was always rubbed up the
wrong way by contact with the outer world: and he withdrew
into the circle of his own absurd little brain: and he told himself stories. He had a burning, almost feminine, longing to
love and be loved: and, living alone, away from boys of his
own age, he had invented two or three imaginary friends: one
was called Jean, another Étienne, another François: he was
always with them. He never slept well, and he was always
dreaming. In the morning, when he was lifted out of bed, he
would forget himself, and sit with his bare legs dangling
down, or sometimes with two stockings on one leg. He would
go off into a dream with his hands in the basin. He would
forget himself at his desk in the middle of writing or learning
a lesson: he would dream for hours on end: and then he would
suddenly wake up, horrified to find that he had learned nothing.
At dinner he was abashed if any one spoke to him: he would
reply two minutes after he had been spoken to: he would forget
what he was going to say in the middle of a sentence. He
would doze off to the murmuring of his thoughts and the familiar
sensations of the monotonous provincial days that marched so
slowly by: the great half-empty house, only part of which they
occupied: the vast and dreadful barns and cellars: the mysterious closed rooms, the fastened shutters, the covered furniture,
veiled mirrors, and the chandeliers wrapped up: the old family portraits with their haunting smiles: the Empire engravings,
with their virtuous, suave heroism: *Alcibiades and Socrates in
the House of the Courtezan, Antiochus and Stratonice, The Story*

of Epaminondas, Belisarius Begging. . . .   Outside, the sound
of the smith shoeing horses in the smithy opposite, the uneven clink of the hammers on the anvil, the snorting of the
broken-winded horses, the smell of the scorched hoofs, the
slapping of the pats of the washerwomen kneeling by the water,
the heavy thuds of the butcher's chopper next door, the clatter
of a horse's hoofs on the stones of the street, the creaking of
a pump, or the drawbridge over the canal, the heavy barges
laden with blocks of wood, slowly passing at the end of the
garden, drawn along by a rope: the little tiled courtyard, with a
square patch of earth, in which two lilac-trees grew, in the
middle of a clump of geraniums and petunias: the tubs of laurel
and flowering pomegranate on the terrace above the canal:
sometimes the noise of a fair in the square hard by, with peasants in bright blue smocks, and grunting pigs. . . .   And on
Sunday, at church, the precentor, who sang out of tune, and
the old priest, who went to sleep as he was saying Mass: the
family walk along the station road, where all the time he had to
take off his hat politely to other wretched beings, who were under the same impression of the necessity of going for a walk all
together,—until at last they reached the sunny fields, above
which larks soared invisible,—or along by the still mirror of
the canal, on both sides of which were poplars rustling in
line. . . .   And then there was the great provincial Sunday
dinner, when they went on and on eating and talking about
food learnedly and with gusto: for everybody was a connoisseur:
and, in the provinces, eating is the chief occupation, the first
of all the arts.   And they would talk business, and tell spicy
yarns, and every now and then discuss their neighbors' illnesses,
going into endless detail. . . .   And the little boy, sitting
in his corner, would make no more noise than a little mouse,
pick at his food, eat hardly anything, and listen with all his
ears.   Nothing escaped him: and when he did not understand,
his imagination supplied the deficiency.   He had that singular
gift, which is often to be remarked in the children of old
families and an old stock, on which the imprint of the ages is

too strongly marked, of divining thoughts, which have never passed through their minds before, and are hardly comprehensible to them.—Then there was the kitchen, where bloody and succulent mysteries were concocted: and the old servant who used to tell him frightful and droll stories. . . . At last came evening, the silent flitting of the bats, the terror of the monstrous creatures that were known to swarm in the dark depths of the old house: huge rats, enormous hairy spiders: and he would say his prayers, kneeling at the foot of his bed, and hardly know what he was saying: the little cracked bell of the convent hard by would sound the bed-time of the nuns;—and so to bed, the Island of Dreams. . . .

The best times of the year were those that they spent in spring and autumn at their country house some miles away from the town. There he could dream at his ease: he saw nobody. Like most of the children of their class, the little Jeannins were kept apart from the common children: the children of servants and farmers, who inspired them with fear and disgust. They inherited from their mother an aristocratic—or, rather, essentially middle-class—disdain for all who worked with their hands. Olivier would spend the day perched up in the branches of an ash reading marvelous stories: delightful folklore, the *Tales* of Musæus, or Madame d'Aulnoy, or the *Arabian Nights,* or stories of travel. For he had that strange longing for distant lands, "those oceanic dreams," which sometimes possess the minds of boys in the little provincial towns of France. A thicket lay between the house and himself, and he could fancy himself very far away. But he knew that he was really near home, and was quite happy: for he did not like straying too far alone: he felt lost with Nature. Round him the wind whispered through the trees. Through the leaves that hid his nest he could see the yellowing vines in the distance, and the meadows where the straked cows were at pasture, filling the silence of the sleeping country-side with their plaintive ong-drawn lowing. The strident cocks crowed to each other from farm to farm. There came up the irregular beat of the flails in the barns. The fevered life of myriads of creatures swelled and flowed through the peace of inanimate Nature. Uneasily Olivier would watch the ever hurrying columns of the ants, and the bees big with their booty, buzzing like organ-pipes, and the superb and stupid wasps who know not what they want —the whole world of busy little creatures, all seemingly devoured by the desire to reach their destination. . . . Where is it? They do not know. No matter where! Somewhere. . . . Olivier was fearful amid that blind and hostile world. He would start, like a young hare, at the sound of a pine-cone falling, or the breaking of a rotten branch. . . . He would find his courage again when he heard the rattling of the chains of the swing at the other end of the garden, where Antoinette would be madly swinging to and fro.

She, too, would dream: but in her own fashion. She would spend the day prowling round the garden, eating, watching, laughing, picking at the grapes on the vines like a thrush, secretly plucking a peach from the trellis, climbing a plum-tree, or giving it a little surreptitious shake as she passed to bring down a rain of the golden mirabelles which melt in the mouth like scented honey. Or she would pick the flowers, although that was forbidden: quickly she would pluck a rose that she had been coveting all day, and run away with it to the arbor at the end of the garden. Then she would bury her little nose in the delicious scented flower, and kiss it, and bite it, and suck it: and then she would conceal her booty, and hide it in her bosom between her little breasts, at the wonder of whose coming she would gaze in eager fondness. . . . And there was an exquisite forbidden joy in taking off her shoes and stockings, and walking bare-foot on the cool sand of the paths, and on the dewy turf, and on the stones, cold in the shadow, burning in the sun, and in the little stream that ran along the outskirts of the wood, and kissing with her feet, and legs, and knees, water, earth, and light. Lying in the shadow of the pines, she would hold her hands up to the sun, and watch the light play through them, and she would press her lips upon the soft satin skin of her pretty rounded arms. She would make herself crowns and necklets and gowns of ivy-leaves and oak-leaves: and she would deck them with the blue thistles, and barberry and little pine-branches, with their green fruit: and then she looked like a little savage Princess. And she would dance for her own delight round and round the fountain: and, with arms outstretched, she would turn and turn until her head whirled, and she would slip down on the lawn and bury her face in the grass, and shout with laughter for minutes on end, unable to stop herself, without knowing why.

So the days slipped by for the two children, within hail of each other, though neither ever gave a thought to the other,—except when it would suddenly occur to Antoinette to play a prank on her brother, and throw a handful of pine-needles in his face, or shake the tree in which he was sitting, threatening to make him fall, or frighten him by springing suddenly out upon him and yelling:

"Ooh! Ooh! . . ."

Sometimes she would be seized by a desire to tease him. She would make him come down from his tree by pretending that her mother was calling him. Then, when he had climbed down, she would take his place and refuse to budge. Then Olivier would whine and threaten to tell. But there was no danger of Antoinette staying in the tree for long: she could not keep still for two minutes. When she had done with taunting Olivier from the top of his tree, when she had thoroughly infuriated him and brought him almost to tears, then she would slip down, fling her arms round him, shake him, and laugh, and call him a " little muff," and roll him on the ground, and rub his face with handfuls of grass. He would try to struggle: but he was not strong enough. Then he would lie still, flat on his black, like a cockchafer, with his thin arms pinned to the ground by Antoinette's strong little hands: and he would look piteous and resigned. Antoinette could not resist that: she would look at her vanquished prisoner, and burst out laughing and kiss him suddenly, and let him go—not without

the parting attention of a little gag of fresh grass in his mouth:
and that he detested most of all, because it made him sick.
And he would spit and wipe his mouth, and storm at her, while
she ran away as hard as she could, pealing with laughter. She
was always laughing. Even when she was asleep she laughed.
Olivier, lying awake in the next room, would suddenly start
up in the middle of the stories he was telling himself, at the
sound of the wild laughter and the muttered words which she
would speak in the silence of the night. Outside, the trees
would creak with the wind, an owl would hoot, in the distant
villages and the farms in the heart of the woods dogs would
bark. In the dim phosphorescence of the night Olivier would
see the dark, heavy branches of the pines moving like ghosts
outside his window: and Antoinette's laughter would comfort
him.

The two children were very religious, especially Olivier.
Their father used to scandalize them with his anti-clerical
professions of faith, but he did not interfere with them: and,
at heart, like so many men of his class who are unbelievers,
he was not sorry that his family should believe for him: for
it is always good to have allies in the opposing camp, and one
is never sure which way Fortune will turn. He was a Deist,
and he reserved the right to summon a priest when the time
came, as his father had done: even if it did no good, it could
do no harm: one insures against fire, even if one has no reason
to believe that the house will be burned down.

Olivier was morbidly inclined towards mysticism. There
were times when he doubted whether he existed. He was
credulous and soft-hearted, and needed a prop: he took a
sorrowful delight in confession, in the comfort of confiding in
the invisible Friend, whose arms are always open to you, to
whom you can tell everything, who understands and forgives
everything: he tasted the sweetness of the waters of humility
and love, from which the soul issues pure, cleansed, and comforted. It was so natural to him to believe, that he could not

understand how any one could doubt: he thought people did so
from wickedness, and that God would punish them. He used
to pray secretly that his father might find grace: and he was
delighted when, one day, as they went into a little country
church, he saw his father mechanically make the sign of the
cross. The stories of the Gospel were mixed up in his mind
with the marvelous tales of Rübezahl, and Gracieuse and Per-
cinet, and the Caliph Haroun-al-Raschid. When he was a little boy he no more doubted the truth of the one than the
other. And just as he was not sure that he did not know
Shacabac of the cleft lips, and the loquacious barber, and the
little hunchback of Casgar, just as when he was out walking he
used to look about for the black woodpecker which bears in its
beak the magic root of the treasure-seeker, so Canaan and the
Promised Land became in his childish imagination certain
regions in Burgundy or Berrichon. A round hill in the country, with a little tree, like a shabby old feather, at the summit,
seemed to him to be like the mountain where Abraham had
built his pyre. A large dead bush by the edge of a field was the
Burning Bush, which the ages had put out. Even when he was
older, and his critical faculty had been awakened, he loved to
feed on the popular legends which enshrined his faith: and
they gave him so much pleasure, though he no longer accepted
them implicitly, that he would amuse himself by pretending to
do so. So for a long time on Easter Saturday he would look
out for the return of the Easter bells, which went away to
Rome on the Thursday before, and would come floating through
the air with little streamers. He did finally admit that it was
not true: but he did not give up looking skywards when he
heard them ringing: and once—though he knew perfectly well
that it could not be—he fancied he saw one of them disappearing over the house with blue ribbons.

It was vitally necessary for him to steep himself in the world
of legend and faith. He avoided life. He avoided himself.
Thin, pale, puny, he suffered from being so, and could not
bear its being talked about. He was naturally pessimistic,

no doubt inheriting it from his mother, and his pessimism was fed by his morbidity. He did not know it: thought everybody must be like himself: and the queer little boy of ten, instead of romping in the gardens during his play-time, used to shut himself up in his room, and, carefully picking his words, wrote his will.

He used to write a great deal. Every evening he used laboriously and secretly to write his diary—he did not know why, for he had nothing to say, and he said nothing worth saying. Writing was an inherited mania with him, the age-old itch of the French provincial—the old indestructible stock—who every day, until the day of his death, with an idiotic patience which is almost heroic, writes down in detail what he has seen, said, done, heard, eaten, and drunk. For his own pleasure, entirely. It is not for other eyes. No one will ever read it: he knows that: he never reads it again himself.

Music, like religion, was for Olivier a shelter from the too vivid light of day. Both brother and sister were born musicians,—especially Olivier, who had inherited the gift from his mother. Their taste, as it needed to be, was excellent. There was no one capable of forming it in the province, where no music was ever heard but that of the local band, which played nothing but marches, or—on its good days—selections from Adolphe Adam, and the church organist who played romanzas, and the exercises of the young ladies of the town who strummed a few valses and polkas, the overture to the *Caliph of Bagdad, la Chasse du Jeune Henri,* and two or three sonatas of Mozart, always the same, and always with the same mistakes, on instruments that were sadly out of tune. These things were invariably included in the evening's program at parties. After dinner, those who had talent were asked to display it: at first they would blush and refuse, but then they would yield to the entreaties of the assembled company: and they would play their stock pieces without their music. Every one would then admire the artist's memory and her beautiful touch.

The ceremony was repeated at almost every party, and the thought of it would altogether spoil the children's dinner. When they had to play the *Voyage en Chine* of Bazin, or their pieces of Weber as a duet, they gave each other confidence, and were not very much afraid. But it was torture to them to have to play alone. Antoinette, as usual, was the braver of the two. Although it bored her dreadfully,—as she knew that there was no way out of it, she would go through with it, sit at the piano with a determined air, and gallop through her *rondo* at breakneck speed, stumbling over certain passages, make a hash of others, break off, turn her head, and say, with a smile:

"Oh! I can't remember. . . ."

Then she would start off again a few bars farther on, and go on to the end. And she would make no attempt to conceal her pleasure at having finished: and when she returned to her chair, amid the general chorus of praise, she would laugh and say:

"I made such a lot of mistakes."

But Olivier was not so easy to handle. He could not bear making a show of himself in public, and being "the observed of all observers." It was bad enough for him to have to speak in company. But to have to play, especially for people who did not like music—(that was obvious to him)—for people whom music actually bored, people who only asked him to play as a matter of habit, seemed to him to be neither more nor less than tyranny, and he tried vainly to revolt against it. He would refuse obstinately. Sometimes he would escape and go and hide in a dark room, in a passage, or even in the barn, in spite of his horror of spiders. His refusal would make the guests only insist the more, and they would quiz him: and his parents would sternly order him to play, and even slap him when he was too impudently rebellious. And in the end he always had to play,—of course unwillingly and sulkily. And then he would suffer agonies all night because he had played

so badly, partly from vanity, and partly from his very genuin•
love for music.

The taste of the little town had not always been so banal
There had been a time when there were quite good chamber
concerts at several houses. Madame Jeannin used often to
speak of her grandfather, who adored the violoncello, and used
to sing airs of Gluck, and Dalayrac, and Berton. There was
a large volume of them in the house, and a pile of Italian
songs. For the old gentleman was like M. Andrieux, of whom
Berlioz said: " He *loved* Gluck." And he added bitterly: " He
also *loved* Piccinni."—Perhaps of the two he preferred Piccinni. At all events, the Italian songs were in a large majority
in her grandfather's collection. They had been Olivier's first
musical nourishment. Not a very substantial diet, rather like
those sweetmeats with which provincial children are stuffed:
they corrupt the palate, destroy the tissues of the stomach, and
there is always a danger of their killing the appetite for more
solid nutriment. But Olivier could not be accused of greediness. He was never offered any more solid food. Having no
bread, he was forced to eat cake. And so, by force of circumstance, it came about that Cimarosa, Paesiello, and Rossini fed
the mystic, melancholy little boy, who was more than a little
intoxicated by his draughts of the *Asti spumante* poured out
for him, instead of milk, by these bacchanalian Satyrs, and the
two lively, ingenuously, lasciviously smiling Bacchante of
Naples and Catania—Pergolesi and Bellini.

He played a great deal to himself, for his own pleasure. He
was saturated with music. He did not try to understand what
he was playing, but gave himself up to it. Nobody ever thought
of teaching him harmony, and it never occurred to him to learn
it. Science and the scientific mind were foreign to the nature
of his family, especially on his mother's side. All the lawyers,
wits, and humanists of the De Villiers were baffled by any sort
of problem. It was told of a member of the family—a distant
cousin—as a remarkable thing that he had found a post in the
Bureau des Longitudes. And it was further told how he had

gone mad. The old provincial middle-classes, robust and positive in temper, but dull and sleepy as a result of their gigantic meals and the monotony of their lives, are very proud of their common sense: they have so much faith in it that they boast that there is no difficulty which cannot be resolved by it: and they are never very far from considering men of science as artists of a sort, more useful than the others, but less exalted, because at least artists serve no useful purpose, and there is a sort of distinction about their lounging existence.—(Besides, every business man flatters himself that he might have been an artist if he had cared about it.)—While scientists are not far from being manual laborers,—(which is degrading),—just master-workmen with more education, though they are a little cracked: they are mighty fine on paper: but outside their arithmetic factories they're nobody. They would not be much use without the guidance of common-sense people who have some experience of life and business.

Unfortunately, it is not proven that their experience of life and business goes so far as these people like to think. It is only a routine, ringing the changes on a few easy cases. If any unforeseen position arises, in which they have to decide quickly and vigorously, they are always disgruntled.

Antoine Jeannin was that sort of man. Everything was so nicely adjusted, and his business jogged along so comfortably in its place in the life of the province, that he had never encountered any serious difficulty. He had succeeded to his father's position without having any special aptitude for the business: and, as everything had gone well, he attributed it to his own brilliant talents. He loved to say that it was enough to be honest, methodical, and to have common sense: and he intended handing down his business to his son, without any more regard for the boy's tastes than his father had had for his own. He did not do anything to prepare him for it. He let his children grow up as they liked, so long as they were good, and, above all, happy: for he adored them And so the two children were as little prepared for the struggle of life as possible: they

were like hothouse flowers. But, surely, they would always live
like that? In the soft provincial atmosphere, in the bosom of
their wealthy, influential family, with a kindly, gay, jovial
father, surrounded by friends, one of the leading men of the
district, life was so easy, so bright and smiling.

Antoinette was sixteen. Olivier was about to be confirmed.
His mind was filled with all kinds of mystic dreams. In her
heart Antoinette heard the sweet song of new-born hope soaring,
like the lark in April, in the springtime of her life. It was a
joy to her to feel the flowering of her body and soul, to know
that she was pretty, and to be told so. Her father's immoderate
praises were enough to turn her head.

He was in ecstasies over her: he delighted in her little
coquetries, to see her eying herself in her mirror, to watch
her little innocent tricks. He would take her on his knees, and
tease her about her childish love-affairs, and the conquests she
had made, and the suitors that he pretended had come to him
a-wooing: he would tell her their names: respectable citizens,
each more old and ugly than the last. And she would cry out in
horror, and break into rippling laughter, and put her arms about
her father's neck, and press her cheek close to his. And he
would ask which was the happy man of her choice: was it the
District Attorney, who, the Jeannins' old maid used to say,
was as ugly as the seven deadly sins? Or was it the fat notary?
And she would slap him playfully to make him cease, or hold
her hand over his mouth. He would kiss her little hands, and
jump her up and down on his knees, and sing the old song

> " What would you, pretty maid ?
> An ugly husband, eh ? "

And she would giggle and tie his whiskers under his chin,
and reply with the refrain:

> " A handsome husband I,
> No ugly man, madame."

She would declare her intention of choosing for herself.
She knew that she was, or would be, very rich,—(her father

used to tell her so at every turn)—she was a "fine catch."
The sons of the distinguished families of the country were already courting her, setting a wide white net of flattery and
cunning snares to catch the little silver fish. But it looked
as though the fish would elude them all: for Antoinette saw
all their tricks, and laughed at them: she was quite ready to be
caught, but not against her will. She had already made up
her mind to marry.

The noble family of the district—(there is generally one
noble family to every district, claiming descent from the ancient
lords of the province, though generally its origin goes no farther
back than some purchaser of the national estates, some com-
missary of the eighteenth century, or some Napoleonic army-
contractor)—the Bonnivets, who lived some few miles away
from the town, in a castle with tall towers with gleaming slates,
surrounded by vast woods, in which were innumerable fish-
ponds, themselves proposed for the hand of Mademoiselle Jeannin. Young Bonnivet was very assiduous in his courtship of
Antoinette. He was a handsome boy, rather stout and heavy
for his age, who did nothing but hunt and eat, and drink and
sleep: he could ride, dance, had charming manners, and was not
more stupid than other young men. He would ride into the
town, or drive in his buggy and call on the banker, on some
business pretext: and sometimes he would bring some game or a
bouquet of flowers for the ladies. He would seize the opportunity to pay court to Antoinette. They would walk in the
garden together. He would pay her lumbering compliments,
and pull his mustache, and make jokes, and make his spurs
clatter on the tiles of the terrace. Antoinette thought him
charming. Her pride and her affections were both tickled.
She would swim in those first sweet hours of young love.
Olivier detested the young squire, because he was strong, heavy,
brutal, had a loud laugh, and hands that gripped like a vise,
and a disdainful trick of always calling him: "Boy . . ."
and pinching his cheeks. He detested him above all,—without
knowing it,—because he dared to love his sister: . . . his

sister, his very own, his, and she could not belong to any one
else ! . . .

Disaster came. Sooner or later there must come a crisis
in the lives of the old middle-class families which for centuries have vegetated in the same little corner of the earth,
and have sucked it dry. They sleep in peace, and think themselves as eternal as the earth that bears them. But the soil
beneath them is dry and dead, their roots are sapped : just the
blow of an ax, and down they come. Then they talk of accidents and unforeseen misfortunes. There would have been
no accident if there had been more strength in the tree : or, at
least, would have been no more than a sudden storm, wrenching
away a few branches, but never shaking the tree.

Antoine Jeannin was weak, trustful, and a little vain. He
loved to throw dust in people's eyes, and easily confounded
" seeming " and " being." He spent recklessly, though his
extravagance, moderated by fits of remorse as the result of the
age-old habit of economy—(he would fling away pounds, and
haggle over a farthing)—never seriously impaired his capital.
He was not very cautious in business either. He never refused
to lend money to his friends : and it was not difficult to be a
friend of his. He did not always trouble to ask .for a receipt :
he kept a rough account of what was owing to him, and never
asked for payment before it was offered him. He believed in
the good faith of other men, and supposed that they would
believe in his own. He was much more timid than his jocular,
easy-going manners led people to suppose. He would never
have dared to refuse certain importunate borrowers, or to let
his doubts of their solvency appear. That arose from a mixturo
of kindness and pusillanimity. He did not wish to offend anybody, and he was afraid of being insulted. So he was always
giving way. And, by way of carrying it off, he would lend with
alacrity, as though his debtors were doing him a service by
borrowing his money. And he was not far from believing it :

his vanity and optimism had no difficulty in persuading him that every business he touched was good business.

Such ways of dealing were not calculated to alienate the sympathies of his debtors: he was adored by the peasants, who knew that they could always count on his good nature, and never hesitated to resort to him. But the gratitude of men— even of honest men—is a fruit that must be gathered in good season. If it is left too long upon the tree, it quickly rots. After a few months M. Jeannin's debtors would begin to think that his assistance was their right: and they were even inclined to think that, as M. Jeannin had been so glad to help them, it must have been to his interest to do so. The best of them considered themselves discharged—if not of the debt, at least of the obligation of gratitude—by the present of a hare they had killed, or a basket of eggs from their fowlyard, which they would come and offer to the banker on the day of the great fair of the year.

As hitherto only small sums had been lent, and M. Jeannin had only had to do with fairly honest people, there were no very awkward consequences: the loss of money—of which the banker never breathed a word to a soul—was very small. But it was a very different matter when M. Jeannin knocked up against a certain company promoter who was launching a great industrial concern, and had got wind of the banker's easy-going ways and financial resources. This gentleman, who wore the ribbon of the Legion of Honor, and pretended to be intimate with two or three Ministers, an Archbishop, an assortment of senators, and various celebrities of the literary and financial world, and to be in touch with an omnipotent newspaper, had a very imposing manner, and most adroitly assumed the authoritative and familiar tone most calculated to impress his man. By way of introduction and recommendation, with a clumsiness which would have aroused the suspicions of a quicker man than M. Jeannin, he produced certain ordinary complimentary letters which he had received from the illustrious persons of his acquaintance, asking him to dinner, or thanking him for some

invitation they had received: for it is well known that the
French are never niggardly with such epistolary small change,
nor particularly chary of shaking hands with, and accepting invitations from, an individual whom they have only known for
an hour—provided only that he amuses them and does not ask
them for money: and even as regards that, there are many who
would not refuse to lend their new friend money so long as
others did the same. And it would be a poor lookout for a
clever man bent on relieving his neighbor of his superfluous
money if he could not find a sheep who could be induced to
jump the fence so that all the rest would follow.—If other
sheep had not taken the. fence before him, M. Jeannin would
have been the first. He was of the woolly tribe which is made
to be fleeced. He was seduced by his visitor's exalted connections, his fluency and his trick of flattery, and also by the first
fine results of his advice. He only risked a little at first, and
won: then he risked much: finally he risked all: not only his
own money, but that of his clients as well. He did not tell
them about it: he was sure he would win: he wanted to overwhelm them with the great thing he had done for them.

The venture collapsed. He heard of it ·indirectly through
one of his Parisian correspondents who happened to mention
the new crash, without ever dreaming that Jeannin was one
of the victims: for the banker had not said a word to anybody: with incredible irresponsibility, he had not taken the
trouble—even avoided—asking the advice of men who were in
a position to give him information: he had done the whole
thing secretly, in the infatuated belief in his infallible common sense, and he had been satisfied with the vaguest knowledge
of what he was doing. There are such moments of aberration
in life: moments, it would seem, when a man is marked out
for ruin, when he is fearful lest any one should come to his aid,
when he avoids all advice that might save him, hides away, and
rushes headlong, madly, shaking himself free for the fatal
plunge.

M. Jeannin rushed to the station, utterly sick at heart, and took train for Paris. He went to look for his man. He flattered himself with the hope that the news might be false, or, at least, exaggerated. Naturally he did not find the fellow, and received further news of the collapse, which was as complete as possible. He returned distracted, and said nothing. No one had any idea of it yet. He tried to gain a few weeks, a few days. In his incurable optimism, he tried hard to believe that he would find a way to make good, if not his own losses, at least those of his clients. He tried various expedients, with a clumsy haste which would have removed any chance of succeeding that he might have had. He tried to borrow, but was everywhere refused. In his despair, he staked the little he had left on wildly speculative ventures, and lost it all. From that moment there was a complete change in his character. He relapsed into an alarming state of terror: still he said nothing: but he was bitter, violent, harsh, horribly sad. But still, when he was with strangers, he affected his old gaiety: but no one could fail to see the change in him: it was attributed to his health. With his family he was less guarded: and they saw at once that he was concealing some serious trouble. They hardly knew him. Sometimes he would burst into a room and ransack a desk, flinging all the papers higgledy-piggledy on to the floor, and flying into a frenzy because he could not find what he was looking for, or because some one offered to help him. Then he would stand stock still in the middle of it all, and when they asked him what he was looking for, he did not know himself. He seemed to have lost all interest in his family: or he would kiss them with tears in his eyes. He could not sleep. He could not eat.

Madame Jeannin saw that they were on the eve of a catastrophe: but she had never taken any part in her husband's affairs, and did not understand them. She questioned him: he repulsed her brutally: and, hurt in her pride, she did not persist. But she trembled, without knowing why.

The children could have no suspicion of the impending disaster. Antoinette, no doubt, was too intelligent not, like her mother, to have a presentiment of some misfortune: but she was absorbed in the delight of her budding love: she refused to think of unpleasant things: she persuaded herself that the clouds would pass—or that it would be time enough to see them when it was impossible to disregard them.

Of the three, the boy Olivier was perhaps the nearest to understanding what was going on in his unhappy father's soul. He felt that his father was suffering, and he suffered with him in secret. But he dared not say anything: naturally he could do nothing, and he was helpless. And then he, too, thrust back the thought of sad things, the nature of which he could not grasp: like his mother and sister, he was superstitiously inclined to believe that perhaps misfortune, the approach of which he did not wish to see, would not come. Those poor wretches who feel the imminence of danger do readily play the ostrich: they hide their heads behind a stone, and pretend that Misfortune will not see them.

Disturbing rumors began to fly. It was said that the bank's credit was impaired. In vain did the banker assure his clients that it was perfectly all right, on one pretext or another the more suspicious of them demanded their money. M. Jeannin felt that he was lost: he defended himself desperately, assum· ing a tone of indignation, and complaining loftily and bitterly of their suspicions of himself: he even went so far as to be violent and angry with some of his old clients, but that only let him down finally. Demands for payment came in a rush. On his beam-ends, at bay, he completely lost his head. He went away for a few days to gamble with his last few banknotes at a neighboring watering-place, was cleaned out in a quarter of an hour, and returned home. His sudden departure set the little town by the ears, and it was said that he had cleared out: and Madame Jeannin had had great difficulty in coping with the wild, anxious inquiries of the people: she begged them to be patient, and swore that her husband would return. They did not believe her, although they would have been only

too glad to do so.   And so, when it was known that he had
returned, there was a general sigh of relief: there were many
who almost believed that their fears had been baseless, and
that the Jeannins were much too shrewd not to get out of a
hole by admitting that they had fallen into it.   The banker's
attitude confirmed that impression.   Now that he no longer had
any doubt as to what he must do, he seemed to be weary, but
quite calm.   He chatted quietly to a few friends whom he met
in the station road on his way home, talking about the drought
and the country not having had any water for weeks, and the
superb condition of the vines, and the fall of the Ministry, announced in the evening papers.

When he reached home he pretended not to notice his
wife's excitement, who had run to meet him when she heard
him come in, and told him volubly and confusedly what had
happened during his absence.   She scanned his features to
try and see whether he had succeeded in averting the unknown
danger: but, from pride, she did not ask him anything: she
was waiting for him to speak first.   But he did not say a word
about the thing that was tormenting them both.   He silently
disregarded her desire to confide in him, and to get him to confide in her.   He spoke of the heat, and of how tired he was,
and complained of a racking headache: and they sat down to
dinner as usual.

He talked little, and was dull, lost in thought, and his
brows were knit: he drummed with his fingers on the table:
he forced himself to eat, knowing that they were watching
him, and looked with vague, unseeing eyes at his children,
who were intimidated by the silence, and at his wife, who sat
stiffly nursing her injured vanity, and, without looking at him,
marking his every movement.   Towards the end of dinner he
seemed to wake up: he tried to talk to Antoinette and Olivier,
and asked them what they had been doing during his absence:
but he did not listen to their replies, and heard only the
sound of their voices· and although he was staring at them,
his gaze was elsewhere.   Olivier felt it: he stopped in the

middle of his prattle, and had no desire to go on. But, after a moment's embarrassment, Antoinette recovered her gaiety: she chattered merrily, like a magpie, laid her head on her father's shoulder, or tugged his sleeve to make him listen to what she was saying. M. Jeannin said nothing: his eyes wandered from Antoinette to Olivier, and the crease in his forehead grew deeper and deeper. In the middle of one of his daughter's stories he could bear it no longer, and got up and went and looked out of the window to conceal his emotion. The children folded their napkins, and got up too. Madame Jeannin told them to go and play in the garden: in a moment or two they could be heard chasing each other down the paths and screaming. Madame Jeannin looked at her husband, whose back was turned towards her, and she walked round the table as though to arrange something. Suddenly she went up to him, and, in a voice hushed by her fear of being over-heard by the servants and by the agony that was in her, she said:

"Tell me, Antoine, what is the matter? There is something the matter. . . . You are hiding something. . . . Has something dreadful happened? Are you ill?"

But once more M. Jeannin put her off, and shrugged his shoulders, and said harshly:

"No! No, I tell you! Let me be!"

She was angry, and went away: in her fury, she declared that, no matter what happened to her husband, she would not bother about it any more.

M. Jeannin went down into the garden. Antoinette was still larking about, and tugging at her brother to make him run. But the boy declared suddenly that he was not going to play any more: and he leaned against the wall of the terrace a few yards away from his father. Antoinette tried to go on teasing him: but he drove her away and sulked: then she called him names: and when she found she could get no more fun out of him, she went in and began to play the piano.

M. Jeannin and Olivier were left alone.

"What's the matter with you, boy? Why won't you play?" asked the father gently

"I'm tired, father."

"Well, let us sit here on this seat for a little."

They sat down. It was a lovely September night. A dark, clear sky. The sweet scent of the petunias was mingled with the stale and rather unwholesome smell of the canal sleeping darkly below the terrace wall. Great moths, pale and sphinx-like, fluttered about the flowers, with a little whirring sound. The even voices of the neighbors sitting at their doors on the other side of the canal rang through the silent air. In the house Antoinette was playing a florid Italian cavatina. M. Jeannin held Olivier's hand in his. He was smoking. Through the darkness behind which his father's face was slowly disappearing the boy could see the red glow of the pipe, which gleamed, died away, gleamed again, and finally went out. Neither spoke. Then Olivier asked the names of the stars. M. Jeannin, like almost all men of his class, knew nothing of the things of Nature, and could not tell him the names of any save the great constellations, which are known to every one: but he pretended that the boy was asking their names, and told him. Olivier made no objection: it always pleased him to hear their beautiful mysterious names, and to repeat them in a whisper. Besides, he was not so much wanting to know their names as instinctively to come closer to his father. They said nothing more. Olivier looked at the stars, with his head thrown back and his mouth open: he was lost in drowsy thoughts: he could feel through all his veins the warmth of his father's hand. Suddenly the hand began to tremble. That seemed funny to Olivier, and he laughed and said sleepily:

"Oh, how your hand is trembling, father!"

M. Jeannin removed his hand.

After a moment Olivier, still busy with his own thoughts, said:

"Are you tired, too, father?"

" Yes, my boy."

The boy replied affectionately :

" You must not tire yourself out so much, father."

M. Jeannin drew Olivier towards him, and held him to his breast and murmured :

" My poor boy ! . . ."

But already Olivier's thoughts had flown off on another tack. The church clock chimed eight o'clock. He broke away, and said :

" I'm going to read."

On Thursdays he was allowed to read for an hour after dinner, until bedtime : it was his greatest joy : and nothing in the world could induce him to sacrifice a minute of it.

M. Jeannin let him go. He walked up and down the terrace for a little in the dark. Then he, too, went in.

In the room his wife and the two children were sitting round the lamp. Antoinette was sewing a ribbon on to a blouse, talking and humming the while, to Olivier's obvious discomfort, for he was stopping his ears with his fists so as not to hear, while he pored over his book with knitted brows, and his elbows on the table. Madame Jeannin was mending stockings and talking to the old nurse, who was standing by her side and giving an account of her day's expenditure, and seizing the opportunity for a little gossip : she always had some amusing tale to tell in her extraordinary lingo, which used to make them roar with laughter, while Antoinette would try to imitate her. M. Jeannin watched them silently. No one noticed him. He wavered for a moment, sat down, took up a book, opened it at random, shut it again, got up : he could not sit still. He lit a candle and said good-night. He went up to the children and kissed them fondly : they returned his kiss absently without looking up at him,—Antoinette being absorbed in her work, and Olivier in his book. Olivier did not even take his hands from his ears, and grunted " Good-night," and went on reading :—(when he was reading even if one of his family had fallen into the fire, he would not have looked up).—M. Jeannin left the room. He lingered in the next room, for a moment. His wife came out soon, the old nurse having gone to arrange the linen-cupboard. She pretended not to see him. He hesitated, then came up to her, and said:

"I beg your pardon. I was rather rude just now."

She longed to say to him:

"My dear, my dear, that is nothing: but, tell me, what is the matter with you? Tell me, what is hurting you so?"

But she jumped at the opportunity of taking her revenge, and said:

"Let me be! You have been behaving odiously. You treat me worse than you would a servant."

And she went on in that strain, setting forth all her grievances volubly, shrilly, rancorously.

He raised his hands wearily, smiled bitterly, and left her.

No one heard the report of the revolver. Only, next day, when it was known what had happened, a few of the neighbors remembered that, in the middle of the night, when the streets were quiet, they had noticed a sharp noise like the cracking of a whip. They did not pay any attention to it. The silence of the night fell once more upon the town, wrapping both living and dead about with its mystery.

Madame Jeannin was asleep, but woke up an hour or two later. Not seeing her husband by her side she got up and went anxiously through all the rooms, and downstairs to the offices of the bank, which were in an annex of the house: and there, sitting in his chair in his office, she found M. Jeannin huddled forward on his desk in a pool of blood, which was still dripping down on to the floor. She gave a scream, dropped her candle, and fainted. She was heard in the house. The servants came running, picked her up, took care of her, and laid the body of M. Jeannin on a bed. The door of the children's room was locked. Antoinette was sleeping happily. Olivier heard the sound of voices and footsteps: he wanted to go and see what it was all about: but he was afraid of waking his sister, and presently he went to sleep again.

Next morning the news was all over the town before they knew anything. Their old nurse came sobbing and told them. Their mother was incapable of thinking of anything: her condition was critical. The two children were left alone in the presence of death. At first they were more fearful than sorrowful. And they were not allowed to weep in peace. The cruel legal formalities were begun the first thing in the morning. Antoinette hid away in her room, and with all the force of her youthful egoism clung to the only idea which could help her to thrust back the horror of the overwhelming reality: the thought of her lover: all day long she waited for him to come. Never had he been more ardent than the last time she had seen him, and she had no doubt that, as soon as he heard of the catastrophe, he would hasten to share her grief.—But nobody came, or wrote, or gave one sign of sympathy. As soon as the news of the suicide was out, people who had intrusted their money to the banker rushed to the Jeannins' house, forced their way in, and, with merciless cruelty, stormed and screamed at the widow and the two children.

In a few days they were faced with their utter ruin: the loss of a dear one, the loss of their fortune, their position, their public esteem, and the desertion of their friends. A total wreck. Nothing was left to provide for them. They had all three an uncompromising feeling for moral purity, which made their suffering all the greater from the dishonor of which they were innocent. Of the three Antoinette was the most distraught by their sorrow, because she had never really known suffering. Madame Jeannin and Olivier, though they were racked by it, were more inured to it. Instinctively pessimistic, they were overwhelmed but not surprised. The idea of death had always been a refuge to them, as it was now, more than ever: they longed for death. It is pitiful to be so resigned, but not so terrible as the revolt of a young creature, confident and happy, loving every moment of her life, who suddenly finds herself face to face with such unfathomable, irremediable sorrow, and death which is horrible to her. . . .

Antoinette discovered the ugliness of the world in a flash. Her eyes were opened: she saw life and human beings as they are: she judged her father, her mother, and her brother. While Olivier and Madame Jeannin wept together, in her grief she drew into herself. Desperately she pondered the past, the present, and the future: and she saw that there was nothing left for her, no hope, nothing to support her: she could count on no one.

The funeral took place, grimly, shamefully. The Church refused to receive the body of the suicide. The widow and orphans were deserted by the cowardice of their former friends. One or two of them came for a moment: and their embarrassment was even harder to bear than the absence of the rest. They seemed to make a favor of it, and their silence was big with reproach and pitying contempt. It was even worse with their relations: not only did they receive no single word of sympathy, but they were visited with bitter reproaches. The banker's suicide, far from removing ill-feeling, seemed to be hardly less criminal than his failure. Respectable people cannot forgive those who kill themselves. It seems to them monstrous that a man should prefer death to life with dishonor: and they would fain call down all the rigor of the law on him who seems to say:

" There is no misery so great as that of living with you."

The greatest cowards are not the least ready to accuse him of cowardice. And when, in addition, the suicide, by ending his life, touches their interests and their revenge, they lose all control.—Not for one moment did they think of all that the wretched Jeannin must have suffered to come to it. They would have had him suffer a thousand times more. And as he had escaped them, they transferred their fury to his family. They did not admit it to themselves: for they knew they were unjust. But they did it all the same, for they needed a victim.

Madame Jeannin, who seemed to be able to do nothing but

weep and moan, recovered her energy when her husband was
attacked. She discovered then how much she had loved him:
and she and her two children, who had no idea what would
become of them in the future, all agreed to renounce their claim
to her dowry, and to their own personal estate, in order, as
far as possible, to meet M. Jeannin's debts. And, since it had
become impossible for them to stay in the little town, they decided to go to Paris.

Their departure was something in the nature of a flight.

On the evening of the day before,—(a melancholy evening
towards the end of September: the fields were disappearing
behind the white veil of mist, out of which, as they walked
along the road, on either side the fantastic shapes of the dripping, shivering bushes started forth, looking like the plants in
an aquarium),—they went together to say farewell to the grave
where he lay. They all three knelt on the narrow curbstone
which surrounded the freshly turned patch of earth. They
wept in silence; Olivier sobbed. Madame Jeannin mopped her
eyes mournfully. She augmented her grief and tortured herself by saying to herself over and over again the words she
had spoken to her husband the last time she had seen him alive.
Olivier thought of that last conversation on the seat on the
terrace. Antoinette wondered dreamily what would become of
them. None of them ever dreamed of reproaching the wretched
man who had dragged them down in his own ruin. But Antoinette thought:

"Ah! dear father, how we shall suffer!"

The mist grew more dense, the cold damp pierced through
to their bones. But Madame Jeannin could not bring herself
to go. Antoinette saw that Olivier was shivering and she said
to her mother:

"I am cold."

They got up. Just as they were going, Madame Jeannin
turned once more towards the grave, gazed at it for the last
time, and said:

" My dear, my dear! "

They left the cemetery as night was falling. Antoinette held Olivier's icy hand in hers.

They went back to the old house. It was their last night under the roof-tree where they had always slept, where their lives and the lives of their parents had been lived—the walls, the hearth, the little patch of earth were so indissolubly linked with the family's joys and sorrows, as almost themselves to be part of the family, part of their life, which they could only leave to die.

Their boxes were packed. They were to take the first train next day before the shops were opened: they wanted to escape their neighbors' curiosity and malicious remarks.—They longed to cling to each other and stay together: but they went instinctively to their rooms and stayed there: there they remained standing, never moving, not even taking off their hats and cloaks. touching the walls, the furniture, all the things they were going to leave, pressing their faces against the window-panes. trying to take away with them in memory the contact of the things they loved. At last they made an effort to shake free from the absorption of their sorrowful thoughts and met in Madame Jeannin's room,—the family room, with a great recess at the back, where, in old days. they always used to fore-gather in the evening, after dinner. when there were no visitors. In old days! . . . How far off they seemed now!—They sat silently round the meager fire: then they all knelt by the bed and said their prayers: and they went to bed very early, for they had to be up before dawn. But it was long before they slept.

About four o'clock in the morning Madame Jeannin, who had looked at her watch every hour or so to see whether it was not time to get ready, lit her candle and got up. Antoinette, who had hardly slept at all, heard her and got up too. Olivier was fast asleep. Madame Jeannin gazed at him tenderly and could not bring herself to wake him. She stole away on tiptoe and said to Antoinette:

" Don't make any noise: let the poor boy enjoy his last mo
ments here!"

The two women dressed and finished their packing. About
the house hovered the profound silence of the cold night, such
a night as makes all living things, men and beasts, cower away
for warmth into the depths of sleep. Antoinette's teeth were
chattering: she was frozen body and soul.

The front door creaked upon the frozen air. The old nurse,
who had the key of the house, came for the last time to serve
her employers. She was short and fat, short-winded, and slow-
moving from her portliness, but she was remarkably active for
her age: she appeared with her jolly face muffled up, and her
nose was red, and her eyes were wet with tears. She was
heart-broken when she saw that Madame Jeannin had got up
without waiting for her, and had herself lit the kitchen fire.—
Olivier woke up as she came in. His first impulse was to close
his eyes, turn over, and go to sleep again. Antoinette came and
laid her hand gently on her brother's shoulder, and she said in a
low voice:

" Olivier, dear, it is time to get up."

He sighed, opened his eyes, saw his sister's face leaning
over him: she smiled sadly and caressed his face with her hand.
She said:

" Come!"

He got up.

They crept out of the house, noiselessly, like thieves. They
all had parcels in their hands. The old nurse went in front
of them trundling their boxes in a wheelbarrow. They left
behind almost all their possessions, and took away, so to speak,
only what they had on their backs and a change of clothes. A
few things for remembrance were to be sent after them by
goods-train: a few books, portraits, the old grandfather's clock,
whose tick-tock seemed to them to be the beating of their
hearts.—The air was keen. No one was stirring in the town:
the shutters were closed and the streets empty. They said
nothing: only the old servant spoke. Madame Jeannin was

striving to fix in her memory all the images which told her of all her past life.

At the station, out of vanity, Madame Jeannin took second-class tickets, although she had vowed to travel third: but she had not the courage to face the humiliation in the presence of the railway clerks who knew her. She hurried into an empty compartment with her two children and shut the door. Hiding behind the curtains they trembled lest they should see any one they knew. But no one appeared: the town was hardly awake by the time they left: the train was empty: there were only a few peasants traveling by it, and some oxen, who hung their heads out of their trucks and bellowed mournfully. After a long wait the engine gave a slow whistle, and the train moved on through the mist. The fugitives drew the curtains and pressed their faces against the windows to take a last long look at the little town, with its Gothic tower just appearing through the mist, and the hill covered with stubby fields, and the meadows white and steaming with the frost; already it was a distant dream-landscape, fading out of existence. And when the train turned a bend and passed into a cutting, and they could no longer see it, and were sure there was no one to see them, they gave way to their emotion. With her handkerchief pressed to her lips Madame Jeannin sobbed. Olivier flung himself into her arms and with his head on her knees he covered her hands with tears and kisses. Antoinette sat at the other end of the compartment and looked out of the window and wept in silence. They did not all weep for the same reason. Madame Jeannin and Olivier were thinking only of what they had left behind them. Antoinette was thinking rather of what they were going to meet: she was angry with herself: she, too, would gladly have been absorbed in her memories. . . .—She was right to think of the future: she had a truer vision of the world than her mother and brother. They were weaving dreams about Paris. Antoinette herself had little notion of what awaited them there. They had never been there. Madame Jeannin imagined that, though their position would be sad enough, there would be no reason for anxiety. She had a sister in Paris, the wife of a wealthy magistrate: and she counted on her assistance. She was convinced also that with the education her children had received and their natural gifts, which, like all mothers, she overestimated, they would have no difficulty in earning an honest living.

Their first impressions were gloomy enough. As they left the station they were bewildered by the jostling crowd of people in the luggage-room and the confused uproar of the carriages outside. It was raining. They could not find a cab, and had to walk a long way with their arms aching with their heavy parcels, so that they had to stop every now and then in the middle of the street at the risk of being run over or splashed by the carriages. They could not make a single driver pay any attention to them. At last they managed to stop a man who was driving an old and disgustingly dirty barouche. As they were handing in the parcels they let a bundle of rugs fall into the mud. The porter who carried the trunk and the cabman traded on their ignorance, and made them pay double. Madame Jeannin gave the address of one of those second-rate expensive hotels patronized by provincials who go on going to them, in spite of their discomfort, because their grandfathers went to them thirty years ago. They were fleeced there. They were told that the hotel was full, and they were accommodated with one small room for which they were charged the price of three. For dinner they tried to economize by avoiding the table d'hôte: they ordered a modest meal, which cost them just as much and left them famishing. Their illusions concerning Paris had come toppling down as soon as they arrived. And, during that first night in the hotel, when they were squeezed into one little, ill-ventilated room, they could not sleep: they were hot and cold by turns, and could not breathe, and started at every footstep in the corridor, and the banging of the doors, and the furious ringing of the electric bells: and their heads throbbed with the incessant roar of the carriages and heavy drays: and altogether they felt terrified of the monstrous city into which they had plunged to their utter bewilderment.

Next day Madame Jeannin went to see her sister, who lived in a luxurious flat in the *Boulevard Hausmann.* She hoped, though she did not say so, that they would be invited to stay there until they had found their feet. The welcome she received was enough to undeceive her. The Poyet-Delormes were furious at their relative's failure: especially Madame Delorme, who was afraid that it would be set against her, and might injure her husband's career, and she thought it shameless of the ruined family to come and cling to them, and compromise them even more. The magistrate was of the same opinion: but he was a kindly man: he would have been more inclined to help, but for his wife's intervention—to which he knuckled under. Madame Poyet-Delorme received her sister with icy coldness. It cut Madame Jeannin to the heart: but she swallowed down her pride: she hinted at the difficulty of her position and the assistance she hoped to receive from the Poyets. Her sister pretended not to understand, and did not even ask her to stay to dinner: they were ceremoniously invited to dine at the end of the week. The invitation did not come from Madame Poyet either, but from the magistrate, who was a little put out at his wife's treatment of her sister, and tried to make amends for her curtness: he posed as the good-natured man: but it was obvious that it did not come easily to him and that he was really very selfish. The unhappy Jeannins returned to their hotel without daring to say what they thought of their first visit.

They spent the following days in wandering about Paris, looking for a flat: they were worn out with going up stairs, and disheartened by the sight of the great barracks crammed full of people, and the dirty stairs, and the dark rooms, that seemed so depressing to them after their own big house in the country. They grew more and more depressed. And they were always shy and timid in the streets, and shops, and restaurants, so that they were cheated at every turn. Everything they asked

for cost an exorbitant sum: it was as though they had the
faculty of turning everything they touched into gold: only, ft
was they who had to pay out the gold. They were incredibly simple and absolutely incapable of looking after themselves.

Though there was little left to hope for from Madame Jeannin's sister, the poor lady wove illusions about the dinner to
which they were invited. They dressed for it with fluttering
hearts. They were received as guests, and not as relations—
though nothing more was expended on the dinner than the
ceremonious manner. The children met their cousins, who
were almost the same age as themselves, but they were not much
more cordial than their father and mother. The girl was very
smart and coquettish, and spoke to them with a lisp and a politely superior air, with affectedly honeyed manners which disconcerted them. The boy was bored by this duty-dinner with
their poor relations: and he was as surly as could be. Madame
Poyet-Delorme sat up stiffly in her chair, and, even when she
handed her a dish, seemed to be reading her sister a lesson.
Madame Poyet-Delorme talked trivialities to keep the conversation from becoming serious. They never got beyond talking of
what they were eating for fear of touching upon any intimate
and dangerous topic. Madame Jeannin made an effort to bring
them round to the subject next her heart: Madame Poyet-
Delorme cut her short with some pointless remark, and she
had not the courage to try again.

After dinner she made her daughter play the piano by way
of showing off her talents. The poor girl was embarrassed and
unhappy and played execrably. The Poyets were bored and
anxious for her to finish. Madame Poyet exchanged glances
with her daughter, with an ironic curl of her lips: and as the
music went on too long she began to talk to Madame Jeannin
about nothing in particular. At last Antoinette, who had quite
lost her place, and saw to her horror that, instead of going
on, she had begun again at the beginning, and that there was
no reason why she should ever stop, broke off suddenlv. and

ended with two inaccurate chords and a third which was absolutely dissonant. Monsieur Poyet said:

" Bravo ! "

And he asked for coffee.

Madame Poyet said that her daughter was taking lessons
with Pugno: and the young lady " who was taking lessons with
Pugno " said:

" Charming, my dear . . ."

And asked where Antoinette had studied.

The conversation dropped. They had exhausted the knick-
knacks in the drawing-room and the dresses of Madame and
Mademoiselle Poyet. Madame Jeannin said to herself:

" I must speak now. I must . . ."

And she fidgeted. Just as she had pulled herself together to
begin, Madame Poyet mentioned casually, without any attempt
at an apology, that they were very sorry but they had to go
out at half-past nine: they had an invitation which they had
been unable to decline. The Jeannins were at a loss, and got
up at once to go. The Poyets made some show of detaining
them. But a quarter of an hour later there was a ring at the
door: the footman announced some friends of the Poyets,
neighbors of theirs, who lived in the flat below. Poyet and
his wife exchanged glances, and there were hurried whisperings
with the servants. Poyet stammered some excuse, and hurried the Jeannins into the next room. (He was trying to hide
from his friends the existence, and the presence in his house,
of the compromising family.) The Jeannins were left alone in
a room without a fire. The children were furious at the affront.
Antoinette had tears in her eyes and insisted on their going.
Her mother resisted for a little: but then, after they had waited
for some time, she agreed. They went out. In the hall they
were caught by Poyet, who had been told by a servant, and
he muttered excuses: he pretended that he wanted them to
stay: but it was obvious that he was only eager for them to go.
He helped them on with their cloaks, and hurried them to the
loor with smiles and handshakes and whispered pleasantries. and

closed the door on them. When they reached their hotel the children burst into angry tears. Antoinette stamped her foot, and swore that she would never enter their house again.

Madame Jeannin took a flat on the fourth floor near the *Jardin des Plantes.* The bedrooms looked on to the filthy walls of a gloomy courtyard: the dining-room and the drawing-room—(for Madame Jeannin insisted on having a drawing-room)—on to a busy street. All day long steam-trams went by and hearses crawling along to the Ivry Cemetery. Filthy Italians, with a horde of children, loafed about on the seats, or spent their time in shrill argument. The noise made it impossible to have the windows open: and in the evening, on their way home, they had to force their way through crowds of bustling, evil-smelling people, cross the thronged and muddy streets, pass a horrible pothouse, that was on the ground floor of the next house, in the door of which there were always fat, frowsy women with yellow hair and painted faces, eying the passers-by.

Their small supply of money soon gave out. Every evening with sinking hearts they took stock of the widening hole in their purse. They tried to stint themselves: but they did not know how to set about it: that is a science which can only be learned by years of experimenting, unless it has been practised from childhood. Those who are not naturally economical merely waste their time in trying to be so: as soon as a fresh opportunity of spending money crops up, they succumb to the temptation: they are always going to economize next time: and when they do happen to make a little money, or to think they have made it, they rush out and spend ten times the amount on the strength of it.

At the end of a few weeks the Jeannins' resources were exhausted. Madame Jeannin had to gulp down what was left of her pride, and, unknown to her children, she went and asked Poyet for money. She contrived to see him alone at his office, and begged him to advance her a small sum until they had found work to keep them alive. Poyet, who was weak and human enough, tried at first to postpone the matter, but finally acceded to her request. He gave her two hundred francs in a moment of emotion, which mastered him, and he repented of it immediately afterwards,—when he had to make his peace with Madame Poyet, who was furious with her husband's weakness, and her sister's slyness.

All day and every day the Jeannins were out and about in Paris, looking for work. Madame Jeannin, true to the prejudices of her class, would not hear of their engaging in any other profession than those which are called "liberal"—no doubt because they leave their devotees free to starve. She would even have gone so far as to forbid her daughter to take a post as a family governess. Only the official professions, in the service of the State, were not degrading in her eyes. They had to discover a means of letting Olivier finish his education so that he might become a teacher. As for Antoinette, Madame Jeannin's idea was that she should go to a school to teach, or to the Conservatoire to win the prize for piano playing. But the schools at which she applied already had teachers enough, who were much better qualified than her daughter with her poor little elementary certificate: and, as for music, she had to recognize that Antoinette's talent was quite ordinary compared with that of so many others who did not get on at all. They came face to face with the terrible struggle for life, and the blind waste of talent, great and small, for which Paris can find no use.

The two children lost heart and exaggerated their uselessness: they believed that they were mediocre, and did their best to convince themselves and their mother that it was so. Olivier, who had had no difficulty in shining at his provincial school, was crushed by his various rebuffs: he seemed to have lost possession of all his gifts. At the school for which he won a scholarship, the results of his first examinations were so disastrous that his scholarship was taken away from him. He thought himself utterly stupid. At the same time he had a horror of Paris, and its swarming inhabitants, and the disgusting immorality of his schoolfellows, and their shameful conversation, and the bestiality of a few of them who did not spare him from their abominable proposals. He was not even strong enough to show his contempt for them. He felt degraded by the mere thought of their degradation. With his mother and sister, he took refuge in the heartfelt prayers which they used to say every evening after the day of deceptions and private humiliations, which to their innocence seemed to be a taint, of which they dared not tell each other. But, in contact with the latent spirit of atheism which is in the air of Paris, Olivier's faith was beginning to crumble away, without his knowledge, like whitewash trickling down a wall under the beating of the rain. He went on believing: but all about him God was dying.

His mother and sister pursued their futile quest. Madame Jeannin turned once more to the Poyets, who were anxious to be quit of them, and offered them work. Madame Jeannin was to go as reader to an old lady who was spending the winter in the South of France. A post was found for Antoinette as governess in a family in the West, who lived all the year round in the country. The terms were not bad, but Madame Jeannin refused. It was not so much for herself that she objected to a menial position, but she was determined that Antoinette should not be reduced to it, and unwilling to part with her. However unhappy they might be, just because they were unhappy, they wished to be together.—Madame Poyet took it very badly. She said that people who had no means of living had no business to be proud. Madame Jeannin could not refrain from crying out upon her heartlessness. Madame Poyet spoke bitterly of the bankruptcy and of the money that Madame Jeannin owed her. They parted, and the breach between them was final. All relationship between them was broken off. Madame Jeannin had only one desire left: to pay back the money she had borrowed. But she was unable to do that.

They resumed their vain search for work. Madame Jeannin went to see the deputy and the senator of her department, men whom Monsieur Jeannin had often helped. Everywhere she was brought face to face with ingratitude and selfishness. The deputy did not even answer her letters, and when she called on him he sent down word that he was out. The senator commiserated her ponderously on her unhappy position, which he attributed to "the wretched Jeannin," whose suicide he stigmatized harshly. Madame Jeannin defended her husband. The senator said that of course he knew that the banker had acted, not from dishonesty, but from stupidity, and that he was a fool, a poor gull, who knew nothing, and would go his own way without asking anybody's advice or taking a warning from any one. If he had only ruined himself, there would have been nothing to say: that would have been his own affair. But—not to mention the ruin that he had brought on others,— that he should have reduced his wife and children to poverty and deserted them and left them to get out of it as best they could . . . it was Madame Jeannin's own business if she chose to forgive him, if she were a saint, but for his part, he, the senator, not being a saint—(s, a, i, n, t),—but, he flattered himself, just a plain man—(s, a, i, n),—a plain, sensible, reasonable human being,—he could find no reason for forgiveness: a man who, in such circumstances, could kill himself, was a wretch. The only extenuating circumstance he could find in Jeannin's case was that he was not responsible for his actions. With that he begged Madame Jeannin's pardon for having expressed himself a little emphatically about her husband: he pleaded the sympathy that he felt for her: and he opened his drawer and offered her a fifty-franc note,—charity—which she refused.

She applied for a post in the offices of a great Government department. She set about it clumsily and inconsequently, and all her courage oozed out at the first attempt. She returned home so demoralized that for several days she could not stir. And, when she resumed her efforts, it was too late. She did

not find help either with the church-people, either because they
saw there was nothing to gain by it, or because they took no
interest in a ruined family, the head of which had been notoriously anti-clerical. After days and days of hunting for work
Madame Jeannin could find nothing better than a post as music-
teacher in a convent—an ungrateful task, ridiculously ill-paid.
To eke out her earnings she copied music in the evenings for
an agency. They were very hard on her. She was severely
called to task for omitting words and whole lines, as she did
in spite of her application, for she was always thinking of so
many other things and her wits were wool-gathering. And so,
after she had stayed up through the night till her eyes and her
back ached, her copy was rejected. She would return home utterly downcast. She would spend days together moaning, unable to stir a finger. For a long time she had been suffering
from heart trouble, which had been aggravated by her hard
struggles, and filled her with dark forebodings. Sometimes
she would have pains, and difficulty in breathing as though she
were on the point of death. She never went out without her
name and address written on a piece of paper in her pocket
in case she should collapse in the street. What would happen
if she were to disappear? Antoinette comforted her as best she
could by affecting a confidence which she did not possess: she
begged her to be careful and to let her go and work in her
stead. But the little that was left of Madame Jeannin's pride
stirred in her, and she vowed that at least her daughter should
not know the humiliation she had to undergo.

In vain did she wear herself out and cut down their expenses: what she earned was not enough to keep them alive.
They had to sell the few jewels which they had kept. And
the worst blow of all came when the money, of which they were
in such sore need, was stolen from Madame Jeannin the very
day it came into her hands. The poor flustered creature took
it into her head while she was out to go into the *Bon Marché*,
which was on her way: it was Antoinette's birthday next day,
and she wanted to give her a little present. She was carrying

her purse in her hand so as not to lose it. She put it down mechanically on the counter for a moment while she looked at something. When she put out her hand for it the purse was gone. It was the last blow for her.

A few days later, on a stifling evening at the end of August, —a hot steaming mist hung over the town,—Madame Jeannin came in from her copying agency, whither she had been to deliver a piece of work that was wanted in a hurry. She was late for dinner, and had saved her three sous' bus fare by hurrying home on foot to prevent her children being anxious. When she reached the fourth floor she could neither speak nor breathe. It was not the first time she had returned home in that condition: the children took no notice of it. She forced herself to sit down at table with them. They were both suffering from the heat and did not eat anything: they had to make an effort to gulp down a few morsels of food, and a sip or two of stale water. To give their mother time to recover they did not talk—(they had no desire to talk)—and looked out of the window.

Suddenly Madame Jeannin waved her hands in the air, clutched at the table, looked at her children, moaned, and collapsed. Antoinette and Olivier sprang to their feet just in time to catch her in their arms. They were beside themselves, and screamed and cried to her:

"Mother! Mother! Dear, dear mother!"

But she made no sound. They were at their wit's end. Antoinette clung wildly to her mother's body, kissed her, called to her. Olivier ran to the door of the flat and yelled:

"Help! Help!"

The housekeeper came running upstairs, and when she saw what had happened she ran for a doctor. But when the doctor arrived, he could only say that the end had come. Death had been instantaneous—happily for Madame Jeannin—although it was impossible to know what thoughts might have been hers during the last moments when she knew that she was dying and leaving her children alone in such misery.

They were alone to bear the horror of the catastrophe, alone to weep, alone to perform the dreadful duties that follow upon death. The porter's wife, a kindly soul, helped them a little: and people came from the convent where Madame Jeannin had taught: but they were given no real sympathy.

The first moments brought inexpressible despair. The only thing that saved them was the very excess of that despair, which made Olivier really ill. Antoinette's thoughts were distracted from her own suffering, and her one idea was to save her brother: and her great, deep love filled Olivier and plucked him back from the violent torment of his grief. Locked in her arms near the bed where their mother was lying in the glimmer of a candle, Olivier said over and over again that they must die, that they must both die, at once: and he pointed to the window. In Antoinette, too, there was the dark desire: but she fought it down: she wished to live. . . .

"Why? Why?"

"For her sake," said Antoinette—(she pointed to her mother).—"She is still with us. Think . . . after all that she has suffered for our sake, we must spare her the crowning sorrow, that of seeing us die in misery. . . . Ah!" (she went on emphatically). . . . "And then, we must not give way. I will not! I refuse to give in. You must, you shall be happy, some day!"

"Never!"

"Yes. You shall be happy. We have had too much unhappiness. A change will come: it must. You shall live your life. You shall have children, you shall be happy, you shall, you shall!"

"How are we to live? We cannot do it. . . ."

"We can. What is it, after all? We have to live somehow until you can earn your living. I will see to that. You will see: I'll do it. Ah! If only mother had let me do it, as I could have done. . . ."

"What will you do? I will not have you degrading yourself. You could not do it."

"I can. . . . . And there is nothing humiliating in working for one's living—provided it be honest work. Don't you worry about it, please. You will see, everything will come right. You shall be happy, we shall be happy: dear Olivier, *she* will be happy through us. . . ."

The two children were the only mourners at their mother's grave. By common consent they agreed not to tell the Poyets: the Poyets had ceased to exist for them: they had been too cruel to their mother: they had helped her to her death. And, when the housekeeper asked them if they had no other relations, they replied:

"No. Nobody."

By the bare grave they prayed hand in hand. They set their teeth in desperate resolve and pride and preferred their solitude to the presence of their callous and hypocritical relations.—They returned on foot through the throng of people who were strangers to their grief, strangers to their thoughts, strangers to their lives, and shared nothing with them but their common language. Antoinette had to support Olivier.

They took a tiny flat in the same house on the top floor— two little attics, a narrow hall, which had to serve as a dining-room, and a kitchen that was more like a cupboard. They could have found better rooms in another neighborhood: but it seemed to them that they were still with their mother in that house. The housekeeper took an interest in them for a time: but she was soon absorbed in her own affairs and nobody bothered about them. They did not know a single one of the other tenants: and they did not even know who lived next door.

Antoinette obtained her mother's post as music-teacher at the convent. She procured other pupils. She had only one idea: to educate her brother until he was ready for the *École Normale*. It was her own idea, and she had decided upon it after mature reflection: she had studied the syllabus and asked about it, and had also tried to find out what Olivier thought:— but he had no ideas, and she chose for him. Once at the *École Normale* he would be sure of a living for the rest of his life,

and his future would be assured. He must get in, somehow;
whatever it cost, they would have to keep alive till then. It
meant five or six terrible years: they would win through. The
idea possessed Antoinette, absorbed her whole life. The poor
solitary existence which she must lead, which she saw clearly
mapped out in front of her, was only made bearable through
the passionate exaltation which filled her, her determination, by
all means in her power, to save her brother and make him
happy. The light-hearted, gentle girl of seventeen or eighteen
was transfigured by her heroic resolution: there was in her an
ardent quality of devotion, a pride of battle, which no one had
suspected, herself least of all. In that critical period of a
woman's life, during the first fevered days of spring, when love
fills all her being, and like a hidden stream murmuring beneath
the earth, laves her soul, envelops it, floods it with tenderness,
and fills it with sweet obsessions, love appears in divers shapes:
demanding that she should give herself, and yield herself up
to be its prey: for love the least excuse is enough, and for its
profound yet innocent sensuality any sacrifice is easy. Love
made Antoinette the prey of sisterly devotion.

Her brother was less passionate and had no such stay. Besides, the sacrifice was made for him, it was not he who was
sacrificed—which is so much easier and sweeter when one loves.
He was weighed down with remorse at seeing his sister wearing
herself out for him. He would tell her so, and she would reply:

"Ah! My dear! . . . But don't you see that that is what
keeps me going? Without you to trouble me, what should I
have to live for?"

He understood. He, too, in Antoinette's position, would
have been jealous of the trouble he caused her: but to be the
cause of it! . . . That hurt his pride and his affection.
And what a burden it was for so weak a creature to bear such
a responsibility, to be bound to succeed, since on his success
his sister had staked her whole life! The thought of it was intolerable to him, and, instead of spurring him on, there were
times when it robbed him of all energy. And yet she forced

him to struggle on, to work, to live, as he never would have done without her aid and insistence. He had a natural predisposition towards depression,—perhaps even towards suicide: —perhaps he would have succumbed to it had not his sister wished him to be ambitious and happy. He suffered from the contradiction of his nature: and yet it worked his salvation. He, too, was passing through a critical age, that fearful period when thousands of young men succumb, and give themselves up to the aberrations of their minds and senses, and for two or three years' folly spoil their lives beyond repair. If he had had time to yield to his thoughts he would have fallen into discouragement or perhaps taken to dissipation: always when he turned in upon himself he became a prey to his morbid dreams, and disgust with life, and Paris, and the impure fermentation of all those millions of human beings mingling and rotting together. But the sight of his sister's face was enough to dispel the nightmare: and since she was living only that he might live, he would live, yes, he would be happy, in spite of himself.

So their lives were built on an ardent faith fashioned of stoicism, religion, and noble ambition. All their endeavor was directed towards the one end: Olivier's success. Antoinette accepted every kind of work, every humiliation that was offered her: she went as a governess to houses where she was treated almost as a servant: she had to take her pupils out for walks, like a nurse, wandering about the streets with them for hours together under pretext of teaching them German. In her love for her brother and her pride she found pleasure even in such moral suffering and weariness.

She would return home worn out to look after Olivier, who was a day-boarder at his school and only came home in the evening. She would cook their dinner—a wretched dinner— on the gas-stove or over a spirit-lamp. Olivier had never any appetite and everything disgusted him, and his gorge would rise at the food: and she would have to force him to eat, or cudgel her brains to invent some dish that would catch his fancy, and poor Antoinette was by no means a good cook. And when

she had taken a great deal of trouble she would have the mortification of hearing him declare that her cooking was uneatable.
It was only after moments of despair at her cooking-stove,—
those moments of silent despair which come to inexperienced
young housekeepers and poison their lives and sometimes their
sleep, unknown to everybody—that she began to understand it
a little.

After dinner, when she had washed up the dishes—(he would
offer to help her, but she would never let him),—she would
take a motherly interest in her brother's work. She would hear
him his lessons, read his exercises, and even look up certain
words in the dictionary for him, always taking care not to ruffle
up his sensitive little soul. They would spend the evening at
their one table at which they had both to eat and write. He
would do his homework, she would sew or do some copying.
When he had gone to bed she would sit mending his clothes
or doing some work of her own.

Although they had difficulty in making both ends meet,
they were both agreed that every penny they could put by should
be used in the first place to settle the debt which their mother
owed to the Poyets. It was not that the Poyets were importunate creditors: they had given no sign of life: they never gave
a thought to the money, which they counted as lost: they
thought themselves very lucky to have got rid of their undesirable relatives so cheaply. But it hurt the pride and filial
piety of the young Jeannins to think that their mother should
have owed anything to these people whom they despised. They
pinched and scraped: they economized on their amusements, on
their clothes, on their food, in order to amass the two hundred
francs—an enormous sum for them. Antoinette would have
liked to have done the saving by herself. But when her brother
found out what she was up to, nothing could keep him from
doing likewise. They wore themselves out in the effort, and
were delighted when they could set aside a few sous a day.

In three years, by screwing and scraping, sou by sou, they
had succeeded in getting the sum together. It was a great joy

to them. Antoinette went to the Poyets one evening. She
was coldly received, for they thought she had come to ask for
help. They thought it advisable to take the initiative: and
reproached her for not letting them have any news of them: and
not having even told them of the death of her mother, and not
coming to them when she wanted help. She cut them short
calmly by telling them that she had no intention of incommoding them: she had come merely to return the money which had
been borrowed from them: and she laid two banknotes on the
table and asked for a receipt. They changed their tone at once,
and pretended to be unwilling to accept it: they were feeling
for her that sudden affection which comes to the creditor for
the debtor, who, after many years, returns the loan which he
had ceased to reckon upon. They inquired where she was living with her brother, and how they lived. She did not reply,
asked once more for the receipt, said that she was in a hurry,
bowed coldly, and went away. The Poyets were horrified at
the girl's ingratitude.

Then, when she was rid of that obsession, Antoinette went on
with the same sparing existence, but now it was entirely for her
brother's sake. Only she concealed it more to prevent his
knowing it: she economized on her clothes and sometimes on
her food, to keep her brother well-dressed and amused, and to
make his life pleasanter and gayer, and to let him go every now
and then to a concert, or to the opera, which was Olivier's
greatest joy. He was unwilling to go without her, but she
would always make excuses for not going so that he should
feel no remorse: she would pretend that she was too tired and
did not want to go out: she would even go so far as to say
that music bored her. Her fond quibbles would not deceive
him: but his boyish selfishness would be too strong for him.
He would go to the theater: once inside, he would be filled
with remorse, and it would haunt him all through the piece,
and spoil his pleasure. One Sunday, when she had packed
him off to the *Châtelet* concert, he returned half an hour later,
and told Antoinette that when he reached the Saint Michel

Bridge he had not the heart to go any farther: the concert did
not interest him: it hurt him too much to have any pleasure
without her. Nothing was sweeter to Antoinette, although
she was sorry that her brother should be deprived of his Sunday
entertainment because of her. But Olivier never regretted it:
when he saw the joy that lit up his sister's face as he came in, a
joy that she tried in vain to conceal, he felt happier than the
most lovely music in the world could ever have made him.
They spent the afternoon sitting together by the window, he
with a book in his hand, she with her work, hardly reading at all,
hardly sewing at all, talking idly of things that interested
neither of them. Never had they had so delightful a Sunday.
They agreed that they would never go alone to a concert again:
they could never enjoy anything alone.

She managed secretly to save enough money to surprise
and delight Olivier with a hired piano, which, on the hire-
purchase system became their property at the end of a certain
number of months. The payments for it were a heavy burden
for her to shoulder! It often haunted her dreams, and she
ruined her health in screwing together the necessary money.
But, folly as it was, it did assure them both so much happiness.
Music was their Paradise in their hard life. It filled an
enormous place in their existence. They steeped themselves
in music so as to forget the rest of the world. There was danger
in it too. Music is one of the great modern dissolvents. Its
languorous warmth, like the heat of a stove, or the enervating
air of autumn, excites the senses and destroys the will. But it
was a relaxation for a creature forced into excessive, joyless
activity as was Antoinette. The Sunday concert was the only
ray of light that shone through the week of unceasing toil.
They lived in the memory of the last concert and the eager
anticipation of the next, in those few hours spent outside Paris
and out of the vile weather. After a long wait outside in the
rain, or the snow, or the wind and the cold, clinging together,
and trembling lest all the places should be taken, they would
pass into the theater, where they were lost in the throng, and

sit on dark uncomfortable benches. They were crushed and stifling, and often on the point of fainting from the heat and discomfort of it all:—but they were happy, happy in their own and in each other's pleasure, happy to feel coursing through their veins the flood of kindness, light, and strength, that surged forth from the great souls of Beethoven and Wagner, happy, each of them, to see the dear, dear face light up—the poor, pale face worn by suffering and premature anxieties. Antoinette would feel so tired and as though loving arms were about her, holding her to a motherly breast! She would nestle in its softness and warmth: and she would weep quietly. Olivier would press her hand. No one noticed them in the dimness of the vast hall, where they were not the only suffering souls taking refuge under the motherly wing of Music.

Antoinette had her religion to support her. She was very pious, and every day never missed saying her prayers fervently and at length, and every Sunday she never missed going to Mass. Even in the injustice of her wretched life she could not help believing in the love of the divine Friend, who suffers with you, and, some day, will console you. Even more than with God, she was in close communion with the beloved dead, and she used secretly to share all her trials with them. But she was of an independent spirit and a clear intelligence: she stood apart from other Catholics, who did not regard her altogether favorably: they thought her possessed of an evil spirit: they were not far from regarding her as a Free Thinker, or on the way to it, because, like the honest little Frenchwoman she was, she had no intention of renouncing her own independent judgment: she believed not from obedience, like the base rabble, but from love.

Olivier no longer believed. The slow disintegration of his faith, which had set in during his first months in Paris, had ended in its complete destruction. He had suffered cruelly: for he was not of those who are strong enough or commonplace enough to dispense with faith: and so he had passed through crises of mental agony. But he was at heart a mystic: and, though he had lost his belief, yet no ideas could be closer to his own than those of his sister. They both lived in a religious atmosphere. When they came home in the evening after the day's parting their little flat was to them a haven, an inviolable refuge, poor, bitterly cold, but pure. How far removed they felt there from the noise and the corrupt thoughts of Paris! . . .

They never talked much of their doings: for when one comes home tired one has hardly the heart to revive the memory of a painful day by the tale of its happenings. Instinctively they set themselves to forget it. Especially during the first hour when they met again for dinner they avoided questions of all kinds. They would greet each other with their eyes: and sometimes they would not speak a word all through the meal. Antoinette would look at her brother as he sat dreaming, just as he used to do when he was a little boy. She would gently touch his hand:

" Come! " she would say, with a smile. " Courage! "

He would smile too and go on eating. So dinner would pass without their trying to talk. They were hungry for silence. Only when they had done would their tongues be loosed a little, when they felt rested, and when each of them in the comfort of the understanding love of the other had wiped out the impure traces of the day.

Olivier would sit down at the piano. Antoinette was out of practice from letting him play always: for it was the only relaxation that he had: and he would give himself up to it wholeheartedly. He had a fine temperament for music: his feminine nature, more suited to love than to action, with loving sympathy could catch the thoughts of the musicians whose works he played, and merge itself in them and with passionate fidelity render the finest shades,—at least, within the limitations of his physical strength, which gave out before the Titanic effort of *Tristan,* or the later sonatas of Beethoven. He loved best to take refuge in Mozart or Gluck, and theirs was the music that Antoinette preferred.

Sometimes she would sing too, but only very simple songs, old melodies. She had a light mezzo voice, plaintive and delicate. She was so shy that she could never sing in company, and hardly even before Olivier: her throat used to contract. There was an air of Beethoven set to some Scotch words, of which she was particularly fond: *Faithful Johnnie:* it was calm, so calm . . . and with what a depth of tenderness! . . . It was like herself. Olivier could never hear her sing it without the tears coming to his eyes.

But she preferred listening to her brother. She would hurry through her housework and leave the door of the kitchen open the better to hear Olivier: but in spite of all her care he would complain impatiently of the noise she made with her pots and pans. Then she would close the door; and, when she had finished, she would come and sit in a low chair, not near the piano —(for he could not bear any one near him when he was playing),—but near the fireplace: and there she would sit curled up like a cat, with her back to the piano, and her eyes fixed on the golden eyes of the fire, in which a lump of coal was smoldering, and muse over her memories of the past. When nine o'clock rang she would have to pull herself together to remind Olivier that it was time to stop. It would be hard to drag him, and to drag herself, away from dreams: but Olivier would still have some work to do. And he must not go to bed too late. He would not obey her at once: he always needed a certain time in which to shake free of the music before he could apply himself seriously to his work. His thoughts would be off wandering. Often it would be half-past nine before he could shake free of his misty dreams. Antoinette, bending over her work at the other side of the table, would know that he was doing nothing: but she dared not look in his direction too often for fear of irritating him by seeming to be watching him.

He was at the ungrateful age—the happy age—when a boy saunters dreamily through his days. He had a clear forehead, girlish eyes, deep and trustful, often with dark circles round them, a wide mouth with rather thick pouting lips, a rather

crooked smile, vague, absent, taking: he wore his hair long
so that it hung down almost to his eyes, and made a great bunch
at the back of his neck, while one rebellious lock stuck up at
the back: a neckerchief loosely tied round his neck—(his sister
used to tie it carefully in a bow every morning) :—a waistcoat
which was always buttonless, although she was for ever sewing
them on: no cuffs: large hands with bony wrists. He had a
heavy, sleepy, bantering expression, and he was always wool-
gathering. His eyes would blink and wander round Antoinette's room:—(his work-table was in her room) :—they
would light on the little iron bed, above which hung an ivory
crucifix, with a sprig of box,—on the portraits of his father
and mother,—on an old photograph of the little provincial town
with its tower mirrored in its waters. And when they reached
his sister's pallid face, bending in silence over her work, he
would be filled with an immense pity for her and anger with
himself: then he would shake himself in annoyance at his own
indolence: and he would work furiously to make up for lost
time.

He spent his holidays in reading. They would read together
each with a separate book. In spite of their love for each
other they could not read aloud. That hurt them as an offense
against modesty. A fine book was to them as a secret which
should only be murmured in the silence of the heart. When
a passage delighted them, instead of reading it aloud, they
would hand the book over, with a finger marking the place: and
they would say:

" Read that."

Then, while the other was reading, the one who had already
read would with shining eyes gaze into the dear face to see
what emotions were roused and to share the enjoyment of it.

But often with their books open in front of them they would
not read: they would talk. Especially towards the end of the
evening they would feel the need of opening their hearts, and
they would have less difficulty in talking. Olivier had sad
thoughts: and in his weakness he had to rid himself of all that

tortured him by pouring out his troubles to some one else. He was a prey to doubt. Antoinette had to give him courage, to defend him against himself: it was an unceasing struggle, which began anew each day. Olivier would say bitter, gloomy things: and when he had said them he would be relieved: but he never troubled to think how they might hurt his sister. Only very late in the day did he see how he was exhausting her: he was sapping her strength and infecting her with his own doubts. Antoinette never let it appear how she suffered. She was by nature valiant and gay, and she forced herself to maintain a show of gaiety, even when that gracious quality was long since dead in her. She had moments of utter weariness, and revolt against the life of perpetual sacrifice to which she had pledged herself. But she condemned such thoughts and would not analyze them: they came to her in spite of herself, and she would not accept them. She found help in prayer, except when her heart could not pray—(as sometimes happens)—when it was, as it were, withered and dry. Then she could only wait in silence, feverish and ashamed, for the return of grace. Olivier never had the least suspicion of the agony she suffered. At such times Antoinette would make some excuse and go away and lock herself in her room: and she would not appear again until the crisis was over: then she would be smiling, sorrowful, more tender than ever, and, as it were, remorseful for having suffered.

Their rooms were adjoining. Their beds were placed on either side of the same wall: they could talk to each other through it in whispers: and when they could not sleep they would tap gently on the wall to say:

"Are you asleep? I can't sleep."

The partition was so thin that it was almost as though they shared the same room. But the door between their rooms was always locked at night, in obedience to an instinctive and profound modesty,—a sacred feeling:—it was only left open when Olivier was ill, as too often happened.

He did not gain in health. Rather he seemed to grow

weaker. He was always ailing: throat, chest, head or heart: if
he caught the slightest cold there was always the danger of its
turning to bronchitis: he caught scarlatina and almost died of
it: but even when he was not ill he would betray strange symptoms of serious illnesses, which fortunately did not come to anything: he would have pains in his lungs or his heart. One day
the doctor who examined him diagnosed pericarditis, or
peripneumonia, and the great specialist who was then consulted
confirmed his fears. But it came to nothing. It was his
nerves that were wrong, and it is common knowledge that disorders of the nerves take the most unaccountable shapes: they
are got rid of at the cost of days of anxiety. But such days
were terrible for Antoinette, and they gave her sleepless nights.
She would lie in a state of terror in her bed, getting up every
now and then to listen to her brother's breathing. She would
think that perhaps he was dying, she would feel sure, convinced
of it: she would get up, trembling, and clasp her hands, and
hold them fast against her lips to keep herself from crying out.
    "Oh! God! Oh! God!" she would moan. "Take him not
from me! Not that . . . not that. You have no right!
. . . Not that, oh! God, I beg! . . . Oh, mother, mother!
Come to my aid! Save him: let him live! . . ."
    She would lie at full stretch.
    "Ah! To die by the way, when so much has been done,
when we were nearly there, when he was going to be happy . . .
no: that could not be: it would be too cruel! . . ."

    It was not long before Olivier gave her other reasons for
anxiety.
    He was profoundly honest, like herself, but he was weak
of will and too open-minded and too complex not to be uneasy,
skeptical, indulgent towards what he knew to be evil, and attracted by pleasure. Antoinette was so pure that it was some
time before she understood what was going on in her brother's
mind. She discovered it suddenly, one day.
    Olivier thought she was out. She usually had a lesson at

that hour: but at the last moment she had received word from her pupil, telling her that she could not have her that day. She was secretly pleased, although it meant a few francs less in that week's earnings: but she was very tired and she lay down on her bed: she was very glad to be able to rest for once without reproaching herself. Olivier came in from school bringing another boy with him. They sat down in the next room and began to talk. She could hear everything they said: they thought they were alone and did not restrain themselves. Antoinette smiled as she heard her brother's merry voice. But soon she ceased to smile, and her blood ran cold. They were talking of dirty things with an abominable crudity of expression: they seemed to revel in it. She heard Olivier, her boy Olivier, laughing: and from his lips, which she had thought so innocent, there came words so obscene that the horror of it chilled her. Keen anguish stabbed her to the heart. It went on and on: they could not stop talking, and she could not help listening. At last they went out, and Antoinette was left alone. Then she wept: something had died in her: the ideal image that she had fashioned of her brother—of her boy— was plastered with mud: it was a mortal agony to her. She did not say anything to him when they met again in the evening. He saw that she had been weeping and he could not think why. He could not understand why she had changed her manner towards him. It was some time before she was able to recover herself.

But the worst blow of all for her was one evening when he did not come home. She did not go to bed, but sat up waiting for him. It was not only her moral purity that was hurt: her suffering went down to the most mysterious inner depths of her heart—those same depths where there lurked the most awful feelings of the human heart, feelings over which she cast a veil, to hide them from her sight.

Olivier's first aim had been the declaration of his independence. He returned in the morning, casting about for the proper attitude and quite prepared to fling some insolent remark at his

sister if she had said anything to him. He stole into the flat
on tiptoe so as not to waken her. But when he saw her standing there, waiting for him, pale, red-eyed from weeping, when
he saw that, instead of making any effort to reproach him, she
only set about silently cooking his breakfast, before he left
for school, and that she had nothing to say to him, but was
overwhelmed, so that she was, in herself, a living reproach, he
could hold out no longer: he flung himself down before her,
buried his face in her lap, and they both wept. He was
ashamed of himself, sick at the thought of what he had done:
he felt degraded. He tried to speak, but she would not let him
and laid her hand on his lips: and he kissed her hand. They
said no more: they understood each other. Olivier vowed that
he would never again do anything to hurt Antoinette, and that
he would be in all things what she wanted him to be. But
though she tried bravely she could not so easily forget so sharp
a wound: she recovered from it slowly. There was a certain
awkwardness between them. Her love for him was just the
same: but in her brother's soul she had seen something that
was foreign to herself, and she was fearful of it.

She was the more overwhelmed by the glimpse she had had
into Olivier's inmost heart, in that, about the same time, she
had to put up with the unwelcome attentions of certain men.
When she came home in the evening at nightfall, and especially
when she had to go out after dinner to take or fetch her copying, she suffered agonies from her fear of being accosted, and
followed (as sometimes happened) and forced to listen to insulting advances. She took her brother with her whenever
she could under pretext of making him take a walk: but he only
consented grudgingly and she dared not insist: she did not like
to interrupt his work. She was so provincial and so pure that
she could not get used to such ways. Paris at night was to her
like a dark forest in which she felt that she was being tracked
by dreadful, savage beasts: and she was afraid to leave the
house. But she had to go out. She would put off going out

as long as possible: she was always fearful. And when she thought that her Olivier would be—was perhaps—like one of those men who pursued her, she could hardly hold out her hand to him when she came in. He could not think what he had done to change her so, and she was angry with herself.

She was not very pretty, but she had charm, and attracted attention though she did nothing to do so. She was always very simply dressed, almost always in black: she was not very tall, graceful, frail-looking; she rarely spoke: she tripped quietly through the crowded streets, avoiding attention, which, however, she attracted in spite of herself by the sweetness of the expression of her tired eyes and her pure young lips. Sometimes she saw that she had attracted notice: and though it put her to confusion she was pleased all the same. Who can say what gentle and chaste pleasure in itself there may be in so innocent a creature at feeling herself in sympathy with others? All that she felt was shown in a slight awkwardness in her movements, a timid, sidelong glance: and it was sweet to see and very touching. And her uneasiness added to her attraction. She excited interest, and, as she was a poor girl, with none to protect her, men did not hesitate to tell her so.

Sometimes she used to go to the house of some rich Jews, the Nathans, who took an interest in her because they had met her at the house of some friends of theirs where she gave lessons: and, in spite of her shyness, she had not been able to avoid accepting invitations to their parties. M. Alfred Nathan was a well-known professor in Paris, a distinguished scientist, and at the same time he was very fond of society, with that strange mixture of learning and frivolity which is so common among the Jews. Madame Nathan was a mixture in equal proportions of real kindliness and excessive worldliness. They were both generous, with loud-voiced, sincere, but intermittent sympathy for Antoinette.—Generally speaking Antoinette had found more kindness among the Jews than among the members of her own sect. They have many faults: but they have one great quality—perhaps the greatest of all: they are alive, and human: nothing human is foreign to them and they are interested in every living being. Even when they lack real, warm sympathy they feel a perpetual curiosity which makes them seek out men and ideas that are of worth, however different from themselves they may be. Not that, generally speaking, they do anything much to help them, for they are interested in too many things at once and much more a prey to the vanities of the world than other people, while they pretend to be immune from them. But at least they do something: and that is saying a great deal in the present apathetic condition of society. They are an active balm in society, the very leaven of life.—Antoinette who, among the Catholics, had been brought sharp up against a wall of icy indifference, was keenly alive to the worth of the interest, however superficial it might be, which the Nathans took in her. Madame Nathan had marked Antoinette's life of devoted sacrifice: she was sensible of her physical and moral charm: and she made a show of taking her under her protection. She had no children: but she loved young people and often had gatherings of them in her house: and she insisted on Antoinette's coming also, and breaking away from her solitude, and having some amusement in her life. And as she had no difficulty in guessing that Antoinette's shyness was in part the result of her poverty, she even went so far as to offer to give her a pretty frock or two, which Antoinette refused proudly: but her kindly patroness found a way of forcing her to accept a few of those little presents which are so dear to a woman's innocent vanity. Antoinette was both grateful and embarrassed. She forced herself to go to Madame Nathan's parties from time to time: and being young she managed to enjoy herself in spite of everything.

But in that rather mixed society of all sorts of young people Madame Nathan's protégée, being poor and pretty, became at once the mark of two or three young gentlemen, who with perfect confidence in themselves picked her out for their attentions. They calculated how far her timidity would go: they even made bets about her.

One day she received certain anonymous letters—or rather letters signed with a noble pseudonym—which conveyed a declaration of love: at first they were love-letters, flattering, ardent, appointing a rendezvous: then they quickly became bolder, threatening, and soon insulting and basely slanderous: they stripped her, exposed her, besmirched her with their coarse expressions of desire: they tried to play upon Antoinette's simplicity by making her fearful of a public insult if she did not go to the appointed rendezvous. She wept bitterly at the thought of having called down on herself such base proposals: and these insults scorched her pride. She did not know what to do. She did not like to speak to her brother about it: she knew that he would feel it too keenly and that he would make the affair even more serious than it was. She had no friends. The police? She would not do that for fear of scandal. But somehow she had to make an end of it. She felt that her silence would not sufficiently defend her, that the blackguard who was pursuing her would hold to the chase and that he would go on until to go farther would be dangerous.

He had just sent her a sort of ultimatum commanding her to meet him next day at the Luxembourg. She went.—By racking her brains she had come to the conclusion that her persecutor must have met her at Madame Nathan's. In one of his letters he had alluded to something which could only have happened there. She begged Madame Nathan to do her a great favor and to drive her to the door of the gallery and to wait for her outside. She went in. In front of the appointed picture her tormentor accosted her triumphantly and began to talk to her with affected politeness. She stared straight at him without a word. When he had finished his remark he asked her jokingly why she was staring at him. She replied:

"You are a coward."

He was not put out by such a trifle as that, and became familiar in his manner. She said:

"You have tried to threaten me with a scandal. Very well, I have come to give you your scandal. You have asked for it!"

She was trembling all over, and she spoke in a loud voice to show him that she was quite equal to attracting attention to themselves. People had already begun to watch them. He felt that she would stick at nothing. He lowered his voice. She said once more, for the last time:

"You are a coward," and turned her back on him.

Not wishing to seem to have given in he followed her. She left the gallery with the fellow following hard on her heels. She walked straight to the carriage waiting there, wrenched the door open, and her pursuer found himself face to face with Madame Nathan, who recognized him and greeted him by name. His face fell and he bolted.

Antoinette had to tell the whole story to her companion. She was unwilling to do so, and only hinted roughly at the facts. It was painful to her to reveal to a stranger the intimate secrets of her life, and the sufferings of her injured modesty. Madame Nathan scolded her for not having told her before. Antoinette begged her not to tell anybody. That was the end of it: and Madame Nathan did not even need to strike the fellow off her visiting list: for he was careful not to appear again.

About the same time another sorrow of a very different kind came to Antoinette.

At the Nathans' she met a man of forty, a very good fellow, who was in the Consular service in the Far East, and had come home on a few months' leave. He fell in love with her. The meeting had been planned unknown to Antoinette, by Madame Nathan, who had taken it into her head that she must find a husband for her little friend. He was a Jew. He was not good-looking and he was no longer young. He was rather bald and round-shouldered: but he had kind eyes, an affectionate way with him, and he could feel for and understand suffering, for he had suffered himself. Antoinette was no longer the romantic girl, the spoiled child, dreaming of life as a lovely day's walk on her lover's arm: now she saw the hard struggle of life, which began again every day, allowing no time for rest, or, if rest were taken, it might be to lose in one moment all the ground that had been gained, inch by inch, through years of striving: and she thought it would be very sweet to be able to lean on the arm of a friend, and share his sorrows with him, and be able to close her eyes for a little, while he watched over her. She knew that it was a dream: but she had not had the courage to renounce her dream altogether. In her heart she knew quite well that a dowerless girl had nothing to hope for in the world in which she lived. The old French middle-classes are known throughout the world for the spirit of sordid interest in which they conduct their marriages. The Jews are far less grasping with money. Among the Jews it is no uncommon thing for a rich young man to choose a poor girl, or a young woman of fortune to set herself passionately to win a man of intellect. But in the French middle-classes, Catholic and provincial in their outlook, almost always money woos money. And to what end? Poor wretches, they have none but dull commonplace desires: they can do nothing but eat, yawn, sleep—save. Antoinette knew them. She had observed their ways from her childhood on. She had seen them with the eyes of wealth and the eyes of poverty. She had no illusions left about them, nor about the treatment she had to expect from them. And so the attentions of this man who had asked her to marry him came as an unhoped for treasure in her life. At first she did not think of him as a lover, but gradually she was filled with gratitude and tenderness towards him. She would have accepted his proposal if it had not meant following him to the colonies and consequently leaving her brother. She refused: and though her lover understood the magnanimity of her reason for doing so, he could not forgive her: love is so selfish, that the lover will not hear of being sacrificed even to those virtues which are dearest to him in the beloved. He gave up seeing her: when he went away he never wrote: she had no news of him at all until, five or six months later, she received a printed intimation, addressed in his hand, that he had married another woman.

Antoinette felt it deeply. She was broken-hearted, and she

offered up her suffering to God: she tried to persuade herself that she was justly punished for having for one moment lost sight of her one duty, to devote herself to her brother: and she grew more and more wrapped up in it.

She withdrew from the world altogether. She even dropped going to the Nathans', for they were a little cold towards her after she refused the marriage which they had arranged for her: they too refused to see any justification for her. Madame Nathan had decided that the marriage should take place, and her vanity was hurt at its missing fire through Antoinette's fault. She thought her scruples certainly quite praiseworthy, but exaggerated and sentimental: and thereafter she lost interest in the silly little goose. It was necessary for her always to be helping people, with or without their consent, and she quickly found another protégée to absorb, for the time being, all the interest and devotion which she had to expend.

Olivier knew nothing of his sister's sad little romance. He was a sentimental, irresponsible boy, living in his dreams and fancies. It was impossible to depend on him in spite of his intelligence and charm and his very real tenderheartedness. Often he would fling away the results of months of work by his irresponsibility, or in a fit of discouragement, or by some boyish freak, or some fancied love affair, in which he would waste all his time and energy. He would fall in love with a pretty face, that he had seen once, with coquettish little girls, whom perhaps he once met out somewhere, though they never paid any attention to him. He would be infatuated with something he had read, a poet, or a musician: he would steep himself in their works for months together, to the exclusion of everything else and the detriment of his studies. He had to be watched always, though great care had to be taken that he did not know it, for he was easily wounded. There was always a danger of a seizure. He had the feverish excitement, the want of balance, the uneasy trepidation, that are often found in those who have a consumptive tendency. The doctor had not concealed the danger from Antoinette. The sickly plant, transplanted from the provinces

to Paris, needed fresh air and light. Antoinette could not provide them. They had not enough money to be able to go away
from Paris during the holidays. All the rest of their year every
day in the week was full, and on Sundays they were so tired that
they never wanted to go out, except to a concert.

There were Sundays in the summer when Antoinette would
make an effort and drag Olivier off to the woods outside Paris,
near Chaville or Saint-Cloud. But the woods were full of noisy
couples, singing music-hall songs, and littering the place with
greasy bits of paper: they did not find the divine solitude which
purifies and gives rest. And in the evening when they turned
homewards they had to suffer the roar and clatter of the trains,
the dirty, crowded, low, narrow, dark carriages of the suburban
lines, the coarseness of certain things they saw, the noisy, singing, shouting, smelly people, and the reek of tobacco smoke.
Neither Antoinette nor Olivier could understand the people, and
they would return home disgusted and demoralized. Olivier
would beg Antoinette not to go for Sunday walks again:
and for some time Antoinette would not have the heart to go
again. And then she would insist, though it was even more
disagreeable to her than to Olivier: but she thought it necessary
for her brother's health. She would force him to go out once
more. But their new experience would be no better than the
last, and Olivier would protest bitterly. So they stayed shut
up in the stifling town, and, in their prison-yard, they sighed
for the open fields.

Olivier had reached the end of his schooldays. The examinations for the *École Normale* were over. It was quite time.
Antoinette was very tired. She was counting on his success:
her brother had everything in his favor. At school he was
regarded as one of the best pupils: and all his masters were
agreed in praising his industry and intelligence, except for a
certain want of mental discipline which made it difficult for him
to bend to any sort of plan. But the responsibility of it
weighed on Olivier so heavily that he lost his head as the exam-

ination came near. He was worn out, and paralyzed by the fear of failure, and a morbid shyness that crept over him. He trembled at the thought of appearing before the examiners in public. He had always suffered from shyness: in class he would blush and choke when he had to speak: at first he could hardly do more than answer his name. And it was much more easy for him to reply impromptu than when he knew that he was going to be questioned: the thought of it made him ill: his mind rushed ahead picturing every detail of the ordeal as it would happen: and the longer he had to wait, the more he was obsessed by it. It might be said that he passed every examination at least twice: for he passed it in his dreams on the night before and expended all his energy, so that he had none left for the real examination.

But he did not even reach the *viva voce,* the very thought of which had sent him into a cold sweat the night before. In the written examination on a philosophical subject, which at any ordinary time would have sent him flying off, he could not even manage to squeeze out a couple of pages in six hours. For the first few hours his brain was empty; he could think of nothing, nothing. It was like a blank wall against which he hurled himself in vain. Then, an hour before the end, the wall was rent and a few rays of light shone through the crevices. He wrote an excellent short essay, but it was not enough to place him. When Antoinette saw the despair on his face as he came out, she foresaw the inevitable blow, and she was as despairing as he: but she did not show it. Even in the most desperate situations she had always an inexhaustible capacity for hope.

Olivier was rejected.

He was crushed by it. Antoinette pretended to smile as though it were nothing of any importance: but her lips trembled. She consoled her brother, and told him that it was an easily remedied misfortune, and that he would be certain to pass next year, and win a better place. She did not tell him how vital it was to her that he should have passed, that year,

or how utterly worn out she felt in soul and body, or how uneasy she felt about fighting through another year like that.
But she had to go on. If she were to go away before Olivier
had passed he would never have the courage to go on fighting
alone : he would succumb.

She concealed her weariness from him, and even redoubled
her efforts. She wore herself to skin and bone to let him have
amusement and change during the holidays so that he might
resume work with greater energy and confidence. But at the
very outset her small savings had to be broken into, and, to
make matters worse, she lost some of her most profitable pupils.

Another year! . . . Within sight of the final ordeal they
were almost at breaking-point. Above all, they had to live, and
discover some other means of scraping along. Antoinette accepted a situation as a governess in Germany which had been
offered her through the Nathans. It was the very last thing she
would have thought of, but nothing else offered at the time, and
she could not wait. She had never left her brother for a single
day during the last six years : and she could not imagine what
life would be like without seeing and hearing him from day to
day. Olivier was terrified when he thought of it : but he dared
not say anything : it was he who had brought it about : if he
had passed Antoinette would not have been reduced to such
an extremity : he had no right to say anything, or to take
into account his own grief at the parting : it was for her to
decide.

They spent the last days together in dumb anguish, as
though one of them were about to die : they hid away from each
other when their sorrow was too much for them. Antoinette
gazed into Olivier's eyes for counsel. If he had said to her :
" Don't go! " she would have stayed, although she had to go.
Up to the very last moment, in the cab in which they drove to
the station, she was prepared to break her resolution : she felt
that she could never go through with it. At a word from him,
one word! . . . But he said nothing. Like her, he set his
teeth and would not budge.—She made him promise to write to

her every day, and to conceal nothing from her, and to send for her if he were ever in the least danger.

They parted. While Olivier returned with a heavy heart to his school, where it had been agreed that he should board, the train carried Antoinette, crushed and sorrowful, towards Germany. Lying awake and staring through the night they felt the minutes dragging them farther and farther apart, and they called to each other in whispering voices.

Antoinette was fearful of the new world to which she was going. She had changed much in six years. She who had once been so bold and afraid of nothing had grown so used to silence and isolation that it hurt her to go out into the world again. The laughing, gay, chattering Antoinette of the old happy times had passed away with them. Unhappiness had made her sensitive and shy. No doubt living with Olivier had infected her with his timidity. She had had hardly anybody to talk to except her brother. She was scared by the least little thing, and was really in a panic when she had to pay a call. And so it was a nervous torture to her to think that she was now going to live among strangers, to have to talk to them, to be always with them. The poor girl had no more real vocation for teaching than her brother: she did her work conscientiously, but her heart was not in it, and she had not the support of feeling that there was any use in it. She was made to love and not to teach. And no one cared for her love.

Nowhere was her capacity for love less in demand than in her new situation in Germany. The Grünebaums, whose children she was engaged to teach French, took not the slightest interest in her. They were haughty and familiar, indifferent and indiscreet: they paid fairly well: and, as a result, they regarded everybody in their payment as being under an obligation to them, and thought they could do just as they liked. They treated Antoinette as a superior sort of servant and allowed her hardly any liberty. She did not even have a room to herself: she slept in a room adjoining that of the children and had to leave the door open all night. She was never alone. They had no respect for her need of taking refuge every now and then within herself—the sacred right of every human being to preserve an inner sanctuary of solitude. The only happiness she had lay in correspondence and communion with her brother: she made use of every moment of liberty she could snatch. But even that was encroached upon. As soon as she began to write they would prowl about in her room and ask her what she was writing. When she was reading a letter they would ask her what was in it: by their persistent impertinent curiosity they found out about her "little brother." She had to hide from them. Too shameful sometimes were the expedients to which she had to resort, and the holes and crannies in which she had to hide, in order to be able to read Olivier's letters unobserved. If she left a letter lying in her room she was sure it would be read: and as she had nothing she could lock except her box, she had to carry any papers she did not want to have read about with her: they were always prying into her business and her intimate affairs, and they were always fishing for her secret thoughts. It was not that the Grünebaums were really interested in her, only they thought that, as they paid her, she was their property. They were not malicious about it: indiscretion was with them an incurable habit: they were never offended with each other.

Nothing could have been more intolerable to Antoinette than such espionage, such a lack of moral modesty, which made it impossible for her to escape even for an hour a day from their curiosity. The Grünebaums were hurt by the haughty reserve with which she treated them. Naturally they found highly moral reasons to justify their vulgar curiosity, and to condemn Antoinette's desire to be immune from it.

"It was their duty," they thought, "to know the private life of a girl living under their roof, as a member of their household, to whom they had intrusted the education of their children: they were responsible for her."—(That is the sort of thing that so many mistresses say of their servants, mistresses whose "responsibility" does not go so far as to spare the unhappy girls any fatigue or work that must revolt them, but is entirely limited to denying them every sort of pleasure.)— "And that Antoinette should refuse to acknowledge that duty, imposed on them by conscience, could only show," they concluded, "that she was conscious of being not altogether beyond reproach: an honest girl has nothing to conceal."

So Antoinette lived under a perpetual persecution, against which she was always on her guard, so that it made her seem even more cold and reserved than she was.

Every day her brother wrote her a twelve-page letter: and she contrived to write to him every day even if it were only a few lines. Olivier tried hard to be brave and not to show his grief too clearly. But he was bored and dull. His life had always been so bound up with his sister's that, now that she was torn from him, he seemed to have lost part of himself: he could not use his arms, or his legs, or his brains, he could not walk, or play the piano, or work, or do anything, not even dream—except through her. He slaved away at his books from morning to night: but it was no good: his thoughts were elsewhere: he would be suffering, or thinking of her, or of the morrow's letter: he would sit staring at the clock, waiting for the day's letter: and when it arrived his fingers would tremble with joy— with fear, too—as he tore open the envelope. Never did lover tremble with more tenderness and anxiety at a letter from his mistress. He would hide away, like Antoinette, to read his letters: he would carry them about with him: and at night he always had the last letter under his pillow, and he would touch it from time to time to make sure that it was still there, during the long, sleepless nights when he lay awake dreaming of his dear sister. How far removed from her he felt! He felt that most dreadfully when Antoinette's letters were delayed by the post and came a day late. Two days, two nights, between them! . . . He exaggerated the time and the distance because he had never traveled. His imagination would take fire:

"Heavens! If she were to fall ill! There would be time for her to die before he could see her. . . . Why had she not written to him, just a line or two, the day before? . . . Was she ill? . . . Yes. She was surely ill. . . ." He would choke.—More often still he would be terrified of dying away from her, dying alone, among people who did not care, in the horrible school, in grim, gray Paris. He would make himself ill with the thought of it. . . . "Should he write and tell her to come back?"—But then he would be ashamed of his cowardice. Besides, as soon as he began to write to her it gave him such joy to be in communion with her that for a moment he would forget his suffering. It seemed to him that he could see her, hear her voice: he would tell her everything: never had he spoken to her so intimately, so passionately, when they had been together: he would call her "my true, brave, dear, kind, beloved, little sister," and say, "I love you so." Indeed they were real love-letters.

Their tenderness was sweet and comforting to Antoinette: they were all the air she had to breathe. If they did not come in the morning at the usual time she would be miserable. Once or twice it happened that the Grünebaums, from carelessness, or —who knows?—from a wicked desire to tease, forgot to give them to her until the evening, and once even until the next morning: and she worked herself into a fever.—On New Year's Day they had the same idea, without telling each other: they planned a surprise, and each sent a long telegram—(at vast expense)—and their messages arrived at the same time.—Olivier always consulted Antoinette about his work and his troubles: Antoinette gave him advice, and encouragement, and fortified him with her strength, though indeed she had not really enough for herself.

She was stifled in the foreign country, where she knew nobody, and nobody was interested in her, except the wife of a professor, lately come to the town, who also felt out of her element. The good creature was kind and motherly, and sympathetic with the brother and sister who loved each other so

and had to live apart—(for she had dragged part of her story
out of Antoinette) :—but she was so noisy, so commonplace, she
was so lacking—though quite innocently—in tact and discretion that aristocratic little Antoinette was irritated and drew
back. She had no one in whom she could confide and so all
her troubles were pent up, and weighed heavily upon her: sometimes she thought she must give way under them: but she set
her teeth and struggled on. Her health suffered: she grew
very thin. Her brother's letters became more and more downhearted. In a fit of depression he wrote:

"Come back, come back, come back! . . ."

But he had hardly sent the letter off than he was ashamed
of it and wrote another begging Antoinette to tear up the first
and give no further thought to it. He even pretended to be in
good spirits and not to be wanting his sister. It hurt his umbrageous vanity to think that he might seem incapable of doing
without her.

Antoinette was not deceived: she read his every thought: but
she did not know what to do. One day she almost went to him:
she went to the station to find out what time the train left for
Paris. And then she said to herself that it was madness: the
money she was earning was enough to pay for Olivier's board:
they must hold on as long as they could. She was not strong
enough to make up her mind: in the morning her courage would
spring forth again: but as the day dragged towards evening her
strength would fail her and she would think of flying to him.
She was homesick,—longing for the country that had treated
her so hardly, the country that enshrined all the relics of her
past life,—and she was aching to hear the language that her
brother spoke, the language in which she told her love for
him.

Then it was that a company of French actors passed through
the little German town. Antoinette, who rarely visited the
theater—(she had neither time nor taste for it)—was seized
with an irresistible longing to hear her own language spoken,
to take refuge in France.

The rest is known.[1]

There were no seats left in the theater: she met the young musician, Jean-Christophe, whom she did not know, and he, seeing her disappointment, offered to share with her a box which he had to give away: in her confusion she accepted. Her presence with Christophe set tongues wagging in the little town: and the malicious rumors came at once to the ears of the Grüne-baums, who, being already inclined to believe anything ill of the young Frenchwoman, and furious with Christophe as a result of certain events which have been narrated elsewhere, dismissed Antoinette without more ado.

She, who was so chaste and modest, she, whose whole life had been absorbed by her love for her brother and never yet had been besmirched with one thought of evil, nearly died of shame, when she understood the nature of the charge against her. Not for one moment was she resentful against Christophe. She knew that he was as innocent as she, and that, if he had injured her, he had meant only to be kind: she was grateful to him. She knew nothing of him, save that he was a musician, and that he was much maligned: but, in her ignorance of life and men, she had a natural intuition about people, which unhappiness had sharpened, and in her queer, boorish companion she had recognized a quality of candor equal to her own, and a sturdy kindness, the mere memory of which was comforting and good to think on. The evil she had heard of him did not at all affect the confidence which Christophe had inspired in her. Being herself a victim she had no doubt that he was in the same plight, suffering, as she did, though for a longer time, from the malevolence of the townspeople who insulted him. And as she always forgot herself in the thought of others the idea of what Christophe must have suffered distracted her mind a little from her own torment. Nothing in the world could have induced her to try to see him again, or to write to him: her modesty and pride forbade it. She told herself that he did

[1] See *Jean-Christophe*—I, " Revolt "

not know the harm he had done, and, in her gentleness, she hoped that he would never know it.

She left Germany. An hour away from the town it chanced that the train in which she was traveling passed the train by which Christophe was returning from a neighboring town where he had been spending the day.

For a few minutes their carriages stopped opposite each other, and in the silence of the night they saw each other, but did not speak. What could they have said save a few trivial words? That would have been a profanation of the indefinable feeling of common pity and mysterious sympathy which had sprung up in them, and was based on nothing save the sureness of their inward vision. During those last moments, when, still strangers, they gazed into each other's eyes, they saw in each other things which never had appeared to any other soul among the people with whom they lived. Everything must pass: the memory of words, kisses, passionate embraces: but the contact of souls, which have once met and hailed each other amid the throng of passing shapes, that never can be blotted out. Antoinette bore it with her in the innermost recesses of her heart—that poor heart, so swathed about with sorrow and sad thoughts, from out the midst of which there smiled a misty light, which seemed to steal sweetly from the earth, a pale and tender light like that which floods the Elysian Shades of Gluck.

She returned to Olivier. It was high time she returned to him. He had just fallen ill: and the poor, nervous, unhappy little creature who trembled at the thought of illness before it came—now that he was really ill, refused to write to his sister for fear of upsetting her. But he called to her, prayed for her coming as for a miracle.

When the miracle happened he was lying in the school infirmary, feverish and wandering. When he saw her he made no sound. How often had he seen her enter in his fevered fancy! . . . He sat up in bed, gaping, and trembling lest it should be once more only an illusion. And when she sat down

on the bed by his side, when she took him in her arms and he
had taken her in his, when he felt her soft cheek against his
lips, and her hands still cold from traveling by night in his,
when he was quite, quite sure that it was his dear sister he began to weep.   He could do nothing else: he was still the " little
cry-baby " that he had been when he was a child.   He clung
to her and held her close for fear she should go away from
him again.   How changed they were!   How sad they looked!
. . .   No matter!   They were together once more: everything
was lit up, the infirmary, the school, the gloomy day: they clung
to each other, they would never let each other go.   Before she
had said a word he made her swear that she would not go
away again.   He had no need to make her swear: no, she would
never go away again: they had been too unhappy away from
each other: their mother was right: anything was better than
being parted.   Even poverty, even death, so only they were
together.

They took rooms.   They wanted to take their old little flat,
horrible though it was: but it was occupied.   Their new rooms
also looked out on to a yard: but above a wall they could see
the top of a little acacia and grew fond of it at once, as a
friend from the country, a prisoner like themselves, in the
paved wilderness of the city.   Olivier quickly recovered his
health, or rather, what he was pleased to call his health:—
(for what was health to him would have been illness to a
stronger boy).—Antoinette's unhappy stay in Germany had
helped her to save a little money: and she made some more by
the translation of a German book which a publisher accepted.
For a time, then, they were free of financial anxiety: and all
would be well if Olivier passed his examination at the end of the
year.—But if he did not pass?

No sooner had they settled down to the happiness of being
together again than they were once more obsessed by the prospect of the examination.   They tried hard not to think about
it, but in vain, they were always coming back to it.   The fixed
idea haunted them, even when they were seeking distraction

from their thoughts: at concerts it would suddenly leap out
at them in the middle of the performance: at night when they
woke up it would lie there like a yawning gulf before them. In
addition to his eagerness to please his sister and repay her for
the sacrifice of her youth that she had made for his sake,
Olivier lived in terror of his military service which he could
not escape if he were rejected:—(at that time admission to the
great schools was still admitted as an exemption from service).—
He had an invincible disgust for the physical and moral
promiscuity, the kind of intellectual degradation, which, rightly
or wrongly, he saw in barrack-life. Every pure and aristocratic
quality in him revolted from such compulsion, and it seemed
to him that death would be preferable. In these days it is permitted to make light of such feelings, and even to decry them
in the name of a social morality which, for the moment, has
become a religion: but they are blind who deny it: there is no
more profound suffering than that of the violation of moral
solitude by the coarse liberal Communism of the present
day.

The examinations began. Olivier was almost incapable of
going in: he was unwell, and he was so fearful of the torment
he would have to undergo, whether he passed or not, that he
almost longed to be taken seriously ill. He did quite well in
the written examination. But he had a cruel time waiting to
hear the results. Following the immemorial custom of the
country of Revolutions, which is the worst country in the world
for red-tape and routine, the examinations were held in July
during the hottest days of the year, as though it were deliberately intended to finish off the luckless candidates, who were
already staggering under the weight of cramming a monstrous
list of subjects, of which even the examiners did not know a
tenth part. The written examinations were held on the day
after the holiday of the 14th July, when the whole city was
upside down, and making merry, to the undoing of the young
men who were by no means inclined to be merry, and asked for
nothing but silence. In the square outside the house booths

were set up, rifles cracked at the miniature ranges, merry-go-rounds creaked and grunted, and hideous steam organs roared from morning till night. The idiotic noise went on for a week. Then a President of the Republic, by way of maintaining his popularity, granted the rowdy merry-makers another three days' holiday. It cost him nothing: he did not hear the row. But Olivier and Antoinette were distracted and appalled by the noise, and had to keep their windows shut, so that their rooms were stifling, and stop their ears, trying vainly to escape the shrill, insistent, idiotic tunes which were ground out from morning till night and stabbed through their brains like daggers, so that they were reduced to a pitiful condition.

The *viva voce* examination began immediately after the publication of the first results. Olivier begged Antoinette not to go. She waited at the door,—much more anxious than he. Of course he never told her what he thought of his performance. He tormented her by telling her what he had said and what he had not said.

At last the final results were published. The names of the candidates were posted in the courtyard of the Sorbonne. Antoinette would not let Olivier go alone. As they left the house, they thought, though they did not say it, that when they came back they would *know,* and perhaps they would regret their present fears, when at least there was still hope. When they came in sight of the Sorbonne they felt their legs give way under them. Brave little Antoinette said to her brother:

" Please not so fast. . . ."

Olivier looked at his sister, and she forced a smile. He said: " Shall we sit down for a moment on the seat here? "

He would gladly have gone no further. But, after a moment, she pressed his hand and said:

" It's nothing, dear. Let us go on."

They could not find the list at first. They read several others in which the name of Jeannin did not appear. When at last they saw it, they did not take it in at first: they read it several times and could not believe it. Then when they were quite sure that it was true that Jeannin was Olivier, that Jeannin had passed, they could say nothing: they hurried home: she took his arm, and held his wrist, and leaned her weight on him: they almost ran, and saw nothing of what was going on about them: as they crossed the boulevard they were almost run over. They said over and over again:

"Dear. . . . Darling. . . . Dear. . . . Dear. . . ."

They tore upstairs to their rooms and then they flung their arms round each other. Antoinette took her brother's hand and led him to the photographs of their father and mother, which hung on the wall near her bed, in a corner of her room, which was a sort of sanctuary to her: they knelt down before them: and with tears in their eyes they prayed.

Antoinette ordered a jolly little dinner: but they could not eat a morsel: they were not hungry. They spent the evening, Olivier kneeling by his sister's side while she petted him like a child. They hardly spoke at all. They could not even be happy, for they were too worn out. They went to bed before nine o'clock and slept the sleep of the just.

Next day Antoinette had a frightful headache, but there was such a load taken from her heart! Olivier felt, for the first time in his life, that he could breathe freely. He was saved, she was saved, she had accomplished her task: and he had shown himself to be not unworthy of his sister's expectations! . . . For the first time for years and years they allowed themselves a little laziness. They stayed in bed till twelve talking through the wall, with the door between their rooms open: when they looked in the mirror they saw their faces happy and tired-looking: they smiled, and threw kisses to each other, and dozed off again, and watched each other's sleep, and lay weary and worn with hardly the strength to do more than mutter tender little scraps of words.

Antoinette had always put by a little money, sou by sou, so as to have some small reserve in case of illness. She did not tell her brother the surprise she had in store for him. The day after his success she told him that they were going to spend a month in Switzerland to make up for all their years of trouble and hardship. Now that Olivier was assured of three years at the *École Normale* at the expense of the State, and then, when he left the *École,* of finding a post, they could be extravagant and spend all their savings. Olivier shouted for joy when she told him. Antoinette was even more happy than he,—happy in her brother's happiness,—happy to think that she was going to see the country once more: she had so longed for it.

It took them some time to get ready for the journey, but the work of preparation was an unending joy. It was well on in August when they set out. They were not used to traveling. Olivier did not sleep the night before. And he did not sleep in the train. The whole day they had been fearful of missing the train. They were in a feverish hurry, they had been jostled about at the station, and finally huddled into a second-class carriage, where they could not even lean back to go to sleep:— (that is one of the privileges of which the eminently democratic French companies deprive poor travelers, so that rich travelers may have the pleasure of thinking that they have a monopoly of it).—Olivier did not sleep a wink: he was not sure that they were in the right train, and he looked out for the name of every station. Antoinette slept lightly and woke up very frequently: the jolting of the train made her head bob. Olivier watched her by the light of the funereal lamp, which shone at the top of the moving sarcophagus: and he was suddenly struck by the change in her face. Her eyes were hollow: her childish lips were half-open from sheer weariness: her skin was sallow, and there were little wrinkles on her cheeks, the marks of the sad years of sorrow and disillusion. She looked old and ill.— And, indeed, she was so tired! If she had dared she would have postponed their journey. But she did not like to spoil her brother's pleasure: she tried to persuade herself that she was only tired, and that the country would make her well again. She was fearful lest she should fall ill on the way.—She felt that he was looking at her: and she suddenly flung off the drowsiness that was creeping over her, and opened her eyes,—eyes still young, still clear and limpid, across which, from time to time, there passed an involuntary look of pain, like shadows on a little lake. He asked her in a whisper, anxiously and tenderly, how she was: she pressed his hand and assured him that she was well. A word of love revived her.

Then, when the rosy dawn tinged the pale country between Dôle and Pontarlier, the sight of the waking fields, and the gay sun rising from the earth,—the sun, who, like themselves, had escaped from the prison of the streets, and the grimy houses, and the thick smoke of Paris:—the waving fields wrapped in the light mist of their milk-white breath: the little things they passed: a little village belfry, a glimpse of a winding stream, a blue line of hills hovering on the far horizon: the tinkling, moving sound of the angelus borne from afar on the wind, when the train stopped in the midst of the sleeping country: the solemn shapes of a herd of cows browsing on a slope above the railway,—all absorbed Antoinette and her brother, to whom it all seemed new. They were like parched trees, drinking in ecstasy the rain from heaven.

Then, in the early morning, they reached the Swiss Customs. where they had to get out. A little station in a bare country-side. They were almost worn out by their sleepless night, and the cold, dewy freshness of the dawn made them shiver: but it was calm, and the sky was clear, and the fragrant air of the fields was about them, upon their lips, on their tongues, down their throats, flowing down into their lungs like a cooling stream: and they stood by a table, out in the open air, and drank comforting hot coffee with creamy milk, heavenly sweet, and tasting of the grass and the flowers of the fields.

They climbed up into the Swiss carriage, the novel arrangement of which gave them a childish pleasure. But Antoinette was so tired! She could not understand why she should feel so ill. Why was everything about her so beautiful, so absorbing, when she could take so little pleasure in it? Was it not all just what she had been dreaming for years: a journey with her brother, with all anxiety for the future left behind, dear mother Nature? . . . What was the matter with her? She was annoyed with herself, and forced herself to admire and share her brother's naïve delight.

They stopped at Thun. They were to go up into the mountains next day. But that night in the hotel, Antoinette was stricken with a fever, and violent illness, and pains in her head. Olivier was at his wits' ends, and spent a night of frightful anxiety. He had to send for a doctor in the morning —(an unforeseen expense which was no light tax on their slender purse).—The doctor could find nothing immediately serious, but said that she was run down, and that her constitution was undermined. There could be no question of their going on. The doctor forbade Antoinette to get up all day: and he thought they would perhaps have to stay at Thun for some time. They were very downcast—though very glad to have got off so cheaply after all their fears. But it was hard to have come so far to be shut up in a nasty hotel-room into which the sunlight poured so that it was like a hothouse. Antoinette insisted on her brother going out. He went a few yards from the hotel, saw the beautiful green Aar, and, hovering in the distance against the sky, a white peak: he bubbled over with joy: but he could not keep it to himself. He rushed back to his sister's room, and told her excitedly what he had just seen: and when she expressed her surprise at his coming back so soon and made him promise to go out again, he said, as once before he had said when he came back from the *Châtelet* concert:

"No, no. It is too beautiful: it hurts me to see it without you."

That feeling was not new to them: they knew that they had to be together to enjoy anything wholly. But they always loved to hear it said. His tender words did Antoinette more good than any medicine. She smiled now, languidly, happily. —And after a good night, although it was not very wise to go on so soon, she decided that they would get away very early, without telling the doctor, who would only want to keep them back.

The pure air and the joy of seeing so much beauty made her stronger, so that she did not have to pay for her rashness, and without any further misadventure they reached the end of their journey—a mountain village, high above the lake, some distance away from Spiez.

There they spent three or four weeks in a little hotel. Antoinette did not have any further attack of fever, but she never got really well. She still felt a heaviness, an intolerable weight, in her head, and she was always unwell. Olivier often asked her about her health: he longed to see her grow less pale: but he was intoxicated by the beauty of the country, and instinctively avoided all melancholy thoughts: when she assured him that she was really quite well, he tried to believe that it was true,— although he knew perfectly well that it was not so. And she enjoyed to the full her brother's exuberance and the fine air, and the all-pervading peace. How good it was to rest at last after those terrible years!

Olivier tried to induce her to go for walks with him: she would have been happy to join him: but on several occasions when she had bravely set out, she had been forced to stop after twenty minutes, to regain her breath, and rest her heart. So he went out alone,—climbing the safe peaks, though they filled her with terror until he came home again. Or they would go for little walks together: she would lean on his arm, and walk slowly, and they would talk, and he would suddenly begin to chatter, and laugh, and discuss his plans, and make quips and jests. From the road on the hillside above the valley they would watch the white clouds reflected in the still lake, and the boats moving like insects on the surface of a pond: they would drink in the warm air and the music of the goat-bells, borne on the gusty wind, and the smell of the new-mown hay and the warm resin. And they would dream together of the past and the future, and the present which seemed to them to be the most unreal and intoxicating of dreams. Sometimes Antoinette would be infected with her brother's jolly childlike humor: they would chase each other and roll about on the grass. And one day he saw her laughing as she used to do when they were children, madly, carelessly, laughter clear and bubbling as a spring, such as he had not heard for many years.

But, most often, Olivier could not resist the pleasure of going for long walks. He would be sorry for it at once, and later he had bitterly to regret that he had not made enough of those dear days with his sister. Even in the hotel he would often leave her alone. There was a party of young men and girls in the hotel, from whom they had at first kept apart. Then Olivier was attracted by them, and shyly joined their circle. He had been starved of friendship: outside his sister he had hardly known any one but his rough schoolfellows and their girls, who repelled him. It was very sweet to him to be among well-mannered, charming, merry boys and girls of his own age. Although he was very shy, he was naïvely curious, sentimental, and affectionate, and easily bewitched by the little burning, flickering fires that shine in a woman's eyes. And in spite of his shyness, women liked him. His frank longing to love and be loved gave him, unknown to himself, a youthful charm, and made him find words and gestures and affectionate little attentions, the very awkwardness of which made them all the more attractive. He had the gift of sympathy. Although in his isolation his intelligence had taken on an ironical tinge which made him see the vulgarity of people and their defects, which he often loathed,—yet in their presence he saw nothing but their eyes, in which he would see the expression of a living being, who one day would die, a being who had only one life, even as he, and, even as he, would lose it all too soon: then of that creature he would involuntarily be fond: in that moment nothing in the world could make him do anything to hurt: whether he liked it or not, he had to be kind and amiable. He was weak: and, in being so, he was sure to please the "world" which pardons every vice, and even every virtue,— except one: force, on which all the rest depend.

Antoinette did not join them. Her health, her tiredness, her apparently causeless moral collapse, paralyzed her. Through

the long years of anxiety and ceaseless toil, exhausting body and
soul, the positions of the brother and sister had been inverted:
now it was she who felt far removed from the world, far
from everything and everybody, so far! . . . She could not
break down the wall between them: all their chatter, their
noise, their laughter, their little interests, bored her, wearied
her, almost hurt her. It hurt her to be so: she would have loved
to go with the other girls, to share their interests and laugh
with them. . . . But she could not! . . . Her heart
ached; she seemed to be as one dead. In the evening she would
shut herself up in her room; and often she would not even
turn on the light: she would sit there in the dark, while downstairs Olivier would be amusing himself, surrendering to the
current of one of those romantic little love affairs to which he
so easily succumbed. She would only shake off her torpor when
she heard him coming upstairs, laughing and talking to the
girls, hanging about saying good-night outside their rooms, being unable to tear himself away. Then in the darkness Antoinette would smile, and get up to turn on the light. The
sound of her brother's laughter revived her.

Autumn was setting in. The sun was dying down. Nature
was a-weary. Under the thick mists and clouds of October
the colors were fading fast; snow fell on the mountains: mists
descended upon the plains. The visitors went away one by
one, and then several at a time. And it was sad to see even
the friends of a little while going away, but sadder still to see
the passing of the summer, the time of peace and happiness
which had been an oasis in their lives. They went for a last
walk together, on a cloudy autumn day, through the forest on
the mountain-side. They did not speak: they mused sadly, as
they walked along with the collars of their cloaks turned up,
clinging close together: their hands were locked. There was
silence in the wet woods, and in silence the trees wept. From
the depths there came the sweet plaintive cry of a solitary bird
who felt the coming of winter. Through the mist came the
clear tinkling of the goat-bells, far away, so faint they could

hardly hear it, so faint it was as though it came up from their inmost hearts. . . .

They returned to Paris. They were both sad. Antoinette was no better.

They had to set to work to prepare Olivier's wardrobe for the *École*. Antoinette spent the last of her little store of money, and even sold some of her jewels. What did it matter? He would repay her later on. And then, she would need so little when he was gone from her! . . . She tried not to think of what it would be like when he was gone: she worked away at his clothes, and put into the work all the tenderness she had for her brother, and she had a presentiment that it would be the last thing she would do for him.

During the last days together they were never apart: they were fearful of wasting the tiniest moment. On their last evening they sat up very late by the fireside, Antoinette occupying the only armchair, and Olivier a stool at her feet, and she made a fuss of him like the spoiled child he was. He was dreading—though he was curious about it, too—the new life upon which he was to enter. Antoinette thought only that it was the end of their dear life together, and wondered fearfully what would become of her. As though he were trying to make the thought even more bitter for her, he was more tender than ever he had been, with the innocent instinctive coquetry of those who always wait until they are just going to show themselves at their best and most charming. He went to the piano and played her their favorite passages from Mozart and Gluck—those visions of tender happiness and serene sorrow with which so much of their past life was bound up.

When the time came for them to part, Antoinette accompanied Olivier as far as the gates of the *École*. Then she returned. Once more she was alone. But now it was not, as when she had gone away to Germany, a separation which she could bring to an end at will when she could bear it no longer. Now it was she who remained behind, he who went away: it was

he who had gone away, for a long, long time—perhaps for life.
And yet her love for him was so maternal that at first she
thought less of herself than of him: she thought only of how
different the first few days would be for him, of the strict rules
of the *École,* and was preoccupied with those harmless little
worries which so easily assume alarming proportions in the
minds of people who live alone and are always tormenting
themselves about those whom they love. Her anxiety did at
least have this advantage, that it distracted her thoughts from
her own loneliness. She had already begun to think of the half-
hour when she would be able to see him next day in the visitors' room. She arrived a quarter of an hour too soon. He
was very nice to her, but he was altogether taken up with all
the new things he had seen. And during the following days,
when she went to see him, full of the most tender anxiety, the
contrast between what those meetings meant for her and what
they meant for him was more and more marked. For her they
were her whole life. For Olivier—no doubt he loved Antoinette
dearly: but it was too much to expect him to think only of her,
as she thought of him. Once or twice he came down late to the
visitors' room. One day, when she asked him if he were at all
unhappy, he said that he was nothing of the kind. Such little
things as that stabbed Antoinette to the heart.—She was angry
with herself for being so sensitive, and accused herself of
selfishness: she knew quite well that it would be absurd, even
wrong and unnatural, for him to be unable to do without her,
and for her to be unable to do without him, and to have no
other object in life. Yes: she knew all that. But what was
the good of her knowing it? She could not help it if for the
last ten years her whole life had been bound up in that one idea:
her brother. Now that the one interest of her life had been torn
from her, she had nothing left.

She tried bravely to keep herself occupied and to take up
her music and read her beloved books. . . . But alas!
how empty were Shakespeare and Beethoven without Olivier!
. . .—Yes: no doubt they were beautiful. . . . But Olivier

was not there. What is the good of beautiful things if the eyes of the beloved are not there to see them? What is the use of beauty, what is the use even of joy, if they cannot be won through the heart of the beloved?

If she had been stronger she would have tried to build up her life anew, and give it another object. But she was at the end of her tether. Now that there was nothing to force her to hold on, at all costs, the effort of will to which she had subjected herself snapped: she collapsed. The illness, which had been gaining grip on her for over a year, during which she had fought it down by force of will, was now left to take its course.

She spent her evenings alone in her room, by the spent fire, a prey to her thoughts: she had neither the courage to light the fire again, nor the strength to go to bed: she would sit there far into the night, dozing, dreaming, shivering. She would live through her life again, and summon up the beloved dead and her lost illusions: and she would be terribly sad at the thought of her lost youth, without love or hope of love. A dumb, aching sorrow, obscure, unconfessed. . . . A child laughed in the street: its little feet pattered up to the floor below. . . . Its little feet trampled on her heart. . . . She would be beset with doubts and evil thoughts; her soul in its weakness would be contaminated by the soul of that city of selfish pleasure.— She would fight down her regrets, and burn with shame at certain longings which she thought evil and wicked: she could not understand what it was that hurt her so, and attributed it to her evil instincts. Poor little Ophelia, devoured by a mysterious evil, she felt with horror dark and uneasy desires mounting from the depths of her being, from the very pit of life. She could not work, and she had given up most of her pupils: she, who was so plucky, and had always risen so early, now lay in bed sometimes until the afternoon: she had no more reason for getting up than for going to bed: she ate little or nothing. Only on her brother's holidays—Thursday afternoons and Sunday »-she would make an effort to be her old self with him.

He saw nothing. He was too much taken up with his new life to notice his sister much. He was at that period of boyhood when it was difficult for him to be communicative, and he always seemed to be indifferent to things outside himself which would only be his concern in later days.—People of riper years sometimes seem to be more open to impressions, and to take a simpler delight in life and Nature, than young people between twenty and thirty. And so it is often said that young people are not so young in heart as they were, and have lost all sense of enjoyment. That is often a mistaken idea. It is not because they have no sense of enjoyment that they seem less sensitive. It is because their whole being is often absorbed by passion, ambition, desire, some fixed idea. When the body is worn and has no more to expect from life, then the emotions become disinterested and fall into their place; and then once more the source of childish tears is reopened.—Olivier was preoccupied with a thousand little things, the most outstanding of which was an absurd little passion,—(he was always a victim to them),—which so obsessed him as to make him blind and indifferent to everything else.—Antoinette did not know what was happening to her brother: she only saw that he was drawing away from her. That was not altogether Olivier's fault. Sometimes when he came he would be glad to see her and start talking. He would come in. Then all of a sudden he would dry up. Her affectionate anxiety, the eagerness with which she clung to him, and drank in his words, and overwhelmed him with little attentions,—all her excess of tenderness and querulous devotion would deprive him utterly of any desire to be warm and open with her. He might have seen that Antoinette was not in a normal condition. Nothing could be farther from her usual tact and discretion. But he never gave a thought to it. He would reply to her questions with a curt " Yes " or " No." He would grow more stiff and surly, the more she tried to win him over: sometimes even he would hurt her by some brusque reply. Then she would be crushed and silent. Their day together would slip by, wasted. But hardly had he set foot outside the house on his way back to the *École* than he would be heartily ashamed of his treatment of her. He would torture himself all night as he lay awake thinking of the pain he had caused her. Sometimes even, as soon as he reached the *École*, he would write an effusive letter to his sister.—But next morning, when he read it through, he would tear it up. And Antoinette would know nothing at all about it. She would go on thinking that he had ceased to love her.

She had—if not one last joy—one last flutter of tenderness and youth, when her heart beat strongly once more; one last awakening of love in her, and hope of happiness, hope of life. It was quite ridiculous, so utterly unlike her tranquil nature! It could never have been but for her abnormal condition, the state of fear and over-excitement which was the precursor of illness.

She went to a concert at the *Châtelet* with her brother. As he had just been appointed musical critic to a little Review, they were in better places than those they occupied in old days, but the people among whom they sat were much more apathetic. They had stalls near the stage. Christophe Krafft was to play. Neither of them had ever heard of the German musician. When she saw him come on, the blood rushed to her heart. Although her tired eyes could only see him through a mist, she had no doubt when he appeared: he was the unknown young man of her unhappy days in Germany. She had never mentioned him to her brother: and she had hardly even admitted his existence to her thoughts: she had been entirely absorbed by the anxieties of her life since then. Besides, she was a reasonable little Frenchwoman, and refused to admit the existence of an obscure feeling which she could not trace to its source, while it seemed to lead nowhere. There was in her a whole region of the soul, of unsuspected depths, wherein there slept many other feelings which she would have been ashamed to behold: she knew that they were there: but she looked away from them in a sort of religious terror of that Being within herself which lies beyond the mind's control.

When she had recovered a little, she borrowed her brother's glasses to look at Christophe: she saw him in profile at the conductor's stand, and she recognized his expression of forceful concentration. He was wearing a shabby old coat which fitted him very badly.—Antoinette sat in silent agony through the vagaries of that lamentable concert when Christophe joined issue with the unconcealed hostility of his audience, who were at the time ill-disposed towards German artists, and actively bored by his music. And when he appeared, after a symphony which had seemed unconscionably long, to play some piano music, he was received with cat-calls which left no room for doubt as to their displeasure at having to put up with him again. However, he began to play in the face of the bored resignation of his audience: but the uncomplimentary remarks exchanged in a loud voice by two men in the gallery went on, to the great delight of the rest of the audience. Then he broke off: and in a childish fit of temper he played *Malbrouck s'en va t'en guerre* with one finger, got up from the piano, faced the audience, and said:

"That is all you are fit for."

The audience were for a moment so taken aback that they did not quite take in what the musician meant. Then there was an outburst of angry protests. Followed a terrible uproar. They hissed and shouted:

"Apologize! Make him apologize!"

They were all red in the face with anger, and they blew out their fury—tried to persuade themselves that they were really enraged: as perhaps they were, but the chief thing was that they were delighted to have a chance of making a row, and letting themselves go: they were like schoolboys after a few hours in school.

Antoinette could not move: she was petrified: she sat still tugging at one of her gloves. Ever since the last bars of the symphony she had had a growing presentiment of what would happen: she felt the blind hostility of the audience, felt it growing: she read Christophe's thoughts, and she was sure he would not go through to the end without an explosion: she sat waiting for the explosion while agony grew in her: she stretched every nerve to try to prevent it; and when at last it came, it was so exactly what she had foreseen that she was overwhelmed by it, as by some fatal catastrophe against which there was nothing to be done. And as she gazed at Christophe, who was staring insolently at the howling audience, their eyes met. Christophe's eyes recognized her, greeted her, for the space of perhaps a second: but he was in such a state of excitement that his mind did not recognize her (he had not thought of her for long enough). He disappeared while the audience yelled and hissed.

She longed to cry out: to say or do something: but she was bound hand and foot, and could not stir; it was like a nightmare. It was some comfort to her to hear her brother at her side, and to know that, without having any idea of what was happening to her, he had shared her agony and indignation. Olivier was a thorough musician, and he had an independence of taste which nothing could encroach upon: when he liked a thing, he would have maintained his liking in the face of the whole world. With the very first bars of the symphony, he had felt that he was in the presence of something big, something the like of which he had never in his life come across. He went on muttering to himself with heartfelt enthusiasm:

"That's fine! That's beautiful! Beautiful!" while his sister instinctively pressed close to him, gratefully. After the symphony he applauded loudly by way of protest against the ironic indifference of the rest of the audience. When it came to the great fiasco, he was beside himself: he stood up, shouted that Christophe was right, abused the booers, and offered to fight them: it was impossible to recognize the timid Olivier. His voice was drowned in the uproar: he was told to shut up: he was called a "snotty little kid," and told to go to bed. An-

toinette saw the futility of standing up to them, and took his
arm and said:

"Stop! Stop! I implore you! Stop!"

He sat down in despair, and went on muttering:

"It's shameful! Shameful! The swine! . . ."

She said nothing and bore her suffering in silence: he thought
she was insensible to the music, and said:

"Antoinette, don't *you* think it beautiful?"

She nodded. She was frozen, and could not recover herself.
But when the orchestra began another piece, she suddenly got
up, and whispered to her brother in a tone of savage hatred:

"Come, come! I can't bear the sight of these people!"

They hurried out. They walked along arm-in-arm, and
Olivier went on talking excitedly. Antoinette said nothing.

All that day and the days following she sat alone in her
room, and a feeling crept over her which at first she refused
to face: but then it went on and took possession of her thoughts,
like the furious throbbing of the blood in her aching temples.

Some time afterwards Olivier brought her Christophe's collection of songs, which he had just found at a publisher's. She
opened it at random. On the first page on which her eyes fell
she read in front of a song this dedication in German:

"*To my poor dear little victim,*" together with a date.

She knew the date well.—She was so upset that she could
read no farther. She put the book down and asked her brother
to play, and went and shut herself up in her room. Olivier,
full of his delight in the new music, began to play without remarking his sister's emotion. Antoinette sat in the adjoining
room, striving to repress the beating of her heart. Suddenly
she got up and looked through a cupboard for a little account-
book in which was written the date of her departure from Germany, and the mysterious date. She knew it already: yes, it
was the evening of the performance at the theater to which she
had been with Christophe. She lay down on her bed and closed
her eyes, blushing, with her hands folded on her breast, while

she listened to the dear music. Her heart was overflowing with gratitude. . . . Ah! Why did her head hurt her so?

When Olivier saw that his sister had not come back, he went into her room after he had done playing, and found her lying there. He asked her if she were ill. She said she was rather tired, and got up to keep him company. They talked: but she did not answer his questions at once: her thoughts seemed to be far away: she smiled, and blushed, and said, by way of excuse, that her headache was making her stupid. At last Olivier went away. She had asked him to leave the book of songs. She sat up late reading them at the piano, without playing, just lightly touching a note here and there, for fear of annoying her neighbors. But for the most part she did not even read: she sat dreaming: she was carried away by a feeling of tenderness and gratitude towards the man who had pitied her, and had read her mind and soul with the mysterious intuition of true kindness. She could not fix her thoughts. She was happy and sad—sad! . . . Ah! How her head ached!

She spent the night in sweet and painful dreams, a crushing melancholy. During the day she tried to go out for a little to shake off her drowsiness. Although her head was still aching, to give herself something to do, she went and made a few purchases at a great shop. She hardly gave a thought to what she was doing. Her thoughts were always with Christophe, though she did not admit it to herself. As she came out, worried and mortally sad, through the crowd of people she saw Christophe go by on the other side of the street. He saw her, too, at the same moment. At once,—(suddenly and without thinking), she held out her hands towards him. Christophe stopped: this time he recognized her. He sprang forward to cross the road to Antoinette: and Antoinette tried to go to meet him. But the insensate current of the passing throng carried her along like a windlestraw, while the horse of an omnibus, falling on the slippery asphalt, made a sort of dyke in front of Christophe, by which the opposing streams of carriages were

dammed, so that for a few moments there was an impassable
barrier. Christophe tried to force his way through in spite of
everything: but he was trapped in the middle of the traffic, and
could not move either way. When at last he did extricate himself and managed to reach the place where he had seen Antoinette, she was gone: she had struggled vainly against the
human torrent that carried her along: then she yielded to it—
gave up the struggle. She felt that she was dogged by some
fatality which forbade the possibility of her ever meeting Christophe: against Fate there was nothing to be done. And when
she did succeed in escaping from the crowd, she made no attempt to go back: she was suddenly ashamed: what could she
dare to say to him? What had she done? What must he have
thought of her? She fled away home.

She did not regain assurance until she reached her room.
Then she sat by the table in the dark, and had not even the
strength to take off her hat or her gloves. She was miserable
at having been unable to speak to him: and at the same time
there glowed a new light in her heart: she was unconscious of
the darkness, and unconscious of the illness that was upon her.
She went on and on turning over and over every detail of the
scene in the street: and she changed it about and imagined
what would have happened if certain things had turned out differently. She saw herself holding out her arms to Christophe,
and Christophe's expression of joy as he recognized her, and she
laughed and blushed. She blushed: and then in the darkness
of her room, where there was no one to see her, and she could
hardly see herself, once more she held out her arms to him.
Her need was too strong for her: she felt that she was losing
ground, and instinctively she sought to clutch at the strong
vivid life that passed so near her, and gazed so kindly at her.
Her heart was full of tenderness and anguish, and through the
night she cried:

"Help me! Save me!"

All in a fever she got up and lit the lamp, and took pen
and paper. She wrote to Christophe. Her illness was full

upon her, or she would never even have thought of writing to him, so proud she was and timid. She did not know what she wrote. She was no longer mistress of herself. She called to him, and told him that she loved him. . . . In the middle of her letter she stopped, appalled. She tried to write it all over again: but her impulse was gone: her mind was a blank, and her head was aching: she had a horrible difficulty in finding words: she was utterly worn out. She was ashamed. . . . What was the good of it all? She knew perfectly well that she was trying to trick herself, and that she would never send the letter. . . . Even if she had wished to do so, how could she? She did not know Christophe's address. . . . Poor Christophe! And what could he do for her? Even if he knew all and were kind to her, what could he do? . . . It was too late! No, no: it was all in vain, the last dying struggle of a bird, blindly, desperately beating its wings. She must be resigned to it. . . .

So for a long time she sat there by the table, lost in thought, unable to move hand or foot. It was past midnight when she struggled to her feet—bravely. Mechanically she placed the loose sheets of her letter in one of her few books, for she had the strength neither to put them in order nor to tear them up. Then she went to bed, shivering and shaking with fever. The key to the riddle lay near at hand: she felt that the will of God was to be fulfilled.—And a great peace came upon her.

On Sunday morning when Olivier came he found Antoinette in bed, delirious. A doctor was called in. He said it was acute consumption.

Antoinette had known how serious her condition was: she had discovered the cause of the moral turmoil in herself which had so alarmed her. She had been dreadfully ashamed, and it was some consolation to her to think that not she herself but her illness was the cause of it. She had managed to take a few precautions and to burn her papers and to write a letter to Madame Nathan: she appealed to her kindness to look after

her brother during the first few weeks after her "death"—
(she dared not write the word). . . .

The doctor could do nothing: the disease was too far gone,
and Antoinette's constitution had been wrecked by the years of
hardship and unceasing toil.

Antoinette was quite calm. Since she had known that there
was no hope her agony and torment had left her. She lay
turning over in her mind all the trials and tribulations through
which she had passed: she saw that her work was done and her
dear Olivier saved: and she was filled with unutterable joy.
She said to herself:

"I have achieved that."

And then she turned in shame from her pride and said:

"I could have done nothing alone. God has given me His
aid."

And she thanked God that He had granted her life until she
had accomplished her task. There was a catch at her heart as
she thought that now she had to lay down her life: but she
dared not complain: that would have been to feel ingratitude
towards God, who might have called her away sooner. And
what would have happened if she had passed away a year
sooner?—She sighed, and humbled herself in gratitude.

In spite of her weakness and oppression she did not complain,—except when she was sleeping heavily, when every now
and then she moaned like a little child. She watched things and
people with a calm smile of resignation. It was always a joy
to her to see Olivier. She would move her lips to call him,
though she made no sound: she would want to hold his hand in
hers: she would bid him lay his head on the pillow near hers,
and then, gazing into his eyes, she would go on looking at him
in silence. At last she would raise herself up and hold his face
in her hands and say:

"Ah! Olivier! . . . Olivier! . . ."

She took the medal that she wore round her neck, and hung
it on her brother's. She commended her beloved Olivier to
the care of her confessor, her doctor, everybody. It seemed as

though she was to live henceforth in him, that, on the point of death, she was taking refuge in his life, as upon some island in uncharted seas. Sometimes she seemed to be uplifted by a mystic exaltation of tenderness and faith, and she forgot her illness, and sadness changed to joy in her,—a joy divine indeed that shone upon her lips and in her eyes. Over and over again she said:

"I am happy. . . ."

Her senses grew dim. In her last moments of consciousness her lips moved and it seemed that she was repeating something to herself. Olivier went to her bedside and bent down over her. She recognized him once more and smiled feebly up at him: her lips went on moving and her eyes were filled with tears. They could not make out what she was trying to say. . . . But faintly Olivier heard her breathe the words of the dear old song they used to love so much, the song she was always singing:

"*I will come again, my sweet and bonny, I will come again.*"

Then she relapsed into unconsciousness. So she passed away.

Unconsciously she had aroused a profound sympathy in many people whom she did not even know: in the house in which she lived she did not even know the names of the other tenants. Olivier received expressions of sympathy from people who were strangers to him. Antoinette was not taken to her grave unattended as her mother had been. Her body was followed to the cemetery by friends and schoolfellows of her brother, and members of the families whose children she had taught, and people whom she had met without saying a word of her own life or hearing a word from them, though they admired her secretly, knowing her devotion, and many of the poor, and the housekeeper who had helped her, and even many of the small tradesmen of the neighborhood. Madame Nathan had taken Olivier under her wing on the day of his sister's death, and she had carried him off in spite of himself, and done her best to turn his thoughts away from his grief.

If it had come later in his life he could never have borne
up against such a catastrophe,—but now it was impossible for
him to succumb absolutely to his despair. He had just begun a
new life; he was living in a community, and had to live the
common life whatever he might be feeling. The full busy life
of the *École,* the intellectual pressure, the examinations, the
struggle for life, all kept him from withdrawing into himself:
he could not be alone. He suffered, but it proved his salvation.
A year earlier, or a few years earlier, he must have succumbed.

And yet he did as far as possible retire into isolation in
the memory of his sister. It was a great sorrow to him that he
could not keep the rooms where they had lived together: but
he had no money. He hoped that the people who seemed to
be interested in him would understand his distress at not being
able to keep the things that had been hers. But nobody seemed
to understand. He borrowed some money and made a little
more by private tuition and took an attic in which he stored all
that he could preserve of his sister's furniture: her bed, her
table, and her armchair. He made it the sanctuary of her
memory. He took refuge there whenever he was depressed.
His friends thought he was carrying on an intrigue. He would
stay there for hours dreaming of her with his face buried in his
hands: unhappily he had no portrait of her except a little photograph, taken when she was a child, of the two of them together.
He would talk to her and weep. . . . Where was she? Ah!
if she had been at the other end of the world, wherever she
might be and however inaccessible the spot,—with what great
joy and invincible ardor he would have rushed forth in search
of her, though a thousand sufferings lay in wait for him,
though he had to go barefoot, though he had to wander for
hundreds of years, if only it might be that every step would
bring him nearer to her! . . . Yes, even though there were
only one chance in a thousand of his ever finding her. . . .
But there was nothing. . . . Nowhere to go. . . . No way
of ever finding her again. . . . How utterly lonely he was
now! Now that she was no longer there to love and counsel

and console him, inexperienced and childish as he was, he was
flung into the waters of life, to sink or swim! . . . He who
has once had the happiness of perfect intimacy and boundless
friendship with another human being has known the divinest
of all joys,—a joy that will make him miserable for the remainder of his life. . . .

*Nessun maggior dolore che ricordarsi del tempo felice nella
miseria.* . . .

For a weak and tender soul it is the greatest of misfortunes
ever to have known the greatest happiness.

But though it is sad indeed to lose the beloved at the beginning of life, it is even more terrible later on when the springs
of life are running dry. Olivier was young: and, in spite of his
inborn pessimism, in spite of his misfortune, he had to live his
life. As often seems to happen after the loss of those dear to
us, it was as though when Antoinette passed away she had
breathed part of her soul into her brother's life. And he believed it was so. Though he had not such faith as hers, yet he
did arrive at a vague conviction that his sister was not dead,
but lived on in him, as she had promised. There is a Breton
superstition that those who die young are not dead, but stay and
hover over the places where they lived until they have fulfilled
the normal span of their existence.—So Antoinette lived out
her life in Olivier.

He read through the papers he had found in her room. Unhappily she had burned most of them. Besides, she was not the
sort of woman to keep notes and tallies of her inner life. She
was too modest to uncloak her inmost thoughts in morbid
babbling indiscretion. She only kept a little notebook which
was almost unintelligible to anybody else—a bare record in
which she had written down without remark certain dates, and
certain small events in her daily life, which had given her joys
and emotions, which she had no need to write down in detail
to keep alive. Almost all these dates were connected with some
event in Olivier's life. She had kept every letter he had ever
written to her, without exception.—Alas! He had not been so

careful: he had lost almost all the letters she had written to him. What need had he of letters? He thought he would have his sister always with him: that dear fount of tenderness seemed inexhaustible: he thought that he would always be able to quench his thirst of lips and heart at it: he had most prodigally squandered the love he had received, and now he was eager to gather up the smallest drops. . . . What was his emotion when, as he skimmed through one of Antoinette's books, he found these words written in pencil on a scrap of paper:

"Olivier, my dear Olivier! . . . ."

He almost swooned. He sobbed and kissed the invisible lips that so spoke to him from the grave.—Thereafter he took down all her books and hunted through them page by page to see if she had not left some other words of him. He found the fragment of the letter to Christophe, and discovered the unspoken romance which had sprung to life in her: so for the first time he happed upon her emotional life, that he had never known in her and never tried to know: he lived through the last passionate days, when, deserted by himself, she had held out her arms to the unknown friend. She had never told him that she had seen Christophe before. Certain words in her letter revealed the fact that they had met in Germany. He understood that Christophe had been kind to Antoinette, in circumstances the details of which were unknown to him, and that Antoinette's feeling for the musician dated from that day, though she had kept her secret to the end.

Christophe, whom he loved already for the beauty of his art, now became unutterably dear to him. She had loved him: it seemed to Olivier that it was she whom he loved in Christophe. He moved heaven and earth to meet him. It was not an easy matter to trace him. After his rebuff Christophe had been lost in the wilderness of Paris: he had shunned all society and no one gave a thought to him.—After many months it chanced that Olivier met Christophe in the street: he was pale and sunken from the illness from which he had only just recovered. But Olivier had not the courage to stop him. He followed him home at a distance. He wanted to write to him, but could not screw himself up to it. What was there to say? Olivier was not alone: Antoinette was with him: her love, her modesty had become a part of him: the thought that his sister had loved Christophe made him as bashful in Christophe's presence as though he had been Antoinette. And yet how he longed to talk to him of her!—But he could not. Her secret was a seal upon his lips.

He tried to meet Christophe again. He went everywhere where he thought Christophe might be. He was longing to shake hands with him. And when he saw him he tried to hide so that Christophe should not see him.

At last Christophe saw him at the house of some mutual friends where they both happened to be one evening. Olivier stood far away from him and said nothing: but he watched him. And no doubt the spirit of Antoinette was hovering near Olivier that night: for Christophe saw her in Olivier's eyes: and it was her image, so suddenly evoked, that made him cross the room and go towards the unknown messenger, who, like a young Hermes, brought him the melancholy greeting of the blessed dead.

THE HOUSE

I

I have a friend! . . . Oh! The delight of having found a kindred soul to which to cling in the midst of torment, a tender and sure refuge in which to breathe again while the fluttering heart beats slower! No longer to be alone, no longer never to unarm, no longer to stay on guard with straining, burning eyes, until from sheer fatigue he should fall into the hands of his enemies! To have a dear companion into whose hands all his life should be delivered—the friend whose life was delivered into his! At last to taste the sweetness of repose, to sleep while the friend watches, watch while the friend sleeps. To know the joy of protecting a beloved creature who should trust in him like a little child. To know the greater joy of absolute surrender to that friend, to feel that he is in possession of all secrets, and has power over life and death. Aging, worn out, weary of the burden of life through so many years, to find new birth and fresh youth in the body of the friend, through his eyes to see the world renewed, through his senses to catch the fleeting loveliness of all things by the way, through his heart to enjoy the splendor of living. . . . Even to suffer in his suffering. . . . Ah! Even suffering is joy if it be shared!

I have a friend! . . . Away from me, near me, in me always. I have my friend, and I am his. My friend loves me. I am my friend's, the friend of my friend. Of our two souls love has fashioned one.

Christophe's first thought, when he awoke the day after the Roussins' party, was for Olivier Jeannin. At once he felt an irresistible longing to see him again. He got up and went out. It was not yet eight o'clock. It was a heavy and rather oppressive morning. An April day before its time: stormy clouds were hovering over Paris.

Olivier lived below the hill of Sainte-Geneviève, in a little street near the *Jardin des Plantes*. The house stood in the narrowest part of the street. The staircase led out of a dark yard, and was full of divers unpleasant smells. The stairs wound steeply up and sloped down towards the wall, which was disfigured with scribblings in pencil. On the third floor a woman, with gray hair hanging down, and in petticoat-bodice, gaping at the neck, opened the door when she heard footsteps on the stairs, and slammed it to when she saw Christophe. There were several flats on each landing, and through the ill-fitting doors Christophe could hear children romping and squalling. The place was a swarming heap of dull base creatures, living as it were on shelves, one above the other, in that low-storied house, built round a narrow, evil-smelling yard. Christophe was disgusted, and wondered what lusts and covetous desires could have drawn so many creatures to this place, far from the fields, where at least there is air enough for all, and what it could profit them in the end to be in the city of Paris, where all their lives they were condemned to live in such a sepulcher.

He reached Olivier's landing. A knotted piece of string was his bell-pull. Christophe tugged at it so mightily that at the noise several doors on the staircase were half opened. Olivier came to the door. Christophe was struck by the careful simplicity of his dress: and the neatness of it, which at any other time would have been little to his liking, was in that place an agreeable surprise: in such an atmosphere of foulness there was something charming and healthy about it. And at once he felt just as he had done the night before when he gazed into Olivier's clear, honest eyes. He held out his hand: but Olivier was overcome with shyness, and murmured:

"You. . . . You here!"

Christophe was engrossed in catching at the lovable quality of the man as it was revealed to him in that fleeting moment of embarrassment, and he only smiled in answer. He moved forward and forced Olivier backward, and entered the one room in which he both slept and worked. An iron bedstead stood against the wall near the window; Christophe noticed the pillows heaped up on the bolster. There were three chairs, a black-painted table, a small piano, bookshelves and books, and that was all. The room was cramped, low, ill-lighted: and yet there was in it a ray of the pure light that shone in the eyes of its owner. Everything was clean and tidy, as though a woman's hands had dealt with it: and a few roses in a vase brought spring-time into the room, the walls of which were decorated with photographs of old Florentine pictures.

"So. . . . You. . . . You have come to see me?" said Olivier warmly.

"Good Lord, I had to!" said Christophe. "You would never have come to me?"

"You think not?" replied Olivier.

Then, quickly:

"Yes, you are right. But it would not be for want of thinking of it."

"What would have stopped you?"

"Wanting to too much."

"That's a fine reason!"

"Yes. Don't laugh. I was afraid you would not want it as much as I."

"A lot that's worried me! I wanted to see you, and here I am. If it bores you, I shall know at once."

"You will have to have good eyes."

They smiled at each other.

Olivier went on:

"I was an ass last night. I was afraid I might have offended you. My shyness is absolutely a disease: I can't get a word out."

"I shouldn't worry about that. There are plenty of talkers

in your country: one is only too glad to meet a man who is silent occasionally, even though it be only from shyness and in spite of himself."

Christophe laughed and chuckled over his own gibe.

"Then you have come to see me because I can be silent?"

"Yes. For your silence, the sort of silence that is yours. There are all sorts: and I like yours, and that's all there is to say."

"But how could you sympathize with me? You hardly saw me."

"That's my affair. It doesn't take me long to make up my mind. When I see a face that I like in the crowd, I know what to do: I go after it: I simply have to know the owner of it."

"And don't you ever make mistakes when you go after them?"

"Often."

"Perhaps you have made a mistake this time."

"We shall see."

"Ah! In that case I'm done! You terrify me. If I think you are watching me, I shall lose what little wits I have."

With fond and eager curiosity Christophe watched the sensitive, mobile face, which blushed and went pale by turns. Emotion showed fleeting across it like the shadows of clouds on a lake.

"What a nervous youngster it is!" he thought. "He is like a woman."

He touched his knee.

"Come, come!" he said. "Do you think I should come to you with weapons concealed about me? I have a horror of people who practise their psychology on their friends. I only ask that we should both be open and sincere, and frankly and without shame, and without being afraid of committing ourselves finally to anything or of any sort of contradiction, be true to what we feel. I ask only the right to love now, and next minute, if needs must, to be out of love. There's loyalty and manliness in that, isn't there?"

Olivier gazed at him with serious eyes, and replied:

" No doubt. It is the more manly part, and you are strong enough. But I don't think I am."

" I'm sure you are," said Christophe; "but in a different way. And then, I've come just to help you to be strong, if you want to be so. For what I have just said gives me leave to go on and say, with more frankness than I should otherwise have had, that—without prejudice for to-morrow—I love you."

Olivier blushed hotly. He was struck dumb with embarrassment, and could not speak.

Christophe glanced round the room.

" It's a poor place you live in. Haven't you another room?"

" Only a lumber-room."

" Ugh! I can't breathe. How do you manage to live here?"

" One does it somehow."

" I couldn't—never."

Christophe unbuttoned his waistcoat and took a long breath. Olivier went and opened the window wide.

" You must be very unhappy in a town, M. Krafft. But there's no danger of my suffering from too much vitality. I breathe so little that I can live anywhere. And yet there are nights in summer when even I am hard put to it to get through. I'm terrified when I see them coming. Then I stay sitting up in bed, and I'm almost stifled."

Christophe looked at the heap of pillows on the bed, and from them to Olivier's worn face: and he could see him struggling there in the darkness.

" Leave it," he said. " Why do you stay?"

Olivier shrugged his shoulders and replied carelessly:

" It doesn't matter where I live."

Heavy footsteps padded across the floor above them. In the

room below a shrill argument was toward. And always, without ceasing, the walls were shaken by the rumbling of the buses in the street.

"And the house!" Christophe went on. "The house reeking of filth, the hot dirtiness of it all, the shameful poverty—how can you bring yourself to come back to it night after night? Don't you lose heart with it all? I couldn't live in it for a moment. I'd rather sleep under an arch."

"Yes. I felt all that at first, and suffered. I was just as disgusted as you are. When I went for walks as a boy, the mere sight of some of the crowded dirty streets made me ill. They gave me all sorts of fantastic horrors, which I dared not speak of. I used to think: 'If there were an earthquake now, I should be dead, and stay here for ever and ever'; and that seemed to me the most appalling thing that could happen. I never thought that one day I should live in one of them of my own free-will, and that in all probability I shall die there. And then it became easier to put up with: it had to. It still revolts me: but I try not to think of it. When I climb the stairs I close my eyes, and stop my ears, and hold my nose, and shut off all my senses and withdraw utterly into myself. And then, over the roof there, I can see the tops of the branches of an acacia. I sit here in this corner so that I don't see anything else: and in the evening when the wind rustles through them I fancy that I am far away from Paris: and the mighty roar of a forest has never seemed so sweet to me as the gentle murmuring of those few frail leaves at certain moments."

"Yes," said Christophe. "I've no doubt that you are always dreaming; but it's all wrong to waste your fancy in such a struggle against the sordid things of life, when you might be using it in the creation of other lives."

"Isn't it the common lot? Don't you yourself waste energy in anger and bitter struggles?"

"That's not the same thing. It's natural to me: what I was born for. Look at my arms and hands! Fighting is the breath of life to me. But you haven't any too much strength: that's obvious."

Olivier looked sadly down at his thin wrists, and said:

"Yes. I am weak: I always have been. But what can I do? One must live?"

"How do you make your living?"

"I teach."

"Teach what?"

"Everything—Latin, Greek, history. I coach for degrees. And I lecture on Moral Philosophy at the Municipal School."

"Lecture on what?"

"Moral Philosophy."

"What in thunder is that? Do they teach morality in French schools?"

Olivier smiled:

"Of course."

"Is there enough in it to keep you talking for ten minutes?"

"I have to lecture for twelve hours a week."

"Do you teach them to do evil, then?"

"What do you mean?"

"There's no need for so much talk to find out what good is."

"Or to leave it undiscovered either."

"Good gracious, yes! Leave it undiscovered. There are worse ways of doing good than knowing nothing about it. Good isn't a matter of knowledge: it's a matter of action. It's only your neurasthenics who go haggling about morality: and the first of all moral laws is not to be neurasthenic. Rotten pedants! They are like cripples teaching people how to walk."

"But they don't do their talking for such as you. You know: but there are so many who do not know!"

"Well, let them crawl like children until they learn how to walk by themselves. But whether they go on two legs or on all fours, the first thing, the only thing you can ask is that they should walk somehow."

He was prowling round and round and up and down the room, though less than four strides took him across it. He stopped in front of the piano, opened it, turned over the pages of some music, touched the keys, and said:

"Play me something."

Olivier started.

"I!" he said. "What an idea!"

"Madame Roussin told me you were a good musician. Come: play me something."

"With you listening? Oh!" he said, "I should die."

The sincerity and simplicity with which he spoke made Christophe laugh: Olivier, too, though rather bashfully.

"Well," said Christophe, "is that a reason for a Frencchman?"

Olivier still drew back.

"But why? Why do you want me to?"

"I'll tell you presently. Play!"

"What?"

"Anything you like."

Olivier sat down at the piano with a sigh, and, obedient to the imperious will of the friend who had sought him out, he began to play the beautiful *Adagio in B Minor* of Mozart. At first his fingers trembled so that he could hardly make them press down the keys: but he regained courage little by little: and, while he thought he was but repeating Mozart's utterance, he unwittingly revealed his inmost heart. Music is an indiscreet confidant: it betrays the most secret thoughts of its lovers to those who love it. Through the godlike scheme of the *Adagio* of Mozart Christophe could perceive the invisible lines of the character, not of Mozart, but of his new friend sitting there by the piano: the serene melancholy, the timid, tender smile of the boy, so nervous, so pure, so full of love, so ready to blush. But he had hardly reached the end of the air, the topmost point where the melody of sorrowful love ascends and snaps, when a sudden irrepressible feeling of shame and modesty overcame Olivier, so that he could not go on: his fingers would not move, and his voice failed him. His hands fell by his side, and he said:

"I can't play any more. ... ."

Christophe was standing behind him, and he stooped and reached over him and finished the broken melody: then he said:

"Now I know the music of your soul."

He held his hands, and stayed for a long time gazing into his face. At last he said:

"How queer it is! . . . I have seen you before. . . . I know you so well, and I have known you so long! . . ."

Olivier's lips trembled: he was on the point of speaking. But he said nothing.

Christophe went on gazing at him for a moment or two longer. Then he smiled and said no more, and went away.

He went down the stairs with his heart filled with joy. He passed two ugly children going up, one with bread, the other with a bottle of oil. He pinched their cheeks jovially. He smiled at the scowling porter. When he reached the street he walked along humming to himself until he came to the Luxembourg. He lay down on a seat in the shade, and closed his eyes. The air was still and heavy: there were only a few passers-by. Very faintly he could hear the irregular trickling of the fountain, and every now and then the scrunching of the gravel as footsteps passed him by. Christophe was overcome with drowsiness, and he lay basking like a lizard in the sun: his face had been out of the shadow of the trees for some time: but he could not bring himself to stir. His thoughts wound about and about: he made no attempt to hold and fix them: they were all steeped in the light of happiness. The Luxembourg clock struck: he did not listen to it: but, a moment later, he thought it must have been striking twelve. He jumped up to realize that he had been lounging for a couple of hours, had missed an appointment with Hecht, and wasted the whole morning. He laughed, and went home whistling. He composed a *Rondo* in canon on the cry of a peddler. Even sad melodies now took on the charm of the gladness that was in him. As he passed the laundry in his street, as usual, he glanced into the shop, and saw the little red-haired girl, with her dull complexion flushed with the heat, and she was ironing with her thin arms bare to the shoulder and her bodice open at the neck: and, as usual, she ogled him brazenly: for the first time he was not irritated by her eyes meeting his. He laughed once more. When he reached his room he was free of all the obsessions from which he had suffered. He flung his hat, coat, and vest in different directions, and sat down to work with an all-conquering zest. He gathered together all his scattered scraps of music, which were lying all over the room, but his mind was not in his work: he only read the script with his eyes: and a few minutes later he fell back into the happy somnolence that had been upon him in the Luxembourg Gardens; his head buzzed, and he could not think. Twice or thrice he became aware of his condition, and tried to shake it off: but in vain. He swore light-heartedly, got up. and dipped his head in a basin of cold water. That sobered him a little. He sat down at the table again, sat in silence, and smiled dreamily. He was wondering:

"What is the difference between that and love?"

Instinctively he had begun to think in whispers, as though he were ashamed. He shrugged his shoulders.

"There are not two ways of loving. . . . Or, rather, yes, there are two ways: there is the way of those who love with every fiber of their being, and the way of those who only give to love a part of their superfluous energy. God keep me from such cowardice of heart!"

He stopped in his thought, from a sort of shame and dread of following it any farther. He sat for a long time smiling at his inward dreams. His heart sang through the silence:

Du bist mein, und nun ist das Meine Meiner als jemals . . .

("Thou art mine, and now I am mine, more mine than I have ever been. . . .")

He took a sheet of paper, and with tranquil ease wrote down the song that was in his heart.

They decided to take rooms together. Christophe wanted to take possession at once without worrying about the waste of half a quarter. Olivier was more prudent, though not less ardent in their friendship, and thought it better to wait until their respective tenancies had expired. Christophe could not understand such parsimony. Like many people who have no money, he never worried about losing it. He imagined that Olivier was even worse off than himself. One day when his friend's poverty had been brought home to him he left him suddenly and returned a few hours later in triumph with a few francs which he had squeezed in advance out of Hecht. Olivier blushed and refused. Christophe was put out and made to throw them to an Italian who was playing in the yard. Olivier withheld him. Christophe went away, apparently offended, but really furious with his own clumsiness to which he attributed Olivier's refusal. A letter from his friend brought balm to his wounds. Olivier could write what he could not express by word of mouth: he could tell of his happiness in knowing him and how touched he was by Christophe's offer of assistance. Christophe replied with a crazy, wild letter, rather like those which he wrote when he was fifteen to his friend Otto: it was full of *Gemüth* and blundering jokes: he made puns in French and German, and even translated them into music.

At last they went into their rooms. In the Montparnasse quarter, near the *Place Denfert,* on the fifth floor of an old house they had found a flat of three rooms and a kitchen, all very small, and looking on to a tiny garden inclosed by four high walls. From their windows they looked out over the opposite wall, which was lower than the rest, on to one of those large convent gardens which are still to be found in Paris, hidden and unknown. Not a soul was to be seen in the deserted avenues. The old trees, taller and more leafy than those in the Luxembourg Gardens, trembled in the sunlight: troops of birds sang: in the early dawn the blackbirds fluted, and then there came the riotously rhythmic chorus of the sparrows: and in summer in the evening the rapturous cries of the swifts cleaving the luminous air and skimming through the heavens. And at night, under the moon, like bubbles of air mounting to the surface of a pond, there came up the pearly notes of the toads.   Almost they might have forgotten the surrounding presence of Paris but that the old house was perpetually shaken by the heavy vehicles rumbling by, as though the earth beneath were shivering in a fever.

One of the rooms was larger and finer than the rest, and there was a struggle between the friends as to who should not have it.   They had to toss for it: and Christophe, who had made the suggestion, contrived not to win with a dexterity of which he found it hard to believe himself capable.

Then for the two of them there began a period of absolute happiness.   Their happiness lay not in any one thing, but in all things at once: their every thought, their every act, were steeped in it, and it never left them for a moment.

During this honeymoon of their friendship, the first days of deep and silent rejoicing, known only to him "who in all the universe can call one soul his own" . . . *Ja, wer auch nur eine Seele sein nennt auf dem Erdenrund . . .* they hardly spoke to each other, they dared hardly breathe a word; it was enough for them to feel each other's nearness, to exchange a look, a word in token that their thoughts, after long periods of silence, still ran in the same channel.   Without probing or inquiring, without even looking at each other, yet unceasingly they watched each other.   Unconsciously the lover takes for model the soul of the beloved: so great is his desire to give no hurt, to be in all things as the beloved, that with mysterious and sudden intuition he marks the imperceptible movements in the depths of his soul.   One friend to another is crystal-clear: they exchange entities.   Their features are assimilated.   Soul imitates soul,—until that day comes when deep-moving force, the spirit of the race, bursts his bonds and rends asunder the web of love in which he is held captive.

Christophe spoke in low tones, walked softly, tried hard to make no noise in his room, which was next to that of the silent Olivier: he was transfigured by his friendship: he had an expression of happiness, confidence, youth, such as he had never worn before. He adored Olivier. It would have been easy for the boy to abuse his power if he had not been so timorous in feeling that it was a happiness undeserved: for he thought himself much inferior to Christophe, who in his turn was no less humble. This mutual humility, the product of their great love for each other, was an added joy. It was a pure delight—even with the consciousness of unworthiness— for each to feel that he filled so great a room in the heart of his friend. Each to other they were tender and filled with gratitude.

Olivier had mixed his books with Christophe's: they made no distinction. When he spoke of them he did not say "*my* book," but "*our* book." He kept back only a few things from the common stock: those which had belonged to his sister or were bound up with her memory. With the quick perception of love Christophe was not slow to notice this: but he did not know the reason of it. He had never dared to ask Olivier about his family: he only knew that Olivier had lost his parents: and to the somewhat proud reserve of his affection, which forbade his prying into his friend's secrets, there was added a fear of calling to life in him the sorrows of the past. Though he might long to do so, yet he was strangely timid and never dared to look closely at the photographs on Olivier's desk, portraits of a lady and a gentleman stiffly posed, and a little girl of twelve with a great spaniel at her feet.

A few months after they had taken up their quarters Olivier caught cold and had to stay in bed. Christophe, who had become quite motherly, nursed him with fond anxiety: and the doctor, who, on examining Olivier, had found a little inflammation at the top of the lungs, told Christophe to smear the invalid's chest with tincture of iodine. As Christophe was gravely acquitting himself of the task he saw a confirmation medal hanging from Olivier's neck. He was familiar enough with Olivier to know that he was even more emancipated in matters of religion than himself. He could not refrain from showing his surprise. Olivier colored and said:

"It is a souvenir. My poor sister Antoinette was wearing it when she died."

Christophe trembled. The name of Antoinette struck him like a flash of lightning.

"Antoinette?" he said.

"My sister," said Olivier.

Christophe repeated:

"Antoinette . . . Antoinette Jeannin. . . . She was your sister? . . . But," he said, as he looked at the photograph on the desk, "she was quite a child when you lost her?"

Olivier smiled sadly.

"It is a photograph of her as a child," he said. "Alas! I have no other. . . . She was twenty-five when she left me."

"Ah!" said Christophe, who was greatly moved. "And she was in Germany, was she not?"

Olivier nodded.

Christophe took Olivier's hands in his.

"I knew her," he said.

"Yes, I know," replied Olivier.

And he flung his arms round Christophe's neck.

"Poor girl! Poor girl!" said Christophe over and over again.

They were both in tears.

Christophe remembered then that Olivier was ill. He tried to calm him, and made him keep his arms inside the bed, and tucked the clothes up round his shoulders, and dried his eyes for him, and then sat down by the bedside and looked long at him.

"You see," he said, "that is how I knew you. I recognized you at once, that first evening."

(It were hard to tell whether he was speaking of the present or the absent friend.)

"But," he went on a moment later, "you knew? . . . Why didn't you tell me?"

And through Olivier's eyes Antoinette replied:

"I could not tell you. You had to see it for yourself."

They said nothing for some time: then, in the silence of the night, Olivier, lying still in bed, in a low voice told Christophe, who held his hand, poor Antoinette's story:—but he did not tell him what he had no right to tell; the secret that she had kept locked,—the secret that perhaps Christophe knew already without needing to be told.

From that time on the soul of Antoinette was ever near them. When they were together she was with them. They had no need to think of her: every thought they shared was shared with her too. Her love was the meeting-place wherein their two hearts were united.

Often Olivier would conjure up the image of her: scraps of memory and brief anecdotes. In their fleeting light they gave a glimpse of her shy, gracious gestures, her grave, young smile, the pensive, wistful grace that was so natural to her. Christophe would listen without a word and let the light of the unseen friend pierce to his very soul. In obedience to the law of his own nature, which everywhere and always drank in life more greedily than any other, he would sometimes hear in Olivier's words depths of sound which Olivier himself could not hear: and more than Olivier he would assimilate the essence of the girl who was dead.

Instinctively he supplied her place in Olivier's life: and it was a touching sight to see the awkward German hap unwittingly on certain of the delicate attentions and little mothering ways of Antoinette. Sometimes he could not tell whether it was Olivier that he loved in Antoinette or Antoinette in Olivier. Sometimes on a tender impulse, without saying anything, he would go and visit Antoinette's grave and lay flowers on it. It was some time before Olivier had any idea

of it. He did not discover it until one day when he found
fresh flowers on the grave: but he had some difficulty in proving
that it was Christophe who had laid them there. When he tried
bashfully to speak about it Christophe cut him short roughly
and abruptly. He did not want Olivier to know: and he stuck
to it until one day when they met in the cemetery at Ivry.

Olivier, on his part, used to write to Christophe's mother
without letting him know. He gave Louisa news of her son,
and told her how fond he was of him and how he admired him.
Louisa would send Olivier awkward, humble letters in which
she thanked him profusely: she used always to write of her
son as though he were a little boy.

After a period of fond semi-silence—" a delicious time of
peace and enjoyment without knowing why,"—their tongues
were loosed. They spent hours in voyages of discovery, each
in the other's soul.

They were very different, but they were both pure metal.
They loved each other because they were so different though so
much the same.

Olivier was weak, delicate, incapable of fighting against difficulties. When he came up against an obstacle he drew back,
not from fear, but something from timidity, and more from
disgust with the brutal and coarse means he would have to employ to overcome it. He earned his living by giving classes,
and writing art-books, shamefully underpaid, as usual, and
occasionally articles for reviews, in which he never had a free
hand and had to deal with subjects in which he was not
greatly interested:—there was no demand for the things that
did interest him: he was never asked for the sort of thing he
could do best: he was a poet and was asked for criticism: he
knew something about music and he had to write about painting:
he knew quite well that he could only say mediocre things,
which was just what people liked, for there he could speak to
mediocre minds in a language which they could understand.
He grew disgusted with it all and refused to write. He had
no pleasure except in writing for certain obscure periodicals,

which never paid anything, and, like so many other young men, he devoted his talents to them because they left him a free hand. Only in their pages could he publish what was worthy of publicity.

He was gentle, well-mannered, seemingly patient, though he was excessively sensitive. A harsh word drew blood: injustice overwhelmed him: he suffered both on his own account and for others. Certain crimes, committed ages ago, still had the power to rend him as though he himself had been their victim. He would go pale, and shudder, and be utterly miserable as he thought how wretched he must have been who suffered them, and how many ages cut him off from his sympathy. When any unjust deed was done before his eyes he would be wild with indignation and tremble all over, and sometimes become quite ill and lose his sleep. It was because he knew his weakness that he drew on his mask of calmness: for when he was angry he knew that he went beyond all limits and was apt to say unpardonable things. People were more resentful with him than with Christophe, who was always violent, because it seemed that in moments of anger Olivier, much more than Christophe, expressed exactly what he thought: and that was true. He judged men and women without Christophe's blind exaggeration, but lucidly and without his illusions. And that is precisely what people do pardon the least readily. In such cases he would say nothing and avoid discussion, knowing its futility. He had suffered from this restraint. He had suffered more from his timidity, which sometimes led him to betray his thoughts, or deprived him of the courage to defend his thoughts conclusively, and even to apologize for them, as had happened in the argument with Lucien Lévy-Cœur about Christophe. He had passed through many crises of despair before he had been able to strike a compromise between himself and the rest of the world. In his youth and budding manhood, when his nerves were not hopelessly out of order, he lived in a perpetual alternation of periods of exaltation and periods of depression which came and went with horrible suddenness. Just when

he was feeling most at his ease and even happy he was very
certain that sorrow was lying in wait for him. And suddenly
it would lay him low without giving any warning of its coming.
And it was not enough for him to be unhappy: he had to blame
himself for his unhappiness, and hold an inquisition into his
every word and deed, and his honesty, and take the side of other
people against himself. His heart would throb in his bosom, he
would struggle miserably, and he would scarcely be able to
breathe.—Since the death of Antoinette, and perhaps thanks to
her, thanks to the peace-giving light that issues from the beloved dead, as the light of dawn brings refreshment to the
eyes and soul of those who are sick, Olivier had contrived, if
not to break away from these difficulties, at least to be resigned
to them and to master them. Very few had any idea of his inward struggles. The humiliating secret was locked up in his
breast, all the immoderate excitement of a weak, tormented
body, surveyed serenely by a free and keen intelligence which
could not master it, though it was never touched by it,—
*" the central peace which endures amid the endless agitation of
the heart."*

Christophe marked it. This it was that he saw in Olivier's
eyes. Olivier had an intuitive perception of the souls of
men, and a mind of a wide, subtle curiosity that was open to
everything, denied nothing, hated nothing, and contemplated
the world and things with generous sympathy: that freshness
of outlook, which is a priceless gift, granting the power to taste
with a heart that is always new the eternal renewal and re-birth.
In that inward universe, wherein he knew himself to be free,
vast, sovereign, he could forget his physical weakness and
agony. There was even a certain pleasure in watching from
a great height, with ironic pity, that poor suffering body which
seemed always so near the point of death. So there was no
danger of his clinging to *his* life, and only the more passionately
did he hug life itself. Olivier translated into the region of
love and mind all the forces which in action he had abdicated.
He had not enough vital sap to live by his own substance

He was as ivy: it was needful for him to cling. He was never
so rich as when he gave himself. His was a womanish soul
with its eternal need of loving and being loved. He was born
for Christophe, and Christophe for him. Such are the aristocratic and charming friends who are the escorts of the great
artists and seem to have come to flower in the lives of their
mighty souls: Beltraffio, the friend of Leonardo: Cavalliere of
Michael Angelo: the gentle Umbrians, the comrades of young
Raphael: Aërt van Gelder, who remained faithful to Rembrandt in his poor old age. They have not the greatness of the
masters: but it is as though all the purity and nobility of
the masters in their friends were raised to a yet higher spiritual
power. They are the ideal companions for men of genius.

Their friendship was profitable to both of them. Love lends
wings to the soul. The presence of the beloved friend gives
all its worth to life: a man lives for his friend and for his
sake defends his soul's integrity against the wearing force of
time.

Each enriched the other's nature. Olivier had serenity of
mind and a sickly body. Christophe had mighty strength and
a stormy soul. They were in some sort like a blind man and a
cripple. Now that they were together they felt sound and
strong. Living in the shadow of Christophe Olivier recovered
his joy in the light: Christophe transmitted to him something
of his abounding vitality, his physical and moral robustness,
which, even in sorrow, even in injustice, even in hate, inclined
to optimism. He took much more than he gave, in obedience
to the law of genius, which gives in vain, but in love always
takes more than it gives, *quia nominor leo,* because it is genius,
and genius half consists in the instinctive absorption of all
that is great in its surroundings and making it greater still.
The vulgar saying has it that riches go to the rich. Strength
goes to the strong. Christophe fed on Olivier's ideas: he impregnated himself with his intellectual calmness and mental detachment, his lofty outlook, his silent understanding and mastery
of things. But when they were transplanted into him, the

richer soil, the virtues of his friend grew with a new and other energy.

They both marveled at the things they discovered in each other. There were so many things to share! Each brought vast treasures of which till then he had never been conscious: the moral treasure of his nation: Olivier the wide culture and the psychological genius of France: Christophe the innate music of Germany and his intuitive knowledge of nature.

Christophe could not understand how Olivier could be a Frenchman. His friend was so little like all the Frenchmen he had met! Before he found Olivier he had not been far from taking Lucien Lévy-Cœur as the type of the modern French mind, Lévy-Cœur who was no more than the caricature of it. And now through Olivier he saw that there might be in Paris minds just as free, more free indeed than that of Lucien Lévy-Cœur, men who remained as pure and stoical as any in Europe. Christophe tried to prove to Olivier that he and his sister could not be altogether French.

"My poor dear fellow," said Olivier, "what do you know of France?"

Christophe avowed the trouble he had taken to gain some knowledge of the country: he drew up a list of all the Frenchmen he had met in the circle of the Stevens and the Roussins: Jews, Belgians, Luxemburgers, Americans, Russians, Levantines, and here and there a few authentic Frenchmen.

"Just what I was saying," replied Olivier. "You haven't seen a single Frenchman. A group of debauchees, a few beasts of pleasure, who are not even French, men-about-town, politicians, useless creatures, all the fuss and flummery which passes over and above the life of the nation without even touching it. You have only seen the swarms of wasps attracted by a fine autumn and the rich meadows. You haven't noticed the busy hives, the industrious city, the thirst for knowledge."

"I beg pardon," said Christophe, "I've come across your intellectual élite as well."

"What? A few dozen men of letters? They're a fine lot!

Nowadays when science and action play so great a part literature has become superficial, no more than the bed where the thought of the people sleeps. And in literature you have only come across the theater, the theater of luxury, an international kitchen where dishes are turned out for the wealthy customers of the cosmopolitan hotels. The theaters of Paris? Do you think a working-man even knows what is being done in them? Pasteur did not go to them ten times in all his life! Like all foreigners you attach an exaggerated importance to our novels, and our boulevard plays, and the intrigues of our politicians. . . . If you like I will show you women who never read novels, girls in Paris who have never been to the theater, men who have never bothered their heads about politics,—yes, even among our intellectuals. You have not come across either our men of science or our poets. You have not discovered the solitary artists who languish in silence, nor the burning flame of our revolutionaries. You have not seen a single great believer, or a single great skeptic. As for the people, we won't talk of them. Outside the poor woman who looked after you, what do you know of them? Where have you had a chance of seeing them? How many Parisians have you met who have lived higher than the second or third floor? If you do not know these people, you do not know France. You know nothing of the brave true hearts, the men and women living in poor lodgings, in the garrets of Paris, in the dumb provinces, men and women who, through a dull, drab life, think grave thoughts, and live in daily sacrifice,—the little Church, which has always existed in France—small in numbers, great in spirit, almost unknown, having no outward or apparent force of action, though it is the very force of France, that might which endures in silence, while the so-called élite rots away and springs to life again unceasingly. . . . You are amazed when you find a Frenchman who lives not for the sake of happiness, happiness at all costs, but to accomplish or to serve his faith? There are thousands of men like myself, men more worthy than myself, more pious, more humble, men who to their dying day live unfailingly to serve an ideal, a God, who vouchsafes them no reply. You know nothing of the thrifty, methodical, industrious, tranquil middle-class living with a quenchless dormant flame in their hearts—the people betrayed and sacrificed who in old days defended 'my country' against the selfish arrogance of the great, the blue-eyed ancient race of Vauban. You do not know the people, you do not know the élite. Have you read a single one of the books which are our faithful friends, the companions who support us in our lives? Do you even know of the existence of our young reviews in which such great faith and devotion are expressed? Have you any idea of the men of moral might and worth who are as the sun to us, the sun whose voiceless light strikes terror to the army of the hypocrites? They dare not make a frontal attack: they bow before them, the better to betray them. The hypocrite is a slave, and there is no slave but he has a master. You know only the slaves: you know nothing of the masters. . . . You have watched our struggles and they have seemed to you brutish and unmeaning because you have not understood their aim. You see the shadow, the reflected light of day: you have never seen the inward day, our age-old immemorial spirit. Have you ever tried to perceive it? Have you ever heard of our heroic deeds from the Crusades to the Commune? Have you ever seen and felt the tragedy of the French spirit? Have you ever stood at the brink of the abyss of Pascal? How dare you slander a people who for more than a thousand years have been living in action and creation, a people that has graven the world in its own image through Gothic art, and the seventeenth century, and the Revolution,—a people that has twenty times passed through the ordeal of fire, and plunged into it again, and twenty times has come to life again and never yet has perished! . . . —You are all the same. All your countrymen who come among us see only the parasites who suck our blood, literary, political, and financial adventurers, with their minions and their hangers-on and their harlots: and they judge France by these wretched creatures who prey on her. Not one of you has

any idea of the real France living under oppression, or of the
reserve of vitality in the French provinces, or of the great
mass of the people who go on working heedless of the uproar
and pother made by their masters of a day. . . . Yes: it is
only natural that you should know nothing of 'all this: I do
not blame you: how could you? Why, France is hardly at all
known to the French. The best of us are bound down and
held captive to our native soil. . . . No one will ever know
all that we have suffered, we who have guarded as a sacred
charge the light in our hearts which we have received from
the genius of our race, to which we cling with all our might,
desperately defending it against the hostile winds that strive
blusteringly to snuff it out;—we are alone and in our nostrils
stinks the pestilential atmosphere of these harpies who have
swarmed about our genius like a thick cloud of flies, whose
hideous grubs gnaw at our minds and defile our hearts:—we are
betrayed by those whose duty it is to defend us, our leaders, our
idiotic and cowardly critics, who fawn upon the enemy, to win
pardon for being of our race:—we are deserted by the people who
give no thought to us and do not even know of our existence. . . .
By what means can we make ourselves known to them? We
cannot reach them. . . . Ah! that is the hardest thing of
all! We know that there are thousands of men in France who
all think as we do, we know that we speak in their name, and we
cannot gain a hearing! Everything is in the hands of the
enemy: newspapers, reviews, theaters. . . . The Press scur-
ries away from ideas or admits them only as an instrument of
pleasure or a party weapon. The cliques and coteries will only
suffer us to break through on condition that we degrade ourselves. We are crushed by poverty and overwork. The politicians, pursuing nothing but wealth, are only interested in that
section of the public which they can buy. The middle-class
is selfish and indifferent, and unmoved sees us perish. **The
people know nothing of our existence: even those who are fighting the same fight like us are cut off by silence and do not
know that we exist, and we do not know that they exist. . . .**

Ill-omened Paris! No doubt good also has come of it—by gathering together all the forces of the French mind and genius. But the evil it has done is at least equal to the good: and in a time like the present the good quickly turns to evil. A pseudo-élite fastens on Paris and blows the loud trumpet of publicity and the voices of all the rest of France are drowned. More than that: France herself is deceived by it: she is scared and silent and fearfully locks away her own ideas. . . . There was a time when it hurt me dreadfully. But now, Christophe, I can bear it calmly. I know and understand my own strength and the might of my people. We must wait until the flood dies down. It cannot touch or change the bed-rock of France. I will make you feel that bed-rock under the mud that is borne onward by the flood. And even now, here and there, there are lofty peaks appearing above the waters. . . ."

Christophe discovered the mighty power of idealism which animated the French poets, musicians, and men of science of his time. While the temporary masters of the country with their coarse sensuality drowned the voice of the French genius, it showed itself too aristocratic to vie with the presumptuous shouts of the rabble and sang on with burning ardor in its own praise and the praise of its God. It was as though in its desire to escape the revolting uproar of the outer world it had withdrawn to the farthest refuge in the innermost depths of its castle-keep.

The poets—that is, those only who were worthy of that splendid name, so bandied by the Press and the Academies and doled out to divers windbags greedy of money and flattery— the poets, despising impudent rhetoric and that slavish realism which nibbles at the surface of things without penetrating to reality, had intrenched themselves in the very center of the soul, in a mystic vision into which was drawn the universe of form and idea, like a torrent falling into a lake, there to take on the color of the inward life. The very intensity of this idealism, which withdrew into itself to recreate the universe, made it inaccessible to the mob. Christophe himself did not understand it at first. The transition was too abrupt after the market-place. It was as though he had passed from a furious rush and scramble in the hot sunlight into silence and the night. His ears buzzed. He could see nothing. At first, with his ardent love of life, he was shocked by the contrast. Outside was the roaring of the rushing streams of passion overturning France and stirring all humanity. And at the first glance there was not a trace of it in this art of theirs. Christophe asked Olivier:

"You have been lifted to the stars and hurled down to the depths of hell by your Dreyfus affair. Where is the poet in whose soul the height and depth of it were felt? Now, at this very moment, in the souls of your religious men and women there is the mightiest struggle there has been for centuries between the authority of the Church and the rights of conscience. Where is the poet in whose soul this sacred agony is reflected? The working classes are preparing for war, nations are dying, nations are springing to new life, the Armenians are massacred, Asia, awaking from its sleep of a thousand years, hurls down the Muscovite colossus, the keeper of the keys of Europe: Turkey, like Adam, opens its eyes on the light of day: the air is conquered by man: the old earth cracks under our feet and opens: it devours a whole people. . . . All these prodigies, accomplished in twenty years, enough to supply material for twenty *Iliads:* but where are they, where shall their fiery traces be found in the books of your poets? Are they of all men unable to see the poetry of the world?"

"Patience, my friend, patience!" replied Olivier. "Be silent, say nothing, listen. . . ."

Slowly the creaking of the axle-tree of the world died away and the rumbling over the stones of the heavy car of action was lost in the distance. And there arose the divine song of silence. . . .

The hum of bees, and the perfume of the limes. . . .
The wind,
With his golden lips kissing the earth of the plains. . . .
The soft sound of the rain and the scent of the roses.

There rang out the hammer and chisel of the poets carving the sides of a vase with

> *The fine majesty of simple things,*

solemn, joyous life,

> *With its flutes of gold and flutes of ebony,*

religious joy, faith welling up like a fountain of souls

> *For whom the very darkness is clear, . . .*

and great sweet sorrow, giving comfort and smiling,

> *With her austere face from which there shines*
> *A clearness beyond nature, . . .*

and

> *Death serene with her great, soft eyes.*

A symphony of harmonious and pure voices. Not one of them had the full sonorousness of such national trumpets as were Corneille and Hugo: but how much deeper and more subtle in expression was their music! The richest music in Europe of to-day.

Olivier said to Christophe, who was silent:

" Do you understand now? "

Christophe in his turn bade him be silent. In spite of himself, and although he preferred more manly music, yet he drank in the murmuring of the woods and fountains of the soul which came whispering to his ears. Amid the passing struggles of the nations they sang the eternal youth of the world, the

> *Sweet goodness of Beauty.*

While humanity,

> *Screaming with terror and yelping its complaint*
> *Marched round and round a barren gloomy field,*

while millions of men and women wore themselves out in wrangling for the bloody rags of liberty, the fountains and the woods sang on:

" Free! . . . Free! . . . *Sanctus, Sanctus.* . . ."

And yet they slept not in any dream selfishly serene. In the choir of the poets there were not wanting tragic voices: voices of pride, voices of love, voices of agony.

A blind hurricane, mad, intoxicated

With its own rough force or gentleness profound,

tumultuous forces, the epic of the illusions of those who sing the wild fever of the crowd, the conflicts of human gods, the breathless toilers,

Faces inky black and golden peering through darkness and
     mist,
Muscular backs stretching, or suddenly crouching
Round mighty furnaces and gigantic anvils . . .

forging the City of the Future.

In the flickering light and shadow falling on the glaciers of the mind there was the heroic bitterness of those solitary souls which devour themselves with desperate joy.

Many of the characteristics of these idealists seemed to the German more German than French. But all of them had the love for the "fine speech of France" and the sap of the myths of Greece ran through their poetry. Scenes of France and daily life were by some hidden magic transformed in their eyes into visions of Attica. It was as though antique souls had come to life again in these twentieth-century Frenchmen, and longed to fling off their modern garments to appear again in their lovely nakedness.

Their poetry as a whole gave out the perfume of a rich civilization that has ripened through the ages, a perfume such as could not be found anywhere else in Europe. It were impossible to forget it once it had been breathed. It attracted foreign artists from every country in the world. They became French poets, almost bigotedly French: and French classical art had no more fervent disciples than these Anglo-Saxons and Flemings and Greeks.

Christophe, under Olivier's guidance, was impregnated with the pensive beauty of the Muse of France, while in his heart he found the aristocratic lady a little too intellectual for his liking, and preferred a pretty girl of the people, simple, healthy, robust, who thinks and argues less, but is more concerned with love.

The same *odor di bellezza* arose from all French art, as the scent of ripe strawberries and raspberries ascends from autumn woods warmed by the sun. French music was like one of those little strawberry plants, hidden in the grass, the scent of which sweetens all the air of the woods. At first Christophe had passed it by without seeing it, for in his own country he had been used to whole thickets of music, much fuller and bearing more brilliant fruits. But now the delicate perfume made him turn: with Olivier's help among the stones and brambles and dead leaves which usurped the name of music, he discovered the subtle and ingenuous art of a handful of musicians. Amid the marshy fields and the factory chimneys of democracy, in the heart of the Plaine-Saint-Denis, in a little magic wood fauns were dancing blithely. Christophe was amazed to hear the ironic and serene notes of their flutes which were like nothing he had ever heard:

> " A little reed sufficed for me
> To make the tall grass quiver,
> And all the meadow,
> The willows sweet,
> And the singing stream also :
> A little reed sufficed for me
> To make the forest sing."

Beneath the careless grace and the seeming dilettantism of their little piano pieces, and songs, and French chamber-music, which German art never deigned to notice, while Christophe himself had hitherto failed to see the poetic accomplishment of it all, he now began to see the fever of renovation, and the uneasiness,—unknown on the other side of the Rhine,—with

which French musicians were seeking in the untilled fields
of their art the germs from which the future might grow.
While German musicians sat stolidly in the encampments of
their forebears, and arrogantly claimed to stay the evolution
of the world at the barrier of their past victories, the world
was moving onwards: and in the van the French plunged onward to discovery: they explored the distant realms of art,
dead suns and suns lit up once more, and vanished Greece,
and the Far East, after its age-long slumber, once more opening its slanting eyes, full of vasty dreams, upon the light of
day. In the music of the West, run off into channels by the
genius of order and classic reason, they opened up the sluices
of the ancient fashions: into their Versailles pools they turned
all the waters of the universe: popular melodies and rhythms,
exotic and antique scales, new or old beats and intervals. Just
as, before them, the impressionist painters had opened up a new
world to the eyes,—Christopher Columbuses of light,—so the
musicians were rushing on to the conquest of the world of
Sound; they pressed on into mysterious recesses of the world of
Hearing: they discovered new lands in that inward ocean. It
was more than probable that they would do nothing with their
conquests. As usual the French were the harbingers of the
world.

Christophe admired the initiative of their music born of
yesterday and already marching in the van of art. What
valiance there was in the elegant tiny little creature! He
found indulgence for the follies that he had lately seen in her.
Only those who attempt nothing never make mistakes. But
error struggling on towards the living truth is more fruitful and
more blessed than dead truth.

Whatever the results, the effort was amazing. Olivier showed
Christophe the work done in the last thirty-five years, and the
amount of energy expended in raising French music from the
void in which it had slumbered before 1870: no symphonic
school, no profound culture, no traditions, no masters, no
public: the whole reduced to poor Berlioz, who died of suf-

focation and weariness. And now Christophe felt a great respect for those who had been the laborers in the national revival: he had no desire now to jeer at their esthetic narrowness
or their lack of genius. They had created something much
greater than music: a musical people. Among all the great
toilers who had forged the new French music one man was especially dear to him: César Franck, who died without seeing the
victory for which he had paved the way, and yet, like old Schütz,
through the darkest years of French art, had preserved intact
the treasure of his faith and the genius of his race. It was
a moving thing to see: amid pleasure-seeking Paris, the angelic
master, the saint of music, in a life of poverty and work
despised, preserving the unimpeachable serenity of his patient
soul, whose smile of resignation lit up his music in which is
such great goodness.

To Christophe, knowing nothing of the depths of the life of
France, this great artist, adhering to his faith in the midst
of a country of atheists, was a phenomenon, almost a miracle.
But Olivier would gently shrug his shoulders and ask if
any other country in Europe could show a painter so wholly
steeped in the spirit of the Bible as François Millet;—a man
of science more filled with burning faith and humility than the
clear-sighted Pasteur, bowing down before the idea of the infinite, and, when that idea possessed his mind, " in bitter agony "
—as he himself has said—" praying that his reason might be
spared, so near it was to toppling over into the sublime madness of Pascal." Their deep-rooted Catholicism was no more
a bar in the way of the heroic realism of the first of these two
men, than of the passionate reason of the other, who, sure of
foot and not deviating by one step, went his way through " the
circles of elementary nature, the great night of the infinitely
little, the ultimate abysses of creation, in which life is born."
It was among the people of the provinces, from which they
sprang, that they had found this faith, which is for ever brooding on the soil of France, while in vain do windy demagogues

struggle to deny it. Olivier knew well that faith: it had lived
in his own heart and mind.

He revealed to Christophe the magnificent movement towards
a Catholic revival, which had been going on for the last twenty-
five years, the mighty effort of the Christian idea in France to
wed reason, liberty, and life: the splendid priests who had the
courage, as one of their number said, " to have themselves
baptized as men," and were claiming for Catholicism the right
to understand everything and to join in every honest idea:
for " every honest idea, even when it is mistaken, is sacred and
divine ": the thousands of young Catholics banded by the generous vow to build a Christian Republic, free, pure, in brotherhood, open to all men of good-will: and, in spite of the odious
attacks, the accusations of heresy, the treachery on all sides, right
and left,—(especially on the right),—which these great Christians had to suffer, the intrepid little legion advancing towards
the rugged defile which leads to the future, serene of front,
resigned to all trials and tribulations, knowing that no enduring
edifice can be built, except it be welded together with tears
and blood.

The same breath of living idealism and passionate liberalism
brought new life to the other religions in France. The vast
slumbering bodies of Protestantism and Judaism were thrilling
with new life. All in generous emulation had set themselves
to create the religion of a free humanity which should sacrifice
neither its power for reason, nor its power for enthusiasm.

This religious exaltation was not the privilege of the religious:
it was the very soul of the revolutionary movement. There it
assumed a tragic character. Till now Christophe had only seen
the lowest form of socialism,—that of the politicians who
dangled in front of the eyes of their famished constituents the
coarse and childish dreams of Happiness, or, to be frank, of
universal Pleasure, which Science in the hands of Power could,
according to them, procure. Against such revolting optimism
Christophe saw the furious mystic reaction of the élite arise to
lead the Syndicates of the working-classes on to battle. It

was a summons to " war, which engenders the sublime," to heroic
war " which alone can give the dying worlds a goal, an aim, an
ideal." These great Revolutionaries, spitting out such
" bourgeois, peddling, peace-mongering, English " socialism,
set up against it a tragic conception of the universe, " whose
law is antagonism," since it lives by sacrifice, perpetual sacrifice,
eternally renewed.—If there was reason to doubt that the army,
which these leaders urged on to the assault upon the old world,
could understand such warlike mysticism, which applied both
Kant and Nietzsche to violent action, nevertheless it was a stirring sight to see the revolutionary aristocracy, whose blind pessimism, and furious desire for heroic life, and exalted faith in
war and sacrifice, were like the militant religious ideal of some
Teutonic Order or the Japanese Samurai.

And yet they were all Frenchmen : they were of a French
stock whose characteristics have endured unchanged for centuries. Seeing with Olivier's eyes Christophe marked them in
the tribunes and proconsuls of the Convention, in certain of the
thinkers and men of action and French reformers of the *Ancien
Régime*. Calvinists, Jansenists, Jacobins, Syndicalists, in all
there was the same spirit of pessimistic idealism, struggling
against nature, without illusions and without loss of courage :—
the iron bands which uphold the nation.

Christophe drank in the breath of these mystic struggles, and
he began to understand the greatness of that fanaticism, into
which France brought uncompromising faith and honesty, such
as were absolutely unknown to other nations more familiar
with *combinazioni*. Like all foreigners it had pleased him at
first to be flippant about the only too obvious contradiction between the despotic temper of the French and the magic formula
which their Republic wrote up on the walls of their buildings.
Now for the first time he began to grasp the meaning of the
bellicose Liberty which they adored as the terrible sword of
Reason. No : it was not for them, as he had thought, mere
sounding rhetoric and vague ideology. Among a people for
whom the demands of reason transcend all others the fight for

reason dominated every other. What did it matter whether
the fight appeared absurd to nations who called themselves practical? To eyes that see deeply it is no less vain to fight for
empire, or money, or the conquest of the world: in a million
years there will be nothing left of any of these things. But
if it is the fierceness of the fight that gives its worth to life,
and uplifts all the living forces to the point of sacrifice to a
superior Being, then there are few struggles that do more
honor life than the eternal battle waged in France for or against
reason. And for those who have tasted the bitter savor of it
the much-vaunted apathetic tolerance of the Anglo-Saxons is
dull and unmanly. The Anglo-Saxons paid for it by finding
elsewhere an outlet for their energy. Their energy is not in
their tolerance, which is only great when, between factions, it
becomes heroism. In Europe of to-day it is most often indifference, want of faith, want of vitality. The English, adapting a
saying of Voltaire, are fain to boast that " diversity of belief
has produced more tolerance in England " than the Revolution
has done in France.—The reason is that there is more faith
in the France of the Revolution than in all the creeds of
England.

From the circle of brass of militant idealism and the battles
of Reason,—like Virgil leading Dante, Olivier led Christophe by
the hand to the summit of the mountain where, silent and
serene, dwelt the small band of the elect of France who were
really free.

Nowhere in the world are there men more free. They have
the serenity of a bird soaring in the still air. On such a height
the air was so pure and rarefied that Christophe could hardly
breathe. There he met artists who claimed the absolute and
limitless liberty of dreams,—men of unbridled subjectivity, like
Flaubert, despising " the poor beasts who believe in the reality
of things " :—thinkers, who, with supple and many-sided minds,
emulating the endless flow of moving things, went on " cease-
lessly trickling and flowing," staying nowhere, nowhere coming

in contact with stubborn earth or rock, and "depicted not the
essence of life, but the *passage*," as Montaigne said, "the
eternal passage, from day to day, from minute to minute";—
men of science who knew the emptiness and void of the universe, wherein man has builded his idea, his God, his art, his
science, and went on creating the world and its laws, that vivid
day's dream. They did not demand of science either rest, or
happiness, or even truth:—for they doubted whether it were at-
tainable: they loved it for itself, because it was beautiful, because it alone was beautiful, and it alone was real. On the topmost pinnacles of thought these men of science, passionately
Pyrrhonistic, indifferent to all suffering, all deceit, almost indifferent to reality, listened, with closed eyes, to the silent music
of souls, the delicate and grand harmony of numbers and
forms. These great mathematicians, these free philosophers,—
the most rigorous and positive minds in the world,—had reached
the uttermost limit of mystic ecstasy: they created a void about
themselves, they hung over the abyss, they were drunk with its
dizzy depths: into the boundless night with joy sublime they
flashed the lightnings of thought.

Christophe leaned forward and tried to look over as they
did: and his head swam. He who thought himself free because
he had broken away from all laws save those of his own
conscience, now became fearfully conscious of how little he was
free compared with these Frenchmen who were emancipated
from every absolute law of mind, from every categorical imperative, from every reason for living. Why, then, did they
live?

"For the joy of being free," replied Olivier.

But Christophe, who was unsteadied by such liberty, thought
regretfully of the mighty spirit of discipline and German
authoritarianism: and he said:

"Your joy is a snare, the dream of an opium-smoker. You
make yourselves drunk with liberty, and forget life. Absolute
liberty means madness to the mind, anarchy to the State . . .
Liberty! What man is free in this world? What man in your

Republic is free?—Only the knaves. You, the best of the nation, are stifled. You can do nothing but dream. Soon you will not be able even to dream."

"No matter!" said Olivier. "My poor dear Christophe, you cannot know the delight of being free. It is worth while paying for it with so much danger, and suffering, and even death. To be free, to feel that every mind about you—yes, even the knave's—is free, is a delicious pleasure which it is impossible to express: it is as though your soul were soaring through the infinite air. It could not live otherwise. What should I do with the security you offer me, and your order and your impeccable discipline, locked up in the four walls of your Imperial barracks? I should die of suffocation. Air! give me air, more and more of it! Liberty, more and more of that!"

"There must be law in the world," replied Christophe. "Sooner or later the master cometh."

But Olivier laughed and reminded Christophe of the saying of old Pierre de l'Estoile:

> It is as little in the power of all the
> dominions of the earth to curb the French
> liberty of speech, as
> to bury the sun in the earth
> or to shut it up
> inside a
> hole.

Gradually Christophe grew accustomed to the air of boundless liberty. From the lofty heights of French thought, where those minds dream that are all light, he looked down upon the slopes of the mountain at his feet, where the heroic elect, fighting for a living faith, whatever faith it be, struggle eternally to reach the summit:—those who wage the holy war against ignorance, disease, and poverty: the fever of invention, the mental delirium of the modern Prometheus and Icarus conquering the light and marking out roads in the air: the

Titanic struggle between Science and Nature, being tamed;—
lower down, the little silent band, the men and women of good
faith, those brave and humble hearts, who, after a thousand
efforts, have climbed half-way, and can climb no farther, being
held bound in a dull and difficult existence, while in secret
they burn away in obscure devotion:—lower still, at the foot
of the mountain, in a narrow gorge between rocky crags, the
endless battle, the fanatics of abstract ideas and blind instincts,
fiercely wrestling, with never a suspicion that there may be
something beyond, above the wall of rocks which hems them in:
—still lower, swamps and brutish beasts wallowing in the mire.
—And everywhere, scattered about the sides of the mountain,
the fresh flowers of art, the scented strawberry-plants of music,
the song of the streams and the poet birds.

And Christophe asked Olivier:

"Where are your people?   I see only the elect, all sorts, good
and bad."

Olivier replied:

"The people?   They are tending their gardens.   They never
bother about us.   Every group and faction among the elect
strives to engage their attention.   They pay no heed to any
one.   There was a time when it amused them to listen to the
humbug of the political mountebanks.   But now they never
worry about it.   There are several millions who do not even
make use of their rights as electors.   The parties may break
each other's heads as much as they like, and the people don't
care one way or another so long as they don't trample the crops
in their wrangling: if that happens then they lose their tempers,
and smash the parties indiscriminately.   They do not act: they
react in one way or another against all the exaggerations which
disturb their work and their rest.   Kings, Emperors, republics,
priests, Freemasons, Socialists, whatever their leaders may be,
all that they ask of them is to be protected against the great
common dangers: war, riots, epidemics,—and, for the rest, to be
allowed to go on tending their gardens.   When all is said and
done they think:

" ' Why won't these people leave us in peace? '

" But the politicians are so stupid that they worry the people, and won't leave off until they are pitched out with a fork,— as will happen some day to our members of Parliament. There was a time when the people were embarked upon great enterprises. Perhaps that will happen again, although they sowed their wild oats long ago: in any case their embarkations are never for long: very soon they return to their age-old companion: the earth. It is the soil which binds the French to France, much more than the French. There are so many different races who for centuries have been tilling that brave soil side by side, that it is the soil which unites them, the soil which is their love. Through good times and bad they cultivate it unceasingly: and it is all good to them, even the smallest scrap of ground."

Christophe looked down. As far as he could see, along the road, around the swamps, on the slopes of rocky hills, over the battlefields and ruins of action, over the mountains and plains of France, all was cultivated and richly bearing: it was the great garden of European civilization. Its incomparable charm lay no less in the good fruitful soil than in the blind labors of an indefatigable people, who for centuries have never ceased to till and sow and make the land ever more beautiful.

A strange people! They are always called inconstant: but nothing in them changes. Olivier, looking backward, saw in Gothic statuary all the types of the provinces of to-day: and so in the drawings of a Clouet and a Dumoustier, the weary ironical faces of worldly men and intellectuals: or in the work of a Lenain the clear eyes of the laborers and peasants of Île-de-France or Picardy. And the thoughts of the men of old days lived in the minds of the present day. The mind of Pascal was alive, not only in the elect of reason and religion, but in the brains of obscure citizens or revolutionary Syndicalists. The art of Corneille and Racine was living for the people even more than for the elect, for they were less attainted by foreign influences: a humble clerk in Paris would feel more sympathy with a tragedy of the time of Louis XIV than with a novel of Tolstoi or a drama of Ibsen. The chants of the Middle Ages, the old French *Tristan,* would be more akin to the modern French than the *Tristan* of Wagner. The flowers of thought, which since the twelfth century have never ceased to blossom in French soil, however different they may be, were yet kin one to another, though utterly different from all the flowers about them.

Christophe knew too little of France to be able to grasp how these characteristics had endured. What struck him most of all in all the wide expanse of country was the extremely small divisions of the earth. As Olivier said, every man had his garden : and each garden, each plot of land, was separated from the rest by walls, and quickset hedges, and inclosures of all sorts. At most there were only a few woods and fields in common, and sometimes the dwellers on one side of a river were forced to live nearer to each other than to the dwellers on the other. Every man shut himself up in his own house : and it seemed that this jealous individualism, instead of growing weaker after centuries of neighborhood, was stronger than ever. Christophe thought :

" How lonely they all are ! "

In that sense nothing could have been more characteristic than the house in which Christophe and Olivier lodged. It was a world in miniature, a little France, honest and industrious, without any bond which could unite its divers elements. A five-storied house, a shaky house, leaning over to one side, with creaking floors and crumbling ceilings. The rain came through into the rooms under the roof in which Christophe and Olivier lived : they had had to have the workmen in to botch up the roof as best they could : Christophe could hear them working and talking overhead. There was one man in particular who amused and exasperated him : he never stopped talking to himself, and laughing, and singing, and babbling nonsense, and whistling inane tunes, and holding long conversations with himself all the time he was working: he was incapable of doing anything without proclaiming exactly what it was:

"I'm going to put in another nail. Where's my hammer? I'm putting in a nail, two nails. One more blow with the hammer! There, old lady, that's it. . . ."

When Christophe was playing he would stop for a moment and listen, and then go on whistling louder than ever: during a stirring passage he would beat time with his hammer on the roof. At last Christophe was so exasperated that he climbed on a chair, and poked his head through the skylight of the attic to rate the man. But when he saw him sitting astride the roof, with his jolly face and his cheek stuffed out with nails, he burst out laughing, and the man joined in. And not until they had done laughing did he remember why he had come to the window:

"By the way," he said, "I wanted to ask you: my playing doesn't interfere with your work?"

The man said it did not: but he asked Christophe to play something faster, because, as he worked in time to the music, slow tunes kept him back. They parted very good friends. In a quarter of an hour they had exchanged more words than in six months Christophe had spoken to the other inhabitants of the house.

There were two flats on each floor, one of three rooms, the other of only two. There were no servants' rooms: each household did its own housework, except for the tenants of the ground floor and the first floor, who occupied the two flats thrown into one.

On the fifth floor Christophe and Olivier's next-door neighbor was the Abbé Corneille, a priest of some forty years old, a learned man, an independent thinker, broad-minded, formerly a professor of exegesis in a great seminary, who had recently been censured by Rome for his modernist tendency. He had accepted the censure without submitting to it, in silence: he made no attempt to dispute it and refused every opportunity

)ffered to him of publishing his doctrine: he shrank from a noisy publicity and would rather put up with the ruin of his ideas than figure in a scandal. Christophe could not understand that sort of revolt in resignation. He had tried to talk to the priest, who, however, was coldly polite and would not speak of the things which most interested him, and seemed to prefer as a matter of dignity to remain buried alive.

On the floor below in the flat corresponding to that of the two friends there lived a family of the name of Elie Elsberger: an engineer, his wife, and their two little girls, seven and ten years old: superior and sympathetic people who kept themselves very much to themselves, chiefly from a sort of false shame of their straitened means. The young woman who kept her house most pluckily was humiliated by it: she would have put up with twice the amount of worry and exhaustion if she could have prevented anybody knowing their condition: and that too was a feeling which Christophe could not understand. They belonged to a Protestant family and came from the East of France. Both man and wife, a few years before, had been bowled over by the storm of the Dreyfus affair: both of them had taken the affair passionately to heart, and, like thousands of French people, they had suffered from the frenzy brought on by the turbulent wind of that exalted fit of hysteria which lasted for seven years. They had sacrificed everything to it, rest, position, relations: they had broken off many dear friendships through it: they had almost ruined their health. For months at a time they did not sleep nor act, but went on bringing forward the same arguments over and over again with the monotonous insistence of the insane: they screwed each other up to a pitch of excitement: in spite of their timidity and their dread of ridicule, they had taken part in demonstrations and spoken at meetings, from which they returned with minds bewildered and aching hearts, and they would weep together through the night. In the struggle they had expended so much enthusiasm and passion that when at last victory was theirs they had not enough of either to rejoice: it left them dry of energy and broken for life. Their hopes had been so high, their eagerness for sacrifice had been so pure, that triumph when it came had seemed a mockery compared with what they had dreamed. To such single-minded creatures for whom there could exist but one truth, the bargaining of politics, the compromises of their heroes had been a bitter disappointment. They had seen their comrades in arms, men whom they had thought inspired with the same single passion for justice,—once the enemy was overcome, swarming about the loot, catching at power, carrying off honors and positions, and, in their turn, trampling justice underfoot. Only a mere handful of men held steadfast to their faith, and, in poverty and isolation, rejected by every party, rejecting every party, they remained in obscurity, cut off one from the other, a prey to sorrow and neurasthenia, left hopeless and disgusted with men and utterly weary of life. The engineer and his wife were among these wretched victims.

They made no noise in the house: they were morbidly afraid of disturbing their neighbors, the more so as they suffered from their neighbors' noises, and they were too proud to complain. Christophe was sorry for the two little girls, whose outbursts of merriment, and natural need of shouting, jumping about and laughing, were continually being suppressed. He adored children, and he made friendly advances to his little neighbors when he met them on the stairs. The little girls were shy at first, but were soon on good terms with Christophe, who always had some funny story to tell them or sweetmeats in his pockets: they told their parents about him: and, though at first they had been inclined to look askance at his advances, they were won over by the frank open manners of their noisy neighbor, whose pianoplaying and terrific disturbance overhead had often made them curse:—(for Christophe used to feel stifled in his room and take to pacing up and down like a caged bear).—They did not find it easy to talk to him. Christophe's rather boorish and abrupt manners sometimes made Elie Elsberger shudder. But it was all in vain for the engineer to try to keep up the wall of reserve, behind which he had taken shelter, between himself and the German: it was impossible to resist the impetuous good humor of the man whose eyes were so honest and affectionate and so free from any ulterior motive. Every now and then Christophe managed to squeeze a little confidence out of his neighbor. Elsberger was a queer man, full of courage, yet apathetic, sorrowful, and yet resigned. He had energy enough to bear a life of difficulty with dignity, but not enough to change it. It was as though he took a delight in justifying his own pessimism. Just at that time he had been offered a post in Brazil as manager of an undertaking: but he had refused as he was afraid of the climate and fearful of the health of his wife and children.

"Well, leave them," said Christophe. "Go alone and make their fortune."

"Leave them!" cried the engineer. "It's easy to see that you have no children."

"I assure you that, if I had, I should be of the same opinion."

"Never! Never! . . . Leave the country! . . . No. I would rather suffer here."

To Christophe it seemed an odd way of loving one's country and one's wife and children to sit down and vegetate with them. Olivier understood.

"Just think," he said, "of the risk of dying out there, in a strange unknown country, far away from those you love! Anything is better than the horror of that. Besides, it isn't worth while taking so much trouble for the few remaining years of life! . . ."

"As though one had always to be thinking of death!" said Christophe with a shrug. "And even if that does happen, isn't it better to die fighting for the happiness of those one loves than to flicker out in apathy?"

On the same landing in the smaller flat on the fourth floor lived a journeyman electrician named Aubert.—If he lived en-

tirely apart from the other inhabitants of the house it was not
altogether his fault. He had risen from the lower class and
had a passionate desire not to sink back into it. He was small
and weakly-looking; he had a harsh face, and his forehead
bulged over his eyes, which were keen and sharp and bored into
you like a gimlet: he had a fair mustache, a satirical mouth, a
sibilant way of speaking, a husky voice, a scarf round his neck,
and he had always something the matter with his throat, in
which irritation was set up by his perpetual habit of smoking:
he was always feverishly active and had the consumptive temperament. He was a mixture of conceit, irony, and bitterness,
cloaking a mind that was enthusiastic, bombastic, and naïve,
while it was always being taken in by life. He was the bastard
of some burgess whom he had never known, and was brought up
by a mother whom it was impossible to respect, so that in his
childhood he had seen much that was sad and degrading. He
had plied all sorts of trades and had traveled much in France.
He had an admirable desire for education, and had taught himself with frightful toil and labor: he read everything: history,
philosophy, decadent poets: he was up-to-date in everything:
theaters, exhibitions, concerts: he had a touching veneration for
art, literature, and middle-class ideas: they fascinated him. He
had imbibed the vague and ardent ideology which intoxicated the
middle-classes in the first days of the Revolution. He had a
definite belief in the infallibility of reason, in boundless
progress,—*quo non ascendam?*—in the near advent of happiness on earth, in the omnipotence of science, in Divine Humanity, and in France, the eldest daughter of Humanity. He
had an enthusiastic and credulous sort of anti-clericalism which
made him lump together religion—especially Catholicism—and
obscurantism, and see in priests the natural foe of light. Socialism, individualism, Chauvinism jostled each other in his
brain. He was a humanitarian in mind, despotic in temperament, and an anarchist in fact. He was proud and knew the
gaps in his education, and, in conversation, he was very cautious:
he turned to account everything that was said in his presence,

but he would never ask advice: that humiliated him; now, though he had intelligence and cleverness, these things could not altogether supply the defects of his education. He had taken it into his head to write. Like so many men in France who have not been taught, he had the gift of style, and a clear vision: but he was a confused thinker. He had shown a few pages of his productions to a successful journalist in whom he believed, and the man made fun of him. He was profoundly humiliated, and from that time on never told a soul what he was doing. But he went on writing: it fed his need of expansion and gave him pride and delight. In his heart he was immensely pleased with his eloquent passages and philosophic ideas, which were not worth a brass farthing. And he set no store by his observation of real life, which was excellent. It was his crank to fancy himself as a philosopher, and he wished to write sociological plays and novels of ideas. He had no difficulty in solving all sorts of insoluble questions, and at every turn he discovered America. When in due course he found that America was already discovered, he was disappointed, humiliated, and rather bitter: he was never far from scenting injustice and intrigue. He was consumed by a thirst for fame and a burning capacity for devotion which suffered from finding no means or direction of employment: he would have loved to be a great man of letters, a member of that literary élite, who in his eyes were adorned with a supernatural prestige. In spite of his longing to deceive himself he had too much good sense and was too ironical not to know that there was no chance of its coming to pass. But he would at least have liked to live in that atmosphere of art and middle-class ideas which at a distance seemed to him so brilliant and pure and chastened of mediocrity. This innocent longing had the unfortunate result of making the society of the people with whom his condition in life forced him to live intolerable to him. And as the middle-class society which he wished to enter closed its doors to him, the result was that he never saw anybody. And so Christophe had no difficulty in making his acquaintance. On the contrary he had very soon

to bolt and bar against him: otherwise Aubert would more often
have been in Christophe's rooms, than Christophe in his. He
was only too happy to find an artist to whom he could talk about
music, plays, etc. But, as one would imagine, Christophe did
not find them so interesting: he would rather have discussed the
people with a man who was of the people. But that was just
what Aubert would not and could not discuss.

In proportion as he went lower in the house relations between Christophe and the other tenants became naturally more
distant. Besides, some secret magic, some *Open Sesame,* would
have been necessary for him to reach the inhabitants of the
third floor.—In the one flat there lived two ladies who were under the self-hypnotism of grief for a loss that was already some
years old: Madame Germain, a woman of thirty-five who had
lost her husband and daughter, and lived in seclusion with her
aged and devout mother-in-law.—On the other side of the landing there dwelt a mysterious character of uncertain age, anything between fifty and sixty, with a little girl of ten. He was
bald, with a handsome, well-trimmed beard, a soft way of speaking, distinguished manners, and aristocratic hands. He was
called M. Watelet. He was said to be an anarchist, a revolutionary, a foreigner, from what country was not known, Russia
or Belgium. As a matter of fact he was a Northern Frenchman and was hardly at all revolutionary: but he was living on
his past reputation. He had been mixed up with the Commune of '71 and condemned to death: he had escaped, how he
did not know: and for ten years he had lived for a short time
in every country in Europe. He had seen so many ill-deeds
during the upheaval in Paris, and afterwards, and also in exile,
and also since his return, ill-deeds done by his former comrades
now that they were in power, and also by men in every rank of
the revolutionary parties, that he had broken with them, peacefully keeping his convictions to himself useless and untarnished.
He read much, wrote a few mildly incendiary books, pulled—
(so it was said)—the wires of anarchist movements in distant
places, in India or the Far East, busied himself with the uni-

versal revolution, and, at the same time, with researches no
less universal but of a more genial aspect, namely with a universal language, a new method of popular instruction in music.
He never came in contact with anybody in the house: when he
met any of its inmates he did no more than bow to them with
exaggerated politeness. However, he condescended to tell Christophe a little about his musical method. Christophe was not
the least interested in it: the symbols of his ideas mattered very
little to him: in any language he would have managed somehow to express them. But Watelet was not to be put off, and
went on explaining his system gently but firmly: Christophe
could not find out anything about the rest of his life. And so
he gave up stopping when he met him on the stairs and only
looked at the little girl who was always with him: she was
fair, pale, anemic: she had blue eyes, rather a sharp profile,
a thin little figure—she was always very neatly dressed—and she
looked sickly and her face was not very expressive. Like
everybody else he thought she was Watelet's daughter. She
was an orphan, the daughter of poor parents, whom Watelet had
adopted when she was four or five, after the death of her father
and mother in an epidemic. He had an almost boundless love
for the poor, especially for poor children. It was a sort of
mystic tenderness with him as with Vincent de Paul. He distrusted official charity, and knew exactly what philanthropic institutions were worth, and therefore he set about doing charity
alone: he did it by stealth, and took a secret joy in it. He had
learned medicine so as to be of some use in the world. One
day when he went to the house of a working-man in the district
and found sickness there, he turned to and nursed the invalids:
he had some medical knowledge and turned it to account. He
could not bear to see a child suffer: it broke his heart. But,
on the other hand, what a joy it was when he had succeeded in
tearing one of these poor little creatures from the clutches of
sickness, and the first pale smile appeared on the little pinched
face! Then Watelet's heart would melt. Those were his moments of Paradise. They made him forget the trouble he often

had with his protégés: for they very rarely showed him much gratitude. And the housekeeper was furious at seeing so many people with dirty boots going up her stairs, and she would complain bitterly. And the proprietor would watch uneasily these meetings of anarchists, and make remarks. Watelet would contemplate leaving his flat: but that hurt him: he had his little whimsies: he was gentle and obstinate, and he put up with the proprietor's observations.

Christophe won his confidence up to a certain point by the love he showed for children. That was their common bond. Christophe never met the little girl without a catch at his heart: for, though he did not know why, by one of those mysterious similarities in outline, which the instinct perceives immediately and subconsciously, the child reminded him of Sabine's little girl. Sabine, his first love, now so far away, the silent grace of whose fleeting shadow had never faded from his heart. And so he took an interest in the pale-faced little girl whom he never saw romping, or running, whose voice he hardly ever heard, who had no little friend of her own age, who was always alone, mum, quietly amusing herself with lifeless toys, a doll or a block of wood, while her lips moved as she whispered some story to herself. She was affectionate and a little offhanded in manner: there was a foreign and uneasy quality in her, but her adopted father never saw it: he loved her too much. Alas! Does not that foreign and uneasy quality exist even in the children of our own flesh and blood? . . .— Christophe tried to make the solitary little girl friends with the engineer's children. But with both Elsberger and Watelet he met with a polite but categorical refusal. These people seemed to make it a point of honor to bury themselves alive, each in his own mausoleum. If it came to a point each would have been ready to help the other: but each was afraid of it being thought that he himself was in need of help: and as they were both equally proud and vain,—and the means of both were equally precarious,—there was no hope of either of them being the first to hold out his hand to the other.

The larger flat on the second floor was almost always empty. The proprietor of the house reserved it for his own use: and he was never there. He was a retired merchant who had closed down his business as soon as he had made a certain fortune, the figure of which he had fixed for himself. He spent the greater part of the year in some hotel on the Riviera, and the summer at some watering-place in Normandy, living as a gentleman with private means who enjoys the illusion of luxury cheaply by watching the luxury of others, and, like them, leading a useless existence.

The smaller flat was let to a childless couple: M. and Madame Arnaud. The husband, a man of between forty and forty-five, was a master at a school. He was so overworked with lectures, and correcting exercises, and giving classes, that he had never been able to find time to write his thesis: and at last he had given it up altogether. The wife was ten years younger, pretty, and very shy. They were both intelligent, well read, in love with each other: they knew nobody, and never went out. The husband had no time for it. The wife had too much time: but she was a brave little creature, who fought down her fits of depression when they came over her, and hid them, by occupying herself as best she could, trying to learn, taking notes for her husband, copying out her husband's notes, mending her husband's clothes, making frocks and hats for herself. She would have liked to go to the theater from time to time: but Arnaud did not care about it: he was too tired in the evening. And she resigned herself to it.

Their great joy was music. They both adored it. He could not play, and she dared not although she could: when she played before anybody, even before her husband, it was like a child strumming. However, that was good enough for them: and Gluck, Mozart, Beethoven, whom they stammered out, were as friends to them: they knew their lives in detail, and their sufferings filled them with love and pity. Books, too, beautiful, fine books, which they read together, gave them happiness. But there are few such books in the literature of to-day: authors do not worry about those people who can bring them neither reputation, nor pleasure, nor money, such humble readers who are never seen in society, and do not write in any journal, and can only love and say nothing. The silent light of art, which in their upright and religious hearts assumed almost a supernatural character, and their mutual affection, were enough to make them live in peace, happy enough, though a little sad— (there is no gainsaying that),—very lonely, a little bruised in spirit. They were both much superior to their position in life. M. Arnaud was full of ideas: but he had neither the time nor enough courage left to write them down. It meant such a lot of trouble to get articles and books published: it was not worth it: futile vanity! Anything he could do was so small in comparison with the thinkers he loved! He had too true a love for the great works of art to want to produce art himself: it would have seemed to him pretentious, impertinent, and ridiculous. It seemed to be his lot to spread their influence. He gave his pupils the benefit of his ideas: they would turn them into books later on,—without mentioning his name of course.—Nobody spent more money than he in subscribing to various publications. The poor are always the most generous: they do buy their books: the rich would take it as a slur upon themselves if they did not somehow manage to get them for nothing. Arnaud ruined himself in buying books: it was his weakness—his vice. He was ashamed of it, and concealed it from his wife. But she did not blame him for it: she would have spent just as much.—And with it all they were always making fine plans for saving, with a view to going to Italy some day—though, as they knew quite well, they never would go: and they were the first to laugh at their incapacity for keeping money. Arnaud would console himself. His dear wife was enough for him, and his life of work and inward joys. Was it not also enough for her?—She said it was. She dared not say how dear it would have been to her if her husband could have some reputation, which would in some sort be reflected

upon herself, and brighten her life, and give her ease and
comfort: inward joys are beautiful: but a little ray of light
from without shining in from time to time is sweet, and does so
much good! . . . But she never said anything, because she
was timid: and besides, she knew that even if he wished to
make a reputation it was by no means certain that he would succeed: it was too late! . . . Their greatest sorrow was that
they had no children. Each hid that sorrow from the other:
and they were only the more tender with each other: it was as
though the poor creatures were striving to win one another's
forgiveness. Madame Arnaud was kind and affectionate: she
would gladly have been friends with Madame Elsberger. But
she dared not: she was never approached. As for Christophe,
husband and wife would have asked nothing better than to
know him: they were fascinated by the music that they could
hear faintly when he was playing. But nothing in the world
could have induced them to make the first move: they would
have thought it indiscreet.

The whole of the first floor was occupied by M. and Madame
Félix Weil. They were rich Jews, and had no children, and
they spent six months of the year in the country near Paris.
Although they had lived in the house for twenty years—(they
stayed there as a matter of habit, although they could easily
have found a flat more in keeping with their fortune)—they
were always like passing strangers. They had never spoken
a word to any of their neighbors, and no one knew any more
about them than on the day of their arrival. But that was no
reason why the other tenants should not pass judgment on
them: on the contrary. They were not liked. And no doubt
they did nothing to win popularity. And yet they were worthy
of more acquaintance: they were both excellent people and remarkably intelligent. The husband, a man of sixty, was an As-
syriologist, well known through his famous excavations in Central Asia: like most of his race he was open-minded and curious, and did not confine himself to his special studies: he was

interested in an infinite number of things: the arts, social
questions, every manifestation of contemporary thought. But
these were not enough to occupy his mind: for they all amused
him, and none of them roused passionate interest. He was
very intelligent, too intelligent, too much emancipated from
all ties, always ready to destroy with one hand what he had
constructed with the other: for he was constructive, always
producing books and theories: he was a great worker: as a
matter of habit and spiritual health he was always patiently
plowing his deep furrow in the field of knowledge, without having any belief in the utility of what he was doing. He had
always had the misfortune to be rich, so that he had never had
the interest of the struggle for life, and, since his explorations
in the East, of which he had grown tired after a few years,
he had not accepted any official position. Outside his own personal work, however, he busied himself with clairvoyance, contemporary problems, social reforms of a practical and pressing
nature, the reorganization of public education in France: he
flung out ideas and created lines of thought: he would set great
intellectual machines working, and would immediately grow disgusted with them. More than once he had scandalized people,
who had been converted to a cause by his arguments, by producing the most incisive and discouraging criticisms of the
cause itself. He did not do it deliberately: it was a natural
necessity for him: he was very nervous and ironical in temper,
and found it hard to bear with the foibles of things and people
which he saw with the most disconcerting clarity. And, as
there is no good cause, nor any good man, who, seen at a certain
angle or with a certain distortion, does not present a ridiculous
aspect, there was nothing that, with his ironic disposition, he
could go on respecting for long. All this was not calculated to
make him friends. And yet he was always well-disposed
towards people, and inclined to do good: he did much good:
but no one was ever grateful to him: even those whom he had
helped could not in their hearts forgive him, because they
had seen that they were ridiculous in his eyes. It was necessary

for him not to see too much of men if he were to love them.
Not that he was a misanthrope. He was not sure enough of
himself to be that. Face to face with the world at which he
mocked, he was timid and bashful: at heart he was not at all sure
that the world was not right and himself wrong: he endeavored
not to appear too different from other people, and strove to base
his manners and apparent opinions on theirs. But he strove in
vain: he could not help judging them: he was keenly sensible
of any sort of exaggeration and anything that was not simple:
and he could never conceal his irritation. He was especially
sensible of the foibles of the Jews, because he knew them best:
and as, in spite of his intellectual freedom, which did not admit of barriers between races, he was often brought up sharp
against those barriers which men of other races raised against
him,—as, in spite of himself, he was out of his element among
Christian ideas, he retired with dignity into his ironic labors
and the profound affection he had for his wife.

Worst of all, his wife was not secure against his irony. She
was a kindly, busy woman, anxious to be useful, and always
taken up with various charitable works. Her nature was much
less complex than that of her husband, and she was cramped
by her moral benevolence and the rather rigidly intellectual,
though lofty, idea of duty that she had begotten. Her whole
life, which was sad enough, without children, with no great joy
nor great love, was based on this moral belief of hers, which
was more than anything else the will to believe. Her husband's irony had, of course, seized on the element of voluntary
self-deception in her faith, and—(it was too strong for him)—
he had made much fun at her expense. He was a mass of contradictions. He had a feeling for duty no less lofty than his
wife's, and, at the same time, a merciless desire to analyze, to
criticize, and to avoid deception, which made him dismember
and take to pieces his moral imperative. He could not see
that he was digging away the ground from under his wife's
feet: he used cruelly to discourage her. When he realized that
he had done so, he suffered even more than she: but the harm

was done. It did not keep them from loving each other faithfully, and working and doing good. But the cold dignity of the wife was not more kindly judged than the irony of the husband: and as they were too proud to publish abroad the good they did, or their desire to do good, their reserve was regarded as indifference, and their isolation as selfishness. And the more conscious they became of the opinion that was held of them, the more careful were they to do nothing to dispute it. Reacting against the coarse indiscretion of so many of their race they were the victims of an excessive reserve which covered a vast deal of pride.

As for the ground floor, which was a few steps higher than the little garden, it was occupied by Commandant Chabran, a retired officer of the Colonial Artillery: he was still young, a man of great vigor, who had fought brilliantly in the Soudan and Madagascar: then suddenly, he had thrown the whole thing up, and buried himself there: he did not even want to hear the army mentioned, and spent his time in digging his flower-beds, and practising the flute without making any progress, and growling about politics, and scolding his daughter, whom he adored: she was a young woman of thirty, not very pretty, but quite charming, who devoted herself to him, and had not married so as not to leave him. Christophe used often to see them leaning out of the window: and, naturally, he paid more attention to the daughter than the father. She used to spend part of the afternoon in the garden, sewing, dreaming, digging, always in high good humor with her grumbling old father. Christophe could hear her soft clear voice laughingly replying to the growling tones of the Commandant, whose footsteps ground and scrunched on the gravel-paths: then he would go in, and she would stay sitting on a seat in the garden, and sew for hours together, never stirring, never speaking, smiling vaguely, while inside the house the bored old soldier played flourishes on his shrill flute, or, by way of a change, made a broken-winded old harmonium squeal and groan, much to Christophe's amusement—or exasperation—(which, depended on the day and his mood).

All these people went on living side by side in that house with its walled-in garden sheltered from all the buffets of the world, hermetically sealed even against each other. Only Christophe, with his need of expansion and his great fullness of life, unknown to them, wrapped them about with his vast sympathy, blind, yet all-seeing. He could not understand them. He had no means of understanding them. He lacked Olivier's psychological insight and quickness. · But he loved them. Instinctively he put himself in their place. Slowly, mysteriously, there crept through him a dim consciousness of these lives so near him and yet so far removed, the stupefying sorrow of the mourning woman, the stoic silence of all their proud thoughts, the priest, the Jew, the engineer, the revolutionary: the pale and gentle flame of tenderness and faith which burned in silence in the hearts of the two Arnauds: the naïve aspirations towards the light of the man of the people: the suppressed revolt and fertile activity which were stifled in the bosom of the old soldier: and the calm resignation of the girl dreaming in the shade of the lilac. But only Christophe could perceive and hear the silent music of their souls: they heard it not: they were all absorbed in their sorrow and their dreams.

They all worked hard, the skeptical old scientist, the pessimistic engineer, the priest, the anarchist, and all these proud or dispirited creatures. And on the roof the mason sang.

In the district round the house among the best of the people Christophe found the same moral solitude—even when the people were banded together.

Olivier had brought him in touch with a little review for which he wrote. It was called *Ésope,* and had taken for its motto this quotation from Montaigne:

"*Æsop was put up for sale with two other slaves. The purchaser inquired of the first what he could do: and he, to put a price upon himself, described all sorts of marvels; the second said as much for himself, or more. When it came to Æsop's turn, and he was asked what he could do:—Nothing, he said, for these two have taken everything: they can do everything."*

Their attitude was that of pure reaction against "the impudence," as Montaigne says, "of those who profess knowledge and their overweening presumption!" The self-styled skeptics of the *Ésope* review were at heart men of the firmest faith. But their mask of irony and haughty ignorance, naturally enough, had small attraction for the public: rather it repelled. The people are only with a writer when he brings them words of simple, clear, vigorous, and assured life. They prefer a sturdy lie to an anemic truth. Skepticism is only to their liking when it is the covering of lusty naturalism or Christian idolatry. The scornful Pyrrhonism in which the *Ésope* clothed itself could only be acceptable to a few minds—"*aeme sdegnose*,"—who knew the solid worth beneath it. It was force absolutely lost upon action and life.

There was no help for it. The more democratic France became, the more aristocratic did her ideas, her art, her science seem to grow. Science securely lodged behind its special languages, in the depths of its sanctuary, wrapped about with a triple veil, which only the initiate had the power to draw, was less accessible than at the time of Buffon and the Encyclopedists. Art,—that art at least which had some respect for itself and the worship of beauty,—was no less hermetically sealed: it despised the people. Even among writers who cared less for beauty than for action, among those who gave moral ideas precedence over esthetic ideas, there was often a strange dominance of the aristocratic spirit. They seemed to be more intent upon preserving the purity of their inward flame than to communicate its warmth to others. It was as though they desired not to make their ideas prevail but only to affirm them.

And yet among these writers there were some who applied themselves to popular art. Among the most sincere some hurled into their writings destructive anarchical ideas, truths of the distant future, which might be beneficent in a century or so, but, for the time being, corroded and scorched the soul : others wrote bitter or ironical plays, robbed of all illusion, sad to the last degree. Christophe was left in a state of collapse, ham-strung, for a day or two after he read them.

" And you give that sort of thing to the people? " he would ask, feeling sorry for the poor audiences who had come to forget their troubles for a few hours, only to be presented with these lugubrious entertainments. " It's enough to make them all go and drown themselves ! "

" You may be quite easy on that score," said Olivier, laughing. " The people don't go."

" And a jolly good thing too! You're mad. Are you trying to rob them of every scrap of courage to live? "

" Why? Isn't it right to teach them to see the sadness of things, as we do, and yet to go on and do their duty without flinching? "

" Without flinching? I doubt that. But it's very certain that they'll do it without pleasure. And you don't go very far when you've destroyed a man's pleasure in living."

" What else can one do? One has no right to falsify the truth."

" Nor have you any right to tell the whole truth to everybody."

" *You* say that? You who are always shouting the truth aloud, you who pretend to love truth more than anything in the world ! "

" Yes: truth for myself and those whose backs are strong enough to bear it. But it is cruel and stupid to tell it to the rest. Yes. I see that now. At home that would never have occurred to me: in Germany people are not so morbid about the truth as they are here: they're too much taken up with living: very wisely they see only what they wish to see. I love you for not being like that: you are honest and go straight ahead. But you are inhuman. When you think you have unearthed a truth, you let it loose upon the world, without stopping to think whether, like the foxes in the Bible with their burning tails, it will not set fire to the world. I think it is fine of you to prefer truth to your happiness. But when it comes to the happiness of other people. . . . Then I say, 'Stop!' You are taking too much upon yourselves. Thou shalt love truth more than thyself, but thy neighbor more than truth."

"Is one to lie to one's neighbor?"

Christophe replied with the words of Goethe:

"We should only express those of the highest truths which will be to the good of the world. The rest we must keep to ourselves: like the soft rays of a hidden sun, they will shed their light upon all our actions."

But they were not moved by these scruples. They never stopped to think whether the bow in their hands shot "*ideas or death,*" or both together. They were too intellectual. They lacked love. When a Frenchman has ideas he tries to impose them on others. He tries to do the same thing when he has none. And when he sees that he cannot do it he loses interest in other people, he loses interest in action. That was the chief reason why this particular group took so little interest in politics, save to moan and groan. Each of them was shut up in his faith, or want of faith.

Many attempts had been made to break down their individualism and to form groups of these men: but the majority of these groups had immediately resolved themselves into literary clubs, or split up into absurd factions. The best of them were mutually destructive. There were among them some first-rate men of force and faith, men well fitted to rally and guide those of weaker will. But each man had his following, and would not consent to merging it with that of other men. So they were split up into a number of reviews, unions, associations, which had all the moral virtues, save one: self-denial; for not one of them would give way to the others: and, while they wrangled over the crumbs that fell from an honest and well-meaning public, small in numbers and poor in purse, they vegetated for a short time, starved and languished, and at last collapsed never to rise again, not under the assault of the enemy, but—(most pitiful!)—under the weight of their own quarrels. —The various professions,—men of letters, dramatic authors, poets, prose writers, professors, members of the Institute, journalists—were divided up into a number of little castes, which they themselves split up again into smaller castes, each one of which closed its doors against the rest. There was no sort of mutual interchange. There was no unanimity on any subject in France, except at those very rare moments when unanimity assumed an epidemic character, and, as a rule, was in the wrong: for it was morbid. A crazy individualism predominated in every kind of French activity: in scientific research as well as in commerce, in which it prevented business men from combining and organizing working agreements. This individualism was not that of a rich and bustling vitality, but that of obstinacy and self-repression. To be alone, to owe nothing to others, not to mix with others for fear of feeling their inferiority in their company, not to disturb the tranquillity of their haughty isolation: these were the secret thoughts of almost all these men who founded " outside " reviews, " outside " theaters, " outside " groups: reviews, theaters, groups, all most often had no other reason for existing than the desire not to be with the general herd, and an incapacity for joining with other people in a common idea or course of action, distrust of other people, or, at the very worst, party hostility, setting one against the other the very men who were most fitted to understand each other.

Even when men who thought highly of each other were united in some common task, like Olivier and his colleagues on the *Ésope* review, they always seemed to be on their guard with each other: they had nothing of that open-handed geniality so common in Germany, where it is apt to become a nuisance. Among these young men there was one especially who attracted Christophe because he divined him to be a man of exceptional force: he was a writer of inflexible logic and will, with a passion for moral ideas, in the service of which he was

absolutely uncompromising and ready in their cause to sacrifice
the whole world and himself: he had founded and conducted
almost unaided a review in which to uphold them: he had sworn
to impose on Europe and on France the idea of a pure, heroic,
and free France: he firmly believed that the world would one
day recognize that he was responsible for one of the boldest
pages in the history of French thought:—and he was not mistaken. Christophe would have been only too glad to know him
better and to be his friend. But there was no way of bringing it
about. Although Olivier had a good deal to do with him
they saw very little of each other except on business: they never
discussed any intimate matter, and never got any farther than
the exchange of a few abstract ideas: or rather—(for, to be
exact, there was no exchange, and each adhered to his own
ideas)—they soliloquized in each other's company in turn. However, they were comrades in arms and knew their worth.

There were innumerable reasons for this reservedness, reasons
difficult to discern, even for their own eyes. The first reason
was a too great critical faculty, which saw too clearly the un-
alterable differences between one mind and another, backed by
an excessive intellectualism which attached too much importance
to those differences: they lacked that puissant and naïve sympathy whose vital need is of love, the need of giving out its
overflowing love. Then, too, perhaps overwork, the struggle
for existence, the fever of thought, which so taxes strength
that by the evening there is none left for friendly intercourse,
had a great deal to do with it. And there was that terrible
feeling, which every Frenchman is afraid to admit, though too
often it is stirring in his heart, the feeling of *not being of one
race,* the feeling that the nation consists of different races
established at different epochs on the soil of France, who,
though all bound together, have few ideas in common, and
therefore ought not, in the common interest, to ponder them
too much. But above all the reason was to seek in the intoxicating and dangerous passion for liberty, to which, when a
man has once tasted it, there is nothing that he will not

sacrifice. Such solitary freedom is all the more precious for having been bought by years of tribulation. The select few have taken refuge in it to escape the slavishness of the mediocre. It is a reaction against the tyranny of the political and religious masses, the terrific crushing weight which overbears the individual in France: the family, public opinion, the State, secret societies, parties, coteries, schools. Imagine a prisoner who, to escape, has to scale twenty great walls hemming him in. If he manages to clear them all without breaking his neck, and, above all, without losing heart, he must be strong indeed. A rough schooling for free-will! But those who have gone through it bear the marks of it all their life in the mania for independence, and the impossibility of their ever living in the lives of others.

Side by side with this loneliness of pride, there was the loneliness of renunciation. There were many, many good men in France whose goodness and pride and affection came to nothing in withdrawal from life! A thousand reasons, good and bad, stood in the way of action for them. With some it was obedience, timidity, force of habit. With others human respect, fear of ridicule, fear of being conspicuous, of being a mark for the comments of the gallery, of meddling with things that did not concern them, of having their disinterested actions attributed to motives of interest. There were men who would not take part in any political or social struggle, women who declined to undertake any philanthropic work, because there were too many people engaged in these things who lacked conscience and even common sense, and because they were afraid of the taint of these charlatans and fools. In almost all such people there are disgust, weariness, dread of action, suffering, ugliness, stupidity, risks, responsibilities: the terrible " What's the use? " which destroys the good-will of so many of the French of to-day. They are too intelligent,— (their intelligence has no wide sweep of the wings),—they are too intent upon reasons for and against. They lack force. They lack vitality. When a man's life beats strongly he never wonders why he goes

THE HOUSE 361

on living: he lives for the sake of living,—because it is a splendid thing to be alive!

In fine, the best of them were a mixture of sympathetic and average qualities: a modicum of philosophy, moderate desires, fond attachment to the family, the earth, moral custom: discretion, dread of intruding, of being a nuisance to other people: modesty of feeling, unbending reserve. All these amiable and charming qualities could, in certain cases, be brought into line with serenity, courage, and inward joy: but at bottom there was a certain connection between them and poverty in the blood, the progressive ebb of French vitality.

The pretty garden, beneath the house in which Christophe and Olivier lived, tucked away between the four walls, was symbolical of that part of the life of France. It was a little patch of green earth shut off from the outer world. Only now and then did the mighty wind of the outer air, whirling down, bring to the girl dreaming there the breath of the distant fields and the vast earth.

Now that Christophe was beginning to perceive the hidden resources of France he was furious that she should suffer the oppression of the rabble. The half-light, in which the select and silent few were huddled away, stifled him. Stoicism is a fine thing for those whose teeth are gone. But he needed the open air, the great public, the sunshine of glory, the love of thousands of men and women: he needed to hold close to him those whom he loved, to pulverize his enemies, to fight and to conquer.

"You can," said Olivier. "You are strong. You were born to conquer through your faults—(forgive me!)—as well as through your qualities. You are lucky enough not to belong to a race and a nation which are too aristocratic. Action does not repel you. If need be you could even become a politician. —Besides, you have the inestimable good fortune to write music. Nobody understands you, and so you can say anything and everything. If people had any idea of the contempt for themselves which you put into your music, and your faith in what they deny, and your perpetual hymn in praise of what they are always trying to kill, they would never forgive you, and you would be so fettered, and persecuted, and harassed, that you would waste most of your strength in fighting them: when you had beaten them back you would have no breath left for going on with your work: your life would be finished. The great men who triumph have the good luck to be misunderstood. They are admired for the very opposite of what they are."

"Pooh!" said Christophe. "You don't understand how cowardly your masters are. At first I thought you were alone, and I used to find excuses for your inaction. But, as a matter of fact, there's a whole army of you all of the same mind. You are a hundred times stronger than your oppressors, you are a thousand times more worthy, and you let them impose on you with their effrontery! I don't understand you. You live in a most beautiful country, you are gifted with the finest intelligence and the most human quality of mind, and with it all you do nothing: you allow yourselves to be overborne and outraged and trampled underfoot by a parcel of fools. Good Lord! Be yourselves! Don't wait for Heaven or a Napoleon to come to your aid! Arise, band yourselves together! Get to work, all of you! Sweep out your house!"

But Olivier shrugged his shoulders, and said, wearily and ironically:

"Grapple with them? No. That is not our game: we have better things to do. Violence disgusts me. I know only too well what would happen. All the old embittered failures, the young Royalist idiots, the odious apostles of brutality and hatred, would seize on anything I did and bring it to dishonor. Do you want me to adopt the old device of hate: *Fuori Barbari*, or: *France for the French?*"

"Why not?" asked Christophe.

"No. Such a device is not for the French. Any attempt to propagate it among our people under cover of patriotism must fail. It is good enough for barbarian countries! But our country has no use for hatred. Our genius never yet asserted itself by denying or destroying the genius of other countries, but by absorbing them. Let the troublous North and the loquacious South come to us. . . ."

" And the poisonous East? "

" And the poisonous East: we will absorb it with the rest: we have absorbed many others! I just laugh at the air of triumph they assume, and the pusillanimity of some of my fellow-countrymen. They think they have conquered us, they strut about our boulevards, and in our newspapers and reviews, and in our theaters and in the political arena. Idiots! It is they who are conquered! They will be assimilated after having fed us. Gaul has a strong stomach: in these twenty centuries she has digested more than one civilization. We are proof against poison. . . . It is meet that you Germans should be afraid! You must be pure or impure. But with us it is not a matter of purity but of universality. You have an Emperor: Great Britain calls herself an Empire: but, in fact, it is our Latin Genius that is Imperial. We are the citizens of the City of the Universe. *Urbis, Orbis."*

" That is all very well," said Christophe, " as long as the nation is healthy and in the flower of its manhood. But there will come a day when its energy declines: and then there is a danger of its being submerged by the influx of foreigners. Between ourselves, does it not seem as though that day had arrived ? "

" People have been saying that for ages. Again and again our history has given the lie to such fears. We have passed through many different trials since the days of the Maid of Orleans, when Paris was deserted, and bands of wolves prowled through the streets. Neither in the prevalent immorality, nor the pursuit of pleasure, nor the laxness, nor the anarchy of the present day, do I see any cause for fear. Patience! Those who wish to live must endure in patience. I am sure that presently there will be a moral reaction,—which will not be much better, and will probably lead to an equal degree of folly; those

who are now living on the corruptness of public life will not
be the least clamorous in the reaction! . . . But what does
that matter to us? All these movements do not touch the real
people of France. Rotten fruit does not corrupt the tree. It
falls. Besides, all these people are such a small part of the
nation! What does it matter to us whether they live or die?
Why should I bother to organize leagues and revolutions against
them? The existing evil is not the work of any form of government. It is the leprosy of luxury, a contagion spread by
the parasites of intellectual and material wealth. Such parasites will perish."

"After they have sapped your vitality."

"It is impossible to despair of such a race. There is in it
such hidden virtue, such a power of light and practical idealism, that they creep into the veins even of those who are exploiting and ruining the nation. Even the grasping, self-seeking politicians succumb to its fascination. Even the most
mediocre of men when they are in power are gripped by the
greatness of its Destiny: it lifts them out of themselves: the
torch is passed on from hand to hand among them: one after
another they resume the holy war against darkness. They are
drawn onward by the genius of the people: willy-nilly they fulfil
the law of the God whom they deny, *Gesta Dei per Francos.*
. . . O my beloved country, I will never lose my faith in
thee! And though in thy trials thou didst perish, yet would I
find in that only a reason the more for my proud belief, even
to the bitter end, in our mission in the world. I will not have
my beloved France fearfully shutting herself up in a sick-
room, and closing every inlet to the outer air. I have no mind
to prolong a sickly existence. When a nation has been so
great as we have been, then it were far better to die rather
than to sink from greatness. Therefore let the ideas of the
world rush into the channels of our minds! I am not afraid.
The flood will go down of its own accord after it has enriched
the soil of France with its ooze."

"My poor dear fellow," said Christophe, "but it's a grim

prospect in the meanwhile. Where will you be when your France emerges from the Nile? Don't you think it would be better to fight against it? You wouldn't risk anything except defeat, and you seem inclined to impose that on yourself as long as you like."

" I should be risking much more than defeat," said Olivier. " I should be running the risk of losing my peace of mind, which I prize far more than victory. I will not be a party to hatred. I will be just to all my enemies. In the midst of passion I wish to preserve the clarity of my vision, to understand and love everything."

But Christophe, to whom this love of life, detached from life, seemed to be very little different from resignation and acceptance of death, felt in his heart, as in Empedocles of old, the stirring of a hymn to Hatred and to Love, the brother of Hate, fruitful Love, tilling and sowing good seed in the earth He did not share Olivier's calm fatalism: he had no such confidence in the continuance of a race which did not defend itself, and his desire was to appeal to all the healthy forces of the nation, to call forth and band together all the honest men in the whole of France.

Just as it is possible to learn more of a human being in one minute of love than in months of observation, so Christophe had learned more about France in a week of intimacy with Olivier, hardly ever leaving the house, than during a whole year of blind wandering through Paris, and standing at attention at various intellectual and political gatherings. Amid the universal anarchy in which he had been floundering, a soul like that of his friend seemed to him veritably to be the " Île de France "— the island of reason and serenity in the midst of the ocean. The inward peace which was in Olivier was all the more striking, inasmuch as it had no intellectual support,—as it existed amid unhappy circumstances,—(in poverty and solitude, while the country of its birth was decadent),—and as its body was weak.

sickly, and nerve-ridden. That serenity was apparently not the
fruit of any effort of will striving to realize it,—(Olivier had
little will);—it came from the depths of his being and his
race. In many of the men of Olivier's acquaintance Christophe perceived the distant light of that σωφροσύνη,—" the
silent calm of the motionless sea ";—and he, who knew, none
better, the stormy, troublous depths of his own soul, and how
he had to stretch his will-power to the utmost to maintain the
balance in his lusty nature, marveled at its veiled harmony.

What he had seen of the inner France had upset all his preconceived ideas about the character of the French. Instead of
a gay, sociable, careless, brilliant people, he saw men of a headstrong and close temper, living in isolation, wrapped about with
a seeming optimism, like a gleaming mist, while they were in
fact steeped in a deep-rooted and serene pessimism, possessed
by fixed ideas, intellectual passions, indomitable souls, which it
would have been easier to destroy than to alter. No doubt these
men were only the select few among the French: but Christophe wondered where they could have come by their stoicism
and their faith. Olivier told him:

" In defeat. It is you, my dear Christophe, who have forged
us anew. Ah! But we suffered for it, too. You can have no
idea of the darkness in which we grew up in a France humiliated
and sore, which had come face to face with death, and still felt
the heavy weight of the murderous menace of force. Our life,
our genius, our French civilization, the greatness of a thousand years,—we were conscious that France was in the hands
of a brutal conqueror who did not understand her, and hated
her in his heart, and at any moment might crush the life out
of her for ever. And we had to live for that and no other
destiny! Have you ever thought of the French children born
in houses of death in the shadow of defeat, fed with ideas of
discouragement, trained to strike for a bloody, fatal, and perhaps futile revenge: for even as babies, the first thing they
learned was that there was no justice, there was no justice in the
world: might prevailed against right! For a child to open its

eyes upon such things is for its soul to be degraded or uplifted
for ever. Many succumbed: they said: 'Since it is so, why
struggle against it? Why do anything? Everything is nothing.
We'll not think of it. Let us enjoy ourselves.'—But those who
stood out against it are proof against fire: no disillusion can
touch their faith: for from their earliest childhood they have
known that their road could never lead them near the road to
happiness, and that they had no choice but to follow it: else
they would suffocate. Such assurance is not come by all at
once. It is not to be expected of boys of fifteen. There is
bitter agony before it is attained, and many tears are shed. But
it is well that it should be so. It must be so. . . .

   " O Faith, virgin of steel . . .
   " Dig deep with thy lance into the downtrodden hearts of the
peoples ! . . ."
   In silence Christophe pressed Olivier's hand.
   " Dear Christophe," said Olivier, " your Germany has made
us suffer indeed."
   And Christophe begged for forgiveness almost as though he
had been responsible for it.
   " There's nothing for you to worry about," said Olivier, smiling. " The good it has unintentionally done us far outweighs
the ill. You have rekindled our idealism, you have revived in
us the keen desire for knowledge and faith, you have filled our
France with schools, you have raised to the highest pitch the
creative powers of a Pasteur, whose discoveries are alone worth
more than your indemnity of two hundred million; you have
given new life to our poetry, our painting, our music: to you
we owe the new awakening of the consciousness of our race.
We have reward enough for the effort needed to learn to set our
faith before our happiness: for, in doing so, we have come
by a feeling of such moral force, that, amid the apathy of the
world, we have no doubt, even of victory in the end. Though
we are few in number, my dear Christophe, though we seem
so weak,—a drop of water in the ocean of German power—we
believe that the drop of water will in the end color the whole

ocean.   The Macedonian phalanx will destroy the mighty armies of the plebs of Europe."

Christophe looked down at the puny Olivier, in whose eyes there shone the light of faith, and he said:

" Poor weakly little Frenchmen!   You are stronger than we are."

" O beneficent defeat," Olivier went on.   " Blessed be that disaster!   We will no more deny it!   We are its children."

II

DEFEAT new-forges the chosen among men: it sorts out the people: it winnows out those who are purest and strongest, and makes them purer and stronger.   But it hastens the downfall of the rest, or cuts short their flight.   In that way it separates the mass of the people, who slumber or fall by the way, from the chosen few who go marching on.   The chosen few know it and suffer: even in the most valiant there is a secret melancholy, a feeling of their own impotence and isolation.   Worst of all,— cut off from the great mass of their people, they are also cut off from each other.   Each must fight for his own hand.   The strong among them think only of self-preservation.   *O man, help thyself!* . . .   They never dream that the sturdy saying means: *O men, help yourselves!*   In all there is a want of confidence, they lack free-flowing sympathy, and do not feel the need of common action which makes a race victorious, the feeling of overflowing strength, of reaching upward to the zenith.

Christophe and Olivier knew something of all this.   In Paris, full of men and women who could have understood them, in the house peopled with unknown friends, they were as solitary as in a desert of Asia.

They were very poor.   Their resources were almost nil. Christophe had only the copying and transcriptions of music given him by Hecht.   Olivier had very unwisely thrown up his

post at the University during the period of depression following on his sister's death, which had been accentuated by an
unhappy love affair with a young lady he had met at Madame
Nathan's:—(he had never mentioned it to Christophe, for he
was modest about his troubles: part of his charm lay in the
little air of mystery which he always preserved about his private affairs, even with his friend, from whom, however, he made
no attempt to conceal anything).—In his depressed condition
when he had longed for silence his work as a lecturer became intolerable to him. He had never cared for the profession, which
necessitates a certain amount of showing off, and thinking aloud,
while it gives a man no time to himself. If teaching in a
school is to be at all a noble thing it must be a matter of a sort
of apostolic vocation, and that Olivier did not possess in the
slightest degree: and lecturing for any of the Faculties means
being perpetually in contact with the public, which is a grim
fate for a man, like Olivier, with a desire for solitude. On
several occasions he had had to speak in public: it gave him a
singular feeling of humiliation. At first he loathed being exhibited on a platform. He *saw* the audience, felt it, as with
antennæ, and knew that for the most part it was composed of
idle people who were there only for the sake of having something to do: and the rôle of official entertainer was not at all to
his liking. Worst of all, speaking from a platform is almost
bound to distort ideas: if the speaker does not take care there
is a danger of his passing gradually from a certain theatricality
in gesture, diction, attitude, and the form in which he presents
his ideas—to mental trickery. A lecture is a thing hovering
in the balance between tiresome comedy and polite pedantry.
For an artist who is rather bashful and proud, a lecture, which
is a monologue shouted in the presence of a few hundred unknown, silent people, a ready-made garment warranted to fit all
sizes, though it actually fits no one, is a thing intolerably false.
Olivier, being more and more under the necessity of withdrawing into himself and saying nothing which was not wholly the
expression of his thought, gave up the profession of teaching,

which he had had so much difficulty in entering: and, as he no longer had his sister to check him in his tendency to dream, he began to write. He was naïve enough to believe that his undoubted worth as an artist could not fail to be recognized without his doing anything to procure recognition.

He was quickly undeceived. He found it impossible to get anything published. He had a jealous love of liberty, which gave him a horror of everything that might impinge on it, and made him live apart, like a poor starved plant, among the solid masses of the political churches whose baleful associations divided the country and the Press between them. He was just as much cut off from all the literary coteries and rejected by them. He had not, nor could he have, a single friend among them. He was repelled by the hardness, the dryness, the egoism of the intellectuals—(except for the very few who were following a real vocation, or were absorbed by a passionate enthusiasm for scientific research). That man is a sorry creature who has let his heart atrophy for the sake of his mind—when his mind is small. In such a man there is no kindness, only a brain like a dagger in a sheath: there is no knowing but it will one day cut your throat. Against such a man it is necessary to be always armed. Friendship is only possible with honest men, who love fine things for their own sake, and not for what they can make out of them,—those who live outside their art. The majority of men cannot breathe the atmosphere of art. Only the very great can live in it without loss of love, which is the source of life.

Olivier could only count on himself. And that was a very precarious support. Any fresh step was a matter of extreme difficulty to him. He was not disposed to accept humiliation for the sake of his work. He went hot with shame at the base and obsequious homage which young authors forced themselves to pay to a well-known theater manager, who took advantage of their cowardice, and treated them as he would never dare to treat his servants. Olivier could never have done that to save his life. He just sent his manuscripts by post, or left them

at the offices of the theaters or the reviews, where they lay
for months unread. However, one day by chance he met one
of his old schoolfellows, an amiable loafer, who had still a sort
of grateful admiration for him for the ease and readiness with
which Olivier had done his exercises: he knew nothing at all
about literature: but he knew several literary men, which was
much better: he was rich and in society, something of a snob,
and so he let them, discreetly, exploit him. He put in a word
for Olivier with the editor of an important review in which he
was a shareholder: and at once one of his forgotten manuscripts
was disinterred and read: and, after much temporization,—(for,
if the article seemed to be worth something, the author's name,
being unknown, was valueless),—they decided to accept it.
When he heard the good news Olivier thought his troubles were
over. They were only just beginning.

It is comparatively easy to have an article accepted in Paris:
but getting it published is quite a different matter. The unhappy writer has to wait and wait, for months, if need be for
life, if he has not acquired the trick of flattering people, or
bullying them, and showing himself from time to time at the
receptions of these petty monarchs, and reminding them of his
existence, and making it clear that he means to go on being a
nuisance to them as long as they make it necessary. Olivier
just stayed at home, and wore himself out with waiting. At best
he would write a letter or two which were never answered. He
would lose heart, and be unable to work. It was quite absurd,
but there was nothing to be done. He would wait for post after
post, sitting at his desk, with his mind blanketed by all sorts of
vague injuries: then he would get up and go downstairs to the
porter's room, and look hopefully in his letter-box, only to meet
with disappointment: he would walk blindly about with no
thought in his head but to go back and look again: and when
the last post had gone, when the silence of his room was broken
only by the heavy footsteps of the people in the room above,
he would feel strangled by the cruel indifference of it all. Only
a word of reply, only a word! Could that be refused him if only

in charity? And yet those who refused him that had no idea
of the hurt they were dealing him. Every man sees the world
in his own image. Those who have no life in their hearts see
the universe as withered and dry: and they never dream of the
anguish of expectation, hope, and suffering which rends the
hearts of the young: or if they give it a thought, they judge them
coldly, with the weary, ponderous irony of those who are surfeited and beyond the freshness of life.

At last the article appeared. Olivier had waited so long that
it gave him no pleasure: the thing was dead for him. And yet
he hoped desperately that it would be a living thing for others.
There were flashes of poetry and intelligence in it which could
not pass unnoticed. It fell upon absolute silence.—He máde
two or three more attempts. Being attached to no clique he met
with silence or hostility everywhere. He could not understand
it. He had thought simply that everybody must be naturally
well-disposed towards the work of a new man, even if it was
not very good. It always represents such an amount of work,
and surely people would be grateful to a man who has tried
to give others a little beauty, a little force, a little joy. But he
only met with indifference or disparagement. And yet he knew
that he could not be alone in feeling what he had written, and
that it must be in the minds of other good men. He did not
know that such good men did not read him, and had nothing to
do with literary opinion, or with anything, or with anything.
If here and there there were a few men whom his words had
reached, men who sympathized with him, they would never
tell him so: they remained immured in their unnatural silence.
Just as they refrained from voting, so they took no share in
art: they did not read books, which shocked them: they did
not go to the theater, which disgusted them: but they let their
enemies vote, elect their enemies, engineer a scandalous success and a vulgar celebrity for books and plays and ideas which
only represented an impudent minority of the people of
France.

Since Olivier could not count on those who were mentally

akin to himself, as they did not read, he was delivered up to the hosts of the enemy, to the mercy of men of letters, who were for the most part hostile to his ideas, and the critics who were at their beck and call.

His first bouts with them left him bleeding. He was as sensitive to criticism as old Bruchner, who could not bear to have his work performed, because he had suffered so much from the malevolence of the Press. He did not even win the support of his former colleagues at the University, who, thanks to their profession, did preserve a certain sense of the intellectual traditions of France, and might have understood him. But 'for the most part these excellent young men, cramped by discipline, absorbed in their work, often rather embittered by their thankless duties, could not forgive Olivier for trying to break away and do something else Like good little officials, many of them were inclined only to admit the superiority of talent when it was consonant with hierarchic superiority.

In such a position three courses were open to him : to break down resistance by force : to submit to humiliating compromises : or to make up his mind to write only for himself. Olivier was incapable of the two first : he surrendered to the third. To make a living he went through the drudgery of teaching and went on writing, and as there was no possibility of his work attaining full growth in publicity, it became more and more involved, chimerical, and unreal.

Christophe dropped like a thunderbolt into the midst of his dim crepuscular life. He was furious at the wickedness of people and Olivier's patience.

"Have you no blood in your veins?" he would say. "How can you stand such a life? You know your own superiority to these swine, and yet you let them squeeze the life out of you without a murmur!"

"What can I do?" Olivier would say. "I can't defend myself. It revolts me to fight with people I despise : I know that they can use every weapon against me : and I can't. Not only should I loathe to stoop to use the means they employ, but I

should be afraid of hurting them. When I was a boy I used
to let my schoolfellows beat me as much as they liked. They
used to think me a coward, and that I was afraid of being hit.
I was more afraid of hitting than of being hit. I remember
some one saying to me one day, when one of my tormentors
was bullying me: ' Why don't you stop it once and for all,
and give him a kick in the stomach? ' That filled me with
horror. I would much rather be thrashed."

"There's no blood in your veins," said Christophe. " And
on top of that, all sorts of Christian ideas! . . . Your religious education in France is reduced to the Catechism: the
emasculate Gospel, the tame, boneless New Testament. . . .
Humanitarian clap-trap, always tearful. . . . And the
Revolution, Jean-Jacques, Robespierre, '48, and, on top of that,
the Jews! . . . Take a dose of the full-blooded Old Testament every morning."

Olivier protested. He had a natural antipathy for the Old
Testament, a feeling which dated back to his childhood, when
he used secretly to pore over an illustrated Bible, which had
been in the library at home, where it was never read, and the
children were even forbidden to open it. The prohibition was
useless! Olivier could never keep the book open for long. He
used quickly to grow irritated and saddened by it, and then he
would close it: and he would find consolation in plunging into
the *Iliad,* or the *Odyssey,* or the *Arabian Nights.*

"The gods of the *Iliad* are men, beautiful, mighty, vicious:
I can understand them," said Olivier. " I like them or dislike
them: even when I dislike them I still love them: I am in love
with them. More than once, with Patroclus, I have kissed the
lovely feet of Achilles as he lay bleeding. But the God of the
Bible is an old Jew, a maniac, a monomaniac, a raging madman,
who spends his time in growling and hurling threats, and howling like an angry wolf, raving to himself in the confinement of
that cloud of his. I don't understand him. I don't love him;
his perpetual curses make my head ache, and his savagery fills
me with horror:

" The burden of Moab. . . .
" The burden of Damascus. . . .
" The burden of Babylon. . . .
" The burden of Egypt. . . .
" The burden of the desert of the sea. . . .
" The burden of the valley of vision. . . .

He is a lunatic who thinks himself judge, public prosecutor, and executioner rolled into one, and, even in the courtyard of his prison, he pronounces sentence of death on the flowers and the pebbles. One is stupefied by the tenacity of his hatred, which fills the book with bloody cries . . .—' a cry of destruction, . . . the cry is gone round about the borders of Moab: the howling thereof unto Eglaim, and the howling thereof unto Beerelim. . . .'

" Every now and then he takes a rest, and looks round on his massacres, and the little children done to death, and the women outraged and butchered: and he laughs like one of the captains of Joshua, feasting after the sack of a town:

" ' *And the Lord of hosts shall make unto all people a feast of fat things, a feast of wine on the lees, of fat things full of marrow, of wine on the lees well refined. . . . The sword of the Lord is filled with blood, it is made fat with fatness, with the fat of the kidneys of rams. . . .'*

" But worst of all is the perfidy with which this God sends his prophet to make men blind, so that in due course he may have a reason for making them suffer:

" ' *Make the heart of this people fat, and make their ears heavy and shut their eyes: lest they see with their eyes and hear with their ears and understand with their heart, and convert, and be healed.—Lord, how long?—Until the cities be wasted without inhabitants, and the houses without men, and the land be utterly desolate. . . .'* Oh! I have never found a man so evil as that! . . .

" I'm not so foolish as to deny the force of the language. But I cannot separate thought and form: and if I do occasionally admire this Hebrew God, it is with the same sort of admiration that I feel for a viper, or a . . .—(I'm trying in vain to find a Shakespearean monster as an example : I can't find one : even Shakespeare never begat such a hero of Hatred— saintly and virtuous Hatred). Such a book is a terrible thing. Madness is always contagious. And that particular madness is all the more dangerous inasmuch as it sets up its own murderous pride as an instrument of purification. England makes me shudder when I think that her people have for centuries been nourished on no other fare. . . . I'm glad to think that there is the dike of the Channel between them and me. I shall never believe that a nation is altogether civilized as long as the Bible is its staple food."

"In that case," said Christophe, "you will have to be just as much afraid of me, for I get drunk on it. It is the very marrow of a race of lions. Stout hearts are those which feed on it. Without the antidote of the Old Testament the Gospel is tasteless and unwholesome fare. The Bible is the bone and sinew of nations with the will to live. A man must fight, and he must hate."

"I hate hatred," said Olivier.

"I only wish you did!" retorted Christophe.

"You're right. I'm too weak even for that. What would you? I can't help seeing the arguments in favor of my ene- mies. And I say to myself over and over again, like Chardin: 'Gentleness! Gentleness!' . . ."

"What a silly sheep you are!" said Christophe. "But whether you like it or not, I'm going to make you leap the ditch you're shying at, and I'm going to drag you on and beat the big drum for you."

In the upshot he took Olivier's affairs in hand and set out to do battle for him. His first efforts were not very successful. He lost his temper at the very outset, and did his friend much harm by pleading his cause: he recognized what he had done very quickly, and was in despair at his own clumsiness.

Olivier did not stand idly by. He went and fought for Christophe. In spite of his fear and dislike of fighting, in spite of his lucid and ironical mind, which scorned any sort of exaggeration in word and deed, when it came to defending Christophe he was far more violent than anybody else, and even than Christophe himself. He lost his head. Love makes a man irrational, and Olivier was no exception to the rule.—However, he was cleverer than Christophe. Though he was uncompromising and clumsy in handling his own affairs, when it came to promoting Christophe's success he was politic and even tricky: he displayed an energy and ingenuity well calculated to win support: he succeeded in interesting various musical critics and Mæcenases in Christophe, though he would have been utterly ashamed to approach them with his own work.

In spite of everything they found it very difficult to better their lot. Their love for each other made them do many stupid things. Christophe got into debt over getting a volume of Olivier's poems published secretly, and not a single copy was sold. Olivier induced Christophe to give a concert, and hardly anybody came to it. Faced with the empty hall, Christophe consoled himself bravely with Handel's quip: " Splendid! My music will sound all the better. . . ." But these bold attempts did not repay the money they cost: and they would go back to their rooms full of indignation at the indifference of the world.

In their difficulties the only man who came to their aid was a Jew, a man of forty, named Taddée Mooch. He kept an art-photograph shop: but although he was interested in his trade and brought much taste and skill to bear on it, he was interested in so many things outside it that he was apt to neglect his business for them. When he did attend to his business he was chiefly engaged in perfecting technical devices, and he would lose his head over new reproduction processes, which, in spite of their ingenuity, hardly ever succeeded, and always cost him a great deal of money. He was a voracious reader, and was always hard on the heels of every new idea in philosophy, art, science, and politics: he had an amazing knack of finding out men of originality and independence of character: it was as though he answered to their magnetism. He was a sort of connecting-link between Olivier's friends, who were all as isolated as himself, and all working in their several directions. He used to go from one to the other, and through him there was established between them a complete circuit of ideas, though neither he nor they had any notion of it.

When Olivier first proposed to introduce him to Christophe, Christophe refused: he was sick of his experiences with the tribe of Israel. Olivier laughed and insisted on it, saying that he knew no more of the Jews than he did of France. At last Christophe consented, but when he saw Taddée Mooch he made a face. In appearance Mooch was extraordinarily Jewish: he was the Jew as he is drawn by those who dislike the race: short, bald, badly built, with a greasy nose and heavy eyes goggling behind large spectacles: his face was hidden by a rough, black, scrubby beard: he had hairy hands, long arms, and short bandy legs: a little Syrian Baal. But he had such a kindly expression that Christophe was touched by it. Above all, he was very simple, and never talked too much. He never paid exaggerated compliments, but just dropped the right word, pat. He was very eager to be of service, and before any kindness was asked of him it would be done. He came often, too often; and he almost always brought good news: work for one or other of them, a commission for an article or a lecture for Olivier, or music-lessons for Christophe. He never stayed long. It was a sort of affectation with him never to intrude. Perhaps he saw Christophe's irritation, for his first impulse was always towards an ejaculation of impatience when he saw the bearded face of the Carthaginian idol,—(he used to call him " Moloch ")—appear round the door: but the next moment it would be gone, and he would feel nothing but gratitude for his perfect kindness.

Kindness is not a rare quality with the Jews: of all the virtues it is the most readily admitted among them, even when they do not practise it. Indeed, in most of them it remains negative or neutral: indulgence, indifference, dislike for hurting anybody, ironic tolerance. With Mooch it was an active passion. He was always ready to devote himself to some cause or person: to his poor co-religionists, to the Russian refugees, to the oppressed of every nation, to unfortunate artists, to the alleviation of every kind of misfortune, to every generous cause. His purse was always open: and however thinly lined it might be, he could always manage to squeeze a mite out of it: when it was empty he would squeeze the mite out of some one else's purse: if he could do any one a service no pains were too great for him to take, no distance was too far for him to go. He did it simply—with exaggerated simplicity. He was a little apt to talk too much about his simplicity and sincerity: but the great thing was that he was both simple and sincere.

Christophe was torn between irritation and sympathy with Mooch, and one day he said an innocently cruel thing, though he said it with the air of a spoiled child. Mooch's kindness had touched him, and he took his hands affectionately and said:

"What a pity! . . . What a pity it is that you are a Jew!"

Olivier started and blushed, as though the shaft had been leveled at himself. He was most unhappy, and tried to heal the wound his friend had dealt.

Mooch smiled, with sad irony, and replied calmly:

"It is an even greater misfortune to be a man."

To Christophe the remark was nothing but the whim of a moment. But its pessimism cut deeper than he imagined: and Olivier, with his subtle perception, felt it intuitively. Beneath the Mooch of their acquaintance there was another different Mooch, who was in many ways exactly the opposite. His apparent nature was the result of a long struggle with his real nature. Though he was apparently so simple he had a distorted mind: when he gave way to it he was forced to complicate simple things and to endow his most genuine feelings with a deliberately ironical character. Though he was apparently modest and, if anything, too humble, at heart he was proud,

and knew it, and strove desperately to whip it out of himself.
His smiling optimism, his incessant activity, his perpetual business in helping others, were the mask of a profound nihilism, a
deadly despondency which dared not see itself face to face.
Mooch made a show of immense faith in all sorts of things: in
the progress of humanity, in the future of the pure Jewish spirit,
in the destiny of France, the soldier of the new spirit—(he was
apt to identify the three causes). Olivier was not taken in by
it, and used to say to Christophe:

" At heart he believes in nothing."

With all his ironical common sense and calmness Mooch was
a neurasthenic who dared not look upon the void within himself.
He had terrible moments when he felt his nothingness: sometimes he would wake suddenly in the middle of the night
screaming with terror. And he would cast about for things
to do, like a drowning man clinging to a life-buoy.

It is a costly privilege to be a member of a race which is exceeding old. It means the bearing of a frightful burden of the
past, trials and tribulations, weary experience, disillusion of
mind and heart,—all the ferment of immemorial life, at the
bottom of which is a bitter deposit of irony and boredom. . . .
Boredom, the immense boredom of the Semites, which has
nothing in common with our Aryan boredom, though that, too,
makes us suffer; while it is at least traceable to definite causes,
and vanishes when those causes cease to exist: for in most cases
it is only the result of regret that we cannot have what we want.
But in some of the Jews the very source of joy and life is tainted
with a deadly poison. They have no desire, no interest in anything: no ambition, no love, no pleasure. Only one thing continues to exist, not intact, but morbid and fine-drawn, in these
men uprooted from the East, worn out by the amount of energy
they have had to give out for centuries, longing for quietude,
without having the power to attain it: thought, endless analysis,
which forbids the possibility of enjoyment, and leaves them no
courage for action. The most energetic among them set themselves parts to play, and play them, rather than act on their

own account. It is a strange thing that in many of them—
and not in the least intelligent or the least seriously minded—
this lack of interest in life prompts the impulse, or the unavowed desire, to act a part, to play at life,—the only means
they know of living!

Mooch was an actor after his fashion. He rushed about to
try to deaden his senses. But whereas most people only bestir
themselves for selfish reasons, he was restlessly active in procuring the happiness of others. His devotion to Christophe was
both touching and a bore. Christophe would snub him and
then immediately be sorry for it. But Mooch never bore him
any ill-will. Nothing abashed him. Not that he had any
ardent affection for Christophe. It was devotion that he loved
rather than the men to whom he devoted himself. They were
only an excuse for doing good, for living.

He labored to such effect that he managed to induce Hecht to
publish Christophe's *David* and some other compositions. Hecht
appreciated Christophe's talent, but he was in no hurry to
reveal it to the world. It was not until he saw that Mooch
was on the point of arranging the publication at his own expense with another firm that he took the initiative out of vanity.

And on another occasion, when things were very serious and
Olivier was ill and they had no money, Mooch thought of going
to Félix Weil, the rich archeologist, who lived in the same
house. Mooch and Weil were acquainted, but had little sympathy with one another. They were too different: Mooch's restlessness and mysticism and revolutionary ideas and " vulgar "
manners, which, perhaps, he exaggerated, were an incentive to
the irony of Félix Weil, with his calm, mocking temper, his distinguished manners and conservative mind. They had only one
thing in common: they were both equally lacking in any profound interest in action: and if they did indulge in action, it
was not from faith, but from their tenacious and mechanical
vitality. But neither was prepared to admit it: they preferred
to give their minds to the parts they were playing, and their
different parts had very little in common. And so Mooch was

quite coldly received by Weil: when he tried to interest him in the artistic projects of Olivier and Christophe, he was brought up sharp against a mocking skepticism. Mooch's perpetual embarkations for one Utopia or another were a standing joke in Jewish society, where he was regarded as a dangerous visionary. But on this occasion, as on so many others, he was not put out: and he went on speaking about the friendship of Christophe and Olivier until he roused Weil's interest. He saw that and went on.

He had touched a responsive chord. The friendless solitary old man worshiped friendship: the one great love of his life had been a friendship which he had left behind him: it was his inward treasure: when he thought of it he felt a better man. He had founded institutions in his friend's name, and had dedicated his books to his memory. He was touched by what Mooch told him of the mutual tenderness of Christophe and Olivier. His own story had been something like it. His lost friend had been a sort of elder brother to him, a comrade of youth, a guide whom he had idolized. That friend had been one of those young Jews, burning with intelligence and generous ardor, who suffer from the hardness of their surroundings, and set themselves to uplift their race, and, through their race, the world, and burn hotly into flame, and, like a torch of resin, flare for a few hours and then die. The flame of his life had kindled the apathy of young Weil. He had raised him from the earth. While his friend was alive Weil had marched by his side in the shining light of his stoical faith,—faith in science, in the power of the spirit, in a future happiness,—the rays of which were shed upon everything with which that messianic soul came in contact. When he was left alone, in his weakness and irony, Weil fell from the heights of that idealism into the sands of that Book of Ecclesiastes, which exists in the mind of every Jew and saps his spiritual vitality. But he had never forgotten the hours spent in the light with his friend: jealously he guarded its clarity, now almost entirely faded. He had never spoken of him to a soul, not even to his wife, whom he loved: it was a sacred thing. And the old man, who was considered prosaic and dry of heart, and nearing the end of his life, used to say to himself the bitter and tender words of a Brahmin of ancient India:

" The poisoned tree of the world puts forth two fruits sweeter than the waters of the fountain of life: one is poetry, the other, friendship."

From that time on he took an interest in Christophe and Olivier. He knew how proud they were, and got Mooch, without saying anything, to send him Olivier's volume of poems, which had just been published: and, without the two friends having anything to do with it, without their having even the smallest idea of what he was up to, he managed to get the Academy to award the book a prize, which came in the nick of time to help them in their difficulty.

When Christophe discovered that such unlooked-for assistance came from a man of whom he was inclined to think ill, he regretted all the unkind things he had said or thought of him: he gulped down his dislike of calling, and went and thanked him. His good intentions met with no reward. Old Weil's irony was excited by Christophe's young enthusiasm, although he tried hard to conceal it from him, and they did not get on at all well.

That very day, when Christophe returned, irritated, though still grateful, to his attic, after his interview with Weil, he found Mooch there, doing Olivier some fresh act of service, and also a review containing a disparaging article on his music by Lucien Lévy-Cœur;—it was not written in a vein of frank criticism, but took the insultingly kindly line of chaffing him and banteringly considering him alongside certain third-rate and fourth-rate musicians whom he loathed.

"You see," said Christophe to Olivier, after Mooch had gone, "we always have to deal with Jews, nothing but Jews! Perhaps we're Jews ourselves? Do tell me that we're not. We seem to attract them. We're always knocking up against them, both friends and foes."

"The reason is," said Olivier, "that they are more intelligent than the rest. The Jews are almost the only people in France to whom a free man can talk of new and vital things. The rest are stuck fast in the past among dead things. Unfortunately the past does not exist for the Jews, or at least it is not the same for them as for us. With them we can only talk about the things of to-day: with our fellow-countrymen we can only discuss the things of yesterday. Look at the activity of the Jews in every kind of way: commerce, industry, education, science, philanthropy, art. . . ."

"Don't let's talk about art," said Christophe.

"I don't say that I am always in sympathy with what they do: very often I detest it. But at least they are alive, and can understand men who are alive. It is all very well for us to criticise and make fun of the Jews, and speak ill of them. We can't do without them."

"Don't exaggerate," said Christophe jokingly. "I could do without them perfectly."

"You might go on living perhaps. But what good would that be to you if your life and your work remained unknown, as they probably would without the Jews? Would the members of your own religion come to your assistance? The Catholic Church lets the best of its members perish without raising a hand to help them. Men who are religious from the very bottom of their hearts, men who give their lives in the defense of God,—if they have dared to break away from Catholic dominion and shake off the authority of Rome,—at once find the unworthy mob who call themselves Catholic not only indifferent, but hostile: they condemn them to silence, and abandon them to the mercy of the common enemy. If a man of independent spirit, be he never so great and Christian at heart, is not a Christian as a matter of obedience, it is nothing to the Catholics that in him is incarnate all that is most pure and most truly divine in their faith. He is not of the pack, the blind and deaf sect which refuses to think for itself. He is cast out, and the rest rejoice to see him suffering alone, torn to pieces by the

enemy, and crying for help to those who are his brothers, for
whose faith he is done to death.   In the Catholicism of to-day
there is a horrible, death-dealing power of inertia.   It would
find it far easier to forgive its enemies than those who wish to
awake it and restore it to life. . . .   My dear Christophe,
where should we be, and what should we do—we, who are
Catholics by birth, we, who have shaken free, without the little
band of free Protestants and Jews?   The Jews in Europe of
to-day are the most active and living agents of good and evil.
They carry hither and thither the pollen of thought.   Have not
your worst enemies and your friends from the very beginning
been Jews?"

"That's true," said Christophe.   "They have given me encouragement and help, and said things to me which have given
me new life for the struggle, by showing me that I was understood.   No doubt very few of my friends have remained faithful to me: their friendship was but a fire of straw.   No matter!
That fleeting light is a great thing in darkness.   You are right:
we mustn't be ungrateful."

"We must not be stupid, either," replied Olivier.   "We must
not mutilate our already diseased civilization by lopping off
some of its most living branches.   If we were so unfortunate as
to have the Jews driven from Europe, we should be left so poor
in intelligence and power for action that we should be in danger
of utter bankruptcy.   In France especially, in the present condition of French vitality, their expulsion would mean a more
deadly drain on the blood of the nation than the expulsion of
the Protestants in the seventeenth century.—No doubt, for the
time being, they do occupy a position out of all proportion to
their true merit.   They do take advantage of the present moral
and political anarchy, which in no small degree they help to
aggravate, because it suits them, and because it is natural to
them to do so.   The best of them, like our friend Mooch, make
the mistake, in all sincerity, of identifying the destiny of France
with their Jewish dreams, which are often more dangerous than
useful.   But you can't blame them for wanting to build France

in their own image: it means that they love the country. **If** their love becomes a public danger, all we have to do is to defend ourselves and keep them in their place, which, in France, is the second. Not that I think their race inferior to ours:— (all these questions of the supremacy of races are idiotic and disgusting).—But we cannot admit that a foreign race which has not yet been fused into our own, can possibly know better than we do what suits us. The Jews are well off in France: I am glad of it: but they must not think of turning France into Judea! An intelligent and strong Government which was able to keep the Jews in their place would make them one of the most useful instruments for the building of the greatness of France: and it would be doing both them and us a great service. These hypernervous, restless, and unsettled creatures need the restraint of law and the firm hand of a just master, in whom there is no weakness, to curb them. The Jews are like women: admirable when they are reined in; but, with the Jews as with women, their use of mastery is an abomination, and those who submit to it present a pitiful and absurd spectacle."

In spite of their love for each other, and the intuitive knowledge that came with it, there were many things which Christophe and Olivier could not understand in each other, things, too, which shocked them. In the beginning of their friendship, when each tried instinctively only to suffer the existence of those qualities in himself which were most like the qualities of his friend, they never remarked them. It was only gradually that the different aspects of their two nationalities appeared on the surface again, more sharply defined than before: for being in contrast, each showed the other up. There were moments of difficulty, moments when they clashed, which, with all their fond indulgence, they could not altogether avoid.

Sometimes they misunderstood each other. Olivier's mind was a mixture of faith, liberty, passion, irony, and universal doubt, for which Christophe could not find any working formula. Olivier, on his part, was distressed by Christophe's lack **of** psychology: being of an old intellectual stock, and therefore aristocratic, he was moved to smile at the awkwardness of such a vigorous, though lumbering and single mind, which had no power of self-analysis, and was always being taken in by others and by itself. Christophe's sentimentality, his noisy outbursts, his facile emotions, used sometimes to exasperate Olivier, to whom they seemed absurd. Not to speak of a certain worship of force, the German conviction of the excellence of fist-morality, *Faustrecht,* to which Olivier and his countrymen had good reason for not subscribing.

And Christophe could not bear Olivier's irony, which used sometimes to make him furious with exasperation: he could not bear his mania for arguing, his perpetual analysis, and the curious intellectual immorality, which was surprising in a man who set so much store by moral purity as Olivier, and arose from the very breadth of his mind, to which every kind of negation was detestable,—so that he took a delight in the contemplation of ideas the opposite of his own. Olivier's outlook on things was in some sort historical and panoramic: it was so necessary for him to understand everything that he always saw reasons both for and against, and supported each in turn, according as the opposite thesis was put forward: and so amid such contradictions he lost his way. He would leave Christophe hopelessly perplexed. It was not that he had any desire to contradict or any taste for paradox: it was an imperious need in him for justice and common sense: he was exasperated by the stupidity of any assumption, and he had to react against it. The crudeness with which Christophe judged immoral men and actions, by seeing everything as much coarser and more brutal than it really was, distressed Olivier, who was just as moral, but was not of the same unbending steel; he allowed himself to be tempted, colored, and molded by outside influences. He would protest against Christophe's exaggerations and fly off into exaggeration in the opposite direction. Almost every day this perverseness of mind would make him take up the cudgels for his adversaries against his friends. Christophe would lose his temper. He would cry out upon Olivier's sophistry and his indulgence of hateful things and people. Olivier would smile: he knew the utter absence of illusion that lay behind his indulgence: he knew that Christophe believed in many more things than he did, and had a greater power of acceptance! But Christophe would look neither to the right hand nor the left, but went straight ahead. He was especially angry with Parisian "kindness."

"Their great argument, of which they are so proud, in favor of 'pardoning' rascals, is," he would say, "that all rascals are sufficiently unhappy in their wickedness, or that they are irresponsible or diseased. . . . In the first place, it is not true that those who do evil are unhappy. That's a moral idea in action, a silly melodramatic idea, stupid, empty optimism, such as you find in Scribe and Capus,—(Scribe and Capus, your Parisian great men, artists of whom your pleasure-seeking, vulgar society is worthy, childish hypocrites, too cowardly to face their own ugliness).—It is quite possible for a rascal to be a happy man. He has every chance of being so. And as for his irresponsibility, that is an idiotic idea. Do have the courage to face the fact that Nature does not care a rap about good and evil, and is so far malevolent that a man may easily be a criminal and yet perfectly sound in mind and body. Virtue is not a natural thing. It is the work of man. It is his duty to defend it. Human society has been built up by a few men who were stronger and greater than the rest. It is their duty to see that the work of so many ages of frightful struggles is not spoiled by the cowardly rabble."

At bottom there was no great difference between these ideas and Olivier's: but, by a secret instinct for balance and proportion, he was never so dilettante as when he heard provocative words thrown out.

"Don't get so excited, my friend," he would say to Christophe. "Let the world hug its vices. Like the friends in the 'Decameron,' let us breathe in peace the balmy air of the gardens of thought, while under the cypress-hill and the tall, shady pines, twined about with roses, Florence is devastated by the black plague."

He would amuse himself for days together by pulling to pieces art, science, philosophy, to find their hidden wheels: so he came by a sort of Pyrrhonism, in which everything that was became only a figment of the mind, a castle in the air, which had not even the excuse of the geometric symbols, of being necessary to the mind. Christophe would rage against his pulling the machine to pieces:

"It was going quite well: you'll probably break it. Then how will you be better off? What are you trying to prove? That nothing is nothing? Good Lord! I know that. It is because nothingness creeps in upon us from every side that we fight. Nothing exists? I exist. There's no reason for doing anything? I'm doing what I can. If people like death, let them die! For my part, I'm alive, and I'm going to live. My life is in one scale of the balance, my mind and thought in the other. . . . To hell with thought!"

He would fly off with his usual violence, and in their argument he would say things that hurt. Hardly had he said them than he was sorry. He would long to withdraw them: but the harm was done. Olivier was very sensitive: his skin was easily barked: a harsh word, especially if it came from some one he loved, hurt him terribly. He was too proud to say anything, and would retire into himself. And he would see in his friend those sudden flashes of unconscious egoism which appear in every great artist. Sometimes he would feel that his life was no great thing to Christophe compared with a beautiful piece of music:— (Christophe hardly troubled to disguise the fact).—He would understand and see that Christophe was right: but it made him sad.

And then there were in Christophe's nature all sorts of disordered elements which eluded Olivier and made him uneasy. He used to have sudden fits of a freakish and terrible humor. For days together he would not speak: or he would break out in diabolically malicious moods and try deliberately to hurt.

Sometimes he would disappear altogether and be seen no more for the rest of the day and part of the night. Once he stayed away for two whole days. God knows what he was up to! He was not very clear about it himself. . . . The truth was that his powerful nature, shut up in that narrow life, and those small rooms, as in a hen-coop, every now and then reached bursting-point. His friend's calmness maddened him: then he would long to hurt him, to hurt some one. He would have to rush away, and wear himself out. He would go striding through the streets of Paris and the outskirts in the vague quest of adventure, which sometimes he found: and he would not have been sorry to meet with some rough encounter which would have given him the opportunity of expending some of his superfluous energy in a brawl. . . . It was hard for Olivier, with his poor health and weakness of body, to understand. Christophe was not much nearer understanding it. He would wake up from his aberrations as from an exhausting dream,—a little uneasy and ashamed of what he had been doing and might yet do. But when the fit of madness was over he would feel like a great sky washed by the storm, purged of every taint, serene, and sovereign of his soul. He would be more tender than ever with Olivier, and bitterly sorry for having hurt him. He would give up trying to account for their little quarrels. The wrong was not always on his side: but he would take all the blame upon himself, and put it down to his unjust passion for being right; and he would think it better to be wrong with his friend than to be right, if right were not on his side.

Their misunderstandings were especially grievous when they occurred in the evening, so that the two friends had to spend the night in disunion, which meant that both of them were morally upset. Christophe would get up and scribble a note and slip it under Olivier's door: and next day as soon as he woke up he would beg his pardon. Sometimes, even, he would knock at his door in the middle of the night: he could not bear to wait for the day to come before he humbled himself. As a rule, Olivier would be just as unable to sleep. He knew

that Christophe loved him, and had not wished to hurt him: but
he wanted to hear him say so. Christophe would say so, and
then the whole thing would be forgotten. Then they would be
pacified. Delightful state! How well they would sleep for the
rest of the night!

"Ah!" Olivier would sigh. "How difficult it is to understand each other!"

"But is it necessary always to understand each other?"
Christophe would ask. "I give it up. We only need love each
other."

All these petty quarrels which, with anxious tenderness, they
would at once find ways of mending, made them almost dearer
to each other than before. When they were hotly arguing Antoinette would appear in Olivier's eyes. The two friends would
pay each other womanish attentions. Christophe never let
Olivier's birthday go by without celebrating it by dedicating a
composition to him, or by the gift of flowers, or a cake, or a
little present, bought Heaven knows how!—(for they often had
no money in the house)—Olivier would tire his eyes out with
copying out Christophe's scores at night and by stealth.

Misunderstandings between friends are never very serious so
long as a third party does not come between them.—But that
was bound to happen: there are too many people in this world
ready to meddle in the affairs of others and make mischief between them.

Olivier knew the Stevens, whom Christophe rarely visited,
and he too had been attracted by Colette. The reason why
Christophe had not met him in the girl's little court was that
just at that time Olivier was suffering from his sister's death,
and had shut himself up with his grief and saw no one. Colette,
on her part, did not go out of her way to see him: she liked
Olivier, but she did not like unhappy people: she used to declare that she was so sensitive that she could not bear the sight
of sorrow: she waited until Olivier's sorrow was over before she
remembered his existence. When she heard that he seemed to

be himself again, and that there was no danger of infection, she made bold to beckon him to her. Olivier did not need much inducement to go. He was shy but he liked society, and he was easily led: and he had a weakness for Colette. When he told Christophe of his intention of going back to her, Christophe, who had too much respect for his friend's liberty to express any adverse opinion, just shrugged his shoulders and said jokingly:

" Go, dear boy, if it amuses you."

But nothing would have induced him to follow his example. He had made up his mind to have nothing more to do with a coquette like Colette or the world she lived in. Not that he was a misogynist: far from it. He had a very tender feeling for all the young women who worked for their living, the factory-hands, and typists, and Government clerks, who are to be seen every morning, half awake, always a little late, hurrying to their workshops and offices. It seemed to him that a woman was only in possession of all her senses when she was working and struggling for her own individual existence, by earning her daily bread and her independence. And it seemed to him that only then did she possess all her charm, her alert suppleness of movement, the awakening of all her senses, her integrity of life and will. He detested the idle, pleasure-seeking woman, who seemed to him to be only an overfed animal, perpetually in the act of digestion, bored, browsing over unwholesome dreams. Olivier, on the contrary, adored the *far niente* of women, their charm, like the charm of flowers, living only to be beautiful and to perfume the air about them. He was more of an artist: Christophe was more human. Unlike Colette, Christophe loved other people in proportion as they shared in the suffering of the world. So, between him and them there was a bond of brotherly compassion.

Colette was particularly anxious to see Olivier again, after she heard of his friendship with Christophe: for she was curious to hear the details. She was rather angry with Christophe for the disdainful manner in which he seemed to have forgotten her: and, though she had no desire for revenge,—(it was not worth the trouble: and revenge does mean a certain amount of trouble),—she would have been very glad to pay him out. She was like a cat that bites the hand that strokes it. She had an ingratiating way with her, and she had no difficulty in getting Olivier to talk. Nobody could be more clear-sighted than he, or less easily taken in by people, when he was away from them: but nobody could be more naïvely confiding than he when he was with a woman whose eyes smiled kindly at him. Colette displayed so genuine an interest in his friendship with Christophe that he went so far as to tell her the whole story, and even about certain of their amicable misunderstandings, which, at a distance, seemed amusing, and he took the whole blame for them on himself. He also confided to Colette Christophe's artistic projects, and also some of his opinions—which were not altogether flattering—concerning France and the French. Nothing that he told her was of any great importance in itself, but Colette repeated it all at once, and adapted it partly to make the story more spicy, and partly to satisfy her secret feeling of malice against Christophe. And as the first person to receive her confidence was naturally her inseparable Lucien Lévy-Cœur, who had no reason for keeping it secret, the story went the rounds, and was embellished by the way: a note of ironic pity for Olivier, who was represented as a victim, was introduced, and he cut rather a sorry figure. It seemed unlikely that the story could be very interesting to anybody, since the heroes of it were very little known: but a Parisian takes an interest in everything that does not concern him. So much so, that one day Christophe heard the story from the lips of Madame Roussin. She met him one day at a concert, and asked him if it were true that he had quarreled with that poor Olivier Jeannin: and she asked about his work, and alluded to things which he believed were known only to himself and Olivier. And when he asked her how she had come by her information, she said she had had it from Lucien Lévy-Cœur, who had had it direct from Olivier.

The blow overwhelmed Christophe. Violent and uncritical as he was, it never occurred to him to think how utterly fantastic the story was: he only saw one thing: his secrets which he had confided to Olivier had been betrayed—betrayed to Lucien Lévy-Cœur. He could not stay to the end of the concert: he left the hall at once. Around him all was blank and dark. In the street he narrowly escaped being run over. He said to himself over and over again: " My friend has betrayed me! . . ."

Olivier was with Colette. Christophe locked the door of his room, so that when Olivier came in he could not have his usual talk with him. He heard him come in a few moments later and try to open the door, and whisper " Good-night " through the keyhole: he did not stir. He was sitting on his bed in the dark, holding his head in his hands, and saying over and over again: " My friend has betrayed me! . . .": and he stayed like that half through the night. Then he felt how dearly he loved Olivier: for he was not angry with him for having betrayed him: he only suffered. Those whom we love have absolute rights over us, even the right to cease loving us. We cannot bear them any ill-will; we can only be angry with ourselves for being so unworthy of love that it must desert us. There is mortal anguish in such a state of mind—anguish which destroys the will to live.

Next morning, when he saw Olivier, he did not tell him anything: he so detested the idea of reproaching him,—reproaching him for having abused his confidence and flung his secrets into the enemy's maw,—that he could not find a single word to say to him. But his face said what he could not speak: his expression was icy and hostile. Olivier was struck dumb: he could not understand it. He tried timidly to discover what Christophe had against him. Christophe turned away from him brutally, and made no reply. Olivier was hurt in his turn, and said no more, and gulped down his distress in silence. They did not see each other again that day.

Even if Olivier had made him suffer a thousand times more,

Christophe would never have done anything to avenge himself, and he would have done hardly anything to defend himself: Olivier was sacred to him. But it was necessary that the indignation he felt should be expended upon some one: and since that some one could not be Olivier, it was Lucien Lévy-Cœur. With his usual passionate injustice he put upon him the responsibility for the ill-doing which he attributed to Olivier: and he suffered intolerable pangs of jealousy in the thought that such a man as that could have robbed him of his friend's affection, just as he had previously ousted him from his friendship with Colette Stevens. To bring his exasperation to a head, that very day he happened to see an article by Lucien Lévy-Cœur on a performance of *Fidelio*. In it he spoke of Beethoven in a bantering way, and poked fun at his heroine. Christophe was as alive as anybody to the absurdities of the opera, and even to certain mistakes in the music. He had not always displayed an exaggerated respect for the acknowledged master himself. But he set no store by always agreeing with his own opinions, nor had he any desire to be Frenchily logical. He was one of those men who are quite ready to admit the faults of their friends, but cannot bear anybody else to do so. And, besides, it was one thing to criticise a great artist, however bitterly, from a passionate faith in art, and even—(one may say)— from an uncompromising love for his fame and intolerance of anything mediocre in his work,—and another thing, as Lucien Lévy-Cœur did, only to use such criticism to flatter the baseness of the public, and to make the gallery laugh, by an exhibition of wit at the expense of a great man. Again, free though Christophe was in his judgments, there had always been a certain sort of music which he had tacitly left alone and shielded: music which was not to be tampered with: that music, which was higher and better than music, the music of an absolutely pure soul, a great health-giving soul, to which a man could turn for consolation, strength, and hope. Beethoven's music was in the category. To see a puppy like Lévy-Cœur insulting Beethoven made him blind with anger. It was no longer a question of art, but a question of honor; everything that makes life rare, love, heroism, passionate virtue, the good human longing for self-sacrifice, was at stake. The Godhead itself was imperiled! There was no room for argument. It is as impossible to suffer that to be besmirched as to hear the woman you respect and love insulted: there is but one thing to do, to hate and kill. . . . What is there to say when the insulting blackguard was, of all men, the one whom Christophe most despised?

And, as luck would have it, that very evening the two men came face to face.

To avoid being left alone with Olivier, contrary to his habit, Christophe went to an At Home at the Roussins'. He was asked to play. He consented unwillingly. However, after a moment or two he became absorbed in the music he was playing, until, glancing up, he saw Lucien Lévy-Cœur standing in a little group, watching him with an ironical stare. He stopped short in the middle of a bar: he got up and turned away from the piano. There was an awkward silence. Madame Roussin came up to Christophe in her surprise and smiled forcedly; and, very cautiously,—for she was not sure whether the piece was finished or not,—she asked him:

"Won't you go on, Monsieur Krafft?"

"I've finished," he replied curtly.

He had hardly said it than he became conscious of his rudeness: but, instead of making him more restrained, it only excited him the more. He paid no heed to the amused attention of his auditors, but went and sat in a corner of the room from which he could follow Lucien Lévy-Cœur's movements. His neighbor, an old general, with a pinkish, sleepy face, light-blue eyes, and a childish expression, thought it incumbent on him to compliment him on the originality of his music. Christophe bowed irritably, and growled out a few inarticulate sounds. The general went on talking with effusive politeness and a gentle, meaningless smile: and he wanted Christophe to explain how he

:ould play such a long piece of music from memory. Christophe
fidgeted impatiently, and thought wildly of knocking the old gentleman off the sofa. He wanted to hear what Lucien Lévy-Cœur
was saying: he was waiting for an excuse for attacking him.
For some moments past he had been conscious that he was going
to make a fool of himself: but no power on earth could have
kept him from it.—Lucien Lévy-Cœur, in his high falsetto
voice, was explaining the aims and secret thoughts of great
artists to a circle of ladies. During a moment of silence Christophe heard him talking about the friendship of Wagner and
King Ludwig, with all sorts of nasty innuendoes.

"Stop!" he shouted, bringing his fist down on the table by
his side.

Everybody turned in amazement. Lucien Lévy-Cœur met
Christophe's eyes and paled a little, and said:

"Were you speaking to me?"

"You hound! . . . Yes," said Christophe.

He sprang to his feet.

"You soil and sully everything that is great in the world,"
he went on furiously. "There's the door! Get out, you cur,
or I'll fling you through the window!"

He moved towards him. The ladies moved aside screaming.
There was a moment of general confusion. Christophe was
surrounded at once. Lucien Lévy-Cœur had half risen to his
feet: then he resumed his careless attitude in his chair. He
called a servant who was passing and gave him a card: and he
went on with his remarks as though nothing had happened: but
his eyelids were twitching nervously, and his eyes blinked as he
looked this way and that to see how people had taken it. Roussin had taken his stand in front of Christophe, and he took him
by the lapel of his coat and urged him in the direction of the
door. Christophe hung his head in his anger and shame, and
his eyes saw nothing but the wide expanse of shirt-front, and
kept on counting the diamond studs: and he could feel the big
man's breath on his cheek.

"Come, come, my dear fellow!" said Roussin. "What's the

matter with you? Where are your manners? Control your-self! Do you know where you are? Come, come, are you mad?"

"I'm damned if I ever set foot in your house again!" said Christophe, breaking free: and he reached the door.

The people prudently made way for him. In the cloak-room a servant held out a salver. It contained Lucien Lévy-Cœur's card. He took it without understanding what it meant, and read it aloud: then, suddenly, snorting with rage, he fumbled in his pockets: mixed up with a varied assortment of things, he pulled out three or four crumpled dirty cards:

"There! There!" he said, flinging them on the salver so violently that one of them fell to the ground.

He left the house.

Olivier knew nothing about it. Christophe chose as his wit-nesses the first men of his acquaintance who turned up, the musical critic, Théophile Goujart, and a German, Doctor Barth, an honorary lecturer in a Swiss University, whom he had met one night in a café; he had made friends with him, though they had little in common: but they could talk to each other about Germany. After conferring with Lucien Lévy-Cœur's wit-nesses, pistols were chosen. Christophe was absolutely ignorant about the use of arms, and Goujart told him it would not be a bad thing for him to go and have a few lessons: but Christophe refused, and while he was waiting for the day to come went on with his work.

But his mind was distracted. He had a fixed idea, of which he was dimly conscious, while it kept buzzing in his head like a bad dream. . . . "It was unpleasant, yes, very unpleasant. . . . What was unpleasant?—Oh! the duel to-morrow. . . . Just a joke! Nobody is ever hurt. . . . But it was pos-sible. . . . Well, then, afterwards? . . . Afterwards, that was it, afterwards. . . . A cock of the finger by that swine who hates me may wipe out my life. . . . So be it! . . . Yes, to-morrow, in a day or two, I may be lying in the loathsome soil of Paris. . . .—Bah! Here or anywhere, what does it matter! . . . Oh! Lord: I'm not going to play the coward!— No, but it would be monstrous to waste the mighty world of ideas that I feel springing to life in me for a moment's folly. . . . What rot it is, these modern duels in which they try to equalize the chances of the two opponents! That's a fine sort of equality that sets the same value on the life of a mountebank as on mine! Why don't they let us go for each other with fists and cudgels? There'd be some pleasure in that. But this cold-blooded shooting! . . . And, of course, he knows how to shoot, and I have never had a pistol in my hand. . . . They are right: I must learn. . . . He'll try to kill me. I'll kill him."

He went out. There was a range a few yards away from the house. Christophe asked for a pistol, and had it explained how he ought to hold it. With his first shot he almost killed his instructor: he went on with a second and a third, and fared no better: he lost patience, and went from bad to worse. A few young men were standing by watching and laughing. He paid no heed to them. With his German persistency he went on trying, and was so indifferent to their laughter and so determined to succeed that, as always happens, his blundering patience roused interest, and one of the spectators gave him advice. In spite of his usual violence he listened to everything with childlike docility; he managed to control his nerves, which were making his hand tremble: he stiffened himself and knit his brows: the sweat was pouring down his cheeks: he said not a word: but every now and then he would give way to a gust of anger, and then go on shooting. He stayed there for a couple of hours. At the end of that time he hit the bull's-eye. Few things could have been more absorbing than the sight of such a power of will mastering an awkward and rebellious body. It inspired respect. Some of those who had scoffed at the outset had gone, and the others were silenced one by one, and had not been able to tear themselves away. They took off their hats to Christophe when he went away.

When he reached home Christophe found his friend Mooch waiting anxiously. Mooch had heard of the quarrel, and had come at once: he wanted to know how it had originated. In spite of Christophe's reticence and desire not to attach any blame to Olivier, he guessed the reason. He was very cool-headed, and knew both the friends, and had no doubt of Olivier's innocence of the treachery ascribed to him. He looked into the matter, and had no difficulty in finding out that the whole trouble arose from the scandal-mongering of Colette and Lucien Lévy-Cœur. He rushed back with his evidence to Christophe, thinking that he could in that way prevent the duel. But the result was exactly the opposite of what he expected: Christophe was only the more rancorous against Lévy-Cœur when he learned that it was through him that he had come to doubt his friend. To get rid of Mooch, who kept on imploring him not to fight, he promised him everything he asked. But he had made up his mind. He was quite happy now: he was going to fight for Olivier, not for himself!

A remark made by one of the seconds as the carriage was going along a road through the woods suddenly caught Christophe's attention. He tried to find out what they were think-ing, and saw how little they really cared about him. Professor Barth was wondering when the affair would be over, and whether he would be back in time to finish a piece of work he had be-gun on the manuscripts in the *Bibliothèque Nationale*. Of Christophe's three companions, he was the most interested in the result of the encounter as a matter of German national pride. Goujart paid no attention either to Christophe or the other Ger-man, but discussed certain scabrous subjects in connection with the coarser branches of physiology with Dr. Jullien, a young physician from Toulouse, who had recently come to live next door to Christophe, and occasionally borrowed his spirit-lamp, or his umbrella, or his coffee-cups, which he invariably returned broken. In return he gave him free consultations, tried medi-cines on him, and laughed at his simplicity. Under his im-passive manner, that would have well become a Castilian hidalgo,

there was a perpetual love of teasing. He was highly delighted
with the adventure of the duel, which struck him as sheer
burlesque: and he was amusing himself with fancying the mess
that Christophe would make of it. He thought it a great joke
to be driving through the woods at the expense of good old
Krafft.—That, clearly, was what was in the minds of the trio:
they regarded it as a jolly excursion which cost them nothing.
Not one of them attached the least importance to the duel. But,
on the other hand, they were just as calmly prepared for anything that might come of it.

They reached the appointed spot before the others. It was a
little inn in the heart of the forest. It was a pleasure-resort,
more or less unclean, to which Parisians used to resort to cleanse
their honor when the dirt on it became too apparent. The
hedges were bright with the pure flowers of the eglantine. In
the shade of the bronze-leaved oak-trees there were rows of little
tables. At one of these tables were seated three bicyclists: a
painted woman, in knickerbockers, with black socks: and two
men in flannels, who were stupefied by the heat, and every now
and then gave out growls and grunts as though they had forgotten how to speak.

The arrival of the carriage produced a little buzz of excitement in the inn. Goujart, who knew the house and the people
of old, declared that he would look after everything. Barth
dragged Christophe into an arbor and ordered beer. The air
was deliciously warm and soft, and resounding with the buzzing
of bees Christophe forgot why he had come. Barth emptied
the bottle, and said, after a short silence:

" I know what I'll do."

He drank and went on:

" I shall have plenty of time: I'll go on to Versailles when
it's all over."

Goujart was heard haggling with the landlady over the price
of the dueling-ground. Jullien had not been wasting his time:
as he passed near the bicyclists he broke into noisy and ecstatic
comment on the woman's bare legs: and there was exchanged a

perfect deluge of filthy epithets in which Jullien did not come off worst. Barth said in a whisper:

"The French are a low-minded lot. Brother, I drink to your victory."

He clinked his glass against Christophe's. Christophe was dreaming: scraps of music were floating in his mind, mingled with the harmonious humming of insects. He was very sleepy.

The wheels of another carriage crunched over the gravel of the drive. Christophe saw Lucien Lévy-Cœur's pale face, with its inevitable smile: and his anger leaped up in him. He got up, and Barth followed him.

Lévy-Cœur, with his neck swathed in a high stock, was dressed with a scrupulous care which was strikingly in contrast with his adversary's untidiness. He was followed by Count Bloch, a sportsman well known for his mistresses, his collection of old pyxes, and his ultra-Royalist opinions,—Léon Mouey, another man of fashion, who had reached his position as Deputy through literature, and was a writer from political ambition: he was young, bald, clean-shaven, with a lean bilious face: he had a long nose, round eyes, and a head like a bird's,—and Dr. Emmanuel, a fine type of Semite, well-meaning and cold, a member of the Academy of Medicine, a chief-surgeon in a hospital, famous for a number of scientific books, and the medical skepticism which made him listen with ironic pity to the plaints of his patients without making the least attempt to cure them.

The newcomers saluted the other three courteously. Christophe barely responded, but was annoyed by the eagerness and the exaggerated politeness with which they treated Lévy-Cœur's seconds. Jullien knew Emmanuel, and Goujart knew Mouey, and they approached them obsequiously smiling. Mouey greeted them with cold politeness and Emmanuel jocularly and without ceremony. As for Count Bloch, he stayed by Lévy-Cœur, and with a rapid glance he took in the condition of the clothes and linen of the three men of the opposing camp, and, hardly opening his lips, passed abrupt humorous comment on them with his friend,—and both of them stood calm and correct.

Lucien Lévy-Cœur stood at his ease waiting for Count Bloch, who had the ordering of the duel, to give the signal. He regarded the affair as a mere formality. He was an excellent shot, and was fully aware of his adversary's want of skill. He would not be foolish enough to make use of his advantage and hit him, always supposing, as was not very probable, that the seconds did not take good care that no harm came of the encounter: for he knew that nothing is so stupid as to let an enemy appear to be a victim, when a much surer and better method is to wipe him out of existence without any fuss being made. But Christophe stood waiting, stripped to his shirt, which was open to reveal his thick neck, while his sleeves were rolled up to show his strong wrists, head down, with his eyes glaring at Lévy-Cœur: he stood taut, with murder written implacably on every feature: and Count Bloch, who watched him carefully, thought what a good thing it was that civilization had as far as possible suppressed the risks of fighting.

After both men had fired, of course without result, the seconds hurried forward and congratulated the adversaries. Honor was satisfied.—Not so Christophe. He stayed there, pistol in hand, unable to believe that it was all over. He was quite ready to repeat his performance at the range the evening before, and go on shooting until one or other of them had hit the target. When he heard Goujart proposing that he should shake hands with his adversary, who advanced chivalrously towards him with his perpetual smile, he was exasperated by the pretense of the whole thing. Angrily he hurled his pistol away, pushed Goujart aside, and flung himself upon Lucien Lévy-Cœur. They were hard put to it to keep him from going on with the fight with his fists.

The seconds intervened while Lévy-Cœur escaped. Christophe broke away from them, and, without listening to their laughing expostulation, he strode along in the direction of the forest, talking loudly and gesticulating wildly. He did not even notice that he had left his hat and coat on the dueling-ground. He plunged into the woods. He heard his seconds laughing and calling him: then they tired of it, and did not worry about him any more. Very soon he heard the wheels of the carriages rumbling away and away, and knew that they had gone. He was left alone among the silent trees. His fury had subsided. He flung himself down on the ground and sprawled on the grass.

Shortly afterwards Mooch arrived at the inn. He had been pursuing Christophe since the early morning. He was told that his friend was in the woods, and went to look for him. He beat all the thickets, and awoke all the echoes, and was going away in despair when he heard him singing: he found his way by the voice, and at last came upon him in a little clearing with his arms and legs in the air, rolling about like a young calf. When Christophe saw him he shouted merrily, called him "dear old Moloch," and told him how he had shot his adversary full of holes until he was like a sieve: he made him tuck in his tuppenny, and then join him in a game of leap-frog: and when he jumped over him he gave him a terrific thump. Mooch was not very good at it, but he enjoyed the game almost as much as Christophe.—They returned to the inn arm-in-arm, and caught the train back to Paris at the nearest station.

Olivier knew nothing of what had happened. He was surprised at Christophe's tenderness: he could not understand his sudden change. It was not until the next day, when he saw the newspapers, that he knew that Christophe had fought a duel. It made him almost ill to think of the danger that Christophe had run. He wanted to know why the duel had been fought. Christophe refused to tell him anything. When he was pressed he said with a laugh:

"It was for you."

Olivier could not get a word more out of him. Mooch told him all about it. Olivier was horrified, quarreled with Colette, and begged Christophe to forgive his imprudence. Christophe

was incorrigible, and quoted for his benefit an old French
saying, which he adapted so as to infuriate poor Mooch, who
was present to share in the happiness of the friends:

"My dear boy, let this teach you to be careful. . . .

> *"From an idle chattering girl,*
> *From a wheedling, hypocritical Jew,*
> *From a painted friend,*
> *From a familiar foe,*
> *And from flat wine,*
> *Libera Nos, Domine!"*

Their friendship was re-established. The danger of losing
it, which had come so near, made it only the more dear. Their
small misunderstandings had vanished: the very differences between them made them more attractive to each other. In his
own soul Christophe embraced the souls of the two countries,
harmoniously united. He felt that his heart was rich and
full: and, as usual with him, his abundant happiness expressed
itself in a flow of music.

Olivier marveled at it. Being too critical in mind, he was
never far from believing that music, which he adored, had
said its last word. He was haunted by the morbid idea that
decadence must inevitably succeed a certain degree of progress:
and he trembled lest the lovely art, which made him love life,
should stop short, and dry up, and disappear into the ground.
Christophe would scoff at such pusillanimous ideas. In a
spirit of contradiction he would pretend that nothing had been
done before he appeared on the scene, and that everything remained to be done. Olivier would instance French music,
which seemed to have reached a point of perfection and ultimate
civilization beyond which there could not possibly be anything.
Christophe would shrug his shoulders:

"French music? . . . There has never been any. . . .
And yet you have such fine things to do in the world! You
can't really be musicians, or you would have discovered that.
Ah! if only I were a Frenchman! . . ."

And he would set out all the things that a Frenchman might turn into music:

" You involve yourselves in forms which do not suit you, and you do nothing at all with those which are admirably fitted for your use. You are a people of elegance, polite poetry, beautiful gestures, beautiful walking movements, beautiful attitudes, fashion, clothes, and you never write ballets nowadays, though you ought to be able to create an inimitable art of poetic dancing. . . .—You are a people of laughter and comedy, and you never write comic operas, or else you leave it to minor musicians, the confectioners of music. Ah! if I were a Frenchman I would set Rabelais to music, I would write comic epics. . . .—You are a people of story-tellers, and you never write novels in music: (for I don't count the feuilletons of Gustave Charpentier). You make no use of your gift of psychological analysis, your insight into character. Ah! if I were a Frenchman I would give you portraits in music. . . . (Would you like me to sketch the girl sitting in the garden under the lilac?). . . . I would write you Stendhal for a string quartet. . . .—You are the greatest democracy in Europe, and you have no theater for the people, no music for the people. Ah! if I were a Frenchman, I would set your Revolution to music: the 14th July, the 10th August, Valmy, the Federation, I would express the people in music! Not in the false form of Wagnerian declamation. I want symphonies, choruses, dances. Not speeches! I'm sick of them. There's no reason why people should always be talking in a music drama! Bother the words! Paint in bold strokes, in vast symphonies with choruses, immense landscapes in music, Homeric and Biblical epics, fire, earth, water, and sky, all bright and shining, the fever which makes hearts burn, the stirring of the instincts and destinies of a race, the triumph of Rhythm, the emperor of the world, who enslaves thousands of men, and hurls armies down to death. . . . Music everywhere, music in everything! If you were musicians you would have music for every one of your public holidays, for your official ceremonies, for the trades

unions, for the student associations, for your family festivals.
. . . But, above all, above all, if you were musicians, you
would make pure music, music which has no definite meaning,
music which has no definite use, save only to give warmth,
and air, and life. Make sunlight for yourselves! *Sat prata*.
. . . (What is that in Latin?). . . . There has been rain
enough. Your music gives me a cold. One can't see in it:
light your lanterns. . . . You complain of the Italian
porcherie, who invade your theaters and conquer the public,
and turn you out of your own house? It is your own fault!
The public are sick of your crepuscular art, your harmonized
neurasthenia, your contrapuntal pedantry. The public goes
where it can find life, however coarse and gross. Why do you
run away from life? Your Debussy is a bad man, however
great he may be as an artist. He aids and abets you in your
torpor. You want roughly waking up."

"What about Strauss?"

"No better. Strauss would finish you off. You need the
digestion of my fellow-countrymen to be able to bear such immoderate drinking. And even they cannot bear it. . . .
Strauss's *Salome!* . . . A masterpiece. . . . I should not
like to have written it. . . . I think of my old grandfather and uncle Gottfried, and with what respect and loving
tenderness they used to talk to me about the lovely art of
sound! . . . But to have the handling of such divine powers
and to turn them to such uses! . . . A flaming, consuming
meteor! An Isolde, who is a Jewish .prostitute. Bestial and
mournful lust. The frenzy of murder, pillage, incest, and untrammeled instincts which is stirring in the depths of German
decadence. . . . And, on the other hand, the spasm of a
voluptuous and melancholy suicide, the death-rattle which sounds
through your French decadence. . . . On the one hand, the
beast: on the other, the prey. Where is man? . . . Your
Debussy is the genius of good taste: Strauss is the genius of
bad taste. Debussy is rather insipid. But Strauss is very unpleasant. One is a silvery thread of stagnant water, losing it⸗

self in the reeds, and giving off an unhealthy aroma. The
other is a mighty muddy flood. . . . Ah! the musty base
Italianism and neo-Meyerbeerism, the filthy masses of sentiment which are borne on by the torrent! . . . An odious
masterpiece! . . . Salome, the daughter of Ysolde. . . .
And whose mother will Salome be in her turn?"

"Yes," said Olivier, "I wish we could jump fifty years.
This headlong gallop towards the precipice must end one way
or another: either the horse must stop or fall. Then we shall
breathe again. Thank Heaven, the earth will not cease to
flower, nor the sky to give light, with or without music! What
have we to do with an art so inhuman! . . . The West is
burning away. . . . Soon. . . . Very soon. . . . I see
other stars arising in the furthest depths of the East."

"Bother the East!" said Christophe. "The West has not
said its last word yet. Do you think I am going to abdicate?
I have enough to say to keep you going for centuries. Hurrah
for life! Hurrah for joy! Hurrah for the courage which
drives us on to struggle with our destiny! Hurrah for love
which màketh the heart big! Hurrah for friendship which re-
kindles our faith,—friendship, a sweeter thing than love!
Hurrah for the day! Hurrah for the night! Glory be to the
sun! *Laus Deo,* the God of joy, the God of dreams and actions,
the God who created music! Hosannah! . . ."

With that he sat down at his desk and wrote down everything that was in his head, without another thought for what
he had been saying.

At that time Christophe was in a condition in which all
the elements of his life were perfectly balanced. He did not
bother his head with esthetic discussions as to the value of
this or that musical form, nor with reasoned attempts to create
a new form: he did not even have to cast about for subjects for
translation into music. One thing was as good as another.
The flood of music welled forth without Christophe knowing
exactly what feeling he was expressing. He was happy: that

was all: happy in expanding, happy in having expanded, happy in feeling within himself the pulse of universal life.

His fullness of joy was communicated to those about him.

The house with its closed garden was too small for him. He had the view out over the garden of the neighboring convent with the solitude of its great avenues and century-old trees: but it was too good to last. In front of Christophe's windows they were building a six-story house, which shut out the view and completely hemmed him in. In addition, he had the pleasure of hearing the creaking of pulleys, the chipping of stones, the hammering of nails, all day long from morning to night. Among the workmen he found his old friend the slater, whose acquaintance he had made on the roof. They made signs to each other, and once, when he met him in the street, he took the man to a wineshop, and they drank together, much to the surprise of Olivier, who was a little scandalized. He found the man's drollery and unfailing good-humor very entertaining, but did not curse him any the less, with his troop of workmen and stupid idiots who were raising a barricade in front of the house and robbing him of air and light. Olivier did not complain much: he could quite easily adapt himself to a limited horizon: he was like the stove of Descartes, from which the suppressed ideas darted upward to the free sky. But Christophe needed more air. Shut up in that confined space, he avenged himself by expanding into the lives of those about him. He drank in their inmost life, and turned it into music. Olivier used to tell him that he looked like a lover.

"If I were in love," Christophe would reply, "I should see nothing, love nothing, be interested in nothing outside my love."

"What is the matter with you, then?"

"I'm very well. I'm hungry."

"Lucky Christophe!" Olivier would sigh. "I wish you could hand a little of your appetite over to us."

Health, like sickness, is contagious. The first to feel the benefit of Christophe's vitality was naturally Olivier. Vitality

was what he most lacked.   He retired from the world because
its vulgarity revolted him.   Brilliantly clever though he was,
and in spite of his exceptional artistic gifts, he was too delicate
to be a great artist.   Great artists do not feel disgust: the first
law for every healthy being is to live: and that law is even more
imperative for a man of genius: for such a man lives more.
Olivier fled from life: he drifted along in a world of poetic fic-
tions that had no body, no flesh and blood, no relation to reality.
He was one of those literary men who, in quest of beauty, have
to go outside time, into the days that are no more, or the days
that have never been.   As though the wine of life were not as
intoxicating, and its vintages as rich nowadays as ever they
were!   But men who are weary in soul recoil from direct contact with life: they can only bear to see it through the veil of
visions spun by the backward movement of time, and hear it
in the echo which sends back and distorts the dead words of
those who were once alive.—Christophe's friendship gradually
dragged Olivier out of this Limbo of art.   The sun's rays
pierced through to the innermost recesses of his soul in which he
was languishing.

Elsberger, the engineer, also succumbed to Christophe's contagious optimism.   It was not shown in any change in his
habits: they were too inveterate: and it was too much to expect
him to become enterprising enough to leave France and go and
seek his fortune elsewhere.   But he was shaken out of his
apathy: he recovered his taste for research, and reading, and
the scientific work which he had long neglected.   He would
have been much astonished had he been told that Christophe
had something to do with his new interest in his work: and
certainly no one would have been more surprised than
Christophe.

But of all the inhabitants of the house, Christophe was the
soonest intimate with the little couple on the second floor.
More than once as he passed their door he had stopped to listen

to the sound of the piano which Madame Arnaud used to play quite well when she was alone. Then he gave them tickets for his concert, for which they thanked him effusively. And after that he used to go and sit with them occasionally in the evening. He had never heard Madame Arnaud playing again: she was too shy to play in company: and even when she was alone, now that she knew she could be heard on the stairs, she kept the soft pedal down. But Christophe used to play to them, and they would talk about it for hours together. The Arnauds used to speak of music with such eagerness and freshness of feeling that he was enchanted with them. He had not thought it possible for French people to care so much for music.

"That," Olivier would say, "is because you have only come across musicians."

"I'm perfectly aware," Christophe would reply, "that professed musicians are the very people who care least for music: but you can't make me believe that there are many people like you in France."

"A few thousands at any rate."

"I suppose it's an epidemic, the latest fashion."

"It is not a matter of fashion," said Arnaud. "*He who does not rejoice to hear a sweet accord of instruments, or the sweetness of the natural voice, and is not moved by it, and does not tremble from head to foot with its sweet ravishment, and is not taken completely out of himself, does thereby show himself to have a twisted, vicious, and depraved soul, and of such an one we should beware as of a man ill-born. . . .*"

"I know that," said Christophe. "It is my friend Shakespeare."

"No," said Arnaud gently. "It is a Frenchman who lived before him, Ronsard. That will show you that, if it is the fashion in France to care for music, it is no new thing."

But what astonished Christophe was not so much that people in France should care for music, as that almost without exception they cared for the same music as the people in Germany.

In the world of Parisian snobs and artists, in which he had moved at first, it had been the mode to treat the German masters as distinguished foreigners, by all means to be admired, but to be kept at a distance: they were always ready to poke fun at the dullness of a Gluck, and the barbarity of a Wagner: against them they set up the subtlety of the French composers. And in the end Christophe had begun to wonder whether a Frenchman could have the least understanding of German music, to judge by the way it was rendered in France. Only a short time before he had come away perfectly scandalized from a performance of an opera of Gluck's: the ingenious Parisians had taken it into their heads to deck the old fellow up, and cover him with ribbons, and pad out his rhythms, and bedizen his music with impressionistic settings, and charming little dancing girls, forward and wanton. . . . Poor Gluck! There was nothing left of his eloquent and sublime feeling, his moral purity, his naked sorrow. Was it that the French could not understand these things?—And now Christophe could see how deeply and tenderly his new friends loved the very inmost quality of the Germanic spirit, and the old German *lieder,* and the German classics. And he asked them if it was not the fact that the great Germans were as foreigners to them, and that a Frenchman could only really love the artists of his own nationality.

"Not at all!" they protested. "It is only the critics who take upon themselves to speak for us. They always follow the fashion, and they want us to follow it too. But we don't worry about them any more than they worry about us. They're funny little people, trying to teach us what is and is not French—us, who are French of the old stock of France! . . . They come and tell us that our France is in Rameau,—or Racine,—and nowhere else. As though we did not know,—(and thousands like us in the provinces, and in Paris). How often Beethoven, Mozart, and Gluck, have sat with us by the fireside, and watched with us by the bedside of those we love, and shared our troubles, and revived our hopes, and been one of ourselves! If we dared say exactly what we thought, it is much more likely that the French artists, who are set up on a pedestal by our Parisian critics, are strangers among us."

"The truth is," said Olivier, "that if there are frontiers in art, they are not so much barriers between races as barriers between classes. I'm not so sure that there is a French art or a German art: but there is certainly one art for the rich and another for the poor. Gluck was a great man of the middle-classes: he belongs to our class. A certain French artist, whose name I won't mention, is not of our class: though he was of the middle-class by birth, he is ashamed of us, and denies us: and we deny him."

What Olivier said was true. The better Christophe got to know the French, the more he was struck by the resemblance between the honest men of France and the honest men of Germany. The Arnauds reminded him of dear old Schulz with his pure, disinterested love of art, his forgetfulness of self, his devotion to beauty. And he loved them in memory of Schulz.

At the same time as he realized the absurdity of moral frontiers between the honest men of different nationalities, Christophe began to see the absurdity of the frontiers that lay between the different ideas of honest men of the same nationality. Thanks to him, though without any deliberate effort on his part, the Abbé Corneille and M. Watelet, two men who seemed very far indeed from understanding each other, made friends.

Christophe used to borrow books from both of them and, with a want of ceremony which shocked Olivier, he used to lend their books in turn to the other. The Abbé Corneille was not at all scandalized: he had an intuitive perception of the quality of a man: and, without seeming to do so, he had marked the generous and even unconsciously religious nature of his young neighbor. A book by Kropotkin, which had been borrowed from M. Watelet, and for different reasons had given great pleasure to all three of them, began the process of bringing them together. It chanced one evening that they met in Christophe's room. At first Christophe was afraid that they might be rude to each other: but, on the contrary, they were perfectly polite. They discussed various sage subjects: their travels, and their experience of men. And they discovered in each other a fund of gentleness and the spirit of the Gospels, and chimerical hopes, in spite of the many reasons that each had for despair. They discovered a mutual sympathy, mingled with a little irony. Their sympathy was of a very discreet nature. They never revealed their fundamental beliefs. They rarely met and did not try to meet: but when they did so they were glad to see each other.

Of the two men the Abbé Corneille was not the least independent of mind, though Christophe would never have thought it. He gradually came to perceive the greatness of the religious and yet free ideas, the immense, serene, and unfevered mysticism which permeated the priest's whole mind, the every action of his daily life, and his whole outlook on the world,—leading him to live in Christ, as he believed that Christ had lived in God.

He denied nothing, no single element of life. To him the whole of Scripture, ancient and modern, lay and religious, from Moses to Berthelot, was certain, divine, the very expression of God. Holy Writ was to him only its richest example, just as the Church was the highest company of men united in the brotherhood of God: but in neither of them was the spirit confined in any fixed, unchanging truth. Christianity was the living Christ. The history of the world was only the history of the perpetual advance of the idea of God. The fall of the Jewish Temple, the ruin of the pagan world, the repulse of the Crusades, the humiliation of Boniface VIII, Galileo flinging the world back into giddy space, the infinitely little becoming more mighty than the great, the downfall of kingdoms, and the end of the Concordats, all these for a time threw the minds of men out of their reckoning. Some clung desperately to the passing order: some caught at a plank and drifted. The Abbé Cor-

neille only asked: " Where do we stand as men? Where is that
which makes us live? " For he believed: " Where life is, there
is God."—And that was why he was in sympathy with Christophe.

For his part, Christophe was glad once more to hear the
splendid music of a great religious soul. It awoke in him
echoes distant and profound. Through the feeling of perpetual
reaction, which is in vigorous natures a vital instinct, the instinct of self-preservation, the stroke which preserves the quivering balance of the boat, and gives it a new drive onward,—
his surfeit of doubts and his disgust with Parisian sensuality
had for the last two years been slowly restoring God to his
place in Christophe's heart. Not that he believed in God. He
denied God. But he was filled with the spirit of God. The
Abbé Corneille used to tell him with a smile, that like his
namesake, the sainted giant, he bore God on his shoulders without knowing it.

" How is it that I don't see it then? " Christophe would ask.

" You are like thousands of others: you see God every day,
and never know that it is He. God reveals Himself to all, in
every shape,—to some He appears in their daily life, as He
did to Saint Peter in Galilee,—to others (like your friend M.
Watelet), as He did to Saint Thomas, in wounds and suffering
that call for healing,—to you in the dignity of your ideal: *Noli
me tangere.* . . . Some day you will know it."

" I will never surrender," said Christophe. " I am free.
Free I shall remain."

" Only the more will you live in God," replied the priest
calmly.

But Christophe would not submit to being made out a
Christian against his will. He defended himself ardently and
simply, as though it mattered in the least whether one label
more than another was plastered on to his ideas. The Abbé
Corneille would listen with a faint ecclesiastical irony, that was
hardly perceptible, while it was altogether kindly. He had an
inexhaustible fund of patience, based on his habit of faith. It

had been tempered by the trials to which the existing Church had exposed him: while it had made him profoundly melancholy, and had even dragged him through terrible moral crises, he had not really been touched by it all. It was cruel to suffer the oppression of his superiors, to have his every action spied upon by the Bishops, and watched by the free-thinkers, who were endeavoring to exploit his ideas, to use him as a weapon against his own faith, and to be misunderstood and attacked both by his co-religionists and the enemies of his religion. It was impossible for him to offer any resistance: for submission was enforced upon him. It was impossible for him to submit in his heart: for he knew that the authorities were wrong. It was agony for him to hold his peace. It was agony for him to speak and to be wrongly interpreted. Not to mention the soul for which he was responsible, he had to think of those, who looked to him for counsel and help, while he had to stand by and see them suffer. . . . The Abbé Corneille suffered both for them and for himself, but he was resigned. He knew how small a thing were the days of trial in the long history of the Church.—Only, by dint of being turned in upon himself in his silent resignation, slowly he lost heart, and became timid and afraid to speak, so that it became more and more difficult for him to do anything, and little by little the torpor of silence crept over him. Meeting Christophe had given him new courage. His neighbor's youthful ardor and the affectionate and simple interest which he took in his doings, his sometimes indiscreet questions, did him a great deal of good. Christophe forced him to mix once more with living men and women.

Aubert, the journeyman electrician, once met him in Christophe's room. He started back when he saw the priest, and found it hard to conceal his feeling of dislike. Even when he had overcome his first inclination, he was uncomfortable and oddly embarrassed at finding himself in the company of a man in a cassock, a creature to whom he could attach no exact definition. However, his sociable instincts and the pleasure he always found in talking to educated men were stronger than his anti-clericalism. He was surprised by the pleasant relations existing between M. Watelet and the Abbé Corneille: he was no less surprised to find a priest who was a democrat, and a revolutionary who was an aristocrat: it upset all his preconceived ideas. He tried vainly to classify them in any social category: for he always had to classify people before he could begin to understand them. It was not easy to find a pigeon-hole for the peaceful freedom of mind of a priest who had read Anatole France and Renan, and was prepared to discuss them calmly, justly, and with some knowledge. In matters of science the Abbé Corneille's way was to accept the guidance of those who knew, rather than of those who laid down the law. He respected authority, but in his eyes it stood lower than knowledge. The flesh, the spirit, and charity: the three orders, the three rungs of the divine ladder, the ladder of Jacob. —Of course, honest Aubert was far, indeed, from understanding, or even from dreaming, of the possibility of such a state of mind. The Abbé Corneille used to tell Christophe that Aubert reminded him of certain French peasants whom he had seen one day. A young Englishwoman had asked them the way, in English. They listened solemnly, but did not understand. Then they spoke in French. She did not understand. Then they looked at each other pityingly, and wagged their heads, and went on with their work, and said:

"What a pity! What a pity! Such a pretty girl, too! . . ."

As though they had thought her deaf, or dumb, or soft in the head. . . .

At first Aubert was abashed by the knowledge and distinguished manners of the priest and M. Watelet, and sat mum, listening intently to what they said. Then, little by little, he joined in the conversation, giving way to the naïve pleasure that he found in hearing himself speak. He paraded his generous store of rather vague ideas. The other two would listen politely, and smile inwardly. Aubert was delighted, and could not hold himself in: he took advantage of, and presently abused, the inexhaustible patience of the Abbé Corneille. He read his literary productions to him. The priest listened resignedly; and it did not bore him overmuch, for he listened not so much to the words as to the man. And then he would reply to Christophe's commiseration:

"Bah! I hear so many of them!"

Aubert was grateful to M. Watelet and the Abbé Corneille: and, without taking much trouble to understand each other's ideas, or even to find out what they were, the three of them became very good friends without exactly knowing why. They were very surprised to find themselves so intimate. They would never have thought it.—Christophe was the bond between them.

He had other innocent allies in the three children, the two little Elsbergers and M. Watelet's adopted daughter. He was great friends with them: they adored him. He told each of them about the other, and gave them an irresistible longing to know each other. They used to make signs to each other from the windows, and spoke to each other furtively on the stairs. Aided and abetted by Christophe, they even managed to get permission sometimes to meet in the Luxembourg Gardens. Christophe was delighted with the success of his guile, and went to see them there the first time they were together: they were shy and embarrassed. and hardly knew what to make of their new happiness. He broke down their reserve in a moment, and invented games for them, and races, and played hide-and-seek: he joined in as keenly as though he were a child of ten: the passers-by cast amused and quizzical glances at the great big fellow. running and shouting and dodging round trees, with three little girls after him. And as their parents were still suspicious of each other, and showed no great readiness to let these excursions to the Luxembourg Gardens occur very often—(because it kept them too far out of sight)—Christophe managed to get Commandant Chabran, who lived on the ground floor, to invite the children to play in the garden belonging to the house.

Chance had thrown Christophe and the old soldier together: —(chance always singles out those who can turn it to account). —Christophe's writing-table was near his window. One day the wind blew a few sheets of music down into the garden. Christophe rushed down, bareheaded and disheveled, just as he was, without even taking the trouble to brush his hair. He thought he would only have to see a servant. However, the daughter opened the door to him. He was rather taken aback, but told her what he had come for. She smiled and let him in: they went into the garden. When he had picked up his papers he was for hurrying away, and she was taking him to the door, when they met the old soldier. The Commandant gazed at his odd visitor in some surprise. His daughter laughed, and introduced him.

"Ah! So you are the musician?" said the old soldier. "We are comrades."

They shook hands. They talked in a friendly, bantering tone of the concerts they gave together, Christophe with his piano, the Commandant with his flute. Christophe tried to go, but the old man would not let him: and he plunged blindly into a disquisition on music. Suddenly he stopped short, and said:

"Come and see my canons."

Christophe followed him, wondering how anybody could be interested in anything he might think about French artillery. The old man showed him in triumph a number of musical canons, amazing productions, compositions that might just as well be read upside down, or played as duets, one person playing the right-hand page, and the other the left. The Commandant was an old pupil of the Polytechnic, and had always had a taste for music: but what he loved most of all in it was the mathematical problem: it seemed to him—(as up to a point it is)—a magnificent mental gymnastic: and he racked his brains in the invention and solution of puzzles in the construction of music, each more useless and extravagant than the last. Of course, his military career had not left him much time for the development

of his mania: but since his retirement he had thrown himself
into it with enthusiasm: he expended on it all the energy and
ingenuity which he had previously employed in pursuing the
hordes of negro kings through the deserts of Africa, or avoiding
their traps. Christophe found his puzzles quite amusing, and
set him a more complicated one to solve. The old soldier was
delighted: they vied with one another: they produced a perfect
shower of musical riddles. After they had been playing the
game for some time, Christophe went upstairs to his own room.
But the very next morning his neighbor sent him a new problem,
a regular teaser, at which the Commandant had been working
half the night: he replied with another: and the duel went on
until Christophe, who was getting tired of it, declared himself
beaten: at which the old soldier was perfectly delighted. He
regarded his success as a retaliation on Germany. He invited
Christophe to lunch. Christophe's frankness in telling the old
soldier that he detested his musical compositions, and shouting
in protest when Chabran began to murder an *andante of* Haydn
on his harmonium, completed the conquest. From that time
on they often met to talk. But not about music. Christophe
could not summon up any great interest in his neighbor's
crotchety notions about it, and much preferred getting him to
talk about military subjects. The Commandant asked nothing
better: music was only a forced amusement for the unhappy
man: in reality, he was fretting his life out.

He was easily led on to yarn about his African campaigns.
Gigantic adventures worthy of the tales of a Pizarro and a
Cortez! Christophe was delighted with the vivid narrative of
that marvelous and barbaric epic, of which he knew nothing,
and almost every Frenchman is ignorant: the tale of the twenty
years during which the heroism, and courage, and inventive-
ness, and superhuman energy of a conquering handful of Frenchmen were spent far away in the depths of the Black Continent,
where they were surrounded by armies of negroes, where they
were deprived of the most rudimentary arms of war, and yet, in
the face of public opinion and a panic-stricken Government, in

spite of France, conquered for France an empire greater than
France itself.   There was the flavor of a mighty joy, a flavor
of blood in the tale, from which, in Christophe's mind's eye,
there sprang the figures of modern *condottieri,* heroic adventurers, unlooked for in the France of to-day, whom the France
of to-day is ashamed to own, so that she modestly draws a veil
over them.   The Commandant's voice would ring out bravely as
he recalled it all: and he would jovially recount, with learned
descriptions—(oddly interpolated in his epic narrative)—of
the geological structure of the country, in cold, precise terms,
the story of the tremendous marches, and the charges at full
gallop, and the man-hunts, in which he had been hunter and
quarry, turn and turn about, in a struggle to the death.—
Christophe would listen and watch his face, and feel a great
pity for such a splendid human animal, condemned to inaction,
and forced to spend his time in playing ridiculous games.   He
wondered how he could ever have become resigned to such a lot.
He asked the old man how he had done it.   The Commandant
was at first not at all inclined to let a stranger into his confidence as to his grievances.   But the French are naturally
loquacious, especially when they have a chance of pitching into
each other:

"What on earth should I do," he said, "in the army as it is
to-day?   The marines write books.   The infantry study
sociology.   They do everything but make war.   They don't even
prepare for it: they prepare never to go to war again: they
study the philosophy of war. . . .   The philosophy of war!
That's a game for beasts of burden wondering how much thrashing they are going to get! . . .   Discussing, philosophizing,
no, that's not my work.   Much better stay at home and go on
with my canons!"

He was too much ashamed to air the most serious of his
grievances: the suspicion created among the officers by the
appeal to informers, the humiliation of having to submit to the
insolent orders of certain crass and mischievous politicians, the
army's disgust at being put to base police duty, taking inventories

of the churches, putting down industrial strikes, at the bidding
of capital and the spite of the party in power—the petty burgess
radicals and anti-clericals—against the rest of the country.
Not to speak of the old African's disgust with the new Colonial
Army, which was for the most part recruited from the lowest
elements of the nation, by way of pandering to the egoism and
cowardice of the rest, who refuse to share in the honor and the
risks of securing the defense of " greater France "—France beyond the seas.

Christophe was not concerned with these French quarrels:
they were no affair of his: but he sympathized with the old soldier. Whatever he might think of war, it seemed to him that
an army was meant to produce soldiers, as an apple-tree to
produce apples. and that it was a strange perversion to graft on
to it politicians, esthetes, and sociologists. And yet he could
not understand how a man of such vigor could give way to his
adversaries. It is to be his own worst enemy for a man not to
fight his enemies. In all French people of any worth at all there
was a spirit of surrender, a strange temper of renunciation.—
To Christophe it was even more profound, and even more
touching as it existed in the old soldier's daughter.

Her name was Céline. She had beautiful hair, plaited and
braided so as to set off her high, round forehead and her rather
pointed ears, her thin cheeks, and her pretty chin: she was like
a country girl. with fine intelligent dark eyes, very trustful,
very soft, rather shortsighted: her nose was a little too large,
and she had a tiny mole on her upper lip by the corner of her
mouth, and she had a quiet smile which made her pout prettily
and thrust out her lower lip, which was a little protruding. She
was kind, active, clever, but she had no curiosity of mind. She
read very little. and never any of the newest books. never went
to the theater, never traveled,—(for traveling bored her father,
who had had too much of it in the old days),—never had anything to do with any polite charitable work,—(her father used
to condemn all such things),—made no attempt to study,—(he
used to make fun of blue stockings),—hardly ever left her little

patch of garden inclosed by its four high walls, so that it was like being at the bottom of a deep well. And yet she was not really bored. She occupied her time as best she could, and was good-tempered and resigned. About her and about the setting which every woman unconsciously creates for herself wherever she may be, there was a Chardinesque atmosphere: the same soft silence, the same tranquil expression, the same attitude of absorption—(a little drowsy and languid)—in the common task: the poetry of the daily round, of the accustomed way of life, with its fixed thoughts and actions, falling into exactly the same place at exactly the same time—thoughts and actions which are cherished none the less with an all-pervading tranquil gentleness: the serene mediocrity of the fine-souled women of the middle-class: honest, conscientious, truthful, calm—calm in their pleasures, unruffled in their labors, and yet poetic in all their qualities. They are healthy and neat and tidy, clean in body and mind: all their lives are sweetened with the scent of good bread, and lavender, and integrity, and kindness. There is peace in all that they are and do, the peace of old houses and smiling souls. . . .

Christophe, whose affectionate trustfulness invited trust, had become very friendly with her: they used to talk quite frankly: and he even went so far as to ask her certain questions, which she was surprised to find herself answering: she would tell him things which she had not told anybody, even her most intimate friends.

"You see," Christophe would say, "you're not afraid of me. There's no danger of our falling in love with each other: we're too good friends for that."

"You're very polite!" she would answer with a laugh.

Her healthy nature recoiled as much as Christophe's from philandering friendship, that form of sentimentality dear to equivocal men and women, who are always juggling with their emotions. They were just comrades one to another.

He asked her one day what she was doing in the afternoons, when he saw her sitting in the garden with her work on her knees, never touching it, and not stirring for hours together. She blushed, and protested that it was not a matter of hours, but only a matter of a few minutes, perhaps a quarter of an hour, during which she " went on with her story."

" What story? "

" The story I am always telling myself."

" You tell yourself stories?   Oh, tell them to me! "

She told him that he was too curious. She would only go so far as to intimate that they were stories of which she was not the heroine.

He was surprised at that:

" If you are going to tell yourself stories, it seems to me that it would be more natural if you told your own story with embellishments, and lived in a happier dream-life."

" I couldn't," she said. " If I did that, I should become desperate."

She blushed again at having revealed even so much of her inmost thoughts: and she went on:

" Besides, when I am in the garden and a gust of wind reaches me, I am happy. Then the garden becomes alive for me. And when the wind blusters and comes from a great distance, he tells me so many things! "

In spite of her reserve, Christophe could see the hidden depths of melancholy that lay behind her good-humor, and the restless activity which, as she knew perfectly well, led nowhere. Why did she not try to break away from her condition and emancipate herself? She would have been so well fitted for a useful and active life!—But she alleged her affection for her father, who would not hear of her leaving him. In vain did Christophe tell her that the old soldier was perfectly vigorous and energetic, and had no need of her, and that a man of his stamp could quite well be left alone, and had no right to make a sacrifice of her. She would begin to defend her father: by a pious fiction she would pretend that it was not her father who was forcing her to stay, but she herself who could not bear to leave him.—And, up to a point, what she said was true. It seemed to have been

accepted from time immemorial by herself, and her father, and
all their friends that their life had to be thus and thus, and not
otherwise. She had a married brother, who thought it quite
natural that she should devote her life to their father in his
stead. He was entirely wrapped up in his children. He loved
them jealously, and left them no will of their own. His love
for his children was to him, and especially to his wife, a voluntary bondage which weighed heavily on their life, and cramped
all their movements: his idea seemed to be that as soon as a
man has children, his own life comes to an end, and he has to
stop short in his own development: he was still young, active,
and intelligent, and there he was reckoning up the years he
would have still to work before he could retire.—Christophe saw
how these good people were weighed down by the atmosphere
of family affection, which is so deep-rooted in France—deep-
rooted, but stifling and destructive of vitality. And it has become all the more oppressive since families in France have been
reduced to the minimum: father, mother, one or two children,
and here and there, perhaps, an uncle or an aunt. It is a
cowardly, fearful love, turned in upon itself, like a miser clinging tightly to his hoard of gold.

A fortuitous circumstance gave Christophe a yet greater interest in the girl, and showed him the full extent of the suppression of the emotions of the French, their fear of life, of letting themselves go, and claiming their birthright.

Elsberger, the engineer, had a brother ten years younger than
himself, likewise an engineer. He was a very good fellow, like
thousands of others, of the middle-class, and he had artistic
aspirations: he was one of those people who would like to practise an art, but are afraid of compromising their reputation and
position. As a matter of fact, it is not a very difficult problem,
and most of the artists of to-day have solved it without any
great danger to themselves. But it needs a certain amount of
will-power: and not everybody is capable of even that much expenditure of energy: such people are not sure enough of wanting
what they really want: and as their position in life grows more

assured, they submit and drift along, without any show of revolt
or protest.   They cannot be blamed if they become good citizens
instead of bad artists.   But their disappointment too often
leaves behind it a secret discontent, a *qualis artifex pereo,* which
as best it can assumes a crust of what is usually called philosophy, and spoils their lives, until the wear and tear of daily
life and new anxieties have erased all trace of the old bitterness.
Such was the case of André Elsberger.   He would have liked
to be a writer: but his brother, who was very self-willed, had
made him follow in his footsteps and enter upon a scientific
career.   André was clever, and quite well equipped for scientific
work—or for literature, for that matter: he was not sure enough
of being an artist, and he was too sure that he was middle-
class: and so, provisionally at first,—(one knows what that
means)—he had bowed to his brother's wishes: he entered the
Centrale, high up in the list, and passed out equally high, and
since then he had practised his profession as an engineer conscientiously, but without being interested in it.   Of course, he
had lost the little artistic quality that he had possessed, and he
never spoke of it except ironically.

"And then," he used to say—(Christophe recognized Olivier's
pessimistic tendency in his arguments)—"life is not good
enough to make one worry about a spoiled career.   What does a
bad poet more or less matter! . . ."

The brothers were fond of one another: they were of the
same stamp morally: but they did not get on well together.
They had both been Dreyfus-mad.   But André was attracted
by syndicalism, and was an anti-militarist: and Elie was a
patriot.

From time to time André would visit Christophe without going to see his brother: and that astonished Christophe: for
there was no great sympathy between himself and André, who
used hardly ever to open his mouth except to gird at something or somebody,—which was very tiresome: and when Christophe said anything, André would not listen.   Christophe made
no effort to conceal the fact that he found his visits a nuisance:

but André did not mind, and seemed not to notice it. At last
Christophe found the key to the riddle one day when he found
his visitor leaning out of the window, and paying much more
attention to what was happening in the garden below than to
what he was saying. He remarked upon it, and André was not
reluctant to admit that he knew Mademoiselle Chabran, and that
she had something to do with his visits to Christophe. And, his
tongue being loosed, he confessed that he had long been attached
to the girl, and perhaps something more than that: the Elsbergers had long ago been in close touch with the Chabrans: but,
though they had been very intimate, politics and recent events
had separated them: and thereafter they saw very little of each
other. Christophe did not disguise his opinion that it was an
idiotic state of things. Was it impossible for people to think
differently, and yet to retain their mutual esteem? André said
he thought it was, and protested that he was very broad-minded:
but he would not admit the possibility of tolerance in certain
questions, concerning which, he said, he could not admit any
opinion different from his own: and he instanced the famous
Affair. On that, as usual, he became wild. Christophe knew
the sort of thing that happened in that connection, and made no
attempt to argue: but he asked whether the Affair was never
going to come to an end, or whether its curse was to go on and
on to the end of time, descending even unto the third and fourth
generation. André began to laugh: and without answering
Christophe, he fell to tender praise of Céline Chabran, and
protested against her father's selfishness, who thought it quite
natural that she should be sacrificed to him.

"Why don't you marry her," asked Christophe, "if you love
her and she loves you?"

André said mournfully that Céline was clerical. Christophe
asked what he meant by that. André replied that he meant
that she was religious, and had vowed a sort of feudal service to
God and His bonzes.

"But how does that affect you?"

"I don't want to share my wife with any one."

"What! You are jealous even of your wife's ideas? Why, you're more selfish even than the Commandant!"

"It's all very well for you to talk: would you take a woman who did not love music?"

"I have done so."

"How can a man and a woman live together if they don't think the same?"

"Don't you worry about what you think! Ah! my dear fellow, ideas count for so little when one loves. What does it matter to me whether the woman I love cares for music as much as I do? She herself is music to me! When a man has the luck, as you have, to find a dear girl whom he loves, and she loves him, she must believe what she likes, and he must believe what he likes! When all is said and done, what do your ideas amount to? There is only one truth in the world, there is only one God: love."

"You speak like a poet. You don't see life as it is. I know only too many marriages which have suffered from such a want of union in thought."

"Those husbands and wives did not love each other enough. You have to know what you want."

"Wanting does not do everything in life. Even if I wanted to marry Mademoiselle Chabran, I couldn't."

"I'd like to know why."

André spoke of his scruples: his position was not assured: he had no fortune and no great health. He was wondering whether he had the right to marry in such circumstances. It was a great responsibility. Was there not a great risk of bringing unhappiness on the woman he loved, and himself,—not to mention any children there might be? . . . It was better to wait—or give up the idea.

Christophe shrugged his shoulders.

"That's a fine sort of love! If she loves you, she will be happy in her devotion to you. And as for the children, you French people are absurd. You would like only to bring them into the world when you are sure of turning them out with comfortable private means, so that they will have nothing to suffer and nothing to fear. . . . Good Lord! That's nothing to do with you: your business is only to give them life, love of life, and courage to defend it. The rest . . . whether they live or die . . . is the common lot. Is it better to give up living than to take the risks of life?"

The sturdy confidence which emanated from Christophe affected André, but did not change his mind. He said:

"Yes, perhaps, that is true. . . ."

But he stopped at that. Like all the rest, his will and power of action seemed to be paralyzed.

Christophe had set himself to fight the inertia which he found in most of his French friends, oddly coupled with laborious and often feverish activity. Almost all the people he met in the various middle-class houses which he visited were discontented. They had almost all the same disgust with the demagogues and their corrupt ideas. In almost all there was the same sorrowful and proud consciousness of the betrayal of the genius of their race. And it was by no means the result of any personal rancor nor the bitterness of men and classes beaten and thrust out of power and active life, or discharged officials, or unemployed energy, nor that of an old aristocracy which has returned to its estates, there to die in hiding like a wounded lion. It was a feeling of moral revolt, mute, profound, general: it was to be found everywhere, in a greater or less degree, in the army, in the magistracy, in the University, in the officers, and in every vital branch of the machinery of government. But they took no active measures. They were discouraged in advance: they kept on saying:

"There is nothing to be done:"

or

"Let us try not to think of it."

Fearfully they dodged anything sad in their thoughts and conversation: and they took refuge in their home life.

If they had been content to refrain only from political action!

But even in their daily lives these good people had no interest in doing anything definite. They put up with the degrading, haphazard contact with horrible people whom they despised, because they could not take the trouble to fight against them, thinking that any such revolt must of necessity be useless. Why, for instance, should artists, and, in particular, the musicians with whom Christophe was most in touch, unprotestingly put up with the effrontery of the scaramouches of the Press, who laid down the law for them? There were absolute idiots among them, whose ignorance *in omni re scibili* was proverbial, though they were none the less invested with a sovereign authority *in omni re scibili.* They did not even take the trouble to write their articles and books: they had secretaries, poor starving creatures, who would have sold their souls, if they had had such things, for bread or women. There was no secret about it in Paris. And yet they went on riding their high horse and patronizing the artists. Christophe used to roar with anger sometimes when he read their articles.

" They have no heart! " he would say. " Oh! the cowards! "

" Who are you screaming at? " Olivier would ask. " The idiots of the market-place? "

" No. The honest men. These rascals are plying their trade: they lie, they steal, they rob and murder. But it is the others—those who despise them and yet let them go on—that I despise a thousand times more. If their colleagues on the Press, if honest, cultured critics, and the artists on whose backs these harlequins strut and poise themselves, did not put up with it, in silence, from shyness or fear of compromising themselves, or from some shameful anticipation of mutual service, a sort of secret pact made with the enemy so that they may be immune from their attacks,—if they did not let them preen themselves in their patronage and friendship, their upstart power would soon be killed by ridicule. There's the same weakness in everything, everywhere. I've met twenty honest men who have said to me of so-and-so: ' He is a scoundrel.' But there is not one of them who would not refer to him as his ' dear colleague,' and, if he

met him, shake hands with him.—'There are too many of
them!' they say.—Too many cowards. Too many flabby honest
men."

"Eh! What do you want them to do?"

"Be every man his own policeman! What are you waiting
for? For Heaven to take your affairs in hand? Look you, at
this very moment. It is three days now since the snow fell.
Your streets are thick with it, and your Paris is like a sewer of
mud. What do you do? You protest against your Municipal
Council for leaving you in such a state of filth. But do you
yourselves do anything to clear it away? Not a bit of it! You
sit with your arms folded. Not one of you has energy enough
even to clean the pavement in front of his house. Nobody does
his duty, neither the State nor the members of the State: each
man thinks he has done as much as is expected of him by
laying the blame on some one else. You have become so used,
through centuries of monarchical training, to doing nothing
for yourselves that you all seem to spend your time in star-gazing
and waiting for a miracle to happen. The only miracle that
could happen would be if you all suddenly made up your minds
to do something. My dear Olivier, you French people have
plenty of brains and plenty of good qualities: but you lack blood.
You most of all. There's nothing the matter with your mind
or your heart. It's your life that's all wrong. You're sputter-
ing out."

"What can we do? We can only wait for life to return
to us."

"You must want life to return to you. You must want to be
cured. You must *want,* use your will! And if you are to do
that you must first let in some pure air into your houses. If
you won't go out of doors, then at least you must keep your
houses healthy. You have let the air be poisoned by the unwholesome vapors of the market-place. Your art and your
ideas are two-thirds adulterated. And you are so dispirited
that it hardly occasions you any surprise, and rouses you to no
sort of indignation. Some of these good people—(it is pitiful

to see)—are so cowed that they actually persuade themselves that they are wrong and the charlatans are right. Why—even on your *Ésope* review, in which you profess not to be taken in by anything,—I have found unhappy young men persuading themselves that they love an art and ideas for which they have not a vestige of love. They get drunk on it, without any sort of pleasure, simply because they are told to do so: and they are dying of boredom—boredom with the monstrous lie of the whole thing!"

Christophe passed through these wavering and dispirited creatures like a wind shaking the slumbering trees. He made no attempt to force them to his way of thinking: he breathed into them energy enough to make them think for themselves. He used to say:

"You are too humble. The grand enemy is neurasthenia, doubt. A man can and must be tolerant and human. But no man may doubt what he believes to be good and true. A man must believe in what he thinks. And he should maintain what he believes. Whatever our powers may be, we have no right to forswear them. The smallest creature in the world, like the greatest, has his duty. And—(though he is not sufficiently conscious of it)—he has also a power. Why should you think that your revolt will carry so little weight? A sturdy upright conscience which dares assert itself is a mighty thing. More than once during the last few years you have seen the State and public opinion forced to reckon with the views of an honest man, who had no other weapons but his own moral force, which, with constant courage and tenacity, he had dared publicly to assert. . . .

"And if you must go on asking what's the good of taking so much trouble, what's the good of fighting, *what's the good of it all?* . . . Then, I will tell you:—Because France is dying, because Europe is perishing—because, if we did not fight, our civilization, the edifice so splendidly constructed, at the cost of centuries of labor, by our humanity, would crumble away. These are not idle words. The country is in danger, our European mother-country,—and more than any, yours, your own native country, France. Your apathy is killing her. Your silence is killing her. Each of your energies as it dies, each of your ideas as it accepts and surrenders, each of your good intentions as it ends in sterility, every drop of your blood as it dries up, unused, in your veins, means death to her. . . . Up! up! You must live! Or, if you must die, then you must die fighting like men."

But the chief difficulty lay not in getting them to do something, but in getting them to act together. There they were quite unmanageable. The best of them were the most obstinate, as Christophe found in dealing with the tenants in his own house: M. Félix Weil, Elsberger, the engineer, and Commandant Chabran, lived on terms of polite and silent hostility. And yet, though Christophe knew very little of them, he could see that, underneath their party and racial labels, they all wanted the same thing.

There were many reasons particularly why M. Weil and the Commandant should have understood each other. By one of those contrasts common to thoughtful men, M. Weil, who never left his books and lived only in the life of the mind, had a passion for all things military. "We are all cranks," said the half-Jew Montaigne, applying to mankind in general what is perfectly true of certain types of minds, like the type of which M. Weil was an example. The old intellectual had the craze for Napoleon. He collected books and relics which brought to life in him the terrible dream of the Imperial epic. Like many Frenchmen of that crepuscular epoch, he was dazzled by the distant rays of that glorious sun. He used to go through the campaigns, fight the battles all over again, and discuss operations: he was one of those chamber-strategists who swarm in the Academies and the Universities, who explain Austerlitz and declare how Waterloo should have been fought. He was the first to make fun of the "Napoleonite" in himself: it tickled his irony: but none the less he went on reading the splendid stories with the wild enthusiasm of a child playing a game: he would weep over certain episodes: and when he realized that he had been weak enough to shed tears, he would roar with laughter, and call himself an old fool. As a matter of fact, he was a Napoleonite not so much from patriotism as from a romantic interest and a platonic love of action. However, he was a good patriot, and much more attached to France than many an actual Frenchman. The French anti-Semites are stupid and actively mischievous in casting their insulting suspicions on the feeling for France of the Jews who have settled in the country. Outside the reasons by which any family does of necessity, after a generation or two, become attached to the land of its adoption, where the blood of the soil has become its own, the Jews have especial reason to love the nation which in the West stands for the most advanced ideas of intellectual and moral liberty. They love it because for a hundred years they have helped to make it so, and its liberty is in part their work. How, then, should they not defend it against every menace of feudal reaction? To try—as a handful of unscrupulous politicians and a herd of wrong-headed people would like—to break the bonds which bind these Frenchmen by adoption to France, is to play into the hands of that reaction.

Commandant Chabran was one of those wrong-headed old Frenchmen who are roused to fury by the newspapers, which make out that every immigrant into France is a secret enemy, and, in a human, hospitable spirit, force themselves to suspect and hate and revile them, and deny the brave destiny of the race, which is the conflux of all the races. Therefore, he thought it incumbent on him not to know the tenant of the first floor, although he would have been glad to have his acquaintance. As for M. Weil, he would have been very glad to talk to the old soldier: but he knew him for a nationalist, and regarded him with mild contempt.

Christophe had much less reason than the Commandant for being interested in M. Weil. But he could not bear to hear ill

spoken of anybody unjustly.   And he broke many a lance in de-
fence of M. Weil when he was attacked in his presence.

One day, when the Commandant, as usual, was railing against
the prevailing state of things, Christophe said to him:

"It is your own fault.   You all shut yourselves up inside
yourselves.   When things in France are not going well, to your
way of thinking, you submit to it and send in your resignation.
One would think it was a point of honor with you to admit yourselves beaten.   I've never seen anybody lose a cause with such
absolute delight.   Come, Commandant, you have made war; is
that fighting, or anything like it?"

"It is not a question of fighting," replied the Commandant.
"We don't fight against France.   In such struggles as these we
have to argue, and vote, and mix with all sorts of knaves and
low blackguards: and I don't like it."

"You seem to be profoundly disgusted!   I suppose you had
to do with knaves and low blackguards in Africa!"

"On my honor, that did not disgust me nearly so much.   Out
there one could always knock them down!   Besides, if it's a
question of fighting, you need soldiers.   I had my sharpshooters
out there.   Here I am all alone."

"It isn't that there is any lack of good men."

"Where are they?"

"Everywhere.   All round us."

"Well: what are they doing?"

"Just what you're doing.   Nothing.   They say there's nothing
to be done."

"Give me an instance."

"Three, if you like, in this very house."

Christophe mentioned M. Weil,—(the Commandant gave an
exclamation),—and the Elsbergers,—(he jumped in his seat):

"That Jew?   Those Dreyfusards?"

"Dreyfusards?" said Christophe.   "Well: what does that
matter?"

"It is they who have ruined France."

"They love France as much as you do."

"They're mad, mischievous lunatics."

"Can't you be just to your adversaries?"

"I can get on quite well with loyal adversaries who use the same weapons. The proof of that is that I am here talking to you, Monsieur German. I can think well of the Germans, although some day I hope to give them back with interest the thrashing we got from them. But it is not the same thing with our enemies at home: they use underhand weapons, sophistry, and unsound ideas, and a poisonous humanitarianism. . . ."

"Yes. You are in the same state of mind as that of the knights of the Middle Ages, when, for the first time, they found themselves faced with gunpowder. What do you want? There is evolution in war too."

"So be it. But then, let us be frank, and say that war is war."

"Suppose a common enemy were to threaten Europe, wouldn't you throw in your lot with the Germans?"

"We did so, in China."

"Very well, then: look about you. Don't you see that the heroic idealism of your country and every other country in Europe is actually threatened? Don't you see that they are all, more or less, a prey to the adventurers of every class of society? To fight that common enemy, don't you think you should join with those of your adversaries who are of some worth and moral vigor? How can a man like you set so little store by the realities of life? Here are people who uphold an ideal which is different from your own! An ideal is a force, you cannot deny it: in the struggle in which you were recently engaged, it was your adversaries' ideal which defeated you. Instead of wasting your strength in fighting against it, why not make use of it, side by side with your own, against the enemies of all ideals, the men who are exploiting your country and your wealth of ideas, the men who are bringing European civilization to rottenness?"

"For whose sake? One must know where one is. To make our adversaries triumph?"

"When you were in Africa, you never stopped to think whether you were fighting for the King or the Republic. I fancy that not many of you ever gave a thought to the Republic."

"They didn't care a rap."

"Good! And that was well for France. You conquered for her, as well as for yourselves, and for the honor and the joy of it. Why not do the same here? Why not widen the scope of the fight? Don't go haggling over differences in politics and religion. These things are utterly futile. What does it matter whether your nation is the eldest daughter of the Church or the eldest daughter of Reason? The only thing that does matter is that it should live! Everything that exalts life is good. There is only one enemy, pleasure-seeking egoism, which fouls the sources of life and dries them up. Exalt force, exalt the light, exalt fruitful love, the joy of sacrifice, action, and give up expecting other people to act for you. Do, act, combine! Come! . . ."

And he laughed and began to bang out the first bars of the march in *B minor* from the *Choral Symphony*.

"Do you know," he said, breaking off, "that if I were one of your musicians, say Charpentier or Bruneau (devil take the two of them!), I would combine in a choral symphony *Aux armes, citoyens!, l'Internationale, Vive Henri IV,* and *Dieu Protège la France!,*—(You see, something like this.)—I would make you a soup so hot that it would burn your mouth! It would be unpleasant,—(no worse in any case than what you are doing now):—but I vow it would warm your vitals, and that you would have to set out on the march!"

And he roared with laughter.

The Commandant laughed too:

"You're a fine fellow, Monsieur Krafft. What a pity you're not one of us!"

"But I am one of you! The fight is the same everywhere Let us close up the ranks!"

The Commandant quite agreed: but there he stayed. Then

Christophe pressed his point and brought the conversation back to M. Weil and the Elsbergers. And the old soldier no less obstinately went back to his eternal arguments against Jews and Dreyfusards, and nothing that Christophe had said seemed to have had the slightest effect on him.

Christophe grew despondent. Olivier said to him:

"Don't you worry about it. One man cannot all of a sudden change the whole state of mind of a nation. That's too much to expect! But you have done a good deal without knowing it."

"What have I done?" said Christophe.

"You are Christophe."

"What good is that to other people?"

"A great deal. Just go on being what you are, my dear Christophe. Don't you worry about us."

But Christophe could not surrender. He went on arguing with Commandant Chabran, sometimes with great vehemence. It amused Céline. She was generally present at their discussions, sitting and working in silence. She took no part in the argument: but it seemed to make her more lively: and quite a different expression would come into her eyes: it was as though it gave her more breathing-space. She began to read, and went out a little more, and found more things to interest her. And one day, when Christophe was battling with her father about the Elsbergers, the Commandant saw her smile: he asked her what she was thinking, and she replied calmly:

"I think M. Krafft is right."

The Commandant was taken aback, and said:

"You . . . you surprise me! . . . However, right or wrong, we are what we are. And there's no reason why we should know these people. Isn't it so, my dear?"

"No, father," she replied. "I would like to know them."

The Commandant said nothing, and pretended that he had not heard. He himself was much less insensible of Christophe's influence than he cared to appear. His vehemence and narrow-mindedness did not prevent his having a proper sense of justice and very generous feelings. He loved Christophe, he loved his frankness and his moral soundness, and he used often bitterly to regret that Christophe was a German. Although he always lost his temper in these discussions, he was always eager for more, and Christophe's arguments did produce an effect on him, though he would never have been willing to admit it. But one day Christophe found him absorbed in reading a book which he would not let him see. And when Céline took Christophe to the door and found herself alone with him, she said:

"Do you know what he was reading? One of M. Weil's books."

Christophe was delighted.

"What does he say about it?"

"He says: 'Beast!' . . . But he can't put it down."

Christophe made no allusion to the fact with the Commandant. It was he who asked:

"Why have you stopped hurling that blessed Jew at my head?"

"Because I don't think there's any need to," said Christophe.

"Why?" asked the Commandant aggressively.

Christophe made no reply, and went away laughing.

Olivier was right. It is not through words that a man can influence other men: but through his life. There are people who irradiate an atmosphere of peace from their eyes, and in their gestures, and through the silent contact with the serenity of their souls. Christophe irradiated life. Softly, softly, like the moist air of spring, it penetrated the walls and the closed windows of the somnolent old house: it gave new life to the hearts of men and women, whom sorrow, weakness, and isolation had for years been consuming, so that they were withered and like dead creatures. What a power there is in one soul over another! Those who wield that power and those who feel it are alike ignorant of its working. And yet the life of the world is in the ebb and flow controlled by that mysterious power of attraction.

On the second floor, below Christophe and Olivier's room, there lived, as we have seen, a young woman of thirty-five, a Madame Germain, a widow of two years' standing, who, the year before, had lost her little girl, a child of seven. She lived with her mother-in-law, and they never saw anybody. Of all the tenants of the house, they had the least to do with Christophe. They had hardly met, and they had never spoken to each other.

She was a tall woman, thin, but with a good figure; she had fine brown eyes, dull and rather inexpressive, though every now and then there glowed in them a hard, mournful light. Her face was sallow and her complexion waxy: her cheeks were hollow and her lips were tightly compressed. The elder Madame Germain was a devout lady, and spent all her time at church. The younger woman lived in jealous isolation in her grief. She took no interest in anything or anybody. She surrounded herself with portraits and pictures of her little girl, and by dint of staring at them she had ceased to see her as she was: the photographs and dead presentments had killed the living image of the child. She had ceased to see her as she was, but she clung to it: she was determined to think of nothing but the child: and so, in the end, she reached a point at which she could not even think of her: she had completed the work of death. There she stopped, frozen, with her heart turned to stone, with no tears to shed, with her life withered. Religion was no aid to her. She went through the formalities, but her heart was not in them, and therefore she had no living faith: she gave money for Masses, but she took no active part in any of the work of the Church: her whole religion was centered in the one thought of seeing her child again. What did the rest matter? God? What had she to do with God? To see her child again, only to see her again. . . . And she was by no means sure that she would do so. She wished to believe it,

willed it hardly, desperately: but she was in doubt. . . . She
could not bear to see other children, and used to think:

"Why are they not dead too?"

In the neighborhood there was a little girl who in figure and
manner was like her own. When she saw her from behind, with
her little pigtails down her back, she used to tremble. She would
follow her, and, when the child turned round and she saw that it
was not *she,* she would long to strangle her. She used to complain that the Elsberger children made a noise below her, though
they were very quiet, and even very subdued by their up-bringing: and when the unhappy children began to play about their
room, she would send her maid to ask her neighbors to make
them be quiet. Christophe met her once as he was coming in
with the little girls, and was hurt and horrified by the hard
way in which she looked at them.

One summer evening when the poor woman was sitting in the
dark in the self-hypnotized condition of the utter emptiness of
her living death, she heard Christophe playing. It was his habit
to sit at the piano in the half-light, musing and improvising.
His music irritated her, for it disturbed the empty torpor into
which she had sunk. She shut the window angrily. The music
penetrated through to her room. Madame Germain was filled
with a sort of hatred for it. She would have been glad to stop
Christophe, but she had no right to do so. Thereafter, every
day at the same time she sat waiting impatiently and irritably
for the music to begin: and when it was later than usual her
irritation was only the more acute. In spite of herself, she
had to follow the music through to the end, and when it was
over she found it hard to sink back into her usual apathy.—And
one evening, when she was curled up in a corner of her dark
room, and, through the walls and the closed window, the distant
music reached her, that light-giving music . . . she felt a
thrill run through her, and once more tears came to her eyes.
She went and opened the window, and stood there listening and
weeping. The music was like rain drop by drop falling upon
her poor withered heart, and giving it new life. Once more she

could see the sky, the stars, the summer night: within herself she felt the dawning of a new interest in life, as yet only a poor, pale light, vague and sorrowful sympathy for others. And that night, for the first time for many months, the image of her little girl came to her in her dreams.—For the surest road to bring us near the beloved dead, the best means of seeing them again, is not to go with them into death, but to live. They live in our lives, and die with us.

She made no attempt to meet Christophe. Rather she avoided him. But she used to hear him go by on the stairs with the children: and she would stand in hiding behind her door to listen to their babyish prattle, which so moved her heart.

One day, as she was going out, she heard their little padding footsteps coming down the stairs, rather more noisily than usual, and the voice of one of the children saying to her sister:

" Don't make so much noise, Lucette. Christophe says you mustn't because of the sorrowful lady."

And the other child began to walk more quietly and to talk in a whisper. Then Madame Germain could not restrain herself: she opened the door, and took the children in her arms, and hugged them fiercely. They were afraid: one of the children began to cry. She let them go, and went back into her own room.

After that, whenever she met them, she used to try to smile at them, a poor withered smile,—(for she had grown unused to smiling) :—she would speak to them awkwardly and affectionately, and the children would reply shyly in timid, bashful whispers. They were still afraid of the sorrowful lady, more afraid than ever: and now, whenever they passed the door, they used to run lest she should come out and catch them. She used to hide to catch sight of them as they passed. She would have been ashamed to be seen talking to the children. She was ashamed in her own eyes. It seemed to her that she was robbing her own dead child of some of the love to which she only was entitled. She would kneel down and pray for her forgiveness. But now that the instinct for life and love was newly awakened in her, she could not resist it: it was stronger than herself.

One evening, as Christophe came in, he saw that there was an unusual commotion in the house. He met a tradesman, who told him that the tenant of the third floor, M. Watelet, had just died suddenly of angina pectoris. Christophe was filled with pity, not so much for his unhappy neighbor as for the child who was left alone in the world. M. Watelet was not known to have any relations, and there was every reason to believe that he had left the girl almost entirely unprovided for. Christophe raced upstairs, and went into the flat on the third floor, the door of which was open. He found the Abbé Corneille with the body, and the child in tears, crying to her father: the housekeeper was making clumsy efforts to console her. Christophe took the child in his arms and spoke to her tenderly. She clung to him desperately: he could not think of leaving her: he wanted to take her away, but she would not let him. He stayed with her. He sat near the window in the dying light of day, and went on rocking her in his arms and speaking to her softly. The child gradually grew calmer, and went to sleep, still sobbing. Christophe laid her on her bed, and tried awkwardly to undress her and undo the laces of her little shoes. It was nightfall. The door of the flat had been left open. A shadow entered with a rustling of skirts. In the fading light Christophe recognized the fevered eyes of the sorrowful lady. He was amazed. She stood by the door, and said thickly:

"I came. . . . Will you . . . will you let me take her?"

Christophe took her hand and pressed it. Madame Germain was in tears. Then she sat by the bedside. And, a moment later, she said:

"Let me stay with her. . . ."

Christophe went up to his own room with the Abbé Corneille. The priest was a little embarrassed, and begged his pardon for coming up. He hoped, he said, humbly, that the dead man would have nothing to reproach him with: he had gone, not as a priest, but as a friend. Christophe was too much moved to speak, and left him with an affectionate shake of the hand.

Next morning, when Christophe went down, he found the child with her arms round Madame Germain's neck, with the naïve confidence which makes children surrender absolutely to those who have won their affection. She was glad to go with her new friend. . . . Alas! she had soon forgotten her adopted father. She showed just the same affection for her new mother. That was not very comforting. Did Madame Germain, in the egoism of her love, see it? . . . Perhaps. But what did it matter? The thing is to love. That way lies happiness. . . .

A few weeks after the funeral Madame Germain took the child into the country, far away from Paris. Christophe and Olivier saw them off. The woman had an expression of contentment and secret joy which they had never known in her before. She paid no attention to them. However, just as they were going, she noticed Christophe, and held out her hand, and said:

"It was you who saved me."

"What's the matter with the woman?" asked Christophe in amazement, as they were going upstairs after her departure.

A few days later the post brought him a photograph of a little girl whom he did not know, sitting on a stool, with her little hands sagely folded in her lap, while she looked up at him with clear, sad eyes. Beneath it were written these words:

"With thanks from my dear, dead child."

Thus it was that the breath of life passed into all these people. In the attic on the fifth floor was a great and mighty flame of humanity, the warmth and light of which were slowly filtered through the house.

But Christophe saw it not. To him the process was very slow.

"Ah!" he would sigh, "if one could only bring these good

people together, all these people of all classes and every kind of belief, who refuse to know each other! Can't it be done?"

"What do you want?" said Olivier. "You would need to have mutual tolerance and a power of sympathy which can only come from inward joy,—the joy of a healthy, normal, harmonious existence,—the joy of having a useful outlet for one's activity, of feeling that one's efforts are not wasted, and that one is serving some great purpose. You would need to have a prosperous country, a nation at the height of greatness, or— (better still)—on the road to greatness. And you must also have—(the two things go together)—a power which could employ all the nation's energies, an intelligent and strong power, which would be above party. Now, there is no power above party save that which finds its strength in itself—not in the multitude, that power which seeks not the support of anarchical majorities,—as it does nowadays when it is no more than a well-trained dog in the hands of second-rate men, and bends all to its will by service rendered: the victorious general, the dictatorship of Public Safety, the supremacy of the intelligence . . . what you will. It does not depend on us. You must have the opportunity and the men capable of seizing it: you must have happiness and genius. Let us wait and hope! The forces are there: the forces of faith, knowledge, work, old France and new France, and the greater France. . . . What an upheaval it would be, if the word were spoken, the magic word which should let loose these forces all together! Of course, neither you nor I can say the word. Who will say it? Victory? Glory? . . . Patience! The chief thing is for the strength of the nation to be gathered together, and not to rust away, and not to lose heart before the time comes. Happiness and genius only come to those peoples who have earned them by ages of stoic patience, and labor, and faith."

"Who knows?" said Christophe. "They often come sooner than we think—just when we expect them least. You are counting too much on the work of ages. Make ready. Gird your loins. Always be prepared with your shoes on your feet and your staff in your hand. . . . For you do not know that the Lord will not pass your doors this very night."

The Lord came very near that night. His shadow fell upon the threshold of the house.

Following on a sequence of apparently insignificant events, relations between France and Germany suddenly became strained: and, in a few days, the usual neighborly attitude of banal courtesy passed into the provocative mood which precedes war. There was nothing surprising in this, except to those who were living under the illusion that the world is governed by reason. But there were many such in France: and numbers of people were amazed from day to day to see the vehement Gallophobia of the German Press becoming rampant with the usual quasi-unanimity. Certain of those newspapers which, in the two countries, arrogate to themselves a monopoly of patriotism, and speak in the nation's name, and dictate to the State, sometimes with the secret complicity of the State, the policy it should follow, launched forth insulting ultimatums to France. There was a dispute between Germany and England; and Germany did not admit the right of France not to interfere: the insolent newspapers called upon her to declare for Germany, or else threatened to make her pay the chief expenses of the war: they presumed that they could wrest alliance from her fears, and already regarded her as a conquered and contented vassal,—to be frank, like Austria. It only showed the insane vanity of German Imperialism, drunk with victory, and the absolute incapacity of German statesmen to understand other races, so that they were always applying the simple common measure which was law for themselves: Force, the supreme reason. Naturally, such a brutal demand, made of an ancient nation, rich in its past ages of a glory and a supremacy in Europe, such as Germany had never known, had had exactly the opposite effect to that which Germany expected. It had provoked their slum-

bering pride: France was shaken from top to base: and even
the most diffident of the French roared with anger.

The great mass of the German people had nothing at all to
do with the provocation: they were shocked by it: the honest
men of every country ask only to be allowed to live in peace: and
the people of Germany are particularly peaceful, affectionate,
anxious to be on good terms with everybody, and much more inclined to admire and emulate other nations than to go to war
with them. But the honest men of a nation are not asked for
their opinion: and they are not bold enough to give it. Those
who are not virile enough to take public action are inevitably
condemned to be its pawns. They are the magnificent and unthinking echo which casts back the snarling cries of the Press
and the defiance of their leaders, and swells them into the *Marseillaise,* or the *Wacht am Rhein.*

It was a terrible blow to Christophe and Olivier. They were
so used to living in mutual love that they could not understand
why their countries did not do the same. Neither of them could
grasp the reasons for the persistent hostility, which was now so
suddenly brought to the surface, especially Christophe, who, being a German, had no sort of ground for ill-feeling against the
people whom his own people had conquered. Although he himself was shocked by the intolerable vanity of some of his fellow-
countrymen, and, up to a certain point, was entirely with the
French against such a high-handed Brunswicker demand, he
could not understand why France should, after all, be unwilling
to enter into an alliance with Germany. The two countries
seemed to him to have so many deep-seated reasons for being
united, so many ideas in common, and such great tasks to accomplish together, that it annoyed him to see them persisting in
their wasteful, sterile ill-feeling. Like all Germans, he regarded
France as the most to blame for the misunderstanding: for,
though he was quite ready to admit that it was painful for
her to sit still under the memory of her defeat, yet that was,
after all, only a matter of vanity, which should be set aside in
the higher interests of civilization and of France herself. He

had never taken the trouble to think out the problem of Alsace and Lorraine. At school he had been taught to regard the annexation of those countries as an act of justice, by which, after centuries of foreign subjection, a German province had been restored to the German flag. And so, he was brought down with a run, and he discovered that his friend regarded the annexation as a crime. He had never even spoken to him about these things, so convinced was he that they were of the same opinion: and now he found Olivier, of whose good faith and broadmindedness he was certain, telling him, dispassionately, without anger and with profound sadness, that it was possible for a great people to renounce the thought of vengeance for such a crime, but quite impossible for them to subscribe to it without dishonor.

They had great difficulty in understanding each other. Olivier's historical argument, alleging the right of France to claim Alsace as a Latin country, made no impression on Christophe: there were just as good arguments to the contrary: history can provide politics with every sort of argument in every sort of cause. Christophe was much more accessible to the human, and not only French, aspect of the problem. Whether the Alsatians were or were not Germans was not the question. They did not wish to be Germans: and that was all that mattered. What nation has the right to say: "These people are mine: for they are my brothers"? If the brothers in question renounce that nation, though they be a thousand times in the wrong, the consequences of the breach must always be borne by the party who has failed to win the love of the other, and therefore has lost the right to presume to bind the other's fortunes up with his own. After forty years of strained relations, vexations, patent or disguised, and even of real advantage gained from the exact and intelligent administration of Germany, the Alsatians persist in their refusal to become Germans: and, though they might give in from sheer exhaustion, nothing could ever wipe out the memory of the sufferings of the generations, forced to live in exile from their native land, or, what is even more pitiful, unable to leave it, and compelled to bend under a yoke which was hateful to them, and to submit to the seizure of their country and the slavery of their people.

Christophe naïvely confessed that he had never seen the matter in that light: and he was considerably perturbed by it. And honest Germans always bring to a discussion an integrity which does not always go with the passionate self-esteem of a Latin, however sincere he may be. It never occurred to Christophe to support his argument by the citation of similar crimes perpetrated by all nations all through the history of the world. He was too proud to fall back upon any such humiliating excuse: he knew that, as humanity advances, its crimes become more odious, for they stand in a clearer light. But he knew also that if France were victorious in her turn she would be no more moderate in the hour of victory than Germany had been, and that yet another link would be added to the chain of the crimes of the nations. So the tragic conflict would drag on for ever, in which the best elements of European civilization were in danger of being lost.

Though the subject was terribly painful for Christophe, it was even more so for Olivier. It meant for him, not only the sorrow of a great fratricidal struggle between the two nations best fitted for alliance together. In France the nation was divided, and one faction was preparing to fight the other. For years pacific and anti-militarist doctrines had been spread and propagated both by the noblest and the vilest elements of the nation. The Government had for a long time held aloof, with the weak-kneed dilettantism with which it handled everything which did not concern the immediate interests of the politicians: and it never occurred to it that it might be less dangerous frankly to maintain the most dangerous doctrines than to leave them free to creep into the veins of the people and ruin their capacity for war, while armaments were being prepared. These doctrines appealed to the Free Thinkers who were dreaming of founding a European brotherhood, working all together to make the world more just and human. They appealed also to the selfish cowardice of the rabble, who were unwilling to endanger their skins for anything or anybody.—These ideas had been taken up by Olivier and many of his friends. Once or twice, in his rooms, Christophe had been present at discussions which had amazed him. His friend Mooch, who was stuffed full of humanitarian illusions, used to say, with eyes blazing, quite calmly, that war must be abolished, and that the best way of setting about it was to incite the soldiers to mutiny, and, if necessary, to shoot down their leaders: and he would insist that it was bound to succeed. Elie Elsberger would reply, coldly and vehemently, that, if war were to break out, he and his friends would not set out for the frontier before they had settled their account with the enemy at home. André Elsberger would take Mooch's part. . . . One day Christophe came in for a terrible scene between the two brothers. They threatened to shoot each other. Although their bloodthirsty words were spoken in a bantering tone, he had a feeling that neither of them had uttered a single threat which he was not prepared to put into action. Christophe was amazed when he thought of a race of men so absurd as to be always ready to commit suicide for the sake of ideas. . . . Madmen. Crazy logicians. And yet they are good men. Each man sees only his own ideas, and wishes to follow them through to the end, without turning aside by a hair's breadth. And it is all quite useless: for they crush each other out of existence. The humanitarians wage war on the patriots. The patriots wage war on the humanitarians. And meanwhile the enemy comes and destroys both country and humanity in one swoop.

"But tell me," Christophe would ask André Elsberger, "are you in touch with the proletarians of the rest of the nations?"

"Some one has to begin. And we are the people to do it. We have always been the first. It is for us to give the signal!"

"And suppose the others won't follow!"

"They will."

"Have you made treaties, and drawn up a plan?"

" What's the good of treaties? Our force is superior to diplomacy."

" It is not a question of ideas: it's a question of strategy. If you are going to destroy war, you must borrow the methods of war. Draw up your plan of campaign in the two countries. Arrange that on such and such a date in France and Germany your allied troops shall take such and such a step. But, if you go to work without a plan, how can you expect any good to come of it? With chance on the one hand, and tremendous organized forces on the other—the result would never be in doubt: you would be crushed out of existence."

André Elsberger did not listen. He shrugged his shoulders and took refuge in vague threats: a handful of sand, he said, was enough to smash the whole machine, if it were dropped into the right place in the gears.

But it is one thing to discuss at leisure, theoretically, and quite another to have to put one's ideas into practice, especially when one has to make up one's mind quickly. . . . Those are frightful moments when the great tide surges through the depths of the hearts of men! They thought they were free and masters of their thoughts! But now, in spite of themselves, they are conscious of being dragged onwards, onwards. . . . An obscure power of will is set against their will. Then they discover that it is not they who exist in reality, not they, but that unknown Force, whose laws govern the whole ocean of humanity. . . .

Men of the firmest intelligence, men the most secure in their faith, now saw it dissolve at the first puff of reality, and stood turning this way and that, not daring to make up their minds, and often, to their immense surprise, deciding upon a course of action entirely different from any that they had foreseen. Some of the most eager to abolish war suddenly felt a vigorous passionate pride in their country leap into being in their hearts. Christophe found Socialists, and even revolutionary syndicalists, absolutely bowled over by their passionate pride in a duty utterly foreign to their temper. At the very beginning of the upheaval, when as yet he hardly believed that the affair could be serious, he said to André Elsberger, with his usual German want of tact, that now was the moment to apply his theories, unless he wanted Germany to take France. André fumed, and replied angrily:

"Just you try! . . . Swine, you haven't even guts enough to muzzle your Emperor and shake off the yoke, in spite of your thrice-blessed Socialist Party, with its four hundred thousand members and its three million electors. We'll do it for you! Take us? We'll take you. . . ."

And as they were held on and on in suspense, they grew restless and feverish. André was in torment. He knew that his faith was true, and yet he could not defend it! He felt that he was infected by the moral epidemic which spreads among the people of a nation the collective insanity of their ideas, the terrible spirit of war! It attacked everybody about Christophe, and even Christophe himself. They were no longer on speaking terms, and kept themselves to themselves.

But it was impossible to endure such suspense for long. The wind of action willy-nilly sifted the waverers into one group or another. And one day, when it seemed that they must be on the eve of the ultimatum,—when, in both countries, the springs of action were taut, ready for slaughter, Christophe saw that everybody, including the people in his own house, had made up their minds. Every kind of party was instinctively rallied round the detested or despised Government which represented France. Not only the honest men of the various parties: but the esthetes, the masters of depraved art, took to interpolating professions of patriotic faith in their work. The Jews were talking of defending the soil of their ancestors. At the mere mention of the flag tears came to Hamilton's eyes. And they were all sincere: they were all victims of the contagion. André Elsberger and his syndicalist friends, just as much as the rest, and even more: for, being crushed by necessity and pledged to a party that they detested, they submitted with a grim fury and a stormy pessimism which made them crazy for action. Aubert, the artisan, torn between his cultivated humanitarian ism and his instinctive chauvinism, was almost beside himself. After many sleepless nights he had at last found a formula which could accommodate everything: that France was synonymous with Humanity. Thereafter he never spoke to Christophe. Almost all the people in the house had closed their doors to him. Even the good Arnauds never invited him. They went on playing music and surrounding themselves with art: they tried to forget the general obsession. But they could not help thinking of it. When either of them alone happened to meet Christophe alone, he or she would shake hands warmly, but hurriedly and furtively. And if, the very same day, Christophe met them together, they would pass him by with a frigid bow. On the other hand, people who had not spoken to each other for years now rushed together. One evening Olivier beckoned to Christophe to go near the window, and, without a word, he pointed to the Elsbergers talking to Commandant Chabran in the garden below.

Christophe had no time to be surprised at such a revolution in the minds of his friends. He was too much occupied with his own mind, in which there had been an upheaval, the consequences of which he could not master. Olivier was much calmer than he, though he had much more reason to be upset. Of all Christophe's acquaintance, he seemed to be the only one to escape the contagion. Though he was oppressed by the anxious waiting for the outbreak of war, and the dread of schism at home, which he saw must happen in spite of everything, he knew the greatness of the two hostile faiths which sooner or later would come to grips: he knew also that it is the part of France to be the experimental ground in human progress, and that all new ideas need to be watered with her blood before they can come to flower. For his own part, he refused to take part in the skirmish. While the civilized nations were cutting each other's throats he was fain to repeat the device of Antigone: "*I am made for love, and not for hate.*"—For love and for understanding, which is another form of love. His fondness for Christophe was enough to make his duty plain to him. At a time when millions of human beings were on the brink of hatred, he felt that the duty and happiness of friends like himself and Christophe was to love each other, and to keep their reason uncontaminated by the general upheaval. He remembered how Goethe had refused to associate himself with the liberation movement of 1813, when hatred sent Germany to march out against France.

Christophe felt the same: and yet he was not easy in his mind. He who in a way had deserted Germany, and could not return thither, he who had been fed with the European ideas of the great Germans of the eighteenth century, so dear to his old friend Schulz, and detested the militarist and commercial spirit of New Germany, now found himself the prey of gusty passions: and he did not know whither they would lead him. He did not tell Olivier, but he spent his days in agony, longing for news. Secretly he put his affairs in order and packed his trunk. He did not reason the thing out. It was too strong for him. Olivier watched him anxiously, and guessed the struggle which was going on in his friend's mind: and he dared not question him. They felt that they were impelled to draw closer to each other than ever, and they loved each other more: but they were afraid to speak: they trembled lest they should discover some difference of thought which might come between them and divide them, as their old misunderstanding had done. Often their eyes would meet with an expression of tender anxiety, as though they were on the eve of parting for ever. And they were silent and oppressed.

But still on the roof of the house that was being built on the other side of the yard, all through those days of gloom, with the rain beating down on them, the workmen were putting the finishing touches: and Christophe's friend, the loquacious slater, laughed and shouted across:

" There! The house is finished! "

Happily, the storm passed as quickly as it had come. The chancelleries published bulletins announcing the return of fair

weather, barometrically as it were. The howling dogs of the
Press were despatched to their kennels. In a few hours the tension was relieved. It was a summer evening, and Christophe
had rushed in breathless to convey the good news to Olivier.
He was happy, and could breathe again. Olivier looked at him
with a little sad smile. And he dared not ask him the question
that lay next his heart. He said:

"Well: you have seen them all united, all these people who
could not understand each other."

"Yes," said Christophe good-humoredly, "I have seen them
united. You're such humbugs! You all cry out upon each
other, but at bottom you're all of the same mind."

"You seem to be glad of it," remarked Olivier.

"Why not? Because they were united at my expense? . . .
Bah! I'm strong enough for that. . . . Besides, it's a fine
thing to feel the mighty torrent rushing you along, and the
demons that were let loose in your hearts. . . ."

"They terrify me," said Olivier. "I would rather have
eternal solitude than have my people united at such a cost."

They relapsed into silence: and neither of them dared approach the subject which was troubling them. At last Olivier
pulled himself together, and, in a choking voice, said:

"Tell me frankly, Christophe: you were going away?"

Christophe replied:

"Yes."

Olivier was sure that he would say it. And yet his heart
ached for it. He said:

"Tell me, Christophe: could you . . . could you . . . ?"

Christophe drew his hand over his forehead and said:

"Don't let's talk of it. I don't like to think of it."

Olivier went on sorrowfully:

"You would have fought against us?"

"I don't know. I never thought about it."

"But, in your heart, you had decided?"

Christophe said:

"Yes."

" Against me? "

" Never against you. You are mine. Where I am, you are too."

" But against my country? "

" For my country."

" It is a terrible thing," said Olivier. " I love my country, as you do. I love France: but could I slay my soul for her? Could I betray my conscience for her? That would be to betray her. How could I hate, having no hatred, or, without being guilty of a lie, assume a hatred that I did not feel? The modern State was guilty of a monstrous crime—a crime which will prove its undoing—when it presumed to impose its brazen laws on the free Church of those spirits the very essence of whose being is to love and understand. Let Cæsar be Cæsar, but let him not assume the Godhead! Let him take our money and our lives: over our souls he has no rights: he shall not stain them with blood. We are in this world to give it light, not to darken it: let each man fulfil his duty! If Cæsar desires war, then let Cæsar have armies for that purpose, armies as they were in olden times, armies of men whose trade is war! I am not so foolish as to waste my time in vainly moaning and groaning in protest against force. But I am not a soldier in the army of force. I am a soldier in the army of the spirit: with thousands of other men who are my brothers-in-arms I represent France in that army. Let Cæsar conquer the world if he will! We march to the conquest of truth."

" To conquer," said Christophe, " you must vanquish, you must live. Truth is no hard dogma, secreted by the brain, like a stalactite by the walls of a cave. Truth is life. It is not to be found in your own head, but to be sought for in the hearts of others. Attach yourself to them, be one with them. Think as much as you like, but do you every day take a bath of humanity. You must live in the life of others and love and bow to destiny."

" It is our fate to be what we are. It does not depend on us whether we shall or shall not think certain things, even though they be dangerous. We have reached such a pitch of civilization that we cannot turn back."

"Yes, you have reached the farthest limit of the plateau of civilization, that dizzy height to which no nation can climb without feeling an irresistible desire to fling itself down. Religion and instinct are weakened in you. You have nothing left but intelligence. You are machines grinding out philosophy. Death comes rushing in upon you."

"Death comes to every nation: it is a matter of centuries."

"Have done with your centuries! The whole of life is a matter of days and hours. If you weren't such an infernally metaphysical lot, you'd never go shuffling over into the absolute, instead of seizing and holding the passing moment."

"What do you want? The flame burns the torch away. You can't both live and have lived, my dear Christophe."

"You must live."

"It is a great thing to have been great."

"It is only a great thing when there are still men who are alive enough and great enough to appreciate it."

"Wouldn't you much rather have been the Greeks, who are dead, than any of the people who are vegetating nowadays?"

"I'd much rather be myself, Christophe, and very much alive."

Olivier gave up the argument. It was not that he was without an answer. But it did not interest him. All through the discussion he had only been thinking of Christophe. He said, with a sigh:

"You love me less than I love you."

Christophe took his hand and pressed it tenderly:

"Dear Olivier," he said, "I love you more than my life. But you must forgive me if I do not love you more than Life, the sun of our two races. I have a horror of the night into which your false progress drags me. All your sentiments of renunciation are only the covering of the same Buddhist Nirvana. Only action is living, even when it brings death. In this world we can only choose between the devouring flame and night. In spite of the sad sweetness of dreams in the hour of twilight,

I have no desire for that peace which is the forerunner of death. The silence of infinite space terrifies me. Heap more fagots upon the fire! More! And yet more! Myself too, if needs must. I will not let the fire dwindle. If it dies down, there is an end of us, an end of everything."

"What you say is old," said Olivier; "it comes from the depths of the barbarous past."

He took down from his shelves a book of Hindoo poetry, and read the sublime apostrophe of the God Krishna:

"Arise, and fight with a resolute heart. Setting no store by pleasure or pain, or gain or loss, or victory or defeat, fight with all thy might. . . ."

Christophe snatched the book from his hands and read:

". . . I have nothing in the world to bid me toil: there is nothing that is not mine: and yet I cease not from my labor. If I did not act, without a truce and without relief, setting an example for men to follow, all men would perish. If for a moment I were to cease from my labors, I should plunge the world in chaos, and I should be the destroyer of life."

"Life," repeated Olivier,—"what is life?"

"A tragedy," said Christophe.   "Hurrah!"

The panic died down. Every one hastened to forget, with a hidden fear in their hearts. No one seemed to remember what had happened. And yet it was plain that it was still in their thoughts, from the joy with which they resumed their lives, the pleasant life from day to day, which is never truly valued until it is endangered. As usual when danger is past, they gulped it down with renewed avidity.

Christophe flung himself into creative work with tenfold vigor. He dragged Olivier after him. In reaction against their recent gloomy thoughts they had begun to collaborate in a Rabelaisian epic. It was colored by that broad materialism which follows on periods of moral stress. To the legendary heroes—Gargantua, Friar John, Panurge—Olivier had added, on Christophe's inspiration, a new character, a peasant, Jacques

Patience, simple, cunning, sly, resigned, who was the butt of
the others, putting up with it when he was thrashed and
robbed,—putting up with it when they made love to his wife,
and laid waste his fields,—tirelessly putting his house in order
and cultivating his land,—forced to follow the others to war,
bearing the burden of the baggage, coming in for all the kicks,
and still putting up with it,—waiting, laughing at the exploits
of his masters and the thrashings they gave him, and saying,
" They can't go on for ever," foreseeing their ultimate downfall,
looking out for it out of the corner of his eye, and silently
laughing at the thought of it, with his great mouth agape.
One fine day it turned out that Gargantua and Friar John
were drowned while they were away on a crusade. Patience
honestly regretted their loss, merrily took heart of grace, saved
Panurge, who was drowning also, and said:

" I know that you will go on playing your tricks on me: you
don't take me in: but I can't do without you: you drive away
the spleen, and make me laugh."

Christophe set the poem to music with great symphonic pictures, with soli and chorus, mock-heroic battles, riotous country
fairs, vocal buffooneries, madrigals à la Jannequin, with tremendous childlike glee, a storm at sea, the Island of Bells, and,
finally, a pastoral symphony, full of the air of the fields, and the
blithe serenity of the flutes and oboes, and the clean-souled folk-
songs of Old France.—The friends worked away with boundless delight. The weakly Olivier, with his pale cheeks, found
new health in Christophe's health. Gusts of wind blew through
their garret. The very intoxication of Joy! To be working
together, heart to heart with one's friend! The embrace of
two lovers is not sweeter or more ardent than such a yoking
together of two kindred souls. They were so near in sympathy
that often the same ideas would flash upon them at the same
moment. Or Christophe would write the music for a scene for
which Olivier would immediately find words. Christophe im-
petuously dragged Olivier along in his wake. His mind
swamped that of his friend, and made it fruitful.

The joy of creation was enhanced by that of success. Hecht had just made up his mind to publish the *David:* and the score, well launched, had had an instantaneous success abroad. A great Wagnerian *Kapellmeister,* a friend of Hecht's, who had settled in England, was enthusiastic about it: he had given it at several of his concerts with considerable success, which, with the *Kapellmeister's* enthusiasm, had carried it over to Germany, where also the *David* had been played. The *Kapellmeister* had entered into correspondence with Christophe, and had asked him for more of his compositions, offered to do anything he could to help him, and was engaged in ardent propaganda in his cause. In Germany, the *Iphigenia,* which had originally been hissed, was unearthed, and it was hailed as a work of genius. Certain facts in Christophe's life, being of a romantic nature, contributed not a little to the spurring of public interest. The *Frankfurter Zeitung* was the first to publish an enthusiastic article. Others followed. Then, in France, a few people began to be aware that they had a great musician in their midst. One of the Parisian conductors asked Christophe for his Rabelaisian epic before it was finished: and Goujart, perceiving his approaching fame, began to speak mysteriously of a friend of his who was a genius, and had been discovered by himself. He wrote a laudatory article about the admirable *David,*—entirely forgetting that only the year before he had decried it in a short notice of a few lines. Nobody else remembered it either or seemed to be in the least astonished at his sudden change. There are so many people in Paris who are now loud in their praises of Wagner and César Franck, where formerly they roundly abused them, and actually use the fame of these men to crush those new artists whom to-morrow they will be lauding to the skies!

Christophe did not set any great store on his success. He knew that he would one day win through: but he had not thought that the day could be so near at hand: and he was distrustful of so rapid a triumph. He shrugged his shoulders, and said that he wanted to be left alone. He could have under-

stood people applauding the *David* the year before, when he
wrote it: but now he was so far beyond it; he had climbed higher.
He was inclined to say to the people who came and talked about
his old work:

"Don't worry me with that stuff. It disgusts me. So do you."

And he plunged into his new work again, rather annoyed at
having been disturbed. However, he did feel a certain secret
satisfaction. The first rays of the light of fame are very
sweet. It is good, it is healthy, to conquer. It is like the open
window and the first sweet scents of the spring coming into a
house.—Christophe's contempt for his old work was of no avail,
especially with regard to the *Iphigenia:* there was a certain
amount of atonement for him in seeing that unhappy production, which had originally brought him only humiliation, belauded by the German critics, and in great request with the
theaters, as he learned from a letter from Dresden, in which
the directors stated that they would be glad to produce the piece
during their next season.

The very day when Christophe received the news, which, after
years of struggling, at last opened up a calmer horizon, with
victory in the distance, he had another letter from Germany.

It was in the afternoon. He was washing his face and talking
gaily to Olivier in the next room, when the housekeeper slipped
an envelope under the door. His mother's writing. . . . He
had been just on the point of writing to her, and was happy at
the thought of being able to tell her of his success, which
would give her so much pleasure. He opened the letter. There
were only a few lines. How shaky the writing was!

*"My dear boy, I am not very well. If it were possible, I
should like to see you again. Love.*
                                "MOTHER."

Christophe gave a groan. Olivier, who was working in the
next room, ran to him in alarm. Christophe could not speak,
and pointed to the letter on the table. He went on groaning.

and did not listen to what Olivier said, who took in the letter at a glance, and tried to comfort him. He rushed to his bed, where he had laid his coat, dressed hurriedly, and without waiting to fasten his collar,—(his hands were trembling too much)— went out. Olivier caught him up on the stairs: what was he going to do? Go by the first train? There wasn't one until the evening. It was much better to wait there than at the station. Had he enough money?—They rummaged through their pockets, and when they counted all that they possessed between them, it only amounted to thirty francs. It was September. Hecht, the Arnauds, all their friends, were out of Paris. They had no one to turn to. Christophe was beside himself, and talked of going part of the way on foot. Olivier begged him to wait for an hour, and promised to procure the money somehow. Christophe submitted: he was incapable of a single idea himself. Olivier ran to the pawnshop: it was the first time he had been there: for his own sake, he would much rather have been left with nothing than pledge any of his possessions, which were all associated with some precious memory: but it was for Christophe, and there was no time to lose. He pawned his watch, for which he was advanced a sum much smaller than he had expected. He had to go home again and fetch some of his books, and take them to a bookseller. It was a great grief to him, but at the time he hardly thought of it: his mind could grasp nothing but Christophe's trouble. He returned, and found Christophe just where he had left him, sitting by his desk, in a state of collapse. With their thirty francs the sum that Olivier had collected was more than enough. Christophe was too upset to think of asking his friend how he had come by it, or whether he had kept enough to live on during his absence. Olivier did not think of it either: he had given Christophe all he possessed. He had to look after Christophe, just like a child, until it was time for him to go. He took him to the station, and never left him until the train began to move.

In the darkness into which he was rushing Christophe sat wide-eyed, staring straight in front of him and thinking:

" Shall I be in time? "

He knew that his mother must have been unable to wait for her to write to him. And in his fevered anxiety he was impatient of the jolting speed of the express. He reproached himself bitterly for having left Louisa. And at the same time he felt how vain were his reproaches: he had no power to change the course of events.

However, the monotonous rocking of the wheels and springs of the carriage soothed him gradually, and took possession of his mind, like tossing waves of music dammed back by a mighty rhythm. He lived through all his past life again from the far-distant days of his childhood: loves, hopes, disillusion, sorrows, —and that exultant force, that intoxication of suffering, enjoying, and creating, that delight in blotting out the light of life and its sublime shadows, which was the soul of his soul, the living breath of the God within him. Now as he looked back on it all was clear. His tumultuous desires, his uneasy thoughts, his faults, mistakes, and headlong struggles, now seemed to him to be the eddy and swirl borne on by the great current of life towards its eternal goal. He discovered the profound meaning of those years of trial: each test was a barrier which was burst by the gathering waters of the river, a passage from a narrow to a wider valley, which the river would soon fill: always he came to a wider view and a freer air. Between the rising ground of France and the German plain the river had carved its way, not without many a struggle, flooding the meadows, eating away the base of the hills, gathering and absorbing all the waters of the two countries. So it flowed between them, not to divide, but to unite them: in it they were wedded. And for the first time Christophe became conscious of his destiny, which was to carry through the hostile peoples, like an artery, all the forces of life of the two sides of the river.—A strange serenity, a sudden calm and clarity, came over him, as sometimes happens in the darkest hours. . . . Then the vision faded, and he saw nothing but the tender, sorrowful face of his old mother.

It was hardly dawn when he reached the little German town. He had to take care not to be recognized, for there was still a warrant of arrest out against him. But nobody at the station took any notice of him: the town was asleep: the houses were shut up and the streets deserted: it was the gray hour when the lights of the night are put out and the light of day is not yet come,—the hour when sleep is sweetest and dreams are lit with the pale light of the east. A little servant-girl was taking down the shutters of a shop and singing an old German folk-song. Christophe almost choked with emotion. O Fatherland! Beloved! . . . He was fain to kiss the earth as he heard the humble song that set his heart aching in his breast; he felt how unhappy he had been away from his country, and how much he loved it. . . . He walked on, holding his breath. When he saw his old home he was obliged to stop and put his hand to his lips to keep himself from crying out. How would he find his mother, his mother whom he had deserted? . . . He took a long breath and almost ran to the door. It was ajar. He pushed it open. No one there. . . . The old wooden stair-case creaked under his footsteps. He went up to the top floor. The house seemed to be empty. The door of his mother's room was shut.

Christophe's heart thumped as he laid his hand on the door-knob. And he had not the strength to open it. . . .

Louisa was alone, in bed, feeling that the end was near. Of her two other sons, Rodolphe, the business man, had settled in Hamburg, the other, Ernest, had emigrated to America, and no one knew what had become of him. There was no one to attend to her except a woman in the house, who came twice a day to see if Louisa wanted anything, stayed for a few minutes, and then went about her business: she was not very punctual, and was often late in coming. To Louisa it seemed quite natural that she should be forgotten, as it seemed to her quite natural to be ill. She was used to suffering, and was as patient as an angel. She had heart disease and palpitations, during which

she would think she was going to die: she would lie with her eyes
wide open, and her hands clutching the bedclothes, and the sweat
dripping down her face. She never complained. She knew
that it must be so. She was ready: she had already received
the sacrament. She had only one anxiety: lest God should find
her unworthy to enter into Paradise. She endured everything
else in patience.

In a dark corner of her little room, near her pillow, on the
wall of the recess, she had made a little shrine for her relics and
trophies: she had collected the portraits of those who were dear
to her: her three children, her husband, for whose memory
she had always preserved her love in its first freshness, the old
grandfather, and her brother, Gottfried: she was touchingly devoted to all those who had been kind to her, though it were never
so little. On her coverlet, close to her eyes, she had pinned
the last photograph of himself that Christophe had sent her: and
his last letters were under her pillow. She had a love of neatness and scrupulous tidiness, and it hurt her to know that
everything was not perfectly in order in her room. She listened
for the little noises outside which marked the different moments
of the day for her. It was so long since she had first heard
them! All her life had been spent in that narrow space. . . .
She thought of her dear Christophe. How she longed for him
to be there, near her, just then! And yet she was resigned even
to his absence. She was sure that she would see him again on
high. She had only to close her eyes to see him. She spent
days and days, half-unconscious, living in the past. . . .

She would see once more the old house on the banks of the
Rhine. . . . A holiday. . . . A superb summer day. The
window was open: the white road lay gleaming under the sun.
They could hear the birds singing. Melchior and the old grandfather were sitting by the front-door smoking, and chatting
and laughing uproariously. Louisa could not see them: but she
was glad that her husband was at home that day, and that grandfather was in such a good temper. She was in the basement,
cooking the dinner: an excellent dinner: she watched over it as

the apple of her eye: there was a surprise: a chestnut cake. already she could hear the boy's shout of delight. . . . The boy, where was he? Upstairs: she could hear him practising at the piano. She could not make out what he was playing, but she was glad to hear the familiar tinkling sounds, and to know that he was sitting there with his grave face. . . . What a lovely day! The merry jingling bells of a carriage went by on the road. . . . Oh! good heavens! The joint! Perhaps it had been burned while she was looking out of the window! She trembled lest grandfather, of whom she was so fond, though she was afraid of him, should be dissatisfied, and scold her. . . . Thank Heaven! there was no harm done. There, everything was ready, and the table was laid. She called Melchior and grandfather. They replied eagerly. And the boy? . . . He had stopped playing. His music had ceased a moment ago without her noticing it. . . .—" Christophe!" . . . What was he doing? There was not a sound to be heard. He was always forgetting to come down to dinner: father was going to scold him. She ran upstairs. . . .— " Christophe!" . . . He made no sound. She opened the door of the room where he was practising. No one there. The room was empty, and the piano was closed. . . . Louisa was seized with a sudden panic. What had become of him? The window was open. Oh, Heaven! Perhaps he had fallen out! Louisa's heart stops. She leans out and looks down. . . .— " Christophe!" . . . He is nowhere to be found. She rushes all over the house. Downstairs grandfather shouts to her: " Come along; don't worry; he'll come back." She will not go down: she knows that he is there: that he is hiding for fun, to tease her. Oh, naughty, naughty boy! . . . Yes, she is sure of it now: she heard the floor creak: he is behind the door. She tries to open the door. But the key is gone. The key! She rummages through a drawer, looking for it in a heap of keys. This one, that. . . . No, not that. . . . Ah, that's it! . . . She cannot fit it into the lock, her hand is trembling so. She is in such haste: she must be quick. Why?

She does not know, but she knows that she must be quick, and that if she doesn't hurry she will be too late. She hears Christophe breathing on the other side of the door. . . . Oh, bother the key! . . . At last! The door is opened. A cry of joy. It is he. He flings his arms round her neck. . . . Oh, naughty, naughty, good, darling boy! . . .

She has opened her eyes. He is there, standing by her.

For some time he had been standing looking at her; so changed she was, with her face both drawn and swollen, and her mute suffering made her smile of recognition so infinitely touching: and the silence, and her utter loneliness. . . . It rent his heart. . . .

She saw him. She was not surprised. She smiled all that she could not say, a smile of boundless tenderness. She could not hold out her arms to him, nor utter a single word. He flung his arms round her neck and kissed her, and she kissed him: great tears were trickling down her cheeks. She said in a whisper:

" Wait. . . ."

He saw that she could not breathe.

Neither stirred. She stroked his head with her hands, and her tears went on trickling down her cheeks. He kissed her hands and sobbed, with his face hidden in the coverlet.

When her attack had passed she tried to speak. But she could not find words: she floundered, and he could hardly understand her. But what did it matter? They loved each other, and were together, and could touch each other: that was the main thing.—He asked indignantly why she was left alone. She made excuses for her nurse:

" She cannot always be here: she has her work·to do. . . ."

In a faint, broken voice,—she could hardly pronounce her words,—she made a little hurried request about her burial. She told Christophe to give her love to her two other sons who had forgotten her. And she sent a message to Olivier, knowing his love for Christophe. She begged Christophe to tell him that she sent him her blessing—(and then, timidly, she recol-

lected herself, and made use of a more humble expression),—
" her affectionate respects. . . ."

Once more she choked. He helped her to sit up in her bed.
The sweat dripped down her face. She forced herself to smile.
She told herself that she had nothing more to wish for in the
world, now that she had her son's hand clasped in hers.

And suddenly Christophe felt her hand stiffen in his. Louisa
opened her lips. She looked at her son with infinite tenderness :—so the end came.

III

In the evening of the same day Olivier arrived. He had
been unable to bear the thought of leaving Christophe alone in
those tragic hours of which he had had only too much experience. He was fearful also of the risks his friend was running in
returning to Germany. He wanted to be with him, to look after
him. But he had no money for the journey. When he returned
from seeing Christophe off he made up his mind to sell the few
family jewels that he had left: and as the pawnshop was closed
at that hour, and he wanted to go by the next train, he was
just going out to look for a broker's shop in the neighborhood
when he met Mooch on the stairs. When the little Jew heard
what he was about he was genuinely sorry that Olivier had not
come to him: he would not let Olivier go to the broker's, and
made him accept the necessary money from himself. He was
really hurt to think that Olivier had pawned his watch and sold
his books to pay Christophe's fare, when he would have been
only too glad to help them. In his zeal for doing them a service
he even proposed to accompany Olivier to Christophe's home,
and Olivier had great difficulty in dissuading him.

Olivier's arrival was a great boon to Christophe. He had
spent the day, prostrated with grief, alone by his mother's body.
The nurse had come, performed certain offices, and then had
gone away and had never come back. The hours had passed

in the stillness of death. Christophe sat there, as still as the body: he never took his eyes from his mother's face: he did not weep, he did not think, he was himself as one dead.— Olivier's wonderful act of friendship brought him back to tears and life.

> *" Getrost! Es ist der Schmerzen werth dies haben,*
> *So lang . . . mit uns ein treues Auge weint."*

(" Courage! Life is worth all its suffering as long as there are faithful friends to weep with us.")

They clasped each other in a long embrace, and then sat by the dead woman's side and talked in whispers. Night had fallen. Christophe, with his arms on the foot of the bed, told random tales of his childhood's memories, in which his mother's image ever recurred. He would pause every now and then for a few minutes, and then go on again, until there came a pause when he stopped altogether, and his face dropped into his hands: he was utterly worn out: and when Olivier went up to him, he saw that he was asleep. Then he kept watch alone. And presently he, too, was overcome by sleep, with his head leaning against the back of the bed. There was a soft smile on Louisa's face, and she seemed happy to be watching over her two children.

In the early hours of the morning they were awakened by a knocking at the door. Christophe opened it. It was a neighbor, a joiner, who had come to warn Christophe that his presence in the town had been denounced, and that he must go, if he did not wish to be arrested. Christophe refused to fly: he would not leave his mother before he had taken her to her last resting-place. But Olivier begged him to go, and promised that he would faithfully watch over her in his stead: he induced him to leave the house: and, to make sure of his not going back on his decision, went with him to the station. Christophe refused point-blank to go without having a sight of the great river, by which he had spent his childhood, the mighty echo of

which was preserved for ever within his soul as in a sea-shell.
Though it was dangerous for him to be seen in the town, yet
for his whim he disregarded it. They walked along the steep
bank of the Rhine, which was rushing along in its mighty peace,
between its low banks, on to its mysterious death in the sands of
the North. A great iron bridge, looming in the mist, plunged
its two arches, like the halves of the wheels of a colossal chariot,
into the gray waters. In the distance, fading into the mist,
were ships sailing through the meadows along the river's windings. It was like a dream, and Christophe was lost in it.
Olivier brought him back to his senses, and, taking his arm,
led him back to the station. Christophe submitted : he was like
a man walking in his sleep. Olivier put him into the train as it
was just starting, and they arranged to meet next day at the
first French station, so that Christophe should not have to go
back to Paris alone.

The train went, and Olivier returned to the house, where
he found two policemen stationed at the door, waiting for Christophe to come back. They took Olivier for him, and Olivier
did not hurry to explain a mistake so favorable to Christophe's
chances of escape. On the other hand, the police were not in
the least discomfited by their blunder, and showed no great
zest in pursuing the fugitive, and Olivier had an inkling that
at bottom they were not at all sorry that Christophe had gone.

Olivier stayed until the next morning, when Louisa was
buried. Christophe's brother, Rodolphe, the business man, came
by one train and left by the next. That important personage
followed the funeral very correctly, and went immediately it
was over, without addressing a single word to Olivier, either to
ask him for news of his brother or to thank him for what he had
done for their mother. Olivier spent a few hours more in the
town, where he did not know a soul, though it was peopled
for him with so many familiar shadows : the boy Christophe,
those whom he had loved, and those who had made him suffer ;
—and dear Antoinette. . . . What was there left of all those
human beings, who had lived in the town, the family of the

Krafft's, that now had ceased to be? Only the love for them that lived in the heart of a stranger.

In the afternoon Olivier met Christophe at the frontier station as they had arranged. It was a village nestling among wooded hills. Instead of waiting for the next train to Paris, they decided to go part of the way on foot, as far as the nearest town. They wanted to be alone. They set out through the silent woods, through which from a distance there resounded the dull thud of an ax. They reached a clearing at the top of a hill. Below them, in a narrow valley, in German territory, there lay the red roof of a forester's house, and a little meadow like a green lake amid the trees. All around there stretched the dark-blue sea of the forest wrapped in cloud. Mists hovered and drifted among the branches of the pines. A transparent veil softened the lines and blurred the colors of the trees. All was still. Neither footsteps nor voices were to be heard. A few drops of rain rang out on the golden copper leaves of the beeches, which had turned to autumn tints. A little stream ran tinkling over the stones. Christophe and Olivier stood still and did not stir. Each was dreaming of those whom he had lost. Olivier was thinking:

" Antoinette, where are you? "

And Christophe:

" What is success to me, now that she is dead? "

But each heard the comforting words of the dead:

" Beloved, weep not for us. Think not of us. Think of Him. . . ."

They looked at each other, and each ceased to feel his own sorrow, and was conscious only of that of his friend. They clasped their hands. In both there was sad serenity. Gently, while no wind stirred, the misty veil was raised: the blue sky shone forth again. The melting sweetness of the earth after rain. . . . So near to us, so tender! . . . The earth takes us in her arms, clasps us to her bosom with a lovely loving smile, and says to us:

" Rest.   All is well. . . ."

The ache in Christophe's heart was gone. He was like a little child. For two days he had been living wholly in the memory of his mother, the atmosphere of her soul: he had lived over again her humble life, with its days one like unto another, solitary, all spent in the silence of the childless house, in the thought of the children who had left her: the poor old woman, infirm but valiant in her tranquil faith, her sweetness of temper, her smiling resignation, her complete lack of selfishness. . . . And Christophe thought also of all the humble creatures he had known. How near to them he felt in that moment! After all the years of exhausting struggle in the burning heat of Paris, where ideas and men jostle in the whirl of confusion, after those tragic days when there had passed over them the wind of the madness which hurls the nations, cozened by their own hallucinations, murderously against each other, Christophe felt utterly weary of the fevered, sterile world, the conflict between egoisms and ideas, the little groups of human beings deeming themselves above humanity, the ambitious, the thinkers, the artists who think themselves the brain of the world, and are no more than a haunting evil dream. And all his love went out to those thousands of simple souls, of every nation, whose lives burn away in silence, pure flames of kindness, faith, and sacrifice,—the heart of the world.

" Yes," he thought, " I know you; once more I have come to you; you are blood of my blood; you are mine. Like the prodigal son, I left you to pursue the shadows that passed by the wayside. But I have come back to you; give me welcome. We are one; one life is ours, both the living and the dead; where I am there are you also. Now I bear you in my soul, O mother, who bore me. You, too, Gottfried, and you Schulz, and Sabine, and Antoinette, you are all in me, part of me, mine. You are my riches, my joy. We will take the road together. I will never more leave you. I will be your voice. We will join forces: so we shall attain the goal."

A ray of sunlight shot through the dripping branches of the

trees. From the little field down below there came up the voices of children singing an Old German folk-song, frank and moving: the singers were three little girls dancing round the house: and from afar the west wind brought the chiming of the bells of France, like a perfume of roses. . . .

"O peace, Divine harmony, serene music of the soul set free, wherein are mingled joy and sorrow, death and life, the nations at war, and the nations in brotherhood. I love you, I long for you, I shall win you. . . ."

The night drew down her veil. Starting from his dream, Christophe saw the faithful face of his friend by his side. He smiled at him and embraced him. Then they walked on through the forest in silence: and Christophe showed Olivier the way.

> "*Taciti, soli e senza compagnia,*
> *N'andavan l' un dinnanzi, e l' altro dopo,*
> *Come i frati minor vanno per via. . .*

BOOK III

LOVE AND FRIENDSHIP

JEAN-CHRISTOPHE

JOURNEY'S END

I

IN spite of the success which was beginning to materialize outside France, the two friends found their financial position very slow in mending. Every now and then there recurred moments of penury when they were obliged to go without food. They made up for it by eating twice as much as they needed when they had money. But, on the whole, it was a trying existence.

For the time being they were in the period of the lean kine. Christophe had stayed up half the night to finish a dull piece of musical transcription for Hecht: he did not get to bed until dawn, and slept like a log to make up for lost time. Olivier had gone out early: he had a lecture to give at the other end of Paris. About eight o'clock the porter came with the letters, and rang the bell. As a rule he did not wait for them to come, but just slipped the letters under the door. This morning he went on knocking. Only half awake, Christophe went to the door growling: he paid no attention to what the smiling, loquacious porter was saying about an article in the paper, but just took the letters without looking at them, pushed the door to without closing it, went to bed, and was soon fast asleep once more.

An hour later he woke up with a start on hearing some one in his room: and he was amazed to see a strange face at the foot of his bed, a complete stranger bowing gravely to him. It was a journalist, who, finding the door open, had entered without ceremony. Christophe was furious, and jumped out of bed:

"What the devil are you doing here?" he shouted.

He grabbed his pillow to hurl it at the intruder, who skipped back. He explained himself. A reporter of the *Nation* wished to interview M. Krafft about the article which had appeared in the *Grand Journal*.

"What article?"

"Haven't you read it?"

The reporter began to tell him what it was about.

Christophe went to bed again. If he had not been so sleepy he would have kicked the fellow out: but it was less trouble to let him talk. He curled himself up in the bed, closed his eyes, and pretended to be asleep. And very soon he would really have been off, but the reporter stuck to his guns, and in a loud voice read the beginning of the article. At the very first words Christophe pricked up his ears. M. Krafft was referred to as the greatest musical genius of the age. Christophe forgot that he was pretending to be asleep, swore in astonishment, sat up in bed, and said:

"They are mad! Who has been pulling their legs?"

The reporter seized the opportunity, and stopped reading to ply Christophe with a series of questions, which he answered unthinkingly. He had picked up the paper, and was gazing in utter amazement at his own portrait, which was printed as large as life on the front page: but he had no time to read the article, for another journalist entered the room. This time Christophe was really angry. He told them to get out: but they did not comply until they had made hurried notes of the furniture in the room, and the photographs on the wall, and the features of the strange being who, between laughter and anger, thrust them out of the room, and, in his nightgown, took them to the door and bolted it after them.

But it was ordained that he should not be left in peace that day. He had not finished dressing when there came another knock at the door, a prearranged knock which was only known to a few of their friends. Christophe opened the door, and found himself face to face with yet another stranger, whom he was just about to dismiss in a summary fashion, when the man protested that he was the author of the article. . . . How are you to get rid of a man who regards you as a genius! Christophe had grumpily to submit to his admirer's effusions. He was amazed at the sudden notoriety which had come like a bolt from the blue, and he wondered if, without knowing it, he had had a masterpiece produced the evening before. But he had no time to find out. The journalist had come to drag him, whether he liked it or not, there and then, to the offices of the paper where the editor, the great Arsène Gamache himself, wished to see him: the car was waiting downstairs. Christophe tried to get out of it: but, in spite of himself, he was so naïvely responsive to the journalist's friendly protestations that in the end he gave way.

Ten minutes later he was introduced to a potentate in whose presence all men trembled. He was a sturdy little man, about fifty, short and stout, with a big round head, gray hair brushed up, a red face, a masterful way of speaking, a thick, affected accent, and every now and then he would break out into a choppy sort of volubility. He had forced himself on Paris by his enormous self-confidence. A business man, with a knowledge of men, naïve and deep, passionate, full of himself, he identified his business with the business of France, and even with the affairs of humanity. His own interests, the prosperity of his paper, and the *salus publica,* all seemed to him to be of equal importance and to be narrowly associated. He had no doubt that any man who wronged him, wronged France also: and to crush an adversary, he would in perfectly good faith have overthrown the Government. However, he was by no means incapable of generosity. He was an idealist of the after-dinner order, and loved to be a sort of God Almighty, and to lift some poor devil or other out of the mire, by way of demonstrating the greatness of his power, whereby he could make something out of nothing, make and unmake Ministers, and, if he had cared to, make and unmake Kings. His sphere was the universe. He would make men of genius, too, if it so pleased him.

That day he had just "made" Christophe.

It was Olivier who in all innocence had belled the cat.

Olivier, who could do nothing to advance his own interests, and had a horror of notoriety, and avoided journalists like the plague, took quite another view of these things where his friend was in question. He was like those loving mothers, the right-living women of the middle-class, those irreproachable wives, who would sell themselves to procure any advantage for their rascally young sons.

Writing for the reviews, and finding himself in touch with a number of critics and dilettanti, Olivier never let slip an opportunity of talking about Christophe: and for some time past he had been surprised to find that they listened to him. He could feel a sort of current of curiosity, a mysterious rumor flying about literary and polite circles. What was its origin? Were there echoes of newspaper opinion, following on the recent performances of Christophe's work in England and Germany? It seemed impossible to trace it to any definite source. It was one of those frequent phenomena of those men who sniff the air of Paris, and can tell the day before, more exactly than the meteorological observatory of the tower of Saint-Jacques, what wind is blowing up for the morrow, and what it will bring with it. In that great city of nerves, through which electric vibrations pass, there are invisible currents of fame, a latent celebrity which precedes the actuality, the vague gossip of the drawing-rooms, the *nescio quid majus nascitur Iliade,* which, at a given moment, bursts out in a puffing article, the blare of the trumpet which drives the name of the new idol into the thickest heads. Sometimes that trumpet-blast alienates the first and best friends of the man whose glory it proclaims. And yet they are responsible for it.

So Olivier had a share in the article in the *Grand Journal.* He had taken advantage of the interest displayed in Christophe, and had carefully stoked it up with adroitly worded information. He had been careful not to bring Christophe directly into touch with the journalists, for he was afraid of an outburst. But at the request of the *Grand Journal* he had slyly introduced Christophe to a reporter in a café without his having any suspicion. All these precautions only pricked curiosity, and made Christophe more interesting. Olivier had never had anything to do with publicity before: he had not stopped to consider that he was setting in motion a machine which, once it got going, it was impossible to direct or control.

He was in despair when, on his way to his lecture, he read the article in the *Grand Journal.* He had not foreseen such a calamity. Above all, he had not expected it to come so soon.

He had reckoned on the paper waiting to make sure and verify its facts before it published anything. He was too naïve. If a newspaper takes the trouble to discover a new celebrity, it is, of course, for its own sake, so that its rivals may not have the honor of the discovery. It must lose no time, even if it means knowing nothing whatever about the person in question. But an author very rarely complains: if he is admired, he has quite as much understanding as he wants.

The *Grand Journal,* after setting out a few ridiculous stories about Christophe's struggles, representing him as a victim of German despotism, an apostle of liberty, forced to fly from Imperial Germany and take refuge in France, the home and shelter of free men,—(a fine pretext for a Chauvinesque tirade!) —plunged into lumbering praise of his genius, of which it knew nothing,—nothing except a few tame melodies, dating from Christophe's early days in Germany, which Christophe, who was ashamed of them, would have liked to have seen destroyed. But if the author of the article knew nothing at all about Christophe's work, he made up for it in his knowledge of his plans—or rather such plans as he invented for him. A few words let fall by Christophe or Olivier, or even by Goujart, who pretended to be well-informed, had been enough for him to construct a fanciful Jean-Christophe, "a Republican genius,—the great musician of democracy." He seized the opportunity to decry various contemporary French musicians, especially the most original and independent among them, who set very little store by democracy. He only excepted one or two composers, whose electoral opinions were excellent in his eyes. It was annoying that their music was not better. But that was a detail. And besides, his eulogy of these men, and even his praise of Christophe, was of not nearly so much account as his criticism of the rest. In Paris, when you read an article eulogizing a man's work, it is always as well to ask yourself:

"Whom is he decrying?"

Olivier went hot with shame as he read the paper, and said to himself:

"A fine thing I've done!"

He could hardly get through his lecture. As soon as he had finished he hurried home. What was his consternation to find that Christophe had already gone out with the journalists! He delayed lunch for him. Christophe did not return. Hours passed, and Olivier grew more and more anxious and thought: "What a lot of foolish things they will make him say!"

About three o'clock Christophe came home quite lively. He had had lunch with Arsène Gamache, and his head was a little muzzy with the champagne he had drunk. He could not understand Olivier's anxiety, who asked him in fear and trembling what he had said and done.

"What have I been doing? I've had a splendid lunch. I haven't had such a good feed for a long time."

He began to recount the menu.

"And wine. . . . I had wine of every color."

Olivier interrupted him to ask who was there.

"Who was there? . . . I don't know. There was Gamache, a little round man, true as gold: Clodomir, the writer of the article, a charming fellow: three or four journalists whom I didn't know, very jolly, all very nice and charming to me—the cream of good fellows."

Olivier did not seem to be convinced. Christophe was astonished at his small enthusiasm.

"Haven't you read the article?"

"Yes. I have. Have you read it?"

"Yes. . . . That is to say, I just glanced at it. I haven't had time."

"Well: read it."

Christophe took it up. At the first words he spluttered.

"Oh! The idiot!" he said.

He roared with laughter.

"Bah!" he went on. "These critics are all alike. They know nothing at all about it."

But as he read farther he began to lose his temper: it was too stupid, it made him look ridiculous. What did they mean by calling him "a Republican musician"; it did not mean anything. . . . Well, let the fib pass. . . . But when they set his "Republican" art against the "sacristy art" of the masters who had preceded him,—(he whose soul was nourished by the souls of those great men),—it was too much. . . .

"The swine! They're trying to make me out an idiot! . . ."

And then, what was the sense of using him as a cudgel to thwack talented French musicians, whom he loved more or less, —(though rather less than more),—though they knew their trade, and honored it? And—worst of all—with an incredible want of tact he was credited with odious sentiments about his country! . . . No, that, that was beyond endurance. . . .

"I shall write and tell them so," said Christophe.

Olivier intervened.

"No, no," he said, "not now! You are too excited. To-morrow, when you are cooler. . . ."

Christophe stuck to it. When he had anything to say he could not wait until the morrow. He promised Olivier to show him his letter. The precaution was useful. The letter was duly revised, so as to be confined practically to the rectification of the opinions about Germany with which he had been credited, and then Christophe ran and posted it.

"Well," he said, when he returned, "that will save half the harm being done: the letter will appear to-morrow."

Olivier shook his head doubtfully. He was still thoughtful, and he looked Christophe straight in the face, and said:

"Christophe, did you say anything imprudent at lunch?"

"Oh no," said Christophe with a laugh.

"Sure?"

"Yes, you coward."

Olivier was somewhat reassured. But Christophe was not. He had just remembered that he had talked volubly and un-guardedly. He had been quite at his ease at once. It had never for a moment occurred to him to distrust any of them: they seemed so cordial, so well-disposed towards him! As, in fact, they were. We are always well-disposed to people when we have done them a good turn, and Christophe was so frankly delighted with it all that his joy infected them. His affection-ate easy manners, his jovial sallies, his enormous appetite, and the celerity with which the various liquors vanished down his throat without making him turn a hair, were by no means displeasing to Arsène Gamache, who was himself a sturdy trencherman, coarse, boorish, and sanguine, and very contemptu-ous of people who had ill-health, and those who dared not eat and drink, and all the sickly Parisians. He judged a man by his prowess at table. He appreciated Christophe. There and then he proposed to produce his *Gargantua* as an opera at the Opéra.—(The very summit of art was reached for these bourgeois French people in the production on the stage of the *Damnation of Faust,* or the *Nine Symphonies.*)—Christophe, who burst out laughing at the grotesqueness of the idea, had great difficulty in preventing him from telephoning his orders to the directors of the Opéra, or the Minister of Fine Arts.— (If Gamache were to be believed, all these important people were apparently at his beck and call.)—And, the proposal reminding him of the strange transmutation which had taken place in his symphonic poem, *David,* he went so far as to tell the story of the performance organized by Deputy Roussin to introduce his mistress to the public. Gamache, who did not like Roussin, was delighted: and Christophe, spurred on by the generous wines and the sympathy of his hearers, plunged into other stories, more or less indiscreet, the point of which was not lost on those present. Christophe was the only one to forget them when the party broke up. And now, on Olivier's question, they rushed back to his memory. He felt a little shiver run down his spine. For he did not deceive himself: he had enough experience to know what would happen: now that he was sober again he saw it as clearly as though it had actually happened: his indiscretions would be twisted and distorted, and scattered broadcast as malicious blabbing, his artistic sallies would be turned into weapons of war. As for his letter correcting the article, he knew as well as Olivier how much that would avail him: it is a waste of ink to answer a journalist, for he always has the last word.

Everything happened exactly to the letter as Christophe had foreseen it would. His indiscretions were published, his letter was not. Gamache only went so far as to write to him that he recognized the generosity of his feelings, and that his scruples were an honor to him: but he kept his scruples dark: and the falsified opinions attributed to Christophe went on being circulated, provoking biting criticism in the Parisian papers, and later in Germany, where much indignation was felt that a German artist should express himself with so little dignity about his country.

Christophe thought he would be clever, and take advantage of an interview by the reporter of another paper to protest his love for the *Deutsches Reich,* where, he said, people were at least as free as in the French Republic.—He was speaking to the representative of a Conservative paper, who at once credited him with anti-Republican views.

"Better and better!" said Christophe. "But what on earth has my music to do with politics?"

"It is usual with us," said Olivier. "Look at the battles that have taken place over Beethoven. Some people will have it that he was a Jacobin, others a mountebank, others still a Père Duchesne, and others a prince's lackey."

"He'd knock their heads together."

"Well, do the same."

Christophe only wished he could. But he was too amiable with people who were friendly towards him. Olivier never felt happy when he left him alone. For they were always coming to interview him : and it was no use Christophe promising to be guarded : he could not help being confidential and unreserved. He said everything that came into his head. Women journalists would come and make a fuss of him, and get him to talk about his sentimental adventures. Others would make use of him to speak ill of such-an-one, or so-and-so. When Olivier came in he would find Christophe utterly downcast.

"Another howler?" he would ask.

"Of course," Christophe would reply in despair.

"You are incorrigible!"

"I ought to be locked up. . . . But I swear that it is the last time."

"Yes, I know. Until the next. . . ."

"No. This really is the last."

Next day Christophe said triumphantly to Olivier:

"Another one came to-day. I shut the door in his face."

"Don't go too far," said Olivier. "Be careful with them. 'This animal is dangerous.' He will attack you if you defend yourself. . . . It is so easy for them to avenge themselves! They can twist the least little thing you may have said to their uses "

Christophe drew his hand across his forehead:

" Oh ! Good Lord ! "

" What's the matter ? "

" When I shut the door in his face I told . . ."

" What ? "

" The Emperor's joke."

" The Emperor's ? "

" Yes. His or one of his people's. . . ."

" How awful ! You'll see it to-morrow on the front page ! "

Christophe shuddered. But, next day, what he saw was a description of his room, which the journalist had not seen, and a report of a conversation which he had not had with him.

The facts were more and more embellished the farther they spread. In the foreign papers they were garnished out of all recognition. Certain French articles having told how in his poverty he had transposed music for the guitar, Christophe learned from an English newspaper that he had played the guitar in the streets.

He did not only read eulogies. Far from it. It was enough for Christophe to have been taken up by the *Grand Journal,* for him to be taken to task by the other papers. They could not as a matter of dignity allow the possibility of a rival's discovering a genius whom they had ignored. Some of them were rabid about it. Others commiserated Christophe on his ill-luck. Goujart, annoyed at having the ground cut away from under his feet, wrote an article, as he said, to set people right on certain points. He wrote familiarly of his old friend Christophe, to whom, when he first came to Paris, he had been guide and comforter: he was certainly a highly gifted musician, but— (he was at liberty to say so, since they were friends)—very deficient in many ways, ill-educated, unoriginal, and inordinately vain; so absurdly to flatter his vanity, as had been done, was to serve him but ill at a time when he stood in need of a mentor who should be wise, learned, judicious, benevolent, and severe, etc.—(a fancy portrait of Goujart).—The musicians made bitter fun of it all. They affected a lofty contempt for an artist who had the newspapers at his back: and, pretending to be disgusted with the *vulgum pecus,* they refused the presents of Artaxerxes. which were not offered them. Some of them

abused Christophe: others overwhelmed him with their commiseration. Some of them—(his colleagues)—laid the blame
on Olivier.—They were only too glad to pay him out for his
intolerance and his way of holding aloof from them,—rather,
if the truth were known, from a desire for solitude than from
scorn of any of them. But men are least apt to pardon those
who show that they can do without them.—Some of them almost
went so far as to hint that he had made money by the articles
in the *Grand Journal*. There were others who took upon themselves to defend Christophe against him: they appeared to be
broken-hearted at Olivier's callousness in dragging a sensitive
artist, a dreamer, ill-equipped for the battle of life,—Christophe,
—into the turmoil of the market-place, where he could not but
be ruined: for they regarded Christophe as a little boy not
strong enough in the head to be allowed to go out alone. The
future of this man, they said, was being ruined, for, even if
he were not a genius, such good intentions and such tremendous
industry deserved a better fate, and he was being intoxicated
with incense of an inferior brand. It was a great pity. Why
could they not leave him in his obscurity to go on working
patiently for years?

Olivier might have had the answer pat:

"A man must eat to work. Who will give him his bread?"

But that would not have abashed them. They would have
replied with their magnificent serenity:

"That is a detail. An artist must suffer. And what does
a little suffering matter?"

Of course, they were men of the world, quite well off, who
professed these Stoic theories. As the millionaire once said to
the simple person who came and asked him to help a poverty-
stricken artist:

"But, sir, Mozart died of poverty."

They would have thought it very bad taste on Olivier's part
if he had told them that Mozart would have asked nothing
better than to go on living, and that Christophe was determined
to do so.

Christophe was getting heartily sick of the vulgar tittle-tattle.
He began to wonder if it were going on forever.—But it was all

over in a fortnight. The newspapers gave up talking about him. However, he had become known. When his name was mentioned, people said, not:

" The author of *David* or *Gargantua*,"

but:

" Oh yes! The *Grand Journal* man! . . ."

He was famous.

Olivier knew it by the number of letters that came for Christophe. and even for himself, in his reflected glory: offers from librettists, proposals from concert-agents, declarations of friendship from men who had formerly been his enemies, invitations from women. His opinion was asked, for newspaper inquiries, about anything and everything: the depopulation of France, idealist art, women's corsets, the nude on the stage,— and did he believe that Germany was decadent, or that music had reached its end, etc., etc. They used to laugh at them all. But, though he laughed, lo and behold! Christophe, that Huron, steadily accepted the invitations to dinner! Olivier could not believe his eyes.

" You? " he said.

" I! Certainly," replied Christophe jeeringly. " You thought you were the only man who could go and see the beautiful ladies? Not at all, my boy! It's my turn now. I want to amuse myself! "

" You? Amuse yourself? My dear old man! "

The truth was that Christophe had for so long lived shut up in his own room that he felt a sudden longing to get away from it. Besides, he took a naïve delight in tasting his new fame. He was terribly bored at parties, and thought the people idiotic. But when he came home he used to take a malicious pleasure in telling Olivier how much he had enjoyed himself. He would go to people's houses once, but never again: he would invent the wildest excuses, with a frightful want of tact, to get out of their renewed invitations. Olivier would be scandalized, and Christophe would shout with laughter. He did not go to their houses to spread his fame, but to replenish his store of life, his collection of expressions and tones of voice—all the material of form, and sound, and color, with which an artist has periodically to enrich his palette. A musician does not

feed only on music. An inflection of the human voice, the
rhythm of a gesture, the harmony of a smile, contain more
suggestion of music for him that another man's symphony.
But it must be said that the music of faces and human souls
is as stale and lacking in variety in polite society as the music
of polite musicians. Each has a manner and becomes set in it.
The smile of a pretty woman is as stereotyped in its studied
grace as a Parisian melody. The men are even more insipid
than the women. Under the debilitating influence of society,
their energy is blunted, their original characters rot away and
finally disappear with a frightful rapidity. Christophe was
struck by the number of dead and dying men he met among
the artists: there was one young musician, full of life and
genius, whom success had dulled, stupefied, and wiped out of
existence: he thought of nothing but swallowing down the
flattery in which he was smothered, enjoying himself, and sleeping. What he would be like twenty years later was shown
in another corner of the room, in the person of an old pomaded
maestro, who was rich, famous, a member of all the Academies,
at the very height of his career, and, though apparently he had
nothing to fear and no more wires to pull, groveled before
everything and everybody, and was fearful of opinion, power,
and the Press, dared not say what he thought, and thought
nothing at all—a man who had ceased to exist, showing
himself off, an ass saddled with the relics of his own past
life.

Behind all these artists and men of intellect who had been
great, or might have been great, there was certain to be some
woman preying upon them. They were all dangerous, both
the fools and those who were by no means fools: both those
who loved and those who loved themselves: the best of them
were the worst: for they were all the more certain to snuff out
the artist with their immoderate affection, which made them in
all good faith try to domesticate genius, turn it to their own
uses, drag it down, prune it, pare it down, scent it, until they
had brought it into line with their sensibility, their petty vanity,
their mediocrity, and the mediocrity of the world they lived in.

Although Christophe only passed through that section of
society, he saw enough of it to feel its danger. More than one

woman, of course, tried to take possession of him for her circle, to press him into her service: and, of course, Christophe nibbled at the hook baited with friendly words and alluring smiles. But for his sturdy common sense and the disquieting spectacle of the transformations already effected in the men about them by these modern Circes, he would not have escaped uncontaminated. But he had no mind to swell the herd of these lovely goose-girls. The danger would have been greater for him if there had not been so many of them angling for him. Now that everybody, men and women, were properly convinced that they had a genius in their midst, as usual, they set to work to stifle him. Such people, when they see a flower, have only one idea: to put it in a pot,—a bird: to put it in a cage,— a free man: to turn him into a smooth lackey.

Christophe was shaken for a moment, pulled himself together, and sent them all packing.

Fate is ironical. Those who do not care slip through the meshes of the net: but those who are suspicious, those who are prudent, and forewarned, are never suffered to escape. It was not Christophe who was caught in the net of Paris, but Olivier.

He had benefited by his friend's success: Christophe's fame had given him a reflected glory. He was better known now, for having been mentioned in a few papers as the man who had discovered Christophe, than for anything he had written during the last six years. He was included in many of the invitations that came for Christophe: and he went with him, meaning carefully and discreetly to look after him. No doubt he was too much absorbed in doing so to look after himself. Love passed by and caught him.

She was a little fair girl, charmingly slender, with soft hair waving in little ripples about her pure narrow forehead: she had fine eyebrows and rather heavy eyelids, eyes of a periwinkle blue, a delicately carved nose with sensitive nostrils; her temples were slightly hollowed: she had a capricious chin, and a mobile, witty, and rather sensual mouth, turning up at the corners, and the *Parmigianninesque* smile of a pure faun. She had a long, delicate throat, a pretty waist, a slender, elegant figure, and a happy, pensive expression in her girlish face, in every line of which there was the disturbing poetic mystery of the waking spring,—*Frühlingserwachen.* Her name was Jacqueline Langeais.

She was not twenty. She came of a rich Catholic family, of great distinction and broad-mindedness. Her father was a clever engineer, a man of some invention, clear-headed and open to new ideas, who had made a fortune, thanks to his own hard work, his political connections, and his marriage. He had married both for love and money—(the proper marriage for love for such people)—a pretty woman, very Parisian, who was bred in the world of finance. The money had stayed: but love had gone. However, he had managed to preserve a few sparks of it, for it had been very ardent on both sides: but they did not stickle for any exaggerated notion of fidelity. They went their ways and had their pleasures: and they got on very well together, as friends, selfishly, unscrupulously, warily.

Their daughter was a bond between them, though she was the object of an unspoken rivalry between them: for they both loved her jealously. They both saw themselves in her with their pet faults idealized by the grace of childhood: and each strove cunningly to steal her from the other. And the child had in due course become conscious of it, with the artful candor of such little creatures, who are only too ready to believe that the universe gravitates round themselves: and she turned it to good account. She had them perpetually outbidding each other for her affection. She never had a whim but she was sure that one of them would indulge it if the other refused: and the other would be so vexed at being outdone that she would at once be offered an even greater indulgence than the first. She had been dreadfully spoiled: and it was very fortunate for her that there was no evil in her nature,—outside the egoism common to almost all children, though in children who are too rich and too much pampered it assumes various morbid shapes, due to the absence of difficulties and the want of any goal to aim at.

Though they adored her, neither M. nor Madame Langeais ever thought of sacrificing their own personal convenience to her. They used to leave the child alone, for the greater part

of the day, to gratify her thousand and one fancies. She had
plenty of time for dreaming, and she wasted none of it. She
was precocious and quick to grasp at incautious remarks let
fall in her presence—(for her parents were never very guarded
in what they said),—and when she was six years old she used
to tell her dolls love-stories, the characters in which were husband, wife, and lover. It goes without saying that she saw
no harm in it. Directly she began to perceive a shade of feeling
underlying the words it was all over for the dolls: she kept
her stories to herself. There was in her a strain of innocent
sensuality, which rang out in the distance like the sound of
invisible bells, over there, over there, on the other side of the
horizon. She did not know what it was. Sometimes it would
come wafted on the wind: it came she did not know from
whence, and wrapped her round and made the blood mount to
her cheeks, and she would lose her breath in the fear and
pleasure of it. She could not understand it. And then it
would disappear as strangely as it had come. There was never
another sound. Hardly more than a faint buzzing, an imperceptible resonance, fainter and fainter, in the blue air. Only
she knew that it was yonder, on the other side of the mountain,
and thither she must go, go as soon as possible: for there lay
happiness. Ah! If only she could reach it! . . .

In the meanwhile, until she should reach that land of happiness, she wove strange dreams of what she would find there.
For the chief occupation of the child's mind was guessing at
its nature. She had a friend of her own age, Simone Adam,
with whom she used often to discuss these great subjects. Each
brought to bear on them the light of her twelve years' experience,
conversations overheard and stolen reading. On tip-toe, clinging to the crannies in the stones, the two little girls strained
to peer over the old wall which hid the future from them. But
it was all in vain, and it was idle for them to pretend that
they could see through the chinks: they could see nothing at all.
They were both a mixture of innocence, poetic salaciousness,
and Parisian irony. They used to say the most outrageous things
without knowing it, and they were always making mountains
out of molehills. Jacqueline, who was always prying, without
anybody to find fault with her, used to burrow in all her

father's books. Fortunately, she was protected from coming
to any harm by her very innocence and her own young, healthy
instincts: an unduly described scene or a coarse word disgusted
her at once: she would drop the book at once, and she passed
through the most infamous company, like a frightened cat
through puddles of dirty water,—without so much as a splash.

As a rule, novels did not attract her: they were too precise,
too dry. But books of poetry used to make her heart flutter
with emotion and hope of finding the key to the riddle,—love-
poems, of course. They coincided to a certain extent with her
childish outlook on things. The poets did not see things as
they were, they imagined them through the prism of desire or
regret: they seemed, like herself, to be peering through the
chinks of the old wall. But they knew much more, they knew
all the things which she was longing to know, and clothed them
with sweet, mysterious words, which she had to unravel with
infinite care to find . . . to find . . . Ah! She could find
nothing, but she was always sure that she was on the very brink
of finding it. . . .

Their curiosity was indomitable. They would thrill as they
whispered verses of Alfred de Musset and Sully Prudhomme,
into which they read abyss on abyss of perversity: they used
to copy them out, and ask each other about the hidden meanings
of passages, which generally contained none. These little
women of thirteen, who knew nothing of love, used, in their
innocent effrontery, to discuss, half in jest, half in earnest, love
and the sweets of love: and, in school, under the fatherly eye
of the master—a very polite and mild old gentleman—verses
like the following, which he confiscated one day, when they
made him gasp:

> "Let, oh! let me clasp you in my arms,
> And in your kisses drink insensate love
> Drop by drop in one long draught. . . ."

They attended lectures at a fashionable and very prosperous
school, the teachers of which were Masters of Art of the
University. There they found material for their sentimental
aspirations. Almost all the girls were in love with their masters. If they were young and not too ugly, that was quite

enough for them to make havoc of their pupils' hearts—who would work like angels to please their sultan. And they would weep when he gave them bad marks in their examinations: though they did not care when anybody else did the same. If he praised them, they would blush and go pale by turns, and gaze at him coquettishly in gratitude. And if he called them aside to give them advice or pay them a compliment, they were in Paradise. There was no need for him to be an eagle to win their favor. When the gymnastic instructor took Jacqueline in his arms to lift her up to the trapeze, she would be in ecstasies. And what furious emulation there was between them! How coaxingly and with what humility they would make eyes at the master to attract his attention from a presumptuous rival! At lectures, when he opened his lips to speak, pens and pencils would be hastily produced to take down what he said. They made no attempt to understand: the chief thing was not to lose a syllable. And while they went on writing and writing without ceasing, with stealthy glances to take in their idol's play of expression and gestures, Jacqueline and Simone would whisper to each other:

" Do you think he would look nice in a tie with blue spots?"

Then they had a chromo-lithographic ideal, based on romantic and fashionable books of verses, and poetic fashion-plates,—they fell in love with actors, virtuosi, authors, dead and alive—Mounet-Sully, Samain, Debussy,—they would exchange glances with young men at concerts, or in a drawing-room, or in the street, and at once begin to weave fanciful and passionate love-affairs,—they could not help always wanting to fall in love, to have their lives filled with a love-affair, to find some excuse for being in love. Jacqueline and Simone used to confide everything to each other: proof positive that they did not feel anything much: it was the best sort of preventive to keep them from ever having any deep feeling. On the other hand, it became a sort of chronic illness with them: they were the first to laugh at it, but they used lovingly to cultivate it. They excited each other. Simone was more romantic and more cautious, and used to invent wilder stories. But Jacqueline, being more sincere and more ardent, came nearer to realizing them. She was twenty times on the brink of the most hopeless folly.—However, she did not commit herself, as is the way with young people. There are times when these poor little crazy creatures—(such as we have all been)—are within an ace, some of suicide, others of flinging themselves into the arms of the first man who comes along. Only, thank God, almost all of them stop short at that. Jacqueline wrote countless rough drafts of passionate letters to men whom she hardly knew by sight: but she never sent any of them, except one enthusiastic letter, unsigned, to an ugly, vulgar, selfish critic, who was as cold-hearted as he was narrow-minded. She fell in love with him over a few lines in which she had discovered a rare wealth of sensibility. She was fired also by a great actor, who lived near her: whenever she passed his door she used to say to herself:

"Shall I go in?"

And once she made so bold as to go up to the door of his flat. When she found herself there, she turned and fled. What could she have talked to him about? She had nothing, nothing at all to say to him. She did not love him. And she knew it. In the greater part of her folly she was deceiving herself. And for the rest it was the old, old, delicious, stupid need of being in love. As Jacqueline was naturally intelligent, she knew that quite well, and it kept her from making a fool of herself. A fool who knows his folly is worth two who don't.

She went out a good deal. There were many young men who felt her charm, and more than one of them was in love with her. She did not care what harm she did. A pretty girl makes a cruel game of love. It seems to her quite natural that she should be loved, and never considers that she owes anything to those who love her: she is apt to believe that her lover is happy enough in loving her. It must be said, by way of excuse, that she has no idea of what love is, although she thinks of nothing else all day long. One is inclined to think that a young girl in society, brought up in the hot-house atmosphere of a great town, would be more precocious than a country girl: but the opposite is the case. Her reading and conversation have made her obsessed by love, so obsessed that in her idle life it often borders on mania: and sometimes it happens that she has read the play beforehand, and knows it word for word by heart.

But she never feels it. In love, as in art, it is useless to read what others have said: we can but say what we feel: and those who make haste to speak before they have anything to say are as likely as not to say nothing.

Jacqueline, like most young people, lived in an atmosphere clouded by the dust of the feelings of others, which, while it kept her in a perpetual fever, with her hands burning, and her throat dry, and her eyes sore, prevented her seeing anything. She thought she knew everything. It was not that she lacked the wish to know. She read and listened. She had picked up a deal of information, here and there, in scraps, from conversation and books. She even tried to read what was written in herself. She was much better than the world in which she lived, for she was more sincere.

There was one woman who had a good influence—only too brief—over her. This was a sister of her father's, a woman of between forty and fifty, who had never married. Tall, with regular features, though sad and lacking in beauty, Marthe Langeais was always dressed in black: she had a sort of stiff distinction of feature and movement: she spoke very little, and she had a deep voice, almost like a man's. But for the clear light in her intelligent gray eyes and the kind smile on her sad lips she would have passed unnoticed.

She only appeared at the Langeais' on certain days, when they were alone. Langeais had a great respect for her, though she bored him. Madame Langeais made no attempt to disguise from her husband how little pleasure his sister's visits gave her. However, they faced their duty, and had her to dinner once a week, and they did not let it appear too glaringly that they regarded it as a duty. Langeais used to talk about himself, which she always found interesting. Madame Langeais would think of something else, and, as a matter of habit, smile affably when she was spoken to. The dinner always went off very well, and she was invariably polite. Sometimes, even, she would be effusively affectionate when her tactful sister-in-law went away earlier than she had hoped: and Madame Langeais's charming smile would be most radiant when she had any particularly pleasant memories to think of. Marthe saw through

it all: very little escaped her eyes: and she saw many things
in her brother's house which shocked and distressed her. But
she never let it appear: what was the good? She loved her
brother, and had been proud of his cleverness and success, like
the rest of the family, who had not thought the triumph of the
eldest son too dear a price to pay for their poverty. She, at
least, had preserved her independence of opinion. She was as
clever as he was, and of a finer moral fiber, more virile—(as
the women of France so often are; they are much superior to
the men),—and she knew him through and through: and when
he asked her advice she used to give it frankly. But for a long
time he had not asked it of her! He found it more prudent
not to know, or—(for he knew the truth as much as she did),—
to shut his eyes. She was proud, and drew aside. Nobody
ever troubled to look into her inward life, and it suited the
others to ignore her. She lived alone, went out very little, and
had only a few not very intimate friends. It would have been
very easy to her to turn her brother's influence and her own
talents to account: but she did not do so. She had written a few
articles for the leading reviews in Paris, historical and literary
portraits, which had attracted some attention by their sober,
just, and striking style. But she had gone no farther. She
might have formed interesting friendships with certain distinguished men and women, who had shown a desire to know her,
whom also she would, perhaps, have been glad to know. She
did not respond to their advances. Though she had a reserved
seat for a theater when the program contained music that she
loved, she did not go: and though she had the opportunity of
traveling to a place where she knew that she would find much
pleasure, she preferred to stay at home. Her nature was a
curious compound of stoicism and neurasthenia, which, however,
in no wise impaired the integrity of her ideas. Her life was
impaired, but not her mind. An old sorrow, known only to
herself, had left its mark on her heart. And even more profound, even less suspected—unknown to herself, was the secret
illness which had begun to prey upon her.—However, the
Langeais saw only the clear expression of her eyes, which
sometimes made them feel embarrassed.

Jacqueline used to take hardly any notice of her aunt in

the days when she was careless and gay—which was her usual
condition when she was a child. But when she reached the
age at which there occurs a mysterious change and growth in
body and soul, which bring agony, disgust, terror, and fearful
moments of depression in their train, and moments of absurd,
horrible dizziness, which, happily, do not last, though they make
their victim feel at the point of death,—the child, sinking and
not daring to cry for help, found only her Aunt Marthe standing
by her side and holding out her hand. Ah! the others were
so far away! Her father and mother were as strangers to her,
with their selfish affection, too satisfied with themselves to
think of the small troubles of a doll of fourteen! But her
aunt guessed them, and comforted her. She did not say anything. She only smiled: across the table she exchanged a
kindly glance with Jacqueline, who felt that her aunt understood her, and she took refuge by her side. Marthe stroked
Jacqueline's head and kissed her, and spoke no word.

The little girl trusted her. When her heart was heavy she
would go and see her friend, who would know and understand
as soon as she arrived; she would be met always with the same
indulgent eyes, which would infect her with a little of their
own tranquillity. She told her aunt hardly anything about her
imaginary love-affairs: she was ashamed of them, and felt that
there was no truth in them. But she confessed all the vague,
profound uneasiness that was in her, and was more real, her
only real trouble.

"Aunt," she would sigh sometimes, "I do so long to be
happy!"

"Poor child!" Marthe would say, with a smile.

Jacqueline would lay her head in her aunt's lap, and kiss
her hands as they caressed her face:

"Do you think I shall be happy? Aunt, tell me; do you
think I shall be happy?"

"I don't know, my dear. It rather depends on yourself. . . .
People can always be happy if they want to be."

Jacqueline was incredulous.

"Are you happy?"

Marthe smiled sadly:

"Yes."

" No? Really? Are you happy? "

" Don't you believe it? "

" Yes. But . . ."

Jacqueline stopped short.

" What is it? "

" I want to be happy, but not like you."

" Poor child! I hope so, too! " said Marthe.

" No." Jacqueline went on shaking her head decisively. " But I couldn't be."

" I should not have thought it possible, either. Life teaches one to be able to do many things."

" Oh! But I don't want to learn," protested Jacqueline anxiously. " I want to be happy in the way I want."

" You would find it very hard to say how! "

" I know quite well what I want."

She wanted many things. But when it came to saying what they were, she could only mention one, which recurred again and again, like a refrain:

" First of all, I want some one to love me."

Marthe went on sewing without a word. After a moment she said:

" What good will it be to you if you do not love? "

Jacqueline was taken aback, and exclaimed:

" But, aunt, of course I only mean some one I loved! All the rest don't count."

" And suppose you did not love anybody? "

" The idea! One loves always, always."

Marthe shook her head doubtfully.

" No," she said. " We don't love. We want to love. Love is the greatest gift of God. Pray to Him that He may grant it you."

" But suppose my love is not returned? "

" Even if your love is not returned, you will be all the happier."

Jacqueline's face fell: she pouted a little:

" I don't want that," she said. " It wouldn't give me any pleasure."

Marthe laughed indulgently, looked at Jacqueline, sighed, and then went on with her work.

" Poor child! " she said once more.

" Why do you keep on saying: ' Poor child '? " asked Jacque-line uneasily. " I don't want to be a poor child. I want—I want so much to be happy! "

" That is why I say: ' Poor child!' "

Jacqueline sulked for a little. But it did not last long. Marthe laughed at her so kindly that she was disarmed. She kissed her, pretending to be angry. But in their hearts children of that age are secretly flattered by predictions of suffering in later life, which is so far away. When it is afar off there is a halo of poetry round sorrow, and we dread nothing so much as a dull, even life.

Jacqueline did not notice that her aunt's face was growing paler and paler. She observed that Marthe was going out less and less, but she attributed it to her stay-at-home disposition, about which she used often to tease her. Once or twice, when she called, she had met the doctor coming out. She had asked her aunt:

" Are you ill? "

Marthe replied:

" It's nothing."

But now she had even given up her weekly dinner at the Langeais'. Jacqueline was hurt, and went and reproached her bitterly.

" My dear," said Marthe gently, " I am rather tired."

But Jacqueline would not listen to anything. That was a poor sort of excuse!

" It can't be very exhausting for you to come to our house for a couple of hours a week! You don't love me," she would say. " You love nothing but your own fireside."

But when at home she proudly told them how she had scolded her aunt, Langeais cut her short with:

" Let your aunt be! Don't you know that the poor creature is very ill! "

Jacqueline grew pale: and in a trembling voice she asked what was the matter with her aunt. They tried not to tell her. Finally, she found out that Marthe was dying of cancer: she had had it for some months.

For some days Jacqueline lived in a state of terror. She

was comforted a little when she saw her aunt. Marthe was mercifully not suffering any great pain. She still had her tranquil smile, which in her thin transparent face seemed to shine like the light of an inward lamp. Jacqueline said to herself:

" No. It is impossible. They must be mistaken. She would not be so calm. . . ."

She went on with the tale of her little confidences, to which Marthe listened with more interest than heretofore. Only, sometimes, in the middle of a conversation, her aunt would leave the room, without giving any sign to show that she was in pain: and she would not return until the attack was over, and her face had regained its serenity. She did not like anybody to refer to her condition, and tried to hide it: she had a horror of the disease that held her in its grip, and would not think of it: all her efforts were directed towards preserving the peace of her last months. The end came sooner than it was expected. Very soon she saw nobody but Jacqueline. Then Jacqueline's visits had to be curtailed. Then came the day of parting. Marthe was lying in her bed, which she had not left for some weeks, when she took a tender farewell of her little friend with a few gentle, comforting words. And then she shut herself up, to die.

Jacqueline passed through months of despair. Marthe's death came at the same time as the very worst hours of her moral distress, against which Marthe had been the only person who could help her. She was horribly deserted and alone. She needed the support of a religion. There was apparently no reason why she should have lacked that support: she had always been made to practise the duties of religion: her mother practised them regularly. But that was just the difficulty: her mother practised them, but her Aunt Marthe did not. And how was she to avoid comparison? The eyes of a child are susceptible to many untruths, to which her elders never give a thought, and children notice many weaknesses and contradictions. Jacqueline noticed that her mother and those who said that they believed had as much fear of death as though there had been no faith in them. No: religion was not a strong enough support. . . . And in addition there were certain

personal experiences, feelings of revolt and disgust, a tactless
confessor who had hurt her. . . .   She went on practising,
but without faith, just as she paid calls, because she had been
well brought up.   Religion, like the world, seemed to her to
be utterly empty.   Her only stay was the memory of the dead
woman, in which she was wrapped up.   She had many grounds
for self-reproach in her treatment of her aunt, whom in her
childish selfishness she had often neglected, while now she called
to her in vain.   She idealized her image: and the great example
which Marthe had left upon her mind of a profound life of
meditation helped to fill her with distaste for the life of the
world, in which there was no truth or serious purpose.   She
saw nothing but its hypocrisy, and those amiable compromises,
which at any other time would have amused her, now revolted
her.   She was in a condition of moral hypersensitiveness, and
everything hurt her: her conscience was raw.   Her eyes were
opened to certain facts which hitherto had escaped her in her
heedlessness.

One afternoon she was in the drawing-room with her mother.
Madame Langeais was receiving a caller,—a fashionable painter,
a good-looking, pompous man, who was often at the house, but
not on terms of intimacy.   Jacqueline had a feeling that she
was in the way, but that only made her more determined to
stay.   Madame Langeais was not very well; she had a headache,
which made her a little dull, or perhaps it was one of those
headache preventives which the ladies of to-day eat like sweets,
so that they have the result of completely emptying their pretty
heads, and she was not very guarded in what she said.   In
the course of the conversation she thoughtlessly called her
visitor:
"My dear . . ."
She noticed the slip at once.   He did not flinch any more
than she, and they went on talking politely.   Jacqueline, who
was pouring out tea, was so amazed that she almost dropped
a cup.   She had a feeling that they were exchanging a meaning
smile behind her back.   She turned and intercepted their privy
looks, which were immediately disguised.—The discovery upset
her completely.   Though she had been brought up with the
utmost freedom, and had often heard and herself laughed and

talked about such intrigues, it hurt her so that she could hardly bear it when she saw that her mother . . . Her mother: no, it was not the same thing! . . . With her habitual exaggeration she rushed from one extreme to the other. Till then she had suspected nothing. Thereafter she suspected everything. Implacably she read new meanings into this and that detail of her mother's behavior in the past. And no doubt Madame Langeais's frivolity furnished only too many grounds for her suppositions: but Jacqueline added to them. She longed to be more intimate with her father, who had always been nearer to her, his quality of mind having a great attraction for her. She longed to love him more, and to pity him. But Langeais did not seem to stand in much need of pity: and a suspicion more dreadful even than the first, crossed the girl's heated imagination,—that her father knew nothing, but that it suited him to know nothing, and that, so long as he were allowed to go his own way, he did not care.

Then Jacqueline felt that she was lost. She dared not despise them. She loved them. But she could not go on living in their house. Her friendship with Simone Adam was no help at all. She judged severely the foibles of her former boon companion. She did not spare herself: everything that was ugly and mediocre in herself made her suffer terribly: she clung desperately to the pure memory of Marthe. But that memory was fading: she felt that the stream of time, one day following another, would cover it up and wash away all trace of it. And then there would be an end of everything: she would be like the rest, sunk deep in the mire. . . . Oh! if she could only escape from such a world, at any cost! Save me! Save me! . . .

It was just when she was in this fever of despair, feeling her utter destitution, filled with passionate disgust and mystic expectancy, holding out her arms to an unknown saviour, that she met Olivier.

Madame Langeais, of course, invited Christophe, who, that winter, was the musician of the hour. Christophe accepted, and, as usual, did not take any trouble to make himself pleasant. However, Madame Langeais thought him charming:—he could do anything he liked, as long as he was the fashion: everybody would go on thinking him charming, while the fashion ran its allotted course of a few months.—Jacqueline, who, for the time being, was outside the current, was not so charmed with him: the mere fact that Christophe was belauded by certain people was enough to make her diffident about him. Besides, Christophe's bluntness, and his loud way of speaking, and his noisy gaiety, offended her. In her then state of mind the joy of living seemed a coarse thing to her: her eyes were fixed on the twilight melancholy of the soul, and she fancied that she loved it. There was too much sunlight in Christophe.

But when she talked to him he told her about Olivier: he always had to bring his friend into every pleasant thing that happened to him: it would have seemed to him a selfish use of a new friendship if he had not set aside a part of it for Olivier. He told Jacqueline so much about him, that she felt a secret emotion in thus catching a glimpse of a soul so much in accordance with her ideas, and made her mother invite him too. Olivier did not accept at first, so that Christophe and Jacqueline were left to complete their imaginary portrait of him at their leisure, and, of course, he was found to be very like it when at last he made up his mind to go.

He went, but hardly spoke a word. He did not need to speak. His intelligent eyes, his smile, his refined manners, the tranquillity that was in and inundated by his personality, could not but attract Jacqueline. Christophe, by contrast, stood as a foil to Olivier's shining qualities. She did not show anything, for she was fearful of the feeling stirring in her: she confined herself to talking to Christophe, but it was always about Olivier. Christophe was only too happy to talk about his friend, and did not notice Jacqueline's pleasure in the subject of their conversation. He used to talk about himself, and she would listen agreeably enough, though she was not in the least interested: then, without seeming to do so, she would bring the conversation round to those episodes in his life which included Olivier.

Jacqueline's pretty ways were dangerous for a man who was not on his guard. Without knowing it Christophe fell in love with her: it gave him pleasure to go to the house again:

he took pains with his dress: and a feeling, which he well knew, began to tinge all his ideas with its tender smiling languor. Olivier was in love with her too, and had been from their first meeting: he thought she had no regard for him, and suffered in silence. Christophe made his state even worse by telling him joyously, as they left the Langeais' house, what he had said to Jacqueline and what she had said to him. The idea never occurred to Olivier that Jacqueline should like him. Although, by dint of living with Christophe, he had become more optimistic, he still distrusted himself: he could not believe that any woman would ever love him, for he saw himself too clearly, and with eyes that saw too truthfully:—what man is there would be worthy to be loved, if it were for his merits, and not by the magic and indulgence of love?

One evening when he had been invited to the Langeais', he felt that it would make him too unhappy to feel Jacqueline's indifference: he said that he was too tired and told Christophe to go without him. Christophe suspected nothing, and went off in high delight. In his naïve egoism he thought only of the pleasure of having Jacqueline all to himself. He was not suffered to rejoice for long. When she heard that Olivier was not coming, Jacqueline at once became peevish, irritable, bored, and dispirited: she lost all desire to please: she did not listen to Christophe, and answered him at random: and he had the humiliation of seeing her stifle a weary yawn. She was near tears. Suddenly she went away in the middle of the evening, and did not appear again.

Christophe went home discomfited. All the way home he tried to explain this sudden change of front: and the truth began dimly to dawn on him. When he reached his rooms he found Olivier waiting for him, and then, with a would-be indifferent air, Olivier asked him about the party. Christophe told him of his discomfiture, and he saw Olivier's face brighten as he went on.

" Still tired?" he asked. "Why didn't you go to bed?"

"Oh! I'm much better," said Olivier. "I'm not the least tired now."

"Yes," said Christophe slyly, "I fancy it has done you a lot of good not going."

He looked at him affectionately and roguishly, and went away into his own room: and then, when he was alone, he began to laugh quietly, and laughed until he cried:

" Little minx! " he thought. " She was making a game of me! And he was deceiving me, too. What a secret they made of it! "

From that moment he plucked out every personal thought of Jacqueline from his heart: and, like a broody hen hatching her eggs, he hatched the romance of the young lovers. Without seeming to know their secret, and without betraying either to the other, he helped them, though they never knew it.

He thought it his solemn duty to study Jacqueline's character to see if Olivier could be happy with her. And, being very tactless, he horrified Jacqueline with the ridiculous questions he put to her about her tastes, her morality, etc., etc.

" Idiot! What does he mean? " Jacqueline would think angrily, and refuse to answer him, and turn her back on him.

And Olivier would be delighted to see Jacqueline paying no more attention to Christophe. And Christophe would be over-joyed at seeing Olivier's happiness. His joy was patent, and revealed itself much more obstreperously than Olivier's. And as Jacqueline could not explain it, and never dreamed that Christophe had a much clearer knowledge of their love than she had herself, she thought him unbearable: she could not understand how Olivier could be so infatuated with such a vulgar, cumbersome friend. Christophe divined her thoughts, and took a malicious delight in infuriating her: then he would step aside, and say that he was too busy to accept the Langeais' invitations, so as to leave Jacqueline and Olivier alone together.

However, he was not altogether without anxiety concerning the future. He regarded himself as responsible in a large measure for the marriage that was in the making, and he worried over it, for he had a fair insight into Jacqueline's character, and he was afraid of many things: her wealth first of all, her up-bringing, her surroundings, and, above all, her weakness. He remembered his old friend Colette, though, no doubt, he admitted that Jacqueline was truer, more frank, more passionate: there was in the girl an ardent aspiration towards a life of courage, an almost heroic desire for it.

" But desiring isn't everything," thought Christophe, remembering a jest of Diderot's: " the chief thing is a straight backbone."

He would have liked to warn Olivier of the danger. But when he saw him come back from being with Jacqueline, with his eyes lit with joy, he had not the heart to speak, and he thought:

" The poor things are happy. I won't disturb their happiness."

Gradually his affection for Olivier made him share his friend's confidence. He took heart of grace, and at last began to believe that Jacqueline was just as Olivier saw her and as she wished to appear in her own eyes. She meant so well! She loved Olivier for all the qualities which made him different from herself and the world she lived in: because he was poor, because he was uncompromising in his moral ideas, because he was awkward and shy in society. Her love was so pure and so whole that she longed to be poor too, and, sometimes, almost . . . yes, almost to be ugly, so that she might be sure that he loved her for herself, and for the love with which her heart was so full, the love for which her heart was so hungry. . . . Ah! Sometimes, when he was not with her, she would go pale and her hands would tremble. She would seem to scoff at her emotion, and pretend to be thinking of something else, and to take no notice of it. She would talk mockingly of things. But suddenly she would break off, and rush away and shut herself up in her room: and then, with the doors locked, and the curtains drawn over the window, she would sit there, with her knees tight together. and her elbows close against her sides, and her arms folded across her breast, while she tried to repress the beating of her heart: she would sit there huddled together, never stirring, hardly breathing: she dared not move for fear lest her happiness should escape if she so much as lifted a finger. She would sit holding her love close, close to her body in silence.

And now Christophe was absolutely determined that Olivier should succeed in his wooing. He fussed round him like a mother, supervised his dressing, presumed to give him advice as to what he should wear, and even—(think of it!)—tied his tie for him. Olivier bore with him patiently at the cost of having to retie his tie on the stairs when Christophe was no longer present. He smiled inwardly, but he was touched by such great affection. Besides, his love had made him timid, and he was not sure of himself, and was glad of Christophe's advice. He used to tell him everything that happened when he was with Jacqueline, and Christophe would be just as moved by it as himself, and sometimes at night he would lie awake for hours trying to find the means of making the path of love smoother for his friend.

It was in the garden of the Langeais' villa, near Paris, on the outskirts of the forest of Isle-Adam, that Olivier and Jacqueline had the interview which was the turning-point in their lives.

Christophe had gone down with his friend, but he had found a harmonium in the house, and sat playing so as to leave the lovers to walk about the garden in peace.—Truth to tell, they did not wish it. They were afraid to be left alone. Jacqueline was silent and rather hostile. On his last visit Olivier had been conscious of a change in her manner, a sudden coldness, an expression in her eyes which was strange, hard, and almost inimical. It froze him. He dared not ask her for an explanation, for he was fearful of hearing cruel words on the lips of the girl he loved. He trembled whenever he saw Christophe leave them, for it seemed to him that his presence was his only safeguard against the blow which threatened to fall upon him.

It was not that Jacqueline loved Olivier less. Rather she was more in love with him, and it was that that made her hostile. Love, with which till then she had only played, love, to which she had so often called, was there, before her eyes: she saw it gaping before her like an abyss, and she flung back in terror: she could not understand it, and wondered:

"Why? Why? What does it mean?"

Then she would look at Olivier with the expression which so hurt him, and think:

"Who is this man?"

And she could not tell. He was a stranger.

"Why do I love him?"

She could not tell.

" Do I love him? "

She could not tell. . . . She did not know: and yet she knew that she was caught: she was in the toils of love: she was on the point of losing herself in love, losing herself utterly; her will, her independence, her egoism, her dreams of the future, all were to be swallowed up by the monster. And she would harden herself in anger, and sometimes she would feel that she almost hated Olivier.

They went to the very end of the garden, into the kitchen-garden, which was cut off from the lawns by a hedge of tall trees. They sauntered down the paths bordered on either side with gooseberry bushes, with their clusters of red and golden fruit, and beds of strawberries, the fragrance of which scented the air. It was June: but there had been storms, and the weather was cold. The sky was gray and the light dim: the low-hanging clouds moved in a heavy mass, drifting with the wind, which blew only in the higher air, and never touched the earth; no leaf stirred: but the air was very fresh. Everything was shrouded in melancholy, even their hearts, swelling with the grave happiness that was in them. And from the other end of the garden, through the open windows of the villa, out of sight, there came the sound of the harmonium, grinding out the Fugue in E Flat Minor of Johann Sebastian Bach. They sat down on the coping of a well, both pale and silent. And Olivier saw tears trickling down Jacqueline's cheeks.

" You are crying? " he murmured, with trembling lips.

And the tears came to his own eyes.

He took her hand. She laid her head on Olivier's shoulder. She gave up the struggle: she was vanquished, and it was such sweet comfort to her! . . . They wept silently as they sat listening to the music under the moving canopy of the heavy clouds, which in their noiseless flight seemed to skim the tops of the trees. They thought of all that they had suffered, and perhaps—who knows?—of all that they were to suffer in the future. There are moments when music summons forth all the sadness woven into the woof of a human being's destiny. . . .

After a moment or two Jacqueline dried her eyes and looked

at Olivier. And suddenly they kissed. O boundless happiness!
Religious happiness! So sweet and so profound that it is almost
sorrow!

Jacqueline asked:
" Was your sister like you? "
Olivier felt a sudden pang. He said:
" Why do you ask me about her? Did you know her? "
She replied:
" Christophe told me. . . . You have suffered? "
Olivier nodded: he was too much moved to speak.
" I have suffered too," she said.
She told him of the friend who had been taken from her,
her beloved Marthe: and with her heart big with emotion she
told him how she had wept, wept until she thought she was
going to die.
" You will help me? " she said, in a beseeching tone. " You
will help me to live, and be good, and to be a little like her?
Poor Marthe: you will love her too? "
" We will love them both, as they both love each other."
" I wish they were here."
" They are here."
They sat there locked in each other's arms: they hardly
breathed, and could feel heart beating to heart. A gentle drizzle
was falling, falling. Jacqueline shivered.
" Let us go in," she said.
Under the trees it was almost dark. Olivier kissed Jacque-
line's wet hair: she turned her face up to him, and, for the
first time, he felt loving lips against his, a girl's lips, warm and
parted a little. They were nigh swooning.
Near the house they stopped once more:
" How utterly alone we were! " he said.
He had already forgotten Christophe.
They remembered him at length. The music had stopped.
They went in. Christophe was sitting at the harmonium with
his head in his hands, dreaming, he too, of many things in the

past. When he heard the door open, he started from his dream, and turned to them affectionately with a solemn, tender smile lighting up his face. He saw in their eyes what had happened, pressed their hands warmly, and said:

" Sit down, and I'll play you something."

They sat down, and he played the piano, telling in music all that was in his heart, and the great love he had for them. When he had done they all three sat in silence. Then he got up and looked at them. He looked so kind, and so much older, so much stronger than they! For the first time she began to appreciate what he was. He hugged them both, and said to Jacqueline:

" You will love him dearly, won't you? You will love him dearly?"

They were filled with gratitude towards him. But at once he turned the conversation, laughed, went to the window, and sprang out into the garden.

During the days following he kept urging Olivier to go and propose his suit to Jacqueline's parents. Olivier dared not, dreading the refusal which he anticipated. Christophe also insisted on his setting about finding work, for even supposing the Langeais accepted him, he could not take Jacqueline's fortune unless he were himself in a position to earn his living. Olivier was of the same opinion, though he did not share his violent and rather comic distrust of wealthy marriages. It was a rooted idea in Christophe's mind that riches are death to the soul. It was on the tip of his tongue to quote the saying of a wise beggar to a rich lady who was worried in her mind about the next life:

" What, madame, you have millions, and you want to have an immortal soul into the bargain?"

" Beware of women," he would say to Olivier—half in jest, half in earnest—" beware of women, but be twenty times more wary of rich women. Women love art, perhaps, but they strangle the artist. Rich women poison both art and artists. Wealth is a disease. And women are more susceptible to it than men. Every rich man is an abnormal being. . . . You laugh? You don't take me seriously? Look you: does a rich man know

what life is? Does he keep himself in touch with the raw
realities of life? Does he feel on his face the stinging breath
of poverty, the smell of the bread that he must earn, of the
earth that he must dig? Can he understand, does he even see
people and things as they are? . . . When I was a little boy
I was once or twice taken for a drive in the Grand Duke's
landau. We drove through fields in which I knew every blade
of grass, through woods that I adored, where I used to run
wild all by myself. Well: I saw nothing at all. The whole
country had become as stiff and starched as the idiots with whom
I was driving. Between the fields and my heart there was not
only the curtain of the souls of those formal people. The
wooden planks beneath my feet, the moving platform being rolled
over the face of Nature, were quite enough. To feel that the
earth is my mother, I must have my feet firmly planted on her
womb, like a newborn child issuing to the light. Wealth severs
the tie which binds men to the earth, and holds the sons of the
earth together. And then how can you expect to be an artist?
The artist is the voice of the earth. A rich man cannot be a
great artist. He would need a thousand times more genius
to be so under such unfavorable conditions. Even if he succeeds his art must be a hot-house fruit. The great Goethe
struggled in vain: parts of his soul were atrophied, he lacked
certain of the vital organs, which were killed by his wealth.
You have nothing like the vitality of a Goethe, and you would
be destroyed by wealth, especially by a rich woman, a fate which
Goethe did at least avoid. Only the man can withstand the
scourge. He has in him such native brutality, such a rich
deposit of rude, healthy instincts binding him to the earth,
that he alone has any chance of escape. But the woman is
tainted by the poison, and she communicates the taint to others.
She acquires a taste for the reeking scent of wealth, and cannot
do without it. A woman who can be rich and yet remain sound
in heart is a prodigy as rare as a millionaire who has genius. . . .
And I don't like monsters. Any one who has more than enough
to live on is a monster—a human cancer preying upon the lives
of the rest of humanity."

  Olivier laughed:

  "What do you want?" he said. "I can't stop loving Jacque-

line because she is not poor, or force her to become poor for
love of me."

"Well, if you can't save her, at least save yourself. That's
the best way of saving her. Keep yourself pure. Work."

Olivier did not need to go to Christophe for scruples. He
was even more nicely sensitive than he in such matters. Not
that he took Christophe's diatribes against money seriously: he
had been rich himself, and did not loathe riches, and thought
them a very good setting for Jacqueline's pretty face. But it
was intolerable to think that his love might in any way be
contaminated with an imputation of interest. He applied to
have his name restored to the University list. For the time
being he could not hope for anything better than a moderate
post in a provincial school. It was a poor wedding-present to
give to Jacqueline. He told her about it timidly. Jacqueline
found it difficult at first to see his point of view: she attributed
it to an excessive pride, put into his head by Christophe, and
she thought it ridiculous: was it not more natural between lovers
to set no store by riches or poverty, and was it not rather shabby
to refuse to be indebted to her when it would give her such
great joy? . . . However, she threw herself in with Olivier's
plans: their austerity and discomfort were the very things that
brought her round, for she found in them an opportunity of
gratifying her desire for moral heroism. In her condition of
proud revolt against her surroundings which had been induced
by the death of her aunt, and was exalted by her love, she had
gone so far as to deny every element in her nature which was
in contradiction to her mystic ardor: in all sincerity her whole
being was strained, like a bow, after an ideal of a pure and
difficult life, radiant with happiness. . . . The obstacles, the
very smallness and dullness of her future condition in life, were
a joy to her. How good and beautiful it would all be! . . .

Madame Langeais was too much taken up with herself to
pay much attention to what was going on about her. For some
time past she had been thinking of little outside her health:
she spent her whole time in treating imaginary illnesses, and
trying one doctor after another: each of them in turn was
her saviour, and went on enjoying that position for a fortnight:
then it was another's turn. She would stay away from home

for months in expensive sanatoria, where she religiously carried out all sorts of preposterous prescriptions to the letter. She had forgotten her husband and daughter.

M. Langeais was not so indifferent, and had begun to suspect the existence of the affair. His paternal jealousy made him feel it. He had for Jacqueline that strange pure affection which many fathers feel for their daughters, an elusive, indefinable feeling, a mysterious, voluptuous, and almost sacred curiosity, in living once more in the lives of fellow-creatures who are of their blood, who are themselves, and are women. In such secrets of the heart there are many lights and shadows which it is healthier to ignore. Hitherto it had amused him to see his daughter making calfish young men fall in love with her: he loved her so, romantic, coquettish, and discreet—(just as he was himself).—But when he saw that this affair threatened to become more serious, he grew anxious. He began by making fun of Olivier to Jacqueline, and then he criticised him with a certain amount of bitterness. Jacqueline laughed at first, and said:

" Don't say such hard things, father: you would find it awkward later on, supposing I wanted to marry him."

M. Langeais protested loudly, and said she was mad: with the result that she lost her head completely. He declared that he would never let her marry Olivier. She vowed that she would marry him. The veil was rent. He saw that he was nothing to her. In his fatherly egoism it had never occurred to him, and he was angry. He swore that neither Olivier nor Christophe should ever set foot inside his house again. Jacqueline lost her temper, and one fine morning Olivier opened the door to admit a young woman, pale and determined looking, who rushed in like a whirlwind, and said:

"Take me away with you! My father and mother won't hear of it. I *will* marry you. You must compromise me."

Olivier was alarmed though touched by it, and did not even try to argue with her. Fortunately Christophe was there. Ordinarily he was the least reasonable of men, but now he reasoned with them. He pointed out what a scandal there would be, and how they would suffer for it. Jacqueline bit her lip angrily, and said:

"Very well. We will kill ourselves."

So far from frightening Olivier, her threat only helped to make up his mind to side with her. Christophe had no small difficulty in making the crazy pair have a little patience: before taking such desperate measures they might as well try others: let Jacqueline go home, and he would go and see M. Langeais and plead their cause.

A queer advocate! M. Langeais nearly kicked him out on the first words he said: but then the absurdity of the situation struck him, and it amused him. Little by little the gravity of his visitor and his expression of honesty and absolute sincerity began to make an impression: however, he would not fall in with his contentions, and went on firing ironical remarks at him. Christophe pretended not to hear: but every now and then as a more than usually biting shaft struck home he would stop and draw himself up in silence; then he would go on again. Once he brought his fist down on the table with a thud, and said:

"I beg of you to believe that it has given me no pleasure to call on you: I have to control myself to keep from retaliating on you for certain things you have said: but I think it my duty to speak to you, and I am doing so. Forget me, as I forget myself, and weigh well what I am telling you."

M. Langeais listened: and when he heard of the project of suicide, he shrugged his shoulders and pretended to laugh: but he was shaken. He was too clever to take such a threat as a joke: he knew that he had to deal with the insanity of a girl in love. One of his mistresses, a gay, gentle creature, whom he had thought incapable of putting her boastful threat into practice, had shot herself with a revolver before his eyes: she did not kill herself at once, but the scene lived in his memory. . . . No, one can never be sure with women. He felt a pang at his heart. . . . "She wishes it? Very well: so be it, and so much the worse for her, little fool! . . ." He would have granted anything rather than drive his daughter to extremes. In truth he might have used diplomacy, and pretended to give his consent to gain time, gently to wean Jacqueline from Olivier. But doing so meant giving himself more trouble than he could or would be bothered with. Besides, he was weak: and the mere fact that he had angrily said "No!"

to Jacqueline, now inclined him to say "Yes." After all, what does one know of life? Perhaps the child was right. The great thing was that they should love each other. M. Langeais knew quite well that Olivier was a serious young man, and perhaps had talent. . . . He gave his consent.

The day before the marriage the two friends sat up together into the small hours. They did not wish to lose the last hours of their dear life together.—But already it was in the past. It was like those sad farewells on the station platform when there is a long wait before the train moves: one insists on staying, and looking and talking. But one's heart is not in it: one's friend has already gone. . . . Christophe tried to talk. He stopped in the middle of a sentence, seeing the absent look in Olivier's eyes, and he said, with a smile:

"You are so far away!"

Olivier was confused and begged his pardon. It made him sad to realize that his thoughts were wandering during the last intimate moments with his friend. But Christophe pressed his hand, and said:

"Come, don't constrain yourself. I am happy. Go on dreaming, my boy."

They stayed by the window, leaning out side by side, and looking through the darkness down into the garden. After some time Christophe said to Olivier:

"You are running away from me. You think you can escape me? You are thinking of your Jacqueline But I shall catch you up. I, too, am thinking of her."

"Poor old fellow," said Olivier, "and I was thinking of you! And even . . ."

He stopped.

Christophe laughed and finished the sentence for him.

". . . And even taking a lot of trouble over it! . . ."

Christophe turned out very fine, almost smart, for the wedding. There was no religious ceremony: neither the indifferent Olivier nor the rebellious Jacqueline had wished it. Christophe had written a symphonic fragment for the ceremony at the *mairie*, but at the last moment he gave up the idea when he

realized what a civil marriage is: he thought such ceremonies
absurd. People need to have lost both faith and liberty before
they can have any belief in them. When a true Catholic takes
the trouble to become a free-thinker he is not likely to endow
a functionary of the civil State with a religious character. Between God and his own conscience there is no room for a State
religion. The State registers, it does not bind man and wife
together.

The marriage of Olivier and Jacqueline was not likely to
make Christophe regret his decision. Olivier listened with a
faintly ironical air of aloofness to the Mayor ponderously fawn-
ing upon the young couple, and the wealthy relations, and the
witnesses who wore decorations. Jacqueline did not listen: and
she furtively put out her tongue at Simone Adam, who was
watching her: she had made a bet with her that being " married "
would not affect her in the least, and it looked as though she
would win it: it hardly seemed to occur to her that it was she
who was being married: the idea of it tickled her. The rest
were posing for the onlookers: and the onlookers were taking
them all in. M. Langeais was showing off: in spite of his
sincere affection for his daughter, he was chiefly occupied in
taking stock of the guests to find out whether he had left any
gaps in his list of invitations. Only Christophe was moved: not
one of the rest, relations, bride, and bridegroom, or the Mayor
officiating, showed any emotion: he stood gazing hungrily at
Olivier, who did not look at him.

In the evening the young couple left for Italy. Christophe
and M. Langeais went with them to the station. They seemed
happy, not at all sorry to be going, and did not conceal their
impatience for the train to move. Olivier looked like a boy,
and Jacqueline like a little girl. . . . What a tender, melancholy charm is in such partings! The father is a little sad
to see his child taken away by a stranger, and for what! . . .
and to see her go away from him forever. But they feel nothing
but a new intoxicating sense of liberty. There are no more
hindrances to life: nothing can stop them ever again: they seem
to have reached the very summit: now might they die readily,
for they have everything, and nothing to fear. . . . But soon
they see that it was no more than a stage in the journey. The

road still lies before them, and winds round the mountain:
and there are very few who reach the second stage. . . .

The train bore them away into the night. Christophe and
M. Langeais went home together. Christophe said with naïve
archness:

"Now we are both widowed!"

M. Langeais began to laugh. He liked Christophe now that
he knew him better. They said good-by, and went their ways.
They were both unhappy, with an odd mixture of sadness and
sweetness. Sitting alone in his room Christophe thought:

"The best of my soul is happy."

Nothing had been altered in Olivier's room. They had
arranged that until Olivier returned and settled in a new house
his furniture and belongings should stay with Christophe. It
was as though he himself was still present. Christophe looked
at the portrait of Antoinette, placed it on his desk, and said
to it:

"My dear, are you glad?"

He wrote often—rather too often—to Olivier. He had a few
vaguely written letters, which were increasingly distant in tone.
He was disappointed, but not much affected by it. He persuaded
himself that it must be so, and he had no anxiety as to the
future of their friendship.

His solitude did not trouble him. Far from it: he did not
have enough of it to suit his taste. He was beginning to suffer
from the patronage of the *Grand Journal*. Arsène Gamache had
a tendency to believe that he had proprietary rights in the
famous men whom he had taken the trouble to discover: he
took it as a matter of course that their fame should be associated
with his own, much as Louis XIV. grouped Molière, Le Brun,
and Lulli about his throne. Christophe discovered that the
author of the *Hymn to Ægis* was not more imperial or more of
a nuisance to art than his patron of the *Grand Journal*. For
the journalist, who knew no more about art than the Emperor,
had opinions no less decided about it: he could not tolerate the
existence of anything he did not like: he decreed that it was
bad and pernicious: and he would ruin it in the public interest.
It is both comic and terrible to see such coarse-grained uncul-

tivated men of affairs presuming to control not only politics
and money, but also the mind, and offering it a kennel with a
collar and a dish of food, or, if it refuses, having the power to
let loose against it thousands of idiots whom they have trained
into a docile pack of hounds!—Christophe was not the sort of
man to let himself be schooled and disciplined. It seemed to
him a very bad thing that an ignoramus should take upon himself to tell him what he ought and ought not to do in music:
and he gave him to understand that art needed a much more
severe training than politics. Also, without any sort of polite
circumlocution, he declined a proposal that he should set to
music a libretto, which the author, a leading member of the
staff of the paper, was trying to place, while it was highly recommended by his chief. It had the effect of cooling his relations with Gamache.

Christophe did not mind that in the least. Though he had
so lately risen from his obscurity, he was longing to return to
it. He found himself "exposed to that great light in which a
man is lost among the many." There were too many people
bothering their heads about him. He pondered these words of
Goethe:

"When a writer has attracted attention by a good piece of
work, the public tries to prevent his producing another. . . .
The brooding talent is dragged out into the hurly-burly of the
world, in spite of itself, because every one thinks he will be able
to appropriate a part of it."

He shut his door upon the outside world, and began to seek
the company of some of his old friends in his own house. He
revisited the Arnauds, whom he had somewhat neglected.
Madame Arnaud, who was left alone for part of the day, had
time to think of the sorrows of others. She thought how empty
Christophe's life must be now that Olivier was gone: and she
overcame her shyness so far as to invite him to dinner. If she
had dared, she would even have offered to go in from time to
time and tidy his rooms: but she was not bold enough: and no
doubt it was better so: for Christophe did not like to have
people worrying about him. But he accepted the invitation to
dinner, and made a habit of going in to the Arnauds' every
evening.

He found them just as united, living in the same atmosphere of rather sad, sorrowful tenderness, though it was even grayer than before. Arnaud was passing through a period of depression, brought on by the wear and tear of his life as a teacher,—a life of exhausting labor, in which one day is like unto another, and each day's work is like that of the next, like a wheel turning in one place, without ever stopping, or ever advancing. Though he was very patient, the good man was passing through a crisis of discouragement. He let certain acts of injustice prey upon him, and was inclined to think that all his zeal was futile. Madame Arnaud would comfort him with kind words: she seemed to be just as calm and peaceful as in the old days: but her face was thinner. In her presence Christophe would congratulate Arnaud on having such a sensible wife.

"Yes." Arnaud would say, "she is a good little creature; nothing ever puts her out. She is lucky: so am I. If she had suffered in this cursed life, I don't see how I could have got through."

Madame Arnaud would blush and say nothing. Then in her even tones she would talk of something else.—Christophe's visits had their usual good effect: they brought light in their train: and he, for his part, found it very pleasant to feel the warmth of their kind, honest hearts.

Another friend, a girl, came into his life. Or rather he sought her out: for though she longed to know him, she could not have made the effort to go and see him. She was a young woman of a little more than twenty-five, a musician, and she had taken the first prize at the Conservatoire: her name was Cécile Fleury. She was short and rather thick-set. She had heavy eyebrows, fine, large eyes, with a soft expression, a short, broad, turned-up nose, inclined to redness, like a duck's beak, thick lips, kind and tender, an energetic chin, heavy and solid, and her forehead was broad, but not high. Her hair was done up in a large bun at the back of her neck. She had strong arms and a pianist's hands, very long, with a splayed thumb and square finger-tips. The general impression she gave was one of a rather sluggish vitality and of rude rustic health. She lived with her mother, who was very dear to her: a good, kind woman, who took not the smallest interest in music, though she used to talk about it, because she was always hearing about it, and knew everything that happened in Musicopolis. She had a dull, even life, gave lessons all day long, and sometimes concerts, of which nobody took any notice. She used to go home late at night, on foot or in an omnibus, worn out, but quite good-tempered: and she used to practise her scales bravely and trim her own hats, talking a great deal, laughing readily, and often singing for nothing.

She had not been spoiled by life. She knew the value of a little comfort when she had earned it by her own efforts,—the joy of a little pleasure, or a little scarcely perceptible advance in her position or her work. Indeed, if one month she could only earn five francs more than in the last, or if she could at length manage to play a certain passage of Chopin which she had been struggling with for weeks,—she would be quite happy. Her work, which was not excessive, exactly fitted her aptitude for it, and gave her a healthy satisfaction. Playing, singing, giving lessons gave her a pleasant feeling of satisfied activity, normal and regular, and at the same time a modest competence and a comfortable placid success. She had a healthy appetite, ate much, slept well, and was never ill.

She was clear-headed, sensible, modest, perfectly balanced, and never worried about anything: for she always lived in and for the present, without bothering her head about what had happened or what was going to happen in the future. And as she was always well, and as her life was comparatively secure from the sudden turns of fate, she was almost always satisfied. She took the same pleasure in practising her piano as in keeping house, or talking about things domestic, or doing nothing. She had the art of living, not from day to day—(she was economical and provident)—but from minute to minute. She was not possessed of any sort of idealism: the only ideal she had, if it could be called so, was bourgeois, and was unostentatiously expressed in her every action, and evenly distributed through every moment of the day: it consisted in peacefully loving everything she was doing, whatever it might be. She went to church on Sundays: but the feeling of religion had practically no place in her life. She admired enthusiasts, like Christophe, who had faith or genius: but she did not envy them: what could she have done with their uneasiness and their genius?

How came it, then, that she could feel their music? She would have found it hard to say. But it was very certain that she did feel it. She was superior to other virtuosi by reason of her sturdy quality of balance, physical and moral: in her abounding vitality, in the absence of personal passion, the passions of others found a rich soil in which to come to flower. She was not touched by them. She could translate in all their energy the terrible passions which had consumed the artist without being tainted by their poison: she only felt their force and the great weariness that came after its expression. When it was over, she would be all in a sweat, utterly exhausted: she would smile calmly and feel very happy.

Christophe heard her one evening, and was struck by her playing. He went and shook hands with her after the concert. She was grateful to him for it: there were very few people at the concert, and she was not so used to compliments as to take no delight in them. As she had never been clever enough to throw in her lot with any musical coterie, or cunning enough to surround herself with a group of worshipers, and as she never attempted to make herself particular, either by technical mannerisms or by a fantastic interpretation of the hallowed compositions, or by assuming an exclusive right to play some particular master, such as Johann Sebastian Bach, or Beethoven, and as she had no theories about what she played, but contented herself with playing simply what she felt—nobody paid any attention to her, and the critics ignored her: for nobody told them that she played well, and they were not likely to find it out for themselves.

Christophe saw a good deal of Cécile. Her strength and tranquillity attracted him as a mystery. She was vigorous and apathetic. In his indignation at her not being better known he proposed that he should get his friends of the *Grand Journal* to write about her. But although she would have liked to be praised, she begged him not to do anything to procure it. She did not want to have the struggle or the bother or the jealousies it would entail: she wanted to be left in peace. She was not talked about: so much the better! She was not envious, and she was the first to be enthusiastic about the technique of other virtuosi. She had no ambition, and no desire for anything.

She was much too lazy in mind! When she had not any immediate and definite work to do, she did nothing, nothing; she did
not even dream, not even at night, in bed: she either slept or
thought of nothing. She had not the morbid preoccupation with
marriage, which poisons the lives of girls who shiver at the
thought of dying old maids. When she was asked if she would
not like to have a husband, she would say:

"Why not throw in fifty thousand a year? One has to take
what comes. If any one offers, so much the better! If not,
one goes without. Because one can't have cake, I don't see why
one shouldn't be glad of honest bread. Especially when one
has had to eat stale bread for so long!"

"Besides," her mother would say, "there are plenty of people
who never get any bread to eat at all!"

Cécile had good reason to fight shy of men. Her father, who
had been dead some years, was a weak, lazy creature: he had
wronged his wife and his family. She had also a brother who
had turned out badly and did not know what had become of
him: every now and then he would turn up and ask for money:
she and her mother were afraid of him and ashamed of him,
and fearful of what they might hear about him any day: and
yet they loved him. Christophe met him once. He was at
Cécile's house: there was a ring at the door: and her mother
answered it. He heard a conversation being carried on in the
next room, and the voices were raised every now and then.
Cécile seemed ill at ease, and went out also, leaving Christophe
alone. The discussion went on, and the stranger's voice assumed
a threatening tone: Christophe thought it time to intervene, and
opened the door. He hardly had time to do more than catch a
glimpse of a young and slightly deformed man, whose back was
turned towards him, for Cécile rushed towards him and implored
him to go back. She went with him, and they sat in silence. In
the next room the visitor went on shouting for a few minutes
longer, and then took his leave and slammed the door. Then
Cécile sighed, and said to Christophe:

"Yes. . . . He is my brother."

Christophe understood:

"Ah!" he said. . . . "I know. . . . I have a brother,
too. . . ."

Cécile took his hand with an air of affectionate commiseration:
" You too? "

" Yes," he said. . . .   " These are the joys of a family."

Cécile laughed, and they changed the conversation. No, the
joys of a family had no enchantment for her, nor had the idea
of marriage any fascination: men were rather a worthless lot
on the whole. Her independent life had many advantages: her
mother had often sighed after her liberty: she had no desire to
lose it. The only day-dream in which she indulged was that
some day—Heaven knows when!—she would not have to give
lessons any more, and would be able to live in the country. But
she did not even take the trouble to imagine such a life in detail·
she found it too fatiguing to think of anything so uncertain: it
was better to sleep,—or do her work. . . .

In the meanwhile, in default of her castle in Spain, she used
to hire a little house in the outskirts of Paris for the summer,
and lived there with her mother. It was twenty minutes' journey
by train. The house was some distance away from the station,
standing alone in the midst of a stretch of waste lands which
were called " fields," and Cécile used often to return late at
night. But she was not afraid, and did not believe there was
any danger. She had a revolver, but she always used to leave
it at home. Besides, it was doubtful if she would have known
how to use it.

Sometimes, when he went to see her, Christophe would make
her play. It amused him to see her keen perception of the
music, especially when he had dropped a hint which put her on
the track of a feeling that called for expression. He had discovered that she had an excellent voice, but she had no idea of it.
He made her practise it, and would give her old German *lieder*
or his own music to sing: it gave her pleasure, and she made
such progress as to surprise herself as much as him. She was
marvelously gifted. The fire of music had miraculously descended upon this daughter of Parisian middle-class parents who
were utterly devoid of any artistic feeling. Philomela—(for so
he used to call her)—used sometimes to discuss music with
Christophe, but always in a practical, never in a sentimental,
way: she seemed only to be interested in the technique of singing
and the piano. Generally, when they were together and were

not playing music, they talked of the most commonplace things, and Christophe, who could not for a moment have tolerated such conversations with an ordinary woman, would discuss these subjects as a matter of course with Philomela.

They used to spend whole evenings alone together, and were genuinely fond of each other, though their affection was perfectly calm and even almost cold. One evening, when he had dined with her, and had stayed talking longer than usual, a violent storm came on: she said:

"You can't go now! Stay until to-morrow morning."

He was fitted up with an improvised bed in the little sitting-room. Only a thin partition was between it and Cécile's bedroom, and the doors were not locked. As he lay there he could hear her bed creaking and her soft, regular breathing. In five minutes she was asleep: and very soon he followed her example without either of them having had the faintest shadow of an uneasy thought.

At the same time there came into his life a number of other unknown friends, drawn to him by reading his works. Most of them lived far away from Paris or shut up in their homes, and never met him. Even a vulgar success does a certain amount of good: it makes the artist known to thousands of good people in remote corners whom he could never have reached without the stupid articles in the papers. Christophe entered into correspondence with some of them. There were lonely young men, living a life of hardship, their whole being aspiring to an ideal of which they were not sure, and they came greedily to slake their thirst at the well of Christophe's brotherly spirit. There were humble people in the provinces who read his *lieder* and wrote to him, like old Schulz, and felt themselves one with him. There were poor artists,—a composer among others,—who had not, and could not attain, not only success, but self-expression, and it made them glad to have their ideas realized by Christophe. And dearest of all, perhaps,—there were those who wrote to him without giving their names, and, being thus more free to speak, naïvely laid bare their touching confidence in the elder brother who had come to their assistance. Christophe's heart would grow big at the thought that he would never know these charming people whom it would have given him such joy to love: he would kiss some of these anonymous letters as the writers of them kissed his *lieder;* and each to himself would think:

" Dear written sheets, what a deal of good you have done me! "

So, according with the unvaried rhythm of the universe, there was formed about him the little family of genius, grouped about him, giving him food and taking it from him, which grows little by little, and in the end becomes one great collective soul, of which he is the central fire, like a gleaming world, a moral planet moving through space, mingling its chorus of brotherhood with the harmony of the spheres.

And as these mysterious links were forged between Christophe and his unseen friends, a revolution took place in his artistic faculty: it became larger and more human. He lost all interest in music which was a monologue, a soliloquy. and even more so in music which was a scientific structure built entirely for the interest of the profession. He wished his music to be an act of communion with other men. There is no vital art save that which is linked with the rest of humanity. Johann Sebastian Bach, even in his darkest hours of isolation, was linked with the rest of humanity by his religious faith. which he ex-pressed in his art. Handel and Mozart, by dint of circumstances, wrote for an audience, and not for themselves. Even Beethoven had to reckon with the multitude. It is salutary. It is good for humanity to remind genius every now and then:

" What is there for us in your art? If there is nothing, out you go! "

In such constraint genius is the first to gain. There are, indeed, great artists who express only themselves. But the greatest of all are those whose hearts beat for all men. If any man would see the living God face to face. he must seek Him, not in the empty firmament of his own brain, but in the love of men.

The artists of that time were far removed. from that love. They wrote only for a more or less anarchical and vain group, uprooted from the life of the country, who preened themselves on not sharing the prejudices and passions of the rest of human-ity, or else made a mock of them. It is a fine sort of fame that is won by self-amputation from life, so as to be unlike other

men! Let all such artists perish! We will go with the living,
be suckled at the breasts of the earth, and drink in all that is
most profound and sacred in our people, and all its love from
the family and the soil. In the greatest age of liberty, among
the people with the most ardent worship of beauty, the young
Prince of the Italian Renaissance, Raphael, glorified maternity
in his transteverine Madonnas. Who is there now to give us in
music a *Madonna à la Chaise?* Who is there to give us music
meet for every hour of life? You have nothing, you have
nothing in France. When you want to give your people songs,
you are reduced to bringing up to date the German masters
of the past. In your art, from top to bottom, everything remains to be done, or to be done again. . . . .

Christophe corresponded with Olivier, who was now settled
in a provincial town. He tried to maintain in correspondence
that collaboration which had been so fruitful during the time
when they had lived together. He wanted him to write him
fine poetic words closely allied with the thoughts and deeds of
everyday life, like the poems which are the substance of the old
German *lieder.* Short fragments from the Scriptures and the
Hindoo poems, and the old Greek philosophers, short religious
and moral poems, little pictures of Nature, the emotions of love
or family life, the whole poetry of morning, evening, and night,
that is in simple, healthy people. Four lines or six are enough
for a *lied:* only the simplest expressions, and no elaborate development or subtlety of harmony. What have I to do with your
esthetic tricks? Love my life, help me to love it and to live
it. Write me the *Hours of France,* my *Great* and *Small Hours.*
And let us together find the clearest melody. Let us avoid like
the plague any artistic language that belongs to a caste like
that of so many writers, and especially of so many French musicians of to-day. We must have the courage to speak like men,
and not like " artists." We must draw upon the common fund
of all men, and unashamedly make use of old formulæ, upon
which the ages have set their seal, formulæ which the ages
have filled with their spirit. Look at what our forefathers
have done. It was by returning to the musical language of
all men that the art of the German classics of the eighteenth
century came into being. The melodies of Gluck and the cre-

ators of the symphony are sometimes trivial and commonplace
compared with the subtle and erudite phrases of Johann Sebastian Bach and Rameau.   It is their raciness of the soil that
gives such zest to, and has procured such immense popularity
for the German classics.   They began with the simplest musical
forms, the *lied* and the *Singspiel,* the little flowers of everyday
life which impregnated the childhood of men like Mozart and
Weber.—Do you do the same.   Write songs for all and sundry.
Upon that basis you will soon build quartettes and symphonies.
What is the good of rushing ahead?   The pyramids were not
begun at the top.   Your symphonies at present are trunkless
heads, ideas without any stuffing.   Oh, you fair spirits, become
incarnate!   There must be generations of musicians patiently
and joyously and piously living in brotherhood with these people.
No musical art was ever built in a day.

Christophe was not content to apply these principles in music:
he urged Olivier to set himself at the head of a similar movement in literature:

"The writers of to-day," he said, "waste their energy in
describing human rarities, or cases that are common enough
in the abnormal groups of men and women living on the fringe
of the great society of active, healthy human beings.   Since they
themselves have shut themselves off from life, leave them and
go where there are men.   Show the life of every day to the men
and women of every day: that life is deeper and more vast than
the sea.   The smallest among you bears the infinite in his soul.
The infinite is in every man who is simple enough to be a man,
in the lover, in the friend, in the woman who pays with her
pangs for the radiant glory of the day of childbirth, in every
man and every woman who lives in obscure self-sacrifice which
will never be known to another soul: it is the very river of
life, flowing from one to another, from one to another, and
back again and round. . . .   Write the simple life of one of
these simple men, write the peaceful epic of the days and nights
following, following one like to another, and yet all different, all
sons of the same mother, from the dawning of the first day in
the life of the world.   Write it simply, as simple as its own
unfolding.   Waste no thought upon the word, and the letter, and
the subtle vain researches in which the force of the artists of

to-day is turned to nought. You are addressing all men: use
the language of all men. There are no words noble or vulgar;
there is no style chaste or impure: there are only words and styles
which say or do not say exactly what they have to say. Be
sound and thorough in all you do: think just what you think,—
and feel just what you feel. Let the rhythm of your heart
prevail in your writings! The style is the soul."

Olivier agreed with Christophe, but he replied rather ironically:

"Such a book would be fine: but it would never reach the
people who would care to read it. The critics would strangle
it on the way."

"There speaks my little French bourgeois!" replied Christophe. "Worrying his mind about what the critics will or will
not think of his work! . . . . The critics, my boy, are only
there to register victory or defeat. The great thing is to be
victor. . . . I have managed to get along without them! You
must learn how to disregard them, too. . . . ."

But Olivier had learned how to disregard something entirely
different! He had turned aside from art, and Christophe, and
everybody. At that time he was thinking of nothing but Jacqueline, and Jacqueline was thinking of nothing but him.

The selfishness of their love had cut them off from everything
and everybody: they were recklessly destroying all their future
resources.

They were in the blind wonder of the first days, when man
and woman, joined together, have no thought save that of losing
themselves in each other. . . . With every part of themselves,
body and soul, they touch and taste and seek to probe into the
very inmost depths. They are alone together in a lawless universe, a very chaos of love, when the confused elements know
not as yet what distinguishes one from the other, and strive
greedily to devour each other. Each in other finds nothing
save delight: each in other finds another self. What is the
world to them? Like the antique Androgyne slumbering in
his dream of voluptuous and harmonious delights, their eyes
are closed to the world. All the world is in themselves. . . .

O days, O nights, weaving one web of dreams, hours fleeting like the floating white clouds in the heavens, leaving nought but a shimmering wake in dazzled eyes, the warm wind breathing the languor of spring, the golden warmth of the body, the sunlit arbor of love, shameless chastity, embraces, and madness, and sighs, and happy laughter, happy tears, what is there left of the lovers, thrice happy dust? Hardly, it seems, that their hearts could ever remember to beat: for when they were one then time had ceased to exist.

And all their days are one like unto another. . . . Sweet, sweet dawn. . . . Together, embracing, they issue from the abyss of sleep: they smile and their breath is mingled, their eyes open and meet, and they kiss. . . . There is freshness and youth in the morning hours, a virgin air cooling their fever. . . . There is a sweet languor in the endless day still throbbing with the sweetness of the night. . . . Summer afternoons, dreams in the fields, on the velvety sward, beneath the rustling of the tall white poplars. . . . Dreams in the lovely evenings, when, under the gleaming sky, they return, clasping each other, to the house of their love. The wind whispers in the bushes. In the clear lake of the sky hovers the fleecy light of the silver moon. A star falls and dies,— hearts give a little throb—a world is silently snuffed out. Swift silent shadows pass at rare intervals on the road near by. The bells of the town ring in the morrow's holiday. They stop for a moment, she nestles close to him, they stand so without a word. . . . Ah! if only life could be so forever, as still and silent as that moment! . . . She sighs and says:

" Why do I love you so much? . . ."

After a few weeks' traveling in Italy they had settled in a town in the west of France, where Olivier had gained an appointment. They saw hardly anybody. They took no interest in anything. When they were forced to pay calls, their scandalous indifference was so open that it hurt some, while it made others smile. Anything that was said to them simply made no impression. They had the impertinently solemn manner common to young married people, who seem to say:

" You people don't know anything at all. . . ."

Jacqueline's pretty pouting face, with its absorbed expression, Olivier's happy eyes that looked so far away, said only:
"If you knew how boring we find you! . . . When shall we be left alone?"

Even the presence of others could not embarrass them. It was hard not to see their exchange of glances as they talked. They did not need to look to see each other: and they would smile: for they knew that they were thinking of the same things at the same time. When they were alone once more, after having suffered the constraint of the presence of others, they would shout for joy—indulge in a thousand childish pranks. They would talk baby-language, and find grotesque nicknames for each other. She used to call him Olive, Olivet, Olifant, Fanny, Mami, Mime, Minaud, Quinaud, Kaunitz, Cosima, Cobourg, Panot, Nacot, Ponette, Naquet, and Canot. She would behave like a little girl; but she wanted to be all things at once to him, to give him every kind of love: mother, sister, wife, sweetheart, mistress.

It was not enough for her to share his pleasures: as she had promised herself, she shared his work: and that, too, was a game. At first she brought to bear on it the amused ardor of a woman to whom work is something new: she seemed really to take a pleasure in the most ungrateful tasks, copying in the libraries, and translating dull books: it was part of her plan of life, that it should be pure and serious, and wholly consecrated to noble thoughts and work in common. And all went well as long as the light of love was in them: for she thought only of him, and not of what she was doing. The odd thing was that everything she did in that way was well done. Her mind found no difficulty in taking in abstract ideas, which at any other time of her life she would have found it hard to follow: her whole being was, as it were, uplifted from the earth by love; she did not know it; like a sleep-walker moving easily over roofs, gravely and gaily, without seeing anything at all, she lived on in her dream. . . .

And then she began to see the roofs: but that did not give her any qualms: only she asked what she was doing so high up, and became herself again. Work bored her. She persuaded herself that it stood in the way of her love: no doubt because

her love had already become less ardent. But there was no
evidence of that. They could not bear to be out of each other's
sight. They shut themselves off from the world, and closed
their doors and refused all invitations. They were jealous of
the affections of other people, even of their occupations, of
everything which distracted them from their love. Olivier's
correspondence with Christophe dwindled. Jacqueline did not
like it: he was a rival to her, representing a part of Olivier's
past life in which she had had no share; and the more room
he filled in Olivier's life, the more she sought, instinctively,
to rob him of it. Without any deliberate intention, she gradually and steadily alienated Olivier from his friend: she made
sarcastic comments on Christophe's manners, his face, his way
of writing, his artistic projects: there was no malice in what
she said, nor slyness: she was too good-natured for that. Olivier
was amused by her remarks, and saw no harm in them: he
thought he still loved Christophe as much as ever, but he loved
only his personality: and that counts for very little in friendship: he did not see that little by little he was losing his understanding of him, and his interest in his ideas, and the heroic
idealism in which they had been so united. . . . Love is too
sweet a joy for the heart of youth: compared with it, what other
faith can hold its ground? The body of the beloved and the
soul that breathes in it are all science and all faith. With
what a pitying smile does a lover regard the object of another's
adoration and the things which he himself once adored! Of all
the might of life and its bitter struggles the lover sees nothing
but the passing flower, which he believes must live forever. . . .
Love absorbed Olivier. In the beginning his happiness was
not so great but it left him with the energy to express it in
graceful verse. Then even that seemed vain to him: it was a
theft of time from love. And Jacqueline also set to work to
destroy their every source of life, to kill the tree of life, without
the support of which the ivy of love must die. Thus in their
happiness they destroyed each other.

Alas! we so soon grow used to happiness! When selfish
happiness is the sole aim of life, life is soon left without an
aim. It becomes a habit, a sort of intoxication which we cannot

do without. And how vitally important it is that we should do without it. . . . Happiness is an instant in the universal rhythm, one of the poles between which the pendulum of life swings: to stop the pendulum it must be broken. . . .

They knew the "boredom of well-being which sets the nerves on edge." Their hours of sweetness dragged, drooped, and withered like flowers without water. The sky was still blue for them, but there was no longer the light morning breeze. All was still: Nature was silent. They were alone, as they had desired.—And their hearts sank.

An indefinable feeling of emptiness, a vague weariness not without a certain charm, came over them. They knew not what it was, and they were darkly uneasy. They became morbidly sensitive. Their nerves, strained in the close watching of the silence, trembled like leaves at the least unexpected clash of life. Jacqueline was often in tears without any cause for weeping, and although she tried hard to convince herself of it, it was not only love that made them flow. After the ardent and tormented years that had preceded her marriage the sudden stoppage of her efforts as she attained—attained and passed—her end,—the sudden futility of any new course of action—and perhaps of all that she had done in the past,—flung her into a state of confusion, which she could not understand, so that it appalled and crushed her. She would not allow that it was so: she attributed it to her nerves, and pretended to laugh it off: but her laughter was no less uneasy than her tears. She tried bravely to take up her work again: but as soon as she began she could not understand how she could ever have taken any interest in such stupid things, and she flung them aside in disgust. She made an effort to pick up the threads of her social life once more: but with no better success: she had committed herself, and she had lost the trick of dealing with the commonplace people and their commonplace remarks that are inevitable in life: she thought them grotesque; and she flung back into her isolation with her husband, and tried hard to persuade herself, as a result of these unhappy experiences, that there was nothing good in the world save love. And for a time she seemed really to be more in love than ever.

Olivier, being less passionate and having a greater store of tenderness, was less susceptible to these apprehensions: only every now and then he would feel a qualm of uneasiness. Besides, his love was preserved in some measure by the constraint of his daily occupation, his work, which was distasteful to him. But as he was highly strung and sensitive, and everything that happened in the heart of the woman he loved affected him also, Jacqueline's secret uneasiness infected him.

One fine afternoon they went for a walk together in the country. They had looked forward to the walk eagerly and happily. All the world was bright and gay about them. But as soon as they set out gloom and heavy sadness descended upon them: they felt chilled to the heart. They could find nothing to say to each other. However, they forced themselves to speak, but every word they said rang hollowly, and made them feel the emptiness of their lives at that moment. They finished their walk mechanically, seeing nothing, feeling nothing. They returned home sick at heart. It was twilight: their rooms were cold, black, and empty. They did not light up at once, to avoid seeing each other. Jacqueline went into her room, and, instead of taking off her hat and cloak, she sat in silence by the window. Olivier sat. too, in the next room with his arms resting on the table. The door was open between the two rooms; they were so near that they could have heard each other's breathing. And in the semi-darkness they both wept, in silence, bitterly. They held their hands over their mouths, so that they should make no sound. At last, in agony, Olivier said:

"Jacqueline. . . ."

Jacqueline gulped down her sobs, and said:

"What is it?"

"Aren't you coming?"

"Yes, I'm coming."

She took off her hat and cloak, and went and bathed her eyes. He lit the lamp. In a few minutes she came into the room. They did not look at each other. Each knew that the other had been weeping. And they could not console each other, for they knew not why it was.

Then came a time when they could no longer conceal their unhappiness. And as they would not admit the true cause of

it, they cast about for another, and had no difficulty in finding
it. They set it down to the dullness of provincial life and
their surroundings. They found comfort in that. M. Langeais
was informed of their plight by his daughter, and was not
greatly surprised to hear that she was beginning to weary of
heroism. He made use of his political friends, and obtained a
post in Paris for his son-in-law.

When the good news reached them, Jacqueline jumped for
joy and regained all her old happiness. Now that they were
going to leave it, they found that they were quite fond of the
dull country: they had sown so many memories of love in it!
They occupied their last days in going over the traces of their
love. There was a tender melancholy in their pilgrimage.
Those calm stretches of country had seen them happy. An
inward voice murmured:

" You know what you are leaving behind you. Do you know
what lies before you? "

Jacqueline wept the day before they left. Olivier asked her
why. She would not say. They took a sheet of paper, and
as they always did when they were fearful of the sound of
words, wrote:

" My dear, dear Olivier. . . ."

" My dear, dear Jacqueline. . . ."

" I am sorry to be going away."

" Going away from what? "

" From the place where we have been lovers."

" Going where? "

" To a place where we shall be older."

" To a place where we shall be together."

" But never so loving."

" Always more loving."

" Who can tell? "

" I know."

" I will be."

Then they drew two circles at the bottom of the paper for
kisses. And then she dried her tears, laughed, and dressed him
up as a favorite of Henri III. by putting her toque on his head
and her white cape with its collar turned up like a ruff round
his shoulders.

In Paris they resumed all their old friendships, but they did not find their friends just as they had left them. When he heard of Olivier's arrival, Christophe rushed to him delightedly. Olivier was equally rejoiced to see him. But as soon as they met they felt an unaccountable constraint between them. They both tried to break through it, but in vain. Olivier was very affectionate, but there was a change in him, and Christophe felt it. A friend who marries may do what he will: he cannot be the friend of the old days. The woman's soul is, and must be, merged in the man's. Christophe could detect the woman in everything that Olivier said and did, in the imperceptible light of his expression, in the unfamiliar turn of his lips, in the new inflections of his voice and the trend of his ideas. Olivier was oblivious of it: but he was amazed to find Christophe so different from the man he had left. He did not go so far as to think that it was Christophe who had changed: he recognized that the change was in himself, and ascribed it to normal evolution, the inevitable result of the passing years; and he was surprised not to find the same progress in Christophe: he thought reproachfully that he had remained stationary in his ideas, which had once been so dear to him, though now they seemed naïve and out of date. The truth was that they did not sort well with the stranger soul which, unknown to himself, had taken up its abode in him. He was most clearly conscious of it when Jacqueline was present when they were talking: and then between Olivier's eyes and Christophe there was a veil of irony. However, they tried to conceal what they felt. Christophe went often to see them, and Jacqueline innocently let fly at him her barbed and poisoned shafts. He suffered her. But when he returned home he would feel sad and sorry.

Their first months in Paris were fairly happy for Jacqueline, and consequently for Olivier. At first she was busy with their new house: they had found a nice little flat looking on to a garden in an old street at Passy. Choosing furniture and wall-papers kept her time full for a few weeks. Jacqueline flung herself into it energetically, and almost passionately and exaggeratedly: it was as though her eternal happiness depended on the color of her hangings or the shape of an old chest. Then she resumed intercourse with her father and mother and

her friends. As she had entirely forgotten them during her
year of love, it was as though she had made their acquaintance
for the first time: just as part of her soul was merged in
Olivier's, so part of Olivier's soul was merged in hers, and she
saw her old friends with new eyes. They seemed to her to
have gained much. Olivier did not lose by it at first. They
were a set-off to each other. The moral reserve and the poetic
light and shade of her husband made Jacqueline find more
pleasure in those worldly people who only think of enjoying
themselves, and of being brilliant and charming: and the seductive but dangerous failings of their world, which she knew so
much better because she belonged to it, made her appreciate
the security of her lover's affection. She amused herself with
these comparisons, and loved to linger over them, the better
to justify her choice.—She lingered over them to such an extent
that sometimes she could not tell why she had made that choice.
Happily, such moments never lasted long. She would be sorry
for them, and was never so tender with Olivier as when they
were past. Thereupon she would begin again. By the time it
had become a habit with her it had ceased to amuse her: and
the comparison became more aggressive: instead of complement-
ing each other, the two opposing worlds declared war on each
other. She began to wonder why Olivier lacked the qualities,
if not some of the failings, which she now admired in her
Parisian friends. She did not tell him so: but Olivier often
felt his wife looking at him without any indulgence in her eyes,
and it hurt him and made him uneasy.

However, he had not lost the ascendancy over Jacqueline
which love had given him: and they would have gone on quite
happily living their life of tender and hard-working intimacy
for long enough had it not been for circumstances which altered
their material condition and destroyed its delicate balance.

Quivi trovammo Pluto il gran nemico. . . .

A sister of Madame Langeais died. She was the widow of a
rich manufacturer, and had no children. Her whole estate
passed to the Langeais. Jacqueline's fortune was more than
doubled by it. When she came in for her legacy, Olivier remembered what Christophe had said about money, and remarked:

"We were quite well off without it: perhaps it will be a bad thing for us."

Jacqueline laughed at him:

"Silly!" she said. "As though money could ever do any harm! We won't make any change in our way of living just yet."

Their life remained the same to all appearances: so much the same that after a certain time Jacqueline began to complain that they were not well enough off: proof positive that there was a change somewhere. And, in fact, although their income had been doubled or tripled, they spent the whole of it without knowing how they did it. They began to wonder how they had managed to live before. The money flew, and was swallowed up by a thousand new expenses, which seemed at once to be habitual and indispensable. Jacqueline had begun to patronize the great dressmakers: she had dismissed the family sempstress who came by the day, a woman she had known since she was a child. The days of the little fourpenny hats made out of nothing, though they were quite pretty all the same, were gone,— gone the days of the frocks which were not impeccably smart, though they had much of her own grace, and were, indeed, a part of herself! The sweet intimate charm which shone upon all about her grew fainter every day. The poetry of her nature was lost. She was becoming commonplace.

They changed their flat. The rooms which they had furnished with so much trouble and pleasure seemed narrow and ugly. Instead of the cozy little rooms, all radiant with her spirit, with a friendly tree waving its delicate foliage against the windows, they took an enormous, comfortable, well-arranged flat which they did not, could not, love, where they were bored to death. Instead of their old friendly belongings, they obtained furniture and hangings which were strangers to them. There was no place left for memories. The first years of their married life were swept away from their thoughts. . . . It is a great misfortune for two people living together to have the ties which bind them to their past love broken! The image of their love is a safeguard against the disappointment and hostility which inevitably succeed the first years of tenderness. . . . The power to spend largely had brought Jacqueline, both in Paris and abroad—(for now that they were rich they often traveled) —into touch with a class of rich and useless people, whose society gave her a sort of contempt for the rest of mankind, all those who had work to do. With her marvelous power of adaptation, she very quickly caught the color of these sterile and rotten men and women. She could not fight against it. At once she became refractory and irritable, regarding the idea that it was possible—and right—to be happy in her domestic duties and the *aurea mediocritus* as mere " vulgar manners." She had lost even the capacity to understand the bygone days when she had so generously given herself in love.

Olivier was not strong enough to fight against it. He, too, had changed. He had given up his work, and had no fixed and compulsory occupation. He wrote, and the balance of his life was adjusted by it. Till then he had suffered because he could not give his whole life to art. Now that he could do so he felt utterly lost in the cloudy world. Art which is not also a profession, and supported by a healthy practical life, art which knows not the necessity of earning the daily bread, loses the best part of its force and its reality. It is only the flower of luxury. It is not—(what in the greatest, the only great, artists it is)—the sacred fruit of human suffering.—Olivier felt a dis-inclination to work, a desire to ask: " What is the good of it? " There was nothing to make him write: he would let his pen run on, he dawdled about, he had lost his bearings. He had lost touch with his own class of men and women patiently plow-ing the hard furrow of their lives. He had fallen into a differ-ent world, where he was ill at ease, though on the whole he did not find it unpleasant. Weak, amiable, and curious, he fell complacently to observing that world which was entirely lacking in consistency, though it was not without charm; and he did not see that little by little he was becoming contaminated by it: it was undermining his faith.

No doubt the transformation was not so rapid in him as it was in Jacqueline.—Women have the terrible privilege of being able suddenly to undergo a complete change. The way in which they suddenly die and then as suddenly come to life again is appalling to those who love them. And yet it is perfectly natural for a human being who is full of life without the curb of the will not to be to-morrow what it is to-day. A woman is like running water. The man who loves her must follow the stream or divert it into the channel of his own life. In both cases there must be change. But it is a dangerous experience, and no man really knows love until he has gone through it. And its harmony is so delicate during the first years of married life that often the very smallest change in either husband or wife is enough to destroy their whole relationship. How much more perilous, then, is a sudden change of fortune or of circumstance! They must needs be very strong—or very indifferent to each other—to withstand it.

Jacqueline and Olivier were neither indifferent nor strong. They began to see each other in a new light: and the face of the beloved became strange to them. When first they made the sad discovery, they hid it from each other in loving pity: for they still loved each other. Olivier took refuge in his work, and by applying himself to it regularly, though with even less conviction than before, won through to tranquillity. Jacqueline had nothing. She did nothing. She would stay in bed for hours, or dawdle over her toilette, sitting idly, half dressed, motionless, lost in thought: and gradually a dumb misery crept over her like an icy mist. She could not break away from the fixed idea of love. . . . Love! Of things human the most Divine when it is the gift of self, a passionate and blind sacrifice. But when it is no more than the pursuit of happiness, it is the most senseless and the most elusive. . . . It was impossible for her to conceive any other aim in life. In moments of benevolence she had tried to take an interest in the sorrows of other people: but she could not do it. The sufferings of others filled her with an ungovernable feeling of repulsion: her nerves were not strong enough to bear them. To appease her conscience she had occasionally done something which looked like philanthropy: but the result had been tame and disappointing.

"You see," she would say to Christophe, "when one tries to do good one does harm. It is much better not to try. I'm not cut out for it."

Christophe would look at her: and he would think of a girl he had met, a selfish, immoral little grisette, absolutely incapable of real affection, though, as soon as she saw anybody suffering, she was filled with motherly pity for him, even though she had not cared a rap for him before, even though he were a stranger to her. She was not abashed by the most horrible tasks, and she would even take a strange pleasure in doing those which demanded the greatest self-denial. She never stopped to think about it: she seemed to find in it a use for her obscure, hereditary, and eternally unexpressed idealism: her soul was atrophied as far as the rest of her life was concerned, but at such rare moments it breathed again: it gave her a sense of wellbeing and inward joy to be able to allay suffering: and her joy was then almost misplaced.—The goodness of that woman, who was selfish, the selfishness of Jacqueline, who was good in spite of it, were neither vice nor virtue, but in both cases only a matter of health. But the first was in the better case.

Jacqueline was crushed by the mere idea of suffering. She would have preferred death to physical illness. She would have preferred death to the loss of either of her sources of joy: her beauty or her youth. That she should not have all the happiness to which she thought herself entitled,—(for she believed in happiness, it was a matter of faith with her, wholeheartedly and absurdly, a religious belief),—and that others should have more happiness than herself, would have seemed to her the most horrible injustice. Happiness was not only a religion to her; it was a virtue. To be unhappy seemed to her to be an infirmity. Her whole life gradually came to revolve round that principle. Her real character had broken through the veils of idealism in which in girlish bashful modesty she had enshrouded herself. In her reaction against the idealism of the past she began to see things in a hard, crude light. Things were only true for her in proportion as they coincided with the opinion of the world and the smoothness of life. She had reached her mother's state of mind: she went to church, and practised religion punctiliously and indifferently. She never stopped to ask herself whether there was any real truth in it: she had other more positive mental difficulties: and she would think of the mystical revolt of her childhood with pitying irony.—And yet her new positivism was no more real than her old idealism. She forced it. She was neither angel nor brute. She was just a poor bored woman.

She was bored, bored, bored: and her boredom was all the greater in that she could not excuse herself on the score of not being loved, or by saying that she could not endure Olivier. Her life seemed to be stunted, walled up, with no future prospect: she longed for a new happiness that should be perpetually renewed; her longing was utterly childish, for it never took into account her indifferent capacity for happiness. She was like so many women living idle lives with idle husbands, who have every reason to be happy, and yet never cease torturing themselves. There are many such couples, who are rich and blessed with health and lovely children, and clever and capable of feeling fine things, and possessed of the power to keep themselves employed and to do good, and to enrich their own lives and the lives of others. And they spend their time in moaning and groaning that they do not love each other, that they love some one else, or that they do not love somebody else—perpetually taken up with themselves, and their sentimental or sensual relations, and their pretended right to happiness, their conflicting egoism, and arguing, arguing, arguing, playing with their sham grand passion, their sham great suffering, and in the end believing in it, and—suffering. . . . If only some one would say to them:

"You are not in the least interesting. It is indecent to be so sorry for yourselves when you have so many good reasons for being happy!"

If only some one would take away their money, their health, all the marvelous gifts of which they are so unworthy! If only some one would once more lay the yoke of poverty and real suffering on these slaves who are incapable of being free and are driven mad by their liberty! If they had to earn their bread in the sweat of their brows, they would be glad enough to eat it. And if they were to come face to face with grim suffering, they would never dare to play with the sham. . . .

But, when all is said and done, they do suffer. They are ill. How, then, are they not to be pitied?—Poor Jacqueline was quite innocent, as innocent in drifting apart from Olivier as Olivier was in not holding her. She was what Nature had made her. She did not know that marriage is a challenge to Nature, and that, when one has thrown down the gauntlet to Nature, it is only to be expected that she will arise and begin valiantly to wage the combat which one has provoked. She saw that she had been mistaken, and she was exasperated with herself; and her disillusion turned to hostility towards the thing she had loved, Olivier's faith, which had also been her own. An intelligent woman has, much more than a man, moments of an intuitive perception of things eternal: but it is more difficult for her to maintain her grip on them. Once a man has come by the idea of the eternal, he feeds it with his life-blood. A woman uses it to feed her own life: she absorbs it, and does not create it. She must always be throwing fresh fuel into her heart and mind: she cannot be self-sufficing. And if she cannot believe and love, she must destroy—except she possess the supreme virtue of serenity.

Jacqueline had believed passionately in a union based on a common faith, in the happiness of struggling and suffering together in accomplishment. But she had only believed in that endeavor, that faith, while they were gilded by the sun of love: and as the sun died down she saw them as barren, gloomy mountains standing out against the empty sky: and her strength failed her, so that she could go no farther on the road: what was the good of reaching the summit? What was there on the other side? It was a gigantic phantom and a snare! . . . Jacqueline could not understand how Olivier could go on being taken in by such fantastic notions which consumed life: and she began to tell herself that he was not very clever, nor very much alive. She was stifling in his atmosphere, in which she could not breathe, and the instinct of self-preservation drove her on to the attack, in self-defense. She strove to scatter and bring to dust the injurious beliefs of the man she still loved: she used every weapon of irony and seductive pleasure in her armory: she trammeled him with the tendrils of her desires and her petty cares: she longed to make him a reflection of herself, . . . herself who knew neither what she wanted nor what she was! She was humiliated by Olivier's want of success: and she did not care whether it were just or unjust; for she had come to believe that the only thing which saves a man of talent from failure is success. Olivier was oppressed by his consciousness of her doubts, and his strength was sapped by it. However, he struggled on as best he could, as so many men have struggled, and will struggle, for the most part vainly, in the unequal conflict in which the selfish instinct of the woman upholds itself against the man's intellectual egoism by playing upon his weakness, his dishonesty, and his common sense, which is the name with which he disguises the wear and tear of life and his own cowardice.—At least, Jacqueline and Olivier were better than the majority of such combatants. For he would never have betrayed his ideal, as thousands of men do who drift with the demands of their laziness, their vanity, and their loves, into renunciation of their immortal souls. And, if he had done so, Jacqueline would have despised him. But, in her blindness, she strove to destroy that force in Olivier, which was hers also, their common safeguard : and by an instinctive strategical movement she undermined the friendship by which that force was upheld.

Since the legacy Christophe had become a stranger in their household. The affectation of snobbishness and a dull practical outlook on life which Jacqueline used wickedly to exaggerate in her conversations with him were more than he could bear. He would lash out sometimes, and say hard things, which were taken in bad part. They could never have brought about a rupture between the two friends : they were too fond of each other. Nothing in the world would have induced Olivier to give up Christophe. But he could not make Jacqueline feel the same about him ; and, his love making him weak, he was incapable of hurting her. Christophe, who saw what was happening to him, and how he was suffering, made the choice easy by a voluntary withdrawal. He saw that he could not help Olivier in any way by staying, but rather made things worse. He was the first to give his friend reasons for turning from him : and Olivier, in his weakness, accepted those inadequate reasons, while he guessed what the sacrifice must have cost Christophe, and was bitterly sorry for it.

Christophe bore him no ill-will. He thought that there was much truth in the saying that a man's wife is his better half For a man married is but the half of a man.

He tried to reconstruct his life without Olivier. But it was all in vain, and it was idle for him to pretend that the separation would only be for a short time: in spite of his optimism, he had many hours of sadness. He had lost the habit of loneliness. He had been alone, it is true, during Olivier's sojourn in the provinces: but then he had been able to pretend and tell himself that his friend was away for a time, and would return. Now that his friend had come back he was farther away than ever. His affection for him, which had filled his life for a number of years, was suddenly taken from him: it was as though he had lost his chief reason for working. Since his friendship for Olivier he had grown used to thinking with him and bringing him into everything he did. His work was not enough to supply the gap: for Christophe had grown used to weaving the image of his friend into his work. And now that his friend no longer took any interest in him, Christophe was thrown off his balance: he set out to find another affection to restore it.

Madame Arnaud and Philomela did not fail him. But just then such tranquil friendship as theirs was not enough.

However, the two women seemed to divine Christophe's sorrow, and they secretly sympathized with him. Christophe was much surprised one evening to see Madame Arnaud come into his room. Till then she had never ventured to call on him. She seemed to be somewhat agitated. Christophe paid no heed to it, and set her uneasiness down to her shyness. She sat down, and for some time said nothing. To put her at her ease, Christophe did the honors of his room. They talked of Olivier, with memories of whom the room was filled. Christophe spoke of him gaily and naturally, without giving so much as a hint of what had happened. But Madame Arnaud, knowing it, could not help looking at him pityingly and saying:

"You don't see each other now?"

He thought she had come to console him, and felt a gust of impatience, for he did not like any meddling with his affairs. He replied:

"Whenever we like."

She blushed, and said:

"Oh! it was not an indiscreet question!"

He was sorry for his gruffness, and took her hands:

"I beg your pardon," he said. "I am always afraid of his being blamed. Poor boy! He is suffering as much as I. . . . No, we don't see each other now."

"And he doesn't write to you?"

"No," said Christophe, rather shamefacedly. . . .

"How sad life is!" said Madame Arnaud, after a moment.

"No; life is not sad," he said. "But there are sad moments in it."

Madame Arnaud went on with veiled bitterness:

"We love, and then we love no longer. What is the good of it all?"

Christophe replied:

"It is good to have loved."

She went on:

"You have sacrificed yourself for him. If only our self-sacrifice could be of any use to those we love! But it makes them none the happier!"

"I have not sacrificed myself," said Christophe angrily. "And if I have, it is because it pleased me to do so. There's no room for arguing about it. One does what one has to do. If one did not do it, one would be unhappy, and suffer for it! There never was anything so idiotic as this talk of sacrifice! Clergymen, in the poverty of their hearts, mix it up with a cramped and morose idea of Protestant gloom. Apparently, if an act of sacrifice is to be good, it must be besotted. . . . Good Lord! if a sacrifice means sorrow to you, and not joy, then don't do it; you are unworthy of it. A man doesn't sacrifice himself for the King of Prussia, but for himself. If you don't feel the happiness that lies in the gift of yourself, then get out! You don't deserve to live."

Madame Arnaud listened to Christophe without daring to look at him. Suddenly she got up and said:

"Good-by."

Then he saw that she had come to confide in him, and said:

"Oh! forgive me. I'm a selfish oaf, and can only talk about myself. Please stay. Won't you?"

She said:

"No: I cannot. . . . Thank you. . . ."

And she left him.

It was some time before they met again. She gave no sign of life; and he did not go to see either her or Philomela. He was fond of both of them: but he was afraid of having to talk to them about things that made him sad. And, besides, for the time being, their calm, dull existence, with its too rarefied air, was not suited to his needs. He wanted to see new faces; it was imperative that he should find a new interest, a new love, to occupy his mind.

By way of being taken out of himself he began to frequent the theaters which he had neglected for a ·long time. The theater seemed to him to be an interesting school for a musician who wishes to observe and take note of the accents of the passions.

It was not that he had any greater sympathy with French plays than when he first came to live in Paris. Outside his small liking for their eternal stale and brutal subjects connected with the psycho-physiology of love, it seemed to him that the language of the French theater, especially in poetic drama, was ultra-false. Neither their prose nor their verse had anything in common with the living language and the genius of the people. Their prose was an artificial language, the language of a polite chronicle with the best, that of a vulgar feuilletonist with the worst. Their poetry justified Goethe's gibe:

"*Poetry is all very well for those who have nothing to say.*"

It was a wordy and inverted prose: the profusion of metaphors clumsily tacked on to it in imitation of the lyricism of other nations produced an effect of utter falsity upon any sincere person. Christophe set no more store by these poetic dramas than he did by the Italian operas with their shrill mellifluous airs and their ornamental vocal exercises. He was much more interested in the actors than the plays. And the authors had tried hard to imitate them. "*It was hopeless to think that a play could be performed with any success unless the author had looked to it that his characters were modeled on the vices of the actors.*" The situation was hardly at all changed since the time when Diderot wrote those lines. The actors had become the models of the art of the theater. As soon as any one of them reached success, he had his theater, his compliant tailor-authors, and his plays made to measure.

Among these great mannikins of literary fashions Françoise Oudon attracted Christophe. Paris had been infatuated with her for a couple of years or so. She, too, of course, had her theater and her purveyors of parts: however, she did not only act in plays written for her: her mixed repertory ranged from Ibsen to Sardou, from Gabriele d'Annunzio to Dumas *fils,* from Bernard Shaw to the latest Parisian playwrights. Upon occasion she would even venture into the Versailles' avenues of the classic hexameter, or on to the deluge of images of Shakespeare. But she was ill at ease in that galley, and her audience was even more so. Whatever she played, she played herself, nothing but herself, always. It was both her weakness and her strength. Until the public had been awakened to an interest in her personality, her acting had had no success. As soon as that interest was roused, everything she did appeared marvelous. And, indeed, it was well worth while in watching her to forget the usually pitiful plays which she betrayed by endowing and adorning them with her vitality. The mystery of the woman's body, swayed by a stranger soul, was to Christophe far more moving than the plays in which she acted.

She had a fine, clear-cut, rather tragic profile. She had not the marked heavy lines of the Roman style: on the contrary, her lines were delicate and Parisian, *à la* Jean Goujon—as much like a boy's as a woman's. A short, finely-modeled nose. A beautiful mouth, with thin lips, curling rather bitterly. Bright cheeks, girlishly thin, in which there was something touching, the light of inward suffering. A strong chin. Pale complexion. One of those habitually impassive faces which are transparent in spite of themselves, and reveal the soul quivering behind it, as though it were exposed in its nakedness; one of those faces in which the soul seems to be ever, in every part of it, just beneath the skin. She had very fine hair and eyebrows, and her changing eyes were gray and amber-colored. passing quickly from one light to another, greenish and golden, like the eyes of a cat. And there was something catlike in all her nature, in her apparent torpor, her semi-somnolence, with eyes wide open, always on the watch, always suspicious, while suddenly she would nervously and rather cruelly relax her watchfulness. She was not so tall as she appeared, nor so slender; she had beautiful shoulders, lovely arms, and fine, long hands. She was very neat in her dress, and her coiffure, always trim and tasteful, with none of the Bohemian carelessness or the exaggerated smartness of many artists—even in that she was catlike, instinctively aristocratic, although she had risen from the gutter. At bottom she was incurably shy and wild.

She must have been a little less than thirty. Christophe had heard people speak of her at Gamache's with coarse admiration, as a woman of great freedom, intelligence, and boldness, tremendous and inflexible energy, and burning ambition, but bitter, fantastic, perplexing, and violent, a woman who had waded through a deal of mud before she had reached her present pinnacle of fame, and had since avenged herself.

One day, when Christophe was going by train to see Philomela at Meudon, as he opened the door of a compartment, he saw the actress sitting there. She seemed to be agitated and perturbed, and Christophe's appearance annoyed her. She turned her back on him, and looked obstinately out of the opposite window. But Christophe was so struck by the changed expression in her face, that he could not stop gazing at her with a naïve and embarrassing compassion. It exasperated her, and she flung an angry look at him which he did not understand. At the next station she got out and went into another compartment. Then for the first time it occurred to him—rather late in the day—that he had driven her away: and he was greatly distressed. A few days later, at a station on the same line, he was sitting on the only seat in the platform, waiting for the train back to Paris. She appeared, and came and sat by his side. He began to move, but she said:

" Stay."

They were alone. He begged her pardon for having forced her to go to another compartment the other day, saying that if he had had any idea that he was incommoding her he would have got out himself. She smiled ironically, and only replied:

" You were certainly unbearable with your persistent staring." He said:

"I begged your pardon: I could not help it. . . . You looked so unhappy."

"Well, what of it?" she said.

"It was too strong for me. If you saw a man drowning, wouldn't you hold out your hand to him?"

"I? Certainly not," she said. "I would push him under water, so as to get it over quickly."

She spoke with a mixture of bitterness and humor: and, when he looked at her in amazement, she laughed.

The train came in. It was full up, except for the last carriage. She got in. The porter told them to hurry up. Christophe, who had no mind to repeat the scene of a few days before, was for finding another compartment, but she said:

"Come in."

He got in, and she said:

"To-day i don't mind."

They began to talk. Christophe tried very seriously to prove to her that it was not right not to take an interest in others, and that people could do so much for each other by helping and comforting each other. . . .

"Consolation," she said, "is not much in my line. . . ."

And as Christophe insisted:

"Yes," she said, with her impertinent smile; "the part of comforter is all very well for the man who plays it."

It was a moment or two before he grasped her meaning. When he understood, when he fancied that she suspected him of seeking his own interest, while he was only thinking of her, he got up indignantly and opened the door, and made as though to climb out, although the train was moving. She prevented him, though not without difficulty. He sat down again angrily, and shut the door just as the train shot into a tunnel.

"You see," she said, "you might have been killed."

"I don't care," he said.

He refused to speak to her again.

"People are so stupid," he said. "They make each other suffer, they suffer, and when a man goes to help another fellow-creature. he is suspected. It is disgusting. People like that are not human."

She laughed and tried to soothe him. She laid her gloved

hand on his: she spoke to him gently, and called him by his name.

"What?" he said. "You know me?"

"As if everybody didn't know everybody in Paris! We're all in the same boat. But it was horrid of me to speak to you as I did. You are a good fellow. I can see that. Come; calm yourself. Shake hands! Let us make peace!"

They shook hands, and went on talking amicably. She said:

"It is not my fault, you know. I have had so many experiences with men that I have become suspicious."

"They have deceived me, too, many a time," said Christophe. "But I always give them credit for something better."

"I see; you were born to be gulled."

He began to laugh:

"Yes; I've been taken in a good many times in my life; I've gulped down a good many lies. But it does me no harm. I've a good stomach. I can put up with worse things, hardship, poverty, and, if necessary, I can gulp down with their lies the poor fools who attack me. It does me good, if anything."

"You're in luck," she said. "You're something like a man."

"And you. You're something like a woman."

"That's no great thing."

"It's a fine thing," he said, "and it may be a good thing, too!"

She laughed:

"To be a woman!" she said. "But what does the world make of women?"

"You have to defend yourself."

"But goodness never lasts long."

"Then you can't have much of it."

"Possibly. And then, I don't think one ought to suffer too much. There is a point beyond which suffering withers you up."

He was just about to tell her how he pitied her, but he remembered how she had received it a short while before. . . .

"You'll only talk about the advantages of the part of comforter. . . ."

"No," she said, "I won't say it again. I feel that you are

kind and sincere. Thank you. Only, don't say anything. You cannot know. . . . Thank you."

They had reached Paris. They parted without exchanging addresses or inviting each other to call.

A few months later she came of her own accord and knocked at Christophe's door.

" I came to see you. I want to talk to you. I have been thinking of you sometimes since our meeting."

She took a seat.

" Only for a moment. I shan't disturb you for long."

He began to talk to her. She said:

" Wait a moment, please."

They sat in silence. Then she said with a smile:

" I couldn't bear it any longer. I feel better now."

He tried to question her.

" No," she said. " Not that! "

She looked round the room, examined and appraised the things in it, and saw the photograph of Louisa:

" Your mother? " she said.

" Yes."

She took it and looked at it sympathetically.

" What a good old woman! " she said. " You are lucky! "

" Alas! she is dead."

" That is nothing. You have had the luck to have her for your mother."

" Yes. And you? "

But she turned the subject with a frown. She would not let him question her about herself.

" No; tell me about yourself. Tell me. . . . Something about your life. . . ."

" How can it be of any interest to you? "

" Tell me, all the same. . . ."

He would not tell her: but he could not avoid answering her questions. for she cross-examined him very skilfully: so much so, that he told her something of what he was suffering, the story of his friendship, and how Olivier had left him. She listened with a pitying ironical smile. . . . Suddenly she asked:

"What time is it? Oh! good Heavens! I've been here two whole hours! . . . Please forgive me. . . . Ah! what a rest it has been! . . ."

She added:

"Will you let me come again? . . . Not often. . . . Sometimes. . . . It would do me good. But I wouldn't like to bore you or waste your time. . . . Only a minute or two every now and then. . . ."

"I'll come and see you," said Christophe.

"No, don't do that. I would much rather come to see you. . . ."

But she did not come again for a long time. One evening he heard by accident that she was seriously ill, and had not been acting for some weeks. He went to see her, although she had forbidden it. She was not at home: but when she heard who it was, she sent and had him brought back as he was going down the stairs. She was in bed, but much better: she had had pneumonia, and looked altered: but she still had her ironical manner and her watchful expression, which there was no disarming. However, she seemed to be really pleased to see Christophe. She made him sit by her bedside, and talked about herself in a mocking, detached way, and said that she had almost died. He was much moved, and showed it. Then she teased him. He reproached her for not having let him know.

"Let you know? And have you coming to see me? Never!"

"I bet you never even thought of me."

"You've won," she said, with her sad little mocking smile. "I didn't think of you for a moment while I was ill. To be precise, I never thought of you until to-day. There's nothing to be glum about, come. When I am ill I don't think of anybody. I only ask one thing of people; to be left alone in peace. I turn my face to the wall and wait: I want to be alone. I want to die alone, like a rat in a hole."

"And yet it is hard to suffer alone."

"I'm used to it. I have been unhappy for years. No one ever came to my assistance. Now it has become a habit. . . . Besides, it is better so. No one can do anything for you. A noise in the room, worrying attentions, hypocritical jeremiads. . . . No; I would rather die alone."

"You are very resigned!"

"Resigned? I don't even know what the word means. No: I set my teeth and I hate the illness which makes me suffer."

He asked her if she had no one to see her, no one to look after her. She said that her comrades at the theater were kind enough,—idiots,—but obliging and compassionate (in a superficial sort of way).

"But I tell you, I don't want to see them. I'm a surly sort of customer."

"I would put up with it," he said.

She looked at him pityingly:

"You, too! You're going to talk like the rest?"

He said:

"Pardon, pardon. . . . Good Heavens! I'm becoming a Parisian! I am ashamed. . . . I swear that I didn't even think what I was saying. . . ."

He buried his face in the bedclothes. She laughed frankly, and gave him a tap on the head!

"Ah! that's not Parisian! That's something like! I know you again. Come, show your face. Don't weep all over my bed."

"Do you forgive me?"

"I forgive you. But don't do it again."

She talked to him a little more, asked him what he was doing, and was then tired, bored, and dismissed him.

He had arranged to go and see her again the following week. But just as he was setting out he received a telegram from her telling him not to come: she was having a bad day.—Then, the next day but one, she sent for him. He went, and found her convalescent, sitting by the window, with her feet up. It was early spring, with a sunny sky and the young buds on the trees. She was more gentle and affectionate than he had yet seen her. She told him that she could not see anybody the other day, and would have detested him as much as anybody else.

"And to-day?"

"To-day I feel young and fresh, and I feel fond of everything else about me that feels young and fresh—as you do."

"And yet I am neither very young nor very fresh."

"You will be both until the day of your death."

They talked about what he had been doing since their last meeting, and about the theater in which she was going to resume her work soon: and on that she told him what she thought of the theater, which disgusted her, while it held her in its grip.

She did not want him to come again, and promised to resume her visits to his flat. He told her the times when she would be least likely to disturb his work. They arranged a counter-sign. She was to knock at the door in a certain way, and he was to open or not as he felt inclined. . . .

She did not go beyond bounds at first. But once, when she was going to a society At Home, where she was to recite, the idea of it bored her at the last moment: she stopped on the way and telephoned to say that she could not come, and she told her man to drive to Christophe's. She only meant to say good-night to him as she passed. But, as it turned out, she began to confide in him that night, and told him all her life from her childhood on.

A sad childhood! An accidental father whom she had never known. A mother who kept an ill-famed inn in a suburb of a town in the north of France: the carters used to go and drink there, use the proprietress, and bully her. One of them married her because she had some small savings: he used to beat her and get drunk. Françoise had an elder sister who was a servant in the inn: she was worked to death; the proprietor made her his mistress in the sight and knowledge of her mother; she was consumptive, and had died. Françoise had grown up amid scenes of violence and shameful things. She saw her mother and sister weep, suffer, accept, degrade themselves, and die. And desperately she made up her mind not to submit to it, and to escape from her infamous surroundings: she was a rebel by instinct: certain acts of injustice would set her beside her-self: she used to scratch and bite when she was thrashed. Once she tried to hang herself. She did not succeed: she had hardly set about it than she was afraid lest she might succeed only too well; and, even while she was beginning to choke and desperately clutching at the rope and trying to loosen it with stiff fumbling fingers, there was writhing in her a furious desire to live. And since she could not escape by death,—(Christophe smiled sadly, remembering his own experiences,)—she swore that she would win, and be free, rich, and trample under foot all those who oppressed her. She had made it a vow in her lair one evening, when in the next room she could hear the oaths of the man, and the cries of her mother as he beat her, and her sister's sobs. How utterly wretched she felt! And yet her vow had been some solace. She clenched her teeth and thought:

"I will crush the lot of you."

In that dark childhood there had been one ray of light:

One day, one of the little grubby boys with whom she used to lark in the gutter, the son of the stage-door keeper of the theater, got her in to the rehearsal, although it was strictly forbidden. They stole to the very back of the building in the darkness. She was gripped by the mystery of the stage, gleaming in the darkness, and by the magnificent and incomprehensible things that the actors were saying, and by the queenly bearing of the actress,—who was, in fact, playing a queen in a romantic melodrama. She was chilled by emotion: and at the same time her heart thumped. . . . "That—that is what I must be some day!" . . . Oh! if she could ever be like that! . . . —When it was over she wanted at all costs to see the evening performance. She let her companion go out, and pretended to follow him: and then she turned back and hid herself in the theater: she cowered away under a seat, and stayed there for three hours without stirring, choked by the dust: and when the performance was about to begin and the audience was arriving, just as she was creeping out of her hiding-place, she had the mortification of being pounced on, ignominiously expelled amid jeers and laughter, and taken home, where she was whipped. She would have died that night had she not known now what she must do later on to master these people and avenge herself on them.

Her plan was made. She took a situation as a servant in the *Hôtel et Café du Théâtre,* where the actors put up. She could hardly read or write: and she had read nothing, for she had nothing to read. She wanted to learn, and applied herself

to it with frantic energy. She used to steal books from the
guests' rooms, and read them at night by moonlight or at dawn,
so as not to use her candle. Thanks to the untidiness of the
actors, her larcenies passed unnoticed or else the owners put
up with cursing and swearing. She used to restore their books
when she had read them,—except one or two which had moved
her too much for her to be able to part with them;—but she
did not return them intact. She used to tear out the pages
which had pleased her. When she took the books back, she used
carefully to slip them under the bed or the furniture, so as
to make the owners of them believe that they had never left
the room. She used to glue her ears to the door to listen to
the actors going over their parts. And when she was alone,
sweeping the corridor, she would mimic their intonations in a
whisper and gesticulate. When she was caught doing so she
was laughed at and jeered at. She would say nothing, and boil
with rage.—That sort of education might have gone on for a
long time had she not on one occasion been imprudent enough
to steal the script of a part from the room of an actor. The
actor stamped and swore. No one had been to his room except
the servant: he accused her. She denied it boldly: he threatened to have her searched: she threw herself at his feet and
confessed everything, even to her other pilferings and the pages
she had torn out of the books: the whole boiling. He cursed
and swore frightfully: but he was not so angry as he seemed.
He asked why she had done it. When she told him that she
wanted to become an actress he roared with laughter. He questioned her, and she recited whole pages which she had learned
by heart: he was struck by it, and said:

"Look here, would you like me to give you lessons?"

She was in the highest heaven of delight, and kissed his hands.

"Ah!" she said to Christophe, "how I should have loved
him!"

But at once he added:

"Only, my dear, you know you can't have anything for
nothing. . . ."

She was chaste, and had always been scared and modest with
those who had pursued her with their overtures. Her absolute
chastity, her ardent need of purity, her disgust with things

unclean and ignoble loveless sensuality, had been with her always from her childhood on, as a result of the despair and nausea of the sad sights which she saw about her on all sides at home:— and they were with her still. . . . Ah! unhappy creature! She had borne much punishment! . . . What a mockery of Fate! . . .

"Then," asked Christophe, "you consented?"

"Ah!" she said, "I would have gone through fire to get out of it. He threatened to have me arrested as a thief. I had no choice.—That was how I was initiated into art—and life."

"The blackguard!" said Christophe.

"Yes, I hated him. But I have met so many men since that he does not seem to me to be one of the worst. He did at least keep his word. He taught me what he knew—(not much!)— of the actor's trade. He got me into his company. At first I was everybody's servant. I played little scraps of parts. Then one night, when the soubrette was ill, they risked giving me her part. I went on from that. They thought me impossible, grotesque, uncouth. I was ugly then. I remained ugly until I was decreed,—if not 'divine' like the other Woman,—the highest, the ideal type of woman, . . .'Woman.' . . . Idiots! As for my acting, it was thought extravagant and incorrect. The public did not like me. The other players used to make fun of me. I was kept on because I was useful in spite of everything, and was not expensive. Not only was I not expensive, but I paid! Ah! I paid for every step, every advance, rung by rung, with my suffering, with my body. Fellow-actors, the manager, the impresario, the impresario's friends. . . ."

She stopped: her face was very pale, her lips were pressed together, there was a hard stare in her eyes: no tears came, but it was plain to see that her soul was shedding tears of blood. In a flash she was living through the shameful past, and the consuming desire to conquer which had upheld her— a desire that burned the more with every fresh stain and degradation that she had had to endure. She would sometimes have been glad to die: but it would have been too abominable to succumb in the midst of humiliation and to go no farther. Better to take her life before—if so it must be—or after victory. But not when she had degraded herself and not enjoyed the price of it. . . .

She said no more. Christophe was pacing up and down the room in anger: he was in a mood to slay these men who had made this woman suffer and besmirched her. Then he looked at her with the eyes of pity: and he stood near her and took her face in his hands and pressed it fondly, and said:

" Poor little woman! "

She made to thrust him away. He said:

" You must not be afraid of me. I love you."

Then the tears trickled down her pale cheeks. He knelt down by her and kissed—

" *La lunga man d'ogni bellezza piena. . . .*"

—the long delicate hands on which two tears had fallen.

He sat down again, and she recovered herself and calmly went on with her story:

An author had at last launched her. He had discovered in the strange little creature a daimon, a genius,—and, even better for his purpose, " a dramatic type, a new woman, representative of an epoch." Of course, he made her his mistress after so many others had done the same. And she let him take her, as she had suffered the others, without love, and even with the opposite of love. But he had made her famous: and she had done the same for him.

" And now," said Christophe, " the others cannot do anything to you: you can do what you like with them."

" You think so? " she said bitterly.

Then she told him of Fate's other mockery,—her passion for a knave whom she despised: a literary man who had exploited her, had plucked out the most sorrowful secrets of her soul, and turned them into literature, and then had left her.

" I despise him," she said, " as I despise the dirt on my boots: and I tremble with rage when I think that I love him, that he has but to hold up his finger, and I should go running to him, and humble myself before such a cur. But what can I do? I have a heart that will never love what my mind

desires.   And I am compelled alternately to sacrifice and humiliate one or the other.   I have a heart: I have a body.   And they
cry out and cry out and demand their share of happiness.   And
I have nothing to curb them with, for I believe in nothing.
I am free. . . .   Free?   I am the slave of my heart and my
body, which often, almost always, in spite of myself, desire
and have their will.   They carry me away, and I am ashamed.
But what can I do? . . ."

She stopped for a moment, and mechanically moved the cinders
in the fire with the tongs.

"I have read in books," she said, "that actors feel nothing.
And, indeed, those whom I meet are nearly all conceited, grown-
up children who are never troubled by anything but petty questions of vanity.   I do not know if it is they who are not true
comedians, or myself.   I fancy it must be I.   In any case, I
pay for the others."

She stopped speaking.   It was three in the morning.   She
got up to go.   Christophe told her to wait until the morning
before she went home, and proposed that she should go and
lie down on his bed.   She preferred to stay in the arm-chair by
the dead fire, and went on talking quietly while all the house
was still.

"You will be tired to-morrow."

"I am used to it.   But what about you? . . .   What are
you doing to-morrow?"

"I am free.   I have a lesson to give about eleven. . . .
Besides, I am strong."

"All the more reason why you should sleep soundly."

"Yes; I sleep like a log.   Not even pain can stand out
against it.   I am sometimes furious with myself for sleeping
so well.   So many hours wasted! . . .   I am delighted to be
able to take my revenge on sleep for once in a way, and to
cheat it of a night."

They went on talking in low tones, with long intervals of
silence.   And Christophe went to sleep.   Françoise smiled and
supported his head to keep him from falling. . . .   She sat
by the window dreaming and looking down into the darkness of
the garden, which presently was lit up.   About seven o'clock
she woke Christophe gently, and said good-by.

In the course of the month she came at times when Christophe was out, and found the door shut. Christophe sent her a key to the flat, so that she could go there when she liked. She went more than once when Christophe was away, and she would leave a little bunch of violets on the table, or a few words scribbled on a sheet of paper, or a sketch, or a caricature—just to show that she had been.

And one evening, when she left the theater, she went to the flat to resume their pleasant talk. She found him at work, and they began to talk. But at the very outset they both felt that the friendly comfortable mood of the last occasion was gone. She tried to go: but it was too late. Not that Christophe did anything to prevent her. It was her own will that failed her and would not let her go. They stayed there with the gathering consciousness of the desire that was in them.

Following on that night she disappeared for some weeks. In him there had been roused a sensual ardor that had lain dormant for months before, and he could not live without her. She had forbidden him to go to her house: he went to see her at the theater. He sat far back, and he was aflame with love and devotion: every nerve in his body thrilled: the tragic intensity which she brought to her acting consumed him also in its fire. At last he wrote to her:

" MY DEAR,—Are you angry with me? Forgive me if I have hurt you."

When she received his humble little note she hastened to him and flung herself into his arms.

" It would have been better to be just friends, good friends. But since it is impossible, it is no good holding out against the inevitable. Come what may! "

They lived together. They kept on in their separate flats, and each of them was free. Françoise could not have submitted to living openly with Christophe. Besides, her position would not allow it. She used to go to Christophe's flat and spend part of the day and night with him; but she used to return to her own place every day and also sleep there.

During the vacation, when the theater was closed, they took a house together outside Paris, near Gif. They had many happy days there, though there were clouds of sadness too. They were days of confidence and work. They had a beautiful light room, high up, with a wide view over the fields. At night through the window they could see the strange shadows of the clouds floating across the clear, dull darkness of the sky. Half asleep, they could hear the joyous crickets chirping and the showers falling; the breath of the autumn earth—honeysuckle, clematis, glycine, and new-mown hay—filled the house and soothed their senses. The silence of the night. In the distance dogs barked. Cocks crowed. Dawn comes. The tinkling angelus rings in the distant belfry, through the cold, gray twilight, and they shiver in the warmth of their nest, and yet more lovingly hold each other close. The voices of the birds awake in the trellis on the wall. Christophe opens his eyes, holds his breath, and his heart melts as he looks down at the dear tired face of his sleeping beloved, pale with the paleness of love. . . .

Their love was no selfish passion. It was a profound love in comradeship, in which the body also demanded its share. They did not hinder each other. They both went on with their work. Christophe's genius and kindness and moral fiber were dear to Françoise. She felt older than he in many ways, and she found a maternal pleasure in the relation. She regretted her inability to understand anything he played: music was a closed book to her, except at rare moments, when she would be overcome by a wild emotion, which came less from the music than from her own inner self, from the passion in which she was steeped at that time, she and everything about her, the country, people, color, and sound. But she was none the less conscious of Christophe's genius, because it was expressed in a mysterious language which she did not understand. It was like watching a great actor playing in a foreign language. Her own genius was rekindled by it. Christophe, thanks to love, could project his ideas and body forth his passions in the mind of the woman and her beloved person: they seemed to him more beautiful there than they were in himself—endowed with

an antique and seemingly eternal beauty. Intimacy with such
a soul, so feminine, so weak and kind and cruel, and genial in
flashes, was a source of boundless wealth. She taught him much
about life, and men—about women, of whom he knew very little,
while she judged them with swift, unerring perception. But
especially he was indebted to her for a better understanding
of the theater; she helped him to pierce through to the spirit
of that admirable art, the most perfect of all arts, the fullest
and most sober. She revealed to him the beauty of that magic
instrument of the human dream,—and made him see that he
must write for it and not for himself, as he had a tendency to
do,—(the tendency of too many artists, who, like Beethoven,
refuse to write *"for a confounded violin when the Spirit speaks
to them "*).—A great dramatic poet is not ashamed to work
for a particular theater and to adapt his ideas to the actors at
his disposal : he sees no belittlement in that : but he knows that
a vast auditorium calls for different methods of expression than
those necessary for a smaller space, and that a man does not
write trumpet-blares for the flute. The theater, like the fresco,
is art fitted to its place. And therefore it is above all else the
human art, the living art.

Françoise's ideas were in accordance with Christophe's, who,
at that stage in his career, was inclined towards a collective art,
in communion with other men. Françoise's experience helped
him to grasp the mysterious collaboration which is set up between the audience and the actor. Though Françoise was a
realist, and had very few illusions, yet she had a great perception
of the power of reciprocal suggestion, the waves of sympathy
which pass between the actor and the multitude, the great silence
of thousands of men and women from which arises the single
voice of their interpreter. Naturally she could only feel it in
intermittent flashes, very, very rare, which were hardly ever
reproduced at the same passages in the same play. For the
rest her work was a soulless trade, an intelligent and coldly
mechanical routine. But the interest of it lay in the exception
—the flash of light which pierced the darkness of the abyss,
the common soul of millions of men and women whose living
force was expressed in her for the space of a second of
eternity.

It was this common soul which it was the business of the great artist to express.   His ideal should be a living objectivism, in which the poet should throw himself into those for whom he sings, and denude himself of self, to clothe the collective passions which are blown over the world like a mighty wind. Françoise was all the more keenly conscious of the necessity, inasmuch as she was incapable of such disinterestedness, and always played herself.—For the last century and a half the disordered efflorescence of individual lyricism has been tinged with morbidity. Moral greatness consists in feeling much and controlling much, in being sober in words and chaste in thought, in not making a parade of it, in making a look speak and speak profoundly, without childish exaggeration or effeminate effusiveness, to those who can grasp the half-spoken thought, to men.   Modern music, which is so loquaciously introspective, dragging in indiscreet confidences at every turn, is immodest and lacking in taste.   It is like those invalids who can think of nothing but their illnesses, and never weary of discussing them with other people and going into repulsive petty details. This travesty of art has been growing more and more prevalent for the last century.   Françoise, who was no musician, was disposed to see a sign of decadence in the development of music at the expense of poetry, like a polypus sucking it dry.   Christophe protested : but, upon reflection, he began to wonder whether there might not be some truth in it.   The first *lieder* written to poems of Goethe were sober and apt : soon Schubert came and infused his romantic sentimentality into them and gave them a twist : Schumann introduced his girlish languor : and, down to Hugo Wolf, the movement had gone on towards more stress in declamation, indecent analysis, a presumptuous endeavor to leave no smallest corner of the soul unlit.   Every veil about the mysteries of the heart was rent.   Things said in all earnestness by a man were now screamed aloud by shameless girls who showed themselves in their nakedness.

Christophe was rather ashamed of such art, by which he was himself conscious of being contaminated : and, without seeking to go back to the past,—(an absurd, unnatural desire),—he steeped himself in the spirit of those of the masters of the past who had been haughtily discreet in their thought and had possessed

the sense of a great collective art: like Handel, who, scorning
the tearful piety of his time and country, wrote his colossal
Anthems and his oratorios, those heroic epics which are songs
of the nations for the nations. The difficulty was to find inspiring subjects, which, like the Bible in Handel's time, could
arouse emotions common to all the nations of modern Europe.
Modern Europe had no common book: no poem, no prayer, no
act of faith which was the property of all. Oh! the shame that
should overwhelm all the writers, artists, thinkers, of to-day!
Not one of them has written, not one of them has thought, for
all. Only Beethoven has left a few pages of a new Gospel of
consolation and brotherhood: but only musicians can read it,
and the majority of men will never hear it. Wagner, on the
hill at Bayreuth, has tried to build a religious art to bind all
men together. But his great soul had too little simplicity and
too many of the blemishes of the decadent music and thought
of his time: not the fishers of Galilee have come to the holy
hill, but the Pharisees.

Christophe felt sure what he had to do: but he had no poet,
and he was forced to be self-sufficing and to confine himself
to music. And music, whatever people say, is not a universal
language: the bow of words is necessary to send the arrow of
sound into the hearts of all men.

Christophe planned to write a suite of symphonies inspired
by everyday life. Among others he conceived a Domestic Symphony, in his own manner, which was very different from that
of Richard Strauss. He was not concerned with materializing
family life in a cinematograph picture, by making use of a
conventional alphabet, in which musical themes expressed arbi-
trarily the various characters whom, if the auditor's eyes and
ears could stand it, were presently to be seen going through
divers evolutions together. That seemed to him a pedantic and
childish game for a great contrapuntist. He did not try to
describe characters or actions, but only to express emotions
familiar to every man and woman, in which they could find
the echo of their own souls, and perhaps comfort and relief.
The first movement expressed the grave and simple happiness
of a loving young couple, with its tender sensuality, its confidence in the future, its joy and hopes. The second movement

was an elegy on the death of a child. Christophe had avoided
with horror any effort to depict death, and realistic detail in
the expression of sorrow: there was only the utter misery of
it,—yours, mine, everybody's, of being face to face with a misfortune which falls or may fall to the lot of everybody. The
soul, prostrate in its grief, from which Christophe had banned
the usual effects of sniveling melodrama, recovered bit by bit,
in a sorrowful effort, to offer its suffering as a sacrifice to God.
Once more it set bravely out on the road, in the next movement,
which was linked with the second,—a headstrong fugue, the
bold design and insistent rhythm of which captivated, and,
through struggles and tears, led on to a mighty march, full of
indomitable faith. The last movement depicted the evening of
life. The themes of the opening movement reappeared in it
with their touching confidence and their tenderness which could
not grow old, but riper, emerging from the shadow of sorrow,
crowned with light, and, like a rich blossoming, raising a religious hymn of love to life and God.

Christophe also rummaged in the books of the past for great,
simple, human subjects speaking to the best in the hearts of
all men. He chose two such stories: *Joseph* and *Niobe*. But
then Christophe was brought up not only against his need of
a poet, but against the vexed question, which has been argued
for centuries and never solved, of the union of poetry and
music. His talks with Françoise had brought him back to
his idea, sketched out long ago with Corinne, of a form of
musical drama, somewhere between recitative opera and the
spoken drama,—the art of the free word united with free music,
—an art of which hardly any artist of to-day has a glimmering,
an art also which the routine critics, imbued with the Wagnerian
tradition, deny, as they deny every really new work: for it is
not a matter of following in the footsteps of Beethoven, Weber,
Schumann, Bizet, although they used the melodramatic form
with genius: it is not a matter of yoking any sort of speaking
voice to any sort of music, and producing, at all costs, with
absurd tremolos, coarse effects upon coarse audiences: it is a
matter of creating a new form, in which musical voices will be
wedded to instruments attuned to those voices, discreetly
mingling with their harmonious periods the echo of dreams and

the plaintive murmur of music. It goes without saying that such a form could only be applied to a narrow range of subjects, to intimate and introspective moments of the soul, so as to conjure up its poetic perfume. In no art should there be more discretion and aristocracy of feeling. It is only natural, therefore, that it should have little chance of coming to flower in an age which, in spite of the pretensions of its artists, reeks of the deep-seated vulgarity of upstarts.

Perhaps Christophe was no more suited to such an art than the rest: his very qualities, his plebeian force, were obstacles in the way. He could only conceive it, and with the aid of Françoise realize a few rough sketches.

In this way he set to music passages from the Bible, almost literally transcribed,—like the immortal scene in which Joseph makes himself known to his brothers, and, after so many trials, can no longer contain his emotion and tender feeling, and whispers the words which have wrung tears from old Tolstoy, and many another:

" Then Joseph could not refrain himself. . . . I am Joseph; doth my father yet live? I am Joseph, your brother, whom ye sold into Egypt. I am Joseph. . . ."

Their beautiful and free relation could not last. They had moments splendid and full of life: but they were too different. They were both strong-willed, and then often clashed. But their differences were never of a vulgar character: for Christophe had won Françoise's respect. And Françoise, who could sometimes be so cruel, was kind to those who were kind to her; no power on earth could have made her do anything to hurt them. And besides, both of them had a fund of gay humor. She was always the first to laugh at herself. She was still eating her heart out: for the old passion still had its grip on her: she still thought of the blackguard she loved: and she could not bear to be in so humiliating a position or, above all, to have Christophe suspecting what she was feeling.

Christophe would sometimes find her for days together silent and restless and given up to melancholy, and could not understand how she could be unhappy. She had achieved her end: she was a great artist, admired, flattered. . . .

"Yes," she would say; "that would be all very well if I were one of those famous actresses, with no soul above shop-keeping, who run the theater just as they would run any other business. They are quite happy when they have 'realized' a good position, a commonplace, wealthy marriage, and—the *ne plus ultra*—been decorated. I wanted more than that. Unless one is a fool, success is even more empty than failure. You must know that!"

"I know," said Christophe. "Ah! Dear God, that is not what I imagined fame to be when I was a child. How I longed for it, and what a shining thing it seemed to be! It was almost a religion to me then. . . . No matter! There is one divine virtue in success: the good it gives one the power to do."

"What good? One has conquered. But what's the good of it? Nothing is altered. Theaters, concerts, everything is just the same. A new fashion succeeds the old: that is all. They do not understand one, or only superficially: and they begin to think of something else at once. . . . Do you yourself understand other artists? In any case, they don't understand you. The people you love best are so far away from you! Look at your Tolstoy. . . ."

Christophe had written to him: he had been filled with enthusiasm for him, and had wept over his books: he wanted to set one of the peasant tales to music, and had asked for his authority, and had sent him his *lieder*. Tolstoy did not reply, any more than Goethe replied to Schubert or Berlioz when they sent him their masterpieces. He had had Christophe's music played to him, and it had irritated him: he could make nothing of it. He regarded Beethoven as a decadent, and Shakespeare as a charlatan. On the other hand, he was infatuated with various little pretty-pretty masters, and the harpsichord music which used to charm the *Roi-Perruque*: and he regarded *La Confession d'une Femme de Chambre* as a Christian book. . . .

"Great men have no need of us," said Christophe. "We must think of the others."

"Who? The dull public, the shadows who hide life from us? Act, write for such people? Give your life for them? That would be bitter indeed!"

"Bah!" said Christophe. "I see them as they are just

as you do: but I don't let it make me despondent. They are not as bad as you say."

" Dear old German optimist! "

" They are men, like myself. Why should they not understand me? . . . —And suppose they don't understand me, why should I despair? Among all the thousands of people there will surely be one or two who will be with me: that is enough for me, and gives me window enough to breathe the outer air. . . . Think of all the simple playgoers, the young people, the old honest souls, who are lifted out of their tedious everyday life by your appearance, your voice, your revelation of tragic beauty. Think of what you were yourself when you were a child! Isn't it a fine thing to give to others—perhaps even only to one other—the happiness that others gave you, and to do to them the good that others did to you? "

" Do you really believe that there is one such in the world? I have come to doubt it. . . . Besides, what sort of love do we get from the best of those who love us? How do they see us? They see so badly! They admire you while they degrade you: they get just as much pleasure out of watching any old stager act: they drag you down to the level of the idiots you despise. In their eyes all successful people are exactly the same."

" And yet, when all is told, it is the greatest of all who go down to posterity with the greatest."

" It is only the backward movement of time. Mountains grow taller the farther you go away from them. You see their height better: but you are farther away from them. . . . And besides, who is to tell us who are the greatest? What do you know of the men who have disappeared? "

" Nonsense! " said Christophe. " Even if nobody were to feel what I think and what I am, I think my thoughts and I am what I am just the same. I have my music, I love it, I believe in it: it is the truest thing in my life."

" You are free in your art,—you can do what you like. But what can I do? I am forced to act in the plays they give me, and go on acting until I am sick of it. We are not yet, in France, such beasts of burden as those American actors who play *Rip* or *Robert Macaire* ten thousand times, and for twenty

five years of their lives go on grinding out and grinding out an
idiotic part. But we are on the road to it. Our theaters are
so poverty-stricken! The public will only stand genius in in-
finitesimal doses, sprinkled with mannerisms and fashionable
literature. . . . A ' fashionable genius'! Doesn't that make
you laugh? . . ᛉ What waste of power! Look at what they
have made of a Mounet. What has he had to play the whole
of his life? Two or three parts that are worth the struggle
for life: the *Oedipus* and *Polyeucte*. The rest has been rot!
Isn't that enough to disgust one? And just think of all the
great and glorious things he might have had to do! . . .
Things are no better outside France? What have they made
of a Duse? What has her life been given up to? Think of
the futile parts she has played?"

"Your real task." said Christophe, "is to force great works
of art on the world."

"We should exhaust ourselves in a vain endeavor. It isn't
worth it. As soon as a great work of art is brought into the
theater it loses its great poetic quality. It becomes a hollow
sham. The breath of the public sullies it. The public consists
of people living in stifling towns and they have lost all knowledge
of the open air, and Nature, and healthy poetry: they must have
their poetry theatrical, glittering, painted, reeking.—Ah! And
besides . . . besides, even suppose one did succeed . . . no,
that would not fill one's life, it would not fill my life. . . ."

"You are still thinking of him."

"Who?"

"You know. That man."

"Yes."

"Even if you could have him and he loved you, confess that
you would not be happy even then: you would still find some
means of tormenting yourself."

"True. . . . Ah! What is the matter with me? . . .
I think I have had too hard a fight. I have fretted too much:
I can't ever be calm again: there is always an uneasiness in me,
a sort of fever. . . ."

"It must have been in you even before your struggles."

"Possibly. Yes. It was in me when I was a little girl, as
far back as I can remember. . . . It was devouring me then."

" What do you want? "

" How do I know?   More than I can have."

" I know that," said Christophe.   " I was like that when I was a boy."

" Yes, but you have become a man.   I shall never be grown-up as long as I live.   I am an incomplete creature."

" No one is complete.   Happiness lies in knowing one's limitations and loving them."

" I can't do that.   I've lost it.   Life has cheated me, tricked me, crippled me.   And yet I fancy that I could never have been a normal and healthy and beautiful woman without being like the rest of the gang."

" There's no reason why you shouldn't be all these things.   I can see you being like that! "

" Tell me how you can see me."

He described her, in conditions under which she might have developed naturally and harmoniously, and been happy, loved, and loving.   And it did her good to hear it.   But when he had done, she said:

" No.   It is impossible now."

" Well," he said, " in that case you must say to yourself, like dear old Handel when he went blind:

What e-ver is,   *is right."*

He went to the piano and sang it for her.   She kissed him and called him her dear, crazy optimist.   He did her good. But she did him harm: or at least, she was afraid of him.   She had violent fits of despair, and could not conceal them from him: her love made her weak.   At night she would try to choke down her agony, he would guess, and beg the beloved creature who was so near and yet so far, to share with him the burden which lay so heavy on her: then she could not hold out any longer, and she would turn weeping to his arms; and he would spend hours in comforting her, kindly, without a spark of anger: but in the long-run her perpetual restlessness was bound to tell on him. Françoise trembled lest the fever that was in her should infect him. She loved him too much to be able to bear the idea that he should suffer because of her. She was offered an engagement in America, and she accepted it, so as to tear herself away from him. She left him a little humiliated. She was as humiliated as he, in the knowledge that they could not make each other happy!

"My poor dear," she said to him, smiling sadly and tenderly. "Aren't we stupid? We shall never have such a friendship again, never such a glorious opportunity. But it can't be helped, it can't be helped. We are too stupid!"

They looked at each other mournfully and shamefacedly. They laughed to keep themselves from weeping, kissed, and parted with tears in their eyes. Never had they loved so well as when they parted.

And after she was gone he returned to art, his old companion. . . . Oh, the peace of the starry sky!

It was not long before Christophe received a letter from Jacqueline. It was only the third time she had written to him, and her tone was very different from that to which she had accustomed him. She told him how sorry she was not to have seen him for so long, and very nicely invited him to come and see her, unless he wished to hurt two friends who loved him. Christophe was delighted, but not greatly surprised. He had been inclined to think that Jacqueline's unjust disposition towards him would not last. He was fond of quoting a jest of his old grandfather's:

"Sooner or later women have their good moments: one only needs the patience to wait for them."

He went to see Olivier, and was welcomed with delight. Jacqueline was most attentive to him: she avoided the ironical manner which was natural to her, took care not to say anything that might hurt Christophe, showed great interest in what he was doing, and talked intelligently about serious subjects. Christophe thought her transformed. But she was only so to please him. Jacqueline had heard of Christophe's affair with the popular actress, the tale of which had gone the rounds of

Parisian gossip: and Christophe had appeared to her in an altogether new light: she was filled with curiosity about him. When she met him again she found him much more sympathetic. Even his faults seemed to her to be not without attraction. She realized that Christophe had genius, and that it would be worth while to make him love her.

The position between the young couple was no better, but rather worse. Jacqueline was bored, bored, bored: she was bored to death. . . . How utterly lonely a woman is! Except children, nothing can hold her: and children are not enough to hold her forever: for when she is really a woman, and not merely a female, when she has a rich soul and an abounding vitality, she is made for so many things which she cannot accomplish alone and with none to help her! . . . A man is much less lonely, even when he is most alone: he can people the desert with his own thoughts: and when he is lonely in married life he can more easily put up with it, for he notices it less, and can always live in the soliloquy of his own thoughts. And it never occurs to him that the sound of his voice going on imperturbably babbling in the desert, makes the silence more terrible and the desert more frightful for the woman by his side, for whom all words are dead that are not kindled by love. He does not see it: he has not, like the woman, staked his whole life on love: his life has other occupations. . . . What man is there can fill the life of a woman and satisfy her immense desire, the millions of ardent and generous forces that, through the forty thousand years of the life of humanity, have burned to no purpose, as a holocaust offered up to two idols: passing love and motherhood, that sublime fraud, which is refused to thousands of women and never fills more than a few years in the lives of the rest?

Jacqueline was in despair. She had moments of terror that cut through her like swords. She thought:

"Why am I alive? Why was I ever born?" And her heart would ache and throb in agony.

"My God, I am going to die! My God, I am going to die!"

That idea haunted her, obsessed her through the night. She used to dream that she was saying:

"It is 1889."

"No," the answer would come. "It is 1909." And the thought that she was twenty years older than she imagined would make her wretched.

"It will all be over, and I have never lived! What have I done with these twenty years? What have I made of my life?"

She would dream that she was *four* little girls, all four lying in the same room in different beds. They were all of the same figure and the same face: but one was eight, one was fifteen, one was twenty, and the fourth was thirty. There was an epidemic. Three of them had died. The fourth looked at herself in the mirror, and she was filled with terror: she saw herself with the skin drawn tight over her nose, and her features pinched and withered . . . she was going to die too—and then it would be all over. . . .

". . . What have I done with my life? . . ."

She would wake up in tears; and the nightmare would not vanish with the day: the nightmare was real. What had she done with her life? Who had robbed her of it? . . . She would begin to hate Olivier, the innocent accomplice—(innocent! What did it matter if the harm done was the same!)— of the blind law which was crushing her. She would be sorry for it at once, for she was kind of heart: but she was suffering too much: and she could not help wreaking her vengeance on the man who was bound to her and was stifling her life, by making him suffer more than he was indeed suffering. Then she would be more sorry than ever: she would loathe herself and feel that if she did not find some way of escape she would do things even more evil. She groped blindly about to find some way of escape: she clutched at everything like a drowning woman: she tried to take an interest in something, work, or another human being, that might be in some sort her own, her work, a creature belonging to herself. She tried to take up some intellectual work, and learned foreign languages: she began an article, a story: she began to paint, to compose. . . . In vain: she grew tired of everything, and lost heart the very first day. They were too difficult. And then, "books, works of art! What are they? I don't know whether I love them, I don't even know whether they exist. . . ."—Sometimes she would talk excitedly and laugh with Olivier, and seem to be keenly interested in the things they talked about, or in what he was doing: she would try to bemuse and benumb herself. . . . In vain: suddenly her excitement would collapse, her heart would go icy cold, she would hide away, with never a tear, hardly a breath, utterly prostrate.—She had in some measure succeeded in destroying Olivier. He was growing skeptical and worldly. She did not mind: she found him as weak as herself. Almost every evening they used to go out: and she would go in an agony of suffering and boredom from one fine house to another, and no one would ever guess the feeling that lay behind the irony of her unchanging smile. She was seeking for some one to love her and keep her back from the edge of the abyss. . . . In vain, in vain, in vain. There was nothing but silence in answer to her cry of despair.

She did not love Christophe: she could not bear his rough manner, his painful frankness, and, above all, his indifference. She did not love him: but she had a feeling that he at least was strong,—a rock towering above death. And she tried to clutch hold of the rock, to cling to the swimmer whose head rose above the waves, to cling to him or to drown with him. . . .

Besides, it was not enough for her to have cut her husband off from his friends: now she was driven on to take them from him. Even the best of women sometimes have an instinct which impels them to try and see how far their power goes, and to go beyond it. In that abuse of their power their weakness proves its strength. And when the woman is selfish and vain she finds a malign pleasure in robbing her husband of the friendship of his friends. It is easily done: she has but to use her eyes a little. There is hardly a single man, honorable or otherwise, who is not weak enough to nibble at the bait. Though the friend be never so true and loyal, he may avoid the act, but he will almost always betray his friend in thought. And if the other man sees it, there is an end of their friendship: they no longer see each other with the same eyes.—The woman who plays such a dangerous game generally stops at that and asks no more: she has them both, disunited, at her mercy.

Christophe observed Jacqueline's new graces and charming treatment of himself, but he was not surprised. When he had

an affection for any one he had a naïve way of taking it as a
matter of course that the affection should be returned without
any ulterior thought. He responded gladly to Jacqueline's advances: he thought her charming, and amused himself thoroughly
with her: and he thought so well of her that he was not far
from thinking Olivier rather a bungler not to be able to be
happy with her and to make her happy.

He went with them for a few days' tour in a motor-car: and
he was their guest at the Langeais' country house in Burgundy
—an old family mansion which was kept because of its associations, though they hardly ever went there. It was in a lovely
situation, in the midst of vineyards and woods: it was very
shabby inside, and the windows were loose in their frames: there
was a moldy smell in it, a smell of ripe fruit, of cold shadow,
and resinous trees warmed by the sun. Living constantly in
Jacqueline's company for days together, a sweet insidious feeling
crept into Christophe's veins, without in the least disturbing his
peace of mind: he took an innocent, though by no means immaterial, delight in seeing her, hearing her, feeling the contact
of her beautiful body, and sipping the breath of her mouth.
Olivier was a little anxious and uneasy, but said nothing. He
suspected nothing: but he was oppressed by a vague uneasiness
which he would have been ashamed to admit to himself: by way
of punishing himself for it he frequently left them alone together. Jacqueline saw what he was thinking, and was touched
by it: she longed to say to him:

" Come, don't be anxious, my dear. I still love you the best."

But she did not say it: and they all three went on drifting:
Christophe entirely unconscious, Jacqueline not knowing what
she really wanted, and leaving it to chance to tell her, and
Olivier alone seeing and feeling what was in the wind, but in
the delicacy of vanity and love, refusing to think of it. When
the will is silent, instinct speaks: in the absence of the soul, the
body goes its own way.

One evening, after dinner, the night seemed to them so lovely
—a moonless, starry night,—that they proposed to go for a walk
in the garden. Olivier and Christophe left the house. Jacqueline went up to her room to fetch a shawl. She did not come
down. Christophe went to look for her, fuming at the eternal

dilatoriness of woman.—(For some time without knowing it
he had slipped into playing the part of the husband.)—He heard
her coming.   The shutters of her room were closed and he could
not see.

"Come along, you dilly-dallying madam," cried Christophe
gaily. "You'll wear your mirror out if you look at yourself
so much."

She did not reply.   She had stopped still.   Christophe felt
that she was in the room : but she did not stir.

"Where are you?" he said.

She did not reply.   Christophe said nothing either, and began
groping in the dark, and suddenly his heart grew big and began
to thump, and he stood still.   Near him he could hear Jacqueline
breathing lightly.   He moved again and stopped once more.
She was near him : he knew it, but he could not move.   There
was silence for a second or two.   Suddenly he felt her hands
on his, her lips on his.   He held her close.   They stood still
and spoke no word.—Their lips parted ; they wrenched away
from each other.   Jacqueline left the room.   Christophe followed her, trembling.   His legs shook beneath him.   He stopped
for a moment to lean against the wall until the tumult in his
blood died down.   At last he joined them again.   Jacqueline
was calmly talking to Olivier.   They walked on a few yards in
front.   Christophe followed them in a state of collapse.   Olivier
stopped to wait for him.   Christophe stopped too.   Olivier,
knowing his friend's temper and the capricious silence in which
he would sometimes bar himself, did not persist, and went on
walking with Jacqueline.   And Christophe followed them mechanically, lagging ten yeards behind them like a dog.   When
they stopped, he stopped.   When they walked on, he walked on.
And so they went round the garden and back into the house.
Christophe went up to his room and shut himself in.   He did
not light the lamp.   He did not go to bed.   He could not think.
About the middle of the night he fell asleep, sitting, with his
head resting in his arms on the table.   He woke up an hour
later.   He lit a candle, feverishly flung together his papers and
belongings, packed his bag, and then flung himself on the bed
and slept until dawn.   Then he went down with his luggage
and left the house.   They waited for him all morning, and spent

the day looking for him. Jacqueline hid her furious anger beneath a mask of indifference, and sarcastically pretended to go over her plate. It was not until the following evening that Olivier received a letter from Christophe:

" *My dear Old Fellow,*
    "*Don't be angry with me for having gone away like a mad-man. I am mad, you know. But what can I do? I am what I am. Thanks for your dear hospitality. I enjoyed it much. But, you know, I am not fit to live with other people. I'm not so sure either that I am fit to live. I am only fit to stay in my corner and love people—at a distance: it is wiser so. When I see them at too close quarters, I become misanthropic. And I don't want to be that. I want to love men and women, I want to love you all. Oh! How I long to help you all! If I could only help you to be—to be happy! How gladly would I give all the happiness I may have in exchange! . . . But that is forbidden. One can only show others the way. One cannot go their way in their stead. Each of us must save him-self. Save yourself! Save yourselves! I love you.*
                                                                "CHRISTOPHE.
    "*My respects to Madame Jeannin.*"

    "Madame Jeannin" read the letter with a smile of contempt and her lips tightly pressed together, and said dryly:
    "Well. Follow his advice. Save yourself."
    But when Olivier held out his hand for the letter, Jacqueline crumpled it up and flung it down, and two great tears welled up into her eyes. Olivier took her hands.
    "What's the matter?" he asked, with some emotion.
    "Let me be!" she cried angrily.
    She went out. As she reached the door she cried:
    "Egoists!"

    Christophe had contrived to make enemies of his patrons of the *Grand Journal,* as was only likely. Christophe had been endowed by Heaven with the virtue extolled by Goethe: *non-gratitude.*

" *The horror of showing gratitude*," wrote Goethe ironically, " *is rare, and only appears in remarkable men who have risen from the poorest class, and at every turn have been forced to accept assistance, which is almost invariably poisoned by the churlishness of the benefactor. . . .*"

Christophe was never disposed to think himself obliged to abase himself in return for service rendered, nor—what amounted to the same thing—to surrender his liberty. He did not lend his own benefactions at so much per cent.: he gave them. His benefactors, however, were of a very different way of thinking. Their lofty moral feeling of the duties of their debtors was shocked by Christophe's refusal to write the music for a stupid hymn for an advertising festivity organized by the paper. They made him feel the impropriety of his conduct. Christophe sent them packing. And finally he exasperated them by the flat denial which he gave shortly afterwards to certain statements attributed to him by the paper.

Then they began a campaign against him. They used every possible weapon. They dragged out once more the old petti-fogging engine of war which has always served the impotent against creative men, and, though it has never killed anybody, yet it never fails to have an effect upon the simple-minded and the fools: they accused him of plagiarism. They went and picked out artfully selected and distorted passages from his compositions and from those of various obscure musicians, and they proved that he had stolen his inspiration from others. He was accused of having tried to stifle various young artists. It would have been well enough if he had only had to deal with those whose business it is to bark, with those critics, those man-nikins, who climb on the shoulders of a great man and cry:

" I am greater than you ! "

But no : men of talent must be wrangling among themselves : each man does his best to make himself intolerable to his col-leagues : and yet, as Christophe said, the world was large enough for all of them to be able to work in peace : and each of them in his own talent had quite enough to struggle against.

In Germany he found artists so jealous of him that they were ready to furnish his enemies with weapons against him, and even, if need be, to invent them. He found the same thing in France. The nationalists of the musical press—several of whom were foreigners,—flung his nationality in his teeth as an insult. Christophe's success had grown widely; and as he had a certain vogue, they pretended that his exaggeration must irritate even those who had no definite views—much more those who had. Among the concert-going public, and among people in society and the writers on the young reviews, Christophe by this time had enthusiastic partisans, who went into ecstasies over everything he did, and were wont to declare that music did not exist before his advent. Some of them explained his music and found philosophic meanings in it which simply astounded him. Others would see in it a musical revolution, an assault on the traditions which Christophe respected more than anybody. It was useless for him to protest. They would have proved to him that he did not know what he had written. They admired themselves by admiring him. And so the campaign against Christophe met with great sympathy among his colleagues, who were exasperated by the "log-rolling" to which he was no party. They did not need to rely on such reasons for not liking his music: most of them felt with regard to it the natural irritation of the man who has no ideas and no difficulty in expressing them according to parrot-like formulæ, with the man who is full of ideas and employs them clumsily in accordance with the apparent disorder of his creative faculty. How often he had had to face the reproach of not being able to write hurled at him by scribes, for whom style consisted in recipes concocted by groups or schools, kitchen molds into which thought was cast! Christophe's best friends, those who did not try to understand him, and were alone in understanding him, because they loved him, simply, for the pleasure he gave them, were obscure auditors who had no voice in the matter. The only man who could have replied vigorously in Christophe's name—Olivier—was at that time out of friends with him, and had apparently forgotten him. Thus Christophe was delivered into the hands of his adversaries and admirers, who vied with each other in doing him harm. He was too disgusted to reply. When he read the pronunciamentos directed against him in the pages of an important newspaper by one of those presumptuous critics who usurp the sovereignty of art with all the in-

solence of ignorance and impunity, he would shrug his shoulders
and say:

" Judge me. I judge you. Let us meet in a hundred years! "

But meanwhile the outcry against him took its course: and
the public, as usual, gulped down the most fatuous and shameful
accusations.

As though his position was not already difficult enough,
Christophe chose that moment to quarrel with his publisher.
He had no reason at all to complain of Hecht, who published
each new work as it was written, and was honest in business.
It is true that his honesty did not prevent his making contracts
disadvantageous to Christophe: but he kept his contracts. He
kept them only too well. One day Christophe was amazed to
see a septette of his arranged as a quartette, and a suite of
piano pieces clumsily transcribed as a duet, without his having
been consulted. He rushed to Hecht's office and thrust the
offending music under his nose, and said:

" Do you know these? "

" Of course," said Hecht.

" And you dared . . . you dared tamper with my work
without asking my permission! . . ."

" What permission? " said Hecht calmly. " Your compositions are mine."

" Mine, too, I suppose? "

" No," said Hecht quietly.

Christophe started.

" My own work does not belong to me? "

" They are not yours any longer. You sold them to me."

" You're making fun of me! I sold you the paper. Make
money out of that if you like. But what is written on it is my
life-blood; it is mine."

" You sold me everything. In exchange for these particular
pieces, I gave you a sum of three hundred francs in advance
of a royalty of thirty centimes on every copy sold of the original
edition. Upon that consideration, without any restriction or
reserve, you have assigned to me all your rights in your work."

" Even the right to destroy it? "

Hecht shrugged his shoulders, rang the bell, and said to a
clerk.

"Bring me M. Krafft's account."

He gravely read Christophe the terms of the contract, which he had signed without reading—from which it appeared, in accordance with the ordinary run of contracts signed by music publishers in those very distant times—"that M. Hecht was the assignee of all the rights, powers, and property of the author, and had the exclusive right to edit, publish, engrave, print, translate, hire, sell to his own profit, in any form he pleased, to have the said work performed at concerts, café-concerts, balls, theaters, etc., and to publish any arrangement of the said work for any instrument and even with words, and also to change the title . . . etc., etc."

"You see," he said, "I am really very moderate."

"Evidently," said Christophe. "I ought to thank you. You might have turned my septette into a café-concert song."

He stopped in horror and held his head in his hands.

"I have sold my soul," he said over and over again.

"You may be sure," said Hecht sarcastically, "that I shall no abuse it."

"And to think," said Christophe, "that your Republic authorizes such practices! You say that man is free. And you put ideas up to public auction."

"You have had your money," said Hecht.

"Thirty pieces of silver. Yes," said Christophe. "Take them back."

He fumbled in his pockets, meaning to give the three hundred francs back to Hecht. But he had nothing like that sum. Hecht smiled a little disdainfully. His smile infuriated Christophe.

"I want my work back," he said. "I will buy them back from you."

"You have no right to do so," said Hecht. "But as I have no desire to keep a man against his will, I am quite ready to give them back to you,—if you are in a position to pay the indemnity stated in the contract."

"I will do it," said Christophe, "even if I have to sell myself."

He accepted without discussion the conditions which Hecht submitted to him a fortnight later. It was an amazing act of folly, and he bought back his published compositions at a price five times greater than the sum they had brought him, in, though it was by no means exorbitant: for it was scrupulously calculated on the basis of the actual profits which had accrued to Hecht. Christophe could not pay, and Hecht had counted on it. He had no intention of squeezing Christophe, of whom he thought more highly, both as a musician and as a man, than of any other young musician: but he wanted to teach him a lesson: for he could not permit his clients to revolt against what was after all within his rights. He had not made the laws: they were those of the time, and they seemed to him equitable. Besides, he was quite sincerely convinced that they were to the benefit of the author as much as to the benefit of the publisher, who knows better than the author how to circulate his work, and is not, like the author, hindered by scruples of a sentimental, respectable order, which are contrary to his real interests. He had made up his mind to help Christophe to succeed, but in his own way, and on condition that Christophe was delivered into his hands, tied hand and foot. He wanted to make him feel that he could not so easily dispense with his services. They made a conditional bargain: if, at the end of six months, Christophe could not manage to pay, his work should become Hecht's absolute property. It was perfectly obvious that Christophe would not be able to collect a quarter of the sum requisite.

However, he stuck to it, said good-by to the rooms which were so full of memories for him, and took a less expensive flat,—selling a number of things, none of which, to his great surprise, were of any value,—getting into debt, and appealing to Mooch's good nature, who, unfortunately, was at that time very badly off and ill, being confined to the house with rheumatism,—trying to find another publisher, and everywhere finding conditions as grasping as Hecht's, and in some cases a point-blank refusal.

It was just at the time when the attack on him in the musical press was at its height. One of the leading Parisian papers was especially implacable: he was like a red rag to a bull to one of the staff who did not sign his name; not a week passed but there appeared in the column headed *Échos* a spiteful para-

graph ridiculing him. The musical critic completed the work
of his anonymous colleague: the very smallest pretext served
him as an opportunity of expressing his animosity. But that
was only the preliminary skirmishing: he promised to return
to the subject and deal with it at leisure, and to proceed in due
course to execution. They were in no hurry, knowing that a
definite accusation has nothing like the same effect on the
public as a succession of insinuations repeated persistently. They
played with Christophe like a cat with a mouse. The articles
were all sent to Christophe, and he despised them, though they
made him suffer for all that. However, he said nothing: and,
instead of replying—(could he have done so, even if he had
wanted to?)—he persisted in the futile and unequal fight with
his publisher, provoked by his own vanity. He wasted his time,
his strength, his money, and his only weapons, since in the
lightness of his heart he was rash enough to deprive himself
of the publicity which his music gained through Hecht.

Suddenly there was a complete change. The article announced
in the paper never appeared. The insinuations against him
were dropped. The campaign stopped short. More than that:
a few weeks later, the critic of the paper published incidentally
a few eulogistic remarks which seemed to indicate that peace
was made. A great publisher at Leipzig wrote to Christophe
offering to publish his work, and the contract was signed on
terms very advantageous to him. A flattering letter, bearing
the seal of the Austrian Embassy, informed Christophe that it
was desired to place certain of his compositions on the programs
of the galas given at the Embassy. Philomela, whom Christophe
was pushing forward, was asked to sing at one of the galas:
and, immediately afterwards, she was in great demand in the
best houses of the German and Italian colonies in Paris. Christophe himself, who could not get out of going to one of the
concerts, was very well received by the Ambassador. However,
a very short conversation showed him that his host, who knew
very little about music, was absolutely ignorant of his work.
How, then, did this sudden interest come about? An invisible
hand seemed to be protecting him, removing obstacles, and making the way smooth for him. Christophe made inquiries. The

Ambassador alluded to friends of Christophe—Count and Countess Berény, who were very fond of him. Christophe did not even know their name: and on the night of his visit to the Embassy he had no opportunity of being introduced to them. He did not make any effort to meet them. He was passing through a period of disgust with men, in which he set as little store by his friends as by his enemies: friends and enemies were equally uncertain: they changed with the wind: he would have to learn how to do without them, and say, like the old fellow of the seventeenth century:

" *God gave me friends: He took them from me. They have* *left me. I will leave them and say no more about it.*"

Since the day when he left Olivier's house, Olivier had given no sign of life: all seemed over between them. Christophe had no mind to form new friendships. He imagined Count and Countess Berény to be like the rest of the snobs who called themselves his friends: and he made no attempt to meet them. He was more inclined to avoid them. He longed to be able to escape from Paris. He felt an urgent desire to take refuge for a few weeks in soothing solitude. If only he could have a few days, only a few days, to refresh himself in his native country! Little by little that idea became a morbid obsession. He wanted once more to see his dear river, his own native sky, the land of his dead kinsfolk. He felt that he must see them. He could not without endangering his freedom: he was still subject to the warrant of arrest issued against him at the time of his flight from Germany. But he felt that he was prepared to go to any lengths if he could return, though it were only for one day.

As good luck would have it, he spoke of his longing to one of his new patrons. A young attaché of the German Embassy, whom he met at an At Home where he was playing, happened to say to him that his country was proud of so fine a musician as himself, to which Christophe replied bitterly:

" Our country is so proud of me that she lets me die on her doorstep rather than open to me."

The young diplomatist asked him to explain the situation, and, a few days later, he came to see Christophe, and said:

" People in high places are interested in you. A very great

personage who alone has the power to suspend the consequence of the sentence which is the cause of your wretchedness has been informed of your position: and he deigns to be touched by it. I don't know how it is that your music can have given him any pleasure: for—(between ourselves)—his taste is not very good: but he is intelligent, and he has a generous heart. Though he cannot, for the moment, remove the sentence passed upon you, the police are willing to shut their eyes, if you care to spend forty-eight hours in your native town to see your family once more. Here is a passport. You must have it endorsed when you arrive and when you leave. Be wary, and do not attract attention to yourself."

Once more Christophe saw his native land. He spent the two days which had been granted him in communion with the earth and those who were beneath it. He visited his mother's grave. The grass was growing over it: but flowers had lately been laid on it. His father and grandfather slept side by side. He sat at their feet. Their grave lay beneath the wall of the cemetery. It was shaded by a chestnut-tree growing in the sunken road on the other side of the low wall, over which he could see the golden crops, softly waving in the warm wind: the sun was shining in his majesty over the drowsy earth: he could hear the cry of the quails in the corn, and the soft murmuring of the cypress-trees above the graves. Christophe was alone with his dreams. His heart was at peace. He sat there with his hands clasping his knees, and his back against the wall, gazing up at the sky. He closed his eyes for a moment. How simple everything was! He felt at home here with his own people. He stayed there near them, as it were hand in hand. The hours slipped by. Towards evening he heard footsteps scrunching on the gravel paths. The custodian passed by and looked at Christophe sitting there. Christophe asked him who had laid the flowers on the grave. The man answered that the farmer's wife from Buir came once or twice a year.

" Lorchen? " said Christophe.

They began to talk.

" You are her son? " said the man.

" She had three," said Christophe.

" I mean the one at Hamburg. The other two turned out badly."

Christophe sat still with his head thrown back a little, and said nothing. The sun was setting.

" I'm going to lock up," said the custodian.

Christophe got up and walked slowly round the cemetery with him. The custodian did the honors of the place. Christophe stopped every now and then to read the names carved on the gravestones. How many of those he knew were of that company! Old Euler,—his son-in-law,—and farther off, the comrades of his childhood, little girls with whom he had played, —and there, a name which stirred his heart: Ada . . . Peace be with all of them. . . .

The fiery rays of the setting sun put a girdle round the calm horizon. Christophe left the cemetery. He went for a long walk through the fields. The stars were peeping. . . .

Next day he came again, and once more spent the afternoon at his vigil. But the fair silent calm of the day before was broken and thrilling with life. His heart sang a careless, happy hymn. He sat on the curb of the grave, and set down the song he heard in pencil in a notebook resting on his knees. So the day passed. It seemed to him that he was working in his old little room, and that his mother was there on the other side of the partition. When he had finished and was ready to go—he had moved a little away from the grave,—he changed his mind and returned, and buried the notebook in the grass under the ivy. A few drops of rain were beginning to fall. Christophe thought:

" It will soon be blotted out. So much the better! . . . For you alone. For nobody else."

And he went to see the river once more, and the familiar streets where so many things were changed. By the gates of the town along the promenade of the old fortifications a little wood of acacia-trees which he had seen planted had overrun the place, and they were stifling the old trees. As he passed along the wall surrounding the Von Kerichs' garden, he recognized the post on which he used to climb when he was a little boy, to look over into the grounds: and he was surprised to see how small the tree, the wall, and the garden had become

He stopped for a moment before the front gateway. He was going on when a carriage passed him. Mechanically he raised his eyes: and they met those of a young lady, fresh, plump, happy-looking, who stared at him with a puzzled expression. She gave an exclamation of surprise. She ordered the carriage to stop, and said:

"Herr Krafft!"

He stopped.

She said laughingly:

"Minna . . ."

He ran to her almost as nervous as he had been on the day when he first met her.* She was with a tall, stout, bald gentleman, with mustachios brushed up belligerently, whom she introduced as "Herr Reichsgerichtsrat von Brombach"—her husband. She wanted Christophe to go home with her. He tried to excuse himself. But Minna exclaimed:

"No, no. You must come; come and dine with us."

She spoke very loud and very quickly, and, without waiting to be asked, began to tell him her whole life. Christophe was stupefied by her volubility and the noise she made, and only heard half what she said, and stood looking at her. So that was his little Minna. She looked blooming, healthy, well-fed: she had a pretty skin and pink complexion, but her features were rather coarse, and her nose in particular was thick and heavy. Her gestures, manners, pretty little ways, were just the same; but her size was greatly altered.

However, she never stopped talking: she told Christophe all the stories of her past; her whole private history, and how she had come to love her husband and her husband her. Christophe was embarrassed. She was an uncritical optimist, who found everything belonging to herself perfect and superior to other people's possessions—(at least, when she was with other people) —her town, her house, her family, her husband, her cooking, her four children, and herself. She said of her husband in his presence that he was "the most splendid man she had ever seen," and that there was in him "a superhuman force." "The most splendid man" pinched Minna's cheeks laughingly, and assured Christophe that she "was a very remarkable woman"

* See "Jean-Christophe: Morning."

It seemed that *Herr Reichsgerichtsrat* was informed of Christophe's position, and did not exactly know whether he ought to treat him with or without respect, having regard on the one hand to the warrant out against him, and on the other to the august protection which shielded him: he solved the difficulty by affecting a compromise between the two manners. As for Minna, she went on talking. When she had talked her fill about herself to Christophe, she began to talk about him: she battered him with questions as intimate as her answers had been to the supposititious questions which he had never asked. She was delighted to see Christophe again: she knew nothing about his music: but she knew that he was famous: it flattered her to think that she had loved him,—(and that she had rejected him).—She reminded him of it jokingly without much delicacy. She asked him for his autograph for her album. She pestered him with questions about Paris. She showed a mixture of curiosity and contempt for that city. She pretended that she knew it, having been to the Folies-Bergère, the Opéra, Montmartre, and Saint-Cloud. According to her, the women of Paris were all *cocottes,* bad mothers, who had as few children as possible, and did not look after them, and left them at home while they went to the theater or the haunts of pleasant vice. She did not suffer contradiction. In the course of the evening she asked Christophe to play the piano. She thought it charming. But at bottom she admired her husband's playing just as much, for she thought him as superior all round as she was herself.

Christophe had the pleasure of meeting Minna's mother once more, Frau von Kerich. He still had a secret tenderness for her because she had been kind to him. She had not lost any of her old kindness, and she was more natural than Minna: but she still treated Christophe with that ironical affection which used to irritate him in the old days. She had stayed very much where he had left her: she liked the same things; and it did not seem possible for her to admit that any one could do better or differently: she set the Jean-Christophe of the old days against the new Jean-Christophe, and preferred the former.

Of those about her no one had changed in mind save Christophe. The rigidity of the little town, and its narrowness of

outlook, were painful to him. His hosts spent part of the evening in talking scandal about people he did not know. They
picked out the ridiculous points of their neighbors, and they
decreed everything ridiculous which was different from themselves or their own way of doing things. Their malicious curiosity, which was perpetually occupied with trifles, at last made
Christophe feel quite sick. He tried to talk about his life
abroad. But at once he became conscious of the impossibility
of making them understand French civilization which had made
him suffer, and now became dear to him when he stood for it
in his own country—the free Latin spirit, whose first law is
understanding: to understand as much as possible of life and
mind, at the risk of cheapening moral codes. In his hosts,
especially in Minna, he found once more the arrogant spirit
with which he had come into such violent contact in the old
days, though he had almost forgotten it since,—the arrogance
of weakness as much as of virtue,—honesty without charity,
pluming itself on its virtue, and despising the weaknesses which
it could not understand, a worship of the conventional, and a
shocked disdain of " irregular " higher things. Minna was
calmly and sententiously confident that she was always right.
There were no degrees in her judgment of others. For the rest,
she never made any attempt to understand them, and was only
occupied with herself. Her egoism was thinly coated with a
blurred metaphysical tinge. She was always talking of her
" ego " and the development of her " ego." She may have been
a good woman, one capable of loving. But she loved herself too
much. And, above all, her respect for herself was too great.
She seemed to be perpetually saying a *Paternoster* and an *Ave* to
her " ego." One felt that she would have absolutely and forever
ceased to love the man she might have loved the best, if for a
single instant he had failed—(even though he were to regret
it a thousand times when it was done)—to show a due and
proper respect for the dignity of her " ego." . . . Hang your
" ego "! Think a little of the second person singular! . . .

However, Christophe did not regard her severely. He who
was ordinarily so irritable listened to her chatter with the
patience of an archangel. He would not judge her. He surrounded her, as with a halo, with the religious memory of his

childish love, and he kept on trying to find in her the image
of his little Minna. It was not impossible to find her in certain
of her gestures: the quality of her voice had certain notes which
awoke echoes that moved him. He was absorbed in them, and
said nothing, and did not listen to what she was saying, though
he seemed to listen and always treated her with tender gentle
respect. But he found it hard to concentrate his thoughts: she
made too much noise, and prevented his hearing Minna. At
last he got up, and thought a little wearily:

"Poor little Minna! They would like me to think that you
are there, in that comely, stout woman, shouting at the top of
her voice, and boring me to death. But I know that it is not
so. Come away, Minna. What have we to do with these
people?"

He went away, giving them to understand that he would return on the morrow. If he had said that he was going away
that very night, they would not have let him go until it was
time to catch the train. He had only gone a few yards in the
darkness when he recovered the feeling of well-being which he
had had before he met the carriage. The memory of his tiresome evening was wiped out as though a wet sponge had been
over it: nothing was left of it: it was all drowned in the voice
of the Rhine. He walked along its banks by the house where
he was born. He had no difficulty in recognizing it. The
shutters were closed: all were asleep in it. Christophe stopped
in the middle of the road: and it seemed to him that if he
knocked at the door, familiar phantoms would open to him.
He went into the field round the house, near the river, and came
to the place where he used to go and talk to Gottfried in the
evening. He sat down. And the old days came to life again.
And the dear little girl who had sipped with him the dream
of first love was conjured up. Together they lived through their
childish tenderness again, with its sweet tears and infinite hopes.
And he thought with a simple smile:

"Life has taught me nothing. All my knowledge is vain. . . .
All my knowledge is vain. . . . I have still the same old
illusions."

How good it is to love and to believe unfailingly! Everything that is touched by love is saved from death.

"Minna, you are with me,—with me, not with *the other*,—Minna, you will never grow old! . . ."

The veiled moon darted from her clouds, and made the silver scales on the river's back gleam in her light. Christophe had a vague feeling that the river never used to pass near the knoll where he was sitting. He went near it. Yes. Beyond the pear-tree there used to be a tongue of sand, a little grassy slope, where he had often played. The river had swept them away: the river was encroaching, lapping at the roots of the pear-tree. Christophe felt a pang at his heart: he went back towards the station. In that direction a new colony—mean houses, sheds half-built, tall factory chimneys—was in course of construction. Christophe thought of the acacia-wood he had seen in the afternoon, and he thought:

"There, too, the river is encroaching. . . ."

The old town, lying asleep in the darkness, with all that it contained of the living and the dead, became even more dear to him: for he felt that a menace hung over it. . . .

Hostis habet muros. . . .

Quick, let us save our women and children! Death is lying in wait for all that we love. Let us hasten to carve the passing face upon eternal bronze. Let us snatch the treasure of our motherland before the flames devour the palace of Priam.

Christophe scrambled into the train as it was going, like a man fleeing before a flood. But, like those men who saved the gods of their city from the wreck, Christophe bore away within his soul the spark of life which had flown upwards from his native land, and the sacred spirit of the past.

Jacqueline and Olivier had come together again for a time. Jacqueline had lost her father, and his death had moved her deeply. In the presence of real misfortune she had felt the wretched folly of her other sorrows: and the tenderness which Olivier showed towards her had revived her affection for him. She was taken back several years to the sad days which had followed on the death of her Aunt Marthe—days which had been followed by the blessed days of love. She told herself that she was ungrateful to life, and that she ought to be thankful that the little it had given her was not taken from her. She hugged that little to herself now that its worth had been revealed to her. A short absence from Paris, ordered by her doctor to distract her in her grief, travel with Olivier, a sort of pilgrimage to the places where they had loved each other during the first year of her marriage, softened her and filled her with tenderness. In the sadness of seeing once more at the turn of the road the dear face of the love which they thought was gone forever, of seeing it pass and knowing that it would vanish once more,—for how long? perhaps forever?—they clutched at it passionately and desperately. . . .

"Stay, stay with us!"

But they knew that they must lose it. . . .

When Jacqueline returned to Paris she felt a little new life, kindled by love, thrilling in her veins. But love had gone already. The burden which lay so heavy upon her did not bring her into sympathy with Olivier again. She did not feel the joy she expected. She probed herself uneasily. Often when she had been so tormented before she had thought that the coming of a child might be her salvation. The child had come, but it brought no salvation. She felt the human plant rooted in her flesh growing, and sucking up her blood and her life. She would stay for days together lost in thought, listening with vacant eyes, all her being exhausted by the unknown creature that had taken possession of her. She was conscious of a vague buzzing, sweet, lulling, agonizing. She would start suddenly from her torpor—dripping with sweat, shivering, with a spasm of revolt. She fought against the meshes in which Nature had entrapped her. She wished to live, to live freely, and it seemed to her that Nature had tricked her. Then she was ashamed of such thoughts, and seemed monstrous in her own eyes, and asked herself if she were more wicked than, or made differently from, other women. And little by little she would grow calm again, browsing like a tree over the sap, and the dream of the living fruit ripening in her womb. What was it? What was it going to be? . . .

When she heard its first cry to the light, when she saw its pitiable touching little body, her heart melted. In one dazzling moment she knew the glorious joy of motherhood, the mightiest in all the world: in her suffering to have created of her own flesh a living being, a man. And the great wave of love which moves the universe, caught her whole body, dashed her down, rushed over her, and lifted her up to the heavens. . . . O God, the woman who creates is Thy equal: and Thou knowest no joy like unto hers: for Thou hast not suffered. . . .

Then the wave rolled back, and her soul dropped back into the depths.

Olivier, trembling with emotion, stooped over the child: and, smiling at Jacqueline, he tried to understand what bond of mysterious life there was between themselves and the wretched little creature that was as yet hardly human. Tenderly, with a little feeling of disgust, he just touched its little yellow wrinkled face with his lips. Jacqueline watched him: jealously she pushed him away: she took the child and hugged it to her breast, and covered it with kisses. The child cried and she gave it back, and, with her face turned to the wall, she wept. Olivier came to her and kissed her, and drank her tears: she kissed him too, and forced herself to smile: then she asked to be left alone to rest with the child by her side. . . . Alas! what is to be done when love is dead? The man who gives more than half of himself up to intelligence never loses a strong feeling without preserving a trace, an idea, of it in his brain. He cannot love any more, but he cannot forget that he has loved. But the woman who has loved wholly and without reason, and without reason ceases wholly to love, what can she do? Will? Take refuge in illusions? And what if she be too weak to will, too true to take refuge in illusions? . . .

Jacqueline, lying on her side with her head propped up by her hand, looked down at the child with tender pity. What was he? Whatever he was, he was not entirely hers. He was also something of "the other." And she no longer loved "the other." Poor child! Dear child! She was exasperated with the little creature who was there to bind her to the dead past: and she bent over him and kissed and kissed him. . . .

It is the great misfortune of the women of to-day that they are too free without being free enough. If they were more free, they would seek to form ties, and would find charm and security in them. If they were less free, they would resign themselves to ties which they would not know how to break: and they would suffer less. But the worst state of all is to have ties which do not bind, and duties from which it is possible to break free.

If Jacqueline had believed that her little house was to be her lot for the whole of her life, she would not have found it so inconvenient and cramped, and she would have devised ways of making it comfortable: she would have ended as she began, by loving it. But she knew that it was possible to leave it, and it stifled her. It was possible for her to revolt, and at last she came to think it her duty to do so.

The present-day moralists are strange creatures. All their qualities have atrophied to the profit of their faculties of observation. They have given up trying to see life, hardly attempt to understand it, and never by any chance WILL it When they have observed and noted down the facts of human nature, they seem to think their task is at an end, and say:

"That is a fact."

They make no attempt to change it. In their eyes, apparently, the mere fact of existence is a moral virtue. Every sort of weakness seems to have been inserted with a sort of Divine right. The world is growing democratic. Formerly only the King was irresponsible. Nowadays all men, preferably the basest, have that privilege. Admirable counselors! With infinite pains and scrupulous care they set themselves to prove to the weak exactly how weak they are, and that it has been decreed that they should be so and not otherwise from all eternity What can the weak do but fold their arms? We may think ourselves lucky if they do not admire themselves! By dint of hearing it said over and over again that she is a sick child, a woman soon takes a pride in being so. It is encouraging cowardice, and making it spread. If a man were to amuse himself by telling children complacently that there is an age in adolescence when the soul, not yet having found its balance, is capable of crimes, and suicide, and the worst sort of physical and moral depravity, and were to excuse these things—at once these offenses would spring into being. And even with men it is quite enough to go on telling them that they are not free to make them cease to be so and descend to the level of the beasts. Tell a woman that she is a responsible being, and mistress of her body and her will, and she will be so. But you moralists are cowards, and take good care not to tell her so: for you have an interest in keeping such knowledge from her! . . .

The unhappy surroundings in which Jacqueline found herself led her astray. Since she had broken with Olivier she had returned to that section of society which she despised when she was a girl. About her and her friends, among married women, there gathered a little group of wealthy young men and women, smart, idle, intelligent, and licentious. They enjoyed absolute liberty of thought and speech, tempered only by the seasoning of wit. They might well have taken for their motto the device of the Rabelaisian abbey:

" Do what thou wilt."

But they bragged a little: for they did not will anything much: they were like the enervated people of Thelema. They would complacently profess the freedom of their instincts: but their instincts were faded and faint; and their profligacy was chiefly cerebral. They delighted in feeling themselves sink into the great piscina of civilization, that warm mud-bath in which human energy, the primeval and vital forces, primitive animalism, and its blossom of faith, will, duties, and passions, are liquefied. Jacqueline's pretty body was steeped in that bath of gelatinous thought. Olivier could do nothing to keep her from it. Besides, he too was touched by the disease of the time: he thought he had no right to tamper with the liberty of another human being: he would not ask anything of the woman he loved that he could not gain through love. And Jacqueline did not in the least resent his non-interference, because she regarded her liberty as her right.

The worst of it was that she went into that amphibious section of society with a wholeness of heart which made anything equivocal repulsive to her: when she believed she gave herself: in the generous ardor of her soul, even in her egoism, she always burned her boats; and, as a result of living with Olivier, she had preserved a moral inability to compromise, which she was apt to apply even in immorality.

Her new friends were too cautious to let others see them as

they were. In theory they paraded absolute liberty with regard
to the prejudices of morality and society, though in practice
they so contrived their affairs as not to fall out with any one
whose acquaintance might be useful to them: they used morality
and society, while they betrayed them like unfaithful servants,
robbing their masters. They even robbed each other for want
of anything better to do, and as a matter of habit. There was
more than one of the men who knew that his wife had lovers.
The wives were not ignorant of the fact that their husbands
had mistresses. They both put up with it. Scandal only begins
when one makes a noise about these things. These charming
marriages rested on a tacit understanding between partners—between accomplices. But Jacqueline was more frank, and played
to win or lose. The first thing was to be sincere. Again, to
be sincere. Again and always, to be sincere. Sincerity was
also one of the virtues extolled by the ideas of that time. But
herein it is proved once again that everything is sound for the
sound in heart, while everything is corrupt for the corrupt.
How hideous it is sometimes to be sincere! It is a sin for
mediocre people to try to look into the depths of themselves.
They see their mediocrity: and their vanity always finds something to feed on.

Jacqueline spent her time in looking at herself in her mirror:
she saw things in it which it were better she had never seen:
for when she saw them she could not take her eyes off them:
and instead of struggling against them she watched them grow:
they became enormous and in the end captured her eyes and
her mind.

The child was not enough to fill her life. She had not been
able to nurse it: the baby pined with her. She had to procure
a wet nurse. It was a great grief to her at first. . . . Soon
it became a solace. The child became splendidly healthy: he
grew lustily, and became a fine little fellow, gave no trouble,
spent his time in sleeping, and hardly cried at all at night.
The nurse—a strapping Nivernaise who had fostered many children, and always had a jealous and embarrassing animal affection for each of them in turn—was like the real mother. Whenever Jacqueline expressed an opinion, the woman went her own
way: and if Jacqueline tried to argue, in the end she always

found that she knew nothing at all about it. She had **never** really recovered from the birth of the child: a slight attack **of** phlebitis had dragged her down, and as she had to lie still for several weeks she worried and worried: she was feverish, and her mind went on and on indefinitely beating out the same monotonous deluded complaint:

" I have not lived, I have not lived: and now my life is finished. . . ."

For her imagination was fired: she thought herself crippled for life: and there rose in her a dumb, harsh, and bitter rancor, which she did not confess to herself, against the innocent cause of her illness, the child. The feeling is not so rare as is generally believed: but a veil is drawn over it: and even those who feel it are ashamed to submit to it in their inmost hearts. Jacqueline condemned herself: there was a sharp conflict between her egoism and her mother's love. When she saw the child sleeping so happily, she was filled with tenderness: but a moment later she would think bitterly:

" He has killed me."

And she could not suppress a feeling of irritation and revolt against the untroubled sleep of the creature whose happiness she had bought at the price of her suffering. Even after she had recovered, when the child was bigger, the feeling of hostility persisted dimly and obscurely. As she was ashamed of it, she transferred it to Olivier. She went on fancying herself ill: and her perpetual care of her health, her anxieties, which were bolstered up by the doctors, who encouraged the idleness which was the prime cause of it all,—(separation from the child, forced inactivity, absolute isolation. weeks of emptiness spent in lying in bed and being stuffed with food, like a beast being fatted for slaughter),—had ended by concentrating all her thoughts upon herself. The modern way of curing neurasthenia is very strange, being neither more nor less than the substitution of hypertrophy of the ego for a disease of the ego! Why not bleed their egoism, or restore the circulation of the blood from head to heart, if they do not have too much, by some violent, moral reagent!

Jacqueline came out of it physically stronger, plumper, and rejuvenated,—but morally she was more ill than ever. Her months of isolation had broken the last ties of thought which bound her to Olivier. While she lived with him she was still under the ascendancy of his idealism, for, in spite of all his failings, he remained constant to his faith: she struggled in vain against the bondage in which she was held by a mind more steadfast than her own, against the look which pierced to her very soul, and forced her sometimes to condemn herself, however loath she might be to do so. But as soon as chance had separated her from her husband—as soon as she ceased to feel the weight of his all-seeing love—as soon as she was free—the trusting friendship that used to exist between them was supplanted by a feeling of anger at having broken free, a sort of hatred born of the idea that she had for so long lived beneath the yoke of an affection which she no longer felt.—Who can tell the hidden, implacable, bitter feelings that seethe and ferment in the heart of a creature he loves, by whom he believes that he is loved? Between one day and the next, all is changed. She loved the day before, she seemed to love, she thought she loved. She loves no longer. The man she loved is struck out from her thoughts. She sees suddenly that he is nothing to her: and he does not understand: he has seen nothing of the long travail through which she has passed: he has had no suspicion of the secret hostility towards himself that has been gathering in her: he does not wish to know the reasons for her vengeful hatred. Reasons often remote, complex, and obscure,—some hidden deep in the mysteries of their inmost life,—others arising from injured vanity, secrets of the heart surprised and judged,—others . . . What does she know of them herself? It is some hidden offense committed against her unwittingly, an offense which she will never forgive. It is impossible to find out, and she herself is not very sure what it is: but the offense is marked deep in her flesh: her flesh will never forget it.

To fight against such an appalling stream of disaffection called for a very different type of man from Olivier—one nearer nature, a simpler man and a more supple one not hampered with sentimental scruples, a man of strong instincts, capable, if need be, of actions which his reason would disavow. He lost the fight before ever it began, for he had lost heart: his perception was too clear, and he had long since recognized in Jacqueline a form of heredity which was stronger than her will, her mother's soul reappearing in her: he saw her falling like a stone down to the depths of the stock from which she sprang: and his weak and clumsy efforts to stay her only accelerated her downfall. He forced himself to be calm. She, from an unconsciously selfish motive, tried to break down his defenses and make him say violent, brutal, boorish things to her so as to have a reason for despising him. If he gave way to anger, she despised him If at once he were ashamed and became apologetic, she despised him even more. And if he did not, would not, give way to anger—then she hated him. And worst of all was the silence which for days together would rise like a wall between them. A suffocating, crushing, maddening silence which brings even the gentlest creatures to fury and exasperation, and makes them have moments when they feel a savage desire to hurt, to cry out, or make the other cry out. The black silence in which love reaches its final stage of disintegration, and the man and the woman, like the worlds, each following its own orbit, pass onward into the night. . . . They had reached a point at which everything they did, even an attempt to come together again, drove them farther and farther apart. Their life became intolerable. Events were precipitated by an accident.

During the past year Cécile Fleury had often been to the Jeannins'. Olivier had met her at Christophe's: then Jacqueline had invited her to the house; and Cécile went on seeing them even after Christophe had broken with them. Jacqueline had been kind to her: although she was hardly at all musical and thought Cécile a little common, she felt the charm of her singing and her soothing influence. Olivier liked playing with her, and gradually she became a friend of the family. She inspired confidence: when she came into the Jeannins' drawing-room with her honest eyes and her air of health and high spirits, and her rather loud laugh which it was good to hear, it was like a ray of sunlight piercing the mist. She brought a feeling of inexpressible relief and solace to Olivier and Jacqueline. When she was leaving they longed to say to her:

" No. Stay, stay a little while longer, for I am cold!"

During Jacqueline's absence Olivier saw Cécile more often: and he could not help letting her see something of his troubles

He did it quite unthinkingly, with the heedlessness of a weak and tender creature who is stifling and has need of some one to confide in, with an absolute surrender. Cécile was touched by it: she soothed him with motherly words of comfort. She pitied both of them, and urged Olivier not to lose heart. But whether it was that she was more embarrassed than he by his confidences, or that there was some other reason, she found excuses for going less often to the house. No doubt it seemed to her that she was not acting loyally towards Jacqueline, for she had no right to know her secrets. At least, that was how Olivier interpreted her estrangement: and he agreed with her, for he was sorry that he had spoken. But the estrangement made him feel what Cécile had become to him. He had grown used to sharing his ideas with her, and she was the only creature who could deliver him from the pain he was suffering. He was too much skilled in reading his own feelings to have any doubt as to the name of what he felt for her. He would never have said anything to Cécile. But he could not resist the imperative desire to write down what he felt. For some little time past he had returned to the dangerous habit of communing with his thoughts on paper. He had cured himself of it during the years of love: but now that he found himself alone once more, his inherited mania took possession of him: it was a relief from his sufferings, and it was the artist's need of self-analysis. So he described himself. and set his troubles down in writing, as though he were telling them to Cécile—more freely indeed; since she was never to read it. And as luck would have it the manuscript came into Jacqueline's hands. It happened one day when she was feeling nearer Olivier than she had been for years. As she was clearing out her cupboard she read once more the old love-letters he had sent her: she had been moved to tears by them. Sitting in the shadow of the cupboard, unable to go on with her tidying, she lived through the past once more: and then was filled with sorrow and remorse to think that she had destroyed it. She thought of the grief it must be to Olivier; she had never been able to face the idea of it calmly: she could forget it: but she could not bear to think that he had suffered through her. Her heart ached. She longed to throw herself into his arms and say:

"Oh! Olivier, Olivier, what have we done? We are mad, we are mad! Don't let us ever again hurt each other!"

If only he had come in at that moment!

And it was exactly at that moment that she found his letters to Cécile. . . . It was the end.—Did she think that Olivier had really deceived her? Perhaps. But what does it signify? To her the betrayal was not so much in the act as in the thought and intention. She would have found it easier to forgive the man she loved for taking a mistress than for secretly giving his heart to another woman. And she was right.

"A pretty state of things!" some will say . . . —(They are poor creatures who only suffer from the betrayal of love when it is consummated! . . . When the heart remains faithful, the sordid offenses of the body are of small account. When the heart turns traitor, all the rest is nothing.) . . .

Jacqueline did not for a moment think of regaining Olivier's love. It was too late! She no longer cared for him enough. Or perhaps she cared for him too much. All her trust in him crumbled away, all that was left in her secret heart of her faith and hope in him. She did not tell herself that she had scorned him, and had discouraged him, and driven him to his new love, or that his love was innocent: and that after all we are not masters of ourselves sufficiently to choose whether we will love or not. It never occurred to her to compare his sentimental impulse with her flirtation with Christophe: she did not love Christophe, and so he did not count! In her passionate exaggeration she thought that Olivier was lying to her, and that she was nothing to him. Her last stay had failed her at the moment when she reached out her hand to grasp it. . . . It was the end.

Olivier never knew what she had suffered that day. But when he next saw her he too felt that it was the end.

From that moment on they never spoke to each other except in the presence of strangers. They watched each other like trapped beasts fearfully on their guard. Jeremias Gotthelf somewhere describes, with pitiless simplicity, the grim situation of a husband and a wife who no longer love each other and watch each other, each carefully marking the other's health, looking for symptoms of illness, neither actually thinking of hasten·

ing or even wishing the death of the other, but drifting along
in the hope of some sudden accident: and each of them living
in the flattering thought of being the healthier of the two.
There were moments when both Jacqueline and Olivier almost
fancied that such thoughts were in the other's mind. And they
were in the mind of neither: but it was bad enough that they
should attribute them to each other, as Jacqueline did at night
when she would lie feverishly awake and tell herself that her
husband was the stronger, and that he was wearing her down
gradually, and would soon triumph over her. . . . The monstrous delirium of a crazy heart and brain!—And to think that
in their heart of hearts, with all that was best in them, they
loved each other! . . .

Olivier bent beneath the weight of it, and made no attempt
to fight against it; he held aloof and dropped the rudder of
Jacqueline's soul. Left to herself with no pilot to steer her,
her freedom turned her dizzy: she needed a master against
whom to revolt: if she had no master she had to make one.
Then she was the prey of a fixed idea. Till then, in spite of
her suffering, she had never dreamed of leaving Olivier. From
that time on she thought herself absolved from every tie. She
wished to love, before it was too late:—(for, young as she was,
she thought herself an old woman).—She loved, she indulged
in those imaginary devouring passions, which fasten on the first
object they meet, a face seen in a crowd, a reputation, sometimes
merely a name, and, having laid hold of it cannot let go, telling
the heart that it cannot live without the object of its choice,
laying it waste, and completely emptying it of all the memories
of the past that filled it; other affections, moral ideas, memories,
pride of self, and respect for others. And when the fixed idea
dies in its time for want of anything to feed it, after it has
consumed everything, who can tell what the new nature may
be that will spring from the ruins, a nature often without kindness, without pity, without youth, without illusions, thinking of
nothing but devouring life as grass smothers and devours the
ruins of monuments!

In this case, as usual, the fixed idea fastened on a creature
of the type that most easily tricks the heart. Poor Jacqueline
fell in love with a philanderer, a Parisian writer, who was

neither young nor handsome, a man who was heavy, red-faced, dissipated, with bad teeth, absolutely and terribly heartless, whose chief merit was that he was a man of the world and had made a great many women unhappy.   She had not even the excuse that she did not know how selfish he was: for he paraded it in his art. He knew perfectly what he was doing: egoism enshrined in art is like a mirror to larks, like a candle to moths.   More than one woman in Jacqueline's circle had been caught: quite recently one of her friends, a young, newly-married woman, whom he had had no great difficulty in seducing, had been deserted by him.   Their hearts were not broken by it, though they found it hard to conceal their discomfiture from the delight of the gossips.   Even those who were most cruelly hurt were much too careful of their interests and their social interests not to keep their perturbation within the bounds of common sense. They made no scandal.   Whether they deceived their husbands or their lovers, or whether they were themselves deceived and suffered, it was all done in silence.   They were the heroines of scandalous rumors.

But Jacqueline was mad: she was capable not only of doing what she said, but also of saying what she did.   She brought into her folly an absolute lack of selfish motive, and an utter disinterestedness.   She had the dangerous merit of always being frank with herself and of never shirking the consequences of her own actions.   She was a better creature than the people she lived with: and for that reason she did worse.   When she loved, when she conceived the idea of adultery, she flung herself into it headlong with desperate frankness.

Madame Arnaud was alone in her room, knitting with the feverish tranquillity with which Penelope must have woven her famous web.   Like Penelope, she was waiting for her husband's return.   M. Arnaud used to spend whole days away from home. He had classes in the morning and evening.   As a rule he came back to lunch.   Although he was a slow walker and his school was at the other end of Paris, he forced himself to take the long walk home, not so much from affection, as from habit, and for the sake of economy.   But sometimes he was detained by lectures, or he would take advantage of being in the neighborhood of a

library to go and work there. Lucile Arnaud would be left
alone in the empty flat. Except for the charwoman who came
from eight to ten to do the cleaning, and the tradesmen who
came to fetch and bring orders, no one ever rang the bell. She
knew nobody in the house now. Christophe had removed, and
there were newcomers in the lilac garden. Céline Chabran
had married André Elsberger. Élie Elsberger had gone away
with his family to Spain, where he had been appointed manager
of a mine. Old Weil had lost his wife and hardly ever lived
in his flat in Paris. Only Christophe and his friend Cécile had
kept up their relations with Lucile Arnaud: but they lived far
away, and they were busy and hard at work all day long, so
that they often did not come to see her for weeks together.
She had nothing outside herself.

She was not bored. She needed very little to keep her interest
in things alive: the very smallest daily task was enough, or a
tiny plant, whose delicate foliage she would clean with motherly
care every morning. She had her quiet gray cat, who had lost
something of his manners, as is apt to happen with domestic
animals who are loved by their masters: he used to spend the
day, like herself, sitting by the fire, or on the table near the
lamp watching her fingers as she sewed, and sometimes gazing
at her with his strange eyes, which watched her for a moment
and then closed again. Even the furniture was company to her.
Every piece was like a familiar face. She took a childlike
pleasure in looking after them, in gently wiping off the dust
which settled on their sides, and in carefully replacing them in
their usual corners. She would hold silent conversations with
them. She would smile at the fine Louis XVI. round-topped
bureau, which was the only piece of old furniture she had.
Every day she would feel the same joy in seeing it. She was
always absorbed in going over her linen, and she would spend
hours standing on a chair, with her hands and arms deep in the
great country cupboard, looking and arranging, while the
cat, whose curiosity was roused, would spend hours watching
her.

But her real happiness came when, after her work was done
and she had lunched alone, God knows how—(she never had
much of an appetite)—and had gone the necessary errands, and

her day was at an end, she would come in about four and sit
by the window or the fire with her work and her cat. Sometimes
she would find some excuse for not going out at all; she was
glad when she could stay indoors, especially in the winter when
it was snowing. She had a horror of the cold, and the wind,
and the mud, and the rain, for she was something of a cat
herself, very clean, fastidious, and soft. She would rather not
eat than go and procure her lunch when the tradespeople forgot
to bring it. In that case she would munch a piece of chocolate
or some fruit from the sideboard. She was very careful not to
let Arnaud know. These were her escapades. Then during the
days when the light was dim, and also sometimes on lovely sunny
days,—(outside the blue sky would shine, and the noise of the
street would buzz round the dark silent rooms; like a sort of
mirage enshrouding the soul),- she would sit in her favorite
corner, with her feet on her hass·ck, her knitting in her hands,
and go off into day-dreams while her fingers plied the needles.
She would have one of her favorite books by her side: as a rule
one of those humble, red-backed volumes, a translation of an
English novel. She would read very little, hardly more than a
chapter a day; and the book would lie on her knees open at
the same page for a long time together, or sometimes she would
not even open it: she knew it already, and the story of it would
be in her dreams. So the long novels of Dickens and Thackeray
would be drawn out over weeks, and in her dreams they would
become years. They wrapped her about with their tenderness.
The people of the present day, who read quickly and carelessly,
do not know the marvelous vigor irradiated by those fine books
which must be taken in slowly. Madame Arnaud had no doubt
that the lives of the characters in the novels were not as real
as her own. There were some for whom she would have laid
down her life: the tender jealous creature, Lady Castlewood, the
woman who loved in silence with her motherly virginal heart,
was a sister to her: little Dombey was her own dear little boy:
she was Dora, the child-wife, who was dying: she would hold
out her arms to all those childlike souls which pass through
the world with the honest eyes of purity: and around her there
would pass a procession of friendly beggars and harmless eccen-
trics, all in pursuit of their touchingly preposterous cranks and

whims,—and at their head the fond genius of dear Dickens, laughing and crying together at his own dreams. At such times, when she looked out of the window, she would recognize among the passers-by the beloved or dreaded figure of this or that personage in that imaginary world. She would fancy similar lives, the same lives, being lived behind the walls of the houses. Her dislike for going out came from her dread of that world with its moving mysteries. She saw around her hidden dramas and comedies being played. It was not always an illusion. In her isolation she had come by the gift of mystical intuition which in the eyes of the passers-by can perceive the secrets of their lives of yesterday and to-morrow, which are often unknown to themselves. She mixed up what she actually saw with what she remembered of the novels and distorted it. She felt that she must drown in that immense universe. And she would have to go home to regain her footing.

But what need had she to read or to look at others? She had but to gaze in upon herself. Her pale, dim existence—seeming so when seen from without—was gloriously lit up within. There was abundance and fullness of life in it. There were memories, and treasures, the existence of which lay unsuspected. . . . Had they ever had any reality?—No doubt they were real, since they were real to her. . . . Oh! the wonder of such lowly lives transfigured by the magic wand of dreams!

Madame Arnaud would go back through the years to her childhood: each of the little frail flowers of her vanished hopes sprang silently into life again. . . . Her first childish love for a girl, whose charm had fascinated her at first sight: she loved her with the love which is only possible to those who are infinitely pure: she used to think she would die at the touch of her: she used to long to kiss her feet, to be her little girl, to marry her: the girl had married, had not been happy, had had a child which died, and then she too had died. . . . Another love, when she was about twelve years old, for a little girl of her own age, who tyrannized over her: a fair-haired madcap, gay and imperious, who used to amuse herself by making her cry, and then would devour her with kisses: she laid a thousand romantic plans for their future together: then, suddenly, the girl became a Carmelite nun, without anybody knowing why: she was said to be happy. . . . Then there had been a great passion for a man much older than herself. No one had ever known anything about it, not even the object of it. She had given to it a great and ardent devotion and untold wealth of tenderness. . . . Then another passion: this time she was loved. But from a strange timidity, and mistrust of herself, she had not dared to believe that she was loved. or to let the man see that she loved him. And happiness passed without her grasping it. . . . Then . . . But what is the use of telling others what only has a meaning for oneself? So many trivial facts which had assumed a profound significance: a little attention at the hands of a friend: a kind word from Olivier, spoken without his attaching any importance to it: Christophe's kindly visits, and the enchanted world evoked by his music: a glance from a stranger: yes, and even in that excellent woman, so virtuous and pure, certain involuntary infidelities in thought, which made her uneasy and feel ashamed, while she would feebly thrust them aside, though all the same—being so innocent—they brought a little sunshine into her heart. . . . She loved her husband truly. although he was not altogether the husband of her dreams. But he was kind, and one day when he said to her: "My darling wife, you do not know all you are to me; you are my whole life," her heart melted: and that day she felt that she was one with him, wholly and forever. without any possibility of going back on it. Each year brought them closer to each other, and tightened the bond between them. They had shared lovely dreams: of work, traveling. children. What had become of them? . . . Alas! . . . Madame Arnaud was still dreaming them. There was a little boy of whom she had so often and so profoundly dreamed, that she knew him almost as well as though he really existed. She had slowly begotten him through the years, always adorning him with all the most beautiful things she saw, and the things she loved most dearly. . . . Silence! . . .

That was all. It meant worlds to her. There are so many tragedies unknown, even the most intimate, in the depths of the most tranquil and seemingly most ordinary lives! And the greatest tragedy of all perhaps is:—*that nothing happens* in such lives of hope crying for what is their right, their just due promised, and refused, by Nature—wasting away in passionate anguish—showing nothing of it all to the outside world!

Madame Arnaud, happily for herself, was not only occupied with herself. Her own life filled only a part of her dreams. She lived also in the lives of those she knew, or had known, and put herself in their place: she thought much of Christophe and his friend Cécile. She was thinking of them now. The two women had grown fond of one another. The strange thing was that of the two it was the sturdy Cécile who felt most need to lean on the frail Madame Arnaud. In reality the healthy, high-spirited young woman was not so strong as she seemed to be. She was passing through a crisis. Even the most tranquil hearts are not immune from being taken by surprise. Unknown to herself, a feeling of tenderness had crept into her heart: she refused to admit it at first: but it had grown so that she was forced to see it:—she loved Olivier. His sweet and affectionate disposition, the rather feminine charm of his personality, his weakness and inability to defend himself, had attracted her at once:—(a motherly nature is attracted by the nature which has need of her).—What she had learned subsequently of his marital troubles had inspired her with a dangerous pity for Olivier. No doubt these reasons would not have been enough. Who can say why one human being falls in love with another? Neither counts for anything in the matter, but often it merely happens that a heart which is for the moment off its guard is taken by surprise, and is delivered up to the first affection it may meet on the road.—As soon as she had no room left for doubt as to her state of mind, Cécile bravely struggled to pluck out the barb of a love which she thought wicked and absurd: she suffered for a long time and did not re·cover. No one would have suspected what was happening to her: she strove valiantly to appear happy. Only Madame Arnaud knew what it must have cost her. Not that Cécile had told her her secret. But she would sometimes come and lay her head on Madame Arnaud's bosom. She would weep a little, without a word, kiss her, and then go away laughing. She adored this friend of hers, in whom, though she seemed so fragile, she felt a moral energy and faith superior to her own. She did not confide in her. But Madame Arnaud could guess

volumes on a hint. The world seemed to her to be a sad misunderstanding. It is impossible to dissolve it. One can only
love, have pity, and dream.

And when the swarm of her dreams buzzed too loudly, when
her thoughts stopped, she would go to her piano and let her
hands fall lightly on the keys, at random, and play softly to
wreathe the mirage of life about with the subdued light of
music. . . .

But the good little creature would not forget to perform her
everyday duties: and when Arnaud came home he would find
the lamp lit, the supper ready, and his wife's pale, smiling face
waiting for him. And he would have no idea of the universe in
which she had been living.

The great difficulty was to keep the two lives going side
by side without their clashing: her everyday life and that other,
the great life of the mind, with its far-flung horizons. It was
not always easy. Fortunately Arnaud also lived to some extent
in an imaginary life, in books, and works of art, the eternal fire
of which fed the flickering flames of his soul. But during the
last few years he had become more and more preoccupied with
the petty annoyances of his profession, injustice and favoritism,
and friction with his colleagues or his pupils: he was embittered: he began to talk politics, and to inveigh against the Government and the Jews: and he made Dreyfus responsible for his
disappointments at the university. His mood of soreness infected Madame Arnaud a little. She was at an age when her
vital force was upset and uneasy, groping for balance. There
were great gaps in her thoughts. For a time they both lost
touch with life, and their reason for existence: for they had
nothing to which to bind their spider's web, which was left hanging in the void. Though the support of reality be never so
weak, yet for dreams there must be one. They had no sort of
support. They could not contrive any means of propping each
other up. Instead of helping her, he clung to her. And she
knew perfectly well that she was not strong enough to hold him
up, for she could not even support herself. Only a miracle could
save her. She prayed for it to come. It came from the depths
of her soul. In her solitary pious heart Madame Arnaud felt

the irony of the sublime and absurd hunger for creation in spite of everything, the need of weaving her web in spite of everything, through space, for the joy of weaving, leaving it to the wind, the breath of God, to carry her whithersoever it was ordained that she should go. And the breath of God gave her a new hold on life, and found her an invisible support. Then the husband and wife both set patiently to work once more to weave the magnificent and vain web of their dreams, a web fashioned of their purest suffering and their blood.

Madame Arnaud was alone in her room. . . . It was near evening.

The door-bell rang. Madame Arnaud, roused from her reverie before the usual time, started and trembled. She carefully arranged her work and went to open the dor. Christophe came in. He was in a great state of emotion. She took his hands affectionately.

"What is it, my dear?" she asked.

"Ah!" he said. "Olivier has come back."

"Come back?"

"He came this morning and said: 'Christophe, help me!' I embraced him. He wept. He told me: I have nothing but you now. She has gone."

Madame Arnaud gasped, and clasped her hands and said:

"Poor things!"

"She has gone," said Christophe. "Gone with her lover."

"And her child?" asked Madame Arnaud.

"Husband, child—she has left everything."

"Poor thing!" said Madame Arnaud again.

"He loved her," said Christophe. "He loved her, and her alone. He will never recover from the blow. He keeps on saying: 'Christophe, she has betrayed me. . . . My dearest friend has betrayed me.' It is no good my saying to him, 'Since she has betrayed you, she cannot have been your friend. She is your enemy. Forget her or kill her!'"

"Oh! Christophe, what are you saying! It is too horrible!"

'Yes, I know. You all think it barbaric and prehistoric to kill! It is jolly to hear these Parisians protesting against the brutal instincts which urge the male to kill the female if she deceives him, and preaching indulgence and reason! They're splendid apostles! It is a fine thing to see the pack of mongrel dogs waxing wrath against the return to animalism. After outraging life, after having robbed it of its worth, they surround it with religious worship. . . . What! That heartless, dishonorable, meaningless life, the mere physical act of breathing, the beating of the blood in a scrap of flesh, these are the things which they hold worthy of respect! They are never done with their niceness about the flesh: it is a crime to touch it. You may kill the soul if you like, but the body is sacred. . . . "

" The murderers of the soul are the worst of all: but one crime is no excuse for another. You know that."

" I know it. Yes. You are right. I did not think what I was saying. . . . Who knows? I should do it, perhaps."

" No. You are unfair to yourself. You are so kind."

" If I am roused to passion, I am as cruel as the rest. You see how I had lost control of myself! . . . But when you see a friend brought to tears, how can you not hate the person who has caused them? And how can one be too hard on a woman who leaves her child to run after her lover? "

" Don't talk like that, Christophe. You don't know."

" What! You defend her? "

" I pity her, too."

" I pity those who suffer. Not those who cause suffering."

" Well! Do you think she hasn't suffered too? Do you think she has left her child and wrecked her life out of lightness of heart? For her life is wrecked too. I hardly know her, Christophe. I have only seen her a few times, and that only in passing: she never said a friendly word to me, she was not in sympathy with me. And yet I know her better than you. I am sure she is not a bad woman. Poor child! I can guess what she has had to go through. . . . "

" You. . . . You whose life is so worthy and so right and sensible! . . . "

" Yes, Christophe, I. You do not know. You are kind, but you are a man and, like all men, you are hard, in spite of your kindness—a man hard and set against everything which is not in and of yourself. You have no real knowledge of the women who live with you. You love them, after your fashion;

but you never take the trouble to understand them. You are so easily satisfied with yourselves! You are quite sure that you know us. . . . Alas! If you knew how we suffer sometimes when we see, not that you do not love us, but how you love us, and that that is all we are to those we love the best! There are moments, Christophe, when we clench our fists so that the nails dig into our hands to keep ourselves from crying to you: 'Oh! Do not love us, do not love us! Anything rather than love us like that!'. . . Do you know the saying of a poet: 'Even in her home, among her children, surrounded with sham honors, a woman endures a scorn a thousand times harder to bear than the most utter misery'? Think of that, Christophe. They are terrible words."

"What you say has upset me. I don't rightly understand. But I am beginning to see. . . . Then, you yourself. . . ."

"I have been through all these torments."

"Is it possible? . . . But, even so, you will never make me believe that you would have done the same as that woman."

"I have no child, Christophe. I do not know what I should have done in her place."

"No. That is impossible. I believe in you. I respect you too much. I swear that you could not."

"Swear nothing! I have been very near doing what she has done. . . . It hurts me to destroy the good idea you had of me. But you must learn to know us a little if you do not want to be unjust. Yes, I have been within an ace of just such an act of folly. And you yourself had something to do with my not going on with it. It was two years ago. I was going through a period of terrible depression, that seemed to be eating my life away. I kept on telling myself that I was no use in the world, that nobody needed me, that even my husband could do without me, that I had lived for nothing. . . . I was on the very point of running away, to do Heaven knows what! I went up to your room. . . . Do you remember? . . . You did not understand why I came. I came to say good-bye to you. . . . And then, I don't know what happened, I can't remember exactly . . . but I know that something you said . . . (though you had no idea of it . . .) . . . was like a flash of light to me. . . . Perhaps it was not what you

said. . . . Perhaps it was only a matter of opportunity; at
that moment the least thing was enough to make or mar
me. . . . When I left you I went back to my own room,
locked myself in, and wept the whole day through. . . . I
was better after that: the crisis had passed."

"And now," asked Christophe, "you are sorry?"

"Now?" she said. "Ah! If I had been so mad as to do
it I should have been at the bottom of the Seine long ago. I
could not have borne the shame of it, and the injury I should
have done to my poor husband."

"Then you are happy?"

"Yes. As happy as one can be in this life. It is so rare
for two people to understand each other, and respect each
other, and know that they are sure of each other, not merely
with a simple lover's belief, which is often an illusion, but as
the result of years passed together, gray, dull, commonplace
years even—especially with the memory of the dangers through
which they have passed together. And as they grow older their
trust grows greater and finer."

She stopped and blushed suddenly.

"Oh, Heavens! How could I tell you that? . . . What
have I done? . . . Forget it, Christophe, I beg of you. No
one must know."

"You need not be afraid," said Christophe, pressing her
hand warmly. "It shall be sacred to me."

Madame Arnaud was unhappy at what she had said, and
turned away for a moment.

Then she went on:

"I ought not to have told you. . . . But, you see, I
wanted to show you that even in the closest and best marriages,
even for the women . . . whom you respect, Christophe . . .
there are times, not only of aberration, as you say, but of real,
intolerable suffering, which may drive them to madness, and
wreck at least one life, if not two. You must not be too hard.
Men and women make each other suffer terribly even when
they love each other dearly."

"Must they, then, live alone and apart?"

"That is even worse for us. The life of a woman who has
to live alone, and fight like men (and often against men), is

a terrible thing in a society which is not ready for the idea of it, and is, in a great measure, hostile to it. . . . ”

She stopped again, leaning forward a little, with her eyes fixed on the fire in the grate; then she went on softly, in a rather hushed tone, hesitating every now and then, stopping, and then going on:

“And yet it is not our fault when a woman lives like that, she does not do so from caprice, but because she is forced to do so; she has to earn her living and learn how to do without a man, since men will have nothing to do with her if she is poor. She is condemned to solitude without having any of its advantages, for in France she cannot, like a man, enjoy her independence, even in the most innocent way, without provoking scandal: everything is forbidden her. I have a friend who is a school-mistress in the provinces. If she were shut up in an airless prison she could not be more lonely and more stifled. The middle-classes close their doors to women who struggle to earn their living by their work; they are suspected and contemned; their smallest actions are spied upon and turned to evil. The masters at the boys’ school shun them, either because they are afraid of the tittle-tattle of the town, or from a secret hostility, or from shyness, and because they are in the habit of frequenting cafés and consorting with low women, or because they are too tired after the day’s work and have a dislike, as a result of their work, for intellectual women. And the women themselves cannot bear each other, especially if they are compelled to live together in the school. The head-mistress is often a woman absolutely incapable of understanding young creatures with a need of affection, who lose heart during the first few years of such a barren trade and such inhuman solitude; she leaves them with their secret agony and makes no attempt to help them; she is inclined to think that they are only vain and haughty. There is no one to take an interest in them. Having neither fortune nor influence, they cannot marry. Their hours of work are so many as to leave them no time in which to create an intellectual life which might bind them together and give them some comfort. When such an existence is not supported by an exceptional religious or moral feeling,—(I might even say abnormal and morbid; for such absolute self-sacrifice is

not natural),—it is a living death. . . .—In default of intellectual work, what resources does charity offer to women?
What great disappointments it holds out for those women who
are too sincere to be satisfied with official or polite charity,
philanthropic twaddle, the odious mixture of frivolity, benefi-
cence, and bureaucracy, the trick of dabbling in poverty in the
intervals of flirtation! And if one of them in disgust has the
incredible audacity to venture out alone among the poor or the
wretched, whose life she only knows by hearsay, think of what
she will see! Sights almost beyond bearing! It is a very hell.
What can she do to help them? She is lost, drowned in such
a sea of misfortune. However, she struggles on, she tries hard
to save a few of the poor wretches, she wears herself out for
them, and drowns with them. She is lucky if she succeeds in
saving one or two of them! But who is there to rescue her?
Who ever dreams of going to her aid? For she, too, suffers,
both with her own and the suffering of others: the more faith
she gives, the less she has for herself; all these poor wretches
cling desperately to her, and she has nothing with which to
stay herself. No one holds out a hand to her. And sometimes she is stoned. . . . You knew, Christophe, the splendid
woman who gave herself to the humblest and most meritorious
charitable work; she took pity on the street prostitutes who
had just been brought to child-bed, the wretched women with
whom the Public Aid would have nothing to do, or who were
afraid of the Public Aid; she tried to cure them physically
and morally, to look after them and their children, to wake
in them the mother-feeling, to give them new homes and a life
of honest work. She taxed her strength to the utmost in her
grim labors, so full of disappointment and bitterness—(so
few are saved, so few wish to be saved! And think of all
the babies who die! Poor innocent little babies, condemned
in the very hour of their birth! . . .).—That woman
who had taken upon herself the sorrows of others, the
blameless creature who of her own free will expiated the crimes
of human selfishness—how do you think she was judged, Christophe? The evil-minded public accused her of making money
out of her work, and even of making money out of the poor
women she protected. She had to leave the neighborhood, and

go away, utterly downhearted. '. . . .—You cannot conceive the cruelty of the struggles which independent women have to maintain against the society of to-day, a conservative, heartless society, which is dying and expends what little energy it has left in preventing others from living."

"My dear creature, it is not only the lot of women. We all know these struggles. And I know the refuge."

"What is it?"

"Art."

"All very well for you, but not for us. And even among men, how many are there who can take advantage of it?"

"Look at your friend Cécile. She is happy."

"How do you know? Ah! You have jumped to conclusions! Because she puts a brave face on it, because she does not stop to think of things that make her sad, because she conceals them from others, you say that she is happy! Yes. She is happy to be well and strong, and to be able to fight. But you know nothing of her struggles. Do you think she was made for that deceptive life of art? Art! Just think of the poor women who long for the glory of being able to write or play or sing as the very summit of happiness! Their lives must be bare indeed, and they must be so hard pressed that they can find no affection to which to turn! Art! What have we to do with art, if we have all the rest with it? There is only one thing in the world which can make a woman forget everything else, everything else: and that is the child."

"And when she has a child, you see, even that is not enough."

"Yes. Not always. . . . Women are not very happy. It is difficult to be a woman. Much more difficult than to be a man. You men never realize that enough. You can be absorbed in an intellectual passion or some outside activity. You mutilate yourselves, but you are the happier for it. A healthy woman cannot do that without suffering for it. It is inhuman to stifle a part of yourself. When we women are happy in one way, we regret that we are not happy in another. We have several souls. You men have but one, a more vigorous soul, which is often brutal and even monstrous. I admire you.

But do not be too selfish. You are very selfish without knowing it. You hurt us often, without knowing it."

" What are we to do? It is not our fault."

" No, it is not your fault, my dear Christophe. It is not your fault, nor is it ours. The truth is, you know, that life is not a simple thing. They say that there we only need to live naturally. But which of us is natural? "

" True. Nothing is natural in our way of living. Celibacy is not natural. Nor is marriage. And free love delivers the weak up to the rapaciousness of the strong. Even our society is not a natural thing: we have manufactured it. It is said that man is a sociable animal. What nonsense! He was forced to be so to live. He has made himself sociable for the purposes of utility, and self-defence, and pleasure, and the rise to greatness. His necessity has led him to subscribe to certain compacts. Nature kicks against the constraint and avenges herself. Nature was not made for us. We try to quell her. It is a struggle, and it is not surprising that we are often beaten. How are we to win through it? By being strong."

" By being kind."

" Heavens! To be kind, to pluck off one's armor of selfishness, to breathe, to love life, light, one's humble work, the little corner of the earth in which one's roots are spread. And if one cannot have breadth to try to make up for it in height and depth, like a tree in a cramped space growing upward to the sun."

" Yes. And first of all to love one another. If a man would feel more that he is the brother of a woman, and not only her prey, or that she must be his! If both would shed their vanity and each think a little less of themselves, and a little more of the other! . . . We are weak: help us. Let us not say to those who have fallen: ' I do not know you.' But: ' Courage. friend. We'll pull through.' "

They sat there in silence by the hearth, with the cat between them, all three still, lost in thought, gazing at the fire It was nearly out; but a little flame flickered up, and with its wing lightly touched Madame Arnaud's delicate face, which was suffused with the rosy light of an inward exaltation which

was strange to her. She was amazed at herself for having
been so open. She had never said so much before, and she
would never say so much again.

She laid her hand on Christophe's and said:
" What will you do with the child?"

She had been thinking of that from the outset. She talked
and talked and became another woman, excited and exalted.
But she was thinking of that and that only. With Christophe's first words she had woven a romance in her heart. She
thought of the child left by its mother, of the happiness of
bringing it up, and weaving about its little soul the web of her
dreams and her love. And she thought:
" No. It is wicked of me: I ought not to rejoice in the misfortunes of others."

But the idea was too strong for her. She went on talking
and talking, and her silent heart was flooded with hope.

Christophe said:
" Yes, of course we have thought it over. Poor child!
Both Olivier and I are incapable of rearing it. It needs a
woman's care. I thought perhaps one of our friends would
like to help us. . . ."

Madame Arnaud could hardly breathe.

Christophe said:
" I wanted to talk to you about it. And then Cécile came
in just as we were talking about it. When she heard of our
difficulty, when she saw the child, she was so moved, she
seemed so delighted, she said: ' Christophe . . .' "

Madame Arnaud's heart stopped; she did not hear what else
he said: there was a mist in front of her eyes. She was fain to
cry out:
" No, no. Give him to me. . . ."

Christophe went on speaking. She did not hear what he
was saying. But she controlled herself. She thought of what
Cécile had told her, and she thought:
" Her need is greater than mine. I have my dear Arnaud . . .
and . . . and everything . . . and besides, I am older. . . ."

And she smiled and said:
" It is well."

But the flame in the dying fire had flickered out: so too

had the rosy light in her face. And her dear tired face wore
only its usual expression of kindness and resignation.

"My wife has betrayed me."

Olivier was crushed by the weight of that idea. In vain
did Christophe try affectionately to shake him out of his
torpor.

"What would you?" he said. "The treachery of a friend
is an everyday evil like illness, or poverty, or fighting the
fools. We have to be armed against it. It is a poor sort of
man that cannot bear up against it."

"That's just what I am. I'm not proud of it . . . a poor
sort of man: yes: a man who needs tenderness, and dies if it
is taken from him."

"Your life is not finished: there are other people to love."

"I can't believe in any one. There are none who can be
friends."

"Olivier!"

"I beg your pardon. I don't doubt you, although there
are moments when I doubt everybody—myself included. . . .
But you are strong: you don't need anybody: you can do
without me."

"So can she—even better."

"You are cruel, Christophe."

"My dear fellow. I'm being brutal to you just to make
you lash out. Good Lord! It is perfectly shameful of you
to sacrifice those who love you, and your life, to a woman who
doesn't care for you."

"What do I care for those who love me? I love her."

"Work. Your old interests . . ."

". . . Don't interest me any longer. I'm sick of it all.
I seem to have passed out of life altogether. Everything
seems so far away. . . . I see, but I don't understand. . . .
And to think that there are men who never grow tired of
winding up their clockwork every day, and doing their dull
work, and their newspaper discussions, and their wretched
pursuit of pleasure, men who can be violently for or against
a Government, or a book, or an actress. . . . Oh! I feel so
old! I feel nothing, neither hatred, nor rancor against any-

body. I'm bored with everything. I feel that there is nothing in the world. . . . Write? Why write? Who understands you? I used to write only for one person: everything
that I did was for her. . . . There is nothing left: I'm worn
out, Christophe, fagged out. I want to sleep."

" Sleep, then, old fellow. I'll sit by you."

But sleep was the last thing that Olivier could have. Ah!
if only a sufferer could sleep for months until his sorrow is
no more and has no part in his new self; if only he could
sleep until he became a new man! But that gift can never
be his: and he would not wish to have it. The worst suffering of all were to be deprived of suffering. Olivier was like
a man in a fever, feeding on his fever: a real fever which
came in regular waves, being at its height in the evening when
the light began to fade. And the rest of the day it left him
shattered, intoxicated by love, devoured by memory. turning
the same thought over and over like an idiot chewing the same
mouthful again and again without being able to swallow it,
with all the forces of his brain paralyzed, grinding slowly on
with the one fixed idea.

He could not, like Christophe, resort to cursing his injuries
and honestly blackguarding the woman who had dealt them.
He was more clear-sighted and just, and he knew that he had
his share of the responsibility, and that he was not the only
one to suffer: Jacqueline also was a victim:—she was his victim. She had trusted herself to him: how had he dealt with
his trust? If he was not strong enough to make her happy,
why had he bound her to himself? She was within her rights
in breaking the ties which chafed her.

" It is not her fault," he thought. " It is mine. I have
not loved her well. And yet I loved her truly. But I did
not know how to love since I did not know how to win her
love."

So he blamed himself: and perhaps he was right. But it
is not much use to hold an inquest on the past: if it were
all to do again, it would be just the same, inquiry or no inquiry: and such probing stands in the way of life. The
strong man is he who forgets the injury that has been done
him—and also, alas! that which he has done himself, as soon

as he is sure that he cannot make it good. But no man is strong from reason, but from passion. Love and passion are like distant relations: they rarely go together. Olivier loved: he was only strong against himself. In the passive state into which he had fallen he was an easy prey to every kind of illness. Influenza, bronchitis, pneumonia, pounced on him. He was ill for part of the summer. With Madame Arnaud's assistance, Christophe nursed him devotedly: and they succeeded in checking his illness. But against his moral illness they could do nothing: and little by little they were overcome by the depression and utter weariness of his perpetual melancholy, and were forced to run away from it.

Illness plunges a man into a strange solitude. Men have an instinctive horror of it. It is as though they were afraid lest it should be contagious: and at the very least it is boring, and they run away from it. How few people there are who can forgive the sufferings of others! It is always the old story of the friends of Job. Eliphaz the Temanite accuses Job of impatience. Bildad the Shuhite declares that Job's afflictions are the punishment of his sins. Sophar of Naamath charges him with presumption. *"Then was kindled the wrath of Elihu, the son of Barachel the Buzite, of the kindred of Ram: against Job was his wrath kindled, because he justifieth himself, rather than God."*—Few men are really sorrowful. Many are called, but few are chosen. Olivier was one of these. As a misanthrope once observed: "He seemed to like being maltreated. There is nothing to be gained by playing the part of the unhappy man. You only make yourself detested."

Olivier could not tell even his most intimate friends what he felt. He saw that it bored them. Even his friend Christophe lost patience with such tenacious and importunate grief. He knew that he was clumsy and awkward in remedying it. If the truth must be told, Christophe, whose heart was generous, Christophe who had gone through much suffering on his own account, could not feel the suffering of his friend. Such is the infirmity of human nature. You may be kind, full of pity, understanding, and you may have suffered a thousand deaths, but you cannot feel the pain of your friend if he has but a toothache. If illness goes on for a long time, there is a temptation to think that the sufferer is exaggerating his complaint. How much more, then, must this be so when the illness is invisible and seated in the very depths of the soul! A man who is outside it all cannot help being irritated by seeing his friend moaning and groaning about a feeling which does not concern him in the very least. And in the end he says: by way of appeasing his conscience:

"What can I do? He won't listen to reason, whatever I say."

To reason: true. One can only help by loving the sufferer, by loving him unreasoningly, without trying to convince him, without trying to cure him, but just by loving and pitying him. Love is the only balm for the wounds of love. But love is not inexhaustible even with those who love the best: they have only a limited store of it. When the sick man's friends have once written all the words of affection they can find, when they have done what they consider their duty, they withdraw prudently, and avoid him like a criminal. And as they feel a certain secret shame that they can help him so little, they help him less and less: they try to let him forget them and to forget themselves. And if the sick man persists in his misfortune and, indiscreetly, an echo of it penetrates to their ears, then they judge harshly his want of courage and inability to bear up against his trials. And if he succumbs, it is very certain that lurking beneath their really genuine pity lies this disdainful under-thought:

"Poor devil! I had a better opinion of him."

Amid such universal selfishness what a marvelous amount of good can be done by a simple word of tenderness, a delicate attention, a look of pity and love! Then the sick man feels the worth of kindness. And how poor is all the rest compared with that! . . . Kindness brought Olivier nearer to Madame Arnaud than anybody else, even his friend Christophe. However, Christophe most meritoriously forced himself to be patient, and in his affection for him, concealed what he really thought of him. But Olivier, with his natural keenness of perception sharpened by suffering, saw the conflict in his friend, and what a burden he was upon him with his unending sorrow. It was enough to make him turn from Christophe, and fill him with a desire to cry:

"Go away. Go."

So unhappiness often divides loving hearts. As the winnower sorts the grain, so sorrow sets on one side those who have the will to live, and on the other those who wish to die. It is the terrible law of life, which is stronger than love! The mother who sees her son dying, the friend who sees his friend drowning,—if they cannot save them, they do not cease their efforts to save themselves: they do not die with them. And yet, they love them a thousand times better than their lives. . . .

In spite of his great love, there were moments when Christophe had to leave Olivier. He was too strong, too healthy, to be able to live and breathe in such airless sorrow. He was mightily ashamed of himself! He would feel cold and dead at heart to think that he could do nothing for his friend: and as he needed to avenge himself on some one, he visited his wrath upon Jacqueline. In spite of Madame Arnaud's words of understanding and sympathy, he still judged her harshly, as a young, ardent, and whole-hearted man must, until he has learned enough of life to have pity on its weaknesses.

He would go and see Cécile and the child who had been entrusted to her. That refreshed his soul. Cécile was transfigured by her borrowed motherhood: she seemed to be young again, and happy, more refined and tender. Jacqueline's departure had not given her any unavowed hope of happiness. She knew that the memory of Jacqueline must leave her farther away from Olivier than her presence. Besides, the little puff of wind that had set her longing had passed: it had been a moment of crisis, which the sight of poor Jacqueline's frenzied mistake had helped to dissipate: she had returned to her normal tranquillity, and she could not rightly understand what it was that had dragged her out of it. All that was best in her need of love was satisfied by her love for the child. With the marvelous power of illusion—of intuition—of women, she found the man she loved in the little child: in that way she could have him, weak and utterly dependent, utterly her own: he belonged to her: and she could love him, love him passionately, with a love as pure as the heart of the

innocent child, and his clear blue eyes, like little drops of
light. . . . True, there was mingled with her tenderness a re-
gretful melancholy. Ah! It could never be the same thing
as a child of her own blood! . . . But it was good, all the same.

Christophe now regarded Cécile with very different eyes.
He remembered an ironic saying of Françoise Oudon:
" How is it that you and Philomela, who would do so well
as husband and wife, are not in love with each other? "

But Françoise knew the reason better than Christophe: it
is very rarely that a man like Christophe loves those who can
do him good: rather he is apt to love those who can do him
harm. Opposites meet: his nature seeks its own destruction,
and goes to the burning and intense life rather than to the
cautious life which is sparing of itself. And a man like
Christophe is quite right, for his law is not to live as long
as possible, but as mightily as possible.

However, Christophe, having less penetration than Françoise, said to himself that love is a blind, inhuman force, throwing those together who cannot bear with each other. Love joins
those together who are like each other. And what love inspires
is very small compared with what it destroys. If it be happy
it dissolves the will. If unhappy it breaks hearts. What good
does it ever do?

And as he thus maligned love he saw its ironic, tender smile
saying to him:
" Ingrate! "

Christophe had been unable to get out of going to one of
the At Homes given at the Austrian Embassy. Philomela
was to sing *lieder* by Schumann, Hugo Wolf, and Christophe.
She was glad of her success and that of her friend, who was
now made much of by a certain set. Christophe's name was
gaining ground from day to day, even with the great public: it
had become impossible for the Lévy-Cœurs to ignore him any
longer. His works were played at concerts: and he had had
an opera accepted by the Opéra Comique. The sympathies of
some person unknown were enlisted on his behalf. The mysterious friend, who had more than once helped him, was still
forwarding his claims. More than once Christophe had been

conscious of that fondly helping hand in everything he did: some one was watching over him and jealously concealing his or her identity. Christophe had tried to discover it: but it seemed as though his friend were piqued by his not having attempted sooner to find out who he was, and he remained unapproachable. Besides, Christophe was absorbed by other preoccupations: he was thinking of Olivier, he was thinking of Françoise: that very morning he had just read in the paper that she was lying seriously ill at San Francisco: he imagined her alone in a strange city, in a hotel bedroom, refusing to see anybody, or to write to her friends, clenching her teeth, and waiting, alone, for death.

He was obsessed by these ideas and avoided the company present: and he withdrew into a little room apart: he stood leaning against the wall in a recess that was half in darkness, behind a curtain of evergreens and flowers, listening to Philomela's lovely voice, with its elegiac warmth, singing *The Lime-tree* of Schubert: and the pure music called up sad memories. Facing him on the wall was a large mirror which reflected the lights and the life of the next room. He did not see it: he was gazing in upon himself: and the mist of tears swam before his eyes. . . . Suddenly, like Schubert's rustling tree, he began to tremble for no reason. He stood so for a few seconds, very pale, unable to move. Then the veil fell from before his eyes, and he saw in the mirror in front of him his " friend," gazing at him. . . . His " friend " ? Who was she? He knew nothing save that she was his friend and that he knew her: and he stood leaning against the wall, his eyes meeting hers, and he trembled. She smiled. He could not see the lines of her face or her body, nor the expression in her eyes, nor whether she was tall or short, nor how she was dressed. Only one thing he saw: the divine goodness of her smile of compassion.

And suddenly her smile conjured up in Christophe an old forgotten memory of his early childhood. . . . He was six or seven, at school, unhappy: he had just been humiliated and bullied by some older, stronger boys, and they were all jeering at him, and the master had punished him unjustly: he was crouching in a corner, utterly forlorn, while the others were playing: and he wept softly. There was a sad-faced little girl who was not playing with the others,—(he could see her now, though he had never thought of her since then; she was short, and had a big head, fair, almost white hair and eyebrows, very pale blue eyes, broad white cheeks, thick lips, a rather puffy face, and small red hands),—and she came close up to him, then stopped, with her thumb in her mouth and stood watching him cry: then she laid her little hand on Christophe's head and said hurriedly and shyly, with just the same smile of compassion:

"Don't cry! Don't cry!"

Then Christophe could not control himself any longer, and he burst into sobs, and buried his face in the little girl's pinafore, while, in a quavering, tender voice, she went on saying:

"Don't cry. . . ."

She died soon afterwards, a few weeks perhaps: the hand of death must have been upon her at the time of that little scene. . . . Why should he think of her now? There was no connection between the child who was dead and forgotten, the humble daughter of the people in a distant German town, and the aristocratic young lady who was gazing at him now. But there is only one soul for all: and although millions of human beings seem to be all different one from another, different as the worlds moving in the heavens, it is the same flash of thought or love which lights up the hearts of men and women though centuries divide them. Christophe had just seen once more the light that he had seen shining upon the pale lips of the little comforter. . . .

It was all over in a second. A throng of people filled the door and shut out Christophe's view of the other room. He stepped back quickly into the shade, out of sight of the mirror: he was afraid lest his emotion should be noticed. But when he was calm again he wanted to see her once more. He was afraid she would be gone. He went into the room and he found her at once in the crowd, although she did not look in the least like what he had seen in the mirror. Now he saw her in profile sitting in a group of finely dressed ladies: her elbow was resting on the arm of her chair, she was leaning forward a little, with her head in her hand, and listening to what they were saying with an intelligent absent smile: she had the expression and features of the young St. John, listening and looking through half-closed eyes, and smiling at his own thoughts, of *The Dispute* of Raphael. . . . Then she raised her eyes, saw him, and showed no surprise. And he saw that her smile was for himself. He was much moved, and bowed, and went up to her.

" You don't recognize me? " she said.

He knew her again that very moment.

" Grazia " . . . he said.*

At the same moment the ambassador's wife passed by, and smiled with pleasure to see that the long-sought meeting had at last come about: and she introduced Christophe to " Countess Berény." But Christophe was so moved that he did not even hear her, and he did not notice the new name. She was still his little Grazia to him.

Grazia was twenty-two. She had been married for a year to a young attaché of the Austrian Embassy, a nobleman, a member of a great family, related to one of the Emperor's chief ministers, a snob, a man of the world, smart, prematurely worn out; with whom she had been genuinely in love, while she still loved him, though she judged him. Her old father was dead. Her husband had been appointed to the Embassy in Paris. Through Count Berény's influence, and her own charm and intelligence, the timid little girl, whom the smallest thing used to set in a flutter, had become one of the best-known women in Parisian society, though she did nothing to procure that distinction, which embarrassed her not at all. It is a great thing to be young and pretty, and to give pleasure, and to know it. And it is a thing no less great to have a tranquil heart, sound and serene, which can find happiness in the harmonious coincidence of its desires and its fate. The lonely flower of her life had unfolded its petals: but she had lost some of the calm music of her Latin soul, fed by the light and the mighty peace of Italy. Quite naturally

* See " Jean-Christophe in Paris: The Market Place."

she had acquired a certain influence in Parisian society: it did not surprise her, and she was discreet and adroit in using it to further the artistic or charitable movements which turned to her for aid: she left the official patronage of these movements to others: for although she could well maintain her rank, she had preserved a secret independence from the days of her rather wild childish days in the lonely villa in the midst of the fields, and society wearied while it amused her, though she always disguised her boredom by the amiable smile of a courteous and kind heart.

She had not forgotten her great friend Christophe. No doubt there was nothing left of the child in whom an innocent love had burned in silence. This new Grazia was a very sensible woman, not at all given to romance. She regarded the exaggerations of her childish tenderness with a gentle irony. And yet she was always moved by the memory of it. The thought of Christophe was associated with the purest hours of her life. She could not hear his name spoken without feeling pleasure: and each of his successes delighted her as though she had shared in it herself: for she had felt that they must come to him. As soon as she arrived in Paris she tried to meet him again. She had invited him to her house, and had appended her maiden name to her letter. Christophe had paid no attention to it, and had flung the invitation into the waste-paper basket unanswered. She was not offended. She had gone on following his doings and, to a certain extent, his life, without his knowing it. It was she whose helping hand had come to his aid in the recent campaign against him in the papers. Grazia was in all things correct and had hardly any connection with the world of the Press: but when it came to doing a friend a service, she was capable of a malicious cunning in wheedling the people whom she most disliked. She invited the editor of the paper which was leading the snarling pack, to her house: and in less than no time she turned his head: she skilfully flattered his vanity: and she gained such an ascendancy over him, while she overawed him, that it needed only a few careless words of contemptuous astonishment at the attacks on Christophe for the campaign to be stopped short. The editor suppressed the insulting article which was to appear next day: and when the writer asked why it was suppressed he rated him soundly. He did more: he gave orders to one of his factotums to turn out an enthusiastic article about Christophe within a fortnight: the article was turned out to order; it was enthusiastic and stupid. It was Grazia, too, who thought of organizing performances of her friend's music at the Embassy, and, knowing that he was interested in Cécile, helped her to make her name. And finally, through her influence among the German diplomatists, she began gently, quietly, and adroitly to awaken the interest of the powers that be in Christophe, who was banished from Germany: and little by little she did create a current of opinion directed towards obtaining from the Emperor a decree reopening the gates of his country to a great artist who was an honor to it. And though it was too soon to expect such an act of grace, she did at least succeed in procuring an undertaking that the Government would close its eyes to his two days' visit to his native town.

And Christophe, who was conscious of the presence of his invisible friend hovering about him without being able to find out who she was, at last recognized her in the young St. John whose eyes smiled at him in the mirror.

They talked of the past. Christophe hardly knew what they said. A man hears the woman he loves just as little as he sees her. He loves her. And when a man really loves he never even thinks whether he is loved or no. Christophe never doubted it. She was there: that was enough. All the rest had ceased to exist. . . .

Grazia stopped speaking. A very tall young man, quite handsome, well-dressed, clean-shaven, partly bald, with a bored, contemptuous manner, stood appraising Christophe through his eye-glass, and then bowed with haughty politeness.

"My husband," said she.

The clatter and chatter of the room rushed back to his ears. The inward light died down. Christophe was frozen, said nothing, bowed, and withdrew at once.

How ridiculous and consuming are the unreasonable demands of the souls of artists and the childish laws which gov-

ern their passionate lives! Hardly had he once more found
the friend whom he had neglected in the old days when she
loved him, while he had not thought of her for years, than
it seemed to him that she was his, his very own, and that if
another man had taken her he had stolen her from him: and
she herself had no right to give herself to another. Christophe did not know clearly what was happening to him. But
his creative daimon knew it perfectly, and in those days begat
some of his loveliest songs of sorrowful love.

Some time passed before he saw her again. He was obsessed
by thoughts of Olivier's troubles and his health. At last one
day he came upon the address she had given him and he made
up his mind to call on her.

As he went up the steps he heard the sound of workmen
hammering. The anteroom was in disorder and littered with
boxes and trunks. The footman replied that the Countess
was not at home. But as Christophe was disappointedly going
away after leaving his card, the servant ran after him and asked
him to come in and begged his pardon. Christophe was shown
into a little room in which the carpets had been rolled up and
taken away. Grazia came towards him with her bright smile
and her hand held out impulsively and gladly. All his foolish
rancor vanished. He took her hand with the same happy im-
pulsiveness and kissed it.

"Ah!" she said, "I am glad you came! I was so afraid
I should have to go away without seeing you again!"

"Go away? You are going away!"

Once more darkness descended upon him.

"You see . . ." she said, pointing to the litter in the room.
"We are leaving Paris at the end of the week."

"For long?"

She shrugged:

"Who knows?"

He tried to speak. But his throat was dry.

"Where are you going?"

"To the United States. My husband has been appointed
first secretary to the Embassy."

"And so, and so . . ." he said . . . (his lips trembled) . . .
"it is all over?"

" My dear friend! " she said, touched by his tone. . . . " No:
it is not all over."

" I have found you again only to lose you? "

There were tears in her eyes.

" My dear friend," she said again.

He held his hand over his eyes and turned away to hide
his emotion.

" Do not be so sad," she said, laying her hand on his.

Once more, just then, he thought of the little girl in Germany. They were silent.

" Why did you come so late? " she asked at last. " I tried
to find you. You never replied."

" I did not know. I did not know," he said. . . . " Tell me,
was it you who came to my aid so many times without my
guessing who it was? . . . Do I owe it to you that I was able
to go back to Germany? Were you my good angel, watching
over me? "

She said:

" I was glad to be able to do something for you. I owe
you so much! "

" What do you owe? " he asked. " I have done nothing for
you."

" You do not know," she said, " what you have been to me."

She spoke of the days when she was a little girl and met
him at the house of her uncle, Stevens, and he had given her
through his music the revelation of all that is beautiful in the
world. And little by little, with growing animation she told
him with brief allusions, that were both veiled and transparent,
of her childish feeling for him, and the way in which she had
shared Christophe's troubles, and the concert at which he had
been hissed, and she had wept, and the letter she had written
and he had never answered: for he had not received it. And
as Christophe listened to her, in all good faith, he projected his
actual emotion and the tenderness he felt for the tender face
so near his own into the past.

They talked innocently, fondly, and joyously. And, as he
talked, Christophe took Grazia's hand. And suddenly they
both stopped: for Grazia saw that Christophe loved her. And
Christophe saw it too. . . .

For some time Grazia had loved Christophe without Christophe knowing or caring. Now Christophe loved Grazia: and Grazia had nothing for him but calm friendship: she loved another man. As so often happens, one of the two clocks of their lives was a little faster than the other, and it was enough to have changed the course of both their lives. . . .

Grazia withdrew her hand, and Christophe did not stay her. And they sat there for a moment, mum, without a word And Grazia said:

" Good-bye."

Christophe said plaintively once more:

" And it is all over? "

" No doubt it is better that it should be so."

" We shall not meet again before you go."

" No," she said.

" When shall we meet again? "

She made a sad little gesture of doubt.

" Then," said Christophe, " what's the good, what's the good of our having met again? "

Her eyes reproached him, and he said quickly:

" No. Forgive me. I am unjust."

" I shall always think of you," said she.

" Alas! " he replied, " I cannot even think of you. I know nothing of your life."

Very quietly she described her ordinary life in a few words and told him how her days were spent. She spoke of herself and of her husband with her lovely affectionate smile.

" Ah! " he said jealously. " You love him? "

" Yes," she said.

He got up.

" Good-bye."

She got up too. Then only he saw that she was with child. And in his heart there was an inexpressible feeling of disgust, and tenderness, and jealousy, and passionate pity. She walked with him to the door of the little room. There he turned, bent over her hands, and kissed them fervently. She stood there with her eyes half closed and did not stir. At last he drew himself up, turned, and hurried away without looking at her.

. . . E chi allora m'avesse domandato di cosa alcuna, la mia risponsione sarebbe stata solamente AMORE, con viso vestito d'umiltà. . . .

All Saints' Day. Outside, a gray light and a cold wind. Christophe was with Cécile, who was sitting near the cradle, and Madame Arnaud was bending over it. She had dropped in. Christophe was dreaming. He was feeling that he had missed happiness: but he never thought of complaining: he knew that happiness existed. . . . Oh! sun, I have no need to see thee to love thee! Through the long winter days, when I shiver in the darkness, my heart is full of thee: my love keeps me warm: I know that thou art there. . . .

And Cécile was dreaming too. She was pondering the child, and she had come to believe that it was indeed her own. Oh, blessed power of dreams, the creative imagination of life! Life. . . . What is life? It is not as cold reason and our eyes tell us that it is. Life is what we dream, and the measure of life is love.

Christophe gazed at Cécile, whose peasant face with its wide-set eyes shone with the splendor of the maternal instinct,—she was more a mother than the real mother. And he looked at the tender weary face of Madame Arnaud. In it, as in books that moved him, he read the hidden sweetness and suffering of the life of a married woman which, though none ever suspects it, is sometimes as rich in sorrow and joy as the love of Juliet or Ysolde: though it touches a greater height of religious feeling. . . .

Socia rei humanæ atque divinæ. . . .

And he thought that children or the lack of children has as much to do with the happiness or unhappiness of those who marry and those who do not marry as faith and the lack of faith. Happiness is the perfume of the soul, the harmony that dwells, singing, in the depths of the heart. And the most beautiful of all the music of the soul is kindness.

Olivier came in. He was quite calm and reposeful in his movements: a new serenity shone in him. He smiled at the child, shook hands with Cécile and Madame Arnaud, and began to talk quietly. He watched them with a sort of surprised affection. He was no longer the same. In the isolation in which he had shut himself up with his grief, like a caterpillar in the nest of its own spinning, he had succeeded after a hard struggle in throwing off his sorrow like an empty shell. Some day we shall tell how he thought he had found a fine cause to which to devote his life, in which he had no interest save that of sacrifice: and, as it is ordered, on the very day when in his heart he had come to a definite renunciation of life, it was kindled once more. His friends looked at him. They did not know what had happened, and dared not ask him: but they felt that he was free once more, and that there was in him neither regret nor bitterness for anything or against anybody in the whole wide world.

Christophe got up and went to the piano, and said to Olivier:

"Would you like me to sing you a melody of Brahms?"

"Brahms?" said Olivier. "Do you play your old enemy's music nowadays?"

"It is All Saints' Day," said Christophe. "The day when all are forgiven."

Softly, so as not to wake the child, he sang a few bars of the old Schwabian folk-song:

> "... Für die Zeit, wo du g'liebt mi hast,
> Da dank' i dir schön,
> Und i wünsch', dass dir's anders wo
> Besser mag geh'n ..."

> "... For the time when thou did'st love me,
> I do thank thee well;
> And I hope that elsewhere
> Thou may'st better fare. ..."

"Christophe!" said Olivier.

Christophe hugged him close.

"Come, old fellow," he said. "We have fared well."

The four of them sat near the sleeping child. They did not speak. And if they had been asked what they were thinking,— *with the countenance of humility, they would have replied only:*

"Love."

THE BURNING BUSH

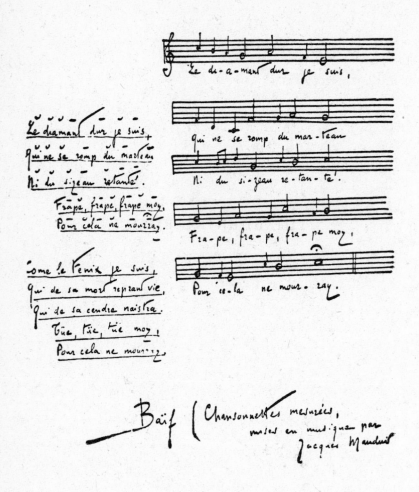

CAME calmness to his heart. No wind stirred. The air was still. . . .

Christophe was at rest: peace was his. He was in a certain measure proud of having conquered it: but secretly, in his heart of hearts, he was sorry for it. He was amazed at the silence. His passions were slumbering: in all good faith he thought that they would never wake again.

The mighty, somewhat brutal force that was his was browsing listlessly and aimlessly. In his inmost soul there was a secret void, a hidden question: "What's the good?": perhaps a certain consciousness of the happiness which he had failed to grasp. He had not force enough to struggle either with himself or with others. He had come to the end of a stage in his progress: he was reaping the fruits of all his former efforts, cumulatively: too easily he was tapping the vein of music that he had opened and while the public was naturally behindhand, and was just discovering and admiring his old work, he was beginning to break away from them without knowing as yet whether he would be able to make any advance on them. He had now a uniform and even delight in creation. At this period of his life art was to him no more than a fine instrument upon which he played like a virtuoso. He was ashamedly conscious of becoming a dilettante.

"If," said Ibsen, "a man is to persevere in his art, he must have something else, something more than his native genius: passions, sorrows, which shall fill his life and give it a direction. Otherwise he will not create, he will write books."

Christophe was writing books. He was not used to it. His books were beautiful. He would have rather had them less beautiful and more alive. He was like an athlete resting, not knowing to what use to turn his muscles, and, yawning in boredom like a caged wild beast, he sat looking ahead at the years and years of peaceful work that awaited him. And as, with his old German capacity for optimism, he had no difficulty in persuading himself that everything was for the best, he thought that such a future was no doubt the appointed inevitable end: he flattered himself that he had issued from his time of trial and tribulation and had become master of himself. That was not saying much. . . . Oh, well! A man is sovereign over that which is his, he is what he is capable of being. . . . He thought that he had reached his haven.

The two friends were not living together. After Jacqueline's flight, Christophe had thought that Olivier would come back and take up his old quarters with him. But Olivier could not. Although he felt keenly the need of intimacy with Christophe, yet he was conscious of the impossibility of resuming their old existence together. After the years lived with Jacqueline, it would have seemed intolerable and even sacrilegious to admit another human being to his most intimate life,—even though he loved and were loved by that other a thousand times more than Jacqueline.—There was no room for argument.

Christophe had found it hard to understand. He returned again and again to the charge, he was surprised, saddened, hurt, and angry. Then his instinct, which was finer and quicker than his intelligence, bade him take heed. Suddenly he ceased, and admitted that Olivier was right.

But they saw each other every day: and they had never been so closely united even when they were living under the same roof. Perhaps they did not exchange their most intimate thoughts when they talked. They did not need to do so. The exchange was made naturally, without need of words, by grace of the love that was in their hearts.

They talked very little, for each was absorbed: one in his art, the other in his memories. Olivier's sorrow was growing less: but he did nothing to mitigate it, rather almost taking a pleasure in it: for a long time it had been his only reason for living. He loved his child: but his child—a puling baby—could occupy no great room in his life. There are men who are more lovers than fathers, and it is useless to cry out against them. Nature is not uniform, and it would be absurd to try

to impose identical laws upon the hearts of all men. No man
has the right to sacrifice his duty to his heart. At least
the heart must be granted the right to be unhappy where a
man does his duty. What Olivier perhaps most loved in his
child was the woman of whose body it was made.

Until quite recently he had paid little attention to the sufferings of others. He was an intellectual living too much shut
up in himself. It was not egoism so much as a morbid habit
of dreaming. Jacqueline had increased the void about him:
her love had traced a magic circle about Olivier to cut him
off from other men, and the circle endured after love had
ceased to be. In addition he was a little aristocratic by temper.
From his childhood on, in spite of his soft heart, he had held
aloof from the mob for reasons rooted in the delicacy of his
body and his soul. The smell of the people and their thoughts
were repulsive to him.

But everything had changed as the result of a commonplace tragedy which he had lately witnessed.

He had taken a very modest lodging at the top of the Montrouge quarter, not far from Christophe and Cécile. The district was rather common, and the house in which he lived was
occupied by little gentlepeople, clerks, and a few working-class
families. At any other time he would have suffered from such
surroundings in which he moved as a stranger: but now it
mattered very little to him where he was: he felt that he was
a stranger everywhere. He hardly knew and did not want to
know who his neighbors were. When he returned from his
work—(he had gone into a publishing-house)—he withdrew
into his memories, and would only go out to see his child and
Christophe. His lodging was not home to him: it was the
dark room in which the images of the past took shape and
dwelling: the darker it was the more clearly did the inward
images emerge. He scarcely noticed the faces of those he
passed on the stairs. And yet unconsciously he was aware of
certain faces that were impressed upon his mind. There is a
certain order of mind which only really sees things after they
have passed. But then, nothing escapes them, the smallest
details are graven on the plate. Olivier's was such a mind: he

bore within himself multitudes of the shadowy shapes of the living. With any emotional shock they would come mounting up in crowds: and Olivier would be amazed to recognize those whom he had never known, and sometimes he would hold out his hands to grasp them. . . . Too late.

One day as he came out of his rooms he saw a little crowd collected in front of the house-door round the housekeeper, who was making a harangue. He was so little interested that he was for going his way without troubling to find out what was the matter: but the housekeeper, anxious to gain another listener, stopped him, and asked him if he knew what had happened to the poor Roussels. Olivier did not even know who " the poor Roussels " were, and he listened with polite indifference. When he heard that a working-class family, father, mother, and five children, had committed suicide to escape from poverty in the house in which he lived, he stopped, like the rest, and looked up at the walls of the building, and listened to the woman's story, which she was nothing loth to begin again from the beginning. As she went on talking, old memories awoke in him, and he realized that he had seen the wretched family: he asked a few questions. . . . Yes, he remembered them: the man—(he used to hear him breathing noisily on the stairs)—a journeyman baker, with a pale face, all the blood drawn out of it by the heat of the oven, hollow cheeks always ill shaven: he had had pneumonia at the beginning of the winter: he had gone back to work only half cured: he had had a relapse: for the last three weeks he had had no work and no strength. The woman had dragged from childbirth to childbirth: crippled with rheumatism, she had worn herself out in trying to make both ends meet, and had spent her days running hither and thither trying to obtain from the Public Charity a meager sum which was not readily forthcoming. Meanwhile the children came, and went on coming: eleven, seven, three—not to mention two others who had died in between:—and, to crown all, twins who had chosen the very dire moment to make their appearance: they had been born only the month before.

—On the day of their birth, a neighbor said, the eldest of the five, a little girl of eleven, Justine—poor little mite!—had begun to cry and asked how ever she could manage to carry both of them.

Olivier at once remembered the little girl,—a large forehead, with colorless hair pulled back, and sorrowful, gray bulging eyes. He was always meeting her, carrying provisions or her little sister: or she would be holding her seven-year-old brother by the hand, a little pinch-faced, cringing boy he was, with one blind eye. When they met on the stairs Olivier used to say, with his absent courteous manner:

" Pardon, mademoiselle."

But she never said anything: she used to go stiffly by, hardly moving aside: but his illusory courtesy used to give her a secret pleasure. Only the evening before, at six o'clock, as he was going downstairs, he had met her for the last time: she was carrying up a bucket of charcoal. He had not noticed it, except that he did remark that the burden seemed to be very heavy. But that is merely in the order of things for the children of the people. Olivier had bowed, as usual, without looking at her. A few steps lower down he had mechanically looked up to see her leaning over the balustrade of the landing, with her little pinched face, watching him go down. She turned away at once, and resumed her climb upstairs. Did she know whither she was climbing?—Olivier had no doubt that she did, and he was obsessed by the thought of the child bearing death in the load that was too heavy for her, death the deliverer— the wretched children for whom to cease to be meant an end of suffering! He was unable to continue his walk. He went back to his room. But there he was conscious of the proximity of the dead. . . . Only a few thin walls between him and them. . . . To think that he had lived so near to such misery!

He went to see Christophe. He was sick at heart: he told himself that it was monstrous for him to have been so absorbed as he had been in vain regrets for love while there were so many creatures suffering misfortunes a thousand times more cruel, and it was possible to help and save them. His emotion was profound: there was no difficulty in communicating it. Christophe was easily impressionable, and he in his turn was moved. When he heard Olivier's story he tore up the page of music he had just been writing, and called himself a selfish brute to be amusing himself with childish games. But, directly after, he picked up the pieces. He was too much under the spell of his music. And his instinct told him that a work of art the less would not make one happy man the more. The tragedy of want was no new thing to him: from his childhood on he had been used to treading on the edge of such abysmal depths, and contriving not to topple over. But he was apt to judge suicide harshly, being conscious as he was of such a fullness of force, and unable to understand how a man, under the pressure of any suffering whatsoever, could give up the struggle. Suffering, struggling, is there anything more normal? These things are the backbone of the universe.

Olivier also had passed through much the same sort of experience: but he had never been able to resign himself to it, either on his own account or for others. He had a horror of the poverty in which the life of his beloved Antoinette had been consumed. After his marriage with Jacqueline, when he had suffered the softening influence of riches and love, he had made haste to thrust back the memory of the sorrowful years when he and his sister had worn themselves out each day in the struggle to gain the right to live through the next, never knowing whether they would succeed or no. The memories of those days would come to him now that he no longer had his youthful egoism to preserve. Instead of flying before the face of suffering he set out to look for it. He did not need to go far to find it. In the state of mind in which he was he was prone to find it everywhere. The world was full of it. the world, that hospital. . . . Oh, the agony, the sorrow! Pains of the wounded body, quivering flesh, rotting away in life. The silent torture of hearts under gnawing grief. Children whom no one loves, poor hopeless girls. women seduced or betrayed, men deceived in their friends, their loves, their faith, the pitiable herd of the unfortunates whom life has broken and forgotten! . . . Not poverty and sickness were the most frightful things to see, but the cruelty of men one to another. Hardly had Olivier raised the cover of the hell of humanity than there rose to his ears the plaint of all the oppressed, the exploited poor, the persecuted peoples, massacred Armenians, Finland crushed and stifled, Poland rent in pieces, Russia martyred, Africa flung

to the rapacious pack of Europe, all the wretched creatures of
the human race. It stifled him: he heard it everywhere, he
could no longer close his ears to it, he could no longer conceive
the possibility of there being people with any other thought.
He was for ever talking about it to Christophe. Christophe
grew anxious, and said:

"Be quiet! Let me work."

And as he found it hard to recover his balance he would lose
his temper and swear.

"Damnation! My day is wasted! And you're a deal the
better for it, aren't you?"

Olivier would beg his pardon.

"My dear fellow," said Christophe, "it's no good always
looking down into the pit. It stops your living."

"One must lend a hand to those who are in the pit."

"No doubt. But how? By flinging ourselves down as well?
For that is what you want. You've got a propensity for seeing
nothing but the sad side of life. God bless you! Your pessimism is charitable, I grant you, but it is very depressing
Do you want to create happiness? Very well, then, be happy."

"Happy! How can one have the heart to be happy when
one sees so much suffering? There can only be happiness in
trying to lessen it and fighting the evil."

"Very good. But I don't help the unfortunate much by
lashing out blindly in all directions. It means only one bad
soldier the more. But I can bring comfort by my art and
spread force and joy. Have you any idea how many wretched
beings have been sustained in their suffering by the beauty of
an idea, by a winged song? Every man to his own trade!
You French people, like the generous scatterbrains that you
are, are always the first to protest against the injustice of, say,
Spain or Russia, without knowing what it is all about. I love
you for it. But do you think you are helping things along?
You rush at it and bungle it and the result is nil,—if not
worse. . . . And, look you, your art has never been more weak
and emaciated than now, when your artists claim to be taking
part in the activities of the world. It is the strangest thing
to see so many little writers and artists, all dilettante and
rather dishonest, daring to set themselves up as apostles! They

would do much better if they were to give the people wine to drink that was not so adulterated.—My first duty is to do whatever I am doing well, and to give you healthy music which shall set new blood coursing in your veins and let the sun shine in upon you."

If a man is to shed the light of the sun upon other men, he must first of all have it within himself. Olivier had none of it. Like the best man of to-day, he was not strong enough to radiate force by himself. But in unison with others he might have been able to do so. But with whom could he unite? He was free in mind and at heart religious, and he was rejected by every party political and religious. They were all intolerant and narrow and were continually at rivalry. Whenever they came into power they abused it. Only the weak and the oppressed attracted Olivier. In this at least he agreed with Christophe's opinion, that before setting out to combat injustice in distant lands, it were as well to fight injustice close at hand, injustice everywhere about, injustice for which each and every man is more or less responsible. There are only too many people who are quite satisfied with protesting against the evil wrought by others, without ever thinking of the evil that they do themselves.

At first he turned his attention to the relief of the poor. His friend, Madame Arnaud, helped to administer a charity. Olivier got her to allow him to help. But at the outset he had more than one setback: the poor people who were given into his charge were not all worthy of interest, or they were unresponsive to his sympathy, distrusted him, and shut their doors against him. Besides, it is hard for a man of intellect to be satisfied with charity pure and simple: it waters such a very small corner of the kingdom of wretchedness! Its effects are almost always piecemeal, fragmentary: it seems to move by chance, and to be engaged only in dressing wounds as fast as it discovers them: generally it is too modest and in too great a hurry to probe down to the roots of the evil. Now it was just this probing that Olivier's mind found indispensable.

He began to study the problem of social poverty. There was no lack of guides to point the way. In those days the social

question had become a society question. It was discussed in
drawing-rooms, in the theater, in novels. Everybody claimed
some knowledge of it. Some of the young men were expending
the best part of their powers upon it.

Every new generation needs to have some splendid mania or
other. Even the most selfish of young people are endowed
with a superfluity of life, a capital sum of energy which has
been advanced to them and cannot be left idle and unpro-
ductive: they are for ever seeking to expend it on a course of
action, or—(more prudently)—on a theory. Aviation or Revolution, a muscular or intellectual exercise. When a man is
young he needs to be under the illusion that he is sharing in
some great movement of humanity and is renewing the life of
the world. It is a lovely thing when the senses thrill in answer to every puff of the winds of the universe! Then a man
is so free, so light! Not yet is he laden with the ballast of a
family, he has nothing, risks next to nothing. A man is very
generous when he can renounce what is not yet his. Besides,
it is so good to love and to hate, and to believe that one is trans-
forming the earth with dreams and shouting! Young people
are like watch-dogs: they are for ever howling and barking at
the wind. An act of injustice committed at the other end of
the world will send them off their heads.

Dogs barking through the night. From one farm to another
in the heart of the forest they were yelping to one another,
never ceasing. The night was stormy. It was not easy to
sleep in those days. The wind bore through the air the echoes
of so many acts of injustice! . . . The tale of injustice is unnum-
bered: in remedying one there is danger of causing others.
What is injustice?—To one man it means a shameful peace,
the fatherland dismembered. To another it signifies war. To
another it means the destruction of the past, the banishment
of princes: to another, the spoliation of the Church: to yet another the stifling of the future to the peril of liberty. For the
people, injustice lies in inequality: for the upper ten, in
equality. There are so many different kinds of injustice that
each age chooses its own,—the injustice that it fights against,
and the injustice that it countenances.

At the present time the mightiest efforts of the world were

directed against social injustice,—and unconsciously were tending to the production of fresh injustice.

And, in truth, such injustice had waxed great and plain to
see since the working-classes, growing in numbers and power,
had become part of the essential machinery of the State. But
in spite of the declamations of the tribunes and bards of the
people, their condition was not worse, but rather better than it
had ever been in the past: and the change had come about not
because they suffered more, but because they had grown
stronger. Stronger by reason of the very power of the hostile
ranks of Capital, by the fatality of economic and industrial development which had banded the workers together in armies
ready for the fight, and, by the use of machinery, had given
weapons into their hands, and had turned every foreman into
a master with power over light, lightning, movement, all the
energy of the world. From this enormous mass of elementary
forces, which only a short time ago the leaders of men were
trying to organize, there was given out a white heat, electric
waves gradually permeating the whole body of human society.

It was not by reason of its justice, or its novelty, or the
force of the ideas bound up in it that the cause of the people
was stirring the minds of the intelligent middle-class, although
they were fain to think so. Its appeal lay in its vitality.

Its justice? Justice was everywhere and every day violated
thousands of times without the world ever giving a thought
to it. Its ideas? Scraps of truth, picked up here and there
and adjusted to the interests and requirements of one class
at the expense of the other classes. Its creed was as absurd
as every other creed,—the Divine Right of Kings, the Infallibility of the Popes. Universal Suffrage, the Equality of Man,—
all equally absurd if one only considers them by their rational
value and not in the light of the force by which they are animated. What did their mediocrity matter? Ideas have never
conquered the world as ideas, but only by the force they represent. They do not grip men by their intellectual contents,
but by the radiant vitality which is given off from them at certain periods in history. They give off as it were a rich scent
which overpowers even the dullest sense of smell. The loftiest
and most sublime idea remains ineffective until the day when

it becomes contagious, not by its own merits, but by the merits
of the groups of men in whom it becomes incarnate by the
transfusion of their blood. Then the withered plant, the rose
of Jericho, comes suddenly to flower, grows to its full height,
and fills all the air with its powerful aroma.—Some of the ideas
which were now the flaming standard under which the working-classes were marching on to the assault upon the capitalistic citadel, emanated from the brains of dreamers of the
comfortable classes. While they had been left in their comfortable books, they had lain dead: items in a museum, mum-
mies packed away in glass cases with no one to look at them.
But as soon as the people laid hands on them, they had become
part and parcel of the people, they had been given their feverish reality, which deformed them while it gave them life, breathing into such abstract reason, their hallucinations, and their
hopes, like a burning wind of Hegira. They were quickly
spread from man to man. Men succumbed to them without
knowing from whom they came or how they had been brought.
They were no respecters of persons. The moral epidemic
spread and spread: and it was quite possible for limited creatures to communicate it to superior men. Every man was unwittingly an agent in the transmission.

Such phenomena of intellectual contagion are to be observed
in all times and in all countries: they make themselves felt even
in aristocratic States where there is the endeavor to maintain
castes hermetically sealed one against the other. But nowhere
are they more electric than in democracies which preserve no
sanitary barrier between the elect and the mob. The elect are
contaminated at once whatever they do to fight against it. In
spite of their pride and intelligence they cannot resist the contagion; for the elect are much weaker than they think. Intelligence is a little island fretted by the tides of humanity, crumbling away and at last engulfed. It only emerges again on
the ebb of the tide.—One wonders at the self-denial of the
French privileged classes when on the night of August 4 they
abdicated their rights. Most wonderful of all, no doubt, is the
fact that they could not do otherwise. I fancy a good many
of them when they returned home must have said to themselves:
"What have I done? I must have been drunk. . . ." A splen-

did drunkenness! Blessed be wine and the vine that gives it
forth! It was not the privileged classes of old France who
planted the vine whose blood brought them to drunkenness.
The wine was extracted, they had only to drink it. He who
drank must lose his wits. Even those who did not drink turned
dizzy only from the smell of the vat that caught them as they
passed. The vintages of the Revolution! . . . Hidden away
in the family vaults there are left only a few empty bottles
of the wine of '89: but our grandchildren's children will remember that their great-grandfathers had their heads turned by it.

It was a sourer wine but a wine no less strong that was
mounting to the heads of the comfortable young people of
Olivier's generation. They were offering up their class as a
sacrifice to the new God, *Deo ignoto:*—the people.

To tell the truth, they were not all equally sincere. Many
of them were only able to see in the movement an opportunity
of rising above their class by affecting to despise it. For the
majority it was an intellectual pastime, an oratorical enthusiasm which they never took altogether seriously. There is a
certain pleasure in believing that you believe in a cause, that
you are fighting, or will fight, for it,—or at least could fight.
There is a by no means negligible satisfaction in the thought
that you are risking something. Theatrical emotions.

They are quite innocent so long as you surrender to them
simply without any admixture of interested motive.—But there
were men of a more worldly type who only played the game
of set purpose: the popular movement was to them only a road
to success. Like the Norse pirates, they made use of the rising
tide to carry their ships up into the land: they aimed at reaching the innermost point of the great estuaries so as to be left
snugly ensconced in the conquered cities when the sea fell back
once more. The channel was narrow and the tide was capricious: great skill was needed. But two or three generations
of demagogy have created a race of corsairs who know every
trick and secret of the trade. They rushed boldly in with
never even so much as a glance back at those who foundered on
the way.

This piratical rabble is made up of all parties: thank Heaven, no party is responsible for it. But the disgust with which such adventurers had inspired the sincere and all men of conviction had led some of them to despair of their class. Olivier came in contact with rich young men of culture who felt very strongly that the comfortable classes were moribund and that they themselves were useless. He was only too much inclined to sympathize with them. They had begun by believing in the reformation of the people by the elect, they had founded Popular Universities, and taken no account of the time and money spent upon them, and now they were forced to admit the futility of their efforts: their hopes had been pitched too high, their discouragement sank too low. The people had either not responded to their appeal or had run away from it. When the people did come, they understood everything all wrong, and only assimilated the vices and absurdities of the culture of the superior classes. And in the end more than one scurvy knave had stolen into the ranks of the burgess apostles, and discredited them by exploiting both people and apostles at the same time. Then it seemed to honest men that the middle-class was doomed, that it could only infect the people who, at all costs, must break free and go their way alone. So they were left cut off from all possibility of action, save to predict and foresee a movement which would be made without and against themselves. Some of them found in this the joy of renunciation, the joy of deep disinterested human sympathy feeding upon itself and the sacrifice of itself. To love, to give self! Youth is so richly endowed that it can afford to do without repayment: youth has no fear of being left despoiled. And it can do without everything save the art of loving.—Others again found in it a pleasurable rational satisfaction, a sort of imperious logic: they sacrificed themselves not to men so much as to ideas. These were the bolder spirits. They took a proud delight in deducing the fated end of their class from their reasoned arguments. It would have hurt them more to see their predictions falsified than to be crushed beneath the weight of circumstance. In their intellectual intoxication they cried aloud to those outside: " Harder! Strike harder! Let there be nothing left of us! "—They had become the theorists of violence.

Of the violence of others. For, as usual, these apostles of brute force were almost always refined and weakly people. Many of them were officials of the State which they talked of destroying, industrious, conscientious, and orderly officials.

Their theoretical violence was the throwback from their weakness, their bitterness, and the suppression of their vitality. But above all it was an indication of the storms brewing all around them. Theorists are like meteorologists: they state in scientific terms not what the weather will be, but what the weather is. They are weathercocks pointing to the quarter whence the wind blows. When they turn they are never far from believing that they are turning the wind.

The wind had turned.

Ideas are quickly used up in a democracy, and the more quickly they are propagated, the more quickly are they worn out. There are any number of Republicans in France who in less than fifty years have grown disgusted with the Republic, with Universal Suffrage, with all the manifestations of liberty won with such blind intoxication! After the fetish worship of numbers, after the gaping optimism which had believed in the sanctity of the majority and had looked to it for the progress of humanity, there came the wind of brute force: the inability of the majority to govern themselves, their venality, their corruption, their base and fearful hatred of all superiority, their oppressive cowardice, raised the spirit of revolt: the minorities of energy—every kind of minority—appealed from the majority to force. A queer, yet inevitable alliance was brought about between the royalists of the *Action Française* and the syndicalists of the C. G. T. Balzac speaks somewhere of the men of his time who " *though aristocrats by inclination, yet became Republicans in spite of themselves, only to find many inferiors among their equals.*"—A scant sort of pleasure. Those who are inferior must be made to accept themselves as such: and to bring that about there is nothing to be done but to create an authority which shall impose the supremacy of the elect—of either class, working or burgess— upon the oppressive majority. Our young intellectuals, being proud and of the better class, became royalists or revolutionaries out of injured vanity and hatred of democratic equality. And the disinterested theorists, the philosophers of brute force, like good little weathercocks, reared their heads above them and were the oriflammes of the storm.

Last of all there was the herd of literary men in search of inspiration—men who could write and yet knew not what to write: like the Greeks at Aulis, they were becalmed and could make no progress, and sat impatiently waiting for a kindly wind from any quarter to come and belly out their sails.— There were famous men among them, men who had been wrenched away from their stylistic labors and plunged into public meetings by the Dreyfus affair. An example which had found only too many followers for the liking of those who had set it. There was now a mob of writing men all engrossed in politics, and claiming to control the affairs of the State. On the slightest excuse they would form societies, issue manifestoes, save the Capitol. After the intellectuals of the advance guard came the intellectuals of the rear: they were much of a muchness. Each of the two parties regarded the other as intellectual and themselves as intelligent. Those who had the luck to have in their veins a few drops of the blood of the people bragged about it: they dipped their pens into it, wrote with it.—They were all malcontents of the burgess class, and were striving to recapture the authority which that class had irreparably lost through its selfishness. Only in rare instances were these apostles known to keep up their apostolic zeal for any length of time. In the beginning the cause meant a certain amount of success to them, success which in all probability was in no wise due to their oratorical gifts. It gave them a delicious flattery for their vanity. Thereafter they went on with less success and a certain secret fear of being rather ridiculous. In the long-run the last feeling was apt to dominate the rest, being increased by the fatigue of playing a difficult part for men of their distinguished tastes and innate skepticism. But they waited upon the favor of the wind and of their escort before they could withdraw. For they were held captive both by wind and escort. These latter-day Voltaires and Joseph de Maistres, beneath their boldness in speech and writing, concealed a dread uncertainty, feeling the ground, being fearful of compromising themselves with the young men,

and striving hard to please them and to be younger than the
young. They were revolutionaries or counter-revolutionaries
merely as a matter of literature, and in the end they resigned
themselves to following the literary fashion which they themselves had helped to create.

The oddest of all the types with which Olivier came in contact in the small burgess advance guard of the Revolution was
the revolutionary who was so from timidity.

The specimen presented for his immediate observation was
named Pierre Canet. He was brought up in a rich, middle-
class, and conservative family, hermetically sealed against any
new idea: they were magistrates and officials who had distinguished themselves by crabbing authority or being dismissed:
thick-witted citizens of the Marais who flirted with the Church
and thought little, but thought that little well. He had married, for want of anything better to do, a woman with an aristocratic name, who had no great capacity for thought, but did her
thinking no less well than he. The bigoted, narrow, and retro-
grade society in which he lived, a society which was perpetually
chewing the cud of its own conceit and bitterness, had finally
exasperated him,—the more so as his wife was ugly and a bore.
He was fairly intelligent and open-minded, and liberal in aspiration, without knowing at all clearly in what liberalism consisted: there was no likelihood of his discovering the meaning
of liberty in his immediate surroundings. The only thing he
knew for certain was that liberty did not exist there: and he
fancied that he had only to leave to find it. On his first move
outwards he was lucky enough to fall in with certain old col-
lege friends, some of whom had been smitten with syndicalistic
ideas. He was even more at sea in their company than in the
society which he had just quitted: but he would not admit it:
he had to live somewhere: and he was unable to find people
of his own cast of thought (that is to say, people of no cast
of thought whatever), though, God knows, the species is by
no means rare in France! But they are ashamed of themselves: they hide themselves, or they take on the hue of one
of the fashionable political colors, if not of several, all at once.
Besides, he was under the influence of his friends.

As always happens, he had particularly attached himself

to the very man who was most different from himself. This Frenchman, French, burgess and provincial to his very soul, had become the *fidus Achates* of a young Jewish doctor named Manousse Heimann, a Russian refugee, who, like so many of his fellow-countrymen, had the twofold gift of settling at once among strangers and making himself at home, and of being so much at his ease in any sort of revolution as to rouse wonder as to what it was that most interested him in it: the game or the cause. His experiences and the experiences of others were a source of entertainment to him. He was a sincere revolutionary, and his scientific habit of mind made him regard the revolutionaries and himself as a kind of madmen. His excited dilettantism and his extreme instability of mind made him seek the company of men the most opposite. He had acquaintances among those in authority and even among the police: he was perpetually prying and spying with that morbid and dangerous curiosity which makes so many Russian revolutionaries seem to be playing a double game, and sometimes reduces the appearance to reality. It is not treachery so much as versatility, and it is thoroughly disinterested. There are so many men of action to whom action is a theater into which they bring their talents as comedians, quite honestly prepared at any moment to change their part! Manousse was as faithful to the revolutionary part as it was possible for him to be: it was the character which was most in accord with his natural anarchy, and his delight in demolishing the laws of the countries through which he passed. But yet, in spite of everything, it was only a part. It was always impossible to know how much was true and how much invented in what he said, and even he himself was never very sure.

He was intelligent and skeptical, endowed with the psychological subtlety of his twofold nationality, could discern quite marvelously the weaknesses of others, and his own, and was extremely skilful in playing upon them, so that he had no difficulty in gaining an ascendancy over Canet. It amused him to drag this Sancho Panza into Quixotic pranks. He made no scruple about using him, disposing of his will, his time, his money,—not for his own benefit, (he needed none, though no one knew how or in what way he lived),—but in the most compromising demonstrations of the cause. Canet submitted to it all: he tried to persuade himself that he thought like Manousse. He knew perfectly well that this was not the case: such ideas scared him: they were shocking to his common sense. And he had no love for the people. And, in addition, he had no courage. This big, bulky, corpulent young man, with his clean-shaven pinkish face, his short breathing, his pleasant, pompous, and rather childish way of speaking, with a chest like the Farnese Hercules, (he was a fair hand at boxing and single-stick), was the most timid of men. If he took a certain pride in being taken for a man of a subversive temper by his own people, in his heart of hearts he used to tremble at the boldness of his friends. No doubt the little thrill they gave him was by no means disagreeable as long as it was only in fun. But their fun was becoming dangerous. His fervent friends were growing aggressive, their hardy pretensions were increasing: they alarmed Canet's fundamental egoism, his deeply rooted sense of propriety, his middle-class pusillanimity. He dared not ask: "Where are you taking me to?" But, under his breath, he fretted and fumed at the recklessness of these young men who seemed to love nothing so much as breaking their necks, and never to give a thought as to whether they were not at the same time running a risk of breaking other people's.—What was it impelled him to follow them? Was he not free to break with them? He had not the courage. He was afraid of being left alone, like a child who gets left behind and begins to whimper. He was like so many men: they have no opinions, except in so far as they disapprove of all enthusiastic opinion: but if a man is to be independent he must stand alone, and how many men are there who are capable of that? How many men are there, even amongst the most clear sighted, who will dare to break free of the bondage of certain prejudices, certain postulates which cramp and fetter all the men of the same generation? That would mean setting up a wall between themselves and others. On the one hand, freedom in the wilderness, on the other, mankind. They do not hesitate: they choose mankind. the herd. The herd is evil smelling, but it gives warmth. Then those who have chosen pretend to think what they do not in fact think. It is not very difficult for them: they know so little what they think! . . . "*Know thy-self!*" . . . How could they, these men who have hardly a *Me* to know? In every collective belief, religious or social, very rare are the men who believe, because very rare are the men who are men. Faith is an heroic force: its fire has kindled but a very few human torches, and even these have often flickered. The apostles, the prophets, even Jesus have doubted. The rest are only reflections,—save at certain hours when their souls are dry and a few sparks falling from a great torch set light to all the surface of the plain: then the fire dies down, and nothing gleams but the glowing embers beneath the ashes. Not more than a few hundred Christians really believe in Christ. The rest believe that they believe, or else they only try to believe.

Many of these revolutionaries were like that. Our friend Canet tried hard to believe that he was a revolutionary: he did believe it. And he was scared at his own boldness.

All these comfortable people invoked divers principles: some followed the bidding of their hearts, others that of their reason, others again only their interests: some associated their way of thinking with the Gospel, others with M. Bergson, others, again, with Karl Marx, with Proudhon, with Joseph de Maistre, with Nietzsche, or with M. Sorel. There were men who were revolutionaries to be in the fashion, some who were so out of snobbishness, and some from shyness: some from hatred, others from love: some from a need of active, hot-headed heroism: and some in sheer slavishness, from the sheeplike quality of their minds. But all, without knowing it, were at the mercy of the wind. All were no more than those whirling clouds of dust which are to be seen like smoke in the far distance on the white roads in the country, clouds of dust foretelling the coming of the storm.

Olivier and Christophe watched the wind coming. Both of them had strong eyes. But they used them in different ways. Olivier, whose clear gaze, in spite of himself, pierced to the very inmost thoughts of men, was saddened by their mediocrity: but he saw the hidden force that sustained them: he was most struck by the tragic aspect of things. Christophe was more sensible of their comic aspect. Men interested him, ideas not at all. He affected a contemptuous indifference towards them. He laughed at Socialistic Utopias. In a spirit of contradiction and out of instinctive reaction against the morbid humanitarianism which was the order of the day, he appeared to be more selfish than he was: he was a self-made man, a sturdy upstart, proud of his strength of body and will, and he was a little too apt to regard all those who had not his force as shirkers. In poverty and alone he had been able to win through: let others do the same! Why all this talk of a social question? What question? Poverty?

"I know all about that," he would say. "My father, my mother, I myself, we have been through it. It's only a matter of getting out of it."

"Not everybody can," Olivier would reply. "What about the sick and the unlucky?"

"One must help them, that's all. But that is a very different thing from setting them on a pinnacle, as people are doing nowadays. Only a short while ago people were asserting the odious doctrine of the rights of the strongest man. Upon my word, I'm inclined to think that the rights of the weakest are even more detestable: they're sapping the thought of to-day, the weakest man is tyrannizing over the strong, and exploiting them. It really looks as though it has become a merit to be diseased, poor, unintelligent, broken,—and a vice to be strong, upstanding, happy in fighting, and an aristocrat in brains and blood. And what is most absurd of all is this, that the strong are the first to believe it. . . . It's a fine subject for a comedy, my dear Olivier!"

"I'd rather have people laugh at me than make other people weep."

"Good boy!" said Christophe. "But, good Lord, who ever said anything to the contrary? When I see a hunchback, my back aches for him. . . . We're playing the comedy, we won't write it."

He did not suffer himself to be bitten by the prevalent dreams of social justice. His vulgar common sense told him and he believed that what had been would be.

"But if anybody said that to you about art you'd be up in arms against him."

"May be. Anyhow, I don't know about anything except art. Nor do you. I've no faith in people who talk about things without knowing anything about them."

Olivier's faith in such people was no greater. Both of them were inclined to push their distrust a little too far: they had always held aloof from politics. Olivier confessed, not without shame, that he could not remember ever having used his rights as an elector: for the last ten years he had not even entered his name at the *mairie*.

"Why," he asked, "should I take part in a comedy which I know to be futile? Vote? For whom should I vote? I don't see any reason for choosing between two candidates, both of whom are unknown to me, while I have only too much reason to expect that, directly the election is over, they will both be false to all their professions of faith. Keep an eye on them? Remind them of their duty? It would take up the whole of my life, with no result. I have neither time, nor strength, nor the rhetorical weapons, nor sufficient lack of scruple, nor is my heart steeled against all the disgust that action brings. Much better to keep clear of it all. I am quite ready to submit to the evil. But at least I won't subscribe to it."

But, in spite of his excessive clear-sightedness, Olivier, to whom the ordinary routine of politics was repulsive, yet preserved a chimerical hope in a revolution. He knew that it was chimerical: but he did not discard it. It was a sort of racial mysticism in him. Not for nothing does a man belong to the greatest destructive and constructive people of the Western world, the people who destroy to construct and construct to destroy,— the people who play with ideas and life, and are for ever making a clean sweep so as to make a new and better beginning, and shed their blood in pledge.

Christophe was endowed with no such hereditary Messianism. He was too German to relish much the idea of a revolution. He thought that there was no changing the world. Why all these theories, all these words, all this futile uproar?

"I have no need," he would say, "to make a revolution—or long speeches about revolution—in order to prove to my own sat-

isfaction that I am strong. I have no need, like these young
men of yours, to overthrow the State in order to restore a King
or a Committee of Public Safety to defend me. That's a queer
way of proving your strength! I can defend myself. I am not
an anarchist: I love all necessary order and I revere the laws
which govern the universe. But I don't want an intermediary
between them and myself. My will knows how to command, and
it knows also how to submit. You've got the classics on the tip
of your tongue. Why don't you remember your Corneille: '*Myself alone, and that is enough.*' Your desire for a master is
only a cloak for your weakness. Force is like the light: only the
blind can deny it. Be strong, calmly, without all your theories,
without any act of violence, and then, as plants turn to the sun,
so the souls of the weak will turn to you."

But even while he protested that he had no time to waste on
political discussions, he was much less detached from it all than
he wished to appear. He was suffering, as an artist, from the
social unrest. In his momentary dearth of strong passion he
would sometimes pause to look around and wonder for what people he was writing. Then he would see the melancholy patrons
of contemporary art, the weary creatures of the upper-classes, the
dilettante men and women of the burgess-class, and he would
think:

"What profits it to work for such people as these?"

In truth there was no lack of men of refinement and culture,
men sensitive to skill and craft, men even who were not incapable of appreciating the novelty or—(it is all the same)—the
archaism of fine feeling. But they were bored, too intellectual,
not sufficiently alive to believe in the reality of art: they were
only interested in tricks,—tricks of sound, or juggling with
ideas; most of them were distraught by other worldly interests,
accustomed to scattering their attention over their multifarious
occupations, none of which was "necessary." It was almost impossible for them to pierce the outer covering of art, to feel its
heart deep down: art was not flesh and blood to them; it was
literature. Their critics built up their impotence to issue from
dilettantism into a theory, an intolerant theory. When it happened that a few here and there were vibrant enough to respond
to the voice of art, they were not strong enough to bear it, and

were left disgruntled and nerve-ridden for life. They were sick
men or dead. What could art do in such a hospital?—And yet
in modern society he was unable to do without these cripples:
for they had money, and they ruled the Press: they only could
assure an artist the means of living. So then he must submit
to such humiliation: an intimate and sorrowful art, music in
which is told the secret of the artist's inmost life, offered up as
an amusement—or rather as a palliative of boredom, or as another sort of boredom—in the theaters or in fashionable drawing-rooms, to an audience of snobs and worn-out intellectuals.

Christophe was seeking the real public, the public which believes in the emotions of art as in those of life, and feels them
with a virgin soul. And he was vaguely attracted by the new
promised world—the people. The memories of his childhood,
Gottfried and the poor, who had revealed to him the living
depths of art, or had shared with him the sacred bread of music,
made him inclined to believe that his real friends were to be
found among such people. Like many another young man of
a generous heart and simple faith, he cherished great plans for
a popular art, concerts, and a theater for the people, which he
would have been hard put to it to define. He thought that a
revolution might make it possible to bring about a great artistic
renascence, and he pretended that he had no other interest in the
social movement. But he was hoodwinking himself: he was
much too alive not to be attracted and drawn onward by the sight
of the most living activity of the time.

In all that he saw he was least of all interested in the middle-
class theorists. The fruit borne by such trees is too often sap-
less: all the juices of life are wasted in ideas. Christophe did
not distinguish between one idea and another. He had nc
preference even for ideas which were his own when he came upon them congealed in systems. With good-humored contempt he
held aloof from the theorists of force as from the theorists of
weakness. In every comedy the one ungrateful part is that of
the *raisonneur*. The public prefers not only the sympathetic
characters to him, but the unsympathetic characters also. Christophe was like the public in that. The *raisonneurs* of the social
question seemed tiresome to him. But he amused himself by
watching the rest, the simple, the men of conviction, those who

believed and those who wanted to believe, those who were tricked and those who wanted to be tricked, not to mention the buccaneers who plied their predatory trade, and the sheep who were made to be fleeced. His sympathy was indulgent towards the pathetically absurd little people like fat Canet. Their mediocrity was not offensive to him as it was to Olivier. He watched them all with affectionate and mocking interest: he believed that he was outside the piece they were playing: and he did not see that little by little he was being drawn into it. He thought only of being a spectator watching the wind rush by. But already the wind had caught him, and was dragging him along into its whirling cloud of dust.

The social drama was twofold. The piece played by the intellectuals was a comedy within a comedy; the people hardly heeded it. The real drama was that of the people. It was not easy to follow it: the people themselves did not always know where they were in it. It was all unexpected, unforeseen.

It was not only that there was much more talk in it than action. Every Frenchman, be he burgess or of the people, is as great an eater of speeches as he is of bread. But all men do not eat the same sort of bread. There is the speech of luxury for delicate palates, and the more nourishing sort of speech for hungry gullets. If the words are the same, they are not kneaded into the same shape: taste, smell, meaning, all are different.

The first time Olivier attended a popular meeting and tasted of the fare he lost his appetite: his gorge rose at it, and he could not swallow. He was disgusted by the platitudinous quality of thought, the drab and uncouth clumsiness of expression, the vague generalizations, the childish logic, the ill-mixed mayonnaise of abstractions and disconnected facts. The impropriety and looseness of the language were not compensated by the raciness and vigor of the vulgar tongue. The whole thing was compounded of a newspaper vocabulary, stale tags picked up from the reach-me-downs of middle-class rhetoric. Olivier was particularly amazed at the lack of simplicity. He forgot that literary simplicity is not natural, but acquired: it is a thing achieved by the people of the elect. Dwellers in towns cannot be simple: they are rather always on the lookout for far-fetched expressions.

Olivier did not understand the effect such turgid phrases might have on their audience. He had not the key to their meaning. We call foreign the languages of other races, and it never occurs to us that there are almost as many languages in our nation as there are social grades. It is only for a limited few that words retain their traditional and age-old meaning: for the rest they represent nothing more than their own experience and that of the group to which they belong. Many of such words, which are dead for the select few and despised by them, are like an empty house, wherein, as soon as the few are gone, new energy and quivering passion take up their abode. If you wish to know the master of the house, go into it.

That Christophe did.

He had been brought into touch with the working-classes by a neighbor of his who was employed on the State Railways. He was a little man of forty-five, prematurely old, with a pathetically bald head, deep-sunken eyes, hollow cheeks, a prominent nose, fleshy and aquiline, a clever mouth, and malformed ears with twisted lobes: the marks of degeneracy. His name was Alcide Gautier. He was not of the people, but of the lower middle-class. He came of a good family who had spent all they had on the education of their only son, but, for want of means, had been unable to let him go through with it. As a very young man he had obtained one of those Government posts which seem to the lower middle-class a very heaven, and are in reality death, —living death.—Once he had gone into it, it had been impossible for him to escape. He had committed the offense—(for it is an offense in modern society)—of marrying for love a pretty workgirl, whose innate vulgarity had only increased with time. She gave him three children and he had to earn a living for them. This man, who was intelligent and longed with all his might to finish his education, was cramped and fettered by poverty. He was conscious of latent powers in himself which were stifled by the difficulties of his existence: he could not take any decisive step. He was never alone. He was a bookkeeping clerk and had to spend his days over purely mechanical work in a room which he had to share with several of his colleagues who were vulgar chattering creatures: they were for ever talking

of idiotic things and avenged themselves for the absurdity of
their existence by slandering their chiefs and making fun of
him and his intellectual point of view which he had not been
prudent enough to conceal from them. When he returned home
it was to find an evil-smelling charmless room, a noisy common
wife who did not understand him and regarded him as a humbug or a fool. His children did not take after him in anything:
they took after their mother. Was it just that it should be so?
Was it just? Nothing but disappointment and suffering and
perpetual poverty, and work that took up his whole day from
morning to night, and never the possibility of snatching an hour
for recreation, an hour's silence, all this had brought him to a
state of exhaustion and nervous irritability.—Christophe, who
had pursued his acquaintance with him, was struck by the
tragedy of his lot: an incomplete nature, lacking sufficient culture and artistic taste, yet made for great things and crushed by
misfortune. Gautier clung to Christophe as a weak man drowning grasps at the arm of a strong swimmer. He felt a mixture
of sympathy and envy for Christophe. He took him to popular
meetings, and showed him some of the leaders of the syndicalist
party to which he belonged for no other reason than his bitterness against society. For he was an aristocrat gone wrong. It
hurt him terribly to mix with the people.

Christophe was much more democratic than he—the more so
as nothing forced him to be so—and enjoyed the meetings. The
speeches amused him. He did not share Olivier's feeling of repulsion: he was hardly at all sensible of the absurdities of the
language. In his eyes a windbag was as good as any other man.
He affected a sort of contempt for eloquence in general. But
though he took no particular pains to understand their rhetoric,
he did feel the music which came through the man who was
speaking and the men who were listening. The power of the
speaker was raised to the hundredth degree by the echo thrown
back from his hearers. At first Christophe only took stock of
the speakers, and he was interested enough to make the acquaintance of some of them.

The man who had the most influence on the crowd was Casi-
mir Joussier,—a little, pale, dark man, between thirty and thirty-
five, with a Mongolian cast of countenance, thin, puny, with cold

burning eyes, scant hair, and a pointed beard. His power lay not so much in his gesture, which was poor, stilted, and rarely in harmony with the words,—not so much in his speech, which was raucous and sibilant, with marked pauses for breathing,—as in his personality and the emphatic assurance and force of will which emanated from it. He never seemed to admit the possibility of any one thinking differently from himself: and as what he thought was what his audience wanted to think they had no difficulty in understanding one another. He would go on saying thrice, four times, ten times, the things they expected him to say: he never stopped hammering the same nail with a tenacious fury: and his audience, following his example, would hammer, hammer, hammer, until the nail was buried deep in the flesh.—Added to this personal ascendancy was the confidence inspired by his past life, the *prestige* of many terms in prison, largely deserved by his violent writings. He breathed out an indomitable energy: but for the seeing eye there was revealed beneath it all an accumulated fund of weariness, disgust with so much continual effort, anger against fate. He was one of those men who every day spend more than their income of vitality. From his childhood on he had been ground down by work and poverty. He had plied all sorts of trades: journeyman glassblower, plumber, printer: his health was ruined: he was a prey to consumption, which plunged him into fits of bitter discouragement and dumb despair of the cause and of himself: at other times it would raise him up to a pitch of excitement. He was a mixture of calculated and morbid violence, of policy and recklessness. He was educated up to a certain point: he had a good knowledge of many things, science, sociology, and his various trades: he had a very poor knowledge of many others: and he was just as cocksure with both: he had Utopian notions, just ideas, ignorance in many directions, a practical mind, many prejudices, experience, and suspicion and hatred of burgess society. That did not prevent his welcoming Christophe. His pride was tickled by being sought out by a well-known artist. He was of the race of leaders, and, whatever he did, he was brusque with ordinary workmen. Although in all good faith he desired perfect equality, he found it easier to realize with those above than with those beneath him.

Christophe came across other leaders of the working-class movement. There was no great sympathy between them. If the common fight—with difficulty—produced unity of action, it was very far from creating unity of feeling. It was easy to see the external and purely transitory reality to which the distinction between the classes corresponded. The old antagonisms were only postponed and marked: but they continued to exist. In the movement were to be found men of the north and men of the south with their fundamental scorn of each other. The trades were jealous of each other's wages, and watched each other with an undisguised feeling of superiority to all others in each. But the great difference lay—and always will lie—in temperament. Foxes and wolves and horned beasts, beasts with sharp teeth, and beasts with four stomachs, beasts that are made to eat, and beasts that are made to be eaten, all sniffed at each other as they passed in the herd that had been drawn together by the accident of class and common interest: and they recognized each other: and they bristled.

Christophe sometimes had his meals at a little creamery and restaurant kept by a former colleague of Gautier's, one Simon, a railway clerk who had been dismissed for taking part in a strike. The shop was frequented by syndicalists. There were five or six of them who used to sit in a room at the back, looking on to an inclosed courtyard, narrow and ill-lit, from which there arose the never-ceasing desperate song of two caged canaries straining after the light. Joussier used to come with his mistress, the fair Berthe, a large coquettish young woman, with a pale face, and a purple cap, and merry, wandering eyes. She had under her thumb a good-looking boy, Léopold Graillot, a journeyman mechanic, who was clever and rather a *poseur:* he was the esthete of the company. Although he called himself an anarchist, and was one of the most violent opponents of the burgess-class, his soul was typical of that class at its very worst. Every morning for years he had drunk in the erotic and decadent news of the halfpenny literary papers. His reading had given him a strongly addled brain. His mental subtlety in imagining the pleasures of the senses was allied in him with an absolute lack of physical delicacy, indifference to cleanliness, and the comparative coarseness of his life. He had acquired a taste for an occasional glass of such adulterated wine—the intellectual alcohol of luxury, the unwholesome stimulants of unhealthy rich men. Being unable to take these pleasures in the flesh, he inoculated his brain with them. That means a bad tongue in the morning and weakness in the knees. But it puts you on an equality with the rich. And you hate them.

Christophe could not bear him. He was more in sympathy with Sébastien Coquard, an electrician, who, with Joussier, was the speaker with the greatest following. He did not overburden himself with theories. He did not always know where he was going. But he did go straight ahead. He was very French. He was heavily built, about forty, with a big red face, a round head, red hair, a flowing beard, a bull neck, and a bellowing voice. Like Joussier, he was an excellent workman, but he loved drinking and laughter. The sickly Joussier regarded his superabundant health with the eyes of envy: and, though they were friends, there was always a simmering secret hostility between them.

Amélie, the manageress of the creamery, a kind creature of forty-five, who must have been pretty once, and still was, in spite of the wear of time, used to sit with them, with some sewing in her hands, listening to their talk with a jolly smile, moving her lips in time to their words: every now and then she would drop a remark into the discussion, and she would emphasize her words with a nod of her head as she worked. She had a married daughter and two children of seven and ten—a little girl and a boy—who used to do their home lessons at the corner of a sticky table, putting out their tongues, and picking up scraps of conversations which were not meant for their ears.

On more than one occasion Olivier tried to go with Christophe. But he could not feel at ease with these people. When these working-men were not tied down by strict factory hours or the insistent scream of a hooter, they seemed to have an incredible amount of time to waste, either after work, or between jobs, in loafing or idleness. Christophe, being in one of those periods when the mind has completed one piece of work and is waiting until a new piece of work presents itself, was in no greater hurry than they were: and he liked sitting there with his elbows on the table, smoking, drinking, and talking. But

Olivier's respectable burgess instincts were shocked, and so were his traditional habits of mental discipline, and regular work, and scrupulous economy of time: and he did not relish such a waste of so many precious hours. Besides that, he was not good at talking or drinking. Above all there was his physical distaste for it all, the secret antipathy which raises a physical barrier between the different types of men, the hostility of the senses, which stands in the way of the communion of their souls, the revolt of the flesh against the heart. When Olivier was alone with Christophe he would talk most feelingly about the duty of fraternizing with the people: but when he found himself face to face with the people, he was impotent to do anything, in spite of his good will. Christophe, on the other hand, who laughed at his ideas, could, without the least effort, meet any workman he chanced to come across in brotherhood. It really hurt Olivier to find himself so cut off from these men. He tried to be like them, to think like them, to speak like them. He could not do it. His voice was dull, husky, had not the ring that was in theirs. When he tried to catch some of their expressions the words would stick in his throat or sound queer and strange. He watched himself; he was embarrassed, and embarrassed them. He knew it. He knew that to them he was a stranger and suspect, that none of them was in sympathy with him, and then, when he was gone, everybody would sigh with relief: "Ouf!" As he passed among them he would notice hard, icy glances, such hostile glances as the working-classes, embittered by poverty, cast at any comfortable burgess. Perhaps Christophe came in for some of it too: but he never noticed it.

Of all the people in that place the only ones who showed any inclination to be friendly with Olivier were Amélie's children. They were much more attracted by their superior in station than disposed to hate him. The little boy was fascinated by the burgess mode of thought: he was clever enough to love it, though not clever enough to understand it: the little girl, who was very pretty, had once been taken by Olivier to see Madame Arnaud, and she was hypnotized by the comfort and ease of it all: she was silently delighted to sit in the fine armchairs, and to feel the beautiful clothes, and to be with lovely ladies: like the little

simpleton she was, she longed to escape from the people and
soar upwards to the paradise of riches and solid comfort. Olivier had no desire or taste for the cultivation of these inclinations in her: and the simple homage she paid to his class by no
means consoled him for the silent antipathy of her companions.
Their ill-disposition towards him pained him. He had such
a burning desire to understand them! And in truth he did
understand them, too well, perhaps: he watched them too closely,
and he irritated them. It was not that he was indiscreet in his
curiosity, but that he brought to bear on it his habit of an-
alyzing the souls of men and his need of love.

It was not long before he perceived the secret drama of Joussier's life: the disease which was undermining his constitution,
and the cruelty of his mistress. She loved him, she was proud
of him: but she had too much vitality: he knew that she was
slipping away from him, would slip away from him: and he
was aflame with jealousy. She found his jealousy diverting:
she was for ever exciting the men about her, bombarding them
with her eyes, flinging around them her sensual provocative atmosphere: she loved to play with him like a cat. Perhaps she
deceived him with Graillot. Perhaps it pleased her to let him
think so. In any case if she were not actually doing so, she
very probably would. Joussier dared not forbid her to love
whomsoever she pleased: did he not profess the woman's right
to liberty equally with the man's? She reminded him of that
slyly and insolently one day when he was upbraiding her. He
was delivered up to a terrible struggle within himself between
his theories of liberty and his violent instincts. At heart he
was still a man like the men of old, despotic and jealous: by
reason he was a man of the future, a Utopian. She was neither
more nor less than the woman of yesterday, to-morrow, and all
time.—And Olivier, looking on at their secret duel, the savagery
of which was known to him by his own experience, was full of
pity for Joussier when he realized his weakness. But Joussier
guessed that Olivier was reading him: and he was very far from
liking him for it.

There was another interested witness, an indulgent spectator of this game of love and hate. This was the manageress,
Amélie. She saw everything without seeming to do so. She

knew life. She was an honest, healthy, tranquil, easy-going woman, and in her youth had been free enough. She had been in a florist's shop: she had had a lover of the class above her own: she had had other lovers. Then she had married a working-man. She had become a good wife and mother. But she understood everything, all the foolish ways of the heart, Joussier's jealousy, as well as the young woman's desire for amusement. She tried to help them to understand each other with a few affectionate words:

"You must make allowances: it is not worth while creating bad blood between you for such a trifle. . . ."

She was not at all surprised when her words produced no result. . . .

"That's the way of the world. We must always be torturing ourselves. . . ."

She had that splendid carelessness of the people, from which misfortune of every sort seems harmlessly to glide. She had had her share of unhappiness. Three months ago she had lost a boy of fifteen whom she dearly loved: it had been a great grief to her: but now she was once more busy and laughing. She used to say:

"If one were to think of these things one could not live."

So she ceased to think of it. It was not selfishness. She could not do otherwise: her vitality was too strong: she was absorbed by the present: it was impossible for her to linger over the past. She adapted herself to things as they were, and would adapt herself to whatever happened. If the revolution were to come and turn everything topsy-turvy she would soon manage to be standing firmly on her feet, and do everything that was there to do; she would be in her place wherever she might be set down. At heart she had only a modified belief in the revolution. She had hardly any real faith in anything whatever. It is hardly necessary to add that she used to consult the cards in her moments of perplexity, and that she never failed to make the sign of the cross when she met a funeral. She was very open-minded and very tolerant, and she had the skepticism of the people of Paris, that healthy skepticism which doubts, as a man breathes, joyously. Though she was the wife of a revolutionary, nevertheless she took up a motherly and ironical attitude to-

wards her husband's ideas and those of his party—and those of
the other parties,—the sort of attitude she had towards the follies of youth—and of maturity. She was never much moved by
anything. But she was interested in everything. And she was
equally prepared for good and bad luck. In fine, she was an
optimist.

"It's no good getting angry. . . . Everything settles itself
so long as your health is good. . . ."

That was clearly to Christophe's way of thinking. They did
not need much conversation to discover that they belonged to
the same family. Every now and then they would exchange
a good-humored smile, while the others were haranguing and
shouting. But, more often, she would laugh to herself as she
looked at Christophe, and saw him being caught up by the argument to which he would at once bring more passion than all
the rest put together.

Christophe did not observe Olivier's isolation and embarrassment. He made no attempt to probe down to the inner workings of his companions. But he used to eat and drink with
them, and laugh and lose his temper. They were never distrustful of him, although they used to argue heatedly enough.
He did not mince his words with them. At bottom he would
have found it very hard to say whether he was with or against
them. He never stopped to think about it. No doubt if the
choice had been forced upon him he would have been a syndicalist as against Socialism and all the doctrines of the State—
that monstrous entity, that factory of officials, human machines.
His reason approved of the mighty effort of the coöperative
groups, the two-edged ax of which strikes at the same time at
the dead abstractions of the socialistic State, and at the sterility
of individualism, that corrosion of energy, that dispersion of collective force in individual frailties,—the great source of modern wretchedness for which the French Revolution is in part
responsible.

But Nature is stronger than reason. When Christophe came
in touch with the syndicates—those formidable coalitions of the
weak—his vigorous individuality drew back. He could not help
despising those men who needed to be linked together before

they could march on to the fight; and if ne admitted that it
was right for them to submit to such a law, he declared that
such a law was not for him. Besides, if the weak and the oppressed are sympathetic, they cease altogether to be so when
they in their turn become oppressors. Christophe, who had only
recently been shouting out to the honest men living in isolation:
"Unite! Unite!" had a most unpleasant sensation when for the
first time he found himself in the midst of such unions of honest
men, all mixed up with other men who were less honest, and
yet were endowed with their force, their rights, and only too
ready to abuse them. The best people, those whom Christophe
loved, the friends whom he had met in The House, on every
floor, drew no sort of profit from these fighting combinations.
They were too sensitive at heart and too timid not to be scared:
they were fated to be the first to be crushed out of existence by
them. Face to face with the working-class movement they were
in the same position as Olivier and the most warmly generous of
the young men of the middle-class. Their sympathies were with
the workers organizing themselves. But they had been brought
up in the cult of liberty: now liberty was exactly what the revolutionaries cared for least of all. Besides, who is there nowadays that cares for liberty? A select few who have no sort of
influence over the world. Liberty is passing through dark days.
The Popes of Rome proscribe the light of reason. The Popes
of Paris put out the light of the heavens. And M. Pataud
puts out the lights of the streets. Everywhere imperialism
is triumphant: the theocratic imperialism of the Church of
Rome: the military imperialism of the mercantile and mystic
monarchies: the bureaucratic imperialism of the republics of
Freemasonry and covetousness: the dictatorial imperialism of
the revolutionary committees. Poor liberty, thou art not in
this world! . . . The abuse of power preached and practised by
the revolutionaries revolted Christophe and Olivier. They had
little regard for the blacklegs who refuse to suffer for the common cause. But it seemed abominable to them that the others
should claim the right to use force against them.—And yet it
is necessary to take sides. Nowadays the choice in fact lies not
between imperialism and liberty, but between one imperialism
and another. Olivier said:

" Neither.   I am for the oppressed."

Christophe hated the tyranny of the oppressors no less.   But he was dragged into the wake of force in the track of the army of the working-classes in revolt.

He was hardly aware that it was so.   He would tell his companions in the restaurant that he was not with them.

" As long as you are only out for material interests," he would say, " you don't interest me.   The day when you march out for a belief then I shall be with you.   Otherwise, what have I to do with the conflict between one man's belly and another's? I am an artist; it is my duty to defend art; I have no right to enroll myself in the service of a party.   I am perfectly aware that recently certain ambitious writers, impelled by a desire for an unwholesome popularity, have set a bad example.   It seems to me that they have not rendered any great service to the cause which they defended in that way: but they have certainly betrayed art.   It is our, the artists', business to save the light of the intellect.   We have no right to obscure it with your blind struggles.   Who shall hold the light aloft if we let it fall? You will be glad enough to find it still intact after the battle. There must always be workers busy keeping up the fire in the engine, while there is fighting on the deck of the ship.   To understand everything is to hate nothing.   The artist is the compass which, through the raging of the storm, points steadily to the north."

They regarded him as a maker of phrases, and said that, if he were talking of compasses, it was very clear that he had lost his: and they gave themselves the pleasure of indulging in a little friendly contempt at his expense.   In their eyes an artist was a shirker who contrived to work as little and as agreeably as possible.

He replied that he worked as hard as they did, harder even, and that he was not nearly so afraid of work.   Nothing disgusted him so much as *sabotage,* the deliberate bungling of work, and skulking raised to the level of a principle.

" All these wretched people," he would say, " afraid for their own skins! . . .   Good Lord! I've never stopped working since I was eight.   You people don't love your work; at heart you're just common men. . . .   If only you were capable of destroying

the Old World! But you can't do it. You don't even want
to. No, you don't even want to. It is all very well for you to
go about shrieking menace and pretending you're going to exterminate the human race. You have only one thought: to get
the upper hand and lie snugly in the warm beds of the middle-
classes. Except for a few hundred poor devils, navvies, who
are always ready to break their bones or other people's bones
for no particular reason,—just for fun—or for the pain, the age-
old pain with which they are simply bursting, the whole lot of
you think of nothing but deserting the camp and going over to
the ranks of the middle-classes on the first opportunity. You
become Socialists, journalists, lecturers, men of letters, deputies,
Ministers. . . . Bah! Bah! Don't you go howling about so-
and-so! You're no better. You say he is a traitor? . . . Good.
Whose turn next? You'll all come to it. There is not one of
you who can resist the bait. How could you? There is not
one of you who believes in the immortality of the soul. You
are just so many bellies, I tell you. Empty bellies thinking of
nothing but being filled."

Thereupon they would all lose their tempers and all talk at
once. And in the heat of the argument it would often happen
that Christophe, whirled away by his passion, would become more
revolutionary than the others. In vain did he fight against it:
his intellectual pride, his complacent conception of a purely
esthetic world, made for the joy of the spirit, would sink deep
into the ground at the sight of injustice. Esthetic, a world in
which eight men out of ten live in nakedness and want, in physical and moral wretchedness? Oh! come! A man must be an
impudent creature of privilege who would dare to claim as
much. An artist like Christophe, in his inmost conscience, could
not but be on the side of the working-classes. What man more
than the spiritual worker has to suffer from the immorality of
social conditions, from the scandalously unequal partition of
wealth among men? The artist dies of hunger or becomes a
millionaire for no other reason than the caprice of fashion and
of those who speculate on fashion. A society which suffers its
best men to die or gives them extravagant rewards is a monstrous society: it must be swept and put in order. Every man,
whether he works or no, has a right to a living minimum.

Every kind of work, good or mediocre, should be rewarded, not according to its real value—(who can be the infallible judge of that?)—but according to the normal legitimate needs of the worker. Society can and should assure the artist, the scientist, and the inventor an income sufficient to guarantee that they have the means and the time yet further to grace and honor it. Nothing more. The *Gioconda* is not worth a million. There is no relation between a sum of money and a work of art: a work of art is neither above nor below money: it is outside it. It is not a question of payment: it is a question of allowing the artist to live. Give him enough to feed him, and allow him to work in peace. It is absurd and horrible to try to make him a robber of another's property. This thing must be put bluntly: every man who has more than is necessary for his livelihood and that of his family, and for the normal development of his intelligence, is a thief and a robber. If he has too much, it means that others have too little. How often have we smiled sadly to hear tell of the inexhaustible wealth of France, and the number of great fortunes, we workers, and toilers, and intellectuals, and men and women who from our very birth have been given up to the wearying task of keeping ourselves from dying of hunger, often struggling in vain, often seeing the very best of us succumbing to the pain of it all,—we who are the moral and intellectual treasure of the nation! You who have more than your share of the wealth of the world are rich at the cost of our suffering and our poverty. That troubles you not at all: you have sophistries and to spare to reassure you: the sacred rights of property, the fair struggle for life, the supreme interests of that Moloch, the State and Progress, that fabulous monster, that problematical Better to which men sacrifice the Good,—the Good of other men.—But for all that, the fact remains, and all your sophistries will never manage to deny it: " You have too much to live on. We have not enough. And we are as good as you. And some of us are better than the whole lot of you put together."

So Christophe was affected by the intoxication of the passions with which he was surrounded. Then he was astonished at his own bursts of eloquence. But he did not attach any importance to them. He was amused by such easily roused excitement, which he attributed to the bottle. His only regret was that the wine was not better, and he would belaud the wines of the Rhine. He still thought that he was detached from revolutionary ideas. But there arose the singular phenomenon that Christophe brought into the discussion, if not the upholding of them, a steadily increasing passion, while that of his companions seemed in comparison to diminish.

As a matter of fact, they had fewer illusions than he. Even the most violent leaders, the men who were most feared by the middle-classes, were at heart uncertain and horribly middle-class. Coquard, with his laugh like a stallion's neigh, shouted at the top of his voice and made terrifying gestures: but he only half believed what he was saying: it was all for the pleasure of talking, giving orders, being active: he was a braggart of violence. He knew the cowardice of the middle-classes through and through, and he loved terrorizing them by showing that he was stronger than they: he was quite ready to admit as much to Christophe, and to laugh over it. Graillot criticized everything, and everything anybody tried to do: he made every plan come to nothing. Joussier was for ever affirming, for he was unwilling ever to be in the wrong. He would be perfectly aware of the inherent weakness of his line of argument, but that would make him only the more obstinate in sticking to it: he would have sacrificed the victory of his cause to his pride of principle. But he would rush from extremes of bullet-headed faith to extremes of ironical pessimism, when he would bitterly condemn the lie of all systems of ideas and the futility of all efforts.

The majority of the working-classes were just the same. They would suddenly relapse from the intoxication of words into the depths of discouragement. They had immense illusions: but they were based upon nothing: they had not won them in pain or forged them for themselves: they had received them ready-made, by that law of the smallest effort which led them for their amusements to the slaughter-house and the blatant show. They suffered from an incurable indolence of mind for which there were only too many excuses: they were like weary beasts asking only to be suffered to lie down and in peace to ruminate over their end and their dreams. But once they had

slept off their dreams there was nothing left but an even greater
weariness and the doleful dumps. They were for ever flaring
up to a new leader: and very soon they became suspicious of him
and spurned him. The sad part of it all was that they were
never wrong: one after another their leaders were dazzled by the
bait of wealth, success, or vanity: for one Joussier, who was kept
from temptation by the consumption under which he was wasting
away, a brave crumbling to death, how many leaders were there
who betrayed the people or grew weary of the fight! They were
victims of the secret sore which was devouring the politicians of
every party in those days: demoralization through women and
money, women and money,—(the two scourges are one and the
same).—In the Government as in the ministry there were men
of first-rate talent, men who had in them the stuff of which great
statesmen are made—(they might have been great statesmen in
the days of Richelieu, perhaps) ;—but they lacked faith and
character: the need, the habit, the weariness of pleasure, had
sapped them: when they were engaged upon vast schemes they
fumbled into incoherent action, or they would suddenly fling
up the whole thing, while important business was in progress,
desert their country or their cause for rest and pleasure. They
were brave enough to meet death in battle: but very few of the
leaders were capable of dying in harness, at their posts, never
budging, with their hands upon the rudder and their eyes un-
swervingly fixed upon the invisible goal.

The revolution was hamstrung by the consciousness of the
fundamental weakness. The leaders of the working-classes spent
part of their time in blaming each other. Their strikes always
failed as a result of the perpetual dissensions between the leaders
and the trades-unions, between the reformers and the revolutionaries—and of the profound timidity that underlay their
blustering threats—and of the inherited sheepishness that made
the rebels creep once more beneath the yoke upon the first legal
sentence,—and of the cowardly egoism and the baseness of those
who profited by the revolt of others to creep a little nearer the
masters, to curry favor and win a rich reward for their disinterested devotion. Not to speak of the disorder inherent in all
crowds, the anarchy of the people. They tried hard to create
corporate strikes which should assume a revolutionary character:

but they were not willing to be treated as revolutionaries. They had no liking for bayonets. They fancied that it was possible to make an omelette without eggs. In any case, they preferred the eggs to be broken by other people.

Olivier watched, observed, and was not surprised. From the very outset he had recognized the great inferiority of these men to the work which they were supposed to be accomplishing: but he had also recognized the inevitable force that swept them on: and he saw that Christophe, unknown to himself, was being carried on by the stream. But the current would have nothing to do with himself, who would have asked nothing better than to let himself be carried away.

It was a strong current: it was sweeping along an enormous mass of passions. interest, and faith, all jostling, pushing, merging into each other, boiling and frothing and eddying this way and that. The leaders were in the van; they were the least free of all, for they were pushed forward, and perhaps they had the least faith of all: there had been a time when they believed: they were like the priests against whom they had so loudly railed, imprisoned by their vows, by the faith they once had had, and were forced to profess to the bitter end. Behind them the common herd was brutal, vacillating, and short-sighted. The great majority had a sort of random faith, because the current had now set in the direction of Utopia: but a little while, and they would cease to believe because the current had changed. Many believed from a need of action, a desire for adventure, from romantic folly. Others believed from a sort of impertinent logic, which was stripped of all common sense. Some believed from goodness of heart. The self-seeking only made use of ideas as weapons for the fight: their eye was for the main chance: they were fighting for a definite sum as wages for a definite number of hours' work. The worst of all were nursing a secret hope of wreaking a brutal revenge for the wretched lives they had led.

But the current which bore them all along was wiser than they: it knew where it was going. What did it matter that at any moment it might dash up against the dyke of the Old World! Olivier foresaw that a social revolution in these days would be squashed. But he knew also that revolution would achieve its end through defeat as well as through victory: for the oppressors only accede to the demands of the oppressed when the oppressed inspire them with fear. And so the violence of the revolutionaries was of no less service to their cause than the justice of that cause. Both violence and justice were part and parcel of the plan of that blind and certain force which moves the herd of human kind. . . .

" For consider what you are, you whom the Master has summoned. If the body be considered there are not many among you who are wise, or strong, or noble. But He has chosen the foolish things of the world to confound the wise; and He has chosen the weak things of the world to confound the strong: and He has chosen the vile things of the world and the despised things, and the things that are not, to the destruction of those things that are. . . ."

And yet, whatever may be the Master who orders all things,— (Reason or Unreason),—and although the social organization prepared by syndicalism might constitute a certain comparative stage in progress for the future, Olivier did not think it worth while for Christophe and himself to scatter the whole of their power of illusion and sacrifice in this earthy combat which would open no new world. His mystic hopes of the revolution were dashed to the ground. The people seemed to him no better and hardly any more sincere than the other classes: there was not enough difference between them and others. In the midst of the torrent of interests and muddy passions, Olivier's gaze and heart were attracted by the little islands of independent spirits, the little groups of true believers who emerged here and there like flowers on the face of the waters. In vain do the elect seek to mingle with the mob: the elect always come together,—the elect of all classes and all parties,—the bearers of the fire of the world. And it is their sacred duty to see to it that the fire in their hands shall never die down.

Olivier had already made his choice.

A few houses away from that in which he lived was a cobbler's booth, standing a little below the level of the street,—a few planks nailed together, with dirty windows and panes of paper.

It was entered by three steps down, and you had to stoop to stand up in it. There was just room for a shelf of old shoes, and two stools. All day long, in accordance with the classic tradition of cobbling, the master of the place could be heard singing. He used to whistle, drum on the soles of the boots, and in a husky voice roar out coarse ditties and revolutionary songs, or chaff the women of the neighborhood as they passed by. A magpie with a broken wing, which was always hopping about on the pavement, used to come from a porter's lodge and pay him a visit. It would stand on the first step at the entrance to the booth and look at the cobbler. He would stop for a moment to crack a dirty joke with the bird in a piping voice, or he would insist on whistling the *Internationale*. The bird would stand with its beak in the air, listening gravely: every now and then it would bob with its beak down by way of salutation, and it would awkwardly flap its wings in order to regain its balance: then it would suddenly turn round, leaving the cobbler in the middle of a sentence, and fly away with its wing and a bit on to the back of a bench, from whence it would hurl defiance at the dogs of the quarter. Then the cobbler would return to his leather, and the flight of his auditor would by no means restrain him from going through with his harangue.

He was fifty-six, with a jovial wayward manner, little merry eyes under enormous eyebrows, with a bald top to his head rising like an egg out of the nest of his hair, hairy ears, a black gap-toothed mouth that gaped like a well when he roared with laughter, a very thick dirty beard, at which he used to pluck in handfuls with his long nails that were always filthy with wax. He was known in the district as Daddy Feuillet, or Feuillette, or Daddy la Feuillette—and to tease him they used to call him La Fayette: for politically the old fellow was one of the reds: as a young man he had been mixed up in the Commune, sentenced to death, and finally deported: he was proud of his memories, and was always rancorously inclined to lump together Badinguet, Galliffet, and Foutriquet. He was a regular attendant at the revolutionary meetings, and an ardent admirer of Coquard and the vengeful idea that he was always prophesying with much beard-wagging and a voice of thunder. He never missed one of his speeches, drank in his words, laughed at his jokes with head thrown back and gaping mouth, foamed at his invective, and rejoiced in the fight and the promised paradise. Next day, in his booth, he would read over the newspaper report of the speeches: he would read them aloud to himself and his apprentice: and to taste their full sweetness he would have them read aloud to him, and used to box his apprentice's ears if he skipped a line. As a consequence he was not always very punctual in the delivery of his work when he had promised it: on the other hand, his work was always sound: it might wear out the user's feet, but there was no wearing out his leather. . . .

The old fellow had in his shop a grandson of thirteen, a hunchback, a sickly, rickety boy, who used to run his errands, and was a sort of apprentice. The boy's mother had left her family when she was seventeen to elope with a worthless fellow who had sunk into hooliganism, and before very long had been caught, sentenced, and so disappeared from the scene. She was left alone with the child, deserted by her family, and devoted herself to the upbringing of the boy Emmanuel. She had transferred to him all the love and hatred she had had for her lover. She was a woman of a violent and jealous character, morbid to a degree. She loved her child to distraction, brutally ill-treated him, and, when he was ill, was crazed with despair. When she was in a bad temper she would send him to bed without any dinner, without so much as a piece of bread. When she was dragging him along through the streets, if he grew tired and would not go on and slipped down to the ground, she would kick him on to his feet again. She was amazingly incoherent in her use of words, and she used to pass swiftly from tears to a hysterical mood of gaiety. She died. The cobbler took the boy, who was then six years old. He loved him dearly: but he had his own way of showing it, which consisted in bullying the boy, battering him with a large assortment of insulting names, pulling his ears, and clouting him over the head from morning to night by way of teaching him his job: and at the same time he grounded him thoroughly in his own social and anti-clerical catechism.

Emmanuel knew that his grandfather was not a bad man: but he was always prepared to raise his arm to ward off his blows: the old fellow used to frighten him, especially on the evenings when he got drunk. For Daddy la Feuillette had not come by his nickname for nothing: he used to get tipsy twice or thrice a month: then he used to talk all over the place, and laugh, and act the swell, and always in the end he used to give the boy a good thrashing. His bark was worse than his bite. But the boy was terrified: his ill-health made him more sensitive than other children: he was precociously intelligent, and he had inherited a fierce and unbalanced capacity for feeling from his mother. He was overwhelmed by his grandfather's brutality, and also by his revolutionary harangues,—(for the two things went together: it was particularly when the old man was drunk that he was inclined to hold forth).—His whole being quivered in response to outside impressions, just as the booth shook with the passing of the heavy omnibuses. In his crazy imagination there were mingled, like the humming vibrations of a belfry, his day-to-day sensations, the wretchedness of his childhood, his deplorable memories of premature experience, stories of the Commune, scraps of evening lectures and newspaper feuilletons, speeches at meetings, and the vague, uneasy, and violent sexual instincts which his parents had transmitted to him. All these things together formed a monstrous grim dream-world, from the dense night, the chaos and miasma of which there darted dazzling rays of hope.

The cobbler used sometimes to drag his apprentice with him to Amélie's restaurant. There it was that Olivier noticed the little hunchback with the voice of a lark. Sitting and never talking to the workpeople, he had had plenty of time to study the boy's sickly face, with its jutting brow and shy, humiliated expression: he had heard the coarse jokes that had been thrown at the boy, jokes which were met with silence and a faint shuddering tremor. During certain revolutionary utterances he had seen the boy's soft brown eyes light up with the chimerical ecstasy of the future happiness,—a happiness which, even if he were ever to realize it, would make but small difference in his stunted life. At such moments his expression would illuminate his ugly face in such a way as to make its ugliness forgotten. Even the fair Berthe was struck by it; one day she told him of it, and, without a word of warning, kissed him on the lips. The boy started back: he went pale and shuddering, and flung away in disgust. The young woman had no time to notice him: she

was already quarreling with Joussier. Only Olivier observed
Emmanuel's uneasiness: he followed the boy with his eyes, and
saw him withdraw into the shadow with his hands trembling,
head down, looking down at the floor, and darting glances of desire and irritation at the girl. Olivier went up to him, spoke to
him gently and politely and soothed him. . . . Who can tell all
that gentleness can bring to a heart deprived of all consideration? It is like a drop of water falling upon parched earth,
greedily to be sucked up. It needed only a few words, a smile,
for the boy Emmanuel in his heart of hearts to surrender to
Olivier, and to determine to have Olivier for his friend. Thereafter, when he met him in the street and discovered that they
were neighbors, it seemed to him to be a mysterious sign from
Fate that he had not been mistaken. He used to watch for
Olivier to pass the booth, and say good-day to him: and if ever
Olivier were thinking of other things and did not glance in his
direction, then Emmanuel would be hurt and sore.

It was a great day for him when Olivier came into Daddy
Feuillette's shop to leave an order. When the work was done
Emmanuel took it to Olivier's rooms; he had watched for him
to come home so as to be sure of finding him in. Olivier was
lost in thought, hardly noticed him, paid the bill, and said nothing: the boy seemed to wait, looked from right to left, and began
reluctantly to move away. Olivier, in his kindness, guessed
what was happening inside the boy: he smiled and tried to talk
to him in spite of the awkwardness he always felt in talking to
any of the people. But now he was able to find words simple
and direct. An intuitive perception of suffering made him see
in the boy—(rather too simply)—a little bird wounded by life,
like himself, seeking consolation with his head under his wing,
sadly huddled up on his perch, dreaming of wild flights into
the light. A feeling that was something akin to instinctive confidence brought the boy closer to him: he felt the attraction of
the silent soul, which made no moan and used no harsh words,
a soul wherein he could take shelter from the brutality of the
streets; and the room, thronged with books, filled with book-
cases wherein there slumbered the dreams of the ages, filled him
with an almost religious awe. He made no attempt to evade
Olivier's questions: he replied readily, with sudden gasps and

starts of shyness and pride: but he had no power of expression. Carefully, patiently, Olivier unswathed his obscure stammering soul: little by little he was able to read his hopes and his absurdly touching faith in the new birth of the world. He had no desire to laugh, though he knew that the dream was impossible, and would never change human nature. The Christians also have dreamed of impossible things, and they have not changed human nature. From the time of Pericles to the time of M. Fallières when has there been any moral progress? . . . But all faith is beautiful: and when the light of an old faith dies down it is meet to salute the kindling of the new: there will never be too many. With a curious tenderness Olivier saw the uncertain light gleaming in the boy's mind. What a strange mind it was! . . . Olivier was not altogether able to follow the movement of his thoughts, which were incapable of any sustained effort of reason, progressing in hops and jerks, and lagging behind in conversation, unable to follow, clutching in some strange way at an image called up by a word spoken some time before, then suddenly catching up, rushing ahead, weaving a commonplace thought or an ordinary cautious phrase into an enchanted world, a crazy and heroic creed. The boy's soul, slumbering and waking by fits and starts, had a puerile and mighty need of optimism: to every idea in art or science thrown out to it, it would add some complacently melodramatic tag, which would link it up with and satisfy its own chimerical dreams.

As an experiment Olivier tried reading aloud to the boy on Sundays. He thought that he was most likely to be interested by realistic and familiar stories: he read him Tolstoy's *Memories of Childhood*. They made no impression on the boy: he said:

"That's quite all right. Things are like that. One knows that."

And he could not understand why anybody should take so much trouble to write about real things. . . .

"He's just a boy," he would say disdainfully, "just an ordinary little boy."

He was no more responsive to the interest of history: and science bored him: it was to him no more than a tiresome intro-

duction to a fairy-tale: the invisible forces brought into the service of man were like terrible genii laid low. What was the use
of so much explanation? When a man finds something it is no
good his telling how he found it, he need only tell what it is
that he has found. The analysis of thought is a luxury of the
upper-classes. The souls of the people demand synthesis, ideas
ready-made, well or ill, or rather ill-made than well, but all
tending to action, and composed of the gross realities of life,
and charged with electricity. Of all the literature open to Emmanuel that which most nearly touched him was the epic pathos
of certain passages in Hugo and the fuliginous rhetoric of the
revolutionary orators, whom he did not rightly understand,
characters who no more understood themselves than Hugo did.
To him as to them the world was not an incoherent collection of
reasons or facts, but an infinite space, steeped in darkness and
quivering with light, while through the night there passed the
beating of mighty wings all bathed in the sunlight. Olivier
tried in vain to make him grasp his cultivated logic. The boy's
rebellious and weary soul slipped through his fingers: and it
sank back with a sigh of comfort and relief into the indeterminate haze and the chafing of its own sensation and hallucinations, like a woman in love giving herself with eyes closed to her
lover.

Olivier was at once attracted and disconcerted by the qualities in the child so much akin to his own:—loneliness, proud
weakness, idealistic ardor,—and so very different,—the unbalanced mind, the blind and unbridled desires, the savage sensuality which had no idea of good and evil, as they are defined in
ordinary morality. He had only a partial glimpse of that sensuality which would have terrified him had he known its full
extent. He never dreamed of the existence of the world of uneasy passions stirring and seething in the heart and mind of his
little friend. Our bourgeois atavism has given us too much wis
dom. We dare not even look within ourselves. If we were
to tell a hundredth part of the dreams that come to an ordinary honest man, or of the desires which come into being in the
body of a chaste woman, there would be a scandal and an outcry. Silence such monsters! Bolt and bar their cage! But
let us admit that they exist, and that in the souls of the young

they are insecurely fettered.—The boy had all the erotic desires
and dreams which we agree among ourselves to regard as perverse: they would suddenly rise up unawares and take him by
the throat: they would come in gusts and squalls: and they only
gained in intensity and heat through the irritation set up by the
isolation to which his ugliness condemned him. Olivier knew
nothing of all this. Emmanuel was ashamed in his presence.
He felt the contagion of such peace and purity. The example
of such a life was a taming influence upon him. The boy felt a
passionate love for Olivier. And his suppressed passions rushed
headlong into tumultuous dreams of human happiness, social
brotherhood, fantastic aviation, wild barbaric poetry—a whole
heroic, erotic, childish, splendid, vulgar world in which his intelligence and his will were tossed hither and thither in mental
loafing and fever.

He did not have much time for indulging himself in this way,
especially in his grandfather's booth, for the old man was never
silent for a minute on end, but was always whistling, hammering, and talking from morning to night; but there is always
room for dreams. How many voyages of the mind one can make
standing up with wide-open eyes in the space of a second!—
Manual labor is fairly well suited to intermittent thought. The
working-man's mind would be hard put to it without an effort
of the will to follow a closely reasoned chain of argument: if he
does manage to do so he is always certain to miss a link here and
there: but in the intervals of rhythmic movement ideas crop up
and mental images come floating to the surface: the regular movements of the body send them flying upwards like sparks under
the smith's bellows. The thought of the people! It is just
smoke and fire, a shower of glittering sparks fading away, glowing, then fading away once more! But sometimes a spark will
be carried away by the wind to set fire to the dried forests and
the fat ricks of the upper-classes. . . .

Olivier procured Emmanuel a place in a printing house. It
was the boy's wish, and his grandfather did not oppose it; he
was glad to see his grandson better educated than himself, and
he had a great respect for printer's ink. In his new trade the
boy found his work more exhausting than in the old: but
he felt more free to think among the throng of workers than

in the little shop where he used to sit alone with his grandfather.

The best time of day was the dinner hour. He would escape
and get right away from the horde of artisans crowding round
the little tables on the pavement and into the wineshops of the
district, and limp along to the square hard by: and there he
would sit astride a bench under a spreading chestnut-tree, near
a bronze dancing faun with grapes in his hands, and untie his
brown-paper parcel of bread and meat, and munch it slowly,
surrounded by a little crowd of sparrows. Over the green turf
little fountains spread the trickling web of their soft rain.
Round-eyed, slate-blue pigeons cooed in a sunlit tree. And all
about him was the perpetual hum of Paris, the roar of the carriages, the surging sea of footsteps, the familiar street-cries, the
gay distant whistle of a china-mender, a navvy's hammer ringing
out on the cobblestones, the noble music of a fountain—all the
fevered golden trappings of the Parisian dream.—And the little hunchback, sitting astride his bench, with his mouth full,
never troubling to swallow, would drowse off into a delicious
torpor, in which he lost all consciousness of his twisted spine and
his craven soul, and was all steeped in an indeterminate intoxicating happiness.

" . . . Soft warm light, sun of justice that art to shine for
us to-morrow, art thou not shining now? It is all so good, so
beautiful! We are rich, we are strong, we are hale, we love . . .
I love, I love all men, all men love me. . . . Ah! How splendid
it all is! How splendid it will be to-morrow! . . ."

The factory hooters would sound: the boy would come to his
senses, swallow down his mouthful, take a long drink at the
Wallace fountain near by, slip back into his hunchbacked shell,
and go limping and hobbling back to his place in the printing
works in front of the cases of magic letters which would one
day write the *Mene, Mene, Tekel, Upharsin,* of the Revolution.

Daddy Feuillet had a crony, Trouillot, the stationer on the
other side of the street. He kept a stationery and haberdashery
shop, in the windows of which were displayed pink and green
bonbons in green bottles, and pasteboard dolls without arms or

legs.   From either side of the street, one standing on his doorstep, the other in his shop, the two old men used to exchange
winks and nods and a whole elaborate code of pantomimic gesture.   At intervals, when the cobbler was tired of hammering,
and had, as he used to say, the cramp in his buttocks, they
would hail each other, La Feuillette in his shrill treble, Trouillot with a muffled roar, like a husky calf; and they would go off
together and take a nip at a neighboring bar.   They were never
in any hurry 'to return.   They were both infernally loquacious.
They had known each other for half a century.   The stationer
also had played a little walking-on part in the great melodrama
of 1871.   To see the fat placid creature with his black cap on
his head and his white blouse, and his gray, heavy-dragoon
mustache, and his dull light-blue bloodshot eyes with heavy
pouches under the lids, and his flabby shining cheeks, always in
a perspiration, slow-footed, gouty, out of breath, heavy of speech,
no one would ever have thought it.   But he had lost none of the
illusions of the old days.   He had spent some years as a refugee
in Switzerland, where he had met comrades of all nations, notably many Russians, who had initiated him in the beauties of an-
archic brotherhood.   On that point he disagreed with La Feuillette, who was a proper Frenchman, an adherent of the strong
line and of absolutism in freedom.   For the rest, they were
equally firm in their belief in the social revolution and the working-class *salente* of the future.   Each was devoted to a leader in
whose person he saw incarnate the ideal man that each would
have liked to be.   Trouillot was for Joussier, La Feuillette for
Coquard.   They used to engage in interminable arguments about
the points on which they were divided, being quite confident that
the thoughts upon which they agreed were definitely decided;—
(and they were so sure of their common ground that they were
never very far from believing, in their cups, that it was a matter of hard fact).—The cobbler was the more argumentative of
the two.   He believed as a matter of reason: or at least he flattered himself that he did, for. Heaven knows, his reason was of
a very peculiar kind, and could have fitted the foot of no other
man.   However, though he was less skilled in argument than in
cobbling, he was always insisting that other minds should be
shod to his own measure.   The stationer was more indolent and

less combative, and never worried about proving his faith. A man only tries to prove what he doubts himself. He had no doubt. His unfailing optimism always made him see things as he wanted to see them, and not see things or forget them immediately when they were otherwise. Whether he did so wilfully or from apathy he saved himself from trouble of any sort: experience to the contrary slipped off his hide without leaving a mark.—The two of them were romantic babies with no sense of reality, and the revolution, the mere sound of the name of which was enough to make them drunk, was only a jolly story they told themselves, and never knew whether it would ever happen, or whether it had actually happened. And the two of them firmly believed in the God of Humanity merely by the transposition of the habits they had inherited from their forbears, who for centuries had bowed before the Son of Man.—It goes without saying that both men were anti-clerical.

The amusing part of it was that the honest stationer lived with a very pious niece who did just what she liked with him. She was a very dark little woman, plump, with sharp eyes and a gift of volubility spiced with a strong Marseilles accent, and she was the widow of a clerk in the Department of Commerce. When she was left alone with no money, with a little girl, and received a home with her uncle, the common little creature gave herself airs, and was more than a little inclined to think that she was doing her shop-keeping relation a great favor by serving in his shop: she reigned there with the airs of a fallen queen, though, fortunately for her uncle's business and his customers, her arrogance was tempered by her natural exuberance and her need of talking. As befitted a person of her distinction, Madame Alexandrine was royalist and clerical, and she used to parade her feelings with a zeal that was all the more indiscreet as she took a malicious delight in teasing the old miscreant in whose house she had taken up her abode. She had set herself up as mistress of the house, and regarded herself as responsible for the conscience of the whole household: if she was unable to convert her uncle—(she had vowed to capture him *in extremis*),—she busied herself to her heart's content with sprinkling the devil with holy water. She fixed pictures of Our Lady of Lourdes and Saint Anthony of Padua on the walls: she decorated the mantelpiece with little painted images in glass cases: and in the proper season she made a little chapel of the months of Mary with little blue candles in her daughter's bedroom. It was impossible to tell which was the predominant factor in her aggressive piety, real affection for the uncle she desired to convert or a wicked joy in worrying the old man.

He put up with it apathetically and sleepily: he preferred not to run the risk of rousing the tempestuous ire of his terrible niece: it was impossible to fight against such a wagging tongue: he desired peace above all things. Only once did he lose his temper, and that was when a little Saint Joseph made a surreptitious attempt to creep into his room and take up his stand above his bed: on this point he gained the day: for he came very near to having an apoplectic fit, and his niece was frightened: she did not try the experiment again. For the rest he gave in, and pretended not to see: the odor of sanctity made him feel very uncomfortable: but he tried not to think of it. On the other hand they were at one in pampering the girl, little Reine, or Rainette.

She was twelve or thirteen, and was always ill. For some months past she had been on her back with hip disease, with the whole of one side of her body done up in plaster of Paris like a little Daphne in her shell. She had eyes like a hurt dog's, and her skin was pallid and pale like a plant grown out of the sun: her head was too big for her body, and her fair hair, which was very soft and very tightly drawn back, made it appear even bigger: but she had an expressive and sweet face, a sharp little nose, and a childlike expression. The mother's piety had assumed in the child, in her sickness and lack of interest, a fervid character. She used to spend hours in telling her beads, a string of corals, blessed by the Pope: and she would break off in her prayers to kiss it passionately. She did next to nothing all day long: needlework made her tired: Madame Alexandrine had not given her a taste for it. She did little more than read a few insipid tracts, or a stupid miraculous story, the pretentious and bald style of which seemed to her the very flower of poetry,—or the criminal reports illustrated in color in the Sunday papers which her stupid mother used to give her. She would perhaps do a little crochet-work, moving her lips, and paying less atten-

tion to her needle than to the conversation she would hold with
some favorite saint or even with God Himself. For it is useless to pretend that it is necessary to be Joan of Arc to have
such visitations: every one of us has had them. Only, as a rule,
our celestial visitors leave the talking to us as we sit by the fireside: and they say never a word. Rainette never dreamed of
taking exception to it: silence gives consent. Besides, she had so
much to tell them that she hardly gave them time to reply: she
used to answer for them. She was a silent chatterer: she had
inherited her mother's volubility: but her fluency was drawn off
in inward speeches like a stream disappearing underground.—
Of course she was a party to the conspiracy against her uncle
with the object of procuring his conversion: she rejoiced over
every inch of the house wrested by the spirit of light from the
spirit of darkness: and on more than one occasion she had sewn
a holy medallion on to the inside of the lining of the old man's
coat or had slipped into one of his pockets the bead of a rosary,
which her uncle, in order to please her, had pretended not to
notice.—This seizure by the two pious women of the bitter foe
of the priests was a source of indignation and joy to the cobbler.
He had an inexhaustible store of coarse pleasantries on the subject of women who wear breeches: and he used to jeer at his
friend for letting himself be under their thumb. As a matter
of fact he had no right to scoff: for he had himself been afflicted for twenty years with a shrewish cross-grained wife, who
had always regarded him as an old scamp and had taken him
down a peg or two. But he was always careful not to mention
her. The stationer was a little ashamed, and used to defend
himself feebly, and in a mealy voice profess a Kropotkinesque
gospel of tolerance.

Rainette and Emmanuel were friends. They had seen each
other every day ever since they were children. To be quite accurate, Emmanuel only rarely ventured to enter the house.
Madame Alexandrine used to regard him with an unfavorable
eye as the grandson of an unbeliever and a horrid little dwarf.
But Rainette used to spend the day on a sofa near the window
on the ground floor. Emmanuel used to tap at the window as
he passed, and, flattening his nose against the panes, he would
make a face by way of greeting. In summer, when the window

was left open, he would stop and lean his arms on the window-sill, which was a little high for him;—(he fancied that this attitude was flattering to himself and that, his shoulders being shrugged up in such a pose of intimacy, it might serve to disguise his actual deformity);—and they would talk. Rainette did not have too many visitors, and she never noticed that Emmanuel was hunchbacked. Emmanuel, who was afraid and mortified in the presence of girls, made an exception in favor of Rainette. The little invalid, who was half petrified, was to him something intangible and far removed, something almost outside existence. Only on the evening when the fair Berthe kissed him on the lips, and the next day too, he avoided Rainette with an instinctive feeling of repulsion: he passed the house without stopping and hung his head: and he prowled about far away, fearfully and suspiciously, like a pariah dog. Then he returned. There was so little woman in her! As he was passing on his way home from the works, trying to make himself as small as possible among the bookbinders in their long working-blouses like nightgowns—busy merry young women whose hungry eyes stripped him as he passed,—how eagerly he would scamper away to Rainette's window! He was grateful for his little friend's infirmity: with her he could give himself airs of superiority and even be a little patronizing. With a little swagger he would tell her about the things that happened in the street and always put himself in the foreground. Sometimes in gallant mood he would bring Rainette a little present, roast chestnuts in winter, a handful of cherries in summer. And she used to give him some of the multi-colored sweets that filled the two glass jars in the shop-window: and they would pore over picture postcards together. Those were happy moments: they could both forget the pitiful bodies in which their childish souls were held captive.

But sometimes they would begin to talk, like their elders, of politics and religion. Then they would become as stupid as their elders. It put an end to their sympathy and understanding. She would talk of miracles and the nine days' devotion, or of pious images tricked out with paper lace, and of days of indulgence. He used to tell her that it was all folly and mummery, as he had heard his grandfather say. But when he in turn tried to tell her about the public meetings to which the old man had taken him, and the speeches he had heard, she would stop him contemptuously and tell him that all such folk were drunken sots. Bitterness would creep into their talk. They would get talking about their relations: they would recount the insulting things that her mother and his grandfather had said of each other respectively. Then they would talk about themselves. They tried to say disagreeable things to each other. They managed that without much difficulty. They indulged in coarse gibes. But she was always the more malicious of the two. Then he would go away: and when he returned he would tell her that he had been with other girls, and how pretty they were, and how they had joked and laughed, and how they were going to meet again next Sunday. She would say nothing to that: she used to pretend to despise what he said: and then, suddenly, she would grow angry, and throw her crochet-work at his head, and shout at him to go, and declare that she loathed him: and she would hide her face in her hands. He would leave her on that, not at all proud of his victory. He longed to pull her thin little hands away from her face and to tell her that it was not true. But his pride would not suffer him to return.

One day Rainette had her revenge.—He was with some of the other boys at the works. They did not like him because he used to hold as much aloof from them as possible and never spoke, or talked too well, in a naïvely pretentious way, like a book, or rather like a newspaper article—(he was stuffed with newspaper articles).—That day they had begun to talk of the revolution and the days to come. He waxed enthusiastic and made a fool of himself. One of his comrades brought him up sharp with these brutal words:

"To begin with, you won't be wanted, you're too ugly. In the society of the future, there won't be any hunchbacks. They'll be drowned at birth."

That brought him toppling down from his lofty eloquence. He stopped short, dumfounded. The others roared with laughter. All that afternoon he went about with clenched teeth. In the evening he was going home, hurrying back to hide away in a corner alone with his suffering. Olivier met him: he was struck by his downcast expression: he guessed that he was suffering.

"You are hurt. Why?"

Emmanuel refused to answer. Olivier pressed him kindly. The boy persisted in his silence: but his jaw trembled as though he were on the point of weeping. Olivier took his arm and led him back to his rooms. Although he too had the cruel and instinctive feeling of repulsion from ugliness and disease that is in all who are not born with the souls of sisters of charity, he did not let it appear.

"Some one has hurt you?"

"Yes."

"What did they do?"

The boy laid bare his heart. He said that he was ugly. He said that his comrades had told him that their revolution was not for him.

"It is not for them, either, my boy, nor for us. It is not a single day's affair. It is all for those who will come after us."

The boy was taken aback by the thought that it would be so long deferred.

"Don't you like to think that people are working to give happiness to thousands of boys like yourself, to millions of human beings?"

Emmanuel sighed and said:

"But it would be good to have a little happiness oneself."

"My dear boy, you mustn't be ungrateful. You live in the most beautiful city, in an age that is most rich in marvels; you are not a fool, and you have eyes to see. Think of all the things there are to be seen and loved all around you."

He pointed out a few things.

The boy listened, nodded his head, and said:

"Yes, but I've got to face the fact that I shall always **have** to live in this body of mine!"

"Not at all. You will quit it."

"And that will be the end."

"How do you know that?"

The boy was aghast. Materialism was part and parcel of his grandfather's creed: he thought that it was only the priest-ridden prigs who believed in an eternal life. He knew that his friend was not such a one: and he wondered if Olivier could be speaking seriously. But Olivier held his hand and expounded at length his idealistic faith, and the unity of boundless life,

that has neither beginning nor end, in which all the millions of
creatures and all the million million moments of time are but
rays of the sun, the sole source of it all.   But he did not put it
to him in such an abstract form.   Instinctively, when he talked
to the boy, he adapted himself to his mode of thought;—ancient
legends, the material and profound fancies of old cosmogonies
were called to mind: half in fun, half in earnest, he spoke of
metempsychosis and the succession of countless forms through
which the soul passes and flows, like a spring passing from pool
to pool.   All this was interspersed with reminiscences of Christianity and images taken from the summer evening, the light of
which was cast upon them both.   He was sitting by the open
window, and the boy was standing by his side, and their hands
were clasped.   It was a Saturday evening.   The bells were ringing.   The earliest swallows, only just returned, were skimming
the walls of the houses.   The dim sky was smiling above the
city, which was wrapped in shadow.   The boy held his breath
and listened to the fairy-tale his man friend was telling him.
And Olivier, warmed by the eagerness of his young hearer, was
caught up by the interest of his own stories.

There are decisive moments in life when, just as the electric
lights suddenly flash out in the darkness of a great city, so the
eternal fires flare up in the darkness of the soul.   A spark darting from another soul is enough to transmit the Promethean
fire to the waiting soul.   On that spring evening Olivier's calm
words kindled the light that never dies in the mind hidden in
the boy's deformed body, as in a battered lantern.   He understood none of Olivier's arguments: he hardly heard them.   But
the legends and images which were only beautiful stories and
parables to Olivier, took living shape and form in his mind, and
were most real.   The fairy-tale lived, moved, and breathed all
around him.   And the view framed in the window of the room,
the people passing in the street, rich and poor, the swallows
skimming the walls, the jaded horses dragging their loads along,
the stones of the houses drinking in the cool shadow of the twilight, and the pale heavens where the light was dying—all the
outside world was softly imprinted on his mind, softly as a kiss.
It was but the flash of a moment.   Then the light died down.
He thought of Rainette, and said:

" But the people who go to Mass, the people who believe in God, are all cracked, aren't they? "

Olivier smiled.

" They believe," he said, " as we do. We all believe the same thing. Only their belief is less than ours. They are people who have to shut all the shutters and light the lamp before they can see the light. They see God in the shape of a man. We have keener eyes. But the light that we love is the same."

The boy went home through the dark streets in which the gas-lamps were not yet lit. Olivier's words were ringing in his head. He thought that it was as cruel to laugh at people because they had weak eyes as because they were hunchbacked. And he thought that Rainette had very pretty eyes: and he thought that he had brought tears into them. He could not bear that. He turned and went across to the stationer's. The window was still a little open: and he thrust his head inside and called in a whisper:

" Rainette."

She did not reply.

" Rainette. I beg your pardon."

From the darkness came Rainette's voice, saying:

" Beast! I hate you."

" I'm sorry," he said.

He stopped. Then, on a sudden impulse, he said in an even softer whisper, uneasily, rather shamefacedly:

" You know, Rainette, I believe in God just as you do."

" Really? "

" Really."

He said it only out of generosity. But, as soon as he had said it, he began to believe it.

They stayed still and did not speak. They could not see each other. Outside the night was so fair, so sweet! . . . The little cripple murmured:

" How good it will be when one is dead! "

He could hear Rainette's soft breathing.

He said:

" Good-night, little one."

Tenderly came Rainette's voice:

" Good-night."

He went away comforted. He was glad that Rainette had forgiven him. And, in his inmost soul, the little sufferer was not
sorry to think that he had been the cause of suffering to the girl.

Olivier had gone into retirement once more. It was not long
before Christophe rejoined him. It was very certain that their
place was not with the syndicalist movement: Olivier could not
throw in his lot with such people. And Christophe would not.
Olivier flung away from them in the name of the weak and the
oppressed; Christophe in the name of the strong and the independent. But though they had withdrawn, one to the bows, the
other to the stern, they were still traveling in the vessel which
was carrying the army of the working-classes and the whole of
society. Free and self-confident, Christophe watched with tingling interest the coalition of the proletarians: he needed every
now and then to plunge into the vat of the people: it relaxed
him: he always issued from it fresher and jollier. He kept up
his relation with Coquard, and he went on taking his meals from
time to time at Amélie's. When he was there he lost all self-
control, and would whole-heartedly indulge his fantastic humor:
he was not afraid of paradox: and he took a malicious delight in
pushing his companions to the extreme consequences of their absurd and wild principles. They never knew whether he was speaking in jest or in earnest: for he always grew warm as he talked,
and always in the end lost sight of the paradoxical point of view
with which he had begun. The artist in him was carried away
by the intoxication of the rest. In one such moment of esthetic
emotion in Amélie's back-shop, he improvised a revolutionary
song, which was at once tried, repeated, and on the very next
day spread to every group of the working-classes. He compromised himself. He was marked by the police. Manousse,
who was in touch with the innermost chambers of authority,
was warned by one of his friends, Xavier Bernard, a young official in the police department, who dabbled in literature and expressed a violent admiration for Christophe's music :—(for dilettantism and the spirit of anarchy had spread even to the watch-
dogs of the Third Republic).

" That Krafft of yours is making himself a nuisance," said

Bernard to Manousse. " He's playing the braggart. We know
what it means: but I tell you that those in high places would
be not at all sorry to catch a foreigner—what's more, a German
—in a revolutionary plot: it is the regular method of discredit-
ing the party and casting suspicion upon its doings. If the
idiot doesn't look out we shall be obliged to arrest him. It's
a bore. You'd better warn him."

Manousse did warn Christophe: Olivier begged him to be careful. Christophe did not take their advice seriously.

" Bah! " he said. " Everybody knows there's no harm in me.
I've a perfect right to amuse myself. I like these people. They
work as I do. and they have faith, and so have I. As a matter
of fact, it isn't the same faith; we don't belong to the same
camp. . . . Very well! We'll fight. Not that I don't like fighting. What would you? I can't do as you do, and stay curled
up in my shell. I must breathe. I'm stifled by the comfortable
classes."

Olivier, whose lungs were not so exacting, was quite at his
ease in his small rooms with the tranquil society of his two
women friends, though one of them, Madame Arnaud, had flung
herself into charitable work, and the other, Cécile, was entirely
taken up with looking after the baby, to such an extent that she
could talk of nothing else and to nobody else, in that twittering,
beatific tone which is an attempt to emulate the note of a little
bird, and to mold its formless song into human speech.

His excursion into working-class circles had left him with
two acquaintances. Two men of independent views, like himself. One of them, Guérin, was an upholsterer. He worked
when he felt so disposed, capriciously, though he was very skilful. He loved his trade. He had a natural taste for artistic
things, and had developed it by observation, work, and visits to
museums. Olivier had commissioned him to repair an old piece
of furniture: it was a difficult job, and the upholsterer had done
it with great skill: he had taken a lot of time and trouble over
it: he sent in a very modest bill to Olivier because he was so
delighted with his success. Olivier became interested in him,
questioned him about his life, and tried to find out what he
thought of the working-class movement. Guérin had no thought

about it: he never worried about it. At bottom he did not belong to the working-class, or to any class. He read very little.
All his intellectual development had come about through his
senses, eyes, hands, and the taste innate in the true Parisian.
He was a happy man. The type is by no means rare among
the working people of the lower middle-class, who are one of
the most intelligent classes in the nation: for they realize a fine
balance between manual labor and healthy mental activity.

Olivier's other acquaintance was a man of a more original
kind. He was a postman, named Hurteloup. He was a tall,
handsome creature, with bright eyes, a little fair beard and
mustache, and an open, merry expression. One day he came
with a registered letter, and walked into Olivier's room. While
Olivier was signing the receipt, he wandered round, looking at
the books, with his nose thrust close up to their backs:

"Ha! Ha!" he said. "You have the classics. . . ."

He added:

"I collect books on history. Especially books about Burgundy."

"You are a Burgundian?" asked Olivier.

> "*Bourguignon salé,*
> *L'épée au côté,*
> *La barbe au menton,*
> *Sante Bourguignon,*"

replied the postman with a laugh. "I come from the Avallon
country. I have family papers going back to 1200 and something. . . ."

Olivier was intrigued, and tried to find out more about him.
Hurteloup asked nothing better than to be allowed to talk. He
belonged, in fact, to one of the oldest families in Burgundy.
One of his ancestors had been on crusade with Philippe Auguste:
another had been secretary of State under Henri II. The
family had begun to decay in the seventeenth century. At the
time of the Revolution, ruined and despairing, they had taken
the plunge into the ocean of the people. Now they were coming to the surface again as the result of honest work and the
physical and moral vigor of Hurteloup the postman, and his
fidelity to his race. His greatest hobby had been collecting his-

torical and genealogical documents relating to his family and their native country. In off hours he used to go to the Archives and copy out old papers. Whenever he did not understand them he would go and ask one of the people on his beat, a Chartist or a student at the Sorbonne, to explain. His illustrious ancestry did not turn his head: he would speak of it laughingly, with never a shade of embarrassment or of indignation at the hardness of fate. His careless sturdy gaiety was a delightful thing to see. And when Olivier looked at him he thought of the mysterious ebb and flow of the life of human families, which for centuries flows burningly, for centuries disappears under the ground, and then comes bubbling forth again, having gathered fresh energy from the depths of the earth. And the people seemed to him to be an immense reservoir into which the rivers of the past plunge, while the rivers of the future spring forth again, and, though they bear a new name, are sometimes the same as those of old.

He was in sympathy with both Guérin and Hurteloup: but it is obvious that they could not be company for him: between him and them there was no great possibility of conversation. The boy Emmanuel took up more of his time: he came now almost every evening. Since their magical talk together a revolution had taken place in the boy. He had plunged into reading with a fierce desire for knowledge. He would come back from his books bewildered and stupefied. Sometimes he seemed even less intelligent than before: he would hardly speak: Olivier could only get him to answer in monosyllables: the boy would make fatuous replies to his questions. Olivier would lose heart: he would try not to let it be seen: but he thought he had made a mistake, and that the boy was thoroughly stupid. He could not see the frightful fevered travail in incubation that was going on in the inner depths of the boy's soul. Besides, he was a bad teacher, and was more fitted to sow the good seed at random in the fields than to weed the soil and plow the furrows. Christophe's presence only served to increase the difficulty. Olivier felt a certain awkwardness in showing his young protégé to his friend: he was ashamed of Emmanuel's stupidity, which was raised to alarming proportions when Jean-Christophe was in the room. Then the boy would withdraw into bashful sul-

lenness. He hated Christophe because Olivier loved him: he
could not bear any one else to have a place in his master's heart.
Neither Christophe nor Olivier had any idea of the love and
jealousy tugging at the boy's heart. And yet Christophe had
been through it himself in old days. But he was unable to see
himself in the boy who was fashioned of such different metal
from that of which he himself was made. In the strange obscure
combination of inherited taints, everything, love, hate, and latent genius, gave out an entirely different sound.

The First of May was approaching. A sinister rumor ran
through Paris. The blustering leaders of the C.G.T. were doing their best to spread it. Their papers were announcing the
coming of the great day, mobilizing the forces of the working-
classes, and directing the word of terror upon the point in which
the comfortable classes were mostly sensitive—namely, upon the
stomach. . . . *Feri ventrem.* . . . They were threatening them
with a general strike. The scared Parisians were leaving for the
country or laying in provisions as against a siege. Christophe
had met Canet, in his motor, carrying two hams and a sack of
potatoes: he was beside himself: he did not in the least know
to which party he belonged: he was in turn an old Republican, a
royalist, and a revolutionary. His cult of violence was like a
compass gone wrong, with the needle darting from north to
south and from south to north. In public he still played the
part of chorus to the wild speeches of his friends: but he would
have taken *in petto* the first dictator who came along and swept
away the red spectre.

Christophe was tickled to death by such universal cowardice.
He was convinced that nothing would come of it all. Olivier
was not so sure. His birth into the burgess-class had given him
something of the inevitable and everlasting tremulation which
the comfortable classes always feel upon the recollection or the
expectation of Revolution.

"That's all right!" said Christophe. "You can sleep in
peace. Your Revolution isn't going to happen to-morrow.
You're all afraid. Afraid of being hurt. That sort of fear is
everywhere. In the upper-classes, in the people, in every nation, in all the nations of the West. There's not enough blood

in the whole lot of them: they're afraid of spilling a little.   For
the last forty years all the fighting has been done in words, in
newspaper articles.   Just look at your old Dreyfus Affair.   You
shouted loud enough: 'Death! Blood! Slaughter!'. . . Oh!
you Gascons! Spittle and ink! But how many drops of
blood?"

"Don't you be so sure," said Olivier.   "The fear of blood is
a secret instinctive feeling that on the first shedding of it the
beast in man will see red, and the brute will appear again under
the crust of civilization: and God knows how it will ever be
muzzled!   Everybody hesitates to declare war: but when the war
does come it will be a frightful thing."

Christophe shrugged his shoulders and said that it was not for
nothing that the heroes of the age were lying heroes, Cyrano the
braggart and the swaggering cock, Chantecler.

Olivier nodded.   He knew that in France bragging is the beginning of action.   However, he had no more faith than Christophe in an immediate movement: it had been too loudly proclaimed, and the Government was on its guard.   There was reason to believe that the syndicalist strategists would postpone the
fight for a more favorable opportunity.

During the latter half of April Olivier had an attack of influenza: he used to get it every winter about the same time, and
it always used to develop into his old enemy, bronchitis.   Christophe stayed with him for a few days.   The attack was only a
slight one, and soon passed.   But, as usual, it left Olivier morally
and physically worn out, and he was in this condition for some
time after the fever had subsided.   He stayed in bed, lying still
for hours without any desire to get up or even to move: he lay
there watching Christophe, who was sitting at his desk, working,
with his back towards him.

Christophe was absorbed in his work.   Sometimes, when he
was tired of writing, he would suddenly get up and walk over to
the piano: he would play, not what he had written, but just
whatever came into his mind.   Then there came to pass a very
strange thing.   While the music he had written was conceived in
a style which recalled that of his earlier work, what he played
was like that of another man.   It was music of a world raucous

and uncontrolled. There were in it a disorder and a violence, and incoherence which had no resemblance at all to the powerful order and logic which were everywhere present in his other music. These unconsidered improvizations, escaping the scrutiny of his artistic conscience, sprang, like the cry of an animal, from the flesh rather than from the mind, and seemed to reveal a disturbance of the balance of his soul, a storm brewing in the depths of the future. Christophe was quite unconscious of it: but Olivier would listen, look at Christophe, and feel vaguely uneasy. In his weak condition he had a singular power of penetration, a far-seeing eye: he saw things that no other man could perceive.

Christophe thumped out a final chord and stopped all in a sweat, and looking rather haggard: he looked at Olivier, and there was still a troubled expression in his eyes; then he began to laugh, and went back to his desk. Olivier asked him:

" What was that, Christophe? "

" Nothing," replied Christophe. " I'm stirring the water to attract my fish."

" Are you going to write that? "

" That? What do you mean? "

" What you've just said."

" What did I say? I don't remember."

" What were you thinking of? "

" I don't know," said Christophe, drawing his hand across his forehead.

He went on writing. Silence once more filled the room. Olivier went on looking at Christophe. Christophe felt that he was looking, and turned. Olivier's eyes were upon him with such a hunger of affection!

" Lazy brute! " he said gaily.

Olivier sighed.

" What's the matter? " asked Christophe.

" Oh! Christophe! To think there are so many things in you, sitting there, close at hand, treasures that you will give to others, and I shall never be able to share! . . ."

" Are you mad? What's come to you? "

" I wonder what your life will be. I wonder what peril and sorrow you have still to go through. . . . I would like to follow you. I would like to be with you. . . . But I shan't see anything of it all. I shall be left stuck stupidly by the wayside."

" Stupid? You are that. Do you think that I would leave you behind even if you wanted to be left?"

" You will forget me," said Olivier.

Christophe got up and went and sat on the bed by Olivier's side: he took his wrists, which were wet with a clammy sweat of weakness. His nightshirt was open at the neck, showing his weak chest, his too transparent skin, which was stretched and thin like a sail blown out by a puff of wind to rending point. Christophe's strong fingers fumbled as he buttoned the neckband of Olivier's nightshirt. Olivier suffered him.

" Dear Christophe! " he said tenderly. " Yet I have had one great happiness in my life! "

" Oh! what on earth are you thinking of? " said Christophe. " You're as well as I am."

" Yes," said Olivier.

" Then why talk nonsense? "

" I was wrong," said Olivier, ashamed and smiling. " Influenza is so depressing."

" Pull yourself together, though! Get up."

" Not now. Later on."

He stayed in bed, dreaming. Next day he got up. But he was only able to sit musing by the fireside. It was a mild and misty April. Through the soft veil of silvery mist the little green leaves were unfolding their cocoons, and invisible birds were singing the song of the hidden sun. Olivier wound the skein of his memories. He saw himself once more as a child, in the train carrying him away from his native town, through the mist, with his mother weeping. Antoinette was sitting by herself at the other end of the carriage. . . . Delicate shapes, fine landscapes, were drawn in his mind's eye. Lovely verses came of their own accord, with every syllable and charming rhythm in due order. He was near his desk: he had only to reach out his hand to take his pen and write down his poetic visions. But his will failed him: he was tired: he knew that the perfume of his dreams would evaporate so soon as he tried to catch and hold them. It was always so: the best of himself could never find expression: his mind was like a little valley full of flowers: but

hardly a soul had access to it: and as soon as they were picked
the flowers faded. No more than just a few had been able
languidly to survive, a few delicate little tales, a few pieces of
verse, which all gave out a fragrant, fading scent. His artistic
impotence had for a long time been one of Olivier's greatest
griefs. It was so hard to feel so much life in himself and to
be able to save none of it! . . .—Now he was resigned. Flowers
do not need to be seen to blossom. They are only the more beautiful in the fields where no hand can pluck them. Happy, happy
fields with flowers dreaming in the sun!—Here in the little
valley there was hardly any sun; but Olivier's dreams flowered
all the better for it. What stories he wove for his own delight
in those days, stories sad and tender and fantastic! They came
he knew not whence, sailing like white clouds in a summer sky,
melted into thin air, and others followed them: he was full of
them. Sometimes the sky was clear: in the light of it Olivier
would sit drowsily until once more, with all sail set, there would
come gliding the silent ships of dreams.

In the evening the little hunchback would come in. Olivier
was so full of stories that he told him one, smiling, eager and
engrossed in the tale. Often he would go on talking to himself,
with the boy breathing never a word. In the end he would altogether forget his presence. . . . Christophe arrived in the middle of the story, and was struck by its beauty, and asked Olivier
to begin all over again. Olivier refused:

" I am in the same position as yourself," he said. " I don't
know anything about it."

" That is not true," said Christophe. " You're a regular
Frenchman, and you always know exactly what you are doing
and saying. You never forget anything."

" Alas! " said Olivier.

" Begin again, then."

" I'm too tired. What's the good? "

Christophe was annoyed.

" That's all wrong," he said. " What's the good of your having ideas? You throw away what you have. It's an utter
waste."

" Nothing is ever lost," said Olivier.

The little hunchback started from the stillness he had maintained during Olivier's story—sitting with his face towards the window, with eyes blankly staring, and a frown on his face and a fierce expression so that it was impossible to tell what he was thinking. He got up and said:

"It will be fine to-morrow."

"I bet," said Christophe to Olivier, "that he didn't even listen."

"To-morrow, the First of May," Emmanuel went on, while his morose expression lighted up.

"That is his story," said Olivier. "You shall tell it me to-morrow."

"Nonsense!" said Christophe.

Next day Christophe called for Olivier to take him for a walk in Paris. Olivier was better: but he still had the same strange feeling of exhaustion: he did not want to go out, he had a vague fear, he did not like mixing with the crowd. His heart and mind were brave: but the flesh was weak. He was afraid of a crush, an affray, brutality of all sorts: he knew only too well that he was fated to be a victim, that he could not, even would not, defend himself: for he had as great a horror of giving pain as of suffering it himself. Men who are sick in body shudder away from physical suffering more readily than others, because they are more familiar with it, because they have less power to resist, and because it is presented more immediately and more poignantly to their heated imagination. Olivier was ashamed of this physical cowardice of his which was in entire contradiction to the stoicism of his will: and he tried hard to fight it down. But this morning the thought of human contact of any sort was painful to him, and he would gladly have remained indoors all day long. Christophe scolded him, rallied him, absolutely insisted on his going out and throwing off his stupor: for quite ten days he had not had a breath of air. Olivier pretended not to pay any attention. Christophe said:

"Very well. I'll go without you. I want to see their First of May. If I don't come back to-night, you will know that I have been locked up."

He went out. Olivier caught him up on the stairs. He would not leave Christophe to go alone.

There were very few people in the streets. A few little work-girls wearing sprays of lily-of-the-valley. Working-people in their Sunday clothes were walking about rather listlessly. At the street corners, and near the Métro stations were groups of policemen in plain clothes. The gates of the Luxembourg were closed. The weather was still foggy and damp. It was a long, long time since the sun had shown himself! . . . The friends walked arm in arm. They spoke but little, but they were very glad of each other. A few words were enough to call up all their tender memories of the intimate past. They stopped in front of a *mairie* to look at the barometer, which had an upward tendency.

" To-morrow," said Olivier, " I shall see the sun."

They were quite near the house where Cécile lived. They thought of going in and giving the baby a hug.

" No. We can do it when we come back."

On the other side of the river they began to fall in with more people. Just ordinary peaceful people taking a walk, wearing their Sunday clothes and faces; poor people with their babies: workmen loafing. A few here and there wore the red eglantine in their buttonholes: they looked quite inoffensive: they were revolutionaries by dint of self-persuasion: they were obviously quite benevolent and optimistic at heart, well satisfied with the smallest opportunities for happiness: whether it were fine or merely passable for their holiday, they were grateful for it . . . they did not know exactly to whom . . . to everything and everybody about them. They walked along without any hurry, expansively admiring the new leaves of the trees and the pretty dresses of the little girls who went by: they said proudly:

" Only in Paris can you see children so well dressed as that."

Christophe made fun of the famous upheaval that had been predicted. . . . Such nice people! . . . He was quite fond of them, although a little contemptuous.

As they got farther along the crowd thickened. Men with pale hangdog faces and horrible mouths slipped into the stream of people, all on the alert, waiting for the time to pounce on their prey. The mud was stirred up. With every inch the river grew more and more turbid. Now it flowed slowly thick, opaque, and heavy. Like air-bubbles rising from the depths to the greasy surface, there came up calling voices, shrill whistles, the cries of the newsboys, piercing the dull roar of the multitude, and made it possible to take the measure of its strata. At the end of a street, near Amélie's restaurant, there was a noise like that of a mill-race. The crowd was stemmed up against several ranks of police and soldiers. In front of the obstacles a serried mass was formed, howling, whistling, singing, laughing, and eddying this way and that. . . . The laughter of the people is the only means they have of expressing a thousand obscure and yet deep feelings which cannot find an outlet in words! . . .

The multitude was not hostile. The people did not know what they wanted. Until they did know they were content to amuse themselves—after their own nervous, brutal fashion, still without malice—to amuse themselves with pushing and being pushed, insulting the police and each other. But little by little, they lost their ardor. Those who came up from behind got tired of being able to see nothing, and were the more provocative inasmuch as they ran little risk behind the shelter of the human barricade in front of them. Those in front, being crushed between those who were pushing and those who were offering resistance, grew more and more exasperated as their position became more and more intolerable: the force of the current pushing them on increased their own force an hundredfold. And all of them, as they were squeezed closer and closer together, like cattle, felt the warmth of the whole herd creeping through their breasts and their loins: and it seemed to them then that they formed a solid block: and each was all, each was a giant with the arms of Briareus. Every now and then a wave of blood would surge to the heart of the thousand-headed monster: eyes would dart hatred, murderous cries would go up. Men cowering away in the third and fourth row began to throw stones. Whole families were looking down from the windows of the houses: it was like being at the play: they excited the mob and waited with a little thrill of agonized impatience for the troops to charge.

Christophe forced his way through the dense throng with elbows and knees, like a wedge. Olivier followed him. The living mass parted for a moment to let them pass and closed again at once behind them. Christophe was in fine fettle. He had entirely forgotten that only five minutes ago he had denied the possibility of an upheaval of the people. Hardly had he set foot inside the stream than he was swept along: though he was a foreigner in this crowd of Frenchmen and a stranger to their demands, yet he was suddenly engulfed by them: little he cared what they wanted: he wanted it too: little he cared whither they were going: he was going too, drinking in the breath of their madness.

Olivier was dragged along after him, but it was no joy to him; he saw clearly, he never lost his self-consciousness, and was a thousand times more a stranger to the passions of these people who were his people than Christophe, and yet he was carried away by them like a piece of wreckage. His illness, which had weakened him, had also relaxed everything that bound him to life. How far removed he felt from these people! . . . Being free from the delirium that was in them and having all his wits at liberty, his mind took in the minutest details. It gave him pleasure to gaze at the bust of a girl standing in front of him and at her pretty, white neck. And at the same time he was disgusted by the sickly, thick smell that was given off from the close-packed heap of bodies.

"Christophe!" he begged.

Christophe did not hear him.

"Christophe!"

"Eh?"

"Let's go home."

"You're afraid?" said Christophe.

He pushed on. Olivier followed him with a sad smile.

A few rows in front of them, in the danger zone where the people were so huddled together as to form a solid barricade, he saw his friend the little hunchback perched on the roof of a newspaper kiosk. He was clinging with both hands, and crouching in a most uncomfortable position, and laughing as he looked over the wall of soldiers: and then he would turn again and look back at the crowd with an air of triumph. He saw Olivier and beamed at him: then once more he began to peer across the soldiers, over the square, with his eyes wide staring in hope and expectation . . . of what?—Of the thing which was to come to pass. . . . He was not alone. There were many, many others all around him waiting for the miracle! And Olivier, looking at Christophe, saw that he too was expecting it.

He called to the boy and shouted to him to come down. Emmanuel pretended not to hear and looked away. He had seen Christophe. He was glad to be in a position of peril in the turmoil, partly to show his courage to Olivier, partly to punish him for being with Christophe.

Meanwhile they had come across some of their friends in the crowd,—Coquard, with his golden beard, who expected nothing more than a little jostling and crushing, and with the eye of an expert was watching for the moment when the vessel would overflow. Farther on they met the fair Berthe, who was slanging the people about her and getting roughly mauled. She had succeeded in wriggling through to the front row, and she was hurling insults at the police. Coquard came up to Christophe. When Christophe saw him he began to chaff him:

"What did I tell you? Nothing is going to happen."

"That remains to be seen!" said Coquard. "Don't you be too sure. It won't be long before the fun begins."

"Rot!" said Christophe.

At that very moment the cuirassiers, getting tired of having stones flung at them, marched forward to clear the entrances to the square: the central body came forward at a double. Immediately the stampede began. As the Gospel has it, the first were last. But they took good care not to be last for long. By way of covering their confusion the runaways yelled at the soldiers following them and screamed: "Assassins!" long before a single blow had been struck. Berthe wriggled through the crowd like an eel, shrieking at the top of her voice. She rejoined her friends; and taking shelter behind Coquard's broad back, she recovered her breath, pressed close up against Christophe, gripped his arm, in fear or for some other reason, ogled Olivier, and shook her fist at the enemy, and screeched. Coquard took Christophe's arm and said:

"Let's go to Amélie's."

They had very little way to go. Berthe had preceded them with Graillot and a few workmen. Christophe was on the point of entering followed by Olivier. The street had a shelving ridge. The pavement, by the creamery, was five or six steps higher than

the roadway. Olivier stopped to take a long breath after his
escape from the crowd. He disliked the idea of being in the
poisoned air of the restaurant and the clamorous voices of these
fanatics. He said to Christophe:

" I'm going home."

" Very well, then, old fellow," said Christophe. " I'll rejoin
you in an hour from now."

" Don't run any risks, Christophe! "

" Coward! " said Christophe, laughing.

He turned into the creamery.

Olivier walked along to the corner of the shop. A few steps
more and he would be in a little by-street which would take him
out of the uproar. The thought of his little protégé crossed his
mind. He turned to look for him. He saw him at the very
moment when Emmanuel had slipped down from his coign of
vantage and was rolling on the ground being trampled underfoot
by the rabble: the fugitives were running over his body: the
police were just reaching the spot. Olivier did not stop to think:
he rushed down the steps and ran to his aid. A navvy saw the
danger, the soldiers with drawn sabers. Olivier holding out his
hand to the boy to help him up, the savage rush of the police
knocked them both over. He shouted out, and in his turn rushed
in. Some of his comrades followed at a run. Others rushed
down from the threshold of the restaurant, and, on their cries,
came those who had already entered. The two bodies of men
hurled themselves at each other's throats like dogs. And the
women, standing at the top of the steps, screamed and yelled.—
So Olivier, the aristocrat, the essentially middle-class nature, released the spring of the battle, which no man desired less than he.

Christophe was swept along by the workmen and plunged into
the fray without knowing who had been the cause of it. Nothing was farther from his thoughts than that Olivier had taken
part in it. He thought him far away in safety. It was impossible to see anything of the fight. Every man had enough to do
in keeping an eye on his opponent. Olivier had disappeared in
the whirlpool like a foundered ship. He had received a jab
from a bayonet, meant for some one else, in his left breast: he
fell: the crowd trampled him underfoot. Christophe had been
swept away by an eddy to the farthest extremity of the field of

battle. He did not fight with any animosity: he jostled and was jostled with a fierce zest as though he was in the throng at a village fair. So little did he think of the serious nature of the affair that when he was gripped by a huge, broad-shouldered policeman and closed with him, he saw the thing in grotesque and said:

"My waltz, I think."

But when another policeman pounced on to his back, he shook himself like a wild boar, and hammered away with his fists at the two of them: he had no intention of being taken prisoner. One of his adversaries, the man who had seized him from behind, rolled down on the ground. The other lost his head and drew his sword. Christophe saw the point of the saber come within a hand's breadth of his chest: he dodged, and twisted the man's wrist and tried to wrench his weapon from him. He could not understand it: till then it had seemed to him just a game. They went on struggling and battering at each other's faces. He had no time to stop to think. He saw murder in the other man's eyes: and murderous desire awoke in him. He saw that the man would slit him up like a sheep. With a sudden movement he turned the man's hand and sword against himself: he plunged the sword into his breast, felt that he was killing him, and killed him. And suddenly the whole thing was changed: he was mad, intoxicated, and he roared aloud.

His yells produced an indescribable effect. The crowd had smelt blood. In a moment it became a savage pack. On all sides swords were drawn. The red flag appeared in the windows of the houses. And old memories of Parisian revolutions prompted them to build a barricade. The stones were torn up from the street, the gas lamps were wrenched away, trees were pulled up, an omnibus was overturned. A trench that had been left open for months in connection with work on the *Métropolitain* was turned to account. The cast-iron railings round the trees were broken up and used as missiles. Weapons were brought out of pockets and from the houses. In less than an hour the scuffle had grown into an insurrection: the whole district was in a state of siege. And, on the barricade, was Christophe, unrecognizable, shouting his revolutionary song, which was taken up by a score of voices.

Olivier had been carried to Amélie's. He was unconscious. He had been laid on a bed in the dark back-shop. At the foot of the bed stood the hunchback, numbed and distraught. At first Berthe had been overcome with emotion: at a distance she had thought it was Graillot who had been wounded, and, when she recognized Olivier, her first exclamation had been:

"What a good thing! I thought it was Léopold."

But now she was full of pity. And she kissed Olivier and held his head on the pillow. With her usual calmness Amélie had undone his clothes and dressed his wound. Manousse Heimann was there, fortunately, with his inseparable Canet. Like Christophe they had come out of curiosity to see the demonstration: they had been present at the affray and seen Olivier fall. Canet was blubbering like a child: and at the same time he was thinking:

"What on earth am I doing here?"

Manousse examined Olivier: at once he saw that it was all over. He had a great feeling for Olivier: but he was not a man to worry about what can't be helped: and he turned his thoughts to Christophe. He admired Christophe though he regarded him as a pathological case. He knew his ideas about the Revolution: and he wanted to deliver him from the idiotic danger he was running in a cause that was not his own. The risk of a broken head in the scuffle was not the only one: if Christophe were taken, everything pointed to his being used as an example and getting more than he bargained for. Manousse had long ago been warned that the police had their eye on Christophe: they would saddle him not only with his own follies but with those of others. Xavier Bernard, whom Manousse had just encountered, prowling through the crowd, for his own amusement as well as in pursuit of duty, had nodded to him as he passed and said:

"That Krafft of yours is an idiot. Would you believe that he's putting himself up as a mark on the barricade! We shan't miss him this time. You'd better get him out of harm's way."

That was easier said than done. If Christophe were to find out that Olivier was dying he would become a raging madman,

he would go out to kill, he would be killed. Manousse said
to Bernard:

" If he doesn't go at once, he's done for. I'll try and take
him away."

" How? "

" In Canet's motor. It's over there at the corner of the
street."

" Please, please . . ." gulped Canet.

" You must take him to Laroche," Manousse went on. " You
will get there in time to catch the Pontarlier express. You
must pack him off to Switzerland."

" He won't go."

" He will. I'll tell him that Jeannin will follow him, or
has already gone."

Without paying any attention to Canet's objections Manousse
set out to find Christophe on the barricade. He was not very
courageous, he started every time he heard a shot: and he
counted the cobble-stones over which he stepped—(odd or
even), to make out his chances of being killed. He did not
stop, but went through with it. When he reached the barricade
he found Christophe, perched on a wheel of the overturned
omnibus, amusing himself by firing pistol-shots into the air.
Round the barricade the riff-raff of Paris, spewed up from the
gutters, had swollen up like the dirty water from a sewer
after heavy rain. The original combatants were drowned by
it. Manousse shouted to Christophe, whose back was turned
to him. Christophe did not hear him. Manousse climbed up
to him and plucked at his sleeve. Christophe pushed him away
and almost knocked him down. Manousse stuck to it, climbed
up again, and shouted:

" Jeannin . . ."

In the uproar the rest of the sentence was lost. Christophe
stopped short, dropped his revolver, and, slipping down from
his scaffolding, he rejoined Manousse, who started pulling him
away.

" You must clear out," said Manousse.

" Where is Olivier? "

" You must clear out." repeated Manousse.

" Why? " said Christophe.

" The barricade will be captured in an hour. You will be arrested to-night."

" What have I done? "

" Look at your hands. . . . Come! . . . There's no room for doubt, they won't spare you. Everybody recognized you. You've not got a moment to lose."

" Where is Olivier? "

" At home."

" I'll go and join him."

" You can't do that. The police are waiting for you at the door. He sent me to warn you. You must cut and run."

" Where do you want me to go? "

" To Switzerland. Canet will take you out of this in his car."

" And Olivier? "

" There's no time to talk. . . ."

" I won't go without seeing him."

" You'll see him there. He'll join you to-morrow. He'll go by the first train. Quick! I'll explain."

He caught hold of Christophe. Christophe was dazed by the noise and the wave of madness that had rushed through him, could not understand what he had done and what he was being asked to do, and let himself be dragged away. Manousse took his arm, and with his other hand caught hold of Canet, who was not at all pleased with the part allotted to him in the affair: and he packed the two of them into the car. The worthy Canet would have been bitterly sorry if Christophe had been caught, but he would have much preferred some one else to help him to escape. Manousse knew his man. And as he had some qualms about Canet's cowardice, he changed his mind just as he was leaving them and the car was getting into its stride and climbed up and sat with them.

Olivier did not recover consciousness. Amélie and the little hunchback were left alone in the room. Such a sad room it was, airless and gloomy! It was almost dark. . . . For one instant Olivier emerged from the abyss. He felt Emmanuel's tears and kisses on his hand. He smiled faintly, and painfully laid his hand on the boy's head. Such a heavy hand it was! . . . Then he sank back once more. . . .

By the dying man's head, on the pillow, Amélie had laid a
First of May nosegay, a few sprays of lily-of-the-valley. A
leaky tap in the courtyard dripped, dripped into a bucket. For
a second mental images hovered tremblingly at the back of
his mind, like a light flickering and dying down . . . a house
in the country with glycine on the walls: a garden where a child
was playing: a boy lying on the turf: a little fountain plashing
in its stone basin: a little girl laughing. . . .

II

THEY drove out of Paris. They crossed the vast plains of
France shrouded in mist. It was an evening like that on which
Christophe had arrived in Paris ten years before. He was a
fugitive then, as now. But then his friend, the man who loved
him, was alive: and Christophe was fleeing towards him. . . .
During the first hour Christophe was still under the excitement of the fight: he talked volubly in a loud voice: in a
breathless, jerky fashion he kept on telling what he had seen
and heard: he was proud of his achievement and felt no remorse. Manousse and Canet talked too, by way of making him
forget. Gradually his feverish excitement subsided, and Christophe stopped talking: his two companions went on making conversation alone. He was a little bewildered by the afternoon's
adventures, but in no way abashed. He recollected the time
when he had come to France, a fugitive then, always a fugitive.
It made him laugh. No doubt he was fated to be so. It gave
him no pain to be leaving Paris: the world is wide: men are
the same everywhere. It mattered little to him where he might
be so long as he was with his friend. He was counting on
seeing him again next day. They had promised him that.
They reached Laroche. Manousse and Canet did not leave
him until they had seen him into the train. Christophe made
them say over the name of the place where he was to get out,
and the name of the hotel. and the post-office where he would
find his letters. In spite of themselves, as they left him. they
both looked utterly dejected. Christophe wrung their hands
gaily.

"Come!" he shouted, "don't look so like a funeral. Good Lord, we shall meet again! Nothing easier! We'll write to each other to-morrow."

The train started. They watched it disappear.

"Poor devil!" said Manousse.

They got back into the car. They were silent. After a short time Canet said to Manousse:

"Bah! the dead are dead. We must help the living."

As night fell Christophe's excitement subsided altogether. He sat huddled in a corner of the carriage, and pondered. He was sobered and icy cold. He looked down at his hands and saw blood on them that was not his own. He gave a shiver of disgust. The scene of the murder came before him once more. He remembered that he had killed a man: and now he knew not why. He began to go over the whole battle from the very beginning; but now he saw it in a very different light. He could not understand how he had got mixed up in it. He went back over every incident of the day from the moment when he had left the house with Olivier: he saw the two of them walking through Paris until the moment when he had been caught up by the whirlwind. There he lost the thread: the chain of his thoughts was snapped: how could he have shouted and struck out and moved with those men with whose beliefs he disagreed? It was not he, it was not he! . . . It was a total eclipse of his will! . . . He was dazed by it and ashamed. He was not his own master then? Who was his master? . . . He was being carried by the express through the night: and the inward night through which he was being carried was no less dark, nor was the unknown force less swift and dizzy. . . . He tried hard to shake off his unease: but one anxiety was followed by another. The nearer he came to his destination, the more he thought of Olivier; and he was oppressed by an unreasoning fear.

As he arrived he looked through the window across the platform for the familiar face of his friend. . . . There was no one. He got out and still went on looking about him. Once or twice he thought he saw . . . No, it was not "he." He went to the appointed hotel. Olivier was not there. There was no reason for Christophe to be surprised: how could Olivier have preceded him? . . . But from that moment on he was in an agony of suspense.

It was morning. Christophe went up to his room. Then he came down again, had breakfast, sauntered through the streets. He pretended to be free of anxiety and looked at the lake and the shop-windows, chaffed the girl in the restaurant, and turned over the illustrated papers. . . . Nothing interested him. The day dragged through, slowly and heavily. About seven o'clock in the evening, Christophe having, for want of anything else to do, dined early and eaten nothing, went up to his room, and asked that as soon as the friend he was expecting arrived, he should be brought up to him. He sat down at the desk with his back turned to the door. He had nothing to busy himself with, no baggage, no books: only a paper that he had just bought: he forced himself to read it: but his mind was wandering: he was listening for footsteps in the corridor. All his nerves were on edge with the exhaustion of a day's anxious waiting and a sleepless night.

Suddenly he heard some one open the door. Some indefinable feeling made him not turn around at once. He felt a hand on his shoulder. Then he turned and saw Olivier smiling at him. He was not surprised, and said:

"Ah, here you are at last!"

The illusion vanished.

Christophe got up suddenly, knocking over chair and table. His hair stood on end. He stood still for a moment, livid, with his teeth chattering.

At the end of that moment—(in vain did he shut his eyes to it and tell himself: "I know nothing")—he knew everything: he was sure of what he was going to hear.

He could not stay in his room. He went down into the street and walked about for an hour. When he returned the porter met him in the hall of the hotel and gave him a letter. *The* letter. He was quite sure it would be there. His hand trembled as he took it. He opened it, saw that Olivier was dead, and fainted.

The letter was from Manousse. It said that in concealing the disaster from him the day before, and hurrying him off, they had only been obeying Olivier's wishes, who had desired to

insure his friend's escape,—that it was useless for Christophe
to stay, as it would mean the end of him also,—that it was his
duty to seek safety for the sake of his friend's memory, and for
his other friends, and for the sake of his own fame, etc.,
etc. . . . Amélie had added three lines in her big, scrawling
handwriting, to say that she would take every care of the poor
little gentleman. . . .

When Christophe came back to himself he was furiously
angry. He wanted to kill Manousse. He ran to the station.
The hall of the hotel was empty, the streets were deserted:
in the darkness the few belated passers-by did not notice his
wildly staring eyes or his furious breathing. His mind had
fastened as firmly as a bulldog with its fangs on to the one
fixed idea: "Kill Manousse! Kill! . . ." He wanted to return to Paris. The night express had gone an hour before.
He had to wait until the next morning. He could not wait.
He took the first train that went in the direction of Paris, a
train which stopped at every station. When he was left alone
in the carriage Christophe cried over and over again:
"It is not true! It is not true!"
At the second station across the French frontier the train
stopped altogether: it did not go any farther. Shaking with
fury, Christophe got out and asked for another train, battering
the sleepy officials with questions, and only knocking up against
indifference. Whatever he did he would arrive too late. Too
late for Olivier. He could not even manage to catch Manousse.
He would be arrested first. What was he to do? Which way
to turn? To go on? To go back? What was the use? What
was the use? . . . He thought of giving himself up to a
gendarme who went past him. He was held back by an obscure
instinct for life which bade him return to Switzerland. There
was no train in either direction for a few hours. Christophe
sat down in the waiting-room, could not keep still, left the station, and blindly followed the road on through the night. He
found himself in the middle of a bare countryside—fields, broken
here and there with clumps of pines, the vanguard of a forest.
He plunged into it. He had hardly gone more than a few steps
when he flung himself down on the ground and cried:

" Olivier ! "

He lay across the path and sobbed.

A long time afterwards a train whistling in the distance roused him and made him get up. He tried to go back to the station, but took the wrong road. He walked on all through the night. What did it matter to him where he went? He went on walking to keep from thinking, walking, walking, until he could not think, walking on in the hope that he might fall dead. Ah! if only he might die! . . .

At dawn he found himself in a French village a long way from the frontier. All night he had been walking away from it. He went into an inn, ate a huge meal, set out once more, and walked on and on. During the day he sank down in the middle of a field and lay there asleep until the evening. When he woke up it was to face another night. His fury had abated. He was left only with frightful grief that choked him. He dragged himself to a farmhouse, and asked for a piece of bread and a truss of straw for a bed. The farmer stared hard at him, cut him a slice of bread, led him into the stable, and locked it. Christophe lay in the straw near the thickly-smelling cows, and devoured his bread. Tears were streaming down his face. Neither his hunger nor his sorrow could be appeased. During the night sleep once more delivered him from his agony for a few hours. He woke up next day on the sound of the door opening. He lay still and did not move. He did not want to come back to life. The farmer stopped and looked down at him for a long time: he was holding in his hand a paper, at which he glanced from time to time. At last he moved forward and thrust his newspaper in front of Christophe. His portrait was on the front page.

" It is I." said Christophe. " You'd better give me up."

" Get up." said the farmer.

Christophe got up. The man motioned to him to follow. They went behind the barn and walked along a winding path through an orchard. They came to a cross, and then the farmer pointed along a road and said to Christophe:

" The frontier is over there."

Christophe walked on mechanically. He did not know why he should go on. He was so tired, so broken in body and soul, that he longed to stop with every stride. But he felt that if he were to stop he would never be able to go on again, never budge from the spot where he fell. He walked on right through the day. He had not a penny to buy bread. Besides, he avoided the villages. He had a queer feeling which entirely baffled his reason, that, though he wished to die, he was afraid of being taken prisoner: his body was like a hunted animal fleeing before its captors. His physical wretchedness, exhaustion, hunger, an obscure feeling of terror which was augmented by his worn-out condition, for the time being smothered his moral distress. His one thought was to find a refuge where he could in safety be alone with his distress and feed on it.

He crossed the frontier. In the distance he saw a town surmounted with towers and steeples and factory chimneys, from which the thick smoke streamed like black rivers, monotonously, all in the same direction across the gray sky under the rain. He was very near a collapse. Just then he remembered that he knew a German doctor, one Erich Braun, who lived in the town, and had written to him the year before, after one of his successes, to remind him of their old acquaintance. Dull though Braun might be, little though he might enter into his life, yet, like a wounded animal, Christophe made a supreme effort before he gave in to reach the house of some one who was not altogether a stranger.

Under the cloud of smoke and rain, he entered the gray and red city. He walked through it, seeing nothing, asking his way, losing himself, going back, wandering aimlessly. He was at the end of his tether. For the last time he screwed up his will that was so near to breaking-point to climb up the steep alleys, and the stairs which went to the top of a stiff little hill, closely overbuilt with houses round a gloomy church. There were sixty red stone steps in threes and sixes. Between each little flight of steps was a narrow platform for the door of a house. On each platform Christophe stopped swaying to take breath. Far over his head, above the church tower, crows were whirling.

At last he came upon the name he was looking for. He knocked.—The alley was in darkness. In utter weariness he closed his eyes. All was dark within him. . . . Ages passed.

The narrow door was opened. A woman appeared on the threshold. Her face was in darkness: but her outline was sharply shown against the background of a little garden which could be clearly seen at the end of a long passage, in the light of the setting sun. She was tall, and stood very erect, without a word, waiting for him to speak. He could not see her eyes: but he felt them taking him in. He asked for Doctor Erich Braun and gave his name. He had great difficulty in getting the words out. He was worn out with fatigue, hunger, and thirst. Without a word the woman went away, and Christophe followed her into a room with closed shutters. In the darkness he bumped into her: his knees and body brushed against her. She went out again and closed the door of the room and left him in the dark. He stayed quite still, for fear of knocking something over, leaning against the wall with his forehead against the soft hangings: his ears buzzed: the darkness seemed alive and throbbing to his eyes.

Overhead he heard a chair being moved, an exclamation of surprise, a door slammed. Then came heavy footsteps down the stairs.

" Where is he ? " asked a voice that he knew.

The door of the room was opened once more.

" What ! You left him in the dark ! Anna ! Good gracious ! A light ! "

Christophe was so weak, he was so utterly wretched, that the sound of the man's loud voice, cordial as it was, brought him comfort in his misery. He gripped the hand that was held out to him. The two men looked at each other. Braun was a little man : he had a red face with a black, scrubby and untidy beard, kind eyes twinkling behind spectacles, a broad, bumpy, wrinkled, worried, inexpressive brow, hair carefully plastered down and parted right down to his neck. He was very ugly: but Christophe was very glad to see him and to be shaking hands with him. Braun made no effort to conceal his surprise.

" Good Heavens ! How changed he is ! What a state he is in ! "

" I'm just come from Paris," said Christophe. " I'm a fugitive."

"I know, I know. We saw the papers. They said you were caught. Thank God! You've been much in our thoughts, mine and Anna's."

He stopped and made Christophe known to the silent creature who had admitted him:

"My wife."

She had stayed in the doorway of the room with a lamp in her hand. She had a taciturn face with a firm chin. The light fell on her brown hair with its reddish shades of color, and on her pallid cheeks. She held out her hand to Christophe stiffly with the elbow close against her side: he took it without looking at her. He was almost done.

"I came . . ." he tried to explain. "I thought you would be so kind . . . if it isn't putting you out too much . . . as to put me up for a day——"

Braun did not let him finish.

"A day! . . . Twenty days, fifty, as long as you like As long as you are in this country you shall stay in our house: and I hope you will stay for a long time. It is an honor and a great happiness for us."

Christophe was overwhelmed by his kind words. He flung himself into Braun's arms.

"My dear Christophe, my dear Christophe!" said Braun. . . . "He is weeping. . . . Well, well what is it? . . . Anna! Anna! . . . Quick, he has fainted. . . ."

Christophe had collapsed in his host's arms. He had succumbed to the fainting fit which had been imminent for several hours.

When he opened his eyes again he was lying in a great bed. A smell of wet earth came up through the open window. Braun was bending over him.

"Forgive me," murmured Christophe, trying to get up.

"He is dying of hunger!" cried Braun.

The woman went out and returned with a cup and gave him to drink. Braun held his head. Christophe was restored to life: but his exhaustion was stronger than his hunger: hardly was his head laid back on the pillow than he went to sleep. Braun and his wife watched over him: then, seeing that he only needed rest, they left him.

He fell into the sort of sleep that seems to last for years, a heavy crushing sleep, dropping like a piece of lead to the bottom of a lake. In such a sleep a man is a prey to his accumulated weariness and the monstrous hallucinations which are forever prowling at the gates of his will. He tried to wake up, burning, broken, lost in the impenetrable darkness: he heard the clocks striking the half hours: he could not breathe, or think, or move: he was bound and gagged like a man flung into water to drown: he tried to struggle, but only sank down again.—Dawn came at length, the tardy gray dawn of a rainy day. The intolerable heat that consumed him grew less: but his body was pinned under the weight of a mountain. He woke up. It was a terrible awakening.

"Why open my eyes? Why wake up? Rather stay, like my poor friend, who is lying under the earth. . . ."

He lay on his back and never moved, although he was cramped by his position in the bed: his legs and arms were heavy as stone. He was in a grave. A dim pale light. A few drops of rain dashed against the windows. A bird in the garden was uttering a little plaintive cry. Oh! the misery of life! The cruel futility of it all! . . .

The hours crept by. Braun came in. Christophe did not turn his head. Seeing his eyes open, Braun greeted him joyfully: and as Christophe went on grimly staring at the ceiling he tried to make him shake off his melancholy: he sat down on the bed and chattered noisily. Christophe could not bear the noise. He made an effort, superhuman it seemed to him, and said:

"Please leave me alone."

The good little man changed his tone at once.

"You want to be alone? Why, of course. Keep quiet. Rest, don't talk, we'll bring you up something to eat, and no one shall say a word."

But it was impossible for him to be brief. After endless explanations he tiptoed from the room with his huge slippers creaking on the floor. Christophe was left alone once more, and sank back into his mortal weariness. His thoughts were veiled by the mist of suffering. He wore himself out in trying to understand. . . . "Why had he known him? Why had

he loved him? What good had Antoinette's devotion been?
What was the meaning of all the lives and generations,—so
much experience and hope—ending in that life, dragged down
with it into the void?" . . . Life was meaningless. Death
was meaningless. A man was blotted out, shuffled out of existence, a whole family disappeared from the face of the earth,
leaving no trace. Impossible to tell whether it is more odious
or more grotesque. He burst into a fit of angry laughter,
laughter of hatred and despair. His impotence in the face of
such sorrow, his sorrow in the face of such impotence, were
dragging him down to death. His heart was broken. . . .

There was not a sound in the house, save the doctor's footsteps as he went out on his rounds. Christophe had lost all
idea of the time, when Anna appeared. She brought him some
dinner on a tray. He watched her without stirring, without
even moving his lips to thank her: but in his staring eyes,
which seemed to see nothing, the image of the young woman
was graven with photographic clarity. Long afterwards, when
he knew her better, it was always thus that he saw her: later
impressions were never able to efface that first memory of her.
She had thick hair done up in a heavy knob, a bulging forehead, wide cheeks, a short, straight nose, eyes perpetually cast
down, and when they met the eyes of another, they would turn
away with an expression in which there was little frankness and
small kindness: her lips were a trifle thick, and closely pressed
together, and she had a stubborn, rather hard expression. She
was tall, apparently big and well made, but her clothes were
very stiff and tight, and she was cramped in her movements.
She came silently and noiselessly and laid the tray on the table
by the bed and went out again with her arms close to her sides
and her head down. Christophe felt no surprise at her strange
and rather absurd appearance: he did not touch his food and
relapsed into his silent suffering.

The day passed. Evening came and once more Anna with
more food. She found the meal she had brought in the morning still untouched: and she took it away without a remark.
She had none of those fond observations which all women seem
instinctively to produce for the benefit of an invalid. It was
as though Christophe did not exist for her, as though she

herself hardly existed. This time Christophe felt a sort of dumb hostility as impatiently he followed her awkward hasty movements. However, he was grateful to her for not trying to talk.—He was even more grateful to her when, after she had gone, he had to put up with the doctor's protestations, when he observed that Christophe had not touched the earlier meal. He was angry with his wife for not having forced Christophe to eat, and now tried to compel him to do so. For the sake of peace, Christophe had to gulp down a little milk. After that he turned his back on him.

The next night was more tranquil. Heavy sleep once more drew Christophe into its state of nothingness. Not a trace of hateful life was left.—But waking up was even more suffocating than before. He went on turning over and over all the details of the fateful day, Olivier's reluctance to leave the house, his urgent desire to go home, and he said to himself in despair:

"It was I who killed him. . . ."

He could not bear to stay there any longer, shut up in that room, lying motionless beneath the claws of the fierce-eyed sphinx that went on battering him with its dizzy rain of questions and its deathlike breath. He got up all in a fever: he dragged himself out of the room and went downstairs: in his instinctive fear he was driven to cling to other human creatures. And as soon as he heard another voice he felt a longing to rush away.

Braun was in the dining-room. He received Christophe with his usual demonstrations of friendship and at once began to ply him with questions as to what had happened in Paris. Christophe seized him by the arm:

"No," he said. "Don't ask me. Later on. . . . You mustn't mind. I can't, now. I'm dead tired, worn out. . . ."

"I know, I know," said Braun kindly. "Your nerves are shaken. The emotions of the last few days. Don't talk. Don't put yourself out in any way. You are free, you are at home here. No one will worry about you."

He kept his word. By way of sparing his guest he went to the opposite extreme: he dared not even talk to his wife in Christophe's presence: he talked in whispers and walked about on tiptoe: the house became still and silent. Exasperated by the whispering and the silence and the affectation of it all, Christophe had to beg Braun to go on living just as he usually did.

For some days no one paid any attention to Christophe. He would sit for hours together in the corner of a room, or he would wander through the house like a man in a dream. What were his thoughts? He hardly knew. He hardly had even strength enough to suffer. He was crushed. The dryness of his heart was a horror to him. He had only one desire: to be buried with " him " and to make an end.—One day he found the garden-door open and went out. But it hurt him so much to be in the light of day that he returned hurriedly and shut himself up in his room with all the shutters closed. Fine days were torture to him. He hated the sun. The brutal serenity of Nature overwhelmed him. At meals he would eat in silence the food that Braun laid before him, and he would sit with never a word staring down at the table. One day Braun pointed to the piano in the drawing-room: Christophe turned from it in terror. Noise of any sort was detestable to him. Silence, silence, and the night! . . . There was nothing in him save an aching void, and a need of emptiness. Gone was his joy in life, gone the splendid bird of joy that once used to soar blithely, ecstatically upwards, pouring out song. There were days when, sitting in his room, he had no more feeling of life than the halting tic-tac of the clock in the next room, that seemed to be beating in his own brain. And yet, the wild bird of joy was still in him, it would suddenly take flight, and flutter against the bars of its cage: and in the depths of his soul there was a frightful tumult of sorrow—" the bitter cry of one living in the wilderness. . . ."

The world's misery lies in this, that a man hardly ever has a companion. Women perhaps, and chance friendships. We are reckless in our use of the lovely word, friend. In reality we hardly have a single friend all through our lives. Rare, very rare, are those men who have real friends. But the happiness of it is so great that it is impossible to live when they are gone. The friend filled the life of his friend, unbeknown to him, unmarked. The friend goes: and life is empty. Not only the beloved is lost, but every reason for loving, every reason for having loved. Why had he lived? Why had either lived?

The blow of Olivier's death was the more terrible to Christophe in that it fell just at a time when his whole nature was in a state of upheaval. There are in life certain ages when there takes place a silently working organic change in a man: then body and soul are more susceptible to attack from without; the mind is weakened, its power is sapped by a vague sadness, a feeling of satiety, a sort of detachment from what it is doing, an incapacity for seeing any other course of action. At such periods of their lives when these crises occur, the majority of men are bound by domestic ties, forming a safeguard for them, which, it is true, deprives them of the freedom of mind necessary for self-judgment, for discovering where they stand, and for beginning to build up a healthy new life. For them so many sorrows, so much bitterness and disgust remain concealed! . . . Onward! Onward! A man must ever be pressing on. . . . The common round, anxiety and care for the family for which he is responsible, keep a man like a jaded horse, sleeping between the shafts, and trotting on and on.—But a free man has nothing to support him in his hours of negation, nothing to force him to go on. He goes on as a matter of habit: he knows not whither he is going. His powers are scattered, his consciousness is obscured. It is an awful thing for him if, just at the moment when he is most asleep, there comes a thunderclap to break in upon his somnambulism! Then he comes very nigh to destruction.

A few letters from Paris, which at last reached him, plucked Christophe for a moment out of his despairing apathy. They were from Cécile and Madame Arnaud. They brought him messages of comfort. Cold comfort. Futile condolence. Those who talk about suffering know it not. The letters only brought him an echo of the voice that was gone. . . . He had not the heart to reply: and the letters ceased. In his despondency he tried to blot out his tracks. To disappear. . . . Suffering is unjust: all those who had loved him dropped out of his existence. Only one creature still existed: the man who was dead. For many weeks he strove to bring him to life again: he used to talk to him, write to him:

" My dear, I had no letter from you to-day. Where are you?
Come back, come back, speak to me, write to me! . . ."

But at night, hard though he tried, he could never succeed
in seeing him in his dreams. We rarely dream of those we
have lost, while their loss is still a pain. They come back to
us later on when we are beginning to forget.

However, the outside world began gradually to penetrate
to the sepulcher of Christophe's soul. At first he became dimly
conscious of the different noises in the house and to take an
unwitting interest in them. He marked the time of day when
the front door opened and shut, and how often during the day,
and the different ways in which it was opened for the various
visitors. He knew Braun's step: he used to visualize the doctor
coming back from his rounds, stopping in the hall, hanging up
his hat and cloak, always with the same meticulous fussy way.
And when the accustomed noises came up to him out of the
order in which he had come to look for them, he could not help
trying to discover the reason for the change. At meals he began
mechanically to listen to the conversation. He saw that Braun
almost always talked single-handed. His wife used only to give
him a curt reply. Braun was never put out by the want of
anybody to talk to: he used to chat pleasantly and verbosely
about the houses he had visited and the gossip he had picked up.
At last, one day, Christophe looked at Braun while he was
speaking: Braun was delighted, and laid himself out to keep
him interested.

Christophe tried to pick up the threads of life again. . . .
It was utterly exhausting! He felt old, as old as the world! . . .
In the morning when he got up and saw himself in the mirror
he was disgusted with his body, his gestures, his idiotic figure.
Get up, dress, to what end? . . . He tried desperately to
work: it made him sick. What was the good of creation, when
everything ends in nothing? Music had become impossible for
him. Art—(and everything else)—can only be rightly judged
in unhappiness. Unhappiness is the touchstone. Only then do
we know those who can stride across the ages, those who are
stronger than death. Very few bear the test. In unhappiness
we are struck by the mediocrity of certain souls upon whom we
had counted—(and of the artists we had loved, who had been

like friends to our lives).—Who survives? How hollow does the beauty of the world ring under the touch of sorrow!

But sorrow grows weary, the force goes from its grip. Christophe's nerves were relaxed. He slept, slept unceasingly. It seemed that he would never succeed in satisfying his hunger for sleep.

At last one night he slept so profoundly that he did not wake up until well on into the afternoon of the next day. The house was empty. Braun and his wife had gone out. The window was open, and the smiling air was quivering with light. Christophe felt that a crushing weight had been lifted from him. He got up and went down into the garden. It was a narrow rectangle, inclosed within high walls, like those of a convent. There were gravel paths between grass-plots and humble flowers; and an arbor of grape-vines and climbing roses. A tiny fountain trickled from a grotto built of stones: an acacia against the wall hung its sweet-scented branches over the next garden. Above stood the old tower of the church, of red sandstone. It was four o'clock in the evening. The garden was already in shadow. The sun was still shining on the top of the tree and the red belfry. Christophe sat in the arbor, with his back to the wall, and his head thrown back, looking at the limpid sky through the interlacing tendrils of the vine and the roses. It was like waking from a nightmare. Everywhere was stillness and silence. Above his head nodded a cluster of roses languorously. Suddenly the most lovely rose of all shed its petals and died: the snow of the rose-leaves was scattered on the air. It was like the passing of a lovely innocent life. So simply! . . . In Christophe's mind it took on a significance of a rending sweetness. He choked: he hid his face in his hands, and sobbed. . . .

The bells in the church tower rang out. From one church to another called answering voices. . . . Christophe lost all consciousness of the passage of time. When he raised his head, the bells were silent and the sun had disappeared. Christophe was comforted by his tears: they had washed away the stains from his mind. Within himself he heard a little stream of music well forth and he saw the little crescent moon glide into the evening sky. He was called to himself by the sound of footsteps entering the house. He went up to his room, locked the door, and let the fountain of music gush forth. Braun summoned him to dinner, knocked at the door, and tried to open it: Christophe made no reply. Anxiously Braun looked through the keyhole and was reassured when he saw Christophe lying half over the table surrounded with paper which he was blackening with ink.

A few hours later, worn out, Christophe went downstairs and found the doctor reading, impatiently waiting for him in the drawing-room. He embraced the little man, asked him to forgive him for his strange conduct since his arrival, and, without waiting to be asked, he began to tell Braun about the dramatic events of the past weeks. It was the only time he ever talked to him about it: he was never sure that Braun had understood him, for he talked disconnectedly, and it was very late, and, in spite of his eager interest, Braun was nearly dead with sleep. At last—(the clock struck two)—Christophe saw it and they said good-night.

From that time on Christophe's existence was reconstituted. He did not maintain his condition of transitory excitement: he came back to his sorrow, but it was normal sorrow which did not interfere with his life. He could not help returning to life! Though he had just lost his dearest friend in the world, though his grief had undermined him and Death had been his most intimate companion, there was in him such an abundant, such a tyrannical force of life, that it burst forth even in his elegies, shining forth from his eyes, his lips, his gestures. But a gnawing canker had crept into the heart of his force. Christophe had fits of despair, transports rather. He would be quite calm, trying to read, or walking: suddenly he would see Olivier's smile, his tired, gentle face. . . . It would tug at his heart. . . . He would falter, lay his hand on his breast, and moan. One day he was at the piano playing a passage from Beethoven with his old zest. . . . Suddenly he stopped, flung himself on the ground, buried his face in the cushions of a chair, and cried:

"My boy. . . ."

Worst of all was the sensation of having "already lived"

that was constantly with him.   He was continually coming across familiar gestures, familiar words, the perpetual recurrence of the same experiences.   He knew everything, had foreseen every-thing.   One face would remind him of a face he had known and the lips would say—(as he was quite sure they would)—exactly the same things as he had heard from the original: beings similar to each other would pass through similar phases, knock up against the same obstacles, suffer from them in exactly the same way.   If it is true that "nothing so much brings weariness of life as the new beginning of love," how much more then the new beginning of everything!   It was elusive and delusive.—Christophe tried not to think of it, since it was nec-essary to do so, if he were to live, and since he wished to live. It is the saddest hypocrisy, such rejection of self-knowledge, in shame or piety, it is the invincible imperative need of living hiding away from itself!   Knowing that no consolation is possi-ble, a man invents consolations.   Being convinced that life has no reason, he forges reasons for living.   He persuades himself that he must live, even when no one outside himself is con-cerned.   If need be he will go so far as to pretend that the dead man encourages him to live.   And he knows that he is putting into the dead man's mouth the words that he wishes him to say. O misery! . . .

Christophe set out on the road once more: his step seemed to have regained its old assurance: the gates of his heart were closed upon his sorrow: he never spoke of it to others: he avoided being left alone with it himself: outwardly he seemed calm.

"*Real sorrows,*" says Balzac, "*are apparently at peace in the deep bed that they have made for themselves, where they seem to sleep, though all the while they never cease to fret and eat away the soul.*"

Any one knowing Christophe and watching him closely, seeing him coming and going, talking, composing, even laughing—(he could laugh now!)—would have felt that for all his vigor and the radiance of life in his eyes, something had been destroyed in him, in the inmost depths of his life.

As soon as he had regained his hold on life he had to

look about him for a means of living. There could be no
question of his leaving the town. Switzerland was the safest
shelter for him : and where else could he have found more devoted hospitality ?—But his pride could not suffer the idea of
his being any further a burden upon his friend. In spite of
Braun's protestations, and his refusal to accept any payment,
he could not rest until he had found enough pupils to permit
of his paying his hosts for his board and lodging. It was not
an easy matter. The story of his revolutionary escapade had
been widely circulated : and the worthy families of the place
were reluctant to admit a man who was regarded as dangerous,
or at any rate extraordinary, and, in consequence, not quite
" respectable," to their midst. However, his fame as a musician
and Braun's good offices gained him access to four or five of
the less timorous or more curious families, who were perhaps
artistically snobbish enough to desire to gain particularity. They
were none the less careful to keep an eye on him, and to maintain a respectable distance between master and pupils.

The Braun household fell into a methodically ordered existence. In the morning each member of it went about his
business : the doctor on his rounds, Christophe to his pupils,
Madame Braun to the market and about her charitable works.
Christophe used to return about one, a little before Braun,
who would not allow them to wait for him ; and he used to sit
down to dinner alone with the wife. He did not like that at
all : for she was not sympathetic to him, and he could never
find anything to say to her. She took no trouble to remove
his impression, though it was impossible for her not to be aware
of it ; she never bothered to put herself out in dress or in mind
to please him : she never spoke to Christophe first : her notable
lack of charm in movement and dress, her awkwardness, her
coldness, would have repelled any man who was as sensitive
as Christophe to the charm of women. When he remembered
the sparkling elegance of the Parisian women, he could not help
thinking, as he looked at Anna :

" How ugly she is ! "

Yet that was unjust : and he was not slow to notice the beauty
of her hair, her hands, her mouth, her eyes,—on the rare
occasions when he chanced to meet her gaze, which she always

averted at once. But his opinion was never modified. As a matter of politeness he forced himself to speak to her: he labored to find subjects of conversation: she never gave him the smallest assistance. Several times he tried to ask her about the town, her husband, herself: he could get nothing out of her. She would make the most trivial answers: she would make an effort to smile: but the effort was painfully evident; her smile was forced, her voice was hollow: she drawled and dragged every word: her every sentence was followed by a painful silence. At last Christophe only spoke to her as little as possible; and she was grateful to him for it. It was a great relief to both of them when the doctor came in. He was always in a good humor, talkative, busy, vulgar, worthy. He ate, drank, talked, laughed, plentifully. Anna used to talk to him a little: but they hardly ever touched on anything but the food in front of them or the price of things. Sometimes Braun would jokingly tease her about her pious works and the minister's sermons. Then she would stiffen herself, and relapse into an offended silence until the end of the meal. More often the doctor would talk about his patients: he would delight in describing repulsive cases, with a pleasant elaboration of detail which used to exasperate Christophe. Then he would throw his napkin on the table and get up, making faces of disgust which simply delighted the teller. Braun would stop at once, and soothe his friend and laugh. At the next meal he would begin again. His hospital pleasantries seemed to have the power to enliven the impassive Anna. She would break her silence with a sudden nervous laugh, which was something animal in quality. Perhaps she felt no less disgust than Christophe at the things that made her laugh.

In the afternoon Christophe had very few pupils. Then, as a rule, he would stay at home with Anna, while the doctor went out. They never saw each other. They used to go about their separate business. At first Braun had begged Christophe to give his wife a few lessons on the piano: she was, he said, an excellent musician. Christophe asked Anna to play him something. She did not need to be pressed, although she disliked doing it: but she did it with her usual ungraciousness: she played mechanically, with an incredible lack of sensibility:

each note was like another: there was no sort of rhythm or expression: when she had to turn the page she stopped short in the middle of a bar, made no haste about it, and went on with the next note. Christophe was so exasperated by it that he was hard put to it to keep himself from making an insulting remark: he could not help going out of the room before she had finished. She was not put out, but went on imperturbably to the very last note, and seemed to be neither hurt nor indignant at his rudeness: she hardly seemed to have noticed it. But the matter of music was never again mentioned between them. Sometimes in the afternoons when Christophe was out and returned unexpectedly, he would find Anna practising the piano, with icy, dull tenacity, going over and over one passage fifty times, and never by any chance showing the least animation. She never played when she knew that Christophe was at home. She devoted all the time that was not consecrated to her religious duties to her household work. She used to sew, and mend, and darn, and look after the servant: she had a mania for tidiness and cleanliness. Her husband thought her a fine woman, a little odd—"like all women," he used to say— but "like all women," devoted. On that last point Christophe made certain reservations *in petto:* such psychology seemed to him too simple; but he told himself that, after all, it was Braun's affair; and he gave no further thought to the matter.

They used to sit together after dinner in the evening. Braun and Christophe would talk. Anna would sit working. On Braun's entreaty, Christophe had consented to play the piano sometimes: and he would occasionally play on to a very late hour in the big gloomy room looking out on to the garden. Braun would go into ecstasies. . . . Who is there that does not know the type that has a passionate love for things they do not understand, or understand all wrong!—(which is why they love them!)—Christophe did not mind: he had met so many idiots in the course of his life! But when Braun gave vent to certain mawkish expressions of enthusiasm, he would stop playing, and go up to his room without a word. Braun grasped the truth at last, and put a stopper on his reflections. Besides, his love for music was quickly sated: he could never listen with any attention for more than a quarter of an hour on end: he would pick up his paper, or doze off, and leave Christophe in peace. Anna would sit back in her chair and say nothing: she would have her work in her lap and seem to be working: but her eyes were always staring and her hands never moved. Sometimes she would go out without a sound in the middle of a piece, and be seen no more.

So the days passed. Christophe regained his strength. Braun's heavy but kindly attentions, the tranquillity of the household, the restful regularity of such a domestic life, the extremely nourishing German food, restored him to his old robustness. His physical health was repaired: but his moral machinery was still out of gear. His new vigor only served to accentuate the disorder of his mind, which could not recover its balance, like a badly ballasted ship which will turn turtle on the smallest shock.

He was profoundly lonely. He could have no intellectual intimacy with Braun. His relations with Anna were reduced, with a few exceptions, to saying good-morning and good-night. His dealings with his pupils were rather hostile than otherwise: for he hardly hid from them his opinion that the best thing for them to do was to give up music altogether. He knew nobody. It was not only his fault, though he had hidden himself away since his loss. People held aloof from him.

He was living in an old town, full of intelligence and vitality, but also full of patrician pride, self-contained, and self-satisfied. There was a bourgeois aristocracy with a taste for work and the higher culture, but narrow and pietistic, who were calmly convinced of their own superiority and the superiority of their city, and quite content to live in family isolation. There were enormous families with vast ramifications. Each family had its day for a general gathering of the clan. They were hardly at all open to the outside world. All these great houses, with fortunes generations old, felt no need of showing their wealth. They knew each other, and that was enough: the opinion of others was a thing of no consequence. There were millionaires dressed like humble shopkeepers, talking their raucous dialect with its pungent expressions, going conscientiously to their offices, every day of their lives, even at an age when the most

industrious of men will grant themselves the right to rest.
Their wives prided themselves on their domestic skill. No
dowry was given to the daughters. Rich men let their sons
in their turn go through the same hard apprenticeship that they
themselves had served. They practised strict economy in their
daily lives. But they made a noble use of their fortune in
collecting works of art, picture galleries, and in social work:
they were forever giving enormous sums, nearly always anonymously, to found charities and to enrich the museums. They
were a mixture of greatness and absurdity, both of another age.
This little world, for which the rest of the world seemed not
to exist—(although its members knew it thoroughly through
their business, and their distant relationships, and the long and
extended voyages which they forced their sons to take,)—this
little world, for which fame and celebrity in another land only
were esteemed from the moment when they were welcomed and
recognized by itself,—practised the severest discipline upon itself.
Every member of it kept a watch upon himself and upon the
rest. The result of all this was a collective conscience which
masked all individual differences (more marked than elsewhere
among the robust personalities of the place) under the veil of
religious and moral uniformity. Everybody practised it, everybody believed in it. Not a single soul doubted it or would
admit of doubt. It were impossible to know what took place
in the depths of souls which were the more hermetically sealed
against prying eyes inasmuch as they knew that they were
surrounded by a narrow scrutiny, and that every man took
upon himself the right to examine into the conscience of other
men. It was said that even those who had left the country
and thought themselves emancipated—as soon as they set foot
in it again were dominated by the traditions, the habits, the
atmosphere of the town: even the most skeptical were at once
forced to practise and to believe. Not to believe would have
seemed to them an offense against Nature. Not to believe was
the mark of an inferior caste, a sign of bad breeding. It was
never admitted that a man of their world could possibly be
absolved of his religious duties. If a man did not practise their
religion, he was at once unclassed, and all doors were closed
to him.

Even the weight of such discipline was apparently not enough for them. The men of this little world were not closely bound enough within their caste. Within the great *Verein* they had formed a number of smaller *Vereine* by way of binding their fetters fast. There were several hundred of them: and they were increasing every year. There were *Vereine* for everything: for philanthropy, charitable work, commercial work, work that was both charitable and commercial, for the arts, for the sciences, for singing, music, spiritual exercises, physical exercises, merely to provide excuses for meeting and taking their amusement collectively: there were *Vereine* for the various districts and the various corporations: there were *Vereine* for men of the same position in the world, the same degree of wealth, men of the same social weight, who wore the same handle to their names. It was even said that an attempt had been made to form a *Verein* for the *Vereinlosen* (those who did not belong to any *Verein*) : though not twelve such people had been forth-coming.

Within this triple bandage of town, caste, and union, the soul was cramped and bound. Character was suppressed by a secret constraint. The majority were brought up to it from childhood—had been for centuries: and they found it good: they would have thought it improper and unhealthy to go without these bandages. Their satisfied smiles gave no indication of the discomfort they might be feeling. But Nature always took her revenge. Every now and then there would arise some individual in revolt, some vigorous artist or unbridled thinker who would brutally break his bonds and set the city fathers by the ears. They were so clever that, if the rebel had not been stifled in the embryo, and became the stronger, they never troubled to fight him—(a fight might have produced all sorts of scandalous outbreaks) :—they bought him up. If he were a painter, they sent him to the museum: if he were a thinker, to the libraries. It was quite useless for him to roar out all sorts of outrageous things: they pretended not to hear him. It was in vain for him to protest his independence: they incorporated him as one of themselves. So the effect of the poison was neutralized: it was the homeopathic treatment.—But such cases were rare, most of the rebellions never reached the light of day.

Their peaceful houses concealed unsuspected tragedies. The master of a great house would go quietly and throw himself into the river, and leave no explanation. Sometimes a man would go into retirement for six months, sometimes he would send his wife to an asylum to restore her mind. Such things were spoken of quite openly, as though they were quite natural, with that placidity which is one of the great features of the town, the inhabitants of which are able to maintain it in the face of suffering and death.

These solid burgesses, who were hard upon themselves because they knew their own worth, were much less hard on others because they esteemed them less. They were quite liberal towards the foreigners dwelling in the town like Christophe, German professors, and political refugees, because they had no sort of feeling about them. And, besides, they loved intelligence. Advanced ideas had no terrors for them: they knew that their sons were impervious to their influence. They were coldly cordial to their guests, and kept them at a distance.

Christophe did not need to have these things underlined. He was in a state of raw sensitiveness which left his feelings absolutely unprotected: he was only too ready to see egoism and indifference everywhere, and to withdraw into himself.

To make matters worse, Braun's patients, and the very limited circle to which his wife belonged, all moved in a little Protestant society which was particularly strict. Christophe was ill-regarded by them both as a Papist by origin and a heretic in fact. For his part, he found many things which shocked him. Although he no longer believed, yet he bore the marks of his inherited Catholicism, which was more poetic than a matter of reason, more indulgent towards Nature, and never suffered the self-torment of trying to explain and understand what to love and what not to love: and also he had the habits of intellectual and moral freedom which he had unwittingly come by in Paris. It was inevitable that he should come into collision with the little pious groups of people in whom all the defects of the Calvinistic spirit were marked and exaggerated: a rationalistic religion, which clipped the wings of faith and left it dangling over the abyss: for it started with an *a priori* reason which was open to discussion like all mysticism: it was no longer poetry,

nor was it prose, it was poetry translated into prose. They
had pride of intellect, an absolute, dangerous faith in reason—
in *their* reason. They could not believe in God or in immortality: but they believed in reason as a Catholic believes in the
Pope, or as a fetish-worshiper believes in his idol. They never
even dreamed of discussing the matter. In vain did life contradict it; they would rather have denied life. They had no
psychology, no understanding of Nature, or of the hidden forces,
the roots of humanity, the "Spirit of the Earth." They
fashioned a scheme of life and nature that were childish, silly,
arbitrary figments. Some of them were cultured and practical
people who had seen and read much. But they never saw or
read anything as it actually was: they always reduced it to an
abstraction. They were poor-blooded: they had high moral
qualities: but they were not human enough: and that is the
cardinal sin. Their purity of heart, which was often very real,
noble, and naïve, sometimes comic, unfortunately, in certain
cases, became tragic: it made them hard in their dealings with
others, and produced in them a tranquil inhumanity, self-
confident and free from anger, which was quite appalling.
How should they hesitate? Had they not truth, right, virtue,
on their side? Did they not receive revelation direct from
their hallowed reason? Reason is a hard sun: it gives light,
but it blinds. In that withering light, without shade or mist,
human beings grow pallid, the blood is sucked up from their
hearts.

Now, if there was one thing in the world that was utterly
meaningless to Christophe at that time it was reason. To his
eyes its sun only lit up the walls of the abyss, and neither
showed him the means of escape nor even enabled him to sound
its depths.

As for the artistic world, Christophe had little opportunity
and less desire to mix with it. The musicians were for the
most part worthy conservatives of the neo-Schumann period
and "Brahmins" of the type against which Christophe had
formerly broken many a lance. There were two exceptions:
Krebs, the organist, who kept a famous confectioner's shop, an
honest man and a good musician, who would have been an
even better one if, to adapt the quip of one of his fellow-

countrymen, " he had not been seated on a Pegasus which he
overfed with hay,"—and a young Jewish composer of an original
talent, a man full of a vigorous and turbid sap, who had a
business in the Swiss trade: wood carvings, chalets, and Berne
bears. They were more independent than the others, no doubt
because they did not make a trade of their art, and they would
have been very glad to come in touch with Christophe: and at
any other time Christophe would have been interested to know
them: but at this period of his life, all artistic and human
curiosity was blunted in him: he was more conscious of the
division between himself and other men than of the bond of
union.

His only friend, the confidant of his thoughts, was the river
that ran through the city—the same mighty fatherly river that
washed the walls of his native town up north. In the river
Christophe could recover the memory of his childish dreams. . . .
But in his sorrow they took on, like the Rhine itself, a darkling
hue. In the dying day he would lean against the parapet of
the embankment and look down at the rushing river, the fused
and fusing, heavy, opaque, and hurrying mass, which was always
like a dream of the past, wherein nothing could be clearly seen
but great moving veils, thousands of streams, currents, eddies
twisting into form, then fading away: it was like the blurred
procession of mental images in a fevered mind: forever taking
shape, forever melting away. Over this twilight dream there
skimmed phantom ferry-boats, like coffins, with never a human
form in them. Darker grew the night. The river became
bronze. The lights upon its banks made its armor shine with
an inky blackness, casting dim reflections, the coppery reflections
of the gas lamps, the moon-like reflections of the electric lights,
the blood-red reflections of the candles in the windows of the
houses. The river's murmur filled the darkness with its eternal
muttering that was far more sad than the monotony of the
sea. . . .

For hours together Christophe would stand drinking in the
song of death and weariness of life. Only with difficulty could
he tear himself away: then he would climb up to the house
again, up the steep alleys with their red steps, which were worn
away in the middle: broken in soul and body he would cling

to the iron hand-rail fastened to the walls, which gleamed under the light thrown down from the empty square on the hilltop in front of the church that was shrouded in darkness. . . .

He could not understand why men went on living. When he remembered the struggles he had seen, he felt a bitter admiration for the undying faith of humanity. Ideas succeeded the ideas most directly opposed to them, reaction followed action: —democracy, aristocracy: socialism, individualism: romanticism, classicism: progress, tradition:—and so on to the end of time. Each new generation, consumed in its own heat in less than ten years, believed steadfastly that it alone had reached the zenith, and hurled its predecessors down and stoned them: each new generation bestirred itself, and shouted, and took to itself the power and the glory, only to be hurled down and stoned in turn by its successors and so to disappear. Whose turn next? . . .

The composition of music was no longer a refuge for Christophe: it was intermittent, irregular, aimless. Write? For whom? For men? He was passing through an acute phase of misanthropy. For himself? He was only too conscious of the vanity of art with its impotence to top the void of death. Only now and then the blind force that was in him would raise him on its mighty beating wing and then fall back, worn out by the effort. He was like a storm cloud rumbling in the darkness. With Olivier gone, he had nothing left. He hurled himself against everything that had filled his life, against the feelings that he had thought to share with others, against the thoughts which he had in imagination had in common with the rest of humanity. It seemed to him now that he had been the plaything of an illusion: the whole life of society was based upon a colossal misunderstanding originating in speech. We imagine that one man's thought can communicate with the thought of other men. In reality the connection lies only in words. We say and hear words: not one word has the same meaning in the mouths of two different men. Words outrun the reality of life. We speak of love and hatred. There is neither love nor hatred, friends nor enemies, no faith, no passion, neither good nor evil. There are only cold reflections of the lights falling from vanished suns, stars that have been

dead for ages. . . . Friends? There is no lack of people to
claim that name. But what a stale reality is represented by
their friendship! What is friendship in the sense of the everyday world? How many minutes of his life does he who thinks
himself a friend give to the pale memory of his friend? What
would he sacrifice to him, not of the things that are necessary,
but of his superfluity, his leisure, his waste time? What had
Christophe sacrificed for Olivier?—(For he made no exception
in his own case: he excepted only Olivier from the state of
nothingness into which he cast all human beings).—Art is no
more true than love. What room does it really occupy in life?
With what sort of love do they love it, they who declare their
devotion to it? , . . The poverty of human feeling is in-
conceivable. Outside the instincts of species, the cosmic force
which is the lever of the world, nothing exists save a scattered
dust of emotion. The majority of men have not vitality enough
to give themselves wholly to any passion. They spare themselves
and save their force with cowardly prudence. They are a little
of everything and nothing absolutely. A man who gives himself without counting the cost, to everything that he does, everything that he suffers, everything that he loves, everything that
he hates, is a prodigy, the greatest that is granted to us here
on earth. Passion is like genius: a miracle, which is as much
as to say that it does not exist.

So thought Christophe: and life was on the verge of giving
him the lie in a terrible fashion. The miracle is everywhere,
like fire in stone: friction brings it forth. We have little notion
of the demons who lie slumbering within ourselves. . . .
. . . *Pero non mi destar, deh! parla basso!* . . .

One evening when he was improvising at the piano, Anna
got up and went out, as she often did when Christophe was
playing. Apparently his music bored her. Christophe had
ceased to notice it: he was indifferent to anything she might
think. He went on playing: then he had an idea which he
wished to write down, and stopped short and hurried up to
his room for the necessary paper. As he opened the door into
the next room and, with head down, rushed into the darkness,

he bumped violently against a figure standing motionless just inside. Anna. . . . The shock and the surprise made her cry out. Christophe was anxious to know if he had hurt her, and took her hands in his. Her hands were frozen. She seemed to shiver,—no doubt from the shock. She muttered a vague explanation of her presence there:

" I was looking in the dining-room. . . ."

He did not hear what she was looking for: and perhaps she did not say what it was. It seemed to him odd that she should go about looking for something without a light. But he was used to Anna's singular ways and paid no attention to it.

An hour later he returned to the little parlor where he used to spend the evening with Braun and Anna. He sat at the table near the lamp, writing. Anna was on his right at the table, sewing, with her head bent over her work. Behind them, in an armchair, near the fire, Braun was reading a magazine. They were all three silent. At intervals they could hear the pattering of the rain on the gravel in the garden. To get away from her Christophe sat with his back turned to Anna. Opposite him on the wall was a mirror which reflected the table, the lamp, the two faces bending over their work. It seemed to Christophe that Anna was looking at him. At first he did not pay much attention to it; then, as he could not shake off the idea, he began to feel uneasy and he looked up at the mirror and saw. . . . She *was* looking at him. And in such a way! He was petrified with amazement, held his breath, watched her. She did not know that he was watching her. The light of the lamp was cast upon her pale face, the silent solemnity of which seemed now to be fiercely concentrated. Her eyes—those strange eyes that he had never been able squarely to see—were fixed upon him: they were dark blue, with large pupils, and the expression in them was burning and hard: they were fastened upon him, searching through him with dumb insistent ardor. Her eyes? Could they be her eyes? He saw them and could not believe it. Did he really see them? He turned suddenly. . . . Her eyes were lowered. He tried to talk to her, to force her to look up at him. Impassively she replied without raising her eyes from her work or from their refuge behind the impenetrable shadow of her bluish eyelids with their short thick lashes. If Christophe had not been quite positive of what he had seen, he would have believed that he had been the victim of an illusion. But he knew what he had seen, and he could not explain it away.

However, as his mind was engrossed in his work and he found Anna very uninteresting, the strange impression made on him did not occupy him for long.

A week later Christophe was trying over a song he had just composed, on the piano. Braun, who had a mania, due partly to marital vanity and partly to love of teasing, for worrying his wife to sing and play, had been particularly insistent that evening. As a rule Anna only replied with a curt " No "; after which she would not even trouble to reply to his requests, entreaties, and pleasantries: she would press her lips together and seem not to hear. On this occasion, to Braun's and Christophe's astonishment, she folded up her work, got up, and went to the piano. She sang the song which she had never even read. It was a sort of miracle:—*the* miracle. The deep tones of her voice bore not the faintest resemblance to the rather raucous and husky voice in which she spoke. With absolute sureness from the very first note. without a shade of difficulty. without the smallest effort, she endued the melody with a grandeur that was both moving and pure: and she rose to an intensity of passion which made Christophe shiver: for it seemed to him to be the very voice of his own heart. He looked at her in amazement while she was singing, and at last, for the first time, he saw her as she was. He saw her dark eyes in which there was kindled a light of wildness, he saw her wide, passionate mouth with its clear-cut lips, the voluptuous, rather heavy and cruel smile, her strong white teeth, her beautiful strong hands, one of which was laid on the rack of the piano, and the sturdy frame of her body cramped by her clothes, emaciated by a life of economy and poverty, though it was easy to divine the youth, the vigor, and the harmony, that were concealed by her gown.

She stopped singing, and went and sat down with her hands folded in her lap. Braun complimented her: but to his way of thinking there had been a lack of softness in her singing. Christophe said nothing. He sat watching her. She smiled vaguely, knowing that he was looking at her. All the evening there was a complete silence between them. She knew quite

well that she had risen above herself, or rather, that she had
been "herself," for the first time. And she could not understand why.

From that day on Christophe began to observe Anna closely.
She had relapsed into her sullenness, her cold indifference, and
her mania for work, which exasperated even her husband, while
beneath it all she lulled the obscure thoughts of her troubled
nature. It was in vain that Christophe watched her, he never
found her anything but the stiff ordinary woman of their first
acquaintance. Sometimes she would sit lost in thought, doing
nothing, with her eyes staring straight in front of her. They
would leave her so, and come back a quarter of an hour later
and find her just the same: she would never stir. When her
husband asked her what she was thinking of, she would rouse
herself from her torpor and smile and say that she was thinking
of nothing. And she spoke the truth.

There was nothing capable of upsetting her equanimity. One
day when she was dressing, her spirit-lamp burst. In an instant
Anna was a mass of flames. The maid rushed away screaming
for help. Braun lost his head, flung himself about, shouted and
yelled, and almost fell ill. Anna tore away the hooks of her
dressing-gown, slipped off her skirt just as it was beginning to
burn, and stamped on it. When Christophe ran in excitedly
with a water-bottle which he had blindly seized, he found Anna
standing on a chair, in her petticoat with her arms bare, calmly
putting out the burning curtains with her hands. She got burnt,
said nothing about it, and only seemed to be put out at being
seen in such a costume. She blushed, awkwardly covered her
shoulders with her arms, and with an air of offended dignity
ran away into the next room. Christophe admired her calmness: but he could not tell whether it proved her courage or her
insensibility. He was inclined to the latter explanation. Indeed, Anna seemed to take no interest in anything, or in other
people, or in herself. Christophe doubted even whether she had
a heart.

He had no doubt at all after a little scene which he happened
to witness. Anna had a little black dog, with intelligent soft
eyes, which was the spoiled darling of the household. Braun

adored it. Christophe used to take it to his room when he shut himself up to work; and often, when the door was closed, instead of working, he would play with it. When he went out, the dog was always waiting for him at the door, looking out for him, to follow at his heels: for he always wanted a companion in his walks. She would run in front of him, pattering along with her little paws moving so fast that they seemed to fly. Every now and then she would stop in pride at walking faster than he: and she would look at him and draw herself up archly. She used to beg, and bark furiously at a piece of wood: but directly she saw another dog in the distance she would tear away as fast as she could and tremblingly take refuge between Christophe's legs. Christophe loved her and used to laugh at her. Since he had held aloof from men he had come nearer to the brutes: he found them pitiful and touching. The poor beasts surrender with such absolute confidence to those who are kind to them! Man is so much the master of their life and death that those who are cruel to the weak creatures delivered into their hands are guilty of an abominable abuse of power.

Affectionate though the pretty creature was with every one, she had a marked preference for Anna. She did nothing to attract the dog: but she liked to stroke her and let her snuggle down in her lap, and see that she was fed, and she seemed to love her as much as she was capable of loving anything. One day the dog failed to get out of the way of a motor-car. She was run over almost under the very eyes of her masters. She was still alive and yelping pitiably. Braun ran out of the house bareheaded: he picked up the bleeding mass and tried to relieve the dog's suffering. Anna came up, looked down without so much as stooping, made a face of disgust, and went away again. Braun watched the little creature's agony with tears in his eyes. Christophe was striding up and down the garden with clenched fists. He heard Anna quietly giving orders to the servant. He could not help crying out:

" It doesn't affect you at all ? "

She replied:

" There's nothing to be done. It is better not to think of it."

He felt that he hated her: then he was struck by the grotesque

ness of her reply: and he laughed.   He thought it would be well
if Anna could give him her recipe for avoiding the thought of
sad things, and that life must be very easy for those who are
lucky enough to have no heart.   He fancied that if Braun were
to die, Anna would hardly be put out by it, and he felt glad
that he was not married.   His solitude seemed less sad to him
than the fetters of habit that bind a man for life to a creature
to whom he may be an object of hatred, or worse still, nothing
at all.   It was very certain that this woman loved no one.   She
hardly existed.   The atmosphere of piety had withered her.

   She took Christophe by surprise one day at the end of October.
—They were at dinner.   He was talking to Braun about a crime
of passion which was the sole topic in the town.   In the country
two Italian girls, sisters, had fallen in love with the same man.
They were both unable to make the sacrifice with a good grace,
and so they had drawn lots as to who should yield.   But when
the lot was cast the girl who had lost showed little inclination to
abide by the decision.   The other was enraged by such faithlessness.   From insult they came to blows, and even to fighting
with knives: then, suddenly, the wind changed: they kissed each
other, and wept, and vowed that they could not live without
each other: and, as they could not submit to sharing the lover,
they made up their minds that he should be killed.   This they
did.   One night the two girls invited the lover to their room,
and he was congratulating himself upon such twofold favor; and,
while one girl clasped him passionately in her arms, the other
no less passionately stabbed him in the back.   It chanced that
his cries were heard.   People came and tore him in a pitiable
condition from the embraces of his charmers, and they were
arrested.   They protested that it was no one's business, and that
they alone were interested in the matter, and that, from the
moment when they had agreed to rid themselves of their own
property, it was no one else's concern.   Their victim was not a
little inclined to agree with their line of argument: but the law
was unable to follow it.   And Braun could not understand it
either.

   "They are mad," he said.   "They should be shut up in an
asylum.   Beasts! . . . I can understand a man killing himself for love. I can even understand a man killing the woman

he loves if she deceives him. . . . I don't mean that I would
excuse his doing so: but I am prepared to admit that there is
a remnant of primitive savagery in us: it is barbarous, but it is
logical: you kill the person who makes you suffer. But for a
woman to kill the man she loves, without bitterness, without
hatred, simply because another woman loves him, is nothing but
madness. . . . Can you understand it, Christophe?"

"Peuh!" said Christophe. "I'm quite used to being unable
to understand things. Love is madness."

Anna, who had said nothing, and seemed not to be listening,
said in her calm voice:

"There is nothing irrational in it. It is quite natural.
When a woman loves, she wants to destroy the man she loves
so that no one else may have him."

Braun looked at his wife aghast, thumped on the table, folded
his arms, and said:

"Where on earth did you get that from? . . . What? So
you must put your oar in, must you? What the devil do you
know about it?"

Anna blushed a little, and said no more. Braun went on:

"When a woman loves, she wants to destroy, does she? That's
a nice sort of thing to say! To destroy any one who is dear
to you is to destroy yourself.—On the contrary, when one loves,
the natural feeling is to do good to the person you love, to
cherish him, to defend him, to be kind to him, to be kind to
everything and everybody. Love is paradise on earth."

Anna sat staring into the darkness, and let him talk, and then
shook her head, and said coldly:

"A woman is not kind when she loves."

Christophe did not renew the experiment of hearing Anna
sing. He was afraid . . . of disillusion, or what? He could
not tell. Anna was just as fearful. She would never stay in
the room when he began to play.

But one evening in November, as he was reading by the fire,
he saw Anna sitting with her sewing in her lap, deep in one
of her reveries. She was looking blankly in front of her, and
Christophe thought he saw in her eyes the strangely burning
light of the other evening. He closed his book. She felt his

eyes upon her, and picked up her sewing. With her eyelids down she saw everything. He got up and said:

" Come."

She stared at him, and there was still a little uneasiness in her eyes: she understood, and followed him.

" Where are you going?" asked Braun.

" To the piano," replied Christophe

He played. She sang. At once he found her just as she had been on the first occasion. She entered the heroic world of music as a matter of course, as though it were her own. He tested her yet further, and went on to a second song, then to a third, more passionate, which let loose in her the whole gamut of passion, uplifting both herself and him: then, as they reached a very paroxysm, he stopped short and asked her, staring straight into her eyes:

" Tell me, what woman are you?"

Anna replied:

" I do not know."

He said brutally:

" What is there in you that makes you sing like that?"

She replied:

" Only what you put there to make me sing."

" Yes? Well, it is not out of place. I'm wondering whether I created it or you. How do you come to think of such things?"

" I don't know. I think I am no longer myself when I am singing."

" I think it is only then that you are yourself."

They said no more. Her cheeks were wet with a slight perspiration. Her bosom heaved, but she spoke no word. She stared at the lighted candles, and mechanically scratched away the wax that had trickled down the side of the candlestick. He drummed on the keys as he sat looking at her. They exchanged a few awkward remarks, brusquely and roughly, and then they tried a commonplace remark or two, and finally relapsed into silence, being fearful of probing any farther. . . .

Next day they hardly spoke: they stole glances at each other in a sort of dread. But they made it a habit to play and sing together in the evening. Before long they began in the afternoon, giving a little more time to it each day. Always the same incomprehensible passion would take possession of her with the very first bars, and set her flaming from head to foot, and, while the music lasted, make of the ordinary little woman an imperious Venus, the incarnation of all the furies of the soul. Braun was surprised at Anna's sudden craze for singing, but did not take the trouble to discover any explanation for a mere feminine caprice: he was often present at their little concerts, marked time with his head, gave his advice, and was perfectly happy, although he would have preferred softer, sweeter music: such an expenditure of energy seemed to him exaggerated and unnecessary. Christophe breathed freely in the atmosphere of danger: but he was losing his head: he was weakened by the crisis through which he had passed, and could not resist, and lost consciousness of what was happening to him without perceiving what was happening to Anna. One afternoon, in the middle of a song, with all the frantic ardor of it in full blast, she suddenly stopped, and left the room without making any explanation. Christophe waited for her: she did not return. Half an hour later, as he was going down the passage past Anna's room, through the half-open door he saw her absorbed in grim prayer, with all expression frozen from her face.

However, a slight, very slight, feeling of confidence cropped up between them. He tried to make her talk about her past: only with great difficulty could he induce her to tell him a few commonplace details. Thanks to Braun's easy, indiscreet good nature, he was able to gain a glimpse into her intimate life.

She was a native of the town. Her maiden name was Anna Maria Senfl. Her father, Martin Senfl, was a member of an old commercial house, very old and enormously rich, in whom pride of caste and religious strictness were ingrained. Being of an adventurous temper, like many of his fellow-countrymen, he had spent several years abroad in the East and in South America: he had even made bold exploring expeditions in Central Asia, whither he had gone to advance the commercial interests of his house, for love of science, and for his own pleasure. By dint of rolling through the world, he had not only gathered no moss, but had also rid himself of that which covered him, the moss of his old prejudices. When, therefore, he returned to his own country, being of a warm temper and an obstinate mind, he married, in face of the indignant protests of his family, the daughter of a farmer of the surrounding country, a lady of doubtful reputation who had originally been his mistress. Marriage had been the only available means of keeping the beautiful girl to himself, and he could not do without her. After having exercised its veto in vain, his family absolutely closed its doors to its erring member who had set aside its sacrosanct authority. The town—all those, that is, who mattered, who, as usual. were absolutely united in any matter that touched the moral dignity of the community—sided bodily against the rash couple. The explorer learned to his cost that it is no less dangerous to traverse the prejudice of the people in a country inhabited by the sectaries of Christ, than in a country inhabited by those of the Grand Lama. He had not been strong enough to live without public opinion. He had more than jeopardized his patrimony: he could find no employment: everything was closed to him. He wore himself out in futile wrath against the affronts of the implacable town. His health, undermined by excess and fever, could not bear up against it. He died of a flux of blood five months after his marriage. Four months later, his wife, a good creature, but weak and feather-brained, who had never lived through a day since her marriage without weeping, died in childbirth, casting the infant Anna upon the shores which she was leaving.

Martin's mother was alive. Even when they were dying she had not forgiven her son or the woman whom she had refused to acknowledge as her daughter-in-law. But when the woman died—and Divine vengeance was appeased—she took the child and looked after her. She was a woman of the narrowest piety: she was rich and mean, and kept a draper's shop in a gloomy street in the old town. She treated her son's daughter less as a grandchild than as an orphan taken in out of charity, and therefore occupying more or less the position of a servant by way of payment. However, she gave her a careful education: but she never departed from her attitude of suspicious strictness towards her: it seemed as though she considered the child guilty of her parents' sin, and therefore set herself to chasten and chastise the sin in her. She never allowed her any amusement: she punished everything that was natural in her gestures, words, thoughts, as a crime. She killed all joy in her young life. From a very early age Anna was accustomed to being bored in church and disguising the fact: she was hemmed in by the terrors of hell: every Sunday the child's heavy-lidded eyes used to see them at the door of the old *Münster,* in the shape of the immodest and distorted statues with a fire burning between their legs, while round their loins crawled toads and snakes. She became accustomed to suppressing her instincts and lying to herself. As soon as she was old enough to help her grandmother, she was kept busy from morning to night in the dark gloomy shop. She assimilated the habits of those around her, the spirit of order, grim economy, futile privations, the bored indifference, the contemptuous, ungracious conception of life, which is the natural consequence of religious beliefs in those who are not naturally religious. She was so wholly given up to her piety as to seem rather absurd even to the old woman: she indulged in far too many fasts and macerations: at one period she even went so far as to wear corsets embellished with pins, which stuck into her flesh with every movement. She was seen to go pale, but no one knew what was the matter. At last, when she fainted, a doctor was called in. She refused to allow him to examine her—(she would have died rather than undress in the presence of a man)—but she confessed: and the doctor was so angry about it that she promised not to do it again. To make quite sure her grandmother thereafter took to inspecting her clothes. In such self-torture Anna did not, as might have been supposed, find any mystic pleasure: she had little imagination, she would never have understood the poetry of saints like Francis of Assisi or Teresa. Her piety was sad and materialistic. When she tormented herself, it was not in any hope of advantage to be gained in the next world, but came only from a cruel boredom which rebounded against herself, so that she only found in it an almost angry pleasure in hurting herself. Singularly enough, her hard, cold spirit was, like her grandmother's, open to the influence of music, though she never knew how profound that influence was. She was impervious to all the other arts: probably she had never looked at a picture in her life: she seemed to have no sense of plastic beauty, for she was lacking in taste, owing to her proud and wilful indifference; the idea of a beautiful body only awoke in her the idea of nakedness, that is to say, like the peasant of whom Tolstoy speaks, a feeling of repugnance, which was all the stronger in Anna inasmuch as she was dimly aware, in her relations with other people whom she liked, of the vague sting of desire far more than of the calm impression of esthetic judgment. She had no more idea of her own beauty than of her suppressed instincts: or rather, she refused to have any idea of it: and with her habitual self-deception she succeeded in deluding herself.

Braun met her at a marriage feast at which she was present, quite unusually for her: for she was hardly ever invited because of the evil reputation which clung to her from her improper origin. She was twenty-two. He marked her out; not that she made any attempt to attract attention. She sat next him at dinner: she was very stiff and badly dressed, and she hardly ever opened her mouth. But Braun never stopped talking to her, in a monologue, all through the meal, and he went away in raptures. With his usual penetration, he had been struck by his neighbor's air of original simplicity: he had admired her common sense and her coolness: also he appreciated her healthiness and the solid domestic qualities which she seemed to him to possess. He called on her grandmother, called again, proposed, and was accepted. She was given no dowry: Madame Senfl had left all the wealth of her family to the town to encourage trade abroad.

At no point in her life had the young wife had any love for her husband; the idea of such a thing never seemed to her to play any part in the life of an honest woman, but rather to be properly set aside as guilty. But she knew the worth of Braun's kindness: she was grateful to him, though she never showed it, for having married her in spite of her doubtful origin. Besides, she had a very strong feeling of honor between husband and wife. For the first seven years of their married life nothing had occurred to disturb their union. They lived side by side, as it were, did not understand each other, and never worried about it: in the eyes of the world they were a model couple. They went out very little. Braun had a fairly large practice, but he had never succeeded in making his friends accept his wife. No one liked her: and the stigma of her birth was not yet quite obliterated. Anna, for her part, never put herself out in order to gain admission to society. She was resentful on account of the scorn which had cast a cloud on her childhood. Besides, she was never at her ease in society, and she was not sorry to be left out of it. She paid and received a few inevitable calls, such as her husband's interests made necessary. Her callers were inquisitive and scandalous women of the middle-class. Anna had not the slightest interest in their gossip, and she never took the trouble to conceal her indifference. That is what such people never forgive. So her callers grew fewer and more far between, and Anna was left alone. That was what she wanted: nothing could then come and break in upon the dreams over which she brooded, and the obscure thrill and humming of life that was ever in her body.

Meanwhile for some weeks Anna looked very unwell. Her face grew thin and pale. She avoided both Christophe and Braun. She spent her days in her room, lost in thought, and she never replied when she was spoken to. Usually Braun did not take much notice of her feminine caprices. He would explain them to Christophe at length. Like all men fated to be deceived by women he flattered himself that he knew them through and through. He did know something about them, as a matter of fact, but a little knowledge is quite useless. He knew that women often have fits of persistent moodiness and blindly sullen antagonism: and it was his opinion that it was necessary at such times to leave them alone, and to make no attempt to understand or, above all, to find out what they were doing in the dangerous unconscious world in which their minds were steeped. Nevertheless he did begin to grow anxious about Anna. He thought that her pining must be the result of her mode of life, always shut up, never going outside the town, hardly ever out of the house. He wanted her to go for walks: but he could hardly ever go with her: the whole day on Sunday was taken up with her pious duties, and on the other days of the week he had consultations all day long. As for Christophe, he avoided going out with her. Once or twice they had gone for a short walk together, as far as the gates of the town: they were bored to death. Their conversation came to a standstill. Nature seemed not to exist for Anna: she never saw anything: the country was to her only grass and stones: her insensibility was chilling. Christophe tried once to make her admire a beautiful view. She looked, smiled coldly, and said, with an effort towards being pleasant:

"Oh! yes, it is very mystic. . . ."

She said it just as she might have said:

"The sun is very hot."

Christophe was so irritated that he dug his nails into the palms of his hands. After that he never asked her anything: and when she was going out he always made some excuse and stayed in his room.

In reality it was not true that Anna was insensible to Nature. She did not like what are conventionally called beautiful landscapes: she could see no difference between them and other landscapes. But she loved the country whatever it might be like—just earth and air. Only she had no more idea of it than of her other strong feelings: and those who lived with her had even less idea of it.

Braun so far insisted as to induce his wife to make a day's excursion into the outskirts of the town. She was so bored with him that she consented for the sake of peace. It was arranged that they should go on the Sunday. At the last moment, the doctor, who had been looking forward to it with childlike glee, was detained by an urgent case of illness. Christophe went with Anna.

It was a fine winter day with no snow: a pure cold air, a clear sky, a flaming sun, and an icy wind. They went out on a little local railway which took them to one of the lines of blue hills which formed a distant halo round the town. Their compartment was full: they were separated. They did not speak to each other. Anna was in a gloomy mood: the day before she had declared to Braun's surprise, that she would not go to church on Sunday. For the first time in her life she missed a service. Was it revolt? . . . Who could tell what struggles were taking place in her? She stared blankly at the seat in front of her, she was pale: she was eating her heart out.

They got out of the train. The coldness and antagonism between them did not disappear during the first part of their
walk. They stepped out side by side: she walked with a firm
stride and looked at nothing: her hands were free: she swung
her arms: her heels rang out on the frozen earth.—Gradually her
face quickened into life. The swiftness of their pace brought
the color to her pale cheeks. Her lips parted to drink in the
keen air. At the turn of a zigzag path she began to climb
straight up the hillside like a goat; she scrambled along the edge
of a quarry, where she was in great danger of falling, clinging
to the shrubs. Christophe followed her. She climbed faster
and faster, slipping, stopping herself by clutching at the grass
with her hands. Christophe shouted to her to stop. She made
no reply, but went on climbing on all fours. They passed
through the mists which hung above the valley like a silvery
gauze rent here and there by the bushes: and they stood in
the warm sunlight of the uplands. When she reached the summit she stopped: her face was aglow: her mouth was open, and
she was breathing heavily. Ironically she looked down at Christophe scaling the slope, took off her cloak, flung it at him, then
without giving him time to take his breath, she darted on.
Christophe ran after her. They warmed to the game: the air
intoxicated them. She plunged down a steep slope: the stones
gave way under her feet: she did not falter, she slithered, jumped,
sped down like an arrow. Every now and then she would dart
a glance behind her to see how much she had gained on Christophe. He was close upon her. She plunged into a wood. The
dead leaves crackled under their footsteps: the branches which
she thrust aside whipped back into his face. She stumbled over
the roots of a tree. He caught her. She struggled, lunging
out with hands and feet, struck him hard, trying to knock him
off: she screamed and laughed. Her bosom heaved against him:
for a moment their cheeks touched: he tasted the sweat that lay
on Anna's brow: he breathed the scent of her moist hair. She
pushed away from him and looked at him, unmoved, with
defiant eyes. He was amazed at her strength, which all went
for nothing in her ordinary life.

They went to the nearest village, joyfully trampling the dry
stubble crisping beneath their feet. In front of them whirled

the crows who were ransacking the fields.   The sun was burning, the wind was biting.   He held Anna's arm.   She had on a rather thin dress: through the stuff he could feel the moisture and the tingling warmth of her body.   He wanted her to put on her cloak once more: she refused, and in bravado undid the hooks at her neck.   They lunched at an inn, the sign of which bore the figure of a " wild man " (*Zum wilden Mann*).   A little pine-tree grew in front of the door.   The dining-room was decorated with German quatrains, and two chromolithographs, one of which was sentimental: *In the Spring* (*Im Frühling*), and the other patriotic: *The Battle of Saint Jacques,* and a crucifix with a skull at the foot of the cross.   Anna had a voracious appetite, such as Christophe had never known her to have. They drank freely of the ordinary white wine.   After their meal they set out once more across the fields, in a blithe spirit of companionship.   In neither was there any equivocal thought. They were thinking only of the pleasure of their walk, the singing in their blood, and the whipping, nipping air.   Anna's tongue was loosed.   She was no longer on her guard: she said just whatever came into her mind.

She talked about her childhood, and how her grandmother used to take her to the house of an old friend who lived near the cathedral: and while the old ladies talked they sent her into the garden over which there hung the shadow of the *Münster*.   She used to sit in a corner and never stir: she used to listen to the shivering of the leaves, and watch the busy swarming insects: and she used to be both pleased and afraid.— (She made no mention of her fear of devils: her imagination was obsessed by it: she had been told that they prowled round churches but never dared enter: and she used to believe that they appeared in the shape of animals: spiders, lizards, ants, all the hideous creatures that swarmed about her, under the leaves, over the earth, or in the crannies of the walls).—Then she told him about the house she used to live in, and her sunless room: she remembered it with pleasure: she used to spend many sleepless nights there, telling herself things. . . .

" What things? "

" Silly things."

" Tell me."

She shook her head in refusal.

" Why not? "

She blushed, then laughed, and added:

" In the daytime too, while I was at work."

She thought for a moment, laughed once more, and then said:
" They were silly things, bad things."

He said, jokingly:

" Weren't you afraid? "

" Of what? "

" Of being damned? "

The expression in her eyes froze.

" You mustn't talk of that," she said.

He turned the conversation. He marveled at the strength
she had shown a short while before in their scuffle. She resumed her confiding expression and told him of her girlish
achievements—(she said " boyish," for, when she was a child she
had always longed to join in the games and fights of the boys).—
On one occasion when she was with a little boy who was a head
taller than herself she had suddenly struck him with her fist,
hoping that he would strike her back. But he ran away yelling
that she was beating him. Once, again, in the country she
had climbed on to the back of a black cow as she was grazing:
the terrified beast flung her against a tree, and she had narrowly
escaped being killed. Once she took it into her head to jump
out of a first-floor window because she had dared herself to
do it: she was lucky enough to get off with a sprain. She used
to invent strange, dangerous gymnastics when she was left alone
in the house: she used to subject her body to all sorts of queer
experiments.

" Who would think it of you now, to see you looking so
solemn? . . ."

" Oh! " she said, " if you were to see me sometimes when I
am alone in my room! "

" What! Even now? "

She laughed. She asked him—jumping from one subject to
another—if he were a shot.

He told her that he never shot. She said that she had once
shot at a blackbird with a gun and had wounded it. He waxed
indignant.

"Oh!" she said. "What does it matter?"

"Have you no heart?"

"I don't know."

"Don't you ever think the beasts are living creatures like ourselves?"

"Yes," she said. "Certainly. I wanted to ask you: do you think the beasts have souls?"

"Yes. I think so."

"The minister says not. But I think they have souls. . . . Sometimes," she added, "I think I must have been an animal in a previous existence."

He began to laugh.

"There's nothing to laugh at," she said (she laughed too). "That is one of the stories I used to tell myself when I was little. I used to pretend to be a cat, a dog, a bird, a foal, a heifer. I was conscious of all their desires. I wanted to be in their skins or their feathers for a little while: and it used to be as though I really was. You can't understand that?"

"You are a strange creature. But if you feel such kinship with the beasts how can you bear to hurt them?"

"One is always hurting some one. Some people hurt me. I hurt other people. That's the way of the world. I don't complain. We can't afford to be squeamish in life! I often hurt myself for the pleasure of it."

"Hurt yourself?"

"Myself. One day I hammered a nail into my hand, here."

"Why?"

"There wasn't any reason."

(She did not tell him that she had been trying to crucify herself.)

"Give me your hand," she said.

"What do you want it for?"

"Give it me."

He gave her his hand. She took it and crushed it until he cried out. They played, like peasants, at seeing how much they could hurt each other. They were happy and had no ulterior thought. The rest of the world, the fetters of their ordinary life, the sorrows of the past, fear of the future, the gathering storm within themselves, all had disappeared.

They had walked several miles, but they were not at all tired.
Suddenly she stopped, flung herself down on the ground, and
lay full length on the stubble, and said no more. She lay on
her back with her hands behind her head and looked up at the
sky. Oh! the peace of it, and the sweetness! . . . A few
yards away a spring came bubbling up in an intermittent stream,
like an artery beating, now faintly, now more strongly. The
horizon took on a pearly hue. A mist hung over the purple
earth from which the black naked trees stood out. The late
winter sun was shining, the little pale gold sun sinking down
to rest. Like gleaming arrows the birds cleft the air. The
gentle voices of the country bells called and answered calling
from village to village. . . . Christophe sat near Anna and
looked down at her. She gave no thought to him. She was
full of a heartfelt joy. Her beautiful lips smiled silently. He
thought:

"Is that you? I do not know you."

"Nor I. Nor I. I think I must be some one else. I am no
longer afraid: I am no longer afraid of Him. . . . Ah! How
He stifled me, how He made me suffer! I seemed to have been
nailed down in my coffin. . . . Now I can breathe: this body
and this heart are mine. My body. My dear body. My heart
is free and full of love. There is so much happiness in me!
And I knew it not. I never knew myself! What have you done
to me? . . ."

So he thought he could hear her softly sighing to herself.
But she was thinking of nothing, only that she was happy, only
that all was well.

The evening had begun to fall. Behind the gray and lilac
veils of mist, about four o'clock, the sun, weary of life, was
setting. Christophe got up and went to Anna. He bent down
to her. She turned her face to him, still dizzy with looking
up into the vast sky over which she seemed to have been hanging.
A few seconds passed before she recognized him. Then her eyes
stared at him with an enigmatic smile that told him of the
unease that was in her. To escape the knowledge of it he closed
his eyes for a moment. When he opened them again she was still
looking at him: and it seemed to him that for many days they
had so looked into each other's eyes. It was as though they

were reading each other's soul.   But they refused to admit what
they had read there.

He held out his hand to her.   She took it without a word.
They went back to the village, the towers of which they could
see shaped like the pope's nose in the heart of the valley: one
of the towers had an empty storks' nest on the top of its roof
of mossy tiles, looking just like a toque on a woman's head.
At a cross-roads just outside the village they passed a fountain
above which stood a little Catholic saint, a wooden Magdalene,
graciously and a little mincingly holding out her arms.   With
an instinctive movement Anna responded to the gesture and
held out her arms also, and she climbed on to the curb and filled
the arms of the pretty little goddess with branches of holly and
mountain-ash with such of their red berries as the birds and the
frost had spared.

On the road they passed little groups of peasants and peasant
women in their Sunday clothes: women with brown skins, very
red cheeks, thick plaits coiled round their heads, light dresses,
and hats with flowers.   They wore white gloves and red cuffs.
.They were singing simple songs with shrill placid voices not
very much in tune.   In a stable a cow was mooing.   A child
with whooping-cough was coughing in a house.   A little farther
on there came up the nasal sound of a clarionet and a cornet.
There was dancing in the village square between the little inn
and the cemetery.   Four musicians, perched on a table, were
playing a tune.   Anna and Christophe sat in front of the inn
and watched the dancers.   The couples were jostling and slanging each other vociferously.   The girls were screaming for the
pleasure of making a noise.   The men drinking were beating time
on the tables with their fists.   At any other time such ponderous
coarse joy would have disgusted Anna: but now she loved it:
she had taken off her hat and was watching eagerly.   Christophe
poked fun at the burlesque solemnity of the music and the
musicians.   He fumbled in his pockets and produced a pencil
and began to make lines and dots on the back of a hotel bill:
he was writing dance music.   The paper was soon covered: he
asked for more, and these too he covered like the first with his
big scrawling writing.   Anna looked over his shoulder with her
face near his and hummed over what he wrote: she tried to

guess how the phrases would end, and clapped her hands when
she guessed right or when her guesses were falsified by some
unexpected sally. When he had done Christophe took what
he had written to the musicians. They were honest Suabians
who knew their business, and they made it out without much
difficulty. The melodies were sentimental, and of a burlesque
humor, with strongly accented rhythms, punctuated, as it were,
with bursts of laughter. It was impossible to resist their impetuous fun: nobody's feet could help dancing. Anna rushed
into the throng; she gripped the first pair of hands held out
to her and whirled about like a mad thing; a tortoise-shell pin
dropped out of her hair and a few locks of it fell down and
hung about her face. Christophe never took his eyes off her:
he marveled at the fine healthy animal who hitherto had been
condemned to silence and immobility by a pitiless system of
discipline: he saw her as no one had ever seen her, as she really
was under her borrowed mask: a Bacchante, drunk with life.
She called to him. He ran to her and put his arms round her
waist. They danced and danced until they whirled crashing
into a wall. They stopped, dazed. Night was fully come. They
rested for a moment and then said good-by to the company.
Anna, who was usually so stiff with the common people, partly
from embarrassment, partly from contempt, held out her hand
to the musicians, the host of the inn, the village boys with whom
she had been dancing.

Once more they were alone under the brilliant frozen sky
retracing the paths across the fields by which they had come
in the morning. Anna was still excited. She talked less and
less, and then ceased altogether, as though she had succumbed
to fatigue or to the mysterious emotion of the night. She leaned
affectionately on Christophe. As they were going down the
slope up which they had so blithely scrambled a few hours before, she sighed. They approached the station. As they came
to the first house he stopped and looked at her. She looked up
at him and smiled sadly. The train was just as crowded as it
had been before, and they could not talk. He sat opposite her
and devoured her with his eyes. Her eyes were lowered: she
raised them and looked at him when she felt his eyes upon her
then she glanced away and he could not make her look at him,

again. She sat gazing out into the night. A vague smile hovered about her lips which showed a little weariness at the corners. Then her smile disappeared. Her expression became mournful. He thought her mind must be engrossed by the rhythm of the train and he tried to speak to her. She replied coldly, without turning her head, with a single word. He tried to persuade himself that her fatigue was responsible for the change: but he knew that it was for a very different reason. The nearer they came to the town the more he saw Anna's face grow cold, and life die down in her, and all her beautiful body with its savage grace drop back into its casing of stone. She did not make use of the hand he held out to her as she stepped out of the carriage. They returned home in silence.

A few days later, about four o'clock in the evening, they were alone together. Braun had gone out. Since the day before the town had been shrouded in a pale greenish fog. The murmuring of the invisible river came up. The lights of the electric trams glared through the mist. The light of day was dead, stifled: time seemed to be wiped out: it was one of those hours when men lose all consciousness of reality, an hour which is outside the march of the ages. After the cutting wind of the preceding days, the moist air had suddenly grown warmer, too damp and too soft. The sky was filled with snow, and bent under the load.

They were alone together in the drawing-room, the cold cramped taste of which was the reflection of that of its mistress. They said nothing. He was reading. She was sewing. He got up and went to the window: he pressed his face against the panes, and stood so dreaming: he was stupefied and heavy with the dull light which was cast back from the darkling sky upon the livid earth: his thoughts were uneasy: he tried in vain to fix them: they escaped him. He was filled with a bitter agony: he felt that he was being engulfed: and in the depths of his being, from the chasm of the heap of ruins came a scorching wind in slow gusts. He turned his back on Anna: she could not see him, she was engrossed in her work; but a faint thrill passed through her body: she pricked herself several times with her needle, but she did not feel it. They were both fascinated by the approaching danger.

He threw off his stupor and took a few strides across the room. The piano attracted him and made him fearful. He looked away from it. As he passed it his hand could not resist it, and touched a note. The sound quivered like a human voice. Anna trembled, and let her sewing fall. Christophe was already seated and playing. Without seeing her, he knew that Anna had got up, that she was coming towards him, that she was by his side. Before he knew what he was doing, he had begun the religious and passionate melody that she had sung the first time she had revealed herself to him: he improvised a fugue with variations on the theme. Without his saying a word to her, she began to sing. They lost all sense of their surroundings. The sacred frenzy of music had them in its clutches. . . .

O music, that openest the abysses of the soul! Thou dost destroy the normal balance of the mind. In ordinary life, ordinary souls are closed rooms: within, there droop the unused forces of life, the virtues and the vices to use which is hurtful to us: sage, practical wisdom, cowardly common sense, are the keepers of the keys of the room. They let us see only a few cupboards tidily and properly arranged. But music holds the magic wand which drives back every lock. The doors are opened. The demons of the heart appear. And, for the first time, the soul sees itself naked.—While the siren sings, while the bewitching voice trembles on the air, the tamer holds all the wild beasts in check with the power of the eye. The mighty mind and reason of a great musician fascinates all the passions that he sets loose. But when the music dies away, when the tamer is no longer there, then the passions he has summoned forth are left roaring in their tottering cage, and they seek their prey. . . .

The melody ended. Silence. . . . While she was singing she had laid her hand on Christophe's shoulder. They dared not move: and each felt the other trembling. Suddenly—in a flash—she bent down to him, he turned to her: their lips met: he drank her breath.

She flung away from him and fled. He stayed, not stirring,

in the dark. Braun returned. They sat down to dinner. Christophe was incapable of thought. Anna seemed absent-minded : she was looking " elsewhere." Shortly after dinner she went to her room. Christophe found it impossible to stay alone with Braun, and went upstairs also.

About midnight the doctor was called from his bed to a patient. Christophe heard him go downstairs and out. It had been snowing ever since six o'clock. The houses and the streets were under a shroud. The air was as though it were padded with cotton-wool. Not a step, not a carriage could be heard outside. The town seemed dead. Christophe could not sleep. He had a feeling of terror which grew from minute to minute. He could not stir. He lay stiff in his bed, on his back, with his eyes wide open. A metallic light cast up from the white earth and roofs fell upon the walls of the room. . . . An imperceptible noise made him tremble. Only a man at a feverish tension could have heard it Came a soft rustling on the floor of the passage. Christophe sat up in bed. The faint noise came nearer, stopped ; a board creaked. There was some one behind the door : some one waiting. . . . Absolute stillness for a few seconds, perhaps for several minutes. . . . Christophe could not breathe, he broke out into a sweat. Outside flakes of snow brushed the window as with a wing. A hand fumbled with the door and opened it. There appeared a white form, and it came slowly forward : it halted a few yards away from him. Christophe could see nothing clearly : but he could hear her breathing : and he could hear his own heart thumping. She came nearer to him ; once more she halted. Their faces were so near that their breath mingled. Their eyes sought each other vainly in the darkness. . . . She fell into his arms. In silence, without a word, they hugged each other close, frenziedly. . . .

An hour, two hours, a century later, the door of the house was opened. Anna broke from the embrace in which they were locked, slipped away, and left Christophe without a word, just as she had come. He heard her bare feet moving away, just skimming the floor in her swift flight. She regained her room, and there Braun found her in her bed, apparently asleep.

So she lay through the night, with eyes wide open, breathless, still, in her narrow bed near the sleeping Braun. How many nights had she passed like that!

Christophe could not sleep either. He was utterly in despair. He had always regarded the things of love, and especially marriage, with tragic seriousness. He hated the frivolity of those writers whose art uses adultery as a spicy flavoring. Adultery roused in him a feeling of repulsion which was a combination of his vulgar brutality and high morality. He had always felt a mixture of religious respect and physical disgust for a woman who belonged to another man. The doglike promiscuity in which some of the rich people in Europe lived appalled him. Adultery with the consent of the husband is a filthy thing: without the husband's knowledge it is a base deceit only worthy of a rascally servant hiding away to betray and befoul his master's honor. How often had he not piteously despised those whom he had known to be guilty of such cowardice! He had broken with some of his friends who had thus dishonored themselves in his eyes. . . . And now he too was sullied with the same shameful thing! The circumstances of the crime only made it the more odious. He had come to the house a sick, wretched man. His friend had welcomed him, helped him, given him comfort. His kindness had never flagged. Nothing had been too great a demand upon it. He owed him his very life. And in return he had robbed the man of his honor and his happiness, his poor little domestic happiness! He had basely betrayed him, and with whom? With a woman whom he did not know, did not understand, did not love. . . . Did he not love her? His every drop of blood rose up against him. Love is too faint a word to express the river of fire that rushed through him when he thought of her. It was not love, it was a thousand times a greater thing than love. . . . He was in a whirl all through the night. He got up, dipped his face in the icy water, gasped, and shuddered. The crisis came to a head in an attack of fever.

When he got up, aching all over, he thought that she, even more than he, must be overwhelmed with shame. He went to the window The sun was shining down upon the dazzling snow. In the garden Anna was hanging out the clothes on a line. She was engrossed in her work, and seemed to be in no wise put out. She had a dignity in her carriage and her gesture which was quite new to him, and made him, unconsciously, liken her to a moving statue.

They met again at lunch. Braun was away for the whole day. Christophe could not have borne meeting him. He wanted to speak to Anna. But they were not alone: the servant kept going and coming: they had to keep guard on themselves. In vain did Christophe try to catch Anna's eye. She did not look at him or at anything. There was no indication of inward ferment: and always in her smallest movement there was the unaccustomed assurance and nobility. After lunch he hoped they would have an opportunity of speaking: but the servant dallied over clearing away; and when they went into the next room she contrived to follow them: she always had something to fetch or to bring: she stayed bustling in the passage near the half-open door which Anna showed no hurry to shut: it looked as though she were spying on them. Anna sat by the window with her everlasting sewing. Christophe leaned back in an armchair with his back to the light, and a book on his knee which he did not attempt to read. Anna could only see his profile, and she noticed the torment in his face as he looked at the wall: and she gave a cruel smile. From the roof of the house and the tree in the garden the melting snow trickled down into the gravel with a thin tinkling noise. Some distance away was the laughter of children chasing each other in the street and snow-balling. Anna seemed to be half-asleep. The silence was torture to Christophe: it hurt him so that he could have cried out.

At last the servant went downstairs and left the house. Christophe got up, turned to Anna, and was about to say:

"Anna! Anna! what have we done?"

Anna looked at him: her eyes, which had been obstinately lowered, had just opened: they rested on Christophe, and devoured him hotly, hungrily. Christophe felt his own eyes burn under the impact, and he reeled; everything that he wanted to say was brushed aside. They came together, and once more they were locked in an embrace. . . .

The shades of the evening were falling. Their blood was still in turmoil. She was lying down, with her dress torn her arms outstretched. He had buried his face in the pillow, and was groaning aloud. She turned towards him and raised his head, and caressed his eyes and his lips with her fingers: she brought her face close to his, and she stared into his eyes. Her eyes were deep, deep as a lake, and they smiled at each other in utter indifference to pain. They lost consciousness. He was silent. Mighty waves of feeling thrilled through them. . . .

That night, when he was alone in his room, Christophe thought of killing himself.

Next day, as soon as he was up, he went to Anna. Now it was he whose eyes avoided hers. As soon as he met their gaze all that he had to say was banished from his mind. However, he made an effort, and began to speak of the cowardice of what they had done. Hardly had she understood than she roughly stopped his lips with her hand. She flung away from him with a scowl, and her lips pressed together, and an evil expression upon her face. He went on. She flung the work she was holding down on the ground, opened the door, and tried to go out. He caught her hands, closed the door, and said bitterly that she was very lucky to be able to banish from her mind all idea of the evil they had done. She struggled like an animal caught in a trap, and cried angrily:

" Stop! . . . You coward, can't you see how I am suffer‧ing? . . . I won't let you speak! Let me go!"

Her face was drawn, her expression was full of hate and fear, like a beast that has been hurt: her eyes would have killed him, if they could.—He let her go. She ran to the opposite corner of the room to take shelter. He had no desire to pursue her. His heart was aching with bitterness and terror. Braun came in. He looked at them, and they stood stockishly there. Nothing existed for them‧ outside their own suffering.

Christophe went out. Braun and Anna sat down to their meal. In the middle of dinner Braun suddenly got up to open the window. Anna had fainted.

Christophe left the town for a fortnight on the pretext of having been called away. For a whole week Anna remained shut up in her room except for meal-times. She slipped back into consciousness of herself, into her old habits, the old life from which she had thought she had broken away, from which we never break away. In vain did she close her eyes to what she had done. Every day anxiety made further inroads into her heart, and finally took possession of it. On the following Sunday she refused once more to go to church. But the Sunday after that she went, and never omitted it again. She was conquered, but not submissive. God was the enemy,—an enemy from whose power she could not free herself. She went to Him with the sullen anger of a slave who is forced into obedience. During service her face showed nothing but cold hostility: but in the depths of her soul the whole of her religious life was a fierce, dumbly exasperated struggle against the Master whose reproaches persecuted her. She pretended not to hear. She *had* to hear: and bitterly, savagely, with clenched teeth, hard eyes, and a deep frowning furrow in her forehead, she would argue with God. She thought of Christophe with hatred. She could not forgive him for having delivered her for one moment from the prison of her soul, only to let her fall back into it again, to be the prey of its tormentors. She could not sleep; day and night she went over and over the same torturing thoughts: she did not complain: she went on obstinately doing her household work and all her other duties, and throughout maintaining the unyielding and obstinate character of her will in her daily life, the various tasks of which she fulfilled with the regularity of a machine. She grew thin, and seemed to be a prey to some internal malady. Braun questioned her fondly and anxiously: he wanted to sound her. She repulsed him angrily. The greater her remorse grew for what she had done to him, the more harshly she spoke to him.

Christophe had determined not to return. He wore himself out. He took long runs and violent exercise, rowed, walked, climbed mountains. Nothing was able to quench the fire in him.

He was more the victim of passion than an ordinary man. It is the necessity of the nature of men of genius. Even the most chaste, like Beethoven and Bürchner, must always be in love: every human capacity is raised to a higher degree in them, and as, in them, every human capacity is seized on by their imagination, their minds are a prey to a continual succession of passions. Most often they are only transitory fires: one destroys another, and all are absorbed by the great blaze of the creative spirit. But if the heat of the furnace ceases to fill the soul, then the soul is left defenseless against the passions without which it cannot live: it must have passion, it creates passion: and the passions will devour the soul . . . —and then, besides the bitter desire that harrows the flesh, there is the need of tenderness which drives a man who is weary and disillusioned of life into the mothering arms of the comforter, woman. A great man is more of a child than a lesser man: more than any other, he needs to confide in a woman, to lay his head in the soft hands of the beloved, in the folds of the lap of her gown.

But Christophe could not understand. . . . He did not believe in the inevitability of passion—the idiotic cult of the romantics. He believed that a man can and must fight with all the force of his will. . . . His will! Where was it? Not a trace of it was left. He was possessed. He was stung by the barbs of memory, day and night. The scent of Anna's body was with him everywhere. He was like a dismantled hulk, rolling rudderless, at the mercy of the winds. In vain did he try to escape, he strove mightily, wore himself out in the attempt: he always found himself brought back to the same place, and he shouted to the wind:

"Break me, break me, then! What do you want of me?"

Feverishly he probed into himself. Why, why this woman? . . . Why did he love her? It was not for her qualities of heart or mind. There were any number of better and more intelligent women. It was not for her body. He had had other mistresses more acceptable to his senses. What was it? . . . —"We love because we love."—Yes, but there is a reason, even if it be beyond ordinary human reason. Madness? That means nothing. Why this madness?

Because there is a hidden soul, blind forces, demons, which every one of us bears imprisoned in himself. Our every effort, since the first existence of humanity, has been directed towards the building up against this inward sea of the dykes of our reason and our religions. But a storm arises (and the richest souls are the most subject to storms), the dykes are broken, the demons have free play, they find themselves in the presence of other souls uptorn by similar powers. . . . They hurl themselves at each other. Hatred or love? A frenzy of mutual destruction?—Passion is the soul of prey.

The sea has burst its bounds. Who shall turn it back into its bed? Then must a man appeal to a mightier than himself. To Neptune, the God of the tides.

After a fortnight of vain efforts to escape, Christophe returned to Anna. He could not live away from her. He was stifled.

And yet he went on struggling. On the evening of his return, they found excuses for not meeting and not dining together: at night they locked their doors in fear and dread.—But love was stronger than they. In the middle of the night she came creeping barefooted, and knocked at his door. She wept silently. He felt the tears coursing down her cheeks. She tried to control herself, but her anguish was too much for her and she sobbed. Under the frightful burden of her grief Christophe forgot his own: he tried to calm her and gave her tender, comfortable words. She moaned:

" I am so unhappy. I wish I were dead. . . ."

Her plaint pierced his heart. He tried to kiss her. She repulsed him:

" I hate you! . . . Why did you ever come? "

She wrenched herself away from him. She turned her back on him and shook with rage and grief. She hated him mortally. Christophe lay still, appalled. In the silence Anna heard his choking breathing: she turned suddenly and flung her arms round his neck:

" Poor Christophe! " she said. " I have made you suffer. . . ."

For the first time he heard pity in her voice.

" Forgive me," she said.

He said:

" We must forgive each other."

She raised herself as though she found it hard to breathe. She sat there, with bowed back, overwhelmed, and said:

"I am ruined. . . . It is God's will. He has betrayed me. . . . What can I do against Him?"

She stayed for a long time like that, then lay down again and did not stir. A faint light proclaimed the dawn. In the half-light he saw her sorrowful face so near his. He murmured:

"The day."

She made no movement.

He said:

"So be it. What does it matter?"

She opened her eyes and left him with an expression of utter weariness. She sat for a moment looking down at the floor. In a dull, colorless voice she said:

"I thought of killing him last night."

He gave a start of terror:

"Anna!" he said.

She was staring gloomily at the window.

"Anna!" he said again. "In God's name! . . . **Not** him! . . . He is the best of us! . . ."

She echoed:

"Not him. Very well."

They looked at each other.

They had known it for a long time. They had known where the only way out lay. They could not bear to live a lie. And they had never even considered the possibility of eloping together. They knew perfectly well that that would not solve the problem: for the bitterest suffering came not from the external obstacles that held them apart, but in themselves, in their different souls. It was as impossible for them to live together as to live apart. They were driven into a corner.

From that moment on they never touched each other: the shadow of death was upon them: they were sacred to each other.

But they put off appointing a time for their decision. They kept on saying: "To-morrow, to-morrow. . . ." And they turned their eyes away from their to-morrow. Christophe's mighty soul had wild spasms of revolt: he would not consent to his defeat: he despised suicide, and he could not resign himself to such a pitiful and abrupt conclusion of his splendid life. As

for Anna, how could she, unless she were forced, accept the idea
of a death which must lead to eternal death? But ruthless
necessity was at their heels, and the circle was slowly narrowing
about them.

That morning, for the first time since the betrayal, Christophe
was left alone with Braun. Until then he had succeeded in
avoiding him. He found it intolerable to be with him. He
had to make an excuse to avoid eating at the same table: the
food stuck in his throat. To shake the man's hand, to eat his
bread, to give the kiss of Judas! . . . Most odious for him
to think of was not the contempt he had for himself so much
as the agony of suffering that Braun must endure if he should
come to know. . . . The idea of it crucified him. He knew
only too well that poor Braun would never avenge himself, that
perhaps he would not even have the strength to hate them: but
what an utter wreck of all his life! . . . How would he
regard him! Christophe felt that he could not face the reproach
in his eyes.—And it was inevitable that sooner or later Braun
would be warned. Did he not already suspect something? Seeing him again after his fortnight's absence Christophe was struck
by the change in him: Braun was not the same man. His gaiety
had disappeared, or there was something forced in it. At meals
he would stealthily glance at Anna, who talked not at all, ate
not at all, and seemed to be burning away like the oil in a lamp.
With timid, touching kindness he tried to look after her: she
rejected his attentions harshly: then he bent his head over his
plate and relapsed into silence. Anna could bear it no longer,
and flung her napkin on the table in the middle of the meal and
left the room. The two men finished their dinner in silence,
or pretended to do so, for they ate nothing: they dared not raise
their eyes. When they had finished, Christophe was on the
point of going when Braun suddenly clasped his arm with both
hands and said:

"Christophe!"

Christophe looked at him uneasily.

"Christophe," said Braun again—(his voice was shaking),—
"do you know what's the matter with her?"

Christophe stood transfixed: for a moment or two he could

find nothing to say. Braun stood looking at him timidly: very quickly he begged his pardon:

"You see a good deal of her, she trusts you. . . . ."

Christophe was very near taking Braun's hands and kissing them and begging his forgiveness. Braun saw Christophe's downcast expression, and, at once, he was terrified, and refused to see: he cast him a beseeching look and stammered hurriedly and gasped:

"No, no. You know nothing? Nothing?"

Christophe was overwhelmed and said:

"No."

Oh! the bitterness of not being able to lay bare his offense, to humble himself, since to do so would be to break the heart of the man he had wronged! Oh! the bitterness of being unable to tell the truth, when he could see in the eyes of the man asking him for it, that he could not, would not know the truth! . . .

"Thanks, thank you. I thank you . . ." said Braun.

He stayed with his hands plucking at Christophe's sleeve as though there was something else he wished to ask, and yet dared not, avoiding his eyes. Then he let go, sighed, and went away.

Christophe was appalled by this new lie. He hastened to Anna. Stammering in his excitement, he told her what had happened. Anna listened gloomily and said:

"Oh, well. He knows. What does it matter?"

"How can you talk like that?" cried Christophe. "It is horrible! I will not have him suffer, whatever it may cost us, whatever it may cost."

Anna grew angry.

"And what if he does suffer? Don't I have to suffer? Let him suffer too!"

They said bitter things to each other. He accused her of loving only herself. She reproached him with thinking more of her husband than of herself.

But a moment later, when he told her that he could not go on living like that, and that he would go and tell the whole story to Braun, then she cried out on him for his selfishness, declaring that she did not care a bit about Christophe's conscience, but was quite determined that Braun should never know.

In spite of her hard words she was thinking as much of Braun

as of Christophe. Though she had no real affection for her
husband she was fond of him. She had a religious respect for
social ties and the duties they involve. Perhaps she did not
think that it was the duty of a wife to be kind and to love her
husband: but she did think that she was compelled scrupulously
to fulfil her household duties and to remain faithful. It seemed
to her ignoble to fail in that object as she herself had done.

And even more surely than Christophe she knew that Braun
must know everything very soon. It was something to her credit
that she concealed the fact from Christophe, either because she
did not wish to add to his troubles or more probably because
of her pride.

Secluded though the Braun household was, secret though the
tragedy might remain that was being enacted there, some hint
of it had trickled away to the outer world.

In that town it was impossible for any one to flatter himself
that the facts of his life were hidden. This was strangely true.
No one ever looked at anybody in the streets: the doors and
shutters of the houses were closed. But there were mirrors
fastened in the corners of the windows: and as one passed the
houses one could hear the faint creaking of the venetian shutters
being pushed open and shut again. Nobody took any notice of
anybody else: everything and everybody were apparently ignored:
but it was not long before one perceived that not a single word,
not a single gesture had been unobserved: whatever one did,
whatever one said, whatever one saw, whatever one ate was
known at once: even what one thought was known, or, at least,
everybody pretended to know. One was surrounded by a universal, mysterious watchfulness. Servants, tradespeople, relations,
friends, people who were neither friends nor enemies, passing
strangers, all by tacit agreement shared in this instinctive
espionage, the scattered elements of which were gathered to a
head no one knew how. Not only were one's actions observed,
but they probed into one's inmost heart. In that town no man
had the right to keep the secrets of his conscience, and everybody
had the right to rummage amongst his intimate thoughts, and,
if they were offensive to public opinion, to call him to account.
The invisible despotism of the collective mind dominated the

individual: all his life he remained like a child in a state of tutelage: he could call nothing his own: he belonged to the town.

It was enough for Anna to have stayed away from church two Sundays running to arouse suspicion. As a rule no one seemed to notice her presence at service: she lived outside the life of the place, and the town seemed to have forgotten her existence.—On the evening of the first Sunday when she had stayed away her absence was known to everybody and docketed in their memory. On the following Sunday not one of the pious people following the blessed words in their Bibles or on the minister's lips seemed to be distracted from their solemn attention: not one of them had failed to notice as they entered, and to verify as they left, the fact that Anna's place was empty. Next day Anna began to receive visits from women she had not seen for many months: they came on various pretexts, some fearing that she was ill, others assuming a new interest in her affairs, her husband, her house: some of them showed a singularly intimate knowledge of the doings of her household: not one of them—(with clumsy ingenuity)—made any allusion to her absence from church on two Sundays running. Anna said that she was unwell and declared that she was very busy. Her visitors listened attentively and applauded her: Anna knew that they did not believe a word she said. Their eyes wandered round the room, prying, taking notes, docketing. They did not for a moment drop their cold affability or their noisy affected chatter: but their eyes revealed the indiscreet curiosity which was devouring them. Two or three with exaggerated indifference inquired after M. Krafft.

A few days later—(during Christophe's absence),—the minister came himself. He was a handsome, good-natured creature, splendidly healthy, affable, with that imperturbable tranquillity which comes to a man from the consciousness of being in sole possession of the truth, the whole truth. He inquired anxiously after the health of the members of his flock, politely and absently listened to the excuses she gave him, which he had not asked for, accepted a cup of tea, made a mild joke or two, expressed his opinion on the subject of drink that the wine referred to in the Bible was not alcoholic liquor, produced several quotations, told a story, and, as he was leaving, made a dark allusion to the danger of bad company, to certain excursions in the country, to the spirit of impiety, to the impurity of dancing, and the filthy lusts of the flesh. He seemed to be addressing his remarks to the age in general and not to Anna. He stopped for a moment, coughed, got up, bade Anna give his respectful compliments to M. Braun, made a joke in Latin, bowed, and took his leave.—Anna was left frozen by his allusion. Was it an allusion? How could he have known about her excursion with Christophe? They had not met a soul of their acquaintance that day. But was not everything known in the town? The musician with the remarkable face and the young woman in black who had danced at the inn had attracted much attention: their descriptions had been spread abroad; and, as the story was bandied from mouth to mouth, it had reached the town where the watchful malice of the gossips had not failed to recognize Anna. No doubt it amounted as yet to no more than a suspicion, but it was singularly attractive, and it was augmented by information supplied by Anna's maid. Public curiosity had been a-tip-toe, waiting for them to compromise each other, spying on them with a thousand invisible eyes. The silent crafty people of the town were creeping close upon them, like a cat lying in wait for a mouse.

In spite of the danger Anna would in all probability not have given in: perhaps her consciousness of such cowardly hostility would have driven her to some desperate act of provocation if she had not herself been possessed by the Pharisaic spirit of the society which was so antagonistic to her. Her education had subjugated her nature. It was in vain that she condemned the tyranny and meanness of public opinion: she respected it: she subscribed to its decrees even when they were directed against herself: if they had come into conflict with her conscience, she would have sacrificed her conscience. She despised the town: but she could not have borne the town to despise herself.

Now the time was coming when the public scandal would be afforded an opportunity of discharging itself. The carnival was coming on.

In that city, the carnival had preserved up to the time of the events narrated in this history—(it has changed since then)—a character of archaic license and roughness. Faithfully in accordance with its origin, by which it had been a relaxation for the profligacy of the human mind subjugated, wilfully or involuntarily, by reason, it nowhere reached such a pitch of audacity as in the periods and countries in which custom and law, the guardians of reason, weighed most heavily upon the people. The town in which Anna lived was therefore one of its most chosen regions. The more moral stringency paralyzed action and gagged speech, the bolder did action become and speech the more untrammeled during those few days. Everything that was secreted away in the lower depths of the soul, jealousy, secret hate, lewd curiosity, the malicious instincts inherent in the social animal, would burst forth with all the vehemence and joy of revenge. Every man had the right to go out into the streets, and, prudently masked, to nail to the pillory, in full view of the public gaze, the object of his detestation, to lay before all and sundry all that he had found out by a year of patient industry, his whole hoard of scandalous secrets gathered drop by drop. One man would display them on the cars. Another would carry a transparent lantern on which were pasted in writings and drawings the secret history of the town. Another would go so far as to wear a mask in imitation of his enemy, made so easily recognizable that the very gutter-snipes would point him out by name. Slanderous newspapers would appear during the three days. Even the very best people would craftily take part in the game of *Pasquino*. No control was exercised except over political allusions,—such coarse liberty of speech having on more than one occasion produced fierce conflict between the authorities of the town and the representatives of foreign countries. But there was nothing to protect the citizens against the citizens, and this cloud of public insult, constantly hanging over their heads, did not a little help to maintain the apparently impeccable morality on which the town prided itself.

Anna felt the weight of that dread—which was quite unjustified. She had very little reason to be afraid. She occupied too small a place in the opinion of the town for any one to

think of attacking her. But in the absolute isolation in which
of her own choice she lived, in her state of exhaustion and
nervous excitement brought on by several weeks of sleepless
nights and moral suffering, her imagination was apt to welcome
the most unreasoning terrors. She exaggerated the animosity
of those who did not like her. She told herself that suspicion
was on her track: the veriest trifle was enough to ruin her: and
there was nothing to assure her that it was not already an
accomplished fact. It would mean insult, pitiless exposure, her
heart laid bare to the mockery of the passers-by: dishonor so
cruel that Anna was near dying of shame at the very thought
of it. She called to mind how, a few years before, a girl, who
had been the victim of such persecution, had had to fly the
country with her family. . . . And she could do nothing,
nothing to defend herself, nothing to prevent it, nothing even
to find out if it was going to happen. The suspense was even
more maddening than the certainty. Anna looked desperately
about her like an animal at bay. In her own house she knew
that she was hemmed in.

Anna's servant was a woman of over forty: her name was Bäbi:
she was tall and strong: her face was narrow and bony round
her brow and temples, wide and long in the lower part, fleshy
under the jaw, roughly pear-shaped: she had a perpetual smile
and eyes that pierced like gimlets, sunken, as though they had
been sucked in, beneath red eyelids with colorless lashes. She
never put off her expression of coquettish gaiety: she was always
delighted with her superiors, always of their opinion, worrying
about their health with tender interest: smiling when they gave
her orders: smiling when they scolded her. Braun believed that
she was unshakably devoted. Her gushing manner was strongly
in contrast with Anna's coldness. However, she was like her
in many things: like her she spoke little and dressed in a severe
neat style: like her she was very pious, and went to service
with her, scrupulously fulfilling all her religious duties and
nicely attending to her household tasks: she was clean, methodical, and her morals and her kitchen were beyond reproach. In
a word she was an exemplary servant and the perfect type of
domestic foe. Anna's feminine instinct was hardly ever wrong

in her divination of the secret thoughts of women, and she had no illusions about her. They detested each other, knew it, and never let it appear.

On the night of Christophe's return, when Anna, torn by her desire and her emotion, went to him once more in spite of her resolve never to see him again, she walked stealthily, groping along the wall in the darkness: just as she reached Christophe's door, instead of the ordinary cold smooth polished floor, she felt a warm dust softly crunching under her bare feet. She stooped, touched it with her hands, and understood: a thin layer of ashes had been spread for the space of a few yards across the passage. Without knowing it Bäbi had happed on the old device employed in the days of the old Breton songs by Frocin the dwarf to catch Tristan on his way to Yseult: so true it is that a limited number of types, good and bad, serve for all ages. A remarkable piece of evidence in favor of the wise economy of the universe!—Anna did not hesitate; she did not stop or turn, but went on in a sort of contemptuous bravado: she went to Christophe, told him nothing, in spite of her uneasiness: but when she returned she took the stove brush and carefully effaced every trace of her footsteps in the ashes, after she had crossed over them.—When Anna and Bäbi met next day it was with the usual coldness and the accustomed smile.

Bäbi used sometimes to receive a visit from a relation who was a little older than herself: he fulfilled the function of beadle of the church: during *Gottesdienst* (Divine service) he used to stand sentinel at the church door, wearing a white armlet with black stripes and a silver tassel, leaning on a cane with a curved handle. By trade he was an undertaker. His name was Sami Witschi. He was very tall and thin, with a slight stoop, and he had the clean-shaven solemn face of an old peasant. He was very pious and knew better than any one all the tittle-tattle of the parish. Bäbi and Sami were thinking of getting married: they appreciated each other's serious qualities, and solid faith and malice. But they were in no hurry to make up their minds: they prudently took stock of each other.—Latterly Sami's visits had become more frequent. He would come in unawares. Every time Anna went near the kitchen and looked through the door, she would see Sami sitting near the fire, and Bäbi a few yards away, sewing. However much they talked, it was impossible to hear a sound. She could see Bäbi's beaming face and her lips moving: Sami's wide hard mouth would stretch in a grin without opening: not a sound would come up from his throat: the house seemed to be lost in silence. Whenever Anna entered the kitchen, Sami would rise respectfully and remain standing, without a word, until she had gone out again. Whenever Bäbi heard the door open, she would ostentatiously break off in the middle of a commonplace remark, and turn to Anna with an obsequious smile and wait for her orders. Anna would think they were talking about her: but she despised them too much to play the eavesdropper.

The day after Anna had dodged the ingenious trap of the ashes, as she entered the kitchen, the first thing she saw in Sami's hand was the little broom she had used the night before to wipe out the marks of her bare feet. She had taken it out of Christophe's room, and that very minute, she suddenly remembered that she had forgotten to take it back again; she had left it in her own room, where Bäbi's sharp eyes had seen it at once. The two gossips had immediately put two and two together. Anna did not flinch. Bäbi followed her mistress's eyes, gave an exaggerated smile, and explained:

" The broom was broken: I gave it to Sami to mend."

Anna did not take the trouble to point out the gross falsehood of the excuse: she did not seem even to hear it: she looked at Bäoi's work, made a few remarks, and went out again impassively. But when the door was closed she lost all her pride: she could not help hiding behind the corner of the passage and listening—(she was humiliated to the very depths of her being at having to stoop to such means: but fear mastered her). —She heard a dry chuckle of laughter. Then whispering, so low that she could not make out what was said. But in her desperation Anna thought she heard: her terror breathed into her ears the words she was afraid of hearing: she imagined that they were speaking of the coming masquerades and a charivari. There was no doubt: they would try to introduce the episode of the ashes. Probably she was wrong: but in her state of morbid excitement, having for a whole fortnight been haunted by the fixed idea of public insult, she did not stop to consider whether the uncertain could be possible: she regarded it as certain.

From that time on her mind was made up.

On the evening of the same day—(it was the Wednesday preceding the carnival)—Braun was called away to a consultation twenty miles out of the town: he would not return until the next morning. Anna did not come down to dinner and stayed in her room. She had chosen that night to carry out the tacit pledge she had made with herself. But she had decided to carry it out alone, and to say nothing to Christophe. She despised him. She thought:

" He promised. But he is a man, he is an egoist and a liar. He has his art. He will soon forget."

And then perhaps there was in her passionate heart that seemed so inaccessible to kindness, room for a feeling of pity for her companion. But she was too harsh and too passionate to admit it to herself.

Bäbi told Christophe that her mistress had bade her to make her excuses as she was not very well and wished to rest. Christophe dined alone under Bäbi's supervision, and she bored him with her chatter, tried to make him talk, and protested such an extraordinary devotion to Anna, that, in spite of his readiness to believe in the good faith of men, Christophe became suspicious. He was counting on having a decisive interview with Anna that night. He could no more postpone matters than she. He had not forgotten the pledge they had given each other at the dawn of that sad day. He was ready to keep it if Anna demanded it of him. But he saw the absurdity of their dying together, how it would not solve the problem, and how the sorrow of it and the scandal must fall upon Braun's shoulders. He was inclined to think that the best thing to do was to tear themselves apart and for him to try once more to go right away, —to see at least if he were strong enough to stay away from her: he doubted it after the vain attempt he had made before: but he thought that, in case he could not bear it, he would still have time to turn to the last resort, alone, without anybody knowing.

He hoped that after supper he would be able to escape for

a moment to go up to Anna's room. But Bäbi dogged him. As a rule she used to finish her work early: but that night she seemed never to have done with scrubbing her kitchen: and when Christophe thought he was rid of her, she took it into her head to tidy a cupboard in the passage leading to Anna's room. Christophe found her standing on a stool, and he saw that she had no intention of moving all evening. He felt a furious desire to knock her over with her piles of plates: but he restrained himself and asked her to go and see how her mistress was and if he could say good-night to her. Bäbi went, returned, and said, as she watched him with a malicious joy, that Madame was better and was asleep and did not want anybody to disturb her. Christophe tried irritably and nervously to read, but could not, and went up to his room. Bäbi watched his light until it was put out, and then went upstairs to her room, resolving to keep watch: she carefully left her door open so that she could hear every sound in the house. Unfortunately for her, she could not go to bed without at once falling asleep and sleeping so soundly that not thunder, not even her own curiosity, could wake her up before daybreak. Her sound sleep was no secret. The echo of it resounded through the house even to the lower floor.

As soon as Christophe heard the familiar noise he went to Anna's room. It was imperative that he should speak to her. He was profoundly uneasy. He reached her door, turned the handle: the door was locked. He knocked lightly: no reply. He placed his lips to the keyhole and begged her in a whisper, then more loudly, to open: not a movement, not a sound. Although he told himself that Anna was asleep, he was in agonies. And as, in a vain attempt to hear, he laid his cheek against the door, a smell came to his nostrils which seemed to be issuing from the room: he bent down and recognized it: it was the smell of gas. His blood froze. He shook the door, never thinking that he might wake Bäbi: the door did not give. . . . He understood: in her dressing-room, which led out of her room, Anna had a little gas-stove: she had turned it on. He must break open the door: but in his anxiety Christophe kept his senses enough to remember that at all costs Bäbi must not hear. He leaned against one of the leaves of the door and gave an enormous shove as quietly as he could. The solid, well-fitting door creaked on its hinges, but did not yield. There was another door which led from Anna's room to Braun's dressing-room. He ran to it. That too was locked: but the lock was outside. He started to tug it off. It was not easy. He had to remove the four big screws which were buried deep in the wood. He had only his knife and he could not see: for he dared not light a candle; it would have meant blowing the whole place up. Fumblingly he managed to fit his knife into the head of a screw, then another, breaking the blades and cutting himself; the screws seemed to be interminably long, and he thought he would never be able to get them out: and, at the same time, in the feverish haste which was making his body break out into a cold sweat, there came to his mind a memory of his childhood: he saw himself, a boy of ten, shut up in a dark room as a punishment: he had taken off the lock and run out of the house. . . . The last screw came out. The lock gave with a crackling noise like the sawing of wood. Christophe plunged into the room, rushed to the window, and opened it. A flood of cold air swept in. Christophe bumped into the furniture in the dark and came to the bed, groped with his hands, and came on Anna's body, tremblingly felt her legs lying still under the clothes, and moved his hands up to her waist: Anna was sitting up in bed, trembling. She had not had time to feel the first effects of asphyxiation: the room was high: the air came through the chinks in the windows and the doors. Christophe caught her in his arms. She broke away from him angrily, crying:

"Go away! . . . Ah! What have you done?"

She raised her hands to strike him: but she was worn out with emotion: she fell back on her pillow and sobbed:

"Oh! Oh! We've to go through it all over again!"

Christophe took her hands in his, kissed her, scolded her spoke to her tenderly and roughly:

"You were going to die, to die, alone, without me!"

"Oh! You!" she said bitterly.

Her tone was as much as to say:

"You want to live."

He spoke harshly to her and tried to break down her will.

"You are mad!" he said. "You might have blown the house to pieces!"

"I wanted to," she said angrily.

He tried to play on her religious fears: that was the right note. As soon as he touched on it she began to scream and to beg him to stop. He went on pitilessly, thinking that it was the only means of bringing her back to the desire to live. She said nothing more, but lay sobbing convulsively. When he had done, she said in a tone of intense hatred:

"Are you satisfied now? You've done your work well. You've brought me to despair. And now, what am I to do?"

"Live," he said.

"Live!" she cried. "You don't know how impossible it is! You know nothing! You know nothing!"

He asked:

"What is it?"

She shrugged her shoulders:

"Listen."

In a few brief disconnected sentences she told him all that she had concealed from him: Bäbi's spying on her, the ashes, the scene with Sami, the carnival, the public insult that was before her. As she told her story she was unable to distinguish between the figments of her fear and what she had any reason to fear. He listened in utter consternation, and was no more capable than she of discerning between the real and the imaginary in her story. Nothing had ever been farther from his mind than to suspect how they were being dogged. He tried to understand: he could find nothing to say: against such enemies he was disarmed. Only he was conscious of a blind fury, a desire to strike and to destroy. He said:

"Why didn't you dismiss Bäbi?"

She did not deign to reply. Bäbi dismissed would have been even more venomous than Bäbi tolerated: and Christophe saw the idiocy of his question. His thoughts were in a whirl: he was trying to discover a way out, some immediate action upon which to engage. He clenched his fists and cried:

"I'll kill them?"

"Who?" she said, despising him for his futile words.

He lost all power of thought or action. He felt that he

was lost in such a network of obscure treachery, in which it was impossible to clutch at anything since all were parties to it. He writhed.

"Cowards!" he cried, in sheer despair.

He slipped down on to his knees and buried his face against Anna.—They were silent for a little. She felt a mixture of contempt and pity for the man who could defend neither himself nor her. He felt Anna's limbs trembling with cold against his cheek. The window had been left open, and outside it was freezing: they could see the icy stars shivering in the sky that was smooth and gleaming as a mirror.

When she had fully tasted the bitter joy of seeing him as broken as herself, she said in a hard, weary voice:

"Light the candle."

He did so. Anna's teeth were chattering, she was sitting huddled up, with her arms tight folded across her chest and her knees up to her chin. He closed the window. Then he sat on the bed. He laid his hands on Anna's feet: they were cold as ice, and he warmed them with his hands and lips. She was softened.

"Christophe!" she said.

Her eyes were pitiful to see.

"Anna!" said he.

"What are we going to do?"

He looked at her and replied:

"Die."

She gave a cry of joy.

"Oh! You will? You will? . . . I shall not be alone!"

She kissed him.

"Did you think I was going to let you?"

She replied in a whisper:

"Yes."

A few moments later he questioned her with his eyes. She understood.

"In the bureau," she said. "On the right. The bottom drawer."

He went and looked. At the back of the drawer he found a revolver. Braun had bought it as a student. He had never made use of it. In an open box Christophe found some cartridges. He took them to the bed. Anna looked at them, and at once turned her eyes away to the wall.

Christophe waited, and then asked:

" You don't want to . . . ? "

Anna turned abruptly:

" I will. . . .   Quick! "

She thought:

" Nothing can save me now from the everlasting pit.   A little more or less, it will be just the same."

Christophe awkwardly loaded the revolver.

" Anna," he said, and his voice trembled.   " One of us will see the other die."

She wrenched the pistol out of his hands and said selfishly :

" I shall be the first."

They looked at each other once more. . . .   Alas!   At the very moment when they were to die for each other they felt so far apart! . . .   Each was thinking in terror:

" What am I doing?   What am I doing? "

And each was reading the other's eyes.   The absurdity of the thing was what struck Christophe most.   All his life gone for nothing: vain his struggles: vain his suffering: vain his hopes: all botched, flung to the winds: one foolish act was to wipe all away. . . .   In his normal state he would have wrenched the revolver away from Anna and flung it out of the window and cried:

" No, no!   I will not."

But eight months of suffering, of doubt and torturing grief, and on top of that the whirlwind of their crazy passion, had wasted his strength and broken his will: he felt that he could do nothing now, that he was no longer master of himself. . . .   Ah! what did it matter, after all?

Anna, feeling certain that she was doomed to everlasting death, stretched every nerve to catch and hold the last minute of her life: Christophe's sorrowful face lit by the flickering candle, the shadows on the wall, a footstep in the street, the cold contact of the steel in her hand. . . .   She clung to these sensations, as a shipwrecked man clings to the spar that sinks beneath his weight.   Afterwards all was terror.   Why not prolong the time of waiting?   But she said to herself:

" I must. . . ."

She said good-by to Christophe, with no tenderness, with the haste of a hurried traveler fearful of losing the train: she bared her bosom, felt for her heart, and laid the mouth of the revolver against it. Christophe hid his face. Just as she was about to fire she laid her left hand on Christophe's. It was the gesture of a child dreading to walk in the darkness. . . .

Then a few frightful seconds passed. . . . Anna did not fire. Christophe wanted to raise his head, to take her in his arms: and he was afraid that his very movement might bring her to the point of firing. He heard nothing more: he lost consciousness. . . . A groan from Anna pierced his heart. He got up. He saw Anna with her face distorted in terror. The revolver had fallen down on to the bed. She kept on saying plaintively:

" Christophe! . . . It has missed fire! . . ."

He took the pistol: it had lain long forgotten and had grown rusty: but the trigger was in working order. Perhaps the cartridges had gone bad with exposure to the air.—Anna held out her hand for the revolver.

" Enough! Enough! " he implored her.

She commanded him:

" The cartridges! "

He gave them to her. She examined them, took one, loaded the pistol, trembling, put the pistol to her breast, and fired.— Once more it missed fire.

Anna flung the revolver out into the room.

" Oh! It is horrible, horrible! " she cried. " *He* will not let me die! "

She writhed and sobbed: she was like a madwoman. He tried to touch her: she beat him off, screaming. Finally she had a nervous attack. Christophe stayed with her until morning. At last she was pacified: but she lay still and breathless, with her eyes closed and the livid skin stretched tight over the bones of her forehead and cheeks: she looked like one dead.

Christophe repaired the disorder of her bed, picked up the revolver, fastened on the lock he had wrenched away, tidied up the whole room, and went away: for it was seven o'clock and Bäbi might come at any moment.

When Braun returned next morning he found Anna in the same prostrate condition. He saw that something extraordinary had happened: but he could glean nothing either from Bäbi or Christophe. All day long Anna did not stir: she did not open her eyes: her pulse was so weak that he could hardly feel it: every now and then it would stop, and, for a moment, Braun would be in a state of agony, thinking that her heart had stopped. His affection made him doubt his own knowledge: he ran and fetched a colleague. The two men examined Anna and could not make up their minds whether it was the beginning of a fever, or a case of nervous hysteria: they had to keep the patient under observation. Braun never left Anna's bedside. He refused to eat. Towards evening Anna's pulse gave no signs of fever, but was extremely weak. Braun tried to force a few spoonfuls of milk between her lips: she brought it back at once. Her body lay limp in her husband's arms like a broken doll. Braun spent the night with her, getting up every moment to listen to her breathing. Bäbi, who was hardly at all put out by Anna's illness, played the devoted servant and refused to go to bed and sat up with Braun.

On the Friday Anna opened her eyes. Braun spoke to her: she took no notice of him. She lay quite still with her eyes staring at a mark on the wall. About midday Braun saw great tears trickling down her thin cheeks: he dried them gently: one by one the tears went on trickling down. Once more Braun tried to make her take some food. She took it passively. In the evening she began to talk: loose snatches of sentences. She talked about the Rhine: she had tried to drown herself, but there was not enough water. In her dreams she persisted in attempting suicide, imagining all sorts of strange forms of death; always death was at the back of her thoughts. Sometimes she was arguing with some one, and then her face would take on an expression of fear and anger: she addressed herself to God, and tried obstinately to prove that it was all His fault. Or the flame of desire would kindle in her eyes, and she would say shameless things which it seemed impossible that she should know. Once she saw Bäbi, and gave precise orders for the morrow's washing. At night she dozed. Suddenly she got up: Braun ran to her. She looked at him strangely, and babbled impatient formless words. He asked her:

"My dear Anna, what do you want?"

She said harshly:

"Go and bring him."

"Who?" he asked.

She looked at him once more with the same expression and suddenly burst out laughing: then she drew her hands over her forehead and moaned:

"Oh! my God! Let me forget! . . ."

Sleep overcame her. She was at peace until day. About dawn she moved a little: Braun raised her head to give her to drink: she gulped down a few mouthfuls, and, stooping to Braun's hands, she kissed them. Once more she dozed off.

On the Saturday morning she woke up about nine o'clock. Without saying a word, she began to slip out of bed. Braun went quickly to her and tried to make her lie down again. She insisted. He asked her what she wanted to do. She replied:

"Go to church."

He tried to argue with her and to remind her that it was not Sunday and the church was closed. She relapsed into silence: but she sat in a chair near the bed, and began to put on her clothes with trembling fingers. Braun's doctor-friend came in. He joined Braun in his entreaties: then, seeing that she would not give in, he examined her, and finally consented. He took Braun aside, and told him that his wife's illness seemed to be altogether moral, and that for the time being he must avoid opposing her wishes, and that he could see no danger in her going out, so long as Braun went with her. Braun told Anna that he would go with her. She refused, and insisted on going alone. But she stumbled as soon as she tried to walk across the room. Then, without a word, she took Braun's arm, and they went out. She was very weak, and kept stopping. Several times he asked her if she wanted to go home. She began to walk on. When they reached the church,

as he had told her, they found the doors closed. Anna sat down
on a bench near the door, and stayed, shivering, until the clock
struck twelve. Then she took Braun's arm again, and they
came home in silence. But in the evening she wanted to go
to church again. Braun's entreaties were useless. He had to
go out with her once more.

Christophe had spent the two days alone. Braun was too
anxious to think about him. Only once, on the Saturday morning, when he was trying to divert Anna's mind from her fixed
idea of going out, he had asked her if she would like to see
Christophe. She had looked at him with such an expression
of fear and loathing that he could not but remark it: and he
never pronounced Christophe's name again.

Christophe had shut himself up in his room. Anxiety, love,
remorse, a very chaos of sorrow was whirling in him. He
blamed himself for everything. He was overwhelmed by self-
disgust. More than once he had got up to go and confess the
whole story to Braun—and each time he had immediately been
arrested by the thought of bringing wretchedness to yet another
human being by his self-accusation. At the same time he was
spared nothing of his passion. He prowled about in the passage
outside Anna's room; and when he heard footsteps inside coming to the door he rushed away to his own room.

When Braun and Anna went out in the afternoon, he looked
out for them from behind his window-curtains. He saw Anna.
She who had been so erect and proud walked now with bowed
back, lowered head, yellow complexion: she was an old woman
bending under the weight of the cloak and shawl her husband
had thrown about her: she was ugly. But Christophe did not
see her ugliness: he saw only her misery; and his heart ached
with pity and love. He longed to run to her, to prostrate himself in the mud, to kiss her feet: her dear body so broken and
destroyed by passion, and to implore her forgiveness. And he
thought as he looked after her:

"My work. . . .   That is what I have done!"

But when he looked into the mirror and saw his own face,
he was shown the same devastation in his eyes, in all his
features: he saw the marks of death upon himself, as upon her,
and he thought:

"My work? No. It is the work of the cruel Master who drives us mad and destroys us."

The house was empty. Bäbi had gone out to tell the neighbors of the day's events. Time was passing. The clock struck five. Christophe was filled with terror as he thought of Anna's return and the coming of the night. He felt that he could not bear to stay under the same roof with her for another night. He felt his reason breaking beneath the weight of passion. He did not know what to do, he did not know what he wanted, except that he wanted Anna at all costs. He thought of the wretched face he had just seen going past his window, and he said to himself:

"I must save her from myself! . . ."

His will stirred into life.

He gathered together the litter of papers on the table, tied them up, took his hat and cloak, and went out. In the passage, near the door of Anna's room, he hurried forward in a spasm of fear. Downstairs he glanced for the last time into the empty garden. He crept away like a thief in the night. An icy mist pricked his face and hands. Christophe skirted the walls of the houses, dreading a meeting with any one he knew. He went to the station, and got into a train which was just starting for Lucerne. At the first stopping-place he wrote to Braun. He said that he had been called away from the town on urgent business for a few days, and that he was very sorry to have to leave him at such a time: he begged him to send him news, and gave him an address. At Lucerne he took the St. Gothard train. Late at night he got out at a little station between Altorf and Goeschenen. He did not know the name, never knew it. He went into the nearest inn by the station. The road was filled with pools of water. It was raining in torrents: it rained all night and all next day. The water was rushing and roaring like a cataract from a broken gutter. Sky and earth were drowned, seemingly dissolved and melted like his own mind. He went to bed between damp sheets which smelt of railway smoke. He could not lie still. The idea of the danger hanging over Anna was too much in his mind for him to feel his own suffering as yet. Somehow he must avert public malignity from her, somehow turn it aside upon another track. In his feverish condition a queer idea came to him: he decided to write to one of the few musicians with whom he had been acquainted in the little town, Krebs, the confectioner-organist. He gave him to understand that he was off to Italy upon an affair of the heart, that he had been possessed by the passion when he first took up his abode with the Brauns, and that he had tried to shake free of it, but it had been too strong for him. He put the whole thing clearly enough for Krebs to understand, and yet so veiled as to enable him to improve on it as he liked. Christophe implored Krebs to keep his secret. He knew that the good little man simply could not keep anything to himself, and—quite rightly—he reckoned on Krebs hastening to spread the news as soon as it came into his hands. To make sure of hoodwinking the gossips of the town Christophe closed his letter with a few cold remarks about Braun and about Anna's illness.

He spent the rest of the night and the next day absorbed by his fixed idea . . . Anna . . . Anna. . . . He lived through the last few months with her, day by day: he did not see her as she was, but enveloped her with a passionate atmosphere of illusion. From the very beginning he had created her in the image of his own desire, and given her a moral grandeur, a tragic consciousness which he needed to heighten his love for her. These lies of passion gained in intensity of conviction now that they were beyond the control of Anna's presence. He saw in her a healthy free nature, oppressed, struggling to shake off its fetters, reaching upwards to a wider life of liberty in the open air of the soul, and then, fearful of it, struggling against her dreams, wrestling with them, because they could not be brought into line with her destiny, and made it only the more sorrowful and wretched. She cried to him: "Help me." He saw once more her beautiful body, clasped it to him. His memories tortured him: he took a savage delight in mortifying the wounds they dealt him. As the day crept on, the feeling of all that he had lost became so frightful that he could not breathe.

Without knowing what he was doing, he got up, went out, paid his bill, and took the first train back to the town in which Anna lived. He arrived in the middle of the night: he went straight to the house. There was a wall between the alley and the garden next to Braun's. Christophe climbed the wall, jumped down into the next-door garden, and then into Braun's. He stood outside the house. It was in darkness save for a night-light which cast a yellow glow upon a window—the window of Anna's room. Anna was there. She was suffering. He had only to make one stride to enter. He laid his hand on the handle of the door. Then he looked at his hand, the door, the garden: suddenly he realized what he was doing: and, breaking free of the hallucination which had been upon him for the last seven or eight hours, he groaned, wrenched free of the inertia which held him riveted to the ground whereon he stood, ran to the wall, scaled it, and fled.

That same night he left the town for the second time: and next day he went and buried himself in a mountain village, hidden from the world by driving blizzards.—There he would bury his heart, stupefy his thoughts, and forget, and forget! . . .

> Però leva su, vinci l'ambascia
> Con l'animo che vinca ogni battaglia,
> Se col suo grave corpo non s'accascia.

> " Leva'mi allor, mostrandomi fornito
> Meglio di lena ch'io non mi sentia;
> E dissi: ' Va, ch'io son forte edardito.' "

INF. LXIV.

Oh! God, what have I done to Thee? Why dost Thou overwhelm me? Since I was a little child Thou hast appointed
misery and conflict to be my lot. I have struggled without
complaint. I have loved my misery. I have tried to preserve
the purity of the soul Thou gavest me, to defend the fire which
Thou hast kindled in me. . . . Lord, it is Thou, it is Thou
who art so furious to destroy what Thou hast created. Thou
hast put out the fire, Thou hast besmirched my soul. Thou
hast despoiled me of all that gave me life. I had but two
treasurable things in the world: my friend and my soul. Now
I have nothing, for Thou hast taken everything from me. One
only creature was mine in the wilderness of the world: Thou
hast taken him from me. Our hearts were one. Thou hast torn
them asunder: Thou hast made us know the sweetness of being
together only to make us know the horror of being lost to each
other. Thou hast created emptiness all about me. Thou hast
created emptiness within me. I was broken and sick, unarmed
and robbed of my will. Thou hast chosen that hour to strike
me down. Thou hast come stealthily with silent feet from
behind treacherously, and Thou hast stabbed me: Thou hast let
loose upon me Thy fierce dogs of passion; I was weak, and Thou
knewest it, and I could not struggle: passion has laid me low,
and thrown me into confusion, and befouled me, and destroyed
all that I had. . . . I am left only in self-disgust. If I
could only cry aloud my grief and my shame! or forget them
in the rushing stream of creative force! But my strength is
broken, and my creative power is withered up. I am like a
dead tree. . . . Would I were dead! O God, deliver me,
break my body and my soul, tear me from this earth, leave
me not to struggle blindly in the pit, leave me not in this
endless agony! I cry for mercy. . . . Lord, make an end!

So in his sorrow Christophe cried upon a God in whom his
reason did not believe.

He had taken refuge in a lonely farm in the Swiss Jura
Mountains. The house was built in the woods tucked away
in the folds of a high humpy plateau. It was protected from

the north winds by crags and boulders. In front of it lay a wide stretch of fields, and long wooded slopes: the rock suddenly came to an end in a sheer precipice: twisted pines hung on the edge of it; behind were wide-spreading beeches. The sky was blotted out. There was no sign of life. A wide stretch of country with all its lines erased. The whole place lay sleeping under the snow. Only at night in the forest foxes barked. It was the end of the winter. Slow dragging winter. Interminable winter. When it seemed like to break up, snow would fall once more, and it would begin again.

However, for a week now the old slumbering earth had felt its heart slow beating to new birth. The first deceptive breath of spring crept into the air and beneath the frozen crust. From the branches of the beech-trees, stretched out like soaring wings, the snow melted. Already through the white cloak of the fields there peered a few thin blades of grass of tender green: around their sharp needles, through the gaps in the snow, like so many little mouths, the dank black earth was breathing. For a few hours every day the voice of the waters, sleeping beneath their robe of ice, murmured. In the skeleton woods a few birds piped their shrill clear song.

Christophe noticed nothing. All things were the same to him. He paced up and down, up and down his room. Or he would walk outside. He could not keep still. His soul was torn in pieces by inward demons. They fell upon and rent each other. His suppressed passion never left off beating furiously against the walls of the house of its captivity. His disgust with passion was no less furiously in revolt: passion and disgust flew at each other's throats, and, in their conflict, they lacerated his heart. And at the same time he was delivered up to the memory of Olivier, despair at his death, the hunger to create which nothing could satisfy, and pride rearing on the edge of the abyss of nothingness. He was a prey to all devils. He had no moment of respite. Or, if there came a seeming calm, if the rushing waves did fall back for a moment, it was only that he might find himself alone, and nothing in himself: thought, love, will, all had been done to death.

To create! That was the only loophole. To abandon the wreck of his life to the mercy of the waves! To save himself

by swimming in the dreams of art! . . . To create! He
tried. . . . He could not.

Christophe had never had any method of working. When
he was strong and well he had always rather suffered from his
superabundance than been disturbed at seeing it diminish: he
followed his whim: he used to work first as the fancy took
him, as circumstances chanced, with no fixed rule. As a matter
of fact, he was always working everywhere: his brain was always
busy. Often and often Olivier, who was less richly endowed
and more reflective, had warned him:

"Take care. You are trusting too much to your force. It
is a mountain torrent. Full to-day, perhaps dry to-morrow.
An artist must coax his genius: he must not let it scatter itself
at random. Turn your force into a channel. Train yourself
in habits of mind and a healthy system of daily work, at fixed
hours. They are as necessary to the artist as the practice of
military movements and steps to a man who is to go into battle.
When moments of crisis come—(and they always do come)—
the bracing of steel prevents the soul from destruction. I know.
It is just that that has saved me from death."

But Christophe used to laugh and say:

"That's all right for you, my boy! There's no danger of
my losing my taste for life. My appetite's too good."

Olivier would shrug his shoulders:

"Too much ends in too little. There are no worse invalids
than the men who have always had too much health."

And now Olivier's words had come true. After the death
of his friend the source of his inward life had not all at once
dried up: but it had become strangely intermittent: it flowed
in sudden gushes, then stopped, then disappeared under the
earth. Christophe had paid no heed to it: what did it matter
to him? His grief and his budding passion had absorbed his
mind.—But after the storm had passed, when once more he
turned to the fountain to drink, he could find no trace of it.
All was barren. Not a trickle of water. His soul was dried
up. In vain did he try to dig down into the sand, and force
the water up from the subterranean wells, and create at all
costs: the machine of his mind refused to obey. He could not
invoke the aid of habit, the faithful ally, which, when we

have lost every reason for living, alone, constant and firmly loyal, stays with us, and speaks no word, and makes no sign, but with eyes fixed, and silent lips, with its sure unwavering hand leads us by the hand through the dangerous chasm until the light of day and the joy of life return. Christophe was helpless: and his hand could find no guiding hand in the darkness. He could not find his way back to the light of day.

It was the supreme test. Then he felt that he was on the verge of madness. Sometimes he would wage an absurd and crazy battle with his own brain, maniacal obsessions, a nightmare of numbers: he would count the boards on the floor, the trees in the forest: figures and chords, the choice of which was beyond his reason. Sometimes he would lie in a state of prostration, like one dead.

Nobody worried about him. He lived apart in one wing of the house. He tidied his own room—or left it undone, every day. His meals were laid for him downstairs: he never saw a human face. His host, an old peasant, a taciturn, selfish creature, took no interest in him. Whether Christophe ate or did not eat was his affair. He hardly ever noticed whether Christophe came in at night. Once he was lost in the forest, buried up to his hips in the snow: he was very near never returning. He tried to wear himself out to keep himself from thinking. He could not succeed. Only now and then could he snatch a few hours of troubled sleep.

Only one living creature seemed to take any notice of his existence: this was an old St. Bernard, who used to come and lay his big head with its mournful eyes on Christophe's knees when Christophe was sitting on the seat in front of the house. They would look long at each other. Christophe would not drive him away. Unlike the sick Goethe, the dog's eyes had no uneasiness for him. Unlike him, he had no desire to cry:

"Go away! . . . Thou goblin, thou shalt not catch me. whatever thou doest!"

He asked nothing better than to be engrossed by the dog's suppliant sleepy eyes and to help the beast: he felt that there must be behind them an imprisoned soul imploring his aid.

In those hours when he was weak with suffering, torn alive away from life, devoid of human egoism, he saw the victims

of men, the field of battle in which man triumphed in the bloody
slaughter of all other creatures: and his heart was filled with
pity and horror. Even in the days when he had been happy
he had always loved the beasts: he had never been able to bear
cruelty towards them: he had always had a detestation of sport,
which he had never dared to express for fear of ridicule: perhaps even he had never dared to admit it to himself: but his
feeling of repulsion had been the secret cause of the apparently
inexplicable feeling of dislike he had had for certain men: he
had never been able to admit to his friendship a man who
could kill an animal for pleasure. It was not sentimentality:
no one knew better than he that life is based on suffering and
infinite cruelty: no man can live without making others suffer.
It is no use closing our eyes and fobbing ourselves off with
words. It is no use either coming to the conclusion that we
must renounce life and sniveling like children. No. We must
kill to live, if, at the time, there is no other means of living.
But the man who kills for the sake of killing is a miscreant.
An unconscious miscreant, I know. But, all the same, a miscreant. The continual endeavor of man should be to lessen
the sum of suffering and cruelty: that is the first duty of
humanity.

In ordinary life those ideas remained buried in Christophe's
inmost heart. He refused to think of them. What was the
good? What could he do? He had to be Christophe, he had
to accomplish his work, live at all costs, live at the cost of the
weak. . . . It was not he who had made the universe. . . .
Better not think of it, better not think of it. . . .

But when unhappiness had dragged him down, him, too, to
the level of the vanquished, he had to think of these things
Only a little while ago he had blamed Olivier for plunging into
futile remorse and vain compassion for all the wretchedness
that men suffer and inflict. Now he went even farther: with
all the vehemence of his mighty nature he probed to the depths
of the tragedy of the universe: he suffered all the sufferings
of the world, and was left raw and bleeding. He could not
think of the animals without shuddering in anguish. He looked
into the eyes of the beasts and saw there a soul like his own, a
soul which could not speak: but the eyes cried for it:

"What have I done to you? Why do you hurt me?"

He could not bear to see the most ordinary sights that he had seen hundreds of times—a calf crying in a wicker pen, with its big, protruding eyes, with their bluish whites and pink lids, and white lashes, its curly white tufts on its forehead, its purple snout, its knock-kneed legs:—a lamb being carried by a peasant with its four legs tied together, hanging head down, trying to hold its head up, moaning like a child, bleating and lolling its gray tongue:—fowls huddled together in a basket:—the distant squeals of a pig being bled to death:—a fish being cleaned on the kitchen-table. . . . The nameless tortures which men inflict on such innocent creatures made his heart ache. Grant animals a ray of reason, imagine what a frightful nightmare the world is to them: a dream of cold-blooded men, blind and deaf, cutting their throats, slitting them open, gutting them, cutting them into pieces, cooking them alive, sometimes laughing at them and their contortions as they writhe in agony. Is there anything more atrocious among the cannibals of Africa? To a man whose mind is free there is something even more intolerable in the sufferings of animals than in the sufferings of men. For with the latter it is at least admitted that suffering is evil and that the man who causes it is a criminal. But thousands of animals are uselessly butchered every day without a shadow of remorse. If any man were to refer to it, he would be thought ridiculous.—And that is the unpardonable crime. That alone is the justification of all that men may suffer. It cries vengeance upon all the human race. If God exists and tolerates it, it cries vengeance upon God. If there exists a good God, then even the most humble of living things must be saved. If God is good only to the strong, if there is no justice for the weak and lowly, for the poor creatures who are offered up as a sacrifice to humanity, then there is no such thing as goodness, no such thing as justice. . . .

Alas! The slaughter accomplished by man is so small a thing of itself in the carnage of the universe! The animals devour each other. The peaceful plants, the silent trees, are ferocious beasts one to another. The serenity of the forests is only a commonplace of easy rhetoric for the literary men who only know Nature through their books! . . . In the forest hard by, a few yards away from the house, there were frightful struggles always toward. The murderous beeches flung themselves upon the pines with their lovely pinkish stems, hemmed in their slenderness with antique columns, and stifled them. They rushed down upon the oaks and smashed them, and made themselves crutches of them. The beeches were like Briareus with his hundred arms, ten trees in one tree! They dealt death all about them. And when, failing foes, they came together, they became entangled, piercing, cleaving, twining round each other like antediluvian monsters. Lower down, in the forest, the acacias had left the outskirts and plunged into the thick of it and attacked the pinewoods, strangling and tearing up the roots of their foes, poisoning them with their secretions. It was a struggle to the death in which the victors at once took possession of the room and the spoils of the vanquished. Then the smaller monsters would finish the work of the great. Fungi, growing between the roots, would suck at the sick tree, and gradually empty it of its vitality. Black ants would grind exceeding small the rotting wood. Millions of invisible insects were gnawing, boring, reducing to dust what had once been life. . . . And the silence of the struggle! . . . Oh! the peace of Nature, the tragic mask that covers the sorrowful and cruel face of Life!

Christophe was going down and down. But he was not the kind of man to let himself drown without a struggle, with his arms held close to his sides. In vain did he wish to die: he did everything in his power to remain alive. He was one of those men of whom Mozart said: *"They must act until at last they have no means of action."* He felt that he was sinking, and in his fall he cast about, striking out with his arms to right and left, for some support to which to cling. It seemed to him that he had found it. He had just remembered Olivier's little boy. At once he turned on him all his desire for life: he clung to him desperately. Yes: he must go and find him, claim him, bring him up, love him, take the place of his father, bring Olivier to life again in his son. Why had he not thought of it in the selfishness of his sorrow? He wrote to Cécile, who had charge of the boy. He waited feverishly for her reply. His

whole being was bent upon the one thought. He forced himself
to be calm: he still had reason for hope. He was quite confident about it: he knew how kind Cécile was.

Her answer came. Cécile said that three months after
Olivier's death, a lady in black had come to her house and said:
" Give me back my child!"

It was Jacqueline, who had deserted her child and Olivier,—
Jacqueline, but so changed that she had hardly recognized her.
Her mad love affair had not lasted. She had wearied of her
lover more quickly than her lover had done of her. She had
come back broken, disgusted, aged. The too flagrant scandal of
her adventure had closed many doors to her. The least scrupulous had not been the least severe. Even her mother had been
so offensive and so contemptuous that Jacqueline had found it
impossible to stay with her. She had seen through and through
the world's hypocrisy. Olivier's death had been the last blow.
She seemed so utterly sorrowful that Cécile had not thought
it right to refuse to let her have her boy. It was hard for her
to have to give up the little creature, whom she had grown so
used to regarding as her own. But how could she make things
even harder for a woman who had more right than herself, a
woman who was further more unhappy? She had wanted to
write to Christophe to ask his advice. But Christophe had
never answered the letters she had written him, she did not
know his address, she did not even know whether he was alive
or dead. . . . Joy comes and goes. What could she do?
Only resign herself to the inevitable. The main thing was
for the child to be happy and to be loved. . . .

The letter reached him in the evening. A belated gust of
winter brought back the snow. It fell all night. In the forest,
where already the young leaves had appeared, the trees cracked
and split beneath the weight of it. They went off like a
battery of artillery. Alone in his room, without a light, surrounded only by the phosphorescent darkness, Christophe sat
listening to the tragic sounds of the forest, and started at every
crack: and he was like one of the trees bending beneath its load
and snapping. He said to himself:

" Now the end has come."

Night passed. Day came. The tree was not broken. All through the new day and the following night the tree went on bending and cracking: but it did not break. Christophe had no reason for living left: and he went on living. He had no motive for struggling; and he struggled, body to body, foot to foot, with the invisible enemy who was bending his back. He was like Jacob with the angel. He expected nothing from the fight, he expected nothing now but the end, rest; and he went on fighting. And he cried aloud:

"Break me and have done! Why dost thou not throw me down?"

Days passed. Christophe issued from the fight, utterly lifeless. Yet he would not lie down, and insisted on going out and walking. Happy are those men who are sustained by the fortitude of their race in the hours of eclipse of their lives! Though the body of the son was near breaking-point, the strength of the father and the grandfather held him up: the energy and impetus of his robust ancestors sustained his broken soul, like a dead knight being carried along by his horse.

Along a precipitous road he went with a ravine on either hand: he went down the narrow path, thick with sharp stones, among which coiled the gnarled roots of the little stunted oaks: he did not know where he was going, and yet he was more surefooted than if he had been moving under the lucid direction of his will. He had not slept, he had hardly eaten anything for several days. He saw a mist in front of his eyes. He walked down towards the valley.—It was Easter-week. A cloudy day. The last assault of winter had been overcome The warmth of spring was brooding. From the villages far down the sound of bells came up: first from a village nestling in a hollow at the foot of the mountain, with its dappled thatched roofs, dark and light in patches, covered with thick, velvety moss. Then from another, out of sight, on the other slope of the hill. Then, others down on the plain beyond the river. And the distant hum of a town seen hazily in the mist. Christophe stopped. His heart almost stopped beating. Their voices seemed to be saying:

" Come with us. Here is peace. Here sorrow is dead. Dead, and thought is dead too. We croon so sweetly to the soul that it sleeps in our arms. Come, and rest, and thou shalt not wake again."

He felt so worn out! He was so fain to sleep! But he shook his head and said:

" It is not peace that I seek, but life."

He went on his way. He walked for miles without noticing it. In his state of weakness and hallucination the simplest sensations came to him with unexpected resonance. Over earth and air his mind cast fantastic lights. A shadow, with nothing to cause it that he could see, going before him on the white and sunless road, made him tremble.

As he emerged from a wood he found himself near a village. He turned back: the sight of men hurt him. However, he could not avoid passing by a lonely house above the hamlet: it was built on the side of the mountain, and looked like a sanatorium: it was surrounded by a large garden open to the sun; a few men were wandering with faltering footsteps along the gravel paths. Christophe did not look at it particularly: but at a turn of the path he came face to face with a man with pale eyes and a fat, yellow face, staring blankly, who had sunk down on a seat at the foot of two poplar trees. Another man was sitting by his side: they were both silent. Christophe walked past them. But, a few yards on, he stopped: the man's eyes had seemed familiar to him. He turned. The man had not stirred: he was still staring fixedly at something in front of him. But his companion looked at Christophe, who beckoned to him. He came up.

" Who is he? " asked Christophe.

" A patient in the asylum," said the man, pointing to the house.

" I think I know him," said Christophe.

" Possibly." replied the man. " He was a well-known writer in Germany."

Christophe mentioned a name.—Yes. That was the name.— He had met him once in the days when he was writing for Mannheim's review. Then, they were enemies: Christophe was only just beginning, and the other was already famous. He had been a man of considerable power, very self-confident, very contemptuous of other men's work, a novelist whose realistic and sensual writings had stood out above the mediocrity of the productions of his day. Christophe, who detested the man, could not help admiring the perfection of his materialistic art, which was sincere, though limited.

"He went mad a year ago," said the keeper. "He was treated, regarded as cured, and sent home. Then he went mad again. One evening he threw himself out of the window. At first, when he came here, he used to fling himself about and shout. But now he is quite quiet. He spends his days sitting there, as you see."

"What is he looking at?" asked Christophe.

He went up to the seat, and looked pitifully at the pale face of the madman, with his heavy eyelids drooping over his eyes: one of them seemed to be almost shut. The madman seemed to be unaware of Christophe's presence. Christophe spoke to him by name and took his hand—a soft, clammy hand, which lay limp in his like a dead thing: he had not the courage to keep it in his: the man raised his glazing eyes to Christophe for a moment, then went on staring straight in front of him with his besotted smile. Christophe asked:

"What are you looking at?"

The man said, without moving, in a whisper:

"I am waiting."

"What for?"

"The Resurrection."

Christophe started back. He walked hurriedly away. The word had burnt into his very soul.

He plunged into the forest, and climbed up the hillside in the direction of his own house. In his confusion he missed his way, and found himself in the middle of an immense pine-wood. Darkness and silence. A few patches of sunlight of a pale, ruddy gold, come it was impossible to tell whence, fell aslant the dense shadows. Christophe was hypnotized by these patches of light. Round him everything seemed to be in darkness. He walked along over the carpet of pine-needles, tripping over the roots which stood out like swollen veins. At the foot of the trees were neither plants nor moss. In the branches was

never the song of a bird. The lower branches were dead. All
the life of the place had fled upwards to meet the sun. Soon
even the life overhead would be gone. Christophe passed into a
part of the wood which was visited by some mysterious pesti-
lence. A kind of long, delicate lichen, like spiders' webs, had
fastened upon the branches of the red pines, and wrapped them
about with its meshes, binding them from hand to foot, passing
from tree to tree, choking the life out of the forest. It was
like the deep-sea alga with its subtle tentacles. There was in
the place the silence of the depths of the ocean. High overhead hung the pale sun. Mists which had crept insidiously
through the forest encompassed Christophe. Everything disappeared: there was nothing to be seen. For half an hour
Christophe wandered at random in the web of the white mist,
which grew slowly thicker, black, and crept down into his throat:
he thought he was going straight: but he was walking in a
circle beneath the gigantic spiders' webs hanging from the stifled
pines: the mist, passing through them, left them enriched with
shivering drops of water. At last the meshes were rent asunder,
a hole was made, and Christophe managed to make his way out
of the submarine forest. He came to living woods and the
silent conflict of the pines and the beeches. But everywhere
there was the same stillness. The silence, which had been brooding for hours, was agonizing. Christophe stopped to listen. . . .

Suddenly, in the distance, there came a storm. A premoni-
tory gust of wind blew up from the depths of the forest. Like
a galloping horse it rushed over the swaying tree-tops. It was
like the God of Michael Angelo passing in a water-spout. It
passed over Christophe's head. The forest rustled, and Christophe's heart quivered. It was the Annunciation. . . .

Silence came again. In a state of holy terror Christophe
walked quickly home, with his legs giving way beneath him.
At the door of the house he glanced fearfully behind him, like
a hunted man. All Nature seemed dead. The forests which
covered the sides of the mountain were sleeping, lying heavy
beneath a weight of sadness. The still air was magically clear
and transparent. There was never a sound. Only the melancholy music of a stream—water eating away the rock—sounded
the knell of the earth. Christophe went to bed in a fever. In

the stable hard by the beasts stirred as restlessly and uneasily
as he. . . .

Night. He had dozed off. In the silence the distant storm
arose once more. The wind returned, like a hurricane now,—
the *fœhn* of the spring, with its burning breath warming the
still sleeping, chilly earth, the *fœhn* which melts the ice and
gathers fruitful rains. It rumbled like thunder in the forests
on the other side of the ravine. It came nearer, swelled, charged
up the slopes: the whole mountain roared. In the stable a
horse neighed and the cows lowed. Christophe's hair stood on
end, he sat up in bed and listened. The squall came up screaming, set the shutters banging, the weather-cocks squeaking, made
the slates of the roof go crashing down, and the whole house
shake. A flower-pot fell and was smashed. Christophe's window was insecurely fastened, and was burst open with a bang,
and the warm wind rushed in. Christophe received its blast
full in his face and on his naked chest. He jumped out of bed
gaping, gasping, choking. It was as though the living God
were rushing into his empty soul. The Resurrection! . . .
The air poured down his throat, the flood of new life swelled
through him and penetrated to his very marrow. He felt like
to burst, he wanted to shout, to shout for joy and sorrow: and
there would only come inarticulate sounds from his mouth.
He reeled, he beat on the walls with his arms, while all around
him were sheets of paper flying on the wind. He fell down
in the middle of the room and cried:

" O Thou, Thou! Thou art come back to me at last! "

" Thou art come back to me, Thou art come back to me!
O Thou, whom I had lost! . . . Why didst Thou abandon
me? "

" To fulfil My task, that thou didst abandon."

" What task? "

" My fight."

" What need hast Thou to fight? Art Thou not master
of all? "

" I am not the master."

" Art Thou not All that Is? "

" I am not all that is. I am Life fighting Nothingness. I
am not Nothingness, I am the Fire which burns in the Night

I am not the Night. I am the eternal Light; I am not an eternal destiny soaring above the fight. I am free Will which struggles eternally. Struggle and burn with Me."

" I am conquered. I am good for nothing."

" Thou art conquered? All seems lost to thee? Others will be conquerors. Think not of thyself, think of My army."

" I am alone. I have none but myself. I belong to no army."

" Thou art not alone, and thou dost not belong to thyself. Thou art one of My voices, thou art one of My arms. Speak and strike for Me. But if the arm be broken, or the voice be weary, then still I hold My ground: I fight with other voices, other arms than thine. Though thou art conquered, yet art thou of the army which is never vanquished. Remember that and thou wilt fight even unto death."

" Lord, I have suffered much ! "

" Thinkest thou that I do not suffer also? For ages death has hunted Me and nothingness has lain in wait for Me. It is only by victory in the fight that I can make My way. The river of life is red with My blood."

" Fighting, always fighting ? "

" We must always fight. God is a fighter, even He Himself. God is a conqueror. He is a devouring lion. Nothingness hems Him in and He hurls it down. And the rhythm of the fight is the supreme harmony. Such harmony is not for thy mortal ears. It is enough for thee to know that it exists. Do thy duty in peace and leave the rest to the Gods."

" I have no strength left."

" Sing for those who are strong."

" My voice is gone."

" Pray."

" My heart is foul."

" Pluck it out. Take Mine."

" Lord, it is easy to forget myself, to cast away my dead soul. But how can I cast out the dead? how can I forget those whom I have loved ? "

" Abandon the dead with thy dead soul. Thou wilt find them alive with My living soul."

" Thou hast left me once: wilt Thou leave me again ? "

"I shall leave thee again. Never doubt that. It is for thee never to leave Me more."

"But if the flame of my life dies down?"

"Then do thou kindle others."

"And if death is in me?"

"Life is otherwhere. Go, open thy gates to life. Thou insensate man, to shut thyself up in thy ruined house! Quit thyself. There are other mansions."

"O Life, O Life! I see . . . I sought thee in myself, in my own empty shut-in soul. My soul is broken: the sweet air pours in through the windows of my wounds: I breathe again. I have found Thee once more, O Life! . . ."

"I have found thee again. . . . Hold thy peace, and listen."

And like the murmuring of a spring, Christophe heard the song of life bubbling up in him. Leaning out of his window. he saw the forest, which yesterday had been dead, seething with life under the sun and the wind, heaving like the Ocean. Along the stems of the trees, like thrills of joy, the waves of the wind passed: and the yielding branches held their arms in ecstasy up to the brilliant sky. And the torrent rang out merrily as a bell. The countryside had risen from the grave in which yesterday it had been entombed: life had entered it at the time when love passed into Christophe's heart. Oh! the miracle of the soul touched by grace, awaking to new life! Then everything comes to life again all round it. The heart begins to beat once more. The eye of the spirit is opened. The dried-up fountains begin once more to flow.

And Christophe returned to the Divine conflict. . . . How his own fight, how all the conflicts of men were lost in that gigantic battle, wherein the suns rain down like flakes of snow tossing on the wind! . . . He had laid bare his soul. And, just as in those dreams in which one hovers in space, he felt that he was soaring above himself, he saw himself from above. in the general plan of the world; and the meaning of his efforts. the price of his suffering, were revealed to him at a glance. His struggles were a part of the great fight of the worlds. His overthrow was a momentary episode, immediately repaired. Just as he fought for all, so all fought for him. They shared his trials, he shared their glory.

" Companions, enemies, walk over me, crush me, let me feel the cannons which shall win victory pass over my body! I do not think of the iron which cuts deep into my flesh, I do not think of the foot that tramples down my head, I think of my Avenger, the Master, the Leader of the countless army. My blood shall cement the victory of the future. . . ."

God was not to him the impassive Creator, a Nero from his tower of brass watching the burning of the City to which he himself has set fire. God was fighting. God was suffering. Fighting and suffering with all who fight and for all who suffer. For God was Life, the drop of light fallen into the darkness, spreading out, reaching out, drinking up the night. But the night is limitless, and the Divine struggle will never cease: and none can know how it will end. It was a heroic symphony wherein the very discords clashed together and mingled and grew into a serene whole! Just as the beech-forest in silence furiously wages war, so Life carries war into the eternal peace.

The wars and the peace rang echoing through Christophe. He was like a shell wherein the ocean roars. Epic shouts passed, and trumpet calls, and tempestuous sounds borne upon sovereign rhythms. For in that sonorous soul everything took shape in sound. It sang of light. It sang of darkness, sang of life and death. It sang for those who were victorious in battle. It sang for himself who was conquered and laid low. It sang. All was song. It was nothing but song.

It was so drunk with it that it could not hear its own song. Like the spring rains, the torrents of music disappeared into the earth that was cracked by the winter. Shame, grief, bitterness now revealed their mysterious mission: they had decomposed the earth and they had fertilized it. The share of sorrow, breaking the heart, had opened up new sources of life. The waste land had once more burst into flower. But they were not the old spring flowers. A new soul had been born.

Every moment it was springing into birth. For it was not yet shaped and hardened, like the souls that have come to the end of their belief, the souls which are at the point of death. It was not the finished statue. It was molten metal. Every second made a new universe of it. Christophe had no thought of setting bounds upon himself. He gave himself up to the joy of a man leaving behind him the burden of his past and setting out on a long voyage, with youth in his blood, freedom in his heart, to breathe the sea air, and think that the voyage will never come to an end. Now that he was caught up again by the creative force which flows through the world, he was amazed to the point of ecstasy at the world's wealth. He loved, he *was,* his neighbor as himself. And all things were " neighbors " to him, from the grass beneath his feet to the man whose hand he clasped. A fine tree, the shadow of a cloud on the mountain, the breath of the fields borne upward on the wind, and, at night, the hive of heaven buzzing with the swarming suns . . . his blood raced through him . . . he had no desire to speak or to think, he desired only to laugh and to cry, and to melt away into the living marvel of it all. Write? Why should he write? Can a man write the inexpressible? . . . But whether it were possible or no, he had to write. It was his law. Ideas would come to him in flashes, wherever he might be, most often when he was out walking. He could not wait. Then he would write with anything, on anything that came to hand : and very often he could not have told the meaning of the phrases which came rushing forth from him with irresistible impetuosity : and, as he wrote, more ideas would come, more and more : and he would write and write, on his shirt cuffs, in the lining of his hat. Quickly though he wrote, yet his thoughts would leap ahead, and he had to use a sort of shorthand.

They were only rough notes. The difficulty began when he tried to turn his ideas into the ordinary musical forms : he discovered that none of the conventional molds were in the least suitable : if he wanted to fix his visions with any sort of fidelity, he had to begin by forgetting all the music he had ever heard, everything he had ever written, make a clean sweep of all the formulæ he had ever learned, and the traditional technique ; fling away all such crutches of the impotent mind, the comfortable bed made for the indolence of those who lie back on the thoughts of other men to save themselves the trouble of thinking for themselves. A short while ago, when he thought that he had reached maturity in life and art—(as a matter of fact he had only been at the end of one of his lives and one of his incarnations in art),—he had expressed himself in a pre-existing language: his feelings had submitted without revolt to the logic of a pre-established development, which dictated a portion of his phrases in advance, and had led him, docilely enough, along the beaten track to the appointed spot where the public was awaiting him. Now there was no road marked out, and his feelings had to carve out their own path: his mind had only to follow. It was no longer appointed to describe or to analyze passion: it had to become part and parcel of it, and seek to wed its inward law.

At the same time he shed all the contradictions in which he had long been involved, though he had never willingly submitted to them. For, although he was a pure artist, he had often incorporated in his art considerations which are foreign to art: he had endowed it with a social mission. And he had not perceived that there were two men in him: the creative artist who never worried himself about any moral aim, and the man of action, the thinker, who wanted his art to be moral and social. The two would sometimes bring each other to an awkward pass. But now that he was subject to every creative idea, with its organic law, like a reality superior to all reality, he had broken free of practical reason. In truth, he shed none of his contempt for the flabby and depraved immorality of the age: in truth, he still thought that its impure and unwholesome art was the lowest rung of art, because it is a disease, a fungus growing on a rotting trunk: but if art for pleasure's sake is the prostration of art, Christophe by no means opposed to it the short-sighted utilitarianism of art for morality's sake, that winged Pegasus harnessed to the plow. The highest art, the only art which is worthy of the name, is above all temporary laws: it is a comet sweeping through the infinite. It may be that its force is useful, it may be that it is apparently useless and dangerous in the existing order of the workaday world: but it is force, it is movement and fire: it is the lightning darted from heaven: and, for that very reason, it is sacred, for that very reason it is beneficent. The good it does may be of the practical

order: but its real, its Divine benefits are, like faith, of the
supernatural order. It is like the sun whence it is sprung. The
sun is neither moral nor immoral. It is that which Is. It
lightens the darkness of space. And so does art.

And Christophe, being delivered up to art, was amazed to
find unknown and unsuspected powers teeming in himself:
powers quite apart from his passions, his sorrows, his conscious
soul, a stranger soul, indifferent to all his loves and sufferings,
to all his life, a joyous, fantastic, wild, incomprehensible soul.
It rode him and dug its spurs into his sides. And, in the rare
moments when he could stop to take breath, he wondered as he
read over what he had written:

"How could such things have come out of me?"

He was a prey to that delirium of the mind which is known
to every man of genius, that will which is independent of the
will, "_the ineffable enigma of the world and life,_" which Goethe
calls "_the demoniac,_" against which he was always armed, though
it always overcame him.

And Christophe wrote and wrote. For days and weeks.
There are times when the mind, being impregnated, can feed
upon itself and go on producing almost indefinitely. The faintest contact with things, the pollen of a flower borne by the
wind were enough to make the inward germs, the myriads of
germs put forth and come to blossom. Christophe had no time
to think, no time to live. His creative soul reigned sovereign
over the ruins of his life.

And suddenly it stopped. Christophe came out of that state
broken, scorched, older by ten years—but saved. He had left
Christophe and gone over to God.

Streaks of white hair had suddenly appeared in his black
mane, like those autumn flowers which spring up in the fields
in September nights. There were fresh lines on his cheeks.
But his eyes had regained their calm expression, and his mouth
bore the marks of resignation. He was appeased. He understood now. He understood the vanity of his pride, the vanity
of human pride, under the terrible hand of the Force which
moves the worlds. No man is surely master of himself. A
man must watch. For if he slumbers that Force rushes into

him and whirls him headlong . . . into what dread abysses? or the torrent which bears him along sinks and leaves him on its dry bed. To fight the fight it is not enough to will. A man must humiliate himself before the unknown God, who *flat ubi vult,* who blows where and when He listeth, love, death, or life. Human will can do nothing without God's. One second is enough for Him to obliterate the work of years of toil and effort. And, if it so please Him, He can cause the eternal to spring forth from dust and mud. No man more than the creative artist feels at the mercy of God: for, if he is truly great, he will only say what the Spirit bids him.

And Christophe understood the wisdom of old Haydn who went down on his knees each morning before he took pen in hand. . . . *Vigila et ora.* Watch and pray. Pray to God that He may be with you. Keep in loving and pious communion with the Spirit of life.

Towards the end of summer a Parisian friend of Christophe's, who was passing through Switzerland, discovered his retreat. He was a musical critic who in old days had been an excellent judge of his compositions. He was accompanied by a well-known painter, who was avowedly a whole-hearted admirer of Christophe's. They told him of the very considerable success of his work, which was being played all over Europe. Christophe showed very little interest in the news: the past was dead to him, and his old compositions did not count. At his visitors' request he showed them the music he had written recently. The critic could make nothing of it. He thought Christophe had gone mad.

"No melody, no measure, no thematic workmanship: a sort of liquid core, molten matter which had not hardened, taking any shape, but possessing none of its own: it is like nothing on earth: a glimmering of light in chaos."

Christophe smiled:

"It is quite like that," he said. "The eyes of chaos shining through the veil of order. . . ."

But the critic did not understand Novalis' words:

("He is cleaned out," he thought.)

Christophe did not try to make him understand.

When his visitors were ready to go he walked with them a little, so as to do the honors of his mountain. But he did not go far. Looking down at a field, the musical critic called to mind the scenery of a Parisian theater: and the painter criticised the colors, mercilessly remarking on the awkwardness of their combination, and declaring that to him they had a Swiss flavor, sour, like rhubarb, musty and dull, *à la* Hodler; further, he displayed an indifference to Nature which was not altogether affectation. He pretended to ignore Nature.

"Nature! What on earth is Nature? I don't know. Light, color, very well! But I don't care a hang for Nature!"

Christophe shook hands with them and let them go. That sort of thing had no effect on him now. They were on the other side of the ravine. That was well. He said to nobody in particular:

"If you wish to come up to me, you must take the same road."

The creative fire which had been burning for months had died down. But its comfortable warmth was still in Christophe's heart. He knew that the fire would flare up again: if not in himself, then around him. Wherever it might be, he would love it just the same: it would always be the same fire. On that September evening he could feel it burning throughout all Nature.

He climbed up to the house. There had been a storm. The sun had come out again. The fields were steaming. The ripe fruit was falling from the apple-trees into the wet grass. Spiders' webs, hanging from the branches of the trees, still glittering with the rain, were like the ancient wheels of Mycenean chariots. At the edge of the dripping forest the green woodpecker was trilling his jerky laughter; and myriads of little wasps, dancing in the sunbeams, filled the vault of the woods with their deep, long-drawn organ note.

Christophe came to a clearing, in the hollow of a shoulder of the mountain, a little valley shut in at both ends, a perfect oval in shape, which was flooded with the light of the setting sun: the earth was red: in the midst lay a little golden field of belated crops, and rust-colored rushes. Round about it was a girdle of the woods with their ripe autumn tints: ruddy copper beeches, pale yellow chestnuts, rowans with their coral berries, flaming cherry-trees with their little tongues of fire, myrtle-bushes with their leaves of orange and lemon and brown and burnt tinder. It was like a burning bush. And from the heart of the flaring cup rose and soared a lark, drunk with the berries and the sun.

And Christophe's soul was like the lark. It knew that it would soon come down to earth again, and many times. But it knew also that it would unwearyingly ascend in the fire, singing its " tirra-lirra " which tells of the light of the heavens to those who are on earth below.

THE NEW DAWN

HERE, AT THE END OF THIS BOOK,

I DEDICATE IT:

TO THE FREE SPIRITS—OF ALL NATIONS—

WHO SUFFER, FIGHT, AND

WILL PREVAIL.

R. R.

PREFACE TO THE LAST VOLUME

OF

JEAN-CHRISTOPHE

I HAVE written the tragedy of a generation which is nearing its end. I have sought to conceal neither its vices nor its virtues, its profound sadness, its chaotic pride, its heroic efforts, its despondency beneath the overwhelming burden of a super-human task, the burden of the whole world, the reconstruction of the world's morality, its esthetic principles, its faith, the forging of a new humanity.—Such we have been.

You young men, you men of to-day, march over us, trample us under your feet, and press onward. Be ye greater and happier than we.

For myself, I bid the soul that was mine farewell. I cast it from me like an empty shell. Life is a succession of deaths and resurrections. We must die, Christophe, to be born again.

ROMAIN ROLLAND.

October, 1912.

Du hol-de Kunst, in wie viel grau-en Stun-den..

LIFE passes. Body and soul flow onward like a stream. The years are written in the flesh of the ageing tree. The whole visible world of form is forever wearing out and springing to new life. Thou only dost not pass, immortal music. Thou art the inward sea. Thou art the profound depths of the soul. In thy clear eyes the scowling face of life is not mirrored. Far, far from thee, like the herded clouds, flies the procession of days, burning, icy, feverish, driven by uneasiness, huddling, moving on, on, never for one moment to endure. Thou only dost not pass. Thou art beyond the world. Thou art a whole world to thyself. Thou hast thy sun, thy laws, thy ebb and flow. Thou hast the peace of the stars in the great spaces of the field of night, marking their luminous track—plows of silver guided by the sure hand of the invisible ox-herd.

Music, serene music, how sweet is thy moony light to eyes wearied of the harsh brilliance of this world's sun! The soul that has lived and turned away from the common horse-pond, where, as they drink, men stir up the mud with their feet, nestles to thy bosom, and from thy breasts is suckled with the clear running water of dreams. Music, thou virgin mother, who in thy immaculate womb bearest the fruit of all passions, who in the lake of thy eyes, whereof the color is as the color of rushes, or as the pale green glacier water, enfoldest good and evil, thou art beyond evil, thou art beyond good; he that taketh refuge with thee is raised above the passing of time: the succession of days will be but one day; and death that devours everything on such an one will never close its jaws.

Music, thou who hast rocked my sorrow-laden soul; music, thou who hast made me firm in strength, calm and joyous,— my love and my treasure,—I kiss thy pure lips, I hide my face

349

in thy honey-sweet hair. I lay my burning eyelids upon the cool palms of thy hands. No word we speak, our eyes are closed, and I see the ineffable light of thine eyes, and I drink the smile of thy silent lips: and, pressed close to thy heart, I listen to the throb of eternal life.

CHRISTOPHE loses count of the fleeting years. Drop by drop life ebbs away. But *his* life is elsewhere. It has no history. His history lies wholly in his creative work. The unceasing buzzing song of music fills his soul, and makes him insensible to the outward tumult.

Christophe has conquered. His name has been forced upon the world. He is ageing. His hair is white. That is nothing to him, his heart is ever young: he has surrendered none of his force, none of his faith. Once more he is calm, but not as he was before he passed by the Burning Bush. In the depths of his soul there is still the quivering of the storm, the memory of his glimpse into the abyss of the raging seas. He knows that no man may boast of being master of himself without the permission of the God of battle. In his soul there are two souls. One is a high plateau swept by winds and shrouded with clouds. The other, higher still, is a snowy peak bathed in light. There it is impossible to dwell; but, when he is frozen by the mists on the lower ground, well he knows the path that leads to the sun. In his misty soul Christophe is not alone. Near him he ever feels the presence of an invisible friend, the sturdy Saint Cecilia, listening with wide, calm eyes to the heavens; and, like the Apostle Paul,—in Raphael's picture, —silent and dreaming, leaning on his sword, he is beyond exasperation, and has no thought of fighting: he dreams, and forges his dreams into form.

During this period of his life he mostly wrote piano and chamber music. In such work he was more free to dare and be bold: it necessitated fewer intermediaries between his ideas and their realization; his ideas were less in danger of losing force in the course of their percolation. Frescobaldi, Couperin, Schubert, and Chopin, in their boldness of expression and style, anticipated the revolutionaries in orchestral music by fifty years. Out of the crude stuff shaped by Christophe's strong hands came strange and unknown agglomerations of harmony, bewildering combinations of chords, begotten of the remotest kinships of sounds accessible to the senses in these days; they cast a magical and holy spell upon the mind.—But the public must have time to grow accustomed to the conquests and the trophies which a great artist brings back with him from his quest in the deep waters of the ocean. Very few would follow Christophe in the temerity of his later works. His fame was due to his earlier compositions. The feeling of not being understood, which is even more painful in success than in the lack of it, because there seems to be no way out of it, had, since the death of his only friend, aggravated in Christophe his rather morbid tendency to seek isolation from the world.

However, the gates of Germany were open to him once more. In France the tragic brawl had been forgotten. He was free to go whithersoever he pleased. But he was afraid of the memories that would lie in wait for him in Paris. And, although he had spent a few months in Germany and returned there from time to time to conduct performances of his work, he did not settle there. He found too many things which hurt him. They were not particular to Germany: he found them elsewhere. But a man expects more of his own country than any other, and he suffers more from its foibles. It was true, too, that Germany was bearing the greatest burden of the sins of Europe. The victor incurs the responsibility of his victory, a debt towards the vanquished: tacitly the victor is pledged to march in front of them to show them the way. The conquests of Louis XIV. gave Europe the splendor of French reason. What light has the Germany of Sedan given to the world? The glitter of bayonets? Thought without wings, action without generosity, brutal realism, which has not even the excuse of being the realism of healthy men; force and interest: Mars turned bagman. Forty years ago Europe was led astray into the night, and the terrors of the night. The sun was hidden beneath the conqueror's helmet. If the vanquished are too weak to raise the extinguisher, and can claim only pity mingled with contempt, what shall be given to the victor who has done this thing?

A little while ago, day began to peep: little shafts of light shimmered through the cracks. Being one of the first to see the rising of the sun, Christophe had come out of the shadow of the helmet: gladly he returned to the country in which he had been a sojourner perforce, to Switzerland. Like so many of the spirits of that time, spirits thirsting for liberty, choking in the narrowing circle of the hostile nations, he sought a corner of the earth in which he could stand above Europe and breathe freely. Formerly, in the days of Goethe, the Rome of the free Popes was the island upon which all the winged thought of divers nations came to rest, like birds taking shelter from the storm. Now what refuge is there? The island has been covered by the sea. Rome is no more. The birds have fled from the Seven Hills.—The Alps only are left for them. There, amid the rapacity of Europe, stands (for how long?) the little island of twenty-four cantons. In truth it has not the poetic radiance and glamor of the Eternal City: history has not filled its air with the breath of gods and heroes; but a mighty music rises from the naked Earth; there is an heroic rhythm in the lines of the mountains, and here, more than anywhere else, a man can feel himself in contact with elemental forces. Christophe did not go there in search of romantic pleasure. A field, a few trees, a stream, the wide sky, were enough to make him feel alive. The calm aspect of his native country was sweeter and more companionable to him than the gigantic grandeur of the Alps. But he could not forget that it was here that he had renewed his strength: here God had appeared to him in the Burning Bush; and he never returned thither without a thrill of gratitude and faith. He was not the only one. How many of the combatants of life, ground beneath life's heel, have on that soil renewed their energy to turn again to the fight, and believe once more in its purpose!

Living in that country he had come to know it well. The majority of those who pass through it see only its excrescences: the leprosy of the hotels which defiles the fairest features of that sturdy piece of earth, the stranger cities, the monstrous marts whither all the fatted people of the world come to browse, the *table d'hôte* meals, the masses of food flung into the trough for the nosing beasts: the casino bands with their silly music mingling with the noise of the little horses, the

Italian scum whose disgusting uproar makes the bored wealthy idiots wriggle with pleasure, the fatuous display of the shops—wooden bears, châlets, silly knick-knacks, always the same, repeated time and again, over and over again, with no freshness or invention; the worthy booksellers with their scandalous pamphlets,—all the moral baseness of those places whither every year the idle, joyless millions come who are incapable of finding amusement in the smallest degree finer than that of the multitude, or one tithe as keen.

And they know nothing of the people in whose land they stay. They have no notion of the reserves of moral force and civic liberty which for centuries have been hoarded up in them, coals of the fires of Calvin and Zwingli, still glowing beneath the ashes; they have no conception of the vigorous democratic spirit which will always ignore the Napoleonic Republic, of the simplicity of their institutions, or the breadth of their social undertakings, or the example given to the world by these United States of the three great races of the West, the model of the Europe of the future. Even less do they know of the Daphne concealed beneath this rugged bark, the wild, flashing dreams of Boecklin, the raucous heroism of Hodler, the serene vision and humor of Gottfried Keller, the living tradition of the great popular festivals, and the sap of springtime swelling the trees,—the still young art, sometimes rasping to the palate, like the hard fruits of wild pear-trees, sometimes with the sweetish insipidity of myrtles black and blue, but at least something smacking of the earth, is the work of self-taught men not cut off from the people by an archaic culture, but, with them, reading in the same book of life.

Christophe was in sympathy with these men who strive less to seem than to be, and, under the recent veneer of an ultra-modern industrialism, keep clearly marked the most reposeful features of the old Europe of peasants and townsmen. Among them he had found a few good friends, grave, serious, and faithful, who hold isolated and immured in them regrets for the past; they were looking on at the gradual disappearance of the old Switzerland with a sort of religious fatalism and Calvinistic pessimism; great gray souls. Christophe seldom saw them. His old wounds were apparently healed: but they

had been too deep wholly to be cured. He was fearful of forming new ties with men. It was something for this reason that
he liked to dwell in a country where it was easy to live apart,
a stranger amid a throng of strangers. For the rest he rarely
stayed long in any one place; often he changed his lair: he
was like an old migratory bird which needs space, and has its
country in the air. . . . *"Mein Reich ist in der Luft."*

An evening in summer.

He was walking in the mountains above a village. He was
striding along with his hat in his hand, up a winding road.
He came to a neck where the road took a double turn, and
passed into shadow between two slopes; on either side were nut-
trees and pines. It was like a little shut-in world. On either
hand the road seemed to come to an end, cut off at the edge
of the void. Beyond were blue distance and the gleaming air.
The peace of evening came down like a gentle rain.

They came together each at the same moment turning the
bend at either end of the neck. She was dressed in black,
and stood out against the clear sky: behind her were two
children, a boy and a girl, between six and eight, who were
playing and picking flowers. They recognized each other at a
distance of a few yards. Their emotion was visible in their
eyes; but neither brought it into words; each gave only an
imperceptible movement. He was deeply moved: she . . . her
lips trembled a little. They stopped. Almost in a whisper:

" Grazia ! "

" You here ! "

They held out their hands and stood without a word. Grazia
was the first to make an effort to break the silence. She told
him where she lived, and asked him where he was staying.
Question and answer were mechanical, and they hardly listened,
heard later, when their hands had parted: they were absorbed
in gazing at each other. The children came back to her. She
introduced them. He felt hostile towards them, and looked at
them with no kindness, and said nothing: he was engrossed
with her, occupied only in studying her beautiful face that
bore some marks of suffering and age. She was embarrassed
by his gaze, and said:

" Will you come, this evening? "

And she gave the name of her hotel.

He asked her where her husband was. She pointed to her black dress. He was too much moved to say more, and left her awkwardly. But when he had taken a few strides he came back to the children, who were picking strawberries, and took them roughly in his arms and kissed them, and went away.

In the evening he went to the hotel, and found her on the veranda, with the blinds drawn. They sat apart. There were very few people about, only two or three old people. Christophe was irritated by their presence. Grazia looked at him, and he looked at her, and murmured her name over and over again.

" Don't you think I have changed? " she asked.

His heart grew big.

" You have suffered," he said.

" You too," she answered pityingly, scanning the deep marks of agony and passion in his face.

They were at a loss for words.

" Please," he said, a moment later, " let us go somewhere else. Could we not find somewhere to be alone and talk? "

" No, my dear. Let us stay here. It is good enough here. No one is heeding us at all."

" I cannot talk freely here."

" That is all the better."

He could not understand why. Later, when in memory ne went over their conversation, he thought she had not trusted him. But she was instinctively afraid of emotional scenes: unconsciously she was seeking protection from any surprise of their hearts: the very awkwardness of their intimacy in a public room, so sheltering the modesty of her secret emotions, was dear to her.

In whispers, with long intervals of silence, they sketched their lives in outline. Count Berény had been killed in a duel a few months ago; and Christophe saw that she had not been very happy with him. Also, she had lost a child, her first-born. She made no complaint, and turned the conversation from herself to question Christophe, and, as he told her of his tribulations, she showed the most affectionate compassion. Bells rang. It was Sunday evening. Life stood still.

She asked him to come again next day but one. He was hurt that she should be so little eager to see him again. In his heart happiness and sorrow were mingled.

Next day, on some pretext, she wrote and asked him to come. He was delighted with her little note. This time she received him in her private room. She was with her two children. He looked at them, still a little uneasily, but very tenderly. He thought the little girl—the elder of the two—very like her mother: but he did not try to match the boy's looks. They talked about the country, the times, the books lying open on the table:—but their eyes spoke of other things. He was hoping to be able to talk more intimately when a hotel acquaintance came in. He marked the pleasure and politeness with which Grazia received the stranger: she seemed to make no difference between her two visitors. He was hurt by it, but could not be angry with her. She proposed that they should all go for a walk and he accepted; the presence of the other woman, though she was young and charming, paralyzed him: his day was spoiled.

He did not see Grazia again for two days. During that time he lived but for the hours he was to spend with her.—Once more his efforts to speak to her were doomed to failure. While she was very gentle and kind with him, she could not throw off her reserve. All unconsciously Christophe added to her difficulty by his outbursts of German sentimentality, which embarrassed her and forced her instinct into reaction.

He wrote her a letter which touched her, saying that life was so short! Their lives were already so far gone! Perhaps they would have only a very little time in which to see each other, and it was pitiful, almost criminal, not to employ it in frank converse.

She replied with a few affectionate words, begging him to excuse her for her distrust, which she could not avoid, since she had been so much hurt by life: she could not break her habitual reserve: any excessive display, even of a genuine feeling, hurt and terrified her. But well she knew the worth of the friendship that had come to her once more: and she was as glad of it as he. She asked him to dine with her that evening.

His heart was brimming with gratitude. In his room, lying

on his bed, he sobbed. It was the opening of the flood-gates of ten years of solitude: for, since Olivier's death, he had been utterly alone. Her letter gave the word of resurrection to his heart that was so famished for tenderness. Tenderness! . . . He thought he had put it from him: he had been forced to learn how to do without it! Now he felt how sorely he needed it, and the great stores of love that had accumulated in him. . . .

It was a sweet and blessed evening that they spent to-gether. . . . He could only speak to her of trivial subjects, in spite of their intention to hide nothing from each other. But what goodly things he told her through the piano, which with her eyes she invited him to use to tell her what he had to say! She was struck by the humility of the man whom she had known in his violence and pride. When he went away the silent pressure of their hands told them that they had found each other, and would never lose what they had regained.—It was raining, and there was not a breath of wind. His heart was singing.

She was only able to stay a few days longer, and she did not postpone her departure for an hour. He dared not ask her to do so, nor complain. On their last day they went for a walk with the children; there came a moment when he was so full of love and happiness that he tried to tell her so: but, with a very gentle gesture, she stopped him and smiled:

"Hush! I feel everything that you could say."

They sat down at the turn of the road where they had met. Still smiling she looked down into the valley below: but it was not the valley that she saw. He looked at the gentle face marked with the traces of bitter suffering: a few white tresses showed in her thick black hair. He was filled with a pitying, passionate adoration of this beloved creature who had travailed and been impregnated with the suffering of the soul. In every one of the marks of time upon her the soul was visible.—And, in a low, trembling voice, he craved, as a precious favor, which she granted him, a white hair from her head.

She went away. He could not understand why she would not have him accompany her. He had no doubt of her feeling for him, but her reserve disconcerted him. He could not stay

alone in that place, and set out in another direction. He tried
to occupy his mind with traveling and work. He wrote to
Grazia. She answered him, two or three week later, with very
brief letters, in which she showed her tranquil friendship, knowing neither impatience nor uneasiness. They hurt him and he
loved them. He would not admit that he had any right to reproach her; their affection was too recent, too recently renewed.
He was fearful of losing it. And yet every letter he had from
her breathed a calm loyalty which should have made him feel
secure. But she was so different from him! . . .

They had agreed to meet in Rome, towards the end of the
autumn. Without the thought of seeing her, the journey would
have had little charm for Christophe. His long isolation had
made him retiring: he had no taste for that futile hurrying
from place to place which is so dear to the indolence of modern
men and women. He was fearful of a change of habit, which
is dangerous to the regular work of the mind. Besides, Italy
had no attractions for him. He knew it only in the villainous
music of the Verists and the tenor arias to which every now and
then the land of Virgil inspires men of letters on their travels.
He felt towards Italy the hostility of an advanced artist, who
has too often heard the name of Rome invoked by the worst
champions of academic routine. Finally, the old leaven of
instinctive antipathy which ever lies fermenting in the hearts
of the men of the North towards the men of the South, or at
least towards the legendary type of rhetorical braggart which,
in the eyes of the men of the North, represents the men of the
South. At the mere thought of it Christophe disdainfully curled
his lip. . . . No, he had no desire for the more acquaintance
of the musicless people—(for, in the music of modern Europe,
what is the place of their mandolin tinkling and melodramatic
posturing declamation?).—And yet Grazia belonged to this
people. To join her again, whither and by what devious ways
would Christophe not have gone? He would win through by
shutting his eyes until he came to her.

He was used to shutting his eyes. For so many years the
shutters of his soul had been closed upon his inward life. Now,
in this late autumn, it was more necessary than ever. For

three weeks together it had rained incessantly. Then a gray
pall of impenetrable mists had hung over the valleys and towns
of Switzerland, dripping and wet. His eyes had forgotten the
sunlight. To rediscover in himself its concentrated energy he
had to begin by clothing himself in night, and, with his eyes
closed, to descend to the depths of the mine, the subterranean
galleries of his dreams. There in the seams of coal slept the
sun of days gone by. But as the result of spending his life
crouching there, digging, he came out burned, stiff in back and
knees, with limbs deformed, half petrified, dazed eyes, that, like
a bird's, could see keenly in the night. Many a time Christophe
had brought up from the mine the fire he had so painfully
extracted to warm the chill of heart. But the dreams of the
North smack of the warmth of the fireside and the closed room.
No man notices it while he lives in it: dear is that heavy air,
dear the half-light and the soul's dreams in the drowsy head
We love the things we have. We must be satisfied with
them ! . . .

When, as he passed the barrier of the Alps, Christophe,
dozing in a corner of the carriage, saw the stainless sky and
the limpid light falling upon the slopes of the mountains, he
thought he must be dreaming. On the other side of the wall
he had left a darkened sky and a fading day. So sudden was
the change that at first he felt more surprise than joy. It was
some time before his drowsy soul awoke and began slowly to
expand and burst the crust that was upon it, and his heart
could free itself from the shadows of the past. But as the
day wore on, the mellow light took his soul into its arms, and,
wholly forgetting all that had been, he drank greedily of the
delight of seeing.

Through the plains of Milan. The eye of day mirrored in
the blue canals, a network of veins through the downy ricefields.
Mountains of Vinci, snowy Alps soft in their brilliance, ruggedly
encircling the horizon, fringed with red and orange and greeny
gold and pale blue. Evening falling on the Apennines. A
winding descent by little sheer hills, snakelike curving, in a
repeating, involved rhythm like a farandole.—And suddenly,
at the bottom of the slope, like a kiss, the breath of the sea and
the smell of orange-trees. The sea, the Latin sea and its opal

light, whereon, swaying, were the sails of little boats like wings
folded back. . . .

By the sea, at a fishing-village, the train stopped for a while.
It was explained to the passengers that there had been a landslip,
as a result of the heavy rains, in a tunnel between Genoa and
Pisa: all the trains were several hours late. Christophe, who
was booked through to Rome, was delighted by the accident
which provoked the loud lamentations of his fellow-passengers.
He jumped down to the platform and made use of the stoppage
to go down to the sea, which drew him on and on. The sea
charmed him so that when, a few hours later, the engine
whistled as it moved on, Christophe was in a boat, and, as the
train passed, shouted: "Good-by!" In the luminous night,
on the luminous sea, he sat rocking in the boat, as it passed
along the scented coast with its promontories fringed with tiny
cypress-trees. He put up at a village and spent there five days
of unbroken joy. He was like a man issuing from a long fast,
hungrily eating. With all his famished senses he gulped down
the splendid light. . . . Light, the blood of the world, that
flows in space like a river of life, and through our eyes, our
lips, our nostrils, every pore of our skins, filters through to the
depths of our bodies, light, more necessary to life than bread,—
he who sees thee stripped of thy northern veils, pure, burning,
naked, marvels how ever he could have lived without knowing
thee, and deeply feels that he can never live more without
possessing thee. . . .

For five days Christophe was drunk with the sun. For five
days he forgot—for the first time—that he was a musician. The
music of his soul was merged into light. The air, the sea, the
earth: the brilliant symphony played by the sun's orchestra.
And with what innate art does Italy know how to use that
orchestra! Other peoples paint from Nature: the Italians collaborate with her: they paint with sunlight. The music of
color. All is music, everything sings. A wall by the roadside,
red, fissured with gold: above it, two cypress-trees with their
tufted crests: and all around the eager blue of the sky. A
marble staircase, white, steep, narrow, climbing between pink
walls against the blue front of a church. Any one of their
many-colored houses, apricot, lemon, cedrate, shining among the

olive-trees, has the effect of a marvelous ripe fruit among the leaves. In Italy seeing is sensual: the eyes enjoy color, as the palate and the tongue delight in a juicy, scented fruit. Christophe flung himself at this new repast with eager childlike greed: he made up for the asceticism of the gray visions to which till then he had been condemned. His abounding nature, stifled by Fate, suddenly became conscious of powers of enjoyment which he had never used: they pounced on the prey presented to them; scents, colors, the music of voices, bells and the sea, the kisses of the air, the warm bath of light in which his ageing, weary soul began to expand. . . . Christophe had no thought of anything. He was in a state of beatific delight, and only left it to share his joy with those he met: his boatman, an old fisherman, with quick eyes all wrinkled round, who wore a red cap like that of a Venetian senator;—his only fellow-boarder, a Milanese, who ate macaroni and rolled his eyes like Othello: fierce black eyes filled with a furious hatred; an apathetic, sleepy man;—the waiter in the restaurant, who, when he carried a tray, bent his neck, and twisted his arms and his body like an angel of Bernini;—the little Saint John, with sly, winking eyes, who begged on the road, and offered the passers-by an orange on a green branch. He would hail the carriage-drivers, sitting huddled on their seats, who every now and then would, in a nasal, droning, throaty voice, intone the thousand and one couplets. He was amazed to find himself humming *Cavalleria Rusticana*. He had entirely forgotten the end of his journey. Forgotten, too, was his haste to reach the end and Grazia. . . .

Forgotten altogether was she until the day when the beloved image rose before him. Was it called up by a face seen on the road or a grave, singing note in a voice? He did not know. But a time came when, from everything about him, from the circling, olive-clad hills, from the high, shining peaks of the Apennines, graven by the dense shadows and the burning sun, and from the orange-groves heavy with flowers and fruit, and the deep, heaving breath of the sea, there shone the smiling face of the beloved. Through the countless eyes of the air, her eyes were upon him. In that beloved earth she flowered, like a rose upon a rose-tree.

Then he regained possession of himself. He took the train

for Rome and never stopped. He had no interest in the old memories of Italy, or the cities of the art of past ages. He saw nothing of Rome, nor wanted to: and what he did see at first, in passing, the styleless new districts, the square blocks of buildings, gave him no desire to see more.

As soon as he arrived he went to see Grazia. She asked him:

"How did you come? Did you stop at Milan or Florence?"

"No," he said. "Why should I?"

She laughed.

"That's a fine thing to say! And what do you think of Rome?"

"Nothing," he said. "I haven't seen it!"

"Not yet?"

"Nothing. Not a single monument. I came straight to you from my hotel."

"You don't need to go far to see Rome. . . . Look at that wall opposite. . . . You only need to see its light."

"I only see you," he said.

"You are a barbarian. You only see your own ideas. When did you leave Switzerland?"

"A week ago."

"What have you been doing since then?"

"I don't know. I stopped, by chance, at a place by the sea. I never noticed its name. I slept for a week. Slept, with my eyes open. I do not know what I have seen, or what I have dreamed. I think I was dreaming of you. I know that it was very beautiful. But the most lovely part of it all is that I forgot everything. . . ."

"Thank you!" she said.

(He did not listen.)

". . . Everything," he went on. "Everything that was then, everything that had been before. I am a new man. I am beginning to live again."

"It is true," she said, looking into his laughing eyes. "You have changed since we last met."

He looked at her, too, and found her no less different from his memory of her. Not that she had changed in two months, but he was seeing her with new eyes. Yonder, in Switzerland, the image of old days, the faint shadow of the girl Grazia, had flitted between his gaze and this new actual beloved. Now, in the sun of Italy, the dreams of the North had melted away: in the clear light of day he saw her real soul and body. How far removed she was from the little, wild, imprisoned girl of Paris, how far from the woman with the smile like Saint John, whom he had met one evening, shortly after her marriage, only to lose her again! Out of the little Umbrian Madonna had flowered a lovely Roman lady:

Color verus, corpus solidum et succi plenum.

Her figure had taken on an harmonious fullness: her body was bathed in a proud languor. The very genius of tranquillity hovered in her presence. She had that greed of sunny silence, and still contemplation, the delightful joy in the peace of living which the people of the North will never really know. What especially she had preserved out of the past was her great kindness which inspired all her other feelings. But in her luminous smile many new things were to be read: a melancholy indulgence, a little weariness, much knowledge of the ways of men, a fine irony, and tranquil common sense. The years had veiled her with a certain coldness, which protected her against the illusions of the heart; rarely could she surrender herself; and her tenderness was ever on the alert, with a smile that seemed to know and tell everything, against the passionate impulses that Christophe found it hard to suppress. She had her weaknesses, moments of abandonment to the caprice of the minute, a coquetry at which she herself mocked but never fought against. She was never in revolt against things, nor against herself: she had come to a gentle fatalism, and she was altogether kind, but a little weary.

She entertained a great deal, and—at least, in appearance—not very selectively: but as, for the most part, her intimates belonged to the same world, breathed the same atmosphere, had been fashioned by the same habits, they were homogeneous and harmonious enough, and very different from the polite assemblages that Christophe had known in France and Germany. The majority were of old Italian families, vivified here and there by foreign marriages; they all had a superficial cosmopolitanism and a comfortable mixture of the four chief languages, and the

intellectual baggage of the four great nations of the West.
Each nation brought into the pool its personal characteristic, the
Jews their restlessness and the Anglo-Saxons their phlegm, but
everything was quickly absorbed in the Italian melting-pot.
When centuries of great plundering barons have impressed on a
race the haughty and rapacious profile of a bird of prey, the
metal may change, but the imprint remains the same. Many
of the faces that seemed the most pronouncedly Italian, with a
Luini smile, or the voluptuous, calm gaze of a Titian, flowers
of the Adriatic, or the plains of Lombardy, had blossomed on
the shrubs of the North transplanted to the old Latin soil.
Whatever colors be spread on the palette of Rome, the color
which stands out is always Roman.

Christophe could not analyze his impressions, but he admired
the perfume of an age-old culture, an ancient civilization exhaled
by these people, who were often mediocre, and, in some cases,
less than mediocre. It was a subtle perfume, springing from
the smallest trifles. A graceful courtesy, a gentleness of manners that could be charming and affectionate, and at the same
time malicious and consciously superior, an elegant finesse in the
use of the eyes, the smile, the alert, nonchalant, skeptical, diverse,
and easy intelligence. There was nothing either stiff or familiar.
Nothing literary. Here there was no fear of meeting the psycho-
logues of a Parisian drawing-room, ensconced behind their eye-
glasses, or the corporalism of a German pedant. They were
men, quite simply, and very human men, such as were the
friends of Terence and Scipio the Æmilian. . . .

Homo sum. . . .

It was fine to see. It was a life more of appearance than
reality. Beneath it lay an incurable frivolity which is common
to the polite society of every country. But what made this
society characteristic of its race was its indolence. The frivolity
of the French is accompanied by a fever of the nerves—a perpetual agitation of the mind, even when it is empty. The brain
of the Italian knows how to rest. It knows it only too well.
It is sweet to sleep in the warm shadows, on the soft pillow
of a padded Epicureanism, and a very supple, fairly curious,
and, at bottom, prodigiously indifferent intelligence.

All the men of this society were entirely lacking in decided

opinions. They dabbled in politics and art in the same dilettante
fashion. Among them were charming natures, handsome, fine-
featured patrician, Italian faces, with soft, intelligent eyes, men
with gentle, quiet manners, who, with exquisite taste and affectionate hearts, loved Nature, the old masters, flowers, women,
books, good food, their country, music. . . . They loved everything. They preferred nothing. Sometimes one felt that they
loved nothing. Love played so large a part in their lives, but
only on condition that it never disturbed them. Their love was
indolent and lazy, like themselves; even in their passion it was
apt to take on a domestic character. Their solid, harmonious
intelligence was fitted with an inertia in which all the opposites
of thought met without collision, were tranquilly yoked together,
smiling, cushioned, and rendered harmless. They were afraid of
any thorough belief, of taking sides, and were at their ease in
semi-solutions and half-thoughts. They were conservative-liberal
in temper of mind. They needed politics and art half-way up
the hill, like those health resorts where there is no danger of
asthma or palpitations. They recognized themselves in the lazy
plays of Goldoni, or the equally diffused light of Manzoni.
Their amiable indifference was never disturbed. Never could
they have said like their great ancestors: *" Primum vivere . . ."*
but rather *" Dapprima, quieto vivere."*

To live in peace. That was the secret vow, the aim of even
the most energetic of those who controlled politics. A little
Machiavelli, master of himself and others, with a heart as cold
as his head, a lucid, bored intelligence, knowing how and daring
to use all means to gain his ends, ready to sacrifice all his
friends to his ambition, would be capable of sacrificing his
ambition to one thing only: his *quieto vivere.* They needed
long periods of absolute lassitude. When they issued from them,
as from a good sleep, they were fresh and ready: these grave
men, these tranquil Madonnas would be taken with a sudden
desire to talk, to be gay, to plunge into social life; then they
would break out into a profusion of gestures and words, paradoxical sallies, burlesque humor: they were always playing an
opéra bouffe. In that gallery of Italian portraits rarely would
you find the marks of thought, the metallic brilliance of the
eyes, faces stained with the perpetual labor of the mind, such

as are to be found in the North. And yet, here, as elsewhere, there was no lack of souls turned in upon themselves, to feed upon themselves, concealing their woes, and desires and cares seething beneath the mask of indifference, and, voluptuously, drawing on a cloak of torpor. And, in certain faces there would peep out, queerly, disconcertingly, indications of some obscure malady of the spirit peculiar to very ancient races—like the excavations in the Roman Campagna.

There was great charm in the enigmatic indifference of these people, and their calm, mocking eyes, wherein there slumbered hidden tragedy. But Christophe was in no humor to recognize it. He was furious at seeing Grazia surrounded by worldly people with their courteous, witty, and empty manners. He hated them for it, and he was angry with her. He sulked at her just as he sulked at Rome. His visits to her became less and less frequent, and he began to make up his mind to go.

He did not go. Unknown to himself, he was beginning to feel the attraction of Italian society, though it irritated him so much.

For the time being, he isolated himself and lounged about Rome and the environment. The Roman light, the hanging gardens, the Campagna, encircled, as by a golden scarf, by the sunlit sea, little by little delivered up to him the secret of the enchanted land. He had sworn not to move a step to see the monuments of the dead, which he affected to despise: he used grumblingly to declare that he would wait until they came to look for him. They came; he happened on them by chance on his rambling through the City of many hills. Without having looked for it, he saw the Forum red under the setting sun, and the half-ruined arches of the Palatine and behind them the deep azure vault of heaven, a gulf of blue light. He wandered in the vast Campagna, near the ruddy Tiber, thick with mud, like moving earth,—and along the ruined aqueducts, like the gigantic vertebræ of antediluvian monsters. Thick masses of black clouds rolled across the blue sky. Peasants on horseback goaded across the desert great herds of pearly-gray cattle with long horns; and along the ancient road, straight, dusty, and bare, goat-footed shepherds, clad in thick skins, walked in silence.   On the far horizon, the Sabine Chain, with its Olympian lines, unfolded its hills; and on the other edge of the cup of the sky the old walls of the city, the front of Saint John's Church, surmounted with statues which danced in black silhouette. . . .   Silence. . . .   A fiery sun. . . . The wind passed over the plain. . . .   On a headless, armless statue, almost inundated by the waving grass, a lizard, with its heart beating tranquilly, lay motionless, absorbed, drinking in its fill of light.   And Christophe, with his head buzzing with the sunshine (sometimes also with the *Castelli* wine), sitting on the black earth near the broken statue, smiling, sleepy, lost in forgetfulness, breathed in the calm, tremendous force of Rome.—Until nightfall.—Then, with his heart full of a sudden anguish, he fled from the gloomy solitude in which the tragic light was sinking. . . .   O earth, burning earth, earth passionate and dumb!   Beneath thy fevered peace I still can hear the trumpeting of the legions.   What a fury of life is shining in thy bosom!   What a mighty desire for an awakening!

Christophe found men in whose souls there burned brands of the age-old fire.   Beneath the rust of the dead they had been preserved.   It might be thought that the fire had died down with the closing of Mazzini's eyes.   It was springing to life again.   It was the same.   Very few wished to see it.   It troubled the quiet of those who were asleep.   It gave a clear and brutal light.   Those who bore it aloft,—young men (the eldest was not thirty-five), a little band of the elect come from every point of the horizon, men of free intellect who were all different in temperament, education, opinions, and faith—were all united in worship of this flame of the new life.   The etiquette of parties, systems of thought, mattered not to them: the great thing was to "think with courage."   To be frank, to be brave, in mind and deed.   Rudely they disturbed the sleep of their race.   After the political resurrection of Italy, awakened from death by the summons of her heroes, after her recent economic resurrection, they had set themselves to pluck Italian thought from the grave.   They suffered, as from an insult, from the indolent and timid indifference of the elect, their cowardice of mind and verbolatry.   Their *Voices* rang hollow in the midst of rhetoric and the moral slavery which for centuries had been gathering into a crust upon the soul of their country. They breathed into it their merciless realism and their uncompromising loyalty. Though upon occasion they were capable of sacrificing their own personal intellectual preferences to the duty of discipline which national life imposes on the individual, yet they reserved their highest altar and their purest ardor for the truth. They loved truth with fiery, pious hearts. Insulted by his adversaries, defamed, threatened, one of the leaders of these young men replied, with grand, calm dignity:

"*Respect the truth. I speak to you now, from my heart, with no shade of bitterness. I forget the ill I have received at your hands and the evil that I may have done you. Be true. There is no conscience, there is no noble life, there is no capacity for sacrifice where there is not a religious, a rigid, and a rigorous respect for truth. Strive, then, to fulfil this difficult duty. Untruth corrupts whoever makes use of it before it overcomes him against whom it is used. What does it matter that you gain an immediate success? The roots of your soul will remain withered in the air above the soil that is crumbled away with untruth. We are on a plane superior to our disagreements, even though on your lips your passion brings the name of our country. There is one thing greater than a man's country, and that is the human conscience. There are laws which you must not violate on pain of being bad Italians. You see before you now only a man who is a seeker after truth: you must hear his cry. You have before you now only a man who ardently desires to see you great and pure, and to work with you. For, whether you will or no, we all work in common with all those who in this world work truthfully. That which comes out of our labors (and we cannot foresee what it will be) will bear our common mark, the mark of us all, if we have labored with truth. The essence of man lies in this, in his marvelous faculty for seeking truth, seeing it, loving it, and sacrificing himself to it.—Truth, that over all who possess it spends the magic breath of its puissant health! . . ."* *

The first time Christophe heard these words they seemed to him like an echo of his own voice: and he felt that these men

*The hymn to Truth here introduced is an abridgment of an article by Giuseppe Prezzolini (*La Voce*, April 13, 1911).

and he were brothers.   The chances of the conflict of the nations
and ideas might one day fling them into the position of adversaries in the mêlée; but, friends or enemies, they were, and
would always be, members of the same human family.   They
knew it, even as he.   They knew it, before he did.   They knew
him before he knew them, for they had been friends of Olivier's.
Christophe discovered that his friend's writings—(a few volumes
of verse and critical essays)—which had only been read by a
very few in Paris, had been translated by these Italians, and
were as familiar to them as to himself.

Later on he was to discover the impassable distance which
divided these men from Olivier.   In their way of judging others
they were entirely Italian, incapable of the effort necessary to
see beyond themselves, rooted in the ideas of their race.   At
bottom, in all good faith, in foreign literature they only sought
what their national instinct was willing to find in it; often they
only took out of it what they themselves had unconsciously read
into it.   Mediocre as critics, and as psycho'ogists contemptible,
they were too single-minded, too full of themselves and their
passions, even when they were the most enamored of truth.
Italian idealism cannot forget itself: it is not interested in the
impersonal dreams of the North; it leads everything back to
itself, its desires, its pride of race, and transfigures them.   Consciously or unconsciously, it is always toiling for the *terza Roma*.
It must be said that for many centuries it has not taken much
trouble to realize it.   These splendid Italians, who are cut out
for action, only act through passion, and soon weary of it: but
when the breath of passion rushes in their veins it raises them
higher than all other nations; as has been seen, for example, in
their *Risorgimento*.—Some such great wind as that had begun
to pass over the young men of Italy of all parties: nationalists,
socialists, neo-Catholics, free idealists, all the unyielding Italians,
all, in hope and will, citizens of Imperial Rome, Queen of the
universe.

At first Christophe saw only their generous ardor and the
common antipathies which united him and them.   They could
not but join with him in their contempt for the fashionable
society, against which Christophe raged on account of Grazia's
preferences.   More than he they hated the spirit of prudence,

the apathy, the compromise, and buffoonery, the things half said, the amphibious thoughts, the subtle dawdling of the mind between all possibilities, without deciding on any one, the fine phrases, the sweetness of it all. They were all self-taught men who had pieced themselves together with everything they could lay their hands on, but had had neither means nor leisure to put the finishing touch to their work, and they were prone to exaggerate their natural coarseness and their rather bitter tone fitting to rough *contadini*. They wished to provoke active hostility. Anything rather than indifference. In order to rouse the energy of their race they would gladly have consented to be among the first victims to it.

Meanwhile they were not liked, and they did nothing to gain liking. Christophe met with but small success when he tried to talk to Grazia of his new friends. They were repugnant to her order-loving, peace-loving nature. He had to recognize when he was with her that they had a way of upholding the best of causes which sometimes provoked a desire in the best of people to declare themselves hostile to it. They were ironical and aggressive, in criticism harsh to the point of insult, even with people whom they had no desire to hurt. Having reached the sphere of publication before they had come to maturity, they passed with equal intolerance from one infatuation to another. Passionately sincere, giving themselves unreservedly, without stint or thought of economy, they were consumed by their excessive intellectuality, their precocious and blindly obstinate endeavors. It is not well for young ideas, hardly out of the pod, to be exposed to the raw sunlight. The soul is scorched by it. Nothing is made fruitful save with time and silence. Time and silence these men had not allowed themselves. It is the misfortune of only too many Italian talents. Violent, hasty action is an intoxicant. The mind that has once tasted it is hard put to it to break the habit; and its normal growth is then in great peril of being forced and forever twisted.

Christophe appreciated the acid freshness of such green frankness in contrast with the insipidity of the people who frequented the middle way, the *via di mezzo,* who are in perpetual fear of being compromised, and have a subtle talent for saying neither " Yes " nor " No." But very soon he came to see that such people also, with their calm, courteous minds, have their worth. The perpetual state of conflict in which his new friends lived was very tiring. Christophe began by thinking it his duty to go to Grazia's house to defend them. Sometimes he went there to forget them. No doubt he was like them, too much like them. They were now what he had been twenty years ago. And life never goes back. At heart Christophe well knew that, for his own part, he had forever said good-by to such violence, and that he was going towards peace, whose secret seemed to lie for him in Grazia's eyes. Why, then, was he in revolt against her? . . . Ah! In the egoism of his love he longed to be the only one to enjoy her peace. He could not bear Grazia to dispense its benefits without marking how to all comers she extended the same prodigally gracious welcome.

She read his thoughts, and, with her charming frankness, she said to him one day:

" You are angry with me for being what I am? You must not idealize me, my dear. I am a woman, and no better than another. I don't go out of my way for society; but I admit that I like it, just as I like going sometimes to an indifferent play, or reading foolish books, which you despise, though I find them soothing and amusing. I cannot refuse anything."

" How can you endure these idiots? "

" Life has taught me not to be too nice. One must not ask too much. It is a good deal, I assure you, when one finds honest people, with no harm in them, kindly people . . . (naturally, of course, supposing one expects nothing of them; I know perfectly well that if I had need of them, I should not find many to help me . . .). And yet they are fond of me, and when I find a little real affection, I hold the rest cheap. You are angry with me? Forgive me for being an ordinary person. I can at least see the difference between what is best and what is not so good in myself. And what you have is the best."

" I want everything," he said gloweringly.

However, he felt that what she said was true. He was so

sure of her affection that, after long hesitation, over many weeks,
he asked her one day:

"Will you ever . . . ?"

"What is it?"

"Be mine."

He went on:

". . . and I yours."

She smiled:

"But you are mine, my dear."

"You know what I mean."

She was a little unhappy: but she took his hands and looked
at him frankly:

"No, my dear," she said tenderly.

He could not speak. She saw that he was hurt.

"Forgive me. I have hurt you. I knew that you would
say that to me. We must speak out frankly and in all truth,
like good friends."

"Friends," he said sadly. "Nothing more?"

"You are ungrateful. What more do you want? To marry
me? . . . Do you remember the old days when you had eyes
only for my pretty cousin? I was sad then because you would
not understand what I felt for you. Our whole lives might
have been changed. Now I think it was better as it has been;
it is better that we should never expose our friendship to the
test of common life, the daily life, in which even the purest must
be debased. . . ."

"You say that because you love me less."

"Oh no! I love you just the same."

"Ah! That is the first time you have told me."

"There must be nothing hidden from us now. You see, I
have not much faith in marriage left. Mine, I know, was not
a very good example. But I have thought and looked about me.
Happy marriages are very rare. It is a little against nature.
You cannot bind together the wills of two people without mutilat-
ing one of them, if not both, and it does not even bring the
suffering through which it is well and profitable for the soul
to pass."

"Ah!" he said. "But I can see in it a fine thing—the
union of two sacrifices, two souls merged into one."

"A fine thing, in your dreams. In reality you would suffer more than any one."

"What! You think I could never have a wife, a family, children? . . . Don't say that! I should love them so! You think it impossible for me to have that happiness?"

"I don't know. I don't think so. Perhaps with a good woman, not very intelligent, not very beautiful, who would be devoted to you, and would not understand you."

"How unkind of you! . . . But you are wrong to make fun of it. A good woman is a fine thing, even if she has no mind."

"I agree. Shall I find you one?"

"Please! No. You are hurting me. How can you talk like that?"

"What have I said?"

"You don't love me at all, not at all. You can't if you can think of my marrying another woman."

"On the contrary, it is because I love you that I should be happy to do anything which could make you happy."

"Then, if that is true . . ."

"No, no. Don't go back to that. I tell you, it would make you miserable."

"Don't worry about me. I swear to you that I shall be happy! Speak the truth: do you think that you would be unhappy with me?"

"Oh! Unhappy? No, my dear. I respect and admire you too much ever to be unhappy with you. . . . But, I will tell you: I don't think anything could make me very unhappy now. I have seen too much. I have become philosophical. . . . But, frankly—(You want me to? You won't be angry?)—well. I know my own weakness. I should, perhaps, be foolish enough, after a few months, not to be perfectly happy with you; and I will not have that, just because my affection for you is the most holy thing in the world, and I will not have it tarnished."

Sadly, he said:

"Yes, you say that, to sweeten the pill. You don't like me. There are things in me which are odious to you."

"No, no. I assure you. Don't look so hang-dog. You are the dearest, kindest man. . . ."

"Then I don't understand. Why couldn't we agree?"

"Because we are too different—both too decided, too individual."

"That is why I love you."

"I too. But that is why we should find ourselves conflicting."

"No."

"Yes. Or, rather, as I know that you are bigger than I, I should reproach myself with embarrassing you with my smaller personality, and then I should be stifled. I should say nothing, and I should suffer."

Tears came to Christophe's eyes.

"Oh! I won't have that. Never! I would rather be utterly miserable than have you suffering through my fault, for my sake."

"My dear, you mustn't feel it like that. . . . You know, I say all that, but I may be flattering myself. . . . Perhaps I should not be so good as to sacrifice myself for you."

"All the better."

"But, then, I should sacrifice you, and that would be misery for me. . . . You see, there is no solving the difficulty either way. Let us stay as we are. Could there be anything better than our friendship?"

He nodded his head and smiled a little bitterly.

"Yes. That is all very well. But at bottom you don't love me enough."

She smiled too, gently, with a little melancholy, and said, with a sigh:

"Perhaps. You are right. I am no longer young. I am tired. Life wears one out unless one is very strong, like you. . . . Oh! you, there are times when I look at you and you seem to be a boy of eighteen."

"Alas! With my old face, my wrinkles, my dull skin!"

"I know that you have suffered as much as I—perhaps more. I can see that. But sometimes you look at me with the eyes of a boy, and I feel you giving out a fresh stream of life. I am worn out. When I think of my old eagerness, then—alas! As some one said, 'Those were great days. I was very unhappy!'"

I hold to life only by a thread. I should never be bold enough
to try marriage again. Ah! Then! Then! . . . If you had
only given a sign! . . ."

"Well, then, well, tell me . . ."

"No. It is not worth the trouble."

"Then, if in the old days, if I had . . ."

"Yes. If you had . . .? I said nothing."

"I understood. You are cruel."

"Take it, then, that in the old days I was a fool."

"You are making it worse and worse."

"Poor Christophe! I can't say a word but it hurts you. I
shan't say any more."

"You must. . . . Tell me. . . . Tell me something."

"Something?"

"Something kind."

She laughed.

"Don't laugh."

"Then you must not be sad."

"How can I be anything else?"

"You have no reason to be sad, I assure you."

"Why?"

"Because you have a friend who loves you."

"Truly?"

"If I tell you so, won't you believe me?"

"Tell me, then."

"You won't be sad any longer? You won't be insatiable?
You will be content with our dear friendship?"

"I must."

"Oh! Ungrateful! And you say you love me? Really, I
think I love you better than you love me."

"Ah! If it were possible."

He said that with such an outburst of lover's egoism that she
laughed. He too. He insisted:

"Tell me! . . ."

For a moment she was silent, looking at him, then suddenly
she brought her face close to Christophe's and kissed him. It
was so unexpected! His heart leaped within him. He tried
to take her in his arms. But she had escaped. At the door

of the little room she laid her finger on her lips.—" Hush! "—
and disappeared.

From that moment on he did not again speak to her of his
love, and he was less awkward in his relation with her. Their
alternations of strained silence and ill-suppressed violence were
succeeded by a simple restful intimacy. That is the advantage
of frankness in friendship. No more hidden meanings, no more
illusions, no more fears. Each knew the other's innermost
thoughts. Now when Christophe was with Grazia in the company of strangers who irritated him and he lost patience at
hearing her exchange with them the empty remarks usual in
polite society, she would notice it and look at him and smile.
It was enough to let him know that they were together, and
he would find his peace restored.

The presence of the beloved robs the imagination of its
poisoned dart: the fever of desire is cooled: the soul becomes
absorbed in the chaste possession of the loved presence.—Besides,
Grazia shed on all about her the silent charm of her harmonious
nature. Any exaggeration of voice or gesture, even if it were
involuntary, wounded her, as a thing that was not simple and
beautiful. In this way she influenced Christophe little by little.
Though at first he tugged at the bridle put upon his eagerness, he slowly gained the mastery of himself, and he was
all the stronger since his force was not wasted in useless violence.

Their souls met and mingled. Grazia, who had smilingly
surrendered to the sweetness of living, was awaked from her
slumber by contact with Christophe's moral energy. She took a
more direct and less passive interest in the things of the mind.
She used to read very little, preferring to browse indolently over
the same old books, but now she began to be curious about new
ideas, and soon came to feel their attraction. The wealth of
the world of modern ideas, which was not unknown to her
though she had never cared to adventure in it alone, no longer
frightened her now that she had a companion and guide. Insensibly she suffered herself, while she protested against it, to
be drawn on to an understanding of the young Italians, whose
ardent iconoclasm had always been distasteful to her.

But Christophe profited the more by this mutual perception. It has often been observed in love that the weaker of the two gives the most: it is not that the other loves less, but, being stronger, must take more. So Christophe had already been enriched by Olivier's mind. But this new mystic marriage was far more fruitful; for Grazia brought him for her dowry the rarest treasure. that Olivier had never possessed—joy. The joy of the soul and of the eyes. Light. The smile of the Latin sky, that loves the ugliness of the humblest things, and sets the stones of the old walls flowering, and endows even sadness with its calm radiance.

The budding spring entered into alliance with her. The dream of new life was teeming in the warmth of the slumbering air. The young green was wedding with the silver-gray of the olive-trees. Beneath the dark red arches of the ruined aqueducts flowered the white almond-trees. In the awakening Campagna waved the seas of grass and the triumphant flames of the poppies. Down the lawns of the villas flowed streams of purple anemones and sheets of violets. The glycine clambered up the umbrella-shaped pines, and the wind blowing over the city brought the scent of the roses of the Palatine.

They went for walks together. When she was able to shake off the almost Oriental torpor, in which for hours together she would muse, she became another creature: she loved walking; she was tall, with a fine length of leg, and a strong, supple figure, and she looked like a Diana of Primatice.—Most often they would go to one of the villas, left like flotsam from the shipwreck of the Splendid Rome of the *setticento* under the assault of the flood of the Piedmontese barbarians. They preferred, above all, the Villa Mattei, that promontory of ancient Rome, beneath which the last waves of the deserted Campagna sink and die. They used to go down the avenue of oaks that, with its deep vault, frames the blue, the pleasant chains of the Alban hills, softly swelling like a beating heart. Along the path through the leaves they could see the tombs of Roman husbands and wives, lying sadly there, with hands clasped in fidelity. They used to sit down at the end of the avenue, under an arbor of roses against a white sarcophagus. Behind them the desert   Profound peace. The murmuring of a slow-drop-

ping fountain, trickling languidly, so languidly that it seemed
on the point of dying. They would talk in whispers. Grazia's
eyes would trustfully gaze into the eyes of her friend. Christophe would tell her of his life, his struggles, his past sorrows;
and there was no more sadness in them. In her presence, with
her eyes upon him, everything was simple, everything seemed
inevitable. . . . She, in her turn, would tell of her life. He
hardly heard what she said, but none of her thoughts were lost
upon him. His soul and hers were wedded. He saw with her
eyes. Everywhere he saw her eyes, her tranquil eyes, in the
depths of which there burned an ardent fire; he saw them in
the fair, mutilated faces of the antique statues and in the riddle
of their silent gaze: he saw them in the sky of Rome, loverly
laughing around the matted crests of the cypress-trees and
through the fingers of the *lecci,* black, shining, riddled with the
sun's arrows.

Through Grazia's eyes the meaning of Latin art reached his
heart. Till then Christophe had been entirely indifferent to
the work of the Italians. The barbarian idealist, the great
bear from the German forests, had not yet learned to taste the
delicious savor of the lovely gilded marbles, golden as honey.
The antiques of the Vatican were frankly repulsive to him.
He was disgusted by their stupid faces, their effeminate or
massive proportions, their banal, rounded modeling, all the
Gitons and gladiators. Hardly more than a few portrait-statues
found favor in his sight, and the originals had absolutely no
interest for him. He was no more kindly towards the pale,
grimacing Florentines and their sick Madonnas and pre-Raphael-
ite Venuses, anæmic, consumptive, affected, and tormented. And
the bestial stupidity of the red, sweating bullies and athletes let
loose upon the world by the example of the Sistine Chapel made
him think of cast-iron. Only for Michael Angelo did he have a
secret feeling of pious sympathy with his tragic sufferings, his
divine contempt, and the loftiness of his chaste passions. With
a pure barbaric love, like that of the master, he loved the religious nudity of his youths, his shy, wild virgins, like wild
creatures caught in a trap, the sorrowful Aurora, the wild-eyed
Madonna, with her Child biting at her breast, and the lovely
Lia, whom he would fain have had to wife. But in the soul

of the tormented hero he found nothing more than the echo of his own.

Grazia opened the gates of a new world of art for him. He entered into the sovereign serenity of Raphael and Titian. He saw the imperial splendor of the classic genius, which, like a lion, reigns over the universe of form conquered and mastered. The flashing vision of the great Venetian which goes straight to the heart of life, and with its lightning cleaves the hovering mists that veil it, the masterful might of these Latin minds that cannot only conquer, but also conquer themselves, and in victory impose upon themselves the straitest discipline, and, on the field of battle, have the art exactly to choose their rightful booty from among the spoils of the enemy overthrown—the Olympian portraits and the *stanze* of Raphael filled Christophe's heart with music richer than Wagner's, the music of serene lives, noble architecture, harmonious grouping, the music which shines forth from the perfect beauty of face, hands, feet, draperies, and gestures. Intelligence. Love. The stream of love which springs from those youthful souls and bodies. The might of the spirit and delight. Young tenderness, ironic wisdom, the warm obsessing odor of amorous bodies, the luminous smile in which the shadows are blotted out and passion slumbers. The quivering force of life rearing and reined in, like the horses of the Sun, by the sturdy hand of the master. . . .

And Christophe wondered:

" Is it impossible to unite, as they have done, the force and the peace of the Romans? Nowadays the best men aspire only to force or peace, one to the detriment of the other. Of all men the Italians seem most utterly to have lost the sense of harmony which Poussin, Lorraine, and Goethe understood. Must a stranger once more reveal to them its work? . . . And what man shall teach it to our musicians? Music has not yet had its Raphael. Mozart is only a child, a little German bourgeois, with feverish hands and sentimental soul, who uses too many words, too many gestures, and chatters and weeps and laughs over nothing. And neither the Gothic Bach nor the Prometheus of Bonn, struggling with the vulture, nor his offspring of Titans piling Pelion on Ossa, and hurling imprecations at the Heavens, have ever seen the smile of God. . . ."

After he had seen it, Christophe was ashamed of his own music; his vain agitation, his turgid passions, his indiscreet exclamations, his parade of himself, his lack of moderation, seemed to him both pitiable and shameful. A flock of sheep without a shepherd, a kingdom without a king.—A man must be the king of his tumultuous soul. . . .

During these months Christophe seemed to have forgotten music. He hardly wrote at all, feeling no need for it. His mind, fertilized by Rome, was in a period of gestation. He spent days together in a dreamy state of semi-intoxication. Nature, like himself, was in the early spring-time, when the languor of the awakening is mixed with a voluptuous dizziness. Nature and he lay dreaming, locked in each other's arms, like lovers embracing in their sleep. The feverish enigma of the Campagna was no longer hostile and disturbing to him; he had made himself master of its tragic beauty; in his arms he held Demeter, sleeping.

During April he received an invitation from Paris to go there and conduct a series of concerts. Without troubling to think it over, he decided to refuse, but thought it better to mention it to Grazia. It was very sweet to him to consult her about his life, for it gave him the illusion that she shared it.

This time she gave him a shock of disillusion. She made him explain the whole matter to her, and advised him to accept. He was very hurt, and saw in her advice the proof of her indifference.

Probably Grazia was sorry to give him such advice. But why did Christophe ask her for it? The more he turned to her and asked her to decide for him, the more she thought herself responsible for her friend's actions. As a result of their interchange of ideas she had gained from Christophe a little of his will-power: he had revealed to her duty and the beauty of action. At least she had recognized duty as far as her friend was concerned, and she would not have him fail in it. Better than he, she knew the power of languor given off by the Italian soil, which, like the insidious poison of its warm *scirocco*. creeps into the veins and sends the will to sleep. How

often had she not felt its maleficent charm, and had no power
to resist it! All her friends were more or less tainted by this
malaria of the soul. Stronger men than they had in old days
fallen victim to it: it had rusted away the brass of the Roman
she-wolf. Rome breathes forth death: it is too full of graves.
It is healthier to stay there for a little time than to live there.
Too easily does one slip out of one's own time, a dangerous
taste for the still young forces that have a vast duty to accomplish. Grazia saw clearly that the society about her had not a
life-giving air for an artist. And although she had more friendship for Christophe than for any other . . . (dared she confess it?) . . . she was not, at heart, sorry for him to go.
Alas! He wearied her with the very qualities that she most
loved in him, his overflowing intelligence, his abundance of
vitality, accumulated for years, and now brimming over: her
tranquillity was disturbed by it. And he wearied her, too, perhaps, because she was always conscious of the menace of his
love, beautiful and touching, but ever-present: so that she had
always to be on her guard against it; it was more prudent to
keep him at a distance. She did not admit it to herself, and
thought she had no consideration for anything but Christophe's
interests.

There was no lack of sound reasons at hand. In Italy just
then it was difficult for a musician to live: the air was circumscribed. The musical life of the country was suppressed and
deformed. The factory of the theater scattered its heavy ashes
and its burning smoke upon the soil, whose flowers in old days
had perfumed all Europe. If a man refused to enroll himself
in the train of the brawlers, and could not, or would not, enter
the factory, he was condemned to exile or a stifled existence.
Genius was by no means dried up. But it was left to stagnate
unprofitably and to go to ruin. Christophe had met more than
one young musician in whom there lived again the soul of the
melodious masters of the race and the instinct of beauty which
filled the wise and simple art of the past. But who gave a
thought to them? They could neither get their work played
nor published. No interest was taken in the symphony. There
were no ears for music except it were presented with a painted
face! . . . So discouraged, they sang for themselves, and

soon sang no more. What was the good of it? Sleep . . .
—Christophe would have asked nothing better than to help
them. While they admitted that he could do so, their umbrageous pride would not consent to it. Whatever he did, he
was a foreigner to them; and for Italians of long descent, in
spite of the warm welcome they will give him, every foreigner
is really a barbarian. They thought that the wretched condition
of their art was a question to be threshed out among themselves,
and while they extended all kind of friendly tributes to Christophe, they could not admit him as one of themselves.—What
could he do? He could not compete with them and dispute
with them their meager place in the sun, where they were by no
means secure! . . .

Besides, genius cannot do without its food. The musician
must have music—music to hear, music to make heard. A temporary withdrawal is valuable to the mind by forcing it to
recuperate. But this can only be on condition that it will
return. Solitude is noble, but fatal to an artist who has not
the strength to break out of it. An artist must live the life of his
own time, even if it be clamorous and impure: he must forever
be giving and receiving, and giving, and giving, and again receiving.—Italy, at the time of Christophe's sojourn, was no
longer the great market of the arts that once it was, and perhaps
will be again. Nowadays the meeting-place of ideas, the exchange of the thought and spirit of the nations, are in
the North. He who has the will to live must live in the
North.

Left to himself, Christophe would have shuddered away from
the rout. But Grazia felt his duty more clearly than he could
see it. And she demanded more of him than of herself: no
doubt because she valued him more highly, but also because it
suited her. She delegated her energy upon him, and so maintained her tranquillity.—He had not the heart to be angry with
her for it. Like Mary, hers was the better part. Each of us
has his part to play in life. Christophe's was action. For her
it was enough to be. He asked no more of her.

He asked nothing but to love her, if it were possible, a little
less for himself, and a little more for her. For he did not
altogether like her having so little egoism in her friendship as

to think only of the interests of her friend—who asked only
to be allowed to give no thought to them.

He went away from her. And yet he did not leave her.
As an old trouvère says: *"The lover does not leave his beloved
but with the sanction of his soul."*

II

HE was sick at heart as he reached Paris. It was the first
time he had been there since the death of Olivier. He had
wished never to see the city again. In the cab which took him
from the station to his hotel he hardly dared look out of the
window; for the first few days he stayed in his room and could
not bring himself to go out. He was fearful of the memories
lying in wait for him outside. But what exactly did he dread?
Did he really know? Was it, as he tried to believe, the terror
of seeing the dead spring to life again exactly as they had been?
Or was it—the greater sorrow of being forced to know that
they were dead? . . . Against this renewal of grief all the
half-unconscious ruses of instinct had taken up arms. It was
for this reason—(though perhaps he knew it not)—that he had
chosen a hotel in a district far removed from that in which he
had lived. And when for the first time he went out into the
streets, having to conduct rehearsals at the concert-hall, when
once more he came in contact with the life of Paris, he walked
for a long time with his eyes closed, refusing to see what he did
see, insisting on seeing only what he had seen in old days. He
kept on saying to himself:
  "I know that. I know that. . . ."
  In art as in politics there was the same intolerant anarchy.
The same Fair in the market-place. Only the actors had changed
their parts. The revolutionaries of his day had become bourgeois, and the supermen had become men of fashion. The old
independents were trying to stifle the new independents. The
young men of twenty years ago were now more conservative
than the old conservatives whom they had fought, and their

critics refused the newcomers the right to live. Apparently
nothing was different.

But everything had changed. . . .

*

* *

"My dear, forgive me. It is good of you not to be angry
with me for my silence. Your letter has helped me greatly.
I have been through several weeks of terrible distress. I had
nothing. I had lost you. Here I was feeling terribly the
absence of those whom I have lost. All my old friends of
whom I used to tell you have disappeared—Philomela—(you
remember the singing voice that dear, sad night when, as I
wandered through a gay crowd, I saw your eyes in a mirror
gazing at me)—Philomela has realized her very reasonable
dream: she inherited a little money, and has a farm in Normandy. M. Arnaud has retired and gone back to the provinces
with his wife, to a little town near Angers. Of the famous men
of my day many are dead or gone under; none are left save the
same old puppets who twenty years ago were playing the juvenile
lead in art and politics, and with the same false faces are still
playing it. Outside these masks there are none whom I recognize. They seem to me to be grimacing over a grave. It is a
terrible feeling.—More than this: during the first few days
after my arrival I suffered physically from the ugliness of things,
from the gray light of the North after your golden sun: the
masses of dull houses, the vulgar lines of certain domes
and monuments, which had never struck me before, hurt
me cruelly. Nor was the moral atmosphere any more to my
taste.

"And yet I have no complaint to make of the Parisians.
They have given me a welcome altogether different from that
which I received before. In my absence I seem to have become
a kind of celebrity. I will say nothing of that, for I know
what it is worth. I am touched by all the pleasant things which
these people say and write of me, and am obliged to them.
But what shall I say to you? I felt much nearer the people
who attacked me in old days than I do to the people who laud
me now. . . . It is my own fault, I know. Don't scold me.

I had a moment of uneasiness. It was to be expected. It is done now. I understand. Yes. You are right to have sent me back among men. I was in a fair way to be buried in my solitude. It is unhealthy to play at Zarathustra. The flood of life moves on, moves on away from us. There comes a time when one is as a desert. Many weary days in the burning sun are needed to dig a new channel in the sand, to dig down to the river.—It has been done. I am no longer dizzy. I am in the current again. I look and see.

"My dear, what a strange people are the French! Twenty years ago I thought they were finished. . . . They are just beginning again. My dear comrade, Jeannin, foretold it. But I thought he was deceiving himself. How could one believe it then! France was, like their Paris, full of broken houses, plaster, and holes. I said: 'They have destroyed everything. . . . What a race of rodents!'—a race of beavers. Just when you think them prostrate on their ruins, lo, they are using the ruins to lay the foundations of a new city. I can see it now in the scaffoldings which are springing up on all sides . . .

> *" Wenn ein Ding geschehen*
> *Selbst die Narren es verstehen, . . ."* *

"In truth there is just the same French disorder. One needs to be used to it to see in the rout seething up from all directions, the bands of workmen, each going about his appointed task. There are also people who can do nothing without vilifying what their neighbors are doing. All this is calculated to upset the stoutest head. But when you have lived, as I have, nearly ten years with them, you cannot be deceived by their uproar. You see then that it is their way of spurring themselves on to work. They talk, but they work, and as each builder's yard sets about building a house, in the end you find that the city has been re-builded. What is most remarkable is that, taken together, all these buildings are not discordant. They may maintain opposing theses, but all their minds are cast in the same mold. So that, beneath their anarchy, there are common instincts, a racial logic which takes the place of discipline, and this discipline is,

* " When a thing has happened, even the fools can see it."

when all is told, probably more solid than that of a Prussian regiment.

"Everywhere the same enthusiasm, the same constructive fever: in politics, where Socialists and Nationalists vie with one another in tightening up the wheels of slackened power; in art, which some wish to make into an old aristocratic mansion for the privileged few, and others a vast hall open to the people, a hall where the collective soul can sing; they are reconstructors of the past, or constructors of the future. But whatever they do, these ingenious creatures are forever building the same cells. They have the instincts of beavers or bees, and through the ages are forever doing the same things, returning to the same forms. The most revolutionary among them are perhaps those who most closely cling, though they may not know it, to the most ancient traditions. Among the syndicates and the most striking of the young writers I have found purely medieval souls.

"Now that I have grown used to their tumultuous ways, I can watch them working with pleasure. Let us be frank: I am too old a bear ever to feel at ease in any of their houses: I need the open air. But what good workers they are! That is their highest virtue. It laves the most mediocre and the most corrupt: and then, in their artists, what a sense of beauty! I remarked that much less in the old days. You taught me to see. My eyes were opened in the light of Rome. Your Renaissance men have helped me to understand these. A page of Debussy, a torso of Rodin, a phrase of Suarès, these are all in the direct line from your *cinquecestenti.*

"Not that there is not much that is distasteful to me here. I have found my old friends of the market-place, who used to drive me to fury. They have not changed. But, alas! I have changed. I cannot be severe. When I feel myself wanting to judge one of them harshly I say to myself: 'You have no right. You have done worse than these men, though you thought yourself so strong.' Also, I have learned that nothing exists in vain, and that even the vilest have their place in the scheme of the tragedy. The depraved dilettantists, the fœtid amoralists, have accomplished their termitic task; the tottering ruins must be brought down before they can be built up again. The Jews have been true to their sacred mission, which is, in the midst

of other races, to be a foreign race, the race which, from end to
end of the world, is to link up the network of human unity.
They break down the intellectual barriers between the nations,
to give Divine Reason an open field. The worst agents of corruption, the ironic destroyers who ruin our old beliefs and kill
our well-beloved dead, toil, unwittingly, in the holy work of
new life. So the ferocious self-interest of the cosmopolitan
bankers, whose labors are attended with such and so many
disasters, build, whether they will or no, the future peace of
the world, side by side with the revolutionaries who combat
them, far more surely than the idiotic pacifists.

"You see, I am getting old. I have lost my bite. My teeth
have lost their sharpness. When I go to the theater I am now
only one of those simple spectators who apostrophize the actors
and cry shame on the traitor.

"My tranquil Grace, I am only talking about myself: and
yet I think only of you. If you knew how importunate is my
ego! It is oppressive and absorbing. It 's like a millstone
that God has tied round my neck. How I should have loved
to lay it at your feet! But what would you have done with it?
It is a poor kind of present. . . . Your feet were made
to tread the soft earth and the sand sinking beneath the
tread. I see your feet carelessly passing over the lawns dappled
with anemones. . . . (Have you been again to the Villa
Doria?). . . . And you are tired! I see you now half-
reclining in your favorite retreat, in your drawing-room, propped
up on your elbow, holding a book which you do not read. You
listen to me kindly, without paying much attention to what I
say; for I am tiresome, and, for patience, you turn every now
and then to your own thoughts; but you are courteous, and,
taking care not to upset me, when a chance word brings you
back from your distant journeying, your eyes, so absent before,
quickly take on an expression of interest. And I am as far
from what I am saying as you: I, too, hardly hear the sound
of my words: and while I follow their reflection in your lovely
face, in my heart I listen to other words which I do not speak
to you. Those words, my tranquil Grace, unlike the others, you
hear quite clearly, but you pretend not to hear them.

"Adieu. I think you will see me again in a little while

I shall not languish here. What should I do now that my concerts are over?—I kiss your children on their little cheeks. They are yours and you. I must be content! . . .

" CHRISTOPHE."

*
* *

" Tranquil Grace " replied:

" MY DEAR,

" I received your letter in the little corner of the drawing-room that you remember so well, and I read it, as I am clever at reading, by letting your letter fall every now and then and resting. Don't laugh at me. I did that to make it last a long time. In that way we spent a whole afternoon to-gether. The children asked me what it was I kept on reading. I told them it was a letter from you. Aurora looked at the paper pityingly and said: ' How tiresome it must be to write such a long letter!' I tried to make her understand that it was not an imposition I had set you, but a conversation we were having together. She listened without a word, then ran away with her brother to play in the next room, and a little later, when Lionello began to shout, I heard Aurora say: ' You mustn't make such a noise: mamma is talking to M. Christophe.'

" What you tell me about the French interests me, but it does not surprise me. You remember that I often used to reproach you with being unjust towards them. It is impossible to like them. But what an intelligent people they are! There are mediocre nations who are preserved by their goodness of heart or their physical vigor. The French are saved by their intelligence. It laves all their weaknesses, and regenerates them. When you think they are down, beaten, perverted, they find new youth in the ever-bubbling spring of their minds.

" But I must scold you. You ask my pardon for speaking only of yourself. You are an *ingannatore*. You tell me nothing about yourself. Nothing of what you have been doing. Nothing of what you have been seeing. My cousin Colette—(why did not you go and see her?)—had to send me press-cuttings about your concerts, or I should have known nothing of your success. You only mentioned it by the way. Are you so de-

tached from everything? . . . It is not true. Tell me that
it pleased you. . . . It must please you, if only because it
pleases me. I don't like you to have a disillusioned air. The
tone of your letter is melancholic. That must not be. . . .
It is good that you are more just to others. But that is no
reason why you should abase yourself, as you do, by saying
that you are worse than the worst of them. A good Christian
would applaud you. I tell you it is a bad thing. I am not a
good Christian. I am a good Italian, and I don't like you
tormenting yourself with the past. The present is quite enough.
I don't know exactly what it was that you did. You told me
the story in a very few words, and I think I guessed the rest.
It was not a nice story, but you are none the less dear to me
for it. My poor, dear Christophe, a woman does not reach my
age without knowing that an honest man is often very weak.
If one did not know his weakness one would not love him so
much. Don't think any more about what you have done. Think
of what you are going to do. Repentance is quite useless. Repentance means going back. And in good as in evil, we must
always go forward. *Sempre avanti, Savoia!* . . . So you
think I am going to let you come back to Rome! You have
nothing to do here. Stay in Paris, work, do: play your part
in its artistic life. I will not have you throw it all up. I want
you to make beautiful things, I want them to succeed, I want
you to be strong and to help the new young Christophes who
are setting out on the same struggles, and passing through the
same trials. Look for them, help them, be kinder to your
juniors than your seniors were to you.—In fine, I want you to
be strong because I know that you are strong: you have no
idea of the strength that gives me.

"Almost every day I go with the children to the Villa
Borghese. Yesterday we drove to Ponte Molle, and walked
round the tower of Monte Mario. You slander my powers of
walking and my legs cry out against you: ' What did the fellow
mean by saying at the Villa Doria that we get tired in ten
paces? He knows nothing about it. If we are not prone to
give ourselves trouble. it is because we are lazy, and not because
we cannot. . . .' You forget, my dear, that I am a little
peasant. . . .

"Go and see my cousin Colette. Are you still angry with
her? She is a good creature at heart, and she swears by you!
Apparently the Parisian women are crazy about your music
(Perhaps they were in the old days.) My Berne bear may,
and he will, be the lion of Paris. Have you had letters? And
declarations? You don't mention any woman. Can you be in
love? Tell me. I am not jealous. Your friend,

"G."

*
* *

". . . So you think I am likely to be pleased with your
last sentence! I would to God you were jealous! But don't
look to me to make you so. I have no taste for these mad
Parisiennes, as you call them. Mad? They would like to be
so. But they are nothing like it. You need not hope that they
will turn my head. There would be more chance of it perhaps
if they were indifferent to my music. But it is only too true
that they love it; and how am I to keep my illusions? When
any one tells you that he understands you, you may be very sure
that he will never do so. . . .

"Don't take my joking too seriously. The feeling I have
for you does not make me unjust to other women. I have never
had such true sympathy for them as I have now since I ceased
to look at them with lover's eyes. The tremendous effort they
have been making during the last thirty years to escape from
the degrading and unwholesome semi-domesticity, to which our
stupid male egoism condemned them to their and our unhappiness, seems to me to be one of the most splendid facts of our time.
In a town like this one learns to admire the new generation
of young women, who, in spite of so many obstacles, with so
much fresh ardor rush on to the conquest of knowledge and
diplomas,—the knowledge, the diplomas which, they think, must
liberate them, open to them the arcana of the unknown world
and make them the equals of men. . . .

"No doubt their faith is illusory and rather ridiculous. But
progress is never realized as we expect it to be: it is none the
less realized because it takes entirely different paths from those
we have marked out for it. This effort of the women will not

be wasted. It will make women completer and more human, as they were in the great ages. They will no longer be without interest in the living questions of the world, as most scandalously and monstrously they have been, for it is intolerable that a woman, though she be never so careful in her domestic duties, should think herself absolved from thinking of her civic duties in the modern city. Their great-great-grandmothers of the time of Joan of Arc and Catherine Sforza were not of this way of thinking. Woman has withered. We have refused her air and sun. She is taking them from us again by force. Ah! the brave little creatures! . . . Of course, many of those who are now struggling will die and many will be led astray. It is an age of crisis. The effort is too violent for those whose strength has too much gone to seed. When a plant has been for a long time without water, the first shower of rain is apt to scald it But what would you? It is the price of progress. Those who come after will flourish through their sufferings. The poor little warlike virgins of our time, many of whom will never marry, will be more fruitful for posterity than the generations of matrons who gave birth before them; for, at the cost of their sacrifices, there will issue from them the women of a new classic age.

" I have not found these working bees in your cousin Colette's drawing-room. What whim was it made you send me to her? I had to obey you; but it is not well: you are abusing your power. I had refused three of her invitations, left two of her letters unanswered. She came and hunted me up at one of my rehearsals—(they were going through my sixth symphony). I saw her, during the interval, come in with her nose in the air, sniffing and crying: 'That smacks of love! Ah! How I love such music! . . .'

" She has changed, physically; only her cat-like eyes with their bulging pupils, and her fantastic nose, always wrinkling up and never still, are the same. But her face is wider, big-boned, highly colored, and coarsened. Sport has transformed her. She gives herself up to sport of all kinds. Her husband, as you know, is one of the swells at the Automobile Club and the Aero Club. There is not an aviation meeting, nor a race by air, land, or water, but the Stevens-Delestrades think themselves compelled to be present at it. They are always out on the highways and byways. Conversation is quite impossible; they talk of nothing but Racing, Rowing, Rugby, and the Derby. They belong to a new race of people. The days of *Pelléas* are forever gone for the women. Souls are no longer in fashion. All the girls hoist a red, swarthy complexion, tanned by driving in the open air and playing games in the sun: they look at you with eyes like men's eyes: they laugh and their laughter is a little coarse. In tone they have become more brutal, more crude. Every now and then your cousin will quite calmly say the most shocking things. She is a great eater, where she used to eat hardly anything. She still complains about her digestion, merely out of habit, but she never misses a mouthful for it. She reads nothing. No one reads among these people. Only music has found favor in their sight. Music has even profited by the neglect of literature. When these people are worn out, music is a Turkish bath to them, a warm vapor, massage, tobacco. They have no need to think. They pass from sport to love, and love also is a sport. But the most popular sport among their esthetic entertainments is dancing. Russian dancing, Greek dancing, Swiss dancing, American dancing, everything is set to a dance in Paris: Beethoven's symphonies, the tragedies of Æschylus, the *Clavecin bien Tempéré,* the antiques of the Vatican, *Orpheus,* Tristan, the Passion, and gymnastics. These people are suffering from vertigo.

"The queer thing is to see how your cousin reconciles everything, her estheticism, her sport, and her practical sense (for she has inherited from her mother her sense of business and her domestic despotism). All these things ought to make an incredible mixture, but she is quite at her ease with them all: her most foolish eccentricities leave her mind quite clear, just as she keeps her eyes and hands sure when she goes whirling along in her motor. She is a masterful woman: her husband, her guests, her servants, she leads them all, with drums beating and colors flying. She is also busy with politics: she is for 'Monseigneur'; not that I believe her to be a royalist, but it is another excuse for bestirring herself. And although she is incapable of reading more than ten pages of a book, she arranges the elections to the Academies.—She set about extending her patronage to me. You may guess that that was not at all to my liking. What is most exasperating is that the fact of my having visited her in obedience to you has absolutely convinced her of her power over me. I take my revenge in thrusting home truths at her. She only laughs, and is never at a loss for a reply. ' She is a good creature at heart. . . .' Yes, provided she is occupied. She admits that herself: if the machine has nothing to grind she is capable of anything and everything to keep it going.—I have been to her house twice. I shall not go again. Twice is enough to prove my obedience to you. You don't want me to die? I leave her house broken, crushed, cramped. Last time I saw her I had a frightful nightmare after it: I dreamed I was her husband, all my life tied to that living whirlwind. . . . A foolish dream, and it need not trouble her real husband, for of all who go to the house he is the last to be seen with her, and when they are together they only talk of sport. They get on very well.

" How could these people make my music a success? I try not to understand. I suppose it shocked them in a new way. They liked it for brutalizing them. For the time being they like art with a body to it. But they have not the faintest conception of the soul in the body: they will pass from the infatuation of to-day to the indifference of to-morrow, from the indifference of to-morrow to the abuse of the day after, without ever having known it. That is the history of all artists. I am under no illusion as to my success, and have not been for a long time: and they will make me pay for it.—Meanwhile I see the most curious things going on. The most enthusiastic of my admirers is . . . (I give him you among a thousand) . . . our friend Lévy-Cœur. You remember the gentleman with whom I fought a ridiculous duel? Now he instructs those who used not to understand me. He does it very well too. He is the most intelligent of all the men talking about me. You may judge what the others are worth. There is nothing to be proud of, I assure you.

" I don't want to be proud of it. I am too humiliated when I hear the work for which I am belauded. I see myself in it, and what I see is not beautiful. What a merciless mirror is a piece of music to those who can see into it! Happily they are

blind and deaf. I have put so much of my troubles and weaknesses into my work that sometimes it seems to me wicked to
let loose upon the world such hordes of demons. I am comforted when I see the tranquillity of the audience: they are
trebly armored: nothing can reach them: were it not so, I
should be damned. . . . You reproach me with being too hard
on myself. You do not know me as I know myself. They
see what we are: they do not see what we might have been,
and we are honored for what is not so much the effect of our
qualities as of the events that bear us along, and the forces
which control us. Let me tell you a story. . . .

"The other evening I was in one of the cafés where they
play fairly good music, though in a queer way: with five or
six instruments, filled out with a piano, they play all the
symphonies, the masses, the oratorios. It is just like the stone-
cutters in Rome, where they sell the Medici chapel as an ornament for the mantelpiece. Apparently this is useful to art,
which, if it is to circulate among men, must be turned into base
coin. For the rest there is no deception in these concerts. The
programs are copious, the musicians conscientious. I found a
violoncellist there and entered into conversation with him: his
eyes reminded me strangely of my father's; he told me the
story of his life. He was the grandson of a peasant, the son
of a small official, a clerk in a *mairie* in a village in the North.
They wanted to make him a gentleman, a lawyer, and he was
sent to school in the neighboring town. He was a sturdy country
boy, not at all fitted for being cooped up over the small work
of a notary's office, and he could not stay caged in: he used
to jump over the wall, and wander through the fields, and run
after the girls, and spend his strength in brawling: the rest of
the time he lounged and dreamed of things he would never do.
Only one thing had any attraction for him: music. God knows
why! There was not a single musician in his family, except a
rather cracked great-uncle, one of those odd, provincial characters, whose often remarkable intelligence and gifts are spent,
in their proud isolation, on whims, and cranks, and trivialities.
This great-uncle had invented a new system of notation—(yet
another!)—which was to revolutionize music; he even claimed
to have found a system of stenography by which words, tune,

and accompaniment could be written simultaneously; but he never managed to transcribe it correctly himself. They just laughed at the old man in the family, but all the same, they were proud of him. They thought: 'He is an old madman. Who knows? Perhaps he is a genius.'—It was no doubt from him that the grandnephew had his mania for music. What music could he hear in the little town? . . . . But bad music can inspire a love as pure as good music.

"The unhappy part of it was that there seemed no possibility of confessing to such a passion in such surroundings: and the boy had not his great-uncle's cracked brains. He hid away to read the old lunatic's lucubrations which formed the basis of his queer musical education. Vain and fearful of his father and of public opinion, he would say nothing of his ambitions until he had succeeded. He was crushed by his family, and did as so many French people of the middle-class have to do when, out of weakness or kindness, they dare not oppose the will of their relations: they submit to all appearance, and live their true life in perpetual secrecy. Instead of following his bent, he struggled on, against his inclination, in the work they had marked out for him. He was as incapable of succeeding in it as he was of coming to grief. Somehow or other he managed to pass the necessary examinations. The main advantage to him was that he escaped from the spying of his father and the neighbors. The law crushed him: he was determined not to spend his life in it. But while his father was alive he dared not declare his desire. Perhaps it was not altogether distasteful to him to have to wait a little before he took the decisive step. He was one of those men who all their lives long dazzle themselves with what they will do later on, with the things they could do. For the moment he did nothing. He lost his bearings, and, intoxicated by his new life in Paris, gave himself up with all his young peasant brutality to his two passions, woman and music; he was crazed with the concerts he went to, no less than with pleasure. He wasted years doing this without even turning to account the means at hand of completing his musical education. His umbrageous pride, his unfortunate independent and susceptible character kept him from taking any course of lessons or asking anybody's advice.

"When his father died he sent Themis and Justinian packing. He began to compose without having had the courage to acquire the necessary technique. His inveterate habit of idle lounging and his taste for pleasure had made him incapable of any serious effort. He felt keenly: but his idea, and its form, would at once slip away: when all was told he expressed nothing but the commonplace. The worst of all was that there was really something great in this mediocrity. I read two of his old compositions. Here and there were striking ideas, left in the rough and then deformed. They were like fireflies over a bog. . . . And what a strange mind he had! He tried to explain Beethoven's sonatas to me. He saw them as absurd, childish stories. But such passion as there was in him, such profound seriousness! Tears would come to his eyes as he talked. He would die for the thing he loves. He is touching and grotesque. Just as I was on the point of laughing in his face, I wanted to take him to my arms. . . . He is fundamentally honest, and has a healthy contempt for the charlatanry of the Parisian groups and their sham reputations,—(though at the same time he cannot help having the bourgeois admiration for successful men). . . .

"He had a small legacy. In a few months it was all gone, and, finding himself without resources, he had, like so many others of his kind, the criminal honesty to marry a girl, also without resources, whom he had seduced; she had a fine voice, and played music without any love for it. He had to live on her voice and her mediocre talent until he had learned how to play the 'cello. Naturally it was not long before they saw their mediocrity, and could not bear each other. They had a little girl. The father transferred his power of illusion to the child, and thought that she would be what he had failed to be. The little girl took after her mother: she was made to play the piano, though she had not a shadow of talent; she adored her father, and applied herself to her work to please him. For several years they plied the hotels in the watering-places, picking up more insults than money. The child was ailing and overworked, and died. The wife grew desperate, and became more shrewish every day. So his life became one of endless misery, with no hope of escape, brightened only by an ideal which he knew himself to be incapable of attaining. . . .

"And, my dear, when I saw that poor broken devil, whose life has been nothing but a series of disappointments, I thought: 'That is what I might have been.' There was much in common in our boyhood, and certain adventures in our two lives are the same; I have even found a certain kinship in some of our musical ideas: but his have stopped short. What is it that has kept me from foundering as he has done? My will, no doubt. But also the chances of life. And even taking my will, is that due only to my merits? Is it not rather due to my descent, my friends, and God who has aided me? . . . Such thoughts make a man humble. With such thoughts he feels brotherly to all who love his art, and suffer for it.

"From lowest to highest the distance is not so great. . . .

"On that I thought of what you said in your letter. You are right: an artist has no right to hold aloof, so long as he can help others. So I shall stay: I shall force myself to spend a few months in every year here, or in Vienna, or Berlin, although it is hard for me to grow accustomed to these cities again. But I must not abdicate. If I do not succeed in being of any great service, as I have good reason to think I shall not, perhaps my sojourn in these cities will be useful to me, myself. And I shall console myself with the thought that it was your wish. Besides . . . (I will not lie) . . . I am beginning to find it pleasant. Adieu, tyrant. You have triumphed. I am beginning not only to do what you want me to do, but to love doing it.

"CHRISTOPHE."

* *
*

So he stayed, partly to please her, but also because his artistic curiosity was reawakened, and was drawn on to contemplation of the renewal of art. Everything that he saw and did he presented for Grazia's scrutiny in his letters. He knew that he was deceiving himself as to the interest she would take in it all; he suspected her of a certain indifference. But he was grateful to her for not letting him see it too clearly.

She answered him regularly once a fortnight. Affectionate, composed letters, like her gestures. When she told him of her life she never discarded her tender, proud reserve. She knew the violence with which her words went resounding through Christophe's heart. She preferred that he should think her cold, rather than to send him flying to heights whither she did not wish to follow him. But she was too womanly not to know the secret of not discouraging her friend's love, and of, at once, by gentle words, soothing the dismay and disappointment caused by her indifferent words. Christophe soon divined her tactics, and by a counter-trick tried in his turn to control his warmth and to write more composedly, so that Grazia's replies should not be so studiously restrained.

The longer he stayed in Paris the greater grew his interest in the new activity stirring in that gigantic ant-heap. He was the more interested in it all as in the young ants he found less sympathy with himself. He was not deceived: his success was a Pyrrhic victory. After an absence of ten years his return had created a sensation in Parisian society. But by an ironic turn of events, such as is by no means rare, he found himself patronized by his old enemies the snobs, and people of fashion: the artists were either mutely hostile or distrustful of him. He won his way by his name, which already belonged to the past, by his considerable accomplishment, by his tone of passionate conviction, and the violence of his sincerity. But if people were forced to reckon with him, to admire or respect him, they did not understand or love him. He was outside the art of the time. A monster, a living anachronism. He had always been that. His ten years of solitude had accentuated the contrast. During his absence in Europe, and especially in Paris, a great work of reconstruction had been carried through. A new order was springing to life. A generation was arising, desirous rather of action than of understanding, hungry rather for happiness than for truth. It wished to live, to grasp life, even at the cost of a lie. Lies of pride—all manner of pride: pride of race, pride of caste, pride of religion, pride of culture and art—all were food to this generation, provided that they were armor of steel, provided that they could be turned to sword and buckler, and that, sheltered by them, they could march on to victory

So to this generation it was distasteful to hear the great voice of torment reminding it of the existence of sorrow and doubt, those whirlwinds that had troubled the night that was hardly gone, and, in spite of its denials, went on menacing the universe, the whirlwinds that it wished to forget. These young people turned away in despite, and they shouted at the top of their voices to deafen themselves. But the voice was heard above them all. And they were angry.

Christophe, on the other hand, regarded them with a friendly eye. He hailed the upward movement of the world towards happiness. The deliberate narrowness of its impulse affected him not at all. When a man wishes to go straight to his goal, he must look straight in front of him. For his part, sitting at the turning of the world, he was rejoiced to see behind him the tragic splendor of the night, and, in front of him, the smile of young hope, the uncertain beauty of the fresh, fevered dawn. And he was at the stationary point of the axis of the pendulum while the clock was beginning to go again. Without following its onward march, he listened joyfully to the beating of the rhythm of life. He joined in the hope of those who denied his past agonies. What would be, would be, as he had dreamed. Ten years before, in night and suffering, Olivier—the little Gallic cock—had with his frail song announced the distant day. The singer was no more; but his song was coming to pass. In the garden of France the birds were singing. And, above all the singing, clearer, louder, happier, Christophe suddenly heard the voice of Olivier come to life again.

He was absently reading a book of poems at a bookstall. The name of the author was unknown to him. Certain words struck him and he went on reading. As he read on between the uncut pages he seemed to recognize a friendly voice, the features of a friend. . . . He could not define his feeling, nor could he bring himself to put the book down, and so he bought it. When he reached his room he resumed his reading. At once the old obsession descended on him. The impetuous rhythm of the poem evoked, with a visionary precision, the universe and age-old souls—the gigantic trees of which we are all the leaves and the fruit—the nations. From the pages there arose the superhuman

figure of the Mother—she who was before us, she who will be
after us. She who reigns, like the Byzantine Madonnas, lofty
as the mountains, at whose feet kneel and pray ant-like human
beings. The poet was hymning the homeric struggle of the
great goddesses, whose lances had clashed together since the
beginning of the ages: the eternal Iliad which is to that of
Troy what the Alps are to the little hills of Greece.

Such an epic of warlike pride and action was far removed
from the ideas of a European soul like Christophe's. And yet,
in gleams, in the vision of the French soul—the graceful virgin,
who bears the Ægis, Athena, with blue eyes shining through
the darkness, the goddess of work, the incomparable artist,
sovereign reason, whose glittering lance hurls down the tumultuously shouting barbarians—Christophe perceived an expression,
a smile that he knew and had loved. But just as he was on
the point of fixing it the vision died away. And while he
was exasperated by this vain pursuit, lo! as he turned a page,
he came on a story which Olivier had told him a few days
before his death. . . .

He was struck dumb. He ran to the publishers, and asked
for the poet's address. It was refused, as is the custom. He
lost his temper. In vain. Finally he remembered that he
could find what he wanted in a year-book. He did find it,
and went at once to the author's house. When he wanted anything he found it impossible to wait.

It was in the Batignolles district on the top floor. There
were several doors opening on to a common landing. Christophe
knocked at the door which had been pointed out to him. The
next door opened. A young woman, not at all pretty, very
dark, with low-growing hair and a sallow complexion—a shriveled face with very sharp eyes—asked what he wanted. She
looked suspicious. Christophe told her why he had come, and,
in answer to her next question, gave his name. She came out
of her room and opened the other door with a key which she
had in her pocket. But she did not let Christophe enter immediately. She told him to wait in the corridor, and went in
alone, shutting the door in his face. At last Christophe reached
the well-guarded sanctum. He crossed a half-empty room which
served as a dining-room and contained only a few shabby pieces

of furniture, while near the curtainless window several birds
were twittering in an aviary. In the next room, on a thread-
bare divan, lay a man. He sat up to welcome Christophe. At
once Christophe recognized the emaciated face, lit up by the
soul, the lovely velvety black eyes burning with a feverish flame,
the long, intelligent hands, the misshapen body, the shrill, husky
voice. . . . Emmanuel! The little cripple boy who had been
the innocent cause. . . . And Emmanuel, suddenly rising to
his feet, had also recognized Christophe.

They stood for a moment without speaking. Both of them
saw Olivier. . . . They could not bring themselves to shake
hands. Emmanuel had stepped backward. After ten long years,
an unconfessed rancor, the old jealousy that he had had of
Christophe, leaped forth from the obscure depths of instinct.
He stood still, defiant and hostile.—But when he saw Christophe's emotion, when on his lips he read the name that was
in their thoughts: " Olivier "—it was stronger than he: he
flung himself into the arms held out towards him.

Emmanuel asked:
" I knew you were in Paris. But how did you find me? "
Christophe said:
" I read your last book: through it I heard *his* voice."
" Yes," said Emmanuel. " You recognized it? I owe every-
thing that I am now to him."
(He avoided pronouncing the name.)
After a moment he went on gloomily:
" He loved you more than me."
Christophe smiled:
" If a man loves truly there is neither more nor less: he gives
himself to all those whom he loves."
Emmanuel looked at Christophe: the tragic seriousness of
his stubborn eyes was suddenly lit up with a profound sweet-
ness. He took Christophe's hand and made him sit on the
divan by his side.

Each told the story of his life. From fourteen to twenty-five
Emmanuel had practised many trades: printer, upholsterer,
pedlar, bookseller's assistant, lawyer's clerk, secretary to a politician, journalist. . . . In all of them he had found the
means of learning feverishly, here and there finding the support

of good people who were struck by the little man's energy, more
often falling into the hands of people who exploited his poverty
and his gifts, turning his worst experiences to profit, and succeeding in fighting his way through without too much bitterness,
leaving behind him only the remains of his feeble health. His
singular aptitude for the dead languages (not so rare as one
is inclined to believe in a race imbued with humanistic traditions) gained him the interest and support of an old Hellenizing
priest. These studies, which he had no time to push very far,
served him as mental discipline and a school of style. This
man, who had risen from the dregs of the people, whose whole
education had been won by his own efforts, haphazard, so that
there were great gaps in it, had acquired a gift of verbal expression, a mastery of thought over form, such as ten years of
a university education cannot give to the young bourgeois. He
attributed it all to Olivier. And yet others had helped him more
effectively. But from Olivier came the spark which in the
night of this man's soul had lighted the eternal flame. The
rest had but poured oil into the lamp.

He said:

" I only began to understand him from the moment when
he passed away. But everything he ever said had become a
part of me. His light never left me."

He spoke of his work and the task which he declared had
been left to him by Olivier; the awakening of the French, the
kindling of that torch of heroic idealism of which Olivier had
been the herald : he wished to make himself the resounding voice
which should hover above the battlefield and declare the approaching victory: he sang the epic of the new-birth of his race.

His poems were the product of that strange race that, through
the ages, has so strongly preserved its old Celtic aroma, while
it has ever taken a bizarre pride in clothing its ideas with the
cast-off clothes and laws of the Roman conqueror. There were
to be found in it absolutely pure the Gallic audacity, the spirit
of heroic reason, of irony, the mixture of braggadocio and crazy
bravura, which set out to pluck the beards of the Roman senators,
and pillaged the temple of Delphi, and laughingly hurled its
javelins at the sky. But this little Parisian dwarf had had
to shape his passions, as his periwigged grandfathers had done

and as no doubt his great-grandnephews would do, in the bodies
of the heroes and gods of Greece, two thousand years dead. It
is a curious instinct in these people which accords well with their
need of the absolute: as they impose their ideas on the remains
of the ages, they seem to themselves to be imposing them on
the ages. The constraint of his classic form only gave Emmanuel's passions a more violent impulse. Olivier's calm confidence
in the destinies of France had been transformed in his little
protégé into a burning faith, hungering for action and sure of
triumph. He willed it, he said it, he clamored for it. It was
by his exalted faith and his optimism that he had uplifted the
souls of the French public. His book had been as effective as
a battle. He had made a breach in the ranks of skepticism and
fear. The whole younger generation had thronged to follow
him towards the new destiny. . . .

He grew excited as he talked: his eyes burned, his pale face
glowed pink in patches, and his voice rose to a scream. Christophe could not help noticing the contrast between the devouring
fire and the wretched body that was its pyre. He was only
half-conscious of the irony of this stroke of fate. The singer
of energy, the poet who hymned the generation of intrepid sport,
of action, war, could hardly walk without losing his breath, was
extremely temperate, lived on a strict diet, drank water, could
not smoke, lived without women, bore every passion in his body,
and was reduced by his health to asceticism.

Christophe watched Emmanuel, and he felt a mixture of
admiration and brotherly pity. He tried not to show it: but
no doubt his eyes betrayed his feeling. Emmanuel's pride, which
ever kept an open wound in his side, made him think he read
commiseration in Christophe's eyes, and that was more odious
to him than hatred. The fire in him suddenly died down. He
stopped talking. Christophe tried in vain to win back his
confidence. His soul had closed up. Christophe saw that he
was wounded.

The hostile silence dragged on. Christophe got up. Emmanuel took him to the door without a word. His step declared
his infirmity: he knew it: it was a point of pride with him to
appear indifferent: but he thought Christophe was watching
him, and his rancor grew.

Just as he was coldly shaking hands with his guest, and saying good-by, an elegant young lady rang at the door. She was escorted by a pretentious nincompoop whom Christophe recognized as a man he had seen at theatrical first-nights, smiling, chattering, waving his hand, kissing the hands of the ladies, and from his stall shedding smiles all over the theater: not knowing his name, he had called him "the buck."—The buck and his companion, on seeing Emmanuel, flung themselves on the "*cher maître*" with obsequious and familiar effusiveness. As Christophe walked away he heard Emmanuel in his dry voice saying that he was too busy to see any one. He admired the man's gift of being disagreeable. He did not know Emmanuel's reasons for scowling at the rich snobs who came to gratify him with their indiscreet visits; they were prodigal of fine phrases and eulogy; but they no more thought of helping him in his poverty than the famous friends of César Franck ever dreamed of releasing him from the piano-lessons which he had to give up to the last to make a living.

Christophe went several times again to see Emmanuel. He never succeeded in restoring the intimacy of his first visit. Emmanuel showed no pleasure in seeing him, and maintained a suspicious reserve. Every now and then he would be carried away by the generous need of expansion of his genius: a remark of Christophe's would shake him to the very roots of his being: then he would abandon himself to a fit of enthusiastic confidence: and over his secret soul his idealism would cast the glowing light of a flashing poetry. Then, suddenly, he would fall back: he would shrivel up into sulky silence: and Christophe would find him hostile once more.

They were divided by too many things. Not the least was the difference in their ages. Christophe was on the way to full consciousness and mastery of himself. Emmanuel was still in process of formation and more chaotic than Christophe had ever been. The originality of his face came from the contradictory elements that were at grips in him; a mighty stoicism, struggling to tame a nature consumed by atavistic desires,—(he was the son of a drunkard and a prostitute) ;—a frantic imagination which tugged against the bit of a will of steel; an immense egoism, and an immense love for others, and of the two it were impossible to tell which would be the conqueror; an heroic idealism and a morbid thirst for glory which made him impatient of other superiorities. If Olivier's ideas, and his independence, and his disinterestedness were in him, if Emmanuel was superior to his master by his plebeian vitality which knew not disgust in the face of action, by his poetic genius and his thicker skin, which protected him from disgust of all kinds, yet he was very far from reaching the serenity of Antoinette's brother: his character was vain and uneasy: and the restlessness of other people only augmented his own.

He lived in a stormy alliance with a young woman who was his neighbor, the woman who had received Christophe on his first visit. She loved Emmanuel, and was jealously busy over him, looked after his house, copied out his work, and wrote to his dictation. She was not beautiful, and she bore the burden of a passionate soul. She came of the people, and for a long time worked in a bookbinding workshop, then in the post-office. Her childhood had been spent in the stifling atmosphere common to all the poor workpeople of Paris: souls and bodies all huddled together, harassing work, perpetual promiscuity, no air, no silence, never any solitude, no opportunity for recuperation or of defending the inner sanctuary of the heart. She was proud in spirit, with her mind ever seething with a religious fervor for a confused ideal of truth. Her eyes were worn out with copying out at night, sometimes without a lamp, by moonlight, *Les Misérables* of Hugo. She had met Emmanuel at a time when he was more unhappy than she, ill and without resources; and she had devoted herself to him. This passion was the first, the only living love of her life. So she attached herself to him with a hungry tenacity. Her affection was a terrible trial to Emmanuel, who rather submitted to than shared it. He was touched by her devotion: he knew that she was his best friend, the only creature to whom he was everything, who could not do without him. But this very feeling overwhelmed him. He needed liberty and isolation; her eyes always greedily beseeching a look obsessed him: he used to speak harshly to her, and longed to say: "Go!" He was irritated by her ugliness and her clumsy manners. Though he had seen but little of fashionable society, and though he heartily despised it,—(for he

suffered at appearing even uglier and more ridiculous there),—
he was sensitive to elegance, and alive to the attraction of women
who felt towards him (he had no doubt of it) exactly as he
felt towards his friend. He tried to show her an affection
which he did not possess or, at least, which was continually
obscured by gusts of involuntary hatred. He could not do it:
he had a great generous heart in his bosom, hungering to do
good, and also a demon of violence, capable of much evil. This
inward struggle and his consciousness of his inability to end it
to his advantage plunged him into a state of acute irritation,
which he vented on Christophe.

Emmanuel could not help feeling a double antipathy towards
Christophe; firstly because of his old jealousy (one of those
childish passions which still subsist, though we may forget the
cause of them): secondly, because of his fierce nationalism.
In France he had embodied all the dreams of justice, pity, and
human brotherhood conceived by the best men of the preceding
age. He did not set France against the rest of Europe as an
enemy whose fortune is swelled by the ruin of the other nations,
but placed her at their head, as the legitimate sovereign who
reigns for the good of all—the sword of the ideal, the guide
of the human race. Rather than see her commit an injustice
he would have preferred to see her dead. But he had no doubt
of her. He was exclusively French in culture and in heart,
nourished wholly by the French tradition, the profound reasons
of which he found in his own instinct. Quite sincerely he
ignored foreign thought, for which he had a sort of disdainful
condescension,—and was exasperated if a foreigner did not
accept his lowly position.

Christophe saw all that, but, being older and better versed
in life, he did not worry about it. If such pride of race could
not but be injurious, Christophe was not touched by it: he
could appreciate the illusions of filial love, and never dreamed
of criticising the exaggerations of a sacred feeling. Besides,
humanity is profited by the vain belief of the nations in their
mission. Of all the reasons at hand for feeling himself estranged
from Emmanuel only one hurt him: Emmanuel's voice, which
at times rose to a shrill, piercing scream. Christophe's ears
suffered cruelly. He could not help making a face when it

happened. He tried to prevent Emmanuel's seeing it. He endeavored to hear the music and not the instrument. There was such a beauty of heroism shining forth from the crippled poet when he evoked the victories of the mind, the forerunners of other victories, the conquest of the air, the "flying God" who should upraise the peoples, and, like the star of Bethlehem, lead them in his train, in ecstasies, towards far distant spaces or near revenge. The splendor of these visions of energy did not prevent Christophe's seeing their danger, and foreknowing whither this change and the growing clamor of the new Marseillaise would lead. He thought, with a little irony, (with no regret for past or fear of the future), that the song would find an echo that the singer could not foresee, and that a day would come when men would sigh for the vanished days of the Market-Place.—How free they were then! The golden age of liberty! Never would its like be known again. The world was moving on to the age of strength, of health, of virile action, and perhaps of glory, but also of harsh authority and narrow order. We shall have called it enough with our prayers, the age of iron, the classic age! The great classic ages— Louis XIV. or Napoleon—seem now at a distance the peaks of humanity. And perhaps the nation therein most victoriously realized its ideal State. But go and ask the heroes of those times what they thought of them! Your Nicolas Poussin went to live and die in Rome; he was stifled in your midst. Your Pascal, your Racine, said farewell to the world. And among the greatest, how many others lived apart in disgrace, and oppressed! Even the soul of a man like Molière hid much bitterness.—For your Napoleon, whom you so greatly regret, your fathers do not seem to have had any doubt as to their happiness, and the master himself was under no illusion; he knew that when he disappeared the world would say: "Ouf!" . . . What a wilderness of thought surrounds the *Imperator!* Over the immensity of the sands, the African sun. . . .

Christophe did not say all that was in his mind. A few hints were enough to set Emmanuel in a fury, and he did not try the experiment again. But it was in vain that he kept his thoughts to himself: Emmanuel knew what he was thinking. More than that, he was obscurely conscious that Christophe saw farther than he. And he was only irritated by it. Young people never forgive their elders for forcing them to see what they will see in twenty years' time.

Christophe read his heart, and said to himself:

"He is right. Every man his own faith. A man must believe what he believes. God keep me from disturbing his confidence in the future!"

But his mere presence upset Emmanuel. When two personalities are together, however hard they try to efface themselves, one always crushes the other, and the other always feels rancor and humiliation. Emmanuel's pride was hurt by Christophe's superiority in experience and character. And perhaps also he was keeping back the love which he felt growing in himself for him.

He became more and more shy. He locked his door, and did not answer letters.—Christophe had to give up seeing him.

During the first days of July Christophe reckoned up what he had gained by his few months' stay in Paris: many new ideas, but few friends. Brilliant and derisory successes, in which he saw his own image and the image of his work weakened or caricatured in mediocre minds; and there is but scant pleasure in that. And he failed to win the sympathy of those by whom he would have loved to be understood; they had not welcomed his advances; he could not throw in his lot with them, however much he desired to share their hopes and to be their ally; it was as though their uneasy vanity shunned his friendship and found more satisfaction in having him for an enemy. In short, he had let the tide of his own generation pass without passing with it, and the tide of the next generation would have nothing to do with him. He was isolated, and was not surprised, for all his life he had been accustomed to it. But now he thought he had won the right, after this fresh attempt, to return to his Swiss hermitage, until he had realized a project which for some time past had been taking shape. As he grew older he was tormented with the desire to return and settle down in his own country. He knew nobody there, and would find even less intellectual kinship than in this foreign city: but none the less it was his country: you do not ask those of your blood to think your thoughts: between them and you there are a thousand secret ties; the senses learned to read in the same book of sky and earth, and the heart speaks the same language.

He gaily narrated his disappointments to Grazia, and told her of his intention of returning to Switzerland: jokingly he asked her permission to leave Paris, and assured her that he was going during the following week. But at the end of the letter there was a postscript saying:.

"I have changed my mind. My departure is postponed."

Christophe had entire confidence in Grazia: he gave into her hands the secret of his inmost thoughts. And yet there was a room in his heart of which he kept the key: it contained the memories which did not belong only to himself, but to those whom he had loved. He kept back everything concerning Olivier. His reserve was not deliberate. The words would not come from his lips whenever he tried to talk to Grazia about Olivier. She had never known him. . . .

Now, on the morning when he was writing to his friend, there came a knock on the door. He went to open it, cursing at being interrupted. A boy of fourteen or fifteen asked for M. Krafft. Christophe gruffly bade him come in. He was fair, with blue eyes, fine features, not very tall, with a slender, erect figure. He stood in front of Christophe, rather shyly, and said not a word. Quickly he pulled himself together, and raised his limpid eyes, and looked at him with keen interest. Christophe smiled as he scanned the boy's charming face, and the boy smiled too.

"Well?" said Christophe. "What do you want?"

"I came," said the boy. . . .

(And once more he became confused, blushed, and was silent.)

"I can see that you have come," said Christophe, laughing. "But why have you come? Look at me. Are you afraid of me?"

The boy smiled once more, shook his head, and said:

"No."

"Bravo! Then tell me who you are."

"I am . . ." said the boy.

He stopped once more. His eyes wandered curiously round

the room, and lighted on a photograph of Olivier on the mantel-piece.

"Come!" said Christophe. "Courage!"

The boy said:

"I am his son."

Christophe started: he got up from his chair, took hold of the boy's arm, and drew him to him; he sank back into his chair and held him in a close embrace: their faces almost touched; and he gazed and gazed at him, saying:

"My boy. . . . My poor boy. . . ."

Suddenly he took his face in his hands and kissed his brow, eyes, cheeks, nose, hair. The boy was frightened and shocked by such a violent demonstration, and broke away from him. Christophe let him go. He hid his face in his hand, and leaned his brow against the wall, and sat so for the space of a few moments. The boy had withdrawn to the other end of the room. Christophe raised his head. His face was at rest: he looked at the boy with an affectionate smile.

"I frightened you," he said. "Forgive me. . . . You see, I loved him."

The boy was still frightened, and said nothing.

"How like you are to him!" said Christophe. . . . "And yet I should not have recognized you. What is it that has changed? . . ."

He asked:

"What is your name?"

"Georges."

"Oh! yes. I remember. Christophe Olivier Georges. . . . How old are you?"

"Fourteen."

"Fourteen! Is it so long ago? . . . It is as though it were yesterday—or far back in the darkness of time. . . . How like you are to him! The same features. It is the same, and yet another. The same colored eyes, but not the same eyes. The same smile, the same lips, but not the same voice. You are stronger. You hold yourself more erect: your face is fuller, but you blush just as he used to do. Come, sit down, let us talk. Who sent you to me?"

"No one."

"You came of your own accord? How do you know about me?"

"People have talked to me about you."

"Who?"

"My mother."

"Ah!" said Christophe. "Does she know that you came to see me?"

"No."

Christophe said nothing for a moment; then he asked:

"Where do you live?"

"Near the Parc Monçeau."

"You walked here? Yes? It is a long way. You must be tired."

"I am never tired."

"Good! Show me your arms."

(He felt them.)

"You are a strong boy. . . . What put it into your head to come and see me?"

"My father loved you more than any one."

"Did she tell you so?"

(He corrected himself.)

"Did your mother tell you so?"

"Yes."

Christophe smiled pensively. He thought: "She too! . . . How they all loved him! Why did they not let him see it? . . ."

He went on:

"Why did you wait so long before you came?"

"I wanted to come sooner. But I thought you would not want to see me."

"I!"

"I saw you several weeks ago at the Chevillard concerts: I was with my mother, sitting a little away from you: I bowed to you: you looked through me, and frowned, and took no notice."

"I looked at you? . . . My poor boy, how could you think that? . . . I did not see you. My eyes are tired. That is why I frown. . . . You don't think me so cruel as that?"

"I think you could be cruel too, if you wanted to be."

"Really?" said Christophe. "In that case, if you thought I did not want to see you, how did you dare to come?"

"Because I wanted to see you."

"And if I had refused to see you?"

"I shouldn't have let you do that."

He said this with a little decided air, at once shy and provoking.

Christophe burst out laughing, and Georges laughed too.

"You would have sent me packing! Think of that! You rogue! . . . No, decidedly, you are not like your father."

A shadow passed over the boy's mobile face.

"You think I am not like him? But you said, just now . . .? You don't think he would have loved me? You don't love me?"

"What difference does it make to you whether I love you or not?"

"A great deal of difference."

"Because . . .?"

"Because I love you."

In a moment his eyes, his lips, all his features, took on a dozen different expressions, like the shadows of the clouds on an April day chasing over the fields before the spring winds. Christophe had the most lovely joy in gazing at him and listening to him; it seemed to him that all the cares of the past were washed away; his sorrowful experiences, his trials, his sufferings and Olivier's sufferings, all were wiped out: he was born again in this young shoot of Olivier's life.

They talked on. Georges knew nothing of Christophe's music until the last few months, but since Christophe had been in Paris, he had never missed a concert at which his work was played. He spoke of it with an eager expression, his eyes shining and laughing, with the tears not far behind: he was like a lover. He told Christophe that he adored music, and that he wanted to be a composer. But after a question or two, Christophe saw that the boy knew not even the elements of music. He asked about his work. Young Jeannin was at the lycée; he said cheerfully that he was not a good scholar.

"What are you best at? Literature or science?"

"Very much the same."

" What? What? Are you a dunce? "

The boy laughed frankly and said:

" I think so."

Then he added confidentially:

" But I know that I am not, all the same."

Christophe could not help laughing.

" Then why don't you work? Aren't you interested in any-thing? "

" No. I'm interested in everything."

" Well, then, why? "

" Everything is so interesting that there is no time. . . ."

" No time? What the devil do you do? "

He made a vague gesture:

" Many things. I play music, and games, and I go to ex-hibitions. I read. . . ."

" You would do better to read your school-books."

" We never read anything interesting in school. . . . Be-sides, we travel. Last month I went to England to see the Oxford and Cambridge match."

" That must help your work a great deal! "

" Bah! You learn much more that way than by staying at the lycée."

" And what does your mother say to that? "

" Mother is very reasonable. She does whatever I want."

" You bad boy! . . . You can thank your stars I am not your father. . . ."

" You wouldn't have had a chance. . . ."

It was impossible to resist his banter.

" Tell me, you traveler," said Christophe. " Do you know my country? "

" Yes."

" I bet you don't know a word of German."

" Yes, I do. I know it quite well."

" Let us see."

They began to talk German. The boy jabbered on quite ungrammatically with the most droll coolness; he was very intelligent and wide awake, and guessed more than he under-stood: often he guessed wrong; but he was the first to laugh at his mistakes. He talked eagerly about his travels and his

reading. He had read a great deal, hastily, superficially, skipping half the pages, and inventing what he had left unread,
but he was always urged on by a keen curiosity, forever seeking
reasons for enthusiasm. He jumped from one subject to another, and his face grew animated as he talked of plays or
books that had moved him. There was no sort of order in his
knowledge. It was impossible to tell how he could read right
through a tenth-rate book, and yet know nothing of the greatest
masterpieces.

"That is all very well," said Christophe. "But you will
never do anything if you do not work."

"Oh! I don't need to. We are rich."

"The devil! Then it is a very serious state of things. Do
you want to be a man who does nothing and is good for
nothing?"

"No. I should like to do everything. It is stupid to shut
yourself up all your life in a profession."

"But it is the only means yet discovered of doing any
good."

"So they say!"

"What do you mean? 'So they say!' . . . I say so.
I've been working at my profession for forty years, and I am
just beginning to get a glimmer of it."

"Forty years, to learn a profession! When can you begin
to practise it?"

Christophe began to laugh.

"You little disputatious Frenchman!"

"I want to be a musician," said Georges.

"Well, it is not too early for you to begin. Shall I teach
you?"

"Oh! I should be so glad!"

"Come to-morrow. I'll see what you are worth. If you
are worth nothing, I shall forbid you ever to lay hands on a
piano. If you have a real inclination for it, we'll try and make
something of you. . . . But, I warn you, I shall make you
work."

"I will work," said Georges delightedly.

They said good-by until the morrow. As he was going,
Georges remembered that he had other engagements on the

morrow, and also for the day after. Yes, he was not free until the end of the week. They arranged day and hour.

But when the day and hour came, Christophe waited in vain. He was disappointed. He had been looking forward with child-like glee to seeing Georges again. His unexpected visit had brightened his life. It had made him so happy, and moved him so much that he had not slept the night after it. With tender gratitude he thought of the young friend who had sought him out for his friend's sake. His natural grace, his malicious and ingenuous frankness had delighted him: he sank back into the mute intoxication, the buzzing of happiness, which had filled his ears and his heart during the first days of his friend-ship with Olivier. It was allied now with a graver and almost religious feeling which, through the living, saw the smile of the past.—He waited all the next day and the day after. No-body came. Not even a letter of excuse. Christophe was very mournful, and cast about for excuses for the boy. He did not know where to write to him, and he did not know his address. Had he had it he would not have dared to write. When the heart of an older man is filled with love for a young creature, he feels a certain modesty about letting him see the need he has of him: he knows that the young man has not the same need: they are not evenly matched: and nothing is so much dreaded as to seem to be imposing oneself on a person who cares not a jot.

The silence dragged on. Although Christophe suffered under it, he forced himself to take no step to hunt up the Jeannins. But every day he expected the boy, who never came. He did not go to Switzerland, but stayed through the summer in Paris. He thought himself absurd, but he had no taste for traveling. Only when September came did he decide to spend a few days at Fontainebleau.

About the end of October Georges Jeannin came and knocked at his door. He excused himself calmly, without being in the least put out by his long silence.

"I could not come," he said "And then we went away to stay in Brittany."

"You might have written to me," said Christophe.

" Yes. I did try. But I never had the time. . . . Besides," he said, laughing, " I forgot all about it."

" When did you come back? "

" At the beginning of October."

" And it has taken you three weeks to come? . . . Listen. Tell me frankly: Did your mother prevent you? . . . Does she dislike your seeing me? "

" No. Not at all. She told me to come to-day."

" What? "

" The last time I saw you before the holidays I told her everything when I got home. She told me I had done right, and she asked about you, and pestered me with a great many questions. When we came home from Brittany, three weeks ago, she made me promise to go and see you again. A week ago she reminded me again. This morning, when she found that I had not been, she was angry with me, and wanted me to go directly after breakfast, without more ado."

" And aren't you ashamed to tell me that? Must you be forced to come and see me? "

" No. You mustn't think that. . . . Oh! I have annoyed you. Forgive me. . . . I am a muddle-headed idiot. . . . Scold me, but don't be angry with me. I love you. If I did not love you I should not have come. I was not forced to come. I can't be forced to do anything but what I want to do."

" You rascal! " said Christophe, laughing in spite of himself. " And your musical projects, what about them? "

" Oh! I am still thinking about it."

" That won't take you very far."

" I want to begin now. I couldn't begin these last few months. I have had so much to do! But now you shall see how I will work, if you still want to have anything to do with me. . . ."

(He looked slyly at Christophe.)

" You are an impostor," said Christophe.

" You don't take me seriously."

" No, I don't."

" It is too dreadful. Nobody takes me seriously. I los all heart."

" I shall take you seriously when I see you working."

"At once, then."

"I have no time now. To-morrow."

"No. To-morrow is too far off. I can't bear you to despise me for a whole day."

"You bore me."

"Please! . . ."

Smiling at his weakness, Christophe made him sit at the piano, and talked to him about music. He asked him many questions, and made him solve several little problems of harmony. Georges did not know much about it, but his musical instinct supplied the gaps of his ignorance; without knowing their names, he found the chords Christophe wanted; and even his mistakes in their awkwardness showed a curiosity of taste and a singularly acute sensibility. He did not accept Christophe's remarks without discussion; and the intelligent questions he asked in his turn bore witness to the sincerity of a mind that would not accept art as a devout formula to be repeated with the lips, but desired to live it for its own sake.— They did not only talk of music. In reference to harmony Georges would summon up pictures, the country, people. It was difficult to hold him in check: it was constantly necessary to bring him back to the middle of the road: and Christophe had not always the heart to do so. It amused him to hear the boy's joyous chatter, so full of wit and life. What a difference there was between his nature and Olivier's! With the one life was a subterranean river that flowed silently; with the other all was above ground: a capricious stream disporting itself in the sun. And yet it was the same lovely, pure water, like their eyes. With a smile, Christophe recognized in Georges certain instinctive antipathies, likings and dislikings, which he well knew, and the naïve intolerance, the generosity of heart which gives itself entirely to whatsoever it loves. . . . Only Georges loved so many things that he had no time to love any one thing for long.

He came back the next day and the days following. He was filled with a youthful passion for Christophe, and he worked enthusiastically at his lessons. . . .—Then his enthusiasm palled, his visits grew less frequent. He came less and less often. Then he came no more, and disappeared for weeks.

He was light-hearted, forgetful, naïvely selfish, and sincerely affectionate; he had a good heart and a quick intelligence which he expended piecemeal day by day. People forgave him everything because they were so glad to see him; he was happy. . . .

Christophe refused to judge him. He did not complain. He wrote to Jacqueline to thank her for having sent her son to him. Jacqueline replied with a short letter filled with restrained emotion: she expressed a hope that Christophe would be interested in Georges and help him in his life. Through shame and pride she could not bring herself to see him again. And Christophe thought he could not visit her without being invited.—So they stayed apart, seeing each other at a distance at concerts, bound together only by the boy's infrequent visits.

The winter passed. Grazia wrote but seldom. She was still faithful in her friendship for Christophe. But, like a true Italian, she was hardly at all sentimental, attached to reality, and needed to see people if she were, perhaps not to think of them, but certainly to take pleasure in talking to them. Her heart's memory needed to be supported by having her sight's memory refreshed from time to time. Her letters became brief and distant. She was as sure of Christophe as Christophe was of her. But their security gave out more light than warmth.

Christophe did not feel his new disappointments very keenly. His musical activity was enough to fill his life. When he reaches a certain age a vigorous artist lives much more in his art than in his life; his life has become the dream, his art the reality. His creative powers had been reawakened by contact with Paris. There is no stronger stimulant in the world than the sight of that city of work. The most phlegmatic natures are touched by its fever. Christophe, being rested by years of healthy solitude, brought to his work an enormous accumulation of force. Enriched by the new conquests forever being made in the fields of musical technique by the intrepid curiosity of the French, he hurled himself in his turn along the road to discovery: being more violent and barbarous than they, he went farther. But nothing in his new audacities was left to the hazardous mercies of his instinct. Christophe had begun to feel the need of clarity; all his life his genius had obeyed the rhythm of alternate currents: it was its law to pass from one pole to the other, and to fill everything between them. Having greedily surrendered in his last period to " *the eyes of chaos shining through the veil of order,*" even to rending the veil so as to see them more clearly, he was now striving to tear himself away from their fascination, and once more to th.ow over the face of the sphinx the magic net of the master mind. The imperial inspiration of Rome had passed over him. Like the Parisian art of that time, by the spirit of which he was infected, he was aspiring to order. But not—like the reactionaries who spent what was left of their energies in protecting their slumber—to order in Varsovia; the good people who are always going back to Brahms—the Brahmses of all the arts, the thematics, the insipid neo-classics, in search of solace! Might one not say that they are enfeebled with passion! You are soon done for, my friends. . . . No, it is not of your order that I speak. Mine has no kinship with yours. Mine is the order in harmony of the free passions and the free will. . . . Christophe was studying how in his art to maintain the just balance between the forces of life. These new chords, the new musical daimons that he had summoned from the abyss of sounds, were used to build clear symphonies, vast, sunlit buildings, like the 'talian cupola'd basilicas.

These plays and battles of the mind occupied him all winter. And the winter passed quickly, although, in the evening, as he ended his day's work and looked behind him at the tale of days, he could not have told whether it had been long or short, or whether he was still young or very old.

Then a new ray of human sunshine pierced the veil of his dreams, and once more brought in the springtime. Christophe received a letter from Grazia, telling him that she was coming to Paris with her two children. For a long time she had planned to do so. Her cousin Colette had often invited her. Her dread of the effort necessary to interrupt her habits and to tear herself away from her careless tranquillity and the home she loved in order to plunge into the Parisian whirligig that she knew so well, had made her postpone the journey from year to year. This spring she was filled with melancholy, perhaps with a secret disappointment—(how many unspoken romances there

are in the heart of a woman, unknown to others, often unconfessed to herself!)—and she longed to go right away from
Rome. A threatened epidemic gave her an excuse for hurrying
on her children's departure. She followed her letter to Christophe in a very few days.

Christophe hastened to her as soon as he heard she was at
Colette's. He found her still absorbed and distant. He was
hurt, but did not show it. By now he was almost rid of his
egoism, and that gave him the insight of affection. He saw
that she had some grief which she wished to conceal, and he
suppressed his longing to know its nature. Only he strove to
keep her amused by giving her a gay account of his misadventures and sharing with her his work and his plans, and he
wrapped her round with his affection. Her mournful heart
rested in the heart of her friend, and he spoke to her always
of things other than that which was in both their minds. And
gradually he saw the shadow of melancholy fade from her eyes,
and their expression became nearly, and ever more nearly, intimate. So much so, that one day, as he was talking to her,
he stopped suddenly, and in silence looked at her

" What is it? " she asked.

" To-day," he said, " you have come back to me."

She smiled, and in a low voice she replied:

" Yes."

It was not easy for them to talk quietly together. They were
very rarely alone. Colette gave them the pleasure of her presence more often than they wished. In spite of her eccentricities
she was extremely kind and sincerely attached to Grazia and
Christophe; but she never dreamed that she could be a nuisance
to them. She had, of course, noticed—(for her eyes saw everything)—what she was pleased to call Christophe's flirtation
with Grazia; flirtation was her element, and she was delighted,
and asked nothing better than to encourage it. But that was
precisely what she was not required to do; she was only desired
not to meddle with things that did not concern her It was
enough for her to appear or to make an (indiscreet) discreet
allusion to their friendship to one of them, to make Christophe
and Grazia freeze and turn the conversation. Colette cast about
among all the possible reasons, except one, and that the true one,

for their reserve. Fortunately for them, she could never stay long. She was always coming and going, coming in, going out, superintending everything in her house, doing a dozen things at a time. In the intervals between her appearances Christophe and Grazia, left alone with the children, would resume the thread of their innocent conversation. They never spoke of the feelings that bound them together. Unrestrainedly they confided to each other their little daily happenings. Grazia, with feminine interest, inquired into Christophe's domestic affairs. They were in a very bad way: he was always having ruptures with his housekeepers; he was continually being cheated and robbed by his servants. She laughed heartily but very kindly, and with motherly compassion for the great child's small practical sense. One day, when Colette left them after a longer visitation than usual, Grazia sighed:

"Poor Colette! I love her dearly. . . . But how she bores me!"

"I love her too," said Christophe, "if you mean by that that she bores us."

Grazia laughed:

"Listen. Will you let me . . . (it is quite impossible for us to talk in peace here) . . . will you let me come to your house one day?"

He could hardly speak.

"To my house! You will come?"

"If you don't mind?"

"Mind! Mercy, no!"

"Well, then, will you let me come on Tuesday?"

"Tuesday, Wednesday, Thursday, any day you like."

"Tuesday, at four. It is agreed?"

"How good of you! How good of you!"

"Wait. There is a condition."

"A condition? Why? Anything you like. You know that I will do it, condition or no condition."

"I would rather make a condition."

"I promise."

"You don't know what it is."

"I don't care. I promise. Anything you like."

"But listen. You are so obstinate."

" Tell me ! "

" The condition is that between now and then you make no change in your rooms—none, you understand; everything must be left exactly as it is."

Christophe's face fell. He looked abject.

" Ah ! That's not playing the game."

" You see, that's what comes of giving your word too hastily ! But you promised."

" But why do you want——?"

" But I want to see you in your rooms as you are, every day, when you are not expecting me."

" Surely you will let me——"

" Nothing at all. I shall allow nothing."

" At least——"

" No, no, no ! I won't listen to you, or else I won't come, if you prefer it——"

" You know I would agree to anything if you will only come."

" Then you promise."

" Yes."

, " On your word of honor ? "

" Yes, you tyrant."

" A good tyrant."

" There is no such thing as a good tyrant: there are tyrants whom one loves and tyrants whom one detests."

" And I am both ? "

" No. You are one of the first."

" It is very humiliating."

On the appointed day she came. With scrupulous loyalty Christophe had not dared even to arrange the smallest piece of paper in his untidy rooms: he would have felt dishonored had he done so. But he was in torture. He was ashamed of what his friend would think. Anxiously he awaited her arrival. She came punctually, not more than four or five minutes after the hour. She climbed up the stairs with her light, firm step. She rang. He was at the door and opened it. She was dressed with easy, graceful elegance. Through her veil he could see her tranquil eyes. They said " Good-day " in a whisper and shook hands: she was more silent than usual: he was awkward and emotional and said nothing, to avoid showing his feeling. He led her in without uttering the sentence he had prepared by way of excusing the untidiness of his room. She sat down in the best chair, and he sat near her.

" This is my work-room."

It was all he could find to say to her.

There was a silence. She looked round slowly, with a kindly smile, and she, too, was much moved, though she would not admit it to herself. (Later she told him that when she was a girl she had thought of coming to him, but had been afraid as she reached the door.) She was struck by the solitary aspect and the sadness of the place: the dark, narrow hall, the absolute lack of comfort, the visible poverty, all went to her heart: she was filled with affectionate pity for her old friend, who, in spite of all his work and his sufferings and his celebrity, was unable to shake free of material anxiety. And at the same time she was amused at the absolute indifference revealed by the bareness of the room that had no carpets, no pictures, no bric-à-brac, no armchair; no other furniture than a table, three hard chairs, and a piano: and papers, papers everywhere, mixed up with books, on the table, under the table, on the floor, on the piano, on the chairs—(she smiled as she thought how conscientiously he had kept his word).

After a minute or two she asked him, pointing to his place at the table:

" Is that where you work? "

" No," he said.   " There."

He pointed to the darkest corner of the room, where there stood a low chair with its back to the light. She went and sat in it quietly, without a word. For a few minutes they were silent, for they knew not what to say. He got up and went to the piano. He played and improvised for half an hour; all around him he felt the presence of his beloved and an immense happiness filled his heart; with eyes closed he played marvelous things. Then she understood the beauty of the room, all furnished with divine harmonies: she heard his loving, suffering heart as though it were beating in her own bosom.

When the music had died away, he stopped for a little while, quite still, at the piano: then he turned as he heard the breath of his beloved and knew that she was weeping She came to him.

"Thank you!" she murmured, and took his hand.

Her lips were trembling a little. She closed her eyes. He did the same. For a few seconds they remained so, hand in hand; and time stopped; it seemed to them that for ages, ages, they had been lying pressed close together.

She opened her eyes, and to shake off her emotion, she asked:
"May I see the rest of the flat?"

Glad also to escape from his emotions, he opened the door into the next room; but at once he was ashamed It contained a narrow, hard iron bed.

On the wall there was a cast of the mask of Beethoven, and near the bed, in a cheap frame, photographs of his mother and Olivier. On the dressing-table was another photograph: Grazia herself as a child of fifteen. He had found it in her album in Rome, and had stolen it. He confessed it, and asked her to forgive him. She looked at the face, and said:

"Can you recognize me in it?"

"1 can recognize you, and remember you

"Which of the two do you love best?" she asked, pointing to herself.

"You are always the same. I love you always just the same. I recognize you everywhere. Even in the photograph of you as a tiny child. You do not know the emotion I feel as in this chrysalis I discern your soul. Nothing so clearly assures me that you are eternal. I loved you before you were born, and I shall love you ever after. . . ."

He stopped. She stood still and made no answer: she was filled with the sweet sorrow of love. When she returned to the work-room, and he had shown her through the window his little friendly tree, full of chattering sparrows, she said:

"Now, do you know what we will do? We will have a feast. I brought tea and cakes because I knew you would have nothing of the kind. And I brought something else. Give me your overcoat."

"My overcoat?"

"Yes. Give it me."

She took needles and cotton from her bag.

" What are you going to do? "

" There were two buttons the other day which made me tremble for their fate. Where are they now? "

" True. I never thought of sewing them on. It is so tiresome! "

" Poor boy! Give it me."

" I am ashamed."

" Go and make tea."

He brought the kettle and the spirit-lamp into the room, so as not to miss a moment of his friend's stay. As she sewed she watched his clumsy ways stealthily and maliciously. They drank their tea out of cracked cups, which she thought horrible, dodging the cracks, while he indignantly defended them, because they reminded him of his life with Olivier.

Just as she was going, he asked:

" You are not angry with me? "

" Why should I be? "

" Because of the litter here? "

She laughed.

" I will make it tidy."

As she reached the threshold and was just going to open the door, he knelt and kissed her feet.

" What are you doing? " she said. " You foolish, foolish dear! Good-by! "

They agreed that she should come once a week on a certain day. She had made him promise that there should be no more outbursts, no more kneelings, no more kissing of her feet. She breathed forth such a gentle tranquillity, that even when Christophe was in his most violent mood, he was influenced by it; and although when he was alone, he often thought of her with passionate desire, when they were together they were always like good comrades. Never did word or gesture escape him which could disturb his friend's peace.

On Christophe's birthday she dressed her little girl as she herself had been when they first met in the old days; and she made the child play the piece that Christophe used to make her play.

But all her grace and tenderness and sweet friendship were

mingled with contradictory feelings. She was frivolous, and loved society, and delighted in being courted, even by fools; she was a coquette, except with Christophe,—even with Christophe. When he was very tender with her, she would be deliberately cold and reserved. When he was cold and reserved she would become tender and tease him affectionately. She was the most honest of women. But even in the most honest and the best of women there is always a girl. She insisted on standing well with the world, and conformed to the conventions. She had fine musical gifts, and understood Christophe's work; but she was not much interested in it—(and he knew it).—To a true Latin woman, art is of worth only in proportion as it leads back to life, to life and love. . . . The love which is forever seething, slumbering, in the depths of the voluptuous body. . . . What has she to do with the tragic meditations, the tormented symphonies, the intellectual passions of the North? She must have music in which her hidden desires can unfold, with the minimum of effort, an opera, which is passionate life without the fatigue of the passions, a sentimental, sensual, lazy art.

She was weak and changing: she could only apply herself intermittently to any serious study: she must have amusement; rarely did she do on the morrow what she had decided to do the night before. She had so many childish ways, so many little disconcerting caprices! The restless nature of woman, her morbid and periodically unreasonable character. She knew it and then tried to isolate herself. She knew her weaknesses, and blamed herself for her failure to resist them, since they distressed her friend; sometimes, without his knowing it, she made real sacrifices for him; but, when all was told, her nature was the stronger. For the rest, Grazia could not bear Christophe to seem to be commanding her; and, once or twice, by way of asserting her independence, she did the opposite of what he asked her. At once she regretted it; at night she would be filled with remorse that she could not make Christophe happier; she loved him more than she would let him see; she felt that her friendship with him was the best part of her life. As usually happens with two very different people, they were more united when they were not together. In truth, if they had been thrust apart by a misunderstanding, the **fault** was not altogether Christophe's, as he honestly believed. Even when in the old days Grazia most dearly loved Christophe, would she have married him? She would perhaps have given him her life; but would she have so given herself as to live all her life with him? She knew (though she did not confess it to Christophe) that she had loved her husband, and, even now, after all the harm he had done her, loved him as she had never loved Christophe. . . . The secrets of the heart, the secrets of the body, of which one is not very proud, and hides from those dear to one, as much out of respect for them, as in complacent pity for oneself. . . . Christophe was too masculine to divine them: but every now and then, in flashes, he would see how little the woman he most dearly loved, who truly loved him, belonged to him—and that he could not wholly count on any one, on any one, in life. His love was not quenched by this perception. He even felt no bitterness. Grazia's peace spread over him. He accepted everything. O life, why should I reproach thee for that which thou canst not give? Art thou not very beautiful and very blessed as thou art? I must fain love thy smile, Gioconda. . .

Christophe would gaze at his beloved's beautiful face, and read in it many things of the past and the future. During the long years when he had lived alone, traveling, speaking little but seeing much, he had acquired, almost unconsciously, the power of reading the human face, that rich and complex language formed by the ages. It is a thousand times richer and more complex than the spoken language. The spirit of the race is expressed in it. . . . There are perpetual contrasts between the lines of the face and the words that come from it. Take the profile of a girl, clear-cut, a little hard, in the Burne-Jones style, tragic, consumed by a secret passion, jealousy, a Shakespearian sorrow. . . . She speaks: and, behold, she is a little bourgeois creature, as stupid as an owl, a selfish, commonplace coquette, with no idea of the terrible forces inscribed upon her body. And yet such passion, such violence are in her. In what shape will they one day spring forth? Will it be in the lust of gain, conjugal jealousy, or splendid energy, or morbid wickedness? There is no knowing. It may be that she will transmit them to another creature of her blood before the time comes for the eruption. But it is an element with which we have to reckon as, like a fatality, it hovers above the race.

Grazia also bore the weight of that uneasy heritage, which, of all the patrimony of ancient families, is the least in danger of being dissipated in transit. She, at least, was aware of it. It is a great source of strength to know our weakness, to make ourselves, if not the masters, the pilots of the soul of the race to which we are bound, which bears us like a vessel upon its waters,—to make fate our instrument, to use it as a sail which we furl or clew up according to the wind. When Grazia closed her eyes, she could hear within herself more than one disturbing voice, of a tone familiar to her. But in her healthy soul even the dissonances were blended to form a profound, soft music, under the guiding hand of her harmonious reason.

Unhappily it is not within our power to transmit the best of our blood to the creatures of our blood.

Of Grazia's two children, the little girl, Aurora, who was eleven years old, was like her mother; she was not so pretty, being a little coarser in fiber; she had a slight limp; she was a good little girl, affectionate and gay, with splendid health, abundant good nature, few natural gifts, except idleness, a passion for doing nothing. Christophe adored her. When he saw her with Grazia he felt the charm of a twofold creature, seen at two ages of life, two generations together. . . . Two flowers upon one stem; a Holy Family of Leonardo, the Virgin and Saint Anne, different shades of the same smile. With one glance he could take in the whole blossoming of a woman's soul; and it was at once fair and sad to see: he could see whence it came and whither it was going. There is nothing more natural than for an ardent, chaste heart to love two sisters at one and the same time, or mother and daughter. Christophe would have loved the woman of his love through all her descendants, just as in her he loved the stock of which she came. Her every smile, her every tear, every line in her face, were they not living beings, the memories of a life which was before her eyes opened to the light, the forerunners of a life which was to come, when her eyes should be forever closed?

The little boy, Lionello, was nine. He was much handsomer than his sister, of a finer stock, too fine, worn out and bloodless, wherein he was like his father. He was intelligent, well-endowed with bad instincts, demonstrative, and dissembling. He had big blue eyes, long, girlish, fair hair, a pale complexion, a delicate chest, and was morbidly nervous, which last, being a born comedian and strangely skilled in discovering people's weaknesses, he upon occasion turned to good account. Grazia was inclined to favor him, with the natural preference of a mother for her least healthy child,—and also through the attraction which all kindly, good women feel for the sons who are neither well nor ill (for in them a part of their life which they have suppressed finds solace). In such attraction there is something of the memory of the husbands who have made them suffer, whom they loved even while they despised them, or the strange flora of the soul, which wax strong in the dark, humid hot-house of conscience.

In spite of Grazia's care equally to bestow her tenderness upon her children, Aurora felt the difference, and was a little hurt by it. Christophe divined her feeling, and she divined Christophe's: they came together instinctively; while between Christophe and Lionello there was an antipathy which the boy covered up with exaggerated, lisping, charming ways,—and Christophe thrust from him as a shameful feeling. He wrestled with himself and forced himself to cherish this other man's child as though he were the child whom it would have been ineffably sweet for him to have had by the beloved. He would not allow himself to see Lionello's bad nature or anything that could remind him of the " other man ": he set himself to find in him only Grazia. She, more clear-sighted, was under no illusions about her son, and she only loved him the more.

However, the disease which for years had been lying dormant in the boy broke out. Consumption supervened. Grazia resolved to go and shut herself up in a sanatorium in the Alps with Lionello. Christophe begged to be allowed to go with her. To avoid scandal she dissuaded him. He was hurt by the excessive importance which she attached to the conventions. She went away and left her daughter with Colette. It was

not long before she began to feel terribly lonely among the
sick people who talked of nothing but their illness, surrounded
by the pitiless mountains rising above the rags and tatters of
men. To escape from the depressing spectacle of the invalids
with their spittoons spying upon each other and marking the
progress of death over each one of them, she left the Palace
hospital, and took a chalet, where she lived aloof with her own
little invalid. Instead of improving Lionello's condition, the
high altitude aggravated it. His fever waxed greater. Grazia
spent nights of anguish. Christophe knew it by his keen intuition, although she told him nothing: for she was growing
more and more rigid in her pride; she longed for Christophe
to be with her, but she had forbidden him to follow her, and
she could not bring herself to confess: " I am too weak, I need
you. . . ."

One evening, as she stood in the veranda of the chalet in the
twilight hour, which is so bitter for hearts in agony, she
saw . . . she thought she saw coming up from the station of
the funicular railway . . . a man walking hurriedly: he
stopped, hesitating, with his back a little bowed. She went indoors to avoïd his seeing her: she held her hands over her
heart, and, quivering with emotion, she laughed. Although she
was not at all religious she knelt down, hid her face in her
hands; she felt the need of thanking some one. . . . But he
did not come. She went back to the window, and, hiding behind the curtains, looked out. He had stopped, leaning against
a fence round a field, near the gate of the chalet. He dared
not enter. And, even more perturbed than he, she smiled, and
said in a low voice:

" Come . . ."

At last he made up his mind and rang the bell. Already she
was at the door, and she opened it. His eyes looked at her
like the eyes of a faithful dog, who is afraid of being beaten.
He said:

" I came. . . . Forgive me. . . ."

She said:

" Thank you."

Then she confessed how she had expected him. Christophe
helped her to nurse the boy, whose condition was growing worse

His heart was in the task. The boy treated him with irritable animosity: he took no pains now to conceal it: he said many malicious things to him. Christophe put it all down to his illness. He was extraordinarily patient. He passed many painful days by the boy's bedside, until the critical night, on passing through which, Lionello, whom they had given up for lost, was saved. And they felt then such pure happiness—watching hand in hand over the little invalid—that suddenly she got up, took her cloak and hood, and led Christophe out of doors, along the road, in the snow, the silence and the night, under the cold stars. Leaning on his arm, excitedly breathing in the frozen peace of the world, they hardly spoke at all. They made no allusion to their love. Only when they returned, on the threshold, she said:

" My dear, dear friend! . . ."

And her eyes were lit up by the happiness of having saved her child.

That was all. But they felt that the bond between them had become sacred.

On her return to Paris after Lionello's long convalescence, she took a little house at Passy, and did not worry any more about " avoiding scandal ": she felt brave enough to dare opinion for her friend's sake. Their life henceforth was so intimately linked that it would have seemed cowardly to her to conceal the friendship which united them at the—inevitable—risk of having it slandered. She received Christophe at all hours of the day, and was seen with him out walking and at the theater: she spoke familiarly to him in company. Colette thought they were making themselves too conspicuous. Grazia would stop her hints with a smile, and quietly go her way.

And yet she had given Christophe no new right over her. They were nothing more than friends: he always addressed her with the same affectionate respect. But they hid nothing from each other: they consulted each other about everything: and insensibly Christophe assumed a sort of paternal authority in the house: Grazia listened to and followed his advice. She was no longer the same woman since the winter she had spent in the sanatorium; the anxiety and fatigue had seriously tried her

health, which, till then, had been sturdy. Her soul was affected
by it. In spite of an occasional lapse into her old caprices,
she had become mysteriously more serious, more reflective, and
was more constantly desirous of being kind, of learning and not
hurting any one. Every day saw her more softened by Christophe's affection, his disinterestedness, and the purity of his
heart: and she was thinking of one day giving him the great
happiness of which he no longer dared to dream, that of becoming his wife.

He had never broached the subject again after her first refusal, for he thought he had no right to do so. But regretfully
he clung to his impossible hope. Though he respected what his
friend had said, he was not convinced by her disillusioned attitude towards marriage: he persisted in believing that the union
of two people who love each other, profoundly and devotedly,
is the height of human happiness.—His regrets were revived
by coming in contact once more with the Arnauds.

Madame Arnaud was more than fifty. Her husband was
sixty-five or sixty-six. Both seemed to be older. He had grown
stout: she was very thin and rather shrunken: spare though she
had been in the old days, she was now just a wisp of a woman.
After Arnaud's retirement they had gone to live in a house in
the country. They had no link with the life of the time save
the newspaper, which in the torpor of their little town and
their drowsy life brought them the tardy echo of the voice
of the world. Once they saw Christophe's name. Madame
Arnaud wrote him a few affectionate, rather ceremonious words,
to tell him how glad they were of his fame. He took the train
at once without letting them know.

He found them in the garden, dozing under the round canopy
of an ash, on a warm summer afternoon. They were like
Boecklin's old couple, sleeping hand in hand, in an arbor. Sun,
sleep, old age overwhelm them: they are falling, they are already
half-buried in the eternal dream. And, as the last gleam of
their life, their tenderness persists to the end. The clasp of
their hands, the dying warmth of their bodies. . . .—They
were delighted to see Christophe, for the sake of all the memories
of the past he brought with him. They talked of the old days,
which at that distance seemed brilliant and full of light.

Arnaud loved talking, but he had lost his memory for names.
Madame Arnaud whispered them to him. She liked saying
nothing and preferred listening to talking: but the image of
the old times had been kept alive and clear in her silent heart:
in glimmers they would appear sharply before her like shining
pebbles in a stream. There was one such memory that Christophe more than once saw reflected in her eyes as she looked
at him with affectionate compassion: but Olivier's name was
not pronounced. Old Arnaud plied his wife with touching,
awkward little attentions; he was fearful lest she should catch
cold, or be too hot; he would gaze hungrily with anxious love
at her dear, faded face, and with a weary smile she would try
to reassure him. Christophe watched them tenderly, with a
little envy. . . . To grow old together. To love in the dear
companion even the wear of time. To say: " I know those lines
round her eyes and nose. I have seen them coming. I know
when they came. Her scant gray hair has lost its color, day
by day, in my company, something because of me, alas! Her
sweet face has swollen and grown red in the fires of the weariness
and sorrow that have consumed us. My soul, how much better
I love thee for that thou hast suffered and grown old with me.
Every one of thy wrinkles is to me as music from the past. . . ."
The charm of these old people, who, after the long vigil of life,
spent side by side, go side by side to sleep in the peace of the
night! To see them was both sweet and profitable and sorrowful for Christophe. Oh! How lovely had life and death been
thus! . . .

When he next saw Grazia, he could not help telling her of
his visit. He did not tell her of the thoughts roused in him
by his visit. But she divined them. He was tender and wistful
as he spoke. He turned his eyes away from her and was silent
every now and then. She looked at him and smiled, and
Christophe's unease infected her.

That evening, when she was alone in her room, she lay
dreaming. She went over the story Christophe had told her:
but the image she saw through it was not that of the old couple
sleeping under the ash: it was the shy, ardent dream of her
friend. And her heart was filled with love for him. She lay
in the dark and thought:

"Yes. It is absurd, criminal and absurd, to waste the opportunity for such happiness. What joy in the world can equal the joy of making the man you love happy? . . . What! Do I love him? . . ."

She was silent, deeply moved, listening to the answer of her heart.

"I love him."

Just then a dry, hard, hasty cough came from the next room where the children were sleeping. Grazia pricked her ears: since the boy's illness she had always been anxious. She called out to him. He made no reply, and went on coughing. She sprang from her bed and went to him. He was irritated, and moaned, and said that he was not well, and broke out coughing again.

"What is the matter?"

He did not reply, but only groaned that he was ill.

"My darling, please tell me what is the matter?"

"I don't know."

"Is it here?"

"Yes. No. I don't know. I am ill all over."

On that he had a fresh fit of coughing, violent and exaggerated. Grazia was alarmed: she had a feeling that he was forcing himself to cough: but she was ashamed of her thought, as she saw the boy sweating and choking for breath. She kissed him and spoke to him tenderly: he seemed to grow calmer; but as soon as she tried to leave him he broke out coughing again. She had to stay shivering by his bedside, for he would not even allow her to go away to dress herself, and insisted on her holding his hand; and he would not let her go until he fell asleep again. Then she went to bed, chilled, uneasy, harassed. And she found it impossible to gather up the threads of her dreams.

The boy had a singular power of reading his mother's thoughts. This instinctive genius is often—though seldom in such a high degree—to be found in creatures of the same stock: they hardly need to look at each other to know each other's thoughts: they can guess them by the breathing, by a thousand imperceptible signs. This natural aptness, which is fortified by living together, was in Lionello sharpened and refined by his ever wake-

ful malevolence. He had the insight of the desire to hurt. He
detested Christophe. Why? Why does a child take a dislike
to a person who has never done him any harm? It is often a
matter of chance. It is enough for a child to have begun by
persuading himself that he detests some one, for it to become
a habit, and the more he is argued with the more desperately
he will cling to it. But often, again, there are deeper reasons
for it, which pass the child's understanding: he has no idea of
them. . . . From the first moment when he saw Christophe,
the son of Count Berény had a feeling of animosity towards
the man whom his mother had loved. It was as though he had
instinctively felt the exact moment when Grazia began to think
of marrying Christophe. From that moment on he never ceased
to spy upon them. He was always between them, and refused
to leave the room whenever Christophe came; or he would manage to burst in upon them when they were sitting together.
More than that, when his mother was alone, thinking of Christophe, he seemed to divine her thoughts. He would sit near
her and watch her. His gaze would embarrass her and almost
make her blush. She would get up to conceal her unease.—He
would take a delight in saying unkind things about Christophe
in her presence. She would bid him be silent, but he would
go on. And if she tried to punish him, he would threaten to
make himself ill. That was the strategy he had always used
successfully since he was a child. When he was quite small,
one day when he had been scolded, he had, out of revenge,
undressed himself and lain naked on the floor so as to catch
cold.—Once, when Christophe brought a piece of music that
he had composed for Grazia's birthday, the boy took the manuscript and hid it. It was found in tatters in a wood-box.
Grazia lost her patience and scolded him severely. Then he
wept and howled, and stamped his feet, and rolled on the ground,
and had an attack of nerves. Grazia was terrified, and kissed
and implored him, and promised to do whatever he wanted.

From that day on he was the master: for he knew it: and
very frequently he had recourse to the weapon with which he
had succeeded. There was never any knowing how far his
attacks were natural and how far counterfeit. Soon he was
not satisfied with using them vengefully when he was opposed

in any way, but took to using them out of spite whenever his
mother and Christophe planned to spend the evening together.
He even went so far as to play his dangerous game out of
sheer idleness, or theatricality, to discover the extent of his
power. He was extraordinarily ingenious in inventing strange,
nervous accidents; sometimes in the middle of dinner he would
be seized with a convulsive trembling, and upset his glass or
break his plate; sometimes, as he was going upstairs, he would
clutch at the banisters with his hand: his fingers would stiffen:
he would pretend that he could not open them again; or he would
have a sharp pain in his side and roll about, howling; or he
would choke. Of course, in the end he developed a genuine
nervous illness. Christophe and Grazia were at their wits' end.
Their peaceful meetings—their quiet talks, their readings, their
music, which were as a festival to them—all their humble happiness was henceforth disturbed.

Every now and then, however, the little imp would give them
a respite, partly because he was tired of his play-acting, partly
because his child's nature took possession of him again, and
made him think of something else. (He was sure now that
he had won the day.)

Then, quickly, quietly, they would seize their opportunity.
Every hour that they could steal in this way was the more
precious to them as they could never be sure of enjoying it
to the end. How near they felt to each other! Why could
they not always be so! . . . One day Grazia herself confessed
to her regret. Christophe took her hand.

"Yes. Why?" he asked.

"You know why, my dear," she said, with a miserable smile.

Christophe knew. He knew that she was sacrificing their
happiness to her son: he knew that she was not deceived by
Lionello's lies, that she still adored him: he knew the blind
egoism of such domestic affections which make the best pour
out their reserves of devotion to the advantage of the bad or
mediocre creatures of their blood, so that there is nothing left
for them to give to those who would be more worthy, whom
they love best, but who are not of their blood. And although
he was irritated by it, although there were times when he
longed to kill the little monster who was destroying their lives,

yet he bowed his head in silence, and understood that Grazia could not do otherwise.

So they renounced their life without vain recrimination. But if the happiness which was their right could be snatched from them, nothing could prevent the union of their hearts. Their very renunciation, their common sacrifice, held them by bonds stronger than those of the flesh. Each confided the sorrow of it all to the other, passed over the burden of it, and took on the other's suffering: so even their sorrow became joy. Christophe called Grazia "his confessor." He did not hide from her the weaknesses from which his pride had to suffer: rather he accused himself with too great contrition, and she would smilingly soothe his boyish scruples. He even confessed to her his material poverty; but he could only bring himself to do that after it had been agreed between them that she should neither offer him, nor he accept from her, any help. It was the last barrier of pride which he upheld and she respected. In place of the well-being which she could not bring into her friend's life, she found many ways of filling it with what was infinitely more precious to him—namely, her tenderness. He felt the breath of it all about him, during every hour of the day: he never opened his eyes in the morning, never closed them at night, without a prayer of love and adoration. And when she awoke, or at night, as often happened, lay for hours without sleeping, she thought:

"My dear is thinking of me."

And a great peace came upon them and surrounded them.

However, her health had given way. Grazia was constantly in bed, or had to spend the day lying on a sofa. Christophe used to go every day and read to her, and show her his new work. Then she would get up from the chair, and limp to the piano, for her feet were swollen. She would play the music he had brought. It was the greatest joy she could give him. Of all his pupils she and Cécile were the most gifted. But while Cécile had an instinctive feeling for music, with hardly any understanding of it, to Grazia it was a lovely harmonious language full of meaning for her. The demoniac quality in life and art escaped her altogether: she brought to bear on it

the clarity of her intelligence and heart. Christophe's genius
was saturated with her clarity. His friend's playing helped
him to understand the obscure passions he had expressed. With
closed eyes he would listen, and follow her, and hold her by the
hand, as she led him through the maze of his own thoughts.
By living in his music through Grazia's soul, he was wedded
to her soul and possessed it. From this mysterious conjuga-
tion sprang music which was the fruit of the mingling of their
lives. One day, as he brought her a collection of his works,
woven of his substance and hers, he said:

" Our children."

Theirs was an unbroken communion whether they were together or apart; sweet were the evenings spent in the peace and
quiet of the old house, which was a fit setting for the image of
Grazia, where the silent, cordial servants, who were devoted
to Christophe, extended to him a little of the respectful affection
they had for their mistress. Joyous was it to listen to the
song of the fleeting hours, and to see the tide of life ebbing
away. . . . A shadow of anxiety was thrown on their happiness by Grazia's failing health. But, in spite of her little
infirmities, she was so serene that her hidden sufferings did
but heighten her charm. She was his " *liebe, leidende, und
doch so rührende, heitre Freundin*" ("his dear, suffering,
touching friend, always so bright and cheerful "). And sometimes, in the evening, when he left her with his heart big with
love so that he could not wait until the morrow, he would write:

" Liebe, liebe, liebe, liebe, liebe Grazia. . . ."

Their tranquillity lasted for months. They thought it would
last forever. The boy seemed to have forgotten them: his
attention was distracted by other things. But after this respite
he returned to them and never left them again. The horrible
little boy had determined to part his mother and Christophe.
He resumed his play-acting. He did not set about it upon any
premeditated plan, but, from day to day, followed the whimsies
of his spite. He had no idea of the harm he might be doing:
he only wanted to amuse himself by boring other people. He
never relaxed his efforts until he had made Grazia promise to
leave Paris and go on a long journey. Grazia had no strength
to resist him. Besides, the doctors advised her to pay a visit to

Egypt.   She had to avoid another winter in the northern climate. Too many things had tried her health: the moral upheaval of the last few years, the perpetual anxiety about her son's health, the long periods of uncertainty, the struggle that had taken place in her without her giving any sign of it, the sorrow of sorrows that she was inflicting on her friend.   To avoid adding to the trouble he divined in her, Christophe hid his own grief at the approach of the day of parting: he made no effort to postpone it; and they were outwardly calm, and, though inwardly they were very far from it, yet they succeeded in forcing it upon each other.

The day came.   A September morning.   They had left Paris together in the middle of July, and spent their last weeks in Switzerland in a mountain hotel, near the place where they had met again six years ago.

They were unable to go out the last five days: the rain came down in unceasing torrents: they were almost alone in the hotel, for all the other travelers had fled.   The rain stopped on their last morning, but the mountains were still covered with clouds.   The children went on ahead with the servants in another carriage.   She drove off.   He accompanied her to the place where the road began to descend in steep windings to the plain of Italy.   The mist came in under the hood of the carriage.   They were very close together, and they said no word: they hardly looked at each other.   A strange light, half-day, half-night, wrapped them round. . . .   Grazia's breath left little drops of water on her veil.   He pressed her little hand, warm under her cold glove.   Their faces came together. Through her wet veil he kissed her dear lips.

They came to the turn of the road.   He got down, and the carriage plunged on into the mist and disappeared.   For a long time he could hear the rumbling of the wheels and the horses' hoofs.   Great masses of white mist rolled over the fields. Through the close tracery of the branches the dripping trees dropped water.   Not a breath of wind.   The mist was stifling life.   Christophe stopped, choking. . . .   There was nothing now.   Everything had gone. . . .

He took in a long breath, filling his lungs with the mist, and walked on.   Nothing passes for him who does not pass.

III

ABSENCE adds to the power of those we love. The heart retains only what is dear to us in them. The echo of each word coming through space from the distant friend, rings out in the silence, faithfully answering.

The correspondence of Christophe and Grazia took on the serious and restrained tone of a couple who are no longer in the dangerous period of trial of love, but, having passed it, feel sure of the road and march on hand in hand. Each was strong to sustain and direct the other, weak and yielding to the other's support and direction.

Christophe returned to Paris. He had vowed never to go there again. But what are such vows worth? He knew that he would find there the shade of Grazia. And circumstances, conspiring with his secret desires against his will, showed him a new duty to fulfil in Paris. Colette, well informed as to society gossip, told Christophe that his young friend Jeannin was making a fool of himself. Jacqueline, who had always been weak in her dealings with her son, could not hold him in check. She herself was passing through a strange crisis, and was too much occupied with herself to pay much heed to him.

Since the unhappy adventure which had destroyed Olivier's marriage and life, Jacqueline had lived a very worthy life. She withdrew from Parisian society, which, after imposing on her a hypocritical sort of quarantine, had made fresh advances to her, which she had rejected. She was not at all ashamed of what she had done as far as these people were concerned: she thought she had no reason to account to them for it, for they were more worthless than she: what she had done openly, half the women she knew did by stealth, under cover of their homes. She suffered only from the thought of the wrong she had done her nearest and dearest, the only man she had loved. She could not forgive herself for having, in so poor a world, lost an affection like his.

Her regrets, and her sorrow, grew less acute with time. There were left only a sort of mute suffering, a humiliated contempt for herself and others, and the love of her child. This affection, into which she poured all her need of love, disarmed her before him; she could not resist Georges's caprices. To excuse her weakness she persuaded herself that she was paying for the wrong she had done Olivier. She had alternate periods of exalted tenderness and weary indifference: sometimes she would worry Georges with her exacting, anxious love, and sometimes she would seem to tire of him, and she let him do as he liked. She admitted to herself that she was bringing him up badly, and she would torment herself with the admission; but she made no change. When, as she rarely did, she tried to model her principles of conduct on Olivier's way of thinking, the result was deplorable. At heart she wished to have no authority over her son save that of her affection. And she was not wrong: for between these two, however similar they might be, there were no bonds save those of the heart. Georges Jeannin was sensible of his mother's physical charm: he loved her voice, her gestures, her movements, her grace, her love. But in mind he was conscious of strangerhood to her. She only saw it as he began to grow into a man, when he turned from her. Then she was amazed and indignant, and attributed the estrangement to other feminine influences: and, as she tried awkwardly to combat them, she only estranged him more. In reality, they had always lived, side by side, each preoccupied with totally different interests, deceiving themselves as to the gulf that lay between them, with the aid of their common surface sympathies and antipathies, which disappeared when the man began to spring forth from the boy (that ambiguous creature, still impregnated with the perfume of womanhood). And bitterly Jacqueline would say to her son:

"I don't know whom you take after. You are not like your father or me."

So she made him feel all that lay between them; and he took a secret pride that was yet feverish and uneasy.

The younger generation has always a keener sense than the elder of the things that lie between them; they need to gain assurance of the importance of their existence, even at the cost of injustice or of lying to themselves. But this feeling varies in its acuteness from one period to another. In the classic ages

when, for a time, the balance of the forces of a civilization are
realized,—those high plateaux ending on all sides with steep
slopes—the difference in level is not so great from one generation to another. But in the ages of renascence or decadence.
the young men climbing or plunging down the giddy slopes.
leave their predecessors far behind.—Georges, like the other
young men of his time, was ascending the mountain.

He was superior neither in character nor in mind: he had
many aptitudes, none of which rose above the level of elegant
mediocrity. And yet, without any effort on his part, he found
himself at the outset of his career several grades higher than
his father, who, in his short life, had expended an incalculable
amount of intellect and energy.

Hardly were the eyes of his mind opened upon the light of
day than he saw all round him the heaped-up darkness, pierced
by luminous gleams, the masses of knowledge and ignorance,
warring truths, contradictory errors, in which his father and
the men of his father's generation had feverishly groped their
way. But at the same time he became conscious of a weapon
in his power which they had never known: his force. . . .
Whence did he have it? . . . Who can tell the mystery
of the resurrections of a race, sleeping, worn out, which suddenly
awakes brimming like a mountain torrent in the spring! . . .
What would he do with his force? Use it in his turn to explore
the inextricable thickets of modern thought? They had no
attraction for him. He was oppressed by the menacing dangers
which lurked in them. They had crushed his father. Rather
than renew that experience and enter the tragic forest he would
have set fire to it. He had only to glance at the books of wisdom
or sacred folly which had intoxicated Olivier: the Nihilist pity
of Tolstoi, the somber destructive pride of Ibsen, the frenzy
of Nietzsche, the heroic, sensual pessimism of Wagner. He had
turned away from them in anger and terror. He hated the
realistic writers who, for half a century, had killed the joy
of art. He could not, however, altogether blot out the shadows
of the sorrowful dream in which he had been cradled. He
would not look behind him, but he well knew that the shadow
was there. He was too healthy to seek a counter-irritant to
his uneasiness in the lazy skepticism of the preceding epoch:

he detested the dilettantism of men like Renan and Anatole France, with their degradation of the free intellect, their joyless mirth, their irony without greatness: a shameful method, fit for slaves, playing with the chains which they are impotent to break.

He was too vigorous to be satisfied with doubt, too weak to create the conviction which, with all his soul, he desired. He asked for it, prayed for it, demanded it. And the eternal snappers-up of popularity, the great writers, the sham thinkers at bay, exploited this imperious and agonized desire, by beating the drums and shouting the clap-trap of their nostrum. From trestles, each of these Hippocrates bawled that his was the only true elixir, and decried all the rest. Their secrets were all equally worthless. None of these pedlars had taken the trouble to find a new recipe. They had hunted about among their old empty bottles. The panacea of one was the Catholic Church: another's was legitimate monarchy: yet another's, the classic tradition. There were queer fellows who declared that the remedy for all evils lay in the return to Latin. Others seriously prognosticated, with an enormous word which imposed on the herd, the domination of the Mediterranean spirit. (They would have been just as ready at some other time to talk of the Atlantic spirit.) Against the barbarians of the North and the East they pompously set up the heirs of a new Roman Empire. . . . Words, words, all second-hand. The refuse of the libraries scattered to the winds.—Like all his comrades, young Jeannin went from one showman to another, listened to their patter, was sometimes taken in by it, and entered the booth, only to come out disappointed and rather ashamed of having spent his time and his money in watching old clowns buffooning in shabby rags. And yet, such is youth's power of illusion, such was his certainty of gaining certainty, that he was always taken in by each new promise of each new vendor of hope. He was very French, of a hypercritical temper, and an innate lover of order. He needed a leader and could bear none; his pitiless irony always riddled them through and through.

While he was waiting for the advent of a leader who should give him the key to the riddle . . . he had no time to wait. He was not the kind of man, like his father, to be satisfied with the lifelong search for truth. With or without a motive, he needed always to make up his mind, to act, to turn to account, to use his energy. Traveling, the delight of art, and especially of music, with which he had gorged himself, had at first been to him an intermittent and passionate diversion. He was handsome, ardent, precocious, beset with temptations, and he early discovered the outwardly enchanting world of love, and plunged into it with an unbridled, poetic, greedy joy. Then this impertinently naïve and insatiable cherub wearied of women: he needed action, so he gave himself up uncontrollably to sport. He tried everything, practised everything. He was always going to fencing and boxing matches: he was the French champion runner and high-jumper, and captain of a football team. He competed with a number of other crazy, reckless, rich young men like himself in ridiculous, wild motor races. Finally he threw up everything for the latest fad, and was drawn into the popular craze for flying machines. At the Rheims meetings he shouted and wept for joy with three hundred thousand other men; he felt that he was one with the whole people in a religious jubilation; the human birds flying over their heads bore them upwards in their flight: for the first time since the dawn of the great Revolution the vast multitude had raised their eyes to the heavens and seen them open.—To his mother's terror young Jeannin declared that he was going to throw in his lot with the conquerors of the air. Jacqueline implored him to give up his perilous ambition. She ordered him to do so. He took the bit between his teeth. Christophe, in whom Jacqueline thought she had found an ally, only gave the boy a little prudent advice, which he felt quite sure Georges would not follow (for, in his place, he would not have done so). He did not deem that he had any right,—even had he been able to do so—to fetter the healthy and normal expansion of the boy's vitality, which, if it had been forced into inaction, would have been perverted to his destruction.

Jacqueline could not reconcile herself to seeing her son leave her. She had vainly thought that she had renounced love, for she could not do without the illusion of love; all her affections, all her actions were tinged with it. There are so many mothers who expend on their sons all the secret ardor which they have been unable to give forth in marriage—or out of it! And when they see how easily their sons do without them, when suddenly they understand that they are not necessary to them, they go through the same kind of crisis as befalls them upon the betrayal of a lover, or the disillusion of love.—Once more Jacqueline's whole existence crumbled away. Georges saw nothing. Young people never have any idea of the tragedies of the heart going on around them: they have no time to stop and see them: and they do not wish to see: a selfish instinct bids them march straight on without looking to right or left.

Jacqueline was left alone to gulp down this new sorrow. She only emerged from it when her grief was worn out, worn out like her love. She still loved her son, but with a distant, disillusioned affection, which she knew to be futile, and she lost all interest in herself and him. So she dragged through a wretched, miserable year, without his paying her any heed. And then, poor creature, since her heart could neither live nor die without love, she was forced to find something to love. She fell victim to a strange passion, such as often takes possession of women, and especially, it would seem, of the noblest and most inaccessible, when maturity comes and the fair fruit of life has not been gathered. She made the acquaintance of a woman who, from their first meeting, gained an ascendancy over her through her mysterious power of attraction.

This woman was about her own age, and she was a nun. She was always busy with charitable works. A tall, fine, rather stout woman, dark, with rather bold, handsome features, sharp eyes, a big, sensitive, ever-smiling mouth, and a masterful chin. She was remarkably intelligent, and not at all sentimental; she had the malice of a peasant, a keen business sense, and a southern imagination, which saw everything in exaggeration, though always exactly to scale when necessary: she was a strangely enticing mixture of lofty mysticism and lawyer's cunning. She was used to domination, and the exercise of it was a habit with her. Jacqueline was drawn to her at once. She became enthusiastic over her work, or, at least, believed herself to be so. Sister Angèle knew perfectly what was the object of her passion: she was used to provoking them; and without seeming to notice them, she used skilfully to turn them to account for her work and the glory of God. Jacqueline gave up her money, her will, her heart. She was charitable, so she believed, through love.

It was not long before her infatuation was observed. She was the only person not to realize it. Georges's guardian became anxious. Georges was too generous and too easy to worry about money matters, though he saw his mother's subjection, and was shocked by it. He tried, too late in the day, to resume his old intimacy with her, and saw that a veil was drawn between them; he blamed the occult influence for it, and, both against his mother and the nun, whom he called an intriguer, he conceived a feeling of irritation which he made no attempt to disguise: he could not admit a stranger to his place in a heart that he had regarded as his natural right. It never occurred to him that his place was taken because he had left it. Instead of trying patiently to win it back, he was clumsy and cruel. Quick words passed between mother and son, both of whom were hasty and passionate, and the rupture grew marked. Sister Angèle established her ascendancy over Jacqueline, and Georges rushed away and kicked over the traces. He plunged into a restless, dissipated life; gambled, lost large sums of money; he put a certain amount of exaggeration into his extravagances, partly for his own pleasure and partly to counterbalance his mother's extravagances.—He knew the Stevens-Delestrades. Colette had marked down the handsome boy, and tried the effect on him of her charms, which she never wearied of using. She knew of all Georges's freaks, and was vastly entertained by them. But her sound common sense and the real kindness concealed beneath her frivolity, helped her to see the danger the young idiot was running. And, being well aware that it was beyond her to save him, she warned Christophe, who came at once.

Christophe was the only person who had any influence over young Jeannin. His influence was limited and very intermittent, but all the more remarkable in that it was difficult to explain. Christophe belonged to the preceding generation against which Georges and his companions were violently in reaction. He was one of the most conspicuous representatives

of that period of torment whose art and ideas rouse in them
a feeling of suspicion and hostility. He was unmoved by the
new Gospels and the charms of the minor prophets and the
old cheapjacks who were offering the young men an infallible
recipe for the salvation of the world, Rome and France. He
was faithful to the free faith, free of all religion, free of all
parties, free of all countries, which was no longer the fashion—
or had never been fashionable. Finally, though he was altogether removed from national questions, he was a foreigner in
Paris at a time when all foreigners were regarded by the natives
of the country as barbarians.

And yet, young Jeannin, joyous, easy-going, instinctively
hostile to everything that might make him sad or uneasy, ardent
in pursuit of pleasure, engrossed in violent sports, easily duped
by the rhetoric of his time, in his physical vigor and mental
indolence inclined to the brutal doctrines of French action,
nationalist, royalist, imperialist—(he did not exactly know)—
in his heart reflected only one man: Christophe. His precocious experience and the delicate tact he had inherited from
his mother made him see (without being in the least disturbed
by it) how little worth was the world that he could not live
without, and how superior to it was Christophe. From Olivier
he had inherited a vague uneasiness, which visited him in sudden
fits that never lasted very long, a need of finding and deciding
on some definite aim for what he was doing. And perhaps it
was from Olivier that he had also inherited the mysterious instinct which drew him towards the man whom Olivier had
loved.

He used to go and see Christophe. He was expansive by
nature, and of a rather chattering temper, and he loved indulging in confidences. He never troubled to think whether
Christophe had time to listen to him. But Christophe always
did listen, and never gave any sign of impatience. Only sometimes he would be rather absent-minded when Georges had interrupted him in his work, but never for more than a few
minutes, when his mind would be away putting the finishing
touches to its work: then it would return to Georges, who never
noticed its absence. He used to laugh at the evasion, and come
back like a man tiptoeing into the room, so as not to be heard

But once or twice Georges did notice it, and then he said indignantly:

"But you are not listening!"

Then Christophe was ashamed: and docilely he would listen to Georges's story, and try to win his forgiveness by redoubled attention. The stories were often very funny: and Christophe could not help laughing at the tale of some wild freak: for Georges kept nothing back: his frankness was disarming.

Christophe did not always laugh. Georges's conduct sometimes pained him. Christophe was no saint: he knew he had no right to moralize over anybody. Georges's love affairs, and the scandalous waste of his fortune in folly, were not what shocked him most. What he found it most hard to forgive was the light-mindedness with which Georges regarded his sins: they were no burden to him: he though them very natural. His conception of morality was very different from Christophe's. He was one of those young men who are fain to see in the relation of the sexes nothing more than a game that has no moral aspect whatever. A certain frankness and a careless kindliness were all that was necessary for an honest man. He was not troubled with Christophe's scruples. Christophe would wax wrath. In vain did he try not to impose his way of feeling upon others: he could not be tolerant. and his old violence was only half tamed. Every now and then he would explode. He could not help seeing how dirty were some of Georges's intrigues, and he used bluntly to tell him so. Georges was no more patient than he, and they used to have angry scenes, after which they would not see each other for weeks. Christophe would realize that his outbursts were not likely to change Georges's conduct, and that it was perhaps unjust to subject the morality of a period to the moral ideas of another generation. But his feeling was too strong for him, and on the next opportunity he would break out again. How can one renounce the faith for which one has lived? That were to renounce life. What is the good of laboring to think thoughts other than one's own, to be like one's neighbor or to meddle with his affairs? That leads to self-destruction, and no one is benefited by it. The first duty is to be what one is, to dare to say: "This is good, that bad." One profits the weak more by being strong than by sharing their weakness. Be indulgent, if you like, towards weakness and past sins. But never compromise with any weakness. . . .

Yes: but Georges never by any chance consulted Christophe about anything he was going to do:—(did he know himself?).— He only told him about things when they were done.—And then? . . . Then, what could he do but look in dumb reproach at the culprit, and shrug his shoulders and smile, like an old uncle who knows that he is not heeded?

On such occasions they would sit for several minutes in silence. Georges would look up at Christophe's grave eyes, which seemed to be gazing at him from far away. And he would feel like a little boy in his presence. He would see himself as he was, in that penetrating glance, which was shot with a gleam of malice: and he was not proud of it.

Christophe hardly ever made use of Georges's confidences against him; it was often as though he had not heard them. After the mute dialogue of their eyes, he would shake his head mockingly, and then begin to tell a story without any apparent bearing on the story he had just been told, some story about his life, or some one else's life, real or fictitious. And gradually Georges would see his double (he recognized it at once) under a new light, grotesquely, ridiculously postured, passing through vagaries similar to his own. Christophe never added any commentary. The extraordinary kindliness of the story-teller would produce far more effect than the story. He would speak of himself just as he spoke of others, with the same detachment, the same jovial, serene humor. Georges was impressed by his tranquillity. It was for this that he came. When he had unburdened himself of his light-hearted confession, he was like a man stretching out his limbs and lying at full length in the shade of a great tree on a summer afternoon. The dazzling fever of the scorching day would fall away from him. Above him he would feel the hovering of protecting wings. In the presence of this man who so peacefully bore the heavy burden of his life, he was sheltered from his own inward restlessness. He found rest only in hearing him speak. He did not always listen: his mind would wander, but wheresoever it went, it was surrounded by Christophe's laughter.

However, he did not understand his old friend's ideas. He used to wonder how Christophe could bear his soul's solitude, and dispense with being bound to any artistic, political, or religious party, or any group of men. He used to ask him: "Don't you ever want to take refuge in a camp of some sort?"

"Take refuge?" Christophe would say with a laugh. "It is much too good outside. And you, an open-air man, talk of shutting yourself up?"

"Ah!" Georges would reply. "It is not the same thing for body and soul. The mind needs certainty: it needs to think with others, to adhere to the principles admitted by all the men of the time. I envy the men of old days, the men of the classic ages. My friends are right in their desire to restore the order of the past."

"Milksop!" said Christophe. "What have I to do with such disheartened creatures?"

"I am not disheartened," protested Georges indignantly. "None of us is that."

"But you must be," said Christophe, "to be afraid of yourselves. What! You need order and cannot create it for yourselves? You must always be clinging to your great-grandmother's skirts! Dear God! You must walk alone!"

"One must take root," said Georges, proudly echoing one of the pontiffs of the time.

"But do you think the trees need to be shut up in a box to take root? The earth is there for all of us. Plunge your roots into it. Find your own laws. Look to yourself."

"I have no time," said Georges.

"You are afraid," insisted Christophe.

Georges indignantly denied it, but in the end he agreed that he had no taste for examining his inmost soul: he could not understand what pleasure there could be in it: there was the danger of falling over if you looked down into the abyss.

"Give me your hand," said Christophe.

He would amuse himself by opening the trap-door of his

realistic, tragic vision of life.   Georges would draw away from
it, and Christophe would shut it down again, laughing:

" How can you live like that? " Georges would ask.

" I am alive, and I am happy," Christophe would reply.

" I should die if I were forced to see things like that always."
Christophe would slap him on the shoulder:

" Fine athlete you are! . . .   Well, don't look, if your head
is not strong enough.   There is nothing to make you, after all.
Go ahead, my boy.   But do you need a master to brand your
shoulder, like a sheep?   What is the word of command you
are waiting for?   The signal was given long ago.   The signal
to saddle has sounded, and the cavalry is on the march.   Don't
worry about anything but your horse.   Take your place!   And
gallop! "

" But where to? " asked Georges.

" With your regiment to the conquest of the world.   Conquer
the air, master the elements, dig the last entrenchment of
Nature, set back space, drive back death . . .

" *Expertus vacuum Dædalus aera.* . . ."

" . . . Do you know that, you champion of Latin?   Can you
even tell me what it means?

" *Perrupit Acheronta.* . . ."

" That is your lot, you happy *conquistadores!* "

So clearly did he show the duty of heroic action that had
devolved upon the new generation, that Georges was amazed,
and said:

" But if you feel that, why don't you come with us? "

" Because I have a different task.   Go, my boy, do your
work.   Surpass me, if you can.   But I stay here and watch. . . .
Have you read the Arabian Night in which a genii, as tall as
a mountain, is imprisoned in a bottle sealed with the seal of
Solomon? . . .   The genii is here, in the depths of our soul,
the soul into which you are afraid to look down.   I and the
men of my time spent our lives in struggling with him: we
did not conquer him: he conquered us.   At present we are both
recovering our breath, and, with no rancor nor fear, we are
looking at each other, satisfied with the struggles in which we
have been engaged, waiting for the agreed armistice to expire.
You are profiting by the armistice to gather your strength and

cull the world's beauty. Be happy. Enjoy the lull. But remember that one day, you or your children, on your return from your conquests, will have to come back to the place where I stand and resume the combat, with new forces, against the genii by whose side I watch and wait. And the combat will endure with intervals of armistice until one of the two (perhaps both) will be laid low. It is your duty to be stronger and happier than we! . . .—Meanwhile, indulge in your sport if you like: stiffen your muscles and strengthen your heart: and do not be so foolish as to waste your impatient vigor upon silly trifles: you belong to an age that, if you are patient, will find a use for it."

Georges did not remember much of what Christophe said to him. He was open-minded enough to grasp Christophe's ideas, but they escaped him at once. He forgot everything before he reached the bottom of the stairs. But all the same, he had a feeling of well-being, which endured when the memory of the words that had produced it had long been wiped out. He had a real veneration for Christophe. He believed in nothing that Christophe believed in (at heart he laughed at everything and had no belief). But he would have broken the head of any man who took upon himself to speak ill of his old friend.

Fortunately, no one did speak ill of him in his presence, otherwise he would have been kept busy.

Christophe had accurately forecast the next change of the wind. The new ideal of the new French music was very different from his own; but while that was a reason the more for Christophe to sympathize with it, its exponents had no sympathy with him. His vogue with the public was not likely to reconcile the most hungry for recognition of these young men to him; they were meagerly fed, and their teeth were long, and they bit. Christophe was not put out by their spite.

"How thoroughly they do it!" he would say. "These boys are cutting their teeth. . . ."

He was inclined to prefer them to the other puppies who fawned on him because of his success—those people of whom D'Aubigné writes, who *" when a mastiff plunges his nose into a butter-pot, come and lick his whiskers by way of congratulation."*

He had a piece accepted at the Opéra. Almost at once it was put into rehearsal. Through a newspaper attack Christophe learned that a certain young composer's piece had been postponed for it. The writer of the article waxed indignant over such abuse of power, and made Christophe responsible for it.

Christophe went to see the manager, and said:

" Why didn't you tell me? You must not do it. You must put on the opera you accepted before mine."

The manager protested, began to laugh, refused, covered Christophe's character, work, genius, with flattery, and said that the other man's work was beneath contempt, and assured him that it was worthless and would not make a sou.

" Why did you accept it then? "

" One can't always do as one likes. Every now and then one has to throw a sop to public opinion. Formerly these young men could shout as much as they pleased. And no one listened to them. But now they are able to let loose on us the nationalist Press, which roars ' Treason ' and calls you a disloyal Frenchman because you happen to have the misfortune to be unable to go into ecstasies over the younger school. The younger school! Let's look at it! . . . Shall I tell you what I think of it? I'm sick of it! So is the public. They bore us with their *Oremus!* . . . There's no blood in their veins: they're like sacristans chanting Mass: their love duets are like the *De Profundis.* . . . If I were fool enough to put on the pieces I am compelled to accept, I should ruin my theater. I accept them: that is all they can ask.—Let us talk of something serious. Your work means a full house. . . ."

And he went on with his compliments.

Christophe cut him short, and said angrily:

" I am not taken in. Now that I am old and have ' arrived,' you are using me to suppress the young men. When I was a young man you would have suppressed me in just the same way. You must play this boy's piece, or I shall withdraw my own."

The manager threw up his hands, and said:

" But don't you see that if we did what you want, it would look as if we were giving in to these newspaper attacks? "

" What do I care? " said Christophe.

" As you please! You will be their first victim."

They put the young musician's piece into rehearsal without interrupting the preparation of Christophe's. One was in three acts, the other in two: it was arranged to include them both in one program. Christophe went to see the young man, for he wanted to be the first to give him the news. The musician was loud in his promises of eternal gratitude.

Naturally Christophe could not make the manager not devote all his attention to his piece. The interpretation and the scenery of the other were rather scamped. Christophe knew nothing about it. He asked to be allowed to be present at a few rehearsals of the young man's opera: he thought it very mediocre, as he had been told: he ventured to give a little advice which was ill-received: he gave it up then, and did not interfere again On the other hand, the manager had made the young man admit the necessity for a little cutting to have his piece produced in time. Though the sacrifice was easily consented to at first, it was not long before the author regretted it.

On the evening of the performance the beginner's piece had no success, and Christophe's caused a sensation. Some of the papers attacked Christophe: they spoke of a trick, a plot to suppress a great young French artist: they said that his work had been mutilated to please the German master, whom they represented to be basely jealous of the coming fame of all the new men. Christophe shrugged his shoulders and thought:

" He will reply."

" He " did not reply. Christophe sent him one of the paragraphs with these words:

" Have you read this? "

The other replied:

" How sorry I am! The writer of it has always been so well disposed towards me! Really, I am very sorry. The best thing is to pay no attention to it."

Christophe laughed and thought:

" He is right! The little sneak."

And he decided to forget all about it.

But chance would have it that Georges, who seldom read the papers, and that hastily, except for the sporting articles, should light on the most violent attacks on Christophe. He knew the writer. He went to the café where he knew he would meet him, found him, struck him, fought a duel with him, and gave him a nasty scratch on the shoulder with his rapier.

Next day, at breakfast, Christophe had a letter from a friend telling him of the affair. He was overcome. He left his breakfast and hurried to see Georges. Georges himself opened the door. Christophe rushed in like a whirlwind, seized him by the arms, and shook him angrily, and began to overwhelm him with a storm of furious reproaches.

"You little wretch!" he cried. "You have fought a duel for me! Who gave you leave! A boy, a fly-by-night, to meddle in my affairs! Do you think I can't look after myself? What good have you done? You have done this rascal the honor of fighting him. He asked no more. You have made him a hero. Idiot! And if it had chanced . . . (I am sure you rushed at it like a madman as usual) . . . if you had been wounded, killed perhaps! . . . You wretch! I should never have forgiven you as long as you lived! . . ."

Georges laughed uproariously at this last threat, and was so overcome with merriment, that he cried:

"My dear old friend, how funny you are! Ah! You're unique! Here are you insulting me for having defended you! Next time I shall attack you. Perhaps you'll embrace me then."

Christophe stopped and hugged Georges, and kissed him on both cheeks. and then once more he said:

"My boy! . . . Forgive me. I am an old idiot. . . . But my blood boiled when I heard the news. What made you think of fighting? You don't fight with such people. Promise me at once that you will never do it again."

"I'll promise nothing of the kind," said Georges. "I shall do as I like."

"I forbid it. Do you hear? If you do it again, I'll never see you again. I shall publicly disown you in the newspapers. I shall . . ."

"You will disinherit me, you mean."

" Come, Georges. Please. What's the good of it ? "

" My dear old friend, you are a thousand times a better man than I am, and you know infinitely more: but I know these people better than you do. Make yourself easy. It will do some good. They will think a little now before they let loose their poisonous insults upon you."

" But what can these idiots do to me? I laugh at anything they may say."

" But I don't. And you must mind your own business."

Thereafter Christophe lived on tenterhooks lest some fresh article might rouse Georges's susceptibilities. It was quite comic to see him during the next few days going to a café and devouring the newspapers, which he never read as a rule, ready to go to all lengths (even to trickery) if he found an insulting article, to prevent it reaching Georges. After a week he re-covered his equanimity. The boy was right. His action had given the yelping curs food for a moment's reflection.—And, though Christophe went on grumbling at the young lunatic who had made him waste eight working days, he said to himself that, after all, he had no right to lecture him. He remembered a certain day, not so very long ago, when he himself had fought a duel for Olivier's sake. And he thought he heard Olivier's voice saying:

" Let be, Christophe. I am giving you back what you lent me ! "

Though Christophe took the attacks on himself lightly, there was one other man who was very far from such disinterestedness. This was Emmanuel.

The evolution of European thought was progressing swiftly. It was as though it had been accelerated by mechanical inventions and the new motors. The stock of prejudices and hopes which in old days were enough to feed humanity for twenty years was now exhausted in five years. The generations of the mind were galloping ahead, one behind the other, often one trampling the other down, with Time sounding the charge.—Emmanuel had been left behind.

The singer of French energy had never denied the idealism of his master, Olivier. Passionate as was his national feeling, he identified himself with his worship of moral greatness. If in his poetry he loudly proclaimed the triumph of France, it was because in her, by an act of faith, he adored the loftiest ideas of modern Europe, the Athena Nike, the victorious Law which takes its revenge on Force.—And now Force had awakened in the very heart of Law, and it was springing up in all its savage nakedness. The new generation, robust and disciplined, was longing for combat, and, before its victory was won, had the attitude of mind of the conqueror. This generation was proud of its strength, its thews, its mighty chest, its vigorous senses so thirsting for delight. its wings like the wings of a bird of prey hovering over the plains, waiting to swoop down and try its talons. The prowess of the race, the mad flights over the Alps and the sea, the new crusades, not much less mystic, not much less interested than those of Philip Augustus and Villehardouin, had turned the nation's head. The children of the nation who had never seen war except in books had no difficulty in endowing it with beauty. They became aggressive. Weary of peace and ideas, they hymned the anvil of battle, on which, with bloody fists, action would one day new-forge the power of France. In reaction against the disgusting abuse of systems of ideas, they raised contempt of the idea to the level of a profession of faith. Blusteringly they exalted narrow common sense, violent realism, immodest national egoism, trampling underfoot the rights of others and other nations, when it served the turn of their country's greatness. They were xenophobes, anti-democrats, and—even the most skeptical of them—set up the return to Catholicism. in the practical necessity for " digging channels for the absolute," and shutting up the infinite under the surveillance of order and authority. They were not content to despise—they regarded the gentle dotards of the preceding generation, the visionary idealists, the humanitarian thinkers of the preceding generation, as public malefactors. Emmanuel was among them in the eyes of the young men. He suffered cruelly and was very angry.

The knowledge that Christophe was, like himself,—more than himself—the victim of their injustice, made him sympathetic. His ungraciousness had discouraged Christophe's visits. He was too proud to show his regret by seeking him out. But he

contrived to meet him, as if by chance, and forced Christophe
to make the first advances.   Thereafter his umbrageous susceptibilities were at rest, and he did not conceal the pleasure he
had in Christophe's company.   Thereafter they often met in
each other's rooms.

Emmanuel confided his bitterness to Christophe.   He was
exasperated by certain criticisms, and, thinking that Christophe
was not sufficiently moved by them, he made him read some
of the newspaper appreciations of himself.   Christophe was
accused of not knowing the grammar of his work, of being
ignorant of harmony, of having stolen from other musicians,
and, generally, of dishonoring music.   He was called: " This
old toss-brain. . . ."   They said: " We have had enough
of these convulsionaries.   We are order, reason, classic balance. . . ."

Christophe was vastly entertained.

" It is the law," he said.   " The young bury the old. . . .
In my day, it is true, we waited until a man was sixty before
we called him an old man.   They are going faster, nowadays. . . .   Wireless telegraphy, aeroplanes. . . .   A generation is more quickly exploded. . . .   Poor devils!   They
won't last long!   Let them despise us and strut about in the
sun ! "

But Emmanuel had not his sanity.   Though he was fearless
in thought, he was a prey to his diseased nerves; with his ardent
soul in his rickety body, he was driven on to the fight and
was unfitted for it.   The animosity of certain opinions of his
work drew blood.

" Ah ! " he would say.   " If the critics knew the harm they
do artists by the unjust words they throw out so recklessly,
they would be ashamed of their trade."

" But they do know, my friend.   That is the justification
of their existence.   Everybody must live."

" They are butchers.   One is drenched with the blood of life,
worn out by the struggle we have to wage with art.   Instead
of holding out their hands to us, and compassionately telling
us of our faults, and brotherly helping us to mend them, they
stand there with their hands in their pockets and watch you
dragging your burden up the slope, and say: ' You can't do

it!' And when you reach the top, some of them say: 'Yes, but that is not the way to climb up.' While the others go on blandly saying: 'You couldn't do it! . . .' You're lucky if they don't send great stones rolling down on you to send you flying!'"

"Bah! There are plenty of good men among them, and think of the good they can do! There are bad men everywhere. They're not peculiar to criticism. Do you know anything worse than an ungenerous, vain, and embittered artist, to whom the world is only loot, that he is furious because he cannot grab? You must don patience for your protection. There is no evil but it may be of good service. The worst of the critics is useful to us; he is a trainer: he does not let us loiter by the way. Whenever we think we have reached the goal, the pack hound us on. Get on! Onward! Upward! They are more likely to weary of running after me than I am of marching ahead of them. Remember the Arabian proverb: '*It is no use flogging sterile trees. Only those are stoned whose front is crowned with golden fruit. . . .*' Let us pity the artists who are spared. They will stay half-way, lazily sitting down. When they try to get up their legs will be so stiff that they will be unable to walk. Long live my friend the enemy! They do me more good in my life than the enemy, my friend!'"

Emmanuel could not help smiling. Then he said:

"All the same, don't you think it hard for a veteran like you to be taken to task by recruits who are just approaching their first battle?"

"They amuse me," said Christophe. "Such arrogance is the mark of young, hot blood tingling to be up and doing. I was like that once. They are like the showers of March falling on the new-born soil. . . . Let them take us to task! They are right, after all. Old people must learn from the young! They have profited by us, and are ungrateful: that is in the order of things. But, being enriched by our efforts, they will go farther than we, and will realize what we attempted. If we still have some youth left, let us learn in our turn, and try to rejuvenate ourselves. If we cannot, if we are too old, let us rejoice in them. It is fine to see the perpetual new-flowering of the human soul that seemed exhausted, the vigorous

optimism of these young men, their delight in action and adventures, the races springing to new life for the conquest of the
world."

" What would they be without us? Their joy is the fruit
of our tears. Their proud force is the flower of the sufferings
of a whole generation. *Sic vos non nobis.* . . ."

" The old saying is wrong. It is for ourselves that we
worked, and our reward lies in the creation of a race of men
who shall surpass us. We amassed their treasury, we hoarded
it in a wretched hovel open to all the winds of Heaven: we had
to strain every nerve to keep the doors closed against death.
Our arms carved out the triumphal way along which our sons
shall march. Our sufferings have saved the future. We have
borne the Ark to the threshold of the Promised Land. It will
reach that Land with them, and through us."

" Will they ever remember those who crossed the wilderness,
bearing the sacred fire, the gods of our race, and them, those
children, who now are men? For our share we have had tribulation and ingratitude."

" Do you regret it? "

" No. There is a sort of intoxication in the tragic grandeur
of the sacrifice of a mighty epoch like ours to the epoch that
it has brought into being. The men of to-day would not
be more capable of tasting the sovereign joy of renunciation."

" We have been the happier. We have scaled Mount Nebo,
at whose feet lie stretched the countries that we shall never
enter. But we enjoy them more than those who will enter
them. When you descend to the plain, you lose sight of the
plain's immensity and the far horizon."

The soothing influence that Christophe exercised over Georges
and Emmanuel had the source of its power in Grazia's love.
It was through this love that he felt himself so near to all
young things, and had an inexhaustible fund of sympathy for
every new form of life. Whatever the forces might be that
rekindled the earth, he was always with them, even when they
were against him: he had no fear for the immediate future of
the democracies, that future which caused such an outcry against

the egoism of a handful of privileged men: he did not cling desperately to the paternosters of an old art: he felt quite sure that from the fabulous visions, the realized dreams of science and action, a new art, more puissant than the old, would spring forth: he hailed the new dawn of the world, even though the beauty of the old world were to die with it.

Grazia knew the good that her love did for Christophe: and this consciousness of her power lifted her out of herself. Through her letters she exercised a controlling power over her friend. She was not so absurdly pretentious as to try to control his art: she had too much tact, and knew her limitations. But her true, pure voice was the diapason to which he attuned his soul. Christophe had only to hear her voice echoing his thought to think nothing that was not just, pure, and worthy of repetition. The sound of a beautiful instrument is to a musician like a beautiful body in which his dream at once becomes incarnate. Mysterious is the fusion of two loving spirits: each takes the best from the other, but only to give it back again enriched with love. Grazia was not afraid to tell Christophe that she loved him. Distance gave her more freedom of speech, and also, the certain knowledge that she would never be his. Her love, the religious fervor of which was communicated to Christophe, was a fountain of force and peace to him.

Grazia gave to others more of such force and peace than she had herself. Her health was shattered, her moral balance seriously affected. Her son's condition did not improve. For the last two years she had lived in a perpetual state of anxiety, aggravated by Lionello's fatal skill in playing on it. He had acquired a consummate mastery of the art of keeping those who loved him on tenterhooks: his idle mind was most fertile in inventing ways of rousing interest in himself and tormenting others: it had become a mania with him. And the tragedy of it was, that, while he aped the ravages of disease, the disease did make real inroads upon him, and death peeped forth. Then the expected happened: Grazia, having been tortured by her son for years with his imaginary illness, ceased to believe in it when the illness really came. The heart has its limitations. She had exhausted her store of pity over his lies. She thought Lionello was still a comedian when he spoke the truth. And when the truth was revealed to her, the rest of her life was poisoned by remorse.

Lionello's malice had not laid aside its weapons. Having no love for any one in the world, he could not bear any of those near him to feel love for any one else: jealousy was his only passion. It was not enough for him to have separated his mother and Christophe: he tried to force her to break off the intimacy which subsisted between them. Already he had employed his usual weapon—his illness—to make Grazia swear that she would not marry again. He was not satisfied with her promise. He tried to force his mother to give up writing to Christophe. On this she rebelled; and, being delivered by such an attempted abuse of power, she spoke harshly and severely to Lionello about his habit of lying, and, later on, regarded herself as a criminal for having done so: for her words flung Lionello into a fit of fury which made him really ill. His illness grew worse as he saw that his mother did not believe in it. Then, in his fury, he longed to die so as to avenge himself. He never thought that his wish would be granted.

When the doctor told Grazia that there was no hope for her son, she was dumfounded. But she had to disguise her despair in order to deceive the boy who had so often deceived her. He had a suspicion that this time it was serious, but he refused to believe it; and his eyes watched his mother's eyes for the reproachful expression that had infuriated him when he was lying. There came a time when there was no room for doubt. Then it was terrible, both for him and his mother and sister: he did not wish to die. . . .

When at last Grazia saw him sinking to sleep, she gave no cry and made no moan: she astonished those about her by her silence: she had no strength left for suffering: she had only one desire, to sleep also. However, she went about the business of her life with the same apparent calm. After a few weeks her smile returned to her lips, but she was more silent still. No one suspected her inward distress, Christophe least of all. She had only written to tell him the news, without a word of herself. She did not answer Christophe's anxiously affectionate letters. He wanted to come to her: she begged him not to. At the end of two or three months, she resumed her old grave, serene

tone with him. She would have thought it criminal to put
upon him the burden of her weakness. She knew how the echo
of all her feelings reverberated in him, and how great was his
need to lean on her. She did not impose upon herself the
restraint of sorrow. This discipline was her salvation. In
her weariness of life only two things gave her life: Christophe's
love, and the fatalism, which, in sorrow as in joy, lay at the
heart of. her Italian nature. There was nothing intellectual
in her fatalism: it was the animal instinct, which makes a
hunted beast go on, with no consciousness of fatigue, in a staring
wide-eyed dream, forgetting the stones of the road, forgetting
its own body, until it falls. Her fatalism sustained her body.
Love sustained her heart. Now that her own life was worn out,
she lived in Christophe. And yet she was more scrupulous than
ever never in her letters to tell him of the love she had for
him: no doubt because her love was greater: but also because
she was conscious of the *veto* of the dead boy, who had made
her affection a crime. Then she would relapse into silence, and
refrain from writing for a time.

Christophe did not understand her silence. Sometimes in
the composed and tranquil tone of one of her letters he would
be conscious of an unexpected note that seemed to be quivering
with passionate moaning. That would prostrate him: but he
dared not say anything: he hardly dared to notice it: he was like
a man holding his breath, afraid to breathe, for fear of destroying
an illusion. He knew almost infallibly that in the next letter
such notes as these would be atoned for by a deliberate coldness.
Then, once more, tranquillity . . . *Meeresstille.* . . .

Georges and Emmanuel met at Christophe's one afternoon.
Both were preoccupied with their own troubles: Emmanuel with
his literary disappointments, and Georges with some athletic
failure. Christophe listened to them good-humoredly and teased
them affectionately. There was a ring at the door. Georges
went to open it. A servant had come with a letter from Colette
Christophe stood by the window to read it. His friends went on
with their discussion, and did not see Christophe, whose back
was turned to them. He left the room without their noticing
it. And when they realized that he had done so, they were not

surprised. But as time passed and he did not return, Georges went and knocked at the door of the next room. There was no reply. Georges did not persist, for he knew his old friend's queer ways. A few minutes later Christophe returned without a word. He seemed very calm, very kind, very gentle. He begged their pardon for leaving them, took up the conversation where he had left it, and spoke kindly about their troubles, and said many helpful things. The tone of his voice moved them, though they knew not why.

They left him. Georges went straight to Colette's, and found her in tears. As soon as she saw him she came swiftly to him and asked:

" How did our poor friend take the blow? It is terrible."

Georges did not understand. And Colette told him that she had just sent Christophe the news of Grazia's death.

She was gone, without having had time to say farewell to anybody. For several months past the roots of her life had been almost torn out of the earth: a puff of wind was enough to lay it low. On the evening before the relapse of influenza which carried her off she received a long, kind letter from Christophe. It had filled her with tenderness, and she longed to bid him come to her: she felt that everything else, everything that kept them apart, was absurd and culpable. She was very weary, and put off writing to him until the next day. On the day after she had to stay in bed. She began a letter which she did not finish: she had an attack of giddiness, and her head swam: besides, she was reluctant to speak of her illness, and was afraid of troubling Christophe. He was busy at the time with rehearsals of a choral symphony set to a poem of Emmanuel's: the subject had roused them both to enthusiasm, for it was something symbolical of their own destiny: *The Promised Land*. Christophe had often mentioned it to Grazia. The first performance was to take place the following week. . . . She must not upset him. In her letter Grazia just spoke of a slight cold. Then that seemed too much to her. She tore up the letter, and had no strength left to begin another. She told herself that she would write in the evening. When the evening came it was too late—too late to bid him come, too late even to write. . . . How swiftly everything passes! A few hours are enough to destroy the labor of ages. . . . Grazia hardly had time to give her daughter a ring she wore and beg her to send it to her friend. Till then she had not been very intimate with Aurora. Now that her life was ebbing away, she gazed passionately at the face of the girl: she clung to the hand that would pass on the pressure of her own, and, joyfully, she thought:

" Not all of me will pass away."

" Quid ? hic, inquam. quis est qui complet aures meas tantus et tam dulcis sonus? . . ."—(The Dream of Scipio.)

When he left Colette, on an impulse of sympathy Georges went back to Christophe's. For a long time, through Colette's indiscretions, he had known the place that Grazia filled in his old friend's heart: he had even—(for youth is not respectful)— made fun of it. But now generously and keenly he felt the sorrow that Christophe must be feeling at such a loss; and he felt that he must go to him, embrace him, pity him. Knowing the violence of his passions,—the tranquillity that Christophe had shown made him anxious. He rang the bell. No answer. He rang once more and knocked, giving the signal agreed between Christophe and himself. He heard the moving of a chair and a slow, heavy tread. Christophe opened the door. His face was so calm that Georges stopped still, just as he was about to fling himself into his arms: he knew not what to say. Christophe asked him gently:

" You, my boy. Have you forgotten something? "

Georges muttered uneasily:

" Yes."

" Come in."

Christophe went and sat in the chair he had left on Georges's arrival, near the window, with his head thrown back, looking at the roofs opposite and the reddening evening sky. He paid no attention to Georges. The young man pretended to look about on the table, while he stole glances at Christophe. His face was set: the beams of the setting sun lit up his cheek-bones and his forehead. Mechanically Georges went into the next room—the bedroom—as though he were still looking for something. It was in this room that Christophe had shut himself up with the letter. It was still there on the bed, which bore the imprint of a body. On the floor lay a book that had slipped down. It had been left open with a page crumpled. Georges picked it up, and read the story of the meeting of the Magdalene and the Gardener in the Gospel.

He came back into the living-room, and moved a few things here and there to gain countenance, and once more he looked at Christophe, who had not budged. He longed to tell him how he pitied him. But Christophe was so radiant with light that Georges felt that it was out of place to speak. It was rather himself who stood in need of consolation. He said timidly:

"I am going."

Without turning his head, Christophe said:

"Good-by, my boy."

Georges went away and closed the door without a sound.

For a long time Christophe sat there. Night came. He was not suffering: he was not thinking: he saw no definite image. He was like a tired man listening to some vague music without making any attempt to understand it. The night was far gone when he got up, cramped and stiff. He flung himself on his bed and slept heavily. The symphony went on buzzing all around him. . . .

And now he saw *her,* the well-beloved. . . . She held out her hands to him, and said, smiling:

"Now you have passed through the zone of fire."

Then his heart melted. An indescribable peace filled the starry spaces, where the music of the spheres flung out its great, still, profound sheets of water. . . .

When he awoke (it was day), his strange happiness still endured, with the distant gleam of words falling upon his ears. He got up. He was exalted with a silent, holy enthusiasm.

" . . *Or vedi, figlio,*
    tra Beatrice e te è questo muro . . ."

Between Beatrice and himself, the wall was broken down.

For a long time now more than half his soul had dwelt upon the other side. The more a man lives, the more a man creates, the more a man loves and loses those whom he loves, the more does he escape from death. With every new blow that we have to bear, with every new work that we round and finish, we escape from ourselves, we escape into the work we have created, the soul we have loved, the soul that has left us. When all is told, Rome is not in Rome: the best of a man lies outside himself. Only Grazia had withheld him on this side of the wall. And now in her turn . . . Now the door was shut upon the world of sorrow.

He lived through a period of secret exaltation. He felt the weight of no fetters. He expected nothing of the things of this world. He was dependent upon nothing. He was set free. The struggle was at an end. Issuing from the zone of combat and the circle where reigned the God of heroic conflict, *Dominus Deus Sabaoth,* he looked down, and in the night saw the torch of the Burning Bush put out. How far away it was! When it had lit up his path he had thought himself almost at the summit. And since then, how far he had had to go! And yet the topmost pinnacle seemed no nearer. He would never reach it (he saw that now), though he were to march on to eternity. But when a man enters the circle of light and knows that he has not left those he loves behind him, eternity is not too long a space to be journeying on with them.

He closed his doors. No one knocked. Georges had expended all his compassion and sympathy in the one impulse; he was reassured by the time he reached home, and forgot all about it by the next day. Colette had gone to Rome. Emmanuel knew nothing, and hypersensitive as usual, he maintained an affronted silence because Christophe had not returned his visit. Christophe was not disturbed in his long colloquy with the woman whom he now bore in his soul, as a pregnant woman bears her precious burden. It was a moving intercourse, impossible to translate into words. Even music could hardly express it. When his heart was full, almost overflowing, Christophe would lie still with eyes closed, and listen to its song. Or, for hours together, he would sit at his piano and let his fingers speak. During this period he improvised more than he had done in

the whole of his life. He did not set down his thoughts.
What was the good?

When, after several weeks, he took to going out again and
seeing other men, while none of his friends, except Georges, had
any suspicion of what had happened, the daimon of improvisa-
tion pursued him still. It would take possession of Christophe
just when he was least expecting it. One evening, at Colette's,
Christophe sat down at the piano and played for nearly an
hour, absolutely surrendering himself, and forgetting that the
room was full of strangers. They had no desire to laugh. His
terrible improvisations enslaved and overwhelmed them. Even
those who did not understand their meaning were thrilled and
moved: and tears came to Colette's eyes. . . . When Christophe had finished he turned away abruptly: he saw how everybody was moved, and shrugged his shoulders, and—laughed.

He had reached the point at which sorrow also becomes a
force—a dominant force. His sorrow possessed him no more:
he possessed his sorrow: in vain it fluttered and beat upon its
bars: he kept it caged.

From that period date his most poignant and his happiest
works: a scene from the Gospel which Georges recognized—

*" Mulier. quid ploras? "—" Quia tulerunt Dominum meum, et nescio
ubi posuerunt eum."*

*Et cum hæc dixisset, conversa est retrorsum, et vidit Jesum stantem: et
non sciebat quia Jesus est.*

—a series of tragic *lieder* set to verses of popular Spanish
cantares, among others a gloomy sad love-song, like a black
flame—

" Quisiera ser el sepulcro
Donde á ti te han de enterrar,
Para tenerte en mis brazos
Por toda la eternidad."

("Would I were the grave, where thou art to be buried, that I might
hold thee in my arms through all eternity.")

—and two symphonies, called *The Island of Tranquillity* and
The Dream of Scipio, in which, more intimately than in any
other of the works of Jean-Christophe Krafft, is realized the

union of the most beautiful of the forces of the music of his time: the affectionate and wise thought of Germany with all its shadowy windings, the clear passionate melody of Italy, and the quick mind of France, rich in subtle rhythms and variegated harmonies.

This "enthusiasm begotten of despair at the time of a great loss" lasted for a few months. Thereafter Christophe fell back into his place in life with a stout heart and a sure foot. The wind of death had blown away the last mists of pessimism, the gray of the Stoic soul, and the phantasmagoria of the mystic chiaroscura. The rainbow had shone upon the vanishing clouds. The gaze of heaven, purer, as though it had been laved with tears, smiled through them. There was the peace of evening on the mountains.

IV

THE fire smoldering in the forest of Europe was beginning to burst into flames. In vain did they try to put it out in one place: it only broke out in another: with gusts of smoke and a shower of sparks it swept from one point to another, burning the dry brushwood. Already in the East there were skirmishes as the prelude to the great war of the nations. All Europe, Europe that only yesterday was skeptical and apathetic, like a dead wood, was swept by the flames. All men were possessed by the desire for battle. War was ever on the point of breaking out. It was stamped out, but it sprang to life again. The world felt that it was the mercy of an accident that might let loose the dogs of war. The world lay in wait. The feeling of inevitability weighed heavily even upon the most pacifically minded. And ideologues, sheltered beneath the massive shadow of the cyclops, Proudhon, hymned in war man's fairest title of nobility. . . .

This, then, was to be the end of the physical and moral resurrection of the races of the West! To such butchery they were to be borne along by the currents of action and passionate faith! Only a Napoleonic genius could have marked out a chosen, deliberate aim for this blind, onward rush. But nowhere in Europe was there any genius for action. It was as though the world

had chosen the most mediocre to be its governors. The force
of the human mind was in other things.—So there was nothing
to be done but to trust to the declivity down which they were
moving. This both governors and governed were doing. Europe
looked like a vast armed vigil.

Christophe remembered a similar vigil, when he had had
Olivier's anxious face by his side. But then the menace of war
had been only a passing cloud. Now all Europe lay under its
shadow. And Christophe's heart also had changed. He could
not share in the hatred of the nations. His state of mind was
like that of Goethe in 1813. How could a man fight without
hatred? And how could he hate without youth? He had passed
through the zone of hatred. Which of the great rival nations
was the dearest to him? He had learned to know all their
merits, and what the world owed to them. When a man has
reached a certain stage in the development of the soul *" he
knows no nation, he feels the happiness or unhappiness of the
neighboring peoples as his own."* The storm-clouds are at his
feet. Around him is nothing but the sky—*" the whole Heavens
the kingdom of the eagle."*

And yet Christophe was sometimes embarrassed by this am-
bient hostility. In Paris he was made to feel too clearly that
he was of the hostile race: even his friend Georges could not
resist the pleasure of giving vent, in his presence, to feelings
about Germany which made him sad. Then he rushed away,
on the excuse that he wanted to see Grazia's daughter: and he
went and stayed for a time in Rome. But there the atmosphere
was no more serene. The great plague of national pride had
spread there, and had transformed the Italian character. The
Italians, whom Christophe had known to be indifferent and indolent, were now thinking of nothing but military glory, battle,
conquests, Roman eagles flying over the sands of Libya: they
believed they had returned to the time of the Emperors. The
wonderful thing was that this madness was shared, with the
best faith in the world, by the opposition parties, socialists and
clericals, as well as by the monarchists, and they had not the
least idea that they were being unfaithful to their cause. So
little do politics and human reason count when the great epidemic passions sweep over the nations. Such passions do not

even trouble to suppress individual passions; they use them; and everything converges on the one goal. In the great periods of action it was ever thus. The armies of Henri IV., the Councils of Louis XIV., which forged the greatness of France, numbered as many men of faith and reason as men of vanity, interest, and enjoyment. Jansenists and libertines, Puritans and gallants, served the same destiny in serving their instincts. In the forthcoming wars no doubt internationalists and pacificists will kindle the blaze, in the conviction, like that of their ancestors of the Convention, that they are doing it for the good of the nations and the triumph of peace.

With a somewhat ironical smile, Christophe, from the terrace of the Janiculum, looked down on the disparate and harmonious city, the symbol of the universe which it dominated; crumbling ruins, "baroque" façades, modern buildings, cypress and roses intertwined—every age, every style, merged into a powerful and coherent unity beneath the clear light. So the mind should shed over the struggling universe the order and light that are in it.

Christophe did not stay long in Rome. The impression made on him by the city was too strong: he was afraid of it. Truly to profit by its harmony he needed to hear it at a distance: he felt that if he stayed he would be in danger of being absorbed by it, like so many other men of his race.—Every now and then he went and stayed in Germany. But, when all was told, and in spite of the imminence of a Franco-German war, Paris still had the greatest attraction for him. No doubt this was because his adopted son, Georges, lived there. But he was not only swayed by reasons of affection. There were other reasons of an intellectual order that were no less powerful. For an artist accustomed to the full life of the mind, who generously shares in all the sufferings, all the hopes, and all the passions of the great human family, it was difficult to grow accustomed to life in Germany. There was no lack of artists there. But the artists lacked air. They were isolated from the rest of the nation, which took no interest in them: other preoccupations, social or practical, absorbed the attention of the public. The poets shut themselves up in disdainful irritation in their disdained art: it became a point of honor with them to sever the last ties which bound them to the life of the people: they wrote only for a few, a little aristocracy full of talent, refined and sterile, being itself divided into rival groups of jaded initiates, and they were stifled in the narrow room in which they were huddled together: they were incapable of expanding it, and set themselves to dig down; they turned the soil over until it was exhausted. Then they drifted away into their archaic dreams, and never even troubled to bring their dreams into the common stock. Each man fought for his place in the mist. They had no light in common. Each man had to look for light within himself.

Yonder, on the other hand, on the other side of the Rhine, among their neighbors on the West, the great winds of collective passion, of public turbulence and tribulation, swept periodically over art. And, high above the plain, like their Eiffel Tower above Paris, shone afar off the never-dying light of a classic tradition, handed down from generation to generation, which, while it never enslaved nor constrained the mind, showed it the road followed by past ages, and established the communion of a whole nation in its light. Many a German spirit—like birds strayed in the night—came winging towards the distant beacon. But who is there in France can dream of the power of the sympathy which drives so many generous hearts from the neighboring nation towards France! So many hands stretched out: hands that are not responsible for the aims of the politicians! . . . And you see no more of us, our brothers in Germany, though we say to you: "Here are our hands. In spite of lies and hatred, we will not be parted. We have need of you, you have need of us, to build the greatness of our spirits and our people. We are the two wings of the West. If one be broken, there is an end of flight! Let the war come! It will not break the clasp of our hands or the flight of our genius in brotherhood."

So thought Christophe. He felt the mutual completion which the two races could give each other, and how lame and halting were the spirit, the art, the action of each without the help of the other. For his own part, born in the Rhine-lands where the two civilizations mingle in one stream, from his childhood he had instinctively felt their inevitable union; all through his life the unconscious effort of his genius had been to maintain the balance and equilibrium of the two mighty wings. The greater was his wealth of Germanic dreams, the more he needed the Latin clarity of mind and order. It was for this reason that France was so dear to him. In France he had the joy of better knowledge and mastery of himself. Only in France was he wholly himself.

He turned to account all the elements that were or might be noxious to him. He assimilated foreign energy in his own. A vigorous healthy mind absorbs every kind of force, even that which is hostile to it, and makes it bone and flesh of its bone and flesh. There even comes a time when a man is most attracted by what least resembles him, for therein he finds his most plentiful nourishment.

Christophe did in fact find more pleasure in the work of artists who were set up as his rivals than in the work of his imitators:—for he had imitators who called themselves his disciples, to his great despair. They were honest, laborious, estimable, and altogether virtuous people who were full of respect and veneration for him. Christophe would have given much if he could have liked their music; but—(it was just his luck!)—he could not do it: he found it meaningless. He was a thousand times more pleased with the talent of musicians who were personally antipathetic to him, and in art represented tendencies hostile to his own. . . . Well! What did it matter? These men were at least alive! Life is, in itself, such a virtue, that, if a man be deprived of it, though he possess all the other virtues, he will never be a really good man, for he cannot really be a man. Christophe used jokingly to say that the only disciples he recognized were the men who attacked him. And when a young artist came and talked to him about his musical vocation, and tried to win his sympathy by flattering him, Christophe would say:

"So. My music satisfies you? That is how you would express your love. or your hatred?"

"Yes, master."

"Well. Don't. You have nothing to say."

His horror of the submissive temper of mind, of men born to obey. his need of absorbing other ideas than his own, attracted him to circles whose ideas were diametrically opposed to his own. He had friends among men to whom his art, his idealistic faith, his moral conceptions, were a dead letter: they had absolutely different ways of envisaging life, love, marriage, the family, every social relationship:—but they were good fellows, though they seemed to belong to another stage of moral evolution: the anguish and the scruples that had consumed a part of Christophe's life were incomprehensible to them. No doubt that was all the better for them! Christophe had no desire to make them understand. He did not ask others to confirm his ideas by thinking as he did: he was sure of his own thoughts. He asked them to let him know their thoughts, and to love their souls. He asked always to know and to love more, to see and to learn how to see. He had reached the point not only of admitting in others tendencies of mind that he had once combated, but also of rejoicing in them, for they seemed to him to contribute to the fecundity of the universe. He loved Georges the more because he did not take life tragically, as he did. Humanity would be too poor and too gray in color if it were to be uniformly clad in the moral seriousness, and the heroic restraint with which Christophe was armed. Humanity needed joy, carelessness, irreverent audacity in face of its idols, all its idols, even the most holy. Long live " the Gallic salt which revives the world "! Skepticism and faith are no less necessary. Skepticism, riddling the faith of yesterday, prepares the way for the faith of to-morrow. . . . How clear everything becomes to the man who stands away from life, and, as in a fine picture, sees the contrasting colors merge into a magical harmony, where, when they were closely seen, they clashed.

Christophe's eyes had been opened to the infinite variety of the material, as of the moral, world. It had been one of his greatest conquests since his first visit to Italy. In Paris he especially sought the company of painters and sculptors; it seemed to him that the best of the French genius was in them. The triumphant audacity with which they pursued and captured movement, vibrant color, and tore away the veils that cover life, made his heart leap with delight. The inexhaustible riches that he who has eyes to see can find in a drop of light, a second of life! Against such sovereign delights of the mind what matters the vain tumult of dispute and war? . . . But dispute and war also are a part of the marvelous spectacle. We must embrace everything, and, valiantly, joyously, fling into the crucible of our burning hearts both the forces of denial and the forces of affirmation, enemies and friends, the whole metal of life. The end of it all is the statue which takes shape in us, the divine fruit of our minds; and all is good that helps to make it more beautiful even at the cost of the sacrifice of ourselves. What does the creator matter? Only that which is created is real. . . . You cannot hurt us, ye enemies who seek to reach us with your hostility. We are beyond the reach of your attacks. . . . You are rending the empty cloak. I have been gone this many a day.

His music had found a more serene form. No longer did it show the storms of spring, which gathered, burst, and disappeared in the old days, but, instead, the white clouds of summer, mountains of snow and gold, great birds of light, slowly soaring, and filling the sky. . . . Creation. Ripening crops in the calm August sunlight. . . .

At first a vague, mighty torpor, the obscure joy of the full grape, the swollen ear of corn, the pregnant woman brooding over her ripe fruit. A buzzing like the sound of an organ; the hive all alive with the hum of the bees. . . . Such somber, golden music, like an autumn honeycomb, slowly gives forth the rhythm which shall mark its path: the round of the planets is made plain: it begins to spin. . . .

Then the will appears. It leaps onto the back of the whinnying dream as it passes, and grips it with its knees The mind recognizes the laws of the rhythm which guides it: it tames the disordered forces and fixes the path they shall take, the goal towards which they shall move. The symphony of reason and instinct is organized. The darkness grows bright. On the long ribbon of the winding road, at intervals, there are brilliant fires, which in their turn shall be in the work of creation the nucleus of little planetary worlds linked up in the girdle of their solar system. . . .

The main lines of the picture are henceforth fixed. Now it looms through the uncertain light of dawn. Everything is becoming definite: the harmony of the colors, the outline of the figures. To bring the work to its close all the resources of his being are brought into requisition. The scent-box of memory is opened and exhales its perfumes. The mind unchains the senses: it lets them wax delirious and is silent: but, crouching there, it watches them and chooses its prey. . . .

All is ready: the team of workmen carries out, with the materials snatched from the senses, the work planned by the mind. A great architect must have good journeymen who know their trade and will not spare themselves.—The cathedral is finished.

"And God looked down on his work. And He saw that *it was not yet good.*"

The Master's eyes take in the whole of His creation, and His hand perfects its harmony. . . .

The dream is ended. *Te Deum.* . . .

The white clouds of summer, like great birds of light, slowly soar and hover; and the heavens are filled with their widespread wings.

And yet his life was very far from being one with his art. A man of his kind cannot do without love, not merely that equable love which the spirit of an artist sheds on all things in the world, but a love that knows *preference:* he must always be giving himself to the creatures of his choice. They are the roots of the tree. Through them his heart's blood is renewed.

Christophe's heart's blood was nothing like dried up. He was steeped in a love which was the best part of his joy, a twofold love, for Grazia's daughter and Olivier's son. He united them in thought, and was to unite them in reality.

Georges and Aurora had met at Colette's: Aurora lived in her cousin's house. She spent part of the year in Rome and the rest in Paris. She was eighteen: Georges five years older. She was tall, erect, elegant, with a small head, and an open countenance, fair hair, a dark complexion, a slight down on her lips, bright eyes with a laughing expression behind which lay busy thoughts, a rather plump chin, brown hands, beautiful round strong arms, and a fine bust, and she always looked gay, proud, and worldly. She was not at all intellectual, hardly at all sentimental, and she had inherited her mother's careless indolence. She would sleep eleven hours on end. The rest of the time she spent in lounging and laughing, only half awake. Christophe called her *Dornröschen*—the Sleeping Beauty. She reminded him of his old love, Sabine. She used to sing as she went to bed, and when she got up, and laugh for no reason at all, with merry childish laughter, and then gulp it down with a sort of hiccough. It were impossible to tell how she spent the time. All Colette's efforts to equip her with the brilliant artificiality which is so easily imposed on the mind of a young girl, like a kind of lacquered varnish, had been wasted: the varnish would not hold. She learned nothing: she would take months to read a book, and would like it immensely, though in a week she would forget both its title and its subject: without the least embarrassment she would make mistakes in spelling, and when she spoke of learned matters she would fall into the most comical blunders. She was refreshing in her youth, her gaiety, her lack of intellectuality, even in her faults, her thoughtlessness which sometimes amounted to indifference, and her naïve egoism. She was always so spontaneous. Young as she was, and simple and indolent, she could when she pleased play the coquette, though in all innocence: then she would spread her net for young men and go sketching, or play the nocturnes of Chopin, or carry books of poetry which she had not read, and indulge in conversations and hats that were about equally idealistic.

Christophe would watch her and laugh gently to himself. He had a fatherly tenderness, indulgent and teasing, for Aurora. And he had also a secret feeling of worship for the woman he had loved who had come again with new youth for another love than his. No one knew the depth of his affection. Only Aurora ever suspected it. From her childhood she had almost always been used to having Christophe near her, and she used to regard him as one of her family. In her old sorrow at being less loved than her brother she had instinctively drawn near to Christophe. She divined that he had a similar sorrow; he saw her grief: and though they never exchanged confidences, they shared each other's feelings. Later, when she discovered

the feeling that united her mother and Christophe, it seemed
to her that she was in the secret, though they had never told
her. She knew the meaning of the message with which Grazia
had charged her as she lay dying, and of the ring which was
now on Christophe's hand. So there existed hidden ties between
her and Christophe, ties which she did not need to understand, to feel them in their complexity. She was sincerely
attached to her old friend, although she could never have made
the effort necessary to play or to read his work. Though she
was a fairly good musician, she had never even had the curiosity
to cut the pages of a score he had dedicated to her. She loved
to come and have an intimate talk with him.—She came more
often when she found out that she might meet Georges Jeannin
in his rooms.

And Georges, too, found an extraordinary interest in Christophe's company.

However, the two young people were slow to realize their
real feelings. They had at first looked at each other mockingly. They were hardly at all alike. He was quicksilver, she
was still water. But it was not long before quicksilver tried to
appear more at rest, and sleeping water awoke. Georges would
criticise Aurora's clothes, and her Italian taste—a slight want
of feeling for modulation and a certain preference for crude
colors. Aurora used to delight in teasing Georges, and imitating
his rather hurried and precious way of speaking. And while
they laughed at each other, they both took pleasure . . . in
laughing, or in entertaining each other? They used to entertain
Christophe too, and, far from gainsaying them, he would maliciously transpose these little poisoned darts from one to the
other. They pretended not to care: but they soon discovered
that they cared only too much; and both, especially Georges,
being incapable of concealing their annoyance, as soon as they
met they would begin sparring. Their wounds were slight: they
were afraid of hurting each other: and the hand which dealt
the blow was so dear to the recipient of it that they both found
more pleasure in the hurts they received than in those they
gave. They used to watch each other curiously, and their eyes,
seeking defects, would find only attractions. But they would
not admit it. Each, to Christophe, would declare that the other

was unbearable, but, for all that, they were not slow to seize
every opportunity of meeting that Christophe gave them.

One day when Aurora was with her old friend to tell him
that she would come and see him on the following Sunday in
the morning, Georges rushed in, like a whirlwind as usual,
to tell Christophe that he was coming on Sunday afternoon. On
Sunday morning Christophe waited in vain for Aurora. At the
hour mentioned by Georges she appeared, and asked him to forgive her because it had been impossible for her to come in the
morning: she embroidered her excuses with a circumstantial
story. Christophe was amused by her innocent roguery, and
said:

"It is a pity. You would have seen Georges: he came and
lunched with me; but he would not stay this afternoon."

Aurora was discomfited, and did not listen to anything Christophe said. He went on talking good-humoredly. She replied
absently, and was not far from being cross with him. Came a
ring at the bell. It was Georges. Aurora was amazed. Christophe looked at her and laughed. She saw that he had been
making fun of her, and laughed and blushed. He shook his
finger at her waggishly. Suddenly she ran and kissed him
warmly. He whispered to her:

"*Biricchina, ladroncella, furbetta. . . .*"

And she laid her hand on his lips to silence him.

Georges could make nothing of their kissing and laughter.
His expression of astonishment, almost of vexation, added to
their joy.

So Christophe labored to bring the two young people together.
And when he had succeeded he was almost sorry. He loved
them equally; but he judged Georges more hardly: he knew
his weakness: he idolized Aurora, and thought himself responsible for her happiness even more than for Georges's; for it
seemed to him that Georges was as a son to him, a part of
himself, and he wondered whether it was not wrong to give
Aurora in her innocence a companion who was very far from
sharing it.

But one day as he passed by an arbor where the two young
people were sitting—(a short time after their betrothal)—his
heart sank as he heard Aurora laughingly questioning Georges

about one of his past adventures, and Georges telling her, nothing
loth. Other scraps of conversation, which they made no attempt
to disguise, showed him that Aurora was far more at home
than himself with Georges's moral ideas. Though they were
very much in love with each other it was clear that they did not
regard themselves as bound forever; into their discussions of
questions relating to love and marriage, they brought a spirit
of liberty, which might have a beauty of its own, though it
was singularly at variance with the old ideal of mutual devotion
usque ad mortem. And Christophe would look at them a little
sadly. . . . How far they were from him already! How
swiftly does the ship that bears our children speed on! . . .
Patience! A day will come when we shall all meet in harbor.

Meanwhile the ship paid no heed to the way marked out for
it: it trimmed its sails to every wind.—It would have seemed
natural for the spirit of liberty, which was then tending to
modify morality, to take up its stand also in the other domains
of thought and action. But it did nothing of the kind: human
nature cares little for contradiction. While morality was becoming more free, the mind was becoming less so; it was demanding that religion should restore its yoke. And this twofold
movement in opposite directions was, with a magnificent defiance of logic, taking place in the same souls. Georges and
Aurora had been caught up by the new current of Catholicism
which was conquering many people of fashion and many intellectuals. Nothing could be more curious than the way in
which Georges, who was naturally critical and perfectly irreligious, skepticism being to him as easy as breathing, Georges,
who had never cared for God or devil—a true Frenchman, laughing at everything—suddenly declared that there lay the truth.
He needed truth of some sort, and this sorted well with his
need of action, his atavistic French bourgeois characteristics,
and his weariness of liberty. The young fool had wandered long
enough, and he returned of his own accord to be harnessed to
the plow of his race. The example of a number of his friends
was enough for him. Georges was hypersensitive to the least
atmospheric pressure of the ideas that surrounded him, and
he was one of the first to be caught. And Aurora followed him,
as she would have followed him anywhere. At once they felt

sure of themselves, and despised everybody who did not think as they did. The irony of it! These two frivolous children were sincerely devout, while the moral purity, the serious and ardent efforts of Grazia and Olivier had never helped them to be so, in spite of their desire.

Christophe watched their spiritual evolution with sympathetic curiosity. He did not try to fight against it, as Emmanuel would have done, for Emmanuel's free idealism was up in arms against this return of the ancient foe. It is vain to fight against the passing wind. One can only wait for it to go. The reason of humanity was exhausted. It had just made a gigantic effort. It was overcome with sleep, and, like a child worn out by a long day, before going to sleep, it was saying its prayers. The gate of dreams had reopened; in the train of religion came little puffs of theosophy, mysticism, esoteric faiths, occultism to visit the chambers of the Western mind. Even philosophy was wavering. Their gods of thought, Bergson and William James, were tottering. Even science was attainted, even science was showing the signs of the fatigue of reason. We have a moment's respite. Let us breathe. To-morrow the mind will awake again, more alert, more free. . . . Sleep is good when a man has worked hard. Christophe, who had had little time for it, was happy that these children of his should enjoy it in his stead, and should have rest for the soul, security of faith, absolute, unshakable confidence in their dreams. He would not nor could he have exchanged his lot for theirs. But he thought that Grazia's melancholy and Olivier's distress of mind had found solace in their children, and that it was well.

" All that we have suffered, I, my friends, and so many others whom I never knew, others who lived before us, all has been, that these two might attain joy. . . . The joy, Antoinette, for which thou wast made, the joy that was refused thee! . . . Ah! If only the unhappy could have a foretaste of the happiness that will one day spring forth from the sacrifice of their lives! "

What purpose could be served by his trying to dispute their happiness? We must not try to make others happy in our way, but in their own. At most he only asked Georges and Aurora not to be too contemptuous of those who, like himself, did not share their faith.

They did not even take the trouble to argue with him. They seemed to say to each other:

"He cannot understand. . . ."

In their eyes he belonged to the past. And, to be frank, they did not attach much importance to the past. When they were alone they used often to talk innocently of the things they would do when Christophe "was no longer with them." . . .
—However, they loved him well. . . . How terrible are the children who grow up over us like creepers! How terrible is the force of Nature, hurrying, hurrying, driving us out. . . .

"Go! Go! Remove thyself! It is my turn now! . . ."

Christophe, overhearing their thoughts, longed to say to them:

"Don't be in such a hurry! I am quite happy here. Please regard me still as a living being."

He was amused by their naïve impertinence.

"You may as well say straight out," he observed one day when they had crushed him with their disdainful manner. "You may as well say that I am a stupid old man."

"No, no, my dear old friend," said Aurora, laughing heartily. "You are the best of men, but there are some things that you do not know."

"And that you do know, my girl? You are very wise!"

"Don't laugh at me. I know nothing much. But Georges knows."

Christophe smiled:

"Yes. You are right, my dear. The man you love always knows."

It was much more difficult for him to tolerate their music than to put up with their intellectual superiority. They used to try his patience severely. The piano was given no rest when they were in his rooms. It seemed that love had roused them to song, like the birds. But they were by a long way not so skilled in singing. Aurora had no illusions as to her talent, but she was quite otherwise about her fiancé: she could see no difference between Georges's playing and Christophe's. Perhaps she preferred Georges's style, and Georges, in spite of his ironic

subtlety, was never far from being convinced by his sweetheart's
belief in him.   Christophe never contradicted them: maliciously
he would concur in the girl's opinion (except when, as sometimes happened, he could bear it no longer, and would rush
away, banging the doors).   With an affectionate, pitying smile
he would listen to Georges playing *Tristan* on the piano.   The
unhappy young man would conscientiously apply himself to
the transcription of the formidable pages with all the amiable
sweetness of a young girl, and a young girl's tender feeling.
Christophe used to laugh to himself.   He would never tell the
boy why he laughed.   He would kiss him.   He loved him as he
was.   Perhaps he loved him the more for it. . . .   Poor
boy! . . .   Oh! the vanity of art! . . .

He used often to talk about "his children"—(for so he
called them)—to Emmanuel.   Emmanuel, who was fond of
Georges, used jokingly to say that Christophe ought to hand
him over to him.   He had Aurora, and it was not fair.   He
was grabbing everything.

Their friendship had become almost legendary in Parisian
society, though they lived apart from it.   Emmanuel had grown
passionately devoted to Christophe, though his pride would not
let him show it.   He covered it up with his brusque manners,
and sometimes used to be absolutely rude to Christophe.   But
Christophe was not deceived.   He knew how deeply attached to
him Emmanuel was, and he knew the worth of his affection.
No week went by but they met two or three times.   When they
were prevented by ill-health from going out, they used to write
to each other.   Their letters might have been written from
places far removed from Paris.   They were less interested in
external happenings than in the progress of the mind in science
and art.   They lived in their ideas, pondering their art, or
beneath the chaos of facts perceiving the little undistinguished
gleam which reveals the progress of the history of the human
mind.

Generally it was Christophe who visited Emmanuel.   Although, since a recent illness, he was not much better in health
than his friend, he had grown used to thinking that Emmanuel's
health called for more consideration than his own.   Christophe

could not now ascend Emmanuel's six flights of stairs without difficulty, and when he reached the top he had to wait a moment to recover his breath. They were both incapable of taking care of themselves. In defiance of their weak throats and their fits of despondency, they were inveterate smokers. That was one of the reasons why Christophe preferred that they should meet in Emmanuel's rooms rather than in his own, for Aurora used to declare war on his habit of smoking, and he used to hide away from her. Sometimes they would both break out coughing in the middle of their conversation, and then they would break off and look at each other guiltily like schoolboys, and laugh: and sometimes one would lecture the other while he was coughing; but as soon as he had recovered his breath the other would vigorously protest that smoking had nothing to do with it.

On Emmanuel's table, in a clear space among the papers, a gray cat would sit and gravely look at the smokers with an air of reproach. Christophe used to say that it was their living conscience, and, by way of stifling it, he would cover it up with his hat. It was a wretched beast, of the commonest kind, that Emmanuel had picked up half-dead in the street; it had never really recovered from the brutal handling it had received, and ate very little, and hardly ever played, and never made any noise: it was very gentle, and used to follow its master about with its intelligent eyes, and be unhappy when he was absent, and quite content to sit on the table by his side, only breaking off its musing ecstatically, for hours together, to watch the cage where the inaccessible birds fluttered about, purring politely at the least mark of attention, patiently submitting to Emmanuel's capricious, and Christophe's rough, attentions, and always being very careful not to scratch or bite. It was very delicate, and one of its eyes was always weeping: it used to cough: and if it had been able to speak it would certainly not have had the effrontery, like the two men, to declare that " the smoke had nothing to do with it "; but it accepted everything at their hands, and seemed to think:

" They are men. They know what they are doing."

Emmanuel was fond of the beast because he saw a certain similarity between its lot and his own. Christophe used to declare that the resemblance was even extended to the expression in their eyes.

"Why not?" Emmanuel would say.

Animals reflect their surroundings. Their faces grow refined or the reverse according to the people with whom they live. A fool's cat has a different expression from that of a clever man's cat. A domestic animal will become good or bad, frank or sly, sensitive or stupid, not only according to what its master teaches it, but also according to what its master is. And this is true not only of the influence of men. Places fashion animals in their own image. A clear, bright landscape will light up the eyes of animals.—Emmanuel's gray cat was in harmony with the stuffy garret and its ailing master, who lived under the Parisian sky.

Emmanuel had grown more human. He was not the same man that he had been at the time of his first acquaintance with Christophe. He had been profoundly shaken by a domestic tragedy. His companion, whom, in a moment of exasperation, he had made too clearly feel how tiresome the burden of her affection was to him, had suddenly disappeared. Frantic with anxiety, he spent a whole night looking for her, and at last he found her in a police station where she was being retained. She had tried to throw herself into the Seine; a passer-by had caught hold of her by the clothes, and pulled her back just as she was clambering over the parapet of the bridge; she had refused to give her name and address, and made another attempt on her life. The sight of her grief had overwhelmed Emmanuel; he could not bear the thought that, having suffered so much at the hands of others, he, in his turn, was causing suffering. He brought the poor crazed creature back to his rooms, and did his best to heal the wound he had dealt her, and to win her back to the confidence in his affection she so sorely needed. He suppressed his feeling of revolt, and resigned himself to her absorbing love, and devoted to her the remainder of his life. The whole sap of his genius had rushed back to his heart. The apostle of action had come to the belief that there was only one course of action that was really good—not to do evil. His part was played. It seemed that the Force which raises the great human tides had used him only as an instrument, to

let loose action. Once his orders were carried out, he was
nothing: action pursued its way without him. He watched it
moving on, almost resigned to the injustice which touched him
personally, though not altogether to that which concerned his
faith. For although, as a free-thinker, he claimed to be free
of all religion and used humorously to call Christophe a clerical
in disguise, like every sturdy spirit, he had his altar on which
he deified the dreams to which he sacrificed himself. The altar
was deserted now, and Emmanuel suffered. How could· he
without suffering see the blessed ideas, which he had so hardly
led to victory, the ideas for which, during the last hundred
years, all the finest men had suffered such bitter torment—how
could he see them tramped underfoot by the oncoming generation? The whole magnificent inheritance of French idealism—
the faith in Liberty, which had its saints, martyrs, heroes, the
love of humanity, the religious aspiration towards the brotherhood of nations and races—all, all was with blind brutality
pillaged by the younger generation! What madness is it in
them that makes them sigh for the monsters we had vanquished,
submit to the yoke that we had broken, call back with great
shouts the reign of Force, and kindle Hatred and the insanity
of war in the heart of my beloved France!

"It is not only in France," Christophe would say laughingly.
"it is throughout the entire world. From Spain to China blows
the same keen wind. There is not a corner anywhere for a
man to find shelter from the wind! It is becoming a joke:
even in my little Switzerland, which is turning nationalist!"

"You find that comforting?"

"Certainly. It shows that such waves of feeling are not
due to the ridiculous passions of a few men, but to a hidden
God who controls the universe. And I have learned to bow
before that God. If I do not understand Him, that is my
fault, not His. Try to understand Him. But how many of
you take the trouble to do that? You live from day to day,
and see no farther than the next milestone, and you imagine
that it marks the end of the road. You see the wave that bears
you along, but you do not see the sea! The wave of to-day is
the wave of yesterday; it is the wave of our souls that prepared
the way for it. The wave of to-day will plow the ground for

the wave of to-morrow, which will wipe out its memory as the memory of ours is wiped out. I neither admire nor dread the naturalism of the present time. It will pass away with the present time: it is passing, it has already passed. It is a rung in the ladder. Climb to the top of it! It is the advance-guard of the coming army. Hark to the sound of its fifes and drums! . . ."

(Christophe drummed on the table, and woke the cat, which sprang away.)

". . . Every nation now feels the imperious necessity of gathering its forces and making up its balance-sheet. For the last hundred years all the nations have been transformed by their mutual intercourse and the immense contributions of all the brains of the universe, building up new morality, new knowledge, new faith. Every man must examine his conscience, and know exactly what he is and what he has, before he can enter with the rest into the new age. A new age is coming. Humanity is on the point of signing a new lease of life. Society is on the point of springing into new vigor with new laws. It is Sunday to-morrow. Every one is making up his accounts for the week, setting his house in order, making it clean and tidy, that, with other men, we may go into the presence of our common God and make a new compact of alliance with Him."

Emmanuel looked at Christophe, and his eyes reflected the passing vision. He was silent for some time after Christophe had finished speaking, and then he said:

"You are lucky, Christophe! You do not see the night!"

"I can see in the dark," said Christophe. "I have lived in it enough. I am an old owl."

About this time his friends noticed a change in his manner. He was often distracted and absent-minded. He hardly listened to what was said to him. He had an absorbed, smiling expression. When his absent-mindedness was commented upon he would gently excuse himself. Sometimes he would speak of himself in the third person:

"Krafft will do that for you. . . ."

or,

"Christophe will laugh at that. . . ."

People who did not know him said:

"What extraordinary self-infatuation!"

But it was just the opposite. He saw himself from the outside, as a stranger. He had reached the stage when a man loses interest even in the struggle for the beautiful, because, when a man has done his work, he is inclined to believe that others will do theirs, and that, when all is told, as Rodin says, "the beautiful will always triumph." The malevolence and injustice of men did not repel him.—He would laugh and tell himself that it was not natural, that life was ebbing away from him.

In fact, he had lost much of his old vigor. The least physical effort, a long walk, a fast drive, exhausted him. He quickly lost his breath, and he had pains in his heart. Sometimes he would think of his old friend Schulz. He never told anybody what he was feeling. It was no good. It was useless to upset his friends, and he would never get any better. Besides he did not take his symptoms seriously. He far more dreaded having to take care of himself than being ill.

He had an inward presentiment and a desire to see his country once more. He had postponed going from year to year, always saying—"next year. . . ." Now he would postpone it no longer.

He did not tell any one, and went away by stealth. The journey was short. Christophe found nothing that he had come to seek. The changes that had been in the making on his last visit were now fully accomplished: the little town had become a great industrial city. The old houses had disappeared. The cemetery also was gone. Where Sabine's farm had stood was now a factory with tall chimneys. The river had washed away the meadows where Christophe had played as a child. A street (and such a street!) between black buildings bore his name. The whole of the past was dead, even death itself. . . . So be it! Life was going on: perhaps other little Christophes were dreaming, suffering, struggling, in the shabby houses in the street that was called after him.—At a concert in the gigantic *Tonhalle* he heard some of his music played, all topsyturvy: he hardly recognized it. . . . So be it! Though it were misunderstood it might perhaps arouse new energy. We

sowed the seed. Do what you will with it: feed on us.—At
nightfall Christophe walked through the fields outside the city;
great mists were rolling over them, and he thought of the great
mists that should enshroud his life, and those whom he had
loved, who were gone from the earth, who had taken refuge
in his heart, who, like himself, would be covered up by the
falling night. . . . So be it! So be it! I am not afraid
of thee, O night, thou devourer of suns! For one star that
is put out, thousands are lit up. Like a bowl of boiling milk,
the abysm of space is overflowing with light. Thou shalt not
put me out. The breath of death will set the flame of my
life flickering up once more. . . .

On his return from Germany, Christophe wanted to stop in
the town where he had known Anna. Since he had left it, he
had had no news of her. He had never dared to ask after
her. For years her very name was enough to upset him. . . .
—Now he was calm and had no fear. But in the evening, in
his room in the hotel looking out on the Rhine, the familiar
song of the bells ringing in the morrow's festival awoke the
images of the past. From the river there ascended the faint
odor of distant danger, which he found it hard to understand.
He spent the whole night in recollection. He felt that he was
free of the terrible Lord, and found sweet sadness in the thought.
He had not made up his mind what to do on the following day.
For a moment—(the past lay so far behind!)—he thought of
calling on the Brauns. But when the morrow came his courage
failed him: he dared not even ask at the hotel whether the
doctor and his wife were still alive. He made up his mind
to go. . . .

When the time came for him to go an irresistible force drove
him to the church which Anna used to attend: he stood behind
a pillar from which he could see the seat where in old days
she used to come and kneel. He waited, feeling sure that, if
she were still alive, she would come.

A woman did come, and he did not recognize her. She was
like all the rest, plump, full-faced, with a heavy chin, and an
indifferent, hard expression. She was dressed in black. She
sat down in her place, and did not stir. There was nothing
in the woman to remind Christophe of the woman he was ex-

pecting. Only once or twice she made a certain queer little
gesture as though to smooth out the folds of her skirt about
her knees. In old days, *she* had made such a gesture. . . .
As she went out she passed slowly by him, with her head erect
and her hands holding her prayer-book, folded in front of her.
For a moment her somber, tired eyes met Christophe's. And
they looked at each other. And they did not recognize each
other. She passed on, straight and stiff, and never turned her
head. It was only after a moment that suddenly, in a flash of
memory, beneath the frozen smile, he recognized the lips he
had kissed by a certain fold in them. . . . He gasped for
breath and his knees trembled. He thought:
"Lord, is that the body in which she dwelt whom I loved?
Where is she? Where is she? And where am I, myself?
Where is the man who loved her? What is there left of us
and the cruel love that consumed us?—Ashes. Where is the
fire?"
And his God answered and said:
"In Me."
Then he raised his eyes and saw her for the last time in the
crowd passing through the door into the sunlight.

It was shortly after his return to Paris that he made peace
with his old enemy, Lévy-Cœur, who had been attacking him
for a long time with equal malicious talent and bad faith.
Then, having attained the highest success, glutted with honors,
satiated, appeased, he had been clever enough secretly to recognize Christophe's superiority, and had made advances to him.
Christophe pretended to notice neither attacks nor advances.
Lévy-Cœur wearied of it. They lived in the same neighborhood
and used often to meet. As they passed each other Christophe
would look through Lévy-Cœur, who was exasperated by this
calm way of ignoring his existence.
He had a daughter between eighteen and twenty, a pretty,
elegant girl, with a profile like a lamb, a cloud of curly fair
hair, soft coquettish eyes, and a Luini smile. They used to
go for walks together, and Christophe often met them in the
Luxembourg Gardens; they seemed very intimate, and the girl
would walk arm-in-arm with her father. Absent-minded though

he was, Christophe never failed to notice a pretty face, and he had a weakness for the girl.   He would think of Lévy-Cœur:

" Lucky beast! "

But then he would add proudly:

" But I too have a daughter."

And he used to compare the two.   In the comparison his bias was all in favor of Aurora, but it led him to create in his mind a sort of imaginary friendship between the two girls, though they did not know each other, and even, without his knowing it, to a certain feeling for Lévy-Cœur.

When he returned from Germany he heard that " the lamb " was dead.   In his fatherly selfishness his first thought was:

" Suppose it had been mine! "

And he was filled with an immense pity for Lévy-Cœur. His first impulse was to write to him: he began two letters, but was not satisfied, was ashamed of them, and did not send either.   But a few days later when he met Lévy-Cœur with a weary. miserable face, it was too much for him: he went straight up to the poor wretch and held out both hands to him.   Lévy-Cœur, with a little hesitation, took them in his.   Christophe said:

" You have lost her! . . ."

The emotion in his voice touched Lévy-Cœur.   It was so unexpected!   He felt inexpressibly grateful. . . .   They talked for a little sadly and confusedly.   When they parted nothing was left of all that had divided them.   They had fought: it was inevitable, no doubt: each man must fulfil the law of his nature!   But when men see the end of the tragi-comedy coming, they put off the passions that masked them, and meet face to face,—two men, of whom neither is of much greater worth than the other, who, when they have played their parts to the best of their ability, have the right in the end to shake hands.

The marriage of Georges and Aurora had been fixed for the early spring.   Christophe's health was declining rapidly.   He had seen his children watching him anxiously.   Once he heard them whispering to each other.   Georges was saying:

" How ill he looks!   He looks as though he might fall ill at any moment."

And Aurora replied:

" If only he does not delay our marriage! "

He did not forget it. Poor children! They might be sure that he would not disturb their happiness!

But he was inconsiderate enough on the eve of the marriage— (he had been absurdly excited as the day drew near: as excited as though it were he who was going to be married)—he was stupid enough to be attacked by his old trouble, a recurrence of pneumonia, which had first attacked him in the days of the Market-Place. He was furious with himself, and dubbed himself fool and idiot. He swore that he would not give in until the marriage had taken place. He thought of Grazia as she lay dying, never telling him of her illness because of his approaching concert, for fear lest he should be distracted from his work and pleasure. Now he loved the idea of doing for her daughter—for her—what she had done for him. He concealed his condition, but he found it hard to keep himself going. However, the happiness of his children made him so happy that he managed to support the long ordeal of the religious ceremony without disaster. But he had hardly reached Colette's house than his strength gave out: he had just time enough to shut himself up in a room, and then he fainted. He was found by a servant. When he came to himself Christophe forbade them to say anything to the bride and bridegroom, who were going off on their honeymoon in the evening. They were too much taken up with themselves to notice anything else. They left him gaily, promising to write to him to-morrow, and afterwards. . . .

As soon as they were gone, Christophe took to his bed. He was feverish, and could not shake off the fever. He was alone. Emmanuel was ill too, and could not come. Christophe did not call in a doctor. He did not think his condition was serious. Besides, he had no servant to go for a doctor. The housekeeper who came for two hours in the morning took no interest in him, and he dispensed with her services. He had a dozen times begged her not to touch any of his papers when she was dusting his room. She would do it: she thought she had a fine opportunity to do as she liked, now that he was confined to his bed. In the mirror of his wardrobe door he saw her from his bed

turning the whole room upside down. He was so furious—(no,
assuredly the old Adam was not dead in him!)—that he jumped
out of bed, snatched a packet of papers out of her hands, and
showed her the door. His anger cost him a bout of fever and
the departure of the servant, who lost her temper and never
returned, without even taking the trouble to tell the "old
madman," as she called him. So he was left, ill, with no one
to look after him. He would get up in the morning to take
in the jug of milk left at the door, and to see if the portress
had not slipped under the door the promised letter from the
lovers. The letter did not come: they had forgotten him in
their happiness. He was not angry with them, and thought
that in their place he would have done the same. He thought
of their careless joy, and that it was he had given it to them.

He was a little better and was able to get up when at last a
letter came from Aurora. Georges had been content to add his
signature. Aurora asked very little about Christophe and told
very little, but, to make up for it, she gave him a commission,
begging him to send her a necktie she had left at Colette's.
Although it was not at all important—(Aurora had only thought
of it as she sat down to write to Christophe, and then only
because she wanted something to say),—Christophe was only
too delighted to be of use, and went out at once to fetch it.
The weather was cold and gusty. The winter had taken an
unpleasant turn. Melting snow, and an icy wind. There were
no carriages to be had. Christophe spent some time in a parcels'
office. The rudeness of the clerks and their deliberate slowness
made him irritable, which did not help his business on. His
illness was partly responsible for his gusts of anger, which the
tranquillity of his mind repudiated; they shook his body, like
the last tremors of an oak falling under the blows of an ax.
He returned chilled and trembling. As he entered, the portress
handed him a cutting from a review. He glanced at it. It was
a spiteful attack upon himself. They were growing rare in
these days. There is no pleasure in attacking a man who never
notices the blows dealt him. The most violent of his enemies
were reduced to a feeling of respect for him, which exasperated
them, for they still detested him.

"*We believe*," said Bismarck, almost regretfully, "*that noth*

*ing is more involuntary than love. Respect is even more
so. . . ."*

But the writer of the article was one of those strong men,
who, being better armed than Bismarck, escape both respect
and love. He spoke of Christophe in insulting terms, and
announced a series of attacks during the following fortnight:
Christophe began to laugh, and said as he went to bed again:
" He will be surprised! He won't find me at home! "

They tried to make him have a nurse, but he refused obstinately, saying that he had lived alone so much that he thought
he might at least have the benefit of his solitude at such a time.

He was never bored. During these last years he had constantly been engrossed in dialogues with himself; it was as
though his soul was twofold; and for some months past his
inward company had been considerably augmented: not two
souls, but ten, now dwelt in him. They held converse among
themselves, though more often they sang. He would take part
in their conversation, or he would hold his peace and listen
to them. He had always on his bed, or on the table, within
reach of his hand, music-paper on which he used to take down
their remarks and his own, and laugh at their rejoinders. It
was a mechanical habit: the two actions, thinking and writing,
had become almost simultaneous with him; writing was thinking out loud to him. Everything that took him away from
the company of his many souls exhausted and irritated him,
even the friends he loved best, sometimes. He tried hard not
to let them see it, but such constraint induced an extreme lassitude. He was very happy when he came to himself again, for he
would lose himself: it was impossible to hear the inward voices
amid the chattering of human beings. Divine silence! . . .

He would only allow the portress or one of her children to
come three or four times a day to see if he needed anything.
He used to give them the notes which, up to the last, he exchanged with Emmanuel. They were almost equally ill, and
were under no illusion as to their condition. By different ways
the free religious genius of Christophe and the free irreligious
genius of Emmanuel had reached the same brotherly serenity.
In their wavering handwriting, which they found it more and
more difficult to read, they discoursed, not of their illness, but

of the perpetual subject of their conversations, their **art, and the** future of their ideas.

This went on until the day when, with his failing **hand,** Christophe wrote the words of the King of Sweden, as he **lay** dying on the field of battle:

" Ich habe genug, Bruder: rette dich! " *

As a succession of stages he looked back over the whole **of** his life: the immense effort of his youth to win self-possession, his desperate struggles to exact from others the bare right **to** live, to wrest himself from the demons of his race.   And even after the victory, the forced unending vigil over the fruits **of** conquest, to defend them against victory itself.   The sweetness, the tribulation of friendship opening up the great human family through conflict to the isolated heart.   The fullness of art, the zenith of life.   His proud dominion over his conquered spirit. His belief that he had mastered his destiny.   And then, suddenly at the turn of the road, his meeting with the knights of the Apocalypse, Grief, Passion, Shame, the vanguard of the Lord.   Then laid low, trampled underfoot by the horses, dragging himself bleeding to the heights, where, in the midst of the clouds, flames the wild purifying fire.   His meeting face to face with God.   His wrestling with Him, like Jacob with the Angel.   His issue, broken from the fight.   His adoration of his defeat, his understanding of his limitations, his striving to fulfil the will of the Lord, in the domain assigned to him. Finally, when the labors of seed-time and harvest, the splendid hard work, were at an end, having won the right to rest at the feet of the sunlit mountains, and to say to them:

" Be ye blessed!   I shall not reach your light, but very sweet to me is your shade. . . ."

Then the beloved had appeared to him: she had taken him by the hand; and death, breaking down the barrier of her body, had poured the pure soul of the beloved into the soul of her lover.   Together they had issued from the shadow of days, and they had reached the happy heights where, like the three Graces, in a noble round, the past, the present, and the future, clasped

---

* " I have had my fill, brother: save thyself! "

hands, where the heart at rest sees griefs and joys in one
moment spring to life, flower, and die, where all is Harmony. . . .

He was in too great a hurry. He thought he had already
reached that place. The vise which gripped his panting bosom,
and the tumultuous whirl of images beating against the walls
of his burning brain, reminded him that the last stage and the
hardest was yet to run. . . . Onward! . . .

He lay motionless upon his bed. In the room above him some
silly woman would go on playing the piano for hours. She only
knew one piece, and she would go on tirelessly repeating the
same bars; they gave her so much pleasure! They were a joy,
an emotion to her; every color, every kind of form was in
them. And Christophe could understand her happiness, but
she made him weep with exasperation. If only she would not
hit the keys so hard! Noise was as odious to Christophe as
vice. . . . In the end he became resigned to it. It was hard
to learn not to hear. And yet it was less difficult than he
thought. He would leave his sick, coarse body. How humiliating it was to have been shut up in it for so many years! He
would watch its decay and think:

" It will not go on much longer."

He would feel the pulse of his human egoism and wonder:

" Which would you prefer? To have the name and person
ality of Christophe become immortal and his work disappear,
or to have his work endure and no trace be left of his personality and name? "

Without a moment's hesitation he replied:

" Let me disappear and my work endure! My gain is twofold: for only what is most true of me, the real truth of myself
will remain. Let Christophe perish! . . ."

But very soon he felt that he was becoming as much a stranger
to his work as to himself. How childish was the illusion of
believing that his art would endure! He saw clearly not only
how little he had done, but how surely all modern music was
doomed to destruction. More quickly than any other the language of music is consumed by its own heat; at the end of a
century or two it is understood only by a few initiates. For

how many do Monteverdi and Lully still exist? Already the
oaks of the classic forest are eaten away with moss. Our buildings of sound, in which our passions sing, will soon be empty
temples, will soon crumble away into oblivion.—And Christophe
was amazed to find himself gazing at the ruins untroubled.

"Have I begun to love life less?" he wondered.

But at once he understood that he loved it more. . . . Why
weep over the ruins of art? They are not worth it. Art is
the shadow man casts upon Nature. Let them disappear together, sucked up by the sun's rays! They prevent my seeing
the sun.—The vast treasure of Nature passes through our fingers.
Human intelligence tries to catch the running water in the
meshes of a net. Our music is an illusion. Our scale of sounds
is an invention. It answers to no living sound. It is a compromise of the mind between real sounds, the application of the
metric system to the moving infinite. The mind needs such
a lie as this to understand the incomprehensible, and the mind
has believed the lie, because it wished to believe it. But it is
not true. It is not alive. And the delight which the mind
takes in this order of its own creation has only been obtained
by falsifying the direct intuition of what is. From time to
time, a genius, in passing contact with the earth, suddenly perceives the torrent of reality, overflowing the continents of art.
The dykes crack for a moment. Nature creeps in through a
fissure. But at once the gap is stopped up. It must be done
to safeguard the reason of mankind. It would perish if its eyes
met the eyes of Jehovah. Then once more it begins to strengthen
the walls of its cell, which nothing enters from without, except
it have first been wrought upon. And it is beautiful, perhaps,
for those who will not see. . . . But for me, I will see Thy
face, Jehovah! I will hear the thunder of Thy voice, though
it bring me to nothingness. The noise of art is an hindrance
to me. Let the mind hold its peace! Let man be silent! . . .

But a few minutes after this harangue he groped for one
of the sheets of paper that lay scattered on his bed, and he tried
to write down a few more notes. When he saw the contradiction
of it, he smiled and said:

"Oh, my music, companion of all my days, thou art better

than I. 1 am an ingrate: I send thee away from me. But
thou wilt not leave me: thou wilt not be repulsed at my caprice.
Forgive me. Thou knowest these are but whimsies. I have
never betrayed thee, thou hast never betrayed me; and we are
sure of each other. We will go home together, my friend.
Stay with me to the end.

Bleib bei uns. . . .

He awoke from a long torpor, heavy with fever and dreams.
Strange dreams of which he was still full. And now he looked
at himself, touched himself, sought and could not find himself.
He seemed to himself to be "another." Another, dearer than
himself. . . . Who? . . . It seemed to him that in his
dreams another soul had taken possession of him. Olivier?
Grazia? . . . His heart and his head were so weak! He
could not distinguish between his loved ones. Why should he
distinguish between them? He loved them all equally.

He lay bound in a sort of overwhelming beatitude. He made
no attempt to move. He knew that sorrow lay in ambush for
him, like a cat waiting for a mouse. He lay like one dead.
Already. . . . There was no one in the room. Overhead
the piano was silent. Solitude. Silence. Christophe sighed.

"How good it is to think, at the end of life, that I have never
been alone even in my greatest loneliness! . . . Souls that I
have met on the way, brothers, who for a moment have held out
their hands to me, mysterious spirits sprung from my mind,
living and dead—all living.—O all that I have loved, all that
I have created! Ye surround me with your warm embrace.
ye watch over me. I hear the music of your voices. Blessed
be destiny, that has given you to me! I am rich, I am
rich. . . . My heart is full! . . ."

He looked out through the window. . . . It was one of those beautiful sunless days, which, as old Balzac said, are like a beautiful blind woman. . . . Christophe was passionately absorbed in gazing at the branch of a tree that grew in front of the window. The branch was swelling, the moist buds were bursting, the little white flowers were expanding; and in the flowers, in the leaves, in the whole tree coming to new life, there was such an ecstasy of surrender to the new-born force of spring, that Christophe was no longer conscious of his weariness, his depression, his wretched, dying body, and lived again in the branch of the tree. He was steeped in the gentle radiance of its life. It was like a kiss. His heart, big with love, turned to the beautiful tree, smiling there upon his last moments. He thought that at that moment there were creatures loving each other, that to others this hour, that was so full of agony for him, was an hour of ecstasy, that it is ever thus, and that the puissant joy of living never runs dry. And in a choking voice that would not obey his thoughts—(possibly no sound at all came from his lips, but he knew it not)—he chanted a hymn to life.

An invisible orchestra answered him. Christophe said within himself:

" How can they know? We did not rehearse it. If only they can go on to the end without a mistake! "

He tried to sit up so as to see the whole orchestra, and beat time with his arms outstretched. But the orchestra made no mistake; they were sure of themselves. What marvelous music! How wonderfully they improvised the responses! Christophe was amused.

" Wait a bit, old fellow! I'll catch you out."

And with a tug at the tiller he drove the ship capriciously to left and right through dangerous channels.

" How will you get out of that? . . . And this? Caught! . . . And what about this? "

But they always extricated themselves: they countered all his audacities with even bolder ventures.

" What will they do now? . . . The rascals! . . ."

Christophe cried " bravo! " and roared with laughter.

" The devil! It is becoming difficult to follow them! **Am**

I to let them beat me? . . . But, you know, this is not a game! I'm done, now. . . . No matter! They shan't say that they had the last word. . . ."

But the orchestra exhibited such an overpoweringly novel and abundant fancy that there was nothing to be done but to sit and listen open-mouthed. They took his breath away. . . . Christophe was filled with pity for himself.

"Idiot!" he said to himself. "You are empty. Hold your peace! The instrument has given all that it can give. Enough of this body! I must have another."

But his body took its revenge. Violent fits of coughing prevented his listening:

"Will you hold your peace?"

He clutched his throat, and thumped his chest, wrestled with himself as with an enemy that he must overthrow. He saw himself again in the middle of a great throng. A crowd of men were shouting all around him. One man gripped him with his arms. They rolled down on the ground. The other man was on top of him. He was choking.

"Let me go. I will hear! . . . I will hear! Let me go, or I'll kill you! . . ."

He banged the man's head against the wall, but the man would not let him go.

"Who is it, now? With whom am I wrestling? What is this body that I hold in my grasp, this body warm against me? . . ."

A crowd of hallucinations. A chaos of passions. Fury, lust, murderous desires, the sting of carnal embraces, the last stirring of the mud at the bottom of the pond. . . .

"Ah! Will not the end come soon? Shall I not pluck you off, you leeches clinging to my body? . . . Then let my body perish with them!"

Stiffened in shoulders, loins, knees, Christophe thrust back the invisible enemy. . . . He was free. . . . Yonder, the music was still playing, farther and farther away. Dripping with sweat, broken in body, Christophe held his arms out towards it:

"Wait for me! Wait for me!"

He ran after it. He stumbled. He jostled and pushed his way. . . . He had run so fast that he could not breathe.

His heart beat, his blood roared and buzzed in his ears, like a train rumbling through a tunnel. . . .

"God! How horrible!"

He made desperate signs to the orchestra not to go on without him. . . . At last! He came out of the tunnel! . . . Silence came again. He could hear once more.

"How lovely it is! How lovely! Encore! Bravely, my boys! . . . But who wrote it, who wrote it? . . . What do you say? You tell me that Jean-Christophe Krafft wrote it? Oh! come! Nonsense! I knew him. He couldn't write ten bars of such music as that! . . . Who is that coughing? Don't make such a noise! . . . What chord is that? . . . And that? . . . Not so fast! Wait! . . ."

Christophe uttered inarticulate cries; his hand, clutching the quilt, moved as if it were writing: and his exhausted brain went on mechanically trying to discover the elements of the chords and their consequents. He could not succeed: his emotion made him drop his prize. He began all over again. . . . Ah! This time it was too difficult. . . .

"Stop, stop. . . . I can no more. . . .".

His will relaxed utterly. Softly Christophe closed his eyes. Tears of happiness trickled down from his closed lids. The little girl who was looking after him, unknown to him, piously wiped them away. He lost all consciousness of what was happening. The orchestra had ceased playing, leaving him on a dizzy harmony, the riddle of which could not be solved. His brain went on saying:

"But what chord is that? How am I to get out of it? I should like to find the way out, before the end. . . ."

Voices were raised now. A passionate voice. Anna's tragic eyes. . . . But a moment and it was no longer Anna. Eyes now so full of kindness. . . .

"Grazia, is it thou? . . . Which of you? Which of you? I cannot see you clearly. . . . Why is the sun so long in coming?"

Then bells rang tranquilly. The sparrows at the window chirped to remind him of the hour when he was wont to give them the breakfast crumbs. . . . In his dream Christophe saw the little room of his childhood. . . . The bells. Now it is dawn! The lovely waves of sound fill the light air. They come from far away, from the villages down yonder. . . . The murmuring of the river rises from behind the house. . . . Once more Christophe stood gazing down from the staircase window. All his life flowed before his eyes, like the Rhine. All his life, all his lives, Louisa, Gottfried, Olivier, Sabine. . . .

"Mother, lovers, friends. . . . What are these names? . . . Love. . . . Where are you? Where are you, my souls? I know that you are there, and I cannot take you."

"We are with thee. Peace, O beloved!"

"I will not lose you ever more. I have sought you so long!"

"Be not anxious. We shall never leave thee more."

"Alas! The stream is bearing me on."

"The river that bears thee on, bears us with thee."

"Whither are we going?"

"To the place where we shall be united once more."

"Will it be soon?"

"Look."

And Christophe, making a supreme effort to raise his head—(God! How heavy it was!)—saw the river overflowing its banks, covering the fields, moving on, august, slow, almost still. And, like a flash of steel, on the edge of the horizon there seemed to be speeding towards him a line of silver streams, quivering in the sunlight. The roar of the ocean. . . . And his heart sank, and he asked:

"Is it He?"

And the voices of his loved ones replied:

"It is He!"

And his brain dying, said to itself:

"The gates are opened. . . . That is the chord I was seeking! . . . But it is not the end! There are new spaces! . . .—We will go on, to-morrow."

O joy, the joy of seeing self vanish into the sovereign peace of God, whom all his life he had so striven to serve! . . .

"Lord, art Thou not displeased with Thy servant? I have done so little. I could do no more. . . . I have struggled, I have suffered, I have erred, I have created. Let me draw breath in Thy Father's arms. Some day I shall be born again for a new fight."

And the murmuring of the river and the roaring of the sea sang with him:

"Thou shalt be born again. Rest. Now all is one heart. The smile of the night and the day entwined. Harmony, the august marriage of love and hate. I will sing the God of the two mighty wings. Hosanna to life! Hosanna to death!

> "*Christofori faciem die quacunque tueris,*
> *Illa nempe die non morte mala morieris.*"

Saint Christophe has crossed the river. All night long he has marched against the stream. Like a rock his huge-limbed body stands above the water. On his shoulders is the Child, frail and heavy. Saint Christophe leans on a pine-tree that he has plucked up, and it bends. His back also bends. Those who saw him set out vowed that he would never win through, and for a long time their mockery and their laughter followed him. Then the night fell and they grew weary. Now Christophe is too far away for the cries of those standing on the water's brink to reach him. Through the roar of the torrent he hears only the tranquil voice of the Child, clasping a lock of hair on the giant's forehead in his little hand, and crying: "March on."— And with bowed back, and eyes fixed straight in front of him on the dark bank whose towering slopes are beginning to gleam white, he marches on.

Suddenly the Angelus sounds, and the flock of bells suddenly springs into wakefulness. It is the new dawn! Behind the sheer black cliff rises the golden glory of the invisible sun. Almost falling Christophe at last reaches the bank, and he says to the Child:

"Here we are! How heavy thou wert! Child, who art thou?"

And the Child answers:

"I am the day soon to be born."

THE END